THE LION
AND THE
SCORPION

8BCE-4CE

MARY MUDD

Published by:

 **OMNIBOOK**Co.

OMNIBOOK CO.
99 Wall Street, Suite 118
New York, NY 10005
USA
+1-866-216-9965
www.omnibookcompany.com

For e-book purchase: Kindle on Amazon, Barnes and Noble
Book purchase: Amazon.com, Barnes & Noble, and
www.omnibookcompany.com

Omnibook titles may be purchased in bulk for educational, business,
fund-raising, or sales promotional use. For more information,
please e-mail **info@omnibookcompany.com**

CONTENTS

PREFATORY NOTES

CHARACTERIZATION OF HISTORICAL PERSONS
and significant events in their lives, are derived from meticulous scrutiny of primary sources. As most of these are muckraking in nature, special care was taken to distinguish between valid information and derogatory nonsense. Misrepresentations based upon innuendo are excluded from portrayals of individuals, but are alluded to elsewhere in the text. Examples of such disparagements include Tiberius as sexual deviant and pedophile who cast people off cliffs, his mother Livia as dynastic murderess, his son Drusus as sadistically cruel.

PLACE NAMES
Most cities and geographical districts extant today are represented by their modern names, so the reader can identify them. For those of which only ancient designations or descriptions exist, or the ancient names of which are specifically pertinent to the story, modern equivalents or approximations are given in parentheses.

RECKONING OF HOURS
The Roman day began at first light – essentially 6:00 a.m. This was the first of twelve hours, which ended at sunset. Between sunset and sunrise, the night was divided into four watches of three hours each. Hours and watches varied in length according to the time of year—hours longer in summer, shorter in winter; the opposite for the watches.

CALENDAR DATES
The Romans identified individual days of a month by counting backward from one of three benchmarks:

Calends – first day of every month;

Nones – fifth day of every month except for March, May, July and October, of which the Nones was the seventh day;

Ides – thirteenth day of every month except for March, May, July and October, of which the Ides was the fifteenth day.

Since numeric zero was unknown to the Greeks and Romans, any temporal numeration began with the benchmark numbered as 1. Hence Clytia's birthday of August 19 is the fourteenth day before the Calends of September.

Individuals are usually described in the text as being in or entering a certain year of life, rather than as so many years old. This conceit also arises from lack of numeric zero.

Children were held to be born ten months after being conceived, because the conception month was counted as the first month of gestation.

The modern equivalents of Roman dates are supplied parenthetically in numeric format.

New Year's Day for the Romans was the Calends of March *[3/1]*.

DENUNCIATIONS OF HOMOSEXUALITY

as a vice or perversion reflect specifically ancient Italian attitudes toward this orientation.

DESCRIPTIONS OF MEALS

are derived from the ***De re coquinaria*** *[On Matters Culinary]* by the first century epicure, Marcus Gabius Apicius.

THE RHODIAN MOTHS

described in the text are the Jersey Tiger species. To this day they summer on Rhodes.

ASTROLOGY

Owing to shifts in celestial orbits over time and human ignorance of these movements, the horoscopes of people who lived more than 1000 years ago cannot be accurately plotted. Consequently the horoscopes of characters in the story are necessarily modern conceits. Those of actual historical figures are tailored to support extant descriptions of these individuals' personalities and life experiences.

MEANINGS OF NAMES

The names of the following fictitious characters were deliberately chosen to reflect attributes ascribed to those individuals in the story:

Alcimus – valiant
Anthe – blossom; scum
Anthrakia – charcoal (Greek)
Asellus – little donkey
Bellator – warrior
Carbo – charcoal (Latin)
Clytia – heliotrope; undulating like ocean waves; notable
Cyanea – blue cornflower
Daphne – laurel
Euethia – goodness; fatuity
Eupistus – trustworthy; gullible
Galatea – milky
Heliophanes – sun bright
Hipparion – dobbin
Imperator – military general; emperor
Karyon – walnut
Lampourus – fiery tail
Leo – lion
Leonidas – lion-like
Melambrotus – Black fellow
Miranda – amazing
Nivea – snow
Nomius – nomad
Pericalles – exceptional beauty
Philo – friend; adored one
Plato – broad
Plinthus – brick
Rusticulus – bumpkin
Sannio – buffoon
Scourus – dusky
Sinapeus – mustard colored
Timoleon – esteemed like or by a lion
Timotheus – esteemed like or by a god
Xanthrothix – yellow hair

3

Gaius J

Julia===M. Atius Balbus   Corneli‹

L. Marcius==Atia Major==========Gaius Octavius Thurinus==Ancharia
Philippus

S. Appuleius==Octavia

Atia Minor====L. Marcius
Philippus

Paullus Fabius====Marcia   Quinctilia==Sextus   Marcus
Maximus   Varilla ?   Appuleius   Appuleius

Fabia====M. Plautius
Numan-   Silvanus   Appuleia   S. Appuleius==Fabia Numantina
tina   Varilla

S. Appuleius

Publius========Scribonia===================Augustus=====Livia========T. Claudius   F‹
Cornelius   Nero
Scipio
                                                                                Marce‹
                                                                                Major

P. Cor- Cor-====Paullus   Julia(1)====M. Vipsanius==Caecilia   L. ‹
nelius   nelia   Aemilius   Agrippa
Scipio   Lepidus
                                    Vipsania====Tiberius Drusus====Antonia
                                                                    Minor

                                         Drusus==Livilla   Aelia==Claudi‹

                                                                 Antonia   [
                                    Germanicus Tiberius Julia(3)
                                             Gemellus

L. Aemilius==Julia(2) Gaius Lucius Postumus Agrippina========== Germanicus
Paullus   Major

L. Aemilius   Aemilia==M. Junius Julia(3)==Nero Drusus Caligula Drusilla Julia
Paullus   Lepida   Silanus   Livilla

Marcus   Decius Junius   Lucius Junius   Junia   Junia
Junius   Silanus Torquatus Silanus Torquatus Lepida Calvina
Silanus

ian Dynasty

ded from Augustus and/or Livia, is my invention.

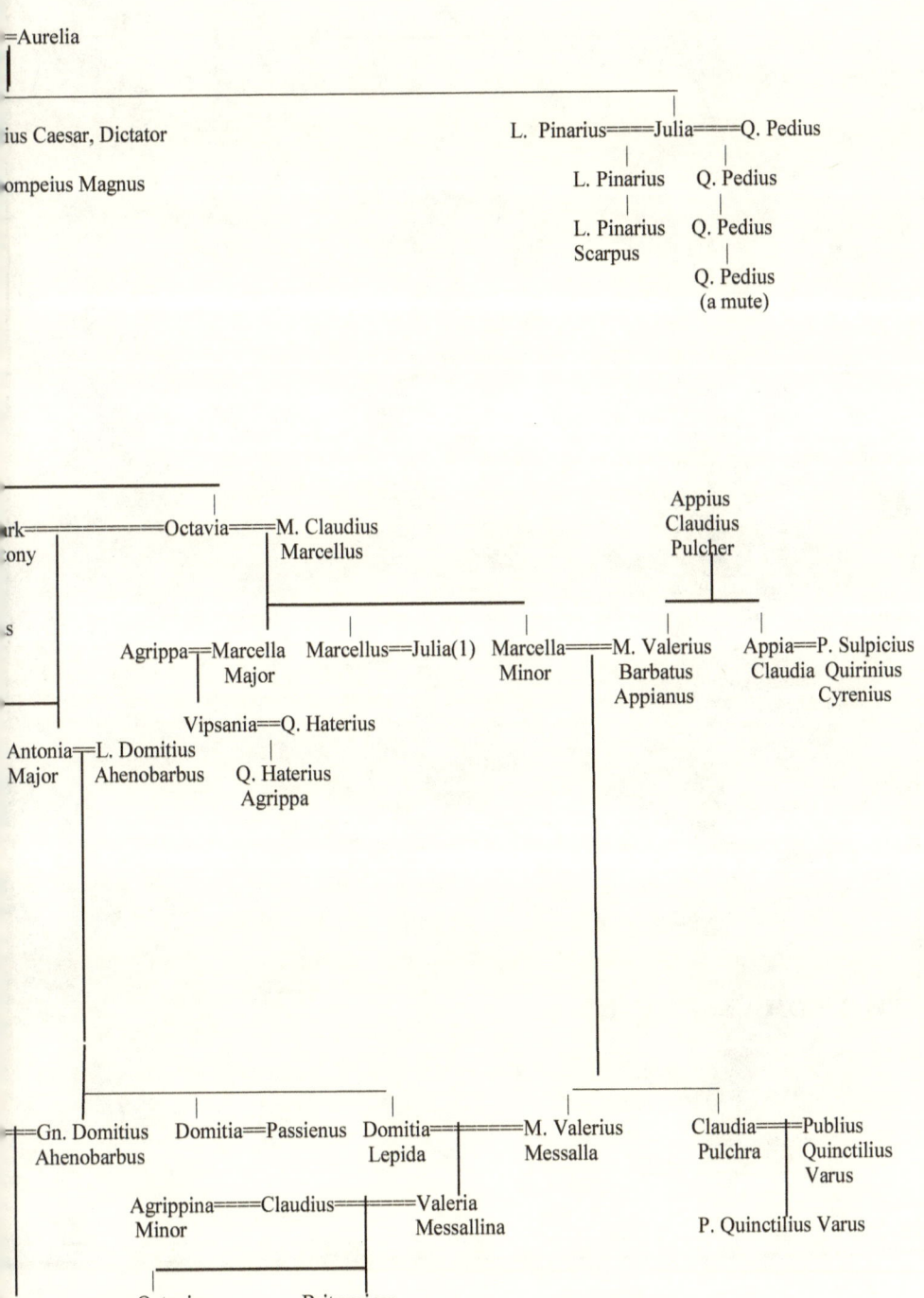

THE ROMAN EMPIRE

UNDER

AUGUSTUS

ROMAN MILES

0   75   150   225   300   375   450

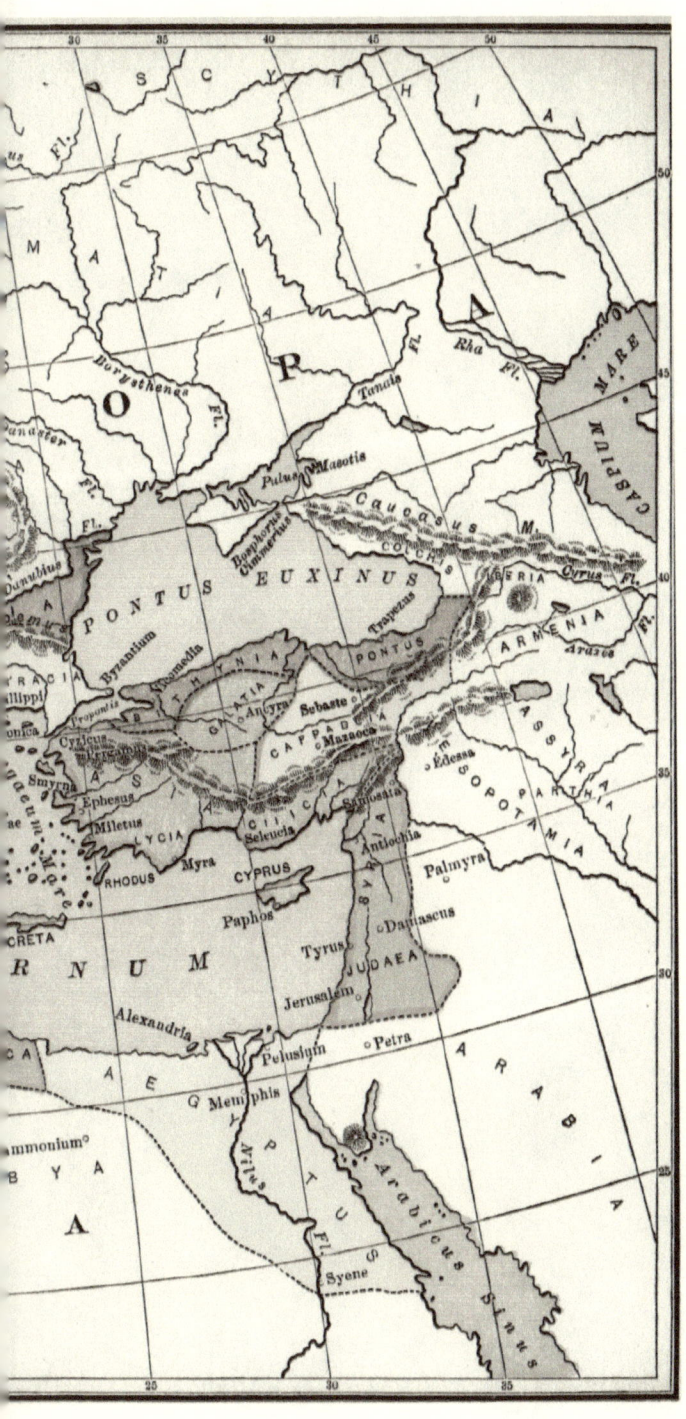

THE ROMAN EMPIRE UNDER AUGUSTUS

A map of the extent of the Roman Empire under Augustus (63 BC to AD 14). The map is color–coded to show the territories, and uses Latin place names such as Mare Internum (Mediterranean Sea), Pontus Euxinus (Black Sea), and Danubius Fl. (Danube River). Important cities of the time are shown, as well as major rivers and terrain.

Place Names: Italy, Africa, Asia, Belgica, Belgium, Hispania, Judea, Lycia, Macedonia, Rome, Sicily, Spain, Syria

Source: Victor Duruy, Edwin A. Grosvenor, & Louis E. Van Norman, Duruy's General History of the World (vol. I) (New York, New York: The Review of Reviews Company, 1912)

Map Credit: Courtesy the private collection of Roy Winkelman

Maps ETC is copyright © 2007–2012 by the University of South Florida.

To Andrew and his family

PROLOGUE

"An intriguing find for sure, Mr. Cymapoulos, and of inestimable value!" The voice of the archaeologist on the telephone was effervescent with excitement.

My cousin and I were remodeling the defunct eighteenth century hotel, which our families had managed until our grandfather's death in 1984. Since then it had stood empty, its exterior an attraction to photographers and bus tours as a prime but dilapidated example of Alexandrian architecture from its era, and its disposition a source of discussions and arguments between relatives. But at last Sotiris and I had turned sufficient profits from our stockbrokerage firm, to set aside savings and procure loans for converting the edifice into a new office for our enterprise. The Alexandrian Ministry of Tourism and Antiquities gave us an outright grant, on condition we restore the exterior to its original condition.

The land on which our hotel stands has belonged to my family since the seventh century. Like Rome, Athens, Istanbul, Damascus—any city in the Mediterranean basin—Alexandria is overbuilt upon successive layers of construction. When our contractors advised us the basement had be breached, for determining where new buttresses and pillars should be placed to support the weight of our office equipment, pursuant to law we had to notify the Ministry of Tourism and Antiquities. They sent over a team of experts to oversee the excavation.

The brick basement of the hotel overlay an earlier basement, also of brick. Scattered through it besides sand were remnants of textiles, pottery shards, pieces of broken furniture, ravaged metal cookware, odds and ends of tableware, shattered storage vessels, and fragmented tools. Slowly and meticulously, the antiquarians scrutinized the leavings. Apart from evincing the previous structure had also been an inn, the relics were unremarkable. The next level was essentially the same in construction and detritus—an inn yet older.

A subsequent level was lined with paving stones. It contained debris analogous to that in the brick levels, but with a greater admixture of shapes, markings, colorations, and designs. This variety suggested the edifice had been a complex of apartments. The diversity of the articles indicated use by multiple occupants according to their individual tastes, in contrast to the stark uniformity of hotel materials.

Since electronic soundings had suggested the paved floor was solid, the team initially presumed the apartment building was the first erected on the site. After all the refuse had been cleared, however, the well-trained eyes of one antiquarian noted a slight variation in the mortar of the floor. Careful removal of pavers opened a small, shallow chamber below. This cavity was filled with clean sand, which upon extraction revealed a stone chest. It was about a meter in length, half a meter in width and height. A relief depicting a hound adorned its lid.

Excitement prevailed among the excavators, and curiosity among the construction workers. Had the sarcophagus of a child or a pet been discovered? Immediately the antiquarians summoned their supervisor—the archaeologist who later telephoned me. He affirmed the style of the hound relief and the frieze bordering the lid were consistent with the fifth century. Another surprise followed. Scrutinizing closely the walls of the little storage chamber, the archaeologist realized it was not a sub-foundational vault but part of a yet earlier foundation. Being filled entirely with sand and sealed off, this region had presented a false impression of being solid. Removal of pavers above it revealed charring. The earliest building on the site had been destroyed by fire. A small section of its foundation had been cleared and cleaned, to create the chamber before the next foundation was laid above. Why?

The archaeologist insisted the stone chest must be opened in the controlled conditions of the Ministry's laboratory. Exposure to ordinary urban air, especially that of an active construction site, could rapidly deteriorate the contents. Fortuitously the chest was not bolted or cemented to the floor. A fascinating process followed. Down the access ramp the construction workers had installed, the excavators wheeled an open cart. It was equipped with a horizontal winch, and its hopper lined with plastic bubble cushioning. The tops of the harness straps were attached to the winch, which was then cranked to raise the chest and position it over the lined hopper. The chest was not lowered all the way into the hopper but left hanging slightly above the bottom. Then the harness straps at the bottom of the chest were attached by tethers to the hopper's sides. The end result was a sling. Gravity kept the chest level, and the tethers and hopper padding retarded its swinging, as the excavation team wheeled the cart up the ramp to the van waiting outside.

"Like moving a live bomb," remarked one of the construction workers.

"Absolutely true, although I prefer the simile of transporting glassware," said the archaeologist.

Three days later came the telephone call. The chest was not a coffin but a storage container. It held eighteen scrolls. The housings thereof, the inks, and the overall condition of the papyri indicated fifth century origin. The text, however, was koine Greek—the first century dialect in which the New Testament is written. The treatise was either a copy of an earlier text, or a fifth century imitation of such. In addition to the scrolls there was a lacquered box, wrapped in linen cloth treated with rosin, and most definitely of the first century. It was lined with the same cloth, and contained the following:

> Two wood pallets, upon which artists of the era painted or sketched;
> Two charcoal sketching pencils;
> Two paintbrushes;
> Three paint vials, each individually holding traces of one of the primary colors;
> An ivory stylus, engraved with stylized plant motifs consistent with Nubian patterns of the era;
> Two leather amulets—the bullae worn by Roman children;
> A pendant necklace of gold and silver with a large aquamarine stone;
> A silver ring set with three rectangular rubies, its small diameter suggesting a woman's;
> A gold ring set with a fire opal, its larger size suggesting a man's;
> A diminutive scroll case;
> A gold Roman aureus, with the image and superscription of the Emperor Tiberius.

My daughter-in-law Christina became euphoric. She had recently begun a master's degree program in ancient languages, and was in search of a thesis topic. Could she edit this manuscript and translate it into modern Greek? Her advisor approved, conditionally of course upon consent of the Ministry. That consent was readily forthcoming. With full cooperation from the conservators who preserved the papyri and the paleographers who transcribed the text, Christina embarked upon her project. After her first few days of work, she declared it was the autobiography of a very talented and proactive woman. A month went by, then another, then still another. We saw little of Christina as she immersed herself in her endeavor.

Early in the fourth month (December), Christina announced she had managed to read the entire text. Now in corroboration with the Roman historian at the university, she was comparing the historical data in the manuscript with bona fide primary sources for the first century. Then quite excitedly, she said the artifacts in the storage box were referred to by the writer. Only one article could not be corroborated. The papyri in the little scroll case were deteriorated beyond any hope of restoration.

Two weeks later, Christina sat at Christmas dinner unwontedly quiet. Finally, as dessert was being served, she spoke up. "Papi Yorgio, my adviser is convinced the manuscript must have some sort of connection with your family. Why else were the materials stored so meticulously on your property at the very time your ancestors came to possess it? The descriptions it includes of first century events are entirely accurate. But whether it is for certain a first century document cannot be established. It could be a fifth century romance, inspired by those first century artifacts and incorporating data from extant primary sources of that era. But if it does date from the first century, and all the persons represented therein are authentic—then it may offer proof that you and Spiros here *[her husband, my son]* and all your clan, are descended from ancient Roman royalty."

"How?" Spiros inquired, clearly intrigued.

"The explanation is rather complicated—for me, at least. To forestall my omitting some essential detail, I prefer you read the actual text. My editing of the first third or so should be finished by March." Her manner brightened. "Dr. El Kharim *[her adviser]* recommends having the entire document translated into English, to facilitate its publication and distribution worldwide!"

"Oh, my dear, how exciting!" exclaimed Petra my wife. "What are you going to call it?"

"How remiss of me!" Christina returned. "I neglected to tell you the author titled it **The Lion and the Scorpion.**"

HOPELESSNESS AND REVOLT

Who am I? Many names have been ascribed to me. My legal designation, which has always been my favorite, is Clytia. My presumed father Eupistus Evandrides consistently maintained he had called me after his favorite blossom. As his wife's name was Anthe, he maintained it was more than appropriate I be named for a particular flower. This may well have been the last independent assertion Eupistus ever made in his lifetime—if, in fact, he even made it at all.

Although I am a native of Alexandria, both my parents came from Colossae in Asia Minor. When I was born—in the fourth summer after the Romans conquered Egypt—my father was pursuing advanced studies in philosophy, rhetoric, and the natural sciences at Alexandria's great Museion. He aspired to become a sophistos—a teacher of higher learning. I have no childhood recollections of my native city. Just after I entered my fourth year, my father completed his course and relocated with his family to Naples. *[24 BCE]*

Southern Italy has a large Greek population. Greeks had colonized Campania—the region in which Naples is located—centuries before our arrival. Naples like Alexandria is a predominantly Greek city and an intellectual center. Greek residents of the environs send their children to Naples to be educated, as do many Romans. At the time of our arrival, the city was undergoing revitalization along with the rest of Italy.

After being wracked by a century of civil and external wars, the country was finally settling into peace. Over the centuries, Rome had brought under her control first the other city-states of Italy, and subsequently the majority of nations in the Mediterranean basin. But Rome's traditional Republican type of government, with its annual rotation of magistrates, was proving too volatile to control a confederation of far-flung dominions. The stability of monarchy was the apparent solution; but the Roman constitution strictly forbade the concentration of power in a single office of long duration. The Republic had been established as the result of a revolt against a monarchy; and the Romans were determined never again to be ruled by kings.

Various politicians had tried, over the years, to make a monarchic solution work within the existing constitutional framework. Not only did these efforts invariably fail: they usually resulted in bloody feuds between political factions. Finally a single young warlord emerged victorious, in full control of all the armies that held sway over Italy and provinces. He was now in a position to exact, from the Roman senate, whatever concessions he desired.

Having learned from the mistakes of his predecessors, this young man demanded the senate grant him the privilege of sharing its powers with the understanding those may be taken back at any time. The war-weary senate hastened to comply. The problem of disrupting the Republican framework had been resolved, and the office of the Roman emperor established. The senate conferred upon the position's originator, Gaius Julius Caesar Octavianus, the special title of Augustus—Latin for Consecrated. All this had occurred in the winter preceding my birth. *[January 27 BCE]*

Those political developments were far away and far removed from us. At Naples my father joined the faculty of a moderately sized academy, at which all levels of education were offered. As a sophistos my father taught the most advanced learning, so his pupils tended to be older: boys in their late teen years, and adult men. The occasional woman who appeared in an audience was almost invariably Italian. The public activities of Greek women were severely restricted. They seldom ventured outside their homes, and then only under the strict supervision of chaperones. Italian women were far less constrained. They might go about freely, provided they were well veiled.

Education was nevertheless prized in women, be they Italian or Greek. Girls attended elementary school side by side with boys. They studied mathematics and rudiments of science, Greek and Latin grammar and composition, history, and the classics of literature. By the time these subjects were mastered, the pupils were around fourteen years of age. At this point academics for girls ceased, and preparations for marriage got underway.

Except in my case.

As soon as I was old enough to retain information, my father poured everything into my head that would stay there. And from what I could tell at my young age he genuinely enjoyed what he did, rejoicing at my devouring interest in whatever material he offered. Astronomy was definitely my favorite. When only in my seventh year, I was able to identify all the constellations by sight and describe the legends behind them. I remember sitting my mother down and giving her an entire lecture on the subject. To celebrate my eighth birthday my father took me on a three-day journey into the hills of Campania, where we stayed in a small village inn. There, away from the lights of Naples, he showed me the night sky in all its glory. The familiar patterns were enhanced by faint, usually invisible stars. We saw the Milky Way, streaming its path across the heaven. And on our last night a meteor streaked across our view, lighting the sky with a momentary burst of sunshine.

And then we came home.

Before we had even removed our wraps, my mother announced that her maiden aunt Euethia was coming all the way from Colossae to live with us. The prospect seemed exciting to me. Surely it would be fun to have someone else to talk to. Coming from a place so far away, she surely must be filled with exciting stories.

And then four days later, my mother announced she was pregnant.

Great-aunt Euethia arrived a few months thereafter, as autumn was painting the trees. She was immediately given my little bedroom in the women's quarters of our house, and I was sequestered into an alcove near the vegetable pantry. All this was temporary I was told; presently things were going to be rearranged for the better. But the months dragged on, and the rearrangement never came. The following April my brother Philo was born. Caring for a new baby offered another exciting prospect; it was like having a live doll. Yet quite promptly after Philo's birth, Euethia and my mother became irascible and unforgiving. Why, they repeatedly demanded of me, did I hate the baby so? Hate the baby? I did not hate the baby!

According to time-honored Greek tradition, my brother ought to have been called Evander after our paternal grandfather. Although they prided themselves on unalloyed adherence to the norms of our culture and sharply criticized anyone else who deviated, Anthe and Euethia decided in this case an exception was justified: the name must be Philo. My father capitulated without a whimper. The name proved most appropriate, for beloved my brother was indeed. From the moment he first saw the light of day, Philo was pampered and indulged. From being overfed he developed colic, and subsequently obesity. Eventually his frequent spells of vomiting impelled my mother to seek a consultation from a leading Neapolitan physician. When this gentleman recommended smaller portions of a leaner diet, the most virulent of complaints about him went on for months. Every time Philo threw up, my mother and her aunt would shriek and wail as though the destruction of the universe were imminent. Their outbursts left me shaking with terror. Until this very day, I cannot hear or witness vomiting without becoming so frantic that I nearly faint.

Philo was never allowed any personal conflicts. He must not exert himself, physically or mentally. Every word he uttered was received as if from an oracle, whether it made sense or not. He was never contradicted or corrected, even when he was clearly wrong. If he coveted something of mine, I must forfeit it immediately. He enjoyed defacing my books and other belongings; and this behavior was condoned as though it were his privilege.

About the time Philo was born, I was considered old enough to attend the Academy at which my father taught. When Philo reached school age, it was decided this pathway was beneath him. His great genius must surely go unrecognized in a crowd of students who were unquestionably his intellectual inferiors. A series of private tutors was engaged at great expense. Whenever Philo found a subject boring or difficult, the tutor was promptly dismissed and replaced with one who offered the promise of a less challenging curriculum.

What irritated me the most about my brother, was that on his account my family started addressing me by a different name. When Philo was very young, he mispronounced Clytia as Pythia. He was never corrected, even after he could pronounce my real name properly and understand he had been applying a misnomer.

Pythia is the title of the prophetess of Apollo at Delphi. You should feel honored to be renamed for her, my father would preach over and over again. Well prophetess or no prophetess, I resented having my identity altered by a foolish and undisciplined child. After growing older and more educated, I eventually challenged the use of this designation as blasphemous. Thereafter I was required to pretend I was not being called after the oracle after all but for the cycle of games designated Pythia, held at Delphi quadrennially in honor of Apollo. Then my father revealed that Pythia derives from Python, the dragon Apollo slew at the site on his temple in Delphi. (The legend commemorates the victory of inspiration and illumination over the darkness of chaos and confusion.) Now my new name was truly appropriate, given my draconian character.

Nothing I said or did seemed acceptable anymore. There was little commendation, but degradation aplenty. Never was I praised for doing well on some school assignment or in the execution of a household task. Instead I was told I had barely met some minimal standard. Failure of any kind resulted in humiliation and punishment for laziness. No one wanted to hear I had not understood instruction, let alone offer to guide and correct me. And the gods forbid I should voice an opinion! Who was I to pass judgments of any kind, frivolous and self-centered as I was?

Everything started to have a price far beyond my ability to pay. I was never sufficiently grateful for the food on my plate, the clothes on my body, the roof over my head, and (this I never quite understood) the unsurpassable privilege of having Philo as my brother. From time to time I would request guidance: what must I do to satisfy the requirement for sufficient gratitude? This question was never answered, only dismissed as evidence of how deep my ingratitude ran.

An occasional remission from the attacks made them all the more devastating. At times my mother became congenial and solicitous, Euethia became jocular, my father would actually talk to me, Philo would receive some discipline. I would begin to hope the crisis had ended and reconciliation was imminent. Then the hostility would return without warning or apparent cause.

What was happening, oh what was happening? I kept trying to be a better person, but to no avail. To my father I tried turning for comfort and support. Instead of the warm affability he had once imparted, I now encountered sharp indifference. This was so intense, at times I felt as though I were walking into a physical wall.

In Naples we lived in a house. Most of the instructors at the Academy— even those with families far larger than ours—resided in apartments, with neither physical discomfort nor financial hardship. We, however, had to have a house. To finance its purchase my father had had to borrow a substantial amount of money. When payments on the mortgage came due, the house was filled with weeping and wailing. And as if the house were not enough of an indulgence, we had to have a country retreat. As the sophistoi did not teach during the summer months, there was no justification for our remaining in Naples. The atmosphere of the countryside had to be far more salubrious for Philo than the fetid air of the city. Never mind the atmosphere at our country house was at times more fetid than in Naples.

Our villa as we were required to call it, was located on a scrubby and rocky piece of property unsuitable for farming or grazing, where the coastal plain rises into the foothills of the Apennines east of Naples. The hills trapped damp air that blew in from the sea and mingled with the dust of the plain. We still had to pretend this atmosphere was less oppressive than that of Naples. My brother did suffer from nasal blockages, which caused him to sniff and snort and slurp when awake and snore like a drunken sailor when asleep. The same physician, who had recommended less food as a cure for Philo's vomiting, advised that relief from the congestion could be achieved if my brother were simply required to blow his nose. This suggestion quite predictably produced the same response as to the counsel regarding the vomiting.

The villa—far better described as a hovel—consisted of a central dayroom flanked by a smaller room on either side. One of these wings served as the women's quarters, where I was jammed cheek by jowl with my mother and her aunt. Space was so sparse we had to sleep on cots, which we set out every night and stored against one wall during the days. My father and brother occupied the other wing. It was slightly larger, and more congenial since it was nicely shaded by a tree. A lean-to abutting against the men's wing contained a hearth, and as such doubled as a kitchen and bathroom. One had to go outside the house entirely in order to enter this structure. On the women's side, a similar but smaller lean-to housed the latrine. It was my duty (whose else?) to dig out its accumulated deposits and haul them to the dung heap at one edge of the property. A well near the front of the house, on ground higher than the latrine, was the only source of potable water. We always traveled to the place by hired carriage because we did not have one of our own, let alone a horse or mule to draw it.

The sophistoi of the Academy were expected to use their summer hiatus for acquiring new knowledge, and developing new insights and interpretations. Not my father. He seldom brought any of his books with him because he yielded to the argument, *You need some respite, Eupistus!* The principal reason intellectual pursuits were discouraged, is that Philo objected to them while we were on vacation. Since I found our retreat the most boring and uncomfortable place on the earth, I was soundly reprimanded for ingratitude. The nearest town was Nola, on the outskirts of which the emperor owned an estate he had inherited from his father. And did we ever visit Nola? No! Such an excursion might have put some variety into the endless monotony of identical, indolent days.

There was a murky little pond on our property. From a straight sturdy branch, a length of stout sewing thread, and an old needle, I fashioned a fishing pole. When I brought home my first catch swimming about in a bucket, you would have thought I had engaged in an unthinkably vicious act of animal cruelty. How could I have been so pitiless, to snatch those poor little fish from their home? And what unthinkable insolence I expressed, when I suggested cleaning and cooking the fish—which had cost us nothing—might bring some relief to our straitened food budget about which everyone kept complaining. Now the incident was yet another example of my abject lack of consideration for my brother: how could I forget he preferred not to eat fish? That is why fish was never served in our home, even though its abundant and inexpensive availability at the Neapolitan marketplace could have lessened our food expenses considerably. Veal and beef, which were served at many of our meals because

Philo preferred them above all other meats, were also the costliest. On this particular occasion I dutifully trudged my bucket back to the pond and released the fish. Following this ruckus I continued to angle for the solitude and access to nature the activity offered, but immediately and always returned whatever I caught to the pond.

Sheep rearing was ubiquitous in the area of our country torture. Campania is renowned for the quality of its wool; hence the women we encountered in the region wove profusely. I loved the sight and touch of their textiles—of the textures, colors, and patterns. One summer, having nothing else to do but fish, I begged to be given a loom. One might have though I asked for some sort of instrument of immorality. *Are you mad? Weaving is beneath people like us! Only menials weave!* When a lady who lived in the area offered to give me a loom she was no longer using, she was politely but firmly turned down. Thereafter I was sharply reprimanded for having demeaned myself before strangers by flaunting my interest in weaving. Of course a great announcement was made to me, whenever another family in the area procured a loom for one of their daughters.

As best I could, I contented myself with watching the sky and land change color with passing clouds or with sunsets. The shifting light I would pretend was a magical loom, revealing the colors and textures of flowers, leaves, and cobwebs, and skittering the patterns of wavering shadows across the landscape.

My excursions into the natural world were denounced and ridiculed. They were interpreted as deliberate attempts to evade the household chores for which I had been made responsible. These consisted for the most part of cooking and housecleaning, the washing of clothes but not their creation or repair. We did not make our own garments as did most families, but entrusted their manufacture and mending to professional tailors or fullers—an extreme expense for which I was never sufficiently grateful. The fabrics selected for our wardrobe were costly but drab, the patterns for the clothing dowdy and unflattering. I became adept at routine sewing, which I was able to justify as necessary to effect immediate mends when a professional was unreachable. This was preferable to not being allowed to touch a textile at all. Of course I was carefully supervised to make sure I did not do any more work of this character than was absolutely necessary, let alone waste time and thread on an embroidery that might bring a little stylishness to an otherwise dreary costume. That is precisely what I longed to do: experiment with weaves and colors and textures to develop unique and flattering designs.

My other chief responsibility was to become as highly educated as possible. Admittedly I enjoyed this, but only to a point. The accusations of inadequacy persisted, diminishing my appreciation for the erudition I was acquiring. If I could not master a subject, it was presumed I was not applying myself. If I did well, then the material was obviously too easy for me; and my father would be ordered to direct me to something more difficult.

The more educated you are, the more your friends will like you, Aunt Euethia pontificated over and over again. How could she speak with authority on this matter, when she could barely read? At any rate, my experience proved her utterly incorrect. My erudition did not impress or inspire other children my age: it intimidated them. They shunned or derided me, leaving me open to the heart-wrenching demand, *What is wrong with you, that you have no friends and everybody bullies you?*

From pursuing the ordinary interests of my contemporaries I was disparagingly prevented. If I tried to discover the most current fashions in hairstyles or clothing, or follow the career of the latest heartthrob actor or charioteer or gymnast, I was accused of wasting my mental energies on frivolities—not to mention monies which could be put to far better purpose. No one was willing or even available to chaperone me to public events. We had no servants: the excuse was that their presence would compromise our privacy. No uncles or other male relatives resided in our area. My father would refuse outrightly, without even stopping to consider the nature of the occasion I wished to attend. Apart from the academic subjects no one else cared about, I had nothing to share with girls my own age. When they scoffed at my lack of worldly knowledge, the question was raised, *Well, why do you not know what they know?*

There was one little girl named Photis, who did befriend me for a number of years. Her father was a bookseller; so like me she was very well read. We used to entertain ourselves by inventing preposterously funny stories about people famous in history. Although affectedly cordial to Photis face-to-face, in private my mother and her aunt took great pains to attempt undermining our relationship. Photis was only permitted visits to our house so long as a member of my family could watch over her. Never was I allowed to attend her home, much less her father's shop; and I was pronounced cravenly selfish, for even thinking my father might take time from his schedule to escort me to either venue.

Anthe and Euethia mercilessly criticized Photis' wardrobe, the way she wore her hair, her use of cosmetics at what they insisted was too early an age, the slimness of her figure. (How dare I defend her svelte by suggesting perhaps I was too fat?) Further depravity was evident in our waste of mental energies, which ought to have been better utilized than in fanciful and entertaining speculations—of the great Athenian leader Pericles trying on different wigs and helmets to conceal the conical shape of his head; of Alexander the Great getting pitched into a prickly bush by his temperamental horse Bucephalus; of the intrepid Roman general Scipio Africanus getting drunk one night, then accidentally stumbling his way into the Carthaginian camp to end up sitting in a pile of elephant dung.

I reached the age of fourteen, at which both Greek and Italian women are customarily first wed. And just as I anticipated, one after another of the girls I knew was spoken for while no man sought my hand. Some of the girls pitied my plight; but far many more gloated and sneered and spread malicious rumors. *She is so ugly, no dowry however large can entice a man. She must be a lover of women. She must be a shrew. What man would want a walking cyclopedia for a wife?* And no one at home offered any comfort, let alone strategies for fending off the attacks or coping with the emotional pain they induced.

When Photis married I was not allowed to attend her wedding (an excuse to evade my personal responsibilities), or even to send her a gift (a waste of my father's money). Thereafter and not surprisingly, I lost all contact with Photis. Before long, all my contemporaries—friend and foe alike—disappeared into the refuge of married life, leaving me to agonize over my spinsterhood.

My father could have arranged a marriage for me. To do so was his legal right and, by the standards of Greek culture, his moral duty. Why, then, was no one selected for me? Did my father not care enough about me, to find a husband to honor and protect me? These questions had three invariable answers. *We have not found anyone with whom we feel you would be happy. We have not found anyone who matches your level of intellect. We have not found anyone who is willing to endure the insolence of your tongue.*

Someday the right man will come along, the never-married Euethia would chant ad nauseam. *Keep up your education. The longer you wait, the better your chances. An education can make you famous. Just look at Apsaisea.*

Aspasia! I would hiss, correcting her incessant mispronunciation of the elegant and learned mistress of the aforementioned Pericles. *She was a hetaera, a courtesan! Shall I follow her example?* This response invariably drove Euethia into a pouty silence, until the day she caught me masturbating. I was not permitted personal privacy. Never mind preservation of this privilege was the justification for our not having servants. My mother and her aunt would enter my quarters without warning, to criticize the manner in which I kept my belongings or to cross-examine me about my activities. When the latter invariably proved innocuous, the discovery I was not up to something sinister always seemed a hugely frustrating disappointment. The revelation I possessed a libido like everyone else was a horror beyond imagination. Now there was little wonder I admired *Apsaisea*, for I was surely well on my way to emulating her.

My youthful tormentors were correct in one respect. At an age when great importance is placed upon personal appearance, I was physically ugly. Being heavily boned, I am somewhat thickset by nature. Our rich and excessive diet, which was primarily intended to entice Philo, fattened me all the more. It caused acne pimples to break out on my face, especially my forehead. My thick and potentially beautiful hair—wavy, and black as nightshade—was never styled (such vanity!), but daily drawn and plated by Euethia into what must have been the most unbecoming arrangement ever conceived. My teeth developed a yellowish hue. They are a bit broad, so this characteristic emphasized their discoloration. Add my unflattering clothes, and you can imagine the sight I presented. And no remedy of any sort was offered: no program for weight loss, no properly styled garments to minimize my dumpy figure, no makeup to cover my acne, no dentifrice to polish my teeth.

Nor did I have much social grace, since no effort was expended on my finishing. What poise I gained was self-learned, and usually at the price of great emotional distress. From the stares and sneers and rebukes of strangers I determined when my voice was too loud, when my conversation was inane or tactless, when my interactions with others were intrusive, when a habit was offensive. Whenever I became anguished over some incident in which I had embarrassed myself, the consensus at home was that I should have known better than to behave as I had. How was I supposed to know acceptable behaviors no one had ever taught me?

When somebody bullied or taunted me and I defended myself, I was informed my conduct was unbecoming and unacceptable. If I ignored an imposition, I was accused of being insipid. Since no one ever intervened for me, I became vituperative toward tormentors. Anybody who insulted my physique, my character, my intellectualism—anything about which I was particularly sensitive—was in for the tongue-lashing of a lifetime. Invariably I felt miserable afterward. My successes at humiliating my assailants led to remorse, my failures to embarrassment and frustration.

As I matured, I became increasingly concerned that I did not menstruate regularly. Was this a sign I may not be able to bear children? Should we not consult a physician, or a midwife at least? My mother or Euethia would only sneer, *Why are you not grateful you do not have to endure that mess every month?*

Eventually I began to wonder whether sterility was the reason a husband was not being sought for me.

I started to cherish my alcove, dark and stuffy as it was. Although it was subject to invasion by family members at any time, the little room gave me as much privacy as I could expect in my home. Occasionally I was ordered out, amid accusations I was being deliberately morose and unsociable, and made to join in some inane family conversation or activity. But for the most part, so long as everyone was satisfied I was buried in my books they left me alone in my closet. There in the shadows, I fought my emotional pain and fears of impending insanity.

I felt as though bursting, with love I aspired to give freely but no one wanted. No longer had I any friends upon whom to bestow my affections: my few childhood chums were all married. My chances of acquiring a husband and children to love were essentially nonexistent. At times I would hold and caress some inanimate object—a doll, a pillow, a bundle of cloth—pretending it was alive and hurting and I was bringing it comfort. Once I set about to see if I could find an outlet for my aspirations by engaging in charitable activities. Upon being discovered, my interest was promptly quashed. *How can you even conceive of demeaning yourself by associating with the scum of the earth?* My family considered the less fortunate an inferior race of mankind.

There was never any forgiveness. If inadvertently I hurt someone's feelings with a thoughtless remark or gesture; if I developed a habit I did not realize was obnoxious; if I committed a breach of etiquette; or I failed to execute some assigned task because I was distracted or had not been properly coached in preparation—then correction came in the form of unmitigated reprisal. Seldom was I subject to corporal punishments like beatings. These I would have preferred, to the degradation of character that came in their stead. No more craven, inconsiderate, mean-spirited, self-centered individual existed on the face of the earth. So frequent and so serious were my mistakes, there was clearly no hope for improvement. I must be punished as fully as possible; for if unrestrained, I would afflict with disgrace and torment the family who loved me beyond what I deserved. The world would be far better off today, if upon my birth I had been exposed to the elements and left to die. Instead my family had chosen to rear me, to their everlasting regret and to the detriment of mankind.

Reminders and reprimands for my real and imagined mistakes went on and on, sometimes for years after the infractions had occurred. I would try to offer amends, hoping assurances I had meant no harm would lessen the hurts I had inflicted unintentionally. Apologies were never accepted, but scoffed at and condemned. How dare I try to defend myself with a hypocritical display of repentance? No amount of regret could undo the damages I should never have inflicted in the first place. In was incumbent upon me to forgive others readily; but to desire the same for myself was to wallow in self-pity. Cheerfulness was a charade to disguise a guilty conscience. Quietude was an expression of groundless hostility toward my family. Anger was ingratitude. Sorrow was an outright admission of guilt.

When very young I tended to cry easily during and after verbal assaults, be they afflicted by family members or outsiders. This reaction only brought more chastisement: tears were an admission of guilt and self-pity for the reproach I so roundly deserved. Eventually I learned to suppress my tears during the actual onslaughts. But alone in my alcove I did weep silently and sorrowfully, during long wakeful periods in the night. Persistent difficulty in sleeping had plagued me since early childhood. Frustration and remorse tortured me. Why did this family of mine refuse to understand, that I wanted to love them and wanted them to love me? Never would I hurt them deliberately; why did they not comprehend this? If they took umbrage at my mistakes, why did they not educate me so I did not make those mistakes? Could no one see how deeply I regretted my errors, how vigorously I was trying to accept correction and become a better person? Were my chances of any kind of reconciliation utterly hopeless? Was evil ingenuous to me, so ingrained that I could not detect and correct it?

With nowhere to turn for solace, I threw myself into my studies with more intensity than ever. In them I found a mental buffer against the hopelessness of my life. This cerebral haven may very well have saved me from suicide. Literature and history provided fantasy worlds into which I escaped, as I imagined myself the companion of some legendary hero or famous real person from a bygone era. The one place to which my father willingly escorted me was the Academy. Almost daily I accompanied him, and was extolled rather than condemned for doing so. Frequenting lecture halls or libraries enabled me to stay away from home without consequence. No chaperone was required once I reached these premises, because everybody there knew who I was. And everyone seemed to appreciate me—faculty and students alike. No one gave my unbecoming appearance or behaviors second thought.

And so I immersed myself in logic, mathematics, rhetoric, natural science, political theory and law, and of course in literature and drama. I perfected my fluency in Latin and studied the writings of Roman thinkers. Philosophy, both Greek and Roman, became my favorite subject. Although I did not embrace any particular school, I found they all had a common objective: to find harmony and personal peace amid the discords and sorrows of human life. Eventually I came to understand I was not alone with my anguish. The greatest thinkers of the world—Thales of Miletus, Heraclitus of Ephesus, Pythagoras of Samos, Xenophanes, Parmenides, Anaxagoras of Clazomenae, Socrates, Plato, Aristotle, Epicurus, Publius Nigidius Figulus, Titus Lucretius Caro—all had been driven to their theories and doctrines by quests for inner peace.

This revelation healed me somewhat, and showed in my comportment at the Academy. With greater awareness and enthusiasm than before, I recognized and acted upon opportunities to help others. Some of the students I encountered were terrified at the prospect of failing their subjects, and of having to face parental fury in consequence. Others were frustrated with their assignments; still others were simply homesick. I began to commiserate and to offer whatever assistance I could, whether that be tutoring, encouragement, or just sympathetic listening.

Now that I was spending the majority of my time out of the house, I found myself able to evaluate my familial situation with detachment and objectivity. My mother, I came to realize, had delusions of grandeur. She had hoped my father would become the director of his own academy, and this institution would develop great renown and wealth. In short she wanted him to become the next Plato; and she harassed him continually for his failure to achieve this goal. She was bitterly jealous of those whom she perceived were living better lives than she was—hence our need for mortgaged houses, and unnecessarily expensive food and clothing.

I also came to understand how Euethia had become part of our lives. In her quest for the extravagant lifestyle to which she felt entitled, my mother had enlisted her aunt as an ally. Legally an unmarried Greek woman is subject to the guardianship of her nearest male relative. After her father died (I was in my third or fourth year), Euethia went to live with her brother—my maternal grandfather Lysander. He had tried to put a stop to her inane conversations, her intrusiveness, her adherence to distorted ideals and her efforts to force others to embrace them. The disdain for weaving was one example of her silliness. Lysander had made Euethia assist him in his business (he was a fuller). Aghast at being subjected to discipline—and worse yet, at being required to work— Euethia turned to her niece Anthe for succor. My mother promptly insisted upon taking Euethia in. My father had no choice in the matter, since Greek law and tradition holds that the domicile of a married couple belongs to the wife. Thereafter whenever my mother pressured my father for some new benefit he could not afford, Euethia promptly and vocally supported the demand.

Every Greek family aspires to have sons because genealogies are traced through the male lines. The euphoria over Philo was typical of Euethia's extremity; and my refusal to comply occasioned the unfounded accusations I hated him. It was well and fine my father had a male heir; but must we treat him like the manifestation of a demigod?

With the birth of the demigod, I became an unnecessary and unwelcome expense. I could redeem myself, however, by becoming renowned and well remunerated for my erudition. Surely I must become a sophista, the feminine version of my father. Such women have been so few and far between in our culture, their fame was assured. With this career, however, there also came a virtual guarantee of spinsterhood, or else of marriage to some gloating dilettante—a collector who craved an educated wife to display like a show animal. Sophistoi themselves tended to marry retiring women, either educated only in rudiments or content to keep their knowledge of advanced subjects to themselves. Who would want to wed a female version of himself, who might prove an intellectual competitor or superior?

My dismal prospects worked well into the scheme of things, since no money had ever been set aside for my dowry. Moreover it was becoming increasingly clear my father would never give his consent, for me to marry any man who was unwilling to submit to my family's control. And in Greek society, such an individual must be a greater rarity than a sophista.

Once I came to understand my family's distorted ideals, my anguish and guilt turned into anger; and my manner at home changed dramatically. Instead of sorrowful and repentant, I became flippant and assertive. This did nothing to improve familial relations, but magnified the hostility toward me instead. Still it gave me a wonderful sense of courage—of independence and self-determination the like of which I had never experienced before. When accused of neglecting my household chores, I suggested the country hellhole be sold and the proceeds used to purchase a slave. To the inevitable, *We have no servants because we value our privacy,* I would respond with *We have no servants because we cannot afford them! When have you ever respected my privacy?* That rejoinder led to accusations of unfathomable selfishness.

At the end of each day, I had been required to provide a detailed accounting of my whereabouts and activities. Now I answered such queries with the likes of, *I have been at the Academy all day: where else do you suppose I went? If you do not believe me, ask Father! He watches my every movement there, and can tell you how often I pissed in the latrine!* That was a sure indication of my filthy mind driving my insolent mouth.

I started to improve my appearance. Amid accusations of ingratitude for the abundance and expense of the food on our table, I began dieting to lose weight. When my mother or Euethia would pressure me to eat more, I would accuse them of force-feeding me. One day I asked a neighbor if she would style my hair. The woman gladly complied; and although she did not have much skill, her efforts produced a distinct improvement. When Euethia predictably objected, I informed her she had the option of closing her eyes. Over the writings of Hippocrates and other physicians I pored, until I found poultices to dry my acne and dentifrices to whiten my teeth. When Philo complained about the odor from the herbs in one prescription I was preparing, I told him he could just hold his nose until the process was complete. I also started to remind him regularly that my name was Clytia and not Pythia.

That autumn, our house in Naples seemed overrun with insects and mice. My mother complained about this to a different neighbor, who suggested we try a cat. Everyone else in the world seemed to have at least one household cat to control vermin: we had to be different. At any rate, this neighbor had a litter of mature kittens and invited us to take one. Since he had a coat like burnished gold and a bit of a mane, I immediately called him Leo. At once I was reprimanded for exhibiting my characteristic selfishness. Not only had I not let Philo name the cat; I had called him after my birth sign. When I retorted the horoscope had not even crossed my mind, I was accused of endeavoring to disguise my self-centeredness with what was assuredly a lie. My choice of name stayed anyway, as did Leo since the vermin disappeared almost overnight. Nevertheless his presence in the house continued to be resented. To keep him from sharing my bed or anyone else's, I was consigned with preparing him a bed of straw and rags in the kitchen and ensuring he utilized it.

Leo had to go outside to relieve himself, and after he got a bit older to visit the area females. When he yowled around the doors for reentry, I was blamed for the noise and required to stop whatever I was doing and let him in. If some household task I was performing had to be interrupted, I faced accusations of reneging my responsibilities to my family in favor of the cat. Feeding Leo was my duty as well. It presented no difficulty so long as there were scraps before or after a meal was prepared. But when no leftovers were available, I had to set aside a portion of my own victuals for Leo. Since I was his caretaker, Leo quite naturally showed greater devotion to me than to anyone else. This partiality I was accused of deliberately soliciting, even though I did not consider the cat my pet and gave him no attention beyond meeting his basic needs.

The neighbor who gave us Leo took care of him whenever we were at our villa. During one such sojourn, Philo adopted a toad. Quite predictably, Leo could not rejoin us when we got back to Naples. It was infinitely more important for Philo to enjoy his toad than for the cat to perform his duty as warden. When the mice and beetles reappeared, this was certainly because I was being sloppy and leaving the doors ajar. I went to the neighbor, retrieved Leo, returned home holding him above my head, and cried, "Behold the solution!"

Once again Leo went to work and got rid of the vermin, and was thereafter allowed to stay. Of course he eventually caught the toad and that was my fault too, because I should have kept Leo under better control. "Why did you not hold Philo accountable?" was my retort on that occasion. "Assuming responsibility for someone or something apart from himself would be an entirely new experience for him. And why is he not being required to improve his choice of pets? A cat is a far cleaner and intelligent and useful animal than a dirty, warty, smelly toad." That night I had to salve and bandage my head before retiring, because my mother in retaliation had pulled a huge shock of my hair out by the roots.

At length I did have to put a stop to my new flippancy, if only to survive. It was not the physical injuries and verbal desecrations that brought me to heel. The decisive blow came from my father. Legally he had the right to kill me; but what he offered was even more devastating than the prospect of death. He threatened never to allow me at the Academy again. I would lose only escape available to me besides my alcove, which remained liable to intrusions at any time.

And so I returned to accounting for all my actions, with the consequent castigations for my indifference to silly and unrealistic mores, and accusations I harbored malicious or self-serving intentions the likes of which I would never conceive. From time to time I became confrontational, calmly but insistently demanding a logical explanation for some unfounded accusation. This strategy often stopped the assault of a particular moment; but it increased the underlying contempt for me and eventually produced more virulent consequences.

I was informed there would be no more correcting my brother about my name. Henceforth at home I would be called Pythia and only Pythia—and by the entire family, not Philo alone! But even worse: at the Academy I must give this as my name to anyone who asked. My very identity had been ripped from me, just to indulge the mental laziness of a spoiled brat. This angered and distressed me, I believe, even more than the punishments for false accusations. I went back to sitting alone for long stretches of time, in my alcove or in some corner of the Academy's library, considering and reconsidering my relationship with my family. Trying to make amends I stopped, and endured the assaults in a stony silence that was invariably interpreted as admission of guilt. Trying to apologize I stopped, and not just because these efforts were futile. No longer had I any remorse; and I rued having been driven to such indifference. In my periods of wakefulness I no longer wept but lay restively in the dark, clenching my fists and teeth in disillusionment and despair. Apparently I continued to do so even when I did manage to sleep, since I started to awaken with headaches and with pain in my jaw.

Because my birthday falls in summer, we were at our Campanian retreat when I entered my twentieth year *[8 BCE]*. The event was celebrated with the same dreary little family party that was invariably carried out on occasions of this sort. My mother was in a snit on three accounts. Earlier in the year the emperor accepted a resolution the Roman senate had passed two decades previously, redesignating my birth month Sextilis as August in his honor. Worse yet the Conscript Fathers now added a day to the newly named month by removing a day from February, the month of my mother's birth. Subsequent to all that, the emperor had mandated an empire-wide census. Our orders to appear before the enumerators in Naples at the end of the month meant we must cut our vacation short.

We served some flavorless, greasy pastries procured from a local woman, whom my mother and Euethia adored like some goddess but I considered a prattling bore. Philo, in his twelfth year a pasty pimply pyramid of soft dough, devoured nearly half the pastries in a thrice. Later on he threw them up. When I recoiled as usual, the entire occurrence was blamed on me. Because of my birthday we had to have pastries. These had caused Philo to vomit. Instead of rushing to pity and fuss over him, I had shrunk from the scene. The pastries had cost good money and were now a terrible waste. How much more selfish could I be?

That night I had more trouble sleeping than usual. The ear-shattering snores of Euethia and Philo assaulted my hearing. The vomiting incident had left me agitated and unsettled; being blamed for it had left me infuriated. Rising from my cot I crept outside, realizing with resignation that I would be certainly questioned and probably penalized if caught. The air was hot and dusty and filled with the clattering of night insects. No rain had fallen for the past month, and the local farmers were in despair over the advancing desiccation of their crops. The drought seemed an uncanny parallel to the hopelessness of my situation.

29

My prospects for being married seemed more remote than ever. The Academy was filled with men. Over the years a good number had shown interest in me; but every relationship that developed had proven short-lived. I attracted a host of lechers, who withdrew dumbfounded and incredulous when I renounced them with loathing. Some of these predators had assumed I was unmarried at my age because I craved the freedom to lie with whomever I wished whenever I wished. Others concluded I was starved for sex and hence ready to succumb to any illicit advance. But there were also men who seriously considered asking my father for my hand. Once they got to know my family, however, they were driven off by my lack of dowry, or by the prospect of having to submit to my mother's domination and adhere unresistingly to her aunt's preposterous notions. Should I follow the path of Aspasia and become a courtesan? The requisite education I possessed; for Greek hetaerae are expected to provide stimulating intellectual conversation along with sexual pleasures. But how could I succeed in such a career, having had absolutely no instruction or experience in the arts of lovemaking? I could not even touch my own body without being castigated for lewdness.

Twice I had fancied myself in love. The first time was with an extremely flirtatious student. He turned out to be devoted to the fiancée to whom he had been betrothed in childhood, but not above toying with the affections of other women. Later I became infatuated with a young sophistos who was utterly engaging, but unmarried and determined to stay that way. Hopelessly naïve, lacking poise and discretion, I made an absolute fool of myself with my blatant endeavors to engage his ardor. At home I was informed I had been a great cause of embarrassment to my father; I ought to have known better; by now everyone at the Academy must surely consider me a hussy or a nitwit or both. So far as I could tell, no one at the Academy held my romantic escapade against me. Nevertheless I kept quite to myself thereafter, and gained a reputation for aloofness and untouchability.

Apparently there was no recourse, apart from suicide, to escape this absurd family that hated me so. They persisted in refusing to see through the malignant fantasies they had created about me, to perceive my true identity, and to acknowledge my affection and good intentions. Why was there no apparent hope of reconciliation? Why? Why? Why? Nothing I did seemed right. When I kept silent in the face of some accusation, my unresponsiveness was taken as an admission of guilt. When I defended myself, I was reprimanded for insolence. If I proved some accusation wrong, I was denounced for discomfiting my accuser.

More than ever I was becoming concerned, that I would finally and inevitably sink into insanity. And there seemed no way out.

On that summer's night I beheld what stars were visible through the haze, and began to reflect upon my philosophical studies. Underlying every school of philosophic thought was the conviction, that behind all the varying and conflicting actions of the universe lay a fundamental Good. Peace and harmony can be reached when one's thought is brought into line with that Principle.

If Good underlies everything, I continued to reason, then any type of evil must eventually yield and dissipate. Suddenly a great calm came over me. Then a thought came to mind so powerfully, that it was almost as if a voice had spoken. It seemed to say, *Endure for now because the future is well worth awaiting.* As I gazed at the horizon, a meteor suddenly traced a horizontal path just above it. I thought about the last time I had seen a meteor, and how immediately thereafter my life had plummeted into disaster. Had I just observed an omen; and did it portend even greater calamity? Or were things finally about to change for the better?

Hold fast to the Good, I thought.

It was not uncommon for some of the Italian students to make believe they were Greeks while attending the Academy. They would substitute chiton for tunic, chlamys or himation for toga, and grow the traditional philosopher's beard that carpeted cheeks, upper lip, chin, and neck. Some assumed Greek pseudonyms. One such pretender emerged when the academic session resumed in the autumn.

He was clearly older than the average student—in his mid-thirties, it appeared. He was moderately tall with broad shoulders, and a firm athletic body attesting to regular physical exercise. His skin was fair and his hair and beard were auburn. Being shy, he tended to direct his gaze at the ground when introduced to people he did not know well. Once you saw them, his large hazel-brown eyes seemed to convey a sense of mournfulness. Oftentimes he wrote with his left hand.

He had registered under the name of Decimus Calvinius Valens. But in keeping with the tradition of other Italians who assumed Greek names while attending the Academy, he insisted upon being called Alcimus. Knowing Latin, I recognized his pseudonym as the Greek translation of his surname. Because he was so reticent, no one knew very much about him. We understood he was a praefectus equitum—a cavalry commander. He had earned some sabbatical time, having served for the past three years in the emperor's wars against rebellious natives in provinces along the Danube frontier. Alcimus had come to Campania for some relaxation, which included his visits to our Academy. No one was really sure where he was staying.

Something about him seemed puzzlingly familiar.

At the beginning of the term he would pass me by without casting a glance. Eventually our eyes would meet and we would nod at each other. Finally one day found us seated beside each other in a lecture hall, waiting for the session to start. He turned to me slowly and said in a measured undertone, "I understand your name is Pythia."

"It is really Clytia," I responded, the exasperation clear in my voice. "But I am known here at the Academy as Pythia. I shall not bore you with the miserable explanation."

"Then perhaps I should call you Plytia." His combining of the names set me to tittering a bit. He returned a slight smile; and a momentary twinkle brightened his melancholy eyes.

We began to chat between lectures. Our conversations focused upon academic matters: the content of a recent lecture, the proper interpretation of some philosophical notion or a point of law, the lesson to be derived from some incident of history. He listened thoughtfully to my conclusions about the eternal Good, and said he would ponder them further. Intrigued that I had studied Hippocrates, he asked me in depth about my research on acne. A friend of his, he said, suffered severely from that ailment.

Then one day, after the conclusion of a discussion had produced a moment of silence, he looked at me intently and said, "I perceive your heart is sore."

There was another silence. Startled, I gazed back at him with what must have surely been a quizzical look. How had he read my thoughts? Before I could answer he continued, "Mine is as well. You need a friend, and you also need to be a friend."

"Thank you," I replied with great sincerity. There was yet another silence. Then I proceeded to explain as concisely as possible, how my family had no use for me but still wanted to keep me under their direct control. This objective, I concluded, together with a gynecological aberration that had never received medical attention, were the reasons I was not married. Immediately I wondered to myself, whatever could have prompted me to be so frank with a man whom I hardly knew?

Nevertheless he listened, pensively and compassionately. After I finished, he remarked that marriage was not necessarily a solution to my predicament. Momentarily I felt a stab of resentment, which faded into sympathy once he began to describe his own distress. His marriage was strained, and his wife wanted a divorce. He would not consent, however, because they had a young son. Under Roman law both spouses must be in agreement to separate, unless one can successfully impute criminal activity to the other. He was also mourning the loss of his closest lifelong friend, who had perished in a dreadful accident. Alcimus had left his family in Rome and come to our Academy, seeking respite from his fractious home and inner peace from the pursuit of philosophy.

Soon we became inseparable at the Academy. Together we attended lectures, perused the collections of the library, conversed in study areas, strolled the grounds—taking care at all times to be in plain sight of my father, or of close acquaintances like the other sophistoi. We were not lovers and had no inclination to be. Nor we did not want a rumor to spread, insinuating we were. Although a liaison with a woman who was not a Roman citizen could not be construed as adulterous, my companion did not want to give his wife any pretext for escalating her complaints. What my family would do to me, I did not venture to imagine.

To have a friend and to be a friend proved a healing experience. It awakened spiritual strengths I did not realize I possessed. I would describe some preposterous opinion or standard of conduct to which my family insisted upon adhering, and the verbal abuse they inflicted upon me when I rejected their cherished notions. My companion would reassure me the fallacies lay with the distorted ideals and not my responses; and I would rejoice in the recognition I was not going mad after all. He predicted Philo would eventually suffer in consequence of the indulgences with which he was being showered, for as an adult he would be unable to think for himself. Suddenly the contempt I had always held for my brother gave way to compassion. Alcimus laughed when I described how my family had reacted after I changed my hair and reduced my weight, and especially over the story of Leo. Then he pointed out that my kin's failure to return me to my previous condition was proof of how little they actually cared for me. He urged me not to be dismayed by this revelation, but rather embrace the independence it implied. Let them rail at me! Once the fuss subsided I should be able to do as I pleased, so long as I did not break a law or a moral precept and thereby disgrace my very gender and race.

Equally if not more rewarding I found to be a listener. When my friend discussed his marital problems, I would simply sit and hear him without offering comment or advice. He was glad of this, for he was not trying to elicit a solution from me. He just wanted a sympathetic ear, so he could gain a better perspective on his difficulties by talking about them. His wife aspired to be a socialite and had taken up with a fast set. She flitted about in provocative clothing, frequented salons and dinner parties, attended theatrical performances and other cultural events more often in the company of her reckless companions than of her husband. And although she was apparently discreet—careful to leave no substantiating evidence—he strongly suspected she was unfaithful to him. His values were very much the opposite of hers. He believed, like our emperor, that the foundation of a civilization's strength and permanence was the morality of its people.

The days shortened and grew colder. A persistent drizzly rain developed. Everyone complained about the dreariness of the weather, notwithstanding the rain was breaking the dryness that everyone had complained about earlier in the year. Such was the atmosphere on the day in early December, when my friend announced his stay at our Academy had drawn to its end. His leave was about to expire. He also felt obligated to spend the Saturnalia festival, which fell later in that month *[December 17 to 23]*, with his family.

He invited me to correspond with him, and assured me he would make arrangements for messengers. His offer I accepted with almost euphoric fervor, but immediately grew glum. My family, I said, would undoubtedly want to scrutinize the letters I received and the ones I wrote in return.

He had already anticipated that prospect. My letters were to be disguised as lesson plans, which he had asked me to prepare for his son. Since our correspondence was supposedly intended for a Roman schoolboy, it must be in Latin. This was an ideal ruse, because my father was the only member of my family beside me who could read Latin, and just barely at that. We might also employ a sort of code, using literary references and allusions and alliterations to represent real people and events. Alcimus' responses would include remunerations for my efforts. Although I protested taking his money, he was adamant. My family, he anticipated, would not try to blockade our arrangement upon discovering I was being reimbursed for it.

Sitting alone in a corner of the library, actually feeling and fighting back tears I so seldom shed, I reflected with gratitude upon the relief and inspiration he had instilled into my miserable existence. The realization this was not goodbye, and we would continue to interact through letters, ameliorated the pain of his departure if only to a degree.

A few days later, one of the Academy schoolboys informed me a lady was asking for me at the main gate. The rain had stopped, but the skies were still overcast and lowering. My caller was bundled against the weather in a palla, the toga-like outer garment worn by Roman women. When I arrived she curtsied and introduced herself as Phoebe, a serving woman of the gentleman I knew as Alcimus. He wanted to see me one more time, to finalize the arrangements we had discussed. Would I please accompany her?

A servant meant he was well off, or at least spent his money more wisely than my family did theirs. Drawing my himation over my head and face, I set out with her into the damp street. At that instant the clouds parted somewhat, and the dreary landscape momentarily became slightly golden with faint sunlight.

Phoebe led me to a small military carriage drawn by a mule. We were transported to the barracks on the outskirts of Naples. The place was bustling with soldiers and civilians, none of whom paid any attention to us. Phoebe led me down a colonnade to an office. The door was shut and flanked by a pair of sentries, one of whom nodded to her. She rapped twice; and from within we heard Alcimus respond, "Come."

When I entered that room I received such a start, its memory can still cause me to tremble.

He was now clean shaven. His hair was cropped short in regular Roman fashion. He wore a standard military tunic, and caligae *[Roman combat boots]*. With his Greek disguise gone I recognized him at once, from the commemorative statues and medallions that adorned the city's public squares and buildings.

The companion I had known as Alcimus was Tiberius Claudius Nero: stepson and son-in-law of Caesar Augustus, regent to the emperor's grandsons and intended successors.

My heart was pounding, my knees weak. I could scarcely breathe. Becoming lightheaded, I kept telling myself I must not faint.

"Clytia," he began in a gentle tone. Flustered as I was, I noted his use of my real name. "If we are going to be correspondents, you need to know my true identity."

"I always wondered why you seemed so strangely familiar," I sputtered, still breathless and now feeling very stupid about my response.

He motioned for me to take a chair. I stood transfixed, however, until Phoebe, who had shut the door behind us, gently grasped my shoulders and eased me toward my destination. Tiberius seated himself beside a small table, on which lay his crimson paludamentum—the distinguishing cloak of a Roman general. *He did not just serve in those brilliant campaigns on the Danube; he planned, organized and led them,* I reflected numbly.

For a long moment he gazed at the floor, not directly in front of him but at somewhat of an angle; this he often did when lost in thought. I wondered if the interview was proving as difficult for him as it was for me. A patch of pimply rash on one cheek caught my attention. Acne: the beard he sported at the Academy had concealed it. Little wonder he had taken such interest in my research on the subject.

At length he looked directly at me and smiled.

"Clytia, I value our acquaintance very, very highly. You have become one of my closest confidants, of which I have had very few over the years. One was my brother; and you have certainly helped fill the void that his death has left in my soul." So that was the bosom companion for whom he had said he was grieving. Tiberius' younger brother, Nero Claudius Drusus, had died a year earlier in a terrible and tragic accident. He had conducted a brilliant military campaign, which had extended the Roman frontier province of Germania into the region between the Rhine and Elbe rivers. On the return march to his headquarters in Gaul his horse had slipped and rolled on him, crushing half his body.

Tiberius continued, "As your confidant, I shall be telling things you must not reveal to anyone under any circumstances. Maintaining secrecy is going to prove formidably difficult at times. Are you prepared to accept that responsibility?"

"I am, my lord."

"And never, *ever* call me that—please." He paused, took a deep breath. "Your family is likely to investigate whether your correspondent exists, and harass you if they do not find a record. Accordingly I have created a false military enrollment for Decimus Calvinius Valens, as a magister equitum in the peacekeeping force at the German front. I shall dispatch messengers to you twice a month—around the Calends and the Ides. Appear diffident about my correspondence when you receive it, and about yours when you write it. Remember, your ostensible task is to prepare and grade schoolboy lessons.

"Do not volunteer information. The only way to keep a secret is not to divulge it. Dissemble whenever possible. If you must disclose, give no more than the barest amount needed to satisfy the inquirer. You may find it necessary to divulge superficial information to keep the more sensitive concealed. Then you must decide, sometimes on a moment's notice, which secrets can be sacrificed and which must be guarded at all costs."

Vigorously I nodded my understanding.

"Feign ignorance if you can do so plausibly. If you must lie, then fabricate stories carefully, lest you run into difficulty if called upon to substantiate them. If you lead some—particularly your relatives—to believe they have succeeded in extracting information from you against your will, they may very well feel satisfied and not make further inquiries. If you can manage to convince your adversaries they are somehow oppressing you, when in reality they are granting you precisely what you want, you will not only succeed at your quest but turn disapproval into sanction. While this may be your greatest challenge, it carries the prospect of the greatest rewards."

"Indeed!" Now it was I who was staring intently at the floor.

"And you, my dear, are more than equal to it." He arose, came to my chair, took my hand and raised me to my feet. We embraced like a brother and sister. "This parting is immensely difficult for me, Clytia. That is why I refuse to say goodbye. I am leaving only your sight, not your life." He then nodded to Phoebe, who opened the door and escorted me out.

When the carriage returned me to the Academy, my father was waiting with the anticipated salvo of questions. "Who was that woman, and where did you go with her?" he demanded indignantly as we began our walk homeward.

I was going to make up a fanciful story about going to interview a prospective student—a little boy from a very wealthy family who could not be brought to the Academy because he was sick; but then I recalled Tiberius' precaution about unsustainable tales. And so I answered, "She is a servant of the Italian cavalryman who was a guest at our Academy—the one who called himself Alcimus." Then before my father could interject, I continued, "He has hired me to prepare lesson plans for his two children." Now I complimented myself for creating a false lead without actually lying. It was a well-known fact Tiberius had fathered two sons. One of them, however, had died in infancy.

"That soulmate of yours," my father harrumphed sarcastically. "A strange bird indeed. He could not come to see you, let alone me about this? You had to go to him?"

My heart began to pound again. I had to take care my voice did not waver and betray my trepidation. "He is back on duty, Father. He could not leave his post—that is why he sent the woman to fetch me."

"Where did she take you?"

"The Roman barracks." He winced; but again I would not let him interrupt me. "Stop worrying! She stayed with me throughout the entire journey and interview. I did nothing inappropriate, and no one did anything to me."

My father fumed but said nothing. Of course my mother and her aunt were thoroughly outraged when he gave them the news. How, oh how, could I have been so brazen? Bad enough that I had gone off with a strange woman; but then to visit a man in a strange locale! Worst of all: I had agreed to accept payment without first seeking the approval of my father! In that respect they did have a point. As a woman, I was legally ineligible to enter into a contract on my own authority. A male guardian must act on my behalf.

Putting on a great show of penitence I did not really feel, I murmured, "If you prefer, I shall call the arrangement off. I had only thought our household could benefit from a little extra income."

On being reminded about the remuneration, everyone at once concurred I should go ahead with this particular agreement, but never enter another without consulting the family first. Then, "How much is he going to pay?"

"We have not yet set an amount."

"Well, be sure it is adequate!"

Into my alcove I withdrew, trembling with anxiety from my close escape and feeling a strangely guilty joy. The ruse had worked flawlessly. My goal had been achieved, and my family satisfied that appropriate censure had been inflicted. I had discovered the art of evasion.

And what an instructor I had! I reflected upon how, as a young girl, to escape my personal torments I had fantasized about being the best friend of an imaginary princess, or of some renowned historical personage the type Photis and I used to poke fun at. Those dreams had escorted me into idyllic worlds unspoiled by conflict and softened with kindness, joy, and unconditional love. Now daydream had suddenly become reality. Moreover I was to discover, rather quickly, that my imperial correspondent's life was hardly the charmed existence most people envisioned and envied.

True to my expectations, I had to show the first few letters I received and the first few I wrote. The combination of routine lesson plans with obscure and convoluted literary allusions, all written in Latin, confounded my father from the start. Soon everyone was persuaded our exchanges were so incomprehensible, they had to be harmless. The inspections stopped; and I was free to correspond without scrutiny.

Much of the content of our letters resembled our conversations at the Academy. We mused about philosophic and ethical matters, compared the successes of the acne treatments with which we experimented, speculated on causes of phenomena in the natural world. Are unusual occurrences in nature actually portents? Tiberius was deeply interested in astrology. He had had to make very clear to his stepfather the emperor, that he was not using it to determine the future of the Roman state. Calculations of this type were considered potentially seditious, and hence were illegal. If you had foreknowledge, say, of the outcome of an election or of when a ruler was destined to die or be overthrown, you could arrange to be in a position to profit from that event. Had Augustus assumed this was the motive behind Tiberius' pursuit of such reckonings, he would certainly have put an immediate stop to it.

Tiberius approached astrology from the standpoint of scientific inquiry. Do the patterns and forces of the universe, which order the movements of the stars and other heavenly bodies, regulate human experience as well? Or do we retrospectively associate these divinations with events already transpired, and from that basis conclude prophecies have been fulfilled? Augustus had had his own horoscope read in his nineteenth year. As the astrologer pursued his calculations, he grew wide-eyed with astonishment. Upon finishing, he had prostrated himself at his young client's feet.

Does this personal experience prove astrology is indeed a window on the future? We already know how to calculate the future of celestial events. You can determine when to expect each phase of the moon, or when a constellation is due to rise. If a cosmic link exists between celestial and terrestrial events, then we may only need more sophisticated calculations to discern the future of both. Tiberius carefully considered my notion that meteors are harbingers of significant change. I had described how, after I saw the meteor on my childhood excursion with my father, my life immediately plunged into misery and despair. A great shower of them had been observed, he wrote, just before his brother's fatal accident.

Subsequently I wrote him about the meteor I had observed on my birthday, that summer before we made our acquaintance at the Academy. His response left me breathless with wonder and amazement. On the very same night at the same hour, he had witnessed a meteor. What a coincidence! If the dual sighting presaged our acquaintance, it hardly portended disaster.

He encouraged me to elaborate upon my relationship with my family—my exasperation with their distorted notions, my bewildered grief at their attacks. His responses, filled with compassion and suggestions for coping and occasionally with humor, strengthened my forbearance and helped increase my detachment from my family's absurdities. He was dumbfounded when I described how my interest in weaving and sewing was decried as degrading. *My own mother weaves!* he wrote back in amazement. *She spins and sews as well. So does my wife, even though these are hardly her favorite activities.* One evening shortly thereafter, I offhandedly mentioned that I understood the emperor's wife and daughter did not think weaving beneath them. The response was precisely what I had anticipated. "Something is gravely wrong with that entire family anyway!" My mother hated the Caesars, covetous as she was of their wealth, fame, and power.

How utterly predictable, Tiberius agreed.

As we continued to correspond, Tiberius became increasingly comfortable with disclosing details of his private life to which he had heretofore either alluded to or left unmentioned.

He was in his thirty-fifth year. His birthday was sixteen days before the Calends of December *[November 16, 42 BCE]*; and he was delighted to learn mine was the fourteenth before the Calends of September *[August 19]*. On this day in the year before his birth, his stepfather for the first time had assumed the consulship, the highest executive magistracy of the Roman senate. *[43 BCE]*

Tiberius belonged by birth to the ancient Roman aristocracy. Both his parents were blood descendants of the gens Claudia, one of the oldest and most politically powerful clans in Rome. Unlike most Romans, who were of Latin origin, the Claudii were descendants of a central Italian people called the Sabini. When I asked Tiberius if he knew any of the Sabine language, he replied that he understood a few phrases. He revealed Nero means powerful or valiant in that tongue. I replied that I appreciated how he had chosen his aliases, Alcimus and Valens. These are respectively the Greek and Latin translations of his surname.

After complimenting my perspicacity and assuring me he had suspected I would arrive at my conclusion all along, Tiberius explained how he had derived the remainder of his Latin pseudonym, Decimus Calvinius Valens. Alfidia was the Volscan gens to which his maternal grandmother belonged. She was very much alive, he wrote, in her seventy-fifth year and living on her family's ancestral estate at Fondi. Lest his identity is tracked through her gentilicum, Tiberius had corrupted its spelling into Calvinius. Decimus Claudius Nero was the original name of his younger brother. At the celebration of his coming of age on his fifteenth birthday, Decimus adopted the name Nero Claudius Drusus in honor of his maternal grandfather, Marcus Livius Drusus Claudianus.

Tiberius' father, after whom he was named, had been a Roman senator of moderate distinction. In his younger days the elder Tiberius Nero had sought the hand of Tullia, daughter of the great statesman Cicero. After his suit failed, this Nero remained unmarried until the daughter of a politically powerful kinsman became nubile. Marcus Livius Drusus Claudianus belonged by birth to the Claudii Pulchri—perhaps the most prominent family of the gens Claudia. As his name indicated, he had been adopted in infancy by another significant politician who lacked a natural male heir.

Tiberius had no recollection of the abject danger in which he passed his first few years of life. A year before his birth, three powerful military leaders seized control of the Roman government. Two were a pair of cousins: Marcus Antonius and Gaius Julius Caesar Octavianus. They were also brothers-in-law. To cement their alliance the widowed Antonius had espoused Octavia, the likewise widowed sister of Octavianus. The third member of the junta, Marcus Aemilius Lepidus, was a retainer and protégé of his colleagues. The trio hoped the Triumvirate as they called their coalition, would solve the current constitutional impasse by providing stable government without concentrating power in the hands of a single individual.

The Triumvirate encountered bitter opposition from the old Roman aristocracy, whose families had controlled the government for centuries. The elder Tiberius Nero and Drusus Claudianus his father-in-law were at the forefront of this resistance. To the public they disseminated hostile propaganda, in an effort to undermine popular approval of the Triumvirate. In the Senate they introduced legislation to block the junta's agendas. Not surprisingly the Triumvirate responded by identifying both men as enemies of the state, liable to prosecution and possible execution. Following a pitched battle at Philippi in Macedonia, during which the Triumviral army routed that of the dissenters, Marcus Livius Drusus Claudianus committed suicide.

Little Tiberius was born only a month later. His father persisted with his activism. During the year following, Nero dragged his family about Italy, challenging the Triumvirate's policies and then fleeing furtively to avoid capture by its agents. On two occasions, the young Tiberius almost disclosed his family's whereabouts with his crying.

With a warrant outstanding for his arrest and the Triumviral authorities closing in, the elder Tiberius Nero fled Italy for Sicily. Here he sought refuge and alliance with Sextus Pompeius Magnus, the youngest son of the great general and statesman Gnaeus Pompeius Magnus—once the ally and later the archenemy of Caesar the Dictator, the maternal granduncle and adoptive father of Caesar Octavianus. From his Sicilian base Sextus was endeavoring to sway public opinion against Octavianus by disrupting shipments of grain from North Africa to Rome, thereby plaguing the capital with food shortages. Disorganized, and threatened by tenacious and superior political and military tactics, many of Octavianus' opponents were rallying about Sextus for leadership despite his often offensive and disreputable behaviors and stratagems. Nero had hoped Sextus would accept him as an ally in their common cause against Octavianus. Instead, Nero found himself rebuffed. Having just concluded a tenuous peace with Octavianus, Sextus was loathe to shelter an active aggressor against Octavianus whom the latter was currently pursuing.

Flight for himself and his family now appeared to be Nero's only alternative. His health was in decline: the exertion, deprivation, and emotional distress of his opposition activities had compromised an already delicate constitution. He knew a warm welcome and personal security awaited him at Sparta, for the Claudii had long been patrons of this pleasant and historic Greek city. This meant members of the gens Claudia represented the interests of the city, its requests for interventions and entitlements, during proceedings of the Roman senate. Nero arranged for Livia and young Tiberius to travel separately from him. He wanted to ensure their escape, should confederates of Octavianus detect and capture him.

During the ensuing winter, Octavianus Caesar rethought and revised his tactics. Replacing military force with gracious and cautious diplomacy, he successfully reconciled the majority of the old Republican aristocracy to the Triumvirate. In the subsequent spring he offered amnesty to those against whom warrants had been issued—including Tiberius Nero. It was the dry season when the Nerones began their return journey. As their carriage entered the woods bordering Sparta, the parched tinder suddenly burst into flames. Tiberius' mother was affected the most, with burns to her hair and garments. Although badly shaken by the incident, she was convinced the event was an omen of the momentous change that was about to occur in her life.

The pleasant environs of Sparta in the company of his young wife and son, and the subsequent relief that the danger from the Triumvirate had abated, brought a measure of revival to the elder Tiberius' spirits and physique. Shortly after their return to Italy, Livia determined she was expecting another child. She also renewed her old acquaintance with Octavianus Caesar.

Livia and Octavianus had known one another since childhood, and had always shared a strong mutual attraction. Duty bound by tradition, however, Livia had agreeably married the husband her father had selected for her. Once committed to the role of a faithful and devoted wife, she conscientiously strove to suppress her feelings for Octavianus. She also became somewhat ambivalent toward him, after he had impugned her father and husband as enemies of his regime. He had tried to forget her as well, by deliberately focusing his attention on other women. His flirtations won him a reputation as a womanizer.

Once the Nerones had returned to Rome from Sparta, an inexorable train of events unfolded. Tiberius Nero, his health in shambles, decided not to return to public life. Meanwhile to emphasize that his quarrel with the aristocracy was over, Octavianus assiduously set about befriending his former enemies during senate meetings and at social gatherings. In the latter he began to encounter and interact with Livia. Their former feelings revived and intensified.

Not being himself an aristocrat by birth, one of the better ways Octavianus could demonstrate his adherence to that order was by marriage to a woman who belonged to it. He already had such a wife: Scribonia. She was five years his senior. Her brother was Lucius Scribonius Libo, the father-in-law of Sextus Pompeius. Octavianus had espoused Scribonia as part of an effort to cement a short-lived treaty between the Triumvirate and Pompeius. Now Libo and Octavianus alike wanted this marital alignment dissolved, lest their continued opposition escalate into outright aggression. Neither side relished facing the social and potentially legal ramifications of declaring war upon a kinsman. Octavianus made the divorce effective the very day Scribonia bore their daughter Julia. They had agreed to this arrangement so the child's legitimacy could not be questioned or challenged.

By now Octavianus was ardently in love with Livia, and she with him. Should he take Livia as his mistress, Octavianus stood to alienate anew the aristocracy to which she belonged—undoing all his labors at reconciliation and reopening the floodgates of civil strife. But as Octavianus' wife, Livia the aristocrat—the daughter of his former enemy—would be the perfect symbol of his reconciliation and alliance with her milieu, especially if her present husband—a fellow aristocrat and former enemy—surrendered her willingly. The pair approached Tiberius Nero: would he be amenable to granting Livia a divorce?

Nero had been observing and carefully assessing the situation unfolding before him. Surely the dynamic and intrepid Octavianus presented a far more congenial companion for the vibrant and intelligent Livia than a declining invalid. And how could that declining invalid properly rear two young sons, let alone introduce them to public life once they came of age? Would he even be alive by then? Nero agreed to release Livia on a strict condition: Octavianus must assume the responsibility of raising Nero's children and promoting their political careers.

For Tiberius and his younger brother, visiting their father had been like going to see any relative who is not a member of one's immediate family. Tiberius recalled a gentle man, soft of speech and slow of movement. Although he was only in his early fifties, the elder Tiberius' frailty made him seem decades older. Oftentimes he was bedridden. When he could, he sat the boys on his knees and listened earnestly as they unfolded the trivial details of their young lives. There were toys and treats and entertainments and much kind solicitude; but there was always a sense of detachment.

Not Tiberius' father but his stepfather was the prevailing paternal influence upon his upbringing. It was Octavianus who planned and supervised Tiberius' education—first in standard childhood generalities, and later in the specifics of Roman law and political theory, military history and strategy. It was Octavianus who reprimanded young Tiberius for infractions of family rules, arbitrated in familial disputes, offered remedies when other children bullied, instilled the senses of responsibility and ethics, developed strengths of character and sought solutions to weaknesses, elucidated the sort of life that must arise from a political career, expounded upon the mysteries of womanhood, and was always available to warn and guard and guide and mentor. It was Octavianus who arranged marriage for him, albeit with the elder Tiberius' approval. In his ninth year Tiberius was betrothed to the daughter of Marcus Vipsanius Agrippa, Octavianus' close childhood friend and retainer. The promised bride was in her fifth year of life.

Not that growing up in the Caesar household was by any means easy. Octavianus was an unrelenting and uncompromising taskmaster, accepting nothing short of excellence in himself and in others. He was obstinate, inconsiderate, impatient with shortcomings, and utterly intolerant of any type of conduct he viewed as insubordinate. Tiberius was in his eleventh year when his father died in his fifty-third. Despite his protests, Tiberius was made to deliver the eulogy from the rostra in Rome's forum. It was customary for a decedent's eldest son to do so; and Octavianus was deeply respectful of Italian traditions. He was also eager to take advantage of this opportunity for giving his naturally reticent stepson an experience in public speaking—a task Tiberius must perform repeatedly as an adult politician. Tiberius received a ready compliment for the successful delivery of his oration, but little sympathy for the tears and headache and nausea that followed.

Nevertheless I received an emphatic denial, when I ventured to suggest that Tiberius' familial life was a parallel to mine. Beneath his stepfather's obduracy, he wrote, ran an equally if not more intense affection. Whenever this manifested itself in some word or deed or gesture, it dispelled the resentments accruing from the more frequently encountered hardheadedness. Tiberius' mother, moreover, was a profoundly mitigating presence, ever willing and available to console and encourage and support. Livia seldom quarreled with her husband, as she took great care to be gracious, cheerful, and obedient. Although she kept conscientiously attentive to Octavianus' activities, she scrupulously avoided meddling in them. Consequently her spouse listened with attention and respect when she did venture a comment or request. Through this method, Livia softened the stringencies of her children's upbringing, and secured the help and favors they dared not seek for themselves.

Because of his unique political position, Octavianus hesitated to send his stepsons to ordinary schools. He anticipated they would become objects of curiosity among fellow pupils and their parents. Several sophistoi, selected from the finest in their profession, were engaged as tutors. Tiberius and his brother were hardly the only charges. Their stepfather's short-lived marriage to his former wife Scribonia had produced Julia. She was a saucy and fun-loving soul, but with a steely side attesting to her paternity. There were also the five children of Octavianus' sister Octavia: her son and two daughters from her first husband Marcus Claudius Marcellus, and two more daughters from her second spouse Marcus Antonius. She also brought four stepchildren to the mix: Iullus Antonius her husband's son from his first marriage, plus the two sons and daughter he had fathered on the Queen of Egypt. The young Tiberius had little contact with children from outside this closed circle. Nor did he miss such interaction, because his own coterie supplied him with schoolmates and playmates aplenty.

Had Roman custom been followed, Marcus Antonius would have assumed responsibility for the education of his children and stepchildren. He only bestowed such attention upon Antyllus, his elder son by his late first wife Fulvia. The others he had ignored because his marriage with Octavia was crumbling—not from personal animosity, but from reorientation of his political intentions.

Since the formation of the Triumvirate, Antonius had spent most of his time in the eastern Mediterranean, solidifying alliances with the vassal kingdoms of Rome that lay in this region. The largest and wealthiest of these was Egypt. Antonius had become infatuated with Cleopatra VII, the ambitious and unscrupulous queen of that nation. Under her influence, Antonius aspired to oust his fellow Triumvirs and seize control of the Roman state for himself. In return for her financial support, for the recruitment and equipment of an army and fleet, Cleopatra would be his consort and hopefully his fellow sovereign. Antyllus would become a primary functionary in his new regime. They miscalculated, and fatally.

Lepidus had been remanded to exile some years earlier, after attempting an abortive insurrection against his two colleagues. Now the xenophobic Romans, terrified at the prospect of foreign domination, unilaterally rallied behind Octavianus as champion of their self-determination. The Roman senate declared war on Cleopatra. There was little contest. By the time Octavianus marched on Alexandria, all but the few most inveterate supporters of Antonius had deserted him. Antonius and Cleopatra took their own lives. When the obstreperous Antyllus remained unflaggingly and outspokenly defiant, Octavianus decided he was dangerous and ordered him executed—along with Cleopatra's eldest son, whose paternity she had attributed to Caesar the Dictator. Antonius and Cleopatra had advanced the conceit, that Caesarion as they called him was more rightfully heir to the Dictator's position and power than the adopted Octavianus.

Tiberius was a prepubescent boy at the time these events were unfolding. He remembered his mother kneeling daily before the shrine to their household gods, praying for her husband's safety and success. When Tiberius tried to ask questions, he was told to mind his studies and not worry. Although victory seemed certain for Octavianus, there was always a possibility the tide of events could turn against him. Cleopatra was as merciless as she was seductive; and she had corrupted Antonius' scruples. He had helped her secure her own throne by murdering her siblings. The couple would hardly hesitate to apply the same treatment to anyone else they considered a threat. Livia was not about to disclose, to the young children of her household, the dire consequences awaiting them should Antonius and Cleopatra prevail in the conflict with Octavianus. His family would be the primary enemies of the new regime. All the adult members would surely be put to death, and the children saved only if they could somehow be exploited.

The suicide of Antonius left Octavianus without a constitutional equal or rival. He was supreme commander of all Roman armies. Every municipality in Italy, along with many provincial cities, had sworn an oath of loyalty to him. In all but name, he was a king.

Tiberius recalled his mother sinking onto a chair in weary relief, her eyes closed but streaming with tears, after the military messenger delivered the news of Alexandria's capitulation. He was filled with boyish pleasure and pride at his stepfather's achievement. Now in his twelfth year, Tiberius was beginning to grasp the implications of that feat for the Roman state and for his family. Over the next few years Octavianus would forge the constitutional system, which resolved the impasse between the critical need for single rulership and the traditional Roman opposition to monarchy. As for his family: they were no longer members of the Roman aristocracy. Now they were royalty.

As Tiberius and Nero his brother entered young manhood, they embarked upon public careers filled with privileges and advantages that could only arise from their stepfather's unique political position. Octavianus—now known as Caesar Augustus—orchestrated their advancement as carefully and forcefully as he had supervised their education. His agreement with the elder Tiberius

Nero was assiduously kept. Augustus had blood relatives who did not enjoy the degree of promotion he accorded his stepsons.

Together and separately, Tiberius and his brother officiated at religious festivals and produced public entertainments. The senate granted both the right to hold regular magistracies five years before reaching the requisite age, and to hold some special offices as well. As part of their legal training, Augustus assigned his stepsons the management of specially selected cases. These were of high profile to draw public notice to the trainees, and graduated in difficulty to develop their skill and comfort with the thorniest of litigations.

Advancement in military service was similarly rapid, intense, and publicized. After reaching his seventeenth year, Tiberius served for several years as a military tribune (squadron commander), a rank customarily exercised by youths of noble birth. The theater was Spain, where war was being waged to subdue bands of marauding natives. In his twenty-second year Tiberius exercised his first full command, which was predictably prestigious. He led an army to Armenia, where he installed a Roman loyalist on that nation's throne. This action proved a deterrent to Parthia, the hostile desert empire bordering Rome's easternmost dominions. During the previous thirty years, the Parthians had inflicted two devastating defeats on the armies of Rome. Now the Parthian king surrendered, to Tiberius, the legion standards captured during those humiliating incidents.

In the decade that followed, Tiberius' military activities were concentrated upon the empire's northern frontiers. For several years he shared command with his brother. Together they put a stop to the inroads, which the Germans had been making across the Rhine into Roman territory. Tiberius assisted his stepfather in restructuring the disorganized province of Gaul, and served there as military governor for a time. His brother succeeded him, and continued the military actions against the Germans. Meanwhile Tiberius moved eastward to suppress the belligerent Pannonians and Dalmatians, thereby establishing the Danube as the empire's northeastern frontier.

Tiberius confessed he was always more comfortable in a military setting than in civilian politics. In the armed forces, one was appreciated solely for his capabilities and accomplishments. No one cared about physical appearance or personal traits; or if he did, such opinions were disregarded or suppressed under military discipline. To succeed in statecraft, however, one had to be obsequious, persuasive, diplomatic, inscrutable, unconscionable, dogged, aggressive, evasive, hypocritical—and capable of concealing that all with charm and personability. These aptitudes came naturally to Augustus and to Tiberius' brother; but Tiberius lacked their gift.

For all his life he had been afflicted with shyness. Starting a conversation or responding to someone else's was always difficult. He tended to stammer as he groped for words, to stare at the ground to avoid eye contact, to fidget by drumming his fingers in the air. When he did manage to assert himself, he frequently did so more forcefully than he intended. Although after many years of practice he had managed to control these propensities to a large extent, he never became completely free of them. He was fond of seclusion, preferring to stand alone and apart rather than mingle with strangers or even at times with his own relatives. He was also loath to disclose information about his private life, and less inclined to express his feelings and opinions or to make any displays of emotion. Characteristics of his physique had heightened his self-consciousness. Through his growth years he was always taller than other youths his age. This engendered a tendency to stoop. There was his acne, of course, and his left-handedness. Nearsightedness caused him to squint at far distant objects, and to overlook or not perceive miniscule details in those perspectives.

While Tiberius' family understood his predispositions, the general public did not. His inability to express himself comfortably led some to regard him as indecisive and wavering, uncertain about his own judgments, unable to commit to an opinion or course of action. Others mistook his introversion for aloofness, petulance, arrogance, and condescension. Augustus frequently and testily took critics to task, assuring them Tiberius' mannerisms were merely unconscious habits and not evidence of conscious disdain. These explanations had little effect; and Tiberius continually endured an exaggerated reputation for being morose, diffident, scornful, and even malicious.

In my reply, I admitted to having noted his introversion during our days at the Academy. Drawing a parallel to his military experience, I described how at the Academy I was accepted for my intellect with little concern for my appearance or comportment. Then I told him about my alcove at home, how I would flee to its dingy seclusion for peace. In conclusion I wrote that a successful general, who had to make and rely upon split-second decisions, could hardly be indecisive by nature. How refreshing, he responded, to find someone apart from his relatives who understood and shared his fondness for detachment. And how special that a woman should have such insight about the peremptory responsibilities of military command.

There was one more widespread public assumption at which Tiberius chafed: the assumption he aspired to succeed to his stepfather's unique political position. Augustus had made clear very early on, that he wanted his newly devised office to devolve upon a member of his own bloodline in the event of his death or abdication. This was due in part to personal inclination, but more to the ingrained nepotism of Roman culture. Augustus was not sure his countrymen would accept a successor who was not genealogically related to him. Unfortunately he had no sons of his own. Much to his deep dismay, Livia had proven unable to bear him a child. The single baby that was conceived did not survive a premature birth.

Augustus had refused to divorce Livia in favor of someone more assuredly fertile, because he loved her, and because the Romans consider it the height of poor taste to repudiate one's wife for barrenness. Right after the fall of Alexandria, Augustus began to indicate his nephew Marcus Claudius Marcellus as successor to his unique political position. In the triumphal procession that celebrated Augustus' return to Rome, Tiberius rode the left trace horse of his stepfather's chariot. Marcellus, however, enjoyed the greater privilege of riding the right trace horse. When the senate voted Tiberius the privilege of holding public office five years before reaching the designated age, they granted Marcellus the right to do so ten years early. And two years later, while Tiberius was still serving as a military tribune in Spain, Marcellus received the hand of Augustus' daughter Julia in marriage.

Two more years passed, and then disaster struck. Having been in my fifth year at that time, I recall only vaguely the plague that ravaged Italy. Confined to the house, not allowed to go outside to play, I was not offered an explanation but only told I was being a naughty and disobedient girl for complaining. I did not realize people were literally collapsing in the streets. Tiberius suffered a mild case, as did several other members of his family; but Augustus became so ill he expected to die. Marcellus was far less fortunate, and succumbed to the malady. He was only six months Tiberius' senior.

Once the period of mourning for Marcellus was over, Augustus gave Julia in marriage to his confidante and advisor, Marcus Vipsanius Agrippa. The latter was merely a year younger than his new father-in-law. In the Roman ruling class, where marriages were arranged to cement political alignments, unions between spouses of far disparate ages were not uncommon. Augustus' brush with death alerted him to the need for someone with training and experience, who could step into the imperial office immediately if circumstances required. Even Marcellus had not been ready. When Augustus feared his end was near, he had handed his signet ring to Agrippa.

As the loss of Marcellus had deprived Augustus of a male heir, he hoped Julia would eradicate this problem by bearing her new husband a son. This is precisely what happened a year later. Not surprisingly the baby was called

Gaius after his grandfather. Julia proved quite satisfactorily fecund. A daughter Vipsania Julia was born after Gaius, and thereafter another son named Lucius. Augustus formally adopted both boys, thereby indicating Gaius as his intended successor, and Lucius as alternate should Gaius prove unable to fulfill his designated mission. By special decree of the senate, Agrippa was invested with powers that made the regency an official office of the state.

And so it had always been clear, right along, that Augustus never aspired to confer the succession upon either of his stepsons. Tiberius and Nero cared little about this, because they understood the rationale behind Augustus' desire for bloodline succession. Both were satisfied to be the especially privileged retainers and functionaries of his regime. This was particularly true for Tiberius, whose shyness made him recoil from the high level of public visibility the imperial office mandated. Nonetheless, people assumed Tiberius' quiet moodiness arose from jealousy of the designated successors and indicated he coveted their future for himself.

Strongly I sympathized. My mother and her aunt, I wrote, based evaluations of public figures—including Tiberius himself at times—on their appearance and mannerisms, their habits and tastes, and in particular on their gaffes and mistakes. Little consideration was given to personal achievements, contributions to society, or political agendas. Once again Tiberius responded he had found my comments refreshing. Throughout his life he had been warned that people were going to form preposterous opinions and cling to them unflinchingly, and this was simply an inevitable aspect of public life to be endured. Now he was pleased to find a purely private person, who had noted the same inanity and shared his distaste for it.

In the spring that followed his tour of duty in the East, Tiberius married Vipsania. He was in his twenty-third year, his bride in her eighteenth. The ceremony took place at Livia's country estate just outside Rome. The new union proved very happy, even though it had been arranged so many years earlier. Tiberius and Vipsania had learned to love each other. Having been betrothed for so long, neither had ever considered anyone else as a potential spouse. They did not have children immediately, because Vipsania did not reach full menarche for several years. She accompanied her husband on his junket to Gaul, and later to Aquileia in northeastern Italy, where his military headquarters for the Danube campaigns was located. Finally on the Nones of October *[10/7/14 BCE]*—hardly more than a month before Tiberius' twenty-eighth birthday—a little boy was born. By now they were back in Rome, where Tiberius would assume his first consulship the following January. Departing from the usual practice of giving a firstborn son the forename of his father, they named the baby Drusus Claudius Nero.

Promptly I ventured to ask Tiberius why he and his brother embraced the surname of Livia's father, especially after she had ceased to apply its feminine diminutive—Drusilla—to herself.

The explanation was long, complex and convoluted; and it gave me considerable food for thought.

Livia had a kinsman by adoption named Marcus Livius Drusus Libo. He was the adopted son of Lucius Livius Drusus, a nephew of Livia's adoptive grandfather. Drusus Libo's natural father, Marcus Scribonius Libo, was first cousin to Augustus' former wife Scribonia and her brother Lucius Scribonius Libo. The sister of Marcus Scribonius Libo had been Livia's father's first wife. She had died of complications from a miscarriage.

By his willing surrender of Livia to Augustus—then still Caesar Octavianus—Tiberius Claudius Nero had demonstrated his decision, if not to support the Triumvirate then at least to abandon his active opposition. Lucius Scribonius Libo proceeded publicly to scorn Nero as something less than a man, unworthy of his rank and a disgrace to his aristocratic ancestry—a flaccid lackey to his former wife and her new husband, whose tryst Nero should have resisted and avenged. This denunciation prompted Tiberius Nero to denounce Lucius Libo with breach of amicitia—absolute estrangement political and personal, without hope of reconciliation, for an offense unforgiveable.

Although he remained an active member of the senate for another twenty-five years, Lucius Scribonius Libo never reconciled himself to the Triumvirate or to Augustus' regime. His namesake son, along with Marcus Livius Drusus Libo, joined the senate at about the time Tiberius entered public life. These younger Libones remained conspicuously ambivalent to the Augustan system—not outrightly hostile, but not openly supportive either. Neither showed any interest in serving within the newly developed imperial administration, even though Augustus would have rewarded them with prestigious and powerful positions in return for their adherence. Owing to the breach of amicitia between their respective fathers, the younger Lucius Scribonius Libo remained unflaggingly hostile to Tiberius and his brother Decimus.

Tiberius and Decimus and Augustus with them feared this enmity would breed insinuations the Libones, being at once aligned to the Drusi and demonstratively resistant to Augustus' system, were following the political intentions of Livia's father while his natural grandsons were defying those very aspirations. Accordingly with financial assistance from his mother and stepfather, Tiberius produced a lavish set of games and stage plays in honor of his father and maternal grandfather. Already I knew that upon coming of age, Decimus Claudius Nero assumed the designation Nero Claudius Drusus. (The transition had actually been easy: Decimus had never cared for his forename, and as a child had insisted upon being called Nero.) While Vipsania was pregnant, Tiberius learned the younger Lucius Scribonius Libo—married to his cousin the daughter of Sextus Pompeius—had named his newborn son Lucius Scribonius Libo Drusus. That was the reason, when Tiberius' first son was born only four days later, he received the name Drusus Claudius Nero. Livia never returned to using her surname Drusilla, because Antonius had once derided it, but more urgently because she now wanted the public to recognize her first and foremost as Livia Caesaris—Caesar Augustus' wife. She nevertheless endorsed the use of Drusilla as a name for female descendants she might have.

And so I discovered that I had something else in common with at least some members of the most powerful family in the world. Our identities were being ripped from us: mine by an enforced change of name, theirs through misrepresentation by political opponents. Our intentions and motives were being falsified. My family routinely accused and punished me for sinister aspirations I would never dream of harboring. Livia and her sons faced falsification of their devotion to their personal heritage. Respect for ancestry is as deeply rooted in Italian culture as it is in Greek, if not more so. Abuse of it is considered reprehensible—a crime against humanity.

I berated myself for taking a bit of comfort, from realizing I was not the only one seething over and fighting against defamation of character. Maybe my family was right in their assessment of me after all. What kind of evil person would take solace from another's distress?

My correspondent suggested I stop being so harsh on myself.

In his twenty-ninth year, Tiberius assumed the office of consul (chief executive). For a season, everything seemed golden. If not popular as a politician, Tiberius was at least renowned and respected for his military exploits. He was happily married with a new son. But in the year that followed, things began to unravel. Agrippa died suddenly. He was only in his fifty-first year. Julia, now in her twenty-seventh year, was expecting their fifth child. While waiting for her to come to term, Augustus considered a host of candidates, one of whom he would ask to become her new husband. With that marriage, of course, would come the regency for Gaius and Lucius. After nearly a year of deliberation, the emperor's choice fell upon Tiberius.

The decision was agonizing for everyone involved. Augustus acknowledged he had no authority to force Tiberius and Julia to wed. Both were legally self-determinate, free of any type of guardianship: each was entitled to refuse the other. Vipsania was once again pregnant; and her condition increased Tiberius' reluctance to leave her. She nevertheless reassured him of her willingness to support any decision he made, even if that meant the end of their marriage. Vipsania was much like her father Agrippa: reserved, dutiful, and compliant.

Tiberius and Julia had always shared a certain fondness. Having grown up together, they knew what to expect in one another. More recently, Julia had become strongly attracted to Tiberius. He had deemed it inappropriate for her to consider him while she was married to Agrippa. Under the present circumstances, however, he felt her affection offered the prospect of a congenial union. In the end, family loyalty prevailed. Having grown up under Augustus' iron tutelage, Julia and Tiberius found they could not resist him.

The wedding took place at Rome during the Saturnalia—on the winter solstice, twelve days before the Calends of January *[December 21]*. On that following Calends—the day on which the newly elected magistrates took office—the senate had formally invested Tiberius with the regency for his new stepsons. Vipsania had miscarried; and while Tiberius grieved for their loss, he had to admit it helped him relinquish their relationship. His new marriage did, in fact, work well for a time. Julia had a perceptive and analytical mind. With her brilliant education and clever wit, she was a stimulating and incisive conversationalist. Graceful and poised, lighthearted and cheerful, she made a truly pleasant companion.

Leaning upon her mother's family, Julia managed to acquire for herself and her new husband the elegant mansion which had been the ancestral home of the inimitable Gnaeus Pompeius Magnus—the former opponent of Caesar the Dictator and father of Sextus Pompeius. (The latter's father-in-law was Julia's maternal uncle.) Julia was a caring and supportive mother, not only to her own children but to Tiberius' son Drusus as well. After three months of marriage, it was clear Julia was going to bear her new husband a child. Augustus and Livia were eminently pleased, and quite understandably. They had been unable to have children of their own; but now they were to share a grandchild.

Tiberius' second and namesake son was born at Aquileia, after revolt among the Dalmatians had necessitated his return to the region. The birth was premature, the baby weak and puny. He lived little more than a month. After his death, Julia seemed inconsolable. Tiberius endeavored to reassure her: they could certainly try for another child. Nero and Antonia had had many

53

children, only two of whom were still living. They were expecting yet another at this very time. When he proved to be a boy, they named him Tiberius in honor of their deceased nephew. Julia nevertheless remained despondent. Finally she asked Tiberius to let her return to Rome before the conclusion of his campaign, insisting the death of their son made her long for the company of her living children. When he arrived home several months later, Tiberius found her very much like her old self; however there was now a restiveness about her.

Julia started to flaunt the fact she was the mother of Gaius, who was indicated to be the next emperor. This assertion blatantly insulted her father and stepmother, pointing up their failure to meet Roman cultural expectations regarding children. Livia was barren in her marriage to Augustus, and he in consequence had no son of his own body. When Augustus rebuked Julia for the embarrassment she was creating, she responded that nothing she said or did could alter the truth. Presently he turned the tables on her, by arranging for the newly completed Altar of Augustan Peace to be dedicated on Livia's birthday. Julia had been particularly proud the ceremony, consecrating the land on which the altar was constructed, had taken place on her own birthday five years earlier.

Julia was undeterred in her defiance. She connected herself with a firm but disorganized resistance to a significant element of her father's regime. Rome's subjugation of the Mediterranean had resulted in a monopoly on trade, which had brought unprecedented prosperity to many Roman families. This, in turn, had encouraged a devotion to indolence and profligacy at the expense of traditional family life. The birth rate of the Roman citizenry had fallen into sharp decline, as its members rejected marriage and childrearing in favor of sensual pursuits. Why spend money on children when there were so many physical pleasures available for purchase? Why tie yourself to a single boring spouse, rather than enjoy the freedom to lie with anyone who caught your fancy?

About a decade earlier, Augustus had endeavored to address this moral lassitude through legislation. The statutes criminalized adultery, abortion, homosexual liaisons, and the intercourse of a married male citizen with any freeborn Roman woman other than a licensed prostitute. Another set of laws imposed financial disabilities upon the unmarried and childless, conversely provided incentives for families with numerous children, and regulated expenditures on luxury goods and pursuits. A fair number of Romans felt these requirements infringed a far more basic human right: that of personal self-determination. For many years this opposition had received little notice, while public attention focused upon the frontier wars in Gaul and Pannonia. But as these conflicts were winding down, awareness of local matters was increasing.

And now with Julia among its ranks, the opposition party became organized and visible.

Julia began to behave as Tiberius had depicted her to me at the Academy, while I was still ignorant of their true identities. She wore racy and extravagantly expensive clothes, attended parties and cultural activities in the company of friends instead of family, and maintained a high degree of independence from her father and husband. Whenever Augustus reprimanded her she returned a flippant and evasive retort. Tiberius never quite knew what to expect. She could be tenderly solicitous and erotic one day, scornful and insolent the next, indifferent and ambivalent thereafter. Was she unfaithful to him? He had no firm evidence and hoped none would surface. He cringed in anticipation of the stupid curiosity, the gossip, the snickering and speculations, which a discovery of this nature must surely produce.

To her credit, Tiberius wrote, Julia put a stop to her posturing and became strongly supportive of her family when his brother died. At the funeral that September she stood with lowered eyes, gently holding her cousin Antonia's hand while the latter sobbed uncontrollably. Through the ensuing winter Julia was respectfully quiet at home, patient and sympathetic with everyone's grief. Tiberius wondered if this tragedy had put an end to her rebelliousness, even as the loss of their son had seemed to engender it. In the spring he accompanied his stepfather back to Gaul. Livia the ever-avid traveler joined them; Julia, however, did not. She insisted her children as well as little Drusus needed her maternal care far more than her husband and father required her company. While Augustus engaged some German tribal leaders in diplomacy, Tiberius ran raids against others. In the end the Germans capitulated, leaving the new frontier province of Germania intact and in a state of submission.

The senate voted Tiberius the honor of a triumph—the special military parade that celebrated the return of a general after the successful conclusion of a war. One tradition associated with this distinction is that its recipient must remain outside the pomerium—the sacred boundary of the city of Rome—until the actual event. This necessity is what brought Tiberius to our Academy. As the date for his triumph had been set for the Calends of January, he had several months in which to absent himself from Rome. He decided to spend this time relaxing at the little villa he owned in Baia. When the time for his triumph became imminent, Tiberius would make ready at his mother's estate on the outskirts of Rome. Julia had declined his invitation to join him at either locale.

In one of his very earliest letters, Tiberius had asked if I were planning to visit Rome to witness his triumph. An honor of this type was a major public celebration. There were going to be feasts and games and street entertainments and other forms of merriment, promising an exhilarating time for all.

In return I wrote that I had never been to Rome and never expected to get there, much as I longed to see the empire's capital. We never traveled anywhere, except to our miserable little villa. The rationale centered upon the usual convoluted logic punctuated with the usual nastiness. *Rome is for the Romans—we are Greek. Ever since you took up with that oddball soldier, you have been fixated on his people. Why are you not content with your own heritage? Those Romans you adore ravaged the proud country of Greece and reduced her to one of their provinces. They pilfered her national art treasures to decorate their capital which you are so eager to see!* I was tempted to point out the weakness and corruption of the Greek government had enabled the Roman conquest; that the Romans so ardently admired and imitated Hellenic culture they had adopted Greek as a second language; that most of the Greek artworks adorning Italian cities were copies of originals still in the motherland. But being tired, and knowing only too well that my comments would be rebuffed and disdained as distorted and naïve, I merely withdrew to my alcove and poured my frustrations into my *lesson plan*.

Patience, Tiberius counseled, patience. Someday the right time would arrive, for him to escort me to Rome as his special guest. He would have preferred to forgo the entire business of his triumph anyway, and slip back into the city incognito. His shyness made him uncomfortable with large gatherings of any type. Being the focus of a crowd's attention was all the more grueling.

By now I had become a bona fide sophista—thoroughly versed in knowledge, and able to interpret what I knew into educated conclusions and judgments. I delivered my own lectures, wrote treatises, and led small study groups in discussions of advanced topics. Presently I gained some fame in academic circles, albeit this renown was limited because I was a newcomer. Nevertheless some scholars came to respect my ideas and theories, considering them all the more remarkable because they emanated from a woman.

For a time I hoped the recognition of fellow academicians would pacify my family and promote reconciliation between us. Maybe now they would feel satisfied I had lived up to their expectations. Maybe now that I had some renown they would let me use my real name again, since I was now living up to its alternate meaning of distinguished. None of these aspirations materialized. No accolade or distinction from fellow academicians was sufficient. Nor were the royalties I received from the publications of my writings. Were I less lazy, more diligent about applying myself to my scholarly efforts, then perhaps I would cease to produce substandard work. When I demanded a precise definition of that standard, my mother responded with the derisive laugh she invariably gave when she had no answer for me. The notion of restoring my true name was dismissed as an indication of incipient insanity. And yet I dutifully tried to do better, tried to work harder, tried in vain to please.

The departure of my companion had made life at the Academy all the more empty and soulless. I was nothing more than an accomplished artisan, executing my craft with skill and precision but deriving little inspiration or satisfaction from it. My entire life to this juncture I had spent in preparation to become an academician. Now I found this role dissatisfying and emotionally sterile. It did not please my family, as they had promised me repeatedly that it would; and it most certainly did not express my true selfhood. What disposition did? Would I ever find out?

Tiberius, who served his second consulship that year, felt similarly mired in the turgid minutiae of government administration. In the summer, growing unrest among the Germans brought him back to that arena. We were at our villa when the messenger arrived with a parcel. It contained a shawl, woven of thick brown wool interspersed with dashes of white. In the very center was a design: a silhouette in white of two stags rearing toward one another. The texture of the cloth, the tension between the warp and woof, the intensity of the colors and way they caught the light, were different from any I had ever seen before. He had remembered my fascination with textiles, and sent me something unique to the area of his military operations.

Predictably as ever, my mother and great-aunt pronounced the shawl ugly. And was he mad, sending a gift of such fabric during the heat of summer? After I retorted that it was obviously intended for the colder seasons, they forbade me to wear it anywhere outside my room once we returned to Naples. I must certainly not sport it at the Academy, as there it would surely draw the wrong sort of attention. Aside from detracting from my appearance, it flaunted the incurable brazenness I had displayed in accepting a gift from a man.

Well: with the onset of cooler weather, wear the shawl at the Academy was precisely what I did. My father never reported the offense. By now he was so indifferent to me, he would not have cared if I showed up naked so long as my doing so had no direct effect upon him. My shawl did attract attention, and not the type Anthe and Euethia would have liked to have seen humiliate me. A larger number of women was frequenting the Academy, drawn by my reputation as a sophista. They were escorted by husbands or brothers or sons or other male relatives, to hear my lectures and to ask questions. One was a hetaera, who came in the company of her lover. Some were genuinely interested in the subject matter I offered, while others were simply curious to meet one of their own sex whose academic stature was considered an anomaly.

The women bombarded me with questions. Yes there were the ones specifically about the shawl, the answers to which required some dissembling. *Where is it from? __ Germania. __ Amazing! How did you acquire it? __ From a friend whose fiancé is in military service there,* I would lie. *__ How is it made; may I touch it? __ Certainly! __ Did your friend's fiancé serve under the command of Tiberius Nero this past summer? __ Indeed he did!*

Then there were the understandable questions about me—far more painful to answer than the ones for my shawl. *How does it feel to be a woman and yet to be so educated? __ I cannot tell. Never having been a man or an uneducated woman, I have no basis for comparison. __ How did you manage to acquire so much knowledge? __ Persistence, dogged persistence. __ Do you engage in feminine activities? Do you spin and weave? __ Yes,* I would lie so I did not have to explain the preposterous rationale for which I was forbidden these activities. *Sew? __ Yes. __ Cook? __ Yes. __ Do you enjoy those? __ Sometimes I do, sometimes not. __ Do you regret not being married? __ Occasionally.* (An evasion: I was not about to disclose how truly embittered I was about my spinsterhood.) *Why did you pursue advanced education instead of marriage? __ I am incapable of bearing children.* This last response usually wrought sufficient discomfiture upon my questioners to put a stop to their inquiries.

On returning to Rome that autumn, Tiberius discovered Julia had resumed her defiance with greater intensity. Her resistance, originally directed at her father and stepmother, now targeted her husband as well. She endeavored to build tension between him and Augustus by insinuating Tiberius approved her fast lifestyle. One day, after Augustus had reprimanded her for yet once again dressing like a siren, she appeared before him in a plain garment with her hair arranged very simply. On this day, she announced, she had dressed for her father, but on the previous (i.e. in her risqué costume) for her husband. When Tiberius tried pleading with Julia to stop, she ordered him to remember whose daughter she was. He responded that the man whose daughter she was shared his distaste for her conduct. She shrugged off his retort with the assertion that while Augustus may forget he was Caesar, she would never forget she was Caesar's daughter.

In mid-September I sent condolences for the anniversary of Tiberius' brother's death, which had occurred eighteen days before the Calends of October *[September 14, 9 BCE]*. The somewhat stiff reply grieved me significantly. While appreciative of my intention he preferred I refrain from offering such sentiments, as they only served to intensify the sharp memories of the sad event. In my effusively apologetic response, I explained how Euethia and my mother persistently maintained I was insensitive to the woes and bereavements of others—most often after I had failed to notice, on account of its triviality, some besetment my brother had suffered. *No need for groveling and self-recrimination,* he answered. Now aware of his preference, I would honor it down the future; and I must stop being so harsh on myself. But harsh on myself I continued to be—not because of this incident per se, but because I had made so much of it when Tiberius was enduring difficulties far more severe.

Julia's friends and adherents had begun to scorn Tiberius openly, with disdainful stares and snickers and derogatory asides that burgeoned and spread as rumors. One of these was that Julia felt marriage to Tiberius was beneath her dignity and social status. This particular insult—coming from a woman whose father was of landed gentry background and patrician only by adoption—was particularly hurtful. Tiberius was deeply, perhaps even inordinately, proud of his uniquely Claudian heritage, since from this long and exceptionally noble ancestry he descended through both parents. Julia's rebuff, he suspected, arose from the hostility of her mother's family, the Scribonii Libones.

Tiberius tried the more forceful approach, of asserting his legal and cultural prerogative as Julia's husband to demand she put a stop to the innuendo. That set off a firestorm of degradation. What kind of a man was he, if he could not tolerate the fact some people disagreed with his opinions and attitudes? Her father had reassured him there would always be those who disapproved: this was a fact of life for their family; Tiberius should feel content when people expressed their hostility verbally without actually inflicting physical harm. Had that counsel eluded him? She was embarrassed to have such a spineless sap for a spouse. Maybe if he were a little less austere, a little less haughty, a little more outgoing, he would be more popular.

Following that argument a rumor began to spread, maintaining Tiberius was pining for his first wife Vipsania. The story went that after encountering her by chance, he had followed her through the streets of Rome with tears in his eyes. Tiberius chafed at this insinuation. Having always been loath to display his emotions in public, he resented having such a behavior ascribed to him. He certainly did see Vipsania from time to time. She was remarried to a young senator named Gaius Asinius Gallus, to whom she had already borne two children. Tiberius did miss her, especially now that his marriage to Julia was strained; but he never considered making any effort to rekindle Vipsania's affections. He contented himself with the memory of their years together.

Yet another rumor began to circulate. Tiberius was fond of fine wine, and able to consume large quantities without becoming intoxicated or ill. Some of the military officers under his command had expressed their admiration for his capacity, by giving him the nickname of Biberius Caldius Mero (from the Latin words bibendum—inclined to drink; caldus—heated, from the practice of warming some wines to enhance their flavors and intoxicating qualities; mero—the term for wine undiluted with water, presumably consumed only by the intemperate). Allegations were spreading that Tiberius' natural temperance was all a sham; that privately he was an inveterate drunkard, and secured political favors for men whose winebibbing habits he esteemed.

Perhaps what concerned Tiberius most, was the growing hostility of Julia's sons toward him. Lucius in his eleventh year was merely an insolent brat; but Gaius in his fourteenth was becoming very much aware of political agendas. Still too young and inexperienced to develop one of his own, he embraced that of his mother and her adherents without examining its validity or potential consequences. Gaius was also becoming the target of flatterers and sycophants, who hoped to gain political advancement or other benefits through his influence, whether now or after he grew older.

From these notions, Gaius derived a sense he was entitled to more independence than he was being allowed. Like many youths his age, Gaius fancied he had a grasp on everything there was to know about life, and his elders were out of touch with reality. Augustus with his morality program was stodgy and unrealistically strict. Julia and her hedonistic friends were so pleasantly plausible, they surely had to be right about everything. Tiberius as regent was a distasteful and unnecessary restraint. Gaius was offended when, at the annual rotation of magistrates the next January, Augustus had the senate renew Tiberius' regency for another five years. The young crown prince began to embellish the already prevalent rumor, which maintained Tiberius' reticence signified he aspired to procure the succession for himself. Surely Tiberius was secretive because he was plotting to persuade Augustus he was far better qualified than Gaius to be the next emperor—or perhaps worse yet to have Gaius murdered.

Tiberius began to fear for his very life, more deeply than he ever had while on the field of war. He was not concerned about his family, being perfectly confident Augustus and Livia and even Julia understood he harbored no intention of challenging Augustus' chosen successors. Nor did Tiberius particularly fear or resent Gaius who was simply young and gullible. As he matured, Gaius could be persuaded to change his opinion of Tiberius; and at present he had no authority to authorize any type of harmful action. What truly worried Tiberius was the prospect of falling victim to the dagger of some toady, hoping to ingratiate himself to Gaius by dispatching the presumed rival. Almost as serious was the possibility of permanent ruin to his political and personal reputation, should detractors succeed in representing him as a genuine rival to Gaius and hence a parricide: an enemy of his own family. Tiberius became increasingly conscious of people who whispered to one another while casting furtive glances at him, and then approached him with clearly affected cordiality. Was he being plotted against? Or had he become so sensitized, he was noticing ordinary behaviors which he had previously overlooked?

Tiberius discussed the matter with his stepfather, reiterating he harbored no designs upon the succession. Augustus doubled the size of Tiberius' bodyguard. He scolded Gaius and then endeavored to pacify him, with investiture in a priesthood and the right to attend proceedings of the senate. But as the ambivalence and hostility of Julia and her adherents persisted, Tiberius took little comfort from his stepfather's interventions. Augustus was neither omniscient nor omnipotent. There were limits to the protection he could offer.

And to think I had spent my life fretting over enforced spinsterhood, over incessant verbal but relatively rare physical abuse, over a peremptory change of name that was emotionally but not physically harmful. How paltry my issues now seemed, as I sat in my alcove assessing Tiberius' situation. I had always believed—and not without a hint of jealousy—that rank, wealth, and privilege offered a cushion of reassurance in the face of those personal crises ordinary mortals must face without any form of consolation. Now I saw through this illusion. Tiberius was fragile with apprehension and anxiety; his prospects seemed to be worsening daily; no solution seemed in sight. Where was that Fundamental Good? Was it all an illusion too; or were we somehow missing it, stumbling and groping like the blind?

That summer at our so-called villa, my concern for my correspondent numbed me to the usual nonsense from my family. I cleaned the house and sewed and prepared meals, fished in the pond, considered subjects for the lectures I would give at the Academy come the fall, and wrote out my *lesson plans* in anticipation of the messenger's arrivals—all in a state of unemotional detachment worthy of the most hardened Cynic.

"Why are you moping now?" my mother demanded. "Have you fallen in love with that weird Roman soldier?"

At last I responded to this now well-worn cliché. "Yes, I have; and if he comes to take me away, I shall most certainly go with him!"

Much to my surprise my mother neither reprimanded me nor brought the subject up again.

On my birthday I sat stone-faced through the routine celebration (we had better pastries this time), and received a firm rebuke for my indifference to the effort and money that had been expended on me. At this point I decided to apologize and concoct an explanation for my moodiness before being pressed to do so, as I could hardly disclose the real reason. Accordingly I confessed to not feeling well because I was beginning to menstruate—for only the second time all year, I emphasized. That I was menstruating was true. That felt ill was a lie: discomfort from my condition was present but minimal. As I hoped, nobody wanted to pursue the matter any further. After a disparaging comment about the poor taste I had displayed in disclosing the details of my bodily function, I was left alone with my preoccupation—to my immense relief.

I went outside to sit in the open air beneath the tree beside the house, taking with me the letter that the messenger delivered earlier that day. Precisely two years had elapsed since the meteors had appeared to us both, on that birthday just before I made Tiberius' acquaintance at the Academy. Our association had honored, thrilled, enriched, and steadied me. Tiberius had helped me gain more perspective, more objectivity, about my relationship with my family than all the philosophical tracts I had ever read and pondered. I felt sure that, had it not been for his influence, by now I might have succumbed to the insanity or suicide I had anticipated for so long.

In my last correspondence I had poured out my gratitude, together with my abject concern for Tiberius' personal safety and peace of mind. His present condition was far more perilous than mine had ever been; yet I could do no more than sympathize and philosophize and commiserate. I felt so frustrated, so incapable of offering any kind of concrete directive or assistance. In the letter before me now, Tiberius thanked me for my compassion. It gave him great spiritual strength, he wrote, in these dark times. He had absolutely no doubt his family cared about his security and wellbeing, and would take whatever steps they could to protect it; but he also found a special reassurance in my consideration.

He continued that he had consulted an astrologer, and had had my horoscope read along with his own. Both revealed increasing distress in the present and immediate future, to be followed by a long period of mitigation. At some point during that easement, each of us would experience monumental change in the directions our lives were taking. He pondered the findings. Without question we were enduring present distress; and it appeared things were going to get worse before they improved. But what was meant by mitigation and monumental change? Were we destined soon to die (the monumental change), and find release (the mitigation) from our troubles through extinction? A flawed conclusion, since it reversed the order of events as the astrologer had given them. Did the prophecy instead point to the future worth waiting for—the ideal I had conceived on the night of the meteor? Speculation is pointless, and will only increase our anxiety. There is nothing to do but wait out the course of events.

The night of the meteor. How uncanny I was reading this on the very anniversary of that occasion. But something even more extraordinary had caught my attention. The predictions of two horoscopes were identical. What did that imply?

That night the powerful Sirocco winds began to blow from the South.

September arrived; and the term at the Academy began uneventfully. Change nevertheless came before the month had passed, in the person of a new student named Lucius Norenas.

He was of Etruscan ancestry, and rich—the scion of a truck farmer with vast landholdings in southern Italy and North Africa. His family had houses and villas throughout Calabria and Campania, including one in Naples. Their chief residence was in Pompeii. When Lucius enrolled his father Publius presented the Academy with an immense endowment, on the condition the school be named in their honor. Entirely predictably, the governing body hastened to comply.

Lucius was in his eighteenth year and a virtual Adonis—delicately boned with creamy skin, fair wavy hair, and limpid green eyes. These physical differences put aside, he was an exact copy of my brother—inane, indulged, and idiotic. There was little wonder his father had hastened to remunerate the Academy so generously: without that inducement the institution would probably have insisted Lucius withdraw. I tutored him a few times, but after finding him so frustratingly poor a student advised I was no longer available to assist him. Our brief contact, however, proved to be all he needed. Although I was nearly five years his senior, he became utterly infatuated with me.

His doting daddy, who had never refused him anything, hastened to approach my father. My lack of dowry was no deterrent: all that mattered was that his baby boy should possess his darling. To prove his sincerity, my prospective father-in-law showered us with material benefits. Within days of his first contact with my father, everyone had a new wardrobe. Our house in Naples was suddenly filled with new furniture. Plans were discussed to renovate and enlarge the little Campanian villa-hovel. We also acquired two servants, both women. They served little purpose because few tasks were assigned to them. Euethia and my mother performed—and complained about—essentially the same complement of chores as before. Nor was I allowed any relief from the household responsibilities with which I was charged. With virtually nothing to do, the two serving women got underfoot and in the way. They gossiped and snickered about the unbalanced distribution of work, and their privileged position as status symbols. To accommodate them I had to abandon my alcove and start sharing my former bedroom with Euethia, whose ear-shattering snores reverberated off the walls. Whatever happened to the argument, that the presence of servants compromised privacy?

My aspiring father-in-law offered yet another inducement. My new husband and I would not live in Pompeii but in Naples, where a house would be purchased or built especially for us. While I continued to pursue my scholarly activities at the Academy, my husband would continue his studies; and our close association with my family (i.e., their continued domination) would be preserved.

Euethia and my mother were euphoric. Their control over me would not be compromised; and they could now extend it to my new partner. My father had no choice but to offer my hand.

My fiancé became an embarrassment for me at the newly designated Academia Norenas. Mornings found him hanging about the main gate, awaiting my arrival. He followed me throughout the day, carrying my belongings and staring at me in rapture with his mouth slightly agape, like the stock character of the lovelorn fool in Atellan farce *[a satirizing theatrical genre analogous to Punch and Judy but with live actors]*. The only way I could escape him was to give or attend lectures and discussions about subjects too difficult for him to comprehend. But whenever a session ended there he would be, waiting for me by the door like a faithful puppy. Every noon and evening he accompanied my father and me to our home. After lunch or supper he would retire with me to the garden, or to a dayroom if the weather were foul.

At first I tried to engage him in conversations that carried a modicum of intelligence, but very quickly found these efforts a waste. He would just gaze at me with his unchanging look of yearning, hanging on every word I uttered without comprehending any; or he would interrupt to tell me I was lovely or had beautiful eyes or that he could hardly wait until we were married; or he would read aloud some disgustingly saccharine poetry he had composed about me, the likes of which would have prompted any grammarian to issue a poor mark to a schoolboy. I began just to sit reading or writing and ignoring him, until it was time to return to the Academy for the afternoon session or until it got dark and he had to go home, and I was left wondering whether suicide might indeed be a better option.

As much as I disliked my fiancé, I loathed his father all the more. Not content with the already sizable business he had inherited, he had enlarged it aggressively through shady transactions perpetrated during the confusion of the civil wars. These had enabled him to procure the properties of others through foreclosure or other pretexts. Eventually—and much to my unexpressed satisfaction—he had lost a moderate portion of his holdings when Augustus as Caesar Octavianus enacted a comprehensive series of land seizures. The confiscated lands were redistributed with careful equity, providing pensions for veterans and compensations for people who had been swindled. The resulting resurgence of small farms increased economic competition in the marketplace, and forced food prices to drop.

Some years later my would-be father-in-law was cited for maintaining substandard living conditions, and for impressing free but indigent citizens into his slave workhouses. Ironically, Tiberius had served as one of the inspectors: this was one of the special political positions Augustus had assigned him as part of his training in statecraft. Norenas was required to pay an expensive fine, and to make immediate improvements at his own expense. To ensure his continued compliance, his workhouses were made subject to unannounced inspections by the regulatory commission.

Needless to say, the head of our government was not precisely Publius Norenas' favorite person. "This Caesar Augustus is going to deprive us of every human freedom there is," he bellowed one evening, pounding his fist on our dining table as I was clearing the remnants of supper. "We cannot spend our own money as we see fit. And who is he to regulate our personal relationships, or dictate the number of children we must have? Especially he, who stole another man's wife! How many brats has he begotten on her?" So my prospective father-in-law decried the moralizing legislation the emperor had enacted a decade earlier. My mother hung on every word, delighted to find someone who shared her contempt for the imperial family. I ventured to suggest the laws might not be arbitrary despotism, but have a rationale behind them. Then I added that some people simply cannot have children no matter how hard they try. "How can you be so educated and yet be so naïve?" came the predictable response.

When a Greek father accepts a bridegroom for his daughter, she has no choice about the matter. But it is also presumed the truly responsible father exercises great care to ensure the son-in-law he selects comes from a good family, and is prepared to take proper care of his new wife and promote her happiness. I had been sold to a mountebank, to satisfy the rapture of a child in a youth's body and my own family's lust for extravagant living.

"Why do you sulk once again?" my mother scolded. "A bride-to-be should be joyous. Behold all his people have done for the Academy and for us, even before you are married. True to expectation you are not the least bit grateful." The usual assault had adopted a new theme. The horoscope was being fulfilled, I wrote Tiberius. Things had indeed gone from bad to worse, just as the astrologer had predicted. I wondered what forms the mitigation and monumental change would take.

It was now early October, and the Sirocco had not abated. The air was oppressively warm and dusty and the constant wind irritating, making everybody slightly sick or slightly irritable or both. One morning a few days after sending my letter I delivered a lecture on Atomism, a doctrine which made little sense to me. Afterward I was gathering my notes and dreading the inevitable encounter with my fiancé outside the lecture hall, when a slim young man approached me. Having never seen him before, I assumed he was a new enrollee. He carried several wax tablets, the type students often use for recording lecture notes. During my talk, he said, he had jotted down some notions about my subject. Would I quickly review these, he asked as he offered me a tablet, and inform him whether I felt they made sense?

When I opened the tablet, I did not find musings on a philosophy, but a terse note in Tiberius' own hand:

> I am preparing to depart for the island of Rhodes, with the intention of remaining there indefinitely. Will you accompany me? Advise the bearer of this message and follow his instructions.
>
> Clytia, I love you. I seek not a casual tryst, but a firm and permanent commitment. Please do not come unless you feel likewise.

With a greater certainty than I had ever felt in my life, I knew how I must respond.

I returned the tablet to the messenger, who promptly rubbed the wax to remove the letter. As he did, I said in the most casual tone I could manage, "My answer to your query is an unqualified *Yes*."

"Thank you," he replied with seemingly equal nonchalance. Handing me a different tablet, he said "I think, then, you will agree with this premise also." The second message read,

> You will receive further instructions within the next few days. Be prepared to leave on a moment's notice, and not to take anything with you. In the meanwhile, carry out your usual activities.

I nodded; and the youth erased this tablet as well.

During those next few and endless days, at the Academy and at home I immersed myself in my books to disguise my anticipation. When my mother demanded an explanation for my quietude, I managed successfully to blame it on the Sirocco. At length my elopement commenced, and from the most unlikely of places. It was midmorning, five days before the Ides of October *[10/11]*. After I had led an early morning study group at the Academy, a call of nature drew me to the women's privy. As I started to leave, I heard someone softly call, "Clytia!" My real name. On turning I perceived a palla-clad figure in the shadows. Phoebe. What better hiding place? Sooner or later I must visit this site.

She drew me back beside her against the wall. "Say nothing," she said in a tense whisper. "Remove your himation." From a satchel she withdrew a palla, which she wrapped about my body and head. Then she stuffed the himation into the satchel. "We must leave no trace." She peered out the doorway and withdrew. After a few moments she again peered out and withdrew. The next time she looked, she gave a slight toss to her head. "Come," she said. "Keep your head and face covered and walk as unhurriedly as you can manage. If you can, change the appearance of your gait a bit."

The head toss was a signal; for as if out of nowhere two men joined us. One was the youth who had delivered Tiberius' original message to me several days before. The other was an older man with graying hair; he was wrapped in a toga. As we sauntered toward a side gate to the grounds, I perceived the effectiveness of our disguise. We appeared for all the world to be a typical Roman family on an excursion to the Academy—to visit a student perhaps, or to consider enrolling one. With a twinge of amusement I noted my father and fiancé, impatiently awaiting me outside the entrance to the main building. Into my walk I took care to put an uncharacteristic steadiness (I had always tended to bounce a bit), and understood the reason Phoebe had urged me to change my gait. That way I could not be recognized from the manner in which I carried myself.

After leaving the Academy campus we crossed two streets and turned a corner. A carriage was waiting. It was larger than the one that had transported Phoebe and me two years earlier, and civilian rather than military. Once we were underway, Phoebe made introductions. "These are my husband Menon and my son Alexias. We are en route to Miseno. There is less chance you will be noticed there than at the harbor in Naples." The driver urged the horses through the narrow city streets at as fast a pace as could be maintained, without toppling the carriage or running over a pedestrian. Once we reached the open road outside the city, he broke the team into full gallop. We reached our destination within an hour.

Lying on a promontory west of Naples, Miseno is one of two ports at which Augustus had established headquarters for the Roman fleet. (The other is Ravenna in northeastern Italy.) A liburna warship was being outfitted in one of the docks. Beside her lay a monotreme: a type of light, swift vessel most frequently used for the transport of government officials. I assumed this ship was our destination, until I noted the diminutive merchant vessel at anchor in the harbor. Tiberius must be traveling as a private citizen, and not a magistrate in office. How true to his ethics. He would not consider exploiting the entitlements of a public position to fulfill a personal agenda. Although he could have utilized the military post system for delivery of our *lesson plans*, he had always sent them with hired messengers or members of his household staff.

My assumption proved correct. Our carriage drew up to a dock at which a launch was tied. As we alighted the crew helped us into the launch, then rowed directly toward the civilian ship.

Filtering through the hazy air, the sunlight fell diffuse and shifting upon the water, which the intense wind whipped into patterns and shapes. The scene made me think of warp and woof; the pitching launch seemed a weaver's shuttle. Textiles. My German shawl I remembered with regret at having to leave it behind. It would likely be given to one of our servants, or possibly to some poverty-stricken family in one of my mother's rare and hypocritical displays of generosity. On a few occasions she would actually render assistance to people she considered inferior, provided she was guaranteed some sort of accolade for her efforts. At any rate, I felt abandoning the shawl a very small price to pay for what lay ahead.

After a short and bumpy but exhilarating voyage, the launch pulled alongside our destination. A crewmember escorted us into a vestibule, then down a staircase and through a door to the passenger cabin aft. This consisted of a dayroom which extended to the stern of the ship. Along its right side lay two bedchambers, and at their end a water closet. This was replete with vats and basins for bathing, shelves with linens for drying, and an alcove with a privy. All the rooms were illuminated by windows near the ceiling, hung with heavy shutters to close out the elements. The dayroom appointments—a writing desk, several chairs, cabinets containing a few books, a low table with couches for dining—were understandably secured to the floor. Beside the entry door was a cot to accommodate an attendant overnight.

Phoebe broke the silence we had kept since leaving Naples. "Alexias, find Master and advise him of our arrival. Lady, are you hungry?"

Lady. My family's servants had never addressed me so. "No, but thank you," I answered.

"Then would you care to wash a bit?"

"That would be most welcome," I returned; for I felt gritty from the carriage ride, and damp from salt spray and nervous anticipation.

Phoebe accompanied me to the bathroom, where she poured water from an urn into a shallow basin. "Regrettably we cannot offer you any more than this," she said as she handed me a washing cloth. "Fresh water has to be carefully conserved on a ship, and saltwater will leave your skin itchy." She removed the palla, and then left me alone in the bathroom. After cleansing my face and underarms, my privates in expectation of what I knew must come, and finally my feet, I rejoined Phoebe in the smaller bedchamber.

Besides the sleeping couch, the bedroom held a small dressing table, a stool, and a travel trunk which Phoebe opened. It contained every type of garment I required. There was even a vial of dentifrice, a bottle of perfume, a small jar of pale rouge, and a little mirror. While I cleaned my teeth and applied the perfume and the rouge to my lips and cheeks, she brushed and rebound my hair. Then she attached a gauzy white veil, which trailed down my shoulders and back and fluttered behind me as I moved. For the first time since I could remember, I actually felt pretty.

Phoebe opened the door to the main dayroom, where Menon was keeping watch. "Lady, the Master is on his way," he said. "May I be so bold to say you look quite fetching?" He spoke with an accent I did not recognize. As he had discarded the toga he had worn during our journey, I could now see the dagger secured to his belt. My heart began to pound in anticipation of the encounter about to take place. Seating myself on one of the chairs, I folded my hands and hoped to appear composed.

The sound of men's voices emanated from the vestibule, and then the door swung open. With Tiberius was a man whose uniform and insignias indicated he was the ship's captain. He was beginning a sentence, "But Sir, the wind..." when he noticed me and bowed. This was the first time a man had ever made such obeisance to me. It made me feel very elegant but also a bit flustered, since I was unsure how I was supposed to respond. Consequently I smiled and nodded but said nothing. Tiberius, however, introduced me as, "My ward Daphne, daughter of Hipparchus."

Having fretted for years about forced use of a pseudonym I now accepted one gladly, without the dreadful sense of lost identity that had accompanied my family's imposition of Pythia upon me. The new nomenclature, applied to protect me, had been bestowed out of love rather than malice. No one on the ship could be compelled to disclose my real identity so long as it remained unknown. And what a magnificent choice, given my interest in astronomy. Hipparchus of Nicaea, the great astronomer of the last century, had pursued most of his academic career at the Academy of Rhodes, and spent his final years at the Museion in Alexandria my birthplace. But why the particular forename of Daphne? Perhaps Tiberius considered our escape a victory, which laurel symbolizes. Or maybe he was thinking of the laurel groves at his mother's estate, which lies along the banks of the Tiber just outside the city limits of Rome. Whatever its source, the new name felt almost like a shelter, a haven, a cocoon in which my life was being transformed. The laurel tree, it seemed, was protecting the heliotrope growing beneath her branches.

The captain bowed again, and then resumed speaking. "The wind is dead contrary. You can feel for yourself how powerful it is. We cannot raise sail under these conditions. I can set oarsmen to work, but fear they will make little headway trying to push the ship against such resistance."

"There can be no further delay." Tiberius' tone was distinctly final. "I shall pay double the price of your charter if you manage to get us underway immediately."

"Thank you, Sir: this will provide the crew with incentive. We shall most likely have to give them shore leave at Messina, however, as they will certainly be fatigued."

"A reasonable request: kindly proceed."

The captain bowed once again and departed. The servants trailed after him.

Tiberius took me in his arms and laid his cheek against mine. "Thank you for joining me," he said, his voice slightly hoarse with intense emotion.

"Thank you for inviting me," I returned, and then continued, "I love you, and am prepared to stand by you down the future no matter what it brings."

As we shared our first kiss, we heard the captain shout, "Extend oars! Lower oars!" The ship began to shudder and pitch, as she pressed forward against the opposing wind.

Tiberius said, "Come, let us go above for now, and gaze upon our homeland from the sea. We may not behold her again for some time."

Standing in the vestibule outside the cabin door was a man armed with dagger and sword. A regular bodyguard: Tiberius was not taking any chances a member of the resistance party had infiltrated the crew. I assumed the guard was a Gaul. He was statuesque with pale skin, blue eyes, and bright red hair. When I caught his eye he smiled and bowed, then followed us up the staircase.

As we reached the deck, a passing crewmember offered me his hand in assistance. I wrapped my little veil tightly about me as the intense wind whipped us without mercy. The island of Ischia was on our right side, the mainland port of Pozzuoli on our left. These gradually receded and Naples came into view. The early afternoon sun, illuminating the haze a brilliant white and bouncing off the water in piercing glints, as well as our distance from the harbor, made the details of the city difficult to see. The familiar sites were discernible—the wharves and warehouses, the forum, the temples, the crags above the city. I could not make out the Academy, however, or our house. An interesting omen, not being able to see the landmarks of the life I was leaving. After Naples we passed the wealthy resort town of Herculaneum, the bustling market city of Pompeii, and eventually the promontory of Sorrento. The deep gray hulk of the extinct volcano Mount Vesuvius, which had dominated the horizon since Naples, now receded into the distance.

We passed between Sorrento and the island of Capri. Tiberius remarked that Capri was among his favorite places in Italy. He related the story of how his stepfather had acquired ownership of the island. For generations the family patrimony of the Octavii had included Ischia, while Capri had been a dependency of Naples. Augustus had halted at Capri on his return to Italy from Egypt after his victory over Cleopatra. During his stay, an apparently dead oak tree suddenly sprang back into life. Considering this a significant omen at such an auspicious time in his career, Augustus successfully petitioned the city of Naples to grant him ownership of Capri in exchange for the larger island of Ischia. Even from our distance, I was struck by Capri's wild beauty. The pale sheer cliffs and rock pinnacles, dotted with sparse vegetation, seemed almost alive as they reflected the changing, shimmering colors of the sea and sky. "Oh, to be able to visit that captivating place," I mused aloud.

"Do not relinquish that thought. Remember how I promised to bring you to Rome as my special guest? I vow to do the same with regard to Capri."

After Sorrento the coastline began to recede into the haze, as we headed through open sea toward the Straits of Messina. "Come," said Tiberius. "There is little to see now; and we have urgent business to attend below." I understood perfectly well what he meant.

As we descended the stairs, my body came to life with familiar driving sensations I had always been required to suppress. Now I had no inclination to stifle them, because a key element was missing. Guilt, the weapon with which my family had consistently forced me to subdue sexual desire, had been replaced by determination to satisfy the yearnings coursing through mind and body. Phoebe was sitting in the dayroom, sewing something. She glanced up at us, collected her work, and hastened to the exit. Tiberius drew an arm about my shoulders and started to ease me toward the larger bedroom. And then he paused. "Why my dearest, I sense you are frightened."

What insight! My trepidation I did not want to admit, even to myself. Laying my head on his shoulder, I sighed. "Here I am in my twenty-second year, and have never been with a man. Surely I will be awkward and clumsy. I am also self-conscious, knowing Phoebe is well aware of what we are about to do."

"You will become accustomed to having the servants about. In time they will seem practically invisible, and you will find yourself relying upon them comfortably. Rest assured: right now they are watching the entry to insure our privacy. As for you: just surrender to whatever feels natural and comfortable and trust me, remembering all the while we are committing an act of love." He escorted me into the main bedchamber and closed the door behind us.

I unbound my hair, which cascaded down my back as the veil fell to the floor. This gesture alone was so erotic and arousing, that I found myself ready far sooner than I had expected to be. As I slipped out of my sandals, I undid the shoulder clasps of my chiton. The garment dropped down to uncover my breasts, which my companion caressed and kissed. While he did so I unfastened my girdle, which along with the chiton fell to my feet. My partner removed his sandals, unfastened his belt, and shed his tunic. With a sudden daring that surprised as much as delighted me, I slipped his loincloth from his hips and caressed his hardening genitals. He took me in his arms; for a long moment we were locked in a kiss. I retreated to the bed, lay down on my back, and drew him onto me as though I were well familiar with the whole procedure.

His physical strength and virile forcefulness enthralled me; a sense he was trying to be gentle dispelled my lingering fear. The stab of pain that accompanied his penetration I found exhilarating. My breath came in shuddering gasps; my breasts tingled; my belly and buttocks tightened as I shifted and writhed, synchronizing my body with the rhythm of his. Ecstasy steadily crept toward frenzy and then dissipated in a glorious burst of spasms, leaving a warm afterglow of satisfaction and joy. I caressed Tiberius' hips and lower back while continuing to match his movements, until he finished with a shudder and settled at my side. We were both panting a bit from our exertions. We kissed. He smiled at me and stroked my hair.

"Your fears were groundless," he said with gentle earnestness. "You were lovely."

"I had the perfect teacher," I replied.

He kissed my forehead in what was to become an all too familiar gesture, and I softly declared, "I love you!"

"And I you," he returned. I hoped my tone had conveyed the same tender sincerity I heard in his.

We dozed in one another's arms until the harsh late afternoon sunlight woke us, blazing through the windows as though from an inferno. In the restrictive conditions of limited water and space we bathed as best we could. With distinct satisfaction I noted the little patches of blood mingled with semen on my inner thighs. Observing these would have sent Euethia into hysteria for sure.

We extracted clean garments from our respective travel trunks. The new chiton I selected draped my upper body and swung gracefully about my ankles. It was pale green—a color my mother and Euethia had always decried without explanation—and unlike the garments of my home, properly designed to flatter me. While we dressed, I inquired about my pseudonym. The connection with Hipparchus I had understood at once and relished. But whence Daphne? From the laurels of Ad Gallinas Albas? That was the name of Livia's farm.

"Actually…ah…Daphne was the name of the pony I had there when a boy."

"You named me for your horse? Is this the image I evoke in you? Granted I am stocky and have broad teeth; but is the similarity really that strong?"

"Why, I was very fond of her! And I am very fond of you! I have thoroughly enjoyed riding both of you!"

"Hopefully not in the same fashion!" Euethia should have heard that rejoinder.

"Rest assured you are far prettier than the other Daphne, teeth and all. You have softer skin, and you smell a lot better. Furthermore you do not have whiskers."

We emerged laughing from the bedchamber to discover a cold supper of cooked vegetables, bread rolls, and fish—a special treat for me—awaiting us on the dining table. Tiberius was right: the servants were becoming invisible. Following the traditional practice for women, I seated myself on one of the couches rather than reclining on it. To my surprise, my companion did as well. "I hate reclining at table," he explained. "It strains my shoulders, inclines me to spill on myself, and induces indigestion. Were these couches not secured to the floor, I would replace them with chairs."

During the meal we chatted and reminisced like old friends reunited after long separation. The absence of flirtatious poses and amorous glances, of fondling and petting, of coquettish banter and shallow small talk, reassured me our relationship was not a superficial one. I began with the latest chapters in the epic of life with the Eupistodoi.

After one of our serving women whacked Leo with a broom, I seized the instrument and applied the same treatment to her. The maid was not reprimanded; but true to expectation, I was. For a day or so I worried the cat would be discarded. He was not, of course, because his presence was essential for the control of vermin. The gods forbid the maid should perform such a service.

Some days later my brother, now in his sixteenth year, was discovered naked with the other servant. Nothing had happened. She had not made any progress with him, because he had never been taught anything at all about sex. His unsurpassed purity must not be sullied with instructions in carnal knowledge. Predictably enough there were no consequences for Philo or for the maid; however I was informed my own lewdness had set the bad example for my brother.

With that I lost my temper for sure. My fiancé was hanging about, gaping and ogling as usual. I announced he was bothering me and ordered him home. He complied with his usual complacent obedience. Thereafter I stormed into the women's quarters with my mother in hot pursuit.

"How dare you mistreat your intended like that?" she bellowed. "Consider all we stand to lose if he repudiates you!"

"See, all you care about is his money and what it has done for you. And to think you call me selfish! Well not to worry: he will not break off our betrothal. He is far too devoted to me, the obsequious little parasite. Should I order him to cut off his testicles and eat them, he will comply without a whimper. Since when is it my fault Philo has a libido? Why do you not educate him about it, so he knows how to respond properly to his own urges, let alone to the solicitations of sluts like Argo? Apparently he is not smart enough to figure any of that out on his own. How do you expect him to marry and produce descendants to this family you venerate like a theogony, when he has no idea of the purpose for which he has a penis dangling between his legs?"

"You sloven, selfish, degenerate bitch!" she retorted. "How unsurprising such filth should emanate from your mouth! Have you no respect for your brother, let alone gratitude for a servant like Argo?"

"Why should I entertain respect for either, seeing Philo has never learned to think for himself, and Argo does absolutely nothing around here but show him her anatomy?"

My mother slapped my face. "Do not think of presenting your despicable self at supper!"

As she strode away I shouted after her, "That suits me quite well, since I am still overstuffed from the forced feeding of this past noon!"

Later that evening a plate of cold, unappetizing, leftover food was shoved under my bedroom door, as though to a prisoner in some dungeon. I shoved the plate right back. For the entire next day I did not receive anything to eat at all. In the days that followed I was served only minuscule portions, barely enough to sustain Leo. Since I was still responsible for feeding him, one evening I forfeited my entire supper. "So, you have no use for the food that nourishes you, that has been provided for you amply!" Euethia derided my relinquishment. Knowing my departure was imminent, and grateful for the opportunity to shed some weight, thereafter I consumed the paltry morsels in silent submission that engendered no less resentment than my original refusal.

Tiberius interrupted me, to inquire for what sort of vocation was my brother being prepared. None whatsoever, I replied. Philo had no skills, no interests, no motivations. My mother and aunt seemed to believe prospective employers would seek him out without being solicited, just because he was who he was. It had also been anticipated that once my father became too old to work, primary responsibility for supporting the family would devolve upon me—upon royalties from my academic achievements (hence these must be phenomenal), and upon my marriage connections. My companion shook his head, incredulous.

Finally there was my prospective father-in-law's latest pronouncement on social issues. My mother and her aunt accepted it with their usual reverence. "The world would be far better off, if all the Jews could be rounded up and exterminated altogether. Little wonder Caesar is in bed with Herod: the one is as treacherous and underhanded as the other." This conclusion evolved after Norenas had ordered a shipment of timber from Judaea, for the construction of storage sheds on one of his farms. When he reneged on payment, the Jewish supplier initiated a lawsuit against him.

By now Tiberius was shaking with laughter. "It sounds as though your Norenas is more like King Herod than he would care to admit. Herod is one of the most despicable individuals alive—cruel, arbitrary, and despotic. He assumes everybody is plotting his overthrow, but cannot comprehend what he is doing to provoke them. What he has inflicted upon his family makes your experiences with yours seem a stroll through Elysium. My stepfather once grumbled he would rather be Herod's pig than his son—the pig, you will recall, is anathema in the Jews' religion. Herod is a loyal vassal to Rome, and an effective ruler of a proud and restive people no Roman quite understands. These are the only reasons we keep him in power. The rest of his family is not like him at all. My mother has a devoted friend and retainer in his sister Salome, who has not been spared unfounded allegations."

I sighed dejectedly. "I realize I should be grateful things are not as bad for me as they are for others."

"Clytia, that is not what I meant to imply at all." His response was patient but emphatic. "Hear me, not your family, in my words. Reminders that others are worse off than you do nothing to lessen your own pain. They only serve to increase your anguish and create groundless guilt."

"Thank you, thank you ever so much. I hope someday to stop responding in this manner."

"You will, my love; in time you will. Believe that you can."

Tiberius proceeded to elucidate the reasons for his withdrawal from public life. One was pure nervous exhaustion. This was the explanation he had offered the public—an assertion he was fatigued from his labors on behalf of the Roman state and required rest. His emotions had indeed been frayed raw, by concerns for his own safety and by the high degree of public scrutiny to which he was being subjected. Being a focus of attention was hard enough for him when that attention was positive. The escalating misrepresentations of his intentions with regard to the succession were anything but positive. He still harbored no designs upon his stepfather's position, and was becoming increasingly frustrated as more and more people seemed inclined to believe just the opposite. Hopefully his departure would help diffuse the increasingly prevalent rumors, that he was trying to persuade Augustus to divert the succession to him, or that he was attempting to build a hostile political party to challenge and diminish Gaius' effectiveness as a ruler.

Another consideration for leaving Rome was that life with Julia had become unbearable. In public she maintained decorum and behaved deferentially toward Tiberius. At family gatherings she put on great displays of affection toward him. At home, however, she was impassive—not really hostile, just stolidly indifferent. Her conversations were usually courteous and pleasant, but oblique and evasive. She cut them short whenever she could. Although she never refused sex with her husband, she seemed thoroughly bored with it. On one occasion, Tiberius confronted her and asked outrightly if she wanted a divorce. She did not answer but walked away, tittering with a clearly affected laugh. I interjected the similarity of my mother's responses to me.

What time Julia spent at home, when she was not flitting about her social circuit, she lavished on her three sons and two daughters. By now they ranged in age from five to fourteen years. Julia dutifully continued to accommodate Tiberius' son Drusus. She always spoke graciously to him, never raised her voice, took pains to make sure his physical needs were met, arranged for him to take his lessons with her own children. But she began to exude the same coolness toward him as she did toward his father. There was no interest in his discoveries, his hobbies, his aspirations, or his fears. Like his father, Drusus was sensitive and shy. Julia's ambivalence, and her unconcealed partiality to her own children, discomfited him. One day he quietly asked Livia if he could come and live with her and Augustus, who promptly demanded an explanation from his daughter and son-in-law. What was transpiring between them, that the boy had found life in their home intolerable? Julia reacted as if dumbfounded by the inquiry and insisted nothing was amiss. And because she was always so confoundedly indirect, Tiberius had no specifics upon which to base a complaint.

The effect of Julia's conduct upon his son solidified Tiberius' determination to leave her. He did not want his departure to hurt her, but instead hoped it would bring her to her senses. Despite all he had endured from Julia, Tiberius retained a measure of affection for her. Perhaps the shock and embarrassment at being abandoned would prompt her to rethink their relationship and become amenable to repairing it. On the other hand maybe Tiberius' absence would induce Julia to persuade Augustus, to select someone else to be her husband and regent for her sons—someone far more to their liking and that of their political adherents. Tiberius was well willing to trade the prestige and power of the regency for peace of mind, and the reassurance his life and reputation were not endangered.

There was yet another reason for his withdrawal: me. As our acquaintance developed through our correspondence, so had Tiberius' determination to bring me into his household—to free me from my family's harassments and cultivate our emergent love. For a Roman aristocrat to have a mistress was so commonplace, that the acquisition of a horse or a slave or a new residence was probably a greater occasion for comment. The law against adultery did not apply, so long as the woman was not a Roman citizen. Augustus had had a number of paramours over the years. Flirtation and sex provided him release from the phenomenal tensions associated with his political position. Because he was so discreet his family never knew the women's identities, much less when or where he saw them. Livia, who understood and loved him more intimately than anybody else, could usually sense when he was involved with someone. All she did was pretend she was unaware; and this tolerance reinforced her husband's devotion to her.

Tiberius was more concerned about what might happen, should my family discover our relationship. Through our correspondence he had come to know them well enough, to anticipate they would raise the ruckus of a millennium. For this insight I complimented him, and agreed. Were I to become involved with a man of ordinary circumstances my kin would punish me inexorably, but most likely run the lover off without consequence and proceed to hush the entire affair up. No scandal must ever be allowed to contaminate the Eupistodoi—unless it happened to involve a public figure. Tiberius' status would have completely reversed the character of their reaction. A thrill not to be missed would be the opportunity to overpower, with humiliation and disgrace, a man of prominence and authority whom they already hated (although they had never even laid eyes on him).

While Tiberius was not really hesitant to bring me to Rome, he felt Rhodes offered the better alternative. Should my family decide to look for me in Rome, they would unquestionably have trouble finding me amid the city's immense population. Nevertheless, there was always the possibility of a chance encounter. Tiberius had also anticipated my family would assume I had eloped to Gaul with my correspondent. They would not even consider the possibility I had departed for Rhodes or any other eastern locale, because they did not realize I had a patron with the ability to arrange my transfer anywhere in the known world. To preclude their pressing kidnapping charges—and finding out in the process that my presumed lover did not exist—Tiberius had altered the bogus military record to show Decimus Calvinius Valens killed in action during a border skirmish.

Again I interrupted. Why had Tiberius selected Rhodes as our destination?

He had fond memories of Rhodes, having first lived there as a youth in his thirteenth and fourteenth years. Following the capitulation of Cleopatra, Augustus spent the next two years reaffirming alliances with the vassal kingdoms that lay along Rome's eastern frontier. After selecting Rhodes as his headquarters for this endeavor, he had had Livia and their children join him there. Years later, after completing his installation of the vassal king of Armenia, Tiberius had halted at Rhodes for several weeks during the long return journey to Rome. On both occasions he had been very much impressed with the salubrious climate of the island, the friendliness of its people, and the abundant opportunities to immerse oneself in Greek learning and culture. I shall enjoy the place thoroughly, he assured me.

The final reason behind Tiberius' retirement was his unfulfilled desire for personal autonomy. In another month he would enter his thirty-seventh year of life. At no time, so far, had he been allowed to make an independent decision or pursue an independent course of action. All the aspects of his personal experience—his education, his marriages, his political and military careers, privileged though they were—had been carefully arranged and manipulated by his stepfather. Tiberius respected Augustus intensely and even loved him, far more than he had the natural father whom he had never really known. He was deeply grateful for the nurturing upbringing and incomparable advantages that had been bestowed upon him. Tiberius nevertheless found himself yearning, with increasing desperation, for self-determination. His mother, his brother, Augustus' now deceased sister, her son and four daughters, all had been content to let the emperor dictate the courses of their lives. Tiberius, however, had come to chafe at this regulation. He had also begun to believe Julia shared his feelings, and surmised the growing friction between them arose from that very desire for independence. They would have never married, Tiberius felt certain, had Augustus' relentlessness not importuned them. The emperor was a phenomenally intelligent man and an astute judge of character; yet he could not perceive how his dogged adherence to his political agendas had compromised the individualities of his family members.

Lack of personal autonomy? How well I understood this condition. The restrictions on my independence had been driven by malice; but more and more clearly, I was perceiving those on my companion had not.

Tiberius had been planning his departure since the summer months. Through agents he had rented a house in the main city of Rhodes, chartered the ship, arranged for my retrieval, and made sure a staff of servants and tutors was in place for Drusus so that burden did not fall upon Livia. Only after all this was settled did he announce his intentions to his family—on the Nones of October *[10/7]*, after they had finished celebrating Drusus' eighth birthday. As Tiberius anticipated, Augustus became furious. The emperor had little patience with behavior he considered insubordinate, especially when it came from his relatives. He was far more concerned, however, about the potential repercussion of Tiberius' departure on his regime.

Knowing peace was more enduring when based upon diplomacy rather than military force, Augustus was in the process of negotiating alliances with the tribal leaders at the German and Danube frontiers. Although the efforts were meeting with success, they were moving slowly. Lingering native resistance might still erupt into revolt against the Roman presence before the treaties could be finalized. If Roman military intervention became necessary, Tiberius' expertise as a general and familiarity with the regions made him the best possible choice for a commander. A similar situation was developing in Armenia. Tigranes II, the client king Tiberius had installed, had died. Diplomatic intervention was now needed here as well, to prevent the Armenian nobility from succumbing to the influence of Parthia and allowing that power to enthrone their vassals. Once again, Tiberius' experience with the Armenian situation made him the most appropriate person to intervene. And finally, perhaps most importantly, was the matter of the regency. Gaius and Lucius were still underage. Should anything happen to Augustus before Gaius reached legal majority, incumbent upon Tiberius would be to assume the leadership of the empire.

Tiberius endeavored to reassure his stepfather. There were other experienced diplomats and military commanders—loyal supporters of the Roman regime—who could handle Armenia and the northern front. The regency would automatically devolve upon him should the need arise, no matter where in the empire he was. Should that situation come about, what difference did it make whether he was on Rhodes or in Germania? To reaffirm he was not going into seclusion to design a plot against Gaius and Lucius, or for some other underhanded reason, Tiberius read his will aloud before his mother and stepfather. The testament merely left the bulk of his property to his son, with smaller portions directed to his wife, his niece and two nephews, and an assortment of remaindermen. There were no unusual provisions, such as plans for disposition of the empire in the event of his death.

Augustus fought back vehemently. Because Tiberius was of legal majority, the emperor could not lawfully force him to remain in Rome. Consequently he made a formal complaint against Tiberius before the senate. The grievance alleged Tiberius was neglecting the responsibilities of the regency, the powers of which the senate had conferred upon him. Tiberius promptly left the senate house for his own and sequestered himself in his bedchamber. For the remainder of that day and the next three, he refused to emerge or to take food or drink. (I had noticed he seemed a bit thinner in the cheeks than I had remembered him.) Even the indifferent Julia, who had neither entreated him to stay nor urged him to leave, now became alarmed. *We have to let him go,* she told her father, *lest he destroy himself.*

Had this situation involved an ordinary politician, the emperor might well have let him starve himself to death. But Tiberius was part of his family, the stepson he had nurtured since childhood. Affection overcame political posturing. For one of the few times in his political career, Caesar Augustus capitulated. He withdrew the complaint. No longer under compulsion to answer to the senate, Tiberius was free to depart.

"And to think people still call you indecisive," I mused aloud, slowly shaking my head from side to side. Tiberius smiled and caressed my hand, then continued his story.

He had had the ship waiting at Ostia, his belongings and servants aboard, from the day he first announced his intentions. Julia stood emotionless with eyes lowered, just inside the front door to their house as he prepared to leave. "Be well," she had murmured as he exited to the litter awaiting him. Before heading to Ostia, he stopped at the Caesars' home to say his goodbyes. Livia and his sister-in-law Antonia begged him to reconsider, even as they kissed him and wished him well. Augustus refused to participate in the farewells. Livia said he was upstairs in his study, pouting. Drusus took the whole business with great forbearance. He had become accustomed to staying with his grandparents whenever his father and stepmother were away from Rome, and now he was living with them at his own request. As Tiberius hugged him Drusus promised to mind his grandmother, to pursue his studies diligently, and to write letters. He made Tiberius promise to bring him souvenirs from his travels.

Another interruption. Had Tiberius not considered bringing Drusus with us? Surely he understood I was more than willing to look after his son; and for certain I was well equipped to educate him. Tiberius shook his head. It was time, even at his early age, for Drusus to start presenting a political presence in Rome. Entry to the senate is not automatic: one must be elected quaestor to gain admission. To secure that election, an aspiring politician must maintain a high public profile for years before he actually ran for the office. Tiberius did not care to jeopardize Drusus' political career by removing him from Rome, at precisely the time he needed to start exhibiting his intentions to enter public life. Augustus could be relied upon, in Tiberius' absence, to supervise Drusus' education and advance his public image.

"He would do that for you, even after you offended him so deeply?"

"Let me remind you again, Clytia: this is my family, not yours. My stepfather is not vindictive, even when he is angry. He never exacts vengeance unless it serves a political purpose. Retribution for its own sake he rightly considers a waste of time and effort, standing only to perpetuate ill will by reinforcing the resentment of its victims and their allies. And he certainly would not victimize Drusus because he is piqued at me. When we halted at Miseno to collect you, our Gaul Arbindus went ashore to gather news. My stepfather has released a public statement, asserting he has sent me to Rhodes to further my education. See how he is trying to obfuscate the dissension between us? And do you notice also, how he is trying to create the impression he is managing this whole affair?

"Unfortunately the rumors continue to fly. Caesar is presently ill with the respiratory ailment that usually plagues him this time of year. The blasted Sirocco is probably aggravating his condition. Because we halted at Miseno, the story has spread that I was waiting to see if he was going to succumb to his malady so I might assume his position. That is one of the reasons we rushed to get you aboard and set sail against the contrary wind. The other, of course, was to keep your family from tracking you." He suddenly looked away from me. "Yes, Menon?" I had not noticed the servant's approach.

"If all is satisfactory, Master, I should like to retire. Alexias will attend you through the night. A glorious sunset is taking place at this moment. May I urge you and Lady to go on the deck and view it?"

"By all means, Menon—rest well. Come, my dear one, let us go behold that sunset."

In the vestibule outside our quarters, the Gallic bodyguard Arbindus had been relieved by a Nubian. He dutifully followed us up the stairs. The ship was now under sail, but still moving slowly because of the contrary wind. The three great expanses of oiled cloth were trimmed at oddly oblique angles, to catch whatever currents of air were useful. The members of the crew attending the sails were hard-pressed to keep them in line. The sunset was indeed glorious, well worth standing in the unremitting Sirocco to watch. The haze made the sky appear like a great curtain, fluttering with shifting bands of pastels that made the water seem like burnished metal. The colors deepened, of course, as the great reddish-gold sun sank lower and lower. Amid the varying shades of red and brown, gray and blue, I thought I detected a flash of green. In the purplish glow that lingered after the sun had set, a few stars became visible through the haze. A crewmember approached, carrying a compass. He acknowledged us with a slight bow, then used the stars to verify the ship's direction. All at once, a meteor streaked downward from the zenith and disappeared below the horizon, leaving a lingering trail of light in its wake.

"By all the gods!" Tiberius exclaimed. "What an omen! It seemed almost close enough to catch!"

"You saw that!" I exclaimed joyously.

He scoffed. "I am nearsighted, not blind!" he asserted sharply. Then his tone softened. "Stars, and distant terrestrial lights like lanterns or fires, appear to me as luminous florets. That meteor seemed a swath of paint, applied by a celestial artist's brush."

In the near future his second simile would prove portentous, although at the time we had no way of knowing this. For the present I was overcome with embarrassment and shame, as the inner voice of my mother harassed me. In meek, contrite tones I said, "Most sincerely I apologize for seeming to derogate your eyesight. That was not my intention whatsoever, no matter how it sounded."

"There was no derogation. You were pleased I saw the meteor despite my limited vision. Your family's castigations are haunting you. Well rest assured, my dearest, I am going to put a stop to all that."

Returning to our quarters, we found the supper dishes had been cleared. Alexias was in the process of lighting the chandelier hanging from the ceiling of the dayroom. It threw its light upward, because the lamp rested in a bowl to prevent oil from spilling during rough voyages. A similar but smaller lamp burned in the main bedroom, suspended from a bracket on the wall beside the bed. The heap of clothes we had left on the floor earlier had been removed, the bed freshened and our night garments laid upon it. We changed into these and cleaned our teeth. After brushing my hair and braiding it loosely for the night, I slipped under the coverlet beside my new bed partner. He put out the lamp, which hung on his side of the bed.

"An eventful day for you, eh my Clytia?" he said as the darkness enveloped us.

"Eventful hardly describes it: more the turning point of a lifetime. How ironic: as a young girl I used to fantasize that someday a princess—*or a prince*—would appear like a deus ex machina and transport me out of my miserable existence."

"A prince I am not, only a regent for a prince. Two princes, to be precise."

"Close enough," I responded. "You are the stepson of a king."

He laughed softly. "My stepfather is not a king, under the strictly legal definition of that term. Nor does he want anyone to think him a king. Anyway, it has been said one should be careful for what one wishes, lest that wish comes true. It may prove not to be quite what was expected. Transport you I can; whether out of misery remains to be seen. Sleep well, my love." He kissed my forehead as I nestled against his side.

For a time I lay awake in the darkness, reflecting and ruminating as I usually did upon retiring. My family were undoubtedly searching for me, that I may be restored to the altruistic home I did not appreciate and there punished relentlessly for my own good and instruction. Would failure to find me annoy and exasperate them? Most certainly, I hoped. Would they wonder if something they had done drove me away? Most likely never; however I would for sure enjoy seeing them tortured with remorse. Would they grieve for me? That would be very nice. Although I never expected this should come to pass, I fancied myself gloating over the bluster, the sputtering outrage, the weeping and wailing the following discoveries must certainly induce: first, I had surrendered my virginity; worse yet, I had done so out of wedlock; and finally, I had given myself to a celebrated man whom they hated, rather than to the insipid worm they had fawned over and forced on me because he was rich. The only member of my family I was going to miss was Leo. For his wellbeing I was not concerned. Should he start to endure mistreatment, he could always seek sanctuary with the neighbor who had reared him or at the home of one of his lady friends. Maybe he will give Philo fleas, or puke up a hairball in the middle of Philo's bed, or bury a tattered mouse or some other trophy of the hunt in that bed. And If Leo did run off, the lazy maids must deal with the mice and vermin. Was I really this vindictive?

My thoughts turned to the meteor we had observed earlier in the evening. When I first contemplated the existence of an Eternal Good—on that dusty, miserable birthday two years ago—the persuasion a better future was forthcoming entered my mind as a meteor shot across the sky. That future had become the present, its arrival announced by another meteor. Misery aplenty had preceded it; but its eventual unfoldment was well worth the struggle to endure. Was there really some Principle behind all this? Can we discover its operation, and use it to bless mankind? All I did was claim the presence of Underlying Eternal Good. Is the secret to the harmonized existence, which has eluded the world's greatest philosophers, really this simple? Were the meteor sightings truly prophetic of the adjustments to my life, or mere coincidences that stimulated my overactive imagination? And what of our horoscopes? Were we entering upon the promised period of mitigation; or must our experience continue to worsen before it improves?

Heretofore I had spent many a wakeful night, considering and reconsidering similar matters that had troubled my mind. Tonight, however, after a yawn I cut my contemplations short. I was far too tired, too thrilled with new freedom, and too enraptured with new love, to concern myself with ineffective deliberations about my family, speculations about the workings of the universe, or about anything else for that matter.

SEA INTERLUDE

The ship was called the Phoenix. Although she was designed to carry multiple passengers as well as cargo, Tiberius had chartered her for our party alone. He and I occupied the luxury quarters. Forward of these ran a hallway with chambers on either side, including a shared bathroom and latrine. Our servants occupied this area when not on duty, as did our bodyguards of which there were four altogether. Beside the Gaul and Nubian was a pair of identical twin Copts from Egypt, whose names I never mastered because I could not tell these two brothers apart. Little could I foresee an eventual significance of twins to my life.

To maintain the appearance I was Tiberius' ward rather than his mistress, that smaller bedroom within our private accommodations was used as my dressing room and to store my belongings. Only our servants knew this arrangement was a sham.

A guard was always within sight or earshot of each of us. Additionally our male servants Menon and Alexias wore daggers at all times. The notion of being under perpetual watch made me uncomfortable for a time. Hardly could I believe I was so special, so valuable, that I must be kept under armed surveillance. Tiberius was mildly amused. Such was part of the price one paid for being the acquaintance of a public figure. Now I had become a potential target, for political opponents or attention seekers or outright lunatics. I might be seized and held for ransom, or worse yet intentionally harmed by someone aspiring to satisfy a grudge or just to gain notoriety.

An extended sea voyage is an inevitably uncomfortable affair, no matter how much effort and expense are devoted to mitigating it. Spaces are cramped. Fresh water is at a premium. Seawater of course is readily available in abundance, for dirty tasks like cleaning floors and flushing out latrines and washing one's linens—even washing one's backside when no fresh water is on hand for this purpose. Nevertheless one certainly cannot drink seawater. Nor can one bathe one's entire body in it without incurring an itchy residue. Shipboard bathing consists of scraping with strigils and sponging off as best one can with the sparse amounts of available fresh water. Washing garments is difficult because there is little place to hang them, and because they dry stubbornly in the humid conditions. Little wonder the regular crewmembers tended to smell like the goats and pigs I used to encounter, during those revolting sojourns at my family's country house.

Since fire poses a formidable danger on a pitching ship, lamps are never allowed to burn unless someone is at hand (and awake) to watch them. The Phoenix had a carefully tended brazier on the deck, to heat water for cooking and bathing. Since it could only be fired when sea and wind were calm, the Sirocco precluded its use.

Foodstuffs are limited to those items most resistant to spoilage and mold from the ever-present humidity: dry hard biscuits, salt-cured meats, boiled eggs, desiccated soft fruits or storable hard fruits like apples, similarly storable vegetables like carrots and dasheens. When these cannot be heated, they must be served cold and raw. A strong set of teeth is essential.

Had this been a pleasure voyage we might have put in at ports every day, for visits to public baths and access to fresh foods. But as such was not the case, we only made stops that were absolutely necessary. The first of these was at Messina in Sicily, which we reached toward the middle of our fourth day out. The crewmembers, worn from pushing the ship into the Sirocco, were truly in need of their promised shore leave. When we first arrived I thought about asking permission to visit the city as well. Then quite immediately, I reconsidered. Tiberius had to remain on the ship, for the obvious purpose of evading public attention. Therefore I decided to stay aboard with him and spend the afternoon engaged in sex, of course because the process was brand new to me and very enjoyable, but principally because I was fast falling ever more deeply in love. Fervent with desire for my partner, I was eager to reassure him of my devotion. I was enthralled that this man of some maturity (he was sixteen years my senior), this man of intelligence and achievement and rank and of unsurpassed fame—a man who could have had his choice of women—had selected me to love and desire and to share his life.

Phoebe stayed aboard while our menservants busied themselves in the city. Menon managed to have a great vat of fresh water delivered for us to bathe in. One had to sit in a cramped position, knees tucked under chin. The ship's little brazier struggled to make the water lukewarm. Nevertheless we were grateful for this distinct improvement over basin bathing. Supper that evening had everything fresh: roasted fowl, soft bread, salad greens, and thin slices of a root with which I was unfamiliar. Tiberius was not: he held up a piece and smiled reflectively. "A hint of home. Elecampane: renowned for its digestive properties. My mother makes sure it is on our table every day. Menon or Alexias must have found it in the marketplace this afternoon." The root was sweetly astringent, and left my palate and throat with a feeling of having been coated with soothing liquor.

While we dined we heard from the wharf outside, "So here you are, Tiberius Nero. Running away from home, you peevish varlet, because you were not chosen to play prince? What happened? Mommy not suck Stepdaddy's cock hard enough? Pimp the wrong cutie for him?"

Tiberius rolled his eyes. "No matter how hard I have tried, I cannot fully inure myself to this sort of thing."

Suddenly a heated hubbub began on the wharf. We peered through a shuttered window that was slightly ajar. Two members of our ship's crew were harassing the heckler, poking and punching at his chest and shaking their hands in the air. The heckler swung his fist at one of the crewmembers, who managed to duck in time to avoid being struck. Just as it appeared a brawl was going to break out, one of our twin Coptic bodyguards strode into the scene with his hand on the hilt of his sword. The heckler took off down the wharf like a scared rabbit. While we tittered, the crewmembers whooped and guffawed and hurled catcalls after the assailant.

When we were back at table I posed the question, "How did the heckler determine you are traveling on this particular ship?"

"Who knows? Maybe a servant of some senator or businessman with interests in this area recognized Menon when he went ashore. The crewmembers seem to be loyal enough; but you never know if one of them started to brag about me after an overload of wine and bravado in a local tavern. Perhaps the heckler simply noticed the lack of passenger activity, and concluded the ship had to be mine. Everyone knows I am en route to Rhodes, and that we must pass through the Straits of Messina to get there. Directly across the strait on the mainland is the city of Reggio Calabria. The Scribonii Libones have strong political and financial interests there. Remember them?"

"The family of Julia's mother—and of your kinsman Drusus Libo. Not exactly your friends."

"Now you have seen, firsthand, why discretion is paramount for us—and also that it is not always effective. News about some things manages to leak out no matter how careful we are, while other secrets are successfully concealed for a lifetime. You also had a demonstration of how loyalties emerge in unanticipated ways. The crewmembers cannot form assessments about my character because they do not converse with me. Yet when the heckler launched his attack, the two on the wharf came to my defense at once. Their loyalty is impelled by their mere association with me."

The next morning I briefly reconsidered going ashore, but even more quickly discarded the notion upon recalling the heckler. Tiberius had not so much as gone up on deck; yet his presence in Messina had been detected. The city was well within the economic territory of Publius Norenas, my once prospective father-in-law. Surely his agents were everywhere. No matter how well I kept myself veiled, I still might be discovered. Moreover I continued to feel sorry for my partner, confined below deck as though under house arrest. He reassured me he did not mind the seclusion, since he had always been reclusive by nature. Our present captivity, however, he felt would be a good test of our liaison. If we were not quarreling by the end of the day, we could rest assured our relationship was sound.

There was nothing we could learn or consider from the rudimentary books in our quarters: a set of silly and boring comedies by Sextus Turpilius, three trite novels, the **Iliad** and **Odyssey** (both of which we knew by heart). We amused ourselves for a while by quizzing each other on the Homeric epics. After one of us read a passage aloud, the other would identify what character uttered it or what situation it described.

Then I discovered, in the minimal library, a book of odes by Quintus Horatius Flaccus. For decades Augustus had engaged the profound talents of this now deceased poet for the dissemination of propaganda. I proceeded to tease Tiberius by scrolling through the book and reading aloud the poems that lauded his military accomplishments. After the fourth ode he growled, "All right, that will do!" through clenched teeth. "Do you not understand how intensely I dislike having my achievements flaunted, especially for no reason?"

"I am so sorry!" So I declared penitently, while mentally flagellating myself for failing to be more considerate of his self-consciousness. "I meant no offense."

"That I realize." His response had a gentler tone. "We are still acclimating ourselves on one another's foibles. But from now on, please refrain from rehearsing accolades about me unless you are specifically asked to do so."

After nodding meekly I returned to the odes in silence. While I read, Tiberius sat chin in hand, lost in thought.

The shutters on the ship's windows were closed for privacy, but not so tightly as to shut out air and light. The sun glinting off the agitated water, the slight rocking of the ship, the shadows cast by moving clouds or by passersby on the wharf, by the crewmembers unlading and taking on cargo, kept altering the illumination of our quarters with an array of continuous shimmers. As the shifting light made reading difficult, I presently decided to abandon the odes and interrupt my partner's reverie.

"You seem so pensive. I hope you are not still aggravated at me."

"Oh, stop being so harsh on yourself. I was thinking about the Phoenix. The name of our ship here reminded me of the legend. You know it."

"Most certainly: a mythical bird with luminous plumage. During its lifetime it lays a single egg. After dying in consuming fire, it emerges anew from the egg. The legend is of Egyptian origin, as I recall."

"I was contemplating the parallel in my life. I left a happy marriage for one that has failed. But without that failure, most likely I would never have been blessed with you."

"What a beautiful thing to say!" I smiled appreciatively, grateful and even a little surprised his earlier irritation at me had dissipated. My mother would still be rehearsing the incident. He smiled back and took my hand. We fell silent once again, continuing to hold hands while the flashes danced about the room.

"Do you still love Vipsania?" I finally ventured, not without trepidation.

He sighed. "Yes, in a way. It is rather like being in love with someone who has died. I should like to have had more children; and she has proven quite fecund. Just this past summer she presented her new husband with a third son. Do my contemplations disturb you?"

"No—I regret you suffered such a loss."

He shrugged. "We both agreed to our divorce."

"Your stepfather coerced you."

"More correctly, we let him persuade us."

"You always seem to defend him."

"I understand him."

"Do you think it was fair of him to marry your mother for love, but then force you to cast aside your feelings for Vipsania?"

"There is no question he loves my mother intensely. You may nonetheless rest assured: he would never have married her had he not stood to benefit from her social position and political connections."

"Would he willingly divorce her and remarry Scribonia?"

"Should he regard that as essential to his political needs, absolutely; and my mother would acquiesce, just as Vipsania did to separation from me. Remember: our new government, which has brought such unprecedented peace and prosperity to the world, is my stepfather's creation—his child, if you will. Once he joked about having two spoiled daughters: Julia and the Roman state. He is perfectly willing to trammel his own emotions and inclinations to ensure the success of his system; and he convinced all three of us—Vipsania, Julia, and me—we could as well. He can be every bit as engaging and persuasive as he is ruthless. Moreover, in our family we care very strongly for each other's aspirations no matter how much we quarrel. Each of us wants to see the regime succeed. I certainly do, despite my present recalcitrance. So does Vipsania; and surely so does Julia, vexatious as she has been. But that desire to support family and government has led all three of us to resist our own inclinations. Now here I am, torn between loyalty to my family, loyalty to tradition, loyalty to the Roman state, and loyalty to myself."

"Please understand I am not trying to be adversarial. On the contrary, I know only too well how difficult refusing a parent can be."

He looked directly at me and smiled. "Thank you for your empathy."

I changed the subject. "Sincerely I regret not being able to you children. They would be illegitimate anyway."

"I am in trouble enough without the added complication of bastard offspring. Right now my stepfather is undoubtedly furious enough to consider chopping me into pieces, for use as bait during one of his fishing expeditions. Why are you suddenly amused?"

I had leaned forward on my elbows and started to smile enthusiastically. "The great Caesar Augustus is an angler?"

"Yes, and quite an avid one—when he can find the time."

"I am as well!"

"You?"

"On our country property there was a miserable little pond, in which I fished for lack of anything else to do. The first catch I brought home was decried as cruelty to the fish." Tiberius rolled his eyes and scoffed. I continued, "Although I returned everything I caught to the pond that first time and thereafter, I continued to fish for the solitude and contact with nature the activity brought me. For this I was pronounced perverse, because my fishing sessions absented me from the rest of the family."

"Perverse for fishing. Where does your family get their distorted ideals? I keep wondering what crazed notion I am going to hear about next."

"Well, I am pleased to discover there is an affable side to your stepfather after all."

"He can be as disarmingly pleasant as he is uncompromisingly ruthless. The two traits conjoined have brought about his phenomenal success in statecraft."

All at once the pattern of light ceased to be random and became a slow horizontal progression across the wall. The motion of the ship changed as well, from an aimless bobbing to a directional pitch. My companion was suddenly attentive. "We are underway," he declared. For a while he peered through the shutter. "As soon as we are clear of the city, I am going directly up on deck. Much as I like solitude, I am starting to feel like a caged beast."

Hardly could I begrudge his hasty escape. After straightening up the book cabinet, I was about to seek a veil to wear outside when Phoebe entered the dayroom.

"Lady, I found this in the marketplace this morning and thought you might enjoy it." She was carrying an immense rectangle of woven cloth. It appeared so coarse and heavy that I wondered how she managed to hold it. On taking it from her I found it soft, and nearly as light as gauze. It was patterned with rows of white circles imposed on a dark blue background. To keep it from unraveling, the woof ends were tied together into a fringe secured with beads. "Nomads of North Africa weave this particular type of cloth," Phoebe explained. "A trader probably brought it to Messina from Carthage."

Phoebe's thoughtfulness impressed me considerably. We had not been acquainted for very long; she only knew me in her capacity as a servant; yet she had recognized my interest in textiles and gone to effort and expense to indulge it. I bubbled, "Why Phoebe, thank you ever so much!" and threw my arms about her. To my surprise she recoiled: clearly my gesture had disturbed her. She recovered, curtsied, then helped me wrap her gift about my head and shoulders. Clutching it I clambered up the staircase to the deck, still puzzled by Phoebe's reaction.

Once again the ship was being slowly rowed, not only because of the Sirocco, but also in consideration of the high volume of ship traffic in the strait. The Sicilian shoreline was uninteresting: a flat coastal plain devoid of the sheer, towering cliffs of the mainland Italian coast south of Naples. Eventually the strait widened. We entered open water; and the sails were unfurled. Like an undulating black carpet, a colony of sea dogs spread over a distant section of beach, safely removed from human interference *[Mediterranean seals, presently endangered]*. A great gray cloud hung in the sky. There was a rumble of noise which I assumed was thunder, until a crewmember pointed at the cloud and exclaimed, "Aetna, Lady!"

Aetna. The celebrated volcano of Sicily was erupting. Straining into the far distance, we could just barely discern the peak from which the ash cloud was emanating. "Oh, to be able to see its glow in the night!" I exclaimed. "The actual rivers of lava or even the crater itself!"

Tiberius shook his head. "It is just like you to put scientific curiosity ahead of personal safety."

"I understand volcanoes arise from the shifting of humors within the earth."

"No matter how they arise, they surely must be dangerous. Have you never visited the volcanic springs at Baia or Stabiae, where my stepfather goes to relieve his rheumatism?"

"Naturally not, even though we lived fairly close by. You know how untraveled my family insisted upon being. Only once did we go to Baia, when I was very young."

"Well, if the temperature of that water is any indication, the heat far below must be unfathomable." He left me for a moment to speak to a crewmember, who nodded and then departed hastily. Presently the ship began to move in a different direction. Instead of heading directly into the open ocean we crept closer to the shoreline—and the volcano.

"Oh, we are approaching Aetna! Did you request a course change?" I asked excitedly. As the ship skirted the shore we started to discern tongues of flame, shooting upward from the peak into the cloud of smoke. On one slope there stretched a black rivulet, flecked with glowing patches of bright red. The air reverberated with sounds like thunder.

"Yes, I did. So long as we are here, we might as well get as close as we can to observe without being roasted alive. Uncanny. A painting on a wall in our townhouse in Rome depicts the Sicilian hero Acis, rescuing his beloved Galatea from the sea monster Polyphemus while Aetna erupts in the background. The locale represented in the picture is just about where we are at this time."

Uncanny indeed. For how many years had Tiberius regarded that painting? Had he—could he—ever surmise, that one day he would transport a love of his own to safety and solace through those very waters represented in the scene? And what an appreciation for my interests, to change the ship's heading to accommodate my fascination with Aetna. Placed in the same circumstances, my family would have made sure they headed in the opposite direction, purposely to frustrate my curiosity. I felt a great surge of gratitude for this wonderful expression of affection, the likes of which still seemed foreign to me. There remained a strange adamant in my psyche, which refused to believe this man whom I loved so fervently was actually in love with me as well.

I sided up against my companion. He drew away from me sharply. "Do not be alarmed," he said, in response to my look of bewildered chagrin, "but please: never do that again. I shall explain later. Meanwhile, enjoy the view of Aetna."

That evening Tiberius invited the captain of our ship to join us for supper. In the earlier years of his reign, Augustus had established colonial cities in North Africa. These he had populated with military veterans in compensation for their service, and with families who had been displaced from their Italian homesteads during the civil wars. From his base in Messina our captain had built a successful maritime transport business—safely and honestly conducting these settlers to their new homes, and subsequently filling their orders for wares of various sorts. At present he owned and ran four transports, of which the Phoenix was the smallest and swiftest. Because he owed his fortune to the settlement program, the captain was unassailably loyal to Augustus and his family. This was the very reason Tiberius' agent had selected him to transport us and Tiberius had approved the choice. The captain was thrilled beyond measure to be our guest.

And I made one of the greatest mistakes of my life.

A robust Sicilian wine was served with the entree of roast lamb shank. The wine I found very tasty, warming, and satisfying. Of the lamb I did not partake because I dislike this meat intensely—not only for its texture and flavor, but because my family had served it with great frequency to pacify my brother. When veal or beef was not available, he could be persuaded to consume lamb. Exulting in my freedom to abstain from this viand and fascinated by the dinner conversation, I continued to sip on the wine without heed to the quantity I was imbibing. Nor did I think to dilute the wine with water as the Romans customarily do.

The captain regaled us with his experiences as a mariner. Originally from Alexandria, he had been second in command of a warship in the fleet of Cleopatra. After becoming disillusioned with the political aspirations she shared with Marcus Antonius, our captain started to leak Egyptian government information to Octavianus. Although his superiors began to suspect him after a while, they never betrayed him because they had become disenchanted with Cleopatra as well. Love for and eventual marriage with the daughter of a Sicilian sea trader ultimately brought our captain to Messina. Octavianus Augustus never forgot the captain's loyalty: hence the lucrative transport contracts. During his seafaring career he had weathered great storms, survived shipwrecks, evaded pirates, observed strange beasts, shipped unusual wares, and encountered a fascinating variety of people and cultures.

While Tiberius interrupted with an occasional question, I sat in silence. The stories intrigued me. Neither of my dinner partners was paying much attention to me. Nor was I paying much attention to what I was doing. Suddenly I felt very strange—became lightheaded and slightly nauseous. The room began to reel. Somehow I managed to stand up, murmur "Gentlemen, I must bid you goodnight," and reach the master bedchamber without falling over myself. I lay down on the bed. The next thing I knew it was morning. I was alone in the bedroom, lying atop rather than under the coverlet, and still clad in my outer garments. My hair though disheveled was still tied with its binding ribbons.

With considerable effort I swung my feet onto the floor and sat on the edge of the bed. My head ached as though it were in the winepress from which the previous night's drink had emerged. Drawing breath I found arduous, as though the cabin were closing in on me. My belly seemed filled to bursting with a portion of the surging sea outside. Whether anyone was in the dayroom I did not notice. Slowly and dizzily I made my way to the water closet, where the simple act of urinating proved a chore of great complexity. Afterward I discovered Phoebe in the dayroom. Ignoring her solicitations I desperately gasped, "I need air!" and without stopping to find a head covering headed for the vestibule. Painfully but urgently, as quickly as I could manage, I stumbled up the staircase to the deck.

Now we were south of Italy, the ship had been turned eastward in the direction of Rhodes. Blowing against our rear, the Sirocco was finally working to our advantage. The sails were filled with wind and the ship was traveling rapidly. In a great swell she pitched suddenly downward, then up just as precipitately. My stomach followed suit. After sinking painfully, the sea within me swelled upward. I stumbled to the rail, leaned over, and vomited.

There was a tug on my chiton just below the girdle. The Nubian bodyguard had seized the garment to ensure I did not follow the contents of my stomach into the water. In a deep and thickly accented but gently compassionate voice he inquired, "Lady, what ailing you?"

Tiberius arrived and got a better grip by extending his arm across my collar. None of the other men present would have dared touch my body. "Drunk!" he declared to the guard, and to the crewmembers who had gathered with concern. These onlookers—all of whom most certainly must have been in my condition themselves at one time or other—smiled with good-natured sympathy. "She had better be no more than that!" Everyone, including Tiberius himself, chuckled over his mock despair at the notion I might be pregnant. "Will someone please find my freedwoman Phoebe?"

I was regurgitating over the rail again when Phoebe arrived and draped my veil over my head and shoulders. "Go ahead, heave it all out—better up here in the open than down below. Serves you right for inebriating yourself!" she scolded. "And look at you: so wasted you could not even dress properly!" She was referring of course to my appearing unveiled in the presence of men. At last the retching ceased and I pulled away from the rail, feeling worse than ever. "Are you finally finished?" Phoebe demanded. I nodded weakly. "Come along, then, back downstairs before you end up in Poseidon's realm along with that puke offering you just gave him." Although I did not want to return below deck, I had neither the strength nor the inclination to argue.

I do not know for how long I sat in one of the chairs with my eyes closed, shaking with my usual agitation about vomiting, my face buried in a damp towel, a basin at my feet just in case. Finally I looked up at the sound of voices. The Nubian was speaking to Phoebe at the door. On noticing what he was wearing I jumped to my feet and rushed over, headache and bilious stomach notwithstanding.

Now off duty, the Nubian had replaced his leather body armor with a great swath of yellowish cloth patterned with little rectangles. Most were yellow; but some were filled with different colors. The rectangles were individual pieces of cloth sewn together with a heavy yellow thread.

"Melambrotus, your garment fascinates me!"

"It is unique to my people. How you feel, Lady, still miserable? Here I have something for your help—also from my people." He handed me a goblet filled with a clear, greenish-brown liquid. "Drink! Nothing to fear! Made from leaves of kindly plants." The infusion was pleasantly fragrant with a mild, almost negligible taste. He had managed to warm it a bit. It removed my nausea immediately. I lay down on one of the dining couches and dozed for a little while. When I awoke the aftereffects of the wine were gone, and I felt refreshed and well.

Tiberius laughed when I refused Menon's offer to serve me wine with supper. "Last night you were so stupefied, you could not be roused to remove your clothes. To maintain appearances—that you are my ward and hence I am honor bound not to molest you—I spent the night not even in the smaller bedchamber but in the forward section with the servants. You began to snore and babble so loudly, I would not have been able to sleep nearby to you anyway."

"While the captain was still present?" I asked in horror.

"Yes; but fortunately he found your reverberations quite amusing." He gazed at me intently. "Clytia, I want you to take this incident very seriously. We are fortunate it occurred among friends. Henceforth you must be prodigiously careful of the image you project. As a member of my household you will become an object of intense public scrutiny. Friends will exaggerate your failings a hundredfold and enemies a thousand. You need to search yourself for weaknesses, inclinations, habits that might compromise you—like drinking too much wine, embracing a female servant as though she were your sister, or charging at a male servant with blatant interest in his garment. Can you imagine what consequences might have arisen, had that scorner from Messina observed you this morning?"

I winced. At least now I understood why Phoebe had shrunk from me when I hugged her earlier.

"The captain and crew know absolutely nothing about you, except that you are a member of my household. When they know nothing, they can divulge nothing. Nevertheless I do not care to encourage their speculating about our relationship. Among the Romans it is considered highly inappropriate for members of a family to display their affection for one another in the presence of strangers—especially if one is a holder of public office. This is the reason I withdrew from you yesterday when we were on deck. None of the crew was about, but Melambrotus was present. He is not one of my servants but an independent hireling."

Now thoroughly dejected, I nodded my understanding.

"After we are settled in Rhodes, Clytia, I should like to arrange for you to have some training in comportment. I hope you are not offended."

My mood changed immediately. "Offended? On the contrary I am delighted at the prospect!" I answered ebulliently. "Never was I taught poise or etiquette while growing up. What manners I have were acquired through trials and errors—mostly errors. You may rest assured I shall be a most willing and enthusiastic pupil."

He took my hand and kissed it. "This is the girl with whom I fell in love, truly a worthy companion. Now: you do not sing or play a musical instrument, do you?"

"Absolutely not. I can describe the harmonic relation of every note in every scale to its fellow, but cannot reproduce a single one. There was never any money for lessons or to purchase a harp or flute. And whenever I did start to sing, I was ordered to stop immediately because my brother objected."

"As I suspected. We shall remedy that deficiency as well. A woman ought to know how to play and sing."

There was a sound at the door, which Menon went to investigate. He returned to our table and said, "Lady, Melambrotus requests permission to speak with you."

Had I been in my family home, I would have been expected to rise and approach the visitor groveling, even though he was of servile status. Suppressing this impulse I gave a slight nod, said "Certainly," and waited for the Nubian to come before me.

He bowed, and then extended his right hand over which lay a small cloth. Like his garment, it was constructed of variegated rectangles. "For you, Lady—please take. Altar covering. On it we place sacred objects when we honor our gods and ancestors." With his left hand he lifted the cloth to reveal three little carvings in dark polished wood. One represented a hippopotamus, the second an elephant, and the third a panther. "For you also: creatures of my homeland."

I smiled, and made a point of responding in a pleasant but steady tone. "Thank you, Melambrotus; I shall treasure your gift always." The Nubian bowed again and departed.

"Well done," Tiberius commented. "A most refined and gracious acceptance."

Melambrotus' altar cloth and animal carvings I possess to this day. Their colors and designs continue to please and inspire. My brief interactions with Melambrotus, his medicine and his artifacts, marked the beginning of another lifelong interest: the cultural diversity of the people I have encountered over the years.

While a few of the crewmembers of the Phoenix were Sicilian, most seemed to have come from everywhere else the world. They presented quite an array of different hair and beard styles and of course of costumes, the textiles of which I particularly enjoyed observing. There were frequent exchanges in foreign tongues between fellow countrymen. One man was especially unusual. From his straight, shiny black hair, yellowish skin, and oddly oblong eyes we concluded he had come all the way from China. I did not approach any of them to inquire about their origins, much as I would have liked. From Tiberius' warning I was now conscious of the unseemliness for a woman to ask personal questions of strange men. Furthermore, most of the foreign crewmembers only understood enough Greek or Latin to follow their commands.

Phoebe was willing to disclose her background. She was a Syro-Phoenician Greek from the seacoasts of the Judaean province of Galilee—and freeborn. In her thirteenth year her father sold her into slavery to raise money for repayment of a bad debt. She had three brothers all younger than she, and was sacrificed because she was female. Since she was advertised as proficient in domestic chores, she was purchased as a house servant by a steward to Princess Salome, the sister of the Judaean king Herod. About five years later, Salome sent Phoebe to Livia as a gift. During Phoebe's voyage to Italy, two members of the transport ship's crew had raped her repeatedly. The consequence was Alexias. He was in his fifth year when Augustus and Livia presented him with his mother to Tiberius, in anticipation of the latter's marriage to Vipsania. In their household Phoebe became acquainted with Tiberius' steward Menon.

Menon was Cappadocian—hence his strange accent. Archelaus, the rather underhanded sovereign of that Asiatic nation, had given Menon to Tiberius as part of a compensation, for Tiberius' successful legal defense of the king before the tribunal of Augustus. Menon promptly befriended the newcomer Phoebe, who was profoundly in need of sympathy and sincerely grateful for his solicitation. A few years later, Menon asked Phoebe to become his spouse and Tiberius to sanction their union. As slaves they did not enjoy the right to marry of their own free will. They did not have any children. For the first year they were together, Phoebe was tense and squeamish about sex—understandably because of her traumatic experience with it. In time she became comfortable with Menon; but by then she was beyond menarche. Eventually Tiberius emancipated Menon, not only in return for many years of unflagging and meritorious service, but so Menon as steward of Tiberius' properties could freely enter into contracts relevant to their maintenance. Tiberius manumitted Phoebe as well, so she could be Menon's legal wife and not his slave concubine. Alexius he retained in servile status. Tiberius was hesitant to confer freedom upon one who had not lived long enough to earn it, whether through years of meritorious service, some particularly noteworthy action, or by amassing sufficient pecuniary earnings to remunerate the master the price the slave would bring if sold. There was a legal limit to the number of slaves a master could manumit during his lifetime.

When I asked Phoebe whether she was bitter about her life experience, she replied her feelings were very mixed. Although offended by her father's action, she had understood the rationale behind it. He had tried without success, to find other ways of settling his debt before resorting to selling his daughter. At first she had resented having to keep house for her masters, until she realized that as a freeborn wife she would be undertaking precisely the same tasks. Although she felt degraded by her ravishment, she delighted in her son—now in his nineteenth year—who had always been lovingly loyal and supportive. The Caesars never separated her from her child as some slave owners do. She and

Menon had united for love, and with their master's blessing. Had she remained in her father's household she may not have been so fortunate, as she would have been required to wed whomever he selected for her. The fact that for many years she had been legally a piece of property like a parcel of land—and that her son was still so—had never disturbed her: legal status cannot affect human individuality. She was grateful for the fairness with which the Caesars had treated her, and was personally fond of each member of the family.

I thanked Phoebe for her candor; but when I started to describe the misery of my own upbringing she stopped me with, "Lady, please, it is not my place to know all that." Tiberius later explained it is inappropriate for a servant to learn the details of one's private life, and equally inappropriate for me to disclose them. The whole purpose of such discretion is to keep servants from gossiping, since they cannot reveal what they do not know. "Do not be abashed," he reminded me. "You are still learning."

During the final days of our voyage we were mostly in the open sea, where there were no landmarks to observe. Nevertheless I found it pleasant enough to stand on the deck (yes, with a settled stomach), and watch the changing patterns in the billowing waves and clouds. Every so often a school of dolphins would appear and escort the ship for a while. A necessary return to minimal bathing prompted Tiberius to voice his determination to find the deepest and hottest bath in all Rhodes, and me to wonder if I were starting to smell like the Daphne for whom I had been named. Rummaging among the books in our dayroom, I found an abandoned writing tablet. After dusting it off I began to jot down the notes, reminiscences, and musings that became the foundation of this journal.

We were back to dining on hard cold rations until one afternoon a crewmember, trailing a line in the water behind the ship, managed to hook a huge swordfish. Within minutes everyone was on deck, to help haul the great fish aboard, participate in the butchering or watch its progress, and to offer advice—mostly the unsolicited type. A throng of seabirds gathered behind the ship, sitting on the water or looping in the air and squawking raucously for tidbits. "The men will find use for virtually every part of that fish," the captain remarked. "The bones will be fashioned into tools. The entrails will be dried and most kept for bait; but some will be used in medicines. The skin will also be dried and cured, and then employed as a waterproof wrap for items stored here on the ship."

After a brief but noisily argumentative discussion about potential danger from the wind, it was decided the brazier could be lit with a minimal fire so long as it was kept under particularly careful supervision. For this responsibility the captain appointed three crewmembers from a host of enthusiastic volunteers. So that evening I had my first taste of fresh swordfish, which has remained to this day one of my favorite viands. My family had never served it because of my brother's refusal to eat fish of any sort. Such was their loss, I mused in my state of drowsy well-stuffed contentment.

"Careful," Tiberius cautioned. "I do not care to see your waistline broadened."

"Enough experience with forced feeding enables me to recognize my limit. I gather your stepfather would have enjoyed the festivities."

"My stepfather would have been right up there on that deck, scraping scales and extracting entrails and throwing refuse to the seabirds alongside the grubbiest of crewmembers."

We made a second and brief stop, primarily to take on fresh water, at Cydonia on the northern coast of Crete. It was in the middle of the night. As we skirted the Cretan coastline I stared out a window at the black landscape, wondering whether I could recognize Mount Ida the legendary birthplace of Zeus against the sky dimly lit by starlight. "Oh, come on back to bed!" my companion chided me sleepily. "You cannot see Ida from here: it is in the middle of the island. Rest assured you will visit Ida, and places even more fascinating. I hope to take you traveling once we have settled on Rhodes. And we shall be there presently. Tomorrow should be our last full day at sea."

Back to bed I went, but not back to sleep. We had been at sea for eight days. Lying awake in the dark, listening to Tiberius' soft snores—more like Leo's purring than Euethia's trumpeting because he was not overweight by some forty pounds—I reflected upon the phenomenal impact the week had had upon my life.

For the first time ever I felt blessed with respect and appreciation, not only by the lover from whom I would expect such consideration, but also by the strangers I had met—our servants, our bodyguards, the ship's captain and crew. These people had imparted me more esteem than I had ever received from my parents, or from the condescending academicians who had been my associates at the Academy. Humanity is no respecter of race or intellect or social status. Of this I had seen more in the past few days than in the past two decades. Here were Phoebe and Melambrotus, who had presented me gifts. Here were the crewmembers who had always been so courteous, who had challenged the heckler at Messina, who had shown me Aetna, who had extended me their friendly concern while I was sick from being drunk.

I had gained a new perspective on forgiveness. The many mistakes I had made in matters of etiquette, Tiberius had pointed out with patient tolerance, corrected or made arrangement for correction, and then dismissed. There were no continual reminders and ongoing punishments.

Phoebe had been sold into slavery by her own father and subsequently raped by two strangers; but now she was rejoicing over husband and son and content with her life of service. Tiberius was fretting over the impositions his stepfather had inflicted upon him throughout his life. Nonetheless he was reminiscing about Augustus with forgiveness and great fondness, even while rejoicing in his newly found independence and relationship with me.

Now I too had embarked upon a new life, out of the reach of my family. Yet I remained overwhelmed with anger, still wishing they would admit to having mistreated me, wishing they would apologize and make amends or else suffer punishment for their actions. Why could I not simply leave all that behind and rejoice in my freedom as well? What was wrong with me?

The dawn was beginning to brighten the bedchamber. As my lover stirred a little beside me, a phrase he had used echoed through my mind. *Stop being so harsh on yourself.* Thereupon I relaxed and began to doze.

THE EXPATRIATES

We reached the capital city of Rhodes as dawn was breaking on the thirteenth day before the Calends of November *[October 20]*. It was the beginning of our tenth day at sea. Ideally the voyage should have taken less time, perhaps six or seven days; but it had been prolonged, of course, by the Sirocco and the stop at Messina. Watching out a window of the dayroom, I tried to imagine the renowned Colossus—the immense statue of Apollo that had graced the city's acropolis centuries ago. A serving of fresh berries procured in Crete mitigated our final breakfast of hard flavorless sea biscuits. Afterward the arrangements for debarkation began. First Tiberius summoned the captain, to whom he remitted payment for our journey. After counting out the coins, the captain expressed effusive thanks for the generosity of the remuneration, wished us well, bowed and departed. Tiberius winced. "Expensive but well worth the price. He got us here safely and discreetly and fought adverse conditions doing so."

Our servants busied themselves with packing up the few odds and ends of belongings that remained scattered about, while we awaited the arrival of the agent who had arranged our accommodations on Rhodes. "Be sure you are well veiled," my companion urged, "and not just because it is bright out there. I do not care to attract public attention right away. We are going to draw plenty of that once we are settled."

When the agent arrived, Tiberius did not make any introductions. "The lady and my steward will accompany us," he said as he motioned to Menon and me, "as will the Gallic bodyguard. The others you will transport later with our belongings." The agent bowed but said nothing. He followed the three of us up the stairs to the deck, where Arbindus was waiting.

Since the Phoenix was too large to enter the inner harbor, we had to reach the wharf by launch. Overnight the Sirocco had abated, replaced by a gently refreshing southerly breeze. Tiberius pulled a petasos onto his head. He was correct about the brightness. The yellow sunlight was strong but pleasantly so. The water reflected the brilliant blue sky in shifting shades of indigo. Because it was so clear we could see the sea floor even at great depth. A carriage was awaiting us at the dock. After settling us inside, the agent climbed beside the driver who directed the vehicle toward the town.

The city of Rhodes reminded me of Naples, but was smaller and cleaner. Rows of identical white houses gleamed in the sunlight. They stood in uniformly sized blocks of three, following the design of the legendary urban architect Hippodamus of Miletus. Children at play and adult pedestrians in the streets waved as we passed.

"It appears our efforts to remain unnoticed have failed," I commented.

"Not necessarily," Tiberius replied. The people here are simply very, very friendly."

Before long we entered a hilly district overlooking the sea. This was clearly a wealthier area, characterized by tree-lined streets and more elaborate homes set within the standardized, three-house blocks. The carriage halted before the unit on the end of one such grouping. Arbindus as guard waited outside while the rest of us explored the residence. It was built about a central court illuminated by immense windows above the doors on either end. There was a stairway at the rear. The walls were painted in different pastels. Dayrooms were on the first floor, bedrooms on the second. A balcony traversing the rear wall allowed passage from one side of the second story to the other. The exterior wall on the opposite side rose directly above the edge of the street. To ensure privacy the windows in both exterior walls were small and near the ceilings. To enhance light and air circulation, each room had large windows opening into the court. The hillside construction had allowed for rooms to be built beneath a portion of the main house. These comprised the servants' quarters and work areas. They were reached by a flight of steps beneath the primary staircase. An exterior door in this area, opening to the rear, allowed the servants to run their errands and retrieve supplies without having to invade the master living areas.

The rear of the first floor opened onto a walled veranda. Roses planted in pots coursed up the walls. An extension to the main house gave the veranda privacy from the property next door. The servants' bath lay in the subterranean part of this section, the kitchen on the first floor, and the master bathroom on the second. Latrines were on all three levels. Since these rooms required access to the water piped from the aqueduct and to heating fires, their separation from the rest of the building evoked a measure of safety as well as sanitation. In the corner of the veranda which was formed by the intersection of the main house with the extension, a pear tree grew in a great pot. A stone bench stood directly before the tree. The veranda overlooked a sharply descending knoll, embedded with stone steps leading up to a gate in the center of the wall. At the bottom of the knoll was a small stable. Just beyond it and across a narrow street was the rear of another house unit. Looking above its rooftops, and at right angles above the street that skirted our property, one had a commanding view of the sea from two perspectives.

Our hitherto taciturn agent now became as loquacious as any broker desperate for a sale. "As you see, Commander, the house is well illumined. There is ample space in which to entertain guests and clients. The library holds a fair collection of old and new philosophical and literary classics. The walls have been cleaned and repainted. All of the furnishings are either new or reconditioned. Household necessities like cookware, window shades, bedlinens, towels, lamp oil, and charcoal, all have been supplied. The kitchen and the root cellar beneath it have been stocked with provisions. Three house servants—a woman and two men—have been purchased, and a chef has been hired. Three men—one bond, two free—have been procured to serve as bodyguards." I already understood the reason for this last arrangement. Arbindus was Tiberius' slave and would stay with us; but Melambrotus and the Copts had been hired solely for the voyage. Although I liked the Egyptian twins, I felt relieved they were not going to remain since I had never been able to tell them apart.

The agent continued his discourse. "The carriage driver is also a hired groom, and owner of the harness team. A litter has been provided for transport as well. You have a sufficient number of able-bodied male servants to serve as bearers. At your request I am in the process of obtaining a riding horse. The neighbors have been thoroughly screened. They are honest and courteous, and delighted at the prospect of having someone of your exalted status in their midst."

He fell silent and turned away from us, apparently seeking some other virtue of the house to extol. Tiberius leaned over my shoulder and whispered, "Is the place to your liking?"

"Very much; it is quite pleasant," I responded as quietly.

Just as the agent appeared poised to resume his exposition, Tiberius forestalled him. "The house and its staff are amply suitable. You may now proceed with delivering the balance of my travel party and my luggage." The agent bowed and departed. He was a diminutive man with dark hair and skin and rugged features.

Menon had been wandering about, acquainting himself with the appointments of the house, locating supplies, and opening windows to freshen the air. He now approached us.

"Menon, I believe you know the first task I wish you to perform." There was a hint of humor in Tiberius' tone.

"Yes, Master. I have located the charcoal, and shall fire the bath furnace at once."

Not only was I to have my own bedroom, but a set of four adjoining rooms that ran along an entire side of the second floor. This area, which comprised the female quarters of the house, was relatively extensive because it was designed to be shared with children. Although I intended to sleep in the master suite on the opposite side of the house, I found quite pleasing the prospect of a personal retreat far larger than an alcove. My haven also provided a place to keep the multiple and fussy appurtenances of female toilette—clothes, cosmetics, hair ribbons and the like—from getting in the way of and becoming an aggravation to my partner. Already I had had a taste of this luxury in the smaller bedchamber of the Phoenix. Now in my new locale I paced the floor, awaiting delivery of my trunk. When it finally arrived, I immediately started to rummage rather recklessly through the few clean garments that remained.

"Such impatience!" Phoebe exclaimed. "You will not even wait for me to assemble a proper wardrobe for you."

"Phoebe, you are far too slow to make a respectable woman of me," I murmured distractedly. After finally locating an unused dressing gown and my bedroom slippers, I managed to find a comb and a clean hair ribbon. Clutching these, I hurried down the hallway to the bathroom. Tiberius was already lying in the rectangular sunken bath, his eyes closed in pleasure. Wisps of steam rose from the water. "Only sex can convey as much blissfully sensual enjoyment as this," he mused as I undressed. He reached up and took my hand to keep me from slipping as I joined him. The hot water and added astringents made my skin prickle pleasantly with the feeling of cleanliness.

"My hair is sticky from salt spray," I said as I removed the soiled winding ribbon and cast it onto the floor beside the bath.

"That is what comes from standing on deck watching dolphins."

I immersed my scalp in the water, letting my unbound tresses float about; then laid my head on his shoulder. "Why did you ask me whether I liked the house? Was it not your decision?"

"Well, you are going to be its mistress, so I am leaving its management to you. Assigning tasks to the servants and making sure these are completed, deciding how furniture should be arranged and utilized, choosing a new appointment or changing an existing one—all that will be up to you. You will be responsible for scrutinizing the household books, to ensure our domestic finances are being properly managed. We can expect visitors. Virtually every bureaucrat and dignitary traveling between Rome and the East puts in at Rhodes. Since I am still regent they will feel duty bound to call on me. Hopefully I shall never have to hold a formal dinner. Should I decide to, however, I shall rely upon you to plan the menu, arrange the placement of guests at table, and select appropriate entertainment. Are you prepared to accept such duties?"

"With far more zeal than I would ever care to devote to the writing of dreadfully dull treatises about philosophical premises with which I do not agree."

He caressed my cheek and kissed my forehead. "The answer I anticipated from you." He had assessed me ever so correctly. Thoroughly delighting me was the prospect of becoming a housewife—the role I had despaired of ever attaining.

We soaked for a time, then washed ourselves and one other with the strigils and sponges Menon had left at the bath's edge. "One could have grown a crop of barley on my back, I imagine," Tiberius mused.

"And I pity anyone who might have been standing downwind of me," I rejoined.

My thick hair I was struggling to dry with the towels, when an alternative occurred to me. Grabbing the comb and hair ribbon and a fresh towel, I made my way to the veranda. With disappointment I discovered the bench before the pear tree was in shade. After placing my accouterments on the bench I returned to the house, retrieved a chair, brought it out to the veranda, and placed it where I could sit with my back to the sun. I shook out my hair, then combed it and rifled it with my fingers, letting the warm rays and air complete the task towel drying had not.

"Clever idea!" Tiberius had seated himself on the bench. "Only take care that the sunlight does not darken your skin. We would not like to see you looking like a peasant." Hearing that, I spread my hair out all the more broadly across my shoulders. This not only allowed it to dry faster, but also provided a shield for my face and arms.

Tiberius looked the pear tree over. "Let us consider this shrub a favorable omen. Pears are my favorite fruit."

Menon approached us. "Master, Eurycles" (the agent) "has returned with two of the new bodyguards. The other man will arrive tomorrow, as will the new domestic staff."

"Ah good, our poor Gaul will have some relief. As soon as the men are installed in their quarters, have one of them replace Arbindus at watch."

"You are still employing private bodyguards," I commented after Menon departed. "Are you not entitled to the protection of the praetorians?" These are the exclusive squadrons, selected and trained specifically to safeguard the emperor and members of his immediate family during excursions outside of Rome.

"Yes; but I do not care to ruffle feathers at home any more than I have already. Remember, my sojourn here is primarily as private citizen rather than regent. Scrupulously I aspire to avoid doing or saying anything that might be construed as abuse of power."

We watched the light play on the ocean in the distance until my hair was dry. While binding it with the ribbon, I moved out of the sunlight and sat on the bench beside my partner. The sky and sea began to darken as the sun set. In the little garden of a house behind ours, two women were watching two small children at play. "Tiberius, now I am becoming unnerved," I confessed. "I have no experience in managing a household. No one ever taught me its intricacies; and my mother was hardly a decent model."

"Why make things more difficult than they have to be? Menon is responsible for the regular operations. Do not take his burdens upon yourself. If you want something initiated or altered in the house, or if you have a grievance against one of the staff, you need to inform him. He will take the appropriate action. Furthermore, he keeps the actual financial records. All I ask you to do is review these regularly for unnecessary or excessive expenditures. Granted I am reasonably wealthy; but I hardly wish to see my fortune squandered. Meanwhile, enjoy yourself. You have an eye for color and order. Let the place reflect your creativity."

Menon returned and bade us to supper. Aware of the peculiar seating preference we shared, he had replaced the dining couches with chairs. While the steward was serving us some of the swordfish from our voyage, Tiberius addressed him. "Should anyone ask the identity of Lady Clytia, you are to follow the same charade as on the Phoenix. Her name is Daphne; she is my ward; and you know nothing about her person or background. Her real name and her origins must not be disclosed to the new servants, the neighbors, or anyone else. Please remind Phoebe, Alexias, and Arbindus."

Menon bowed in acknowledgment. After he left Tiberius said, "We must continue to take every precaution to ensure word of your identity does not make its way back to your family, and to conceal the true nature of your liaison with me. My family is bound to hear about you. Gossip spreads readily; and I suspect my stepfather already has me under surveillance. Therefore I have created a bogus personal history for you. Our relationship is strictly that of retainer to patron, for you are the beneficiary of my philanthropy. Your father was a peripatetic pedagogue from the Campanian countryside. While I was staying at Baia in anticipation of my triumph, he sought my charity. Having been diagnosed with cancer, he asked me to provide care for you in the event of his passing. You are a most unfortunate young woman. Your mother died long ago from complications associated with your birth. Earlier this year, while I was making preparations for retiring to Rhodes, I learned your father had succumbed to his illness. I also discovered you were undergoing a tumultuous divorce, from a rake who had become abusive and threatening upon discovering you could not bear children. I have brought you with me to Rhodes as a member of my household, to protect you from your former husband, to offer you the opportunity to seek solace from your bereavements through the pursuit of philosophy at the Rhodes Academy, and possibly to find a new spouse for you.

"This ruse should satisfy my family along with curious Rhodians. We can help perpetuate it by conveying an appearance of independence from one another—traveling separately to the Academy or other venues for example, or attending different lectures. This arrangement will enable you to pursue interests of your own, as spontaneously as you please. You can go about the city as you wish. Just be sure you have a female servant and a bodyguard accompany you."

"Hopefully the servants will keep quiet about us."

"We can depend upon those who accompanied us from Italy. Having been trained in my household, they know never to ask, speculate, or divulge. Eurycles took great pains to screen the newcomers for discretion. You must do your part as well. Remember not to discuss your background—even the false one we have created for you—or your feelings with any of the servants. If one of them solicits such personal information from you, report the incident to Menon."

"What about Eurycles himself? You certainly place considerable confidence in him."

"I have told him you are my ward, and nothing more. He manages a firm that consolidates small shipments of goods into larger ones and prepares them for transport to markets. I rented a house from him when I sojourned here before, and was quite impressed with his efficiency and reliability as a personal agent. Naturally I contacted him when I started to plan our present stay. He has a special gift for arranging matters effectively. Moreover, he is impeccably discreet. That is why I intend to name him your curator. Beware nonetheless: he may only be loyal so long as he is receiving remuneration. I take care not to reveal to him anything he does not absolutely need to know.

He also understands that if confidential information leaks out, suspicion will fall upon him immediately and my ample compensations will abruptly cease."

"My curator?"

"Guardian of your properties. Clytia, have you stopped to consider what you would do, should I suffer death or some other adversity that renders me incapable of providing for you?"

"To tell the truth, no. But being highly educated, now thanks to you familiar with sex, and incapable of bearing children, I am ideally suited to become a hetaera. With embarrassment I must admit, that in my euphoria over our new relationship I quite naïvely presumed you would always be here for my help."

"In a way you presumed correctly. After reading my will to my parents, I immediately had it altered to include you as a remainderman of second order. If I die, my son receives two-thirds of my entire estate. Two-thirds of the remaining balance goes to my brother's children. Julia receives the standard widow's legacy of a mere 100,000 sesterces—paltry because a widow's dowry automatically reverts to her. The final portion of my estate is divided among the few distant relatives and several friends and retainers whom I particularly wish to honor. One of the latter is the woman known as Daphne Hipparchide. Although your portion may be comparatively small, it will not leave you destitute."

"You would do that for me?"

"Have you forgotten I love you, and am grateful beyond measure to have you as my companion?"

"The entire notion is still quite new to me. I am not sure what to say apart from *Thank you*."

Returning my smile, he took my hand in his. "A finer response you could not have given."

The next day, Eurycles took us by carriage to see the public areas of the city, which were actually a short walk from our townhouse. Afterward he showed us a villa in the suburbs. It was barely larger than the townhouse, also double-storied, but built about an open courtyard adorned with columns, potted shrubs, statuary, and a reflecting pool. To ensure coolness in summer, the actual residence was entirely on the first floor: the dayrooms on one side of the court and the bedrooms on the other. To catch natural breezes, the rooms had windows opening onto the courtyard as well as the exterior. The kitchen was an extension on the rear of the dayroom section, the bath correspondingly on the bedroom side. The servants' quarters were on the second floor, where a slave couple was already in residence. A hallway between the two extensions exited to a formal garden, replete with trees and statuary and flowering plants.

In one corner there stood a small belvedere with a fountain at its center. A high stone fence lined with shrubbery enclosed the garden. The stable and fields were just beyond this wall. Once again Tiberius asked my opinion of the premises, and once again I approved.

Upon our return to our townhouse we met our new servants. Eurycles had acquired the three new housekeepers—Nicanor, his son Ajax and daughter Penelope—from the liquidated estate of a recently deceased local tradesman. Almost immediately they assumed the invisibility that characterized well-trained servants of their type. The slave bodyguard was a Cappadocian named Androcles, who responded with delighted affirmation when I asked if he knew Menon was his fellow countryman. The two hired guards were a local father and son, Chryses and Chrysides. As part of their service they brought with them a pair of excellently trained mastiff guard dogs.

The hired cook Dorotheus, a most pleasant man, was almost as wide as he was tall. There was an oddness about him that I could not identify. He was not exactly effeminate; yet he had a high-pitched voice and a certain delicacy to his movements. Tiberius later explained he was a eunuch. They are common in the easterly regions of the empire, because the practice of castration prevails in the Asiatic kingdoms lying yet farther to the east. With the very first supper he served, Dorotheus introduced me to lobster—yet another culinary delight of which, owing to my brother's refusal to consume fish of any type, I had never partaken despite its commonality at Naples. Over the next several weeks, Dorotheus' efforts would acquaint me with the immense variety of fish and shellfish that teemed in the waters off Rhodes—and much to my appreciation.

On the day after the expansion of my gastronomic horizon began, so did the transformation of my person. Eurycles arrived with two men. One of them—tall and lanky with long gray hair—stared down his nose at me disdainfully through half-closed eyes. The agent introduced him as Demas, a renowned teacher of manners. The other man—short and pudgy with curly brown hair and a warm smile—carried an object concealed in a fine linen sack. He was Erastus, an instructor of singing and of the harp. That is what was in the sack.

We withdrew to the library. While I stood in the center of the room Demas walked around me, looking me up and down with his hand on his chin, as though I were a piece of dilapidated furniture with little hope for restoration. He had me walk back and forth a few times and sniffed as I did. Then he asked me to recite the alphabet, and thereafter to sing the first stanza of a hymn. When I denied knowing any he looked at me with condescending surprise, then asked if by any chance I knew the notes of the scale. After I sang them he again drew up close, studied my face intently, and tugged at my hair. Finally he stepped back, folded his arms, and delivered his assessment.

"Walk has a noticeable bounce. Speech has particularly forceful inflections. Singing voice is gravelly and slightly flat. Hair is thick and poorly trained. Whatever treatment was applied for acne was excessively strong, and left the skin on the forehead scarred and parched."

My response of, "Coarse barley meal, mixed with crushed peppercorns and camellia leaves, and bound with extracts of camphor and lavender," elicited another contemptuous sniff. "It suppressed the acne, did it not?" I snarled.

"Somewhat," he scoffed. "You still have emergent pimples. Facial features are nicely proportioned," he continued, "with the exception of those broad teeth."

"Am I expected to be able to alter their shape at will?"

He paused to glower at me before continuing. "Heavy bone structure, emphasized by excessive weight in the lower abdomen and hips. Impudently defensive. A fair amount of training is in order, my lord Tiberius. I should like to start right away tomorrow midmorning if you are agreeable."

"Certainly!"

Humiliated and angered as I was by the evaluation, I was mortified all the more to discover his lordship smiling gleefully. Before I could react, Demas swept out of the room with his long nose in the air. Then the music master began his first lesson, which had a calming effect on me. Erastus was the precise opposite of Demas—patient, tolerant, and even complimentary. He was intrigued that I could read music but not play an instrument; and he listened with genuine interest, while I explained how I had studied music theory as part of an advanced academic curriculum. He showed me how to correlate the written notes with the strings of the harp, and how to create different notes by placing my fingers in various positions along the strings. He would teach me how to sing, he said; I should not worry over the mannerist's comment about my voice. The harp was mine to borrow. He asked that I familiarize myself with it until he returned for my next lesson.

After Erastus had departed, I confronted my lover for the first time since our relationship began. "How could you sit there and laugh while that horrid man belittled me so? I felt like a substandard heifer being degraded by a livestock trader!"

He grinned again. "Do you not understand he was testing you? He wanted to determine how you would respond to embarrassing situations and insulting or uncouth remarks. Do not let him unnerve you. All that is part of your training."

My heart sank. "I hope to get through this without shedding blood—his or my own," I murmured.

"You will be quite all right: of that I have every confidence. Meanwhile, here is something to console you. Alexias!"

The servant entered the library carrying something in a large, loosely woven satchel. When he set it on the floor, the bag began to move. Then it fell open.

"Leo!" I exclaimed. "What a wonderful surprise!"

The cat uttered an enthusiastic "Brraouh!" as he bounded over to me. He proceeded to rub against my legs.

"Thank you, oh thank you my love!" The now loudly purring Leo I gathered up in my arms.

"I had the steward of my villa at Baia kidnap him shortly after our departure, and send him here on a merchant vessel. It is well Menander intervened when he did; for your family had begun to neglect Leo. They were seldom letting him into the house and only feeding him sporadically. His fur had become dirty and matted. His rescuer paid the ship's crew to feed him well and groom him—a responsibility they accepted with delight, the steward said."

My exhilaration gave way to bitterness. I was seething with anger even more than before, but now not at Demas. "Such I should have anticipated," I fumed cynically. "Hopefully that house is hopelessly overrun again with mice and beetles! Maybe they will get my brother another toad, and pretend it will control the invaders."

"Do not brood; you will only make yourself miserable. Instead, rejoice we were able to rescue your friend Leo."

So touched was I by this expression of kindness and affection, that I resolved to proceed with my finishing no matter how much maltreatment the instructor heaped upon me. Indeed he had been testing me after all. Demas proved to be one of the kindest, most patient, supportive, and encouraging men I have ever encountered—deeply sympathetic about the deficiencies of my upbringing. Hence for the next three weeks or so I spent practically the whole of each day in my bedroom suite, discovering with joy the skills of comportment and etiquette, which had been scorned in my childhood as the province of dandies and courtesans.

Tiberius did not mind my preoccupation, being engrossed in activities of his own. Aspiring to keep abreast of government activities, on many mornings he met with local officials both Roman and Greek, and attended sessions of the municipal council. He also set about acquainting himself with the Rhodes Academy, and with the city's libraries, galleries, and other educational offerings.

Oftentimes he repaired to the city's gymnasium or to the local military barracks. Not to lose his martial skills, he arranged for regular practice with armaments on foot and on horseback. Eurycles had duly procured a gelding, aptly named Sinapeus for the mustard-like color of his coat.

Phoebe sat in on my training, not only as chaperone, but also to learn how she might assist me with specific elements of dress or toilette. Mornings were devoted to my physical refinement. Demas began by teaching me the steps of traditional Greek folk dances, which I had never learned because my family neither hosted nor attended social or religious events of any sort. Rhodians are inveterate dancers, he explained, and my participation in women's dances at functions will be expected. More importantly: from the practice of dance, my ordinary body movements would become controlled and graceful. He spread pebbles on the veranda and made me walk on the stones. After a few days he had me do so while trying to balance a writing tablet on my head. Once I was adept at this, he replaced the tablet with a dasheen that kept rolling off. But by the time a week had passed the bounce to my gait was gone, and I could walk a straight line while balancing a saucer of water on my head without spilling.

I learned how to ascend and descend the staircase while keeping my head level, lowering only my eyes, and holding the skirt of my chiton or gently kicking it in front of me to ensure I did not trip. Demas encouraged me to take the stairs frequently and vigorously as an exercise for losing weight. He also showed me how specifically to reduce my abdomen and hips, by lying on my back and then repeatedly pulling myself into a sitting position. We discussed my eating habits. From having been forced to eat excessively as a child, I had developed a hearty appetite. This I could curb by drinking water or wine before and during meals, consuming my food slowly, and leaving off while still feeling slightly hungry. My description of how I became drunk on Sicilian wine elicited a sympathetic laugh. He recommended several far lighter Rhodian wines, and urged me to make sure I cut them with water.

One morning, Demas arrived with his wife Timoxena. Her first action was to ask Phoebe to draw me a bath. No, I was not offensive; but as a woman of childbearing age, I ought to bathe more than once a day if possible—especially when engaging in sexual activity or planning to do so. Concluding she had surmised the true nature of my liaison with Tiberius, I felt myself turn hot with embarrassment; yet Timoxena took no notice. She was instructing a pupil, not trying to impute something to me. Frequent bathing would reduce my chances of developing vaginal and uterine infections, she continued. After the bath she anointed my body with a fine light oil. Its regular use, she said, would keep my skin clean, supple, and desirable. When I started to clean my teeth, Timoxena inquired from what ingredients the dentifrice was made. Rock salt and macerated pellitory nettle, Phoebe replied, a combination favored by Tiberius' mother. Highly effective, Timoxena acknowledged, as my teeth were thoroughly clean and my mouth free of odor. To keep my breath all the fresher, she recommended I gargle and rinse my mouth with a solution of water, lemon juice, and crushed mint leaves or extract of mint.

She talked with me at some length about wardrobe. A garment should flatter the body, she asserted. It should provide a hint of enticement but not be indecent. And for a woman in an active relationship with a man, it should be designed for easy but graceful removal. Again I turned hot; and again Timoxena paid no heed. After measuring me from shoulder to ankle, and then about the bodice, waist, hips, and thighs, she promised to design several prototype garments as examples for purchase in the marketplace or creation at home. Scarves and veils are essential to ensure modesty in public. Moreover they should complement and enhance a costume. Their colors might match those of my chitons; or they might be different so long as they did not clash. While I sat looking at a mirror, Timoxena held differently colored swaths of material against my face to determine which best complemented my complexion. Shades cool and deep—like blues, greens and grays—proved the most becoming. Reds and yellows if too blatant could make my skin appear waxen. When selecting these particular colors, I should make sure nuances of the cooling hues are in some way present. Hence ochre is preferable to lemony yellow, crimson to scarlet, sapphire blue to azure, mauve or violet or rose to bright pink.

The purpose of cosmetics, Timoxena explained, is to enhance existing features but not to alter them or create new ones. Hence this adornment should be applied sparingly: a woman should look like a woman, not a painted doll. As my bluish-gray eyes are large with naturally dark shadings, they do not require emphasis. I should therefore coordinate the colors of my eye makeup with those of my clothing. Timoxena showed me how to broaden the appearance of my mouth with lip rouge, thereby minimizing the size of my teeth. Since my cheekbones are somewhat low, they must be highlighted by the application of color slightly above the bone line. The acne damage I would always have; my hair, however, could be trimmed and styled to cover or at least draw attention away from the marks. Natural oiliness and further acne breakouts I could control by wiping my face with vinegar or lemon juice. Timoxena added she had observed a correlation between acne eruptions and anguish. What a revelation!

Her conclusion, if true, certainly explained my affliction with this ailment and Tiberius' as well.

Timoxena gave me an assortment of perfume samples in a host of little vials. She instructed me to rub one on my wrist, wear it for an hour, then wash it off and apply a different one. Never choose a perfume for the way it smells in its bottle. Application to the skin and exposure to the air alters a fragrance. I should ask the members of the household what they thought of each scent. What good is a fragrance if it offends the people its wearer encounters? Once I had decided which suited me best, I should use it exclusively. Not only would it become a sort of signature for me. After a particular fragrance has permeated my clothes, the use of a different one might create olfactory havoc by combining two conflicting scents. Care must be taken not to apply too much perfume. After wearing a scent regularly, one cannot detect it on one's self.

She unbound my hair, and commended me for its cleanliness as she combed it. I explained how I had washed it on the afternoon of our arrival and then struggled to get it dry. A proper trim would eliminate that difficulty, she said as she held up swatches to determine thickness and patterns of growth. When she picked up a shears, I intervened. Tiberius' birthday was imminent. I had been struggling with ideas for a gift. How does one find a present for a man who has always had easy access to any object he might desire? Why not give him the gift of a refashioned me? Timoxena was delighted with my idea. She would wait until that day to bring my new wardrobe and style my hair.

Demas worked with me to refine my facial expressions, which I practiced while gazing at myself in a mirror. He had me read aloud in Latin as well as in Greek, and coached me on my enunciation. I should make a point of conversing in Latin regularly, he said—with Tiberius and with those servants who spoke that language—lest I lose my proficiency in it. Remember, I was now living in environs where Greek was spoken almost exclusively.

Demas taught me how to project my voice, to ensure I made myself heard clearly without sounding harsh or excessively loud. To assist me with these declamation exercises, he brought Procne his daughter of ten years. On a little flute she sounded different tones to signal when my voice was too high, too low, too loud, too soft, or abrasive.

We engaged in discussions of various innocuous subjects: our favorite colors, favorite foods, his two daughters, my fascination with textiles, the antics of Leo, our respective opinions of the weather in Rhodes. Demas averred my experience as a tutor and teacher had given me the singular asset, of being able to initiate conversations without appearing ill at ease or making others feel so. My interest in cultural backgrounds presented another advantage. Information of this nature provides ready and pleasing subjects for discussion. People love to talk about their personal histories, even when those are unhappy.

Then one day, he confronted me with a disturbing question. Why was I so irreligious, seeing that I did not even know any hymns or sacred dances?

I started to explain how my family had never engaged in traditional religious rites; that I believed in an incorporeal, underlying cosmic Goodness; how I felt what most people called gods were the various manifestations of this Principle in human experience; that I had no quarrel with the beliefs of others. At this point he stopped me: too many words, too much information. He had not asked me to explicate my religious stance but had challenged it. In such circumstances, he said, shy people like me tend to become immediately defensive of their attitudes.

He advised me to deflect challenges back at the challengers. Why are they asking such questions; do my opinions disturb them; do they really want to listen or just quarrel? I might insist that I preferred not to discuss such matters, change the subject, or merely excuse myself and walk away. Never should I try to belittle such adversaries, or prove them in error and myself right. This only inclines them to challenge all the more. When faced with sarcastic comments or with grunts and sniffs, the likes of which he had expressed at our first meeting, I should try to remain unresponsive. And finally: I might simply choose to ignore an assailant. Demas asked me to insult him. I said his hair was repulsive. He did not respond but looked out the window unperturbed. My lesson was learned.

Above all, I should never become disturbed or frustrated because someone else is being obstreperous. Why punish myself for another's foolishness or lack of breeding? Furthermore, forgiveness might be in order. Not even the most refined, the most rational, the most gracious of people, are exempt from speaking or acting stupidly at one time or another. On finding myself flustered I should take deep breaths, and then turn my thoughts at once to the contemplation of something particularly pleasant—like the ocean on a languid summer's day or my cat curled up on a blanket in winter. This technique momentarily detaches one's attention from the immediate confrontation, and promotes a calmly rational response. Also useful for curbing sudden reactions, it should deter me from making the excessive displays of emotion Tiberius wanted me to control.

No one had ever called me shy before. Little wonder I had always been defying my family—resenting their efforts to turn me into something I was not, trying without success to show them how wrong they were about me. Tiberius commented afterward that even he had not fully perceived this aspect of my nature, most likely because I had always been so outspoken. His family had recognized his shyness and taken steps to remedy it. Mine ever so predictably had done precisely the opposite.

After this revelation I plunged into my finishing with greater enthusiasm than ever. Right at dawn or occasionally even before, I would rise to perform my various exercises and practice my dance steps. For this I was especially glad to have my own rooms, so I did not disturb the rest of the household. At Tiberius' insistence, Leo slept in my boudoir: "Sufficient I rescued that cat; we are not sharing our bed with him!" Leo had laid claim to the couch in my quarters, on which I only intended to sleep during the very rare times I was menstruating. When I arrived on those early mornings Leo would look up at me with groggy incredulity, then turn his head upside down and go back to sleep.

From time to time, Tiberius urged me to engage in some diversion— to accompany him to a lecture or concert or one of the city's many other academic and cultural offerings. Invariably I refused. "Not until I feel sufficiently refurbished!" I would insist as he rolled his eyes.

Erastus the harpist, who was Timoxena's brother, made a point of coming when Tiberius was away and not around to hear us. I learned to extend the range of my voice by controlling my breath and resonating it through my nasal passages. One's voice, Erastus said, sounds different inside one's own head from the way it sounds to bystanders; this was why I sang off key. He taught me how to compensate for flatness by singing slightly higher than the pitch of the music as I perceived it. My voice would never become as refined as a professional singer's, but with practice become acceptably melodious. Erastus felt I showed an aptitude for the harp, and expected I would soon be ready for a more complicated instrument. So for the first time in my life I was enjoying music as it was meant to be enjoyed—played and sung, not studied as dry theory. As part of my preparation for Tiberius' birthday, I had Erastus recommend several simple pieces. These I practiced until I could play them without mistakes, and in a sufficiently polished manner that they did not sound perfunctory and mechanical. I did not venture to prepare any songs because we agreed my voice needed further training.

Timoxena inquired whether I knew how to embroider. Yes, I replied, although I had never really pursued the art. My mother and her aunt had always decried it because, like weaving, they regarded it the work of menial laborers. While that may be true in a professional sense, Timoxena said, the pursuit of embroidery is an excellent way to cultivate one's perception of detail and symmetry. I would find such strengths useful, when deciding how furniture ought to be arranged or a window appointed or a dining table set. Embroidery is also very relaxing, a good way to diffuse stress. *And what a wonderful way, I reflected, to further my appreciation for textiles.* So I began, without guilt, to pursue a pastime I had always desired but never been allowed. Reviewing my initial efforts, Timoxena expressed pleasant surprise and declared I had genuine talent. She said a level of precision and creativity, which many achieved only after months or even years of practice, came to me naturally.

Demas brought several artist's palettes, charcoal pencils and an assortment of paints. He urged me to experiment in mixing colors and drawing shapes. This would train my eye, he said, for the coordination of hues when selecting attire for myself or appointments for the house. I showed him Melambrotus' variegated altar cloth, which he declared an excellent model. He averred its colors, though manifold, are carefully placed so not to clash with those adjacent.

Within a few days we discovered I had even greater aptitude for pictorial art than for embroidery. Demas supplied me almost daily with blank palettes, which quickly became a burgeoning collection of representations. With utmost enthusiasm I began to sketch simple objects like furniture and kitchen utensils. Then I went on to arrangements of dishes and fruits, mastering their more intricate shadings with minimal difficulty. With similar ease I graduated to the next level of complexity: trees and flowers and animals. I began with the roses on the veranda, the potted pear, and the views of the ocean from the bench beneath that tree. Then I turned to Leo and Sinapeus, Hipparion and Bucephalus the carriage horses, the two watchdogs, and the three little wood carvings from Melambrotus. Lastly I began to depict people: Tiberius of course, Phoebe and Menon and Alexias and Timoxena, the new housemaid Penelope, Dorotheus the chef. And ultimately, I began a great gift project. With the aid of descriptions from Phoebe, I managed to sketch a representation of Tiberius' son.

Tiberius and I decided that since his birthday marked our first special occasion since arriving in Rhodes, we should repair to our villa that afternoon and remain for the next few days. Advised of our intentions, Timoxena agreed to meet me there for pursuing my makeover. Dorotheus I enlisted to prepare a special menu of Tiberius' favorite foods: red mullet, long beans, elecampane, Rhaetian wine of which Tiberius had grown fond during his years on the Dalmatian front, or if this was unattainable then a popular Italian variety like Falernian.

On the morning of that sixteenth day before the Calends of December I came to breakfast in my dressing gown with my hair still in its night braid, and made a point of being offhand and nonchalant as though this day were no different from any other. Tiberius was preoccupied anyway. The municipal council of Rhodes had invited him to a noontime banquet in honor of his birthday. As usual he was dreading the inevitable focus of attention which an event of this sort imposed upon him. He called for the litter to convey him to his ordeal.

As soon as he had departed I summoned the carriage and left for the villa with Phoebe and the chef. We arrived to find Timoxena had already arrived, and was awaiting me in the bedchamber I had designated mine. She proceeded to rub a satisfyingly astringent pomade into my scalp and brushed it through my hair. Then she began to trim, not so much to shorten as to sculpt. After cutting, combing, and rebinding, she had me look in the mirror. My face was framed in feathery curls that covered the acne scars, while the bulk of my hair rippled in flowing waves. I had never realized my coiffure could be made to look so soft and pretty and—well, feminine.

Next, Timoxena ordered me a bath. The perfume I had chosen as my signature fragrance was night-blooming jasmine, which to me seemed to convey a nuance of mystery. Timoxena dribbled an oil of this scent into the water. After the bath I returned to the bedchamber. The new chiton Timoxena had selected for me was lavender in color. Owing to the weave of its cloth, it caught the light and shimmered as I walked. She added a pale blue veil trimmed with a brocade of darker blue. The binding ribbons for my hair were of the same brocade. The clothes complimented my complexion and coordinated with my new hairstyle to create a distinct impression of delicacy. We applied makeup (sparingly!) to complete the effect. For perhaps the first time ever I truly felt like a woman instead of an overgrown schoolgirl. Sitting in my room, I breathed deeply and pondered pleasant thoughts to insure my composure. When Tiberius arrived I picked up my representation of Drusus and entered the courtyard in a slow, measured walk. Looking earnestly into his eyes I smiled and said, "Happy birthday, my love."

He stopped short, and gazed at me as though transfixed. "By all the gods!" he finally exclaimed in a breathless undertone. He walked around me as I stood, looking me over the way Demas had on our first meeting. This time, however, I felt flattered instead of demeaned. "You are ravishing—utterly ravishing!" he exclaimed at length.

"Demas and Timoxena have worked very hard to make me so."

"Allow me to correct. YOU worked very hard with them to uncover what was already there. This I insist you recognize and acknowledge."

"Thank you—you always say the kindest things to me."

"And you always respond as though you are not entitled to them."

"Here is a gift I made for you. I hope you find it pleasing." When he looked at the portrait, he gasped.

"What do you mean, you made this? You have never laid eyes on my son."

"Phoebe described him as I sketched. The process came very naturally to me and much to my surprise. My family never encouraged or even allowed me to draw or paint, so I never realized I had artistic potential."

He shook his head from side to side in astonishment. "You are amazing! To think such talent went undetected for all these years. I hope you intend to pursue these endeavors."

"Indeed I do, and with the greatest of zeal!" As I smiled at him he took each of my hands in one of his and kissed my forehead. At last I realized why he performed this gesture so frequently: I stood at precisely the right height.

He led me to the master bedroom where, as I helped him remove his toga, I asked him about the celebration in his honor. He replied it had followed the usual dreary pattern of long-winded tributes from various public officials, extolling his family's distinctions along with his own, and exulting over the fact a personage of his great renown had chosen to sojourn in their city. While pouring water into the basin on the washstand from the storage jar that stood on the floor I said, "Now you can appreciate why I recoil when you bestow praise on me."

He washed his face and rinsed his mouth and dried with the towel I handed him. "You deserve the compliments I give you."

"No less than you deserve the accolades people will always and inevitably confer upon you. You need no reminders that you are a very distinguished man, Tiberius—not only by virtue of your familial connections but also because of your own accomplishments, especially as a military leader."

For a long moment he pondered my words. "We are truly two of a kind, my Clytia, plagued with an inherent self-effacement engendered by our inveterate shyness."

"I prefer to think of it as humility."

After another reflective pause he smiled. "Your last sentence is every bit as magnificent a birthday gift as the others you have given me. And you look so stunning, I am almost afraid to touch you." He glanced toward the bed.

I shut the door. "Do not be afraid," I murmured as I slipped out of my easily removed garments and into his arms.

We had developed the habit of going outside between bath and supper on afternoons when weather permitted—whether to our townhouse veranda or to the villa's garden—to talk about our activities of the day or anything else that came to mind. On this particular occasion I donned Phoebe's North African shawl against a slight, mid-autumn chill. My partner grabbed his favorite homespun cloak. I had planned to bring my harp and play it, but reconsidered since a fog was starting to roll in from the sea. Hardly did I care to risk the damp harming the instrument.

As we were seating ourselves on a bench within the belvedere, the resident house servant Nestor approached with a letter packet. A military messenger, he said, had just delivered it. Although practically all commercial shipping ceased during winter, the operations of the military post continued throughout the year. "Ah, birthday greetings from my family," Tiberius remarked as he opened the packet. After reading the first tablet he smiled and handed it to me. It was inscribed with the large deliberate calligraphy of a child. The first line was in Latin. *We miss you Papa: come home as soon as you can.* The second, in the appropriate language and script, read *See, I am learning to read and write Greek.*

There were greetings from Augustus, from Livia, from Antonia, even from Julia and—to Tiberius' pleasant surprise—from his former wife Vipsania. All of the messages had a common theme: we miss your person and your political presence; we hope you will reconsider your decision and return to Rome; nevertheless we hope you are healthy and happy and enjoying Rhodes.

Although the messages from Julia and Vipsania contained nothing more, the others were replete with chatty personal information. Augustus, whose general health was chronically poor, complained good-naturedly about the various ailments afflicting him, and asked Tiberius to forward any appropriate remedies he might come across while in Rhodes. Amused, I observed Augustus had combined Greek and Latin phrases together in some of his sentences. "He does that all the time in his private letters," Tiberius explained.

Antonia wrote her elder son Nero and Tiberius' son Drusus his first cousin had become inseparable companions. She added that things were far too quiet without Tiberius around. At Augustus' invitation, Antonia had been residing in the emperor's home with her daughter and two sons since the death of her husband.

Livia advised the statue of the goddess Hestia, which Tiberius had purchased from the city of Parium *[Kemer, Turkey]* in northern Asia Minor, was due to arrive in Rome any day. In accordance with his request, preparations were in place for installation of the image in the Temple of Concord. A peace offering of sorts, Tiberius explained, and a profound political statement. Investiture of the Greek goddess of home and hearth, in the Roman temple dedicated to domestic and national harmony, was his way of showing he intended no disruption either to his family or to the state. He had negotiated to buy the statue from the Parians immediately after we had arrived in Rhodes. I was unaware of the transaction because I was preoccupied with my finishing at the time, and he had forgotten to tell me about it.

Owing, I presume, to my three-year association with Tiberius, I felt no sense of awe as I read this private correspondence from Rome's emperor and his kindred. Instead I reveled in the warm familiarity of the messages. Beneath the abrasive politics around which their lives revolved, beneath the trappings of unsurpassed power and privilege and affluence, the Caesars were simply another family and clearly a far more pleasant one than mine. The affability of the communiqués, the lack of sarcastic or cryptically hurtful comments, impressed me strongly. Tiberius was seriously at odds with his family; yet they had put the differences aside to wish him well on this most special personal occasion. My family had always found ways to make me feel guilty for accepting the birthday celebrations they held for me.

My companion grew thoughtfully quiet again, fingering the tablets as he reflected. I sided against him and laid my head on his shoulder. He drew his free arm across my back.

"You miss them," I said, referring of course to his family.

"Truthfully, I do," he sighed. "Even Julia."

"It was nice to see you received a salutation from Vipsania."

"We resolved to remain friends so long as her husband does not object. We take pains to maintain a discreet distance, to avoid words or gestures that might be construed as allusions to intimacy. Although we acknowledge one another's birthdays—hers is the Nones of April *[4/5]*—we do not exchange gifts."

Do you think you will ever return to Rome? A silly question, I suppose."

"So I am resolved, but hardly to those emotionally wrenching and potentially hazardous conditions from which I fled. At this moment I have no solutions for them. Nor, presumably, does my stepfather; otherwise he would have offered them to me."

Although my next inquiry frightened me, I felt all the more uneasy not asking it. "Would you return to Julia?"

"I anticipate having to, sooner or later. Remember, in my milieu a marriage is a statement of political alignment. To divorce Julia, or to remain permanently separated from her, might impel my stepfather to breach amicitia with me. Do you know what that implies?"

"Yes," I replied, recalling my study of Roman political practices. "It is the utter renunciation of one's agreement with and support for the person, ideals, intentions, and proposals of another—as when your father repudiated Lucius Scribonius Libo."

"Precisely. Such disputes can escalate into feuds of major proportions as relatives, retainers, and political adherents of the two opponents align themselves accordingly. Marriages have been dissolved and contracts abrogated by the antagonists and their supporters alike. People have even been killed because of these disagreements, some of which go on for generations. I have grievances against my stepfather, as you well know. Still, I am neither his personal enemy nor an adversary of his government; and I most definitely do not want to be thought of as either. If I must prove this by groveling back to Julia and enduring her scorn, then I am prepared and willing. But I assure you," his tone grew softer but no less determined. "I am resolved to take no direction, no course of action whatsoever, unless you can remain a part of my life."

Raising my head slightly I gazed into his eyes and smiled. He placed the letter packet on the bench and with his free hand caressed my cheek. "Never before have I loved like this," he continued, "with such intensity, such sincerity, such a sense of fulfillment. When I first noticed you at your Academy: brilliantly intelligent, learned and insightful, yet awkward and defensive, pedantic and overly serious—a sad, frightened schoolgirl in a woman's body—you stirred feelings I did not realize I possessed. Never before had I felt so useful, so helpful to and protective of another person. It is as though my being was incomplete until you supplied its missing elements.

"I was delighted to have you as my correspondent, never expecting our relationship to develop into anything more. But when the opportunity came to free you from the ravages of your paternal home and bring you to my hearth, I felt as though an unuttered prayer had been answered. Our voyage and the brief time we have spent here on Rhodes have convinced me my decision was absolutely correct. Since we have been together I have known more joy, more sense of purpose, more inner peace, than at any other time in my life. I respect and love you without limit, without condition. More deeply than my desire to return to Rome and be reconciled to my stepfather runs my continuing hope you will remain with me always, blessing me with your unselfish devotion forever."

I tightened my arms about him, my head still on his shoulder. "Always," I answered, gently but emphatically. "Forever, without reservation, under any and all conditions. If that means crawling through the gutters of the streets or returning to face my mother's retribution, I am yours so long as you will have me, Tiberius. You are right about the sense of completeness. When you asked me to accompany you, not so much the desire to escape my family impelled me as the recognition you make me whole. What you have done for me since—corrected me, finished me, remade me into someone I genuinely like—has made me love you unfathomably. How can I begin to show sufficient gratitude? You have been so kind, so gentle, so infinitely patient with the deficiencies of my character. And no one has ever called me unselfish. Until now, I have always been pronounced the very opposite."

He continued to caress my face. "The personal transformation you have accomplished is unqualified proof of your selflessness. Selfish people lack the humility to change themselves, to admit they require improvement. Can you imagine your mother undertaking the endeavor you just completed? And until now no one has called me gentle or patient. See how love brings out the strengths and better qualities we do not realize we have, and allows us to see them in each other and in ourselves? We need one other, Clytia. I am as prepared to stand by you as you have avowed you will by me. Of this you may rest assured!"

The fog had thickened considerably. It was not the clammy, penetratingly cold sort one might expect for the time of year, but a pleasant cleansing ether that felt almost like protecting gauze. Our kiss was far less an expression of sexual desire than of pure affection, of mutual commitment, of permanent devotion. For a little while we held one other in silence, which I finally broke.

"Not to quarrel, but I am beginning to wonder if Galatea would have been a more appropriate pseudonym for me than Daphne. Like Acis the hero you carried me to safety in the shadow of Aetna. And like Pygmalion the sculptor you have transformed me into someone vibrant and lovable."

He laughed a little. "Too late I fear; too many already know you as Daphne. I do not care to impose another change upon the servants. And you have always been vibrant and lovable: never forget that. Both heliotrope and laurel are sacred to Apollo, my family's patron deity. That is the true reason I chose Daphne for your pseudonym—not because of the horse. My stepfather attributes his victories to his prayers to Mars as Avenging Principle, but ascribes the phenomenal success of his government to his appeals to Apollo as Inspiration and Enlightenment. You are an atheist, I know. Chances are I would be one as well, had I your background. Given mine, however, I cannot help but believe or at least wonder if there is truth to the existence of these divinities."

"I am an atheist only in the sense that I do not believe in anthropomorphic gods. But I view Inspiration and Principle as attributes of Underlying Good, the existence of which I am thoroughly convinced. My own prayer to this Entity brought me to you. It appears your stepfather and I are of similar persuasion. Now I am particularly pleased to be called Daphne."

"And I deeply appreciate your loyalty to my family. Let me warn you: the path to reconciliation with my stepfather will likely prove difficult. So far he has not breached amicitia with me; but should he decide to do so, I shall be roundly and dangerously disgraced."

"I am prepared to stand by you through any and all conditions. This I have said before, and will say again and again until the end of time."

He drew me closer against him. "Thank you," he said fervently. "I love you."

"And I love you—always and forever."

Although it was still relatively early, daylight was fading fast. This was the time of year for short days; and the fog was helping obscure the light. Through the mist we could see the servants beginning to illumine the lamps in the house. My companion rose. "We had better go inside while we can still see," he said as he took my hand. At the door Dorotheus bowed and announced that supper was ready. He had managed to provide the menu selections I had requested right down to the Rhaetian wine. I delighted in the mullet, which like swordfish I had never tasted while living in Naples where it is abundant.

We retired to the library, where I played the harp pieces I had practiced so assiduously. Afterward, Tiberius retrieved from a shelf a large flat box of polished wood. It contained a board of elegantly inlaid wood with a raised edge, a conical cup, and four small cubes of wood. "A birthday calls for dice," he drawled. "Let me guess: you never learned to play."

"Naturally not: games of chance are immoral," I responded sarcastically. "They might engender undeserved pleasure. Worse yet: they might place my brother in a situation where he has to lose."

"Everyone in my family is an inveterate player. Any holiday or special occasion calls for bringing out the board. Julia and I put aside our quarrels to roll dice. Gaming for money is actually illegal in Rome. But so long as it is done in strict privacy the authorities look the other way—especially since Caesar himself is one of the city's most notorious dicers."

He showed me one of the dice. Each side was marked with a number of dots ranging from one to six. The dice were shaken in the cup to ensure that each throw was random. Little shelves within the cup helped with the mixing. The best throw—all sixes—is called the Venus. The worst throw—all ones—is the Dog. Of course that is what I kept rolling. "You will improve with practice," my companion reassured me. "The secret lies in control of the wrist."

We spent the next four days at the villa reveling in one another's company. Immersion in my finishing had allowed me little time to spend with Tiberius during the preceding months, so now I aspired to make up for my absences. Our declaration of the profound love we shared had heightened our desire to be physically near each other. We talked about a host of subjects weighty and mundane; we had sex of course; I embroidered or sketched while he read or watched me; we played at dice (I improved slightly but continued to throw mostly Dogs); and at other times we sat together in silence, exchanging caresses and kisses or simply holding one another. One clear evening we stayed up very late to observe the stars. The villa's suburban location, away from the lights of the city, provided a splendid view of the night sky. No meteors appeared; but the familiar wintertime constellations shone in all their glory. I thought I even detected a bit of reddish coloration in the hazy light of Orion's dagger.

Now I was eager to join Tiberius on his excursions about the city. Rhodes had been an academic and artistic center for more than two centuries. The art galleries and museums, the libraries, the performances of concerts and plays, and the lectures offered by sophistoi at the Rhodes Academy, seemed virtually innumerable. Nevertheless a new fear gripped me. What if a sophistos or student, associated with my father's Academy, should happen to be in Rhodes and recognize me? The solution is so easy, Tiberius remarked, he was surprised I had not thought of it. My physical appearance had already changed: I had lost weight, and learned to carry myself steadily. Why not enhance the transformation by having Timoxena dye my hair?

The process took four days. Each day Timoxena applied a paste of crushed chamomile flowers mixed with lemon juice, and then had me sit in the sun for an hour. She colored my eyebrows as well, and showed Phoebe and me how to reapply the dye as my hair grew out, lest its dark roots betray our deception. One must take care when changing one's hair color, she explained, to make sure the new hue looks natural with one's complexion and eye color.

As we chatted during the dyeing operation, the conversation drifted to my unrequited interest in weaving. Timoxena was just as astounded as Tiberius had been, at my family's incomprehensible prejudice against this activity. She had an extra loom, which she would gladly lend me and show me how to use. Rightly presuming I did not know how to spin thread either, she agreed to teach me this as well. Now Phoebe interjected. She had surmised, from my enthusiasm for textiles, that I was already proficient in both operations. Had she realized my ignorance and desire to learn, she would have offered to teach me on her own distaff and loom.

My initial efforts at spinning and weaving were unqualified disasters. Phoebe worked ever so patiently with me, as did Timoxena and her elder daughter Eunice a girl of sixteen years. But try as they might, they simply could not get me to perform either function correctly. The ability to determine proper tension kept eluding me. Consequently the thread I spun was lumpy and tended to unravel, and the cloth I wove was always of inconsistent density.

With my disguise now complete I felt thoroughly comfortable attending lectures, exhibits, and performances. The lack of pressure to account for or demonstrate what I had learned was new and especially gratifying. And no longer was I deliberately immersing myself in academics to escape the disharmony of a fractious family life. Just as my harp lessons with Erastus had enabled me to appreciate music for the first time in my life, so now for once I was enjoying science, philosophy, and art.

My worries about being identified by someone in the academic community proved well founded, and my masquerade an absolute and effective necessity. At the Rhodes Academy one day we encountered a sophistos from the faculty of the Academia Norenas. He recognized Tiberius immediately and bowed. Then he looked at me, and made similar obeisance without showing the slightest hint of recognition. I felt lightheaded and short of breath, first from anxiety and then from relief. My finishing had proven thorough; for when later I described my response, Tiberius remarked I had betrayed no misgiving but appeared calmly collected and gracious. After learning this sophistos was spending a one-year sabbatical at the Rhodian institution, I felt all the more relieved to be incognito since I stood the chance of encountering him again. Moreover I resisted the temptation to ply him—surreptitiously, of course—for information about my father. Why risk even the slightest chance of disclosing my true identity?

Presently the townspeople began to recognize and accept me as Daphne the regent's ward and quite likely his mistress. Sexual favors in return for protective guardianship was an entirely plausible exchange. Everyone was invariably friendly and cordial. No one stared or whispered or snickered upon seeing me; no one tried to press me for details of my private life. In particular I enjoyed the way parents allowed and even encouraged their children to greet me. Hitherto my experiences with children had almost invariably been unpleasant. My brother had been peevish, spoiled, and contemptuous. No matter how hard I had tried to placate and please him, my efforts were decried as hopelessly insufficient—as firm evidence of my unnatural intolerance and lack of maternal feeling.

My mother and her aunt had always scorned and criticized other people's children as ill-bred, ill-tempered, ill-mannered, or otherwise improperly reared.

My own awkward manners, arising from lack of social training and obligatory adherence to distorted familial values, had prompted the schoolmates of my youth to ridicule and persecute me. My family's requirement I pursue the very highest levels of learning had necessarily kept me separated from the youngest pupils at the Academy. Any inclination to tutor one of these in elementary subjects was construed as intellectual laziness on my part.

Now I found myself rejoicing in the innocence, the spontaneity, the pure joy of living which the children I met expressed, as they mentally imbibed the world around them with wonder and eager curiosity. For the most part they were happy and contented and obedient. The few times I encountered fretfulness or rudeness in children, I was unperturbed. How could these little ones understand—much less control—emotions that adults themselves often struggle to curb and suppress? So I proved to be patient and tolerant and appreciative of children after all. Yet another unfounded guilt my family had imposed on me was exposed and dispelled.

Although he did not expect the members of his family to provide him gifts for his own birthday, Tiberius was particularly diligent about procuring presents for them. More than just commemorations, his bestowals were peace offerings to smooth the hackles his retirement to Rhodes had raised. Three anniversaries fell on successive days in late January. The fourth day before the Calends of February *[January 29]* was the birthday of Tiberius' stepson Lucius—Augustus' second grandson—who reached his twelfth anniversary that year. Livia's followed on the next day, and Antonia's on the day after Livia's. Tiberius elicited my help in finding appropriate gifts.

This enterprise I enjoyed immensely because it enabled me to become acquainted—albeit only indirectly—with members of Tiberius' family. On learning Lucius enjoyed the theater, I naturally suggested an anthology of Greek plays. Unsuitable, Tiberius declared: Lucius was far more physical than studious. We agreed with enthusiasm upon an antique comedic mask. To Tiberius' mother we sent an edition of the works of Phillinus of Cos, an empiricist physician who challenged the methods his fellow Cosian Hippocrates had established two centuries earlier. Livia had a particular interest in medical tracts. Like all Roman housewives she investigated cures and remedies for her household—especially for her often afflicted husband. Moreover she herself suffered from arthritis. For Antonia, who was still struggling with melancholy in the aftermath of her husband's death, we found an unusual anthology of consolation verses by Rhodian poets.

In addition to this slurry of birthday gifts we had to find a suitable wedding present. Julia's elder and namesake daughter was to be married on the Calends of February. Her bridegroom Lucius Aemilius Paullus was also her first cousin. His mother Cornelia was the elder Julia's half-sister—the daughter of her mother Scribonia by a husband prior to Augustus. The younger Julia shared her mother's penchant for items expensive and ostentatious. To the nuptial couple Tiberius sent a serving charger of burnished oak inlaid with a pattern of vines in silver. Likely the pair would have preferred something even more extravagant, but Augustus would have objected. Keeping peace with his stepfather was Tiberius' highest priority.

As Tiberius had predicted, every highly placed civilian magistrate, every officer of the imperial administration, every military commander, putting in at Rhodes felt honor-bound to pay his respects to the regent. The same held true for ambassadors and other officials of foreign governments with ties to Rome. And while he did not accept every caller's overture, Tiberius had to be careful about whom he denied audience. Should his refusal to see someone be interpreted as a deliberate snub, it could unnecessarily and possibly irreparably damage the man's reputation.

Tiberius opened the house to callers on second and fourth Tuesdays and on other days by appointment. On reception days I took special care to render myself invisible. Tiberius hired a young secretary named Galen to keep his calendar and transcribe his official correspondence. Finishing what the secretary could not complete became my task. The dictations consisted primarily of responses to the various petitions Tiberius received, from the townspeople of Rhodes and from virtually everywhere else in the empire.

Many were pleas for arbitration: between soldiers and commanding officers, civil servants and bureau directors, private citizens and judges who had rendered unfavorable decisions. Others were requests for government assistance: seed money to start or improve businesses, loans to repay bad debts, welfare for indigent families whose wage-earners were incapacitated. The vast majority of these Tiberius referred to specifically appropriate authorities: higher-level commanders, bureau supervisors, appellate courts, civic governments. For the most part I found the business tediously boring and repetitious. Why, I wondered aloud one day, did people expend great efforts and vast sums of money to acquire public offices, or otherwise—like my mother—envy those who held such positions? "They are intrigued by the notion of having power over others," Tiberius replied. "The most envious often have the least notion of what government service entails."

Tiberius almost never rejected one particular type of petition; and this kind I never found dreary. He liked to care for sick people—not in actual nursing or the seeking of cures, but in rendering financial assistance, ensuring victims were physically comfortable in their surroundings, and otherwise doing what he could to bring consolation and encouragement to the sufferers and their loved ones. On Rhodes this enterprise had a rather inauspicious beginning. Shortly after our arrival, Tiberius asked the city archons to identify the city's sick. He wanted to review their respective conditions and decide how best to assist them. Instead of presenting him with the list of names he had anticipated, the magistrates had all the invalids transported to a public stoa for him to meet them in person. Annoyed, embarrassed, and chagrined these unfortunates had been so troubled, Tiberius demanded a stool. This he carried to and set before each sufferer, apologized for the imposition, and sat for a time to chat and console and cheer. So he could discuss his beneficiaries' ailments and cures with understanding and empathy, Tiberius perused the writings of ancient and contemporary physicians, and attended medical lectures at the Academy. These I tended to avoid because they usually left me bilious.

So I had the gratification of discovering in my partner an altruism I had hitherto not known about. After making sure the city government clearly understood his intentions, Tiberius proceeded with his efforts on behalf of the sick. He almost never visited an invalid personally, and not simply because his own shyness made encounters with strangers difficult for him. He was afraid the arrival, of so celebrated a person as he at a sick person's home, might create a commotion further distressing the individual he aspired to aid. Therefore he usually sent an agent or servant or hireling, depending upon the service required. When I told him I should like to join him in helping the sick he was delighted. He showed me the list of invalids and their needs and urged me to select what I felt I could accomplish. His admonition, "Just do not weave anything for anybody," elicited a punch to his shoulder.

Out of some odds and ends of cloth I created a doll on which I embroidered facial features, to cheer a little girl recovering from injuries sustained in a fall. With embroidery I trimmed some baby garments Phoebe had made for an incapacitated mother. For a bride-to-be, whose father was injured and unable to work, I purchased and then embroidered some linens for her trousseau. While canvassing the marketplace one day I came across a model of a racing chariot, complete with its four horses and driver, carved from wood. This I brought home and painted to make it appear realistic, and then had it delivered to a sick boy. Presently I took notice: I was engaging in the very type of charitable activities from which my family had debarred me. Why, I kept wondering, had they always emphatically condemned me for these inclinations? Aside from loving one's mate, what could be more satisfying, more uplifting, more gratifying, than helping the less fortunate, especially those who were suffering through no fault of their doing?

One incident was particularly touching. Like Tiberius I refrained from visiting the sick in person—not because I was of exalted status but lest I encounter vomiting. One family, however, had asked specifically for music. Further inquiry revealed they had made the request on behalf of a very elderly relative who was dying. Since I had continued my biweekly harp lessons with Erastus and practiced assiduously all winter, my skill had refined and my repertory of pieces had grown. Moreover by now my singing voice had become acceptable. I spent an afternoon playing and singing for the man as he lay with his eyes closed, barely breathing and apparently taking no notice of me. Several days later a messenger brought a note from his daughter. Her father had died peacefully while humming the very melodies I had performed for him.

By virtue of its location, just off the southwestern coast of Asia Minor, Rhodes is a crossroads between East and West. Here tradesmen bring their wares, not only from the farther reaches of Asia Minor but also from the small kingdoms surrounding this vast province—Cappadocia, Armenia, Pontus, the Cimmerian Bosporus, Judaea, Arabia—and from the imperial duchy of Egypt. Many of these include items acquired from caravans, some of which have traveled as far as India and China. At Rhodes the many small collections of goods are consolidated into large shipments, and then sent on to luxury markets in Rome and other cities in the empire's western regions. Such was the primary occupation of Eurycles our personal agent.

Whenever a cargo ship arrived in port, one could find me with my two mandatory companions—a female servant and armed bodyguard—combing the marketplace for imported spices and foodstuffs and artifacts but primarily for textiles. Here I acquired my first swatch of silk, a fabric I had despaired of ever encountering while living in Naples. *(Too expensive! Shamelessly frivolous! The preference of harlots and homosexuals!)* The majority of fabrics were woven of wool or linen or a combination of the two. What made them fascinating was the seemingly endless array of colors, patterns, and textures. Each culture had its own set of characteristic designs; but the variations on these were manifold. I also procured a food imported from the Far East: an oddly elongated but very tasty and satisfying grain called oryza or risa—something to that effect.

As usual, April brought the rainy season. Since the weather frequently kept us at home and indoors, I spent the majority of those days in an all-out effort to master spinning and weaving once and for all. Neither improved whatsoever. Only my frustration increased, especially when Tiberius laughed at my aggravation. Why, he asked, did I feel I had to master every single endeavor I undertook? A point well taken, I mused, and another unrealistic expectation imposed by my family. Consequently I acknowledged defeat, and returned Timoxena's loom and distaff to her. Nevertheless I valued the experience highly, because from it I gained firsthand understanding of and appreciation for the intricacies of textile manufacturing. And well it was after all, that my family had not given me the loom for which I had implored them so often. As soon as they had noticed my inability to weave, no amount of atonement I offered could have compensated for the abject selfishness of my pleas for that loom.

Timoxena pressed me to devote the time and effort I had been wasting on learning to weave, to training and refining the artistic skills for which I had genuine aptitude. She and Demas could readily supply an instructor, were I interested and Tiberius agreeable. We both assented enthusiastically. For this instructor I anticipated an established artist, or at least a gallery curator or a sophistos specialized in art. Demas instead introduced Timotheus, a retired designer and painter of wall decorations for public buildings and private homes. "While he may not be a profound artistic genius, he thoroughly understands the techniques you need to learn," Demas explained. "Who better to expound them than one whose very livelihood depended upon their proper execution?"

Physically, Timotheus was a piteous sight. About two years before our introduction he had suffered a particularly violent seizure. A slow and painful recovery had followed, leaving his body distorted into a twisted pose. He stood almost bent in half. One shoulder was higher than the other and pointed forward. His neck was nearly horizontal. Barely could he lift his head to look upon someone's face, through the shock of white bangs that hung over his forehead. As the seizure had compromised control of his jaw, his speech was slurred and difficult to understand. Moreover he had a tendency to drool, for which he apologized profusely and kept a handkerchief at hand for mopping. His mental faculties were unimpaired. A twinkle in his eyes betrayed his enthusiasm for his profession whenever he spoke of it. Gracious and complimentary, he examined my work without disdain. He agreed with Demas that I possessed an intrinsic artistic talent which needed only to be groomed and refined.

Timotheus came to instruct me every other week, on those alternate to the ones in which I took my music lessons. He began by having me sit for an hour every other day at a different time of day, and observe the shades of light in my surroundings. Then at the end of the hour I must paint those shades and nothing more on a palette. When I showed him the altar cloth of Melambrotus, he declared it elegant but dangerously contradictory to the purpose of the exercise he prescribed. Each of the panes in the altar cloth was solidly unicolorous, without any shading whatsoever.

My first efforts at fulfilling Timotheus' assignment were drab and uninteresting. The frequency of the rain limited my opportunities to sit on the veranda where illumination was abundant and varied; and the overcast so restricted the light reaching indoors that the house seemed dark and monochromatic. After reviewing my many palettes that had only two or three shades—and listening to me complain about not having access to the profuse light of the veranda—Timotheus gave me a special assignment. Before his next visit I must produce six palettes, each with no less than ten shades derived exclusively from the interior of the house. Thereafter I duly began to notice how a shadow cast on a wall by a lamp or window darkened gradually as it receded from the illumination, how the angle between a wall and ceiling created different hues of the same color, or how the light emitted by a lamp took the form of a sphere. Soon I was well aware of gradations and variations I had always seen but never stopped to observe and contemplate.

After reviewing and approving these efforts, Timotheus gave me leave to paint the shades of the veranda whenever the uncooperative weather permitted. The first time I arrived at the veranda with this purpose in mind, I received quite a surprise. My study of the sparse lighting in the house had so attuned me to the subtle nuances of illumination, that when I walked into the richly variegated light of the veranda I felt as though I had entered a mosaic. On each of the few palettes I managed to produce not ten patches of color but upwards of twenty. Many of these contained blendings and gradations of hues, to illustrate the pulsating and shifting and shimmering of natural light.

Timotheus again approved my endeavors, and set me to work reproducing shapes. Looking at familiar objects—plants and trees, buildings and furniture, animals and people—I must begin by depicting only their geometry—lines and planes, circles and curves. Then without regard to detail I should add only their shadings—their light and dark areas—taking care to represent the natural gradations in the intensity of shadows. Two weeks of these exercises gave me a proper sense of perspective. This accomplished, Timotheus decided my rudimental training was complete. He was confident I possessed sufficient natural talent to develop my art independently, now that his instruction had brought discipline to my methods. In addition to refining my skills with practice I should visit the city's many galleries. There was much to learn from studying the techniques of established artists and applying them to my own endeavors. Timotheus would return monthly to review and mentor my work.

The long warm days of June brought new love. First Eunice, the elder daughter of Demas and Timoxena, was married. Although invited, Tiberius did not attend the wedding for the same reason he did not visit sick people in person. He did not want his presence to create an uproar that detracted from the purpose of the event. I went as Daphne his ward and representative, and enjoyed myself immensely. Demas was correct about Rhodians and their love for dancing. For the lessons he had provided I was most grateful, for I danced with relatives and other guests until my head reeled and my feet hurt. The dancing, and the light Rhodian wine cut with water, rendered me pleasantly silly by the time I departed for home, and prompted Tiberius to insist Phoebe put me to bed in my own quarters. No, I did not get sick. Nevertheless I evicted Leo, and was too inebriated to notice him yowling outside my door until eventually a servant sequestered him elsewhere. "Confound that cat of yours!" my lover fumed at breakfast the next morning. "I am almost considering having Dorotheus turn him into stew!"

Leo proved to be the love gods' next target. From time to time he went prowling, absenting himself from the townhouse for several days at a time. One afternoon he did not return to the kitchen door as usual, but stood mewling at the base of the staircase that connected the veranda with the stable area. A little white female was with him. She ran off when Dorotheus waddled down the stone stairs with a plate of meat scraps; but as soon as the chef departed she promptly reappeared to join Leo at the feast. After a few days she no longer fled, but awaited supper at Leo's side. For the homogeneous texture and snowy whiteness of her fur, I named her Nivea. She never did venture into or even near the house. Proceles the groom reported she had taken up residence in one of his hay cribs. He was delighted to have her. As soon as she became his tenant, the mouse and beetle populations of his barn decreased precipitously.

Alexias followed. He had become enamored of Pericalles, the nursemaid to the two children of the family who lived in the house behind ours. Their love remained unrequited. The girl's owners refused to relinquish her, despite pressure from Tiberius and his offer of a substantial price. They were afraid her departure would upset their children. Eurycles had some reservations as well. Not having not screened Pericalles, he could not guarantee she was not a loquacious tattler who would spread the secrets of our household all over the island. Our other male servants clung to celibate life—if that description can be truly accurate. Arbindus in particular earned a reputation for being one of the most frequent and liberally spending guests at the town's brothels.

Julia's birthday fell on the fourth day before the Nones of July *[7/4]*. Tiberius elicited my help in finding her a present. I came across a bracelet of shells, coral, small gold beads, and glass beads of differing colors. Different, Tiberius remarked, but insufficiently ostentatious to satisfy Julia's fussy extravagance. He told me to keep it for myself; and so I acquired the first piece of jewelry I ever owned. Back to scouring the shops and marketplace, I did not find any other jewelry pieces more elaborate than the bracelet, even though Rhodes is renowned for its goldsmiths. The search for Julia's gift made me ruminate about the members of my family, who had demanded I supply unusual gifts that were difficult to find and then complained about what they received. At length I discovered a large palla-like garment of fine light silk, elaborately embroidered with tiny plant, animal, and human figures, and with strange symbols. The merchant said it was from India, where such garments were worn by women of rank. My companion approved, as (to our relief) did Julia. She promptly thanked him for her gift—in a stiff, tersely formal note.

The Dog Days arrived with their oppressive weather. We chose to spend them at the villa. This structure's thick stone walls and open but shaded interior court kept it cooler than the townhouse. The latter's close proximity to other residences trapped the heat and humidity, stifling what little airflow took place. Sirius, the star after which the season is called, hung like an opaque milky opal in the hazy red morning twilight, belying the blue-white brilliance with which it illumines the skies of winter nights.

For the duration of the summer one wanted to budge, much less pursue regular activities. Occasionally Tiberius received some visiting dignitary; but for the most part we lounged about the villa and its garden. "It is plenty hot in Italy too," he remarked one day while reading a letter from his mother. "No more is happening there than here. My family is passing the season on our yacht. Hopefully this means my stepfather will manage to fit some angling into his schedule. Incidentally, you may be interested to know the yacht is called the Galatea."

"Many times I watched her, as she glided through the Bay of Naples and my mother proclaimed her a frivolous waste of tax money." Tiberius laughed at my response. I continued, "I had always wondered what her name was. From the wall painting?"

"No, actually from the milky whiteness of the summer haze in Italy."

On the Ides of July *[7/15]*, Augustus' eldest grandson Gaius entered his sixteenth year. Ordinarily on his fifteenth birth anniversary (albeit in some circumstances as late as his nineteenth), a Roman youth donned the solid white toga of manhood and was regarded as having come of age. He could now legally own property and enter into contracts without the supervision of a guardian, and was eligible to marry a female Roman citizen. He remained ineligible to vote or hold public office until he attained legal majority a decade later. Gaius on this occasion was going to receive the special designation of princeps iuventutis—principal of youths. This title would reiterate to the public, that Augustus intended Gaius to succeed him as emperor. Augustus was bound to commemorate the event with festive celebrations—prayers, sacrifices, games, banquets, and the distributions of money and goods to the populace.

Since this was so special an anniversary, Tiberius made a point of obtaining a particularly special gift. Gaius did derive pleasure from books and other intellectual pursuits, but was certainly getting his fill of these from the rigorous education Augustus had prescribed for him. Accordingly, Tiberius provided something far more physical: a horse. He had exploited his connections with pro-Roman members of the Armenian nobility to procure a gelding from their finest breed—renowned for health, strength, and swiftness. There was no response from Gaius until Tiberius wrote to ascertain whether the animal had arrived safely. Only thereafter did he receive a brusque answer. It did not even indicate the name Gaius had given the horse, despite Tiberius' inquiry. Tiberius was not certain how to react. Gaius had never been fond of him. Was this present slight a mere breach of etiquette, driven by the spoiled youth's arrogance and lack of consideration? Or was it an indication of political hostility continuing to escalate, perhaps toward breach of amicitia? Although Gaius was yet quite young, he was crown prince nonetheless. A denunciation from him could prove as politically devastating as from Augustus.

On my birthday, Tiberius presented me with a harp of my own. Erastus, he said, had advised I was now ready for a more advanced instrument than the one he had lent me. My new instrument had seven strings, rather than five like the borrowed one. The base was a genuine tortoise shell. The arms and bow were ivory. The sound was hauntingly mellow. It was clearly a very expensive instrument—yet another expression of profound love for which I expressed profuse and ebullient thanks. Of course we brought out the dice board. Now my game was better. I did not get a Venus, but threw far fewer Dogs.

September brought shorter days, and cooler but no less sultry weather. Back at our townhouse I audited the household books and found them in order. Tiberius was reasonably wealthy, albeit not tremendously so. His income arose from rents and the sale of farm products from his landholdings in various regions of Italy and Gaul. One cannot be a senator, he had explained, unless one owned sufficient property to be economically self-sustaining. Senators were forbidden by law to engage in merchandising, lest their attention to commercial matters distract them from affairs of state. Tiberius' assets were sufficient to meet this minimum, and from the balance sustain an ample but hardly extravagant income. The revenue varied slightly from month to month, but was consistently sufficient to let us live comfortably and free from debt. Tiberius appreciated quality, and was willing to purchase expensive goods or services he felt were worth their price. He was equally intolerant of frivolous expenditures. Through the first year of our relationship he required me to justify every purchase I made, until I had learned to evaluate whether I genuinely needed a product and whether its cost reflected its value.

The academic season resumed that month as usual. Many of the lectures and discussions I started to find disappointing. Much of the information and conclusions were becoming repetitious. Soon I began to attend only presentations of material about which I was unfamiliar or uncertain. Tiberius remained an ardent attendee, relishing virtually everything he heard with all the enthusiasm of a new learner. I did take special interest in what he was discovering; and we spent many a pleasant evening reviewing and analyzing his most recently acquired knowledge.

My absences from the Academy allowed me more time to assist the sick, and to practice my music and painting for which my lessons now resumed. To give Erastus and Timotheus vacation time of their own I had not taken lessons during the summer. I decided to redecorate the townhouse a bit, rearranging some of the furniture and hanging my completed tableaux on the walls. One day Tiberius received a pompous sub-legate who had put in at Rhodes while en route to his post in Cilicia. This self-styled authority on everything confidently identified the paintings as early renderings by the renowned Zeuxis of Heraclea. Tiberius promptly disconcerted the braggart by attributing my pieces to an aspiring and still little-known decorative artist: Eutychus of Rhodes.

I relayed the story to Timotheus my instructor. After a hearty laugh he concurred with the pretentious admirer. My work was rapidly developing an excellence, which he was confident should someday enable me to market my efforts. That pseudonym I should not lose, he said. Although female artists have secured recognition and acceptance, I stood a greater chance of gaining success with a male name.

Autumn was another time for birthdays. The tenth day before the Calends of October *[September 23]* was that of Augustus. It had been an empire-wide holiday for two decades. All regular business was suspended. Tiberius honored the request of the municipal council, that he deliver a short speech to open the athletic competition and chariot race they had arranged in celebration. I did not attend, because in Greek locales the presence of women at such events is forbidden. Owing to his distaste for public festivities at which he was on display, Tiberius did not remain for the full duration.

Augustus entered his fifty-ninth year on that day. Over supper I remarked he was truly the political and social genius everyone said he was. At a very young age he had created a monarchy in a king-resistant society by disguising his regime as an extension of the constitutional powers of the Roman Republic. "Sttt, my perceptive one: you are not supposed to notice that!" my companion chided. Tiberius had found a gift of an ancient Scythian dagger to enhance his stepfather's collection of antique weaponry. The blade was engraved with the swirling animal and tree designs characteristic of that culture. The leather scabbard had copper inlays of similar shapes; and the polished wood handle was carved to represent a stag.

Tiberius' son Drusus celebrated his ninth birthday on the Nones of the following month, October. Tiberius sent a ludus latrunculorum. In this militaristic board game each player's object is to take his opponents' men or get them into check. An appropriate offering to a boy who must someday serve as military commander.

October's freshening winds from the north had dispelled the haze and humidity and returned the Rhodian skies to pristine azure. A year had passed since our arrival on the island. Tiberius and I began to take long walks beside the sea—conducting ourselves and conversing with the customary formality we maintained in public, and trailing our regular vanguard of bodyguards and servant chaperones. After commenting that commercial sea traffic was about to diminish for the winter, Tiberius remarked he had reneged on his promise to take me traveling. No matter, I reassured him. For the past year my days had been—and continued to be—so satisfying, so joyous, so filled with new discoveries about others and about myself, that I had not given the least thought to travel. The academic profession my family had sought to force upon me I had abandoned, and become merely a dabbler in intellectual pursuits; but I had become a painter, an embroiderer, a philanthropist, and most gratifying of all a lover.

Although I was generally popular because of my endeavors on behalf of their sick, I had not developed any genuine friendships among the Rhodians. The need to keep my relationship with Tiberius as confidential as possible made me reluctant to develop close camaraderie with anyone else. For most of my life I had been friendless; but now this condition did not disturb me since it was by choice, and not because of parental intrusion or social ineptitude on my part.

"Friends are a potential danger," Tiberius commented after I brought the subject up in casual conversation. "Because they understand your strengths and weaknesses more intimately than do strangers, friends know how best you can be hurt." He proceeded to elaborate. When he was growing up, even though he was raised in a tightly closed coterie of relatives, the only true confidants he had were Nero his brother and Augustus' youngest niece who was to become Nero's wife. Today he regarded his brother's widow Antonia—and me of course—as his only genuine friends. Even his parents failed to fit the criterion he described. His stepfather quite understandably put the interests of his government before any and all personal considerations. While his mother tried to remain cautiously neutral in disagreements between her husband and other members of the family, she inclined almost exclusively on the side of her spouse. Tiberius smiled wistfully and took my hand when I remarked that I understood Livia's dilemma. One's commitment to a lover far surpassed even that to a closest comrade.

Decades later, Tiberius and I both would appreciate only too well the import of these observations on the uncertainty of friendship and the solidity of genuine spousal love. At the time, however, I felt left with the gnawing sense that I must continue to prove my devotion to him was unconditional.

That autumn the labors of love turned out not to be lost after all. Proceles the groom announced one morning that he had just become a grandfather. Since he was only in his twentieth year we were puzzled by this declaration, until he explained that Nivea had produced a litter of kittens. One looked exactly like her, another precisely like Leo; the remaining two were mixed. "How many more of these do you have about the neighborhood?" Tiberius demanded of Leo, who looked up at him quizzically as if to answer, "Hunh?"

Subsequently our neighbors relented, and agreed to relinquish Pericalles in return for our housemaid Penelope. The latter had ingratiated herself to their children through casual conversations over the low backyard wall separating our properties. As a prerequisite to the exchange, Menon interviewed Pericalles to ensure she understood and accepted the secrecy incumbent upon the members of our household. Tiberius gave his sanction to her union with the once lovelorn and now euphoric Alexias. After candidly acknowledging he had no say in the disposition of a slave, Nicanor expressed gratitude his daughter's new owners were both conscientious and nearby. Pericalles seemed a model servant: cheerful, respectful, hardworking, and unobtrusive. Nevertheless there was something about her that made me uncomfortable, and in a very frightening way.

In anticipation of Tiberius' birthday I composed a piece of music to perform on my harp. Since it sounded amateurish and pedestrian, I finally abandoned the effort and prepared to play and sing some of the ebullient Rhodian folksongs I had learned. That evening I finally threw a Venus, in return for which I received a joyously enthusiastic kiss. "You are now a member of a very special family: the successful die casters of this world!"

During that academic season we made the acquaintance of a most remarkable man. Originally from Alexandria, Thrasyllus was a sophistos in residence at the Rhodes Academy. He was an accomplished authority on Pythagoras, and a meticulously analytical reader of all sorts of philosophical tracts. He had already organized and edited the enormous collection of writings by the great Atomist philosopher and ethicist Democritus. At the present, Thrasyllus was engaged in the monumental task of editing the works of Plato. He had determined Plato's writings can be arranged according to Pythagorean principles. They fall readily into nine tetrachords, corresponding to the Pythagorean perfect numbers of four, nine, and thirty-six. Each group of four presents a logical progression of instructional steps for the reader to follow in seeking the moral enlightenment of his soul.

Nevertheless it was Thrasyllus' fame as an astrologer that prompted us to introduce ourselves. We both had long been interested in the scientific study of the heavens. Now Tiberius, having revolted against his stepfather's political agenda, was naturally concerned about his future. Thrasyllus came from a long line of astrologers, well known and highly respected among the ruling families of the East. His wife Aka was a member of the royal house of Commagene. Thrasyllus had made her acquaintance—and subsequently won her heart—while serving as personal astrologer to her cousin Antiochus II, the reigning king of that Asian principality. Her father—the king's uncle—had given his consent to their union without the slightest reservation. For a common academician to receive the hand of a princess was a mark of peculiar honor.

I accompanied Tiberius to his second interview with Thrasyllus. We met in the astrologer's study at the Academy. The room was a typical academic office: cramped, unkempt, and slightly dusty. Cabinets and shelves overflowed with book scrolls and tablets; more of these lay on the desk and on an adjacent table; still others were piled on the floor. A pair of star charts hung on adjoining walls. A celestial sphere of carved wood inlaid with mother-of-pearl stood in the corner where those walls intersected.

Thrasyllus, a man of moderate build, was nearing his forty-third year. His thick black hair and philosopher's beard were edged with gray. Deep brown eyes seemed to glimmer with insight, perspicacity and kindness. Although he exuded a distinct air of confidence in his abilities he was not pretentious about them; and while properly respectful of Tiberius' rank, he did not behave obsequiously.

We exchanged greetings; Thrasyllus invited us to be seated; he offered us refreshments which we declined; he thanked us for honoring him by seeking his services. He then took a chair himself and for some time looked at me in silence, but with a friendly smile. Finally he said, "My dear, I venture you are a Leo born near a cusp. You have the strengths characteristic of your sign: courage, determination, integrity, compassion. But the cusp—be it the setting of Cancer or imminent rising of Virgo—induces uncertainties about yourself. These render you defensive and often confused when interacting with others, incline you toward excessive self-criticism, and promote a tendency to assume unwarranted guilt."

"Astounding!" I exclaimed in genuine awe. "Your reputation is most certainly well deserved!"

He neither exulted in my compliment nor tried to belittle it with false modesty. Instead he responded frankly. "With experience, one gains a certain empathy for people—almost like a sixth sense. I presume to have been correct about your birth sign."

"True to the mark: fourteen days before the Calends of September. And true to my character as well." Despite his offhand dismissal of this insight as something ordinary, I remained astonished.

Thrasyllus glanced back and forth at the two of us in silence for a few moments, and then remarked, "Your feelings for one another run far deeper than those to be anticipated between a guardian and ward."

"Daphne is my mistress," Tiberius said quietly. "For reasons you can appreciate we cannot have this noised about."

"My clients' secrets are also my own," the astrologer returned with a reassuring smile. He proceeded to ask us for the locations of our births, which he wrote on a tablet that had been resting on the table beside him. Rising from his chair, he retrieved from a set of shelves several other tablets which he brought to the table. These contained the records of the stars and planets and their movements in relation to the patterns under which each of us was born. Another group provided the dates and hours at which each pattern could be anticipated down the future. The patterns, Thrasyllus explained, succeed one another like links in a chain. By anticipating how the chain is likely to form, one can predict the future to some extent. Every person has his own peculiar chain; and no two can be identical. You may even have two individuals—say a pair of twins—born simultaneously in the same locale under the same star patterns; yet their destinies will be different.

Tiberius described how he had had our horoscopes charted, and was informed the predictions were identical. Thrasyllus shook his head. Each of us occupies a unique place in time and eternity. Events, however, circulate in currents and eddies about points in time. People are swept together by these swirls—sometimes momentarily, sometimes for long durations—even as dry leaves are carried toward or away from one another on the waters of a stream. As two leaves never merge into a single entity, so no two persons ever have exactly the same destiny. But just as leaves might travel on parallel and intersecting rivulets and sometimes link one to another, so the destinies of two individuals can be so closely intertwined that to a casual or inexperienced observer they seem indistinguishable.

Such was the case with ours. After Thrasyllus completed his calculations he concluded, "Superficially considered, your horoscopes do appear identical. Their differences lie in the finer details specific to each. Now that you have fled the impositions of your respective families, you have duly entered a period of mitigation. This will not bring continuous relief, but only a superficial stability replete with difficulties and contradictions. Each of you will undergo a monumental change, which will require you to assume profound responsibilities you never anticipated. You will both be renowned and influential, but not in ways you would prefer. You will enjoy strong and stable family relations; yet certain fragmenting family conditions will aggrieve you. You will know the loyalty of enduring friendships; but some whom you consider the most trusted of friends will betray you or you will betray them. Women will be a source of vexation to you both. Misinterpretations of your motives and actions will torment you. Neither of you will fulfill the destinies for which your progenitors led you to believe you were intended. You will endure periods of physical separation, some for considerable lengths of time. These separations will strengthen the bond between you. Never will you cease to love one another."

"Is not destiny established at birth?" I inquired.

"Astrologers used to hold this true; but now we find birth indicators represent only part of the picture. The stars unfold one's destiny continually: hence they must be consulted continually. Moreover the stars only reveal your destiny. The manner in which you fulfill it is your responsibility."

Observing my puzzled look, Thrasyllus continued, "Let us say we determine from the stars, that you are destined to kill someone. You could fulfill this prediction by leaving this room, seizing your bodyguard's sword and running him through. But being the ethical woman you are, you instead would go out of your way to avoid placing a fellow human being in danger of losing his life—by not handling weapons of any sort, by scrupulously avoiding situations that might lead to accidents, by ensuring the conditions under which your servants work are safe. Then your destiny must assume a different form. Perhaps one of your guard dogs will attack and kill an intruder. Maybe you will fatally injure someone in an unavoidable mishap. You may find yourself a key witness at the prosecution of a murderer or traitor, who receives a sentence of death as the result of your testimony. Or some lovelorn fool, who has lost his heart to you without your knowledge, may commit suicide because you do not return his affections."

"The gods forbid!" I exclaimed.

"See, there is your morality. You improve it through the continued contemplation of and aspiration after absolute goodness. In doing so you channel the precise form of your predestination toward that goodness."

"My acknowledgment of an underlying eternal Good has already brought harmony to what had been quite a devastating existence."

"Be sure you persist. You will always experience troubles—we all do. You are most fortunate to have discovered a means of coping with them."

Thrasyllus returned to his calculations. "Each of you will be bereft of a child uniquely your own; however the children you engender together will bring you prodigious joy and stabilizing calm—a haven of comfort amid sorrow."

Tiberius startled. "Are you inferring I must face the loss of Drusus, my son and only living child?" His voice quavered with alarm.

"Surely you err, Sir!" I protested. "We cannot engender children together, for I am barren."

"Children do not necessarily take the form of human progeny," the sage returned patiently. "Cherished aspirations or achievements are as much one's children as fleshly offspring. For me to predict the precise time of your son's death—or that of any other living person—would be a gross violation of my profession's ethics."

"Drusus is not uniquely Tiberius' own but shared with Vipsania," I interjected, feeling a certain pride at my deduction.

Thrasyllus smiled but said nothing. He sat back in his chair, folded his arms, and looked at the two of us thoughtfully. "Tiberius, someday your renown will overspread the entire world like the light of the sun. And you, my dear, will bless him with your devotion and bask in his glory—even as the heliotrope flower turns throughout the day to face the sun as he travels across the sky."

The slightest breath of air could have knocked me over. I almost choked, as I fought the impulse to blurt out, *My real name is Clytia!* and risk disclosing my identity. Although I did not believe Thrasyllus knew my father personally,

I presumed the latter was disseminating news of my disappearance throughout academic circles in the hope I would be recognized. As quickly as I could I changed the subject, and asked Thrasyllus for his comments on my notion that sighting a meteor portends a significant change in one's life.

After complimenting me for my interest in so profound a subject, he proceeded to elaborate how the nature of meteors is not fully understood. It has not been determined whether they are stars that have become detached from their orbits as Anaxagoras of Clazomenae maintains, stars blown by winds at high altitudes as Aratus of Soli argues, particles the sun sheds like hairs, sparks from the primordial fire that pervades the heavens, or emanations from some element of the universe yet undiscovered. Like all celestial phenomena, meteors are subject to the same forces that drive the stars. Still, their precise movement remains a mystery. There is some predictability to their appearance. They seem to be most common in April, August, October, November, and December. Nevertheless they also appear randomly throughout the year. Thrasyllus proposed meteors are portents only for those who actually observe them. If your neighbor sees one but you do not, then your neighbor can expect a life-changing event while your experience will remain unaltered.

Tiberius related that many people observed the display of meteors which appeared in August, the month preceding his brother's fatal accident. Many people were affected by Nero's death, Thrasyllus replied. A comet, which is a type of meteor, forecasts an event of worldwide consequence—for example the death of a ruler, the rise of a new nation, the birth of a tyrant, or a large-scale natural catastrophe like a flood or massive earthquake. This is why comets remain in the skies for days or weeks or even months at a time, displaying their warnings to all mankind.

I described the meteor I had observed on my birthday preceding my introduction to Tiberius, and continued that he apparently had observed the same phenomenon at the same time. How could this have occurred when I was in Campania and Tiberius in Gaul? Thrasyllus' answer I could have predicted. The sky is huge. Perhaps we witnessed the same meteor, perhaps two different ones. The portent for us was the concurrence of our sightings, on the same date and same hour.

Tiberius described the meteor we had observed from the deck of the Phoenix. It had appeared like the work of a cosmic paintbrush to him but not to me; yet the emergent talent for painting it had presaged was not his but mine. What had impelled the peculiar selectivity of this meteor? Now I spoke up. Tiberius had unwittingly set in motion activities that precipitated the discovery of my artistry. He had engaged the teacher of etiquette who had required I dabble with paints, merely to hone my perception of color with regard to dress and household appointments. Without this impetus, my artistic aptitude would never have been revealed.

"An analytical mentality for sure," Thrasyllus exclaimed, "worthy of a sophista."

It took every nuance of energy I possessed, every technique of comportment I had learned, to maintain my calm and poise.

Our interview marked the first of many rewarding encounters we were to have with Thrasyllus that winter. We attended virtually every lecture he presented. He invited and even pressed us to visit him in his study whenever we wished, and to discuss whatever we wished—not just philosophy or predictions of the future. He was always pleasant, concerned, sympathetic, and kind, but never intrusive or judgmental. Although quick to discern I was embittered about my personal past and a fugitive from it, he never pressured me to disclose its details or reveal my true identity. "You will feel led to tell me whatever I need to know, in order for me to offer you comfort and guidance. Anything else is irrelevant."

From Thrasyllus I discovered more about the heavens and the earth as a celestial body than I had ever learned on my own, let alone from my father or his colleagues at the Academia Norenas. There I had mastered only the basics. The earth appears to rest at the center of a great rotating vault in which the fixed stars are embedded. Over the course of a year, the zodiac constellations traverse the vault along a pathway called the ecliptic. The seven planets, which include the sun and moon, wander back and forth along the ecliptic in measurable periods. The particular locations of the planets at the time of one's birth determine one's horoscope. There is a second and very visible pathway called the Milky Way, the nature of which is not yet understood.

Now I learned that astrologers divide the earth into six horizontal tropics and two vertical colures. These practitioners measure the celestial vault along projections of these circles. The signs of the zodiac have a variety of characteristics. In accordance with Pythagorean numerology, the odd numbered signs are masculine in nature and the even numbered ones are feminine. Cancer, Pisces, Capricorn, and Aquarius are associated with the changeability of water, the others with the stability of dry land. Cancer, Scorpio, and Pisces promote fertility; Aquarius, Virgo, and Leo are sterile. Each sign is associated with a specific part of the human body. A person born under a particular sign will have traits associated therewith. The zodiacal also links naturally into geometric

147

patterns of three or four. The trigons represent the harmony in a person's human relationships, the tetragons the discord.

One afternoon, Thrasyllus showed me the basic information of my own birth chart. He expressed surprise that my parents had not had my horoscope cast as soon as I was born. Then he laughed when I explained that ours was probably the only family in the known world who did not follow this practice, most likely because there was no money to spare for engaging an astrologer. Thrasyllus' mood switched from humored to disbelieving, after I advised him I knew neither the hour of my birth nor the day of the week on which it had taken place. Whenever I had asked, I was either reprimanded for directing my thought to trivia instead of genuinely important matters or else merely ignored.

Thrasyllus reassured me he could still work with what information he had. The first thing he determined was that I had been born on a Tuesday. We already knew the sun was in Leo. This gives me courage, determination, a somewhat haughty self-assurance, and an inclination to dominate others—the very qualities at which my family took offense. The sign also endows me with leonine loyalty and dependability—qualities so especially important to Tiberius. As governor of the heart and spine, Leo imparts generosity and fortitude.

One's lunar sign is the governor of subjective thought: feelings, emotions, intuition. Although the sun sign remains the more dominant, the moon sign has more significance to persons born at night than for those born during the day. This is why nocturnally born persons frequently use their lunar rather than their solar signs as indicators of their births. I had always wondered why Augustus, whose sun is in the first day of Libra, often gives Capricorn as his birth sign. Lunar Capricorns, Thrasyllus explained, are practical, ambitious, devoted to tradition, and comfortable in positions of tremendous power. For certain Caesar is all of these, and wants his subjects to recognize him as such. Not infrequently, Augustus publicizes the fact that Capricorn is also his conception sign. He does so, Thrasyllus continued, because Asiatic peoples like Commageneans and Cappadocians venerate the conception signs of rulers. Modern astrologers, however, do not place much credence in the power of conception signs. Mine, if I was curious, is Scorpio.

At any rate, my moon sign is Aquarius. It is the source of my stubborn resistance to my family's impositions upon me! Lunar Aquarians are resentful and intractable when subjected to unmerited criticism.

My ascendant—the sign on the horizon at the moment of birth—is Gemini. It renders me highly inquisitive with a virtually insatiable desire for acquiring knowledge. My medium coeli—the sign traversing the zenith of the heavens at time of birth—is the same as my moon sign, Aquarius. It imbues a need to feel forever competent and causes me to fret over failures. This explains why my discovery I could not spin or weave disappointed me so deeply.

Being on the cusp of Virgo strengthens my artistic inclinations. It also drives the inveterate shyness which conflicts with, yet regulates, the regal condescending assertiveness of the lion.

As for the other planets: Mercury in Virgo impels me to be well organized in thought, planning, and action—hence my relentlessly logical reasoning. Venus in Cancer drives me to love intensely and desperately crave reassurance my love is reciprocated—hence those nights of despair in that alcove when I pretended inanimate objects accepted and returned my love, and my present thirst for affirmations of Tiberius' devotion. Mars in Libra impels me to fight for justice and correctness, and in its negative sense to seek vengeance. This is why I persistently challenged my family's nonsense despite the impending consequences. The same alignment is the source of my deep consideration of scholarly subjects.

From Jupiter in Sagittarius comes my appreciation for other cultures and my willingness to learn about them through travel. It is also the source of my affinity for philosophy.

An alignment we found particularly notable is the presence of Saturn in Leo, for it is a source of distress. It drives frustration in general, and specifically the guilt I feel when my leonine pursuit of intelligent self-interest afflicts others with real or imagined chagrins. And even far, far more notably: Saturn is troubled in Leo because it is the ruling planet of Leo's complement Aquarius—my mother's sun sign! This explains the underlying cause of such intense friction between us.

Thrasyllus went on to elucidate the polygons. My trigon consists of Aries, Leo, and Sagittarius. Like the Ram I remain patient, gentle, and tenacious, until pushed to the limits of emotional endurance—at which point I become formidably aggressive. From the Lion of course come my fortitude, resolve, and resistance to being controlled. The centaur Sagittarius—half man and half beast—tempers my animal ferocity with rationality, and uses clever strategy to channel that belligerence into effective applications. My tetragon—the source of ill—is Taurus, Leo, Scorpio, and Aquarius. This discovery alarmed me. I could see how my birth sign of Leo conflicted with that of my mother: Aquarius. But Tiberius is a Scorpio. How could he possibly be a source of distress to me?

The astrologer reminded me Tiberius' tetragon is the same as mine. To our mutual benefit the Bull, Lion, and Scorpion form an alliance, which impugns and weakens the negative influences of Aquarius. For this very reason I need not anticipate every Aquarian I ever encounter will automatically be my enemy. Tiberius had removed me from the physical reach of my family. He continues to provide desperately essential emotional support as I battle the sorrow and anger and frustration their afflictions engendered. My devotion in turn supplies Tiberius with a strong sense of partnership. This is particularly important to him in light of his failed marriages, his uneasy relationship with his stepfather and his stepsons, and the inveterate shyness which makes him appear indecisive. The Bull, Lion, and Scorpion—all bestial earth signs—with fierce and solid determination oppose the vacillating tendencies of the water sign Aquarius. Tiberius' trigon of Cancer, Scorpio, and Pisces includes my Venus sign, which represents one's sentimental side. His moon sign is Libra, and his nocturnal birth enhances its influence. Lunar Librans desperately crave concrete relationships with others. This makes my continued dedication to Tiberius all the more critical. Both stellar polygons reflect our intense need for one other, and guarantee the permanency of our love.

In conclusion Thrasyllus expressed regret he could not calculate the horoscopes of my parents, brother, and great-aunt to see how they affected mine. To do so ethically would require he make their acquaintance and obtain their permission. "Little chance of that!" I scoffed.

By the time our session ended I felt as though my head was spinning from the complexity of the information we had considered. But I came away considerably comforted. At last I had some concrete explanations for my personal idiosyncrasies, and for my family's incessant attacks upon me.

In March, Tiberius again raised the subject of travel. Was I still interested? Most assuredly, I declared. Having reconsidered the matter carefully, he had decided it were better he not escort me in person lest his appearance create a sensation. I should plan an itinerary. He would write official letters, introducing Daphne Hipparchide and her entourage to the municipal governments of the locales I elected to visit. Eurycles would make the arrangements for transportation and accommodations.

My list of famous places in Greece and Asia Minor—places I had read about for most of my life but despaired of ever actually seeing—proved far too long to be encompassed in the course of a single season. Could I possibly visit the southernmost Greek district of Achaea this summer and Asia Minor the next? "Why, of course—a very sound idea," was the response; and how refreshed I felt, not having to plead and defend and justify the solution I had offered.

Everything was finalized by the middle of June. After consulting a type of numerological table designed to calculate outcomes, Thrasyllus predicted a safe and rewarding journey. My travel party included Arbindus, Alexias, and Pericalles. We undertook the three-day voyage to Piraeus on a regular commercial transport vessel, which we shared with a crowd of other passengers. Our quarters were cramped and stuffy, the food decent, and the company pleasant. Fortuitously no one identified me as the regent's ward.

Our entire excursion took about a month and a half. The weather grew hot. From the intense and incessant sunlight I endeavored to keep myself covered as much as possible. Nevertheless the skin on my face and arms turned red and thereafter tan, and my hair developed streaks. In some locales we lodged at inns where we had to wait patiently for the bathrooms and latrines. We were subject to awakening by the shouts of revelers in the establishments' taverns, or when their drunken snores or retchings (worse yet!) emanated from adjacent rooms. In other places we were guests in the homes of irritatingly obsequious local magistrates, falling over themselves with the honor of accommodating a protégé of the imperial family. Pericalles' presence grated on me, with that mysterious eeriness she always seemed to have about her.

What, then, could be my final assessment of the journey? Nothing short of marvelous! The art and architecture of Athens was far more breathtaking than the descriptions I had heard or read. The sculptor Pheidias' immense statue of the goddess Athena in the Parthenon was so lifelike in form and color, that for a moment my skin crawled from the feeling I was beholding a genuine living giant. One of the most intriguing structures was the Horologion, built by the astronomer Andronicus Cyrrhestou about a century ago. This tower of Pentelic marble has eight sides. At the top of each is a frieze depicting in human representation one of the eight winds; and below each frieze is a sundial. On the roof an immense weathervane in the image of a Triton turns freely to indicate the direction of the wind. Inside the tower a great clepsydra is powered by water draining from the adjacent Acropolis.

With awe and humility I pursued the privilege of laying a wreath of laurel on the grave of Plato in the original Academy—the grove sacred to the hero Academus—adjacent to the country house where the master wrote his discourses and taught his first students.

After four days in Athens we traveled toward the northwest. The great sanctuary to the goddesses Demeter and Persephone at Eleusis was of less interest to me than the battleground of Plataea. Here the Greeks had decisively stopped the advance of the Persian army nearly five centuries ago. From Plataea we proceeded to Thebes, the city of the Sphinx and her famous riddle, and of Oedipus who solved the riddle and then unwittingly killed his father and married his mother. On through Chaeronea—site of the Roman victory over Mithridates the king of Pontus—to the pass of Thermopylae. Here three hundred valiant Spartans gave their lives to detain the Persians while the city-states garnered their forces at Plataea, and three centuries later the Romans stopped the advance of invading Syrians.

We now turned southward to Amphissa, and thence proceeded to Delphi. The great sanctuary complex, to the oracle of Apollo on the slopes of Mount Parnassus, is far larger and more beautiful than I had imagined. Although I do not believe in physical gods I could almost feel a sacred presence, so suggestive were the surroundings. The grounds are adorned with hundreds or perhaps thousands, of decorative and votive statues. Within the temple stands the great gold tripod which the Greeks had dedicated to Apollo following their victory at Plataea—the battleground we had just visited. I observed the great gold Epsilon that Livia had dedicated to the temple, and recognized its significance from my philosophical studies. The Pythagoreans hold the number five, to which the letter epsilon corresponds, as a manifestation of the creative harmony of nature. The divine representation of this Principle is Apollo—Augustus' patron deity—to whom the Delphic sanctuary is dedicated. Five, moreover, is symbolic of harmony in marriage. The archon in whose home we lodged escorted me to a thought-provoking performance of Sophocles' tragedy *Antigone*, with its inherent implications of the superiority of divine will over human impulse. It was not the year for those Pythian Games toward which my father had aggrieved me. I could not have attended them anyway since they are forbidden to women.

From Delphi we journeyed west to the port of Naupactus, and thence by ship across the strait to Patras on the Peloponnesus. Our next destination, Olympia, took several days of travel to reach. As at Delphi, the athletic complex was off limits to me as a woman; but I was able to visit the temples. Pheidias' great ivory and gold statue of Zeus, so generally touted as an artistic marvel, I found exaggerated and overly proportioned in contrast to the uncanny lifelikeness of his Athena. The head of the seated Zeus abuts the ceiling of the temple, as though the poor god had been forced to crawl into the edifice on his hands and knees. Far, far more elegant is Praxiteles' statue of Hermes holding an infant Dionysius, which stands in the temple to the goddess Hera.

Several more days of travel brought us to Sparta, which Tiberius had warned would probably prove a disappointment. Indeed it did. For the most part, the ancient Spartans did not erect permanent structures. Consequently all that remains, of the centuries-old military culture for which the city-state is legendary, is an austere temple to Hera and some nondescript monuments.

The Sparta of today is a provincial administrative center and an emporium for sheep traders.

We proceeded directly south to the port of Yithion where we boarded a ship for Crete. From Cydonia, the port at which we had stopped on our initial voyage to Rhodes, the journey to Mount Ida took two days. On the second we had to ride donkeys, as the steep and narrow roads were too dangerous for our carriage. The cave in which Zeus was born according to one legend, according to another only nurtured, contains only a small shrine. Far more impressive was the view of Ida in the distance as we approached—a long ridge of deep bluish gray emerging from a verdant green plateau. With some hope I watched a few white storm clouds gather near the summit, thinking how appropriate the sight of a bolt of lightning would be. My hope was not fulfilled.

We returned to the Rhodian villa shortly before my birthday. As soon as possible I seized my paints and palettes and set about creating a pictorial record of sights and impressions from the trip. On my birthday itself, Tiberius presented me with an ivory stylus for the writing of my journal. After my excursion I would surely be making entries in profusion. The pen was elegantly carved with plant motifs. The merchant had claimed it came from Nubia, Tiberius said.

Phoebe fussed and carped about my darkened complexion. "How can you be appealing to Master while looking as though you have been tilling vegetables all summer?" So she scolded as she hustled me from sunlit areas into shade. "At least Helios has given me a reprieve from having to lighten your hair." Every few hours she brought a basin of lemon juice mixed with basil seed oil and made me rinse my skin. Her ministries were effective. By the time September arrived my flesh had regained its former whiteness.

Now that I was focusing on my complexion, I discovered that my acne had all but disappeared. The emergent pimples Demas had described at our first meeting were completely gone, and the scars on my forehead were barely noticeable. For that matter, Tiberius' blemishes had cleared as well. We appeared to be vindicating Timoxena's theory that emotional distress aggravates acne. Moreover I found myself awakening without pain in my jaw, having ceased to grind my teeth in my sleep. Tiberius and I were almost deliriously happy and calm as we reveled in one another's affections, and pursued interests and vocations we relished rather than those our families had foisted upon us.

September, of course, brought the new academic season and the birthday of Augustus. Since the emperor had complained his left leg was continuing to weaken with rheumatism and increase his limp, Tiberius procured a cane.

Being fashioned of oak made it sturdy; fine tooling rendered it wieldy and easy to manage as well as elegantly graceful in appearance. Although he complained good-naturedly that it served as a sharp reminder of his entry into his sixtieth year, Augustus was delighted with his gift. The emperor extolled the treatise on military maneuvers in forested areas Tiberius had personally authored for Gaius' birthday, and apologized for the recipient's failure to acknowledge this gift. He continued his letter with a far less appreciative reaction to the present Tiberius had sent Julia for her birthday the previous July. While he respected and approved Tiberius' desire to happify Julia, Augustus declared the presentation and acceptance of such a wastefully frivolous gift was unbecoming alike the son-in-law and daughter of Caesar. Tiberius explained that while I was traveling, he had come upon an elaborate and expensive collar of pearls and turquoise and black onyx stones interspersed with gold and silver beads. From Julia it had elicited a far more enthusiastic response than the stiff, cursory acknowledgment she had sent for the gift I had acquired for her the previous year.

Quite predictably I started to apologize for the failure of my selection to please Julia—and just as predictably Tiberius stopped me. "She has excellent tastes, like yours; however you know quite well she prefers the extravagant to the refined. Surely she is in her glory, flaunting that excessive bauble to her profligate friends. Here is our confirmation!" he concluded, holding aloft the tablet bearing Augustus' seal.

We were in my personal suite and I dabbling with my paints while Tiberius read me his stepfather's letter. The coincidence gave him an idea. For Julia's next gift, was I willing to produce a group portrait of her children from his descriptions of them, even as I had rendered the image of Drusus with the assistance of Phoebe? This present was bound to please, Tiberius continued ebulliently. Julia doted on her children, as did their grandfather. So manifest was Julia's devotion, it had prompted the city of Priene on the coast of Asia Minor to hail Julia as *Goddess of Beautiful Children*. My portrait would be a palpable demonstration of Tiberius' respect for the imperial grandchildren and their mother. I could only represent the children as Tiberius remembered them from three years ago, before his departure for Rhodes; but this should not matter. Parents and grandparents everywhere cherish childhood representations of their offspring long after the latter have grown to adulthood. The proposal delighted me immensely, since I had found myself running out of subjects to paint. As we had nearly a year before Julia's next birthday, I could take my time to be sure all the details and nuances were correct. The guidance of Timotheus' I would solicit, to ensure the renderings were artistically sound.

This project I enjoyed tremendously as it unfolded over the ensuing months. Tiberius described the characters as well as the physiognomies of Julia's five children. This gave me, in each case, a sense of the whole person, and helped me provide the representations with—well—a kind of humanity one simply cannot derive from purely physical descriptions. The endeavor also served to remind me the most powerful and respected family in the world had their fair share of personal problems.

Gaius the eldest of Julia's children had the same slight build, fair hair and complexion of the grandfather he was expected to succeed. Intrinsically, Gaius was well intentioned. He had a significant failing, however, which the worried Augustus hoped Gaius would eventually outgrow or overcome through education and experience. The young crown prince was terribly gullible and naïve. He heeded and followed the persuasions of people he found likeable, without evaluating the merits and potential consequences of their suggestions and urgings. The possibility he was being duped never seemed to occur to him, so long as the charlatan who was misleading him did so in a friendly manner. This ingenuousness was the fundamental cause of Gaius' hostility to Tiberius. Gaius had allowed the sycophants and dissenters who had rallied about his mother, to rouse his suspicions that Tiberius might be plotting to secure the succession for himself.

Julia's next child was her namesake daughter, now in her third year of marriage. She was slightly more than a year Gaius' junior. Tiberius maintained she had inherited her mother's love for social activities and extravagant living. The younger Julia was at her happiest when the center of attention. Tiberius recalled with a bit of amusement the consecration of the Altar of Augustan Peace. Little Julia, then in her sixth year, walked in the processing wearing a wreath of flowers and holding a small bouquet. She carried herself with an air of innocent self-importance and grave responsibility, as though she feared the ceremony must certainly fail without her proper participation. The younger Julia had the stocky build of her father Agrippa but the delicate facial features and fine dark hair of her mother.

Tiberius had far less liking for Julia's three youngest children. Slim, swarthy, dark-eyed Lucius was arrogant and headstrong, with little regard for etiquette or the feelings of others. When Augustus reprimanded him for attending a theatrical performance without an escort, he scoffed at the regulation as a stodgy and pointless dictate of an oppressive old man. Volatile, petulant, and hostile, the petite, lithe, sandy-haired Agrippina seemed thoroughly convinced everyone in the world hated her along with her mother and siblings. She was some nine months older than Drusus. And finally the youngest—called Postumus because he was born after his father's death—was perhaps the family's greatest concern. From an early age he showed little interest in the activities of his family, even their leisure pursuits. He seldom spoke; and when he did, he tended to use the same words or phrases over and over again. Often he sat by himself in some corner for long periods, saying nothing but rocking his body to and fro or aimlessly shaking his hands. He threw tantrums when he could not have his way, or was forced to change some routine to which he had become accustomed. These latter outbursts occurred not only when someone refused his demands, but also when something beyond anyone's control thwarted him. He would pitch a fit, for example, if it were raining when he wanted a sunny day.

I did my best to idealize each of the children as I felt Augustus would like to see them. Gaius I made appear serious and contemplative, yet earnest, wise, and confident, as befitting a future ruler. The younger Julia I represented as elegant, refined, and gracious; Lucius as ambitious and determined; Agrippina as caring and brooding like a mother hen. Little Postumus I depicted as a happy, contented child, discovering the world around him with wide-eyed rapture. "Pity we cannot replace their real temperaments with those of your portraits," Tiberius remarked. "My stepfather would be considerably relieved—and Julia too, I dare say."

During this winter's academic session I became acquainted with two men, both of whom were to leave indelible impressions upon me.

One of these characters very proudly bore the name Plato. The designation was certainly an appropriate one, as he was phenomenally obese. Perhaps it was due to his enormous weight that he emitted an offensive odor, like a pot of rancid oil. Surely the venerable philosopher and teacher whose namesake he was would never have accepted him as a follower. The Plato of our acquaintance was a paltry and petty dilettante—a dabbler in academic subjects of which he had the only the slightest comprehension. Nevertheless he fancied himself an expert in everything.

Plato would sit through lectures sneering, snickering, and shaking his head in affected incredulity. Afterward he would press the sophistoi for information they had already presented but he had not understood; or he would harangue them and their audiences with long and pointless discourses which revealed his total misapprehension of the subject matter at hand. He never, ever entertained the notion he could possibly be wrong about anything. The sophistoi and fellow students had to give up trying either to correct him or to throw him out of the lectures. Whenever they did either Plato insinuated they could not accept that they were in error, and that they sought to justify themselves by harassing poor unassailably right Plato.

One day we happened to attend the same lecture on Pythagorean numerology. At its close I asked the sophistos whether I had correctly associated the number five with marital stability, and he replied that I had. Heretofore Plato had ignored me as if I did not exist; but now my remark brought me into his focus. As I was leaving the hall he accosted me with the question, "What in the world do you think you are doing here?" Genuinely confused, I asked him to explain his inquiry. He retorted with, "The presence of women lowers the intellectual standard of this institution!"

Needless to say I was stunned and momentarily flustered. Fortunately an exchange between my assailant and bodyguard granted me a pause in which to collect my thoughts.

"Your remark is inappropriate; move on!" Androcles growled as he tightened his hand about the hilt of his sword.

"Oh, you would threaten me for telling the truth?" came the sarcastic rejoinder.

Remembering Demas' training, I took a deep breath and carefully avoided the temptation to answer defensively. The pause enabled me to compose a rational, well-considered response. Calmly and evenly I returned, "The great master whose name you bear accepted women among his own students. You can verify this by pursuing his personal writings and those of his biographers."

Startled, disconcerted, unprepared to refute my comment, he gaped at me angrily. Then—presumably because he could not find anything else to say—he retorted, "Why is your hair so long?" He was referring, of course, to the fact that practicing hetaerae wear their hair at chin length to signify their profession.

Over my shoulder as I walked away, I answered as collectively as before, "Because I am not a hetaera."

Now Plato was frustrated because he had not succeeded in embarrassing me. Tiberius met me outside the lecture hall. On seeing us together Plato became affectedly obsequious. "Oh forgive me, pardon me!" he exclaimed in a mockingly patronizing tone as he bowed rapidly and repeatedly, eyes lowered but eyebrows raised in disdain.

"I fear you were too harsh on him," Tiberius commented after I had described the incident. "You might have been better off telling him you regret your presence causes him distress, or even ignoring him altogether. Instead you made yourself a sworn enemy."

I had been priding myself for having palpably humiliated my adversary, thereby fulfilling one of my mother's strongest demands upon me. Now I was about to discover, rather painfully, the fallacy of her expectation. For the remainder of the academic term, Plato had a rejoinder for every word I uttered. Even when I remained silent he would goad me with comments like, *Nothing to say? Such is the weakness of female comprehension.* I took great care to make sure my questions and conclusions were carefully thought out and the logic behind them sound. Whenever wrong I accepted correction graciously, in the manner expected of an intellectual. As a consequence the students and sophistoi respected my insights and opinions, and did not take Plato's challenges to them seriously.

Furthermore, I enjoyed the comforting counsel of an experienced politician. "When you are a public figure," Tiberius asserted, "you always encounter people who detest you—some because you say what they do not want to hear, others for no comprehensible reason. Such discontents spread rumors and distortions and exaggerations and outright lies without mercy." He reminded me that Augustus had once advised him not to be disturbed by what people say, but to rest content when they merely talk without causing actual physical harm. Tiberius also reminded me I was not Plato's only victim: Plato had a useless but degrading rejoinder for everybody. The diatribes hurt me nonetheless, no matter how hard I tried to dismiss them as frivolous. They always will, Tiberius warned me. We all have feelings.

Tiberius discovered a way to needle Plato, to the delight of everyone except Plato. Although he had little if any genuine comprehension of subjects the sophistoi presented, Plato went to great lengths to cull highly obscure details from the material—details the sophistoi and competent students tended to overlook or disregard as irrelevant or unrelated to the gist of whatever was being considered. When nobody could identify one of his minutiae, Plato would sit back and beam as though he had just been hailed the Eighth Wise Man of Greece. Well, Tiberius had a remarkable talent for remembering the trivialities of a subject while he was focusing upon its more salient elements. And so whenever Plato posed one of his stumbling blocks and Tiberius glibly supplied the answer, the Eighth Wise Man would bristle while sophistos and audience tittered.

My second new acquaintance was Timoleon, an aspiring young sophistos from Thessaloniki in Macedonia. He was slightly more than three years my senior. Like my father, he had received his academic training from the Museion of Alexandria. At present he was beginning a two-year sabbatical, to broaden his general knowledge and specifically to pursue advanced studies in rhetoric. For this subject the Rhodes Academy was particularly renowned. I found it refreshing to meet someone who aspired to bring higher education to an area of Greece that was predominantly rural and intellectually weak. He seemed genuinely pleased when I told him this.

Courteous toward my person and highly respectful of my learning, Timoleon began to seek my answers to his questions about material he had read or lectures he had attended and not understood. From time to time he asked me to tutor him. He tried for a while to intimidate Plato into leaving me alone, but soon discovered neither he nor anyone else was able to deter Plato. All he could do, he said, was to offer me sympathy and moral support, for which I reassured him I was amply grateful.

One day Timoleon reported an incident which amused me, while I rejoiced that I had not been present at the actual occurrence. During a lecture, somebody in the audience suddenly vomited. He later apologized: against his better judgment he had consumed some food with a suspicious odor and taste. After the victim was escorted from the hall, the remaining members of the audience exited—but not before several had managed to seize Plato and set him down in the puddle of puke. Even the sophistos whose discourse had been interrupted approved the action.

As the term progressed, Timoleon' manner toward me became increasingly familiar. Did I have any interests apart from academics? After I told him about my artistic endeavors he asked me to bring him an example. The sketch of Sinapeus I provided elicited gushing accolades. Timoleon inquired about my personal history, to which I responded with a mixture of fact and fiction. My father was a pedagogue (almost true); I had lived all my life in the countryside of southern Italy (almost true); I had endured a tumultuous marriage which was now ending in divorce (false); and I had discovered to my chagrin that I could not bear children (true). Timoleon expressed regret that my life had been so baneful, but rejoiced that I had acquired such a prestigious and influential guardian. He confessed to having endured a divorce for reasons similar to mine: his wife had left him and their daughter of seven years for another man.

Eventually Timoleon asked whether he might call upon me at home. This request I considered inappropriately forward and was about to rebuke him. Then recalling Tiberius' admonition about creating enemies by responding with unneeded harshness, I advised Timoleon he must submit his request in writing to Tiberius—who refused, as I had anticipated and hoped. Fortunately (and somewhat to my surprise), Timoleon did not hold the rejection against me. He continued to elicit my expertise in academic matters, to defend me against Plato as best he could, and to inquire after my interests, aspirations, health, and moods. After learning meteors were a favorite subject of mine he did independent research about them, but did not arrive at any conclusions Thrasyllus had not already reached.

"It appears you are being courted," Tiberius chuckled one evening while we sat on the veranda before supper.

I groaned. "Now I have to persuade him that he is out of luck, and without disclosing the reason."

April, the month which usually heralds the rainy season, arrived and progressed without a trace of moisture. The drought did not deter me from planning my next excursion abroad—this year to Asia Minor. "You are insatiable!" Tiberius grumbled good-naturedly while he wrote letters of introduction, and I pored over maps and travelogues and turned our library into a mess in the process. Eurycles I set to work making the arrangements, and again selected Arbindus to serve as my bodyguard. As Pericalles was expecting a child, I could not bring her with me this year. Not wishing to separate Alexias from Pericalles while she was in her present condition, I asked Eunice the daughter of Demas and Timoxena if she and her young husband Antenor would care to accompany me. Both accepted at once, since heretofore neither had had means nor opportunity to travel. We departed on the Calends of June.

This journey lasted about as long as the previous year's, and had mostly the same material discomforts. Because of the present drought—about which we heard complaints everywhere—water for drinking and bathing was only available in limited quantities. The decorative fountains in the cities were shut down. After four days at sea we reached our first (and northernmost) destination. This was Ilium, the port city Caesar the Dictator had founded near the reputed site of ancient Troy. On a great bluff near the modern city, I stood facing the sea and imagining Homer's stories—the great siege, the battles and chases, the deception of the Trojan Horse and the ultimate destruction of the city. Having also read the contemporary Latin epic *Aeneid*—commissioned and published by Augustus—I fancied the Trojan prince Aeneas leading his rump of survivors through the chaos of the burning city to the sea. They would journey westward to become the ancestors of the Italian race. The visit particularly stirred my companion Antenor, since he was named for a different Trojan prince.

From Ilium we traveled overland through Alexandria Troas to Assus, where we boarded ship for Mytilene—capital city of the island of Lesbos, birthplace and home of the poetess Sappho, and for a time the residence of Aristotle.

Thence we sailed southward to Clazomenae the birthplace of Anaxagoras, and then traveled by land through Izmir to Colophon and finally to Ephesus. The great temple to Artemis proved quite the disappointment, not only to me but to Antenor who was studying to be an architect. Although immense in size, the building lacked architectural originality: it followed the standard temple design of a rectangle bounded by columns and surmounted by a peaked roof. The paintings on the pediments were garish and unrealistic. The Artemis of Ephesus was not the chaste virgin goddess of the night, the patroness of hunters and of women in childbirth, but an ugly grotesquerie dripping with a multitude of egg-shaped breasts. She seemed a humanized version of those huge, loathsome, waxy-white *cows* I guess one would call them, which one occasionally encounters upon disturbing an insect colony. Our discovery of eunuch priests serving the Ephesian Artemis revealed she must have been some sort of Asiatic divinity, whose identity became fused with that of the traditional Greek goddess.

From Ephesus we sailed to the island of Samos—birthplace of Pythagoras and later of Epicurus. Thence we returned to the mainland at Miletus. This city had been the home of three men who can rightly be called the Fathers of all Greek philosophy. From their work as astronomers and geographers and meteorologists, Thales, Anaximander, and Anaximenes had determined the workings of the universe were not mysterious transcendent forces beyond the ken of man, but natural phenomena discoverable and understandable through observation and thoughtful reasoning. Miletus was also the birthplace of Aspasia, and of Aristides the renowned writer of bawdy sexually explicit tales. The city had the same grid-like layout as Rhodes, and for good reason. Hippodamus, the urban architect who had designed the city of Rhodes, was yet another native of Miletus.

From Miletus we sailed due southward to Halicarnassus—birthplace of the historian Herodotus and home to an architectural marvel: the tomb of Mausolus, King of Caria (the region ruled by Halicarnassus), and of his wife Artemisia. The immense oblong structure, ringed by thirty-six columns and surmounted by a pyramid of twenty-four steps, was so carefully constructed to catch shifting light, that its colors and shadings changed continually. The many sculptures adorning the colonnade seemed almost to come alive in the shimmering shadows. Colorful friezes on the walls of the burial chamber depicted the life and achievements of Mausolus and Artemisia. The couple's alabaster and gold sarcophagi had a milky translucence. Antenor had studied the treatises and designs of Satyrus and Pythius, the architects of the Mausoleum. Now beholding their greatest work firsthand, he was practically in a state of reverence. Our final stop was the island of Cos. Here we toured the medical school and hospital complex, which the pioneering physician Hippocrates had established. Even more fascinating to me was our visit to a mill where silk fibers are extracted from cocoons of a special moth and then woven into cloth. Thereafter we set sail for Rhodes—and to my relief.

This excursion was disappointing in comparison with the previous year's. The city of Athens is committed to preserving the centuries-old architectural and artistic marvels of their Acropolis. Being religious complexes, Olympia and Delphi are subject to embellishment and improvement rather than to destructive change that might insinuate blasphemy. But the inhabitants of Asia Minor, enriched by their region's burgeoning economy in agriculture and trade, have continually built and rebuilt and overbuilt and refurbished their cities with newer and higher levels of modernity and opulence. Except for the Mausoleum there were few extant reminders of the famous people of centuries past. No one was quite sure precisely where the ancient city of Troy had stood. The Mytilene of Sappho and Aristotle, the Miletus of Thales and Aspasia, the Halicarnassus Mausolus had known, and the original medical center of Hippocrates on Cos, had all disappeared under the ceaseless mandate of renovation. Nevertheless I was gratified that Eunice and Antenor had found the trip inspiring and returned to their home in jubilation.

After my less than impressive journey I returned to a less than jovial household. Our servants were in a state of dejection. Pericalles had delivered a little girl who seemed healthy enough at birth. Before a month had passed, however, she was declining rapidly and for no apparent reason. Due to the imminence of her death, Alexias had not even named her. Tiberius was in one of his melancholy moods—pensive, preoccupied, and troubled. Having grown accustomed to these, I knew better than to make inquiries. He was loath to discuss issues disturbing him, especially those he had not resolved; he became testy if pressed; and once ready he voluntarily explained whatever had distressed him. Nevertheless I hoped he was only distraught over the situation with the servants, and not about adverse developments regarding his relationship with his family and his political position in Rome.

Two days before my own birthday, Tiberius finally revealed the cause of his torment. We were in our bedroom at our villa, resting in the physical and mental quietude that follows sex; his distraction had been evident during the act itself. He took my hand and for a time gazed at me in silence. Finally he said quietly, "Clytia, my dearest love, you need to know: your acquaintance Timoleon of Thessaloniki sent me a letter in which he asked for your hand in marriage."

"The silly fool!" I scoffed. "Please let me reassure you: I did not solicit his affections in any way."

"Of that I have no doubt. Anyway, I responded that although I am your guardian, I shall defer to whatever decision you make. If you accept his proposal, then it is my responsibility to provide your dowry." He sighed. "Clytia, should you care to do so I shall not stand in your way."

For a moment I felt as though my heart had turned to stone. I responded with the glum resignation that accompanies acceptance of an unavoidable disaster. "Tiberius, are you trying to tell me you have tired of me?"

"No, oh no, no—not at all!" Now there was great urgency in his voice. "On the contrary, I love you more deeply than ever I have. But precisely because I love you so, I want you carefully to consider this opportunity to attain personal security."

Still holding my hand he rolled on his back and stared pensively at the ceiling. "Clytia, we have been on Rhodes for nearly four years. My future remains highly uncertain and possibly perilous. When the powers of the regency expire at the end of next December, my stepfather may well decide he no longer has any use for me, divorce me from Julia, and breach amicitia. You know he has little tolerance for insubordination, particularly that of family members. I may become an outcast for the rest of my life. What prospects do you have with me, apart from skulking in shadows with the possibility of exposure to ridicule and scorn and even physical harm?"

"What if your stepfather does breach amicitia? You are of legal majority. How can he stop you from returning to Rome strictly as a senator, without any special offices or considerations related to the monarchy?"

"Do not use that word!" he fairly hissed. Then he resumed his straightforward tone. "But to answer your question: although my stepfather cannot deter me legally, he can still ruin me politically and socially. Should someone with a public stature as exalted as his breach amicitia with you, your political career will be over and your prestige and credibility utterly destroyed. No one will dare enter into a contract with you, offer you his support or solicit yours in any manner for any purpose. Many will consider you a sworn enemy."

"What makes you think I will be happy living in a backwater like Thessaloniki?"

"Thessaloniki is hardly a backwater. She is a dynamically developing city with a nascent but enthusiastic academic community. You may find yourself quite content there."

"I do not love Timoleon."

"You could learn to love him as I learned to love Vipsania. Couples do so all the time. If this were not true, our society's time-honored practice of arranging marriages would have been abandoned long ago."

"What must I do when he starts asking me about my past—or worse yet, if he initiates an investigation?"

"He can only know what you tell him. I cannot perceive why he would want to have you investigated so long as you answer his questions plausibly. Nevertheless I will create an *official* record for you, just as I did for Decimus Calvinius Valens."

"How could I leave you for another when I love you so very much?"

"To repeat a phrase I have used before: I would be out of your sight, but not out of your life. I intend never to let you out of my life. We would of course become correspondents again, and would arrange rendezvous. Your guardian is going to demand the pleasure of your visits."

"What if he discovers the true character of our relationship and arraigns me for adultery? He has already done this to his former wife, and so would be especially sensitive if faced with a second occurrence. Think too of how he might damage your reputation."

"We would have to abandon sexual activity and become strictly friends; but this does not mean we must cease loving one another."

"How could I possibly enjoy sex with him while missing you?"

"You close your eyes and pretend you are with me, even as I used to lie with Julia while pretending I was embracing you."

"And should the marriage fail?"

"I will always be ready to take you back." He turned his head and looked at me intently. "Clytia, I swear to respect whatever choice you make, and to love you forever. Please promise me, however, that you will consider this matter very carefully."

From outdoors there came the sound of thunder. "Maybe we will get some relief from the drought," I murmured distractedly as I rose from our bed. Without giving my partner a word or even a glance I dressed quickly and then hastened out to the garden, binding my hair as I walked. I seated myself in the belvedere, the fountain of which was not running due to the lack of rain.

Gray storm clouds were gathering in the distance. After watching them for a moment I buried my face in my hands. Tiberius' logic about my prospects was unassailable. What could I expect from him but a life of hiding, and of possible exposure to denunciation and ignominy? Something I had longed for desperately and despaired of ever attaining suddenly appeared within reach: the stable, respectable state of marriage. Timoleon seemed likeable enough. He could be pleasant to live with, even if I did not love him. Tiberius' comment about couples learning to love each other in arranged marriages was encouraging.

I would not lose Tiberius. He had assured me he would love me always, and make certain we continued to see each other. Thrasyllus had prophesied we would always be together, and yet be separate. My acceptance of Timoleon's suit would certainly validate this prediction. Why, then, did I feel so distraught? Why did I feel pressed to reach a decision immediately? And finally: which choice was the more principled, the more humane, the more benevolent, the more closely aligned with Underlying Good?

The thunder rumbled again, more loudly than before. Darkness had set in, the clouds having shut out the sunlight. A sudden flash of lightning illuminated them. Was that an omen? for just then the answer I sought illumined my thoughts. A statement from Aristotle's **Nicomachean Ethics** flashed into my mind. *It behooves one, not to incline toward human counsels because one is human, nor toward mortal predispositions because one is mortal, but to take upon oneself to be godlike and to do everything to live according to the greatest excellence within oneself.*

Feeling Tiberius draw his arm across my back, I leaned against his shoulder, still at a loss for words. There was yet another roll of thunder. A light rain began to fall, from which the belvedere sheltered us. How selfish of me, I thought, to consider leaving him simply so I might be legally married. Espoused, so I might achieve and display openly the social status from which my family had debarred me until Norenas came along with his money? So I might openly prove wrong the adolescent sneers I had suffered about my spinsterhood? So my life might be free, at least to some extent, of perpetual deception and hiding and wondering what dangers the morrow held?

With a future so uncertain and potentially precarious as his, Tiberius was desperately in need of constancy. How could I provide this as the wife of another man? An exchange of letters and an occasional furtive tryst could hardly impart the steadfastness of continuous physical presence. Timoleon could have his choice of women. Whom did Tiberius have beside me? What were his prospects of finding another helpmeet to understand, accept, and support him, given the present unsettled and unpredictable condition of his life?

I considered the astrologic polygons we shared. For certain my marrying Timoleon would weaken the influence of Pisces in Tiberius' trigon, compromising the sense of partnership it provided him. Would the marriage breach the alliance of Taurus, Leo, and Scorpio against the adversarial Aquarius in the tetragon Tiberius and I shared, and thereby bring calamity upon us both?

And finally: what greater evidence was there of Tiberius' selfless consideration for me, than for him to put concern for my wellbeing and contentment ahead of his own? To abandon him now would hardly be to live according to the greatest excellence within myself.

"Do you want me to marry Timoleon?" I asked acquiescently. "If that is your wish, I shall most willingly comply."

"The choice must be yours."

"Then my answer is no—no, NO, **NO**! Do you remember when we sat in this belvedere on the first birthday you celebrated here in Rhodes? And I declared I was prepared to crawl through the gutters of the streets at your side? Well, my decision has not changed; nor will it ever! I want to be ever-present, to exult in your joys, to offer solicitude for your woes and labor to find solutions for them, to understand and cherish and encourage your aspirations. A life of secrecy and insecurity and vagabondage and outright disgrace with you I find infinitely preferable, to that of a predictably respectable and dutiful wife of Timoleon or of any other man! To you I am devoted, and you alone! You swore to love me always, whatever choice I made. Well, made it I have!"

He took me in his arms. "Oh, my Clytia, thank you," he said fervently. "I had hoped you would give this answer, even while I wanted to provide you the chance to embrace stability."

"And thank you for so wondrous a proof of your love. I feel so helpless, so inadequate to express the full extent of my commitment to you."

We remained in the belvedere, neither caressing nor kissing but just holding one another tightly, until the rain stopped. There had not been nearly enough to ease the drought. The little that fell nevertheless cooled the air and cleansed it of haze, washed the accumulated dust from the foliage and ground. Sunlight reappeared. The clouds moved on and the sound of their thunder waned.

I became conscious of an almost physical sense of relief, which persisted for several days. It was as though some chronic ailment—the type one learns to ignore despite its perpetual and nagging presence—had suddenly disappeared.

My partner was clearly feeling a similar ease. He was quietly pensive—as he had been before our conversation about Timoleon—but with an aura of tranquility rather than melancholy. The experience had exposed and dispelled an underlying fear we had both been harboring but had never admitted to ourselves: the fear that someday one of us would reject the other. Now the dissolution of this concern had reinforced our devotion and our resolve to stay together.

On my birthday Tiberius presented me with a ring: a band of silver in which three rectangular rubies lay embedded side-by-side. "Thrasyllus studies the mystical properties of gemstones," he said pleasantly as he slipped the ring on the third finger of my right hand. "Rubies are the jewels of Leo. They discourage violence in temperament, promote gentleness and bliss, and so improve success in controversies and disputes." He paused, and then continued in tone more fervent, "Clytia, I wish I were presenting this to you as a wedding ring!"

"It is lovely, utterly lovely! And all of silver, the most precious metal in the world!" Trembling, breathless with emotion, I turned my gaze from the ring to his eyes. "But its beauty and worth are enhanced beyond any physical description by what you just said to me. Tiberius, by all that is pure and holy I swear: I would accept your offer of marriage without the slightest hesitation or misgiving."

He had been holding my hand; now he began to caress it. "When you rejected so vehemently my suggestion you consider Timoleon's proposal, I realized that you have truly become my wife in all but name. Who but a genuine spouse would show such fierce and unassailable loyalty tempered by such tenderness and forbearance?"

"Truly I meant every word I uttered during that rainstorm."

"And you can rest assured: I am equally devoted to you." He kissed my hand, then looked at me and smiled. There was a slight twinkle in his eyes. "Please promise me, my beloved, that you will refuse Timoleon gently. We men have such fragile natures, especially in matters of the heart."

His smile I returned. "I promise for sure."

We were about to kiss when suddenly he drew away from me. The villa's resident serving woman Alcmene was hurriedly approaching us; and Tiberius had a strong aversion to displaying his feelings toward me in the presence of our servants. With Alcmene was Ajax from our townhouse. He spoke with great urgency. "Master, there is an emergency at the city house for which your presence is essential. That of Menon and Phoebe is necessary as well. I have summoned the carriage for your transport."

Tiberius was gone for quite some time. Alone I bathed and then consumed the swordfish supper he had ordered for my birthday, wondering all the while whether he would return to the villa that evening. He arrived after dark, as I was preparing to retire. Ajax was with him. Standing in the doorway of our bedroom, Tiberius bellowed, "Nestor!" He then sat on the edge of the bed, gazing at the floor in considerable agitation. Ajax stood beside the door, silent and controlled but apparently distressed as well.

"Pericalles has been poisoning her child!" Tiberius spit out the words as though they were nails. "Alexias discovered her this evening, daubing the tips of her nipples with tincture of hemlock prior to nursing the baby. She has admitted doing this since birth—applying just enough of the toxin to induce the appearance of a naturally compromised constitution."

Suddenly I was painfully short of breath, as though someone had struck my chest with a cudgel. "Why?" I asked dully, wondering if he even had an answer.

He did not respond immediately, but went to the door and impatiently called for Nestor again. The servant appeared dressed in nightclothes and carrying a lamp. "Draw my bath!" Tiberius practically barked the order, but then continued less stridently, "I regret the late hour and the imposition, Nestor. Menon and Phoebe did not return with me. I have brought Ajax to serve as my valet in Menon's place. You must familiarize him with the villa. Alcmene will have to attend Lady Daphne. After drawing the bath, kindly fetch me a bowl of polenta and a small goblet of mead." Nestor bowed and went his way. Ajax followed him without being prompted. Tiberius grabbed his dressing gown and slippers. "I did not get a chance to eat anything; and this whole ghastly business has given me a headache. Come, attend me while I bathe. I am in desperate need of sanity."

While I sat on the bathroom bench brushing and braiding my hair, he washed with forceful and agitated motions. His speech paralleled his movements. "Pericalles declared she was determined not bring a child into a life of slavery. 'By committing murder?' I queried. 'Call it euthanasia,' she sneered, 'like the drowning of unwanted kittens.'"

I winced aloud, thinking of Leo and Nivea and their continually renewing brood. Proceles assiduously found homes for the kittens when the clowder threatened to burgeon beyond control.

Tiberius acknowledged my reaction with a nod, then went on with his narrative. "I continued to confront her. Why, then, did she ever take a spouse in the first place; and once wed, why did she not take precautions to prevent conception? 'I have sexual cravings just like you, Master!' she snarled back at me. 'And oh, you need not worry, my lord Tiberius. I have not exposed the tawdry secret you require we keep about you and whatever-her-name-is. How could I prevent conception when he wanted children so desperately?' She gestured contemptuously toward Alexias with her chin. 'Do you think I could have persuaded him to permit me the use of contraceptives, or to withdraw before ejaculating? I tried to abort the pregnancy. Clearly—ever so clearly—I failed.'"

He emerged from the bath, and I wrapped a towel about him. "Nicanor had summoned a pharmakeutria, who was endeavoring to resuscitate the baby when we arrived. Menon and Phoebe stayed behind to assist the pharmakeutria and the household. Alexias I have excused from his responsibilities until further notice, and brought him here to the villa. Please watch him carefully and offer him your sympathies—as I know you will. I want to make sure he does not try to kill himself, and shall advise the other servants of this concern." I handed him his dressing gown. "Tomorrow I shall return to the townhouse, to see about the baby's condition and the disposition of Pericalles." Seizing the lamp, he escorted me back to our bedroom. Ajax was waiting with a clean shift and the refreshments.

"What will be done with her?" I spoke in a retiring undertone, afraid of what I might hear in response.

"The law specifies crucifixion for slaves who commit murder. However, as of now the baby has not died. If by the time I present the case to the praetor it appears she is going to survive, I shall recommend Pericalles be hanged instead."

We both slept fitfully, awakening repeatedly in the warm darkness, holding hands at times but not speaking to each other. Finally I understood why Pericalles had always discomfited me. Unwittingly I had sensed she harbored the same type of perverse, contradictory morality as my family. Unquestionably hers was far more destructive; yet the underlying distortions were uncannily similar. Having a natural libido is a sign of innate debauchery. A gynecologic aberration is a blessing in disguise. Your son, the future of your family's name, must be carefully shielded from learning anything about sex. His utter gullibility when approached by a seductress is the fault of your daughter, because she recommended he be taught about sex. The only way that daughter can justify having been born a female is to become an academic show animal about whom you can boast. Aspasia should be her ensample; yet aspiration to emulate Aspasia is a sign of abject immorality.

It is wrong to bring a child into slavery; yet you are entitled to engage in sex freely without regard for its consequences. You redeem your child from a life of servitude by killing her. You credit yourself with scruples for not revealing your master has a concubine, all the while you are attempting infanticide. I contemplated the statement of Aristotle that had inspired me so recently. Were these twisted attitudes on which I had been reflecting the greatest excellence my family members and Pericalles felt within themselves? Then these souls deserved my pity far more than the resentment I held against them.

Come morning, neither Tiberius nor I wanted breakfast. After planting a distracted kiss on my forehead, he departed for the townhouse in haste and dread. For a time I moped about the villa idly, without incentive to engage in any particular activity. Since the weather was quite warm I considered ordering a bath, but at once rejected the idea on account of the drought. How could I justify indulging in this creature comfort when people were having trouble conserving drinking water for their children? Finally in early afternoon I grabbed my painting accouterments and ventured out to the garden. There I found Alexias seated in the belvedere with his back to the house, staring at the wall that enclosed the garden. For quite some time I sat beside him without speaking or doing anything. Finally he broke the silence with a question that surprised me considerably.

"Lady, do you still believe meteors signify a life changing event?"

"I believe they might, Alexias. The premise has not been proven. Why do you ask?"

"Three nights ago, before I discovered Pericalles…doing…preparing to poison our child…" He broke into sobs, but regained his self-control quickly although with considerable effort. I rubbed his back and he took a deep breath. "…I…I happened to glance at the night sky. There was a cascade of three meteors. Lady, did you see them?" His voice broke again.

"Three nights before your…"—here I swallowed hard— "…before your dreadful event? No, Alexias, I did not see them, although Master and I were out here in the belvedere. I remember it rained a little, and the skies cleared thereafter. Still, we did not observe any meteors. Maybe we simply went indoors before they appeared; or being distracted with other matters" (as was true) "we did not pay attention to the sky. I strongly suspect meteors have a prophetic nature. The astrologer Thrasyllus said they are common this time of year; but he also affirmed they are harbingers of change. If you saw them but Master and I did not, that may confirm Thrasyllus' notion they are prophetic specifically to those who actually witness them."

We fell silent again for a time. The discussion about the meteors brought me great respect for Alexias. Although he spoke both Greek and Latin fluently, he was not terribly literate in either language. Most of his time and efforts were necessarily devoted to his serving responsibilities. And yet he had learned about and obviously devoted some thought to a subject that has intrigued the intelligentsia for centuries. The words he uttered next moved me all the more. "Lady," he began quietly, his voice tremulous, "it is inappropriate for me to ask this of you. But please, just for today,"—he looked at me earnestly with tear-filled eyes— "would you be ever so kind as to consider playing your harp for me?"

"Why of course!" Picking up my painting materials, I hastily returned to the house and exchanged them for my harp. As I made my way back to the belvedere, tuning the instrument while I walked, Ajax approached me. "Lady, I have reached a lull in my duties. Might I accompany you as you bring comfort to Alexias?" he inquired.

"Ajax, you have no need to ask," I replied. When we reached the belvedere, we found Dorotheus sitting with Alexias. The chef had brought a platter of comfits.

From my repertoire I selected the most quieting, soothing of melodies and songs. Alexias sat stone-faced, still staring again at the perimeter wall, until I began to play and sing one very old Greek lullaby. Immediately I stopped, because he burst into tears. "Pericalles was humming that last night while she anointed her breasts with the poison!" He fairly choked on the words.

"Alexias, I am ever so sorry—I had no idea!"

He regained his composure. "You could not know, Lady. Please, please play again. Now I should like very much to hear the piece. My mother used to sing it to me when I was a boy."

Tiberius and Arbindus arrived as I was concluding the lullaby. Dorotheus and Ajax started to rise to their feet; but with a glance and quick shake of his hand Tiberius motioned to them to remain as they were. Arbindus leaned on his spear, Tiberius against one of the columns that supported the belvedere. He had shed his toga but still wore his long white senatorial tunic with its broad purple stripe down the front. "Alexias, it appears your little girl is going to live," he said gently. "Last night the pharmakeutria administered the antidoting opiate in warm honeyed water, which the baby suckled from a cured kid's udder. By morning the child was groggily awake and fussing a little. The pharmakeutria gave more of the antidote and continued to watch the results. Around noon she concluded the baby could take nourishment, and departed to procure a wetnurse.

"Meanwhile Arbindus and I hauled Pericalles before the praetor's court, but not,"—Tiberius' voice suddenly turned steely as he spoke through clenched teeth, — "...not before I made her wash her breasts before me and nurse that babe unsullied while I watched. And do you know, she actually expressed outrage at my demand? 'Clearly you have no regard for female modesty,' she snarled. 'Get on with it!' was all I returned." He sighed wearily. "I did not bother trying to reason with her about respect for human life. All she would have done was preach me her altruism for aspiring to save a child from a life of slavery."

That perverse morality once again, I reflected dejectedly.

Nestor and Alcmene joined us. Now the belvedere was crowded, in as pleasing a sort of way possible under the present circumstances. Picking up my harp I moved a little to free some space on the bench, then beckoned Alcmene to sit beside me. Although she did not utter a word, she accepted my invitation obviously flattered. Nestor, like Tiberius, stood leaning against a column.

For a long while nobody stirred or said anything. Dapples of sunlight drifting through the trees crept across the dusty, drought-stressed garden. Cicadas sang their antiphonal chant, first in one tree and then another. I pondered the range of social status our little company represented. Two of us were women of low station: the one a slave, the other a fugitive and concubine. Four of the men were slaves as well; the fifth was a eunuch; and the sixth was the second most empowered individual in the entire Roman empire. Yet we were gathered with a common intent that rendered the social boundaries artificial and meaningless. We had assembled to bring comfort and courage to a fellow human who had suffered a devastating event, the nature of which was no respecter of rank.

This incident, moreover, gave me my first glimpse at the ruthless side of Tiberius' nature. I had always known it had to exist: he could not have succeeded in politics, and certainly not as a military commander, without it. To tell the truth, the prospect of seeing it had always frightened me. Now I observed how it was purposeful—not the arbitrary or purely retributive cruelty my family always attributed to people who wielded such power. Pericalles had attempted murder. Her execution was more than punishment: it prevented her from perpetrating the same crime again. Forcing her to nurse her baby properly was a sharp and well-deserved reminder of the maternal obligation she had perverted. Rather than belabor her objections, Tiberius had let his final requirement speak for itself.

Eventually another common essential, with no respect for social order, brought our congregation to an end. Feeling a call of nature, I arose and picked up my harp. "Alexias, my sympathies are ever with you," I said sincerely. As I started to leave the belvedere, Alcmene flashed a sympathetic smile at Alexias and rose to follow me. Dorotheus did so as well. "It is time for me to start preparing supper," he said while shaking Alexias' shoulder reassuringly. The day was indeed waning; the lowering sun was beginning to impart the hazy sky a reddish-golden glow. "And for me to feed Vindex and Victor theirs," Nestor added, referring to the villa's guard dogs.

When I reached the main path to the house, I overheard Tiberius' voice from the belvedere: "Alexias and Ajax, remain with me."

While I made use of the latrine, Alcmene drew my bath. Afterward, Tiberius had Alexias as well as Ajax attend him. During our supper of stewed fowl from the villa's flock, Tiberius described the offer he had made to Alexias during the bath. The fifteenth birthday of Lucius Caesar was imminent at the end of January. The extraordinary gift of a trained personal servant would commemorate the prince's coming-of-age and befit the special nature of the occasion.

"I warned Alexias that Lucius' truculence could prove especially challenging to a steward. But the change of physical locale and manifold responsibilities of the appointment offer opportunity and distractions, to help put the terrible events he has suffered behind him. I advised him if he accepted, I would contact my stepfather at once to make sure the arrangement is viable. Should it prove not to be I shall send Alexias to Rome anyway, and ask my parents to utilize him in some other capacity—perhaps as an attendant to Drusus, or simply a household servant. It appears his little girl is recovering well. For now I shall have Phoebe raise her as a member of my personal household. Once an opportunity presents itself, I shall reunite her with her father."

"I presume he accepted your offer."

"On his knees and with tears in his eyes. Alexias has been an efficient and conscientious servant, but always in a subordinate position. For the next month or so, I shall have Ajax and Menon train him in the specific protocols of stewardship. This entails management of the master's household along with care for his person—as you know from observing Menon. Once his mentors feel he is adequately prepared, I shall send Alexias to Italy. By then my parents will be expecting him."

Augustus responded promptly: the gift of Alexias to Lucius Caesar was entirely appropriate and most appreciated. We returned to our townhouse in early September as usual. As we arrived, Phoebe approached Alexias with the baby in her arms. The little girl was glancing about with bright brown eyes, alert and aware of her surroundings. Phoebe placed her on the floor before Alexias, who recognized the custom at once. A Roman infant, newly born, is laid at its father's feet. Lifting the baby in his arms, the father acknowledges his paternity and his intention to rear the child. "I accept you as mine," Alexias declared through yet more tears as he retrieved the little bundle. "And I hereby name you Miranda, for your rescue and recovery have truly been miraculous."

The imminent departure of Alexias, and the removal (I deliberated considerably before choosing this particular word) of Pericalles, diminished the size of our serving staff at the very time the need to care for Miranda increased their responsibilities. As a remedy Tiberius sought to purchase Nestor and Alcmene from the owner of the villa, who was agreeable. The remuneration from the sale was ample to cover the purchase of a new caretaker for the property.

Nestor and Alcmene were originally from Alexandria—and were Jewish we were surprised to learn. Their Hebrew names were Hezir and Abigail. Like most Diasporic Jews they bore Greek names as well. A sophistos in residence at the Museion had been their original owner. Abigail was born in his household; Hezir was acquired later. His history was similar to Phoebe's. In childhood he had been seized by a creditor and sold into slavery after his parents proved unable to repay their debt. The sophistos master had allowed the pair to observe the customs of their religion, called them by their Hebrew names, and eventually sanctioned their union which produced two daughters.

About a decade after the second girl's birth, the now elderly and widowed sophistos died. His heirs were eager to liquidate his estate, and cared little about the familial feelings of his servants. Abigail and Hezir were sold to an Ephesian real estate magnate who specialized in the renting of luxury properties he owned throughout Asia Minor and its environs—hence his possession of the Rhodian villa. The couple had no idea what happened to their daughters. The girls were in their adolescent years, and consequently considered old enough to be separated from their parents. The couple's new owner feared anti-Semitism among potential clients might dissuade them from renting his properties, should they learn he had Jews among his serving staff. Accordingly he forbade them to disclose they were Jewish, required them to use only their Greek names, and disallowed their religious practices whenever tenants were present—even if this meant engaging in labor on their Sabbaths. Now we understood why on certain days they seemed strangely chagrined while serving us.

One morning soon after he had finalized their purchase, Tiberius summoned Nestor/Hezir and Alcmene/Abigail to the library along with Menon and me. "Unfortunately I must insist you continue to be called by your Greek names, simply because they are easier for the rest of us to pronounce and remember. I doubt any member of the staff will harass you about being Jewish; but should this happen, advise Menon here immediately. Feel free to procure and prepare your own foodstuffs in compliance with your dietary laws. Consult with Menon, moreover, to ensure the days he schedules for your respites coincide with your Sabbaths and other feasts." All of our servants were allocated days on which they were excused from work, to allow them rest from their labors and opportunities to address private matters.

Nestor bowed in acknowledgment but said nothing. Alcmene, however, fell to her knees, clasped her hands and exclaimed "Oh, Master, thank you, thank you so very much!"

Tiberius nodded. "It is quite a pity you had to suffer separation from your daughters. Please try your best not to let the presence of little Miranda sorrow you."

"Contrariwise, Master, we are finding her a great joy, especially in light of her recent escape," Nestor returned.

Alexias' ordeal and the kindness of his fellow servants started me ruminating once again about my past. Our attendants came from differing personal and cultural histories. They had been thrown together into our service by the institution of slavery. Nevertheless, they tried their best to get along with one another. They all had private burdens. Phoebe, Menon, Alexias, and Nestor had all been presented to their owners as gifts, as though they were inanimate objects. The same held true for Arbindus. The chieftain of his tribe had given him with his parents to Livia, in return for her recommendation to Augustus that the tribe be allowed to settle within Roman territory.

Phoebe had suffered rape, Dorotheus castration, Alcmene and Nestor for their ethnic and religious background—even to a mild extent in our household, through the requirement they employ their Greek names. Alexias saw the woman he desperately loved attempt to murder their child; and Miranda likely must someday face the fact her own mother had tried to kill her.

My family's intractable intolerance, and their determination to bend others to their preposterous expectations, had left me friendless and driven away the few suitors (apart from Lucius Norenas) who had shown interest in me. This was all trivial before what our servants had endured. Furthermore, I had escaped my torments and their perpetrators. Why, then, did I continue to chafe? Why did I find myself ruing broken trysts from long, long ago, especially since in the end they had led to the splendid relationship I now enjoyed? What was still required, to make me relinquish this ever-intrusive brooding resentment?

We saw Alexias off on the Calends of November. A few days later I was sitting on the veranda, embroidering a decorative border on a well-made but unadorned cloak of red wool I had purchased as a gift for Tiberius' forthcoming birthday. There was a slight commotion at the base of the knoll behind the house. Looking over the veranda wall, I discovered a very young child—perhaps little more than a year old—awkwardly but determinately pursuing Leo up the stone steps. I opened the gate, retrieved Leo, descended to where the child had halted, and sat down on the step beside him. "Would you like to pet the kitty?" I asked, restraining Leo tightly. "Here, put your hand on his head: very softly now—you do not want to hurt the kitty." After enduring several pats that proved rather hard despite my caution, Leo extricated himself, then bounded up the steps and through the gate to the veranda. "Oh my!" I exclaimed. "The kitty ran to get his supper. You can visit him again someday."

Just then a heavyset woman appeared near the bottom of the stairway, looking about rather frantically. As she was holding Miranda, I realized she was the wetnurse. Taking the little boy by the hand I said, "Let us go to Mama," and led him down the steps.

The nurse was not a slave but a hireling, who came to the servants' section of the house several times each day to suckle Miranda. She looked to be about ten years my senior. Her tired eyes, leathern skin, gnarled hands, and thinning brown hair prematurely streaked with gray, all attested to a life of intense labor. Her hair was knotted atop her head without regard for fashion, but simply to get it out of her way. The homespun chiton she wore was clean, but threadbare from wear and repeated washings and marred with indelible stains.

"So, I finally get to meet the lady of the house!" she exclaimed as she bobbed a slight curtsy. Her warmhearted grin revealed a number of missing teeth. "You and I have the same name: Daphne. Appears we have the same build," she added as she assessed me from head to toe. "Lucky girl you are, to have His Honor for your man."

"I assume you refer to the regent Tiberius Nero, who is my guardian."

"If he is your guardian, then I resemble a Praxiteles Aphrodite," she retorted with cheerful sarcasm. Her recognition of the venerable sculptor attested to a modicum of education. "And what a specimen he is!" she continued with undisguised admiration. "He must be a marvel in bed."

To my immense dismay I felt myself grow warm. My murmured, "I would not know," met with a dismissive snort. "What is this little one's name?" I asked hopelessly as I placed the boy's hand in hers.

"All right, we shall change the subject. Your face is as red as a pomegranate." Now my heart really sank. "His name is Dionides. We called him after one of my husband's granduncles."

"Do you have other children?"

"Five besides this one. The eldest is nearing sixteen years."

"You are most fortunate. I cannot bear children: that is why my husband left me."

"So, you have been married—and to a dimwit, clearly enough. Look how much better off you are now. Keep on trying—you never know. You and His Honor might produce a fine brood yet. He certainly has the right physique—and so do you. And be thankful you have plenty of money for raising children."

"The regent is my guardian!" I repeated emphatically. The declaration made no impression whatsoever. I softened my tone and spoke gently. "What does your husband do for a living, Daphne?"

"He is a mate on a cargo vessel. Runs mostly between here and Alexandria. Bastard owners pay little more than subsistence wages. Our firstborn is a girl. Her father has found her a nice young man. That is why I have to sell my milk—and for a slave baby yet—to raise money for a dowry. At least we are happy. You keep His Honor happy too, you promise me now." She turned away and trudged back toward the servants' entrance, cradling Miranda on one arm and patting the baby's fanny while towing Dionides with her other hand.

If one can imagine a mingling of intense agitation with abject relief, that is the state in which I mounted the steps back to the veranda. At once I summoned Menon, and had him sit with me on the bench beneath the pear tree while I described my encounter in urgent undertones. I was concerned one of the servants had revealed the true nature of my relationship with Tiberius, which they were sworn to keep to themselves. Menon reassured me this was not the case. Not only had the wetnurse made her own deduction; she had tried to persuade every member of Menon's staff to support it.

"Welcome once again to the life of a public figure," was Tiberius' response. "People incessantly draw conclusions about you, some of them true, others utterly preposterous. Moreover it seems the more absurd the notion, the more intently its perpetrators maintain its validity. Do you know who Gaius Maecenas was?"

"Your stepfather's childhood friend. An Etruscan. Great patron of arts and literature supportive of the regime. He died fairly young, like Agrippa."

"That summer before you and I first met. He was only in his sixty-first year. Anyway some years earlier, Maecenas' relationship with my stepfather became strained for a time. They had a disagreement over the level of confidentiality to be maintained with regard to the exposure of government information. Maecenas had discussed, with his wife Terentia, some proposals for new policies which he had believed disclosable, but which my stepfather felt should have been kept secret. The rumor spread, however, that the coolness between them developed because my stepfather had seduced Terentia. Notice if you will, the story emerged shortly after passage of the morality laws. And people still cling to this notion as if it were an unassailable truth. The same holds true for the even older rumor, that my mother perpetrated the death of my stepfather's nephew Marcus Marcellus."

"I thought he died of that plague everyone was contracting."

"He did. But the story circulated that my mother poisoned him, so my stepfather would be forced to name me as his successor and my brother as my auxiliary."

"Well she certainly botched things then. Julia married Agrippa and produced Gaius and Lucius, who assumed those roles at birth."

"See how ludicrous the accusation is? Yet twenty years later, it retains a large number of notoriously intransigent and vocal adherents. It surprises me you have not said your family endorsed either story."

"They probably did, and never told me. Remember, I was considered far too naïve to comprehend their profound assessments of people in positions of power. But returning to today's encounter: I fear that by blushing, I validated the nurse's assumption about our relationship."

"You did nothing to verify her assumption. For all she knew you blushed over her accolades of my sexuality or her assessment of your physique. Notice how she accepted your pseudonym, along with the false story of your ruptured marriage. Purely by chance she stumbled upon a truth you are endeavoring to conceal. This sort of thing is bound to happen to you again. Now that you have had this experience, the next occurrence will unsettle you far less."

Eventually the same sort of thing did happen; but I did not respond with nearly the resilience Tiberius had predicted for me.

That autumn I resisted returning to the Rhodes Academy more vigorously than ever, because I had gotten an idea for a new artistic endeavor. Julia had been absolutely delighted with my composite portrait of her children, which Tiberius had sent to her for her birthday while I was touring Asia Minor. *How fortunate of you to come upon so amazing an artist, this Eutychus. What are the chances of having him brought to Rome that I might set him to adorning the walls of our house, relieving them of their dreariness?* Reflecting on Julia's response one day, I had the impetus to ask Tiberius whether his mother might enjoy receiving a similar portrait of her four grandchildren. His answer surprised me. Livia, he felt, would prefer a rendering of his brother Nero. Would that not sadden her, I queried. Quite the contrary, he assured me. Livia cherished mementos of her deceased son, letting them bring her the same joy his presence had given her.

As it was early November, I could easily have a portrait ready for Livia's birthday in that January immediately forthcoming. But why not prepare it for presentation the following year? With a subject so profoundly meaningful to its recipient, I should like to proceed slowly and insure all the details and nuances were correct. And what of Antonia, I continued: might she like a composite of the three children she had borne to Nero? Since her birthday fell on the day after Livia's, I could complete both projects simultaneously at the same carefully measured pace.

Representing Antonia's children might prove difficult, my partner warned. The elder son Nero was well proportioned above his waist, but afflicted below with short narrow hips and spindly legs. Because he was disarmingly ingratiating and charming, people tended readily to overlook these defects. Nor would they pose any difficulty for me, I replied, as I was only going to render his face and upper torso. Nero's siblings were going to be a different matter. The next child Claudia Livilla was downright ugly—skinny and sinewy with lanky black hair, a long oval face, prominent brow bones, a large aquiline nose, and a small pouty mouth. Self-conscious about her appearance, she was alternately brazenly insolent or timidly retiring. In addition to being fat, the younger son Tiberius had a slightly hunched back. Moreover one leg being slightly shorter than the other caused him to walk with an ungainly limp. Little Tiberius also inclined toward obnoxious and bizarre behaviors—not as severely as Julia's youngest son Postumus, but enough to irritate and disgust onlookers. He was inclined to interrupting conversations, and to bursting out in loud guffaws when nothing humorous was apparent. He often stared aimlessly with his mouth agape and drooling and his tongue protruding slightly. His own mother called him a monster unfinished by nature; and his grandmother Livia could not abide being in the same room with him for more than a few minutes.

Perhaps a challenge, I mused; but let me at least try my hand. We did not have to send my results if they failed to produce suitable likenesses. Very well, my companion assented—I could have my year. He would procure some Rhodian pottery pieces for Antonia's imminent birthday. To his mother he would send a treatise on personal peace and serenity—written by the great Atomist philosopher Democritus, and edited by none other than the sophist Thrasyllus of Rhodes.

Quite excitedly I busied myself with this new artistic endeavor, for which I frequently elicited the advice and criticism of my teacher Timotheus. Furthermore, I was dreading the inevitable encounter with Timoleon. "Sooner or later you will have to face him," Tiberius chided me while we were rolling dice on his birthday. "Remember to treat him kindly. You should also know Thrasyllus misses your visits."

To tell the truth, I missed those visits as well. Accordingly I started to make sporadic trips to the Academy, to attend those occasional lectures that particularly interested me but especially to see Thrasyllus. The resident headache Plato was back, this year with two equally obnoxious companions whose names

179

I did not bother to learn. Timoleon had also returned. He became predictably euphoric upon meeting me, insisting I was lovelier than ever and that he had missed me sorely. Why, he asked, was I present at the Academy so seldom this season? He pouted a bit when I explained that I was devoting more time to my non-academic interests. Then he seemed cheered, after I promised to seek him out and spend time with him whenever I did come to the Academy.

Timoleon became increasingly solicitous—rather like my former fiancé but far less obnoxious. He always had a simple gift for me, like a sweet or a nosegay of winter blooms. Presently he began to make us sit within sight of my bodyguard and chaperone but out of their earshot. This led me to anticipate—correctly as it turned out—that he was preparing to make his proposal. And so he did, one blustery afternoon in late January. His quest had an arrogance that took me a bit by surprise, in the wake of the apparent humility with which he had been approaching me. "Daphne, I should like very much to take you as my wife."

Taking his hands in mine and gazing into his eyes, I presented the prepared response I had held ready since the previous August. "Thank you very, very much for your kind offer. Regrettably I must decline because my divorce is still pending. Once it is concluded I am going to require some distance—some time to be alone and independent—before I enter another relationship. You are a most attractive and likable man, Timoleon, a potential joy for any woman. You should have no trouble finding another."

I expected him to be miffed, crestfallen, even saddened by my refusal. Instead he snatched his hands away from mine, glared at me red-faced, and actually bared his teeth. "So! You are so fascinated with power and privilege that you have set your heart upon that malingerer, rather than someone who can give you a genuinely stable family life! Well, you will pay, I swear you will pay!"

Somehow I managed to retain a sense of calm—that gritty, determined calm which accompanies anger and outrage. I stood up and with one hand beckoned Arbindus and Phoebe, who approached at once. Returning Timoleon' glare I said icily, "Do not dare demean me or my guardian! And never, ever threaten me again!"

We had been sitting on a bench in a hallway of the Academy's main building. As I walked away he tried to follow, but Arbindus blocked his way. Timoleon started to shout a taunt: "Fine, go ahead and live your life of..." and then stopped abruptly. By then Phoebe and I had reached the door of Thrasyllus' study, in which we took refuge.

When Arbindus caught up with us, I asked him how he had deterred Timoleon. The Gaul grinned. "After looking about quickly to make sure no one was watching us, I drew my sword and pressed its point against his throat."

Thrasyllus chuckled as I described my encounter. "He has a mean temper all right, that fellow. Someday it may prove his undoing. Be prepared for a possible reprisal. He deserves an uncompromising termagant for a wife. You are hardly that."

I gave a short, sardonic laugh. "My parents always insisted I was."

Thrasyllus raised his eyebrows. "Portentous you should mention your parents at this particular moment—*Clytia*." I gave a start, and he nodded slowly. "Tiberius told me about you, after he came upon me reading a critique of Atomism by one Pythia of Naples. He wanted to ensure I did not unsettle you with an offhand comment about your scholarship. We said nothing to you, because we wanted to give you a chance to reveal your identity voluntarily, when you felt comfortable doing so. However: I am at present preparing a set of lectures on the Atomist philosophers, in which I shall be quoting you—or Pythia, I should say. This is why I want you to know I am now fully aware of who you are. And please forgive Tiberius for making the disclosure before you yourself intended. He loves you profoundly, Clytia. His only motive was to keep you from being hurt."

"Truthfully I have no qualms about your knowing who I am, and would have gladly divulged my identity long before today. My motive for holding off was to protect myself, and Tiberius as well. I was and still am reluctant to disclose anything to anybody, lest the information somehow filter back to my family; for they will raise a ruckus beyond imagination. One cannot reveal what one does not know. And I am deeply moved and honored to learn the great Thrasyllus of Rhodes has seen fit to consider and quote the conclusions of Pythia of Naples. Just please promise you will not acknowledge me to your audience in person!"

"Hardly should I think of doing so. And now with regard to those conclusions: you are rather harsh on the Atomists."

Suddenly I felt a once familiar sinking feeling, almost a nausea. It had always arisen whenever I was called upon to justify the hypotheses I had derived from my studies and reflections. Furthermore I realized my sojourn on Rhodes, during which I had abandoned academics as a profession, had relieved me of this anxiety. But now that I must defend my anti-Atomist contentions, to the very scholar who had compiled and edited the extensive writings of Democritus, the old familiar disquietude returned. "Please rest assured, I respect the Atomists deeply for their ethics," I began, meekly and nervously, "for their aspirations and efforts to bring comfort and peace of mind to humankind. But I cannot accept the premise they share with the Stoics, that nothing lies beyond the material world and goodness must be found within this world. There is no goodness in matter. Only by reaching beyond matter, and recognizing the presence of an underlying, incorporeal, spiritual goodness, can one find respite from the evils that plague material existence."

"That makes you a disciple of Plato."

"I suppose I am—although I like to think I arrived at my conclusions through independent reasoning, without following a prescribed method." Such was my response to the scholar who was currently editing the works of Plato. "With Plato I agree, that Underlying Good is a living palpitating Presence, occupying the same space and time as our material world. But I do not spend my days engaged in dialectic—trying to achieve serenity or an understanding of the precise character of Good and the mechanics of its operation, through contemplation of the perfect incorporeal Forms of which our material concepts are counterfeits. I am not a practicing philosopher—with all due respect to those who are. Nevertheless I try as much as possible to embrace Good—rather in the way Aristotle outlined in his **Eudemian Ethics**—not on blind faith or through dialectic analysis, but by acknowledging and abidingly trusting its presence and power to govern our lives rightly once we surrender to its action.

"Admittedly this is not an easy task when one is facing danger, or when one feels overwhelmed by terror, grief, anger, or even the mundane problems of human life. Nevertheless I feel I have demonstrated, in my personal experience, that wholehearted acceptance of Underlying Good and willingness to let it do its work brings genuine adjustment and harmony to one's experience. On my nineteenth birthday I felt I had reached my absolute nadir. Obsessed with fear the abuse my family kept heaping upon me would lead me to insanity or suicide, I mentally reached out to Underlying Good as desperately and importunately as a terrified child seeking comfort from a loving adult. Almost at once I gained a tangible sense of peace, and of reassurance my life was going to improve. Then I saw that meteor, which we discussed during our very first conversation. About a month later, as you know, I met Tiberius, who had witnessed a meteor at the same time as I."

While I was speaking, Thrasyllus had been sitting back in his chair with his arms folded across his chest. He usually adopted this pose when whatever he was hearing gave him food for thought. After I had finished he sat for a time in reflective silence without changing his position. Finally he said quietly, "I cannot believe you do not describe yourself as a practicing philosopher.

For twenty years or so I have tried to convince generations of students—and many sophistoi as well—that philosophy is far more than idle speculation or a type of mental gymnastics. Its applications are practical and effective. What a confirmation you have provided! Profound cosmic forces surround us, Clytia, the nature of which we have only the barest comprehension. And we are acquiring that comprehension by stumbling about and feeling our way blindly and desperately—like Homer's Cyclops groping in his cave. Following the method Plato prescribed, you used your powers of reasoning to touch something. The result was far more effective than anything the speculation and theorizing of the last five centuries has accomplished. What brought Tiberius to your Academy when you most needed a friend? What prompted him to retire to Rhodes just when you needed to escape? And how about those meteors?"

"On the first night of our voyage from Italy to Rhodes, Tiberius and I together witnessed yet another meteor—the one he likened to a brush spreading paint. Could they be messages that bridge the gulf between our material sense of things and the spiritual nature of Eternal Good? Are they the angels in whom the Jews and Parthians believe? Or are they just mindless physical sparks, perhaps generated when one's thought properly aligns with Underlying Good—as a latch bolt produces a sound when it enters its receptacle?"

"Little wonder you find meteors so interesting. We may never discover their actual character. You are unquestionably a very profound thinker—now, what is your name?" Thrasyllus' eyes twinkled and I laughed. "I can appreciate why Tiberius loves you so ardently. You could become a significant contributor to the academic community, should you decide to resume the role of a sophista."

"Thank you for the compliment," I answered with great sincerity, "but I prefer to remain as I am. I have far too many painful memories of having been forced into the role of sophista, while my physical and emotional needs were abused and my social refinement ignored. Even the discussion we just had made me uncomfortable because it stirred up those recollections."

"I quite understand. You were a woman long before you became a scholar. It is only natural for a woman to desire husband, home, and children above anything else. Your parents tried to turn you into something unnatural. A sophista is an anomaly; a learned housewife is not. My wife is a royal, and well educated; but the primary emphases of her life are the rearing of our infant daughter Thrasylla and the cultivation of our home. The same holds true for Tiberius' mother Livia."

Feeling a rush of anger and chagrin, I covered my face with one hand. "My family incessantly preached I was never grateful enough for everything they did for me. Strangely enough I do feel profound gratitude, but in a way I resent. Had it not been for their afflictions, I would not be here today. Their maltreatment drove me to accept, first the solace of Tiberius' friendship, and subsequently his love and the opportunity he provided me for escape."

Thrasyllus shook his head. "Do not give your family credit that is not their due. Your courage, your quest for normality, your effective use of philosophy— these are what brought you to where you are. Had you remained in Naples— trying in vain to please, to placate, to meet ever escalating, impossible demands— you might have very likely ended up sharing the fate of your father."

Now I looked at him quizzically. "Sharing the fate of my father?"

His tone became grave. "You do not know, do you? Your father died this past November. He suffered some sort of massive seizure and collapsed—directly in front of the class he was teaching. Please accept my condolences."

I sat in silence, staring downward at an angle—a habit I had picked up from Tiberius. "Thank you," I finally replied, blandly and without looking up, "but there is no need for condolences. I feel no grief—only remorse because I am not grieved. Did you know my father, Thrasyllus?"

"Only by his reputation, which was hardly flattering. His fellow academicians considered him a less than mediocre sophistos—hardly better than an ordinary pedagogue. He, however, viewed himself as a superior intellect whose abilities went unnoticed, and hence unrewarded because nobody else had sufficient insight and intellect to appreciate them. Consequently he had no friends, and quite a few enemies. His arrogance alienated virtually every academic peer with whom he came into contact."

"The effect of my mother's influence."

"She contributed heavily to his lack of popularity. Gossip maintained he had let himself be henpecked to death. Why, his associates wondered, was he so emasculated that did he not exercise his prerogative as a husband, and command your mother and her intrusive aunt to stop harassing him? Equally remarkable was his apparent indifference to the fact his daughter ran off after a married Roman cavalry commander. He did not seem to care a fig that you left."

"Hardly surprising," I reflected ruefully.

Tiberius arrived in a state of bewildered agitation. "Whatever did you say to that erstwhile suitor of yours? Did I not warn you to reject him gently?" He greeted Thrasyllus with a quick handshake and took a chair beside us.

"I thought I had managed to carry the business off quite well," I responded, puzzled. "I told him my divorce is not yet finalized; after its conclusion I shall need time to be alone; I still like him; and he has plenty of charm with which to woo someone else."

"He threatened me just now, and thoroughly insulted you in the process. 'Unless you start keeping that abominable bitch of yours tethered and muzzled in her kennel, Tiberius Nero, you will face dire consequences for sure!' He was red with fury, and had his right fist clenched and raised. He would have struck me, I suspect, had Androcles not been present."

"Arbindus had to defend Phoebe and me." I shook my head from side to side slowly in reflective amazement. "I cannot bear to imagine what he would have done to me in marriage—not that I had entertained any intentions of accepting him. Eternal Good has most assuredly been looking after me!"

"Timoleon has great difficulty accepting rejection," Thrasyllus interjected. "He has started to disrupt lectures and study sessions, taking umbrage when someone challenges or corrects him. I am going to ask the director of the Academy to speak with him about his behavior. The boy has a studious mind. He will make an adequate sophistos if he manages to get his sense of insecurity under control. In the meantime, the two of you ought to keep a safe distance from him with your guards close at hand. Trying to reason with him will most likely prove futile, and may result in someone getting hurt. And Clytia," Thrasyllus continued in a milder tone, "your Mercury in Cancer is prompting you to berate yourself for your lack of grief. Your late father does not deserve your grief, only your forgiveness."

"Forgiveness?" I moaned disconsolately and somewhat irritably. "Oh, Thrasyllus, how can I forgive my father, let alone my mother and her aunt, after all they have done to me?"

As I buried my face in my hands, Tiberius said gently, "Every day she struggles desperately to forgive her family; and she condemns herself bitterly when she finds herself unable to do so."

"That is her Saturn in Leo." Thrasyllus' tone was as sympathetic as it was authoritative. "It is a highly afflictive sign for her, especially as regards her relationship with her mother. Mercury in Cancer troubles her too, albeit not as virulently. The two of you share the latter alignment. Hence you both find forgiving difficult, all the while your innate altruism drives intense desire to forgive. Your mutual understanding of this dilemma prompts you to comfort one another readily. Clytia, the stars explain why forgiveness keeps eluding you. Philosophy provides the tool for finding it. Persist with your contemplations of Underlying Good, and do not become discouraged if forgiveness does not come speedily. You may not reach your goal straightaway; but sooner or later you will."

For the remainder of the winter and well into spring, I pored over the ethical treatises of virtually every philosopher from Pythagoras to Posidonius, seeking a pathway to forgiveness. None of my efforts bore fruit. "My quest is futile—nothing seems to help!" I exploded at Thrasyllus one afternoon.

"Patience, dear one, patience. When you find you cannot forgive, try to pity."

That counsel did help a little. Reflecting anew on my parents and great-aunt, I perceived how their humble and labor-ridden origins had driven their desire for wealth and grandeur. As daughter and sister of a fuller, my mother and her aunt had been required to assist him in his business, waiting upon and making obeisance to his customers. The father/brother proprietor required nothing short of excellence in the delivery of his services. He was bitterly critical of mistakes, and of attitudes like sloth, condescension, or irascibility. In short he was uncompromisingly intolerant of any action on the part of his family which might alienate his clientèle. Little wonder my mother had always depicted him as dictatorial and cruel. As they complained and commiserated to one another, Anthe and Euethia became increasingly resentful and envious. Why should they have to work for and defer to relatives and strangers alike, exerting more than minimal efforts to reach a lofty standard? Why should not others be deferring to and serving them? Little wonder they were so bitterly jealous of people in positions of power. Their background also explained their disdain for sewing and weaving. Stitched or woven repair of garments is a principal service fullers offer.

Little wonder my father had supported my mother's quest for grandiosity. His father had been an ordinary pedagogue—the type who set up makeshift classrooms for young children in corners of public buildings. Embittered by his lowly academic status, the pedagogue had relentlessly pressured his son to become not merely a sophistos, but one of the highest possible caliber and renown. Along came my mother, who alternately idolized him as an academician of unsurpassed brilliance, and belittled him for not achieving the recognition to which they both felt him entitled.

I kept reminding myself that I would not be living my present life, had my family not mistreated me. Had I been properly raised and cared for, had my female affliction been addressed when it first became evident, had marriage been arranged for me when I reached the appropriate age—then today I would be wife to a sophistos or pedagogue of my father's acquaintance, possibly with children, certainly with a coterie of acquaintances from the same milieu. Life would be obvious, predictable, and bland. And if this hypothetical marriage failed, I would return to the custody of my family. The uncannily satisfying excitement, arising from the secrecy, the passion, the uncertain future and potential for danger in my relationship with Tiberius, would never have been mine.

Nevertheless, forgiveness continued to elude me; and pity soon gave way to contempt. "You once spoke of improving one's destiny through adherence to ethics," I carped at Thrasyllus. "Well then, why did my family neglect to apply such principles against their abusive inclinations? My father studied ethics during his academic training. What is more, he later taught them! Please do not suggest my family was unaware their actions were injurious. They knew perfectly well they were hurting me; yet they persisted with their assaults. And what burns me all the more: they enjoyed watching me suffer! Not infrequently my mother upbraided me for no apparent reason. After reducing me to tears or to a state of silent anguish, she would boast to my father and her aunt that she had unsettled me purposely, because my life had been proceeding more harmoniously than I deserved. And the two invariably agreed with her! Do you see why forgiveness is so difficult for me? And as for pity: how can I pity my family for coveting wealth and grandeur? The wetnurse who comes to our house is unrenowned and impoverished; yet she is reveling in happiness and gratitude."

"All the more reason to pity," Thrasyllus responded patiently. "Your relations are miserable because they covet. The nurse is not covetous: hence she does not suffer. This may be the very reason the Jews follow a purportedly divine command not to covet."

I continued to wail. "Sometimes I wonder whether I ought to have been more acquiescent. Should the energies I spent resisting my family's demands and justifying myself for doing so, have been directed toward more diligent compliance with their expectations? Maybe if I had been less insolent about their ridiculous requirements—less *impudently defensive* as my teacher of manners put it—I might have been more successful as a sophista, and so managed to satisfy their aspirations for me."

"You could never have satisfied them, no matter how accomplished or compliant you were. Had you been Sage of the Sages, Queen of the World, Athena herself, they would have continued to find inadequacies."

"And yet you expect me to forgive!" I exploded. "If ever there was inadequacy in me, Thrasyllus, there it is!"

He had cast my horoscope while I intoned my lament. "You may be on the verge of a breakthrough. The stars portend an imminent change—not a monumental one, but something cathartic and ultimately rewarding. Remember, your family put you through a terrible ordeal. It is hardly surprising you are finding it difficult to pity or forgive. Sooner or later, however, you will manage to do both. In the meanwhile: will you ever stop being so harsh on yourself?"

How many times had I heard those words before—and from whom? This answer calmed me more than all the ethical theories I had been pondering. Gone at last was the sense of guilt that had haunted my intense gratitude for the life I had found with Tiberius. He promptly noticed the new gaiety in my demeanor and proceeded to tease me about it. "For years I have been coaxing you in vain to stop flagellating yourself. You hear the same urging once from Thrasyllus, and you become a different person. I am beginning to wonder which of us is foremost in your life."

My temperament now acquired an airiness which became apparent to everyone—including me. I stopped pondering and meditating, and trying to extract solutions to my frustrations from philosophical treatises. Instead I read these for pure enjoyment, accepting or rejecting their authors' premises without feeling pressured to glean some sort of enlightenment from them. The music and songs I elected to play and sing were now predominantly lilting and blithe, instead of brooding and contemplative. Light and its patterns, rather than shadows, began to dominate my paintings. The portrait of Tiberius' late brother suddenly surrendered its masklike woodenness to a lifelike vibrancy. The composite of his children assumed a soulfulness that minimized their physical unattractiveness—a rendering with which I had been struggling unsuccessfully for months.

There was new jollity—even a bit of playful daring—in my interactions with other people. My conversations surrendered turgidly somber seriousness to an ebullient chattiness about lighthearted subjects. Everyone noticed: the families of the sick whom I aided, my fellow attendees of the Academy, even our servants. At last I mustered the nerve to ask Thrasyllus about his own horoscope. "I was wondering how long it would take your curiosity to get the better of you," he retorted cheerfully. "The Ides of December *[12/13]*: sun in Sagittarius, moon and Jupiter in Pisces, Mercury in Cancer, Venus in Libra, and Saturn in Virgo—all of which sum up a naturally born psychic. Plot it yourself if you like." His candor I appreciated immensely, especially since for once there was no inner voice berating me for being naturally inquisitive about a private aspect of someone's life.

Albeit within the boundaries of decency, I began to dress more provocatively. The inevitable salacious glances I returned with coy smiles. My partner enjoyed my new apparel and far more, because now I became intrepid and innovative with sex. So apt was I to initiate encounters, and so eager to experiment with positions and techniques, that he began to call me his lioness of the bedroom. He would wonder aloud whether I had confused him with Priapus, and express hope he had sufficient stamina to meet my demands. We both tittered surreptitiously upon overhearing Ajax utter the comment—certainly not intended for our ears—that he anticipated having to hammer reinforcements onto the frame of our bed.

While courting me, Timoleon had been my ardent champion against the sneers and derisions of Plato. Now the two became fast friends. Following Thrasyllus' advice to keep a safe distance, I purposely sat on the opposite sides of lecture halls from them. Timoleon would glower at me while Plato made presumably snide comments which set their two nameless tagalongs to snickering. On one occasion I did come face to face with this quartet, when we happened to pass in an Academy hallway. Timoleon said nothing, only scowled; but Plato jeeringly inquired, "Why can you not simply disappear from the face of the earth?" My new vivacity prompted a reaction that surprised even me. Smiling back at him I patted his cheek, pinched it, and then walked away in silence. No one in the group uttered a sound.

By now it was late April. Tiberius admonished that if I wanted to travel again come the summer, I ought to start making preparations. My choice of Alexandria prompted him to recuse himself from writing letters of introduction to anyone in that city. Egypt, he reminded me, was not a province but an imperial duchy. Following the surrender of Cleopatra, Augustus had absorbed the entire country into his personal patrimony. Its governor is a prefect appointed by and directly answerable to the emperor. Better to avoid any risk the prefect or a member of his staff might spread the word Tiberius' ward was visiting Alexandria.

Once more I engaged Eurycles to arrange transport and accommodations, and designated Arbindus my bodyguard. To take Nestor and Alcmene as my personal servants I thought natural since they hailed from Alexandria, until I noted the look of dejection on Alcmene's face after I announced my intention. At first she refused to explain her disappointment: it was my privilege as their mistress, she said, to take her and her husband wherever I wished. Finally I realized—correctly, as it turned out—that our passage was scheduled for their Sabbath. Gently I chided Alcmene for not reminding me sooner, and said I would endeavor to find a different set of attendants.

For a time my efforts proved unsuccessful. Eunice was pregnant, and her husband newly employed by a builder of the luxury villas for which Rhodes was renowned. Demas and Timoxena had full schedules of appointments with clients. Menon and Phoebe were busy with Miranda as well as the house. At length, Thrasyllus provided a solution. His wife Aka, he said, could use a change of scenery. If I would accept her as my traveling companion, she would bring her servants to attend us both. You can well imagine my response.

Stop being so harsh on yourself. That simple, oft-repeated phrase, finally embedded in my consciousness, had transformed my outlook on life. Feeling blessed with newfound happiness, confidence, and imperturbability, I was certain the change Thrasyllus had predicted had taken place and the anticipated catharsis passed—until that fateful day in late June.

Tiberius and I were attending the last of Thrasyllus' three lectures on Atomism, sitting apart from one another as we often did to convey the impression of independence. Timoleon, Plato, and their crew were also present, as they had been at the first two sessions. These had proceeded without incident. During the second, Thrasyllus had duly quoted a little-known anti-Atomist named Pythia of Naples. This individual argues Democritus contradicts himself. He avers the constant flow of atoms renders the testimony of the senses unreliable, making truth discoverable only through the exercise of reason. How can the human mind be capable of reason, Pythia asks, if it consists of the same ever-moving atoms that generate the misconceptions of the senses?

Thrasyllus' final lecture examined the beautiful but simplistic theology of the great Atomist Epicurus. This philosopher describes the gods as embodiments of rarefied, self-renewing atoms which produce subtle images. The gods must exist, because generations of men have received indelible images of them—frequently in sleep, or in the form of visions.

Afterward, the audience engaged in the customary post-lecture discussion. It went something like this:

> How can a flow of material atoms produce universal absolutes like mathematical principles, or notions of absolute truth and goodness analogous to Plato's Forms?

> They are the subtle emanations from the gods.

> If one of these emanations, such as goodness, consists of a flow of material atoms, it should be unvarying and we should perceive it as such.

Correct! This is why we comprehend goodness as something universal and absolute.

But we do not always comprehend goodness in this manner. What one man perceives as good, another considers evil.

The sense of evil arises from a misinterpretation of goodness. Random swerves in the flow of the atoms generate differences in the mentalities of individuals. This is why one man may revel in the weather of a sunny day, while another complains it is too hot and bright.

How, then, can each of us determine the difference between an absolute truth like goodness, and a human opinion about that truth?

The fourth criterion of Epicurus is the act of apprehension by which we determine the difference between self-evident truths and subjective opinions.

At this point I interjected a comment. "The fourth criterion is the Achilles heel of Epicurus' confirmation methodology. Its test is largely conjectural and consequently uncertain. Epicurus himself was well aware of this. He never promoted his fourth criterion as an explicit test of truth, but merely as a theory—a possible explanation for a process, the precise mechanics of which remain to be discovered."

Timoleon had been arguing on the side of the Epicurean perspective— rather intelligently, but with belligerently condescending degradations of the opposition's views. Although prepared for a scathing rebuttal, I anticipated merely a defense of the fourth criterion. What I heard took me entirely off guard. Timoleon snarled, "It is quite evident, Tiberius Nero, the criteria of Epicurus are written on the ceiling of your bedchamber." His response set the audience to murmuring, and his own little gang to laughing raucously. And my self-control dissolved completely.

Had not Demas spent weeks, training me to deflect and diffuse hostile and obstreperous remarks and challenges? Had I not successfully applied those instructions in previous encounters? And had not Tiberius warned me—even before my encounter with Daphne the wetnurse—that people were going to surmise the true nature of my relationship with him? Suddenly all these precautions and preparations became elusive, impossible for me to reach and apply—like the legendary ever-retracting grapes that taunted King Tantalus. Unable to evoke a dismissive or diffusive response, yet unable to keep silent, I retorted with, "Why do you lack the manliness to admit you are wrong? Or barring that, at least the courtesy to accept contrary opinions?"

This rejoinder was the worst I could have possibly uttered. Now the exchange became personal—and very ugly.

"Why should any of us take correction from a godless, adulterous bitch?"

"I am neither godless nor adulterous. Nor am I canine but as human as you—and quite obviously far more civilized."

"Oh spare us your prissy, hypocritical decorum. You live with a married man who is not your husband." Another murmur rippled through the audience.

"That does not make me an adulteress," I retorted. "And clearly you lack the breeding and decency, to leave groundless speculations about my private life and that of my guardian out of this academic discussion." Tiberius hastily scribbled something on a tablet and beckoned Arbindus.

Thrasyllus endeavored to intervene. "Timoleon, your behavior is inappropriate, unbecoming a sophistos, and disruptive to this session. Unless you refrain at once, I shall have you removed."

"Hah! You just do so, Thrasyllus, and confirm what everyone already knows: that you are in bed with the slut as well!" Timoleon had learned, from Plato, the technique of forestalling ejections by representing them as reprisals.

The audience continued to murmur, Plato and his fellow miscreants to laugh. Arbindus delivered Tiberius' tablet to me. *Desist at once! Hold your peace!* he had written in Latin to confound the eyes of those seated near me.

Nevertheless I continued the exchange, for I was simply unable to stop. "You disrespectful scum! It is hardly a wonder your wife left you!" I hurled back.

"Now look who is indecently speculating about people's private lives. Nero, you are living proof that like attracts like, seeing this lowlife was all you could get after Caesar's daughter pitched you out on your ass."

The murmur in the audience grew louder. Plato and his companions began to whoop.

Rising to his feet, Tiberius addressed Thrasyllus. "Please accept my sincere apologies for this unnecessary and distasteful disruption. Daphne Hipparchide, you shall join me outside this hall!"

Arbindus, Nestor, and Alcmene—our attendants for the day—met us at the doorway. As we prepared to depart, Timoleon delivered a final entendre. "For once, Nero, you are performing a public service. You are riding this gathering of a pestilential scourge."

"Do not dare say a word!" Tiberius hissed as we left.

Although we had traveled separately to the Academy—Tiberius and Arbindus on foot and I in the carriage with Nestor and Alcmene—we all returned home together in the vehicle. Tiberius said nothing to me during the journey. Upon our arrival he extended his hand to help me out of the carriage. Then without acknowledging or even looking at any of the staff he half led, half dragged me upstairs to my suite. Phoebe was there, putting away some newly washed garments. "Leave us!" Tiberius barked as he flung me down on the bed, so forcefully that it skittered.

For what seemed an eternity he stood with his arms folded, glaring at me with a look more of distress than of outright anger. Finally he spoke in the measured, steely tones he always used when under duress. "Your outburst has left me devastated. My reputation was already shaky enough in consequence of my own doings. Now you have compromised it all the more. You made me appear to that audience, not only incapable of defending myself, but reliant upon a woman to fight my battles for me with flagrant frowardness egregiously inappropriate for her sex. Can you imagine the sort of gossip and innuendo this is going to engender? You embarrassed Thrasyllus as well. Now I am afraid to show my face outside the door of this house, let alone at the Academy, thanks to you and that unruly mouth of yours. The gods only know the extent of the damage you have caused." He fell silent again for a few moments and then departed, slamming the door behind him.

The accusations I had endured as a child and young adult now came rushing back upon me like a horde of grotesque ghosts. What drives me to react so uncontrollably to such situations? And worse than ever: this was not an insignificant or imagined slight to a family that exaggerated my gaffes and bumbles beyond reason. It was a decisive hurt to the one who had become my sole purpose for living—him whom I loved with every fiber of my being, and whose love in return I cherished above anything else. How could I have been so thoughtless, so callous, so selfish? How could I be so perverse, to inflict such harm upon the person for whom I cared so deeply, who maintained he urgently depended upon my affection and support? What was wrong with me, that I could not exercise better judgment? My family was right after all: they had done the entire world a disservice by allowing me to live.

My gaze wandered about the room, resting on the various gifts Tiberius had presented me: the shell and coral bracelet, the pair of earrings similarly set, the lapis lazuli throat pendant from Egypt carved in the shape of a scarab, the ivory stylus lying across the tablet that held my journal, the silk shawl from China draped over the chair, on the bed a wool coverlet from Gaul decorated with traditionally circular Celtic patterns, on the floor a luxuriant carpet from Armenia adorned with stylized animal designs. I felt so abjectly thankless, so incapable of showing the gratitude that filled my heart—gratitude the giver of those offerings so rightly deserved. With a surge of self-loathing I violently jerked the ruby ring from my finger, and placed it with the other jewelry in the tray atop the dressing table. My altercation with Timoleon had proven I was so hopelessly corrupt, the rubies purported to impel harmonious resolution of disputes had no effect upon me.

My head ached and spun. Over and over I felt hot and then alternately cold. Presently I began to tremble violently. My clothing became soaked with perspiration. Sensing I was about to vomit and unable to see the chamber pot, I hastened to the latrine. The nausea passed as quickly as it had come, so all I did was urinate. Afterward I could not return to my rooms, to sit among those gifts so lovingly imparted, which I most assuredly did not deserve. In need I was of solitude, dark solitude—but there was no alcove in the house to which I could flee.

Behind the potted pear tree on the veranda—in the corner it shaded between the main house and the kitchen extension—there was a sizable collection of small pots. Some rested on a stack of shelves abutting against the wall, others directly on the veranda's pavement. In these receptacles, Phoebe and Dorotheus grew herbs for medicinal and culinary use. To this area I now retreated and sat on the edge of the pear's planter, facing the intersecting walls and the potted herbs with my back toward the main portion of the veranda. Still dizzy and shaking, I grasped the pear's trunk with both hands and laid my forehead against it to steady myself.

I recalled the legend of the Erinyes: the three goddesses of vengeance who punish mortals for transgressing natural order. Although I had always dismissed them as allegory they now seemed tangibly real, and afflicting me for my trespasses upon the personal rights of others. In my mind's eye I saw myself hurtling down a tunnel in the earth toward a dark and bottomless abyss, leaving the sunlit happiness of the last five years on the surface of the world above me. For a moment I contemplated suicide, but reconsidered at once. What I had done was bad enough; worse yet would be to burden the household with the disposal of my remains. A solution came to mind. Surreptitiously I would gather some heavy rocks. Subsequently I would steal out of the house by night and drown myself in the sea, after first filling the bodice of my chiton with the rocks so their weight kept my body from washing ashore. Then the world would be free of a pestilential scourge, as my enemy had so aptly described me. But even while I reflected upon my decision, another wave of self-hatred struck me. To my disgust I discovered that although I felt I no longer deserved to live, I was cravenly afraid to die.

As during those periods of repentance I had passed in the alcove of my childhood, I felt impelled to love everyone and everything. I loved the pear tree: the strength and firmness of its trunk, the kindly soothing coolness of its shade, the heady perfume of its emergent blossoms, the promise of the fruit it would bear. I loved the birds twittering in the branches above me, the bees visiting the ivory flowers. The tender and fragrant little plants, in the pots at my knees and feet, seemed to exude the ingenuous unsullied innocence I so cherished in young children. I loved the day laborers who were hammering on the house next door, our groom clucking to the horses while he brushed them, the dog barking in the distance, the neighbor who lived behind us calling her child, a group of pedestrians conversing as they walked along the street. The adversary I had sought to humiliate this morning I now relished taking by the hand, and explaining rationally and kindly that while I took offense at his behavior, I also understood why he was so terribly aggravated at me. Had I not impugned his academic deliberations and conclusions before an audience of his peers? Had I not disdained his person by refusing his offer of marriage? He probably assumed I had been toying with him, accepting his attentions and pleasantries with no regard for the purpose behind them.

Above all I aspired to recompense my beloved: to make whatever amends were necessary to restore balance to his life, no matter what sacrifices or hardships I must endure in the process. Now the prospect of death intimidated me less, so long as I knew it would be for his help and not my justification. Yet I still did not want to die, I realized with another surge of self-loathing. I wanted to live, if only to succor and repair the affliction I had caused.

Mentally I reached out to Underlying Good, asking no longer to be its beneficiary but now its instrument, bringing the blessing of its harmony to all mankind. I envisioned myself approaching an immense gold throne, occupied by someone or something invisible, incorporeal. I bore a chalice, the contents of which I poured before the throne. The oblation was not a physical liquid but a flow of light, vibrantly salubrious yet gentle like sunrise in spring. It spread from the foot of the throne to the farthest distance in every direction. Thereafter I became a dismembered shadow which faded into nothing. The vision, I realized, was a silently uttered prayer. Let my love impersonally and impartially extend goodness and comfort to all humanity; and let my own selfhood—worthless, afflictive, continually erring—dissolve.

From far, far away, the sound of a voice drifted to me. It became closer, louder, more distinct. "Clytia...Clytia...Clytia!" Tiberius was standing at the edge of my improvised alcove. "Clytia, what for all the world are you doing back here?"

I opened my eyes, but did not look up at him. Instead I stared at the intersecting walls before me, gripping the pear's planter so hard my hands hurt as I struggled to respond.

"Please...please,...oh please understand...if you can,...I meant harm to no one today...especially to you." I took a deep, sharp breath. "I realize that...all the best motives in the universe...cannot undo the damage I have caused. But maybe, hopefully,...if you are able to perceive...that no wrong was intended,... the pain I brought you will become a little...a little easier to bear."

How often had I said this to my mother and her aunt? Their responses had always been the same. How dare I attempt to ease my conscience and forestall the punishment I so soundly deserved, by offering such obviously contrived hypocrisy?

"And please know," I continued, "that in spite of what I did, I...I love you more than life itself,...and shall do so always,...forever,...long after this incident...has torn us apart."

"Torn us apart? What kind of nonsense are you talking? And come out from among these confounded plants, will you, before I trip and break my neck?" He took my hand and gently extracted me from my retreat. Only then did I discover the sun was setting. The entire afternoon I had spent in self-recrimination. Tiberius noticed the bruise on my finger, "What did you do to yourself here?" he demanded.

"I am not worthy...of that beautiful jewel you...gave me."

"You let me be the judge of that!" Aggravation was clear in his voice. He lowered me onto the bench before the pear and seated himself at my side. "Now, why are you making such ado over all this? You are acting like a silly, scatterbrained, adolescent girl."

I did not respond, but covered my face with my hands. Still shaking violently and uncontrollably, I kept muttering over and over, "I am sorry, so sorry, so terribly, terribly sorry!"

For a few moments Tiberius sat beside me in silence. When he spoke again, his tone had the quiet wonder of someone who has just made a profound discovery. "Why, my Clytia,…you have never perceived yourself forgiven, have you?"

Slowly I moved my head from side to side. "Never!" I answered emphatically in a hoarse whisper. "How can I expect forgiveness…when I am destined forever…to wrong others irreparably…especially those…those whom I love,… and whose love I crave in return?"

Gingerly he took my hands in his, drew them from my face and kissed them. He took me in his arms and laid my head on his shoulder, his cheek against my temple. "Hold me Clytia, as tightly as you need. Little wonder you are trembling. What an unimaginable burden you have carried all these years! And what a fool I am, not to have discerned sooner the depth of agony it has caused you."

"What I…did today is…unforgivable," I murmured inconsolably.

"Aggravating: yes. Damaging: perhaps. Unforgivable: no, my love, no. What mortal among us is exempt from making mistakes—or from becoming irritated at those others make? Oh my Clytia, I forgave you hours ago. Consider how I chastised you; yet you have forgiven me, have you not?"

"Oh yes, yes, certainly yes!"

"Now you need to forgive yourself—which given your upbringing you likely have never, ever done. And then, let the entire incident pass. You must understand too, that all the while I was angry I never ceased to love you—not even for the briefest instant."

"What about the damages…to your public…image?" I moaned. "Never can I forgive…myself for causing…those."

"We shall address them if we must, in whatever way we must—assuming any damages arose in the first place. Crises can erupt at any time, Clytia; and not from malevolence but pure carelessness. What shall we do if the house catches fire because one of us knocks over a lamp, or Sinapeus goes lame after I ride him over rocks? Why, have the house repaired or the horse treated—not sit here in Phoebe's pot garden, mentally flagellating ourselves for our thoughtlessness."

Although I noted the humor in his last sentence, I could not smile or laugh.

He began to stroke my hair. I felt the familiar kiss on my forehead. "You overflow with love, Clytia. It shines forth in your gentle disposition, your fierce loyalty, your caring concern for others, your fondness for children, kindness to animals, appreciation for the beauty of nature—and above all in your selfless, unconditional devotion to me. To have had such freely offered affection thrown back in your face with contempt, year after year, by the very people you loved and who claimed they loved you, must have been devastating. You do not really wish to hurt halfwits like Timoleon. That is why you feel such intense remorse after encounters such as today's."

Had he sat with me long ago in that alcove, while I pondered those very feelings over and over?

"Ah, my Clytia," he continued, "I love you as you said you love me: more than life itself. The self-hatred so long required of you has created an obstruction—a barricade, which keeps you from accepting my love as thoroughly and implicitly as you ought. It shields your inner self—a self battered and bleeding and crying out in desperation for comfort and aid. You are afraid to expose that self, for fear it will be hurt all the more. Little wonder you strike out with fury when a contestant like Timoleon draws too near. For years I have been trying to reach your hidden self, to soothe and salve and heal it. You have already opened it to me a little. Now the time has come for you to surrender completely. Draw on my love, Clytia, draw and depend on it without the least reservation—for as you do, you will bless us both!"

It has been said that only a genuine lover can read and sense one's most concealed thoughts and feelings. The emotions with which I had been wrestling all that afternoon now reemerged with overwhelming intensity. There was regret, of course, for the foolishness of my behavior at the Academy. Far, far stronger, however, were the relief and gratitude, from the quiet and calming reassurance of being forgiven and loved unconditionally. To an impulse long abandoned I now succumbed. For the first time in more than a decade I began to weep—not in noisy wet blubbers but silent, shuddering, almost convulsive sobs.

Tiberius pulled away from me a bit, called out "Phoebe!" Then he returned my head to his shoulder and continued caressing my hair. His voice reassumed its tenderness. "Clytia, I have known you for seven years and lived with you for five; yet I have never known you to weep until now. It is highly unusual—yea, unnatural—for a woman not to weep. Weeping is a concomitant of feminine tenderness. I surmise you were told it is a sign of selfishness or weakness." I nodded. He brushed the tears from beneath my eyes and kissed my forehead. "Weep freely now, my love, without fear, without shame; and let those tears so long suppressed cleanse away the poisons of your past."

He remained silent for a while, still stroking my hair, and kissing my face along my hairline. At length he spoke again, now in a straightforward tone. He was addressing Phoebe. "Imagine a purportedly educated family, using twaddle as an instrument of torture—claiming to be the quintessence of rationality, while inflicting recriminations beyond comprehension on the very person who least deserved them. Take her upstairs to the bath, and then to her suite. Give her something to calm her and bring sleep. You or Alcmene or the both of you attend her through the night awake, for she is feverish. Phoebe, be very, very gentle. I have opened a deep and putrid wound in her soul, festering there for most of her life. Now the infection is draining." Notwithstanding his aversion to displaying affection in the presence of our servants, he placed a long and tender kiss on my lips before releasing me to Phoebe's embrace.

"Come, Lady, come. We all love you, Clytia, and know you love us." Phoebe gently dabbed my face with a clean kerchief. Drawing one arm across my shoulders, she began to escort me toward the house, very slowly, with Tiberius following. Darkness had fallen. Menon stood near the door, holding a lamp. Above the blue-black expanse of the sea, the last remnants of daylight were fading from the sky and the stars were starting to emerge. There was a bright flash; I began to swoon; my three companions caught me as I sank to my knees. After taking a few deep breaths I managed to stand again.

"Lady, do you need to sit a while longer?" Menon queried kindly. "Shall I fetch a chair?"

"No need, thank you, no need." I continued to inhale deeply. "We can proceed; I am simply tired and overwrought. For a moment I imagined…"

"You imagined nothing, my beloved," Tiberius interrupted. "I too saw the meteor.

CATHARSES

Phoebe treated me as though I were a child. By this I do not mean she applied the condescending criticism to which I was accustomed from my mother, but rather maternal attention and care. She did not simply sit by while I bathed, but actually washed, dried, and dressed me. After brushing and braiding my hair, she inquired, "Would you like something to eat?" Although I had not partaken of anything since the morning, I shook my head. Phoebe responded with "I understand." There was no, *What is wrong with you that you refuse? You have to be hungry by now!* She helped me to my suite, where Alcmene was in the bedroom. Having opened my bed, she was preparing the attendant's cot in the adjoining room. Alcmene had to have received orders from Tiberius or one of the other servants, for Phoebe had been with me the entire time since we left the veranda.

After seating me on the edge of the bed, Phoebe retrieved a goblet from the dressing table. "Infusion of chamomile flowers," she said quietly. "It calms the nerves and promotes sleep." The warm, fragrant, golden liquid did indeed refresh and soothe, and left a pleasant aftertaste. Alcmene assisted me with cleaning my teeth; then I reclined on the bed. Phoebe tucked the sheet about me, leaving the Gallic coverlet folded on the adjacent chair because the weather was warm. Before retiring to her cot, she took special care to place the lamp so the light would not shine in my eyes. I drifted into sleep reflecting upon Phoebe's motherliness. Not only had her manner comforted me, but so had her physique—her delicate bones, crepe-like skin, soft and undulating bosom. Never had I been allowed to lean on my own mother, emotionally or physically. Nor could I recall her ever holding or caressing me or helping me in any manner. Once I was old enough to feed and dress myself, she had never touched me except to inflict corporal punishment.

Although I anticipated a restless night, I slept soundly until late the next morning. Shafts of subdued daylight from the house's interior court were penetrating gaps in the window blind. Alcmene was sitting in the chair, watching me. "How are you Lady, feeling better?" she inquired eagerly. I nodded and smiled, then swung my feet to the floor and sat on the edge of the bed. "Shade your eyes," Alcmene said as she drew open the blind. As the room filled with light, the sense of gaiety I had enjoyed before the altercation with Timoleon started to return.

Now I was quite hungry, and dispatched Alcmene to the kitchen for a tray of food. During her brief absence, I reviewed my wardrobe and selected something particularly enticing. Alcmene returned with a meal of biscuits and coddled eggs. As I started to eat she addressed me nervously. "Lady I hope you will not think me an intrusive busybody; but last night I took the liberty of praying to my God on your behalf. You know my religion prescribes Ten Commandments for us to follow. It also distills these into two: love God with all your heart and soul and strength and mind, and love your neighbor as yourself. Lady, I wish you the peace of mind that comes from loving yourself and others in the manner God loves us all—patient with our shortcomings, sympathetic toward our woes, supportive of our efforts to do good in whatever way we can."

From my breakfast I looked up into Alcmene's eyes. "You have just summed up much of the lesson I learned from yesterday's tribulation. Thank you, Abigail!" She smiled with delight at my use of her Hebrew name. What I said about her comment was true. The terrible burden of self-deprecation I had borne for so many years was finally yielding to self-respect. That, in turn, was engendering in me a greater empathy for the troubles affecting others. There nevertheless remained a nuance of self-doubt. How, I wondered, would I respond when I had to face Timoleon again? Would I demonstrate my new sense of tolerance, or once more surrender my self-control to the impulse to humiliate him? Part of me still wanted to have the final say in the matter between us.

Quite promptly I put my concerns about Timoleon aside, for I did not want them to contaminate the renewed sense of lightness I was feeling. Once bathed and dressed in the mauve chiton I thought alluring, I had Alcmene bind my hair in a provocative style. As my right hand was still slightly swollen I could not wear my ruby ring; however I did don my shell bracelet and its matching ear fobs. After cleaning my teeth I grabbed my writing tablet, stylus, and inkpot. I was preparing lesson plans for the children of a petitioner: a distraught young widower whose wife had recently died from unexpected complications after childbirth. Taking care to be as surreptitious as possible, I crept down the stairs and out to the veranda. The day was a fourth Tuesday, on which Tiberius regularly opened the house to callers.

The veranda, of course, had not changed; but somehow it appeared different to me. Now its brightness instead of its shadows appealed. I sat on the bench beneath the blossoming pear tree, grateful for its fragrance and the shade it provided from the day's heat but not thinking of it as a refuge or guardian. With the tree at my back, I looked out upon the veranda's vistas rather than into its dark recesses. The sea was brilliantly blue and vibrant with waves—today a symbol of life rather than of the death I had considered seeking from it. My erstwhile alcove behind the pear tree—yesterday such a source of security and comfort—today seemed cramped and dank and dirty, a haven for spiders and other crawling things. Presently Leo came along and jumped into my lap. In my anguish of the previous day, I had actually forgotten about him. For all I knew he had shared my bed without my noticing; or perhaps my attendants had sequestered him elsewhere for the night.

Early afternoon arrived, and so did Tiberius. He sat down on the bench beside me and I leaned against him. To his inquiry as to my condition I replied, "Chastened…purified…wonderfully light…as though I have experienced a bona fide catharsis."

"Indeed you have. Self-forgiveness is critical to one's mental wellbeing; but it can be elusive. In times of duress one frequently must fight to retain it. Yesterday we both finally recognized how seriously you have been deprived thereof. It is a wonder you have as much stability as you do."

"Thank you. As you know, I often worried about the possibility of going insane. Even now I feel unsettled, frustrated, unrequited, because I was so hopelessly ineffective against Timoleon. I keep berating myself for having mishandled his challenge, as I try to figure out precisely what I did wrong."

My partner's reply was patient but emphatic. "Your efforts to denounce Timoleon were properly intended. They also required a phenomenal amount of courage. But they were ineffective because they were misplaced. Clytia, my love: YOU ARE A WOMAN! —and a woman coming fully aware of her femininity for perhaps the first time in her life. You must learn to leave bravado to the men. It is for us to strut and posture and bluster—to hurl insults and punches and otherwise make fools of ourselves. You do not understand this, because you have always had to fight your own battles. I am willing to bet your father never once intervened on your behalf in a dispute."

My newly brightened world suddenly became even brighter. Pushing Leo off my lap, I threw my arms about my partner right in front of Dorotheus, who embarrassedly inquired whether we wanted luncheon. Neither of us was particularly interested. Tiberius was a light eater in general, and I was still rather surfeited from my belated breakfast. We opted for a platter of sliced fruit.

After the chef left I spoke contritely, but without self-condemnation. "I sincerely apologize for that display before Dorotheus, knowing full well you object to demonstrations of affection in the presence of our servants. Tiberius, you have just enabled me to identify and release yet another terrible burden I have been carrying all my life. Finally I see why I always felt uncomfortable, when defending myself in situations like the one we encountered yesterday. You are absolutely correct about my father. He enjoyed seeing me embroiled in such conflicts, especially when they resulted in my defeat. Your last words gave me an unspeakable, euphoric sense of relief, for which I could not contain my gratitude. In my excitement I did not notice Dorotheus standing there."

"Do not worry about Dorotheus. The entire staff recognizes you have been through an ordeal, and all are very sympathetic. Little wonder you are bemused by testicular confrontations like that of yesterday; and high is the time you acknowledge that you have a champion upon whom you can rely. In fact, your champion has already taken care of Timoleon. He should never trouble you again.

"Whatever do you mean?"

Tiberius' eyes twinkled, and he grinned mischievously. "After I finished scolding you yesterday, I donned my magisterial garb and repaired to the Roman provincial government building. One of the praetors helped me recruit twelve lictores from among the pages and secretaries. Then he summoned a decury of soldiers. We all proceeded to the Academy, where—as you can well imagine— we made quite a grand entrance. By now Thrasyllus' audience had disbanded. Timoleon and his companions were attending a lecture Diogenes was giving, and which we interrupted. After apologizing to the sophistos the praetor announced that Timoleon of Thessaloniki was under arrest, for having violated with insult and invective the personal sacrosanctity of the regent.

"Timoleon folded his arms and glared back with an air of arrogant confidence. 'Before all these witnesses, Nero, I submit you are placing me under false arraignment, because earlier today I exposed the truth about you and that pseudo-intellectual, acid-tongued, horse-toothed strumpet of yours.'"

"He called me all that in front of everyone?" I interrupted.

"I am afraid he did, the bastard. It took every measure of self-control I possess to keep me from pummeling him myself. At that very moment, however, I recognized Timoleon had just incriminated himself all the more deeply. So did the praetor. He intoned, 'You have just committed the same offense anew. Maintaining without substantiated proof, that the regent is engaged in a liaison legally defined as immoral, is a degradation of his character and hence a trespass upon the sacrosanctity with which his office endows him. I recommend you come along quietly.'

"The audience began to buzz. Timoleon turned his head away from us and stuck his nose in the air. 'I have done nothing amiss, and am not about to move.'

"'You have no choice,' the praetor retorted. He made a motion with one hand. The members of the audience sitting between Timoleon and our retinue bolted out of the way as three of the soldiers rushed upon our adversary. Seizing his arms, they bound his wrists behind his back with a thong. Then they marched him off to the city jail, one soldier on either side gripping a forearm and the third walking behind with his sword drawn. Timoleon made a few futile attempts to struggle free, only to get his bum poked in return.

"Our corpulent friend Plato, not unexpectedly, had a rejoinder to offer. 'This is a gross abuse of power, Nero! I am going to make the most devastating complaint imaginable about you!' 'Go right ahead, Plato,' I answered, 'write my stepfather a letter. I am sure Caesar Augustus is holding his breath in great anticipation of hearing from an undisputed authority on grossness!' Nearly everyone present—the sophistos Diogenes, his audience, the praetor, our lictores, the remaining soldiers—howled with laughter. Plato turned bright red as he sat there, steaming like an oversized beet in a boiler. Next, one of those simian cronies spoke up. 'Nero, you are the worst, the most piteous, despicable...' He stopped short as our party halted. After a moment of silence the praetor said, 'Why do you not finish your sentence? Your friend from Thessaloniki could use some company.' The halfwit sat staring at his feet while more laughter echoed through the lecture hall."

Dorotheus arrived with the fruit platter and some napkins. We moved apart so he could place them on the bench between us.

"How wonderfully clever!" I exclaimed as we dug into the fruit. "And how stupid I was to attack Timoleon in the manner I did. How I wish I had stopped to think things through! I should have noticed he was abusing your sacrosanctity, allowed him to get caught in his own trap, avoided embarrassing you, and kept from making an unabashed idiot of myself."

"When will you ever hearken to Thrasyllus and me and stop flagellating yourself? Remember your sun sign. You are a Leo: your impulse is to roar. I am a Scorpio: I sting." He smiled with roguish satisfaction.

"What will become of poor Timoleon? Violation of magisterial sacrosanctity is a capital offense, is it not?"

"Violation of sacrosanctity is a religious offense—an act of sacrilege for which death is one prescribed penalty. Now, now, do not be alarmed," he added, reading the concern on my face. "Do you not see? Here is yet another example of how your natural femininity, so long repressed, is now emerging. Pythia of Naples sought to bash Timoleon. Clytia Neronis is thinking of his wellbeing. Right now Timoleon is languishing in jail, awaiting sentencing and undoubtedly making life quite unpleasant for his keepers. I shall ask the praetor to have him flogged and fined but nothing more. He did not cause me any real damage."

"Will the Academy ask him to leave?" I inquired, still feeling a bit solicitous about Timoleon' fate.

"They will not have to. There is far more to Timoleon' story than either of us realized. What I learned from the praetor who accompanied me yesterday will astound you as it did me. Timoleon had told us his wife abandoned him and their daughter for a lover. In reality his own volatile temper so upset and frightened her, that she fled with the girl to her father's home. After the father-in-law filed for a divorce on his daughter's behalf, Timoleon refused to repay her dowry as required by law and custom. He attempted to justify his resistance by alleging her motives for leaving him were frivolous—that she complained he had ceased to satisfy her sexually; that he did not earn enough money to indulge her extravagance; that she was indolent and lazy and refused to fulfill her wifely responsibilities; that she was prejudicing the little girl against him. He added that her father had pressured her to abandon him for those same allegations.

"The father-in-law initiated a lawsuit to recover the dowry, to clear his daughter's name along with his own, and to secure custody of his granddaughter. Timoleon fled Thessaloniki for Rhodes to forestall these proceedings. And whom did he discover here but you: a presumably marriageable woman with phenomenal access to influence and wealth. He planned to demand an immense dowry of me. Thereafter he would whisk you off to Thessaloniki, to show he could not only acquire a new wife, but someone extraordinarily educated and with ties to Caesar's family. Your ample dowry would enable him to repay that of his first wife should her father's suit against him succeed, and leave him money to spare.

"The civil authorities in Thessaloniki contacted those in Rhodes, requesting Timoleon be extradited should the Rhodians find any occasion to bring charges against him. And you, my dearest, unwittingly supplied the perfect pretext. Your rejection ignited his temper. Because we followed Thrasyllus' advice and avoided Timoleon, he did not have an opportunity to ventilate his feelings until yesterday. Frustration with that delay surely exacerbated his aggravation. Either he was unaware his outburst would impugn the sacrosanctity of my office, or in his determination to humiliate you he overlooked that consequence."

"Poor fool!" I said reflectively. "And to think you and I seriously—albeit briefly—considered his request for my hand."

Tiberius at once grew pensively quiet, and stared askance at the pavement. His next words explained the sudden shift in his mood.

"Clytia, I wish you to understand: I am enormously embarrassed, deeply sorrowed and even horrified, for having encouraged you to accept Timoleon's offer of marriage. Now I hereby beg your forgiveness."

Somewhat puzzled, I took his hands in mine and looked determinedly into his eyes. "There is nothing to forgive. How could either of us have known what his true intentions were?"

"I am a trained and practiced politician. It is incumbent upon me to be a proper judge of character."

"Now who is engaging in self-flagellation? You may be an experienced politician; but are you truly a natural one? Or are you like Pythia of Naples: convinced by upbringing that such is your proper role, but sensing deep inside yourself that it is not?"

"How perceptive you are—a lover for sure! And correct! Here I am in my fortieth year, having spent half my life in the political arena; and I have yet to decide whether it is truly my calling. Moreover I do not want to admit to myself, that I continue to battle those misgivings."

"Well, if you are seeking a place in which to brood, there is a bower of potted herbs I can recommend." We shared some much needed laughter.

The secretary Galen approached, and handed a written message to each of us. He announced that the next caller—a newly appointed aide to Publius Sulpicius Quirinius Cyrenius the imperial governor of Galatia and Pamphylia—was waiting in the library. "Advise him I shall attend momentarily," Tiberius responded. Galen bowed and departed. "I expect to spend some time with this fellow," Tiberius continued as he read his dispatch. "Cyrenius is a very distant relative of my mother, and one of her political protégés. The aide is likely related to him in turn." He looked up from his letter. "Meanwhile, the sophistos Diogenes accepted my apology for having disrupted his lecture yesterday. I had him sent a jug of your favorite Sicilian wine as compensation." He walked away chuckling while I moaned.

My communiqué was from Thrasyllus' wife Aka. She was not going to accompany me to Alexandria after all. Having just discovered she was pregnant, she did not wish to risk any complications. She would still send her servants to attend me on the journey. Beneath her calligraphy on the tablet I wrote a note of thanks. After I clapped my hands, Ajax appeared. To him I entrusted delivery of my message to Aka Thrasyllou. He bowed compliantly as he took the tablet, along with the empty fruit plate and used napkins. After he left I felt the familiar twinge of guilt that invariably accompanied my acceptance of a favor. Here was yet another element of the conflicting expectations with which my family had tortured me. Whenever I had accepted someone's generosity, I was labeled avaricious and inconsiderate. When I refused, I was ungrateful and stupid.

Immediately and quite forcefully I mentally pushed these notions aside, and returned to the arithmetic lesson I had been preparing. After finishing the assignment I gazed beyond the veranda at the ocean and reflected for a while. A mental dialogue, comforting and healing, coursed through my mind. I am prone to err—so is everyone. A fig for *What you just did is unforgivable!* Who is not prone to err? If I am awkward, uncomfortable, and usually unsuccessful at verbal defenses, this is because I am a woman trying to fight a man's battles and not a craven weakling. If I become overbearing, condescending, contumelious when provoked, this is natural for a Leo and does not indicate malevolence or mental derangement. I feel genuine concern for others because I am inherently compassionate and not a nosy busybody. Gifts and other generosities I accept graciously but readily, because I understand my doing so pleases the givers—not because I am greedy.

For years I had tried without success, to cope with the memories of childhood abuse by telling myself to be thankful for it. Had I not suffered those afflictions, I would not be where I am today. Such is the logic of the Atomists: trouble drives the sufferer to seek pleasures of a higher caliber. Little wonder I chafed at their line of reasoning. For most of my life the corollary had been that I should appreciate the pain my family inflicted upon me, because it forced me to reform my inherent inclinations toward indolence, selfishness, and malice. More recently: I should appreciate that pain all the more, since it had impelled me to leave my family for Tiberius. With a sudden flash of anger and surge of self-confidence I abandoned these false, remorse-ridden senses of gratitude with which for so long I had struggled. Whenever I find myself drifting toward undesirable propensities, I shall most assuredly resist them voluntarily! My outreaches to Underlying Good, rather than those unflagging reproaches, led me to where I am today.

Clytia Neronis. On my last birthday, Tiberius had declared me his wife in all but name. Haunted thereafter by my family's imputations of inveterate self-centeredness, I had wrestled with a woeful feeling of inadequacy—that I was unable to supply the sustaining devotion incumbent upon a spouse; that I had wrongly promised him devotion I was incapable of delivering; that my desire to share his life was purely selfish. Now these misgivings disappeared as well, swept away in a rush of joyous confidence, of determination to love and care, to give and help and depend—yes, depend; for doing so brings my beloved the same sweet satisfaction and wonderful sense of purpose I acquire from supporting him. And I need not be perfect to accomplish these aspirations. I must anticipate committing mistakes and blunders and stumbles. These he will forgive and help me fix, yet still love and understand—not demand unrelentingly I be correct at all times, and punish me for errors arising from conditions beyond my control.

Clytia Neronis. Hardly could I use this designation in public; but the restriction did not disturb me. For perhaps the first time in my life, I felt properly named—imbued with the right identity. Gone was my longing to recover and justify Clytia Eupistide, the confused and sorrowed victim of a tortured upbringing. Gone was Pythia of Naples—the frustrated, angry, defensive product of a forcefully and artificially altered individuality, driven incessantly to satisfy standards deliberately contrived so they were beyond her ability to fulfill. And Daphne Hipparchide was merely a disguise—like the dye that concealed but did not alter the true color of my hair; like a theatrical mask which creates a fictitious character, but changes neither the true appearance nor the selfhood of the actor who wears it.

Little wonder I had seen the meteor from the veranda. Truly I had undergone a catharsis, a life-changing experience. This had begun when Thrasyllus admonished me to stop berating myself and culminated in the encounter with Timoleon, my self-immolation among the potted herbs, my conversation with Tiberius earlier this afternoon, and now my present contemplations. These had unearthed and exposed with decisive clarity the emotional distortions and damages my family had inflicted upon me. Some of the latter I had not fully identified until now, although I had always suffered from their influence. The overwhelming calculus of self-condemnation was at last dissolving—yielding to self-understanding, self-forgiveness, self-appreciation, and self-respect. Furthermore the miserably familiar adamant of disbelief—that nagging suggestion which kept insisting the man I loved with passionate unconditionality could not really love me in return—was dissipating as well.

Tiberius too had witnessed the meteor. What did the sighting portend for him? Did it merely signify my catharsis must inevitably affect him as well as myself? After all, my new insights and the self-confident peace they engendered will unquestionably increase the congeniality of my moods and behaviors. On the other hand, did the meteor indicate Tiberius had experienced a catharsis of

208

his own? He admitted the events of the past two days had enabled him detect frailties in his character. He had not fully perceived how deeply my family's abuses had wounded my psyche; he had failed to discern Timoleon' true nature; he continued to harbor uncertainties about whether he was truly suited for political life. Had these perceptions been life changing for him, as mine had for me? Or was the meteor an omen of something yet to take place?

Feeling stiffness in my joints from long sitting, I arose from the bench and walked to the opposite side of the veranda. Resting my folded arms atop the wall, I gazed across the sea to where it met the sky. A band of wispy, grayish-brown clouds lay along that border, marring the otherwise pristine vista. The neighbor from behind us—the father of the two children to whom the infanticidal Pericalles had once been nursemaid—came by on his horse. He was a member of the Haedoi, one of the oldest and noblest families of Rhodes. On seeing me he halted for a chat. After we had inquired after everyone's health and activities, he pointed to the horizon. When he was a boy, he said, his great-grandfather used to sit daily in front of their house and watch the sea. After years and years of observation, the old man had been able to make certain predictions about the weather. "Do you see those vapors, Lady Daphne, rising from the skyline? The present drought will soon end—not immediately but before long, and rather forcefully with great rains."

May the great rains hold off until after my trip to Alexandria.

For the next few weeks I immersed myself in finalizing the preparations for that journey. At my request Aka's steward brought to our house the two maidservants who were to accompany me, that I might make their acquaintance before our departure. Thrasyllus sent along a prognostication for the trip, cast from his numerology tables. It portended a safe and predominantly harmonious journey, with some trouble toward the very end. *Those great rains,* I presumed.

Tiberius had excused me from helping him find Julia a birthday gift. He had come across a rare original compendium of the love stories by Aristides of Miletus, about a century old. Augustus was likely to object to the item as wastefully extravagant because of its expense, and decadently salacious because of its content. Those very qualities were certain to please Julia. For Gaius' birthday Tiberius acquired a bridle of ornately carved leather, for use on the Armenian gelding which we had finally learned was named Bellator.

My entourage and I departed for Egypt on the Ides of July *[7/15]*. During this journey I fell passionately in love—not with another man, rest assured, but with a city. There was an air of comfortable familiarity about Alexandria because she was similar to Naples—a seaport, an emporium, an intellectual center, a site of government administration. But whatever Naples was, Alexandria was better—larger, wealthier, more beautifully embellished, more sophisticated—and of course free of association with a tormented childhood.

Thrasyllus rather than Tiberius had supplied the necessary letters of introduction. Rather than introducing me as the ward to the regent, the astrologer cleverly represented me as a cousin to his wife. My two female companions added credibility to this ruse, dressing in the blouses and trousers that characterize the traditional costume of Asiatic women. Since Commagenean royals themselves wear Greek dress, I did not appear out of place. And owing to Thrasyllus' intervention, a wealthy Commagenean merchant lent us use of the apartment he maintained in Alexandria.

I began my stay with an exploration of Alexandria's rich cultural offerings. At the theater I attended a performance of Euripides' *The Trojan Women*, and of the satyr tragedy **Eutychus** by Sositheus of Alexandria Troas. At the Odeon I heard a splendid orchestral concert, as well as a fine reading of the epic *Cassandra* by Lycophronus of Chalcis. I visited the fabled Serapeion—temple to Alexandria's patron deity the Egyptian Osiris-Apis, whose name corrupts to Serapis in Greek. Although not as large as the Mausoleum at Halicarnassus, the Serapeion is similarly vibrant with lifelike statuary and rich colors that change with shifts in light. Since healing is a primary attribute of Serapis, the temple houses a library of medical tracts.

Thanks to Thrasyllus' intervention as an academician, I acquired permission to visit the Museion. Although academics were no longer the primary focus of my life, I still found our tour awe-inspiring. A secretary to the director showed us about. The great library was far larger, both in physical structure and in accessions, than I had imagined. Here Callimachus, Rhianus, Aratus, and Nicander had penned their poetry; Clitarchus, Timaeus, and Polybius their histories; the seven playwrights known as the Alexandrine Pleiad their tragedies. Here Zenodotus, Crates, Aristarchus, and Aristophanes of Byzantium had developed the skills of literary criticism; Eratosthenes and Apollodorus the science of geography; Heron, Archimedes, and Euclid their mathematical formulae.

After the library, our guide showed us the astronomical observatory, where Eratosthenes, Hipparchus, and Sosigenes—the astronomer who reformed Rome's calendar—had made their observations and calculations. The Museion was a renowned center for the study and practice of medicine. Here Erasistratus and Herophilus had perfected the understanding of human anatomy, and Herophilus' pupil Phillinus of Cos had developed his empirical methods of diagnosis and treatment. The guide showed us some of the laboratories, and rooms for examining patients. To my relief, these areas were not in use when we saw them.

By far the portion of the Museion I enjoyed most was its art gallery. Ever since I began painting on my own, my interest in and appreciation for the techniques of famous artists had burgeoned. The other collections I had visited in my travels were no match for the size and variety of the Museion's accessions. Here I viewed surrealistic scene sketches by Agatharchus of Samos, and careful gradations and fusions of colors by Apollodorus of Athens. I paid special attention to works by Zeuxis of Heraclea and Parhasius of Ephesus—effusively variegated but devoid of precise detail. My own style, I noted, was indeed strongly similar to theirs: the assessments of Tiberius' pompous caller and of my teacher Timotheus had been correct. In sharp contrast stood the starkly accurate details and subdued colorations by Eupompus of Sicyon, and his disciples Pamphilus of Amphipolis and Protogenes of Caunus. The same two techniques stood united in stately works by Apelles of Cos and Timomachus of Byzantium.

As we prepared to leave the Museion I considered, but only momentarily, inquiring after my father's records there. Doing so would surely arouse the guide's suspicion; and what purpose would it serve anyway?

Thrasyllus had been thorough with his request. After our tour of the Museion, the same guide escorted us to the tomb of Alexander the Great. The youthful king's body lay in its sarcophagus of transparent crystal, still in perfect preservation after four centuries. The guide called our attention to the gold crown. Augustus, he said, had placed it on the deceased ruler's head. So Tiberius had told me; for his stepfather was a profound admirer of Alexander. When asked if he cared to see the other royal tombs of Egypt, Augustus had answered, *I came to see a king—not corpses.* After our guide extended the same invitation to me, I responded with the emperor's exact phrase. The guide took no notice, or at least did not react. I did take special care to observe, albeit from a distance, the tomb shared by Cleopatra VII and Marcus Antonius.

My response to our guide was not mere mimicry of Augustus. The historic and academic aspects of Alexandria offered me a lesser appeal, when compared with the vibrant, palpitating, workaday city. Public and private buildings alike are large and opulently appointed. We saw no slums. So wealthy is this city, even her poorest inhabitants are well off. There is considerable friction between the predominantly Greek populace and the only slightly smaller Jewish sector. The premise of the conflict is hardly original. The Jews complain that the Greeks, who monopolize the civic government, give their own people better physical services and arbitrate in their favor, although the Jews and Greeks pay the same taxes. The Greeks in turn argue Alexandria is a Greek city founded by a Greek king: hence the Jews as interlopers ought to pay a higher premium for a lesser return. Economic competition between the two groups is the real basis for the dispute. It gets set aside whenever a Jew and Greek cooperate to their mutual profit in a matter of trade, for commerce is the lifeblood of Alexandria.

The city's great harbor—protected by the monumental lighthouse on the outlying Pharos Island—bustled with shipping and shipbuilding. The marketplace area, crowded and noisy, teemed with every conceivable item. Its counterpart at Rhodes, replete as it is, seemed paltry by comparison. We came upon shop upon shop, stall upon stall, of foodstuffs, furniture, housewares, works of art, musical instruments, toys, books common and rare, leathers, jewelry, cosmetics, perfumes, and—to my particular delight, of course—textiles. Entire city blocks abounded not only with purveyors of finished goods, but with weavers, dyers, tailors, embroiderers, and fullers. Cloth merchants were so abundant, they could afford to limit their offerings to specific articles. Some sold only clothing, others only household textiles. There were artists too, who specialized in designing custom fabrics for whatever purposes their clients desired. And then there were imports: the brilliant rectangles of Nubia like the altar cloth of Melambrotus, silks from the Far East, ornate carpets and prayer rugs from Parthia and Armenia, blankets and cloaks of broadcloth or camels' hair from Ethiopia, gauzes from the nomads of Numidia and Arabia.

I bought as much as I dared—predominantly textiles but also a myrrhine glass pitcher, a pair of lapis lazuli earrings to complement my scarab pendant, a Nabatean saddle blanket for Tiberius to use on Sinapeus, a small gaming board and dice fashioned from ebony wood and ivory, and a rare edition of the discourse in which Hipparchus describes the precession of the equinoxes. Tiberius had asked me to obtain some sort of artifact relevant to Alexander the Great, for presentation to Augustus on the latter's forthcoming birthday. I duly found a fine ivory statuette of the intrepid young king, drawing his bow while seated astride Bucephalus.

To maintain my disguise as Commagenean royalty, I had prearranged with Thrasyllus to have my purchases shipped to his home on Rhodes. At times I wondered whether I would feel discontent and malaise upon returning there; for the affluence and academic repute of Rhodes seemed sparse and diminutive in comparison with that of Alexandria. My servants, too, enjoyed the great city's offerings. During our voyage, I had presented each with an aureus to spend. The two maidservants bought themselves personal items—a scarf, a vial of perfume, a small brooch, a pair of new sandals. Our bodyguard used his money by night. Apparently the overall excellence we had discovered in Alexandria extended to her brothels. On many a morning, Arbindus appeared for duty with a look of dreamy satisfaction on his face.

After deciding it was best not to acquire another article—lest upon my return I encounter, *Is there anything left in our coffers?* —I began simply to stroll with my servants through the thoroughfares and plazas, delighting in the people we passed. Here the diversity I had briefly encountered among the crewmembers on the Phoenix was well evident on a far grander scale. Beside the native Greeks in their himations or chlamydes and their petasos, and the Jews in their turbans and caftans, were the predictable toga-clad Romans, swarthy Arabs in billowing white robes and headdresses, Commageneans in colorful trousers and hats, dusky Numidians wrapped in pastel gauze, black Nubians and Ethiopians clad in their vibrant multicolored fabrics. We came across squat Thracians with their ivory skin and nightshade hair, statuesque Gauls ruddy and redhaired, and even a few blond blue-eyed Germans. A lady clad in a Roman stola complimented me in halting Greek on my blue shawl, the one Phoebe had acquired for me in Messina. She was surprised and delighted when I thanked her in Latin. I asked her where she was from. A town called Florence, she replied, in the central Italian homeland of the Etruscans.

Having explored Alexandria—albeit not to the extent I would have liked—I decided to book a cruise up the Nile through its delta. My hope was to catch a glimpse of Egypt's country people: the lightly boned, bronze-skinned Copts from whom our twin bodyguards of the Phoenix had derived. Furthermore, I longed to observe the region's fabled animals: hippopotami, gazelles, ibises, fearsome crocodiles, and elusive jackals. Moreover I understood the great pyramid tombs near the old capital of Memphis—together with their guardian, an immense stone sphinx—were masterpieces of ancient art and architecture, a sight well worth seeing.

The morning on which I sent Arbindus to the docks to negotiate our river journey was overcast and damp. This was a significant change from the clear, dry days to which the drought had accustomed everybody, and highly unusual for early August even when there was no drought. No matter, I thought, as boats travel in cloudy weather just as easily as in sunny. Hardly had the bodyguard left, when one of the maids brought me a message. A sailor, she said, had just delivered it. The note was from Tiberius.

Return to Rhodes immediately, as soon as you can make the arrangements.

The communiqué alarmed me. From its terseness I realized something was wrong. When relaxed and comfortable my partner wrote loquaciously, even bombastically. And so when Arbindus returned I dispatched the poor man back to the harbor, to cancel our Nile cruise and secure passage to Rhodes. Then I set the maidservants to work and helped them myself, with packing our belongings and cleaning and organizing the apartment so it was not left to its owner in disarray.

Arbindus managed to obtain passenger space on a grain transport, scheduled to leave for Rhodes in three days. For my last full day in Alexandria the weather resumed its brilliant clarity. In the morning, two crewmembers from the freighter arrived to collect our baggage. Afterward I had the servants accompany me on a final stroll about the city. I was going to miss this elegant metropolis, which I was so happy to acknowledge as my birthplace. Hopefully I would be able to return, and resume the tour I had to cut short. Meanwhile, any inclination I might have had to mope was banished by my worries about Tiberius.

On the morning of our departure the clouds were back. By the time the carriage Arbindus had hired delivered us to our ship, a heavy mist was hanging in the air. A superstructure on the rear of the deck housed passengers and crew alike. The entire area beneath the deck was devoted to cargo. The passenger quarters consisted of a single room, which naturally I shared with my maidservants. Arbindus lodged with the crew. My women and I dined in our room, segregated from the men, on the customary cold hard sea rations. For bathing we were daily allotted a single vat of fresh cold water. We were also supplied the luxury of a chamber pot. There was no latrine on the ship. The men relieved themselves over the sides.

The voyage took longer than expected—four miserable days. The ship was fully laded and hence sluggish. Compounding matters, the weather remained foul and made the sea choppy. The mist restricted visibility, and hence increased the danger of collision with another vessel. The crewmembers were too preoccupied with the difficulties of navigation to pay any attention to us. Although I could not help wondering whether one of them might be the husband of Miranda's wetnurse Daphne, I chose not to distract them with inquiries. Besides, who knows what sort of gossip they might have spread—and how far—upon discovering one of their passengers was the regent's ward.

It was early evening when we docked at Rhodes. When booking our passage, Arbindus had exercised the foresight to send ahead a message with the anticipated date of our arrival. Although we were a day late, Proceles was duly awaiting us with our own carriage. By now rain was falling, lightly but steadily. Our neighbor appeared to have been correct: the drought was beginning to break. After leaving Arbindus and me with our luggage at our townhouse, Proceles departed for the home of Thrasyllus and Aka to return the two maidservants. Our house was shadowy from the late hour. Menon was lighting one of the two lampstands that illuminated the courtyard. "Welcome home, Lady," he said warmly but rather cautiously. "Master awaits you in the library."

Tiberius was seated at the table, attempting to write a letter. Having bathed earlier, he was clad in his dressing gown. He was drumming the fingers of his right hand in the air, a gesture he often performed when groping for just the right words. As I took the other chair he put down the stylus, pushed the lamp aside, and folded his hands on the table. He did not smile, but looked at me gravely, and spoke in the hiss-like whisper he used when distressed. "Clytia,… my stepfather is preparing to arraign Julia before the senate! He has had her sent a bill of divorce in my name, and admonished me not to contest it!"

Four days of damp weather, sea spray, cold quarters, cold food, and cold bathwater had left me well chilled. Suddenly, however, I was far colder. "Why?" I returned in the same breathless undertone. "On what grounds?"

"I do not have a full explanation, only the decree from the praetor. It cites immoral conduct detrimental to the wellbeing of the state. This is why I summoned you to return. We may have to leave for Rome on a moment's notice."

The meteor, I thought. This had to be the change it portended for us. And despite the promises we had exchanged year after year, I needed reassurance. "You would take me with you under such difficult circumstances?"

"Of course! So long as you will have me, I shall never let any circumstance separate us." Then with definite irritation, "I thought you understood this by now." He arose, helped me to my feet, and took me in his arms. "By all the gods, you are shivering; come." Leading me to the door he called out sharply, "Menon, heat Lady a bath at once! Have Phoebe or Alcmene bring a bowl of hot broth to the bathroom!" The harshness of his voice betrayed his agitation, but did not ruffle Menon who was inured to Master's moods. Tiberius softened his tone. "You have no idea how relieved I am to have you back."

While I resuscitated in the warmth of bath and broth, Tiberius explained his quandary. He desperately wanted to know, not only precisely what Julia had done, but also whether his family wanted him back in Rome to lend support at this trying time—hence the letter he had been composing. But with equal urgency he must learn whether Augustus or Gaius—or the both of them—felt Tiberius' separation from Julia had precipitated her misconduct. Returning to Rome under such circumstances, Tiberius could be walking directly into a breach of amicitia. Nevertheless he did not want to risk provoking Augustus, by eliciting the details of Julia's offense before his stepfather was ready to reveal them. Nor did he care to press other family members to provide the information surreptitiously, lest he get Augustus angry with one of them. Hence his inability to complete his letter. Waiting for the emperor to disclose in his own due time seemed the only sensible course of action, nerve-wracking as it may be. So I commented, and so my partner agreed.

And so wait we did, uncertain and edgy, through an August that seemed interminable. The weather cleared somewhat into a warm, humid, dirty haze that had everyone sneezing. The two of us went to see Thrasyllus, who cast our horoscopes and found their prognostications frustratingly contradictory: change amid stagnation, joy amid disappointment. In the weeks that followed, neither of us felt like doing much of anything—not even repairing our villa for a different scene. I tried to paint, but found my efforts tedious and bereft of inspiration. Tiberius became moody: mostly glum and brooding, at times irascible, at others desperately hopeful, at still others apologetic for being out of sorts.

Most gladdening was the discovery I harbored far more patience than I had ever realized. It enabled me to weather my lover's shifting humors without frustration, to be consistently pleasant and supportive. I walked with him on the beach, played my harp for him, held him, lay with him, and sometimes just sat close by without uttering a word—letting my very nearness reassure him that he could lean upon my loyalty for moral strength and upon my love for comfort. I took care not to pressure or chide him for anything—not even about forgetting my birthday, an oversight for which he subsequently apologized with great contrition, and which I reassured him I forgave implicitly.

Despite my outward forbearance, I was no more immune than my partner to the sharp pangs of misgiving about the future. Through sleepless nights they haunted me. Over and over I weighed the potential implications of Tiberius' divorce, and of the impending expiration of his regency at the end of the forthcoming December. Could Tiberius return to Rome and resume his role as the emperor's stepson—a significant yet secondary position within the regime's inner circle? Would he remarry? The most logical choice must be his brother's widow Antonia. Suddenly the prospect of sharing him became distasteful, even though I had always accepted the possibility he might return to Julia. I resolved to assess my behaviors with greater care, making sure I was not being petulant, irascible, tedious, or otherwise annoying. After all, I did not want him to discover he found another more appealing than I.

And then there remained the possibility Augustus would breach amicitia. Tiberius could not reenter public life if he returned to Rome under this stigma—assuming he could return to Rome at all. Repeatedly he had expressed doubt as to whether he was genuinely suited for a political career. Nevertheless I wondered whether he was genuinely suited for life as a private citizen, either in Italy or abroad. I was perfectly content to continue my present life of dabbling in academics, aiding the sick, painting and embroidering, playing my harp, writing my journal, gazing at and consulting the stars. Would my partner remain comfortable, engaging in similar avocations for the remainder of his life? Or would he develop the embittered restlessness of a man whose quintessence—whose very purpose for living—has been suppressed? And what of our relationship itself? Must I remain his secretive mistress, forever contriving ways to conceal the true nature of our liaison? Or dared I hope that if he remained in private life he would make me his legal wife?

As if by rote I found myself acknowledging the presence of Underlying Good, and the ultimate necessity that evil must eventually dissipate. A familiar idea reemerged: *Endure for now because the future is worth awaiting.* Was this a new inspiration, or just a memory? *Whatever the future entails,* I thought, *may Underlying Good grant me the strength to bear its vicissitudes and the grace to discern its blessings.* The confidence I had acquired from my catharsis amid the potted plants now filled me with an iron resolve. With greater conscientiousness than I had ever mustered, I would pursue the counsel of Aristotle and live according to the greatest excellence within me. Whatever misfortunes the future brought I was determined to face with steadfast, unruffled calm—minimizing and suppressing my personal consternations while offering my troubled partner hope and self-reassurance and consolation. Perhaps for the first time ever, I was starting to feel like a lion.

Finally, in the early days of September—after nearly four agitated weeks—the answers to our questions arrived. The lengthy and detailed letter was not from Augustus, but Livia. And it was every bit as dreadful as we had hoped it would not be.

Rumors of Julia's marital infidelity had circulated for years, even while she was married to Agrippa. These had escalated considerably after Tiberius' withdrawal to Rhodes. Augustus had always dismissed such stories as frivolous—arising from the public's natural inclination to invent scandals about the famous, and abetted by Julia's own flamboyant lifestyle and the increasingly obvious indications she and Tiberius were sorely mismatched. She had been with child for most of the ten years she was married to Agrippa. All five of their offspring resembled him. The short-lived infant son she bore Tiberius had looked like Tiberius' father. No children had been born after Tiberius left Italy. The frequency of Julia's pregnancies, the fact that all were unquestionably incurred within wedlock, and the visages of his grandchildren, had satisfied Augustus the innuendo about her adulteries was nothing more than innuendo.

During the third summer of our residence on Rhodes, Julia had sent Augustus a letter in which she accused Tiberius of having brutalized her, verbally and physically, during the time they had lived together. She alleged he had insulted and humiliated her almost daily, frequently struck her, raped and sodomized her and forced her to perform fellatio, and destroyed personal possessions she particularly cherished in the manner of a child throwing a tantrum. Fear of reprisal, she insisted, had prevented her from coming forward sooner. She maintained Tiberius had threatened to inflict yet more abuse if she dared complain to her father. Only after it appeared certain Tiberius intended to remain on Rhodes indefinitely did she garner sufficient courage to report these maltreatments.

After reviewing the letter, Augustus at once contacted Tiberius for an explanation. In his response, Tiberius admitted he and Julia had often quarreled bitterly. At times they had indeed shoved and slapped and thrown things at one another. Presumably Julia considered sex with her incompatible husband as distasteful as he found it with her. Augustus was already aware Julia had angered and embarrassed Tiberius frequently, with those public displays of bawdy conduct Tiberius considered vulgar and unseemly for a woman of her caliber, and with her assertions she considered marriage with him beneath her station in life. But despite the growing antipathy between them, Tiberius had never mistreated Julia in the horrific ways she had described. He suggested Augustus verify these assertions by canvassing the servants Tiberius had left behind in Rome, along with Drusus his own son and Julia's youngest children who were still too naïve to alibi her. I was touring Asia Minor while all this was taking place. By the time I returned, Augustus had been satisfied and the incident closed. Tiberius had never mentioned it to me. This sort of business he preferred keeping to himself, especially once he had moved beyond it.

Although to outward appearances he had let the matter drop, the deeply insightful emperor continued to ponder his daughter's letter with great concern. Without question Tiberius could be frighteningly intimidating when he was angry: this I know only too well myself. Nevertheless the extreme behaviors Julia described were distinctly out of character for the stepson Augustus had raised from childhood. It seemed clear enough Julia was attempting to impute criminal conduct to Tiberius so she could demand a divorce by court order. Far more striking than her accusations, however, was the method by which she had delivered them. Throughout her life, Julia had always been candidly and unhesitatingly conversational with her father. It was highly unlike her to wait so very long before expressing a grievance, then to put it in writing as well. Augustus remembered how before his departure for Rhodes, Tiberius had complained the once readily outspoken Julia was becoming increasingly and unwontedly aloof and diffident. Now her letter confirmed this allegation. What or who was changing her—and why? Augustus decided to place his daughter under surveillance, a task that was bound to prove formidably difficult for his agents. Julia had inherited his cagey attentiveness. She would recognize that she was being shadowed, unless her observers maintained an extraordinary degree of concealment.

The investigation revealed Julia was involved in a plot to overthrow her father. She had five co-conspirators. One was her own half-brother Publius Cornelius Scipio, the son of her mother Scribonia by her second husband (Augustus had been Scribonia's third). Another participant was Tiberius Sempronius Gracchus, descendant and namesake of the great Roman social reformer whose mother had been the daughter of Scipio Africanus. Hence these two conspirators were distant cousins. Tiberius was distantly related to Gracchus as well. Sempronia the long deceased paternal grandmother of Tiberius, was granddaughter of Gaius Sempronius Gracchus, the celebrated Tiberius Gracchus' younger brother and fellow activist.

The third participant in Julia's scheme was Appius Claudius Pulcher, another cousin to Tiberius. Pulcher was the youngest of the conspirators, being the same age of Augustus' second grandson Lucius. Fourth on the list of plotters was Titus Quinctius Crispinus Sulpicianus, a relative of Publius Sulpicius Quirinius Cyrenius the imperial governor of Galatia and Pamphylia whom I mentioned earlier.

The fifth conspirator was Iullus Antonius, the second son of Marcus Antonius. Iullus had been reared by his stepmother, Augustus' now deceased sister Octavia. By her first husband Octavia had two daughters: Marcella and Claudia. The former became the second wife of Agrippa and bore him a daughter. (This was not Tiberius' Vipsania, who was borne to Agrippa by his first wife Caecilia.) When Agrippa at Augustus' request divorced Marcella to espouse Julia, Octavia asked her brother to console Marcella by offering her hand to Iullus. Marcella was contentedly happy with her urbane and cultivated new husband. She bore him three children: two sons separated by a daughter.

Iullus was the ringleader of the plot. He and his collaborators did not aspire to deprive Augustus of life. Rather, their intentions went something like this. Since the powers of the emperor were conferred by decree of the senate, the same process could be utilized to revoke them. The insurgents aspired to persuade a sufficient number of senators to carry a vote, requiring Augustus to surrender his authority to Gaius. The conspirators went so far as to offer members of non-senatorial social orders who were retainers of senators, rewards in return for urging their patrons to support the plan.

The unfoldment of recent events lent credibility to the plotters' persuasions. On the Nones of February just past *[2/5/2 BCE]* the senate had honored Augustus with the designation, *Father of the Country*. Without question he well deserved the title: the eminently successful regime he had created was truly the accomplishment of a millennium. This September the emperor would enter his sixty-second year, an age the Italians considered fraught with potential for misfortune. His chronically fragile health was bound to deteriorate further as his years advanced. Was it not time for him to retire—not only to rest from his phenomenal efforts, but also to ensure well before his death that the transition of his office to his intended successor was secure?

Although he had been carefully and relentlessly groomed for the position he must accept, Gaius was still quite young and inexperienced. A less restrictive regency should therefore be in place, that its holder may protect and guide the youthful new emperor until he reached legal majority on completing his twenty-fifth year. Augustus had clearly erred in choosing Tiberius for this present position, the withdrawal to Rhodes being glaring proof. Now that Tiberius' tenure of the office was drawing to a close, why defer the selection of a new regent to Augustus and risk his making another bad choice? Would it not make better sense to have the senate confer the regency upon someone the prince's mother approved and recommended? Who understood his character—and hence the type of mentor best suited for his temperament—better than she?

Furthermore she was present in Rome and well attuned to current political developments—not sulking incommunicado on a far distant island.

And finally: Julia's mother Scribonia would at last receive the recognition she so sorely deserved as Augustus' partner in the creation of a dynasty. Why must she be remembered as the wife he had discarded—citing her cantankerous temperament as his reason, but in actuality because he no longer had use for her political connections? Why should the rival with whom Augustus had replaced Scribonia receive recognition as Rome's First Lady, when she had never given him a viable child? Why should Livia's sons from her prior marriage enjoy the special advantages of Augustus' patronage, while the son of Scribonia did not? Scipio, after all, was uncle to the future emperor. Gaius was not Livia's grandson but Scribonia's.

Tiberius paused his reading of his mother's letter. We were sitting on the veranda beneath the pear. He stared thoughtfully at the ocean, barely visible through the haze. If successful, he mused, the conspiracy stood to eclipse the political ascendancy of his family. Gaius was at present betrothed to Tiberius' niece, Claudia Livilla. Should the dethronement of Augustus succeed and Julia divorce Tiberius, Gaius would most probably repudiate Livilla. Livia would be living with her husband in retirement. The Claudii Nerones would no longer have a representative within the charmed circle of the ruling emperor's intimates. By the time Drusus reached his twenty-eighth year—the requisite minimum age for admission to the senate—the imperial connections of the Claudii Nerones would have long been severed, and Drusus would become no more than an ordinary senator.

On the other hand if Tiberius remained Julia's husband, he must become her political lackey and give his unequivocal assent to her agenda. Otherwise she would have pretext, if not for divorcing him then at least for continuing to scorn and ridicule him. Either way the Claudii Nerones must suffer political emasculation, and the interests of the Scribonii Libones and their opponents be enhanced. Little wonder Scipio was a participant in the intrigue. I expressed mild surprise that Livia had not mentioned her adoptive cousin Marcus Livius Drusus Libo and his blood relatives—Scribonia's brother Lucius Scribonius Libo and his namesake son. After complimenting my memory, Tiberius agreed with my assessment. Surely the Libones supported the intention of the conspiracy, although they did not originate it nor endorse it overtly. The risks of doing so were enormous. Even if prosecution failed, Augustus was certain to breach amicitia. The Libones were clever and circumspect—and consequently highly dangerous.

Tiberius returned to the letter. Once in power, the conspirators intended to cultivate and maintain their popularity by softening Augustus' legislative curbs on the fiscal and sexual wantonness he had perceived as threats to the institution of the family. Julia had made all the more blatant her defense of hedonistic living, thereby supporting her party's contention the laws infringed personal self-determination. Her mode of dress—always risqué—became more extravagant and provocative than ever. Although not gluttonous, she dined upon rare and expensive luxury foods and wines. Her father's agents started to find her in the Forum at night, among revelers engaged in bouts of winebibbing and sex upon the Rostrum: the oration platform from which Augustus had propounded the very statutes that were being subverted. Julia did not indulge in the debaucheries herself, but by her presence lent approval to the participants. During one such episode Julia placed a laurel wreath upon a statue of Marsyas, the Phrygian god of merriment and excess. The action was replete with the symbolism of rebellion. Marsyas had purportedly challenged Apollo—Augustus' patron divinity—to a competition of lute playing. A laurel crown signifies victory, and the laurel tree is sacred to Apollo.

Julia maintained a lavish and elegant salon to which she invited men and women who had pledged support of the conspiracy's agenda—including those non-senators whose persuasions of senators the conspirators had elicited. Julia's co-conspirators—with the exception of the shy and outwardly staid Crispinus—attended these gatherings and were popular for their manners and wit, their eloquence and erudition. Wags and busybodies who remarked the comings and goings were thoroughly convinced, Julia was rewarding each and every one her male adherents with sexual favors. The agents found no evidence of wholesale promiscuity, especially since the male invitees almost invariably brought female companions—wives, sisters, daughters, nieces, even mistresses. Julia nevertheless let the rumors fly and encouraged them. Satirizing her father's contentment her children's resemblance to her husband Agrippa confirmed her chastity, she had asserted, *I never acquire a passenger unless the hold is full.*

Between these populous gatherings, the conspirators themselves frequented Julia's house—sometimes as a group, sometimes individually, sometimes remaining for several days. Julia took pains to ensure these encounters took the appearance of miniscule salons—innocuous exchanges of news or of intellectual ideas. A female chaperone—a freedwoman coincidentally named Phoebe—was conspicuously present at every meeting any of the other servants witnessed. Only Phoebe herself, and the agents skulking in the narrow alleyways outside the house or crawling amid rafters in the attic, knew the deposition of the emperor was being plotted, and Julia was bedding three of the plotters: Antonius, Gracchus, and Crispinus. Phoebe would distract her fellow servants by sending them on errands or assigning them tasks requiring intense concentration, and only then smuggle lover or lovers into Julia's private chambers. Phoebe also kept diligent watch, lest a family member came to call or a servant insisted upon Julia's attention. She was well poised to get Julia quickly into her clothes or her bath, and paramours from the master suite to a dayroom or closet or out of the house entirely.

Angry and heartbroken, Augustus alternately raged and brooded as the information incriminating his child burgeoned. He must intervene and soon, before Julia and her collaborators garnered sufficient senatorial votes to deprive him of his other child: the regime he had designed and developed and fought to implement over the course of a lifetime. Since the conspirators had not yet made any overt actions construable as insurrectional, concrete grounds for charging them with treason were lacking. At least arraignment for a tangible case of adultery would bring Julia and her lovers under indictment. Once this trial was underway, the evidence pertaining to the nascent coup d'état could be brought forward and witnesses queried.

How was Julia avoiding pregnancy? So I wondered aloud at this point. Now in her thirty-eighth year, Tiberius observed, she might have reached the point in life at which she was no longer capable of bearing children. For certain no child was conceived during the four years he had lived with her after the death of their son. Julia might be employing some potion or liniment or device to obstruct conception. And then there was always the alternative of abortion. At this suggestion I winced and groaned and grimaced while my skin crawled and my stomach turned. Not so much the concept of destroying an aspiring child disturbed me—although I could hardly condone such an action unless it were truly appropriate. Augustus had made abortion illegal to Roman citizens, his purpose being to prevent attrition of their race. Nevertheless in Roman culture as well as Greek, parents have always had an implied right to practice infanticide before or at the exact moment of birth, under circumstances considered warranted and even altruistic—as when rearing the child in time of war or famine offered a prospect of life so miserable that death was the better alternative, when the babe was deformed, or when a husband had sound reason for presuming the infant was not his. Once the precise point of inception into life had passed, destruction of the child was deemed murder—as when Pericalles endeavored to poison Miranda. Still, the very idea of having one's innards shredded and ripped and forced from the body I found nothing short of horrific. All the more revolting was the notion Julia might be employing this life-threatening and presumably painful process to conceal an errant and insurrectional lifestyle.

Tiberius returned to Livia's narrative. Drawing upon his innate steeliness and profound aptitude for dissembling, Augustus assumed an unruffled front of casual nonchalance. He put forth the impression that while he disapproved of Julia's rowdy conduct, he was either unaware of the rumors of her adultery and treasonable aspirations or placed no credence in them. While Rome was sweltering in oppressive heat during the early days of his namesake month, Augustus demanded all the grandchildren who were present in the capital—his and Livia's alike—should repair to Ad Gallinas, for a vacation in cooler and healthier environs. Julia's eldest son Gaius was completing military training at the Danube front in anticipation of assuming command of the troops stationed there. Her namesake daughter was married. Her middle son Lucius was already living with Augustus who was supervising his education; but her two youngest children—Agrippina and Postumus—were still residing with her.

The emperor correctly surmised his daughter would seize this opportunity to be alone in Rome. Surely enough: after two days at her stepmother's estate, Julia excused herself on the pretext she must return to the city, there to oversee some retiling of the roof on her townhouse. Augustus knew this repair was underway and had already exploited it. He had placed one of his agents among the laborers, with instructions to make amorous overtures to Julia's Phoebe.

Eventually on a day of rain—probably that same rain I had encountered in Alexandria—none of the roofers reported for work, with the exception of Phoebe's bogus paramour. Flattered and titillated, desperate to take advantage of the man's presence, Phoebe reassured herself that Augustus was ten miles away at Ad Gallinas, that he was thoroughly hoodwinked with regard to Julia's assignations, that he was currently concentrating his attention and energies upon his youthful guests, and that he was not about to put his delicate health at risk by venturing back to Rome in inclement weather. Phoebe did not know the agent had been watching the house for several hours, and had noted the arrival of Iullus Antonius.

Phoebe was at her usual post in the colonnade outside the master suite; but instead of watching out for her mistress, she was confidently exposing herself to her presumed lover. She did not become aware of Augustus, approaching with two serving women and his six-man personal bodyguard, until the agent clapped his hand over her mouth so she could not cry out. He pulled her away from the door and kicked it open. Together with the women and three of the guards,

Augustus charged the suite, not caring the men may see his daughter naked: they would become witnesses to her crime of adultery. As things turned out, no coupling was taking place. Julia and Iullus Antonius were not in the bedchamber at all but in the adjoining sitting room, seated apart from one another and conversing. Nevertheless, Julia was clad in a filmy and revealing dressing gown with her hair unbound; Antonius was completely naked; the linens on the bed were disheveled, warm, and moist. Never mind this evidence might be arguably circumstantial: so far as Augustus was concerned, it confirmed active adultery. The discovery essential to incrimination had been made.

Augustus had left a decury of soldiers waiting in the street before the house. Once the couple was properly dressed, Augustus had eight members of this contingent escort Antonius to his home and place him under house arrest. The emperor ordered Julia brought to his own house under the guard of the serving women, two bodyguards, one soldier, and the agent. He did not allow this escort to remove Julia, however, until in her presence he had commended the agent for successfully distracting Phoebe with false advances, assured him of a promotion and special commendation (he was a secretary in the imperial civil service), and extended special thanks to the man's wife for tolerating the pretense. That very night, Phoebe hanged herself with a twisted bed sheet. Her deed prompted Augustus to remark he wished he were Phoebe's father instead of Julia's.

Augustus confined Julia to the suite of rooms she had occupied as a girl, to remind her of the origins she had dishonored. He would not permit any man to come near her—not even the male servants who had known her throughout her life. He required she dress in homespun, would not let her wear jewelry, forbade her the use of cosmetics and perfumes, had her served the plainest and coarsest of foods, disallowed her wine.

His inevitable question—*Why had she done what she did?*—Julia answered with the insolent vagary so familiar to Tiberius. Since her father prided himself on being an incisive judge of character, he ought to be able to figure it all out for himself. After a condescending laugh she continued that Augustus was paralyzed by his own law. She was still married to Tiberius. So long as a cuckolded husband refused to divorce his wife she was immune from prosecution for adultery, unless it could be demonstrated her spouse had manifestly taken her in the act or reaped some sort of profit from her escapade. Living on Rhodes, Tiberius had done neither. Nor had he imputed any other criminal activity such as treason to her. Augustus slapped Julia's face with such force, his signet ring left an angry red gouge on her cheek. He quit the house for his office in the government administration building, where he ordered an attendant notary to summon a praetor. This magistrate he had prepare a writ of divorce in Tiberius' name, invoking the legal doctrine that Tiberius' prolonged separation from Julia evinced his consent. The divorce gave Augustus, as Tiberius' father-in-law, the legal right to prosecute Julia for adultery.

Augustus sent his niece—Antonius' wife Marcella—to Ad Gallinas, for consolation from her half-sister Antonia and from Livia. As she arrived, Marcella wryly remarked her uncle was truly looking out for the welfare of his daughter. Had he not insisted Marcella quit Rome, she very probably would have invaded his home and scratched out Julia's eyes. Marcella brought along her children by Antonius: Lucius in his eighteenth year, Iulla in her fifteenth, and Gaius in his twelfth. Marcella's elder daughter by Agrippa was married to a man named Quintus Haterius.

The villa house of her farm was now crowded, Livia wrote in conclusion, its atmosphere somber and tense. Augustus insisted she keep the children of Antonius as well as those of Julia until the inception of the trial. Each of them, with the exception of the young and addlebrained Postumus, now understood the severity of the accusations Julia and Antonius were facing. The senate was preparing to open hearings, during which all that damaging evidence so meticulously gathered was going to be examined and weighed.

Tiberius placed the tablet on the bench. He arose and walked to the opposite side of the veranda. Propping his elbows on the top of the retaining wall, he rested his chin on his hands and again gazed at the sea. As I drew alongside him, I heard him sigh. "I wish it had not ended this way;" he said dejectedly, "that Julia and I could have buried our differences and been reconciled."

"As I recall, you tried quite assiduously to placate her."

"Not assiduously enough, it is plain to see."

"Now you are sounding like me, berating yourself."

"I had hoped my departure would bring Julia to her senses, prompt her to rethink and improve her actions. Apparently it had precisely the opposite effect."

"You did what seemed most right under the circumstances at that time."

"Thank you for understanding. You cannot imagine how much relief your words just brought me."

"It is refreshing to discover you pity and forgive Julia after all she has afflicted upon you."

His response surprised me. "I neither pity nor forgive Julia. On the contrary, I feel nothing but the most abject contempt for her. Any shred of respect I ever had for her is gone; and this grieves me very much." Drawing one arm across my shoulder, he led me toward the house. "Come, I need you." I understood what he meant.

Now it was my turn to be distracted and preoccupied during sex, and for my partner to notice. As we were resting afterward he gently inquired, "Why are you troubled, my love—over Julia?"

"Yes," I answered somewhat nervously. "Tiberius, you know I hardly wish to offend you; but I cannot help wondering about your antipathy toward her. All three of us—Julia, you, and I—are victims of family tyranny. You and I defied such tyranny, and Julia did as well. Like you and like me, she rebelled against an enforced unhappy marriage and sought the comfort of another's love. Now you and I have each other while she faces capital punishment; yet you say you have no sympathy for her."

He caressed my cheek and smiled. "Ah, my ever insightful and compassionate Clytia. Our relationship is not legally adulterous. The statute does not apply because you are not a Roman citizen. Of course your family has legitimate grounds for bringing an indictment against me, alleging I abducted you and corrupted your morals. Precisely for this reason I keep you disguised. But should you be discovered and that charge preferred, I anticipate at the very worst the court would restore you to the custody of your family, and issue me a penalty far less drastic than banishment—most likely a heavy fine. The morality laws are directed at Roman citizens, to preserve the integrity of Roman families. A liaison between a Roman man and a Greek woman is far less destructive to that purpose than the avenue Julia pursued.

"She ruined our marriage—and not solely with that coldness she exhibited toward me. She represented me as her social inferior, and a potential detriment to the political success of her sons. She belittled my mother by stressing her failure to bear my stepfather children. Moreover for the past decade, Julia has been making mockery of her father's morality agenda with that raucous style of living she has pursued so openly. Now there is evidence she has breached his law against adultery: specifically the sexual intercourse of a married Roman woman with any man other than her husband. And worst of all: she appears to have been plotting to wrest control of the government from her father and compromise its standards—his government, his creation. How can we not consider her a parricide?"

With slow steady nods I indicated my understanding. "An appropriate epithet," I agreed. "What terrible suffering your family must be enduring. Still, I cannot help but pity Julia. Her life was replete with power and privilege; yet she let herself be enticed by the lust for even more. Now she faces the dreadful consequences of her mistake."

Tiberius fell pensively silent, toying with a lock of my hair while lost in his thoughts. At length he kissed my forehead. "One of the myriad reasons I love you so intensely, Clytia, is that you soften me. You enable me to recognize—perhaps not as readily as I ought—that people let themselves be driven to extreme behaviors by forces and impulses they do not understand or cannot control. This does not excuse crimes but at least explains them, and may help mitigate one's judgment of offenders. The penalties I demanded for Timoleon were far less harsh than those I had originally considered for him. Your concern for his fate prompted me to rethink his offense, and realize it had not been as damaging as I had inclined to believe at first. Now I am starting to reevaluate my feelings about Julia, because you have offered me a sensible explanation for her motives. Julia has always been an inveterate gambler. The game she chose had precariously high stakes. Unfortunately she pitted her chances against the one opponent, who has been more masterfully successful at that game than possibly anyone else in history: her own father."

"Thank you for your compliment," I replied with great sincerity. "Perhaps my trying over and over, year after year, to fathom why my family afflicted me for no apparent purpose, has sharpened my insights into human nature." I gave a short sardonic laugh. "Ironic: Timoleon and Julia I can comprehend; my family I cannot."

"Your family is simply beyond comprehension."

While we kissed, the room darkened. From outside came the sound of thunder and the scent of rain.

The drizzle persisted on and off throughout most of September. Quite predictably, everyone was complaining the rain was insufficient to break the drought but certainly adequate to make life miserable. The Academy had assumed a different mien. Plato and his two truculent companions did not return—much to everyone's relief. The new students seemed noticeably younger, and unabashedly ebullient, opinionated, argumentative, abounding with fresh notions—most preposterously naïve, but some replete with surprisingly sound perception. Thrasyllus chuckled at my observation. "It is not the students who have changed," he said.

After contemplating his words for a few moments, I buried my face in my hands. "Alas, I am growing older!"

"A biological necessity we all must suffer. Come, reassess yourself," he chided me affably. "You no longer feel in competition with the students—or with your fellow sophistoi. With a maturity of judgment that can only arise from longevity, you have moved beyond frenetic aspirations to revolutionize the entire universe with sophomoric innovations. You have the experience to identify and respect sensible ideas, and the aplomb to dismiss the frivolous without feeling you have to belittle them." Although they could hardly provide a solution for the inevitable process of aging, Thrasyllus' words cheered me. They confirmed what I had been striving and hoping for: the assurance I was leaving the spitefully defensive Pythia of Naples behind.

Tiberius and I attended lectures and a few theatrical performances, but paid virtually no attention to their content as we distractedly awaited the outcome of the trial unfolding in Rome. There was no point in soliciting news. Senatorial hearings were closed: Augustus himself was not at liberty to divulge them. September faded into October. The sporadic rains abated, and the weather cleared into cool, pristine days made golden with the burnished hues of autumn. Now everyone was complaining because the rain had stopped before enough had fallen to break the drought.

Tiberius bombarded his stepfather with letters, urging clemency and even outright pardon for Julia. To keep their highly personal content from Galen, Tiberius had me transcribe these communiques. He much preferred dictating correspondence of particular significance to writing it on his own. Dictation was like public speaking, an art at which he was far more comfortable and adept than written composition. This was my first time to prepare letters addressed to the emperor. In a silly sort of way I felt enthralled, to think he of all people was reading my calligraphy.

The political intent of Tiberius' letters was amply clear. He did not want anyone—but Augustus and Gaius in particular—to assume he considered Julia's debacle a victory for himself: a vindication of his decision to leave her. As his dictation proceeded, the profound depth of Tiberius' affection for his family emerged—the empathy, the understanding, the compassion and forbearance he insisted I had awakened in him, and which I knew could not be awakened were they not inherent in the first place. He was keenly and painfully aware of the sorrow, the bewilderment, and the embarrassment his kin were facing. What a bitter responsibility for Augustus, having to incriminate his own daughter. What agony for Gaius and his siblings, to see their own mother declared a criminal and face the possibility of having her torn from them by the prescribed penalty of banishment. And what a terrible pity Julia fell into wrongdoing in the first place, and that she must now face its terrible consequences. Was there no remedy, no possibility of mitigation? Tiberius closed with a plea, for his family to accept whatever help he could offer at this trying time.

The emperor' only response was a belated and tersely humorless note of thanks for his birthday gift: the statuette of Alexander the Great I had procured in Alexandria. His packet included thanks from Drusus for his birthday gift of a stylus.

At last on the Ides of October *[10/15]*, we received the dreaded news from Rome. Tiberius expressed concern his mother was the author of this report as well as the last. Why was she providing the information, and not Augustus? Was the emperor merely too busy or distracted to write; or was anger impelling his silence? Was a breach of amicitia in the making?

Had this been a routine indictment for adultery, the senate would have designated from among its members a special court of inquiry. These appointees would have examined the available evidence, heard the pleas of prosecutors and defenders, and rendered the final judicial decision. But since the present case involved a contingent of senators as well as members of the imperial family— and since there was due reason to believe the investigation might uncover treasonable activity—the matter was brought before the entire senate. First the written reports of Augustus' agents were reviewed. Then oral testimony was taken from agents, servants, acquaintances of the accused, and former sympathizers who turned state's evidence with the hope of receiving rewards or at least commutations of their own sentences. Thereafter, each of the indicted was questioned.

The investigation, Livia wrote, uncovered the personal motivations which had evolved into conspiracy. Because Augustus had considered, but then not selected him to be regent after Agrippa's death, an embittered and jealous Iullus Antonius had resolved to wrest that office from Tiberius through chicanery. When Julia returned to Rome from Aquileia following the death of her infant, Iullus eagerly joined his wife Marcella in offering consolation. Finding Iullus' polished manners and witty demeanor far more engaging than Tiberius' somber and often moody quietude, Julia readily accepted his friendship and subsequently his sexual advances. Antonius aspired to escalate the nascent friction between Julia and Tiberius, hoping the two would beg Augustus to sanction their divorce, and that the emperor would agree so his family did not have to endure the public embarrassment of an obvious mismatch. This was the cause of the once-mysterious ambivalence Julia had begun to show Tiberius in the aftermath of their son's death. With Julia's approval and encouragement, Antonius ingratiated himself to Gaius and Lucius. As Tiberius' regency approached the end of its five-year duration, Antonius encouraged Julia and her sons to urge Augustus to transfer that authority to Antonius—along with Julia's hand.

At the time neither Augustus nor Tiberius would consider divorce, for neither wanted it interpreted as breach of amicitia with the other. When the powers of the regency expired, Augustus adamantly had the senate confer them upon Tiberius for another five-year term. Not wishing to arouse Augustus' suspicions about her involvement with Antonius, Julia made no effort to change her father's mind.

Recognizing he had miscalculated, Antonius revised his strategy. He endeavored to induce the divorce by discrediting Tiberius in Augustus' eyes—hence Julia's letter denouncing her husband for abuse. Gracchus had actually written the letter, after Julia had introduced him to Antonius and their plan. Gracchus was a man of accomplished literary skill. Moreover he had been Julia's lover for over a decade, having seduced her during her previous marriage to Agrippa. The new alliance with Gracchus prompted Antonius to seek the suggestions and support of others. Upon noting the Scribonii Libones approved Julia' outspoken disparagements of Tiberius, Antonius solicited the adherence of Scipio. Pulcher was an ardent admirer of Antonius and friend of the latter's son Lucius. Crispinus, another retainer of Antonius, concealed a libidinous nature beneath a front of prim propriety. He had desired Julia for years. She accepted him as a paramour at Antonius' request.

Livia's narrative turned to the senate hearings. The findings were discussed and debated and the verdicts reached. All five male conspirators—Gracchus, Antonius, Scipio, Crispinus and Pulcher—were found guilty of attempting to incite an overthrow of the existing government. Julia was convicted of abetting their seditious activities by providing meeting opportunities and promoting social interaction between potential supporters. The senate also declared her guilty of adultery with Antonius, Gracchus, and Crispinus, all of whom reciprocally shared this condemnation.

Augustus had understandably recused himself from the sessions in which the senate interviewed Julia and later passed judgment upon her. The verdicts were presented to the senate on the day preceding the Calends of October *[September 30]*. In his capacity as president of the senate, Augustus read them aloud—until he reached Julia's. Breaking into tears, he handed the document to his fellow consul to finish. When the reading was over, a discussion of appropriate sentencing began. His composure recovered, the emperor startled his fellow senators by asking them to punish his daughter with death.

The prescribed penalties for treason and adultery alike were either execution or deportation from Rome for life, and in both cases forfeiture of two thirds of the offender's property to the state. In the end, the senate decided that since the conspiracy had been detected before its fomenters could implement it— and consequently no damage had befallen the present government—the lesser penalty of banishment was adequate for each of the accused except Antonius. He was at once the originator of the plot and a significant corrupter of Julia, having pimped Crispinus on her in addition to seducing her himself. The senate prescribed execution, offering Antonius the option of taking his own life, which he accepted with calm dignity. When the soldiers guarding him had escorted Antonius to his home after the close of the senate session, their commander granted his request to stab himself in their presence with his own dagger.

As of the date Livia composed her letter, sentencing was not yet complete. For certain, all the surviving conspirators were going to be consigned to small, remote islands in the Tyrrhenian or Mediterranean Seas—locales of limited population, well separated from one another and from the Italian mainland, and away from any spheres of influence the convicts' families might have. The purpose of these arrangements was to deter the group from reorganizing. The senate had to ascertain that accommodations, including provisions for servants and guards, were available at the sites under consideration. Those for Pulcher, Crispinus, and Scipio had not yet been determined. Only Gracchus and Julia had been dispatched to their destinations—Gracchus to Cercina *[Kerkennah Islands, Tunisia]* off the eastern coast of Africa south of Carthage, but Julia much closer to home.

After rejecting the death penalty for Julia, the senate at Augustus' behest banished her to the island of Pandataria *[modern Ventotene]*. Tiberius winced upon reading this, and remarked that Julia was sure to be miserable. Pandataria is a volcanic pinnacle, located considerable distance off the coast of Campania. On clear days one can discern Ischia on the horizon. Pandataria is gloriously scenic, with colorful rock cliffs similar to those of Capri. A large variety of farm crops grows successfully in the rich volcanic soil. Wild regions covered with lush and fragrant vegetation abound with bird life and small game. The warm offshore waters teem with fish and crustaceans. This bounty, from which the island derives its name *[from the Greek Pandoteira—Giver of All Bounteously—an epithet of Hecate, goddess of magic]*, renders the place self-sufficient and in little need of regular contact with the mainland. From time to time a trade ship or yacht puts into the port. The climate is warm, salubrious, and monotonous; the pace of life repetitive, nonchalant, and unhurried. Pandataria is idyllic for someone seeking a rest cure. It consequently has some popularity as a resort, although its remoteness prevents it from becoming a significant one. And after years of dynamic social activity at Rome, Julia is bound to find such tranquility a difficult adjustment.

To make matters even worse for Julia, Augustus required the asceticism he had already imposed on her be continued at Pandataria. For her residence he procured an isolated villa on a remote hilltop. He once again prescribed the plainest of foods, no wine, simple clothing, no adornments, no entertainments, only a sufficient number of female servants to address the most basic of needs. Julia must be denied every conceivable opportunity to develop a new liaison. No man might visit her, unless he made a written application justifying his purpose. After submitting to a scrupulous process of identification, he must be under the constant surveillance of female chaperones for the duration of his stay on Pandataria. In a demonstration of defiant support, Scribonia demanded to join Julia on the island. Under the strict letter of the law, banishment disallows family members from accompanying the convict into exile. For his daughter, however, Augustus asked the senate to relent. She and her irascible mother could divert one another with quarreling he scoffed, to the amusement of his senatorial colleagues. The Conscript Fathers also voted to send Gracchus' family to Cercina—not to cheer the convict, but to vitiate their influence in Rome.

The hearings about the conspiracy were far from over. Once sentencing for the remaining three ringleaders was finalized, the senate must still investigate and prosecute adherents—those who supported and agreed to participate in the coup. This task was certain to prove formidable. Not only must evidence be reviewed and appropriate judgment delivered: false accusations had to be discovered as well. Under Roman law, any citizen of legal majority might bring charges against another, either as the party genuinely injured or as a third party acting on behalf of another. If the case resulted in successful conviction, the accuser was entitled to a significant reward—usually a portion of the property the defendant must surrender to the state. But should the accusation prove false—and especially if the defendant could demonstrate the accuser had levied it for the purpose of satisfying a grudge or profiting from the reward—the accuser must face prosecution for false delation.

Livia closed with an urgent warning. Augustus was intensely angry. Tiberius should remember his stepfather had virtually no tolerance for conduct he considered insubordinate, especially when exhibited by a member of his immediate family. Gaius, however, may be an even greater cause for concern. The crown prince shared his grandfather's opinion, that Tiberius' departure from

Rome had abetted the eventual corruption of Julia. While Tiberius was still living with Julia, Gaius had frequently heard about and occasionally witnessed the couple's domestic and political quarrels. For years Gaius had listened as well, to his mother's denunciations of Tiberius as her social and political inferior.

Although the promulgators of the present conspiracy had been exposed and punished, they still had sympathizers. Now the Libones emerged, no doubt encouraged by Scribonia's defiance. Julia's supporters began rallying under the leadership of the inscrutable younger Lucius Scribonius Libo, the son of Augustus' former brother-in-law. This opposition had begun to insinuate the penalties Augustus had approved for the conspirators were excessive, and were the result of Livia's intervention to bolster Tiberius' sagging public image at the expense of Julia and her adherents. The antagonists were also striving to resuscitate the old notion Tiberius posed a danger to Gaius and Lucius—if not as a rival for the succession, then as the leader of a political party adversarial to the princes' influence and success.

Livia quite strongly suspected her husband did not intend to renew the regency. Gaius was now in his nineteenth year, the precise age at which his grandfather had first entered active politics. Augustus felt the time was at hand for his intended successor to start making independent decisions. Should Gaius choose to breach amicitia or afflict Tiberius with some other gesture of hostility, Augustus could not necessarily be depended upon to intervene and mitigate.

We were sitting in the library. For the next few moments, Tiberius contemplated his mother's words with his eyes closed. On looking up, he asked me to transcribe yet another letter to Augustus. Its legal logic I found quite intriguing. Tiberius used Latin, the language in which the laws were written, to ensure his interpretations were not distorted by translation into another tongue.

He encouraged his stepfather to seek, from the senate, commutation of Julia's sentence from lifelong banishment to the lesser penalty of relegation. Augustus may understandably prefer not to make this request of his own volition, lest he convey the appearance of vacillating. If this be so, then let him introduce the proposal as Tiberius' request. The senate's careful examination of the case clearly revealed the burden of blame lay upon Antonius, Gracchus, and Crispinus. They were the instigators of adultery and conspiracy alike. Julia was only an accomplice who had succumbed to their persuasions; she had initiated nothing herself. After finishing the dictation, Tiberius explained relegation to me. It is a lesser form of banishment, requiring withdrawal from Rome for a delimited period of time. The usual interval is a decade, although shorter durations are allowable. There is no enforced surrender of property; and family members are not restricted from residing with the offender at the specified destination.

The morning of Tiberius' birthday dawned raw, gray, and overcast. He was every bit as gloomy as the weather as he sat at the breakfast table, staring at the food offerings without interest. Rash was emerging along his cheekbones: the tension he had been under for the past few months was causing his acne to recur. "Today marks my fortieth anniversary," he remarked dejectedly in response to my birthday greeting and kiss. "I am entering my fifth decade—the prime years of my life—with no expectations, no sense of direction down the future, none of the self-determination I had hoped to discover upon coming to Rhodes five years ago. Thrasyllus keeps predicting change, unanticipated change, change within stagnation, monumental change. Things keep changing all right—and invariably for the worse! I had hoped my departure from Rome would induce Julia to rethink our relationship and become amenable to reconciliation. Rethink it she did: and behold the outcome of her reflections! I seem destined to be no more than a minion, worse than a slave—a puppet, which cannot think or decide for itself but only respond to the directives of its user! Every motive, every aspiration, every endeavor I have undertaken independently of my stepfather's designs for me has resulted in abject failure! Now I cannot be certain he will let me return to his service."

"You ought to eat something, Tiberius," I urged gently. "You will feel better."

He rested one elbow on the table, placed his chin on his fist, and glared at me. "You had better not worsen things by turning into a shrew!"

"Never would I think of doing so," I returned as steadily as before.

Shaking his head, he seized and bit into a pear our tree had borne. Its juice dribbled into his hand. "Clytia, had I not your devotion and support, I might as well hang myself." His tone had become far softer.

"Always and forever yours, I have said many times. Tiberius, be careful you do not start hating yourself; for if you do, you will come to hate me for loving the object of your hatred—namely, yourself. I cannot and will not endure being hated by you."

Smiling, he reached over and took my hand. "A finer birthday gift than those words I couldn't have asked for, my love. And in return I have made you sticky with pear nectar."

"A price well worth paying to see your mood brighten."

Neither mood nor day brightened much as the hours progressed. In midafternoon a messenger delivered the anticipated and dreaded packet of letters from Rome. The messages were predictably dreary. Augustus' was terse and hurtful: *Our compliments for your birthday, nothing more. The verdicts and sentences will stand unaltered.* Livia explained her husband remained vexed at Tiberius, and now not only on account of Julia. In Armenia the pro-Parthian faction had gained the upper hand, driven out the vassal king whom Augustus' ambassador had installed after the death of Tigranes II, and enthroned the latter's namesake and turncoat son who had become a Parthian sympathizer. Augustus felt this situation would not have occurred if Tiberius, who retired to Rhodes just after Tigranes II died, had instead obeyed his stepfather's wishes and traveled to Armenia to secure Roman influence there.

Livia added that Vipsania was unable to extend greetings this year. Having just presented Gallus with their fourth son (there were no daughters), she was still recovering.

Antonia's letter revealed she was enduring torment of a humorous nature. She had been residing with her children in Augustus' home for the past eight years since her husband's death. Now three of Julia's children—Lucius, Agrippina, and Postumus—were living there as well. Agrippina and Antonia's daughter Claudia Livilla were both in their thirteenth year, the former five months older than the latter. When Augustus withdrew Julia's younger children to his home in the summer, the two girls began assessing one another like a pair of cats. At length they had decided they were irreconcilable enemies. Never mind they were second cousins. Never mind each was betrothed to the other's brother—Livilla to Gaius and Agrippina to Antonia's elder son Nero. Never mind that both having reached a minimal marriageable age, they were expected—and continually admonished—to behave with demeanor befitting their state of maturity. The pair postured and squabbled over anything upon which they could possibly disagree. The more trivial or tenuous the issue, the more heated the argument. *She has dreadful taste in clothing. __ She is hideously ugly, yet she makes no effort to improve her appearance. __ She spends entirely too much time in her bath. __ She distracts Patruus (Augustus) far too often. __She makes disgusting noises with her mouth when she eats. __ She is trying to turn my brother against me. __ That perfume she wears smells like chicken manure. __ I cannot believe she still plays with dolls.* Hopefully they will outgrow all this, Antonia wrote, before her own nerves fray beyond recovery.

Drusus' note was doleful and testy. He had just passed his twelfth birthday, and was feeling like an orphan. His parents had divorced when he was a baby; his mother was now preoccupied with her new husband and their enlarging new family; throughout his childhood his father had been consistently absent from Rome—first in the wars on the northern frontiers and subsequently in voluntary retirement on Rhodes. Drusus dutifully reported gratitude for the advantages he enjoyed growing up in Augustus' household: his fine education, the assurances of privileged political advancement, the material comforts afforded by wealth, kindly affection from all his relatives. Nevertheless, none of these benefits provided the intimacy of a nuclear family—the special sense of security from having one's parents at hand to guard, guide, and govern. Even Drusus' first cousin and best friend Nero, although bereft of his father, at least enjoyed the perpetual presence of his mother Antonia. Furthermore, had Tiberius given thought to procuring a bride for his son—a congenial wife with social and political status befitting his?

Tiberius handed me Drusus' letter, and stared dejectedly across the veranda at the sea while I read it. "Now I know I must return home." He spoke with quiet but intense determination. "I shall wait until after the regency expires at the close of next month. No one will be able to argue I hold an office which enables me to strike against Gaius or anybody else. Then I shall announce my intention to return to Rome strictly as a private citizen." He struck the bench with his fist, as his mood shifted from hopeful to angrily despondent. "Why must every word I utter, every endeavor I undertake in good faith, be misconstrued and misinterpreted as sinister and ill-intentioned—not only by strangers but by my own family? Consider the following Julia amassed by disparaging me! My stepfather is angrier with me than I can ever remember, while Gaius views me as malevolent and dangerous."

For a moment he studied his left hand. Then he removed his wedding ring and placed it in the pocket of his tunic. There was more significance to this action than mere acknowledgment his union with Julia was at an end. The divorce had dissolved Tiberius' primary bond with Augustus and Gaius. Alignments between them did remain, in Augustus' marriage to Livia and Gaius' betrothal to Tiberius' niece. These, however, were secondary alliances, devoid of the immediacy and strength arising from marriage to the woman who was the daughter of one patron and mother of the other. At last I understood why he had not ceased wearing the ring sooner. It had symbolized his hope for possible reconciliation. Even now he did not abandon it altogether.

"My own son—my only child—has come to resent me," Tiberius continued his tirade. "Is it merely a matter of time before things go awry between the two of us?"

I looked steadily into his eyes. "Let us resolve not to let that happen!"

Gratitude was apparent in the slight smile he returned. "My Lioness! Why did I know such would be your answer?" He had recovered some optimism. "Will you take a letter?" he asked earnestly.

"Certainly!" We withdrew to the library, where I procured a tablet and stylus from their cabinet.

The letter was to Augustus. Tiberius began with profuse respects and thanks for the acknowledgment of his birthday. He proposed an alternative conciliation for Julia. Should Augustus decide not to lighten her sentence, would he at least consider remanding her to a locale less restrictive—to Messina perhaps, or to a city on the Italian mainland far removed from Rome? Tiberius then asked that Julia be allowed to keep all the gifts he had ever given her—especially my portrait of her children—in the hope they bring some brightness and small pleasure to her straitened and austere surroundings.

"You Scorpion!" I muttered jocularly as I handed him the completed tablet for his signet, the image of which was a hound.

"Whatever do you mean?" There was surprise and alarm in his voice.

"You aspire to surround Julia with mementos, not only of the luxuriant life she once lived but of the kindnesses you extended her—kindnesses she repaid with domestic unrest and public misrepresentation."

"That is not my objective whatsoever!" he growled through clenched teeth.

After jamming his signet ring against the wax he arose, and abruptly left the library as I realized to my horror what I had done. He headed back to the veranda. Owing to the time of year and the overcast skies, darkness was falling early and the air was turning cold and dank. I bolted upstairs, grabbed a shawl from my room and a cloak from his, and hastened after him. He was leaning against the retaining wall, once again looking out toward the sea which a bank of fog obscured. The fog was beginning to enshroud the street and houses lying beneath the veranda.

"Thank you," he said glumly as I drew the cloak about his shoulders. "Do you now see how I am perpetually misunderstood? Not even you can escape the influence of this curse. All I am seeking is to appease my family and bring Julia a modicum of cheer. Although I still resent what she has done and feel she deserves her punishment, thanks to your moderation I have acquired some pity for her. You, however, assumed the intent of my letter was retributive— and directly after you had expressed your determination not to misconstrue my motives."

"Tiberius, I made a stupid and inconsiderate remark without taking into account your state of mind; and for that I am deeply sorry. You know I love you far beyond my ability to express in words. When you suffer, I suffer; and my own pain escalates beyond description when I realize—as at this moment—that I have been a cause of yours. Your chagrin I appreciate because I bear the same curse as you. You are well familiar with my background: from early childhood accused of harboring malevolence and self-seeking of which I had never conceived, then punished without remission for those imagined offenses and subsequently for proving them non-existent. You assert I am not immune to impulses that prompt people to malign your intentions. Well, my most beloved, neither are you!"

My eyes began to fill with tears, my voice to break. Clenching my fists and teeth I continued as resolutely as I could. "What I said about your gifts to Julia was no more than a jest—a bemused observation your gesture might be interpretable as vengeful. You, however, assumed I was actually attributing that motive to you. Thrasyllus predicted misinterpretations of our intentions will bring us grief. If such misunderstandings arise from a genuine curse, then at least we have uncovered its method and can use that knowledge to evade and thwart and counterattack its assaults. And for my part I swear: if I cannot defeat the scourge, I shall assuredly be its most formidable adversary no matter how much anguish I must face in consequence!"

He turned and regarded me in contemplative silence while the fog began to swirl about our ankles. When he finally spoke, his tone had a mildness bordering on contrition. "You would have made a worthy member of my military council, with sounder insights than many of those fools I had. And you are weeping. Behold the woman in you!" He brushed the tears from my cheeks with his thumb, and then took my hands in his. "And what a woman: who has mustered bravery in the most frightening of circumstances, sanguine joy in the midst of deep sorrow, forgiveness where anger and bitterness would be anticipated and justifiable—so insightful, protective, patient, compassionate; so wonderfully selfless that she finds comfort for herself by bringing comfort to others. What better qualities are there to bless her partner?"

He fell silent again, still holding my hands and gazing at me ardently. For the first time since our relationship began I saw his eyes glisten with tears. "Clytia, I had hoped to gain a better sense of what the future holds for me, before voicing the words I am about to speak. No longer can I wait, however, for such certitude. You are the only constancy in my life right now. More desperately than ever I am in need, not only of your love and devotion, but of reassurance you will continue to accept and depend upon mine. With the clear understanding I am likely leading you into greater hardship and insecurity than you have ever before encountered…Oh, my Clytia!…will you consider giving yourself to me in marriage?"

The manner in which he expressed his request moved me nearly as much as its intent. Timoleon had essentially demanded I marry him; Tiberius was inviting me to make that choice. From his grasp I extracted my right hand and lifted it to display my silver and ruby ring. "Do you remember when you presented this to me, that I promised to accept your offer of marriage should you ever extend it? My pledge still stands. No, Tiberius, I will not consider giving myself to you: I hereby do so without hesitation or reservation!"

By now the both of us were trembling and shedding tears. He took me in his arms and laid his moist cheek against mine. We kissed fervently, again and then once more. As I caressed his cheek he clasped my hand. We exchanged smiles and then more kisses. I laid my head against his chest under his chin and he stroked my hair. The rising fog engulfed the veranda with a kind of peace, muffling sounds and refreshing our nostrils and lungs.

"It is like falling in love anew," I exulted breathlessly in rapturous happiness.

"Far finer, for it reinforces the permanence of our commitment to one another with the sanction and protection of the law."

For a time we stood holding one another in silence. Presently our faces became wet again, but not from tears. The fog had thickened substantially and was beginning to produce light drizzle. Tiberius escorted me back indoors to the library. There he sat in another silence, staring at the floor as he usually did when contemplating something. Finally he drew a deep breath. "Clytia, I must insist our marriage be kept absolutely secret—more imperatively, in fact, than our present relationship. We cannot reveal the slightest inkling of its existence, unless we can be certain our doing so will not have adverse consequences. Even our very servants must be excluded, so they cannot be tempted or forced to disclose.

"With my family already aggravated at me, I do not want to risk the chance my taking a non-Roman wife will offend them further. Remember, one of my stepfather's cardinal political objectives is to protect and promote the integrity and perpetuity of a pure Italian race. We can hardly expect him to condone—at least not publicly—the marriage of his own stepson to a non-Italian. Can you imagine, moreover, what rumors and distortions my political enemies might spread about us—especially if they discover my own kin disapprove of our match? The nature of innuendo never ceases to amaze me. Those very persons, whom you believe least likely to learn of and care about confidentiality, invariably seem to be the ones who most readily discover and disseminate it.

"Our union must be morganatic as well. This means you cannot claim an ordinary widow's legacy from my patrimony. My intent is not to deprive, but to protect you from being challenged. I shall retain you as a remainderman to my will under your pseudonym, which we of course shall continue to employ." His tone became increasingly urgent, pleading. "You understand the purpose behind my demands. I shall not—I CANNOT—risk being placed in any condition which forces us to separate. That would destroy me more readily than the most acute public disgrace—so intense is my love for you."

"We shall not separate, Tiberius. Remember my promise of always and forever. Should your family or some political necessity demand we be legally divorced, I promise to cooperate willingly and discreetly with the hope you will retain me as your mistress."

"I shall find a way to keep from divorcing you."

"Should we not at least tell Thrasyllus our intention? How can we validate our nuptials without a witness?"

He smiled with the confidence of one with sound knowledge of a subject. "We do not require a ceremony with witnesses. Under Roman law an unwed couple can establish a marriage simply by cohabiting for an entire year, so long as the woman does not absent herself from their home for three or more consecutive nights during that year. Usus is the legal term for this arrangement. My divorce became effective upon the Nones of this past August. You were in Alexandria at the time; but you returned to my domicile during the week following and have remained here ever since. By the time your next birthday arrives we can declare ourselves legally married, provided you do not go traveling before then. Secrecy will be most critical during this interval. We cannot afford to be found out and forced apart—by my family or by yours or by anyone else—before that year is over. You are absolutely right, however, regarding Thrasyllus. We ought to have at least one freeborn witness, who can vouch that we have fulfilled our year should ever we must verify having done so. I did confide to Thrasyllus—shortly after our confrontation with Timoleon—that I intended to seek your hand should ever I become divorced from Julia. He will be delighted with our news."

A blissful calm permeated the remainder of the day's routine: sex, bath, supper, a brief recital on my harp, and a discussion of the lecture Tiberius had attended at the Rhodes Academy the previous day. The sophistos had proposed the Great Conflagration, in which the Stoics maintain all must end, does not signify the destruction of the material universe, but rather the improvement of an individual human consciousness—when recognition and acceptance of higher and more practical ideals prompts abandonment of corrupt or useless beliefs and dogmas. A sensible and scientific view, we concluded, as no empirical evidence of a physical conflagration cycle can be perceived in nature. Thereafter we decided to designate for certain my next birthday for celebrating the completion of our nuptial year.

The tranquil joy persisted through the ensuing weeks. It alleviated to some extent the restless discomfort of waiting for the regency to expire, as well as the irritating dreariness of a persistent but rainless overcast. In anticipation of our possibly returning to Italy, I started to distance myself from folk who presently depended—or aspired to become dependent—upon my charity. Any continuous assistance I had hitherto been offering I now terminated, with large but final donations of money or goods. As many new petitions as possible I referred to the civic government or to other philanthropists. At this time I also began a meticulous inventory of our personal belongings, to determine which should be prepared for shipment, which should be left behind and donated to the needy, and which bare essentials should be set aside for our use during our voyage. We could not yet relinquish the leases on the townhouse and villa, however, because as yet we did not have a definite date for our departure.

Thrasyllus indeed became ebullient when we informed him of our decision to wed, and from a perusal of his chartings deduced that we had made it at an auspicious time. But when we went to greet him on his birthday in mid-December, he received us somberly. "Tiberius,…Clytia,…I have just completed a thorough casting of your horoscopes. You have entered a period of upheaval, of turning and change, which will culminate in those monumental outcomes predicted for each of you."

"Our forthcoming marriage!" I concluded triumphantly.

"That is an aspect of the change. It does not mark its beginning.

"My divorce?" Tiberius queried.

"Even earlier to that," Thrasyllus mused as he studied his charts and jotted notes on a tablet. "The process appears to have begun about the time Timoleon disrupted my lecture on Epicurean Atomism."

I sat suddenly upright in my chair. "That was indeed a day of great transformation for me!"

"She spent the entire afternoon in mental self-immolation," Tiberius chuckled, "until I reassured her I still loved her and forgave her in spite of the ruckus she had caused."

I pressed the fingers of one hand against my forehead and shook my head as I reflected upon that experience. "He makes it all sound so simple. But it was a profound catharsis for me, Thrasyllus—phoenix-like, as anger and retributivism, self-condemnation, shame, and remorse burned away in purifying fire. Then from their ashes arose the repentance that impels one to reform one's ways with joy, forgiveness of self as well as of others, and the understanding that reliance upon my companion's love is not a form of selfishness but a demonstration of my own love for him. And as that day closed,"—now I looked directly at Thrasyllus and spoke determinedly, —"the both of us witnessed a meteor."

The astrologer raised his eyebrows and nodded. After a thoughtful pause he returned to his charts. "The changes will unfold over the next six years. Some of them will be identical for you both, your impending marriage being an example. Others will be unique to one partner, but have profound and inextricable effects upon the other—like the personal regeneration you just described, Clytia, which made you a better person and hence a better partner for Tiberius; or your divorce, Tiberius, which did not involve Clytia but made you eligible to become her husband. You will feel the progression of events in extremes—either as direly painful or incredibly rewarding. Many of the hardships will be gravely severe, so do not let them dismay you. The final outcomes will truly be monumental for both of you—and more wondrous than we can presently imagine."

That evening the two of us merely picked at our supper of sea scallops, and reassured Dorotheus his culinary efforts were not the cause of our lackluster appetites. My sleep was haunted by bizarre jumbles of dreams, the details of which I could not remember when I woke with a start in the middle of the night. The pain in my jaw confirmed I had been grinding my teeth. I was alone in our bed. We always kept a lamp burning in the adjoining dressing room. Tiberius, who immediately after wakening could see in the dark like a cat, had little need for this accessory; but it was necessary for me should I have to arise overnight for any reason. The pool of light the lamp cast on the bedroom floor was unfamiliarly distorted by a shadow. Tiberius was seated in the chair, wrapped in his dressing gown, his back toward me. As I drew up behind him he laid his head against my bosom. I stroked his hair. "Frightening, is it not?" I ventured.

"Meaning?"

"The imminence of those monumental changes. We have known about them for years; but they have always seemed distant and abstract. Now that they are upon us, I find myself unnerved by their reality. What is going to befall us that will be so phenomenal?

He sighed and took my hand. "There is no more use to speculating about those prospects than any other unknowns. Even Thrasyllus could not discern their details. You would do better steeling yourself in anticipation of the forthcoming hardships he forecast. When I return to Rome in a few months you absolutely must accompany me, so we do not breach our year of continuous cohabitation. Once we establish a departure date, I want you to have Timoxena remove that execrable dye from your hair, or else teach Phoebe how to perform the process during our voyage. To my family I want to present you with your hair its natural color, which far more becomes you."

"But if I return to Italy with my hair in its actual shade, will I not be in danger of being identified by my relatives or their acquaintances?" This question I posed with a shudder, puzzled by his apparent willingness to risk my exposure. "As your companion, will I not become a focus of public attention, a subject of intense scrutiny and discussion? *Who is she; what is her background; did he leave Julia for her?* Am I not legally under my brother's tutelage; and will I not remain so until I pass into yours upon the fulfillment of our year?"

Again I shuddered. Tiberius turned his head and gazed up at me. "Do not be afraid," he said gently. "You have been absent from Italy for five years. During our stay here, no one ever equated Daphne Hipparchide with Clytia Eupistide. That in itself shows your family did not associate your disappearance with my withdrawal to Rhodes; or if they did, they failed to confirm you accompanied me here. I intend to present you in Rome as a different ward—one whose tutelage I assumed while here on Rhodes. You are the sole pupil of my protégé, the local decorative artist Eutychus—hence your artistic talent. You grew up in Alexandria and there married a fellow practitioner of your teacher's craft. Eventually your husband absconded with your dowry for another woman. This conceit enables us to explain why you have no assets to fall back upon. Eutychus appealed to me, his patron, to make you my ward because he presently lacks adequate means to offer you support. His father's unanticipated death has forced him to make immediate provision for his widowed mother."

"How shall we respond to residents of and visitors to Rhodes who know nothing of a Rhodian artist named Eutychus?"

"You…er…he produces his artwork exclusively for me as his patron."

I laughed a little, now warming with relief.

Tiberius continued. "Although you presumably bear an uncannily strong resemblance to a Clytia or Pythia or Cythpleia—or whatever her name is who fled the Eupistodoi of Naples concurrently with my withdrawal—you are altogether a different person. We come across people who resemble other people all the time; coincidences of this nature are commonplace. And rest assured: you are not going to engender phenomenal public attention and scrutiny, even after I start taking you with me to cultural and academic and social events. Many people will assume you are my mistress, as they have here. No one in Rome pays any more heed to a ward or a mistress than to a servant.

"Suppose your mother or brother do recognize you and attempt to launch an exposé? I shall demand they bring unassailable proof before a praetor's court—no, better yet my stepfather's tribunal. Given all the misleads and confusions and obfuscations and outright lies we have concocted, all your kin will be able to offer is speculative or at best circumstantial evidence. Then I in turn could initiate a countersuit for slander and scare them off for sure."

"The scorpion's sting will prevail where the lion's roar has not. A scorpion lives in a burrow and stings to protect itself and its young. From the burrow of secrecy in which you have hidden me, you can and will keep my family at bay."

He laid his head back against my bosom and I resumed stroking his hair. "You will need to take another pseudonym, now that we are disposing of Daphne," he said.

"I have amassed quite a collection: Pythia of Naples, Daphne Hipparchide, Eutychus of Rhodes. Who shall I become now?"

"You like Galatea. For your new surname, how about using the philosopher Plato's real name?"

"Aristocles. That would make me Galatea Aristoclide. Quite pleasing."

"A pity your alleged husband Aristocles was a cad." He smiled up at me and winked, and I laughed. Laying his head back against my bosom, he continued to unfold his plan. "I shall alter my will to reflect the change. Thrasyllus has already agreed to serve as your curator in lieu of Eurycles. I shall simply advise Eurycles his services in that capacity are no longer required. He does not have to learn the reason."

Suddenly there was a hammering on the roof, as if it were being showered with small pebbles. Tiberius glanced at the ceiling. "Cassander Haidou was correct about those great rains." He rose from the chair and took my hand. "We ought to try and get some sleep." He led me back to the bedchamber. As we were settling under the coverlet, a passing thought made me sit up suddenly. My concerned companion propped himself on one elbow. "Are you all right? Are you taken ill?"

"What will become of Leo and Nivea?" I fretted.

In the half-light I saw him roll his eyes. "By all the gods, Clytia! To you of all people the answer should be self-evident. When the time comes for us to depart, we shall decide what course of action is best: taking them with us, sending for them later, or leaving them behind under someone's care."

"I am so sorry. What a trivial issue to raise, especially at this moment!"

He lay back upon the pillow and yawned. "Frankly, I enjoyed the disruption with its triviality. It was quite wifely."

After that seemingly interminable wait, the Calends of January and the expiration of the regency arrived. We prepared the packet of gifts for the trio of birthdays that occurred at the month's end—for Lucius an elegantly tooled bronze fibula for securing a cloak at one's shoulder, for Livia and Antonia the portraits I had rendered. With these goods Tiberius sent his all-important letter, which he must have dictated to me twenty times before he was finally satisfied with its wording. He explained the primary reason for his retirement had been to remove himself from the direct sight, not only of Gaius and Lucius themselves but of the Roman people as well. Tiberius had aspired to avoid irritating the princes or diminishing their prestige, lest his visibility as regent appear a blatant reminder they had not yet acquired sufficient expertise in statecraft to rule in their own right. Moreover he wanted to relieve the brothers of any fears his presence in Rome might induce Augustus to reconsider intentions for the succession, and transfer it from grandsons to stepson. Tiberius sincerely regretted the distress his sojourn had caused, and was now looking forward to reunion with the family he so sorely missed.

Hardly more than a week later we received a response. I was in my suite with Alcmene and Phoebe, sorting through garments and deciding which I wanted packed for our impending journey. We would send for our household items later, once we had settled in Italy. Little Miranda, now in her nineteenth month, was padding about and *helping* in her own way by disarranging things. All at once Tiberius strode into the room and ordered the servants to leave. He handed me a tablet embossed with the imperial seal, then sat down on the bed and stared at the floor. His face was ashen. Nervously I opened the tablet, and recognized the calligraphy at once. With his own hand Caesar Augustus had written,

> You will remain where you are indefinitely, and do well to forget
> the family you so eagerly abandoned.

After placing the tablet on my dressing table, I sat beside my companion and took his hand. "Oh, my dearest love!" I murmured breathlessly, "Breach of amicitia?" Those last words terrified me utterly as I spoke them. My heart was pounding, my knees weak.

"No," Tiberius answered dryly. "Were that his intention, he would have written it specifically and probably recommended I kill myself." He shook his head and sighed. "I am not quite sure what to make of this. Hardly can I expect him not to be angry with me; yet I know for certain he does not inflict punishment or retribution unless it serves a political purpose. What could the present one be? Hopefully my mother can and will elucidate the matter. If we do not hear from her within the next week, I shall write to her."

The very next day a letter arrived from Livia. She thanked Tiberius profusely for my portrait of his brother, and assured him it had stirred joyous memories. Antonia was equally delighted with my rendering of her children, and Lucius predictably indifferent about his gift. After these acknowledgments, Livia proceeded to explain the reasons for which Tiberius must remain on Rhodes.

Not so much Augustus but Gaius wanted Tiberius kept at a distance. As we had come to suspect, Gaius was convinced Tiberius had a strong following. These adherents might immediately and forcefully rally about Tiberius upon his return to Rome, even if he did not resume a public career. Once organized with their champion in their midst to inspire them, this party could weaken Gaius' own prestige and influence—or so he feared. Tiberius' support was particularly significant in military circles—among veterans who had served under his command or that of his brother, and with men presently in active service as well. Should these adherents take up arms, recruit reinforcements, and then hail Tiberius instead of Gaius as their commander-in-chief, civil war could erupt. Gaius also continued to feel Tiberius' separation from Julia was the fundamental cause of her corruption, and that reconciliation would imply Gaius condoned rather than eschewed his stepfather's breach of the marriage. Augustus for certain was not about to let a condition to develop or exist, with any potential to disrupt the smooth transition of power to his grandson and the alignment of public opinion behind the new sovereign.

"So there you have the explanation." Tiberius placed his mother's tablet on the table in the library.

"How will you convince Gaius that you do not pose a threat to him?"

"Clytia my dearest, you are about to witness how Roman political patronage works. My relatives, friends, and retainers will openly defend me, declare their support, and strive to convince Gaius he is wrong about me. At the same time, my enemies—the Scribonii Libones, sympathizers with Julia's paramours, sycophants aspiring to ingratiate themselves to Gaius by reassuring him he is right about everything—will work with equal intensity to malign and execrate me. If my side wins this war of words—and remember, my mother is using her formidable influence on my behalf—there is hope my stepfather and Gaius will decide I am less dangerous to their interests than they had presumed and will

247

relent. But if the opposition prevails: well, my love, we may have to remain on Rhodes for the rest of our lives, or even find ourselves forced to flee to climes more remote."

News of the rift between Caesar Augustus and his stepson spread swiftly and through all levels of society. Scorn and displays of contempt followed, varying in character and intensity. Many a journeying government functionary, when putting into port at Rhodes, ostentatiously neglected to call upon Tiberius and pay respects. Such snubs were unabashed breaches of protocol; for although Tiberius was presently a private citizen, he was nevertheless a former military commander and civilian official of the highest rank. The sophistos Diogenes, who delivered a lecture at the Academy every Saturday morning, informed Tiberius he was no longer welcome at these events.

When we called upon Thrasyllus at the Academy one day, he advised us to stay away; Diogenes was not the only member of the institution who had become contemptuous of Tiberius. The owner of our villa abruptly terminated our lease. Eurycles announced he could no longer serve as our agent, because association with Tiberius was causing clients to forsake him. For the same reason, Erastus my harp instructor, Timotheus my art teacher, and Dorotheus our chef gave their notices amid effusions of regret. Erastus and Timotheus used the same pretext: satisfaction I was thoroughly trained, and in need of no further instruction from them. Dorotheus prepared and left behind a notebook of recipes and culinary techniques for our servants to follow.

I became a target of hostility as well. Parents who used to let their children greet me on the street now turned them away. Diogenes banned me too from his lectures. Merchants in the marketplace, who had once vied with one another for my patronage, now refused to sell me their wares. Requests for my charity declined precipitously, even as the persistent and heavy rain created new and urgent needs for intervention. We learned of homes and farms damaged or destroyed by floods and mudslides; yet the assistance of Daphne Hipparchide remained unsought.

Acts of physical violence began. Hecklers shouted or chanted insults from the street before the townhouse. *Here is Rhodes, so jump here!* quoted out of context from Aesop, we heard repeatedly. The exterior walls were defaced with derogatory graffiti, pummeled with rocks and feces. Our litter was spat upon; objects were hurled at our carriage; one assailant attempted to cause mayhem and injury by spooking the carriage horse Hipparion. Tiberius abandoned his excursions on Sinapeus, although nothing had happened during one of these as yet. Sitting on horseback nonetheless made him a target all too visible and readily accessible. He also began to practice his exercises at arms in the court of our townhouse with one of our bodyguards as a partner, instead of going to the local barracks for this purpose. Not only did the new arrangement preclude his having to venture into public; it enabled him to avoid a place where others had easy access to weapons.

One morning while we were at breakfast, Proceles and the bodyguard Chryses approached us. Bloodied fists and face and a blackened eye proved the groom had been in a fight. A trio of punks had identified Leo as the pet of Tiberius Nero's ward Daphne. They had cornered the cat, doused him with oil, and were about to set him afire when Proceles came upon them. Chryses arrived to investigate the commotion. He set his mastiffs after the assailants, who immediately decided flight was a far preferable alternative to having an arm or leg chewed off. Proceles assured me Leo was all right, just greasy. He then requested and promptly received my permission, to transport Leo and Nivea and the present litter of kittens to safety at his parents' home. Tiberius asked Proceles to remove the horses as well. They like the cats had become potential targets; and we could no longer use them for their intended purposes anyway. He also terminated the lease of our carriage and litter from the livery service of Proceles' father. It had become impossible for us to venture abroad in either vehicle without being accosted, even when we had the curtains drawn shut.

After warning us not to visit him at the Academy, Thrasyllus had invited us to call at his home. Tiberius declined at once. Not only did he and I wish to avoid being attacked ourselves; we both worried Thrasyllus and his family would become victims of persecution should we be seen entering his residence. Grateful for our concern—and undeterred by the prospect of jeers and insults that did in fact materialize—Thrasyllus started to visit us. He had no new forecasts to offer: we were undergoing his predicted period of upheaval prior to monumental change. Nevertheless he cautioned that we could expect continued duress and—far more seriously—danger to our lives. Neither of us was destined to die, he reassured us, so long as we took precautions to ensure our safety.

Leo's ordeal and Thrasyllus' admonition convinced Tiberius the assaults were becoming too virulent for our private bodyguards to handle. He dictated a letter to Augustus, requesting the protection of praetorian guards. As I handed him the tablet for his signet he addressed me in urgent tones. "Clytia, the time is now definitely at hand for Daphne to disappear. Hopefully Galen will not abandon me before I can have him put out the word I married her off. As for you: except in the most extenuating of circumstances—should the roof collapse or the place catch fire—do not venture out of doors, even onto the veranda. If you require fresh air, stand near an open window or door. If you feel a need for exercise, ascend and descend the stairs. Please do your best to occupy and amuse yourself with what you have at hand. Get Timoxena to change your hair color before she forsakes us as well. Once the praetorians arrive I do not want them spreading word that a woman of Daphne's description is residing with me, after I have announced her departure."

He took my hands in his and regarded me imploringly. "You are going to feel trapped and imprisoned; and for this I am sincerely sorry. I am trying to assure your safety by hiding you—to keep you from being harassed or injured or worst of all kidnapped from my domicile, while we are fulfilling our nuptial year. The only alternative I can suggest is for us to postpone our marriage, and separate until the present calamity subsides. Since we no longer have the villa, we must find another locale to which you can retreat. It would be best, in that case, for you to move elsewhere on the island or perhaps even farther away—say to Ephesus or Athens or Alexandria, where you can disappear amid the crowds. You are too well known in this city."

As he finished speaking I started to shake my head. "If we separate under the present uncertainties, Tiberius, then who knows when we shall be reunited if at all? And what sort of wife would leave her husband when he is most in need of her consolation, her forbearance, her insights into and assessments of his plight, and her suggestions for his help? How many times have I promised to crawl through gutters with you? To that, hiding here in the house is a far preferable alternative. Besides, what inducement to go abroad do these great rains offer me?"

He continued to hold my hands and gaze at me, now smiling. "I love you, my Lioness!" he exclaimed with undisguised gratitude.

"And I you." I returned his smile reassuringly. "And I cannot fathom why total strangers have taken to attacking us!" Now I was angrily bewildered. "Your differences with your family are no one else's concern. And why am I sharing in the abuse, especially since I have an established reputation as a philanthropist?"

"Do you recall how the crewmembers of the Phoenix defended us when we were heckled in Messina? Unsophisticated thinkers adhere unquestioningly to whichever side they perceive as the winning one. They will not differ from the majority for fear of receiving ridicule and persecution from that majority. Why do you suppose your father was so acquiescent to your mother and aunt? He understood that opposing them would prove futile, and only subject him to their scorn and abuse."

As we had anticipated, Timoxena declined our request to change my hair color herself. She nevertheless sent the recipe and instructions for a darkening agent, comprised of nightshade and henna. Phoebe thinned and shortened my hair somewhat so there would be less to treat, but left it well below the chin length that signified a hetaera. We applied the mixture every afternoon and let it set for two hours, dripping onto a towel draped about my shoulders. Thereafter, I would rinse it all out in my bath. The ritual helped fill my days and ease the adjustment to being housebound. Within a week, my hair was restored to a close approximation of its true shade. Natural growth thereafter would restore it completely.

At the end of that same first week the praetorians arrived. Their commandant bore a communiqué from Augustus, as terse and acerbic as the last:

> You are now imperial legate to Rhodes—only because I am so confoundedly in love with your mother.

"Is it possible he made you legate because he plans to send you to settle the situation in Armenia?" This I ventured in an effort to cull some hope from the emperor's words.

"Given the content and tenor of his message, he can hardly have that duty in mind for me. Perhaps it is just as well. Were I to succeed in Armenia, the nobles I leave in power there would be my retainers. My prestige in Rome would soar, leaving Gaius feeling all the more eclipsed. Even as a member of our family, I cannot qualify for praetorian protection unless I am exercising an active field command. This has to be why my stepfather appointed me legate. My mother must have prevailed upon him to grant me the praetorian protection." He sighed and stared downward, clearly chagrined. "Clytia, I now appreciate more than ever how bitterly you suffered—how devastating it is to feel rejected by one's closest and most loved kin."

From virtually the moment of their arrival, the praetorians made me uncomfortable. Having armed soldiers stationed throughout the house and about its exterior made me feel as highly privileged as a queen, and as incarcerated as a felon. Moreover I had the constant impression I was being mentally undressed and ravished, and that my sexuality and relationship with Tiberius were hot topics of speculation at the barracks. My partner concurred. "They are a scruffy crowd," he said. "Many come from the lowest levels of society, seeking to improve their condition through military service. They are selected for their loyalty and their dexterity at arms but assuredly not for their manners. If any of them molests you verbally or physically, advise me or the commandant at once."

The praetorians seldom spoke to me; to be sure, none of them ever touched me; but they continued to unnerve me. Tiberius tried to put me at ease. "Quintus Ostorius Scapula, their supreme prefect in Rome, is my mother's protégé. My stepfather accepted him for his position on her recommendation. Scapula is both loyal retainer and firm disciplinarian. Any guard who disrupts the household of a member of my family must answer directly to him, and expect serious consequences." Nevertheless the invasion of these protectors was motivation aplenty for me to spend the better part of my days upstairs, dividing my time between the master suite and my own. I only ventured downstairs to dine, to select a scroll from the library, or for some special purpose like transcribing a dictation for Tiberius when Galen was not around.

Tiberius dismissed the hired guard Chryses with his son and dogs, once the praetorians had usurped their services. Chryses politely acknowledged he could no longer provide the level of protection our present situation demanded. Tiberius retained our servile bodyguards, and assigned them a new type of duty. They must watch out for and report any inappropriate conduct on the part of the praetorians, especially if directed toward me. Having guards protecting me from guards made me feel all the more exposed and vulnerable and content to remain secluded.

Presently I found myself with yet another incentive for remaining hidden. After having dwindled to a scant few, the number of visitors to the townhouse suddenly began to rebound, albeit not with the volume that had preceded Augustus' denunciation. Requests for appointments increased steadily. Some intrepid souls arrived on the doorstep unscheduled and unannounced. Although these intrusions annoyed him, Tiberius seldom turned the invaders away. Hardly did he wish to alienate allies at the very time he most needed them.

With the exception of one loudmouth whom the praetorians promptly hauled off to the city jail, nobody came to denounce Tiberius. Some were petitioners for his intervention or arbitration as imperial legate. Others were civilian or military officials who called in the line of duty, to pay their respects to him in his present position. Many of the visitors emphatically offered sympathy, and the reassurance of their loyalty and support. These partisans were not insurgents against Augustus and Gaius, flocking to Tiberius as a figurehead for rebellion, but were sincere Augustan loyalists. Some, however, were retainers of Tiberius as well—perhaps because a particular family had always sided with the Nerones in the senate; because Tiberius had used his influence to procure somebody an office or other benefit; because someone felt Tiberius was indispensable to the regime and Gaius was compromising its success by ostracizing him.

One adherent went so far as to demonstrate his support by taking up residence in the city. Marcus Vescularius Atticus had served estimably as a praefectus equitum under Tiberius' command in the Danube wars. In this capacity he had become Tiberius' model for the mythical Decimus Calvinius Valens. Now a pensioned veteran, Atticus had received as compensation for his service a grant of farmland in Gaul. This he had leased out to finance his relocation. Atticus was also a family man. His wife, Tiberius speculated, could hardly have needed much persuasion, to leave the cold and deprivations of farm life on the empire's northern frontier for the warmth and opulence of Rhodes.

These affirmations of loyalty showed me that Gaius' concerns about Tiberius' political ascendancy were considerably more justified than I had at first believed—that Tiberius had far more of an independent political following than I had originally assumed. I also came to appreciate why Tiberius failed to take comfort from such overtures. "Do these fools not understand, that the more they overtly rally about me the more Gaius will consider me dangerous?" He also began to wonder how many professed partisans were false friends—actual enemies aspiring to gain his confidence with the hope he would let down his guard, and say or do something they could represent to Gaius as disparaging or threatening.

Tiberius took pains to keep his conversations affable lest he cause offense to someone, and also scrupulously superficial lest he utter something that might eventually be used against him. Often he agonized over what he had said, especially to callers whom he did not know well or at all. Would a careless remark—or one assiduously thought out for that matter—be misconstrued, and so make its way back to Gaius as proof of Tiberius' contumacy? His natural shyness made the visits all the more trying for him; and in consequence he became edgy and preoccupied. This agitation further elevated his concern, that in his unsettled state of mind he might make a remark or convey a mood at which somebody took umbrage.

In my refuge I pursued my regular activities of reading and writing, sewing and embroidering, drawing and painting. Since my retreat limited my access to real models, I resorted to the imaginary and conjectural—scenes from legends and literature, fantastic people and beasts. This new focus inspired a new project. I decided to create six vignettes of legendary lovers, whose liaisons suffered tribulation but ended in happiness and peace. If I managed to complete them by August—and managed to conceal the effort from Tiberius—I would present him the series in commemoration of the fulfillment of our nuptial year. For my subjects I chose Endymion and Selene, Eros and Psyche, Perseus and Andromeda, Acis and Galatea, Melanion and Atalanta, and Odysseus and Penelope.

Little Miranda helped me endure my confinement by becoming my constant companion. Her mother's attempt to poison her had rendered her unable to speak; in fact, she could not utter any sounds at all. In later years we would discover she was mentally slow as well; but at her present early age this impairment was not yet evident. I told her stories and drew her pictures, and gave her a palette of her own so she could pretend to write and draw. I sang songs and played my harp for her, and from time to time let her pluck its strings. She learned quite readily that everything in the house had its place, that she might not handle an object without first seeking my permission, and that she must restore it to its proper location. Miranda provided something I had despaired of ever attaining: an intimate association with a child. None but Underlying Good, I felt, could have imparted so wondrous a gift. My relationship with this little girl brought me abundant compensation for my barrenness, and without imposing upon Tiberius the burdens of providing for—and perhaps worse yet explaining—a child of our own.

Like all small children, Miranda became obstreperous on occasion—most often when she was tired. Then I would hand her off to Phoebe, who put her to bed or administered discipline if necessary. In view of the abusive manner in which childhood reprimands had been applied to me, I often worried whether I would be able to correct Miranda constructively and benignly should the need arise. Then one day Miranda threw a silent tantrum, kicking her feet and pounding her fists because I had refused to let her play with my jewelry. I could not raise Phoebe, who for some reason was out of earshot. So I took Miranda by the hand, led her into the adjoining room, plunked her onto a chair, and closed the door behind me as I left. When Miranda ran back out and started to remonstrate anew, I repeated the operation.

After several minutes Miranda slowly emerged, head and eyes lowered and bottom lip protruding. "Are you going to be a good girl and not fuss at me, when I do not let you have your way with my things?" I demanded sharply. Without lifting eyes or head nor withdrawing lip, Miranda nodded contritely. "Very well," I said, "you make sure you do not do that again. Now, come and help me put my paints in order." At once her glumness dissipated into joy as she set right to work, cleaning and arranging brushes and palettes. Moreover she kept her promise: there were no more tantrums. And I received an important lesson in forgiveness. Once the child had learned from her mistake and its consequences, there was no reason to keep reminding her of the error. The perpetual punishments my family had inflicted upon me were not purposeful lessons, but abject and unnecessary applications of cruelty.

By now it was late March. For some time Tiberius had been thinking about curtailing the visibility and accessibility that was causing him such anguish, by relocating to the interior of the island: to a small village or the rural countryside. Recent events were inclining him more and more toward this course of action. The landlord of the townhouse was worried about defacement to his property from graffiti and rock throwing, despite Tiberius' assurances he would make repairs. The volume of activity from visitors and praetorians, and the persistent noisy heckling, were beginning to distress the elderly couple who resided in the house immediately adjacent to ours. Cassander Haidou, ever solicitous of his young son and daughter, had complained that their chums and schoolmates were taunting them for being our neighbors. Adversaries and supporters alike were accosting our servants in the streets. Some merchants refused to sell them foodstuffs and household supplies. We did not lack these, because other vendors continued to trade with our staff. Nevertheless the diminution of sources increased the difficulty of obtaining these necessities, and caused us to wonder whether our access to them would eventually disappear altogether.

Tiberius' nerves were fraying from the incessant barrage of attention, good and bad alike. His ever-heightening anxiety made him yearn for solitude with increasing desperation. Frequently he retreated upstairs between callers, if only for a few minutes at a time—sometimes to seek my company, at others to be entirely alone. He began to dine with me in my suite, and to dictate correspondence to me there. The tension began to strain elements of our personal relationship. Not that we quarreled: if anything we were more patiently sympathetic and tenderly solicitous toward one another than ever. But both of us began to chafe at our confinement to the house, despite all our efforts to make the best of this condition.

To make matters worse the persistent rains abated, and gave way to absolutely glorious weather that made remaining indoors all the more difficult.

Bad dreams started to afflict Tiberius' slumber, causing him to moan and cry out and even to kick and punch. Knowing he was disturbing me and fearing he might harm me, he insisted I sleep in my own quarters. There I not only missed the warm and soothing intimacy of feeling him beside me, but even more the ability to wake him from his turmoil and offer my solace and understanding.

The frequency and satisfaction of our sexual encounters declined. His acne worsened; mine reemerged.

Fortuitously at just this time, another loyalist took up residence in Rhodes to demonstrate his support. Sextus Julius Marinus had been chief quartermaster during Tiberius' raids against the Germans along the Gallic border, and like Marcus Atticus was now a pensioned veteran. He was the grandson of a freedman, who as a slave had belonged to one Sextus Julius Caesar—a very distant relative of Augustus' family. A confirmed bachelor who dabbled in letters, Marinus was eager to explore the academic offerings of Rhodes.

While reviewing descriptions of Rhodian properties for purchase, Marinus had noted a small country estate in the craggy hills southwest of the city of Rhodes. Since Tiberius could hardly venture forth without creating a sensation—and most likely an unfavorable one—he sent Marinus and Thrasyllus to evaluate the place. Both disapproved because they felt the level of privacy Tiberius desired was lacking. The farm lay fairly close to the city, on a gentle rise at the edge of the hills; and the house itself stood hard by a busy thoroughfare that passed directly through the property.

To mislead the broker about the identity of their client—lest he or one of the creditors he represented refuse to trade with Tiberius—Thrasyllus maintained he and his companion were seeking a refuge for a highly reclusive widow from Alexandria. The broker replied that he had just such an offering: a small hillside farm measuring only about 165 plethora, and much more remote than the one they had just examined. It was in foreclosure after failing as a commercial venture. Minimal size and restrictive terrain allowed sufficient crop production to sustain the inhabitants of the estate, but only a minimal surplus for sale at markets. Unable or unwilling to understand this limitation, the previous owner had borrowed heavily against the property. He had anticipated bumper harvests that would enable repayment of the debts, and still realize substantial net gains for turning the place into a luxury retreat for himself and multiple guests. Along came the drought; there were no surpluses whatsoever; the loans came due; and the owner fled, leaving the farm at the disposal of his creditors. *That landowner and my mother think similarly,* I reflected. The broker urged our agents to give this prospect serious consideration, because if effectively managed it could be made a viable, self-sustaining residential villa farm.

Tiberius concluded from his friends' reports that the property at least sounded idyllic, and decided I must go and investigate it. After all, as the lady of his household I ought to determine whether the new place suited our needs and tastes. Since the broker had already been led to believe his prospective buyer was a woman, my appearance would affirm that notion. Having surrendered our carriage, we asked Thrasyllus if we could borrow his vehicle so we did not arouse public scrutiny by leasing another. Not only did Thrasyllus assure us he was happy to comply: he offered to accompany me, and thereby eased the trepidations I had been entertaining. In the immense collection of textiles I had amassed over the years I found a large swath of deep gray linen. This Alcmene and I washed and dried and took turns hemming. It made a convincing widow's himation—appropriately plain and dark to suggest mourning.

To minimize the chances of my being noticed upon leaving the townhouse, we decided to depart an hour before dawn on the appointed day—the Calends of April. Alcmene would serve as my female chaperone, and Arbindus as bodyguard since a praetorian would defeat the entire purpose of my disguise. The carriage would come to the rear of the townhouse, to create the impression my departure was the activity of our servants. On the preceding night I retired early to my bedchamber and hardly slept, knowing I must arise unwontedly early, chance the possibility of harassment, and make a decision that must profoundly affect my companion's life and wellbeing by concluding a type of transaction about which I knew absolutely nothing. Never had I purchased property. Suppose I liked the place and considered it well suited to our purposes, only to discover Tiberius felt precisely the opposite? Suppose it lacked the level of inaccessibility he desired? Suppose in my ignorance I paid more than the property was worth, because the broker swindled me and I was too naïve to notice? Suppose, suppose, suppose.... Thanks to Underlying Good that Thrasyllus would be along to offer guidance!

When Alcmene came to rouse me, I was not groggy despite my lack of sleep. Although I had absolutely no appetite, Tiberius insisted I eat breakfast. After I continued to refuse for fear of making myself sick, he ordered Alcmene to make sure I consumed something along the way and sent her to pack a basket of provisions. By the time I reached our destination I would be famished and have a headache, and be too distracted with pain and hunger to form a sound opinion about the prospective purchase.

The carriage arrived, but without Thrasyllus! Aka had gone into labor overnight the driver said, and by the time he departed she had not yet delivered. Concerned about the possibility of further complications, Thrasyllus wanted to be present until the birth was over. Tiberius was adamant: I must proceed alone. No, he would not consider sending a message to the broker, asking to have the appointment rescheduled. Our time was limited: he wanted to escape the city as soon as possible. If the present property proved unsuitable, we must promptly consider others. And no: he was not about to risk alienating Marinus by waking him at this outrageous hour, and pressing him on a moment's notice to accompany me in Thrasyllus' stead. Furthermore, Marinus might make advances to me: Tiberius had noticed him eying me salaciously.

Would I please exercise some self-confidence for once in my life? I understood the type of seclusion Tiberius desired, and would accept or reject the property accordingly. As for the financial arrangements: had I not come to comprehend domestic economics after auditing our household books all these years? He concluded with a precautionary reminder not to divulge information not absolutely necessary. And so with heart pounding and knees weak, my new himation drawn tightly over my head and face, leaning on Arbindus' arm I wobbled as hastily as I could across the veranda, and down the steps to the vehicle awaiting us in the back alley.

We encountered but one incident of heckling before reaching the city gate, when someone yelled out *Fie on you, Nero lover!* After an initial surge of panic—thinking I had been identified—I realized the jeer had been aimed at Thrasyllus whose carriage the perpetrator had recognized. In the dark, with the curtains of the vehicle drawn shut, I was not visible. After we had left the city and were on the road for a while, the sky began to lighten. As the scenery brightened gradually with the shades of dawn—first gray, then pink, and finally the yellowish white of new daylight—my spirits began to lift despite my nervousness. Having been housebound for months, I took pleasure from watching the passing countryside. The great rains that had fallen throughout the winter and early spring had broken the drought, and the refreshment of the land was evident everywhere in the verdant green of grass and trees and the riot of colors in abundant flowers.

Moreover I also found gratifying the discovery of nearby environs hitherto unseen. Although I had lived on Rhodes for six years and traveled abroad, I had never visited any area of the island apart from its namesake capital city. We passed little farmhouses that reminded me of my family's country retreat, and caused me to wonder whether I was about to investigate a similar misery. We also encountered the consequences of mudslides from the recent rains: trees toppled in an orchard, a small vineyard overrun, a house engulfed. I made a mental note of these devastations, for consideration when reviewing my prospective purchase.

Our destination was about eight miles from the city of Rhodes. We had to travel very slowly on the sinuous and sharply ascending road. It was consequently midday before the carriage turned off at the top of a rise. We proceeded through an iron gate in a stone fence, then along a pathway that ran through a fruit orchard. The carriage halted at the base of a natural promontory, where the broker was awaiting us with a saddled donkey. He introduced himself politely, thanked me for my interest in his offering, and extended his condolences for my (supposed) bereavement. After I thanked him for his sympathy, he commented that my widowhood at so young an age was certainly a terrible tragedy. I did not respond at all, but only smiled. My silence startled him for a moment. He collected himself, and proceeded to address the purpose of our encounter without any further digressions. Suddenly Tiberius' emphasis on not disclosing unnecessary information became for me an imperative, which I have endeavored to pursue scrupulously ever since. Not only does such silence prevent misrepresentation of one's intentions: it precludes waste of time, energy, and attention in business matters.

The main house atop the promontory was only accessible by a narrow and steep footpath, which the carriage could not negotiate. For this reason the broker had brought the donkey for my convenience. He assisted me as I settled onto the animal's back, helped poor nervous Alcmene climb up behind me, then led the beast up the path while Arbindus trudged gingerly along on foot. The outer edge of the path was fenced with rocks, to reduce the possibility of one slipping down the cliff to certain injury. Sections of the path where the gradient increased sharply were embedded with steps. Tiberius should appreciate this inaccessibility, as it must assuredly deter all but the most determined of visitors.

The surface of the promontory was level, and abundantly covered with tall shade trees. From a roofed veranda running along the front of the primary house, one could see the remainder of the property below. The farm consisted of seven fields extending over three natural terraces of varying heights. Three fields were currently devoted to crops, two to livestock, one to a vineyard, and the last to the orchard through which we had passed. The broker indicated a little collection of buildings where the six tenant families who worked the farm resided. He pointed out the acropolis of Rhodes gleaming in the distance. In an adjacent direction, a band of dark gray lay along the horizon: the sea. The little brown specks on its surface were ships.

Before proceeding to the interior of the primary residence, the broker showed us about the promontory. There were three outbuildings. One was a moderately sized barn. The second—much to my interest—was an unfinished guesthouse. Having expected to reap substantial profits from the farm, the broker explained, the previous owner had anticipated being able to provide lavish entertainments for numerous invitees. Perfect for housing the praetorians if sufficiently complete to serve as a barracks. The last building, located some distance from the others at the edge of a rise, housed a cistern fed by underground rivulets. The broker pointed out the small aqueducts, through which the water ran to the two residences. Dung was deposited on the far side of the barn, in a lean-to that housed a sunken stone basin. The resident farmhands regularly removed the contents for use as fertilizer.

Beyond the complex of buildings, paved walkways curved beneath the trees, past shrubs and statues. The promontory ended at an escarpment, the top of which marked the boundary of the property. Defensible, I thought: guards posted upon that ridge could see every possible approach to the place. The lush greenery and a pond hidden amid the trees attested to an abundance of water—the consequence of natural drainage from the escarpment. A much larger pond, dotted with waterfowl, was visible on a lower terrace. Recollecting the sights of the morning's journey, I asked the broker if the area was in danger of mudslides. To relieve my concern, he pointed out the surface soil on the promontory was well secured by trees, shrubs, and grasses. The buildings were all anchored in bedrock. They were set well enough back from the edge of the promontory so as not to be in danger from landslides, but also far enough forward of the rear ridge to be out of the way of falling rocks.

Main residence and guesthouse alike were architecturally unremarkable: single-storied rambling rectangles built about small open courtyards, each with a reflecting pool. In both edifices, every room opened onto a covered colonnade skirting the courtyard; however, many of the rooms also adjoined one another through interior doors. I asked the broker the reason for this particular feature. He explained that the coldness of the mountain air—particularly at night and during winter—chilled the interiors when the outside doors were opened, and made traversing from room to room through the courtyard colonnades uncomfortable for the occupants.

The primary house faced north. A broad veranda spread across the entire width of the building. Directly inside, dayrooms extended across the front on either side of the entryway and into the wings. The room on the northeast corner held an altar: it was the household shrine. Behind the shrine lay a parlor, and adjacent to that a library. Behind the library lay the master bedroom suite, which adjoined the female quarters. At the front of the west wing lay another parlor, behind it a dining room and serving pantry. Thereafter a jumble of rooms comprised the servant quarters and workrooms. Along the backside of the house—the bottom of the rectangle—the bath and privy lay to the east of the exit, the kitchen and servants' latrine and bath to the west.

The house appeared to be in sound physical condition, but was predictably dusty and stuffy from lack of occupation. Many of the rooms contained pieces of old furniture, most of which seemed rather dilapidated. The walls were unadorned: the previous owner had run out of money before he could arrange to have them painted. A perfect place and pretext, I thought, to display my own artwork. The rear of the building opened to a paved walkway which divided toward the various outbuildings. Beside the walk lay a kitchen garden, presently neglected and overgrown. The primary house had a kind of melancholy duskiness, being heavily shaded by the abundant trees and somewhat distant from the other buildings. In the city of Rhodes the very opposite of conditions— the scarcity of trees and the close proximity of the adjacent white houses—made everything artificially bright. The guesthouse turned out to be nearly complete. All it required to render it usable were interior doors, bath fixtures, and plastering of several interior walls.

The asking price for the property was 65 Greek gold talents—20,800,000 Roman sesterces—which struck me as reasonable. For a house the figure would have been hefty; but this was a farm. The broker assured me the amount comprised only what the creditors were seeking, plus his own commission: there was no impending profit for the owner or anyone else. Was this true, I began to wonder, or was he deceptively inflating the price? Would Tiberius regard this a sensible purchase or a swindle? Should I haggle? Would doing so induce the broker to lower the price, or merely delay the transaction while making me look stupid? More urgently: would Tiberius like the place? Was it adequately reclusive or excessively so? Would it satisfy his yearning for solitude, or make him feel trapped? Would he find it soothingly restful, or as depressing and mind-numbingly dull as my family's country home in Campania?

There was no time to ruminate. Tiberius wanted to quit the city as soon as possible. A quick and firm decision was in order. The farm was remote, inaccessible, and highly defensible. Its accommodations—particularly with that guesthouse—were peculiarly suited to our needs. I knew from auditing our household books that Tiberius had a cash reserve of just over 340,000 aurei—34,000,000 sesterces—on deposit at the bank in the city of Rhodes. Paying the entire price up front would straiten our coffers for a time; but they would rebound. A self-sustaining farm would preclude our need to purchase food. We no longer had the expense of renting the villa, now that its landlord had revoked our lease. The regular income from Tiberius' Italian and Gallic estates would continue unaffected. I asked the broker about the property taxes on the farm. To my pleasant surprise they turned out to be a single talent—320,000 sesterces—per year. The annual rent on the townhouse we were about to surrender had been 1¼ talents—400,000 sesterces.

Hoping to sound straightforwardly businesslike, I offered the broker the entire asking price in cash—on condition the guesthouse be finished, any necessary repairs made to the main house and barn, all three buildings cleared of debris and old furnishings and along with the cistern thoroughly cleaned. He promptly accepted my offer; whereupon I felt as though the breeze might topple me. Managing to maintain my composure, I averred my curator would contact him to finalize the arrangements on my behalf. The broker bowed in acknowledgment.

After Alcmene and I had availed ourselves of the latrine in the guesthouse—which, the broker advised us, was unused and hence far cleaner than the one in the main residence—we clambered aboard the donkey for the descent to our carriage. By now it was late afternoon: the sun was nearing the western horizon. Would it be dark, I wondered, by the time we reached the city? Although I had not eaten all day I was still not hungry, and encouraged Alcmene to share with Arbindus and the carriage driver my portion of the provisions she had brought. As the carriage began its slow, winding descent toward the coast, I fell asleep.

When Alcmene roused me, I found the carriage parked before the home of Thrasyllus. The driver had brought us here because he had received clear instructions not to approach Tiberius' residence before dark. Although the sun had set the twilight was lingering, for this was the time of year in which the days were lengthening. Engulfing myself in my himation I rushed inside, where Thrasyllus greeted me with somber mien. When Aka continued unable to deliver, the midwife had summoned a physician. After drugging his patient with opium, he had sliced her belly open to extract the baby, and then sutured the incision closed. The child—a boy—was stillborn. He was seriously deformed: his body was misshapen, and one of his legs incomplete below the knee. In response to the condolences I immediately expressed, Thrasyllus said he and Aka were naturally saddened. Nevertheless they were relieved the child did not survive: for certain he had been spared a life of abject misery. Thrasyllus took me to visit Aka. She was awake and in considerable pain from her wound, to which the midwife was applying a salve. Like Thrasyllus she was chagrined but palliated. After reiterating my sympathies and admonishing Aka to follow the physician's instructions carefully for her recovery, I retired with Thrasyllus to his library.

He asked if I should like something to eat, and if he should have my servants fed as well. Both offers I accepted readily and gratefully. As Tiberius had predicted, I was starting to develop a headache from my daylong fast; and I was concerned that Arbindus and Alcmene had partaken of nothing more than the basket in the carriage. After I finished describing my mission and its outcome, Thrasyllus remarked the price I had accepted seemed rather high for a property in foreclosure. My heart sank; and I buried my face in my hands. Noting my reaction, Thrasyllus reminded me not to condemn myself. As Tiberius was in a hurry to move, we lacked the luxury of time to be more selective; so clearly I had taken the best course of action under the circumstances. Thrasyllus affirmed he would gladly serve as curator for this transaction, especially since Aka's horoscope had revealed she was free from danger. Now relieved of this anxiety, he could devote attention to other matters without distraction.

He cast my horoscope while I dined on sole fish and turnips. All at once he raised his eyebrows, looked up at me and smiled. In tones hushed and earnest, he said, "Clytia, that monumental change, predicted to bring you phenomenal joy, will occur in your new domicile before a year has passed."

Journeying homeward after dark, I peered at the night sky as much as I could around the edges of my himation and the drawn curtains of Thrasyllus' carriage. No meteor appeared to validate the forecast he had made about my momentous change. Perhaps there was no reason, I thought as I hurried across the veranda with one eye still on the heavens. The prediction had been made some time ago; all Thrasyllus had done this evening was detect the time of its fulfillment. What event, I wondered, was going to bring me phenomenal joy? I made up my mind not to speculate, as doing so would only unnerve me at the very time my partner most needed unruffled calm. Besides, I was worried enough about his reaction to my new acquisition.

Tiberius had no interest in hearing a detailed discourse about the farm: he had every confidence I had made a suitable selection. He was excited over news he had received from his mother during my excursion. Despite misgivings about Gaius' youth and lack of experience in public affairs, Augustus had decided to send his grandson upon an immensely delicate diplomatic mission. The primary purpose of the junket was to reestablish the Roman vassal government in Armenia, and at the same time placate Parthia about that intervention. Additionally Gaius was going to negotiate with the Nabataean Arabs, to secure the unmolested passage of trade caravans from the Orient to Roman markets in Syria and Egypt. Already the senate had invested Gaius with a special extraordinary military command. At present Augustus was selecting an elite council of advisers for the junket. On the forthcoming Calends of July Gaius would espouse Tiberius' niece Livilla, so he might proceed with the dignity of a married man. (The nuptials could not occur any earlier, Tiberius explained, because Italians consider May and June unlucky months for weddings.) Toward the middle of that same month, Livia anticipated, the prince and his entourage should be underway.

To reach their destination, Gaius and his company must put in at or at least pass near Rhodes. The protocols of public office demanded Tiberius, who as legate exercised an official appointment subordinate to that of Gaius, pay his respects to the latter. If this meeting resulted in reconciliation, then perchance Augustus would yield as well and allow Tiberius' return to Rome. No, no, my efforts to procure the farm had not been a waste: we were still going to move there. The meeting with Gaius was yet several months off; and there was no guarantee either he or Augustus was going to relent.

At breakfast the morning following, Tiberius did not care to hear me describe or defend my purchase any more than he had the night before. What was done was done; he must accept my decision; would I ever stop trying to justify it? Testy, I thought—not surprising in view of his present circumstances. He left to meet with Galen and receive several callers. I went upstairs to my suite, where I busied myself sketching scenes of the farm. When I displayed these to my partner that afternoon, he reacted more irritably than he had to my verbal representations. Why did I persist in sedulously soliciting his unqualified approval of my selection, when I ought to be putting my time and energies to better use? Had I made arrangements for furnishing and stocking the place; or was I expecting us to sleep on bare floors and dine on rabbits and weeds?

Feeling like an abject fool in the wake of this reprimand, I meekly put away my pencils and palettes. Then I summoned Menon and ordered him to inventory anew all the contents of the townhouse, differentiating items that belonged to the owner from those we had purchased ourselves or which Eurycles had obtained on our behalf. Even if the acquisition of this farm failed and we had to find a different retreat, we still needed to identify what we should eventually take with us and what we must relinquish. Next I prepared a memorandum for the broker, revising my offer. Although I still wanted both houses put in repair and thoroughly cleaned, I would not require removal of the abandoned furniture. Instead I asked that the kitchen garden be tilled and planted with edibles, and the main residence supplied with sufficient grain, oil, salt, and charcoal to sustain ten occupants for one month. To demand the guesthouse be similarly stocked seemed excessive, and was unnecessary anyway. There was no need to provide for the praetorians, who had their own military rations.

Tiberius had sent Galen with a trio of praetorians to the bank, to retrieve the funds for the purchase. Far simpler would have been for the bankers to transfer the sum from Tiberius' assets to those of the broker; but that would have revealed the purpose of the transaction. Undoubtedly the bankers were speculating about the reason for this substantial withdrawal; but since Galen had not disclosed that reason, there was nothing they could do besides speculate. Late in that night, under the protection of darkness, Thrasyllus arrived to collect the money chest with two armed menservants of his own. I entrusted him with my new terms for the sale, and admonished him not to forget to present them. His meeting with the broker was scheduled for the day after the morrow. The stars portended a favorable outcome.

For the entire next day I took care not to mention the farm at all, and passed the hours reviewing Menon's inventory. He presented it to me in installments because he had completed it room by room. How, I wondered as I read the lists, had we managed to accumulate so many articles in the few years we had lived on Rhodes? I was glad to have this project, for it kept my mind off my impending purchase as well as my grumpy lover. From Menon's catalogue I created three of my own: the landlord's belongings which we must leave behind, essentials we must bring with us, and uncertainties we needed to think about and decide whether we truly required them. The donation of unwanted but usable items to charity might serve to improve Tiberius' public image.

Undeterred by the inevitable execrations from passersby, Thrasyllus arrived the following morning. I was half expecting him to say, that in reaction to my new requirements the broker had postponed the closing or rejected my offering altogether. Instead he handed me a small scroll: the contract of sale with acceptance of all my specific requirements. The broker' name was Meriones. He had duly signed the document on behalf of the creditors whose names were listed, as had Thrasyllus as curator for the woman known as the Widow Galatea Aristoclide of Alexandria. Beneath was the attestation of Chares, a civic scribe, to the validity of the signatures.

Thrasyllus laughed and Tiberius rolled his eyes, when I displayed my relief that the business was over by slumping in my chair. "May I never, *ever* have to assume such a burden again!"

"You may have to," Tiberius said seriously.

"What?" I sat upright at once.

"Clytia, you know I will make every necessary effort to ensure we remain together until we have fulfilled our marital year come August. Nevertheless, eventual separation has been predicted for us."

He shot a glance at Thrasyllus who raised his eyebrows. In quiet confidence the sage asserted, "The monumental change impending for Tiberius will create occasions when you must separate one from another." I closed my eyes and grimaced as my heart turned to stone.

"When these separations occur," Tiberius continued, "you could face decisions of great importance to your life and the lives of others—alone and independently, without advice or assistance from anyone. I seized this opportunity—the purchase of a homestead—to prepare you with firsthand experience in completing a significant transaction entirely by yourself. And my dearest, you carried it off admirably."

"How can you say I did so, when you have not laid eyes on the place?" I retorted, still devastated over the prospect of separation. "Do you not at least want to investigate it before I transfer ownership to you?"

"And run the risk of being seen, and having my intention to retreat there known before I care to unmask it? I read the cursory description of the property in the bill of sale, and am well satisfied. Clytia, after my stepfather appoints a legate to govern a province, does he travel there to inspect firsthand the outcome of every action that man takes? He relies upon the appointee's expertise and ability to execute the responsibilities of the office. Since I trust your judgment, why do you persist in doubting it? You know my tastes in housing and furnishings; you understand my financial condition; you are well aware of our present need for heightened seclusion; and you realize we must provide accommodations for our servants and for the praetorians. You took all of these elements into careful consideration before making your decision—which, I am fully confident was sound." Tiberius turned to Thrasyllus. "Here you see the result of being told all your life, that every decision you make is wrong and a cause of irreparable harm and hardship to others." He looked again at me. "Now answer me forthrightly, Clytia: do you like the property? Does it suit your tastes?"

"Why...er...yes...does my opinion really matter?" His question puzzled me.

"It matters immensely, because there will be no transfer of ownership. In this time of uncertainty and turmoil, I crave the comfort of knowing I have secured for you a source of sustenance and shelter—a refuge in which you can remain without fear of eviction when those times of separation come upon us."

I sat in stunned silence.

"A beautiful gift, Clytia," Thrasyllus said.

"I am at a loss for words," I murmured. My eyes began to brim with tears.

"All you need to say is *Thank you*," the astrologer returned gently.

"That sounds so hopelessly inadequate." The tears trickled down my face and fell onto my bosom.

Tiberius was sitting with his arms folded, staring reflectively at the floor. "Another childhood anguish. No matter how many professions of gratitude she offered, no matter how profound and profuse, they were never sufficient. I know you are grateful, Clytia—I know."

Early in the afternoon Tiberius conferred with Selvinius, the commandant of the praetorians, about readying the guards for relocation. Lest Selvinius be tempted to noise about that Tiberius was sharing his personal business with a courtesan, I remained in my suite reviewing Menon's inventory. Later in the day, Tiberius summoned me to the library along with all of our servants. Did any of them have private commitments in the city that the move stood to affect? The consensus was no: everyone welcomed the prospect of escaping the jeers and shuns. Nicanor admitted he would miss seeing his daughter who belonged to our neighbors, but was content her owners were happy with her and had sanctioned her union with one of their menservants.

Arbindus remained, however, after the others had departed. With lowered eyes he sheepishly confessed to a reservation he had about leaving the city. He had fallen in love with a Gallic maiden. Although a slave in one of the brothels Arbindus frequented, she was not a prostitute there but a skillful practitioner of healing arts. Tiberius raised his eyebrows and nodded with interest. Owing to the purchase of the farm, he said, his finances were presently straitened. Once they improved he would see about acquiring the girl. Her particular abilities should prove invaluable to us in our new isolation, precluding our need to engage an independent physician or pharmakeutria who might spread gossip. Arbindus sank to his knees, seized Tiberius' right hand and pressed it to his forehead. After he departed, Tiberius wondered aloud to me whether the bordellos of Rhodes would ever recover financially from the loss of this particularly avid customer.

With April came the usual spring showers and more complaining: now that the drought had broken, enough rain was enough. In the fourth week of the month, Thrasyllus sent word he had heard from the broker: the requirements I had specified were now complete. Tiberius dispatched Selvinius and Menon to assess the condition of the property. Both returned with favorable reports. Although minimally finished, the guesthouse indeed made a viable barracks; the guards could add any improvements they deemed necessary. Guesthouse and main house alike had been stocked with provisions, and their courtyards decorated with potted plants. This was presumably a gesture from the broker and his creditor clients to indicate my terms had pleased them, for I had requested supplies only for the main residence. Practically all of that old furniture turned out to be of high quality, and salvageable once cleaned and repaired. There was even a perfectly functioning clepsydra. The kitchen garden had been tilled and duly planted, for seedlings were emerging from the ruptured soil.

Having noted beetles and field mice creeping through the grass and under bushes, Menon recommended we retrieve Leo and his family and bring them with us. Tiberius promptly rejected this suggestion. As he did not want a clowder getting under the feet of the praetorians and their horses and distracting their dogs, only male cats should be allowed. Now I interjected: I did not want Leo parted from Nivea, but preferred he be left behind in her company and under Proceles' care. Tiberius agreed: to separate Leo and Nivea would be unkind. He told Menon to have Proceles select three young males not yet breeding and transport them to the farm.

Our menservants began to take our belongings in batches, loaded into a small, roofed wagon that Proceles brought. He came sometimes by day and at others by night—without any set pattern to his arrivals and departures—to create the impression these movements were random activities of our household staff. Once they had arrived at the farm, Menon, Androcles, Ajax and Nicanor remained there to put the house in order. Menon took Miranda with him, lest she get underfoot as we finalized the arrangements for our departure.

Tiberius insisted we depart as soon as Menon sent word he had a bed ready for us to sleep in. By now it was the first week of May. On the eve of the Nones, toward the end of the first watch, Proceles delivered the new carriage and horses Tiberius had asked him to purchase. A rather heavy drizzle was falling. That it was keeping people off the streets—and hence reducing the possibility of our being recognized—amply compensated for making our journey difficult. We took Phoebe, Arbindus and three of the praetorians with us. Nestor, Alcmene, and another praetorian remained behind to ensure the balance of our belongings was sent to the farm, the items we had indicated for charity dispatched to the civic authorities, and the townhouse left in orderly condition for surrender to its owner. To our relief there were no jeers: that meant no one recognized us. Around the beginning of the third watch we arrived at the base of the promontory, where Nicanor, Ajax, and yet another praetorian were awaiting us with torches. Our servants had learned from my encounter with the broker: they had brought a donkey to accommodate Phoebe and me.

On reaching the house we discovered Menon had our bath and bed waiting. Tiberius fell asleep immediately; but for a long time I lay awake despite my intense fatigue. At last the entire business of acquiring and moving to the farm was over. I found myself at once loving and hating the estate—loving it as the first significant possession I had ever owned, and as the patent symbol of my partner's tender love for me and concern for my wellbeing—but hating it for evoking the familial and public misunderstanding and contempt from which it now shielded him, and the impending separations during which it was to be my shelter. Hardly did I want to end up loathing the place as I did my parents' retreat in Campania. At length I decided one way to express the greatest excellence within oneself is to plan for the future insofar as one can anticipate the course it might take, but neither to fret about it nor seek to address its problems until they become part of the present. Slumber followed.

On the morrow I placed Melambrotus' cloth on the altar in the household shrine. This act did not commemorate any established religious ceremony. It was simply my way of acknowledging my ownership, of the house and the farm in which it stood.

"Clytia, I feel as though we have retreated into a pastoral idyll," Tiberius drawled several mornings later while we breakfasted on the veranda. "Although I cannot make out its details, the sheer expanse of this vista is making me feel as though I had been suffocating and am now relieved."

Idyllic our new environs certainly seemed, in comparison to those we had left behind. After half a year of confinement to the interior of our former townhouse, we now had a covered veranda on which we could sit no matter what the weather. We had a park through which we strolled, exchanging furtive caresses or kisses in those fleeting moments when we could be certain no guard was eyeing us. The promontory was sufficiently spacious and flat for Tiberius to canter about on Sinapeus. At dusk, deer and wild pigs emerged. With clear mountain air and the absence of city lights, more stars were visible in the night skies than either of us could ever recall viewing—except for what I remembered from the excursion to Campania on my eighth birthday, that final occasion on which my father showed me any affection or respect.

To my profound relief we no longer had praetorians stationed inside the house. Tiberius had Androcles or Arbindus attend him whenever he received callers, unless he felt a particular need to show a praetorian presence. Selvinius had decided horse patrols offered the best type of protection for the promontory. He procured six steeds, for which his guards constructed a partially roofed pen because the barn could not hold them all. Foot sentries were kept on duty as well. Four patrolled the complex of buildings—house, barn and guesthouse. A single guard stood at the base of the ascent to the promontory. Here the praetorians erected a booth, to protect the hapless guardian assigned to this position from the elements. Each pair of foot guards kept a mastiff with them, as did their fellow at the promontory base and some of the horse guards. There were five dogs in all.

Several days after our arrival, Proceles brought Alcmene and Nestor with the remainder of our belongings. These of course had to be unloaded from the carriage at the base of the promontory and then transported up the ascent, heaped upon the shoulders of our menservants or on the backs of Sinapeus, the carriage horses, or the donkey to whom we gave the utterly unoriginal name of Asellus. The final delivery consisted of three baskets, which Proceles set down on the floor of the courtyard. "At your request, Lord Tiberius, I brought only males," he said.

"Well done! Their purpose here is to control vermin, not reproduce."

"Proceles, how fare Nivea and Leo?" I inquired.

"Happy and well, Lady." *The hand of eternal Underlying Good,* I mused: my pet cats had been provided for in a way I had not considered.

From the first basket emerged a cat with Leo's burnished gold on his back and face, but Nivea's white on his underbelly and legs. The cat from the second basket was entirely yellow, with alternating stripes of darker and paler hues of that color. The third cat proved to be as black as Nivea was white. He had Leo's golden eyes, a minute sprinkling of white—no more than a nuance—on his chest, and white tips on the two central toes of his left hind foot. "Whence this one?" I asked Proceles. "Surely not from Nivea."

"From Leo's other lady, my mother's pet Anthrakia," Proceles replied.

Tiberius' murmur, "That unabashed bigamist!" set me to giggling.

The cats surveyed their new surroundings with nervous apprehension, shoulders hunched, hissing at any human who approached them. Presently they darted into the shadows of different corners in the courtyard.

Eventually all three cats established territories, and settled into the routine for which they had been brought to the farm. The gold and white cat took over the guesthouse where he befriended the praetorians—and much to their delight. They named their new housemate Imperator and treated him to tidbits from their rations. The black cat, whom the praetorians aptly called Carbo, laid claim to the barn—utterly undeterred by the fact the mastiffs lodged there. The dogs quite quickly discovered that any of them who harassed the newcomer could expect to have his nose perforated. When off-duty mastiffs were out and about, Carbo would jump onto a low-hanging tree branch or atop the roof to the horse pen. There he would sit, just out of reach of the dogs, while they barked and howled to the point of frenzy until a human intervened.

The third cat ensconced himself in the kitchen and adjacent storage rooms, and became fast friends with Phoebe. Within days of establishing his domain he captured the vole that had been ravaging the kitchen garden, and presented it to Phoebe dangling from his mouth. She named him Xanthrothix for the color of his coat.

Galen terminated his secretarial services, as we suspected he might. It was not that he feared adverse consequences from associating with Tiberius. He had simply determined he would expend more time and effort traveling to and from the farm, than in keeping his client's calendar and taking his dictations. These tasks fell upon me for a week or so, until Tiberius was able to replace Galen with a military stenographer who lodged with the praetorians. I only knew him by his praenomen of Quintus. He took care of Tiberius' correspondence and appointments relevant solely to the legature. All private matters I must handle, lest Quintus spread gossip among his fellows.

Since our carriage could not ascend the promontory, Menon had arranged for its storage with the farm's resident slaves, in their compound on the lower terrace. They also cared for our new carriage horses, whom they promptly designated Karyon and Plinthus for their coat colors after learning we had not named them. Menon had introduced himself to these workers shortly after his initial arrival on the estate—well before that of Tiberius and me. At that time he told them their new owner had leased the property to a highly placed functionary of the Roman government, who was under the protection of special military guards because his official responsibilities were covert. As a result the promontory was strictly forbidden to the farmhands. They remained responsible for working the farm and harvesting its produce. Menon or one of his fellow servants would visit their compound weekly, to oversee the workers' activities and to hear and discuss matters of concern to them. Any emergencies requiring immediate attention the farmhands should report to the guard at the base of the ascent. The manure on which the farmhands depended would be shoved off the promontory at a designated place far from the dwellings, into a natural trench which would neatly contain this necessity.

As the group disbanded, its leader—whom Menon described as a little old man with withered skin, white hair, perspicacious brown eyes and an earnest smile—called him aside. By chance was the Roman official to whom Menon had referred, Tiberius Nero? After Menon trepidatiously returned an affirmation, the chief reassured him that his master could rely upon the farmhands' loyalty and discretion. Ordinarily they welcomed a new owner or tenant with a feast, which they carried up the promontory unannounced as a surprise. In this case, however, they would refrain. Instead they hoped Tiberius would accept a cask of the estate's finest wine, produced from the vineyard's premier grapes and cellared in reserve until mellowed to the point of perfection.

"Ingenuous Rhodian hospitality," Tiberius mused as he examined the container of wine. "How refreshing to find we have not lost it entirely." He ordered Menon to summon Quintus. After dictating a brief note of thanks for the wine he affixed his signet to the tablet, and ordered Quintus to deliver it to the farmhands. Quintus later described the reception he had received. The workers bowed and prostrated themselves before him, with obeisance Augustus himself would have rejected as excessive. Since no one in the group was literate, Quintus had to read the message aloud. Everyone listened raptly as though to a sermon. Afterward they passed the tablet about, handling it with the reverence due a sacred object and observing the hound signet as though it were the mark of a divinity. In the end the chief appropriated the tablet. Then he led his fellows in a solemn procession to his house, where he placed the tablet upon a special shelf that held his most honored possessions.

Despite the friendliness of the farm workers, Tiberius would not accept provisions from them beyond what they had placed in the house in anticipation of our arrival. He was afraid to rely upon the farmhands for our sustenance. Once word had spread he was occupying the estate, what was to prevent some enemy from distracting or deceiving the workers and then poisoning our food? We would obtain our supplies through the military rationing system, from markets in the neighboring city of Ialyssos where nobody knew our servants, and of course from our own kitchen garden. Menon did acquire from the farmhands—and housed in the barn—a clutch of chickens for eggs, a nanny goat for milk, and a domestic pig to consume kitchen refuse. For meat the fields and orchard offered plenteous game, which the praetorians and our menservants—particularly Nicanor—started to hunt with pleasure. On learning the farmworkers had a hound bitch recently delivered of a litter, Nicanor requested and was duly promised two male pups upon weaning: these he would train as hunting dogs. The promontory pond abounded with turtles and small fish which the servants and guards netted, and which I adamantly refused to angle despite my partner's bantering encouragement. Too many memories of miserable endless days in Campania were associated with this activity.

We had Menon advise the farm workers their new absentee owner— the Widow Galatea allegedly of Alexandria, from whom Tiberius *leased* the property—wanted any harvest revenues which exceeded the workers' own needs and the farm's annual tax obligation set aside, to enable purchase of necessities and payment of taxes in times of harvest failure. Menon would audit this fund quarterly. Originally I had suggested the workers be allowed to keep these profits for themselves. Although he extolled its altruism, Tiberius rejected my notion. So unusual a display of generosity might engender speculative gossip and encourage reckless squandering. Moreover should we ever find ourselves forced to depend upon provisions from the workers, having to forfeit gains to which they had become accustomed could induce resentment and diminish morale. One intrepid farmhand inquired why the taxes were being taken from the harvest income, rather than from the rent Tiberius was presumed to be paying. Menon deftly lied that the owner was using the rental monies to pay the mortgage she had taken on the property. The real reason was to ensure the self-sufficiency of the farm, lest some untoward event obstruct our access to Tiberius' assets.

Once all of our possessions had been delivered and accounted for, I embarked upon the pleasant task of arranging furnishings and decorations. The furniture salvaged from the farm's previous owner, when combined with that transported from the townhouse, proved more than sufficient to fill our new residence. The excess I had placed in the guesthouse for the praetorians, and for use in the three rooms of this building that lay closest to the bath. Tiberius had insisted the guards leave this area vacant—reserved to accommodate any visitors who could not arrive and leave on the same day. The praetorians lived barracks-style, crammed together into their allotted space with just enough room to pass by one another.

After I started to hang my paintings on the walls of the main house, I discovered to my great delight that its gray light subdued my variegated and brilliant colors and gave them depth. They had always inclined toward a shallow and garish appearance in the paler light of the townhouse. Some of the walls remained bare: there were not enough pictures to decorate them all. *A most welcome incentive to create more.*

Our new isolation effectively deterred hecklers, as well as those equally if not more aggravating well-wishers—they who invariably showed up uninvited and unannounced, precisely when Tiberius was trying to belittle the strength and visibility of his political following. Anyone presently seeking an appointment was given to understand he must negotiate the promontory's arduous ascent. Every hour or so, one of the mounted praetorians descended the promontory to determine whether any visitors were awaiting audience. Tiberius sent Arbindus or one of the other menservants to meet approved callers at the base and assist them on the climb. For those unable to negotiate the path on foot the servants brought Asellus.

Now that we had made reaching us so difficult, our visitors were either government functionaries bringing administrative issues or respects to Tiberius as imperial legate, or genuine friends who refused to let our inaccessibility deter them. During that June—the very first full month of our occupancy— two civilian and four military officials applied for appointments. Thrasyllus showed up after the first week. Marinus subsequently came one afternoon and stayed the night in the guest quarters. We spent most of his visit discussing Herodotus' voluminous and rambling history of the war between Greece and Persia. Thrasyllus returned on the summer solstice with his family, for an outing thoroughly enjoyed by all. Tiberius set Thrasylla and Miranda astride Asellus. Then he and Thrasyllus led the donkey along the paths of the park, conversing as best they could while Miranda smiled and Thrasylla squealed with delight. Aka and I sat beneath the trees and chatted about pleasant trivialities. Our visitors brought a much appreciated gift of fresh red mullet from the fish market of Rhodes: seafood like mullet and swordfish was the one commodity the farm could not supply. The fish from the pond were freshwater types like perch and catfish. We thought them flavorless; however our guests had never savored them and were quite interested. So after a dinner of mullet and perch and fresh greens on the veranda, the adults remained to sit and talk and admire the view. An off-duty praetorian brought one of the mastiffs to romp with the children until departure time arrived.

Quiet walks through the park; stargazing; appreciation for Rhodian country folk; amusement from cats and dogs; entertaining children; a definite increase in our sexual activity—all these were signs Tiberius was beginning to feel the calm and emotional peace he had hoped to claim from our new environs. Nevertheless the undercurrent of distress engendered by Tiberius' precarious political position sullied our tranquility. This unease began to increase with the approach of July. The Calends, upon which Gaius would wed Livilla, was now imminent. Gaius' birthday was also forthcoming in mid-July. Did we have suitable gift offerings? I suggested the ebony and ivory gaming board I had acquired in Alexandria: the new couple could enjoy it during their forthcoming journey. After all within a few weeks of his nuptials, Gaius would embark upon his excursion to the East.

As July progressed, Tiberius began to fret again in somber, brooding quietude. Often he sat on the veranda staring into the distance without uttering a word—or in the library, staring in silence at the floor or out the window. During our strolls through the park he walked with head lowered and shoulders hunched, to appearances paying no heed either to me or to our surroundings. He must meet with Gaius during the latter's forthcoming junket. What would the consequences be, should that interview fail to resolve the conflict surrounding them?

Apart from playing my harp I made little overt effort to cheer or otherwise distract Tiberius, sensing he craved my nearness and constancy, my unspoken reassurance of devotion and support. Finally—during the later days of the month that are invariably the hottest of the year—a message arrived from Marcus Lollius, Gaius' chief of staff. Their party was due to reach the military station at Chios around the Nones of August, and Tiberius was expected to attend Gaius there. To evade detection Tiberius departed in the dead of night from the harbor of Ialyssos, where he would not be identified as readily as in the city of Rhodes. He took Ajax as his valet, Arbindus and Androcles as bodyguards instead of praetorians; for a gift, another cask of the wine produced on the farm. Tiberius wanted Gaius and his retinue to perceive him as a harmless private citizen, his legature a hollow title rather than command position with potential to challenge the authority of his superior.

I expected Tiberius to be away for well over a week. On the very day of his departure I plunged into painting, to distract myself from worrying as much as to generate adornments for the empty walls of our house. His absence gave me a welcome opportunity to complete some more work on my lovers series without the risk of his seeing it. I also scrutinized my new surroundings for models: the vista from the veranda of the house, the hulking rise of the escarpment behind our promontory, the trees of the park, the promontory pond, and the endless variations shifting light and shadow wrought upon them. I contemplated turtles on the pond's edge, ducks and wild geese on its surface, horses, dogs, cats, chickens, goat, pig, servants, and praetorians. One afternoon I sketched a guard while he was grooming the horses in the pen. When I gave him the finished product, he wondered aloud whether Tiberius Nero knew and appreciated that he had so talented a ward. His fellows, however, insisted the rendering was inaccurate because it was insufficiently ugly.

Walking through the park one day after a thunderstorm, I came across a trio of trees upon which the intense afternoon sun was falling. The leaves of each tree differed significantly from those of its companions, in shape, texture, and shade of green. The middle tree had white flowers, which glistened with a silvery patina from the recent rain. The gray backdrop of the receding rainclouds seemed to enhance the vibrancy of the sunlit trees. I painted several versions, each of which emphasized a different aspect—the golden highlights of the sunlight, the silvery sheen of the raindrops, the contrasting hues and textures of the leaves and blossoms, the luminosity of the trees against the dark sky. They seemed somehow protective, almost like guardians—reminders that Eternal Good underlay the superficial pain and chaos of our lives.

How I had hated those vacations in Campania! Yet now I was finding in our present placid serenity a welcome respite after five very frenetic years. In that short time I had grown extraordinarily in personal character, learned deportment and poise, discovered artistic and musical abilities I never realized I possessed, developed a friendship with one of the world's greatest intellectuals, learned to manage a household, engaged in philanthropy, traveled—and above all, established a wondrously satisfying and enduring relationship with a mate. It felt good to step back and be still, to slow one's pace of life amid scenery suggestive of languor. Granted I could no longer pursue one of my favorite pastimes—that of combing the markets for textiles—but this restriction led to a new avocation. I started sorting through my now sizable collection, evaluating the unique characteristics and potential uses of its contents—taking careful note of colors, textures, weaves, and dimensions. How might each piece best be utilized—as a garment, a tablecloth or bed covering, a wall hanging?

At last I was starting to appreciate why my family had valued their Campanian sojourns so highly. From those very conditions I had considered so miserable, they had derived the same sort of relief I was taking from my present circumstances. While my idea of respite is to engage in activities I especially enjoy, theirs had been to shut down one's mind completely. And as I pondered these notions, I suddenly realized I started to fulfill a goal Thrasyllus had urged upon me, and which I had despaired of ever attaining. At last I was beginning to feel some forgiveness toward my family, if only for the duress I had endured during their insipid Campanian retreats.

The lovers' vignettes I could not complete, because Tiberius arrived home sooner than I had anticipated. I was sitting on the veranda, fortuitously working on one of the tree tableaux. Without even looking at me, let alone saying something or bestowing a kiss, he settled dejectedly into the chair beside me and stared at the floor. I did not speak either but continued to paint for a while. Eventually I reached over and took his hand. He looked at me and smiled slightly. Then he glumly shook his head, sighed, and began his narrative.

Gaius had received Tiberius respectfully and even quite cordially. During several private dinners, Gaius and Livilla brought Tiberius up to date on family news and gossip. They thanked him effusively for the gaming board, of which they made assiduous use during these informal encounters. Tiberius also had three serious interviews with Gaius, during which Tiberius endeavored to assuage Gaius' concerns about Tiberius' political aspirations. For a time Tiberius could not comprehend the antipathy Gaius bore him, because the prince—like his mother Julia—spoke in vagaries and evasions. Eventually Tiberius perceived, that although Gaius continued to resent his former stepfather's retirement to Rhodes as a precipitating cause of Julia's corruption, the prince had no desire to breach amicitia. Furthermore, Gaius insisted he entertained no fears Tiberius would initiate efforts to undermine Gaius' authority or challenge him for the succession.

Gaius nevertheless remained leery of Tiberius' political following. Were Tiberius to return to Rome, surely his supporters would organize about him. There could emerge a well-defined opposition party, poised to impugn, weaken, and potentially even dethrone Gaius. Tiberius attempted to offer reassurance: he would personally suppress any such endeavors, and renounce his own adherence to any retainer who indicated hostility toward Gaius. The prince remained unconvinced. Tiberius may find he could not stand alone against the collective will of his following, especially if they were prepared to use military force to achieve their intentions. Gaius dreaded the prospect of discovering his only means of halting this opposition was to seek Tiberius' life.

The entourage moved on to Samos—the next stop in their itinerary—with Tiberius in the company. Here Gaius hosted a banquet for his entire staff. The atmosphere fairly crackled with tension as one after another, members of the group baited Tiberius with potentially incriminating insinuations. If he intended to live on Rhodes strictly as a private citizen, why upon expiration of the regency did he promptly accept from Augustus an imperial legature—an office with military authority? Why did he employ praetorian guards? Had he sequestered himself in the countryside to render his activities difficult to monitor? Why did he readily receive visits from government officers both civilian and military? Why was he actively fraternizing on Rhodes, not only with two formerly significant members of his own military staff but—even more alarmingly—with an astrologer? Was he set upon determining the futures of Gaius and his brother Lucius, and exploiting that information to wrest the succession from them?

Gaius' chief of staff endeavored to intervene, reminding the company this was a convivial occasion and not an inquisition. Nevertheless, the harassment did not abate. At length Tiberius arose from the dining couch on which he had been reclining in considerable discomfort. Fighting his revulsion for displays of emotion, he sank to his knees with arms outstretched and palms turned upward. Before all present he swore that he harbored no designs on the succession, and that Gaius and Lucius could rest assured of his unflagging loyalty. He then left the hall for his quarters, vomited up what little he had eaten, and ordered his servants to prepare for immediate departure on the very next monotreme bound in the direction of Rhodes. Why, he wondered with despair, did Gaius neglect to put a stop to his staff's besetments?

And so in an atmosphere sullied with despondency and concern we made preparations to celebrate, on my birthday, the fulfillment of our nuptial year. Although Tiberius had wanted to keep our marriage secret from the servants so they could not be forced to disclose it, he nonetheless decided to engage Menon as a second witness beside Thrasyllus. The attestation of a single man cannot be corroborated; the testimonies of two automatically confirm one another. Menon and Phoebe both swore, before the altar in our household shrine, to respect and maintain the secrecy of our espousal.

Thrasyllus arrived with his family the preceding afternoon: they spent the night in the guesthouse. In the morning I awoke not feeling entirely well, but achy and oddly sloshy as though I had swallowed a great quantity of liquid. Before long I discovered the cause of my affliction. For the first time in nearly a year, I had started to menstruate. I recalled noting a few days earlier, an unusual distension to my abdomen and some acne eruptions on my face, but had forgotten about these in the excitement of the forthcoming event.

Despite my physical duress, I was eager to participate in the ceremony Thrasyllus had prepared. Having cast the horoscope that morning, he assured us the stars were favorable. At noon our wedding party assembled in the shrine. Phoebe stood guard at the door. From a linen satchel Aka drew a red wedding veil, which she draped over my head and shoulders. Already on the altar were a covered basket, an empty basin, a bowl of water, a towel, and a large knife with a silver handle. The implements rested upon Melambrotus' altar cloth.

Our rite followed the simple Roman formula. From the basket Thrasyllus removed a white hen which Tiberius sacrificed upon the altar, catching the blood in the basin. Slicing open the belly, Thrasyllus determined the alignment of the entrails was normal and hence the auspices for our occasion favorable. Both rinsed their hands in the bowl of water and dried them on the towel. The sacrificial victim would later be removed to the kitchen for roasting. Its consumption was an acknowledgment of the gods' provision for mankind.

Thrasyllus produced two rolls of parchment, each of which bore the same set of inscriptions:

I, Tiberius Claudius Nero, do solemnly aver—on this fourteenth day before the Calends of September in the seven hundred fifty third year since the founding of Rome—that the woman Clytia Eupistide has resided in my domicile for an entire year without absence; and I hereby declare her my legal but morganatic wedded wife.

I, Clytia Eupistide, do solemnly aver—on this fourteenth day before the Calends of September in the seven hundred fifty third year since the founding of Rome—that having resided in the domicile of Tiberius Claudius Nero for an entire year without absence, I willingly give myself to him in morganatic marriage, renouncing for myself and my descendants any rights or privileges associated with his patrimony.

I, Thrasyllus Balbilusides, of freeborn status, attest to the veracity of these declarations and to the signatures affixed thereto.

I, Tiberius Claudius Menon, of manumitted status, attest to the veracity of these declarations and to the signatures affixed thereto.

After each of us had signed beneath our respective attestations, Tiberius turned to me and smiled. Taking my hands in his he asked in archaic Latin, "What is thy name?"

I returned his smile and gave the appropriate reply. "Where thou art Gajus, I Gaja." The formula employs the ancient form of the familiar Roman praenomen which means *Law of the Earth*.

Thrasyllus beckoned to Aka, who opened her hand. On her palm lay two rings. The one was my own of silver inlaid with rubies, for which she had asked me earlier. The other was of gold and set with a single, luminous yellowish-red stone. Tiberius took my ring and placed it on the third finger of my left hand—that single digit of the ten from which a nerve runs directly to the heart. "When I first gave you this," he said, "I wished then I could have presented it as a wedding ring. A promise has been fulfilled, a prayer answered." Aka extended her palm toward me, and I took the gold ring. "The opal is the gem of Scorpio," Tiberius continued. "The rare fire opal represents enduring, unassailable love. It also signifies the phoenix. At my request, Thrasyllus had this fashioned from Julia's old ring. From the ashes of that marriage arose the one we are presently solemnizing."

We took one another's hands; then Aka clasped and held hers about ours. This act of bringing the bride and bridegroom together was incumbent upon the pronuba: a matron especially chosen because she had only been once married. We stood so bound while Aka intoned a prayer to the entire pantheon of gods, for the happiness and prosperity of our union. On finishing she joyously tossed our hands into the air. "Talasse!" Thrasyllus cried and Menon echoed, invoking the Italian god of marriages; then "Eutychia! Feliciter!" The ceremony was over. Together Aka and Phoebe hugged me as I wept and laughed simultaneously, while Thrasyllus and Menon shook Tiberius' hand and patted his shoulder.

Thrasyllus handed each of us one of the signed marriage contracts. "I need not admonish you to guard these well," he said. "When you must separate as the stars portend, you will each possess proof your marriage exists. Moreover should one contract be lost or destroyed, you have a second as safeguard. Be not dismayed," he continued, noting Tiberius had rolled his eyes and I lowered mine. "You will suffer the unhappiness of separation, but never the agony of falling out of love."

Tiberius sighed as he removed his ring and placed it on the third finger of his right hand. I did the same, then folded the veil and returned it to Aka. "Do you think we will ever be able to lift the secrecy from our relationship?" I wondered aloud, not addressing anyone in particular.

"Yes," Thrasyllus responded with a confidence that caught my attention, "and on a day not too far off."

Tiberius teased me about my physical condition as he lifted me over the threshold to the master bedchamber. Here it was our wedding night, and we could not consummate our marriage. His insistence I at least sleep beside him proved disastrous. In the middle of the night, a sequence of painful abdominal spasms woke me abruptly. I was lying in a great pool of blood. Responding to our summons, Phoebe changed the soiled sheets while Alcmene washed and swaddled me. They put me to bed in my own chamber, immediately adjacent to the master bedroom. There I remained for the next three days: weak, bleeding profusely, and enduring more spasms. Finally it all ceased on the fourth day, but left me exhausted for the next two.

My illness reminded Tiberius he had promised to acquire Arbindus' sweetheart, so our household might include someone proficient in curative arts. Before Thrasyllus and Aka departed he asked them to purchase the girl, even if they must procure for her present owners a different servant with similar skills. On the final day of August one of Thrasyllus' menservants delivered Arbindus' love: a buxom young woman with sparkling blue eyes and blonde hair tinged with a nuance of red. She said we should call her Briseis, because no Greek or Italian seemed able to pronounce her Gallic name. We most certainly could not—it was something like Brdgihte or Bridichte. She added that she understood the original Briseis was the beloved slave of a famous Greek hero, but she knew nothing more about their story. Inquisitive, indeed: forthright and pleasant, temperamentally well suited to someone seeking to cure people's ailments, and surprisingly fluent in Greek. Perhaps someday I shall read her the *Iliad*.

In mid-September an ominous letter arrived from Augustus. Among Tiberius' callers of the previous June there had been three centurions, whom he had appointed to their positions during the Danube campaigns. After furlough in Italy, the centurions had passed through Rhodes while returning to their current station in Galatia. During their visit, Tiberius had presented each centurion with a letter of commendation. Word had filtered back to Gaius— now in Alexandria—that Tiberius had given the letters to the centurions for circulation to others, and that the messages urged the subversion of Gaius and his brother. Fortunately for Tiberius, both Augustus and Gaius knew him well enough not to place credence in this story. The incident nevertheless confirmed a definitive movement to incriminate Tiberius was clearly afoot. In his final paragraph, Augustus said not to bother commemorating his forthcoming birthday. Tiberius was facing difficulties enough without having to cast about for a gift to remind his already aged stepfather. Furthermore he and Livia would persuade Drusus, who would enter his fourteenth year in October, that he was now sufficiently mature not to importune his harried father for a present.

In response to his stepfather's warning, Tiberius refused to conduct another interview—especially not with friends—unless at least two witnesses were present to observe and vouch under oath for every word he uttered or action he undertook. To serve as a viable witness whose attestation was legally acceptable in a court of law, a man must be of free status. Thrasyllus, Marinus, and Atticus met this qualification but were not regularly available. All the praetorians were both freeborn and present; but Tiberius was disinclined to use them as witnesses, lest they spread gossip during furloughs or upon transfers to different tours of duty. Menon of course was ever at hand; but as with our marriage, Tiberius craved the stronger assurance of multiple witnesses.

As imperial legate, Tiberius had the right to summon any civic or Roman provincial magistrate of Rhodes to his premises. The very day he received Augustus' letter, he sent a praetorian after one of the praetors. When this official arrived the day following, Tiberius revealed his purpose. Satisfied with the unflagging loyalty and discretion of our servants, he manumitted Nicanor and Arbindus, Nestor and Alcmene. Free status enabled the males to be legally acceptable witnesses and curators of properties. Since the new freedmen—and freedwoman—were now retainers of Tiberius, they owed him absolute loyalty and discretion.

Tiberius gave Arbindus leave to take Briseis as his concubine. Since Briseis was so newly acquired, Tiberius was reluctant to free her until he was better acquainted with her character, and satisfied she merited the honor of freedom. To Ajax and Androcles he maintained he could not offer freedom—at least not at this time—lest he approach at too young an age the maximum number of slaves an owner was allowed to emancipate over the course of a lifetime. Augustus had passed this legislation for the purpose of curtailing the growing number of non-Italians, who through manumission were acquiring Roman citizenship. Tiberius was more determined than ever, to be scrupulously obedient to law in every action he undertook.

The business with the centurions and its aftermath set me considering, yet once again, the differences between Tiberius' family and mine. Augustus and Gaius alike had made amply clear their aggravation with Tiberius over his retirement to Rhodes. Both had expressed their determination to protect—at any and all costs—the security of Gaius' person and political position. But both had also taken pains to apprise Tiberius he was becoming a figurehead for opposition to these endeavors. Thanks to their forewarnings, Tiberius was prepared to counter accusations leveled against him, and seize opportunities for disassociating himself from the resistance movement. Gaius had treated Tiberius deferentially during the private portions of their visit, and Augustus had jovially excused Tiberius from having to seek birthday gifts. My family had never offered opportunities to redeem myself, to right real or imagined offenses I had committed. And they had extended no civility, uttered no kind nor even neutral word, until the need to devote attention to other matters distracted them from exacting penance for my misdeed which must never be forgotten or forgiven. That current of human affection, which underflowed personal and political differences in Tiberius' family, had been glaringly and hurtfully absent from mine.

In the past, I would have rehearsed and reiterated these reflections to my partner—by all the gods as he would say, I must now write *husband*. Now I kept my present musings strictly to myself. It would be inconsiderate and cruel of me to afflict Tiberius with yet more rumination about my history—for which there was no remedy anyway—while he continued to face his present anguish. He needed my consolation and support, not a new version of the same complaints I had been repeating for years.

We could not expect to see Thrasyllus for some time now, because the term at the Academy had begun. He started to send academic items he thought might interest us—treatises on various subjects that the students and sophistoi of the Rhodes Academy had completed, notes to lectures he had delivered or attended, part of the draft of a commentary he was preparing on the *Timaeus* of Plato. Atticus arrived for a visit in early October, and reported yet another damaging rumor that was spreading through the city of Rhodes. It alleged the reason Tiberius, although living in retirement, continued to pursue his exercises with arms on foot and horse, was so he might be at the ready to lead an insurrection as soon as an opportune moment presented itself. Tiberius reacted with a low, anguished cry as though seized with a sudden pain. "The praetorians," he moaned. "Apart from my servants, only they know I practice with arms. I can depend upon Selvinius to admonish them; but he still has little control over what they say once they leave here. I wonder how far this has gone through the regular military establishment."

Tiberius disappeared for a time to discuss the rumor with Selvinius, leaving me to chat with Atticus on the veranda. He said he would like to bring his daughters to our farm for a change of scenery. His wife would make his life miserable, however, were she to discover the patron for whose help and support they had moved to Rhodes kept a mistress. I challenged his assertion somewhat irascibly, insisting I was Tiberius' ward, and demanding whether Atticus and his wife had unassailable proof my relationship with Tiberius was an intimate one. Perceiving my point, Atticus nodded acquiescently and promptly changed the subject to a dilemma his family was facing.

The younger of his two daughters, in her twelfth year, was enthusiastic about academics; but her mother was attempting to suppress these interests. On her forthcoming birthday, Attica would attain marriageable age. Hardly was she ready to assume responsibilities of wedlock. She did not seem to understand that every minute spent reading books took away from mastery of domestic tasks and household management. Girls who placed the former ahead of the latter ended up spinsters, or worse yet hetaerae. Only the most wealthy and influential of women—like Aka or Livia—could afford the luxury of being learned. Attica must face the reality she was hardly one of their peers. Making matters worse for Attica, her elder sister Vescularia—whom they called Vesca for short—was an intrinsic homemaker. Accomplished in all the requisite skills, interested in little else, and in her fourteenth year, she was now pressuring her father to arrange a marriage for her. Not surprisingly, Vesca's blatant domesticity prompted her mother regularly to afflict poor Attica with the remark, *Why can you not be like your sister?*

Atticus' predicament I pondered with mixed feelings. In one sense I agreed with his wife. After all, my parents had forced me to place academics ahead of domesticity in my own life. In consequence I had ended up a spinster, and subsequently a concubine. But I also rued Atticus' wife's efforts to suppress their daughter's academic leanings, since I knew only too well the agony that arises from having one's natural inclinations condemned and suppressed by one's parents.

As Atticus finished speaking, an idea flashed through my mind. "Why not make Attica's book learning a treat at the end of her domestic learning—like a dessert at the end of a meal?" I suggested. "Tell her she can read all she wants, but not until she has finished her domestic chores and lessons. And be fair to her. Do not overwhelm her with so much homemaking that she does not have time to read. One of the traditional duties of a Roman wife is to educate her children insofar as she is able. Think of how well-prepared Attica will be to assume this responsibility, if you let her pursue her scholarly interests within appropriate boundaries."

Slowly he nodded his comprehension. "What a simple solution—and so filled with maternal insight and compassion," he said with obvious admiration. Then, "How many children did you bear your estranged husband?" "None," I returned. "I am incapable of bearing." My response unnerved him a little; and we sat together in silence until Tiberius returned.

Atticus' comments intrigued me. There were only two children with whom I had associated closely in my life: Miranda who was impaired, and my brother who was hardly an exemplification of proper childrearing. All my other contacts with children had been superficial: with pupils at the Academia Norenas, and with beneficiaries of my charities, or else mere passersby in the city of Rhodes. Yet my response to Atticus' problem with his daughter came promptly, naturally, and comfortably; and he—a stranger who knew nothing of me or the nature of my interactions with children—recognized my inclination toward them at once. I was not about to explain any of this to him, nor change his assumption I might be a courtesan. Tiberius joined us anew, bearing his personal sword, shield, and body armor. These he entrusted to Atticus for safekeeping, asserting he was giving up his exercises with armaments immediately. To prevent rumors his intent was insincere, and he was prepared to take up arms again on a moment's notice, he wanted his military accouterments removed from his domicile.

Upon arising the next morning, Tiberius donned the short Doric chiton he had elicited from Menon the night before. He did not shave. After seeing Atticus off, he explained that he had decided to reassume Greek attire and a philosopher's beard—the costume he had sported when I first made his acquaintance at the Academia Norenas. The present change was not a disguise and could hardly serve as one: certainly the first caller to see it would spread word of its use. Its purpose was to reiterate, with greater emphasis than ever, that Tiberius had retired to Rhodes as a private citizen seeking to embrace Greek learning and Greek culture—not to elude detection while he schemed and plotted against Gaius and Lucius.

The packet of letters that arrived from Rome on the morning of Tiberius' birthday was hardly cheering. Livia and Augustus were quarreling. She maintained the continued confinement of Tiberius to Rhodes was reinforcing his identification as a rival to Gaius. This in turn stood to encourage rather than dissuade opponents of the heir-apparent to rally about Tiberius. Let Tiberius return to Rome a private citizen, taking no part in public affairs whatsoever. By such concession, Augustus and Gaius would acknowledge they were satisfied Tiberius harbored no designs upon the succession, but preferred to render himself powerless both politically and militarily—hence an ineffectual champion for an opposition movement.

Although he respected his wife's logic—and appreciated her affection for her son and her desire to see him rehabilitated—Augustus refused to allow Tiberius' return to Rome so long as Gaius remained uncomfortable about it. Moreover the emperor continued to consider Tiberius' original withdrawal to Rhodes an act of gross insubordination, unconscionable and unforgivable. Consequently, Augustus was in no hurry to sanction Tiberius' homecoming.

Drusus was worried more than ever about his future. In less than two years he would come of age; and he was concerned his father's presently discredited reputation may eventually sully his own. Antonia was exasperated with the uncouth and apparently incorrigible conduct of her younger son. The only heartening news was that Lucius Caesar was eminently satisfied with Alexias as his personal manservant; and Postumus—now in his eleventh year—had participated competently with other boys of aristocratic lineage in the equestrian *Game of Troy*, as part of the dedication celebration for the newly completed temple to Mars.

In the afternoon Atticus and Marinus arrived, leading a donkey laden with two great kegs. They had come to help Biberius Caldius Mero celebrate his birthday by mollifying the pangs of his tribulations with Rhaetian wine. After dinner I left the three to their carousals and retired to the master bedroom, where I had a mission to fulfill. At long last I had finished the six lovers vignettes. Now I took advantage of Tiberius' preoccupation with his imbibing to have Ajax hang them. Afterward I withdrew to the female suite, where I read Thrasyllus' commentary on the *Timaeus* for a time and then retired. I was afraid to take my usual place in Tiberius' bed, lest he retire reeking and snoring or worse yet vomiting. In the second watch, shouts awakened me: our visiting revelers' valets were escorting them to the guesthouse. I fell back asleep and awoke just at dawn. Cautiously I crept into the master bedchamber to check on my own reveler, whom I assumed would still be sleeping off the effects of the wine. Instead I found him awake, perfectly sober, dressed, and examining the vignettes.

"Marvelous!" he said under his breath in quiet admiration. "I can hardly wait to behold these in full daylight. Clytia, your style and technique have matured and refined estimably. And such a wonderfully refreshing and uplifting gift to receive after what those two sots gave me."

His mood shifted. Now glum, he sat down on the edge of the bed where I joined him. "I thought Rhaetian wine was your favorite," I said as he took my hand.

"It is. Not the wine, but the news they brought disheartened me. Last month, King Archelaus of Cappadocia met with Gaius in Alexandria. During his journey, Archelaus put in at Rhodes twice: while en route to his destination, and again during his return. His failure to call upon me or even to send a message of greeting is a significant snub, renouncing my defense of him as worthless and even detrimental. Remember, I successfully cleared that scoundrel of accusations he was supporting the pro-Parthian party in Armenia, even though I suspected those allegations were valid. Archelaus is shifty, always striving to be on the winning side. Little wonder he sought to ingratiate himself to Gaius by rejecting me."

"Is this not better than having Archelaus outrightly declare his support for you, and have Gaius assume he is prepared to supply you with an army of mercenaries?"

"Well considered, my Lioness, very well considered; however, I have not given Gaius or Archelaus or anyone else cause to believe I would solicit mercenaries. The event disturbs me seriously, Clytia. Since Archelaus is a king, his rebuff is a considerable blow to my prestige and credibility. It also shows my lack of popularity is neither limited to Rhodes where I am present and visible, nor to the coterie of sycophants whose specific adherence to Gaius automatically renders them my enemies."

It was late morning before our two visitors finally meandered over from the guesthouse. Both were suffering from the same self-induced physical condition of which my own memories were unequivocally agonizing. Again I withdrew to the women's quarters, now to work at embroidering a border on the chlamys Phoebe had fashioned for Tiberius out of one of my textile acquisitions. He remained with his guests in the library, amid their moans and groans and reminiscences of bygone military campaigns. As they were preparing to depart, Atticus—the more sober of the two—with a flimsy joke unintentionally delivered another blow to Tiberius' morale. Eying the steep descent he must negotiate in his unsteadiness, Atticus remarked, "Nero, I can appreciate why people are saying you retreated to this height for the purpose of flinging unwanted visitors over its sides."

"What kind of monster is Gaius making me out to be?" Tiberius lamented as he watched them stagger down the promontory, their nervous menservants carefully guiding each step, their donkey plodding behind them unperturbed by the steepness of the path.

Atticus returned in mid-December to celebrate the Roman Saturnalia. Tiberius was far from a rigorous observer of religious rites and festivals. Ordinarily he did nothing to commemorate this holiday, apart from providing the servants with gifts of money and extra free time for themselves. He nevertheless welcomed the present celebrants out of gratitude for their persistent loyalty. I hoped the occasion would lift his spirits; and for a time it did. Atticus brought his family over the objections of his wife Nevidia. So far as she was concerned, our emphatic insistence I was not Tiberius' mistress was unassailable confirmation I was. *How very like my mother and Euethia*, I thought—but more with amusement than contempt, I noted with some surprise. Nevidia sat silently apart, wearing the same look of condescending disdain my mother had always assumed when forced to interact with people she deemed objectionable.

Tiberius enjoyed the company of Atticus' two daughters. He had deep appreciation for girls and young women—not in a lurid sense by any means. He took refreshment from their grace, their sparkle, their clever insights, their uncontrived spontaneity. The older girl Vesca became enthralled upon meeting the renowned general and member of the emperor's family, whose praises she had heard from her father for her entire life. She sat in silence at her mother's side, listening enraptured to the conversations of the men, and watching Tiberius with a fascination punctuated by a hint of disappointment—as though she were surprised to discover with each passing moment, that he was not a demigod after all but every bit as human as the rest of us. Tiberius enthralled the intellectual Attica as much as he did her sister, but for a different reason. Attica was at present reading the *Aeneid*. She was thrilled to meet someone who had actually known Publius Vergilius Maro, the author of this epic who had succumbed to sunstroke nearly two decades ago.

Despite her reverence for Tiberius, Attica spent most of the day with me. We discussed the Trojan War, first from the perspective of the *Iliad* and subsequently from that of the *Aeneid*. By the time we finished it was late in the afternoon. I departed for my suite to retrieve the gifts I had prepared for the girls and their mother. For each I had embroidered a kerchief with a different design—one a key, the second a leaf motif, and the third a train of rosettes. Upon seeing the presents and learning they were my handiwork, Nevidia exchanged her scowl for a look of inquisitive interest. Vesca for once tore her attention away from Tiberius, and with her mother examined my workmanship with sedulous absorption. Then Nevidia remarked in a preachy, didactic tone, "Do you see, Attica? Even this woman of low station—this courtesan," (she practically spat the word) "who has servants to attend her every need, knows and practices the skills of homemaking." *Nevidia has my mother's tact as well as her manner*, I thought cynically. *At least she approves one of my accomplishments.*

We dined upon grouse and pheasant, the outcome of Nicanor's hunting expertise. Afterward we brought out the gaming board, an activity which also met with Nevidia's objections. She refused to let her girls participate and made them sit apart with her. They squirmed at her side but not for long, because the winter's early nightfall allowed me to rescue them. After making each one don her shawl, I took them outdoors to look at the stars. Following some initial excitement at seeing so many in skies undimmed by city lights, Vesca rather quickly grew bored, complained of being cold, and went back inside to resume ogling Tiberius. Attica, however, who had studied the constellations and the legends behind them, gazed and gasped as I identified each pattern for her. She remained with me in euphoria, until her parents collected her as they proceeded to the guesthouse for the night.

Reentering the main house, I found Tiberius in the bath, and once again in a state of dejection. Atticus had told him of a new report that was circulating. It maintained that in Nimes the capital of Gallia Narbonensis, a mob had toppled the statues which had been erected in Tiberius' honor while he was military governor of that province. This news, if true, confirmed that disdain for Tiberius was spreading throughout the empire, and was not restricted to government circles.

"Some fine friend," I grumbled as I seated myself on the bath bench, to undress and await my turn in the bath. The basin was too small to hold the two of us at once. Since it was elevated rather than sunken like most, getting in and out of it presented a challenging endeavor. "On your birthday he reveals you have developed a reputation for throwing people off our cliff. Now on the Saturnalia—the purpose of which is to bring cheer and not despondency—he reports this calamity in Nimes. He is fortunate not to be here with us, as I might likely drown him."

"We would have learned of both matters sooner or later," Tiberius returned dolefully. He emerged from the little bath, helped me into it, draped himself in a towel, and sat down on the bench.

"My beloved, why do we remain here enduring scorn and invective and combating misrepresentation, when you have no intention of returning to public life? Suppose I sell this farm; you liquidate as much of your estate as you can without compromising provision for your son; and then we flee beyond the reach of Roman influence—past Parthia to India or even to China? You know how I would delight in seeing new and strange places, people, customs, and of course textiles."

At my mention of the final item he rolled his eyes. "You are insatiable—and equally intrepid. Often and carefully I have pondered the very type of flight you just suggested, relishing it like the prospect of retreating into Elysium. But Clytia: unless I clear my name, my son's reputation is likely to suffer irreparable damage. If my present state of dishonor persists, it could prevent Drusus from attaining admission to the senate. The son of a disgraced senator has little hope of winning election to that body.

"I have little reason to assume my stepfather would intervene on Drusus' behalf, or let my mother press him to do so. You realize by now, that he will not hesitate to sacrifice the interests of his kindred to promote those of his regime. He will most certainly allow Drusus' political destruction, should he deem it necessary to promote Gaius' success. Behold the fate of Iullus Antonius' children. They are my stepfather's grandnephews and grandniece; yet he will not allow them any chance of achieving political prominence, lest it imply a softening of his attitude toward their father and his daughter. They removed with their mother Marcella to Marseilles. There Lucius is dabbling in academics at the local university, Gaius is training to become a municipal clerk, and Iulla is betrothed to another clerk. Even worse off is young Gaius Sempronius Gracchus, the son of Julia's co-conspirator. He has to grow up in Cercina the place of his father's exile, among illiterates and savages!"

"Iullus Antonius and Tiberius Gracchus were acknowledged adulterers and traitors—criminals. You are not an outlaw."

"True enough. But should I flee, my enemies are likely to construe that action as an admission of guilt, and cite it as reason to disallow Drusus admission to the senate." He stared askance at the floor. "Clytia, I cannot help wondering whether I will ever succeed at redeeming my reputation. Was moving to this farm my monumental change? Is the worldwide renown Thrasyllus predicted for me this curse of misrepresentation I cannot seem to dispel?"

I extended my hand for him to help me clamber out of the bath—as much to distract him from his desolation as to keep me from breaking my neck. "What then was my monumental change?" I asked. "It was supposed to precede yours. Why do we not write Thrasyllus and find out for certain?"

My words brightened him a little. "A wife indeed, doing her husband's thinking for him." He drew me, naked and dripping, close against his own nude body and enveloped us both in the towel. "I would ravish you here and now were I not so tired and disconsolate, the hour not so late, and this floor not so hard and wet."

"I will gladly accept a kiss instead."

He obliged at once: repeatedly, fervently, tenderly. Considerable time had passed since we had engaged in any form of intimacy; for we both were distracted and edgy from the emotional strain the present course of events was inflicting upon us.

That night I lay awake for a long while. Naturally I shared Tiberius' disappointment and chagrin and irritation about his persistently deteriorating reputation. Attica, however, was the main cause of my wakefulness. She was enduring a turmoil uncannily similar to mine, and yet diametrically different. When I aspired to become an educated housewife, my parents had forced me to become a sophista with little if any prospect of marriage. Attica would like to be a sophista; but her parents were pressing her to become an educated housewife. While my parents' motives had been malicious and self-centered, those of Atticus and Nevidia were benign and intended to protect. Intentions aside, however, Attica faced the very future that had confronted me: frustration, lack of self-fulfillment, lack of self-respect.

My thoughts shifted to Drusus. He had been born into the nexus of power, wealth, and privilege that certainly my family had envied and coveted—as no doubt did thousands of other people as well. Nevertheless, his life was hardly idyllic. Through no fault of his own he had suffered estrangement from his parents. Now through no fault of his own he was facing the prospect of disrepute; and his family—the most powerful in the world—might deny him their aid, sacrificing his reputation to their political agenda. My acceptance of Underlying Good had lifted me out of the predicament I had faced with my family. Was not this same Principle applicable to Attica and to Drusus?

Asellus our donkey could accommodate no more than two riders at a time. The next morning there were four women: Nevidia, her daughters, and a female servant they had brought. All must be delivered to the carriage waiting at the promontory's base. Arbindus said he would take the two girls first, then return for their mother and attendant. As he placed Attica upon the beast's back, she cried out to me, "Galatea, you are my exemplar! I hope to become exactly like you!"

"No!" I exclaimed, so emphatically that even Arbindus turned to stare. "Attica, you are entrusted with the greatest honor and responsibility in the universe: that of producing and rearing the next generation of the human race! Obey your parents, and learn to manage a home! Attica, I am incapable of bearing children! That charge so great and wonderful has eluded me! I am inferior to every woman who ever has borne: to your mother, to my mother, to my freedwomen Alcmene and Phoebe—and hopefully down the future to you! Be educated, Attica, be erudite and learned; but be a proper wife and mother first! Sappho commendably raised a daughter, and Aspasia a son!"

The words could not have flowed more readily from me had they been written in preparation and rehearsed. As Arbindus and the donkey disappeared down the slope, Nevidia turned to me and grabbed both my hands in hers. Tears filled her eyes. "Thank you, oh thank you!" she exclaimed fervently. "And please, please forgive my rudeness and misjudgment of you! Cease from calling yourself inferior—you who are a model for all womankind!"

Toward the very end of December, after the Saturnalia was over, Gaius and his entourage had quit Alexandria for Antioch the capital of Syria. On the Calends of January—the day on which the Roman magistracies rotated to their newly elected holders—Gaius assumed the executive office of consul. He had actually won a redounding election to this position five years earlier.

During his coming of age ceremony, which had occurred in July the month in which the magisterial elections take place, the attendant crowd had vociferously and adamantly demanded his name be listed among the candidates for the consulship. Augustus had allowed Gaius to accept the election, but not assume the office until he had reached his twentieth year. The unique circumstances of his election to Rome's highest magistracy, and now his tenure thereof, reinforced the singularity and supremacy of Gaius not only in Roman politics but within his own family as well.

The ensuing January was the bleakest I could ever recall. Comprehending the reason was not difficult. The mountain air—cooler and drier than that of seaside cities like Naples or Rhodes—and the cold, strong Boreas wind blowing persistently from the North, desiccated the flora and induced the trees to shed their leaves. The hillsides assumed a shade of tan, variegated with splotches of dark brown and crimson, and the deep green of those plants which did not hibernate. The three Guardian Trees—aglow in autumn with amber, bronze and scarlet—now gray, sere, and skeletal seemed to evoke the wandering lemures *[skeletal apparitions]* of Italian folklore.

The number of callers at the farm dwindled sharply because of the winter, and because the continued hostility of Gaius was rendering dignitaries increasingly afraid to associate with Tiberius. Even those obligated by official etiquette to pay respects to him as imperial legate, now shunned him for fear of being branded enemies of the prince. In one sense Tiberius was grateful for this reprieve, because his inveterate shyness had never ceased to render associating with strangers arduous for him. Nevertheless the lack of visitors remained a disheartening symbol, of the degradation that was showing no sign of abatement.

Tiberius sent an apology to Livia and Antonia: living in isolation, he could not procure gifts for their birthdays at the end of the month. He refused quite vigorously my offer to paint or embroider something for each of them. How could he explain having come across such fine items while living in isolation? Both women responded that Tiberius' regrets about the matter were unnecessary: no physical present could offer more gratification than seeing his reputation restored. The family was beginning to wonder why Gaius continued so adamantly to regard Tiberius a potential rival.

Although he still upheld Gaius' wish that Tiberius not be given permission to return to Rome, Augustus had begun to urge his grandson to reassess his opinions. Did Tiberius remain a viable threat to Gaius, with a serious following of opponents to the crown prince? Most of Tiberius' known supporters had abandoned him, lest they be presumed enemies of Gaius. And had not Tiberius by now made sufficiently clear, with his own words and actions, that he would not allow himself to become the figurehead of an opposition movement? Had Gaius considered whether the exalted political prominence, which attainment of the consulship had brought him, lessened the likelihood for an opposition centered upon Tiberius to succeed? Moreover, had Tiberius ever posed such danger to the prince in the first place? Or was Gaius allowing some person or circumstance to mislead him? Did Gaius realize he may be ruining a man's life unnecessarily? Was he prepared to carry that onus upon his conscience?

Thrasyllus advised us the forthcoming year portended a fair share of disappointment, but great joy as well. Tiberius must take special care not to succumb to discouragement, as the temptation to do so will be great. In the end his forbearance would receive ample compensation. His monumental change was not yet imminent; however, mine was now at hand.

What was changing for me so ominously? The Calends of March would bring the New Year; but that was a routine change affecting everyone, not something monumentally specific to me. Toward the middle of February a resurgence of abdominal swelling, of acne pimples, and of general achiness meant another menses was imminent. Although these occurred infrequently and irregularly, they were nothing unusual; after all, I had had them all my adult life. How could any menses, light or severe, be a monumental change if it had a precedent? Hopefully, this one would not be as bad as the last. To alleviate my symptoms Briseis fed me slips of fresh parsley and dandelion, which she had growing in pots because the season was winter.

In the final week of February the wind shifted abruptly from north to east, increased in strength, and brought driving rain. This was the great Euroclydon: more of a menace to sea travel than the Sirocco we had endured upon leaving Italy. With the onset of the storm came that of my menstruation—and quite appropriately, as the two conditions paralleled one another in intensity. More profusely than ever I bled, requiring bathing and a change of swaddling and bedlinen every few hours. My back and lower abdomen and even my thighs ached constantly. There were also spasms of stabbing pains, so severe that often I could not refrain from moaning or crying out. I was too nauseous to bear even the thought of solid food. From time to time I managed to swallow—and only with considerable effort—a few spoonsful of barley gruel and the medicines Briseis prepared. She gave me a tincture of yarrow to check the flow of blood, and infusion of chamomile to ease the spasms and induce sleep. These remedies brought but scant relief.

The first two days I endured with gritty determination as I lay in my bedchamber, listening to the shrieking wind tear through the trees and hurl the rain against the house. My ailment was a menses. Like the storm, it must end eventually. Once it is over I should be free for many months. By the middle of the third day, however, my optimism had fled. My body started to feel hot one moment, then frigidly cold the next. I had become so weak, that one of our menservants had to carry me from my bed to the chamber pot or bathing vat. None of them ever saw me unclothed, for my female attendants always made sure I was covered with a sheet. Nevertheless, to have a man lifting me amid all that blood was mortifyingly embarrassing.

A new fragrance and flavor revealed Briseis had introduced a different tincture. I had entered a state of semi-consciousness from which I awoke, abruptly and briefly with the pain of each spasm but otherwise only sporadically. I tried as best I could to acknowledge Underlying Good, hoping this recognition might harmonize my physical condition as it had my interpersonal relationships. I could not be sure my efforts were effective, however, because I kept relapsing into that daze. My earliest rendering of the Guardian Trees hung on a wall near my bed. In my stupor I imagined the trees at times moving about in the room, at others standing at my immediate bedside overshadowing me with protection and imparting sustenance and strength. With each awakening I noticed Briseis busily attentive. During one I became aware of Tiberius, clasping my hand with both of his. His face was stony with the expressionless demeanor he adopted when deeply troubled, and his beard silvery with tears.

All at once a great spasm began in my lower back and shot forward into my abdomen. I heard myself scream. Then I retched violently but did not vomit. At the same moment, a large gelatinous mass erupted from my vagina. Presently I became aware that it was night because the lamps were lit; that the wind was not quite as forceful as it had been; that Briseis was holding one of my hands and Tiberius the other; that his palm was bleeding where my fingernails had dug into its flesh. My mental acuity had returned. Although weak, exhausted, and lightheaded, I could recognize a distinct feeling of having been internally cleansed.

Tiberius summoned Phoebe and Alcmene, who had to be roused from sleep. They prepared the bathing vat while Briseis stripped me. Then Tiberius extracted me from the warm, sticky, loathsome mess in which I was lying and placed me into the vat, kissing my forehead as he carried me despite the presence of the servants. Over her protests he ordered Briseis to retire. Except to prepare the medications she had not left my bedside for the last three days, he said. Dawn began to lighten the room. I inquired what day it was. The Calends of March, Tiberius answered; we were now in the New Year. Six days and nights had passed since the onset of this menses. During the last two I had been delirious.

After the cleansing of my body and bed, and a draught of chamomile, I fell comfortably asleep. When I awoke the room was filled with pale gray light. The rain had ceased, but the skies remained overcast with heavy clouds. Alcmene was in attendance. "Happy New Year, Lady!" she exclaimed in her usual nervously solicitous manner. "How wonderful to see you have rallied! You had us all very frightened for you."

"Thank you. You and your fellow servants have been so wondrously kind, I cannot imagine how I shall ever manage to reward all of you adequately."

"There is no need to reward us, Lady." There was an element of bewilderment in her voice, as though she thought my notion preposterous.

"Alcmene, did you pray to your God for me?"

My inquiry delighted her. "Oh most assuredly, Lady! So did Nestor," she continued brightly. "And if I may be so bold: Master prayed to the deities whom you and he revere! During one of the few, brief times he was not at your side, I beheld him on his knees before your household altar."

"Thank you for sharing that," I responded with sincere gratitude, "but take care to keep your counsel, and not let Master discover you noticed him.

"Yes, Lady."

She appeared a little crestfallen from my admonition until I added, "You would not want to embarrass him. Remember, his ego is as fragile as every other man's. Where is he now—asleep?"

"Yes, for the first time in days. He left orders for me to offer you nourishment upon your awakening."

"That would be wonderful." Her words had made me realize I was indeed a little hungry. I was glad for her departure, for I did not want her to see my eyes welling with tears. Although he strongly respected the beliefs and practices of others, Tiberius was far from religious himself. Days and sleepless nights of attending me, and prayers for my recovery: these beautiful manifestations of his love moved me deeply. But then I began to wonder. Why did such reassurances of his devotion always seem to take me by surprise?

Alcmene returned with a tureen, which filled the room with an appetizing aroma. After a spoonful of a tincture tasting like red raspberries, she fed me a dark, hearty, savory broth. Venison, she said, very restorative after blood loss. To address my condition, Nicanor had ventured out at the height of the Euroclydon to hunt down a deer. About half an hour after my repast, I had the opportunity to thank him. By then I needed the potty and another bathing. Since I was still too weak to rise from my bed, Alcmene summoned Nicanor to lift me. After accepting my profuse expression of gratitude, he graciously but rather bemusedly insisted I should not view his efforts on my behalf as extraordinary actions, but as execution of duties incumbent upon a proper servant.

The spasms had ceased. Now free of their violence and pain, and soothed by the broth and cleansing, I became contentedly drowsy. I only dozed, however, unable to fall asleep. Nicanor's response had set me to pondering once again. Why should I consider it surprising for others to help me endure and recover from an illness? Why should I feel it strange, for ordinarily religious servants to offer prayers on my behalf? And although it may be unusual for my spouse to pray, why should I feel it odd that in desperation he might seek a solution down a path less traveled?

Either I fell asleep after all, or was so lost in my musings that I became aware only gradually of Tiberius sitting on the bedside holding my hand. The light in the room was more intense, for it was midafternoon. When I smiled up at him he rolled his eyes.

"Have you the slightest conception of the trauma you have put this household through? The next time it becomes apparent you are going to menstruate, I am sending you to see a physician if that entails shipping you all the way to Alexandria! I was about to fetch that crack-bones from Ialyssos, weather notwithstanding, when thank the gods your crisis passed. Briseis advises there is no point in having you examined now, as there is nothing left to detect."

"I apologize for having been such an imposition," I murmured dolefully. His words had stirred recollections of the accusations my mother invariably leveled at me whenever I fell ill: that I induced ailments consciously and intentionally to draw attention to myself and disrupt family harmony.

"Oh Clytia, stop—stop misinterpreting me! We were all terrified as you lay there—bleeding, burning with fever, convulsing, crying out from pain—all the while in a mental haze, recognizing none of us nor your surroundings. Imagine how I felt, watching you in that state. The servants empathized with me—and with you. Even the praetorians became concerned when they did not see you." With his free hand he made a gesture of summons. Briseis approached my bed. "Explain to your mistress what you surmise took place."

"Lady, for many years you had a growth in your womb, creating a stoppage. It kept you from menstruating regularly and properly. Then this growth died; and your body tried to expel it when you menstruated last August. That is why you had those spasms and bleeding as never before. The growth did not dislodge at that time, but with your present menses. If all the debris is gone your next menses, whenever it occurs, should give far less trouble. If residue has remained you may have some difficulty, but not by any means as much as you just suffered. My preparation as a healer included the study of midwifery. When your bleeding and spasms continued unabated for so long, I deduced your womb was attempting to eject something. Therefore I administered tincture of pennyroyal, which induces abortion. The outcome confirmed my assessment. Still, Master is correct: you ought to see a physician, to reevaluate your condition, and prepare you for what to expect."

"Briseis, could all this have been avoided had my irregularity been properly diagnosed and treated when it first became apparent at menarche?

"Yes, Lady, very probably; and the remedy would have been simple. Angelica induces and regulates menstruation. Had you taken that along with red raspberry leaves monthly—while the growth was yet small and your womb unaccustomed to it—you could have coaxed the womb to expel the growth and establish a normal cycle. This regimen is far safer than resorting to pennyroyal, which poisons if too much is consumed."

"Is it possible another such growth will develop?"

"I cannot say, Lady. And I hesitate to start giving you angelica as a preventative unless a physician agrees this remedy is truly appropriate. The condition of your womb has been distorted for many years. Angelica regulates menstrual bleeding, but stimulates it as well. I do not want to bring you back into the state from which you just emerged. I also recommend waiting two or three months before seeing the physician, allowing your body time to adjust to its new condition. If a new growth does start to develop, it will be small and easily arrested. You are truly fortunate, Lady, that the present growth dislodged when it did. Continuation of the spasms and bleeding would have led to fatal exhaustion."

At the door, Arbindus asked Alcmene to inform Master the praetor from the city of Rhodes was waiting in the library. Master raised his eyebrows in surprise as he rose to depart. "Quite prompt: I only summoned him this morning. Briseis, accompany us." She followed him with a look of puzzlement on her face. For a brief moment I too wondered why Tiberius had summoned the praetor; but then Phoebe and Alcmene distracted me. It was time for another bathing. Afterward I lay watching the room darken and brighten, as outside the passing clouds alternately thickened and thinned.

I had just had a brush with death! My affliction had grievously anguished my already troubled husband, and thrown our household in a state of disruption. All of this could have been avoided, had my family provided me with timely treatment from a common weed. Vividly I recalled the looks of smug satisfaction on the faces of my mother and her aunt, whenever I had recoiled disconsolate from platitudes about how grateful I ought to be for infrequent menses, or how selfish I was for daring to suggest I might be in need of medical attention. Once again I wondered whether cure was consciously and deliberately withheld, to make infertility a convenient pretext for keeping me unmarried and under direct familial control. Enraged, I grew hot and slightly nauseous and began to take deep, shuddering, irregular breaths. Noting my discomfort, Alcmene inquired if I was feeling ill and wanted her to fetch Briseis. No, I replied: the room was stuffy from the bathwater and the brazier employed to heat it, and I should like the window opened.

The changes of light became more pronounced as shafts of sunlight began to penetrate the now fragmenting clouds. I lay delighting in the altering hues, the shifting patterns of shadows, the differing perspectives in which the variable light placed objects in the room. Now an unfamiliar calm crept over me—a mellow joy the likes of which I could not recall. Physically I began to feel soothingly relaxed. My spirits lifted; the edgy irritability was fading from my disposition. Noting Alcmene was cold—she was vigorously rubbing her upper arms—I told her to close the window. Then I invited her to take a little time for herself: by now I was feeling well enough to be left alone, and would call her if I needed anything.

As Alcmene departed, my thoughts returned to the kindness our servants had shown me during my affliction—of Briseis never leaving my side; of Alcmene and Phoebe washing my body and blood-soaked linens; of Nicanor stalking a deer at the height of a storm to supply me with curative nourishment; of he and his fellow menservants lifting me in and out of bed amid the loathsome detritus of a peculiarly female ailment. How could I ever show sufficient appreciation? Then I reminded myself once again, that caring for my person and my household was my servants' vocation. Whether I found favor with them or they felt I merited their proper service was irrelevant. They were liable to correction or punishment for contumacious behavior or substandard performance.

Still, our servants over the years had demonstrated genuine affection for me in addition to appropriate deference. They had given me gifts, comforted me in tribulation, prayed for me. Why should this seem so surprising— and undeserved? For that matter, why did I continue to harbor a sense of astonishment that Thrasyllus and Aka should consider me their friend, or that Vescularius Atticus' daughters should admire me and his scornful wife come to respect me? And above all: why did I continue to think it astounding for my husband to love me with the same passion and commitment with which I loved him? I was still clinging to that old childhood shibboleth, of presuming myself unworthy of the kindness and affection of others with no right to expect or accept such benefactions. The time was at hand to cast this canard aside forever. A burst of sunlight, penetrating a break in the passing clouds, brought a golden glow to the room. An appropriate complement to the enlightenments that were filling my consciousness, I thought as I drifted into a pleasant doze.

Ajax delivered my supper: more venison broth this time with minute chunks of flavorful dark meat afloat, a puree of carrots, and a wonderful treat: a loose pudding of milk and that marvelous dagger-shaped grain from the Far East. Phoebe was attending me now. She admonished me to eat as much as I could tolerate. Briseis had said everything was easily digestible and highly nutritious, and I needed solid food. The meat was from the deer's liver, the most resuscitating organ for one who has suffered severe depletion of blood. Tiberius sent regrets he could not join me, Phoebe continued, because he was busy with his guest. I assumed she was referring to the praetor until she elaborated.

To reward Briseis for her excellent and diligent care which quite probably had saved my life, Tiberius had summoned a praetor to free her and recognize her as Arbindus' legal wife. The praetor had brought with him a visitor from Rome. It was this gentleman whom Tiberius was entertaining; the praetor had long since departed. Who is this person, I wondered. Had he brought my troubled spouse yet more despair; or had he come to impart much needed hope?

A radiant Briseis arrived with my medicine; and I congratulated her heartily on her new status. She remained to assist Phoebe with my final bath of the day; this washing revealed the flow of my blood was definitely subsiding. Night was falling. The room began to darken, and Phoebe lit the lamps. Having spent much of the day asleep, I was now rather wakeful. Ordinarily when finding myself in this state, I read or painted or embroidered; but tonight I lacked the mental and physical energy to pursue any of these activities. And so to pass the time—and being ever interested in unfamiliar cultures and customs—I asked Briseis to sit at my bedside and tell me about herself. How had she come to be a pharmakeutria? How had she—a Gaul—ended up in Rhodes? And how had she gained so masterful a command of Greek?

She had not been born in Gaul, but to Gallic parents who were slaves on a truck farm in southern Italy, where Greek is the prevailing language of the servile and freeborn alike. Her parents' fellow servants had given her the sobriquet Briseis. She had learned folk remedies and healing practices from her mother, who had in turn learned them from hers; the skills had been handed down through successive generations of women in her family. From an early age, Briseis had demonstrated a keen aptitude for her vocation. She had anticipated spending her entire life on the farm, tending the health of its workers who, exhausted from overwork and malnourishment, sorely needed her services. Among her patients was the suitor—a young man of North African origin— with whom she had begun to cohabitate with hopes of raising a family.

Her owner, however, was far more interested in monetary gain than either the physical wellbeing or the personal happiness of his slaves. He knew a servant with Briseis' particular talents could fetch a high price. He observed her development carefully, and once satisfied she had reached a proficiency that rendered her suitably marketable, abruptly sold her to a slave trader who similarly anticipated garnering a large return for her. I pushed aside the temptation to ask her whether the owner of the truck farm was Publius Norenas, the father of my former fiancé. What she described certainly sounded like his modus operandi. But discovering he was her seller would do nothing more than rekindle my loathing and resentment toward him, at this very time when I needed peace of mind to help promote my recovery.

The trader brought Briseis to Ephesus, where a grain merchant bought her to provide care for his nonagenarian great-grandfather. The old man was so decrepit, Briseis could do little more than keep him comfortable and free of pain. When he died three summers past, a distant cousin raised suspicion Briseis had poisoned him if only to put him out of his misery. After their application of torture failed to elicit a confession from Briseis, the investigating authorities examined her collection of remedies and found nothing toxic. The subsequent funeral vindicated her altogether. During the cremation, the heart of the corpse was reduced to ashes. When a person dies from poisoning, the heart will not burn.

Having decided they no longer required her service, and wishing to recoup the expense of her purchase, the Ephesian family promptly sold Briseis to another trader who was en route to Rhodes. Here the owners of the brothel acquired her—not as a courtesan but strictly a pharmakeutria, to administer the medicines and contraceptives requisite to keep their working staff healthy and effective. She never mingled with the establishment's clientele, until two of the courtesans introduced her to Arbindus because she was his compatriot. I asked her how old she was. In her twenty-second year, she replied. This made her eight years Arbindus' junior.

One of the lamps began to sputter and smoke. Briseis rose from my bedside and smothered the culprit. As she opened the window to change the air, a line of light streaked across the sky just above the horizon. The sighting hardly moved me at all. I felt no surprise, but rather as though the occurrence was a natural and unremarkable commonplace.

My companion did not regard the event as commonplace. "Lady, did you see that?" she gasped. "A traveling star!"

"A meteor, Briseis. One school of astronomical philosophy maintains they are omens of portentous change to whomever witnesses them. And you have most assuredly undergone significant changes in your life that culminated in today's events. You grew up expecting to live out your life as a rural, countryside slave: the daughter of slaves, the spouse of a slave, potentially the mother of slaves. Now here you are: legally free, and legally married to a man of your own race. Did you ever imagine yourself as such?"

Briseis beamed with ebullience like a delighted child. "Not even in my childhood daydreams. And Lady: now I understand why I beheld a traveling star from the ship that carried me to Ephesus. Today I feel as though all the suffering I endured was a small price to pay for its outcome. But you witnessed tonight's traveling star as well as I, Lady. What change does it bear for you?"

"Well, Briseis, thanks largely to your efforts I have quite clearly experienced a major improvement in my gynecologic health. And perhaps there are more changes yet to unfold for me." I left off with this vagary to avoid being drawn into further discussion. Now relishing solitude, I told Briseis I was ready for sleep and asked her to leave. She shut the window, extinguished the remaining lamps, and pleasantly wished me good night as she withdrew to the adjacent room. Actually I was not sleepy despite the draught of chamomile Briseis had given me; but I wanted to be alone to ponder the gratitude she felt for her vicissitudes.

For years I had been reminding myself almost daily, that my family's oppression had driven me to Tiberius; yet I had not achieved the resilience Briseis enjoyed. Gratitude for my mistreatment always seemed like condonation of it, an admission I deserved it. For a moment I grew warm again, with the old familiar heat of resentment toward my family and self-condemnation for my inability to forgive. Then there was another flash: neither meteor nor lightning nor any other physical phenomenon, but an enlightened thought. Without question I could be grateful—was grateful—for my life with Tiberius, and could continue acknowledging my family's cruelty had impelled me to embrace that life. None of this implied, however, that the abuses my family had inflicted upon me were appropriate or warranted. My anger and resentment and chagrin were not unjustified after all. I need not feel guilt for harboring these feelings.

A sort of peaceful exuberance crept over me. Throughout the day the turmoil and pain of my past had been sinking into perspective. By now it was clear I may never forgive my family, no matter how hard I tried to follow Thrasyllus' urgings to do so. But to continue ruminating and fuming and trying to comprehend their bizarre, irrational justifications for afflicting me, was every bit as futile and pointless as hoping they would someday acknowledge their wrongdoings and offer me apologies or amends. The ordeal through which I had just passed was an unforeseen consequence of their abuse. Perhaps there were others lurking in my future, yet to be revealed. Managing them as they emerged would be sensible and practical. Contemplating and ruing their injustice would constitute waste of the most frivolous sort. Infinitely many are the far better purposes, to which I can devote my mental and physical energies. The presence and power of Underlying Good seemed more real, more palpable to me than ever. We fail to recognize and acknowledge that Good, only because it is more subtle than the evils which seem to dominate our lives.

Thrasyllus had said the monumental change forecast for me was at hand. Over the past week I had been purged and cleansed, physically and emotionally. I felt rejuvenated, reborn. Surely this experience was the anticipated change, its occurrence marked by a meteor. So I mused as I drifted toward sleep.

AN INTERLUDE OF SHIFTING
COLORS AND LIGHT

On awakening the next morning, I discovered Tiberius sitting on the bed at my side and holding my hand. Leaning forward he placed a kiss on my forehead and then several on my lips. None of the servants was present at the moment to see him display his feelings.

"I saw a meteor last night," I said as he sat back upright.

He nodded thoughtfully, caressing my hand as he held it. "I am hardly surprised, for your health has just undergone a remarkable adjustment."

"Briseis opened the window at precisely the right moment. The meteor startled her, until I explained its implication of change and applicability to her new legal status."

"Low in the sky and parallel to the horizon," he continued steadily, "and fairly late, well into the first watch."

"Yes." Suddenly realizing the full meaning of his statement I tried to sit up quickly, but immediately became lightheaded and fell back upon the pillow.

"Be careful!" he cautioned. "Do not undo what we all—including you yourself—have fought to accomplish for your wellbeing."

"You saw it also!"

"Yes; and so did Arbindus."

"His life has certainly undergone a significant change, now that Briseis is his free and legal wife. How did you justify freeing Briseis after asserting to Ajax and Androcles your concern about your quota of emancipations?"

"By maintaining to reward Briseis was worth risking my emancipation quota. Both men heartily approved, after what Briseis did for you. Now let me tell you about our visitor from Rome. He is a senator: Gaius Lucilius Longus. As I was escorting him to the guesthouse when the meteor appeared, he saw it too. Apparently there is a connection between the meteor and his arrival. In his eagerness to demonstrate his support for me, he headed here from Rome in his own vessel. Fortuitously he arrived and got a messenger to notify me just ahead of the Euroclydon. When I summoned the praetor, I asked that he contact Longus and bring him along. His coming to Rhodes may represent the turning point in my fortunes for which I have been striving."

Before I could ask him to elaborate upon his last statement, Alcmene and Phoebe arrived and began the preparations for my morning bath. "Take pains with Lady's appearance to make her particularly presentable," he instructed. "My guest from Rome is most eager to meet her."

"WHAT?" Again I sat up too quickly, and made myself dizzy.

The serving women undressed me, and Tiberius carried me to the bath basin. "To be precise, he is interested in one of your alternate identities: Eutychus of Rhodes. Longus is an art aficionado—connoisseur of and trader in paintings. Your pieces astounded him. He carefully scrutinized one after another, and then pressed me relentlessly. Who is this artist? When and where did I discover *his* works? Could Longus possibly see more of them? What are the chances he might acquire some to grace his personal collection, and others to offer for resale? Eventually I yielded to his importunities, confessing the artist is a member of my own household presently recovering from an illness. But then I found myself adding you may be well enough to receive a visitor for a short while. I surmised—hopefully not wrongly—that his enthusiasm might cheer you and so contribute to your healing."

"I thought Roman senators were not allowed to engage in commercial ventures."

"They may, so long as they do not depend upon the income from such enterprises to meet the property qualification for senatorial membership."

Now in the bathing vat, I smiled up at him. "You surmised most rightly— thank you. I shall receive him with delight."

My bath over, Alcmene swaddled and dressed me, and Tiberius returned me to my bed which Phoebe had just changed. There was a knock on the door: Nestor had brought my medicines and breakfast. He announced that Master's visitor had just come over from the guesthouse. Master departed, leaving orders to summon him once I had been made ready to receive our guest.

The appetizing breakfast Briseis had ordered—coddled eggs, barley porridge, and a compote of mixed cooked fruits—I hardly savored in my excitement. Phoebe admonished me to slow the pace of my consumption lest I give myself indigestion. Longus' assessment of my paintings enthralled me. Had not my teacher Timotheus suggested, that with practice my work might one day achieve marketable quality? Now it had attracted the interest of an enthusiast and purveyor of such art. Could this be the monumental change Thrasyllus had predicted for me, or an element thereof? Was I destined to become—under my male pseudonym—a bona fide professional artist, with the ability to command royalties for my products? Was this the implication of the paintbrush meteor?

Alcmene sent Nestor after some extra pillows so I could be propped up in bed. With her assistance I cleaned my teeth, while Phoebe brushed my hair and bound it in a linen napkin. Then Phoebe sparingly applied some very pale pink rouge to my cheeks and lips. "Just a nuance of color," she said. "You are wan and gaunt as a lemur." My glance into the small mirror Alcmene had handed me confirmed Phoebe's assessment; but oddly enough it also revealed the acne blemishes completely gone, and my complexion smoother and clearer than in many years. "We do not want to scare your caller," Phoebe continued. "Are you ready for him?" After I nodded, she departed to make this fact known.

Phoebe returned shortly with Tiberius, and a man of moderate build with chestnut eyes and dark brown hair shot with wisps of gray. He appeared to be about ten years Tiberius' senior—in his early fifties. Upon noticing me he gave a slight start. At the same moment Tiberius said, "Senator Gaius Lucilius Longus, I give you Galatea Aristoclide, whose artistic pseudonym is Eutychus of Rhodes."

"A woman!" Longus gasped. "Who would have guessed?" After a quick glance about the room he seized the chair, dragged it to my bedside, and sat gazing at me excitedly. "Please tell me, my dear: where and with whom did you train? How did you, being a woman, ever obtain an artistic apprenticeship?"

"I had no apprenticeship, Senator, but took private lessons from Timotheus of Rhodes."

"Decorative artist—a quite splendid one. His profession lost a most worthy member when he died last fall. For how long did you study with him?"

"Consistently for about a year, Sir, and then intermittently over the next three." Carefully I avoided showing reaction to his news of Timotheus' death, but did momentarily reflect that in our isolation on the farm we had not learned of his demise. What other information was eluding us?

"Only for four years, and not continually? Come along now, you must have had training besides this. Your work shows a level of expertise suggestive of many years' preparation."

"No, Sir. I started painting for pleasure about seven years ago, and engaged Timotheus for instruction. Apparently I have a native aptitude for this form of art. Timotheus concurred," I added in the hope of dispelling my listener's suspicion I was withholding particulars about my artistic experience.

Tiberius came to my rescue. "Everything she has told you is absolutely correct, Longus."

The senator exchanged his patronizing skepticism for respectful admiration. "Then you are immensely gifted, my dear. One rarely finds such natural, innate talent. Are you aware that your work is evocative of such greats as Zeuxis of Heraclea?"

"So I have been told, Senator."

He rose from his chair and crossed the room, to admire the painting of the Guardian Trees I had found so evocative during my delirium. "Would you be willing to sell me some of your pieces?"

"How many would you like?"

"Let me forewarn you, I am going to be greedy. Not only do I crave your art for myself: I have agents in Rome, Ephesus, and Alexandria, who I am confident can sell it with ease. While I cannot promise your works will end up in galleries, I can virtually guarantee their popularity as decorative articles in homes and shops." He removed the Guardian Trees. Then upon noting the unadorned wall embedded with the hooks for holding the picture, he returned it to its place. "I cannot bear to leave you here in your sickroom, staring at that void. But beware: you may emerge from your chambers into a very barren house."

"Senator, you may have my pieces gratuitously, as I can always create replacements. But for now, I ask that you do not remove more than, say, ten. After all, it will take me some time to generate those replacements."

"By any chance will you allow me twelve—four for each of my outlets?"

"Very well, twelve but no more."

Tiberius interjected, in a tone somewhat stern. "Since she is surrendering the pieces without remuneration, what percentage will you be paying her in royalties?" His inquiry mortified me: I had to fight a strong impulse to pull the bedcovers over my face. To ask him about the royalties had not occurred to me. I could almost hear my mother and her aunt berating me for my laxity.

Glibly, as though he had anticipated this question, Longus replied, "The standard for any commissioned artist: 40 percent of each sale." As Tiberius nodded approvingly, an odd mix of soothing relief and exhilarating excitement overwhelmed my mortification.

Longus rose from his chair and made a slight bow. "I thank you sincerely for your generosity. Now hoping I have not fatigued you, I wish you a swift and complete recovery."

As they approached the door, Tiberius said, "Longus, the only pieces of Galatea's art which you may not select are scenes that would allow recognition of this farm, and the vignettes hanging in my bedchamber." Longus paused, looked back at me, smiled slightly and then nodded slowly and knowingly before turning to depart. So he acknowledged having surmised, from Tiberius' words, the character of our relationship.

My recovery did proceed swiftly, its momentum driven I am quite sure by my excitement over Longus' interest in my artwork. By that same evening I no longer needed lifting from my bed, but was able to rise from it and walk supported by a servant. During the next three days, I managed to sit for intervals in my bedroom chair. Briseis ordered a more varied menu for me, to balance my nutrition as well as to give me a reprieve from venison. Every morning I noticed an increase in my physical strength. The flow of my blood diminished steadily, so that I required less frequent bathing. Not yet inclined to intellectual pursuits—and still too weak venture out of doors or go rummaging through my textile collection—I wrote in my journal and resumed practicing my harp. But most of my interludes out of bed I spent dabbling with my paints. Remembering my training from the late Timotheus, I recorded on palettes the shades and intensities of light I had observed, when the clouds were thinning and fragmenting as the Euroclydon expired.

During this interim I saw Tiberius only sporadically, because Longus had remained on the farm. Although I sorely missed my husband's company, I encouraged him to attend his guest without reservation about leaving me alone. Hosting a friend and political adherent surely offered him much needed respite after attending me in dire illness. Shortly before sunset on the fourth day of my recovery, after his bath Tiberius came to my quarters to take supper with me. Having had my final bath for the day, which revealed my bleeding had stopped altogether, I was sitting in my chair playing my harp. He sat down on the bed.

"Your visitor has departed?" I queried as I laid the instrument in my lap.

He rolled his eyes. "At last! His loquaciousness defies credibility. But although he can overstay his welcome, talk his listeners into a stupor and make an utter pest of himself, Longus is genuine, honest, and reliable. He makes neither frivolous judgments nor promises he cannot or will not keep. If he avers your artwork is marketable, you can safely assume that it is."

"Never mind my artwork: tell me how Longus' arrival implies improvement to your life."

"As you know, the peace between Rome and the Germans, and with the tribes of the Danube, is extremely tenuous. Longus is one of a group of senators who feel very strongly the present military leadership of the Roman peacekeeping forces is hopelessly inadequate, and will not prevail should war break out. This senatorial coterie is urging my stepfather to recall me to Italy, to have at the ready my military expertise for one or both of those frontiers. Like Marinus and Atticus, Longus has taken up residence on Rhodes in demonstration of support for me. His son is in military service, stationed at the German front; so Longus is particularly sensitive about this matter. His wife remained in Rome, not caring to abandon her friends. She probably relished this opportunity to give her ears a rest as well. But please: continue with your harp."

His quip about Longus' talkativeness made me titter, and not just with amusement. The emergence of Tiberius' intrinsically scant sense of humor, along with his expression of appreciation for my music, meant his spirits were lifting; and at this I rejoiced. He sat with his eyes closed while I played and even after I had finished.

"When do you anticipate returning to Italy?" I ventured as I was putting the harp into its bag.

He laughed gently and opened his eyes, in which was a hint of a twinkle. "Ah my Clytia, such expectations are premature. All Longus can offer me at this time is a glimmer of hope I might be recalled. My stepfather does not readily accept the advice and recommendations of others—not even the counsels of his closest advisers—and quite rightly. Only after he has carefully weighed those judgments, and satisfied himself they are sound, will he implement them. He will want assurance my supporters are not doing precisely what Gaius fears: urging my recall so a party of malcontents can organize about me. Moreover he will have to convince Gaius, that having me on hand to guarantee the safety of the empire's frontiers is worth risking the possibility a political opposition might arise. But at least a tangible necessity for my recall has become apparent. Should that necessity grow in strength and urgency, my stepfather and Gaius will have no choice but to capitulate."

"Hence the meteor. What wonderful news, my love. I am so glad to see it has brightened your mood."

"The recovery of your health is what has brightened my mood. My bed has been forlornly empty and cold without you."

Nicanor and Ajax brought a second chair and a small table upon which they placed our meal: a rabbit Nicanor had caught. He said Briseis had admonished him to remind me I should be sure to consume the liver. While we dined, Tiberius read me the letter from his mother which a courier had brought that afternoon.

The Euroclydon had stricken Augustus with catarrh, an ailment he almost invariably contracted when winds blew from the east. He was also suffering from a recurrence of bladder stones. As if the emperor's indispositions were not enough to render him cantankerous and ornery, two relatives had become a new source of concern. One of the generals, about whom Longus and his senatorial cohorts had reservations, was Lucius Domitius Ahenobarbus the husband of Antonia's sister Prima. He was a phenomenally unemotional man, known to observe the carnage of a battlefield without the slightest flinch of reaction; yet he had a penchant for fast and reckless horseback riding and chariot driving. These oddly contradictory traits had conjoined in the minds of scandalmongers, to give Lucius a reputation for cruelty toward animals and humans alike. Meanwhile after repeated warnings, Gaius had just relieved his entourage of Gnaeus Domitius Ahenobarbus the only child of Prima and her spouse. Gnaeus' persistent drunkenness and rowdy behavior had become embarrassing to the crown prince and discomfiting to his staff. In the most recent escapade—that which had prompted Gaius' reaction—Gnaeus had forced his valet to drink wine in excess. The man became stupefied; then his heart stopped and he died. Like father like son, the wags were saying.

On the happier side, Drusus and his cousin Nero were pursuing their academic training with earnest diligence. One of their tutors had told Livia, that Drusus was starting to demonstrate a distinct interest in and aptitude for the study of architecture, and that Nero was showing a similar inclination for astronomy. To everyone's surprise, Nero's uncouth younger brother Tiberius was starting to show avid enthusiasm toward book learning in any subject, and apparently a nascent aptitude for writing as well. Preparations were underway for two celebrations: Lucius Caesar's betrothal to his distant cousin Aemilia Lepida in early April, and Nero's coming of age in May. The imminence of these happenings meant everybody in the family could expect once again to be on display, since the public invariably found watershed events of this sort deliciously enthralling. Livia concluded with gladness that the weather was turning warmer, and relieving the painful stiffness cold always inflicted upon her arthritic joints and those of Antonia.

The private news of Tiberius' family I always found a source of delight, for which reason he readily shared it with me. He understood my interest was not the luridly prying curiosity of a gossip, but a respectful fascination from someone who cherished the vision of an archetypal family. The Caesars took the besetments of physical illnesses and testy dispositions and obstreperous relatives in stride—oftentimes with humor—and not by carrying on as though theirs was the only family in the world facing problems. They rejoiced at familial achievements like academic proficiencies, and milestones like betrothals and comings of age—instead of scoffing at the former as inadequate, and the latter as wasteful lavishes of money upon the undeserving. Such is genuine family life, I later reflected with refreshment as I dozed off to sleep for the night. More and more I was identifying family life with the Eupistodoi as a distorted caricature, best forgotten like a bad dream.

After breakfast the next morning, I ordered that which I had been craving ever since the onset of my recent menses: a long and thorough soak in the main bath. When my hour of hedonistic saturation was over, Phoebe struggled to dry my hair. Finally I insisted she leave my tresses unbound, and to dry them set a chair for me before a brazier. She delivered a firm admonition. I had better not go outside with my head wet and catch a chill and take ill again, and return the household to a state of turmoil: nobody's nerves could withstand the strain. Briseis, also in attendance, voiced a hearty agreement. Before helping me dress, she carefully examined my genitals and pronounced them healthy. She nevertheless recommended I abstain from sexual activity for another week, just to make sure no latent complications remained.

"Welcome back, my Lioness!" Tiberius exclaimed as I engaged him rapaciously at the end of the prescribed waiting period. After we had finished, and I with eyes half-closed lay reveling in the long-missed sensations of sexual afterglow, he arose to retrieve something from the dresser. Sitting back down on our bed, he read from a small tablet,

> The luster of spring illumines the skies;
> The earth wakes with renewal of life;
> The blossoming heliotrope again regards the sun, healed.

Because he could no longer frequent the academic and cultural venues of Rhodes, he had been avidly pursuing the study of poetry since taking up residence on the farm—reading and rereading every offering in our own library, and sending to Thrasyllus for works our collection lacked. He had also begun to write poetic compositions of his own. Despite my persistent entreaties he had resolutely refused to show or recite these creations to me, insisting I would laugh at them as amateurish and pedestrian. Having a pillow hurled at him was not quite the response he was expecting on this particular afternoon.

"You have been writing such graceful and elegant poetry all these months, and not sharing it with me?" I scolded.

"Do you consider the epigram genuinely well written?" he inquired earnestly. Returning the pillow to its place, he lay back down beside me. "Speak as an academician, Clytia—not as a lover. Constructive criticism I crave—not flattery. I should like to start composing epigrams as gifts to commemorate significant occasions—my nephew's imminent coming of age, for example. Extolling your recovery gave me the idea. Before I implement it, however, I must make sure my efforts are not unrefined banalities, destined to insult their recipients and render me a fool."

I took his hand in mine and lay in silence, reflecting upon his verse. Its inherent love so moved me, that for a time I found pondering its purely technical merits a struggle. At length I managed an evaluation, which to my delight and relief was favorable. "Remember how Longus assessed my painting: not the stuff of great masters, but eminently suitable for public consumption? Well, I feel the same description applies to your poetry. It may not equal the work of Hesiod or Pindar or Sappho; but you need not fear it will be thought ludicrous, my beloved."

He smiled and kissed my forehead.

Several days later I ventured out of doors for the first time since being stricken. It was now the final week of March. Strolling through the park in the direction of the pond, I came upon a small clearing in which a red heliotrope was beginning to bloom. At once I returned to the house as quickly as I could, being still somewhat weak. Grabbing my paint box, and the stool on which I sat when painting out of doors, I hastened back to my subject. Sketching the plant proved pleasantly challenging because it moved as the sun moved, so I must keep repositioning myself to maintain perspective. On finishing the picture, I copied the poem beneath it on the tableau. After I had affixed Tiberius' name he demanded I remove it, lest having to explain his authorship prove awkward for me someday. This counsel, like similar ones he had offered, eventually showed itself well considered. Nevertheless I etched his initials, in cryptically small and ornate calligraphy, on the tableau's backside.

Down the future, Tiberius would achieve renown as a capable writer of epigrams. Many would thank him with gracious admiration, for his poetic commemorations of their special occasions. His favorite style became the succinct yet cryptic Alexandrian epigram as perfected by Euphorion of Chalcis and Rhianus of Crete. He attributed his determination to pursue and refine his skills to my commendation of his early efforts.

March gave way to April, and a most wondrous occurrence. During the third week of that month, I had a menses! There were no warning signs--no lethargy, no abdominal bloating, no pimples. The flow of blood was minimal, easily contained, and only lasted four days. Briseis was euphoric, as were Tiberius and I, over this promise of gynecologic correction. Briseis did recommend I eventually consult a physician about addressing the possibility another growth may develop. Nevertheless at this time there was no urgency for doing so. She would continue to monitor my condition, and advise when a physician's skill might be required if at all.

The attrition Longus had wrought upon my art collection left me with the enticing incentive to replenish it. I began combing the promontory for subjects and patterns and shadings and hues—some new and others quite familiar. New shoots of varying shapes and shades of green emerged beside floral buds of every conceivable color. The blooming foliage became a visual riot of colors and shapes and an olfactory mêlée of fragrances. The Euroclydon had reconfigured one of the Guardian Trees by breaking off a limb. The tree was nonetheless replete with the tender green of nascent leaves. The other two Guardians were bedecked with flowers, yellow on the one and purple on the other. On the distant terraces one could see our farmhands hard at work, plowing and planting. Their furrows livened the once monochromatic tan of winter fields, with variegated ribbons of brown and yellow and pale green.

With the arrival of May, newness of life emerged in the fauna. Birds sang out, and built nests in which hatchlings appeared. On the larger pond, puffy ducklings and goslings swam in single file behind their proud parents; at the smaller, young turtles clambered through the mud along the banks. Occasionally a praetorian with his horse and dog, or Tiberius riding Sinapeus, flushed a spotted fawn from its hiding place, or a wild sow with a stream of piglets behind her. Over the winter the farm workers had bred our goat Galatea. Yes, her name was the same as my pseudonym, and had been bestowed for its evocation of milk. Now she was suckling a kid, whose birth insured her continued provision of milk to our household. The vibrancy surrounding me, along with the prospect of improved health, impelled me to resume my artistic endeavors and imbue my representations with a sense of renewal.

One morning I was seated on my stool, painting a vignette rendition of the Guardian Trees—now nearing full leaf, and with a brilliant blue sky behind them. Suddenly there was a voice at my shoulder: "How now, Mistress Galatea?" Startled, I overturned my paint box. The vials that were open discharged their contents into my lap. "Oh, my deepest apologies!" the voice continued. "Nero said I stood a good chance of finding you in this place." My caller was Longus. He walked around in front of me and winced. "Again, I am so very sorry; may I assist you?"

"Oh, no thank you, Senator; I am quite all right," I mumbled distractedly. In view of the mischief he had just caused, I did not want him any closer to me than he had to be. Using the rag with which I wiped my brushes, I endeavored to sop the sticky and variegated puddle that was enlarging across my thighs and starting to trickle down my legs. "My garment is hardly irreplaceable," I added, recalling the large trove of textiles from which a new chiton could readily be fashioned.

Longus glanced about for a place to sit and selected a large rock for this purpose. Recognizing the Guardian Trees, he gestured to them and said, "One of your favorite subjects. I remember it from the wall of your sick chamber. Furthermore you have some version in a goodly number of your paintings. How wonderful to see you have recovered."

"Thank you," I returned distractedly, still preoccupied with the spill. Although I had managed to contain the spread of the paint, my chiton remained saturated and slimy. The rag was so full it had become useless. "I call them my Guardian Trees, because they always strike me as at once imposing and benign."

"Galatea, the present disaster I have caused is a dreadful prelude to the joyous news I am about to impart. Your twelve paintings I divided evenly among my three agents. The men in Rome and Alexandria promptly sold the four they received and are now asking for more."

His words alarmed me. "Senator Longus, my art is the product of purely leisure pursuit," I said weakly. "I am not sure I can guarantee results of equivalent excellence when working under demand."

"Your concern is quite legitimate, my dear. The pressure of deadlines can certainly compromise the quality of an artist's work. I believe, however, that I have a solution for you." There was a comforting enthusiasm in his tone. "My man from Ephesus had a novel idea. He put his four on display and took orders for reproductions. If you will grant me permission to engage copyists, we can fill those orders and readily take new ones as well. We can do the same for newer works which you produce at your own pace. The prices we set for copies cannot be nearly as high as for originals. Moreover the standard royalty for artists is considerably lower—only 25 percent of the return—because the copyists must receive their portion. The greater sales volume, however, compensates for the lesser profit from individual pieces."

"Which four?" Now my curiosity was aroused.

"The lion in repose," he began.

His answer relaxed me a bit and I laughed a little. "The inspiration was the housecat I once had, sunning himself."

He chuckled before continuing his inventory. "A landscape with deer beside a river flowing along the base of a cliff."

"Imaginary: an interpolation of scenery from this farm. We have cliffs and deer but no river—two ponds instead. Moreover we have broad vistas: the painting represents a narrow defile."

He nodded his comprehension. "Your third piece is Achilles stricken in the heel with Paris' arrow—from the *Iliad*, which I presume you have read."

"Read, reread, analyzed, discussed, and critiqued far many times more than I care to admit."

Again Longus chuckled. "Nero told me you are quite the learned and insightful lady. Your final item is the pair of eagles sparring in flight."

"From chickens squabbling in our barnyard. There are no eagles on Rhodes."

"Nor lions. But you must have observed both; otherwise you could not have depicted them with the accuracy your paintings betray."

"I have duly observed those creatures firsthand as well as many, many artistic representations of them."

My utterance was no lie. Lions abounded in the sculptures and paintings to which I had thrilled during my travels. Moreover during my tour of Asia Minor our carriage passed through a forested area, in which a male lion was standing not far from the edge of the road. The driver sped the team and the footman seized his spear. These precautions proved unnecessary, because the lion just watched nonchalantly while we scurried by. Despite the brevity of that encounter, the physical immensity of the lion, the stately aplomb of his bearing, the shimmering shadings of his golden coat and darker mane so uncannily similar to Leo's, left an indelible impression upon my memory. For all my life, of course, I had observed the eagle—the symbol of Roman authority—on public buildings and commemorative statuary everywhere. At my family's country retreat in Campania, I had watched eagles soar overhead almost daily; and occasionally, while taking one of my frowned-upon and ridiculed excursions through the woods, I had encountered one perched in a tree.

Now I raised the same concern I had, when Tiberius first suggested Eutychus as my alter ego. "Senator, suppose someone familiar with the cultural community on this island asserts no artist named Eutychus exists here? How will you and your agents respond?"

"By declaring Eutychus is under exclusive contract with me—which will be legally true if you accept my proposal."

"You have my permission to copy, Senator."

I had assumed Longus would leave upon hearing those words; but he remained on the rock. We sat in silence for a time. I began to trace patterns in the paint spill with my finger. Finally he broke the quiet with a sigh, and with the question I had been anticipating with great dread. He began hesitantly. "Galatea, I have known and honored Tiberius Nero for nearly two decades. Through the course of our acquaintance, I have come to realize he does not always assess persons wisely. Will you please tell me who you are, how you come to know him, and what motivates you to be his companion?" His tone grew stern, almost threatening. "I crave satisfaction you are not some exploitative courtesan, toying with his emotions purely for physical gratification or monetary gain, and ready to abandon him without regard for his feelings for prospects you find more promising."

I looked up abruptly from my paint spill and responded with similar intensity. "Your concern, Senator, is as commendable as it is legitimate. You may have my sworn word. I am a freeborn woman of purely Greek ancestry, residing under Tiberius' guardianship as his ward by my own free choice. No crime or disgrace has ever been imputed to me; and I am most certainly not a courtesan. My…ah…loyalty…," (I cleared my throat as I stumbled for a suitable word) "…is purely to Tiberius' person. His wealth and position mean nothing to me. And now, Senator: to protect Tiberius in these times of grave uncertainty I resolutely refuse to disclose, without his consent, any more about my background or how his guardianship of me came about. No disrespect to you is implied, Sir. Nor do I insinuate your discretion cannot be relied upon. Already word has spread that he has taken a hetaera for his pleasure. My aspiration is to preclude the full truth about our relationship being distorted into innuendo for enemies to use against us both. Therefore I must assiduously refrain from revealing any more information than I have already."

My assertiveness gave me a pleasant surprise. What a change had come over me, since those days when my family demanded a full accounting of every activity, statement, opinion, mood, and aspiration I entertained—and then responded with censure. No longer was I uncomfortable or guilt-ridden about withholding information, particularly from babblers like Longus. Nor did I feel any need to justify my silence, or to obfuscate it with dissimulations and lies.

"Best you keep your counsel." Longus did not argue with me. "Nor do I imply disrespect to you," he continued graciously. "You are a most courageous and honorable woman, Galatea, to stand by Tiberius so patiently and supportively through all the danger and anguish he is encountering at this time. I am sure he realizes how fortunate he is to have you, not only as his ward but as his friend." Again falling silent he gazed at me thoughtfully, and then averred gently yet confidently, "You love Tiberius." I took a deep breath and swallowed hard but did not respond. Eying me as comprehendingly as though I had blurted out the

316

most forthright of affirmations, Longus continued. "As he endures his present difficulties, he needs more than reassurance that you love him. He needs to love you, and to recognize your acceptance of his love. We men are so very fragile. That is why we have such enormous egos: they shield our innate insecurity."

How often had I sat alone and forlorn in my alcove, desperately hurling love at the inanimate or imaginary? I felt a stab of remorse. How could I have been so selfish, not to be aware my beloved could feel the same need? Had not Tiberius said, while comforting me after my confrontation with Timoleon, *Draw on my love, Clytia, for as you do you will bless us both.?* But self-condemnation quickly gave way to gratitude, to Longus for pointing this out. "Oh Sir," I said, "I know only too well the wondrous solace of…er…realizing another has accepted the…ah…approbation and affection one has extended."

Longus rose from his rock. "I have kept you far too long in the state of disarray with which I afflicted you. May I help you return to the house, or dispatch a servant to accommodate you?"

"Thank you—just please send a servant, if you would."

Longus bowed and took his leave, of which I was glad; Tiberius had been right about his loquaciousness. But although Longus had started to annoy me, I could not resent him. His enthusiasm for my artwork I had found flattering and encouraging, his concern for the validity of my relationship with Tiberius refreshingly ethical and fraternal. While we were speaking, I had left off doodling on my lap with my finger and started to sketch a design in the paint with a brush. Now the picture was complete: it was of Longus' rock with its adjacent foliage but missing Longus. The paint was drying. I had to stretch the chiton out horizontally to keep it from adhering to my thighs.

Phoebe arrived and surveyed my condition with a quizzical eye. "Whatever kind of mess did you create now?" she demanded.

"Never mind; just gather all my paraphernalia here. When you return to the house, draw my bath."

"Of that bath you are most certainly in need. You manage to get into the oddest of predicaments." She collected the scattered vials, brushes, palettes, and the paint-soaked rag into their box, picked up my stool, and headed toward the house. Slowly I made my way there with chiton extended in front of me, like a woman in the final weeks of pregnancy. After undressing, I ordered Phoebe to let the paint dry thoroughly over the course of the next few days. Thereafter she must wash and dry the chiton ten times in succession.

Phoebe carried off the chiton, shaking her head from side to side in apparent exasperation but taking care not to disturb the design. She knew me well enough to surmise what I had in mind. The accident Longus had perpetrated on me had made me aware of an art form I had not previously considered pursuing—that of painting images on textiles. Now I wanted to see, at the end of all those washings, how well the paint had adhered to the chiton and whether the picture had distorted. Paint remained embedded in my wiping cloths after repeated launderings—so thoroughly that over time the rags lost their absorbency and had to be discarded. If the outcome for my chiton proved to be the same, then I would try my hand at similar endeavors.

Tiberius' elder nephew Nero came of age nine days before the Calends of June [May 24]—another occasion for which Tiberius composed an epigram. In his letter of effusive thanks, the recipient announced his first political decision since coming of age. His given name was exactly the same as his late father's: Nero Claudius Drusus. It was extremely similar to that of his first cousin and best friend—Tiberius' son Drusus Claudius Nero. Therefore to avoid confusion and ensure the public identified both of them properly, Nero had chosen henceforth to be designated Nero Claudius Germanicus, in all official documents, correspondence, speeches, inscriptions and proclamations. Germanicus is the hereditary honorarium the senate had conferred upon Tiberius and his late brother alike, to commemorate their military successes against the Germans. Tiberius' feelings about this decision were mixed. For certain its practicality was unassailable; yet it seemed to denigrate his brother's memory by consigning his appellation Nero Claudius Drusus to oblivion. Moreover since Augustus had approved the change in nomenclature, Tiberius was hardly in a position to challenge it.

Six days before the Calends of June [May 27], Briseis made the announcement I invariably received with great joy for its deliverer, but with that pang of self-pity I could never quite repress. "Master and Lady, I am with child!" The very next day, however, my gloom dissipated with the discovery I was menstruating anew. One month had passed since my previous menses. Once again there were no warning signs, and no excessive flow of blood. Dare I presume a normal cycle was developing? Briseis thought this must be happening.

Reflecting upon Longus' admonition and my own bitter memories of unaccepted love, I resolved to be more diligently aware of and responsive to Tiberius' unspoken indications of affection—readier to return a glance or touch with an acknowledging smile or touch. Henceforth I scrutinized his silences with greater care, to recognize when I could offer a loving word or gesture without making him feel intruded upon, or when it was better to remain near to him but in silence. In the night when his sleep was troubled, instead of surreptitiously fleeing our bed I would wake him gently and nestle against him; and he would hold me until morning or until he drifted into more peaceful slumber. Sometimes I deliberately pretended to fall asleep in his arms, knowing he took comfort from sensing I was at rest. In return he became more demonstrative with his expressions of affection. There was greater frequency of smiles, and of gentle caresses and kisses exchanged furtively when no servant nor guard nor visitor was present to see.

A mellow calm began to overlay the ever-present tension and emotional uneasiness, which the uncertainty of Tiberius' political position imposed upon us. Our feelings for one another refreshed and intensified like the burgeoning late spring greenery. The frequency and satisfaction of our sexual encounters assumed new heights of emotional fulfillment. More than ever, the acts were soothing reaffirmations of affection and commitment and devotion, conjoined with the physical gratification of mutual attraction and desire. One particular engagement toward the middle of June was so moving—so fraught with tenderness and sincerity and ineffable joy—that while we lay holding one another afterward, I felt for a moment as though my mind and body were suddenly filled with light.

Our walks through the park became longer, slower, more languorous than had been our wont. Occasionally, Tiberius mounted Sinapeus and lifted me up in front of him. Then he let the horse wander about the promontory, his arms about me while he held the reins, my head on his chest beneath his chin. To avoid excessive show of our feelings whenever we passed a servant or guard, Tiberius would release me and hold the reins to one side. I would either lean forward and hold Sinapeus' mane to steady myself, or slide to the ground and walk alongside.

During our excursions we frequently came across Briseis, gathering blooms and leaves and roots for use in her medicines. Usually she had Miranda with her. We had been wondering what to do about Miranda, whose fourth birth anniversary was now imminent. Since she could not speak, we could not be certain as to what she did or did not comprehend. Could she learn any useful skills? When she reached physical maturity, would she be able to recognize her libido and understand its purpose and potential dangers? Now Briseis was taking her about, showing her the various plants and explaining their curative properties in surprisingly sophisticated language; and Miranda appeared to be absorbing everything. When I asked Briseis what had inspired her to begin teaching Miranda about pharmaceutics, she replied that the fascinations of very young children—and even of older ones for that matter—can be indicators of nascent talents. For example, the child who shows an early interest in textiles is likely to become a proficient clothier, fuller, embroiderer, or weaver. She laughed at my insistence that with regard to weaving I must be the exception to her rule. The standard does not necessarily apply, she continued, to every childhood interest.

Briseis felt my genuine attraction had not been to weaving, nor even to textiles per se, but rather to the colors and shapes and light patterns that textiles reflect. Their appeal was the indicator of my latent artistic abilities. As for Miranda: Briseis had noticed that whenever she prepared compounds or cultivated her potted medicinal plants, Miranda was usually right by her side and watching with rapt attention. When Briseis started to identify the plants and medicines and their uses, Miranda would nod in comprehension. One day Alcmene came to Briseis' workroom in the servants' quarters with a burn—the consequence of a minor kitchen accident. Without hesitation Miranda went right to the appropriate plant, broke off a piece of leaf, crushed it between her fingers and applied it to the afflicted hand. She even knew enough to daub the remedy, as rubbing would have exacerbated the condition.

What a chain of events to verify Underlying Good, worth consideration by the most perspicacious philosopher of any school. A vicissitude—the hostility of Gaius—had necessitated our relocation to this farm; but behold the consequent benefits. Preparations for our relocation had prompted Arbindus to identify Briseis to Tiberius. My gynecologic difficulties had impelled Tiberius to acquire Briseis—to her personal happiness and that of Arbindus. She had proceeded to save my life! For doing so, Tiberius had rewarded her with manumission and legal marriage. Now Briseis was resolving what we had thought an impasse: the determination of a viable future for Miranda. Who in our household beside Briseis could have identified Miranda's affinity for pharmaceutics? And how could I foresee that within the space of a few brief years, Briseis' counsel to observe the proclivities of young children would prove one of the most essential I had ever received?

In the wake of those repeated washings, the painted design on my chiton held fast; but because I had executed it gazing down upon my lap, it was upside down to the viewer of the chiton when worn. Therefore I set to work fashioning a new garment from the old. Applying some creative cutting and hemming, I converted the chiton into a crescent-shaped shawl, with the design right side up at its center. This finished product I considered sending to Vesca, in honor of her forthcoming marriage to a soldier assigned to the Roman garrison at Rhodes; but presently I thought better of that decision. Vesca was very likely to boast, heartily and ubiquitously within her new milieu, that her gift had come from the woman her mother insisted was Tiberius Nero's concubine. A gift of money, we decided, must prove far less controversial.

At the solstice, Thrasyllus brought his family to the farm for a second summertime visit. Thrasylla, now in her fifth year, officiously recited to Miranda the profound knowledge owed to Aka's tutoring—the letters of the alphabet and the spellings of a few simple words, names of colors and geometric shapes, simple arithmetic sums, names of the principal gods and goddesses mostly mispronounced. When I showed Aka the painted shawl, she immediately asked if she might have it. Without the slightest hesitation I agreed, knowing Aka could be depended upon to dissemble its origin.

And Thrasyllus delivered our horoscopes. Tiberius rolled his eyes on hearing his, as it was frustratingly redundant. He should continue to forebear his vicissitudes with patience, in anticipation of the brilliant future awaiting him. Beneath the present veneer of stagnation, unseen forces were at work to redeem his reputation. He must avoid the temptation to compromise their efficacy by undertaking ill-considered and recklessly aggressive efforts to vindicate himself. My monumental change was still unfolding. Its culmination would diametrically redirect the aspirations and objectives of my life with a new purpose, the pursuit of which heretofore I had never given the remotest of thoughts. This same event would have deep significance for Tiberius, but not affect the course of his destiny as inexorably as it would mine.

Lying awake that night pondering the prophecy, I finally concluded the phenomenal reorientation of my life was the new vocation Longus had determined for me. His arrival three days later apparently confirmed my conclusion. He produced a purse of 53 aurei—my first royalties—a modest sum to be sure, but quite exciting nonetheless. My late teacher Timotheus had been correct: with practice my work had reached the marketable quality he had predicted it might. Longus was poised to make another raid on my collection. His representatives in Alexandria and Rome, having sold everything they had received, were clamoring for more. Moreover the Ephesian agent had sold one of the originals—the landscape with deer—and now wanted a replacement.

In reply I offered to lend three new pieces to the three sites, on the strictest condition all sold copies alone. Only upon confirmation sales of a particular copy were dwindling would I release another original for reproduction. Under no circumstances may another original be sold without my prior knowledge and consent. Upon this condition I was adamant. Not that I was averse to selling an original; but only after I had decided the price was suitable, and the loss to the overall collection inconsequential. Longus must please remember:

my collection had taken nearly seven years to build. I did not care to see it diminish faster than I could replenish it. He closed his eyes as he nodded acknowledgment. "A shrewd entrepreneur, Nero—dedicated to her product and to a responsible marketing strategy. I have every confidence our venture will continue to prosper."

He made his selections, conscientiously inquiring whether he had my permission to take them. Without disclosing my reason I denied him one—the Alexander the Great astride his horse—because the statuette I had copied it from was now in the possession of Augustus. Longus opted instead for a scene from the *Aeneid*: the ghost of Creusa exhorting her husband Aeneas to flee the burning city of Troy, and with his retainers establish a new civilization in Italy. The remaining pieces included the legendary Judgment of Paris that precipitated the Trojan War; Phrixus and Helle astride the ram of the golden fleece (our goat Galatea served as my model for the ram); a rural landscape inspired by the Guardian Trees; hippopotami in the Nile (a fusion of turtles in the pond with Melambrotus' wood carving); Odysseus and his men escaping the enraged, blinded Cyclops by clinging to the bellies of his sheep (again, Galatea the goat was my model); and the owl that perched at evening atop our barn.

Not long thereafter Longus presented me with a wondrous proposition, which showed he aspired to cultivate and enhance my art as well as sell it. Near the interior of the island of Rhodes, at about a day's journey from our farm, the river Pelecanus flows through an expansive gorge heavily wooded with sweet-gum trees. Between May and September, this vale is populated in droves by a species of large moth. It intrigues scientists with its arrival and departure at precisely the same time each year, and delights artists with its vibrant and variegated markings. Tiberius and I had known about the place for years, but had never considered venturing there.

The valley lay under jurisdiction of a village called Tholos. To deter the casually and carelessly curious from spoiling this unique environment, the village authorities assiduously restricted access to all but those who could present a legitimate reason for visiting the defile. Submission of an application to the archon was mandatory. Tiberius could have used his authority as regent and subsequently as imperial legate to demand admission; but to do so for apparently idle curiosity constituted an abuse of power the likes of which we both eschewed. Now Longus had managed to supply the justification we could not. As patron of the artist Eutychus of Rhodes, whose record of sales unassailable proved *him* a bona fide professional in his field, Longus had sought and received permission to bring his protégé to the glade, for the purely artistic purpose of observing and sketching the moths.

Was I interested? I would have to disguise myself as a man, of course. The journey portended to be highly uncomfortable. Negotiating the primeval terrain of the glade was certain to prove difficult. There were bound to be stinging plants like nettles, along with mosquitoes and midges and other biting pests. We may have to watch out for serpents. Longus had not yet arranged accommodations in or near the village, but had made some inquiries. He feared the lodgings might be of very dubious ambiance. Nevertheless I ought to give this opportunity very careful consideration, as it was likely to enrich my style of painting with refreshing inspiration and broader dimension.

Was I interested? Bouncing up and down in my chair with enthusiasm, I prompted Longus to laugh and Tiberius to roll his eyes. Even if I must cut my hair and endure looking like the hetaera many already presumed I was, eager and ready was I to depart the moment arrangements were finalized. After seeing Longus off the next day, I engaged Phoebe to prepare my disguise. We decided not to shorten my hair as much as to thin it. Then it could be tied atop my head and hidden under a large and loosely fitting petasos. The shade of this hat would help obscure my face while shielding me from the sun. Procuring Greek male garments for me presented no difficulty, as Tiberius wore them along with all our menservants. We would conceal my breasts under a winding sheet of soft cloth, and a loosely woven chlamys overhanging my chiton ostensibly for protection from insects. What proved a challenge was finding a pair of male sandals small enough to accommodate me, as my feet are diminutive even for a woman—until Menon suggested boots might be more appropriate for the terrain of my destination. Nicanor lent a pair of his hunting boots, which we stuffed with rags until they fit. Their size belied that of my feet, and made me appear all the more masculine.

"Walk with resolute strides!" Tiberius admonished as I modeled my costume for him. "Put aside all the comportment and poise Demas and Timoxena taught you and revert to Pythia of Naples. A man does not walk with wary, mincing steps unless he is homosexual. We are going to have enough trouble passing you off as male without having to address that stigma." He taught me how to bow like a man: bend at the hips, chest forward and back straight.

On learning I had selected Alcmene to attend me on the journey, Briseis pleaded with me to take her instead. I had hesitated because of her pregnancy. She assured me she was perfectly hale, and foresaw no complications from her condition. Her curative skill would enable her to detect and check any unforeseen difficulty. We were only going to be away three days. Would I please take her? She did not want to miss this wondrous opportunity to scour that sweet-gum forest for its pharmaceutics. After considering her purpose along with Tiberius' comments about my bearing, I assented. Since Briseis was some five years my junior, I could convincingly represent her as Eutychus' wife. Alcmene, being older than I and better presentable as *his* mother or aunt, might confirm suspicions of perverse sexuality.

We set off the day before the Nones of July *[7/6]*: Longus and Briseis and Eutychus and Longus' valet Mynes who drove his carriage. The weather had turned fetid with heat and humidity. There was no breeze whatsoever. The air was so oppressively still, I found myself almost wishing a Sirocco would arise. Also I worried about Briseis; but she poked high-spirited fun at my concerns. Struck by the ironic coincidence of the two servants' names, to pass the time I related the story of Briseis from the ***Iliad***. Briseis' husband Mynes was king of the Cilician city-state Lyrnessus. An ally of Troy, Mynes fought on that city-state's behalf during the Trojan War. The Greek hero Achilles killed Mynes in battle and took Briseis for his concubine. Apollo subsequently compelled Agamemnon, the king of Mycenae, to surrender his own mistress Chryseis to her father Chryses who was a priest to the god. Agamemnon demanded Briseis in compensation; and thereupon, Achilles refused to fight in support of his fellow Greeks. When the death of his close friend Patroculus compelled Achilles to take up arms once again, a grateful Agamemnon restored Briseis with the assurance he had not lain with her. My Briseis declared the whole business a stunning tribute to the pigheadedness of men.

Although the archon of Tholos had offered to accommodate us in his home, Longus had arranged lodging at a small roadside inn on a principal byway some distance from the village. In the close quarters of a private residence my ruse might be discovered—especially if the host choose to lodge Eutychus in the male quarters rather than matrimonially with *his wife*. The inn I could enter and depart wrapped head to foot in a female himation and sandals, exchanging these for chlamys and petasos and boots in the seclusion of the carriage. Longus also made the clever suggestion we present Eutychus as a mute—freeing me from the onus of having to lower my voice to the precisely the same pitch each time I spoke, lest its timbre fluctuate and sound obviously contrived.

Our quarters were clean, but cramped and stifling hot. Because of the weather, the proprietors offered a pleasant cold supper of fresh greens, bread, and cooked trout. Since I wanted to see the moth forest in every possible light, we decided to set out the next morning before dawn. Accordingly we retired early, and slept badly on account of the muggy atmosphere and the anticipation of our early departure. While we were en route, Briseis rubbed everyone's face, arms, and legs with yarrow leaves to deter stinging insects. When we arrived at the village of Tholos, a man and a lad both clad in short chitons of goatskin were waiting in the morning twilight to greet us. From their garb I assumed they were farmhands, until the man introduced himself as Nicias the archon and the youth as Asander his son. They offered us breakfast which we refused, having brought provisions of our own; moreover Eutychus was eager to reach *his* destination by dawn. Asander climbed aboard the carriage beside Mynes and directed us away from the village toward the ravine.

We completed the last portion of our journey afoot, as the carriage could not negotiate the narrow path along which Asander led us. Each member of the group carried a piece of the equipment we had brought: stools for sitting, paints and palettes and charcoal for etching, satchels to hold Briseis' medicinal gleanings, a basket of food, jugs of drinking water. Asander advised we could leave the jugs behind in the carriage. There was no need to bother hauling these along, because the water of the river was clean and potable. I was glad for Nicanor's boots; for the path was uneven, muddy from dew, and hedged with brambles. Briseis bound her feet and calves with layers of cloth before donning the clogs she always wore when collecting her medicinals.

When we reached the riverbank, the dawn was turning the sky pink and illuminating the tops of the trees. We started to see what appeared to be blighted leaves of deep gray, their veins white with decay. As the sunlight crept down the tree trunks and the air warmed, the leaves began to stir. They were the moths; and they were everywhere. We had to step gingerly to avoid treading on them. As Asander escorted us along the river's edge, we began to hear the sound of falling water. Presently we arrived at a cataract. Down it the river cascaded partway in a single stream, then branched into two before emptying into the pool below. Asander remarked he had brought us here because he thought this the most scenic region of the glade.

In the early morning shadows the area did not seem terribly interesting. As the day progressed, however, I began to feel as though I had walked into a rainbow. As the light intensified the gray moth wings—dully monochromatic in shade—became luminous with hues of varying intensity and nuance. The moths had underwings essentially of yellowish-red, but actually ranging in hue from near yellow almost to blood-red. These were dotted with splotches the same dark gray as the outer wings. From beneath—as when they flew overhead or perched in trees—the moths appeared altogether red and slightly translucent.

Their colors and markings intensified or faded, depending upon the light and the backgrounds on which the moths sat or through which they flew. At times all one noticed were the white vein stripes, at others the shiny dark gray, at still others only the yellowish-red.

In morning light the waterfalls appeared uniformly blue, the sweet-gum trees similarly gray. As the day progressed the water became white, and the trees a mottled mixture of dusty greens and blues. By noon the waterfall mist gleamed silvery-white, and in the light of midafternoon it produced rainbows. The light crept across the smaller shrubs and little plants on the forest floor, bringing out the colors and shapes of leaves and flowers and berries hitherto undetected, and then moving on to conceal them once again in shadow. When the day declined toward sunset, everything in the valley turned golden—moths, foliage, and water—as though from the touch of King Midas.

Asander remained with us through the day: ostensibly to answer our questions, procure any necessities we required, and keep us from getting lost. I rather suspected he wanted to ensure we did not disrupt the environment as well. For a while he watched me; then since he knew Eutychus could not speak, he directed a question to Longus. Why, if I had come to draw moths, was I only painting differently colored lines on my palettes? Longus explained how artists recorded patterns and shapes and colors before using them in pictures. With that Asander decided art was boring, and began to trail a line in the river to catch fish. I resolved to prepare a vignette of a moth for him. If unable to complete it today, I would do so later and send it to him.

Briseis was in her glory. By midmorning she had one of the satchels stuffed full of medicinals. When she came to retrieve another bag, she reminded me to drink plenteous water as a precaution against the heat. Although we had brought our own lunch of bread, fruit, and boiled eggs, we did not escape Rhodian hospitality. Around noon, Nicias appeared with more of the same fare, plus some cold but very savory cooked fowl. The biggest challenge I faced during the day was being able to relieve myself without compromising my disguise. After holding out as long as possible, I beckoned Longus. With my charcoal I wrote *call of nature* in Latin on a blank palette, and hoped desperately he would catch my drift. He did, and proceeded to distract Asander while I bolted behind a thicket suitably dense to let me squat without detection.

We remained in the glade until the setting sun replicated the light patterns of the dawn. I did manage to complete a moth portrait for Asander. It was hardly profound, because I did not have time to include the great diversity of hues I had observed. Not understanding this, he declared the rendering a masterpiece. After declining Nicias' offer of supper, since we were satiated from his generous lunch, we departed the village for the inn. With considerable relief I shed petasos and chlamys and wrapped myself in my himation: being female again felt grand. After a cooling bath I went directly to bed, where the colors and patterns and lighting of the day flashed through my mind before and throughout my slumber.

Upon awakening I felt rested but not yet hungry, so I only partook of water while my companions breakfasted. Our homeward journey proceeded uneventfully enough until just after midday, when suddenly I became uncomfortably aware of the heat. Presently a violent headache set in. Lightheadedness followed: momentarily I thought I might faint. My stomach churned, then tightened and heaved. "Mynes, stop the carriage!" I cried with such urgency that he drew up immediately and abruptly. Barely did I reach the door in time to vomit pale green bile all over the roadside instead of the carriage floor. Diarrhea followed. Briseis gently drew one arm about me as I recoiled shuddering. In her other hand she held her water jug, from which she urged me in quiet, compassionate tones to sip. When I could not swallow, she had me just rinse my mouth with the water. Wetting a kerchief, she cleaned me as best she could. Back in the carriage she retrieved several yarrow leaves from her sack. These she told me to suck, and swallow any of the nectar I could.

Clenching my fists and teeth, nursing the yarrow as best I was able, I managed to complete the trip without further incident until our arrival. The jolting of the carriage, followed by the swaying of Asellus as I rode him up the promontory, proved too much. Before I could dismount I vomited again, all down the donkey's shoulder and foreleg.

"Whatever did you eat?" Tiberius demanded as Briseis helped me stumble up the veranda.

"It was not our food, Master," she responded patiently. "The rest of us are unaffected."

"Poor Asellus," Tiberius sighed as Ajax, his face contorted in a grimace, led the donkey to the barn. Asellus was not ruffled at all.

It turned out I had contracted an annoying but trivial pestilence, which was making its way about the entire island. Everyone got it: the servants, the praetorians, Tiberius himself. Once stricken, one could expect full recovery around the same hour on the following day. Briseis was kept busy, administering infusions of yarrow or chamomile, spearmint or elecampane, depending upon what each victim felt he or she could swallow and keep down.

My sickness, however, refused to disappear. Often I awakened with severe nausea. Occasionally I vomited, or simply retched. On some days I felt achingly lethargic as though I had not slept in weeks. Other days, however, passed entirely without incident. Presently I noticed my face once again had pimples, my breasts were sore, and my abdomen was beginning to swell. Assuming these symptoms portended another menses, I became frantic with concern. Would this bout revert to the severity of those which had preceded my expulsion of the growth? Already the forty-five or so days that had precisely demarked the intervals between my catharsis and the two subsequent menses had passed. Was another growth developing? Worst yet, would I survive? Briseis and Tiberius concurred: time was at hand to summon the physician from Ialyssos, whose name ironically enough was Eupistus. To evade speculations about my identity, we would present me as one of the servants and have me examined in their quarters.

Eupistus declined to come. He did not attend patients in their homes unless they were hopelessly bedridden. So long as a patient could walk, he or she must see Eupistus in his own establishment; for there he had access to his own medicines and equipment with which he was familiar and comfortable. Tiberius wrote back that the patient was weak from vomiting; there was a pharmakeutria in residence on his farm with a store of medicines; he was willing to double or triple the physician's fee. Eupistus nevertheless remained adamant. "You have no choice but to go to Ialyssos,"Tiberius told me irritably, being unaccustomed to having his orders countermanded. "At least it is only half a day's journey—not nearly so distant as the butterfly glade."

At length an appointment was set, for the tenth day after my illness began. Once again I awoke in a state of weakness, lethargy, and nausea—for which I was actually pleased, because the physician could observe my symptoms firsthand. Briseis, who was to accompany me, helped me don a tunic from the deep brown livery of Tiberius' serving staff. My silver and ruby ring I removed, lest it belie my allegedly servile status. Although I ate no breakfast—the very thought of food turned my stomach—I managed to down a precautionary tumbler of chamomile infusion. Afterward in considerable discomfort but at least without throwing up on Asellus, I negotiated the descent down the promontory to where Arbindus was waiting with the carriage. For the duration of the journey I dozed, but far from contentedly. Foreboding about my impending encounter began to torment me more than my physical discomfort. Would the physician deliver a cure or a dire prognosis?

Around noontime, Arbindus halted the carriage before what appeared to be an ordinary house, located a city block off the broad sunlit agora of Ialyssos. Briseis and I entered a large, high-ceilinged room, shaded with blinds from the brightness and heat of the street, but comfortably airy and well ventilated. In the center stood a low table, long and wide, of highly polished wood. The shelves along two walls replicated those in Briseis' workroom. They were replete with bowls and basins, a stack of neatly folded linens, implements the purposes of which one could only conjecture, and innumerable covered containers of various shapes and sizes. A desk and chair stood in a corner opposite the shelf area. The man who entered limping from an adjacent room was much older than I had anticipated, with white hair and droopy skin. Little wonder, I reflected in view of his age, he refused to be an itinerant physician. He said nothing and did not smile, but folded his arms and looked each of us up and down rather disdainfully.

"You Nero's party?" he grunted at last.

Although Tiberius had warned me this Eupistus had a reputation for gruffness, his manner so rattled me I could not respond. Briseis came to my rescue. "Yes Sir," she said and curtsied. Recalling I was supposed to be a servant I curtsied as well, and then handed Eupistus the tablet bearing Tiberius' letter of introduction.

Eupistus perused the note and then looked up at me. "You Galatea?" I nodded. He returned to the tablet. "Refreshing to see this reprobate cares about the wellbeing of his servants. Have you no tongue, Girl?"

Aggravation over this pronouncement about Tiberius enabled me to find my tongue. "Certainly I do, Sir, and am quite prepared to employ it."

"Feisty," he muttered as he ambled to the desk and placed the tablet on it. Turning to Briseis, he pointed to the chair beside the desk. "You sit there, out of my way." Then he took my hand and seated me on the long table. His touch was gentler than I had expected. Still holding my hand he sat down beside me. "So tell me, Girl, what ails you?"

I described my present symptoms and related my gynecological history, concluding with Briseis' assessment of the growth in my womb and my concern about potential fatality. He nodded comprehendingly and reflectively while he listened. As I concluded he rose, went to a shelf, and from a pitcher poured liquid into a tumbler which he carried to me. "Drink," he commanded. Although thirsty from the heat I hesitated, for my nausea was still making me recoil at having to swallow anything. Noting my stall, Eupistus growled, "It is water, Girl, not poison. I want a sample of your urine." He watched observantly as

I struggled to get the water down, and then said quietly, "Do not try to drink faster than you can comfortably manage."

After I had finally drained the tumbler, Eupistus rose to his feet, brought me to mine and said, "Remove your clothes." As I complied, I became suddenly weaker and hotter—and not on account of my physical condition. With the possible exception of my father during my infancy, no man had ever seen me naked apart from Tiberius; and for him, of course, I shed my garments willingly. Physician or no physician, having to disrobe before a strange man made me feel violated, sullied, forced. At least my malaise disproved those incessant accusations of shameless concupiscence and exhibitionism Euethia had hurled at me year after year, ever since she had caught me masturbating when I was a young girl. That surge of resentment increased my discomfort. As I fumbled with clasps and girdle, my hands trembling, Eupistus said, "Come now, no need for fear or embarrassment." He beckoned Briseis. "Here, you: assist your companion."

Eupistus tugged at my hair a little, examined my ears and eyes and then my mouth. "You are not far from your thirtieth year, eh Girl?"

"Yes, Sir. My twenty-seventh anniversary occurs in this August forthcoming."

He proceeded to knead my breasts. I winced because they were sore, and because having a man other than Tiberius touch them furthered my discomfiture. Leaving off this action, Eupistus slowly slid the palm of one hand down my belly to just below my navel. At the same time drew his other palm down my back to just above my buttocks. He gently but steadily pressed both palms against my body as though he were squeezing a sponge, and then released me.

"Has your back been aching?"

At his mention, I did recall noticing occasional discomfort in my lower back over the last week. "Yes Sir, a little," I said.

"How long have you had acne?"

"My entire life."

"Has it worsened recently?"

"Yes."

He nodded. "You might be able to reduce those blemishes by daubing them with donkey's milk. Do you feel ready to urinate yet?"

"Yes, Sir." I was glad he asked, for this familiar call of nature was becoming increasingly urgent.

What happened next mortified me beyond imagination. Eupistus removed a wide-mouthed jar and a small cloth from a shelf, thrust the jar between my legs and said, "Proceed." As I dried myself with the cloth afterward, he poured the urine onto into a shallow bowl and began to examine it closely, swirling it about. This procedure so repulsed me, I became overwhelmed with nausea and began to retch. Eupistus got an empty basin under my chin—and not a moment too soon—to catch a mixture of bile with the water I had swallowed earlier. Unable to remain standing I sat down on the table, gripping its edges and shaking violently. Eupistus looked at me surprised. "Why this ado, Girl?"

Briseis again intervened for me. "Vomiting terrorizes her, Sir—it always has."

"Whatever for? Vomiting is as natural and healthy a function as urinating. It is the body's mechanism for expelling toxins. The physician's task is to discover and eliminate the source of those toxins." Patting my shoulder, he said mildly, "There, there, sit quietly for now and breathe deeply. Let me get these out of your sight." He gathered up the soiled vessels and carried them from the room. On returning he filled another tumbler, stirred something into it, and then brought it to me along with an empty tumbler. "Rinse your mouth, and expectorate into the empty vial. Take care not to swallow the solution, as it will make you vomit anew. This is simply rock salt dissolved in water. You can prepare it at home. Cleansing your mouth with this mixture after vomiting will protect your teeth." I did not tell him I was already familiar with the procedure because Briseis had urged it on me. Then Eupistus said, "You have particularly splendid teeth—strong, healthy, and clean."

"Thank you, Sir, oh thank you!" I returned, not as demurely as I would have liked. He raised an eyebrow at my effusiveness but said nothing. After enduring ridicule of my teeth throughout childhood, hearing a physician praise them was sweet revenge on their critics. My sense of degradation fled before his compliment. Now I was at ease, and comfortably ready to continue the examination.

I finished with the salt water. "Lie on your back and raise your knees," Eupistus commanded as he took the tumblers away. He returned with a little pillow which he placed under my head. Extending one hand over my lower abdomen, he exerted gentle pressure for what seemed a rather long while. Then he cautioned, "Be neither afraid nor outraged." Continuing to push down on my belly, he inserted the fore and middle fingers of his other hand into my vagina. While holding this position he pressed here and there on my lower abdomen with the fingers of his free hand. Withdrawing his fingers, he said, "Straighten your legs." Once again he spread a hand over my belly and applied the same light but steady pressure as before. As he did so he glanced about attentively but without focusing upon anything, as though listening for a faint noise. Suddenly he nodded his head as if in satisfaction, removed his hand and said, "Rise and dress."

"You have a man to yourself, Girl, or you sleep about?" he grunted as Briseis was helping me back into my tunic.

His query irritated me. "One man exclusively—I am most certainly not promiscuous, Sir!" I retorted testily.

"Now, now, no need for insolence." In my annoyance I had abandoned the reticence expected of a servant. "What about you, pharmakeutria?" the physician continued. "I see you are with child—since early March it appears." It took his experienced eye to notice. Briseis' abdomen had only just begun to bulge, her condition barely apparent beneath the loose drape of her chiton.

"A married freedwoman, Sir!" Briseis proudly displayed her wedding ring, which being gold rather than bronze had presumably diminished Arbindus' savings considerably. "In fact my husband is waiting outside with our carriage."

"Master has his way with either of you?"

"No Sir!" we both exclaimed, practically in unison. My response was no lie, since my intercourse with Tiberius was entirely consensual.

"I hear he keeps a hetaera against her will for that purpose," Eupistus muttered, almost as if thinking aloud.

I was too outraged to say anything; but Briseis ejaculated, "No hetaera, Sir! Those rumors are wholly wrong and unfair!"

Eupistus grunted again and raised his eyebrows. "Hnn—a better character than most presume." On hearing that comment, I started to like the man. After I had finished dressing, he motioned us to sit on the examination table and sat down between us. "Pharmakeutria, your physical appearance reveals you are a Gaul; yet you speak Greek fluently. Most commendable. All the more admirable: your diagnosis of uterine growth expulsion was entirely accurate. And as for you, Girl," he patted my knee almost amiably, "you are not sick; nor are you about to menstruate. You are pregnant as well, due to deliver near the Calends of March."

The room reeled about me, filled with pale light, and disappeared.

REGENERATION

Awakening, I found myself lying on my back upon the physician's examining table. A fragrance, piney and biting, filled my head: to revive me, Eupistus had had me inhale the vapors of camphor. After I had taken several deep breaths of fresh air my head cleared; and with the physician's help I managed to sit up. He had a snack awaiting me: strips of bread moistened with milk and sprinkled with pulverized cassia. Now that the cause of my nausea was known, so was its remedy: food. A few morsels of a soft starch such as polenta, bread with the crusts removed, or a draught of grain water, usually alleviate the nausea associated with early pregnancy, and are regurgitated comfortably if vomiting cannot be resisted. Milk and cassia are particularly helpful in relieving the nausea, which should disappear altogether within a month or so. I could expect the acne blemishes to fade as well.

Nausea or no nausea, I must eat regularly and adequately for the sake of my own health and that of my child. The diet Eupistus recommended was almost identical to what Briseis had provided in the wake of my last grave menses: robust meats, eggs, milk and milk-based foods like custards and cheeses, fruits fresh or stewed, greens and cooked green vegetables like asparagus, and of course soft starches. If I felt too nauseous to swallow solid food, I should substitute meat broth and grain water. I might have wine, but in strict moderation: no more than a single tumbler per meal. Turning to Briseis, he inquired whether she had eaten anything that day. Yes, she averred, she had breakfasted. Upon our departure she would partake of the provisions she had brought along in our carriage—unless, of course, her husband had already devoured them all. Eupistus actually smiled.

He continued with a serious warning. I was undergoing my first pregnancy at a relatively advanced age, and following a uterine complication of many years' duration. My risk for miscarriage was quite high. All movements and exertions must be as minimal as possible. My overseer should arrange for me only the lightest of duties—most preferably those like sewing, which would allow me to remain seated. Whenever possible, I should recline. Alternately sitting and lying on the examining table, Eupistus demonstrated some moderate physical exercises for arms and legs: shrugs, kicks, stretches. He insisted I perform these to ensure my muscles did not atrophy while I kept sedentary and recumbent. The foot of my bed I must elevate, so that I sleep on an incline with my feet higher than my head—and tell my man to find alternate accommodations if he objects. Finally—and possibly most objectionable to my spouse—there must be no intercourse, lest its jostlings and contortions compromise my condition. If I managed to reach December without complication, the baby stood a good chance of being born alive and survivable.

Eupistus left the examining table for his desk, where he prepared his invoice for the day's consultation and a list of the instructions he had just delivered verbally. As he handed me the tablets, he cautioned us to proceed homeward at snail's speed to curtail the jolting of our carriage. While we plodded along, my mind swirled with misgivings as my thoughts and emotions shifted between hope and dread. How would Tiberius react? Certainly not with surprise; for once we were underway, Briseis confessed she had confided to him her strong suspicion I might be pregnant—that at some juncture in my body's adjustment after the expulsion of the uterine growth I had become fertile. She was also rather surprised albeit most pleasantly, having anticipated my tumultuous gynecologic history had rendered me sterile. Reluctant to rely solely upon her own judgment of my condition, she had now urged Tiberius to seek verification of her diagnosis and recommendations for further treatment from a bona fide physician.

Would Eupistus' confirmation mollify, with joyful anticipation, the chagrin and desperation of Tiberius' struggle to redeem his reputation? Or would he consider my condition an added duress, the baby a potential embarrassment for enemies to decry and ridicule? Eventually its presence must become known, certainly to the praetorians if not to visitors. We could hardly sequester the babe inside the house once it had matured beyond infancy. How would Tiberius' family react? And what kind of future could we offer this child, when our own was uncertain and potentially perilous? Who would teach a skill or trade, tender employment or at least sponsorship of a career, propose a marriage alignment, to the offspring of an outcast spurned by his own family along with half the world? Given my distorted upbringing, could I even be a suitable mother? Had I learned from my parents' model what errors to avoid; or would I unconsciously revert to these, and unintentionally afflict another human being with the very distresses and impositions I had suffered and ultimately fled?

Was motherhood the monumental change Thrasyllus had predicted for me? Be this the case, the pregnancy was certain to succeed. But on the other hand, was my condition only another step along the way to a different outcome, and as such doomed to end in the disappointment of miscarriage? I recalled my mother, who had never suffered miscarriage, disdaining those who had as though the bereft were an inferior grade of woman. For a brief but unsettling moment I felt the familiar suffocating despair, which used to overtake me whenever I failed to meet an unreachable goal my family had set for me. Then a notion far more horrific supplanted the memory. Was my monumental change destined to be a state of permanent debility, arising from complications in childbirth? My sense of Underlying Eternal Good, harmonizing the outcome of events, seemed irritatingly abstract and elusive in the face of these impending calamities.

A far more immediate and practical concern began to worry me. The lurching of Asellus was bound to put me at risk; but how else could I ascend the promontory? The solution came in the form of Nicanor astride Sinapeus. He and a mounted praetorian intercepted us on the main roadway while we were yet some distance from the farm. When owing to the slowness of our pace we did not arrive home at the anticipated time, Tiberius had become worried and sent the scouts to determine what had befallen us. The sun had set, and dusk was enshrouding the landscape by the time we reached the base of the promontory. Ajax and another praetorian were awaiting us with torches. An uncharacteristically frantic Briseis explained I could not endure even the slightest jostling. This matter was addressed immediately. As Arbindus helped me from the carriage, Nicanor requested his assistance in lifting me onto Sinapeus' withers. Placing one arm about my shoulders and the other beneath my knees, Nicanor actually held me above Sinapeus while Ajax—torch in one hand and reins in the other—led the horse up the ascent.

A meteor flashed across the darkening sky, and several moments later two more. They did not startle me at all, so natural and appropriate they seemed to this day of astounding discovery. I am unsure whether anyone else in the party noticed them. All eyes except mine were focused upon the promontory path, the precariousness of which the half-light had increased.

When we reached the main house Nicanor handed me down to Ajax, who on Briseis' command carried me to my own quarters and laid me on the bed. Tiberius burst into the room, his look of outrage attesting to his alarm. What by all the gods had the physician ascertained? After sending Ajax after a bowl of barley gruel—not only to be rid of him but because my nausea was returning as well—I reported my condition and its dubious prognosis. As Tiberius listened his features assumed the stony, expressionless mien he always wore when fighting to conceal his emotions. After I had finished, he told Briseis in quiet and measured tones to dispatch Phoebe and Alcmene to my chamber and then retire for the night. Sitting down in the chair, he gazed at the floor in silence.

The two serving women arrived with my supper. When Tiberius soberly informed them I was pregnant, they began to squeal with delight. After hushing them curtly, he ordered them to reinstate the regime they had followed during my grievous menses. They must bathe and feed me in my quarters, and with Briseis develop a schedule allowing a female attendant to sleep in the adjoining room. Additionally they must come up with a means of elevating the foot of my bed, carefully ensuring one side was not higher than the other, and that my stirring in sleep did not cause the bed to slip off the props. Without another word he departed abruptly.

Fatigue and apprehension made me unwontedly testy. I snapped at my attendants to cease the cooing adulation they had begun and get me bathed and bedded as soon as possible. Finding a way to raise the nether end of my bed must wait until the morrow. I needed to be alone, to assess the newest uncertainty besetting me. From Tiberius' behavior I knew he was deeply moved—but how? With anger? Despair? Or perchance with happiness?

On falling asleep, I dreamed my mother was supervising a pair of grotesque figures. As they were clad in heavy, dark, hooded garments I could not see their faces. One of them was restraining my hands, while the other pressed down upon my abdomen as though to force the expulsion of its contents. *You would abort your own grandchild?* I demanded of my mother. *Hold your peace, slut!* she retorted. *We are doing the world a service. Any offspring you produce will be as much a scourge to mankind as you.*

Awakening with a start, I discovered a reality far more benign. The feeble light emanating from the antechamber revealed Tiberius sitting on the edge of my bed, holding both of my hands in in his right and caressing my abdomen with his left.

"Please forgive me—I did not mean to wake you," he said gently.

"I am glad you did," I murmured with relief as I smiled up at him. "The dream I was having was far from pleasant. I shall not torment you with a description of it."

"I have not slept at all but have been lying awake, exulting in your wondrous news."

With that I sat up, drew my arms about him and laid my head beneath his chin. "I was so afraid you would be dismayed or angry."

"For whatever reason?" There was bewilderment in his tone. He stroked my hair as he held me. "My Clytia, I am ecstatic! Of the three children who have been born to me, only one is alive today. The possibility of having another child fills me with exuberant anticipation and joy. Why are you weeping? With happiness, I hope. Do you not see? We have witnessed the fulfillment of a prophecy. Your becoming a mother is most certainly a monumental change."

Between sobs I recited my litany of fears.

"Oh, let the praetorians talk!" he exclaimed after I finished. "How many of them have bastards of their own? Until we can disclose my paternity without concern for adverse consequence, let us maintain your fictitious husband Aristocles engendered your child during a brief and furtive reconciliation. For certain I shall amend my will, acknowledging you and our babe as my legitimate wife and child. And although my future is uncertain, that of our child is not. If nothing else, he will become proprietor of this farm. I cannot bequeath him my patrimony because our marriage is morganatic; but I can and assuredly shall name you both remaindermen. Furthermore, my being his father will give him partial Roman citizenship. Although he will not be able to vote or hold public office, he will still enjoy the rights to own property under the protection of Roman law, to marry a Roman citizen of equivalent rank, and to appeal adverse judicial rulings to Caesar."

He laid me back down upon the bed. From under the pillow I retrieved a kerchief with which I dried my eyes.

"And why do you fear torturing him with your mother's techniques?" he continued. "Your conscience and sense of ethics will prevent you from applying them. And should you do so unawares, you will recognize the mistake and make copious amends. Of all the women I know or have known, there is none I would prefer above you to be the mother of this child."

"Such a beautiful thing to say to me!" My eyes again filled with tears.

"Why, it is absolutely true! Now as for the possibility of miscarriage: Eupistus' declaration you are at risk does not automatically guarantee you are going suffer one. We shall certainly do everything within our power to prevent it. I am going to place you directly under a physician's care. Already this night I penned a letter to Thrasyllus, requesting Aka have one of her relatives in the royal house of Commagene procure one. My family I chose not to ask, so I do not have to offer them any explanations. Until this newcomer arrives, you had best follow the regime Eupistus prescribed. He certainly charged a hefty fee for it—8,000 sesterces."

After wincing about the expense I said, "A clever idea, approaching Aka for a physician."

The room darkened as a human shadow spilled across the floor. "All is well, Phoebe—it is only I," Tiberius called out. The shadow retreated and the room resumed its former soft illumination. Tiberius continued speaking in a lower voice. "If in the end you miscarry after all, do not despair. Let us rejoice that we succeeded in creating a new human being in whom our essences blend. And why do I persist in using masculine pronouns? Perhaps you will bear the little girl I always wanted."

"While we were mounting the ascent earlier this night, I witnessed three meteors," I said reflectively. "They did not startle me, but seemed like the sunrise: natural and unremarkably familiar, but glorious nonetheless."

"Behold the confirmation you have undergone monumental change! This very conclusion I posed to Thrasyllus in the letter I just prepared. Not surprisingly I witnessed the meteors as well, as did many of our staff. Your change affects all of us. Will you let me join you?"

To accommodate him I slid to the far edge of the bed, which was narrower than the matrimonial couch we shared the master bedroom. We drew our arms about one another as much to conserve space as to exchange affection. "Remember, no sex," I said. "Frustrating, eh? I promise not to be jealous if you take a hetaera."

"You shall never know if I do." We shared a kiss, long and languid. "I love you—the both of you," he said tenderly.

"And we both love you," I returned as I began to drift peacefully toward sleep, lulled by his physical presence and by the comfort and confidence his words had instilled.

When the daylight woke us he kissed my forehead. "Being so worried about your condition, I have not even begun to consider a gift to present you on the dual anniversary forthcoming—that of your birth and of our marriage. In my last letter to my mother, I asked her to send several jugs of the Ligurian wine to which my stepfather is partial because it mollifies his nervous stomach. If your digestion can be settled before our auspicious day arrives, I might secrete Dorotheus here to prepare a special supper of swordfish. Concern for your health has prevented me from composing a suitable epigram, although I have been endeavoring to do so for weeks."

Leaning over the side of the bed, I vomited into the chamber pot. My partner leaped to his feet and urgently called out, "Phoebe!"

"Did you...have to mention swordfish...and wine?" I gasped between retches.

Phoebe had arrived from the anteroom. "Honestly, Master, you men are all the same. It never occurred to you that what you said might nauseate her. May I respectfully insist you retire at once to your own chamber before you cause more trouble?" Sheepishly, he retreated.

His reaction I found quite amusing, and started to laugh after he left. The humor dissipated my agitation over the vomiting. By the time I had cleansed my mouth with rock salt solution, I was pleasantly hungry. The breakfast of coddled eggs and milk-soaked bread dusted with cassia I ordered—which Phoebe went to fetch but Briseis brought—left me satisfied and invigorated without a trace of nausea.

Briseis remained, relieving Phoebe as my attendant. She told me Tiberius had visitors; hence I anticipated not seeing him until late in the day if at all. After attending me at my bath, Briseis made my bed and then ordered me to lie upon it, reminding me of the physician's admonition that I should recline as much as possible. I passed the morning watching the changes of light on the ceiling and listening to the cicadas in the trees outside the window. For a time I fretted about my prospects for miscarriage, and the uncertain future my child must face if successfully born—as though I had never heard the encouragements Tiberius had uttered only a few hours earlier. Finally I abandoned these reflections—which were accomplishing nothing besides making me despondent and irritable—and started to consider subjects and themes for new paintings. Additionally I was ready to experiment anew with painting on textiles, to see whether I could perfect this technique and create new renderings with ease and success.

Tiberius visited me around noon. "Are you feeling better?" he inquired contritely. I nodded and smiled. "Longus is here," he declared. "One reason I am visiting you is to give my ears some relief."

"Oh dread! I have nothing new to offer him."

"I surmised you would not care to see him, so I lied that you are in Ialyssos shopping for painting supplies."

"Thank you!" I exhaled with relief.

Suddenly his mood shifted. He sat in the chair and stared at the floor.

"What is wrong, my love?" I inquired.

He buried his face in his hands. "Oh my Clytia! Longus is not my only caller. With him came Quirinius Cyrenius, the imperial legate of Galatia and Pamphylia. Cyrenius reported the movement Longus is spearheading—to recall me to Italy as a precaution should my military leadership on the German front suddenly become necessary—has alarmed Gaius. Now that silly youth feels I have become a danger to his person and position even in my confinement here on Rhodes.

"Within a few days, Cyrenius will be leaving for Rome for routine debriefing. Longus is going to accompany him. They plan to press my stepfather to recall me to Italy over Gaius' objections—to argue that restricting me to Rhodes is pointless, if a faction hostile to Gaius can rally about me as readily here as in Rome. And mark this as well: Cyrenius suspects members of Gaius' staff may be deliberately misrepresenting me as more of a threat than I truly am. In anticipation of this journey, Cyrenius sent out an announcement that in his absence he was delegating the government of his province to his deputy legate. Gaius' chief Marcus Lollius responded with a cryptic warning: if Cyrenius puts in at Rhodes, he can expect to find himself scorned and ridiculed by his fellow commanders as a stupid, gullible, self-destructive fool. Cyrenius plans to bring this to my stepfather's attention, and urge him to caution Gaius against naïve acceptance of unfounded speculation and innuendo."

"Oh but this is wonderful news. Why are you troubled?"

He responded slowly and deliberately, choosing his words with great care. "Clytia, if the suit succeeds and my stepfather allows my recall to Italy, you quite obviously cannot accompany me in your present condition. By the time you and our baby have attained sufficient stamina to make the journey, I could find myself on the German front. Moreover if I return to Italy while Gaius still considers me a menace, I shall be under indescribably close supervision. Every word I utter, letter I write, movement I make—all my activities no matter how private or inconsequential—will be scrutinized with greater diligence than under circumstances less adversarial. I need to be scrupulously above suspicion of any kind: far more so than if I were returning strictly as a private citizen with no stake in political or military affairs.

"My sending to Rhodes for a specific woman and child is certain to be noticed, even if the both of you are disguised as the most unobtrusive of servants. Enemies will snicker and deride; my family will object to my action as indiscreet; you will become a focus of attention that might enable your kin to recognize you. And if your child resembles me—well, I leave the ensuing uproar to your imagination. You are right about the praetorians: they are bound to spread gossip. Hardly can I dismiss their chatter as idle rumor if my actions confirm it.

"And finally, Clytia: my stepfather may demand I make a demonstration of loyalty to Gaius by espousing Agrippina. Never mind she is presently intended for Nero and craves him: well you know political expediency disrupts previous commitments and overwhelms personal inclinations. Once remarried—

particularly to my adversary's sister—I could not show even the slightest nuance of interest in another woman. Opponents with mistresses and bastards aplenty would not hesitate to denounce me as a wayward husband. Agrippina would surely object and quite vociferously: you already know she is self-centered, peevish, and volatile. I cannot afford to give Gaius any pretext, any leverage, for proclaiming my recall to Italy over his objections a mistake. You may have to remain here on Rhodes indefinitely—perhaps permanently. We may not be able to see one another or even to correspond." His voice broke on the edge of a sob. "Thrasyllus has predicted separation for us. Must it be now?"

Reaching over, I took his hand. "This morning you despaired of not having a gift ready for me. You have already given me two gifts. One lies within my womb, the other in my psyche. If I must suffer miscarriage, you said, we can at least rejoice that together we created a child. Now apply the same line of reasoning to the prospect of your recall. We have already anticipated and prepared ourselves, for the possibilities of separation and fleetingly surreptitious encounters. Remember that when Thrasyllus predicted we must endure separation, he also said we would always be together. If we must part permanently—should that envisioned togetherness prove to be nothing more than the wonderful yet bittersweet memories of our years together—then we must take joy from those memories and not sorrow. One philosopher—I forget precisely who—wrote that if you grieve because the myrrhine vase you own has fallen to the floor and shattered, then you love the vase and not its beauty."

He smiled wanly. "I appreciate your effort to comfort me, even though it has failed."

"There is no comfort in the words I just delivered. They merely hedge against emotional devastations like miscarriage and separation. Like you I prefer the reality—the actual vase, the live-born child, the spouse at hand—to an infinitude of memories no matter how beautiful."

He brightened a bit. "Now you are sounding like my Lioness. And Longus and Cyrenius have offered new hope."

"Let us resolve, my beloved, to face each forthcoming day with a detached neutrality—not raising our hopes lest we find them frustrated, but not allowing pessimism to dishearten and demoralize us either. Please let us trust in the prevalence of Underlying Good, despite appearances to the contrary. When events turn to our favor, we can rejoice with pleasure and gratitude. When things go badly, we shall not be disappointed or disillusioned."

He pondered my words for what seemed a long while, holding my hand and staring meditatively at the floor. Finally he said thoughtfully, "The philosophy of detachment you just propounded has imbued my spirits with a wonderful sense of resilience. None of the misrepresentation and scorn I have suffered has altered—nor can alter—my true identity. The best outcome I can expect is rehabilitation, the worst is death. In the meanwhile I give thanks—far beyond my ability to adequately express with word or deed—that you continue to stay by me and extend your commitment and love. Thank you, oh thank you my Clytia!" By now he was squeezing the hand I had offered him. He leaned over the bed and kissed me, again and again until we had to stop to catch our breaths. "An encouraging thought to take with me as I leave you," he whispered as he leaned over me again to kiss my forehead. "I must attend to my guests."

Finding a way to elevate the foot of my bed proved more of a challenge than anticipated. Wood boards, overturned mixing bowls, or piles of tightly bound textiles, all skittered when I stirred and turned. Finally, Androcles hit upon a solution, which Ajax put into effect. First he carefully measured the bottoms of the mixing bowls. Then from a log he fashioned two wooden cylinders of equal height, with a notch at each of their centers. After placing the cylinders in the bottom of the mixing bowls, he set the legs of my bed at its foot into the notches. Then he filled the bowls with a mixture of sand and small rocks. This mortar held the bed legs firm.

Rhathines the Commagenean physician arrived the week following. A eunuch, he was an older version of our former chef Dorotheus: bald, pudgy, slightly effeminate, with a soothing voice pitched between that of man and woman. The perfect physician, I thought, to attend a pair of mothers-to-be— after all, Briseis too was with child. Rhathines approved the regimen Eupistus had proposed for me. Since we did not have a lactating jennet on our farm—and owing to Tiberius' unpopularity we could not expect neighbors to sell us their milk—I was unable to pursue the recommended treatment for my acne. No matter, Rhathines returned: just like the nausea, the blemishes would eventually dissipate of their own accord. He examined me every day; and because he was a eunuch, I did not feel uneasy about his seeing me naked or touching my genitals and breasts.

To facilitate my dining, Ajax fashioned a large tray with long legs to straddle my lap. This device could also be used to accommodate my painting materials. Having learned to keep myself content while confined to my quarters during those last four months we had occupied our townhouse, I did not dread that my present restriction portended to be twice as long. I planned to draw and paint and sew and embroider, to read and ponder, to record in my journal a daily diary of observations and of feelings—physical and emotional—associated with the progress of my condition.

Through the remainder of July and all of August I remained weak, listless, and frequently nauseous—devoid of incentive to engage in any of the activities I had outlined. The slightly sweet Ligurian wine Livia sent was indeed helpful in relieving the nausea. Yet precisely because it was so flavorful and ameliorating, I found myself struggling uncomfortably to limit the amount I consumed. I admit to feeling envious of Briseis in a pleasant sort of way. She flitted about her duties unhindered by nausea or weakness, while I lay uncomfortably abed staring upward at my feet.

My dual anniversary of birth and marriage went uncelebrated that year, for I endured the day bilious and sleepy. Tiberius' gift was to replenish my supply of painting and writing supplies. That he did not provide baby articles I immensely appreciated, and told him so: my pregnancy, after all, was tenuous. His very consideration, he replied. He had accordingly admonished the servants, for which reason they did nothing more for the occasion than decorate my bedchamber.

Tiberius took meals with me and visited as often as he could. It was still summer, the season when appeals to him as imperial legate reached their peak. Although dignitaries no longer came to pay their respects in person for fear of alienating Gaius, the flow of petitions did not dwindle. At present Tiberius was preparing a written explanation of several points of law, for a municipal archon who had sought his guidance. He was also arbitrating a dispute between a group of Roman soldiers barracked in the city of Rhodes and their commanding officer. Recently he had upheld the plea of a village council against a Roman resident. The council had mandated the Roman fence his livestock at his own expense, to keep them from trampling his Greek neighbors' crops. The Roman in turn maintained his particular citizenship exempted him from the council's ruling. Tiberius gave the Roman the options of erecting the fence, of compensating the neighbors financially each time the crops were ruined, or of assuming responsibility for actual replanting of the crops each time they were ruined. Describing the incident to me later, he remarked that the disgruntled Roman will undoubtedly accuse him of pandering to the provincials, and probably declare the incident proof Tiberius well deserved his unsavory reputation. In the end, Tiberius had refused to let this consideration deter him from upholding the fundamental rightness of the Greek council's argument.

Tiberius also considered and responded—readily and generously—to petitions for financial assistance from the sick and destitute. One incident was at once touching, hurtful, and funny. An archon from a financially straitened village brought to the farm two impoverished widows, whom the community could not afford to support. To emphasize the desperation of their situation they made their plea in person, rather than in writing via messenger as did most petitioners. They presented their request with urgent yet gracious respect, and thanked Tiberius with equal deference upon receiving his approval. One of the widows had brought along her son of seven years, who had remained dutifully silent throughout the interview. But as they were preparing to descend the promontory, the boy spoke up and asked Tiberius if this was the cliff off which he hurled the visitors he did not like.

The mortified petitioners glanced one at the other in desperation, undoubtedly wondering how or even if they could diffuse the situation. Squatting to face his interrogator at eye level, Tiberius confidently asserted this was indeed the cliff. Further he understood the questioner was well known as a good boy who always minded his mother, who worked hard in the fields, and studied his lessons diligently. Therefore an exception would be made on this occasion, and no member of the present party would be shoved over the precipice. "I felt like laughing and weeping at the same time," he mused glumly, "charmed by the comedy, but chagrined to discover even children hold me in disrepute. At least I might presume that boy will not disobey his mother for quite some time to come."

The names Tiberius selected for our child were Alcimus if male, Cyanea if female. The former is the closest Greek approximation to Nero, the latter to Livia which derives from the archaic Latin word for dark blue. "I hardly wanted to afflict the child, and us ourselves, with having to endure and explain Cholos or Chole." So he eschewed the Greek equivalents of Claudius or Claudia, which mean lame. In Italian culture a son—ordinarily the firstborn—receives the full name of his father, and any daughter the feminine of her father's gentilicum. But among the Greeks a firstborn son is named for his paternal grandfather, a firstborn daughter for her paternal grandmother.

"How wondrous your selections, my love!" I exulted. "They blend our child's heritages without compromising their secrecy!" Now I waxed sardonic. "Anthe would demand—more accurately, contrive in some way—to ensure the babe was named for her or for my father."

"Will you never desist? Your kindred will never learn of our child. And even if for some obtuse reason they do, I for certain will never allow them to dictate nomenclature."

"You have never encountered Anthe," I murmured petulantly.

"And hopefully never I shall. But if by chance that should happen, she will discover she has met her match." Hardly could either of us realize how prophetic his words would prove to be.

Late in September—around the time of Augustus' birthday—my deportment changed utterly. Energetic dynamism overcame lethargy and nausea. My complexion cleared and my eyes began to sparkle. With renewed determination I set about creating a new set of paintings. For reasons of practicality I decided to produce only vignettes. Because they took little time to complete, I knew I could generate a large number quite quickly. Their compact size made them easy for me to manage while reclining in bed, and for Longus' agents to transport. I suspected he might soon seek replenishments for his stock.

To my surprise and dismay, my efforts were amateurishly devoid of skill and sophistication—almost as though I had never picked up a brush, let alone hearkened to the instructions of my teacher Timotheus. It did not take long for me to realize my newfound vigor was making me restless. Rhathines advised me such vitality was common at my present stage of pregnancy, and encouraged me to spend time out of doors. There was a chaise on the veranda, to which I had Tiberius or a manservant carry me whenever the weather was salubrious. The waning September sky gleamed day after day with a patina of luminous overcast. Cloud bands of white, gray, and blue traversed this shimmering backdrop. The bands were touched with tinges of brown and red and gold and even green. Little wonder, I reflected, that despite imputations of laziness and sloth and consequent punishments I had persisted in wandering about my family's Campanian country property, pretending to see textiles in the patterns of nature. Here was my artistic sense, refreshing and restoring itself. My family had never perceived this inclination in me—or had refused to perceive it.

My inspiration revived, impelling me to produce an imaginary landscape inspired by the butterfly glade, and three renderings of the moths themselves. By now it was October, and the entire earth seemed to have turned golden: the ripened fields, the burnished tree leaves, the reddish-gold haze of the sky which the ponds reflected. Impelled by this particular hue, I had begun work on another legendary scene—Zeus as a shower of gold descending into the prison of his mistress Danae—when Longus arrived. To explain my incapacity and the peculiar elevation of my bed, I lied about having injured my back in such a way that the unusual position was necessary to promote healing. After voicing many effusive regrets I was so dreadfully prone to accidents, he asked me for at least six new pieces. I reminded him of his agreement not to elicit any more originals unless sales were dwindling from copies of originals he already held. He replied that the sales of the present inventory had not diminished at all. Rather, the demand for a larger variety of offerings by the same artist had substantially increased. And he proved his point by handing me a stunning royalty of 170 aurei: more than three times the amount of my first take.

Numb with surprise, I promptly invited him to choose six pieces—two for each of his outlets. He must show these to me for my consent to take them. I wanted to make sure his new selections held no particular emotional meaning for Tiberius and me, and were not so large that I could not reproduce them easily. Accordingly I refused Longus the three leaping dolphins, and Aetna erupting against a sky burnished with the smokey pastels of those hazy sunsets in the Sirocco—both reminiscences of our original voyage to Rhodes. Instead I let him have the following:

> Bellerophon descending from the sky astride Pegasus to slay the Chimera of Lycia (Tiberius riding Sinapeus);
>
> A stern-faced Charon standing aboard his skiff on the River Styx, holding his oar with one hand and restraining the triple-headed dog Cerberus with the other (a praetorian with javelin and mastiff);
>
> Admentus driving his chariot to which Apollo had harnessed lions and boars (cats and our barnyard pig);
>
> Athena with the owl of wisdom perched on her shoulder (Alcmene and the barn owl, neither of whom ever came into actual contact with one another);
>
> Another scene from the Odyssey: Skylla the grotesque six-headed dog, with three rows of fangs in each mouth and the body of a lobster, emerging from her cave while in the sea nearby the whirlpool Charybdis spouts a fountain of blood from its center;
>
> King Midas with his touch of gold turning his daughter Chrysanthe into a statue of that metal.

After my bath I lay atop my bed, wiggling my toes and reflecting while awaiting my supper. I was dining alone, of course, because Tiberius was with Longus. As the artist Eutychus of Rhodes I had become what my family had tried to force me to be as the sophista Pythia of Naples and harassed me for not becoming: well renowned and well remunerated. Success was unquestionably pleasant, but startlingly anticlimactic and trivial. None of my physical requirements had changed: I must still eat, sleep, dress, bathe, and relieve myself. My character was unaltered: I had the same predilections and predispositions to which I had always inclined. My worries had not disappeared: I was still facing the possibility of a miscarriage, and a persistently uncertain and dangerous future for my husband that could lead to my separation from him. My household must continue to function, and I to oversee its operations and finances. Quite palpably the monetary royalties that came with recognition must improve the living standards of artists or sophistoi, or practitioners of any profession who were impecunious before they achieved acclaim. My presently newfound monies were nevertheless irrelevant because—thanks to Tiberius' purchase of the farm for me—I was already financially secure.

Lost in my thoughts, I gazed at Phoebe's turtle and fennel stew indifferently, even though it was one of my favorite dishes. Had not my family maintained—relentlessly, inflexibly, with irritation most vociferous— that the celebrated and affluent occupied a rarefied state of being? Here the majority of human necessities and conflicts and bereavements must not exist at all. The few which did were readily subjugated by resolutions inaccessible to ordinary mortals.

Had I not seen from the very inception of my acquaintance with Tiberius, that celebrity was hardly a cure for distress and often a cause of problems which the unrenowned are spared? New to me now was my discovery firsthand— realizing for myself and sensing directly in my own psyche—that recognition and wealth are by no means gateways to Elysian bliss. The idyllic condition my family had so bitterly coveted, and tormented me for not achieving, does not even exist.

With my spoon I stirred the stew slowly and idly. A surge of irritation had come over me. Why had I gone back to ruminating about my past? While recovering from my menstrual catharsis back at the year's beginning, had I not resolved to put those unhappy memories of my former life behind me? And had I not fulfilled this aim, all through the past spring and summer? Was the idleness of my newly mandated confinement prompting me to fill my time with reflections as useless as they were acrimonious?

All at once it occurred to me, that rather than resenting my kin for their flawed assumptions about affluence and renown, I was pitying them. They had endured the distress of jealousy and rage and disappointment for no reason. Suddenly I was pleased, almost to the point of euphoria. At long last I was extending to my family that compassion, which Thrasyllus had urged upon me as a precursor to forgiving them. Digging into my stew with relish, I recalled Aristotle's directive to embrace excellence of thought and action. Turning from contempt to sympathy for my family, I had managed to follow the philosopher's counsel if only in this small way. Excellence of thought and action. That evening I resolved to pay closer attention to the notions I entertained and the behaviors I exhibited, and inculcate Aristotle's principles to the best of my ability. To be more gracious and patient toward everyone, I set as a cardinal goal.

As subsequent days unfolded, I became aware of harboring a type of vindictiveness I had acquired from my mother. Specifically, this was a sense of approval when someone suffered consequences from making a mistake—a satisfaction the perpetrator was receiving just deserts. Now I felt compassion upon learning an insolent praetorian had incurred a reprimand, that someone had embarrassed Longus for his loquaciousness, that an arrogant debtor had been foreclosed upon after disdaining to seek assistance from Tiberius as legate. What human does not err? The change in my demeanor drew notice. "You have become so equable, my love—so wondrously serene and tranquil," Tiberius declared between kisses one evening. "The servants, too, have noted this in you."

I made my mind up to fill my days with constructive activities, so no time was left for pointless ruminating. With a fresh diligence I resumed my music, not merely to maintain my present proficiency but to improve it. Each new sketch or painting I strove to make better than its predecessors. Whenever work on a product fell short of my expectations for it, I put it aside for a time. Then to the project I found myself returning with refreshment and renewed inspiration. One of my new endeavors was to try my hand at still life representation. The static nature of this genre had hitherto inclined me to neglect it, in favor of the broad perspective of landscapes and the dynamism of animals and growing foliage.

Now I had the servants find a low stool and place it where I could see it easily from my bed, but also situate it to catch the shifting of light in the room. Then I had the staff place an array of small objects on the stool: a few vessels of various shapes, a textile, a scroll, a statuette, and of course the still life standard of vegetables and fruits. As the illumination of the articles changed with the passing hours, I began to perceive the vitality I had been overlooking in still life. After a week of observation, I began work on my first rendering. My ever-patient attendants checked the fruit regularly, and replaced with fresh equivalents any that were starting to rot.

Another venture I undertook at this time was to master the technique of painting on textiles. Not to risk ruining the pieces in my collection—some of which were quite costly—I began my experiments on rags and old garments, bedlinens and similar expendables. Very quickly I discovered that the tighter the weave of the fabric, the thinner the paint must be. Thick paint affixed to a tight weave eventually peeled off; and conversely, thin paint promptly ran when applied to coarse and loosely woven material. The intrinsic long hairs of wool made the spread of paint impossible to control; hence the resultant designs were feathery and blurred, and shimmered when the fabric moved.

My third new undertaking did not follow the course I had anticipated for it. Having planned for some time to read the *Iliad* aloud to Briseis, I finally started to do so. To me, rereading this classic was like visiting an old and dear friend. Briseis, however, found tedious and disconcerting the descriptions of warfare and bloodshed, of quarrels between enemies and allies alike. I was about halfway through the epic, when she requested something less harrowing. Quite naturally I turned to the *Odyssey*, which Briseis considered hardly less macabre. I had only reached the third book when again she stopped me, and asked if I would teach her to read and write.

Her request stunned me. Written Greek, I cautioned her, is extraordinarily difficult to learn and takes years to master. It is fraught with diphthongs that do not sound the way one might infer from they are written, with letters that sound the same but are written differently, with accent marks that vary in shape and placement within each word and sentence. There are various dialects—Ionic, Doric, Attic, Alexandrian—each with unique spellings and grammatical peculiarities. No matter, Briseis returned. Should she acquire no more skill than that of a first-year schoolchild, this was satisfyingly more than she had at present.

Further questioning revealed she knew the letters of the alphabet, and the sound to which each corresponded. So for an impromptu first lesson, I showed her the line in the *Odyssey* at which we had halted—πάντες θεων χατέουσ' άνθρωποι [*pantes theon khateous anthropoi*]— and asked her to make a try at enunciating the words. Slowly and determinedly she stammered out, "Of the gods...in need...are all men," and then looked up at me, wide eyed and smiling slightly agape as though enraptured. The written word had come alive.

Menon's regular schedule for the serving staff relieved Briseis of duty on Sunday mornings, and all day on Wednesdays. When I invited her to come to visit me for lessons during those free times, she accepted my offer promptly and enthusiastically. These opportunities I appreciated as well, and not only

349

because they created an additional distraction to keep me from worrying. Many a year had passed since I instructed so elementary a pupil. This preparation I valued inestimably. Within five years—assuming all went well—I could anticipate again teaching the fundamentals of Greek, along with those of many another subject. Briseis I cautioned and exhorted, neither to hesitate nor feel uncomfortable about telling me I was confusing her, was proceeding too quickly or presenting material too advanced. She proved an avid and diligent pupil, as do most adults who pursue a course of study voluntarily. During the first week I set her to work perfecting her ability to write the alphabet, while I created a compilation of simple sentences for her to read. As she progressed I prepared reading material more complicated, and insisted she attempt to write phrases and then sentences of her own. From the corrections to her many predictable mistakes in spelling and grammar, she began to understand and learn the various cases nouns and verbs assumed.

Meanwhile in the final week of October, dreadful news arrived from Rome. Correspondence had been discovered, which revealed that Lucius Aemilius Paullus the husband of Julia's namesake daughter was endeavoring to resurrect his mother-in-law's conspiracy. Paullus aspired to remove Augustus from power, and set himself up as regent to Gaius. But in lieu of obtaining sufficient senatorial votes to rescind Augustus' authority, Paullus had advocated assassinating the emperor. Additionally, both Paullus and his wife had been practicing and urging upon others the same lifestyle of hedonism and profligate spending in which Julia had engaged—the lifestyle which defied Augustus' efforts to induce his fellow Romans to exercise temperance and frugality.

Tiberius was glum and irritable on his birthday as usual; but this year I could blame him less than ever. He was entering his forty-third year, which the Romans consider the inception of old age. In this same year of life his father's health had begun its precipitous decline, into early invalidism and death a decade later. Was a similar fate in store for Tiberius? Cyrenius had written with enthusiasm, that Augustus had listened receptively to the argument Tiberius should be returned to Italy in case his military expertise became needed on the northern frontier. The only familial news in the packet of otherwise routine birthday greetings, was that Gaius' younger brother Lucius was back in Rome after completing military training at the great garrison of Marseilles, and that Livia's aging mother Alfidia was beginning to go blind. There was no hint—not even the slightest suggestion—a recall might be imminent.

Making matters worse, my condition was presently guarded. Rhathines was concerned about some intermittent but nevertheless frequent vaginal bleeding.

Tiberius reassured me several times, that he was endeavoring to implement our commitment to emotional detachment—neither to raise hopes nor yield to dejection. Nonetheless he still spent most of that afternoon staring expressionless at the floor of my bedchamber. My efforts to hearten him with my harp, with a chlamys newly woven and sewn (Phoebe's handiwork) upon which I had successfully painted a design of moths, and with the suggestion Augustus was too preoccupied with the trial of Paullus to render a firm decision about Tiberius' recall, brought an effusive declaration of loving thanks but no cheer. It took Briseis to elicit that. She presented him with a tablet upon which she had written in the oversized calligraphy of a child, *May you have a very happy birthday, dearest Master Tiberius.* For the first time that day he smiled; and I felt a pang of pleasant jealousy mingled with pride. With her modest efforts at letters, my pupil had succeeded where I had failed.

On the Calends of December, with the birth of her babe now imminent, Menon dismissed Briseis from her work responsibilities altogether. Thereafter she came to me daily, waddling slowly and gingerly, as though beneath her chiton she was standing within a barrel suspended from her shoulders. By now she was reading, in their entirety, short compositions I had prepared for her, along with simple selections from the works of great writers. She was also composing brief paragraphs of her own. At length the day arrived—the third before the Ides *[December 11]*—when Briseis did not appear, and of course I knew the reason why. In a way, I had become a new mother as well. Having meticulously recorded the lessons I had created for Briseis, I now had a primer for the teaching of elementary Greek. Upon this down the future I would rely heavily.

Briseis delivered a boy, upon whom Arbindus bestowed another unpronounceable Gallic name. Phar'hail was about the best I could make of it *[Faerghal]*. Briseis said it means valorous. She beamed when I told her she had selected the Celtic equivalent of Nero, and of the Greek name Tiberius intended for our child if male. The new parents also gave their baby the Greek sobriquet Phoenix, so the household could say it. When I reminded Briseis the charioteer Phoenix was a champion of Briseis in the *Iliad*, she assured me she had not forgotten.

On the first day of Saturnalia a letter arrived from Livia, announcing the senate had sentenced Paullus to execution for high treason. Although Paullus'

351

wife—the younger Julia—was cleared of complicity in her husband's crime, the senate found her in violation of her grandfather's laws against sumptuary expenditure. She was sentenced to exile in the city of Reggio Calabria, on the mainland of Italy opposite Messina. The couple's two small children—a daughter and son—were transferred to the residence of their paternal grandfather—another Paullus Aemilius Lepidus—as he was now by default their legal guardian. Tiberius immediately dictated a letter of condolence to his stepfather, ruing the misfortune for its own sake as well as its occurrence at this festive time of year. Why, I asked, did I not know the guilty pair had children? After some effort at recollection, Tiberius explained the news of the girl's birth had arrived while I was in Alexandria, that of the boy while I was seriously ill. Quite palpably he had forgotten to tell me. Phoebe had prepared appropriate gifts.

The day following, Atticus arrived unexpectedly with his wife and their younger daughter. Attica was eager to see me, and sorely disappointed after Tiberius maintained I had gone to Alexandria for the winter. She was bursting with the news of her betrothal—like that of her sister Vesca—to one of the soldiers of the Roman garrison in Rhodes. Vesca's husband, in fact, had introduced the pair. Attica's intended was a native of Perugia, and shared her intellectual inclinations. Two days later, Marinus and Longus came to celebrate over Rhaetian wine. Tiberius made the same excuse when they inquired after me. Being asked about was distinctly gratifying, in the wake of my family's incessant insistence I was unpopular and their berating for my being so. But would I—could I—*ever* stop ruminating about my past?

Apart from this pang of bitterness, my spirits were soaring. I had reached that all-important month at which the survival of my child could be anticipated even in the event of premature birth. The worrisome bleeding had ceased. My abdomen now resembled a great gourd; and I could feel movements within. Rhathines was pleased and confident as well. The cessation of the bleeding and the internal motions meant the infant was viable and healthy. If prematurely born, it would be puny and require careful ministration and nutrition; but it would definitely live.

January brought its usual bleakness. With the Saturnalia and its callers behind us, and the business of his legature at its slowest owing to the time of year, Tiberius was now free to spend entire days in my company. We embarked upon a lively discussion of my belief in Underlying Good, and in one's ability to harmonize one's life through acknowledgment of and surrender to the action of this Principle. I recalled the three instances during which I had clung most desperately to this view: the hot dusty birthday in Campania that had preceded my first encounter with Tiberius, the aftermath of my confrontation with Timoleon, and finally the cathartic menses that had expelled the growth in my womb. All had profoundly harmonized my life and character; and all had been marked by the sighting of a meteor.

Tiberius put forth another proposition, quite well-worn. If goodness is the fundamental governing Principle of the universe, then how does one account for the existence of evil? And if Good prevails, why are some evil events—like the ghastly death of Tiberius' brother and now the present, seemingly irreversible debasement of his reputation—irresistible and unalterable? Perhaps insufficient trust in the existence and prevalence of Underlying Good impels irremediable disasters, I suggested. A fundamental governing Principle must be absolute by nature, Tiberius continued. Goodness, however, is predominantly if not always relative. What is good for one individual is often at the same time evil for another. The outcome of a battle is good for the victor but evil for the vanquished. Having food to sustain life is good for the eater, yet evil for the plant or animal which must die to become that food. A point well taken I admitted, then added I did not presume to have an answer but only a methodology.

He put forth yet another challenge. How could I be certain the outcomes I attributed to aligning my thought with Underlying Good were not destined to occur anyway—despite rather than because of my surrender to that Force? Again I did not have a ready answer. After some cogitation I brought up our first conversation with Thrasyllus, in which the sage had explained how adherence to ethics can improve the pattern one's destiny takes as it unfolds. Perhaps the acknowledgment of Underlying Good awakens one to goodness already inherent in one's destiny—sharpening one's awareness, and impelling one to make decisions and take actions which channel that intrinsic goodness toward superlative ends. Even if my presumption Good is the ultimate power is incorrect—and the universe is in actuality an eternal confrontation between good and evil in which neither prevails—then at least the deliberate yielding of my thought to the control of Good calms and clarifies my consciousness in times of crisis and helps me address such situations rationally.

Continuing, I now disclosed the servants had revealed Tiberius prayed for me during my purgative menses, even though he has doubts whether the gods exist. After rolling his eyes—presumably annoyed and embarrassed by the revelation—he chuckled that people in desperation will try any remedy whether or not they believe in its efficacy. If his prayers did not help me, they certainly caused no harm. Similarly if my personal system of ethics enabled me to manage past calamities, then I should definitely continue to pursue it. In the decade since we first made our acquaintance at the Academia Norenas, he had watched me grow—almost phenomenally, he asserted—in grace, self-confidence, tolerance, discretion, patience, affability, wisdom, poise, and composure. Much of this, he felt sure, I owed to my unique philosophy.

One day toward the middle of that same January, Miranda ran into my quarters and hurled something against a wall. It turned out to be a textile, which fell silently into a heap on the floor. A clearly exasperated Phoebe entered the room, picked up the discarded article, then grabbed Miranda about one wrist and jerked her arm. "Shame, shame on you," Phoebe scolded, "for intruding on Lady and disrespecting your father's gift!" Miranda stamped her feet and jumped up and down. Her little face was red, wet with tears, and distorted with silent rage. Phoebe started to drag her from the room, until I stopped them and asked what was wrong. Such conduct was highly uncharacteristic of Miranda.

Phoebe explained that Miranda had been obstreperous since receiving the present Alexias had sent her for the Saturnalia. The item was a little hooded cape, pale blue in color and embroidered in darker blue with typically swirling Gallic patterns. Alexias had dispatched it from Marseilles, where he had accompanied his master Lucius Caesar. Every year Alexias provided Miranda with a gift for her birthday in June, and again at Saturnalia. This was the first time she had reacted contemptuously to his generosity. I took the cape from Phoebe and extolled it to Miranda: how pretty, how unusual, how becoming her, how appropriate for the present season to keep her warm. All Miranda did was resume her tirade, pounding with her free hand on that of Phoebe, clenched about her wrist.

Suddenly a thought flashed through my mind like a meteor. The timing of Miranda's behavior had caught my attention. I had been reclining. Now I swung my feet to the floor, sat upright on the edge of my bed, and laid the little cape down beside me. "Miranda," I began softly. When she continued to fret I clapped my hands and raised my voice. "MIRANDA, STOP! LISTEN TO ME!" She ceased to struggle and looked up at me sullenly. "Miranda, are you upset because you see Phoenix with a mother and father right here, while you have no mother and your father is far, far away?" Miranda stood as still and silent as a statue for a few moments. Then she nodded and started to weep anew. I had found the cause of the problem.

"Ah, Miranda," I continued, "I know your father well. He would like to be here with you; but because of forces beyond his control he cannot. He sends you presents to prove he loves you. Miranda, my father and mother hated me. They never gave me presents; and they treated me so cruelly, I had to run away from them. To this day, I would rather have a father far away who loves me than parents at hand who do not. And think, Miranda: you can be a big sister to Phoenix, by helping Briseis care for him and by looking out for his wellbeing yourself—making sure he is clean and comfortable, and letting Briseis know when he needs attention. When he gets a little older, you can start showing and teaching him the things you know. I had a younger brother and wanted to help care for him; but my parents would not let me. And do you know what happened? My brother ended up hating me, just like my parents. Surely you want Phoenix to grow up being your friend."

After thinking the notion over Miranda nodded; yet her expression remained sullen. I took her hand from Phoebe's grip and placed it on my abdomen. "Remember too, Miranda: soon I am going to have a baby of my own, and will need your help. You are going to be a very busy big sister." Now Miranda climbed up on the bed beside me, put her arms about me and laid her head on my bosom. I stroked her hair. Phoebe and I exchanged smiles. All at once Miranda slid onto the floor, picked up the cape, drew it about her shoulders, pulled the hood onto her head, and headed with determination for the courtyard—presumably to test the resilience of the garment against the winter's chill.

One morning some two weeks later, Phoebe seemed unwontedly reticent and sluggish as she went about her tasks. When I told her I was ready to have her brush my hair she responded sharply: could I not see she was embroiled with putting away my newly washed garments? Tiberius, just as surprised as I at her response, retorted sternly he would not have her address me in such a manner; whereupon Phoebe burst into tears. I insisted she sit in the chair at my bedside and explain her distress.

After a struggle for words, Phoebe managed her disclosure. Earlier in the morning, she had watched her beloved Xanthothrix succumb to a ghastly death. This cat was inclined to roam about the farm at night, often to considerable distances from the promontory; but he had always returned at daybreak unscathed. On this particular morning, however, he was injured. Instead of treating and dressing the wounds, Rhathines had administered belladonna mixed into honey.

Tiberius, who had been sitting on my bed at my side, called out to Briseis to summon Rhathines.

Chagrin was obvious in the physician's manner as he accounted for his action. He surmised Xanthothrix had gotten into a tussle with a large and aggressive animal—most likely a wild boar. The cat had been mauled and trampled. Bones were shattered; internal organs were ruptured; sepsis was rapidly setting in. Rhathines was amazed Xanthrothix had managed to drag himself home in his condition. Realizing there was no hope for recovery and death was inevitable, Rhathines had decided a quick and painless end was the far kinder alternative to an extended period of agony.

Turning to Phoebe, Tiberius recounted the parable of the shattered vase. Phoebe had lost the vessel but not its beauty. Memories of Xanthothrix were hers to cherish for a lifetime, even as I was cherishing my recollections of Leo. When Phoebe countered that I did not have to endure watching Leo die, Tiberius urged her to think of Xanthothrix as being merely physically separated from her as Leo was from me. He elaborated how earlier in the year he had risked further damaging his already sullied reputation, by arbitrating against the Roman citizen who was letting his livestock run rampant over his Greek neighbors' crops. There are occasions when a ruler or general must choose between several potential courses of action, none of which is satisfactory. The human invalid or fatally wounded soldier, knowing he is declining toward death, recognizes an end to his ravages is in sight. A suffering animal does not comprehend this: all he knows is physical anguish. The most right, the most altruistic, the most principled—in short the best course of action under the circumstances—must prevail; and this Rhathines had done for Xanthrothix. Concluding, Tiberius told Phoebe to have Menon relieve her of duty until she had expunged her grief.

Pursue that which is most right under the circumstances. Through the remainder of the day I reflected upon this precept for living—simple and straightforward to comprehend and practice, selfless and virtuous in intention, benign to applier and recipient alike. Through intervening years I have implemented it without compunction, and found its effects not necessarily gladdening but always satisfactory.

Several days later, Phoebe opened the door to my bedchamber; and two balls of golden fur bounced across the floor. Ajax had acquired them from the farmhands. They were the get of Xanthothrix, who in his wanderings had thoroughly ingratiated himself to the female residents of the farmhands' compound—human and feline alike. Phoebe pressed me to name the newcomers.

When I suggested Castor and Pollux after the Dioscuri—the celestial twins of the Zodiac constellation—Phoebe recoiled. After nervously reassuring me she meant me no disrespect, she proceeded to reject as blasphemous the conferral of divine names upon mortal beasts. For her admonition I was grateful as it alerted me to watch, lest in my agnosticism I say or do something cavalier or offensive to entrenched believers. Pleasantly chastened, I offered Heliophanes and Lampourus which Phoebe approved with delight. Although they were not littermates but half-brothers with different mothers, I never could tell them apart. Nor could Tiberius or most of the servants. Phoebe nevertheless succeeded admirably. Heliophanes she said had the more elongated face, and Lampourus the thicker tail: hence the name I suggested was particularly appropriate. Nicanor cremated Xanthothrix' remains and sealed them in a little urn, which I painted with his portrait and presented to Phoebe.

As the present year waned toward the new, I found myself in a state of reflective tranquility and calm anticipation. Almost a year had passed since my cathartic menses. Without its occurrence, I would not have been able to conceive. The danger of losing my pregnancy to miscarriage had also passed. When standing I could no longer see my feet—nor when reclining, despite the elevation of the nether end of my bed. Like Briseis two months earlier I now resembled a barrel, which undulated visibly with the stirrings of its occupant.

The servants were making ready for the impending birth, chattering gaily as they turned the anteroom of my bedchamber into a nursery. Ajax installed a new set of shelves, which the serving women promptly filled with swaddling cloths and little blankets, towels and sponges, basins of varying size, jars of different unguents and ointments. They brought in great amphorae for storing water and a brazier for heating it, vats for the washing, and wooden racks for the drying of laundered textiles. Ajax built a crib, for which Phoebe created a mattress from layers of thick but tightly woven wool cloth. Briseis continued to come for reading lessons, bringing Phoenix with her and nursing him to keep him quiet. With my assistance she was making her way, slowly but persistently, through a romance she had selected from our library.

Tiberius did not share my nonchalance. He maintained our philosophy of detachment about the future was gaining in urgency. We must guard against becoming prematurely complacent, and expecting prompt and uncomplicated fulfillment of our expectations. No general declares a strategy successful until the outcome of the battle has been assessed. Our child was yet unborn, its father's reputation as yet unredeemed. Unforeseen complications could still compromise either event. Tiberius was angrier and more frustrated than ever, over the impasse regarding his recall. Why after repeated reassurances did Gaius continue to consider him a threat; and why did Augustus persist in deferring to the wishes of this inexperienced and gullible grandson, especially after having acknowledged the military necessity for bringing Tiberius home?

Rhathines had agreed with the physician Eupistus, that I could expect to give birth on or around New Year's Day. Since everything seemed to be progressing normally, I anticipated an uneventful delivery at the predicted time. How uncanny, how oddly auspicious, the birth was projected for the very anniversary of the expulsion of the growth that had compromised my ability to conceive.

Around the Nones of February the weather turned bitterly cold. Everyone was wrapped in shawls and cloaks. The servants brought a second brazier to my bedroom, but removed it after I complained it made the air stuffy. They buried me under a heap of blankets instead. On the fourth day before the Ides, *[2/10]* the weather became stormy—not with the virulence of a Euroclydon, but with wind and rain aplenty nonetheless. That night I went to bed with mild cramps, which I attributed to the ordinary action of my bowels. They had become sensitive from the pressure of the baby, and would be relieved with my next defecation. In the middle of the night, however, I awoke to find my bed soaked. The fetal water sac had ruptured. The pains were far more intense and coming in waves. At my calling, Briseis my attendant for the night summoned Rhathines, who in turn called for Phoebe. It was the Jewish Sabbath, so Alcmene was excused from her duties.

The physician helped me into the chair, where I sat shivering while he removed my wet shift and draped a clean blanket about me. As the women changed the bedding he had them add additional layers. After they finished he had them retrieve and fire that second brazier: never mind the stuffiness, the room must be warm. He got me back into bed, and proceeded to examine me with the same techniques Eupistus had employed, pressing upon my abdomen with one hand while inserting the fingers of his other hand into my vagina. The lamplight on his face seemed to reveal a look of concern. On releasing me he said gravely, "Lady, it is imperative you resist any temptation to expel the child." Then he placed Briseis' hand on the underside of my abdomen and said, "Push upward steadily and continuously until I return."

Staring at the dimly lit ceiling as the contractions rippled through my body, I wondered whether I was in danger and mentally surrendered to Underlying Good. Within a few minutes Rhathines placed something sticky on my tongue and said, "Chew and swallow all of this, Lady, as quickly as you can without gagging." The tiny cake was soft, slightly granular, sweet and very pleasantly flavored. Why, I wondered, was the physician feeding me a confection? To distract me from some dreadful procedure he was about to inflict? Even before I had finished the lozenge, I became strangely drowsy and lightheaded with a sense of floating. My extremities were devoid of feeling. A scratching pain traversed the surface of my abdomen, as though a nail were being dragged across. I fell asleep, and dreamed again of those hooded figures, extracting a warm entity from my side. Now they were benign rather than ominous, their garments luminous and flowing. Instead of my mother, Tiberius was directing them.

When I awoke, the room was filled with extraordinarily bright white light. During my last menses and subsequently my pregnancy—from and watching the illumination of my quarters change through endless hours and days—I had learned to determine time of day from intensity and angle of light and shadow. At present these seemed to indicate it was midmorning. The brilliance, however, seemed exceptional. Outside the wind and rain had abated and all was quiet. My bed was level: the elevating mechanism had been removed. Beneath the bedsheet and blankets I lay naked. My head ached and my stomach was bilious. These symptoms, however, were negligible before the searing pain spanning my abdomen. Within a few moments that pain began to abate. Reaching under the bedcovers, Rhathines was applying a salve. Noticing I was awake, he smiled and uttered a sentence, the memory of which enthralls me without measure to this day. "Lady you have a son—vigorously healthy, and perfect in every way."

He asked how I was feeling and chuckled at my reply. The last time I felt this way, I murmured, I was shamelessly drunk. The headache and nausea would disappear within the next several hours, he reassured me. They had arisen from the opium he had administered: somewhat rare and hence expensive, and dangerously addictive. To prevent its theft for casual use, he kept his supply in a locked box, along with the belladonna he had given Xanthothrix. This container is hidden in his chamber for only the most severe of emergencies. Should I find myself craving the sedative, I should ask him or Briseis for an antidote. Was the effect of opium, I inquired, making my surroundings seem unnaturally bright? No, Rhathines answered: it was the snow falling outside. He went to the window and opened it, to reveal a shining cascade of white, silver, blue, and even touches of pink, shimmering like a curtain of gossamer. The snow imparted a muffling quietude and a cleansing, clarifying, almost biting, crispness to the cold outside air. As I inhaled the draughts that floated into the room, my head began to clear.

The storm was probably the cause of the early birth, Rhathines continued as he shut the window. Sudden and significant changes in the weather are well known to induce premature labor. Ordinarily a delivery two weeks before its anticipated time is no cause for concern. My case, however, involved a serious complication. The baby had not yet shifted to the usual head-downward position for the final weeks of pregnancy, but was essentially sitting with his buttocks atop my vagina. Rhathines had attempted to turn him by reaching inside my vagina. Failing at that, his only option to save both the child and me was to slice through my abdomen to my womb. The same procedure performed for Aka Thrasyllou when she proved unable to deliver, I remarked; and Rhathines nodded in agreement. And another brush with death, I reflected in silence with a shudder. Had I eluded it through sheer chance, or through my efforts to acknowledge and accept the operation of Underlying Good?

Briseis appeared with a small tumbler. While Rhathines supported my head, she with a spoon administered a dose of the tumbler's contents: a mildly astringent liquor. Tincture of feverfew, the physician explained, to ease my headache and the pain of the incision. He told Briseis to advise Master I was awake; but if Tiberius came to see me I did not know, for I fell back asleep. Upon reawakening in late afternoon, I felt significantly better. The headache and nausea were gone as Rhathines had predicted; the pain in my abdomen, although acute, was tolerable. While I had slept, a plaster had been spread over my abdominal incision, reinforcing the stitches holding it closed. I had been washed, swaddled, and dressed in a clean shift; my hair was brushed and rebraided. My bedlinens had been changed. The infamous second brazier had been removed, and the air in the room thoroughly refreshed. Now I needed the chamber pot. As Phoebe assisted me with this operation, I discovered I could move with greater ease than I had anticipated. Nevertheless when I asked Phoebe to help me to the window so I could behold the snow-covered ground, she refused. Rhathines had issued strict orders: no moving me about that was not absolutely necessary. Besides, practically all of the snow had melted.

A band of cloth, encircling my body just beneath my arms, tightly bound my breasts against my chest. When I asked Phoebe the purpose of this restriction, she said it was to suppress my milk. Already irked at having to miss seeing the snow cover, I now became thoroughly irritated and indignantly demanded an explanation. Startled by my anger, Phoebe explained that women of my station in life usually engage wetnurses. Consequently she, her fellow serving women and Rhathines too, had presumed such was my wish. Briseis, in fact, had already nursed my son while I was yet sleeping. Most certainly not my choice, I responded hotly; whereupon Phoebe curtsied and left the room. Her comment about my social status reminded me I had achieved what my mother had always wanted me to be, and railed at me because I was not: an aristocrat, an elite.

Phoebe returned carrying an article of clothing. After helping me to a sitting position she removed my shift and the breast binding, then dressed me in the garment she had brought. It was a shift that opened down the front and tied just above my bosom. Still testy, I demanded to know when I could expect to see the baby to whom I had given birth half a day earlier. Phoebe answered reticently that he was asleep, but if I wished she would carry him to me in that state. Repenting my anger, in gentle tones I thanked her, told her to let the babe be for now, but to bring him to me for his next feeding. She asked me whether I was hungry, whereupon I noticed and admitted I was.

Tiberius passed Phoebe in the doorway as she departed for the kitchen. He sat on the edge of my bed and leaned over me. We drew our arms about each other and kissed. Sitting back up, he took both my hands in his. We exchanged smiles tender and reflective.

"Thank you for giving me this child," I said, "the most marvelous of all the wonderful gifts you have bestowed upon me."

"It is you who deserves the credit and thanks," he replied. "To bring about this new life you placed your own at severe risk. All I did was engage in an act of intense sensual pleasure some ten months ago." Still holding my hands he leaned over to kiss me again. "Have you seen the babe yet?"

"No. When I asked after him, Phoebe said he was asleep. I told her I did not want him disturbed."

"The ingenuous response of a truly caring mother. And on the matter of mothers: he looks rather like mine."

"Oh how marvelous! The Governance of the Universe be thanked he does not look like my mother! Pity we cannot inform her of his existence. Anthe would be utterly mortified to learn she shares a grandson with Livia, and more so because he resembles Livia rather than any of my kin."

"Now, now, let us not be vindictive on this most auspicious day."

"Have you acknowledged him?"

"Not yet. For now only Menon qualifies to be a witness, since he alone among our free menservants knows of our marriage. We cannot engage any of his colleagues, lest they speculate about why I am acknowledging a bastard or else deduce we are married. I should like to have more than a single witness to this propitious event. Accordingly I have invited Thrasyllus to celebrate the New Year with us. Surely the Academy will excuse him from his duties for the holiday.

"In the meanwhile, I cast our son's horoscope myself. He was born today, Saturday, the third before the Ides in the first hour, just after dawn *[6:00–7:00 a.m. February 11, 2 CE]*. Aquarius has a threefold role, being at once his solar and lunar sign and his medium coeli. His rising sign is Gemini. His Mercury is in Capricorn, Venus and Mars in Pisces, Jupiter in Sagittarius, and Saturn in Scorpio. All indicate a dynamically inventive and creative yet highly responsible individual—practical and hardworking, unselfish, altruistic and ethical, honorable in business, loyal to friends and devoted to family. Like you he will enjoy learning; and like me he will have intense emotions but be disinclined to express them openly. The only negative predisposition I detected will be a tendency toward dogmatic self-righteousness—the influence of Jupiter in Sagittarius. He may take umbrage when he knows he is correct about something but others challenge his assessment. This propensity he should temper with a readiness to forgive. Already I have sent my deductions to Thrasyllus, asking him to confirm them and reveal anything I overlooked."

"Rhathines showed me the snow as it fell. What a subject for painting! I should so like to have seen how it covered the landscape; but alas, Phoebe tells me it has melted."

"You would have been disappointed. It was merely a dusting, hardly more than hoarfrost—a paltry comparison to the lustrous gleam of German winters."

Tiberius seated himself on the chair. From his pocket he took an oval object, which proved to be a leather amulet. "This is a bulla," he explained. "I had Ajax fashion it. Every Roman child of aristocratic lineage receives one at birth. A male surrenders his bulla to his progenitors when he comes of age, a female when she marries. It contains a lock of each parent's hair. While you were sleeping, I trimmed a bit from the very end of your braid, here." He showed me the minor attrition at the end of the plait.

Phoebe arrived, carrying a bolster in one hand and a dish of baked custard in the other. I made a face. Flavorless and slimy, her culinary offering was hardly my favorite dish. "Come along, now," she chided. "Rhathines wants you on the most bland and soft of diets until that slice across your belly has healed a little. You cannot afford to have your bowels disrupting your recovery." She handed the dish to Tiberius so she could slide the bolster under my head and shoulders, elevating them to enable me to take the food without choking.

"Leave us," Tiberius said when she reached to retrieve the dish. He proceeded to feed me the custard with the spoon Phoebe had stuck in it.

"Unfortunately you did not get the little girl for whom you hoped," I managed between mouthfuls.

He laughed gently. "No cause for disappointment, my love—our boy is no less welcome in my home and heart." For a moment he paused, holding the spoon in midair and staring across the room. "Do you know, Clytia," he drawled reflectively as he resumed administering the custard, "I am weary of the secrecy that shrouds our relationship—of the skulking and dissembling and outright lying. And I am weary of trying in vain to redeem my political reputation. What is more, it appears I no longer need to do so for the sake of my son...," he paused and smiled wistfully, "...my *elder* son. From what my mother writes, Drusus is winning public recognition and acclaim without my intervention and despite my tarnished reputation. Since his coming of age last year, my nephew Nero—or Germanicus as he calls himself publicly—has been actively ingratiating himself to the Roman populace, and promoting Drusus his cousin as bosom comrade and future colleague and ally in political affairs. So inseparable are the two becoming in people's minds, many are likening them to the Dioscuri." I considered drawing the comparison with our two kittens but immediately rejected the notion, as I did not think him in the mood for such levity.

He set the empty custard dish on the floor and gazed at it while he continued speaking. "Drusus hardly knows me anymore, we have been separated for so long. Clytia, the time appears ripe for me to stop endeavoring to vindicate myself, to resign my sham legature, and announce my intention to live out my life in seclusion on this farm as a purely private citizen. In that circumstance, for me to have a young Greek wife and a half-Italian son with partial Roman citizenship will be perfectly acceptable. We shall finally be able to end our farce."

A soft, short, nasal wail emanated from the antechamber. Others followed in quick succession, more vociferous and urgent: "Waah, maah, owaahh!" Rhathines entered, smiling broadly and cradling a bundle of swaddling in his arms. "Our young man is thoroughly famished," he said jovially. "As you can hear, he has strong sound lungs. My heartiest of congratulations to you, Master and Lady."

As I untied my shift to expose my breast, Tiberius looked at me almost aghast. "You are nursing him? Like a peasant?"

"Like a mother!" I returned emphatically.

Rolling his eyes, he quit the side of my bed for the chair so Rhathines could lay his bundle beside me. At long last I beheld my newborn child—and not without a bit of shock.

His face was perfectly round, and his wide-open mouth seemed to engulf half of it. His skin was deep red and wrinkled; and his otherwise bald head was crowned with a long swatch of very fine, dark brown hair. Since his eyes were closed I could not see their color. Rhathines gently guided my nipple into the gaping mouth and stroked the little cheek, whereupon the baby started to suck voraciously: *Mfff, mfff, mfff*. At last I saw his eyes. They were pale hazel with the slightest nuance of blue.

"Where do you see he resembles your mother?" I inquired. "To me he looks for all the world like a sun-dried pomegranate, complete with the remnants of the blossom." These last words I added as I gently stirred the thin brown hair with my finger.

"About the eyes," Tiberius managed amid guffaws. "They are large and widely set like hers, and similar in same shape and color. He also has her high forehead."

Rhathines, who had smiled at my remark, responded reassuringly. "Lady, within the next two weeks his skin will lighten and become smooth. He may well develop jaundice, as most babies do. We shall hasten its disappearance by placing him in sunlight. Over the next few months his present hair will fall out. Around his fifth month his permanent hair will emerge. He will grow tall."

The baby ceased to suckle and lay staring straight ahead, mouth slightly open and eyes unfocused as though he were contemplating some difficult concept. Suddenly a loud sound much like the ripping of cloth emanated from the swaddling. A pungent odor followed. Rhathines smiled anew and snatched the babe from my bed. "A welcome sign the elimination system is healthy," he said. Then he hastened with his smelly cargo to the nursery.

"Are you sure you do not want to leave all this to Briseis?" Tiberius asked quizzically while I wiped my breast with the oil moistened cloth Rhathines had left for this purpose.

I nodded as I retied my shift. "Such comes with being a mother."

He rolled his eyes. "I suppose you will be changing and washing baby and swaddling yourself, once you are up and about."

"No, no my dearest: that I shall most certainly leave to the servants."

"The gods be thanked there is hope for her sanity yet," he murmured.

The rapidity with which I recovered proved a pleasant surprise. Within a week I was able to get out of bed and move about my quarters without assistance. My incision ceased to hurt and began to itch instead. My attendants brought the baby for nursing every four hours, by night as well as by day. The joy this process invoked for me dissipated any fatigue or difficulty in awakening. Yes, the babe did develop jaundice; and yes it disappeared after a few days of napping in sunlit areas of the nursery. I made several sketches of him—of the little round face in which I could now perceive resemblance to Livia; and of the chubby, ovoid body which reminded me, I must confess, of a colocynth squash. I also completed several unsatisfactory attempts to capture, on palettes, the scintillations of the snowfall that had distinguished the birth. Reproducing the myriad of colors without losing their pervasive translucence proved a formidable challenge.

Precisely two weeks after the birth, Rhathines declared time was at hand to start giving the child solid food—porridge of finely crushed barley, wheat, or oryza the grain from China, all thinned with goat's milk. On the same day *[February 25]* he scrubbed the plaster from my belly, snipped and removed the sutures, applied a salve, and pronounced the incision healed except for the superficial scratches incurred during excision of the stitches. By now the menstrual-like discharge that follows birth had ended. I asked Rhathines whether I could resume regular bathing and return to Tiberius' bed. The former activity I could reinitiate immediately, the physician replied genially. For the latter I had best wait another two weeks, to ensure I was well healed both superficially and internally. Besides, even though he was starting to sleep through most nights, the baby still required an occasional overnight feeding. Master may object to having his own slumber interrupted for this purpose. I agreed.

Now Rhathines spoke frankly. When he had cut open my womb to remove the child, he had not seen any evidence whatsoever of another growth developing. Given my age, and scarring of my womb from the growth and from the incisions made at time of birth, I shall likely never conceive again. If I do, I will most likely miscarry. I cannot conceive so long as I am nursing. After weaning, however, I would do well to apply contraceptive measures until my childbearing years are clearly over.

After the physician departed I lay on my bed, staring at the shifting light patterns on the ceiling, and fighting once again the all too familiar surge of resentment toward my family. Behold the consequences of their neglecting my gynecologic health! First there was the growth that had rendered me unable to conceive. Then came the expulsion of that growth: an event that nearly cost me my life. It took a harrowing, life-threatening process to achieve the very result, which an uncomplicated medication applied at the appropriate time could have rendered without duress. The birth for which I had so desperately yearned had endangered my life, and that of my child as well. Now I must forestall another birth, lest it cost me my life or at least create complications. I uttered a sardonic laugh at the bitter irony of the whole business.

"WILL YOU EVER STOP REITERATING AND LAMENTING YOUR PAST?" an exasperated Tiberius practically bellowed at me, after I had described my musings over our supper of roasted grouse and root vegetables. "You behave as though you are the only person in the world who has endured mistreatment and familial strife! Behold my ongoing struggle with my family. Consider Phoebe's tumultuous history—those of Briseis, of Alcmene and Nestor. You have heard their accounts. Consider Miranda, whose mother tried to kill her! So what if we must start practicing contraception? Thousands of couples do. It is an annoyance, not a sentence. Now do not go crawling into some corner and imagining yourself suicidal," he added with sarcasm upon noting the tears in my eyes. "You have a tremendous and wonderful new responsibility, Clytia, requiring your undivided attention and clear judgment. As your husband, as father of your child, I command you to curb your memories into proper perspective before they compromise his upbringing, even as you have feared they might!"

He had not raised his voice to me since my altercation with Timoleon, to which he had obliquely referred. His present anger I could not begrudge, because it was unequivocally justified. After all, I had been carping about my history—and quite unremittingly—since the very inception of our acquaintance. Remorse struck me like the rush of a headlong cataract. Was I as abjectly self-centered as my mother? Was inordinate fixation upon my own adversities rendering me unable to discern and appreciate, let alone ameliorate, the sufferings of others? Closing my eyes, holding my breath and clenching my lower lip in my teeth, I succeeded in suppressing my tears. Suddenly I was aware, that as a cataract flushes away obstructions in its path, repentance was dissuading the familiar inclination to wallow in disconsolate self-condemnation. In my imagination I once again stood before that supernal throne, sorrowful and penitent as before. But instead of self-immolation, I was now offering gratitude for reprimand and commitment to improvement—a surrender to Underlying Good for correction and direction of my thoughts and actions.

I felt Tiberius take my hand. With my eyes still lowered I murmured humbly, "I promise, my love, to desist—I promise. And I pray you never refrain from rebuking me whenever I fail to keep this promise." As I looked up at him another wave of chagrin struck me, and my tears emerged anew. "Tiberius, I do not understand why I feel so irresistibly driven, to keep reiterating my past when no one else seems similarly inclined. Every time I believe I am finally beginning to forget my harsh experiences and forgive my family for afflicting me, some hitherto forgotten or undetected anguish from my upbringing surfaces, to start me fretting and ruminating and resenting anew. Talking about these events seems the only way I can reassure myself, that I am not insane and my family correct about me after all."

He daubed my face with his napkin. "Clytia, the only way to prevent one's memories from aggravating or hurting others is to keep them to oneself. If all the rest of us can accomplish this, you can as well; for you are a highly intelligent and altruistic woman. You may also discover the less you talk about your history, the less painful it will seem to you." After a thoughtful pause he inquired, "Clytia, did your mother talk on and on about matters that disgruntled her?"

"Oh yes," I replied effusively, "oftentimes for months and sometimes even for years. Her aunt did as well. One would pick up and carry on where the other left off."

"There, do you see? You acquired your habit from them. And now that this trait has been detected there is no need to discuss it—only to abandon it, let it pass."

Yet another bad attribute from my childhood I reflected, feeling once again the familiar hot flash of anger. Nevertheless I said nothing.

Thrasyllus arrived with his family on the final day of February. With two new infants and two new kittens to encounter, Thrasylla was beside herself with excitement. The venison supper we shared was my first meal in the dining room since the previous August. Following breakfast on the morrow—New Year's Day—we escorted our guests to the nursery. The baby was asleep. Thrasylla obediently complied with her instructions to be absolutely quiet. Phoebe was in attendance. After Thrasylla had peered cautiously and curiously into the crib, in a whisper I asked Phoebe to take her to see Phoenix and Miranda and send Menon to us.

After Menon arrived, I carefully collected my son and laid him on the floor before Tiberius. Smiling, with tears in his eyes, he lifted the babe in his arms and declared in an undertone, "My duly begotten and acknowledged son: Tiberius Claudius Alcimus." Despite his father's quietude the baby awoke and began to fuss: time was at hand for another feeding. Menon bowed and took his leave having uttered nary a word, his silence proving he was deeply moved. Tiberius invited Aka and Thrasyllus to join him in the library. Left behind alone, I proceeded to provide the requisite nourishment.

Presently Phoebe returned, having left her charges with Briseis. After handing the baby off to her, I withdrew to the library as well. The table was strewn with star charts, over which Thrasyllus and Tiberius were poring. They hushed me firmly when I started to chat with Aka, so with one hand I beckoned her to join me in the adjacent parlor. There we compared the details of our respective deliveries by the knife, until Tiberius arrived and asked us to return to the library. Thrasyllus had just finished casting Alcimus' horoscope, along with Tiberius' and mine. His calculations for our son agreed with the prognostications Tiberius had made, but provided greater detail. Alcimus will be to us a source of stability—a solace, a haven. He will excel in areas of endeavor at which his parents failed, and fail at those in which we excelled. He will become very learned but not as an intellectual, very influential and powerful but not as a politician or military leader. His familial relationships will be stable and harmonious for the most part. There will be some great distress, surmounted by joy previously unperceived.

Turning to our horoscopes, Thrasyllus averred I had indeed reached my time of monumental change, and Tiberius was entering a threshold period that will culminate in his. The frustrating stagnation of the past two years was about to end.

For luncheon we feasted on a wild boar Nicanor had caught, dasheens and squash. Our visitors departed shortly afterward, in midafternoon. The morrow was a day of regular business for which everyone had to prepare. Thrasyllus had a lecture to deliver. His daughter now enrolled in school, over her protests had to be made ready for this drudgery. Our praetorian guards were being changed: the present company's two-year tour of duty was at an end. Tiberius was going to debrief Selvinius in the morning and interview the new commandant—a Publius Aelius—in the afternoon.

The remainder of this New Year's Day I spent luxuriating in the bath. "If my monumental change takes no other form than a permanent reprieve from vat bathing, I shall be eternally content," I exclaimed to Tiberius, as he seated himself on the bathroom bench to await his time in the tub. Noting the tablet in his hand I inquired, "What have you there?"

"An inspiration from Thrasyllus' casting of our horoscopes—yours, mine, and our son's." Opening the tablet, he read,

> Dousing with his celestial water
> The fires of fear, doubt and anguish
> The valiant emerges phoenix-like from their ashes,

> Fulfilling hopes thought shattered,
> Rendering the lion's snarl a smile,
> The scorpion's sting a caress.

"How gorgeously written—and how true," I exclaimed.

"My Clytia, I envision you sitting on our veranda with Alcimus on your knees, teaching him the wonders of the universe from your vast stores of knowledge, while I stand by rejoicing he will not become involved in politics. Could his horoscope imply my monumental change will consist of retirement from public life?"

"Would that not be a marvel?" I sighed. "The perfect culmination to a life of struggle and torment, of service to a cause for which your temperament so discomfited you? But now remember, we agreed to remain detached about the future—to be neither hopeful nor hopeless."

He nodded slowly, pensively. "Your change has been truly monumental, my love."

"I never, ever expected to become a mother."

"Motherhood is only one small part. The changes wrought in your character since I have known you are astounding—phoenix-like. Disdain has given way to sympathy and charity, vindictiveness to tolerance and forgiveness, not only for the faults of others but for your own. Gone is your envy of and anxiety to surpass the achievements of others; and in its place are appreciation for, aspiration after, and enjoyment of excellence for its own sake without regard to source or authorship. Instead of defending or deprecating your mistakes, you now strive to learn from them as guideposts toward improvement in thought and action. All of these were forerunners to the culmination which has taken place. Do you realize: since our trivial wrangle of last Saturday, you have not mentioned your family once?"

The present day was a Wednesday.

Suddenly wide-eyed and breathless, my heart pounding with astonishment, I sat upright in the bathtub so abruptly that I must have sent three wine jugs worth of water sloshing over the side. "I HAVE NOT GIVEN A SINGLE THOUGHT TO MY FAMILY SINCE THAT MOMENT—AND WITHOUT ANY CONSCIOUS, DELIBERATELY CALCULATED EFFORT TO SUPPRESS SUCH REFLECTIONS!" After a pause to catch my breath, I continued now more sedately. "Those reminiscences and ruminations had intruded on me daily, oftentimes hourly, for as long as I can remember. Being rid of them is truly a monumental change." Falling silent again I watched the agitation of the bathwater subside, still exulting in my discovery.

From outside the bathroom came Alcmene's characteristically nervous voice: "Lady, your son is calling for another feeding."

Tiberius laid a towel for me to stand upon so I did not slip on the saturated floor. "What a mess you have created," he grumbled as he helped me out of the bath.

"I feel like a milch goat: naahaahaahaahaa!"

"No complaints, now: the decision to nurse was entirely yours. Uncanny how appropriate the pseudonym you choose for yourself turned out to be." His comment referred, of course, to the fact that I shared my sobriquet Galatea with our barnyard goat.

The praetorian commander Aelius offered Tiberius a new glimmer of hope. He had a cousin by adoption—Lucius Aelius Sejanus—whom Augustus had recently designated to join Gaius' entourage. Sejanus and several other new appointees had concurred with Longus and Cyrenius, that Tiberius should be permitted return to Italy in the event he must assume command on the German frontier. Aelius averred these new officers were determined to convince Gaius, that to keep Tiberius in exile was to put the empire's safety at risk.

On the day our son turned one month of age, we engaged in sex for the first time since the previous June. Afterward, while we lay holding hands beneath the coverlet, I asked Tiberius whether he had employed a hetaera during my hiatus from his bed. He reminded me of his promise not to tell me, so I did not press him. It was perfectly understandable for a man to be disinclined to share a matter of this nature with his wife; and unlike my mother, I was willing to appreciate and respect such reticence. After a short silence, however, Tiberius chuckled a little and gently squeezed my hand.

"To tell the truth, Clytia, I considered doing so a number of times. And once I did have someone brought here: a former regular of Arbindus from the brothel that had owned Briseis. But I could not engage her, because thoughts of you kept getting in the way. Embracing her portended to be as distasteful as embracing Julia and despairing all the while she was not you. The courtesan accepted my rejection most amicably. She even tried to decline the payment I offered her, and only agreed to take it after I reminded her she would have to justify to her employer her reason for refusing it. Instead of spending the night with me she passed it with Briseis and Arbindus in their quarters, catching up on gossip and sharing reminiscences. You are overpowering, my Lioness, overwhelming and dispelling my desire for any other woman!"

Drawing my free arm across his chest I nestled against him. "You continue to say the most wonderful things about me!"

"And you continue to receive them as though they are untrue. Were that the case, I would not utter them in the first place. Clytia, you continue to succumb to your family's imprecations. They misled you to mistake humility for humiliation. Humility manifests itself in gratitude, in consideration for others, in the striving for excellence without regard for personal acclaim, and in the gracious acceptance of compliments when acclaim is achieved. These qualities you have always had, despite your family's assertions to the contrary."

"Thank you," I answered ingenuously, hoping as always that he could sense my sincerity in the timbre of my voice.

He kissed me. "Those words just proved my point. Ah, my Clytia!" He kissed me again, now more fervently. "I came to Rhodes seeking self-fulfillment, which I anticipated finding through the pursuit of philosophy. Instead I have found it in you and the child you have given me." Releasing me he rolled onto his back, gazed at the ceiling and sighed pensively. "Clytia, life in the political arena inculcates hypocrisy, aggressive and unscrupulous competition, disregard for the personal feelings and innate predispositions of others. You have seen firsthand how these proclivities impugn and distort the natural affections and aspirations members of a family hold for one another, and lead to frustration, disaster, and regret. Clytia, with you and Alcimus I have established a family which will remain exempt from—unsullied by—those aberrations. The only unconventional element about our relationship at the moment is its secrecy, which I am committed eventually to dispel. As Alcimus matures I shall observe him assiduously, to insure I do not drive him—as I was—into pathways of life for which he is temperamentally unsuited. It appears Thrasyllus was correct once again. My craving for self-determination is satisfied. Is this not a monumental change?"

April arrived with its warming weather and noticeably longer days. By now I was desperate to venture out of doors, having been confined to the house since the discovery of my pregnancy the previous July. I longed to revisit my old favorites about the promontory—the pond, the Guardian Trees, the distant vistas, the heliotrope plants—and hopefully discover new subjects or shadings or hues. Longus was bound to be calling for replenishments, especially now the seas had reopened to regular trade traffic. Rhathines recommended I walk at a brisk pace through the park every day the weather allowed, so long as I was careful not to overexert myself. After being sedentary for over half a year, my muscles were lacking in tone and in urgent need of exercise.

Tiberius often accompanied me, walking with me or sitting beside me as I painted and sketched. He conversed very little, remaining for the most part reflectively silent—not broodingly, but as though relief and peace were passing through his psyche in waves. Never before had I perceived such contentment in him; and I rejoiced as never before. Perhaps it was our elation that made this year's spring seem more vibrant with color and fragrance, than any I could remember on Rhodes or in Italy. Briseis had Ajax deposit a load of clean straw from the barn in one corner of the veranda. She fashioned two depressions in the heap, and then covered it with several clean bedsheets. On balmy days thereafter, one of the serving women would lay Alcimus and Phoenix in the depressions, to partake of the fresh spring air which proved quite soporific to both boys. Briseis started to venture about the promontory with Miranda at her side, replenishing their stock of medicinals.

Within three weeks our euphoria came to an abrupt and distressing end. The Guardian Trees changed slightly in appearance with each new spring. I was painting this year's rendition of their blossoming when Tiberius drew up on Sinapeus. After telling me to leave my paints—he would send a servant for them later—he lifted me onto the horse's withers, told me to hold on tightly, and proceeded at full gallop back to the house. Arbindus was standing on the veranda, fully armed. Lowering me off Sinapeus, Tiberius told me to await him in the library.

The cause of the alarm turned out to be a letter which had just arrived from Gaius. The prince reported he had recently hosted a banquet at his headquarters in Antioch, for his staff and that of the imperial legate of Syria. When everyone was deep in his cups, a member of Gaius' entourage stood up and boasted he was ready to sail for Rhodes and return to Antioch with the head of the exsul.

My initial response was to dismiss the incident as inconsequential—the raving of a drunkard—until Tiberius explained its severity. Even had the perpetrator repented his declaration after sobering up—assuming he remembered making it at all—he could not retract the suggestion it had put forth. Not only had a death threat had been made. Being branded an exsul implied further and significantly deleterious debasement of Tiberius' reputation. Exsul is the Roman epithet for an individual who, by behavior particularly execrable, has rendered himself utterly unworthy of Roman citizenship. Ordinarily an exsul is expelled from Rome, and the populace forbidden to offer him sustenance and shelter—aqua et ignis (water and fire) is the conventional formula—within four hundred miles of the capital.

How many hotheads, aspiring to ingratiate themselves to Gaius, had begun to consider organizing raiding parties to storm our retreat? Could we trust the very praetorians—ostensibly our protectors—not to invade the house while we slept, slaughter us all, and run off to Gaius with Tiberius' head in a basket? By the time a report reached the praetorian prefect Ostorius Scapula in Rome and an investigation undertaken, we would be long past redemption.

Following our discussion we both sat staring at the library floor, lost in thought. At length we raised our eyes to meet one another's. The silence I broke with a question: what recourse was Tiberius contemplating? Flight to the Far East? He shook his head. A possibility, he said, but only as a last resort. Such a journey portended to be not only expensive but risky, taking us across Roman dominions nearby to which Gaius was presently stationed. Should Tiberius be recognized, his present degradation as an exsul and the physical proximity of the prince were bound to encourage aspiring attackers.

Rising from his chair, he retrieved a batch of blank tablets and handed them to me. The letters he dictated to Gaius and Augustus were essentially the same. Tiberius renewed his appeal for permission to return to Rome, reiterating his promise not to take any part whatsoever in public affairs. Such, in fact, was his personal preference. His retirement from Rhodes had convinced him life as a private citizen, devoted to assisting the sick and their families, far better suited his shy temperament than the holding of public office or even the exercise of military command. His only motive at present was to ensure his personal safety, which he had every confidence his recipients did not begrudge him. The movements of a posse comitatus, organized for an assault upon Tiberius, stood a far greater likelihood of succeeding in the hinterlands of Rhodes than in the empire's crowded capital. Moreover a gesture of familial reconciliation might dissuade potential assailants from assuming they could ingratiate themselves to Gaius—or to Augustus too for that matter—by destroying Tiberius.

In the eight years since Tiberius had taken up residence on Rhodes, no faction had rallied about him in opposition to Gaius. Tiberius quite palpably had developed a tangible following of supporters among those who wanted him prepared to assume command in Germania should the need arise. Nevertheless, none of these adherents had proposed him as an adversary or even a colleague to Gaius. Was this not evidence enough that Gaius' fears of political rivalry with Tiberius were groundless?

The next set of letters were to Marinus and Atticus, Longus and Cyrenius, apprising them of the development. Tiberius expressed concern these friends, as known supporters of an exsul, may be in greater danger than ever of verbal or physical attack. The final letter was to Thrasyllus. What did the stars portend? Did they indicate whether the danger we faced was as serious as we believed? Was Tiberius seeking the proper remedy? Could he anticipate rehabilitation; or was flight to the ends of the earth the preferable alternative?

Tiberius proceeded to prescribe a series of precautionary measures for our household. As safety lies in numbers, he gave orders no one—not even the servants—should move about the house unaccompanied. We must be at least in pairs at all times. No woman was to venture out of doors, let along bring a child there. The men must make sure at least one of them was within earshot of women or children at all times. Tiberius ordered Nicanor not to hunt or trap beyond sight of the house, nor venture to the pond to catch fish or turtles, lest someone ambush him. Our supply of fresh meats consequently dwindled, although we had an ample reserve of cured meats which reminded me of sea voyage provisions. Impractical would be to place the kitchen garden outside the rear of the house under guard by day and night, to keep someone from contaminating it. Accordingly Phoebe and Briseis did not replant the garden, but instead cultivated vegetables in pots they set about the courtyard.

Nicanor and Ajax moved the four setting hens and Galatea the goat, from the barn into the courtyard to protect our eggs and milk. This year's kid they remanded to the farm workers, in return for a cured carcass to enhance our meat provisions. Carbo and Nicanor's hunting hounds Therates and Atrestus they brought into the house as well, but left Imperator to his friends the praetorians: any attacker who molested that cat could anticipate an exquisite retribution from his guardians. Carbo objected for several days and quite noisily, hissing and growling at Xanthrothix' two sons and the dogs; but eventually he acquiesced to his new environs after determining he could not expect to be fed anywhere but in the courtyard or kitchen.

The praetorian commander Aelius listened receptively to Tiberius' concerns, about the possibility of a raid on the promontory and the potential for danger from the praetorians themselves. Following their discussion, Aelius sent to the barracks at the city of Rhodes for reinforcements—four additional men, two more horses and as many more mastiffs. Aelius reassured Tiberius he had harangued his guards: the slightest nuance of insubordination would result in corporal punishment, followed by immediate dishonorable dismissal and submission of a scathing report to Scapula. From Aelius Tiberius procured swords, daggers, and shields, a set of which he assigned to each of our menservants and kept for himself. Nicanor and Aelius warned the farmhands and issued them armaments, but advised them to report any sightings of intruders to Aelius immediately and not to engage in fighting except as a last resort.

Safety lies in proximity as well as in numbers. Accordingly we moved Alcimus into the master bedchamber with us, Rhathines into the antechamber that adjoined the master chamber on the opposite side from my quarters, Menon with Phoebe and Miranda into my bedchamber, Arbindus with Briseis and Phoenix into the nursery, Alcmene and Nestor into the room that lay beyond. Nicanor, Ajax, and Androcles remained in the servants' quarters on the west wing, there to guard the kitchen and the storerooms in which our food was kept. We were not concerned about our water being poisoned or cut off. The praetorians had to safeguard the cistern sedulously, their being as dependent upon it as we. The menservants worked out a schedule between themselves, so that two of them were awake and on guard during each of the four watches of the night.

More frightened was I now than during my climactic menses and later my delivery, when semi-consciousness had dulled immediate awareness of the danger in which I had lain. The physical topography of the promontory rendered it highly defensible in the event of a siege. Yet how long could our small garrison hold out against an attacking century, let alone a legion?

Deliberately I turned my ponderings to the decency of Gaius in sending his warning. Mentally I embraced the prince's charity as evidence of Underlying Good, but refrained from mentioning my contemplation aloud. Tiberius could hardly be in a frame of mind to hear me reiterate, how a philosophical system of which he was skeptical might solve our presently life-threatening situation. I lost all inclination to draw or paint or play my harp or even to read. After I offered to help the servants with some of their chores—hoping by engaging in such endeavors to keep from brooding—Phoebe inquired whether I had taken leave of my senses. Fortunately Briseis continued to seek reading lessons from me—a distraction for which I believe she was as grateful as I. From my textile collection I hemmed and embroidered two crib blankets and created a little cape for Alcimus, although many months must pass before he could wear the garment.

For a time, Tiberius maintained a cautious yet hopeful anticipation—the same emotional detachment about the future we had embraced during my pregnancy. Gaius and Augustus may wish to see Tiberius destroyed politically; but they most assuredly did not desire his personal annihilation. Nor were they unfair: neither endorsed his unmerited execration as an exsul. But as the month wore on without a response from anybody, Tiberius' expectations started to dwindle. By day he would sit in the library, if not staring at the floor then out the window at the distant sea. His sleep became troubled once again with distressing dreams, from which I frequently had difficulty waking him.

I spent many a wakeful night myself, wondering what must become of Alcimus and me. If Tiberius secured permission to return to Rome, would he feel comfortable bringing us with him? Reingratiating himself to his family was proving difficult enough; the revelation he had a non-Roman wife and son might compromise this precarious endeavor. Worse yet: suppose as Tiberius had suggested, Augustus or Gaius made marriage with Agrippina a condition of his recall? If Tiberius acquiesced and ended our marriage, he could certainly bring Alcimus and me to Italy as his bastard and mistress. That, however, must relegate us to a life of concealment, of furtive and surreptitious encounters. Roman men are sedulously discreet about their illegitimate offspring. Bastards are sequestered away, and invariably consigned to lives as menials—servants or day laborers—without recognition and without inheritance. For Alcimus and me in particular, detection could result in scandal, in our forced separation from Tiberius, and (worst of all!) the possibility of remission to my kin. Surely better under these circumstances would be for my son and me to remain on Rhodes. Then Tiberius could visit us under the pretext of vacationing on the island and looking up old acquaintances from the Academy.

But what if Tiberius' request to return to Italy were denied? How long must we remain on this fortified hilltop as if under siege, potentially in danger from the very guards assigned to protect us? How could we properly rear a child under such conditions—without contact with the world beyond our confines? And if in the end we must flee to the East, were we condemning our son to grow up a vagabond or a permanent expatriate living among strangers, destined never to encounter his Graeco-Roman heritage firsthand?

And what of Thrasyllus? Had he not foreseen this development? Why all of a sudden did he not answer? Heretofore he had always been prompt with his replies to our inquiries. Had he turned against us as well? We had confessed to him our most private thoughts, our most intimate secrets. Apart from Menon and Phoebe, Thrasyllus and his wife alone knew of our marriage. Thrasyllus as my curator was guardian of my property—this farm. He knew my true identity, my personal history. Was he poised to disclose my whereabouts to my mother?

Not caring to add to Tiberius' already overflowing reservoir of distress, I did not share my misgivings with him. I did set about contemplating anew my presumption that evil, no matter how apparently virulent, must eventually yield to the dominance of Underlying Good.

As if to match our mood, the weather became dreary and rainy as it usually does in late April. Then three days before the Nones of May *[5/5]*, an intriguing event took place. It was late afternoon. Tiberius and I were in the bathroom, with Arbindus standing guard outside. I was preparing to enter the tub, Tiberius having preceded me. He was about to dress, when a shaft of golden sunlight broke through the clouds and penetrated the bathroom window. As the light fell upon Tiberius' chiton, for several moments the garment appeared to glow as though with a radiance of its own.

Precisely on the Nones, a military messenger arrived with a tablet bearing the imperial seal. With the terse sarcasm of his earlier correspondence Augustus had written:

> Again I yield to your mother's entreaties. You may return to
> Italy provided you fulfill two conditions: secure Gaius' approval
> of your return, and scrupulously refrain from participation in
> public affairs of any nature for the remainder of your life.

Half the battle was won, but only half. After ordering the messenger to wait, Tiberius immediately dictated another letter to Gaius: a promise anew to eschew public life, and above all to forestall the development of any faction offering the slightest suggestion of setting him up as a possible rival to the prince.

The following week, on the fifth day before the Ides of May, *[5/11]* Alcimus entered his fourth month. He was now able to roll over, and when prone to prop himself up on his elbows a bit. Auburn fuzz was beginning to cover his head. His eyes sparkled whenever he offered his engaging smile, revealing the stubs of developing teeth. He babbled profusely: *Gagalagamababa.* From time to time he fretted from discomfort in his gums and from bouts of colic. Rhathines assured me both ailments were normal at his age and actually indicators of health. I longed to resume taking him outdoors now that the weather had turned pleasant again, and the earth was filled with the sounds of hatchlings and the heady fragrance of blossoms. Our confinement was beginning to wear on me. With servants and animals in close quarters, this house and farm of which I had been so very fond had started to remind me of my parents' Campanian torture. Although I continued my efforts to acknowledge and rely upon the supremacy of Good to redeem our present condition, I was beginning to wonder whether I had truly accessed a cosmic Principle, or simply conjured a philosophic sophistry from my education and empirical experience. However, no other solution seemed at hand.

On an afternoon some ten days later, a mounted praetorian reigned up before the house to announce Thrasyllus was waiting at the promontory's base.

"I have half a mind to push you directly off this cliff, and if you survive then send you to be drowned in the sea!" Tiberius growled from the veranda as Androcles helped the sage dismount Asellus. Thrasyllus was profuse with apologies. The director of the Rhodes Academy had departed suddenly to accept a position at the Alexandria Museion, and the Academy's governing body had appointed Thrasyllus to succeed him. Our friend disliked his new position intensely. Although the governors had assured him he was only an interim director, he was unpersuaded. In academic institutions, nominally temporary positions almost invariably become permanent. The tedious and time-consuming minutiae of administration were distracting him excessively, not only from his scholarly endeavors but from his family and friends as well. Aka had started to complain that she and Thrasylla were hardly seeing him. Spare moments in which to write to us, let alone cast our horoscopes, kept eluding him. As if this were not enough, Aka's father had suddenly died. Thrasyllus had become all the more preoccupied with seeing his wife and daughter off to Commagene, there to attend the funeral and console her mother.

While retiring with our visitor to the library, we explained our new and uncomfortable sleeping arrangements. Unable to offer Thrasyllus lodging in the former guest quarters as these were presently occupied by the additional praetorians, the best we could provide was a vacant cubicle in the servants' milieu. No matter, Thrasyllus assured us: the ambiance of accommodations did not perturb him so long as they were comfortable and clean. He set right to work examining star charts. My horoscope was the first to become apparent, as it was simple and straightforward. My monumental change had occurred—quite palpably my motherhood; but significant changes for me were still imminent. These would cease upon fulfillment of Tiberius' monumental change, whereupon I would enter the mitigation Thrasyllus had forecast to follow.

Alcimus' future, like mine, was inextricably linked to Tiberius' monumental change. Until that event occurs, Alcimus' life will be in continual flux. He will not suffer from this turmoil, and will have no recollection of it. Following his father's impending climax, Alcimus will undergo the same lifelong mitigation predicted for Tiberius and me. Alcimus will mature steadily and healthily in physique, perspicacity, and emotional stability. He will endure few significant changes in his life, and none monumental. He will fulfill with success the destiny his parents anticipated for him, to their immense satisfaction and to his. As child and adult, he will lead a reasonably contented life. Vexations will arise, but dissipate into profound happiness. Essentially the same forecast Thrasyllus had delivered directly after Alcimus' birth.

Turning to the prognostication for Tiberius, Thrasyllus jotted calculation after calculation in silence. A puzzled look came over his face; and he began to shake his head in bewilderment. Nothing was emerging, as though the stars had nothing to reveal. Tiberius became agitated and pressed Thrasyllus: there had to be an answer. While the sage ran his computations anew, Tiberius began nervously to pace the floor. I sensed what he was deliberating the forecast was so baleful, Thrasyllus was hesitant to deliver it. Tiberius sharply repeated his demand for an answer. Thrasyllus clenched his teeth and flinched as though he had been struck. He returned to the charts, his face contorted in a grimace. The ensuing quarter hour seemed an eternity. Suddenly Thrasyllus drew in his breath through his teeth. "By all the gods!" he exclaimed breathlessly. "A ship bearing news of your deliverance is on the seas at this very moment!"

We passed yet another sleepless night. It seemed highly suspicious that Thrasyllus had stalled and evaded, then upon being pressured delivered so definite a prediction. Was the prognosis genuine, or simply a fabrication to mollify us with false anticipation? After half a week had passed with neither news nor omens to verify the forecast, our doubts about Thrasyllus' sincerity started to escalate. Why would he deliberately delude us? This consideration left Tiberius more distraught than ever—angry and aggrieved that so trusted a friend would resort to circumvention and deception. "Perhaps I should have actually pushed Thrasyllus off this cliff," he murmured facetiously one day while gazing out the library window toward the sea. By now I had entered a state of mental and emotional weariness, in which detachment about the future came without effort. Claiming the governance of Underlying Good had become an exercise in redundancy. Were my philosophic process destined to bring about our rescue, now was the time to step aside and let it do its work.

During the subsequent night we woke with a start. Outside there was shouting, the neighing of horses and barking of dogs. A steady series of rapid flashes appeared through the window shutters. Then a sound like a great number of heavy footfalls became audible, and gradually increased in volume. A projectile struck the house, then many more in succession. Alcimus started to wail in his crib. Tiberius arose abruptly and stood beside our bed, glancing about nervously and straining to hear sounds apart from the baby's din. Realizing he was attempting to determine whether we were under attack, I retrieved Alcimus and silenced him by giving suck. Were marauders with torches moving toward the house?

From the antechamber came the sound of a flint being struck, and then a glow of light: Rhathines had been roused as well. He carried his lamp to the doorway to check on us. Lamplight and the sound of murmuring voices emanated from my bedchamber: Phoebe and Menon were awake and reassuring Miranda. Then came a great clap of thunder. Rhathines opened a door to the courtyard. The three cats and two dogs, all well drenched, rushed into the chamber and shook themselves.

What we had thought torchlight was a series of lightning flashes. Unusually heavy rain was mimicking the sound of footfalls. The missiles turned out to be hailstones. Now we could hear the shouts more distinctly: the praetorians were hustling horses and dogs into the barn or under cover elsewhere. Ajax and Androcles were in the courtyard, calming and sheltering the other animals housed therein. All the adults in our coterie heaved sighs of relief; but Alcimus began to fret anew. Phoebe changed his swaddling. She offered take him into her bed for comfort; but Tiberius refused as he lifted the babe from his crib and placed him in the middle of our bed. The servants withdrew, and we laid down on either side of the baby. Nursing him with my other breast calmed him while the storm raged on and on.

At length the lightning waned and the thunder faded, until both died away in the distance and all was quiet. Tiberius and Alcimus were asleep. A mountain thunderstorm was unusual for this time of year, especially one of such virulence. Was this an omen, I wondered.

Near to noon, Aelius brought to the house two military tribunes newly arrived from Gaius' staff. One was the commandant's adoptive cousin Lucius Aelius Sejanus, the other a Marcus Velleius Paterculus. Of course I promptly withdrew to our bedchamber. After Tiberius had interviewed the pair and dismissed them with Aelius to the guesthouse, he summoned me to the library. The emissaries had brought a collection of fine gifts: dates, apricots, almonds, citrus fruits, sandalwood oil, frankincense, a jug of Syrian wine, a vase decorated with native designs, a compendium of Syrian medicinals translated into Greek— and most significantly, a long and highly apologetic letter from Gaius.

Gaius' diplomatic efforts to reestablish Roman dominance in Armenia had succeeded—apparently more through blind chance than artful diplomacy on the part of the prince. The young Parthian king Phraacetes, whose resistance to the reestablishment of a Roman pretender in Armenia was the primary reason behind Gaius' junket, had completely reversed his stance and capitulated. Phraacetes was facing factional strife and impending civil war within his own realm—a turmoil which would eventually lead to his overthrow and assassination.

He had decided to mollify the Romans so he could concentrate his attention upon internal affairs. On the final day of their negotiations, which had ended in the middle of May, Phraacetes advised Gaius that Marcus Lollius had been accepting immense bribes, from those Parthian and Armenian nobles who opposed Roman control of Armenia. In return for these considerations, Lollius had agreed to recommend, outline, and facilitate implementation of policies, which would promote the interests of his benefactors while emasculating Armenia's new pro-Roman government.

Gaius may not yet have perfected all of the skills essential for an effective ruler. Fortunately the art of dissembling was not among these. After distracting Lollius with the attention-demanding task of deciding which legions should be deployed in Armenia, Gaius ordered a covert investigation of his chief's correspondence, financial transactions, and meetings with associates. The inquiry confirmed Phraacetes' allegations. Before his entire entourage, Gaius confronted Lollius with the evidence, relieved him of his authority, and declared amicitia breached. The startled Lollius retorted that the evidence and report were fabrications of Tiberius' supporters; that Gaius ought to have had better sense than to believe such blatant falsehoods; that in the retirement of his quarters Lollius would prepare an unimpeachable defense. There two days later he was found dead upon his bed. The vein in his left elbow joint had been slit and his blood allowed to drain into a basin. Was the death self-inflicted? There was no way to determine for certain.

The discovery he had allowed Lollius to dupe him, so utterly and so treacherously, left Gaius horrified and chagrined. The prince at present was carefully evaluating the validity of measures he had taken, and the notions he had embraced under the influence of his former chief of staff. One of these was his view of Tiberius as a seriously dangerous rival. Lollius had actually staged the banquet at Chios, during which he had ostensibly endeavored to stop Gaius' staff from assailing Tiberius about his political intentions. Now free of Lollius' persuasions, Gaius perceived quite clearly that no organized opposition movement had rallied about Tiberius. At last, Gaius had abandoned his reservations about Tiberius' returning to Rome. Gaius was pleased and relieved to accept his grandfather's appointment of Quirinius Cyrenius for Lollius' replacement, not only because Cyrenius possessed the requisite military and leadership experience for the position, but because he had risked destruction of his own reputation to remain unassailably loyal to Tiberius.

"What did Lollius have against you?" I inquired cautiously as Tiberius closed Gaius' tablet and deposited it on a shelf with other correspondence.

He walked to the window and gazed pensively at the outdoors. "The only incident I can recall, which might have aggrieved him toward me, occurred nearly two decades ago while Lollius was imperial governor of Gaul. Because he overlooked or misinterpreted his intelligence reports, a band of German marauders managed to overwhelm an undermanned frontier garrison and perpetrate some minor pillaging upon the surrounding farms. Happening to be nearby with a crack squadron at the ready, I came forward and scurried the intruders back across the Rhine before Lollius could manage to assemble a force of his own. My stepfather admonished the embarrassed Lollius to be more attentive to the security of his frontiers, but otherwise did not hold this relatively insignificant incident against him. To all appearances, Lollius accepted the reprimand humbly and graciously. My stepfather subsequently appointed him imperial governor of Galatia, a seriously disrupted province which he reorganized most admirably. That achievement, along with his presumed integrity, prompted my stepfather to select Lollius as chief officer for Gaius' present junket. Apparently for all these years, Lollius has resented the fact I rescued that Gallic garrison he had neglected to reinforce. It also seems likely Lollius was endeavoring to thwart the success of Gaius' mission, by distracting him with fear I was plotting against him.

"Amazing, is it not, my Clytia? The greed and lingering grudge of a single man placed our very lives in danger, besides causing us public execration and abuse. Lollius must have realized he could not mislead my stepfather with regard to my political aspirations: hence his failure to impugn me sooner. But Gaius is naïve and credulous. Lollius foresaw he could exploit these proclivities, not only to defame me but to engage in venality without detection. Sadly I fear sooner or later, Gaius' gullibility will prove his undoing."

Joining him at the window, I leaned my head against his shoulder; we drew our arms about each other's waists. "Even your stepfather misjudged Lollius. Moreover if he recognized or suspected Gaius' misgivings about you were exaggerated, why did he not intervene to correct or at least investigate them? You might have been spared the opprobrium of the last three years."

Tiberius sighed. "My stepfather is no less fallible than any other human. He has also made the mistake of entrusting Gaius with independent judgments and decisions and assessments of character, the likes of which Gaius remains too inexperienced and unsophisticated to make. Now you may see why I am so relieved to become a private citizen. The errors one commits in a position of power have far greater consequence than those of ordinary men, and they weigh heavily upon one's conscience. But enough ruminating and reflecting, my love!" he exclaimed, suddenly brightening. "There is much work to be done in preparation for our journey."

The work began at once, with another round of correspondence. To Augustus: completion of the letter Tiberius had been dictating at the time Gaius' emissaries arrived. To Gaius: Tiberius' sincere forgiveness for the prince's misjudgment of him, relief Gaius no longer considered him a threat, and gratitude of course for the permission to return home. To Livia: would she apprise him when the news he had permission to return to Rome had been well disseminated, that he might depart without fear of being attacked by some uninformed sycophant? To the captain of the Phoenix: when would he next have a ship available for charter? To his unflagging adherents Longus, Atticus, Marinus, and Cyrenius: Tiberius will remain forever indebted to them for their unassailable loyalty, and for their willingness to defend his reputation at the risk of sullying their own. And to Drusus: gratitude for his forbearance and hopes for his forgiveness.

The final letter was a proposal to Thrasyllus, now clearly a beloved and trusted friend, from whom we anticipated a difficult and rueful separation. If Thrasyllus will agree to take Alcimus as his ward—to rear and educate him until such time Tiberius feels comfortable identifying Alcimus as our son and returning him to our household—Tiberius will reimburse Thrasyllus for all expenses associated with Alcimus' upkeep. He will also establish a stipend, large enough to enable Thrasyllus to pursue a career as an independent scholar for the remainder of his life. Tiberius proposed sending four servants with Alcimus: Rhathines because he belonged to Aka's family anyway, Briseis as Alcimus' nurse, Arbindus as his bodyguard, and Phoenix as his playmate and eventual valet. If Thrasyllus' present house in Rhodes is too small to accommodate this retinue, they can remain on the farm until larger quarters can be procured. Thrasyllus was welcome to remove with his enhanced household to another locale if he so desired—Alexandria, for example, or Athens; he need not confine himself to Rhodes. Nevertheless Tiberius' ultimate hope was to bring Thrasyllus to Rome, once it had become clear Tiberius' patronage and promotion of a recognized astrologer was not going to arouse criticism or controversy. This particular transfer would allow Tiberius and me to observe and visit our son—ostensibly as friends—until the appropriate time for us to make our true identities known to him. It would also prevent distance from thwarting the intimacy of our relationship with Thrasyllus as our confidant, our celestial prognosticator and spiritual mentor.

After handing him the tablet for his signet I closed my eyes, and abruptly slumped against the back of my chair as though a rock had struck my chest. Noting my reaction Tiberius continued mildly, "Do not misunderstand my motive, Clytia. Remember, we do not know what sort of reception awaits us. I do not want to bring Alcimus forward until it is clear you have won the acceptance of my family."

"You reassured me on the very day of Alcimus' birth, that having a Greek wife and half-Italian son should be perfectly acceptable so long as you live a strictly private life," I moaned petulantly.

"Were we to remain on Rhodes, yes. In Italy, in the presence of my family, I will be subject to as much public scrutiny as if I were holding the most prominent of public offices. Remember, my stepfather eschews marriages between Italians and other races. We must proceed slowly, gingerly, with introducing you as my ward, first to my family and then to Roman society. If we manage to accomplish this without objection or outrage, we can set about persuading my family to accept you as my wife. Thereafter we can work on revealing Alcimus."

"You would separate me from my child even before he is weaned; part him from his mother at so tender an age? Why can you not present him at Rome as the son of the husband who allegedly deserted me?"

"Everyone would see through that ruse for sure. His visage too closely matches my mother's, and his hair mine."

"Could you not declare those resemblances coincidental, as you plan to do should someone recognize me?"

His voice assumed an air of patient exasperation. "Clytia, your countenance is not known to half the population of the earth. With you we stand a good chance of pulling the stratagem off. But if I show up in Rome with a woman toting a baby who resembles my mother and me, do you think people will believe me if I assert that resemblance is coincidental and I had nothing to do with it? Would you?"

"I suppose not," I conceded.

"And furthermore: once we make known our marriage, having to retract denials of paternity and admit Alcimus is my son after all will be highly awkward for me—and frankly for you too."

"Suppose you leave me behind with him, and send for us both when you feel ready to introduce the two of us at once?"

"Evoke your profound rationality, my love. Briseis is still suckling Phoenix. She can nurse Alcimus perfectly well in your stead; she already has. Alcimus at present does comprehend you are his mother. He cannot differentiate between you and any other adult, and will not be able to for several years. His existence I cannot disclose to my family until after I have justified you to them. Suppose Alcimus is discovered before I accomplish this end. My kin will become disaffected with me anew, and the public will snicker about the bastard I endeavored unsuccessfully to hide. What sort of physical life and moral example does concealment and dissembling offer a little boy? He needs freedom and opportunity to disport himself, to discover the world surrounding him, to encounter and play with children his own age like Thrasylla, Phoenix, and Miranda."

He took my hand. "Clytia, I am resolved: Alcimus is going to have a unified family—know the identity and love of his parents—no matter where we must reside to accomplish this end. For this reason I insist you retain this farm and not sell it. If Alcimus is not welcome in Rome as my legitimate son, at least we have reserved a place to which we can retreat with him. Later we can decide if we should like to live elsewhere."

Just after dawn the next morning, we heard the envoys from Gaius depart. The letter for the prince they would deliver to him directly; the others they would entrust to couriers of the imperial post. Thrasyllus received his missive the same day, and in the early afternoon of the following arrived at the farm. As soon as we three were alone in the library, the sage flung himself prostrate on the floor before Tiberius, shaking with silent sobs. Finally he raised his head and, with solemn mien and tears streaming from half-closed eyes, accepted the proposition in the breathless undertones of intense emotion. Together we helped him to his feet and into a chair where he composed himself, wiping his face with his kerchief and continuing to burble his thanks.

Because Phoebe arrived to fetch me for another suckling, I could not remain to hear the discussion that followed. About an hour later I was idly strumming my harp, when she reemerged to advise me Master wished me to join him in the library. Tiberius asked whether I, as owner of the farm, was amenable to letting Thrasyllus and his family take up residence thereon, following our departure for Rome.

Before I could manage an answer, Thrasyllus explained he agreed to take Alcimus directly into his household concurrently with our departure. But as Tiberius had correctly surmised, Thrasyllus' house in Rhodes was too small to accommodate the newcomer and his entourage. Aka and Thrasylla loved the farm. To Thrasyllus it offered an idyll, in which to continue and hopefully finish his massive project of redaction and commentary on the works of Plato—now fallen into neglect on account of his administrative responsibilities at the

Academy. On the farm, Thrasyllus could resume his ponderings about music and the parallels between tonal, mathematical, and astronomical patterns. He could watch the stars in clear mountain air unsullied by city dust and lights, observe the natural world and record its patterns and cycles manifest in our park. With the farm meeting all physical needs of himself and his family, he could afford to resign his directorship at the Academy.

Tiberius interjected. Quite palpably we must leave my art collection on the farm until we had determined if and when we could transport it to Italy. Its protection during our absence had been giving him great concern. The departure of the praetorians, of Alcimus' serving retinue to Thrasyllus, and of the attendants who were going to accompany us to Italy, portended to reduce the population of the promontory drastically. New staff—hired or servile or both—would have to be acquired, to save the collection should the house catch fire or suffer some other form of damage. Thrasyllus by occupying the promontory would alleviate this problem of attrition by bringing his six servants—three men and as many women—to the farm, and precluding the departure of the four Tiberius had assigned to Alcimus.

The two went on and on, justifying the request. Thrasylla would enjoy clean air and open space, in lieu of the squalor and pollution and cramped quarters of the city. So would Aka, who delighted in nature and who amply deserved a reward for suffering Thrasyllus' preoccupation with the Academy for so many years. Briseis and Rhathines could continue training Miranda in pharmaceutics, that she may become a useful servant as an adult. The addition of new staff would enable Menon and Phoebe—respectively in their seventy-third and sixty-fourth years—to relinquish their duties to others and live in retirement.

As if spellbound I sat listening to the propositions, until at last I had the opportunity to speak. Why, I asked, did Thrasyllus assume he must seek my permission to take up residence on the farm, let alone defend his reasons? His impending occupancy being a single solution to so many different uncertainties and needs, I could not help but consider it a manifestation of Underlying Good.

To my relief actually, Tiberius rolling his eyes broke my euphoria. "That private philosophy of hers," he said rather dismissively.

"Not to be scoffed at, my friend," Thrasyllus answered. "Someday the three of us will spend much time exploring it in great depth."

Thrasyllus did not spend the night but departed that same afternoon, as his duties at the Academy were pressing. The next morning, Tiberius ordered Androcles and Ajax to patrol the house, Alcmene to mind Alcimus, Miranda, and Phoenix. Thereafter he ordered Menon to assemble the remainder of serving staff in the west wing parlor—the larger of the two. I too was present at this meeting, in which Tiberius announced his impending return to Italy and intentions for the disposition of the household.

We were going to take Alcmene and Nestor as our personal attendants on our voyage, Androcles and Ajax as bodyguards. All four would remain with us in Italy. They need not be concerned that they did not know much Latin, as a goodly portion of Tiberius' staff in Rome spoke Greek.

Menon was welcome to continue as manager of the farm for as long as he wished; but in light of his age, Tiberius recommended he train Nicanor to replace him were Nicanor willing to accept the task. Duties included insuring the buildings and other structures were kept in repair, supervising the household staff and farm workers, collecting and auditing harvest revenues, arranging for purchase at market whatever necessities the farm could not produce, paying the property's taxes and other financial obligations, and sending me its owner bimonthly reports. Since the household would no longer be receiving military rations, a way to procure these without causing the farmhands deprivation must be established.

For the present we would continue our straitened sleeping arrangements and heightened security—just in case some lunatic, who had not learned of Tiberius' reprieve or who objected to it, decided to mount an assault. Although Tiberius' removal should preclude the possibility of politically motivated attacks, the place would still be as vulnerable as any other farm to marauding by ordinary ruffians. Thrasyllus and his family were going to bring with them three able-bodied menservants who could assist with defense. Nevertheless, since the promontory was about to lose the protection of the praetorians along with that of Androcles and Ajax, Tiberius recommended Menon and Nicanor assess carefully whether the household was adequately defended and if necessary procure additional guards. They might start by offering this responsibility—and remuneration for it—to the farmhands. Alcimus must have adequate protection, regardless of the expense.

Concluding, Tiberius averred any servant of free status was at liberty to depart the farm and pursue an independent life. He, however, had conferred that freedom. Anyone who left him he would hold to the obligation of finding a replacement, if not for the person then for the services the departee had rendered our household. Now he and I would withdraw to our bedchamber, there to await the assembly's decision.

When I reached our quarters, Alcmene handed me Alcimus who was fussing for another feeding. Tiberius arrived carrying a writing tablet. I seated myself on the edge of our bed and began to suckle the babe. Tiberius dismissed Alcmene with orders to join her fellow servants at their meeting, and have them apprise her of what was discussed. After she left he looked about furtively to make sure no one else was nearby. Then he sat down beside me, opened the tablet and wrote, *Do you know why I am transferring Ajax and Androcles to Italy?*

"No," I said aloud.

He held his forefinger to his lips. Beneath the preceding sentence he wrote, *They are lovers. For this reason I have not manumitted them. Nor do I want our son exposed to this influence so long as I am not present to monitor and curtail it.*

My mouth fell open. Fortunately I did not drop Alcimus onto the floor. I mouthed the words, *I had no idea!*

Tiberius quickly erased and shut the tablet, for Phoebe arrived to announce—as I had anticipated—the group had agreed unanimously to the proffered dispensations. Tiberius dispatched her with orders to deliver his personal thanks to the assenters.

I am going to tell Androcles and Ajax their particular prowess at arms makes them more valuable to me as personal bodyguards than as defenders of this household, he wrote on the tablet after Phoebe left. *Once we have settled in Italy I shall address their sexuality, should doing so even become necessary.* He rubbed the tablet clean once more, kissed my forehead, and departed.

Phoebe returned, took Alcimus from me, and announced my bath was drawn. Lying in the warm water, I pondered the revelation Tiberius had delivered to me. Androcles was hardly a young man—certainly older than Tiberius and closer in age to Nicanor than to Ajax. His practices at arms, with Arbindus and the praetorians and Ajax, evinced formidable skill with weapons. But to be sure: although he had never given me offense, when around me Androcles had always exhibited a reserved and retiring demeanor, which I had attributed to shyness. That my womanhood impelled this discomfiture had never occurred to me.

Ajax was all the more surprising. Never showing the slightest malaise in my presence, he was not only readily conversant but unhesitant to touch me appropriately—as when gripping my hand to prevent me from stumbling. Although trained primarily as a house steward and particularly adept at carpentry, Ajax was no sluggard at arms—hence Tiberius' willingness to utilize him as a guard. The state of quiet euphoria, in which Ajax and Androcles usually returned from their jaunts to Ialyssos, I had assumed was the outcome of visits to taverns and brothels rather than time passed alone with one another. Now I understood why Nicanor often regarded Ajax with a painful reflectiveness that had always puzzled me, and why Androcles had never drawn close to Menon despite their common Cappadocian heritage.

Nicanor and Menon readily concluded an eminently satisfactory arrangement with the farm workers, not only for protection of the estate following the dispersion of the praetorians, but for the physical maintenance of the promontory buildings as well. Between the six families there were twenty-three able-bodied men and boys. All were well equal to fending off marauders with swords and spears, hammers and awls, plowshares and scythes, hoes and rakes, even rocks if necessary. Each month a different group of four would serve as sentries and reside in the guesthouse. By day one member of the company would remain behind, providing maintenance on the buildings and any other assistance the new tenant's household might require. The other three would go about their regular duties in the fields and orchards or in their compound, remaining all the while on special alert for and poised to respond to suspicious occurrences.

When Nicanor offered to remunerate each man an aureus at the end of his designated month—the equivalent of a legionary's pay—the farmhands made a counterproposal. Already at my insistence they were setting aside and accounting for excess harvest revenues. The prospect of having to maintain a second fund was confronting them with a formidable intellectual challenge. Was the Widow Galatea conceivably able to let them keep a portion of the harvest surpluses for themselves without compromising her tax obligation? In return they would gladly provide, without remuneration, not only guardian and maintenance service but any foodstuffs and staples the promontory household should require. The alleged widow was most certainly amenable to this, the arrangement she had originally proposed for the farmhands. The proposition resolved the present quandary of how the household was going to obtain, down the future, the commodities it had been receiving from military rations. I told Nicanor to delay delivering my answer for a week, to convince the farm workers he had to await my response from Alexandria.

Answers to Tiberius' letters began to arrive. Livia reported her publicists were accomplishing their endeavors, and all Rome was abuzz with anticipation of Tiberius' return. Drusus was eagerly awaiting his father's arrival. In continued demonstration of their support for Tiberius, Marinus and Longus were already preparing to return to Italy. Atticus would do so as well—to the immense delight of his wife—but not until after their younger daughter's nuptials had been celebrated in September.

The wife of the captain of the Phoenix wrote his schedule was solidly booked for the next year. Although she was certain her husband would willingly cancel any reservation to accommodate Tiberius, she could not yet confirm this because the captain was presently at sea. Tiberius promptly dictated a response for the messenger waiting on the veranda. The captain should keep his present commitments and not accommodate Tiberius at the expense of somebody else; Tiberius would find an alternative means of transport. "Not only is displacing another unfair," he murmured while we watched from the library as Ajax helped the messenger onto Asellus. "Imagine the innuendo a preempted client might spread."

Tiberius was understandably reluctant to reserve passage in his own name on an unfamiliar ship. He required assurance the captain and crew could be relied upon not to spread gossip or—far worse—assassinate him to satisfy lingering hostility or simply a yen for notoriety. On the Phoenix he had utilized two menservants and four bodyguards. For the presently impending voyage so far he had selected only one valet and two guards. I suggested we have the Widow Galatea book a charter and disguise Tiberius—who still sported his lengthy hair and philosopher's beard—as a member of her household. We could send Nestor to Ialyssos for this purpose. Since he seldom ventured there, he would not be readily recognized as a servant to Tiberius. As another possibility, we might solicit one of our friends to act as agent to the Widow Galatea of Alexandria at the harbor in Rhodes. Tiberius felt the only alternative was for him to ask his mother to send a ship with additional guards. But since he was returning to Rome in private life, he preferred to make his own arrangements if possible.

We were discussing these choices in our bedchamber on the Ides of June, *[6/13]* when Phoebe announced the praetorians had sent word Longus was waiting at the promontory's base. After Tiberius departed to meet his guest I lay back on our bed, gazing at the lovers' vignettes on the wall and wondering whether Longus had come to inquire about the disposition of my art collection. Alcimus was lying on his back in his crib, holding one foot and babbling. Phoebe came again, now with Miranda at her side, to check the condition of the baby's swaddling: "Wet, wet, wet!" she pronounced it. In response to her smiles and clucks and tickles, Alcimus kicked and squeaked and giggled. Miranda looked on, smiling in silence. Picking up and shaking a little earthenware rattle, she elicited yet more giggles. Better indeed, I reflected, to leave Alcimus behind, under the care of servants who loved him and the tutelage of Thrasyllus' family, than subject him to an unnatural life of hiding and deception.

Suddenly a wave of sharp alarm passed through my consciousness like a dark and ominous storm cloud. Despite Tiberius' reassurances and promises, would we ever see Alcimus again? Must he remain forever Thrasyllus' ward, happy with and loved by his foster family but unable to discover his true parentage? Would opportunities for being reunited with and identifying ourselves to him keep eluding Tiberius and me? With a sigh I gazed once more at the vignettes, reaffirmed my acceptance of Underlying Good, and was endeavoring to mollify my misgivings with emotional detachment when Alcmene arrived. Master wished me to attend him and his guest in the library, she said.

"My dear, dear Galatea!" Longus bellowed as he took my right hand in both of his. "Nearly a year has passed since our last encounter. You look ever so well—have gained a little weight, I notice!"

"It is wonderful to see you again, Senator," I murmured demurely as I curtsied with lowered eyes. Although annoyed by his tactless comment, I was grateful he did not surmise my new heaviness was the consequence of pregnancy.

"Sit, sit, sit!" Longus motioned to a vacant chair. "First off, I have more royalties to hand you." He thrust a large purse into my hands. "Two hundred twenty aurei, a stunning take."

Flabbergasted, I stared fixated at the bag without opening it.

"Now I have a proposition you simply must not refuse!"

The swaggering confidence in Longus' tone broke my trance. "And what is that, Senator?" I answered archly, unsure whether I should be frightened or elated.

"Nero informs me he has been unsuccessful at procuring transportation to Italy. Well, I shall be returning thither myself upon my own ship. She is a small swift freighter my agents use for the transport of art stock—including yours. I hereby invite Nero and you to accompany me to Italy aboard her as my guests. You need not concern yourselves any further about bodyguards, or how you will manage to screen a strange crew and keep them from spreading gossip. I vouch for the integrity and discretion of my own men. Our little ship can comfortably accommodate as many as eight passengers. That leaves precisely enough room for the pair of you, the four servants you wish to take, myself and my valet. I shall arrange separate quarters for the two of you, should that be your wish." Tiberius rolled his eyes at this last comment. Longus continued determinedly, "There is a condition, however. You, my Galatea, must surrender to me your entire art collection. Leaving it here on this isolated pinnacle will surely be an insufferable waste."

He had come about the collection indeed. Furthermore, he had raised an important consideration. Hardly could he refresh his stock of copies with new originals if I left them all behind. Under no circumstances, however, was I about to forfeit everything. "Senator, a goodly number of my paintings are highly personal in nature. They are not intended for the eyes of anyone apart from my most intimate of associates." I had no intention of yielding Longus particularly meaningful favorites like my original rendering of the Guardian Trees. Moreover I could hardly surrender the lovers' vignettes hanging in Tiberius' bedchamber, nor the portraits of him and of our child and of the heliotrope plant with his epigram, all of which adorned my own quarters. For certain I could never reveal my representation of Tiberius nude. This I kept sequestered from the servants in a linen satchel, stuffed just inside its mouth with cockleburs, and tied with the special cryptic knot I had devised years ago to frustrate my brother's efforts to rifle through my belongings.

"I understand," Longus acceded. "Let me rephrase my offer. You retain your strictly private articles, but yield everything else to me. Why not let your new environs serve as inspiration for new representations? An artist as prolific as you should be able to create an entirely new collection in hardly any time. You will continue to reside with Nero, I presume."

"Indeed I shall remain a member of his household," I returned reticently, having anticipated this question and carefully prepared its response. Now I resumed my challenge. "Senator, I doubt whether I can be as speedily prolific as you anticipate. Remember please, the present collection was many years in the making. Furthermore, I am pursuing a new medium—the art of painting on textiles—to which I hope to devote considerable endeavor. That will leave me less time, less energy, and less inclination for the painting of tableaux." Following Tiberius' wont I left my chair, to stand staring out the window in silence while I thought the matter through. Longus had raised another salient point. Owing to the limited number of models the farm had to offer, the collection was starting to become redundant. Thinning out duplications and replacing them with renderings inspired by my new locale would provide well needed enrichment.

"Senator, I shall set aside the strictly private tableaux," I continued at length. Longus had begun to squirm with impatience. "Of the remainder you may have half, which I shall choose for you. You will of course create and disseminate copies, and only sell originals with my permission."

"Two thirds."

"Half. Remember, I have already ceded you twenty-four."

Now Longus fell into a deliberative silence. "Very well: half," he finally grumbled, "but I select which articles I take. By experience I am a better judge of their marketability than you." Yet another point well made.

"Then for every piece of a particular genre you remove, Senator, you leave an equivalent behind. For every still life you leave a still life; for every landscape you leave a landscape. The same for legendary scenes, moths—any theme."

"Suppose I want something for which there is no duplicate?"

"I reserve the right to decide whether or not to surrender it. And one final condition: I reserve ownership of all originals."

I returned to my chair. Longus was stroking his chin and frowning, Tiberius struggling to suppress a smirk.

"If I refuse your terms?" Longus baited me.

"The entire collection remains here, and we wait until Tiberius' mother sends a ship."

"And everyone will say Mommy had to rescue him."

"Everyone is going to be saying that anyway."

After another silence Longus finally said wearily, "Mistress Galatea, you drive a harder bargain than many men with whom I do business. Still, I cannot fathom why you insist upon leaving half of your collection behind—more than half, taking into account your private pieces. Why not let me transport everything to Italy, and make our division after we arrive there? If you decide you want to display a particular piece in your new home, you will have it right on hand. You would not have to send Rhodes for it."

"I wish to leave behind an abundant selection, for our new tenant and the servants who remain here to enjoy." Hardly could I tell Longus I wanted the son I had borne Tiberius to grow up surrounded by my art. This was the primary, but not the only reason I did not want to transport the entire collection to Rome. For certain once it arrived, Longus would pressure me unceasingly to relinquish it.

"They are only tenant and servants." Longus' retort had a nuance of testiness.

"Tenant or servile status does not automatically deprive one of sensitivity to and appreciation for art," I returned in a similar tenor. Now Tiberius shot me a warning glance: Longus may withdraw his offer if I continued to impugn his condescension. Softening my tone I continued, "Senator, owing to our need for heightened security, a goodly portion of the collection is distributed throughout an area the servants are presently occupying and utilizing for household operations. Please grant me a week to have everything brought into the foyer and reception rooms. There you can view and make your choices in optimal light and without distraction. Yes, Alcmene?" Although with my words I led Longus to believe this strategy was to accommodate him, its primary purpose was to deter him from invading our private quarters and discovering Alcimus. I had noted Alcmene standing in the doorway, trying to catch my attention with her usual nervous mannerisms.

"Forgive my intrusion, Lady, but your presence is required in your chambers." Her unspoken meaning: it was time to nurse Alcimus. I departed with relief. After I had finished suckling the babe, and Alcmene changed his swaddling and settled him down for his afternoon nap, she asked me whether I would like some of the luncheon Phoebe had prepared for Master and his guest. They were dining on a pheasant Nicanor had managed to trap within sight of the house. Unable to resist this reprieve from eggs and cured meats, I asked her to bring me a generous portion—despite the new concern about my weight with which Longus' comment had afflicted me.

A subsequent visit to the latrine revealed I was bleeding vaginally. Panic-stricken I called out, "Rhathines to the master bedchamber!" as I hastened there myself. The physician turned out to be quite pleased with my discovery. For the first menses after childbirth to occur at the beginning of the fifth month since the birth—as it just had for me—is a standard of normality in feminine health. There had been no ominous warning signs—no swelling, aching, lethargy, nausea. Rhathines was confident my present condition indicated my expulsion of the uterine growth and subsequent pregnancy had adjusted my female cycle, and I should enjoy regular and unremarkable menses from now on. Of course only the passage of time could confirm this assessment.

So long as he had my attention, Rhathines explained the procedure for the transfer of Alcimus to Briseis' breast. I must begin, gradually but steadily, to decrease the amount of milk I offered the babe at each feeding, handing him off to Briseis to insure he received sufficient nourishment. When less milk is demanded of a breast, it is replenished with equally less. Once Alcimus was down to taking only a few sips from me, I should similarly decrease the daily number of these truncated sucklings. When I reached the point at which I was giving him a single sip per day, I could cease nursing altogether and have my women tie back my breasts, as Phoebe had immediately following Alcimus' birth. The entire process would probably take about two weeks. When I asked whether Briseis could produce sufficient milk to satisfy both Phoenix and Alcimus as they grew, Rhathines burst out laughing and then apologized. Although his outburst implied no disrespect, he could not suppress it because the answer was so obvious: how would Briseis manage had she borne twins? For certain he and Briseis would monitor and maintain her health and strength, to ensure she was able to supply both boys adequately. When absolutely necessary, a feeding of goat's milk could be substituted.

His conversation prompted me to pose the other question I had been ruing. Once the transfer of Alcimus to Briseis was complete, how must I go about implementing the contraceptive measures he had recommended for me? To my surprise the regimen proved simple and promised pleasure as well. The most effective contraceptive, Rhathines said, is laser, which I identified at once as a relatively rare and costly food seasoning my family had always eschewed. Correct, the physician averred: gastronomically it is used in far smaller quantities than when employed as a contraceptive. Cyrenican is the preferred variety, but is becoming increasingly difficult to obtain. If Cyrenican is unavailable the Syrian type can be substituted, but the dosages must be doubled. A victoriatus of crushed Cyrenican laser—or a denarius of Syrian— stirred into three cyanthi of wine and swallowed weekly, has proven a successful contraceptive for many women. As an extra precaution, I should insert a wad of lamb's wool saturated with laser seed oil into my vagina immediately before intercourse. Moreover my partner, anointing his penis with the oil prior to penetration, could further the contraceptive effect while increasing our mutual pleasure. At Rhathines' suggestion we repaired to the kitchen to canvass Phoebe's collection of seasonings. We duly found a tiny jar of dried, ground laser. It was pale brownish-green in color. The bit Rhathines placed on my tongue tasted rather like marjoram only much stronger.

In anticipation of Longus' return I set Ajax to work, transferring to the parlors and the entryway lying between them every painting with which I was willing to part. Longus duly arrived on the final day of June to wreak his attrition upon the collection. He marked his selections by draping a strip of red cloth over the top of each. Only now did I realize how prolific an artist I had been. Excluding the six lovers vignettes and the seven pieces I chose to retain for myself, fifty-one were left for Longus to select from. Not only did he hold to his agreement to take half. Since the total could not be evenly divided, he insisted upon twenty-five for himself and allowed me to keep twenty-six. He also insisted I increase the value of each piece in his consignment by signing it— as Eutychus Rhodou, of course. We quarreled about two—Zeus descending to ravish Danae (that shaft of October sunlight), and Heracles wrestling the Lion of Nemea (a praetorian playing with Imperator). I did not want to relinquish these because they had no duplicates, and because their execution had been arduous—to represent in the Nemea the tense musculature of the struggling man and beast, and in the Danae an anthropomorphic specter of Zeus within the shower of gold. I had labored long and hard at creating these, and regarded them as two of my best works. Reproducing them with an equivalent level of expertise portended to be especially difficult.

Longus, concurring about the quality of those pieces, considered them the most potentially marketable of the entire collection. For this very reason I did not want them copied and sold in abundance: doing so would belie their value, and render them commonplace and cheap. We reached a compromise. Longus would transport the originals to Italy and have his best copyist render three reproductions of each for his Roman gallery and his other outlets, all to be numbered and affixed with a facsimile of Eutychus Rhodou's signature. The copies would be marketed as unique collectibles, to the most discerning of connoisseurs who were willing to pay a higher price for artwork fine and singular. The originals would be returned to me.

Longus recommended lading in Rhodes, because a shipment of art was unlikely to draw notice in her busy commercial harbor; whereas it might in a less active, less cosmopolitan port like Ialyssos. Contrariwise, Longus felt Tiberius would not be as readily identified in Ialyssos as in Rhodes. For this reason he suggested once the ship was laden, he move her to Ialyssos so we may board her there. Had Tiberius selected a departure date? The Nones of August, Tiberius replied, so long as Longus had no objection: this date would leave us slightly over a month in which to finalize our preparations. Sailing from Ialyssos, however, did not strike Tiberius as a sound idea. A strange ship and the passengers boarding her were more likely to draw notice in a smaller, slower port than in a more bustling one, where everyone was too preoccupied with his own tasks to pay attention to surrounding activities. Departing the farm in late afternoon would enable us to reach the port of Rhodes and board the ship under cover of darkness. We could set sail that same night or at dawn the next morning, whichever Longus' captain preferred.

After some lengthy and irrelevant digressions, Longus finally agreed to Tiberius' requested arrangements and took his leave. Thereafter Tiberius had me transcribe two letters: the one to his stepfather, tendering his resignation as imperial legate to Rhodes effective the Calends of August; the other to his mother, announcing this date for his impending departure and asking her to make sure his house staff was prepared to receive him. He also gave Livia the name of the ship—the Murex—and requested she make sure his steward prearranged transportation for us from Ostia to Rome.

The month of July passed in a flurry of selecting and packing articles for our journey. Deciding what to leave behind proved more arduous than choosing what to take along. Tiberius admonished me to select only enough clothing for the sea voyage and a few days following our arrival. The same for painting and sewing supplies, toiletries, medicines, even the contraceptives to which I must become acclimated. After all we were traveling to Rome, where everything one could possibly need or desire was available. Of course I should take my harp. No pictures of Alcimus, however, lest these arouse troublesome speculations and questions. Anything else—textiles from my collection, additional paintings, other reminiscences, jewelry except for my ring—we could always have the servants who remained behind send to us. Although I verbalized nothing, I mentally reminded myself to include Tiberius' nude in its satchel, lest one of those remaining servants come across it and manage to elude its knot.

As he watched me rummage through my wardrobe, trying to decide what I should or should not take with me, Tiberius advised me to choose garments flattering to my appearance yet demure and unadorned. He added I ought to start wearing makeup again—a practice I had abandoned while living in isolation on the farm—but sparingly: only enough to enhance my natural features. The finishing Timoxena had imparted me I should recall and practice, that I may convey an impression of elegant poise and serenity. Once in Rome, I should have the ornatrix of his household trim and style my hair in accord with current fashion there. I assured him I was already hard at work modulating my voice and motions, and trying to lose some of the weight Longus had imputed to me.

On the Ides of July *[7/15]*, Briseis approached me and announced it was time to initiate the transfer of Alcimus to her breast. We should begin the process in three days. This interim was essential, Briseis explained, to let her adjust the times at which she nursed Phoenix so they did not coincide with those when Alcimus suckled. Feeding the two babes simultaneously might deplete her milk before both were adequately supplied; staggering the feedings would forestall this problem.

Later that same day I suddenly realized I had not menstruated in more than a month, and in a panic sought out Rhathines in his workroom. Was the growth in my womb reemerging? The physician took my hands in his and smiled with a comforting confidence. Although my concern was legitimate, my fear was not. When he had sliced my belly open to remove the baby, he had sought and not seen any evidence a new growth was developing. To be sure, menstrual regularity is the benchmark of gynecologic health. Given my history, however, my menses may never be regular; or they may assume an unconventional regularity—bi- or trimonthly, for example. Nothing but the passage of time can reveal whether a pattern has been established. Over this I must steel myself not to fret. Many years—yea, decades—had elapsed before the condition of the original growth became critical. There would be ample time to intervene and arrest a recurrence, should the symptoms of a growth begin to recur.

My intrusion could not have had better timing, he continued, for he had something to show me. From a shelf he took a linen satchel and laid it on the table. The sack held a large, dried stalk—ribbed, brownish-green, with a batch feathery leaves much like those of parsley—the laser. Rhathines pulverized a section with a pestle, then scraped up the powder with the knife and heaped it onto one platform of a small scale. On the other platform lay a victoriatus weight. Rhathines continued this procedure until the scale balanced; then he scraped the powder into a flask. From a jug he poured wine into the flask, carefully noting the amount, and then stirred the concoction with a spoon. Handing me the flask he said, enthusiastically, "Drink!" I took a sip and gagged. The mixture of laser with wine was not offensive, only far more pungent than I had anticipated. Rhathines chuckled. "You will become accustomed to it. For now, sip slowly." Once I had drained the flask, I found the contraceptive had left a pleasantly cleansing aftertaste.

After crushing the remainder of the laser stalk, he gathered the powder into a jar to which he affixed a lid. The amount was sufficient to last me several months. I need not worry about weighing the laser: the spoon he had just employed for mixing the solution held exactly a victoriatus. He wiped this instrument with a cloth and laid it beside the sealed jar. Next he showed me a bottle of laser seed oil and a bag of clean carded lamb's wool. From the wool mass he pulled a ball about the size of an unshelled walnut, and moistened it with the oil until it was saturated but not dripping. This was the pessary he had recommended. Immediately after intercourse I should sit or stand upright and remove the wad; these motions would further reduce the possibility of conception by promptly evacuating semen from my body. Rhathines cautioned me against consuming preparations of wild carrot or pennyroyal following sex—contraceptive methods which I may hear recommended. Both are powerful abortifacients and can induce excessive bleeding. Having already suffered severely from this condition on two occasions, I must scrupulously avoid substances that could reinduce it. If my forthcoming menses do prove irregular, I should consult a physician or pharmakeutria about initiating monthly consumption of angelica infusion or another substance to promote regularity.

On the morning of the final day of that month, I administered to Alcimus the final sip of milk from each of my breasts. Afterward Phoebe bound me with the winding sheet, chiding me in her inimitable way: "First you object to this thing, now you want it." That same afternoon, Longus arrived with four men and as many donkeys. The beasts were laden with bolts of sailcloth, slats of wood, and an assortment of tools. Under Longus' loquacious direction his crew set right to work, packing his selection of paintings into the materials they had brought and transporting them on the donkeys to a wagon waiting at the base of the promontory. Tiberius admonished me not to interfere. Longus' people, skilled at what they were doing, could be trusted not to injure my artworks; Longus was supervising them; they might spread gossip about the woman who intruded upon their efforts. The men proceeded meticulously yet speedily, stopping only for about half an hour to consume the provisions they had brought along. Within three hours they were finished. Longus declined our invitation to join us for our supper and allow us to feed his men theirs: he wanted to reach his warehouse in Rhodes while it was yet light. Although daylight was prolonged owing to the time of year, they must proceed slowly to minimize the wagon's jostling of their precious cargo.

Four days before our departure, Thrasyllus arrived with four of his six servants. Their wagon was filled with household and wardrobe items, but mostly books and writing materials and instruments for measuring celestial movements. The two remaining servants—an espoused couple—had accompanied Aka to Commagene. She and her entourage were on their way home. After she had read aloud her husband's letter, in which he announced the family's impending move to the farm, Thrasylla became so excited about the transfer and so obstreperous about being in Commagene, Aka had no choice but to cut their visit short.

After greeting Thrasyllus' four attendants, Menon sent Ajax and Arbindus with Asellus and Sinapeus to help them deliver the contents of their wagon to the house. During this operation Thrasyllus sat with Tiberius and me on the veranda, that he might be nearby to answer questions about the disposition of his belongings. From his numerological table he had deduced our voyage to Italy would be harmonious and uneventful. The astrological prognostications, however, remained vague. The most Thrasyllus could determine from them was what we already knew: a myriad of changes, significant for Alcimus and me, monumental for Tiberius, and all with long mitigation to follow.

Meanwhile, Nicanor came trudging nonchalantly around one corner. Since the risk of attack had diminished, Tiberius decided it was safe for Nicanor to hunt and trap on the promontory beyond sight of the house. In one hand he held the pole affixed with net and hook, which he used for catching turtles at the pond. With his other hand he gripped a sack, inside which several of these creatures were crawling over one another. He halted abruptly and stood motionless, looking upward at the roof of the house. Turning his eyes to us he put the forefinger of his hand with the pole to his lips, then beckoned to us and pointed upward. Creeping cautiously down the steps we joined him and turned to view the roof.

"An eagle!" Tiberius whispered excitedly. "By all the gods! This is the first time I have ever beheld one on Rhodes."

"They are not endemic to our island, Master," Nicanor whispered in return. "I was unsure what it was until you identified it."

A breeze ruffled the eagle's feathers, disclosing an array of brown hues from near black to burnished gold to pale yellow. There were also reds, tans, and grays. The fish writhing in its talons evinced it had visited one of our ponds. The bird sat for some time glancing about, with a contented demeanor as though approving the surroundings. It extended its long broad wings and held them vertically above its body for a time. Finally it extended them horizontally, and with its quarry glided off the roof, down the promontory and across fields below, then westward in the direction of the sea. Needless to say, I hastened into the house after pencil and palette that had not been packed. As I was returning to the veranda, while yet in the foyer of the house, I overheard Thrasyllus say, "I cannot be certain, Tiberius, with the stars at this moment being cryptic and evasive. What seems amply clear is that after you have returned to Italy, the authority of Rome will in some fashion come to rest upon your house."

Before retiring on the night preceding our departure I stood watching Alcimus sleep in his crib, which had been moved into the nursery so he was accessible to Briseis. Despair suddenly overwhelmed me. Pummeled I felt, as though rocks had rained down upon me. Clenching my teeth and fists I ran into the master bedchamber and threw myself prone on the bed, burying my face in the pillows. I was shaking uncontrollably and sobbing silently and convulsively, as I had beneath the pear tree after my fracas with Timoleon. Eventually I became aware Tiberius was sitting beside me and stroking my hair. "He will be safe and well," he said with great tenderness.

"Why cannot we just remain here, with our child and the servants we trust?" I shouted angrily into the pillow. After a moment I raised my head and breathed deeply to regain my composure. "With utmost sincerity I beg your forgiveness for that outburst, my love." This I said while struggling to maintain a calm tone. "Hopefully, the servants did not overhear. You have made amply clear to me not only the reasons you must return to Rome, but those for which we cannot bring Alcimus with us. The decision to leave him behind could not have been easy for you."

He continued to stroke my hair. "What genuine, truly selfless mother, would not feel devastated upon being forced to relinquish her babe?" His voice was choked, hoarse with emotion.

Rolling onto my back, I took his outstretched hand in mine and kissed it. Looking up at his face, I discovered him weeping. Abruptly I sat up beside him, threw my arms about him, and pressed my forehead against the front of his shoulder. He resumed stroking my hair.

"Ah, my Clytia! For a second time I am abandoning my child, and persuading myself that my doing so is in his best interests!"

"You did not abandon Drusus!" I exclaimed into his chest. Then I raised my head and spoke softly. "The man who abandoned him was the lackey, who allowed his stepfather to tear Drusus from his mother and place him in a home where he was belittled and disdained. For the first time in his life, Drusus is going to meet his real father: the man who repudiated authority, power, prerogative, and prestige, to reveal the intellectual, the aesthetic, the contemplative, the philanthropist. And by your example you have taught Drusus a lesson most crucial. Should he choose to rebel against your stepfather's intentions for him, the consequences could be devastating. As for Alcimus: you are merely entrusting him to Thrasyllus' protection temporarily while you ascertain the way before you—reconnoitering to determine whether you can safely sally forth with him and me into the acceptance and approval of your family and Roman society; or whether retreat and pursuit of a different strategy is the wiser course. When making decisions for Drusus you have always carefully chosen the best course of action under the given circumstances. Now you are doing the same for Alcimus."

He took several deep breaths, kissed my forehead, and then raised his head, continuing to hold me against him. Finally he said, "Your pseudonym fits you well, Galatea."

"What do you mean?"

"Acis and Galatea. What happened to him after he rescued her from the monster Polyphemus?"

Now realizing he had been gazing at the lovers' vignettes on the wall, I turned to face them myself. "Polyphemus pursued Acis and crushed him with a boulder. To save him from death and make him immortal, Galatea transformed him into the Sicilian river which bears his name. What has that to do with me?"

"A river is phenomenally resilient and irresistible. Droughts dry it up; but sooner or later rains restore it. Ice in winter staunches its flow; but the warmth of spring reawakens it. Obstructed by a dam whether natural or man-made, the river diverts its course, overflows the blockade, or with patient persistence wears the impediment away. A river can be placid and benign, or unrelentingly destructive when a rushing torrent. Treat it with respect for its power, cooperate with it, understand and honor its boundaries, and it will irrigate your fields with its floodwaters, slake your thirst, provide you with excellent foods, cool and cleanse your body at the end of a hot day, permit you the pleasures of swimming, angling, or boating. But oppose a river, strike out against its currents or attempt to curtail or suppress its flow, and it will resist your efforts unrelentingly with destructive force—not consciously let alone premeditatively, but merely from being what it is by nature.

"You, Clytia, have made me realize I am a river. No one—not even my stepfather with all his authority—can change or channel me into what I am not. Behold the self-determination, for which I came to Rhodes in the hopes of finding! You, Clytia, have uncovered and revealed it to me through your forbearance, your courage, your patience with my moods, your emotional fortitude upon which I lean in times of self-doubt, your weaknesses which awaken compassion and forgiveness in me. You have made me feel regenerated, reborn!"

"You have simply come to recognize and respect what you have always been, my love."

"As have you, my Lioness, as have you."

He lowered me back onto the bed, lay down beside me, put out the lamp and took my hand. "Remember, Alcimus will only be out of our sight, not out of our lives."

I expected to lie awake, pondering the conversation that had just transpired. Instead I started to doze straightaway, with that sense of joyous relief and accomplishment one savors when a goal has been attained. I assume Tiberius felt similarly, since I heard him begin to snore as I was drifting off.

The Nones of August *[8/5]* fell on Sunday that year. One of the reasons Tiberius had selected this date for our departure, was so Alcmene and Nestor would not be forced to travel on their Sabbath. We would leave an hour or so before sunset. This would allow us to descend the promontory and mountain roads while it was yet light, but reach the port of Rhodes under cover of darkness.

In early afternoon the praetorians departed, except for the four who in plainclothes were going to escort us to the wharf. They streamed down the promontory, their horses laden with gear and their dogs trotting obediently alongside them. Imperator watched puzzled from the safety of his favorite branch; but to the relief of all he made no effort to follow. Aelius and Tiberius inspected the guesthouse to ensure the guards left it clean and in order, which they had. When the shadows began to lengthen and the sky turn golden, Tiberius declared our time was at hand. Thrasyllus and the servants assembled on the veranda to bid us farewell; Rhathines held Alcimus, and Briseis Phoenix. After Alcmene and I were mounted upon Asellus, Phoebe rushed forward and tearfully hugged and kissed each of us including Tiberius. Nicanor led the donkey down the promontory. Tiberius, Nestor, Ajax, and Androcles followed on foot. At the promontory's base Arbindus was waiting with the carriage and the four undercover praetorians, one of whom was Aelius.

Once those of us headed for Rome were sequestered in the carriage, Tiberius reminded everyone not to disclose my real name—not to Longus, to the crew of his ship, to the staff of Tiberius' Roman household, to members of his family nor to anyone else. Tiberius himself would henceforth address me as Galatea in the presence of others. Settling into a new life in Italy portended to be challenging enough without having to explain my pseudonym.

We duly managed to reach Longus' little ship without detection. Tiberius' assessment had been correct: the wharf at Rhodes was so busy even after nightfall, that no one expended time or interest in scrutinizing us. The captain set sail as soon as we were aboard. The Murex was a far fleeter version of the grain freighter upon which I had sailed from Alexandria. A superstructure devoted to passengers included an opulently appointed dayroom, a galley, a water closet with privy, and four small but comfortable bedchambers. Crew quarters and cargo holds lay below. Tiberius and Nestor lodged together, I with Alcmene, Ajax with Androcles, and Longus with his manservant. These arrangements, together with Tiberius' decision to retain his beard and Greek dress until after our arrival in Rome, worked well to obfuscate his identity from the crew. Longus had told them Tiberius and I were brother and sister, Greek business clients of his traveling with their servants.

The weather was hot and hazy but fair, the winds mild yet favorable. Every day, dolphins escorted the Murex as they had the Phoenix. Whereas the Sirocco had driven great dancing and foaming billows, suggestive of a weaver's shuttle active upon a loom, the present Zephyrs evoked a great expanse of glistering blue-gray fabric, disclosing hidden yellows and greens and even tans and reds as it undulated in the breeze. On days when the haze cleared, leaving the sky pristine blue, the sea duly appeared wine-dark as Homer describes it. Looking directly down through the clear waters, one could see fish and rays and eels swimming, shellfish and bizarre plants strewn across the bottom sand—all with colors rendered mute and subtle by the deep.

Longus spent most of each day with Tiberius, talking about virtually every subject under the sun. Fortunately I managed to excuse myself on the pretext their discussions covered political matters I could not comprehend, and passed the hours by myself outside on the deck. Sitting beneath the ship's two sails, upon a chest in which spare rigging was stored, I recorded on the palettes I had brought the surrounding shades and hues and sketched the sea life I observed. At Tiberius' request and Longus' orders the sailors improvised an awning from unused sail fabric, to keep the sun and its fierce reflections off the water from darkening my complexion. My endeavors puzzled some of the crewmembers and intrigued others. A pair of them—nervously conscientious about the impropriety of accosting a female passenger—mustered the courage to ask me about my efforts. When in need of a reprieve from painting, I perused the Syrian medicinal Gaius had given Tiberius, wrote in my journal, or just sat observing the sea.

On our fourth day at sea I began to menstruate, and became almost euphoric with relief and hope. The present onset of this condition precisely two months after the preceding seemed to hold the promise of improved gynecological health. It also confirmed the contraceptives, which Tiberius and I had implemented in the few days preceding our departure, apparently were having their desired regulatory effect.

That same day Tiberius disclosed our marriage to the four servants who accompanied us, and explained why we had kept it from them until now. He demanded they maintain its secrecy even from members of his family, and certainly from the servants of his Roman household. Ostensibly I was still Tiberius' ward whom he was sheltering from a reprobate husband, until such time Tiberius saw fit to reveal the truth. All reassured us of their compliance, Alcmene adding she rejoiced we had taken this step toward morality and legitimacy for our son. When Tiberius returned we had been married going on three years, and Alcimus had been conceived as well as born in wedlock, she rushed across the room and threw her arms about him.

We might have reached our destination on our seventh day of travel, had not Longus insisted upon stopping along the way—at Crete, Cephalonia, Messina (where Aetna stood dormant), and finally Naples—to take on fresh foodstuffs and allow excursions ashore to public baths. Our host was determined to avoid sea rations and vat bathing as much as possible. Tiberius and I remained aboard during these lacunae—he to avoid being identified; I to be with him; because for several days I was menstruating; and because once we reached Italy, I wanted to avoid the possibility, however remote, that a member or acquaintance of my family might recognize me. The summer's heat, Tiberius' assurance of evading recognition, and my delight over my menses, rendered our restrictive cold baths tolerable and even refreshing.

Owing to Longus' dalliance, we reached Ostia in midmorning on the tenth day of our voyage—the nineteenth before the Calends of September [*August 14*]. Tiberius did not want to disembark until after dark. Fortuitously the Jewish Sabbath had passed. Had we arrived thereon, we would have had to find a pretext for leaving Nestor and Alcmene aboard or in some local lodgment the following evening. While Alcmene was packing up the sundries we had utilized during the voyage, I wrapped myself up in my North African shawl and went outside onto the deck. Although I had grown up in Italy, I had never seen Ostia. Like other seaports I had visited, the place fascinated me with its ever-changing array of faces and languages, of costumes and textiles, of wares being laded and unladed. Ostia was as bustling as Alexandria, as dirty as Naples, as cramped and crowded as Piraeus but lacking the rigid symmetry of that city. On the horizon beyond the shipyards, the public edifices and towering apartment buildings of Ostia loomed in a haphazard yet closely packed jumble.

After a delightful final luncheon aboard the Murex—of swordfish, bread rolls and fresh greens—a middle-aged man with thick black hair arrived to confer with Tiberius. An hour or so later the man departed, and returned shortly with two companions. Together this trio removed our travel trunks from the ship. When the sun was setting the man returned once again, whereupon Tiberius introduced us. "Lady Galatea, I present you my steward Demetrius." He and his confreres were clad in unembellished homespun tunics rather than the livery of Tiberius' household, certainly to keep their master from being recognized. After bowing to me, Demetrius turned to Tiberius and said, "Master, your carriage awaits." We gave our thanks and said our good-byes to Longus. By the time he ended his responses, night had fallen. To help prevent us from drawing notice as we transferred from the Murex to the carriage, Demetrius had had his driver bring the vehicle directly onto the wharf beside the ship.

To avoid being recognized as Tiberius' steward, Demetrius sat in the carriage with us. Once we were underway, Demetrius asserted Tiberius' requirements with regard to my identity had been carried out. Responding to my puzzled look, Tiberius explained he had written Demetrius from Rhodes, advising he was bringing with him to Rome a woman whom he would allege was his ward. Continuing his letter, Tiberius had ordered Demetrius to select, for our personal attendants in addition to Nestor and Alcmene, members of his household staff who could be fully trusted to keep secret the intimate character of our relationship—not only from outsiders but from members of Tiberius' family, and of course from fellow servants.

Shining through the haze, the nearly full moon cast a pallor which imbued the flat landscape of the Tiber river delta with the color of bone, and landmarks with shadows that rendered details indistinct. The roadside was lined with small structures: statues, inscriptions, altars, sacraria, herms marking gateways to farms and villas. From time to time we came upon a tomb, hulking mountainous amid the diminutive monuments. Presently a yellow glow appeared on the horizon before us, increasing steadily in size and intensity. Suddenly the city wall loomed before us, the roadside artifacts having obscured view of it from a distance. The carriage slowed precipitously as it approached and then passed through a great portal. "Draw shut the curtains!" Tiberius said urgently. At once I perceived the reason for his precaution. The carriage began to tip and sway as it crept through the sinuous city streets. Passersby could easily identify the passengers in any vehicle proceeding at this slow a pace. The curtains alternately glowed and darkened as we passed different sources of illumination without.

The carriage halted. Tiberius and Nestor exited first, and then helped Alcmene and me. We hurried up four stone steps and through a narrow vestibule into the atrium of the house. Here a host of servants was assembled. Several of the men were armed. Demetrius declared ebulliently in Latin, "We rejoice at your homecoming, Master; and to you we extend a most hearty welcome, Lady Galatea." The company broke into applause.

Although they had never laid eyes on me, the staff was eminently prepared to accommodate. After the applause subsided, four serving women approached. The eldest of them, who appeared to be about ten years my senior, curtsied and said in Greek, "Lady, I am called Alexandra. If you please, may we have the honor of escorting you to your chambers? Do you prefer we speak to you in Greek or in Latin?"

"You may address me in either language, Alexandra; however, Alcmene here only understands Greek."

Turning to Alcmene, Alexandra nodded and repeated the words, "If you please." With her companions following she led us down a lamplit corridor to a stairway, and thence to a sitting room on the second floor. Adjacent thereto was a bedchamber, and beyond it a dressing room and a servants' alcove. A night shift and dressing gown were already laid out on the bed, a pair of slippers on the floor. "Lady, your bath awaits," Alexandra said softly; and I nodded. Alexandra picked up the dressing gown and slippers and escorted me down the corridor to the bath, where a sunken tub lay filled with lukewarm water. Having just completed a sea voyage, I would like to have washed my hair; but knowing it would never dry at so late an hour, I settled for having it thoroughly brushed and then bound with a clean kerchief.

After robing me, Alexandra said, "The Master awaits you, Lady." She led me back down the corridor to the sitting room, halting before a closed door in the alternate side from my bedchamber. In the dark I found Master already snoring quite loudly. Deciding there was no point to joining him, I found my way back to my own bedroom. Here I informed Alcmene, who had remained as my night attendant, of the reason for my return. We shared a giggle.

As usual in the aftermath of a transition, I lay awake pondering the circumstances surrounding it. Fully had I expected to witness a meteor during our voyage, confirming our transfer to Italy and validating Thrasyllus' forecasts of significant change for Tiberius, Alcimus, and me. Our relocation did not fulfill those predictions: hence no meteor. A larger process of change was still unfolding, into which the portent of the eagle somehow fit. Speculation could accomplish nothing apart from heightening fear and agitation. Reaffirming the existence of Underlying Good, I became aware the misgivings I had been harboring about our future in Italy—that public disdain for Tiberius might persist, that I might prove a public embarrassment for him, that I might be rejected by his family or identified by mine—were yielding to an enticing sense of adventure. Then as I considered Alcimus was safely sequestered away from these uncertainties, a wave of comfort passed through mind and body alike and brought sleep immediately.

The next morning, I took considerable care with my toilette. Recalling Tiberius' instructions to dress with subdued elegance, I seized upon this opportunity to practice. After evaluating the clean garments in my trunk, I decided a chiton of pale gray linen might evoke a sense of coolness in the present heat of August. Thereafter I spent maybe a good quarter hour working at applying just the right amount of makeup, while a quietly exasperated Alcmene bound and rebound my hair until I considered it flattering but not provocative. Alexandra arrived with her fellow serving women: Gallina who seemed about my own age, Phaedra who was somewhat younger, and Nausicaa who was just emerging into womanhood. As I presented Alcmene to them, I thought I noted a flicker of concern in Alexandra's eyes. In a somewhat sulky manner she told me Master and breakfast were awaiting me in the dining room downstairs, to which I followed her.

On entering the dining room I stopped short. Tiberius was seated at the table, in the center of which lay a charger heaped with an assortment of biscuits and fruits. So accustomed I had become to seeing him in Greek costume, that beholding him in a Roman tunic with hair cropped and beard shaven momentarily startled me. With a twinge of sadness I noted the ravaged condition of his now bare cheeks. Considering the distress under which we had lived for the past month, I was surprised my own acne had not recurred.

"I almost didn't recognize you!" I said as I twirled about before him. "Like you, I have been busy with my couture. What do you think of it?"

"Most becoming. Living on that farm has not diminished your finishing. Be sure you continue to dress in like manner, as you cannot foresee whom you might encounter. Already I have set Alexandra to work enlarging your wardrobe. Have her style your hair, for she was Julia's ornatrix."

Suddenly his manner grew intense. After glancing about furtively to ensure no servants were present, he took my hand and gazed at me imploringly. "My dearest, I profoundly regret having to incarcerate you once again—consign you to hiding here in this house while the greatest city on the face of the earth beckons. Nevertheless I want you to remain out of the sight, not only of outsiders but of the members of my family too, until I have introduced you to them. Once they realize you are a woman of character, intellect, and refinement—not an empty-headed tart or vulgar tramp who must prove an embarrassment—I shall feel comfortable bringing you before the public. My kin will be undisturbed by the inevitable innuendo and ready to defend you against it. Hopefully your present confinement will be of short duration. In the meanwhile, please explore and acquaint yourself with this dwelling, miserable as it is; for after all you are now its lady. I am going to spend the morning with Demetrius, reviewing the financial records of my properties."

I returned to my chambers, where I wanted some adjustments implemented. The walls were not adorned with specific pictures but with featureless panels, separated by representations of architectural constructs like columns and plinths. The predominating colors were pale blues, grays and greens, punctuated by touches of lavender. Against this background a bedcover of bright, intense pink clashed raucously. When I ordered it replaced with a counterpane of more appropriate hue, Alexandra to my immense surprise protested. "But Lady, those colors make the room drab; the vibrant pink livens it." As Nausicaa left to seek a new coverlet, Alexandra gazed upon me with the air of condescending pity one might assume when listening to a person whose sanity might be questionable.

Next I ordered my bedroom furniture rearranged, so that when I lay abed the windows were on either side of me, rather than the one at my head and the other at my feet. Alexandra countered with another challenge. "But Lady, with things as they are you will see daylight upon first awakening. Move your bed, and you will awake gazing at a wall." I had found the early morning light shining directly into my eyes irritating, but the painted wall—drab as it was—hardly offensive. Another doleful look ensued, then a stall, and ultimately a markedly antagonistic glare after I exclaimed, "Well, see to it!" At Alexandra's nod Phaedra hastily departed, returning shortly with two menservants to address my requirement. While they were at work, Nausicaa arrived with a deep blue coverlet bordered with a crimson key. It was darker than what I had hoped for and its red somewhat out of place; but it was nevertheless more appropriate to the room's decor than the dazzling pink. "Well done!" I exclaimed. Nausicaa's visage beamed, while Alexandra's assumed the sulky pout my mother had always worn whenever circumstances beyond her control deterred her from imposing her will on me.

We repaired to the sitting room, where I started to unpack the trunk that held the painting and writing materials I had brought along: palettes and vials, my stylus, my journal of which I refused to leave any part behind on Rhodes, a blank writing tablet, and of course the scroll with Rhathines' prescription for my contraceptives. Handing this to Alexandra I said, "For immediate implementation." Now Alexandra looked at me with an expression of bewildered misgiving, as though I had handed her orders to poison somebody or instructions for reconstructing the Trojan Horse. She opened the scroll, perused its calligraphy, rerolled it and then—still bearing a perplexed mien—curtsied and departed without a word. Noticing Phaedra and Gallina smirking, trying to hide their reactions from Nausicaa, I caught their meaning at once. Beckoning to Alcmene I wrote on the tablet, *Alexandra was endeavoring to belie the fact she cannot read that document.*

As I began to explore the house, my spirits lifted and I stopped fretting over Alexandra. The dwelling was designed along the lines of typical Roman domestic architecture. Grouped about the atrium, with its perpluvium open to the sky above an impluvium inlaid with a mosaic of a hippocamp, were rooms used for the transaction of public business. Along one side lay an office and a reception room, on the opposite another reception room that opened onto a sizable formal dining room. These two rooms were deeper than those opposite, because the atrium did not lie precisely in the center of its wing but to one side.

At its far end, the atrium opened to the private living quarters. These were laid out much like the villa we had leased in the suburb of Rhodes, but on a larger scale. This rectangular wing, two stories in height, enclosed an uninteresting peristyle garden. Its primary features were a large and disheveled grayish shrub

I later learned was ligustrum, an equally unkempt rosebush, two overgrown beds of ivy, a small reflection pool now cracked and hence waterless, and a weathered statue of Pan. Why, I wondered, had the servants not maintained the peristyle's condition? Tiberius told me later that Julia—diametrically unlike her father—had little appreciation for gardens. She was content to let the peristyle deteriorate, and distracted the servants from its upkeep.

About the interior perimeter of the house there ran a colonnade with open archways on each floor facing the peristyle. As the doors and principal windows of the individual rooms opened only to the colonnade, it was their primary source of light. The only other illumination came from small, rectangular windows in the exterior wall just below the ceiling in each room—so designed to minimize the influx of noise and dust from the street. This architecture gave the house a dark and cavernous character.

Workrooms and dayrooms, which included a library, an office for private affairs, and the more casual dining room in which we had breakfasted, lay on the first floor. The kitchen was located at the farthest end along the short side of the rectangle. Here I nearly tripped, as a trio of cats darted directly across my pathway. "Ooh, Lady, do watch your step!" boomed a huge blackamoor cook as he seized my hand to keep me from falling. With satisfaction I noted the cats were fat and had sleek, glossy coats—quite obviously well treated.

There were two stairways, diagonally opposite one another across the rectangle. The second story held bedchambers and sitting rooms, a children's playroom, and a suite for guests. The short end of the rectangle above the kitchen held a privy and bath. One entire long side of the rectangle was devoted to servants' quarters. I had not realized Tiberius' domestic staff was so large, with so many attendants of every age. Their responsibilities were commensurate with their particular strengths and abilities. The elderly performed the less strenuous tasks like sewing. The heaviest work of course fell to those in the prime of life. Older children assisted the adults, learning and perfecting the skills they would eventually contribute to the operations of the household. There were nine younger children who scampered about the house naked. They were ever ready to approach with a smile and a bow, to inquire if anything was needed or amiss, or simply to offer an ebullient greeting and pleasant conversation. In addition to preparing them for their servile future—overcoming shyness and developing sensitivity to their masters' requirements—their function imbued the household with cheer and charm: hence their Latin designation of delicia.

The master suite, separated from my quarters by the common sitting room, lay across the short side of the rectangle that abutted the atrium wing. It included its own bath and latrine. It also opened upon the most delightful feature of the house. Above the broader side of the atrium wing—that which held the formal dining room—lay a covered veranda, open on the sides, its roof supported by columns, and hung with awnings which could be raised and lowered to shield one from sunlight or rain or nosy neighbors. It was furnished with a weathered wood table and benches, upon one of which I sat to exult in the view. Before me lay the city of Rome!

Since I had never been here before, I could not identify most of what I saw. The view was hardly an unobstructed one. I had to peer through openings between towering apartment buildings—taller than any residences I had observed anywhere else. As a consequence I could only see portions of the more distant edifices. Nevertheless from descriptions I had read and heard, I thought I recognized the Forum and adjacent Capitoline Hill. The River Tiber I could not see.

The immediate neighborhood in which the house was located was called the Carinae, because it lay adjacent to an outcropping of rock that resembled keels of ships. This feature I looked for but could not discern from my present perspective, and so returned to observing the panorama before me. The city was a jumble of geometric shapes: rectangles and squares, circles and semicircles, trapezoids and other irregular constructions with oblique angles conforming to the pattern of the streets. Colors abounded: on walls the coruscate white of marble, the creamy hue of travertine, deep gray of volcanic tuff, dark red of brick, grayish brown of wood. On roofs lay the gleaming reds, blues, greens, and grays of tiles. Here and there the deep greens and browns of a garden or copse, or the bright colors of a flower box or awning, softened the cityscape's stony mien.

The house stood at a confluence of five streets, three of which seemed scarcely wider than doorways. They teemed with people and animals. Two dogs romped with a group of boys playing with a ball. They dutifully stepped aside and pressed their backs hard against a building's wall to let a litter pass. Pedestrians strolled singly or in groups toward different directions at varying rates of speed—some hurrying, others ambling. One man led a donkey laden with baskets, the contents of which I could not see. Pigs poked in the gutters, and cats darted after vermin and insects. After a while a trio of street musicians gathered at a corner, with a bagpipe, harp, tambourine, and a monkey that danced. Upon the pavement before them they placed a basket into which passersby obligingly tossed coins.

Because the buildings were so closely adjacent to one another, sounds reverberated off their walls with surprising clarity. I caught portions of conversations: pedestrians discussing which charioteer was the best bet at a forthcoming race, a woman comforting a child, the boys keeping score of their game, the dogs barking and the boys hushing them, the cries of the man with the donkey selling kitchen wares, the repetitive rhythms of the musicians, the grunting of a pig, from somewhere in an apartment building a domestic quarrel. After some time I was able to determine the source of a persistent and redundant *Ti-wit ti-woo, ti-wit ti-woo.* It was a birdcage, suspended from the ceiling of a veranda on a house in an adjacent block.

Eventually I became aware the sun was approaching its zenith. Now I was hot, thirsty, and in need of the privy. After refreshing myself I noted through an open archway that Tiberius was in the peristyle, to which I now descended. So rapt as I was after my morning of observation from the veranda, so eager to tell him thereof, I did not think to ascertain whether he was alone. My view as I entered the peristyle was partially obscured by the ligustrum; and a cicada singing in this shrub prevented me from detecting conversation. Upon approaching I discovered Tiberius was with callers; and before I could retreat, I was detected.

Tiberius' visitors were a petite plump woman of mature years, and a delicately boned stripling youth. The woman wore a stola of pale yellow and a light white veil. Her auburn hair, thick and wavy, was just beginning to gray. The boy, clad in a white tunic hemmed with the narrow purple stripe of youth, had eyes and hair the hue of burnished wood. Although I had never met them or even seen them face to face, I knew precisely who they were. And because I was not clad in servants' garb, the woman at once inferred my place in Tiberius' household and life.

"Oh, how now my dear!" she exclaimed in flawless Greek. From my dress she had also deduced my nationality. As she spoke her hazel eyes sparkled. With a surge of emotion I noted they had the precise shape and hue as Alcimus'. "Come, come, no need for embarrassment or fear!" Her perception of my discomfiture dispelled it.

Walking steadily with my head slightly lowered, yet keeping my eyes on hers and smiling, I came before her and curtsied. "Lady, I am called Galatea," I stated in a tone pleasantly modulated with a nuance of self-effacement. Now my finishing came more naturally than I could ever recall, as if by second nature.

"Galatea; what a delightful name!" She took my right hand in both of hers. They were delicate and soft and well manicured, but free of adornment except for two rings. On her right hand was a brilliant blue sapphire; and on her left a broad wedding ring of hammered gold, embedded with a sardonyx that changed hue with the shifts in light as though it were alive. "Is this your first time coming to Rome?" she continued.

"Yes, Lady."

"We hope you will become well familiar with our great city and find it to your liking."

"I am sure I shall, Lady; I am very excited about coming to live here."

"Well, we bid you the warmest welcome. I am Livia, and this," she placed her right hand on the shoulder of the youth, "is Drusus: Tiberius' son." I curtsied again; and Drusus, smiling shyly yet graciously, returned that slight bow at the hips that is customary for Italian men. Although his hair and eyes were lighter than his father's, he strongly resembled Tiberius in physiognomy and mannerisms. "Unfortunately, we are just now departing," Livia continued. "A pity you did not come upon us earlier, so we could become better acquainted. But no matter: we shall be seeing much more of one another anon." After I curtsied once more, Tiberius escorted the guests toward the atrium. I repaired to the dining room, where the blackamoor cook was laying a luncheon suited to the hot weather: slices of cold fowl and salad greens.

"I sincerely apologize for my intrusion!" I exclaimed contritely as Tiberius joined me. "Over the noise of cicadas I could not hear your conversations; and I was so enthralled with the sights of my new home here, I forgot to peek ahead."

"No harm whatsoever, but on the contrary a most auspicious encounter. I had been deliberating when and how first to introduce you to my family. You just solved my problem, and quite satisfactorily."

While we were dining a messenger from Longus arrived, and reported the entire shipment of art had survived the voyage unscathed. After luncheon, Tiberius dictated letters: to Cyrenius, announcing he had arrived safely and wishing him well in his new position as Gaius' chief of staff; to Atticus, announcing we had arrived safely; and to Thrasyllus, announcing we had arrived safely and requesting news of the farm and any new prognostications he had to offer. There was no sense in preparing a similar message for Marinus, until we had ascertained his whereabouts. Tiberius handed the completed tablets to a manservant whose name I did not yet know, with instructions to arrange for their delivery. He then turned to me with that enticing smile of his, the meaning of which I knew right well. "How did I miss you last night?"

"You were fast asleep when I came to join you."

"Why did you not join me anyway?"

"To save my ears. You were snoring loudly enough to be heard in Ostia. Besides, it was awfully hot last night."

"It is awfully hot right now. But since we are both fully awake, why not make ourselves all the hotter?"

He took my hand and gently led me up the stairs to our sitting room, where with a glance he dismissed the attendant manservant. The walls of his bedchamber were adorned like those of mine, with monochromatic panels. Of these the predominating hues were reds, browns, and golds—far more vibrant than the somber hues of my quarters, and perhaps a good backdrop for the lovers' vignettes.

"Never mind the walls; you can gawk at them later!" Tiberius exclaimed. As he loosened my waist girdle, my womb convulsed with desire.

"I have not yet rinsed the sea out of my hair," I said as he unbound it.

"So let us make it all the grubbier with perspiration. Have you been following Rhathines' laser regimen?" He removed his tunic and took me in his arms.

"The wine mixture I consumed yesterday morning while aboard the Murex; however, the oil and lambswool are still packed," I managed between kisses.

"Then I shall make sure to withdraw precisely at climax and spew all over your belly. That will make you good and grubby."

"And foul your bedlinens, and prompt our attendants to snicker while they prepare our bath."

"My man Valens—yes, that is his name—has not yet changed my bed for the night. He will have a good laugh when he does. Already he has drawn us a tepid bath, and procured your dressing gown from Gallina. Oh come now, no need for embarrassment," he continued on feeling me start. "Gallina is his spouse. Stop making excuses, will you?"

Without loosening our embrace we sidled into his bedchamber where we finished undressing one another, crawled upon the bed, and proceeded with our grubbying. "Now you can look at the walls," Tiberius exclaimed while we were resting afterward, holding hands but because of the heat lying some distance apart in our wallow of perspiration and semen.

Presently a cry reverberated from the street. "Whom—or rather what—are you fucking in there, Tiberius Nero?"

Startled, I abruptly sat upright, grabbed the sheet lying folded at the foot of the bed, and cast it over me like a tent. Tiberius sat up at my side. "I see my arrival has become known," he said, his tone sardonic. "Amazing, is it not? I hate this house. It is dark and dreary; and it stands in an area with far too much public activity to suit me. It holds too many bad memories; and it does not even belong to me! Julia acquired it for us from the relatives of her mother, because she relished precisely the very prominent exposure which so disconcerts me. She never let me forget her maternal uncle's daughter married the son of the great and honorable and woefully unfortunate Gnaeus Pompeius Magnus, who once hallowed these halls with his presence. The place was always hers, part of her dowry; I was only its curator; when we were divorced its ownership reverted to my stepfather. To her credit, Julia never embarrassed me by making my lack of ownership known to the public. Nevertheless she had such a sense of having condescended to let me live here, that she took this the master suite to herself and put me in the female quarters you presently occupy. Drusus got the worst room in the children's section: between the shared playroom and shared bath, with all the consequent noise. At least this is not the bed upon which Julia defiled our marriage. I had Demetrius replace all the furniture here in the master chambers."

I pulled the sheet off my head, then mopped myself with it while leaning against him. "The obscure crave fame, and the famous crave obscurity," I mused, sharing his gloomy pensiveness, "Except for types like Julia. And behold the end her frowardness brought her."

"Well said, my Lioness, well said. How many eminent philosophers have written volumes trying to express that very conclusion?"

"Did you not inherit your father's house?"

"The ancestral home of the Nerones, near to the Quirinal Hill, was too small, too old, and too remote to suit Julia. At present a man named Aulus Plautius Silvanus is occupying it with his wife. His kindred have been staunchly loyal retainers of the Claudii Nerones for generations."

"Certainly I appreciate your not wanting to evict them."

Suddenly he started to chuckle. "Look at you, all wrapped up! Do you think that heckler actually saw you? He would have had to scale the walls." Struck by the absurdity of my reaction, I started to laugh as well.

The bath basin in the master suite was sunken, but like the raised tub in our Rhodian farmhouse was too small to accommodate more than one person at a time. The bath itself was wonderfully refreshing. Valens had added enough warm water to loosen soil and prevent the cold from shocking our bodies, yet not so much that the cooling effect was compromised. I duly washed my hair. As I approached my own suite after the bath, with a towel bound loosely about my dripping tresses, I heard Alexandra's raised voice. "How can you presume she will be displeased with my efforts?" I discovered her scowling at an abashed Alcmene who appeared almost in tears. They had unpacked the remaining contents of my clothing trunk, which a manservant was in the process of loading onto his back to carry away for storage. The soiled garments had been heaped into a basket, the few clean ones folded in neat piles upon shelves in the wardrobe. As I entered the man bowed as best he could under his burden, the two women composed themselves and curtsied.

"Why this ado?" I demanded after the man had left.

Alcmene spoke first. "Alexandra has arranged your garments according to their weight: the heavier in one section, the lighter in another. I was attempting to explain that you prefer they be grouped with regard to color, Lady: reds with reds, blues with blues, and so forth."

"Lady, can you not appreciate the logic of having your clothes grouped according to their weight? This saves you the trouble of sorting through heavy garments on hot days and light ones on cold."

"Your suggestion is well taken, Alexandra; however, I prefer the distribution by color. The weight of a garment I can discern simply by looking at its texture and weave, or else by touching it even while it is folded. Alcmene, you know my inclination well. Rearrange the closet accordingly, and then remove that basket downstairs for laundering. Alexandra, prepare to comb out my hair."

The process might have been pleasant, had Alexandra not been my attendant. While drying my hair with the towel, she urged upon me a variety of pomades. These to her blatant dismay I refused, because coatings on my skin and in my hair make me uncomfortable in hot weather. While brushing my hair she noted several strands of gray and would have pulled them out, had I not felt the first tug and stopped her.

"But Lady, are you sure? In hair so dark as yours, the gray stands out sharply. And do you realize, Lady, the styling of your hair is hopelessly out of fashion? You must let me redesign it at once!"

"Not at this time."

"But I am an accomplished ornatrix. I styled the Lady Julia's hair for years before misfortune overtook her. Will you then allow me to dye it, to conceal the gray?"

"NOT UNTIL I AM READY!!"

By now it was midafternoon and hotter than ever. I announced my intention to return to the veranda, and remain there in my dressing gown with my hair unbound. When Alexandra regarded me as though my sanity were questionable, I responded testily, "Where else in this house will I find sufficient breeze to dry my hair?" Another question followed: before my departure, would I not like to be anointed with perfumed astringent to help cool my body? "Did I not just say I dislike such applications in hot weather?" I retorted through clenched teeth.

Presently Alexandra and Nausicaa joined me on the veranda with a great stack of textiles. With an air of accomplishment, Alexandra averred she had spent the entire morning procuring these fabrics to enlarge my wardrobe. As Nausicaa held them up one by one, Alexandra declared the purpose she had decided upon for each: this must become a chiton, that a himation, the next a shawl. At the fourth selection I ordered her to desist, and return the fabrics to my suite. At my leisure I would go through them, choose which I wanted to keep, and thereafter decide the type of garment into which each piece should be made. Down the future I would state when I wished to make additions or alterations to my wardrobe—not only to clothing but to accessories like hair ribbons, jewelry, and cosmetics. I may seek Alexandra's opinion with regard to my appearance: whether a color or texture suited my physique or blended well with other elements of my couture, whether my hair was properly styled. In the end, however, the final decision as to what I required, retained, and utilized would be mine. Alexandra gazed at me with an air of surprised indignation as though I had breached some protocol.

My next requirements gave Alexandra further surprise. In my exploration of the house that morning, I had come upon an unused workroom on the first floor—well illumined and ventilated, and with ample shelving. This I decided to use as my art studio. Now I ordered Alexandra to locate my painting accouterments in our luggage yet unpacked. She should bring me three palettes, as many assorted paint vials as she could carry, several brushes, and a small rag, and have the remaining materials delivered to the workroom. Regarding me as though I must for certain be hopelessly deranged, Alexandra sent Nausicaa on this errand. In doing so, she unwittingly provided me with the opportunity for which I had been hoping.

Speaking vehemently, and in Latin in case Alcmene happened back within earshot, I reminded Alexandra that Alcmene had been my personal servant for eight years. In consequence Alcmene understood my tastes, habits, idiosyncrasies, and preferences far better than Alexandra possibly could, having only known me for two days. I expected Alexandra to defer to Alcmene's decisions and instructions regarding matters of this nature. Furthermore Alcmene was not Alexandra's fellow slave but a freedwoman, serving Master Tiberius and me of her own volition. As such she must be addressed and treated with proper deference to her status. All this being said, I dismissed Alexandra for the remainder of the day. Anger flared in her eyes; but she only curtsied and departed in silence. Nausicaa had returned toward the end of my speech.

Wide-eyed with trepidation, she handed me the painting accouterments and then promptly withdrew again.

Opening the paints, I began to record the hues of the city before me; but without the usual joy and fascination that accompanied this process. Had I not learned from my scrap with Timoleon so many years before, the consequences of letting anger impel my judgments, words, and actions? Had I so allowed Alexandra's conduct to irritate me, that I reprimanded and dismissed her sharply without considering potential consequences? Would she take retribution: destroy a favorite garment or artifact of mine, or inflict some sort of harm upon my person directly? Worse yet: would she betray the secret Demetrius had entrusted to her, about the true nature of my relationship with Tiberius?

And had I been truly fair? How could I pass judgment on Alexandra, when we had been acquainted for so short a time? She may not have known Alcmene was a freedwoman, and for this reason treated her as a servile equivalent. Would merely informing Alexandra of Alcmene's status have evoked the proper respect, and precluded the need for the reprimand? Moreover, had I unilaterally taken Alcmene's side without determining whether she had provoked Alexandra to justified annoyance? And what of the challenges at which I had taken offense? Were they simply unfamiliar yet well-intentioned mannerisms—Alexandra's way of ensuring I was not making decisions I would later regret?

Tiberius rolled his eyes and chuckled as I described my ordeal, over our supper of cold sausage slices, salad greens, and bread rolls. "Alexandra's character could benefit from a little comeuppance. She is overseer of the household's serving women, and is Demetrius' wife. Both I emancipated for precisely the same reasons I freed Menon and Phoebe. The pair have a son whose name is Alexander, but whom everyone calls Nomius because as a young child he was a notorious wanderer. They also have two daughters. Nausicaa the elder is one of your personal attendants; the younger, Calypso, was born during my absence and is presently a delicium. You are accustomed to the warm camaraderie we shared with our servants on Rhodes. This is your first encounter with one who is obstreperous."

My stomach tightened. I closed my eyes and drew my breath through clenched teeth. "Assuming Alexandra was a slave, I ordered her to treat Alcmene with the deference due a superior. And Nausicaa witnessed a portion of my harangue."

"No matter: Alexandra still owes Alcmene civility despite their equality of station. And a good lesson for Nausicaa in the potential consequences of following her mother's example." He chuckled anew. "You derived a lesson as well, and most admirably; for you perceived how irritation can warp one's perceptions and so impel rash and unjust actions. As if supervisory responsibilities are not enough to encourage Alexandra's bossiness, Julia thrived on those challenges at which you chafed. *Lady, are you sure you do not like this garment; Lady, for certain you must try this perfume; Lady, we must extract this gray hair*—of which Julia had many from an early age. She had Alexandra yank them out sedulously, until the day her father suggested she might find remaining gray-headed preferable to letting herself be made bald.

"Have Demetrius remove Alexandra from your service altogether. If you are uncomfortable approaching him, I shall do so for you. Such is your privilege, and the most peaceful solution for you and Alexandra alike. Unless you distance yourself she will continue to offer challenges, hoping you will succumb so she can congratulate herself for having brought you under control. Once she discovers you will not accede, she will end up hating you. Then having to serve you properly and courteously, with the intimacy of a personal servant, will grate upon her and continue to escalate the tensions between the two of you. No need to concern yourself about retribution: Alexandra is far too proud of her sense of ethics to resort to retaliation."

Comforted by his insights and his willingness to intervene, I smiled and took his hand. "Thank you for your offer; but I shall speak with Demetrius myself."

"A wise idea, for it will show you are not afraid to face him after confronting Alexandra."

I reflected upon my encounter with Alexandra and the lesson I had learned. With any position of authority—in my particular case, that of a mistress over a servant—comes the grave responsibility not to wield one's authority arbitrarily or unnecessarily. Resolving a conflict peaceably, without succumbing to anger and without humiliating or otherwise damaging one's adversary: is not that a pursuit of higher excellence within oneself?

Owing to the heat we decided to sleep apart again, lest the natural warmth of our bodies increase the distress the weather was inflicting instead of heightening the pleasure of sharing a bed. The nighttime atmosphere was oppressively warm, clammy, and fetid. Rome enjoys neither the sea breezes that freshened the city of Rhodes, nor the crisply pristine mountain air of our hillside farm. By night, Rome is noisy as well. As a protection to pedestrians, wheeled vehicles are not allowed on the city streets during daylight hours. Consequently farm produce and trade wares—anything requiring transport by cart and wagon—has to be delivered after dark. As I lay listening to the rumble of wheels in the distance, the baying of animals and shouting of men, I thought about the heckler we had heard in the afternoon. By virtue of his family connections and his own personal history, Tiberius must ever be the target of curiosity and derision no matter how privately he lived.

My thoughts drifted to my own reaction to the taunt. Upon first hearing it I had actually taken offense at the heckler's reference to Tiberius' partner as *what*—as though he knew me personally and was intentionally scorning me with that epithet. Oddly enough I began to recall the nasty condescending girls I had known in my youth, who had married young and sneered triumphantly at my persistent spinsterhood. How would they respond to learning I was the consort of a royal, mistress of his household, a sophista with some recognition in academic circles, a renowned decorative artist albeit under a pseudonym? Would they offer apologies and newfound respect, or find ways to belittle my achievements? Did I still feel after all these years, that I must justify myself to these women? What difference did it make whether they approved me or not? For all I knew they did not even remember me. Why at this time was I suddenly recalling these painful incidents so distantly past and long forgotten?

Presently I started to acknowledge the taunts and sneers of my adolescent tormentors had inflicted no genuine damages: the type for which compensation can be recovered through lawsuit. Those cruel words and posturings had ultimately proved harmless. The self-consciousness and shame my family had foisted upon me—their blatant contempt for my characteristics, interests, enjoyments, and fears—had sensitized me to the disdain of others. Driven to rue every mistake or pratfall—every obtuse thought or motive entertained or ridiculous action taken—I had until now lacked the ability to recognize my foibles as intrinsically human and laugh at them accordingly. Sparing Alcimus an upbringing of this nature—teaching him early to correct yet forgive his own mistakes, to discern the difference between genuine and conjectural injury—would empower him to endure without suffering and countermand intrusive prying, undeserved censure, scathing ridicule. As if to match the joyous tranquility these contemplations brought to my mind, a night breeze arose and brought a modicum of refreshment to my body.

The next morning I was thoroughly irritated by Alexandra's vociferous sanction—sanction, mind you, not deprecation! —of the grass-green chiton I had chosen to wear. I was about to order her to desist from giving me her opinions unsolicited even then they were favorable, when Tiberius burst into our sitting room. Seizing my hand he said, "Come!" with breathless urgency, and led me hastily through the corridor to the stairs. As we descended he continued,

"I want you to witness what is about to transpire." When we reached the main floor he drew me into the atrium and thence into the office. From here a door opened directly into the adjacent reception room. "Stay carefully out of sight, but watch and listen. Either keep the door so barely ajar that from a distance it appears to be closed, or else look through the keyhole." He strode across the reception room and into the atrium, leaving the door between these rooms well open so I could see and hear.

Although I heard the atrium resound with the footsteps of many persons, I could see no one apart from Tiberius. He bowed, and upon straightening with one hand beckoned the still unseen visitors to enter the reception room. Two tall, fair-haired men entered. Over their civilian tunics they wore body armor, like that of Ajax and Androcles and Arbindus when on guard duty. Both carried spears and shields, and had daggers and swords strapped to their hips. One of them headed directly toward my barely opened door, which with my heart pounding I promptly and silently closed before he could notice. Unable to find a key, I leaned my entire weight against the door to hold it shut while the guard tried it. When no longer feeling his pressure, I peered through the keyhole. My ruse had succeeded. Assuming the door was locked, the guard had turned away. He was now standing a good pace beyond the door, which very surreptitiously I reopened ever so slightly.

The man who had followed the guards into the reception room was diminutive but well proportioned. He walked with a slight limp. His fair, sandy hair was riddled with streaks of white, which imparted a slight glimmer like the touch of hoarfrost. A broad forehead and prominent cheekbones, descending to a well-defined but relatively small chin, gave his face a noticeably triangular appearance. Beneath merging eyebrows I saw brilliant, blue-gray eyes. They dazzled with a verve and intensity and dynamic intelligence, which I found awesome and slightly unnerving. He was dressed like an ordinary magistrate—in a white senatorial tunic with its vertical purple stripe and a white toga with a purple border—but no ordinary magistrate was he.

"I am not quite sure what to say to you," he said testily as Tiberius and two more guards—blond and statuesque like their fellows—entered the room behind him.

"What about, *Welcome home*?" Tiberius ventured.

Caesar Augustus returned an aggravated glance as he settled onto the settee. With a wave of his hand he signaled the guards to leave. My muscles relaxed as I heaved an inaudible sigh of relief.

"You still owe me a satisfactory explanation for retiring to Rhodes when your presence in Rome was most needed," Augustus continued, his tone still sharp. "Suppose I had lost my life, or become incapacitated before Gaius reached his twentieth year? There is no need to describe what became of Julia, after you withdrew the restraining influence of your presence in her life."

"I was as much regent in Rhodes as I would have been here," Tiberius replied with a complacent weariness as he took an adjacent chair. "Moreover I never exercised any influence upon Julia. That you had recognized right well, Stepfather, but refused to accept. I made quite plain my reason for withdrawing was not to appear a potential political rival to Gaius or his brother."

"Oh come now, Tiberius! No one seriously considered you their rival until you put forth that paltry excuse, giving credence to innuendo and raising genuine suspicions about your motives. Behold the result: your political and personal credibility destroyed; for several years your safety more at risk than in any previous time or condition of your life; we your family beside ourselves with worry about your personal security and wellbeing. Then when the truth finally emerged it made Gaius—the very individual you were ostensibly trying to protect and honor—appear a naïve and credulous simpleton. You have always been an abysmally poor liar, my Tiberius. What was the real reason you left? Was it Julia after all?"

Tiberius was staring at the floor. "Our life together had become unbearable, for Julia as much as for me," he began ruefully. "Yet we both realized implicitly you would never have allowed us a voluntary divorce. Little wonder Julia set about finding other ways to break us apart: insinuating our marriage was beneath her dignity, that I approved her racy lifestyle, that I indulged in winebibbing, and—worst of all—that I subjected her to perverse sexual abuse."

"I would have put a stop to all that."

"You endeavored to do so and failed—remember?"

"You did not allow me sufficient time to intervene effectively before you headed off to Rhodes, nursing your bruised ego like an overly sensitive child sulking over the fatuous taunts of a sibling."

"Although untrue, Julia's taunts were hardly fatuous: they put me in fear for my life. It seemed only a matter of time before one of her quislings succeeded in lodging a dagger between my ribs. Admittedly I entertained a faint hope that absenting myself might induce her to reconsider her behaviors and become amenable to reconciliation. But in the end it was not Julia's conduct that impelled me to leave, Caesar, so much as yours!"

As Tiberius uttered these last few words the intensity of his tone increased. "For the past half century you have relentlessly devoted the entire energy of your life to the redevelopment of the Roman state. In doing so you enlisted—no, required, demanded, according to designs you rigidly outlined—the participation of those who love and support you the most: your family and friends. And because we love and support you, we your family and friends have responded and acquiesced to those designs at great expense to our personal autonomies. Remember how my brother, in the last letter he wrote you before his death, urged you to uphold respect for individual opinions: for the right of persons to disagree without consequence—prescripts which had epitomized the mores of the Roman Republic. Recall the deep, brooding dejection that haunted Agrippa in his final year of life. Granted he was ill with gout; however Julia told me he had felt stifled and abjectly subservient, disallowed any opportunity to make a decision or take an action independent of your dictates. You so alienated Maecenas that he ceased speaking with you several years before his death; yet in the end he still loved you enough to bequeath you his opulent and priceless villa and gardens.

"When to fit your designs you made me repudiate Vipsania for Julia, you neglected to take into account that Julia's nature and mine—natures you had known from our childhood—stood to render us incompatible spouses. Legally, of course, Vipsania and I could have refused to divorce and Julia and I refused to wed, being we were all sui juris. Nevertheless we all three complied—Vipsania and Julia and I—because we too loved you and were dedicated to the success of your intentions. Julia and I honestly tried for a time to make our marriage work. I rather suspect she would not have spurned me so readily and aggressively had our son survived. But ultimately, your oppressive disregard for her individuality and mine undid your goals for us and for your regime, and forced Julia to pay a terrible, terrible price."

"Why, Tiberius, do you not yet perceive our family and most immediate friends—those closest and dearest to us—and myself as well, are all slaves to this arbitrary and fickle monster: this Chimera I have created?" There was a sort of patient exasperation and even a touch of remorse in the emperor's tone. "It is she who suppresses human individuality, not I. Resist or oppose her, and she will respond with unimaginable severity—far more acutely than any human taskmaster no matter how cruel could render. So Julia and you discovered firsthand. Now she is a convicted criminal, and you a public laughingstock for destroying a glorious public career. I was painfully aware you and Julia were mismatched, that I was probably inflicting upon you the same sort of marriage I endured with her mother. Do you not recall how I spent nearly a year, considering different candidates for Julia's hand? In the end, however, the Chimera dictated my selection. No one was more skilled in political and military leadership, more trustworthy and reliable, to serve as regent than you."

"Oh, I perceive the ways of your Chimera, Stepfather—apparently far better than you realize or wish to acknowledge. Why else do you suppose I left Drusus in your care? I wanted him to mature in your milieu, observing and discovering firsthand the life for which his genealogy destines him. His grandmother is your wife. That ensures him a place in your system, even though mine has been lost. You do not understand why I made those vague and lame excuses for withdrawing to Rhodes, and now agree to permanent retirement from public life. To protect you and your regime—your Chimera—I chose to keep people guessing about my motives, rather than embarrass you by disclosing the truth: that I could no longer abide your emasculation of my self-determination, and that your demands were making me feel I had lost my own identity. Imagine the consequent innuendo. You would have been ridiculed for conferring the regency upon a self-centered, spineless ninny; and public confidence in my ability to exercise the powers of that office would have been seriously compromised if not lost altogether."

Now Augustus was staring at the floor, resting his right elbow on his knee and chin in his right palm. After a short silence he raised his piercing eyes. "It pleases me to see you comprehend the Chimera's modes better than I had assumed," he said pensively. "Consider nonetheless: if I secure commutation of Julia's sentence and allow you to return to public life as though nothing at all had happened, does that not imply I forgive the insubordination the both of you displayed? What message will be sent to the rising generation of the Chimera's slaves—not only to Gaius and Lucius and to their brother and sisters, but to your own son and to your brother's children? Will it lead them to assume they can follow your examples, upon finding themselves in the untoward conditions the Chimera imposes? That they are free to rebel against her mandates as Julia did or withdraw into sequestration like you, and leave the Chimera foundering without their contributions to her support and sustentation? Chaos would ensue. Its threat is the Chimera's means of assuring she receives unflagging and uninterrupted servitude."

"Drusus comes of age in October." Now there was a nervous hesitancy in Tiberius' voice. "I should like to bring him to live with me here, that I may spend the intervening months preparing him for the responsibilities he must afterward assume: training as a military officer, broader and deeper understanding of the letter and application of law, the modes and expectations of patronage, betrothal and marriage—and ultimately, of course, election to public office and admission to the senate."

"Legally I cannot prevent you; however, I recommend you let Drusus remain in my household. Surrendering him to yours stands to convey the impression I have forgiven your defiance and all is concordant between us." Augustus' tone was threatening. "For the same reason, I expect you to be careful of the company you keep, and choose wisely those with whom you associate. The slightest nuance, the most subtle suggestion of dissent—no matter how innocuous or unintentional—I cannot and will not countenance, Tiberius!" After a moment of silence he continued, "I shall assuredly send Drusus to call upon you here, that you may instruct him." His tone had become far milder.

"Will you allow me to attend the ceremony commemorating Drusus' coming of age?"

"Tiberius, you are legally and ethically obligated as Drusus' father to officiate. Why do you assume I would impugn or obstruct your doing so?" Augustus practically snarled with exasperation. Once again he averted his eyes to the floor. After another pause he said, "As a remedy for my disaffection with you, I ask that you counsel me privately on military matters." His tone was calmer, but demanding rather than solicitous.

"I am more than pleased to comply."

The emperor rose to his feet, as did Tiberius. "I must be off; already I am late to the senate." Laying his right hand on Tiberius' shoulder, Augustus for the first time in their interview smiled. "I believe I know you well enough to venture you are far more relieved than chagrined to become a private citizen." Now his tone was congenial and engaging. "Be scrupulously discreet, my stepson; bear in mind what I have just said. Your mother informed me you have brought a disarmingly winsome and ingratiating companion with you from Rhodes. Take special precaution to protect and nurture that happiness."

"She is my ward."

"Is she? Why then are your cheeks and ears coloring?"

Tiberius did not answer but bowed again, as Augustus swept into the atrium where his guards at once surrounded him.

After watching until his visitors had exited the house, Tiberius turned to face my door. I opened it and entered the reception room. He smiled and inhaled deeply with relief. "Were you able to hear and see anything?"

"The entire interview."

"Good! Before introducing you to him, I wanted to prepare you with a glimpse of his character. Hopefully it has given you an idea of how drivingly demanding he is. Once he has made your acquaintance, he will for certain importune you in one way or another." He sat down on the couch Augustus had occupied, and I joined him.

"He is formidable for sure," I mused as I took his hand.

"That adjective hardly begins to describe him."

"He neither apologized for underestimating your discernment of his regime—his Chimera—nor thanked you for anticipating the potential calamity of publicizing the real reason for your retirement. And by what legal authority can he prohibit your participation in political affairs?

"None—breach of amicitia, rather. You saw how sharply public opinion turned against me after he ordered me to remain on Rhodes. That was merely a coolness between us: imagine the effect of an actual breach. Remember too, he is my stepfather—a parent who raised me. I do have considerable respect and affection for him. And of course I want to see his regime succeed. I am more than happy to comply with his request for my military advice."

"It impressed me as more a demand than a request."

"Now you are starting to comprehend him."

"He called you an abysmally poor liar; yet behold how successfully you have obfuscated my identity and concealed Alcimus."

"He does not understand me as well as he presumes. And in one sense his accusation is absolutely correct. I lack the disingenuous guile—the ability to be persuasively hypocritical—so essential for a successful politician."

"He did not merely allow, but insisted you introduce Drusus to public life. Moreover he approved—even sanctioned—our relationship."

"His affection for his family and friends is very, very strong; it runs very, very deep. Nevertheless still deeper—far more intense and intimate—is his liaison with his Chimera. The Roman state he has reformed, reshaped, and revitalized, is his very soul—his very being, from which he cannot detach himself consciously or emotionally. He recognizes the attrition he has wrought upon the self-determination of his intimates, sympathizes with and regrets the anguish he has caused us; but he is incapable of truly comprehending why we have suffered from his impositions and resisted them. Such is the slavery under which I have labored all my life, for which Drusus must be prepared, and from which I am determined to spare Alcimus. And I continue daring to hope the monumental change Thrasyllus predicts for me is utter emancipation."

"How does your mother endure him? They have been married a long while."

"Four decades. Since my mother is as passionately in love with him as he is with her, I suspect her affinity renders her less inclined than others to chafe under his demands. Also I venture the popular assumption women by nature are more acquiescent than men is quite valid, your mother and Julia being stark exceptions. My stepfather's kindly sister Octavia, who died so pitifully young of diseased breasts, was always more than happy to do his bidding, even as her daughters—his nieces—are to this day. We men let our overblown egos compromise successful cooperation. Moreover my stepfather over the years has placed as much if not more reliance upon my mother's keen political insights than on those of his male counselors. People are grossly mistaken, who pity them for being childless. The Chimera is their scion, as much her creation as his; and she is as dedicated as he is to the nurturing of its development and success. Like him she loves it, and like him she is conscientious of its propensity to enslave. She aspires at times to deny, and on other occasions to justify, that propensity—like a mother defending the shortcomings of a difficult human child."

"Remember how Thrasyllus said one's children do not necessarily take the form of fellow humans," I mused, suddenly realizing only now did I truly comprehend the sage's meaning. "The bodyguards are Gauls?" I now ventured, almost without thinking. After momentarily wondering why I had felt impelled to change the subject to this triviality, I understood that I needed reprieve from the intensity of our discussion.

"German allies—Ubii—members of their nobility. There are six in all—the last two must have remained in the entryway." Tiberius had not left the intensity.

From the atrium we heard a knock on the door and then a voice: "It is I, Master: Canulus."

"Come!" Tiberius returned, still distracted.

The ostiarius entered the reception room and said, "Quintus Ostorius Scapula waits to pay his respects."

"Advise I shall greet him momentarily, but detain him in the atrium. Send someone to fetch Valens." He escorted me back into the office. "Behold the very type of dilemma about which you just heard my stepfather warn me. Since Scapula is my mother's protégé, I am obliged to receive him. Since he is prefect of the praetorian guards, his visit could be interpreted as an effort on my part to garner military support. This is why I want Valens present during the encounter, so he can attest that nothing subversive transpired. Wait here until I bring Scapula into the reception room; then you can make your escape." He kissed my forehead and returned to the reception room. Once voices emanated therefrom I departed for my quarters, passing Valens who was descending the stairs as I mounted them.

On reaching my chambers I received quite a start. Alcmene was conversing with a person whom I thought might be a wrestler or gladiator clad in a woman's chiton. "Oh, Lady, this is Chloe!" Alcmene exclaimed upon seeing me.

Chloe was somewhat younger than I, as tall and quite possibly as heavy as Tiberius. At first I had thought her light brown hair was cropped short like a man's. It turned out to be so thin, that when pulled back and bound it seemed to disappear. Her brown eyes being asymmetrical, I could not be certain whether she was looking directly at me or beyond. Her smile revealed immense teeth, some set at differing angles, some discolored. By comparison my own dentition suddenly bore closer resemblance to that of Daphne the laurel nymph than of Daphne the horse. Chloe curtsied and said, in a voice evocative of the honking of a goose, "Lady, I am honored and delighted Alexandra has sent me to replace her as your attendant! I am ever so excited to become a personal servant to Master Tiberius' well-beloved!"

For a fleeting moment I wondered whether Alexandra had perpetrated a cruel and ugly taunt. Then with a surge of self-loathing, I recognized and acknowledged the cruelty and ugliness lay within me. I took note of the sparkle in those asymmetrical eyes, the ingenuous warmth in that toothy smile, the high-spirited affability and complimentary intention of that tactless greeting. All inclination to deplore, to belittle, to ridicule, even to pity this woman's physical appearance and artless manner disappeared from my thought. With genuine sincerity I replied, "Why thank you, Chloe, and welcome; may serving me bring you minimal despair."

"Chloe is the household's pharmakeutria and midwife, Lady," Alcmene declared with uncharacteristic exuberance. Clearly she was pleased with her new work-fellow. I was pleased as well, and touched with a sense of indulgent patience and protective love; for by now I had concluded Tiberius had mandated replacement of the troublesome Alexandra with this skilled person, indubitably willing and able to scrutinize my health and keep it in order.

"We were just discussing your use of laser," Alcmene continued.

"Finest and safest contraceptive there is," Chloe asserted with the confidence of a savant. "Cyrenican is the best variety but getting scarce. Be not worried, Lady: I have contacts with procurers most physicians in public practice do not know about. And if the supply does run out, I can and shall find you a suitable substitute. For now we have plenty on hand—for the wine mixture which I shall prepare for you weekly, and for the oil. With your permission, I shall maintain two stocks of pessaries and oil—one in your chamber here and the other in Master Tiberius.' If I may be so bold to inquire, Lady, how many children do you have?"

"Er...none," I murmured, feeling as though a rock had struck my abdomen as I glanced at Alcmene, who reassured me of her discretion with raised eyebrows and an almost imperceptible shake of her head.

"Really? The configuration of your hips and abdomen are consistent with those of a woman who has borne."

"Someday, Chloe, I shall relate to you my tortured gynecological history, which I am sure you will find quite interesting. At the moment, however, I feel a headache coming on: kindly procure me a remedy."

"The weather for certain," Chloe squawked. She curtsied once more and departed on her errand. Alcmene could not suppress a giggle as I slumped in my chair and heaved an audible sigh of relief.

Although burdened with my headache, I proceeded to evaluate the textiles Alexandra had procured for my wardrobe. My present supply of wearable clothing was limited to the few items I had brought with me from Rhodes. Tiberius' arrival raised my spirits, especially since he brought a brief note from Thrasyllus. Anticipating we would be concerned, the sage wanted to assure us all was well on the farm. Having himself already lunched with his guest, Tiberius asked whether I wanted a tray brought to me. His offer I declined, not having any appetite. When I thanked him for having Demetrius replace Alexandra with Chloe, he was surprised. He had said nothing to Demetrius, having assumed I was going to address this matter. Thereupon I recalled that upon introducing herself to me, Chloe had said Alexandra had sent her to be my new attendant. At the time I had assumed Alexandra had acted upon orders Demetrius received from Tiberius. Now it occurred to me that Alexandra had taken upon herself to effect this change.

An hour passed. My headache began to abate thanks to Chloe's spirea infusion, and to Tiberius' engaging description of the visitors who had called as the praetorian prefect Scapula was leaving. Livia Ocellina, a distant cousin of his mother, was a flamboyant soul—loud and loquacious, gaudy in makeup and dress, not terribly knowledgeable but highly appreciative of literature and the arts. She was gentle, kindhearted, and fiercely devoted to endowing charities out of her vast financial resources. Her recent remarriage, following a tumultuous prior union and bitter divorce, was for the present heightening her natural exuberance. Ocellina had brought along her newly acquired stepson, Servius Sulpicius Galba, who portended to grow up quite her opposite. Mature beyond his four years—more a minuscule man than a boy—he had followed the adult conversation attentively and seriously, as though weighing every word for every possible inference and implication.

Alcmene answered a knock on my sitting room door. She announced that Pallas, Florentinus, and Chloris had arrived to attend Lady. Tiberius inquired whether I had summoned barber, cobbler, and seamstress; and of course I denied. He had Alcmene bring the newcomers before us, and posed the same question. Alexandra had sent them, they replied. The three set about their respective tasks with the gracious reticence to which I was accustomed from servants, particularly those who were first making my acquaintance. They listened attentively and tolerantly to my opinions, and prefaced their recommendations and comments with, *Lady, if I may be so bold...* There were no arguments, no challenges, no *But Lady, are you really sure this is how you wish to proceed?*

Pallas was a slim man of about my age. With razor and shears he thinned and shaped my hair. As he went about his work I became aware of how oppressively heavy my hair had been in the hot weather, and luxuriated in the relief his trimmings brought. After he had finished cutting, he asked if I might summon whichever of my serving women dressed my hair. When Alcmene and Phaedra and Gallina arrived, Pallas showed them how to fashion the coiffure. His design was so well executed, that when simply drawn back and bound just above my nape, my hair fell precisely into place. Pallas held up a mirror to show me his handiwork. The nuances of soft femininity with which Timoxena had imbued my coiffure were restored—nay, enhanced. Wispy curls cascaded over my forehead concealing its acne scars. The gray hairs about which Alexandra had raised such a fuss fit into the design as though intentionally lightened for its purpose.

While Pallas was at work on my head, Florentinus tended to my feet. He was a squat man, bald except for a gray fringe along his hairline. After measuring length, width, and girth with a marked thong, he gently squeezed each foot between both his hands as though he were kneading dough, working his way downward from ankle to toes. He was evaluating the bone and muscular structure, he explained, so the sandals and shoes he designed were not only comfortable on my feet but lent support to my entire body.

After measuring the remainder of that body, Chloris sat on the floor beside my chair. Together we examined the textiles. She listened earnestly as I described my intention for each, and approved my selection of muted colors. Afterward she disputed several of my decisions—not with challenge, but with frank yet respectfully offered explanations justified by her expertise. One fabric will not drape properly if fashioned into a chiton but will be eminently serviceable as a veil. Another is too dense for a suitable chiton: by day's end I will feel as though I am wearing a carpet. It will serve well, however, as a himation. The texture of yet another piece will make me appear, er, unnecessarily large.

"Fat, you mean."

"Let us say replete." Since Chloris' back was to him, Tiberius grinned. Chloris herself was short and rotund with tightly curled gray hair, and hands so pudgy as to make me wonder how she managed to thread a needle. She had a soft soothing voice evocative of a dove's coo.

Upon finishing, Chloris clambered to her feet, curtsied, and announced she expected to have at least part of my wardrobe ready within five days. Would I be interested in her bringing along her daughter Leda, a skilled cosmetician, when she returned with the completed garments? Leda could apprise me of current fashions in cosmetics, and help me coordinate makeup colors with my new clothes. I thanked Chloris for the suggestion, and assured her I would welcome Leda's recommendations. With the assistance of Gallina and Phaedra, Chloris bore away the great stack of textiles.

Although my experience with the couturiers was pleasant enough, it left me fuming. How did Pallas know that I had just washed my hair, Florentinus that I had brought only a single pair of sandals from Rhodes, Chloris that I was examining the textile collection? Quite clearly Alexandra was spying and reporting on me—a task not difficult, given the number of servants and delicia whose paths crossed mine throughout the day. Without consulting me or anyone else she had replaced herself with Chloe as my personal serving woman, and sent the others to address my couture. From a distance, without any direct contact or interaction, Alexandra was continuing to impose her will upon me. Natural order seemed reversed, with me subordinate to Alexandra rather than the other way around.

Tiberius expressed mild surprise at my reaction after we were alone. What justification did I have for suspecting Alexandra's surreptitious interventions were a ploy to bring me under her control? Perhaps this was her intention, perhaps not: for all we knew it was her method of offering apology. There is no way to fathom another person's motives, unless and until that individual or someone else discloses them. I should accept Alexandra's efforts on my behalf without troubling myself about her aspirations. Unquestionably the service she had provided me was of highest caliber. She had recognized the emergent friction between us, and before it could escalate replaced herself in my entourage with the highly proficient Chloe. Alexandra had identified and promptly addressed the needs of my hair and wardrobe. The textiles she had procured for my costumes were not merely those of finest quality. Quite palpably when selecting them, she had taken my physique into careful consideration—my stature, the shape of my face, the hues of my hair, skin, and eyes—and had made eminently suitable choices. Nevertheless her taking actions without even telling me, let alone seeking my permission, did constitute a breach of protocol and merited correction if not reprimand. To inform Demetrius was my right.

I thanked Tiberius for his counsel but did not disclose, that I found myself in disagreement with him although I fully understood his premise. He was a military commander, accustomed to the tacit obedience of men chastened by unrelenting discipline and brutal punishments, both delivered without the slightest regard for personal feeling. Servants are subject to a similar rigor. A home, however, is not a field of war, where human emotion becomes a frivolous and potentially fatal distraction. Lying alone once again in the mercilessly hot and humid night, I reasoned that if Alexandra hated me already, subjecting her to reprimand would only heighten her hostility. Were her motive apologetic, to respond with rebuke would be grievous and cruel. Furthermore if I complained about Alexandra's serving me from a distance, what alternative would this leave Demetrius but to restore her to my direct service, where the friction between us had arisen in the first place?

After dressing the next morning I sent Nausicaa to fetch her mother. When Alexandra arrived I announced to her fellow serving women—including Nausicaa—that I would speak to her alone. Alexandra gazed at me with the look of sullen foreboding my mother had always adopted, whenever she anticipated I was about to say something she did not want to hear. This demeanor changed to one of stunned surprise, when I declared the services Alexandra was providing me in absentia were eminently satisfactory. Then I asserted that so long as she continued her present ministrations without deviation, I would overlook her offense of taking actions without my knowledge and consent.

Dear Reader, I beg your indulgence for the belabored account of my adjustments to my new surroundings and servants during those initial days of our sojourn in Rome. In themselves the incidents are trivial; yet they marked a major watershed in the development of my character. From my reaction to the heckler and memories of my childhood tormentors, I had discovered grief and self-condemnation over my peccadilloes were yielding to self-appreciation. My initial encounter with Chloe demonstrated I had mastered the art of dissembling without causing harm to others. My interaction with Alexandra showed I was capable of diffusing personal hostility, and revealed I could issue directives effectively but fairly—without compromising my requirements, yet without oppressing or humiliating those answerable to me. From assuming the aim of Alexandra's surreptitious service was to manipulate me—until Tiberius prompted me to consider the possibility she had other motives—I had learned to watch that haste, anger, preconceptions or other emotions did not warp my assessments of people and their actions.

Now more than ever I was aware of how people are driven, not only by their emotional strengths but by the sensitivities and emotional vulnerabilities with which they struggle. And with great joy I realized this enlarged perspective was wreaking atrophy upon my much hated inclination to justify myself by belittling others. This propensity I had harbored since childhood because it had been the only means whereby I could get my family to lay off their niggling me. It had precipitated my wrangle with Timoleon, and had caused me days of unnecessary resentment and fretting about Alexandra.

These discoveries brought immense personal satisfaction. So much for my alleged artlessness and naïveté, about which my family had hammered me with censure but never provided instruction for overcoming. Within a few short years I would find my newly recognized supervisory abilities more critical to my wellbeing and that of my son, than I could possibly have imagined at the time of their initial discovery. A more immediate effect was to become evident within the week. On the morning of my birthday that year I would find, upon the table in my sitting room, a neatly arranged platter of apricots candied in honey and dusted with pepper. Beside it lay a tablet, on which was inscribed, *To our Lady Galatea on this auspicious day, with honor and affection from Alexandra, Nausicaa, and Calypso.*

THE FAMILY GLORIOUS

After exhorting Alexandra I joined Tiberius in the office. While I wrote in my journal he reviewed, with the resident secretary Fulgens, correspondence which had arrived that morning and on the preceding day.

There were messages from Briseis and Thrasyllus, Marinus and Longus. Briseis' was brief and simplistic as befit the level of her literary skill, and absolutely charming. She was continuing to pursue reading and writing under the tutelage of Aka, and had herself started to teach the rudiments to Miranda. Thrasyllus reported everyone on the farm was well and missed us sorely. Aka was doting upon Alcimus and Phoenix, and Thrasylla reveling in the open spaces and the abundance and proximity of animals domestic and wild. Marinus announced he was in Rome, and inquired whether he could safely call upon Tiberius without raising controversy. The chronology in Marinus' note revealed that although he had quit Rhodes after we had, he had reached Rome before us. Hardly a surprise, given Longus' prolongation of our voyage with his dalliance. That worthy wrote his copyists were hard at work. Visitors to his gallery were duly admiring the pieces I had surrendered, and were placing orders for duplicates.

While we were lunching in the adjacent dining room, Fulgens brought yet another letter tablet. After perusing it Tiberius said nonchalantly, "Advise my mother's servant I accept her invitation." Fulgens bowed and departed, and Tiberius continued in the same offhand tenor, "She has asked you and me to supper this very evening at the twelfth hour." *[5:00 p.m.]*

"WHAT?!!" The spoonful of polenta I was carrying to my mouth dropped from its spoon into my lap. Tiberius rolled his eyes as he handed me an unused napkin. After cleaning up my mess I jumped to my feet and started to depart. "I must get ready!" I declared, hot and breathless with agitation.

Tiberius caught me by my wrist. "Finish your meal first!" he commanded. I settled back into my chair, scarfed the remaining polenta and eggs on my plate, and then bolted for my suite while my partner rolled his eyes anew.

In my chambers I came upon Alcmene and Phaedra, whom I sent after Chloris. No, the seamstress responded to my query, none of my new garments was ready. "With all due respect, Lady, you only ordered them yesterday afternoon." After thanking and dismissing Chloris I told Phaedra and Alcmene to locate every chiton I had brought from Rhodes that was clean, and lay it out on my bed; the same for every clean veil. Meanwhile in my sitting room, I spent perhaps the next hour practicing my finishing—walking, rising and sitting, reciting poems and singing songs to adjust the modulation of my voice. All the while I worried and fretted and attempted to acknowledge the control of Underlying Good.

Suppose I made an unfavorable impression upon Tiberius' family—came across too brash, too loud, too familiar; or contrariwise too demure, too retiring, too obsequious? Suppose they decided I was a potential detriment to his character, to his public image or to theirs, and demanded he repudiate me? He had reassured me, that in this event he would quit Rome and live out his life with me and our son, on Rhodes or elsewhere should the need for greater seclusion arise. But would he be able to keep his promise? He had defied his family once before, when he originally withdrew to Rhodes; but did he have the mettle to do so a second time? Only too well I knew from my own experience how difficult resisting a parental demand could be.

And would Tiberius' family use this forthcoming social occasion to berate him? This consideration unsettled me every bit as much as the prospect of possible repudiation. Roaring back into my mind came those painful memories of sitting at table, accounting to my mother for my inability to fulfill some impossible expectation she had set for me, and afterward listening in silence as she attributed my failure to disrespect, disloyalty, fractiousness, self-centeredness, sloth, immorality, and a host of other conceits I had never considered entertaining—all the while her aunt and my father nodded approvingly and my brother snickered with delight at my discomfiture. Could I manage to sit by in polite silence while my beloved endured like vexation; and would I end up loathing his family as I did mine?

Returning to my bedchamber, I reviewed the array of garments with despair. Each and every one was tatterdemalion or faded or both—including my beloved blue and white North African shawl. Undecided as to which I should wear, I ordered a tepid bath and—contrary to my usual inclination—bath salts, since I wanted to insure suppression of my natural body odors as much as possible. While sitting in my dressing gown afterward I had Phaedra unbind my hair, and instructed her to refresh it by wetting her fingers and running them over my scalp and through my locks. I requested a tweezers and hand mirror. While my hair dried I plucked spiky stray strands from my eyebrows and from around my mouth and chin. Still unable to decide upon a costume, I elected to leave that choice to Tiberius and asked Alcmene to invite him to my suite. On returning she announced he was in his own bath, but she had left word of my request with Nestor.

After cleaning my teeth with my usual dentifrice I sent for Chloe and Leda. From the pharmakeutria I solicited a solution I might gargle or swallow to keep my breath from developing a foul odor; from the cosmetician makeup, and the night jasmine scent I had selected back on Rhodes as a signature fragrance. My hair had dried, so Phaedra began to brush it. Tiberius arrived, and rolled his eyes at my lament that I had nothing suitable to wear. He fumbled through the pile of garments on my bed. "I see nothing wrong with any of these!"

"They are all wear-worn," I protested. "Your family will think me sloven."

He selected a beige linen chiton slightly faded and worn, a pale blue veil bereft of embroidery or any other embellishments, and plain hair ribbons of the same hue. "Bind her hair in a simple, comfortable fashion," he told Phaedra. "And none of all this," he added to Leda who had opened her immense box of cosmetics. "Nothing more than a little pale lip rouge, sparingly applied." He sniffed the air, for Leda had unstopped the bottle of jasmine perfume. "That scent is far too strong; find something lighter!" Leda capped the bottle and opened another, from which emanated a fragrance reminiscent of rain on the wildflowers of our promontory on Rhodes. "Far more suitable," he assented. "And what are you contributing to this folderol?" he demanded of Chloe who had arrived with the tiniest vial I had ever seen.

"Tincture of spearmint, Master," she cackled. "A droplet on her tongue will insure the freshness of her breath." She inverted the vial onto the tip of her index finger and then thrust her finger into my mouth, which immediately felt wonderfully fresh and filled with a pleasantly minty sweetness. Chloe recapped the vial and slipped it into the binding of my hair. "Now you can avail yourself of this whenever you sense the need," she said.

Tiberius shook his head and rolled his eyes. "The Altar of Augustan Peace was dedicated a decade ago," he said. As I gazed back at him bewildered, he shook his head anew and pursed his lips. "Tonight's occasion is not an affair of state," he continued with slight exasperation, as if to a doltish schoolchild. "It is an ordinary family supper." Only then did I notice he was clad in a tan homespun tunic as wear-worn as any of my chitons.

"Unless you calm and compose yourself, you are going to end up making precisely the unfavorable impression you are so desperate to avoid!" Tiberius admonished as I reclined beside him in our litter, breathing heavily and clenching and unclenching my hands while we journeyed to the Palatine Hill. "You will know how to behave, what to do and to say, so long as you simply are yourself!"

"I am not sure who I am anymore," I whined, my eyes closed.

Lowering his voice so the litter-bearers could not hear, he whispered, "Clytia Neronis."

His reminder of my commitment to him imbued me with a gritty resolve, to remain unruffled and amiable in the face of whatever transpired, to speak only when spoken to, and discreetly to refrain from disclosing any more information than was absolutely necessary. Although more nervous than ever, I would manage to conduct myself with grace and poise—or so I hoped.

The dwelling of Caesar Augustus I had expected to have an exterior facade of marble or at least of travertine, elaborately adorned with statuary and carvings, as befitted its owner's political and social status. The house turned out to be faced with the ubiquitous plain, dark gray stone quarried in the Alban Hills. To reduce or hopefully eliminate our chances of attracting public notice, Tiberius had us brought up a narrow alleyway to the rear of the house. Even so a gaggle of pedestrians peered around a corner at our litter, until a mounted guard drew up and bellowed, "Move along!"

The pair of armed guards, standing one on either side of the plain wood door, snapped to attention as we exited the litter. The door swung open, and a youthful ostiarius greeted us with a bow. "Welcome, Master Tiberius!" he exclaimed. "Your family awaits you and your companion in your parents' chambers."

We proceeded down a corridor, broad and lengthy. Servants bowed as we passed them. An ancillary hallway, bisecting the main artery perpendicularly, opened on the right to a staircase, and on the left to a colonnade beyond which a peristyle garden was visible. It was replete with several small trees, narrow walkways of variegated gravel lined with potted flowering plants, a pergola draped with vines shading a bench. Beside the pergola stood a double-tiered fountain, its upper basin supported by the statue of a youthful Triton astride a dolphin. The walls of both primary and subsidiary corridors were elegantly painted with a continuous pattern of architectural and floral motifs.

Presently we turned to our right down another short hallway lying perpendicular to the main. We entered the colonnade surrounding the peristyle at a corner where a long and short side of the rectangle it created intersected. At this juncture another staircase rose. Tiberius drew me by the hand up the stair, then into the nearer short side of the rectangle where an adjacent door stood open. Now fully conscious we were in the personal living quarters of Rome's foremost family, I took a deep breath and momentarily shut my eyes.

From within the room there came a cry of, "Here he is!" A woman perhaps a decade older than I, clad in an unadorned stola of pale blue homespun cloth, burst through the doorway. She flung her arms about Tiberius and kissed him repeatedly. Laying her head on his shoulder she persisted with her embrace; and as he tightened his free arm about her waist, I felt a fleeting surge of jealousy. With a broad forehead and cheeks but narrow chin she looked somewhat like Augustus. She had gray eyes, which seemed to convey a nuance of sorrow despite their sparkle. Her sandy hair was tightly curled and quite unruly, as the ringlets escaping from their bindings and cascading about her ears and upon her shoulders attested.

"Salutation upon this house!" Tiberius exclaimed as he struggled through the doorway with his two feminine appendages. We entered a spacious sitting room. It was illuminated by windows opening to the colonnade on one end and a door to a balcony on the other. At its center a settee and pair of chairs were grouped about a low rectangular table. The walls were decorated with a repetitive pattern of vines and caryatids, interspersed with panels depicting the labors of Heracles, which made me momentarily wonder whether Longus would live up to his agreement to return my **Lion of Nemea** and **Zeus Descending to Danae**. Across the floor of tan, green, and white tiles spread a thick carpet, the gold, brown, and green hues of which complemented those of the floor and walls.

"I give you Galatea Aristoclide," Tiberius continued jubilantly. Turning to look at me, he said, "My stepfather you know by reputation." His assurance I would sense precisely how to act proved true. Continuing to grasp his hand for balance, lowering my eyes and head and keeping my back straight, I sank to one knee before the ruler of the known world. As I stood upright, to my delight Augustus who was himself standing bowed as he took my free hand. "You have already made the acquaintance of my mother," Tiberius continued; and Livia from her chair acknowledged my curtsy with an ingenious warm smile. Now inclining his head toward the fair-haired woman, who in her enthusiasm had started to rock him slightly, Tiberius concluded his introductions with, "And this very strange creature, who appears intent upon crawling inside my skin with me, is my sister-in-law Antonia."

"Welcome!" exclaimed the youngest daughter of Marcus Antonius and Augustus' sister Octavia, as she extended her right hand to me. "We understand this is your first visit to Rome."

"Yes, Lady."

"Come, come now, you must address me by my name. Here, let me take your veil!"

"I was beginning to wonder if I were ever going to be free again," Tiberius murmured after Antonia released him in order to assist me with my garment.

"I shall pretend I did not hear that!" Antonia retorted as she handed my veil to an attendant serving woman. I was the only member of the gathering not clad in homespun. Now I felt uncomfortably overdressed in my chiton of linen commercially loomed and dyed despite its slightly faded and threadbare state.

Something cold and wet brushed against my left hand. It was the muzzle of a gray and white, drooping eyed mastiff whose head I began to pet. "Sannio, hence!" Augustus commanded in Latin; whereupon the dog retired to a corner, lay down on the floor, and uttered an amiable woof. They had aptly named him, I noted, for his face resembled the grimace of an actor's mask representing a buffoon.

"Sannio was a puppy barely the size of a lamb when last I saw him," Tiberius mused. Glancing about the room he inquired, "No one else saw fit to join us?" dismay clear in his tone.

"Lucius departed for Spain and his first military command the day before your arrival," said Livia. "Nero and Drusus have gone to Ad Gallinas to practice cavalry maneuvers, and taken Postumus and Tiberius Drusus with them. We tried to invite Pina but she insisted upon dining alone, lest being in the presence of Tiberius cause her profound gastric distress."

Tiberius guffawed at this second comment, and Augustus rolled his eyes. So it was from him that Tiberius had acquired the gesture. "We have rather exasperating grandchildren," he said with a nuance of irritation.

"In some respects I can empathize with Pina," Antonia murmured. Now Tiberius rolled his eyes.

"Come, come, let us dine; I am famished!" Antonia urged brightly. We adjourned to the grouping of dining furniture in a spacious alcove, created by a partition extending halfway down the far wall. A door opening directly to the colonnade allowed dishes to be brought and serviced behind the partition, thereby precluding disruption of the main sitting area. A manservant was tending chafing dishes atop a brazier. Antonia gestured to Tiberius with her head. "Do you recline at a table like the rest of us, Galatea, or sit upright like this oddball? We have provided a chair for you, but you are welcome to share my couch." The dining couches were designed to hold two people.

"I…er…am actually accustomed to the chair, but will gladly recline…if you prefer I do so," I stammered awkwardly.

Tiberius rescued me. "Remember, she is a Greek: a member of the race to which the world owes civilization. Their women sit at table."

"Then sit you must!" declared Augustus; and so the matter was settled.

Our fare was as simple as a peasant's and served almost as unimpressively. From platters the waiter placed in mid-table we helped ourselves to perch, a coarse but flavorful black bread, a salad of fresh cucumber slices—and of course to elecampane, my familiarity with which thoroughly delighted Livia. An assortment of wines addressed everyone's particular preference: Rhaetian for Tiberius, Ligurian for Augustus, Falernian for Antonia, and for Livia a light yellowish variety slightly but pleasantly astringent. She said it came from grapes indigenous to the hillsides overlooking the Adriatic Sea to the north of Ravenna. To my delighted surprise they had one to which I was partial: the white Atheri of Rhodes. No doubt Tiberius had apprised them of my preference in advance.

I anticipated conversation centering upon government affairs, and of course was dreading the possibility Augustus might afflict Tiberius with diatribe. Instead the table talk was devoted to bringing Tiberius up to date on the news—some sanguine, some doleful, some amusing—of extended family and intimate friends. Whenever the conversation shifted to a particular individual, someone clued me with an explanation like, *He is my cousin,* or *My nephew,* or *Another cousin, and a hopelessly dreary soul,* or *Her family have been retainers of Livia's forever.* One lost his barley crop, because despite advice to the contrary he had insisted upon sowing too early. Another's harvest of plums was presently proving so bountiful and driving prices so low, he could not profit from selling it and had begun distributing the fruits to local paupers. Although this gesture had won him a special acclamation from his civic council, he would have preferred the higher prices of a less prolific take—not to mention that he and his family had consumed so many plums they could no longer abide mention of the fruit, and were wondering whether their eyes were going to turn purple. Another family was rejoicing over the birth of a daughter after three miscarriages, even as they struggled with the vicissitudes of rearing a deafmute son.

Livia's mother Alfidia had become so nearsighted that she was now for all practical purposes blind; but her mind was still sharp, and she was as feisty as ever. Tiberius ought to visit her in Fondi and take me along. "She is the only grandparent I ever knew," he remarked wistfully. "All three of the others died before I was born."

Eventually Antonia mentioned Marcella had come to Rome from Marseilles with her younger daughter. They were staying with her older, married daughter. Turning to me Antonia continued, "As you likely know, I have three sisters..."

"Three sisters?" Tiberius interrupted abruptly. "Since when have you only three? You have four sisters!"

Antonia looked up, startled. "Claudia, Marcella, Prima..." she enumerated.

"And Selene!"

"Oh, of course!"

Augustus calmly interjected to me, "He is referring to Cleopatra Selene, her father's daughter by the late Queen of Egypt, and presently the wife of King Juba of Mauretania."

Meanwhile Tiberius continued his harangue. *"Oh, of course!"* he mimicked in falsetto. After a pause but before Antonia could respond he continued, now in incredulous tenor, "How by all the gods could you forget your own sister?"

Antonia blushed, began to giggle, and made an attempt at recovery. "Well...I have three sisters here in Rome...at the present time."

"Aha, so the moment one crosses the pomerium she ceases to be your sister! Only you can manage reckoning as obtuse as that!"

Now laughing heartily, Antonia buried her face in her hands and shook her head, loosening more ringlets. "Er...I have three sisters...who have the same mother as I!" she groped breathlessly.

"That Selene had the same father as you but a different mother disqualifies her as your sister? Suddenly we men are of no account to you? Have you become an Amazon? Let me see your bosom!"

He reached for the tie-string on the bodice of her stola and she slapped his hand. As he tried again she caught his hand and bit it. "Are you aware he is such a predator?" she asked me.

"Aigh!" he reacted as he retracted his hand. "Call me a predator, do you? Most certainly I do not bite. Have you taken to sleeping under furniture too, alongside Sannio? Rise up and turn your back to us. I want to see if I have grown a tail."

By now Livia was laughing as well. "You had best get accustomed to this," she said. "So they have always cavorted."

"Imagine what raising them was like," Augustus grumbled, but good-naturedly.

Antonia daubed tears from her eyes with a napkin. Attempting to stop herself from laughing she took several sips of wine; whereupon Tiberius worsened her state by muttering, "Now she is going to get herself drunk, and will have to be carried out of here horizontally!"

Simple, affable banter had never been allowed at my family's table. Oh, my brother was permitted and even encouraged to prattle on and on about my shortcomings real or concocted, ostensibly in good-natured fun and because his entitlement to his opinions was unassailable. But for me to chaff him or any other family member was an irreparable offense against the order of the universe. Aware of my sensitivity to teasing, Tiberius had throughout our relationship scrupulously refrained from doing so. Watching and hearing him needle Antonia suddenly verified a conclusion I had reached long ago, and which my family had decried as patently and perversely wrong. Teasing is a natural expression of affection, not an aggressively malicious snipe.

The arrival of the waiter with a bowl of fruit compote for dessert put an end, to the exchange and thankfully to my ruminations. "Pinarius' plums are in this mix?" Tiberius inquired as he picked through the selection on his plate with his spoon. He was referring to the relative with the excessive harvest.

"Most likely," Augustus returned. "He ended up with so many, they are probably flooding markets all the way to Cappadocia, and hopefully afflicting that simian Archelaus with enteritis."

The conversation shifted to Tiberius' aspirations. What intentions did he have for his life, now that he was a private citizen? The bestowal of succor, comfort, encouragement, and consolation upon sick folk and their families had always been his favorite philanthropy. Heretofore he had only dabbled at it, when rare reprieves from his political and military obligations had allowed him brief opportunities. Now he would make this charity his vocation, the primary purpose and objective of his life.

The comment Augustus interjected astounded me. "A new direction for you, my stepson, rising like a phoenix from the ashes of the former." Tiberius and Thrasyllus had repeatedly applied the phoenix metaphor to the changes in our lives. Was the emperor's present choice of the same vocabulary an omen? So engrossed was I in this contemplation, that I only half listened as Tiberius' continued his exposition. Suddenly I was sharply aware the conversation had halted, and everyone was looking at me. But fortunately since Tiberius' concluding words had not eluded me entirely, I knew the reason.

Tiberius had continued that in addition to providing aid to the sick, he intended to promote the careers of aspiring writers and artists. His concluding words were, "In fact the artist, whose portraits of my brother and of your grandchildren I sent you from Rhodes, is sitting right here beside me."

Livia gave a slight start and then smiled excitedly as she grasped his meaning. "YOU executed those splendid pieces!" she declared with exhilaration.

"Yes, Lady. Tiberius described each of the subjects and I depicted them accordingly."

"Livia," she corrected me firmly. Then with renewed ardor she continued, "Why did you employ a male pseudonym? We would have exulted in the rarity of their having been produced by a woman, even as everyone gives special admiration to the poetry of Sappho."

"She was very prolific; and I hung her pieces throughout my houses in Rhodes," Tiberius replied. "I feared the rumors and mischief which might have arisen, had it been noticed the artist was my ward—particularly after Lucilius Longus started marketing copies of her originals."

"That insufferable bellows is promoting her works commercially?" Augustus asked with mild surprise.

"Yes, and with remarkable success."

"The sort of endeavor he would be good at—far better than the expositions about politics with which he afflicts the senate," the emperor mused.

"And allow me to show you a medium she pursues which Longus is not yet marketing," Tiberius continued. "Have you ever beheld the art of painting on fabric?" From his pocket he withdrew a kerchief which, when unfolded upon the table, proved to be a practice piece with three partial renderings of moths. Antonia left her couch and sat down beside Livia, who was reclining on the same couch as her husband. The two women gasped and cooed over the kerchief, tracing the patterns with their fingers. Augustus rolled his eyes, then turned his penetrating gaze directly at me. "Galatea—namesake of the nymph who saved Acis, and also of my yacht," he said pleasantly. "And you hail from Alexandria. What brought you to Rhodes, and the attention of Tiberius?"

Having anticipated this question, I had mentally rehearsed the response Tiberius had recommended: that I was the daughter of a decorative artist originally from Alexandria, a pupil of the renowned Eutychus of Rhodes (although thanks to Tiberius' acknowledgment of my artistic efforts I could no longer make this claim), and an abandoned wife. But now my confidence had fled. With my chest constricted and teeth clenched, I lowered my eyes and swallowed hard. I could not lie, not to this audience. "Actually my name is not Galatea but Clytia," I began steadily enough, and then started to sputter. "I...I... employ a pseudonym because...," I took a sharp, deep breath, "...because—I regret to admit—I am a...a fugitive from my own family!" Fearing Tiberius would be wroth with me for disclosing so readily the truth that could harm us both, I buried my face in my hands. My head swam and my knees started to feel as though they had become disjointed.

From across the table I felt a hand close gently about my own left. "Come now, no need for...," Augustus began soothingly, but then hesitated. Since the beginning of our engagement we had been conversing in Greek. On hearing him ask the company in Latin, "How does one say *malaise?*" I regained my composure.

Raising my head and returning his smile, I said, "Thank you!" in the same tongue, simultaneously sighing with relief. "I simply cannot bring myself to deceive any of you."

"You speak our language," Livia exclaimed admiringly, "and fluently."

"She is a woman of innumerable accomplishments, many of which were very painfully arrived at," said Tiberius.

"Fear not to tell us about yourself," Antonia urged compassionately as she returned to her own couch. "We are well accustomed to keeping secrets; and we do not pass judgment hastily or frivolously."

Bolstered by her encouragement, yet still nervous about how my listeners would react to the story of my life, I described its early halcyon years before my brother's birth, and thereafter the obtuse and unattainable expectations and persecutions for failures to reach them. My family's condemnation of weaving and sewing elicited a vociferous response from Livia. "How perverse!" she exclaimed. "Italian parents are deemed seriously remiss, if they fail to instruct their daughters in those skills. To this day I spin, weave, and sew for pure pleasure, and without the slightest compunction. The very tunic he is wearing is my handiwork," she concluded, pulling at her husband's sleeve.

"Which is why it fits so awkwardly," he quipped.

"Oh, you are impossible!" she retorted as Augustus smiled at me slyly and winked.

Their brief exchange relaxed me. My audience had so accepted me, they felt comfortable bantering one another in my presence. Still a bit nervous but considerably more at ease, I recounted the circumstances under which Tiberius and I had become acquainted at the Academia Norenas. Everyone chuckled when I described how we had disguised our correspondence as school lessons, written in complex Latin my father refused to acknowledge was beyond his ability to read; and how Tiberius solidified my family's approval of our exchange by insisting upon sending me remuneration. "If nothing else they were correct on that count!" Antonia asserted after I said my kin had persistently referred to Tiberius as my weird Roman soldier. A reflective silence followed, while I explained the uncanny timeliness of Tiberius' intervention. Just when I had resigned myself to the inevitability of suicide or insanity or both, he provided the understanding, compassion, cheer, appreciation, respect, and hope of which my life was bereft.

I went on to describe my betrothal to Lucius Norenas, with its grim prospect of more relentless and unfulfillable demands, now from his family as well as my own. When Tiberius offered me the refuge of accompanying him to Rhodes, I felt as though I had met the Savior whose appearance the Jews aver is imminent. Now my apprehension returned. How could I expect sympathy for having abandoned my betrothed? My father had an absolute prerogative—legally, morally, culturally—to arrange marriage for me with whatever man he chose. Would my listeners think me disloyal, wanton, unnatural?

As if he had read my thoughts Tiberius interjected, asserting I was not an obstinate and rebellious child, challenging and defying legitimate parental demands. Instead I was a devoted daughter who had tried assiduously to meet unrealistic requirements, who had grieved deeply and castigated herself because she failed to achieve what she could not possibly accomplish. Imagine what consequences I would have faced once that spoiled, asinine fiancé had tired of me. Tiberius went on to describe how my family's deliberate neglect of my physical appearance and finishing had left me awkward and embarrassed in social settings, and finally how their neglect of my health had nearly cost me my life. "You can appreciate why I offered her solace, and later sanctuary," he stated in conclusion.

The thoughtful silence persisted until Livia said wistfully, "Most touching."

"Indeed," rejoined Augustus. "We were led to understand Tiberius' Rhodian household included a female ward who shared his intellectual pursuits, and from whom he assiduously maintained a proper and respectable distance. She disappeared when he withdrew into seclusion. We presumed she was one of his philanthropies. Were you and she the same person?"

"Yes, Caesar," I answered meekly, hoping he would not take offense on discovering he had been duped by the very man he had called an abysmally poor liar. The disguise Tiberius had invented for me was so effective, it had successfully obfuscated my identity to the very agents who gathered intelligence for the emperor.

Tiberius came to my aid a second time. "To keep her family and their acquaintances from recognizing her, I gave her a pseudonym and created a false personal history, dyed her hair, and engaged instructors in comportment to correct and improve her bearing. When she agreed to remain with me after

I fell into disfavor, I changed her name and appearance again—giving out I had found a husband for the first ward—lest any of my newly made enemies aspire to afflict me by hunting her down for harm. At present she is undisguised, her hair its natural color. I loathe the notion of altering her appearance anew. Thanks to her own diligence and persistence she is far more refined—more elegant and poised—than when I took her from Naples; so I am willing to take the chance her family will not recognize her. Should they, I am prepared to maintain they mistook a similarly featured person for their daughter. Nevertheless at present I am facing a grievous quandary. I long to begin showing her about Rome; but my doing so will surely start the rumors flying. Lingering public antipathy toward me could cast unfavorable attention upon her. Waiting, however, until my reputation is redeemed or at least improved may necessitate imprisoning her in my house for months."

"She requires an authoritative escort of impeccable reputation," drawled Augustus. His eyes were now fastened upon Antonia. "High time you were out and about more, my niece." While Livia smiled and nodded her approval, Antonia lowered her eyes and nodded her comprehension. Augustus resumed looking at me. "So what then is your actual name, my dear; how shall we address you?"

Again the truth got in my way. "I wish I could ask you to call me Clytia, as that is my given name and my preference. But since I must be known to the public as Galatea, to avoid confusion I suppose it is best you address me as that."

"Clytia—that beautiful blossom. Privately we shall call you by your proper name, but leave your pseudonym to public presentation by Tiberius and our publicists." Augustus spoke with a gentle frankness that imbued the matter with finality.

Augustus swung his feet to the floor, affixed his slippers and stood up; the rest of us followed suit. With a smirk Tiberius started surreptitiously to lift the back of Antonia's stola, ostensibly seeking the tail discussed earlier. "Will you ever desist?" she demanded as she snapped her skirt from his hand. Drawing her head close to mine she murmured, "Come with me if you require the necessary." Through a door in the sitting room she led me along the interior balcony. To reach the bath with latrine we passed two bedchambers and a servants' room. Such were the personal quarters of Augustus and Livia. Despite all their wealth and power, they lived very simply. With Tiberius they passed Antonia and me as we returned from our mission.

In the sitting room the lamps were lit, and an expansive gaming board laid upon the low table. "You do play, do you not?" Livia presumed as she beckoned me to sit beside her. Given our close proximity, I was glad I had had the chance to avail myself of Chloe's spearmint while visiting the privy.

"Another area where her family was remiss!" Tiberius exclaimed. "I had to teach her myself."

"Then she has been properly corrupted," said Augustus as he collected the dice. He handed me the cup. "As our newest player, you must make the first toss."

My throw turned out to be a Dog. "A fine teacher you were!" Antonia scoffed at Tiberius.

"She will improve once the lot of you stop unnerving her!" he retorted.

Improve I did, and eventually managed a Venus throw. We played merrily and vociferously. Even Sannio joined the festivities, sidling alongside each player, wagging his tail and contributing an occasional bark. In the end I finished tied with Livia in third place; Antonia was first, Augustus second, and Tiberius last. Night had fallen; and in the flickering of lamplight the figures on the painted walls seemed to come alive. Tiberius dispatched an attendant manservant for our litter; a serving woman retrieved my veil; I curtsied to Augustus, to Livia, and would have to Antonia had she not intervened with, "Oh, none of that for me! Tomorrow is the city's weekly day of respite. Business is suspended; government offices and most shops are closed; people are moving at a leisurely pace: a good time to view the sights, free of the numbers and frenetic bustle of workaday crowds. May I collect you at the second hour *[7:00 a.m.]*, before the day becomes too hot?"

"I shall be waiting with joyous expectancy."

"And may I keep this?" Livia interjected as she held up the kerchief.

"Certainly; although please bear in mind it is only an unfinished sketch cloth."

"We shall send to Rhodes for her finest renderings, Mother," said Tiberius. "And to her credit, she has yet one more achievement about which you may like to know. She is an angler."

"Are you now?" Augustus was smiling engagingly with interest.

"Oh, Caesar, I have neither baited a hook nor cast a line since I fled Naples," I hedged as I felt my cheeks turn warm.

"No matter: once an angler, always an angler. Here is something you and I shall assuredly discuss further."

Back through the corridors, now brilliantly lit with lamps suspended from the ceilings, we departed the house by the way we had entered. A pair of torches, one affixed on either side of the exterior door, illumined the guards, our litter, and four armed torch-bearers waiting to escort us through the dark streets. As soon the curtains were closed and the lurching of the litter indicated we were underway, my emotional stolidity dissolved. Anticipating Tiberius would be annoyed as I had so readily admitted the truth about myself, I buried my face in his chest and wept sorely.

"Why the chagrin? You were stunning this evening!"

"What happened to me?" I moaned, carefully keeping my voice low. "After successfully maintaining pretense all these years, tonight I went ahead and disclosed my real identity! I could not lie, I simply could not lie! Not to your family! Down the future, what will I go blathering about that I should not reveal?"

He stroked my hair. "No one can lie to them easily, not even I. But did I not promise earlier you would sense what you should or should not say? Come now: we want my family eventually to learn of our marriage and of Alcimus. Tonight you disclosed only enough to win their sympathy and respect, to explain and justify your false identity. You presented nothing to bring anger or grief or distress upon them or us. Persist with the intent of coming to the full truth, but gradually—revealing no more than what is necessary to clarify and satisfy a particular situation. Then you need not fear you will reveal more than you ought. You have more discretion than you realize, because it is becoming a second nature to you. Give yourself credit for your perceptions, and me for teaching you. And rejoice that my family has accepted you so readily. Had they found you objectionable, they would not have pressed Antonia to show you about the city. She has lived a virtual recluse since my brother's death. My stepfather would not admonish her to change her ways for someone unworthy of her attention—or of his."

I started to calm down. "It was truly a splendid evening. I was dreading one of criticism and browbeating."

"They are my kin, not yours. You know right well from our correspondence and have witnessed firsthand, how adversarial we can be over our political differences. But we do not let those disagreements diminish or compromise our affection for one another, and certainly not ruin convivial family gatherings. You never knew camaraderie with your relatives."

"The rendering of Acis rescuing Galatea I did not notice. And did you advise them of my partiality to white Rhodian wines?"

We had reached our house. In the half-light I saw him roll his eyes as he helped me from the litter. "How women manage to change moods abruptly, and recall the slightest details of conversations long forgotten, will never cease to amaze me. Yes, I sent word of your wine preference to their steward. And that picture is in an area of the house used for receiving the public. You will see it anon." As we crossed the peristyle, a meteor streaked across the sky. "By all the gods!" Tiberius exclaimed. "I wonder what it imports."

Divulging no more of the truth than what befits a specific situation is an evasion poised to mislead, but certainly more honest than dissembling or outright lying. Abed alone and uncomfortable again in the hot, oppressive, and noisome night, I wondered in bitter irony how much anger and anguish, deprecation and despair I might have spared myself had I not accounted to my family so readily and fully for every action, aspiration, purpose, and opinion I undertook or entertained—mistakenly hoping they would determine from that volume of information my motives were not misplaced. Dire for sure would have been the consequences, had they ascertained I had withheld any information.

As I deliberately—yea, forcefully—banished these considerations from my mind, I found myself wondering about the meteor we had witnessed. What did it signify for Tiberius and me? Suddenly a horrendous feeling of foreboding came over me, causing me to sit upright in bed. Was Alcimus in danger, I wondered with terror so intense I became lightheaded. Lying back down, I endeavored to acknowledge and accept the governance of Underlying Good. Now sleep overwhelmed me a great rush of blackness.

Later I became aware of torchlight flickering in the colonnade outside my bedchamber, and then of my mother's voice laughing with malevolent satisfaction! "We have found her at last! Not even Caesar Augustus with all his authority and power can protect or defend her. The crime of deceiving parents by withholding truth to which they are entitled is a violation of nature— unforgivable, inexpiable, and inescapable! We have her back; and for her perversity we shall punish her forever!" The sound of many footsteps emanated from the corridor. After all these years, after all the disguises and obfuscations and lies, my family had managed to locate me! They had brought a company of reinforcements to haul me away. Again I sat upright. I tried to cry out for Tiberius, for Gallina my attendant for the night, for the guards patrolling the house; but although I was shouting with all my might, my voice was absolutely silent.

All at once I was not sitting after all at all but lying on my back. My heart was pounding and I was short of breath. What I had thought was my mother's voice was only thunder. The torchlight in the hall was lightning and the footfalls the patter of rain. Now I did sit up in bed for sure, and sighed half from relief and half from dismay. Would the memories of my family and my fear of their discovering me ever cease? I remembered exulting at the beginning of the year, that I had managed to drive daily recollection and rumination from my conscious thought. Quite palpably and forcefully, these considerations were still pervading my unconscious mind. And why did I continue letting these memories of events so long past disturb me, when there was a portent of present concern? The feeling of foreboding returned, but not as intense and grievous as before. It was assuaged by a new strong confidence Alcimus was safe.

I dozed back to sleep, and awoke shortly after dawn to find myself slightly but pleasantly chilled. The storm had cleansed the air and reduced its warmth to a tolerable level. Peering through the window in my bedchamber, across the colonnade to the peristyle, I saw the sky was brilliantly blue. No longer self-conscious about my clothing—more concerned about concealing my visage from onlookers than about the condition of my coverings—I selected a thin yellow himation to cover the pale gray chiton newly washed. (The day before I had rejected both garments because the chiton was slightly faded in places and the himation had a small, barely-noticeable stain on its lower hem.) Four bodyguards accompanied Antonia's litter, which the bearers had brought hard up against the rear entrance to the house—not only so I could not be readily seen passing from house to litter, but because the alleyway was barely wide enough to admit the vehicle. (Now I recalled our own bearers had followed this very procedure the previous afternoon. In my state of unrest about the impression I was about to convey, I had taken no notice.) Despite the precaution a few observers gathered, whom the guards drove away.

"Since there will be no petitioners today, would you show her the Acis/ Galatea panel in the central tablinum?" Tiberius called out to Antonia as I settled into the litter beside her. This morning she wore a statelier costume: a white palla embroidered with a narrow red key over a pale reddish-yellow stola, both too well finished not to have been manufactured professionally.

She nodded acknowledgement and waved. "Have we you to thank for this glorious change in the weather?" she inquired genially. "Last night's rain was the first we have had this month." Then in a commanding but hardly unpleasant tone she addressed the escort: "Proceed!" As we departed I finally managed to glimpse the rock formation that gave our neighborhood its designation. It truly did look like the keels of ships berthed one beside the other.

Quite clearly, Antonia had carefully planned our itinerary and discussed it with the guards and litter-bearers, for they required no directives as to where to take us. First she showed me the newly completed Forum of Augustus: an immense rectangular portico of government offices, enclosing at one end the temple to Mars the Avenger. The portico was richly decorated with marbles of different colors, and painted statues of victorious Roman generals from Aeneas to Caesar the Dictator. The litter halted before the temple. Although the offices were closed, the temple was not. As we exited the litter, Antonia drew her palla over her head and closely about her face, as I did with my himation. The bodyguards gathered tightly about us as we proceeded into the temple. The ten or so visitors within drew quietly aside and exchanged whispers, but did not accost Antonia or create any ado over the presence of a member of Augustus' family. Instead they listened respectfully as with moist eyes, Antonia related the history of the temple. At the beginning of his political career, when he set out to suppress the faction of oligarchs who had opposed Caesar the Dictator and engineered his assassination, Augustus had besought the intervention of Mars and vowed construction of this temple in return.

The three statues in the apse commemorated the fulfillment of Augustus' prayer. In the center stood the god Mars, brandishing his avenging sword. To his right stood the goddess Venus, legendary ancestress of the gens Julia to which the Caesar family belongs. On Mars' left stood Caesar the Dictator, his forehead crowned with a comet. By uncanny coincidence if not by divine mandate, a comet had appeared in the sky at the very time Augustus had induced the senate to declare the Dictator a deity. The statuary group was breathtaking, as much in political and religious significance as in artistic excellence. I was intrigued to discover Augustus—calculating, opportunistic, ruthless, almost indifferently callous at times—had a spiritual side. Antonia pointed out to me the legionary standards, captured by Parthia during the disastrous campaigns of Marcus Licinius Crassus and Marcus Antonius, and subsequently recovered through the masterful diplomacy of Augustus. These were the standards Tiberius had retrieved from the surrendering Parthian commander. Tiberius was bound to inquire whether I had seen them, Antonia forewarned me. Indeed he did, as soon as I arrived home that afternoon.

As we settled back into her litter, Antonia apologized she must show me most of the sights on the remainder of our journey from within the vehicle. Otherwise we could expect to be mobbed by more spectators and adulators than her escort could manage to keep away. The people in the temple had refrained from making overtures because they were in a place of worship. She indicated the equestrian statue of Augustus in the center of his forum with a good-natured laugh. In actuality her uncle disliked horseback riding. The fatigue it induced so compromised his attentiveness, that he had often had himself carried onto battlefields in a litter.

Adjacent and perpendicular to the Forum of Augustus lay the elongated Forum of Caesar the Dictator, at its end nearest the Capitoline Hill the temple to Venus the Ancestress. We traveled next to the Esquiline Hill. There a sprawling, pleasant portico was named for Livia because she had provided the funds for its construction and overseen its design. Devoted to horticulture and features of the natural world, the Porticus Liviae included a great lapidary of gemstones, a section devoted to astronomy and the seasons, and a library of works on agriculture. In its exterior garden plots, shade trees sheltered a display of food plants. Adjacent lay the villa and formal gardens of the late Gaius Maecenas, now the property of Augustus. The gardens were open to the public on Wednesdays and Saturdays, the villa's art collection by appointment. Of course I could see both at any time I chose.

We proceeded past another structure Livia had sponsored: a great macellum or market hall, in which produce and wares could be traded regardless of season or weather. Our next destination was the Field of Mars. We halted at the Altar of Augustan Peace, standing in a grove beside the Tiber. The procession represented in relief on the structure's exterior depicts the ceremony, consecrating the ground upon which the altar was subsequently constructed. Antonia pointed out the members of her family, including those I would never meet: her late husband Nero, her mother Octavia, her infamous brother Iullus Antonius, his co-conspirator Julia and her former husband Agrippa. "Was I ever that young, and lithe?" she giggled when we came upon her own portrait. "Actually I was pregnant when this ceremony took place: the artists obscured that feature." She gestured to a nearby conical building, ringed with a planting of cypress trees. Her family mausoleum, she said. Her uncle would want her to indicate it to me. But if I did not mind, could we quit this place? It evoked too many sad memories. Within that sepulcher lay the ashes of her mother, her husband, her brother Marcus Marcellus.

Our journey took us past the Pantheon: the temple Agrippa had raised to venerate all the gods as one. *How intriguing,* I thought. *Did Augustus believe, as did I, that the innumerable individual deities whom mankind worships are really attributes of a single divinity or universal Principle—which I hold to be Underlying Good? Would he be interested in discussing this concept?* My sublime musings were short-lived; they came to an abrupt halt when Antonia precipitously drew shut the curtains of the litter. "Make way, make way!" one of the bodyguards growled.

"So farewell, a somebody!" came a taunt from the street. A second voice rang out: "If that is you in there, Caesar, will you sign me up for the bread dole?"

Then a third voice: "Behind drapes suddenly closed, eh? How well does she measure up against Livia?" Raucous laughter followed.

Antonia smiled wryly. "We are passing the Saepta Julia, where gladiatorial contests are held. None is scheduled for today. Our greeters must be the day laborers, engaged to prepare the arena for the forthcoming Ludi Romani. Since today is Saturday they are not at work, but relaxing at the adjacent taverns."

We passed a great theater. Antonia said its construction had been ordered and financed by Gnaeus Pompeius Magnus, originally the ally and later the archenemy of Caesar the Dictator. Had Tiberius told me, she asked, that his house was the former home of the same Pompeius Magnus? He had indeed, I replied.

Presently we halted. Peering around the curtains, I saw we were before the entrance to a portico of pink marble. Across the street was another theater. Antonia sent one of the bearers into the portico to announce our arrival. While we awaited his return, she explained this building was the Porticus Octaviae. Her mother had financed its construction and specified its purpose: to make the viewing of fine art easy and readily available, for the people of Rome and for visitors from other climes. The portico housed a great gallery of paintings and sculptures: originals, and carefully rendered reproductions of masterworks from elsewhere. Occasionally special exhibitions were mounted. At present, however, only the regular collection was on display. Given my special interest in art, Antonia had assumed—and rightly, I reassured her quite excitedly—that I should like to see the exhibit. The adjacent theater, Antonia continued, was that of Marcellus, named in memory of her late brother. It had been erected in conjunction with the portico for a similar purpose: to encourage public attendance of and appreciation for the dramatic arts.

The litter-bearer returned with a middle-aged man clad in a toga. "All is ready for you, Lady Antonia," he said as he helped her from the vehicle. When he took my hand, Antonia said, "Gaius Octavius Pappus, curator of the art collection, I give you Galatea Aristoclide," and nothing more. How chaste, how uncomplicated: no need to manufacture and remember the details of a false identity or bogus personal history.

Escorted by Pappus and our guards we entered the portico: a great rambling square enclosing a courtyard. At the center there rose a pair of free-standing buildings. They are libraries, Antonia said, the one devoted to Greek literature, the other to Latin. A small crowd of people was milling about the quadrangle. To accommodate us, the staff had temporarily ejected regular visitors from the gallery, which is immense. It comprises two entire sides of the square and half of the side bisected by the entrance, and took us a good hour to peruse even though we did so apace. (The remainder of the portico is devoted to offices, studios and storage.) The reproductions of paintings and sculptures were so well executed, that I could not tell what was copied unless I had seen the original elsewhere or knew it was so located. Two fabled originals I identified entirely by their reputation: Timomachus of Byzantium's *Ajax Aroused from his Madness* and *Medea Contemplating Killing her Children.* Caesar the Dictator had paid 18 talents for this dark and disconcerting pair.

As we were returning to the litter, Antonia drew my attention to the island in the River Tiber, just beyond the Theater of Marcellus. The complex of buildings thereon comprises a sanctuary to Aesculapius and the healing arts. We proceeded past the Capitoline Hill with its towering temple to Jupiter, through the presently empty Forum Boarium where livestock is traded, to the Roman Forum itself. Once again Antonia shut the curtains against the prying eyes of pedestrians, although we heard no catcalls at this place. She identified our location as the Comitium: the great square in which the populace assembles to hear the speeches of magistrates and candidates and to cast votes. Through openings in the drapery she showed me the Curia or senate house, the Niger Lapis (a small Etruscan shrine said to be the legendary tomb of Romulus), the Rostrum from which the speeches were delivered; the Lacus Curtius (a puteal enclosing a sacred spring, beside an altar upon which citizens leave monetary offerings for the health and safety of Augustus). Adjacent to the Curia stands the Basilica Aemilia, a meeting hall for financial transactions and the exchange of money. Directly beside the Basilica Amelia stands the diminutive temple to Janus: the god of passing years who has a face on either side of his head. The gates of this temple stand open in time of war. Antonia remarked (and I agreed) Augustus was justifiably proud, that his defeat of Cleopatra had brought about closure of the gates for the first time in two centuries. Unfortunately they were open at present, owing to ongoing skirmishes with invasive Germans along the Gallic border. Behind these edifices lies the forum of Caesar the Dictator. Across the Comitium from the Basilica Aemilia rises the Basilica Julia—also erected by the Dictator—in which civil cases are tried. Near the base to the Capitoline Hill lies the Temple to Saturn. On the Capitoline itself stand the Tabularium in which the public records are kept, and behind it the Temple to Jupiter.

Antonia commanded the litter to proceed toward the Palatine. We traveled through the center of the Forum on the Sacred Road. The row of buildings on our left, she said, houses the embassies of client states and independent provincial cities. The rise beyond is called the Ringmakers' Stairs, because owing to the steepness of the gradient, steps are embedded in the hillside. Its name attests to the artisans whose studios occupy the district at the top of the stairs. We passed beneath the three-passage arch honoring the triple triumph of Augustus. To our right lay the temple to Divus Julius, the deified Caesar the Dictator. Behind it stand the temple to Castor and Pollux and beside it the Regia. Once the palace of Rome's Etruscan kings, the Regia under the Republic became the official residence of the chief pontiff. Augustus, however, has never used it for either purpose, but converted it into a set of offices devoted to state religious affairs. Behind the Regia stands the circular temple to Vesta, and beside that the expansive residence of the Vestal Virgins: nuns consecrated to the service of the Roman goddess of hearth and home. Next on our right we passed the Diribitorium for the casting and counting of votes. Its great arched windows made the roof appear almost afloat in the air above the building.

The road ascending the Palatine Hill beside the Diribitorium is also embedded in places with stairs. We passed elegant mansions and gardens: for centuries the Palatine has been the traditional habitat of the Roman aristocracy. Antonia with obvious pride described a building at some distance as the Palatine Library. Planned by Caesar the Dictator and established by Augustus, it was Rome's first library open to the public.

When again we halted, the two great laurels before the gray stone facade revealed we were at the front of Augustus' residence. The trees had been planted nearly thirty years earlier by order of the Roman senate, in recognition of Augustus' special service to his country. Above the entry door—as plain and unadorned as that on the rear of the house—hung a crown of fresh oak leaves. This corona civilis, replaced daily, served the same intent as the laurels. I had heard about these honors repeatedly for virtually my entire life and invariably in a pejorative way. My mother had always insisted the senate should have ejected Augustus as a tyrant and suppressor of personal independence, instead of conferring upon him the specific and limited powers that legalized his ability to rule as the senate's special designate. Never mind the system Augustus had implemented put an end to a century of political strife and civil war.

"You have all had a most grueling morning; and I commend each of you for your excellent efforts," Antonia addressed our escort after we had quit the litter. "The six of you may retire for the remainder of the day," she told the litter-bearers. "Advise your commandant I desire the same for you four," she continued to the guards who had accompanied us. "He should contact me at once if he has any reservation. You are witness to this," she added to the pair of guards standing beside the entrance to the house.

Because it was constructed against the hillside like our townhouse in Rhodes, the ground floor of Augustus' home lay below the street onto which the main entrance opened, and had to be reached by descending a short stairway. The attendant ostiarius admitted us to a spacious and airy inner court, two stories in height, illumined and ventilated by the windows of an elevated clerestory in the center of the ceiling. The walls of the court were painted in imitation of marble and alabaster panels. To our right lay a large formal dining room with a small service pantry. Directly across the court from the entryway three reception rooms of equal size lay parallel. Each was furnished with a table and several chairs. Above these rooms extended the continuous balcony that traversed Augustus' private domain. There were no rooms in the walls to the left of the entryway, where the house lay embedded in the hill.

"Come, behold that picture Tiberius wanted you to see!" Antonia beckoned me to the central of the three parallel rooms. Adorning its rear wall was an Acis rescuing Galatea far beyond comparison to mine. It was a superb copy of a painting by Nicias of Athens, the original of which I had beheld in Alexandria. On the wall to our right was Nicias' depiction of Hermes rescuing the nymph Io from the captivity of the multi-eyed monster Argos, by lulling the latter to sleep with a boring and pointless story. The original of this I had seen in Alexandria as well. The wall to our left held Nicias' rendering of Orpheus leading his beloved Eurydice earthward from the realm of the dead, the original of which I saw in the artist's native city. The placement of all three scenes amid renderings of intricate architectural edicula replete with caryatids and fanciful cityscapes, imparted the viewer a reverential sense the artist's work was enshrined. Crimson was the predominant color of the Io/Hermes panel, azure and sea green of the Acis/Galatea, brown and ivory of the Orpheus/Eurydice.

Antonia patiently showed me the other rooms. The reception room closest to the hallway was adorned, like the court, with representations of stone inlays. Here blues and greens prevailed, instead of reds and yellows as in the court. In the farther reception room, gray, ivory, and purple were the predominant colors. Columns rising from a marble socle were interspersed with porphyry orthostates, atop which panels represented pairs of human and animal figures facing one another against an ivory colored background. Brightening the two longer walls were panels representing the story of Philemon and Baucis: the impoverished elderly couple offering what hospitality they could manage to strangers they did not realize were Zeus and Hermes, the gleaming temple into which the gods transformed their hut, the two trees into which the couple themselves were translated as they died. From the panels' style I suspected they were copies of originals by Euphranor of Corinth or one of his pupils.

My least favorite was the dining room, which I found surprisingly garish in comparison with the others. The walls were decorated with still lifes which, although thematically appropriate to the room's use, were garishly oversized. White and intense yellow predominated. The floor was paved in rose and white tesserae, rather than the black and white of the court and reception rooms. Although attractive in itself, its association with the rest of the room's décor rendered it rather raucous.

When she saw I had finished viewing the artwork, Antonia said engagingly, "Now come with me; I have something else for you to behold." Through an entryway adjacent to the rightmost parallel room, she led me into familiar territory: that long corridor traversing the length of the house. We proceeded to the ancillary corridor through which Tiberius and I had entered the private sector, and ascended the staircase to the third story. The landing opened to a narrow colonnade, beyond which a rectangular roof garden extended. It was landscaped with potted shrubs and flowering plants, benches and small statuary. A portion was shaded by a grape arbor. The colonnade delineated one of the garden's longer sides. Along the parallel side directly across the garden from where we stood, ran a socle from which marble columns rose to a horizontal entablature; this side overlooked the peristyle. To our right the shorter, perpendicular side of the garden held an enclosed room at which the colonnade and socle ended. The room had windows and a door giving onto the garden, and another door opening directly to the colonnade. The opposite short side immediately to our left, to which Antonia escorted me, ended in a raised belvedere reached by ascending a few steps.

"My uncle calls this space Syracuse, our retreat on high," Antonia declared. "He withdraws to that study," she gestured with her head to the room, "whenever he craves absolute privacy." She laughed delightedly when I gasped in wonderment upon reaching the belvedere. From this vista one could see almost the entire city of Rome without obstruction. Views blocked by the enclosed room, and by the clerestory above the public section of the house, one could acquire by moving to different sectors of the belvedere or garden. Only a small portion of the Forum and of the Esquiline region beyond were completely obstructed by the rise of the Palatine itself.

Antonia pointed out the places we had passed or visited that morning, as well as other notable sites we had missed. Months are required to acquaint oneself with every element of the city, she said. One building in the immediate foreground, standing directly before the house, Antonia identified as the temple to the Mother of the Gods. Suddenly my tedious studies of Rome's Carthaginian wars became vibrantly tangible. The worship of this goddess was initiated in Rome during her second engagement with Carthage, to fulfill a prophecy in the ancient books of the Sibyl of Cumae suggesting the introduction of the cult would turn the war in Rome's favor. The Romans duly prevailed, so the goddess remained in their pantheon. Beyond the temple extended a rambling two-story building, which Antonia said housed the offices of the imperial bureaucracy.

Near the rear of the house stood another temple, behind which was a story as amusing as reverential. In the year of Antonia's birth, her uncle had decided his house near the Ringmakers' Stairs was too cramped to accommodate his growing family. Feeling a residence in Rome's most exclusive locale better befit his dominant political position as Triumvir, he had purchased a vacant plot of land on the Palatine with the intention of constructing a new residence. Three days after the conclusion of the sale, lightning struck a tree on the property. Augustus regarded the event a portent: a message from Apollo. Out of gratitude for his own protection while traveling in a thunderstorm, during which a lightning bolt had killed one of his attendants, Augustus had acknowledged Apollo as a patron deity. To this day, Augustus still prays diligently to Apollo for guidance, inspiration, and clarity of thought and judgment. Following the lightning strike on his newly purchased property, Augustus had donated the land to the senate with the stipulation a temple to Apollo be constructed thereon. The senate in turn had compensated him with the house in which he presently dwelt.

Nearly a century earlier this property had been acquired, the house built and occupied, by the distinguished senator and orator Quintus Hortensius Hortalus. Ownership had passed to the senate after Hortensius' heirs had allowed the taxes to fall into arrears. The original residence, Antonia continued, was the section enclosing the peristyle; Augustus had added the other wings. Once again, dull and abstract academics became vital and palpable. I had studied Hortensius' writings for his rhetorical style. Now I was sitting on the roof of the very house, in which he had penned those compositions and reared the descendants who had forfeited their home.

Beyond the Temple of Apollo, at the base of the Palatine stretched the fabled Circus Maximus: site of the chariot races most Romans took more seriously than their politics. Antonia said she intentionally had not shown me this arena during our tour, because our present perspective provided a far superior view. Four chariots were on the track. One was proceeding at full gallop, a second at a walk, the other two at standstill. There were no spectators in the bleachers. I asked Antonia whether we were going to witness an actual heat of races. No, she replied; the charioteers were merely exercising their teams.

Antonia invited me to lunch with her in the belvedere. There would only be we two. Augustus and Livia were spending this Saturday as they did most: sequestered with their respective secretaries, reviewing and finalizing their schedules of meetings and appointments and other obligations for the week forthcoming. Our fare included salad greens, a loose cow's milk cheese served in a pot, and more of the black bread we had consumed the night before. The cheese and bread were particular favorites of her uncle's, Antonia said, since they were easy on his tortured digestion.

While we dined she bombarded me with question after question about my artistic inclinations and achievements. I related their chronologic history: my initial fascination with textiles, which I abandoned for painting after discovering I could not weave; my training with Timotheus; my dogged practice of my art to occupy myself during long periods of confinement; Longus' discovery of my works and of their marketability, which to the present continue to surprise both him and me; and finally how the spill Longus had caused led me to experiment with painting on cloth. How intriguing, Antonia commented, that I had returned to my original love—textiles—with a far finer and certainly unique method of embellishment than woven designs stood to offer. For this insight I thanked her.

I described my brief career as a sophista, including my commentaries on Atomism—all done under duress, in the vain hope of pleasing my family rather than to satisfy my own academic interest. Nevertheless I had this accomplishment to my credit, Antonia countered. Would I lend her the Atomism tracts to read? Impossible, I replied; for I had abandoned them in Naples. No matter, she returned; since they were published, she would have her stenographer procure them from a library or bookseller. After thanking her again, I advised the tracts must be sought under authorship by Pythia of Naples. After I had explained the history of this pseudonym, she was incredulous. I was forced to adopt an alias, simply because my brother refused to pronounce my real name. Why was he not corrected instead?

In the distance below us, the chariots in the Circus Maximus seemed like children's toys come to life. I made a number of attempts to direct the conversation toward Antonia's accomplishments and aspirations and away from my own—mostly because I was genuinely interested to learn about hers, but also because her continuing extolment of my attainments was beginning to discomfit me. Another of my mother's impositions. She had insisted I be accomplished and renowned; yet whenever I described my achievements to others she denounced me as conceited and self-centered.

Antonia kept thwarting my efforts at evasion and resuming her inquiries about me. Finally she exclaimed with a touch of exasperation, "Do you not see? I am enthralled, intrigued, fascinated to make the acquaintance of a woman who by her intrepidity eluded oppression, went on to recognize she is endowed with unique and wondrous abilities, and has since labored diligently and successfully to perfect these. Little wonder Tiberius finds you appealing. What is there to say about me? People think me extraordinary—some sort of superior being—because I am my father's daughter and my uncle's niece. Well thrust aside my genealogy, and you will find me about as remarkable as salt.

"I grew up in my mother's household with four brothers and as many sisters. Being the youngest, I always got pushed about. My father I never knew, because he abandoned my mother and our nation for Queen Cleopatra before my birth. Tiberius, his brother Nero, my brother Marcus Marcellus, and my uncle's young first cousin Marcia, were my closest friends. My own first cousin Julia tended to disdain me. My uncle betrothed me to Nero his stepson when I was in my fifth year and Nero his seventh. I suppose our knowing from so early on we were destined for one enabled us to fall in love readily as we matured. Indeed, Nero was an easy man to love: intelligent, witty and clever, generous, patient and affable, well-intentioned toward everyone. In ten blissful years of marriage we had seven children. Two were premature; one only lived four months, and another for just under a year. Since Nero's death I have concentrated my energies upon rearing our three surviving children. My elder son is of age and poised to begin military training at Marseilles, once he has completed the course of academic studies my uncle has approved for him. My daughter as you know, is married to Gaius Caesar and presently with him in Syria. My younger son, who entered his eleventh year on the Calends just passed, is a cause of great vexation because he is inane and boorish and resistant to correction."

She paused, gazed at me with a look of sadness, and sighed before continuing. "People send me petitions for various sorts of assistance and intervention, the likes of which you must have seen Tiberius receive. I winnow out the obviously preposterous, and refer some of the rest to my uncle but most to Livia. The majority come from women seeking financial assistance or clemency in legal decisions. Since Livia is so heavily burdened with matters of this nature and other affairs of state, I assist her considerably with the management of this household and of her estates and other assets—which are considerable because people bequeath properties to her as they do to my uncle. I am reclusive because I dislike social occasions intensely, finding embarrassing the obeisance and adulation with which I am invariably showered. For amusement I read avidly and am consequently rather learned; but I have never engaged in the sort of profound cogitations you have with regard to philosophy, or Livia has over political principles. I play the harp..."

"I do as well!" I interrupted earnestly.

"See, I cannot surpass you in any way! And you fish, to my uncle's distinct delight. Angling I find abysmally boring."

"Please, I do not mean to offend or compete," I said contritely. "Rather, I am delighted to find a fellow dabbler in the musical arts. I was never particularly fond of fishing, and only engaged in it because there was nothing else to do at my parents' country retreat. Also, please remember you can weave; I cannot."

"Now, now, no more groveling! I am a superior being to those hooters at the Saepta Julia but not to you. When I play my harp, Sannio howls and my uncle retreats into his aerie over there. As for your inability to weave: we all have to fail at something, Galat...Clyt...see how I am struggling with your name? Without weaknesses, my dear, none of us would be human!"

The chariots had withdrawn. An army of attendants was raking the track. The descending sun, now directly at the level of our eyes, was obstructing our view of the city but setting the Tiber aglow. "What a splendid day this has been," Antonia said as we stretched a little. "I suppose, however, I ought to return you to Tiberius before he starts wondering whether you fell into the river."

Tiberius employed precisely the same simile after Antonia's litter (with different bearers) delivered me home. I had found him in the library poring over star charts, attempting to determine what portents the meteor implied. Disaster was at hand, he said; but he had not yet ascertained its precise nature or whom in particular it was to affect. Upon detecting the impending calamity he had cast his own horoscope and mine, those of Drusus and Alcimus, of Augustus and Livia and Antonia. None of these forecasts presaged danger or imminent change. Meanwhile a note had arrived from Augustus. Having witnessed the meteor from the colonnade outside his bedchamber, he requested Tiberius ascertain what it implied.

Although Augustus had seen the meteor, his horoscope had proven unremarkable. From this information, Tiberius had concluded the forthcoming trouble was destined to affect Augustus without causing him direct harm. Although presently at work on Gaius Caesar's prognostication, Tiberius put this endeavor aside to listen—patiently and attentively—to my ebullient account of my adventure. This discourse I concluded with a hopeful question: did he think there was any possibility I might be allowed to return to that belvedere with my paints, and record the great panorama I had beheld this day? Did I ask permission, he inquired. I should know right well what the answer would be.

He immersed himself in his calculations anew. After locating a blank writing tablet I penned a message to Menon, asking him to ship me the entire collection of textiles I had left behind: those already finished with designs as well as those as yet untouched; and my jewelry also. I had decided it would be stupid to waste money purchasing new materials—and setting Roman merchants to speculating about my identity—while leaving the extant collection to molder on the farm. This task completed, I departed with another blank tablet for my studio. There I reviewed my inventory of painting supplies, listing on the tablet what was needed to create a full complement of accouterments. Upon finishing I told a passing delicium to summon Ajax. Him I asked to construct shelves for the walls, easels, and wooden racks for the drying of textiles—like those he had fashioned for me on Rhodes. This task, he assured me, he would undertake with relish.

While I was conversing with Ajax the delicium returned, and told me Master desired I should join him in the library. The ashen appearance of Tiberius' face confirmed my assumption he had found his answer, and that it was quite grievous. In quiet tones he asked me to close the door. After I was seated he somberly declared the stars had revealed both Gaius and Lucius Caesar appeared to be in exceptional peril.

Breathless with concern, I reached across the table and took each of his hands in one of mine. Was he certain? Yes, he replied mournfully. He had repeated his astrologic calculations, hoping in vain to find an error. Turning thereafter to Thrasyllus' numerological procedure, he had forecast outcomes for the journeys the princes were presently undertaking—Gaius into Eastern remotes and Lucius to Spain—and found these calculations corroborated the stellar findings with dire results. He must inform Augustus.

To keep the discovery from our servants, he had me transcribe the letter. Dictating slowly, choosing his words carefully, he elucidated his determinations. This warning was strictly an offering of courtesy to Augustus and his two endangered grandsons. In stringent adherence to astrological ethics, Tiberius had not sought the precise natures of the impending calamities, or whether the princes were destined to die. He harbored no ill will. Nor was he about to exploit his predictions to engineer a revitalization of his own public career. In conclusion he averred his ward respectfully craved permission to frequent the Palatine housetop, for the purpose of drawing and painting its views of the city.

We barely touched our supper, which was roasted kid anyway: a viand I do not really dislike but to this day remain ambivalent toward, because my family had invariably served it in a loathsome stew recipe Euethia venerated. That night I slept fitfully, repeatedly reminding myself to trust the governance of Underlying Good as I wrestled with concerns about the meteor. Clearly enough I could perceive how adversity of any nature—illness, death, disgrace, a decision to rebel or to abdicate—befalling Gaius or Lucius or both could affect Augustus without compromising his own safety and wellbeing, by forcing the emperor to alter his arrangements for the succession. But Tiberius and I had witnessed the meteor as well; and our horoscopes presaged no imminent harm. How did the dangers impending for Gaius and Lucius stand to affect us? Eventually I satisfied myself with the conclusion a rumor might arise, attributing to Tiberius the imminent disasters whatever form they assumed—especially with his reputation as a political rival to Gaius still fresh in public memory. But how did it all affect me?

Owing to my troubled night I slept late into the next morning. As she helped me dress, Alcmene showered me with good wishes for my birthday. On showing me the dish of candied apricots from Alexandra and her daughters, Alcmene apologized profusely for not providing a gift of her own. She had no need for remorse, I assured her; by now she should know I did not expect birthday presents from my servants. The apricots were more a peace offering than a recognition of my anniversary. Descending the stairs, I found the atrium and first floor corridors hung with garlands, and banners of cloth in a variety of pastels. Demetrius' son Nomius informed me Master was with a caller in the reception room.

I asked this young servant to accompany me to my studio. Here we found Ajax hard at work on the shelving I had ordered. After handing Nomius the tablet with my list of needed painting supplies, I told him to take it with a satchel and a denarius to the markets and purchase as many items as he could with the money. As the youth was leaving Tiberius arrived with his caller, who proved to be Longus with my *Lion of Nemea*—or so at first I thought. Longus reported the painting had been unpacked the very morning following our arrival. His chief copyist was so taken with it, he had set right to work creating reproductions. With an initial copy to serve as the model for subsequent versions, the original could now be returned.

After Tiberius and Longus departed I set the tableau on a newly completed easel, and stood contemplating it for a time. It had all the right gradations of color, all the right details. Still, there was something amiss that I could not readily identify. Ajax presently left off his labors and came over to stand beside me. "Lady, I have been eying this ever since you placed it here, and am convinced it is not your original painting."

His words settled the matter for me. Grabbing the tableau, I told Ajax to accompany me. Together we hastened to the library, where Longus was regaling Tiberius with some wordy story. Casting etiquette aside—the impropriety of a woman interrupting a conversation between men—I burst out, "Senator, this is not my painting but a very clever forgery! Ajax here will confirm my assessment!"

Longus challenged me. The lighting in this house was far different from that in our house on Rhodes: surely here was the reason the painting seemed unfamiliar. Suddenly an inspiration struck me. I remembered a chip in the wood surface of the palette had left a small gouge, which I had filled in by applying successive layers of paint. Although the patch was not apparent to the eye, by running a finger over it one could discern a difference in texture from the rest of the painted surface. Furthermore in the woodgrain on the backside of the tableau, a pattern resembling an almond became visible when the tableau was held at precisely the correct angle. One by one the four of us—Tiberius, Longus, Ajax, and I—slowly and meticulously slid our forefingers over the region where the gouge should have been. No one was able to detect a variation in the texture. Next we examined the reverse, tipping it in every possible direction. No almond emerged.

Longus grimaced and his eyes shone with determination. He grabbed the tableau, slipped it under his left arm, and with his right hand seized my wrist. "Come along!" he said, and hastened half dragging me toward the atrium. "You as well!" he commanded Ajax.

"Accompany them!" Tiberius cried out to Alexandra who was passing.

Not having a veil I covered my face with my hands, until Alexandra and I were inside Longus' litter and she had drawn shut the curtains. For the sake of propriety and to keep from overburdening the bearers, Longus did not join us in the vehicle but with Ajax strode alongside it. While we were traveling, Alexandra withdrew a kerchief from her bodice. Nervously she inquired if I should like her to bind the kerchief about my hair; the cloth, she assured me, was clean and unused. Although grateful she did as much as she could under the circumstances to preserve my modesty, I did not thank her but only nodded acceptance of her solicitation. She was a servant performing her duty, I told myself, and I did not want to give her pretext for assuming she could resume her efforts to dominate me.

Our journey ended at Longus' Gallery of the Four Winds, near the Macellum Liviae. As he rushed us through the showroom I again covered my face and right well: through my fingers I noticed the manager and three patrons staring. We entered a large studio, where four copyists were at work on reproductions. Longus approached the oldest—a man of moderate build with brown hair starting to gray—who was copying my *Zeus Descending to Danae*. Thrusting the lion tableau before the man's face, Longus demanded "Where is the original, Myronides?"

"This is the original, Sir," the copyist asserted with pert confidence. "See, it is signed but not numbered."

Longus shut the door to the showroom and cried, "Everyone, gather around!" The other copyists left off their efforts and approached. Two youths entered from an adjacent room. "Mistress Galatea, kindly elucidate your discovery to this company!" Longus continued. "She is the artist's pupil, and so knows his work better than any of us." As I described gouge and almond, the color drained from Myronides' face. He stared at the floor and chewed his lower lip. When I finished, Longus took the *Danae* from its easel, handed it to me and demanded, "Is this the original?"

I needed some unassailable proof, some characteristic of the original or lack thereof, which I could cite as I had with the *Lion of Nemea*. On the backside of this tableau, the grommets on either side and the cord extended between them for the hanging of the piece were all new; there was no tarnish, no embedded dust. The boreholes for the grommets showed the paleness of newly exposed wood. It had not occurred to me to look for this feature on the *Lion* tableau. Nevertheless when I commented that this hardware on the *Danae* was too new to be that of the original, Longus destroyed my argument. "We regularly replace the grommets and cords on all our originals, to insure they do not break from age and cause the pictures to fall from the walls." Disappointed and worried, I continued to turn the piece in my hands. At length I recalled a blood stain on the top edge, from when I had pricked my finger on a splinter. Although I had subsequently planed the edge before painting it, some of the stain had remained embedded in the wood. I requested a scraper and carefully stripped the paint from the area where I remembered the stain, taking care not to disturb the surface of the wood. No stain appeared.

"Without question this is another copy!" I declared resolutely.

"An explanation, Myronides, NOW!" Longus bellowed.

Continuing to stare at the floor the copyist began to speak slowly, and not insolently but mournfully, remorsefully. "Senator and most gracious Lady, I confess to having let egotism get the better of me. I allowed one of our gallery's especially avid and high-spending patrons flatter me into perpetrating a fraud. So like the originals were my copies, this patron had insisted, they could be substituted for the originals in the showroom without detection. In return for the price of copies, I have over the past year shipped the patron six originals by Eutychus of Rhodes." After a pause he turned to one of the youths who had entered from the adjoining room, and said, "Fetch the tableau intended for Lucius Norenas of Pompeii."

Although I did not lose consciousness, I saw the room spin about me and felt my knees give way. Ajax and Alexandra caught me; Myronides leaped up from his chair and helped me into it. "Stand back! Give her air!" Longus barked at his staff, and they retreated. Across the room, one of the other copyists poured water from a pitcher into a tumbler which he carried to me. "Do you know this Norenas?" Longus demanded.

Fortunately I had sufficient presence of mind to reply, "Senator, I swooned because I was overwrought about the loss of my teacher's artwork." After taking a few more minutes to compose myself—and dreading what I might hear—I asked Myronides, "Which of Eutychus' originals beside the *Lion of Nemea* were sent to this Norenas?"

"*Scylla and Charybdis*, a still life, a riverscape with deer by the water, *Daedalus and Icarus*, and three trees atop a berm."

Closing my eyes I nodded coolly without saying anything more, for I had become almost intoxicated with relief. On Rhodes there remained what I considered a better *Scylla and Charybdis*, and representations aplenty of still lifes and the Guardian Trees. The riverscape and the *Daedalus and Icarus* were fantasies easily reproduced. The two presently missing, in fact, I had painted to replace earlier versions sold in Alexandria. The youth returned from the packing room with the other *Danae*. There was no need to remove the paint obscuring the blood stain to prove the piece was original. All I did was show the company the grommets and hanging cord, discolored from tarnish and dust. Myronides burst into sobs as he ran from the room.

Longus cast an aggravated glance about the rest of the company. "Does everyone here understand the gravity of this matter?" he demanded agitatedly. "The artist whose works have been pilfered has grounds for filing suit against us. Our enterprise could be ruined."

"Perhaps we should tell the patron Norenas he was sent the originals by mistake, ask him to return them and accept the copies for which he paid," ventured the youthful packer who had retrieved the *Danae*.

Hardly could I admit to knowing right well that Norenas, having obviously adopted his father's shifty methods, could not be expected to cooperate, particularly when confronted with the truth. But the packer's suggestion set me to thinking. Hoping Norenas was still as stupid and gullible as when I had known him, I said, "Senator, your young man here has offered a worthy proposition. Can we discuss it further in private?" I did not want to take the chance another member of the staff might advise Norenas of the plan that had begun to unfold in my mind.

"Young Myronides, go look after your grandfather," Longus ordered the packer. Ironically, the youth who offered a solution to the theft was the perpetrator's own grandson. "The rest of you, return to your tasks," Longus continued. "Come hither," he said, and directed me to an office.

"Not for your ears, my Alexandra" I said gently. She had begun to follow us for the sake of propriety. "Senator Longus can be trusted to respect my honor. We shall leave the door open." Alexandra stopped short and curtsied, but continued to peer through the doorway while Longus and I retreated out of earshot.

"Senator, why not see if we can contrive to swindle the swindler?" I said in an undertone. "Let the patron be sent the unnumbered copy of the *Lion* tableau, with a letter from Myronides averring this piece to be the original and the genuine tableau a replica someone accidentally neglected to number. Let the letter continue with a request the patron surrender the *inferior version* to the messenger, so it can be restored to the gallery before the artifice is discovered. You might even cite the gouge as evidence of supposedly lesser quality. He can keep the other pieces. Superior versions of those I have, or aspire to create. If we request them as well, he might become overly suspicious and refuse to cooperate."

"Clever, most clever," Longus returned. I shall demand Myronides' collaboration as a partial remedy for his transgression. Meanwhile I hope to console you with yet more royalties: 145 aurei. As the purse is surely too large and heavy for you and your woman to carry, I shall have it delivered to Nero's domicile."

While we traveled homeward in Longus' litter with the authentic *Danae*, Alexandra inquired how I was feeling and whether upon our arrival she should seek out Chloe to attend me. No, I replied: I now felt well recovered. Once again I deliberately neglected to thank her for her solicitation without feeling remiss; however I did acknowledge her gift of the apricots as I felt ethically bound to do so. For the first time in our acquaintance she smiled, and with a self-effacing shyness as though she considered my compliment unexpected and undeserved.

To Alexandra I gave no further thought, as my contemplations centered upon my former fiancé. Without question he had embraced dishonesty. For this propensity I loathed yet forgave him, as there was no question it was mimicry of his father. Nevertheless I marveled that he, whom I had despised as crude and incapable of grasping the simplest of intellectual concepts, had developed an appreciation for art—my art in particular! What an uncanny coincidence! How ironic that he, of all people, should confirm my philosophical notion that if Good underlies all, there must be elements of goodness in every one of us no matter how despicable the outward appearance. So why after all these years of trying, could I still not detect a single iota of good in any member of my own family?

We lunched on turtle stew. Since it was one of my favorites, Tiberius had Scourus the blackamoor cook prepared it especially for my birthday. Although I thought Scourus' recipe distinctly inferior to Phoebe's, I said nothing about this and consumed the version before me with gusto and gratitude for the gesture. Tiberius, however, remarked the deficiency in an undertone, lest the attendants carry the news of our disappointment back to poor Scourus. After listening to my account of what had transpired at the gallery, Tiberius commented with an approving smile that my proposed remedy showed I was learning the ways of the scorpion. He found it quite amusing that I had beaten Norenas of all people at his own game.

Our meal over, Tiberius escorted me to the master suite for a purpose I hardly need mention. The day, after all, was the anniversary of our marriage as well as my birth. In the center of the sitting room floor a large, low object lay under a cloth. Tiberius removed the covering to reveal a rectangular wood planter box with four heliotropes of different colors in full blossom. With this gift, he declared, he aspired to relieve my disappointment with our lackluster peristyle. I assured him he had succeeded. He continued that he had considered presenting me with a pet, but was unsure whether I would like a dog. He was concerned a cat would either be absorbed into, or pick fights with, the clowder the household already had. Actually I was glad he had refrained, I replied, as no animal could ever replace Leo in my affections.

As he led me to the bedchamber I unbound my hair; but before I could disrobe he bade me sit beside him on the edge of the bed. On the wall opposite the window, where they received good illumination and could be well seen from the bed, were my six lovers' vignettes. Tiberius explained he had ordered Menon to send them from Rhodes following our departure, so Longus would not discover them aboard the Murex. They had arrived the preceding day while I was out with Antonia; however Tiberius had deliberately refrained from telling me, as he wanted to surprise me with them on my birthday. Originally he had planned to have Ajax hang them in my presence. Then reconsidering, he decided to take advantage of my absence at Longus' gallery to have them hung while I was away, and present them to me already in situ.

His manner changed abruptly from jovial to serious. He took both my hands in mine. While I was with Longus a message had arrived from Livia, confirming endangerment for Lucius Caesar. A courier of the imperial post had delivered a dispatch from the commandant of the great military complex at Marseilles. The message reported Lucius had fallen gravely and perhaps fatally ill. While en route to Spain, Lucius' monotreme had docked at Marseilles in the afternoon of Thursday just past. Immediately the prince had gone ashore to call upon his cousins Lucius and Gaius Antonius. On Friday he addressed the curia in the morning, then spent the remainder of the day visiting places of interest and greeting the populace. Following a gala banquet in his honor at the garrison Friday evening, with a coterie of companions he had set out again into the city for a night of pleasure. During this excursion he collapsed, and was carried to the post infirmary.

Alexias our former servant now Lucius' valet, attested the prince had been intermittently feverish since Wednesday their third day at sea. The garrison's top physicians, along with the most learned members of the medical faculty of the University of Marseilles, had worked through the night, and were still endeavoring to check the now virulently raging fever. Their efforts were meeting no success. By Saturday dawn, when the commandant penned his communique, Lucius had become delirious. The medical authorities concluded he had precipitously aggravated his condition by gallivanting about when he should have been resting.

Freeing my hands, I drew my arms about Tiberius and felt him enclose me. "Your skill at vaticination leaves me in awe," I said softly, tenderly. "And although I am barely acquainted with your family and fear I may sound as though I aspire to intrude, I nevertheless pity them with deepest sincerity as if their bereavement were mine as well."

He kissed my forehead, then my lips. "Thank you for both commendations. And never, never mistake your innate compassionate empathy for intrusiveness. The former keeps you naturally from engaging in the latter."

From under the pillow he took a small parcel wrapped in white linen, and a letter tablet bearing the imperial seal. "Open the message first," he said.

In his own hand the emperor had written,

> Imperator Caesar Augustus and his family to our Clytia, greeting.
>
> You are welcome to frequent, whenever you wish, the familial sections of our home. You may visit the public reception area as well, unless business is being transacted therein. To evade the possibility of intruding during such usage and to minimize attention in general, we request you utilize the rear entrance to the house at all times. Do not enter the apartments on the first floor. These are presently occupied by the heir to the realm of Commagene, and by two members of the royal house of the Cimmerian Bosporus, all of whom are being educated in the ways of Rome. The reason for your restriction from this area you assuredly appreciate.
>
> Given the present crisis facing our family we have concurred, that to offer a gala celebration for your birthday as if nothing were amiss would be hypocritical of us and unfair to you. We beg your indulgence, and hope you will not think trivial this little token of the esteem and affection we hold for you.

Livia and Antonia had affixed their signatures below the message.

"When did you tell them about my birthday?" I queried as I unwrapped the parcel.

"Yesterday I appended a postscript to the letter you transcribed, before affixing my signet. You had already quit the library for your bath."

The gift was a compendium, also written in Augustus' calligraphy, of anecdotes and observations and recommendations to ensure successful and enjoyable angling. I was astounded. "He would send me a private, personal notebook as a gift?" I inquired wide-eyed. "And after only having met me once?"

With a gentle laugh Tiberius replied, "He keeps a number of copies, and maintains a master to which he makes additions and emendations. Nevertheless, that he sent you a version in his own handwriting and not that of a stenographer shows he has considerable regard for you."

"What an honor! He barely knows me!"

"Over the years he has perfected an ability to assess people quickly yet accurately at first acquaintance—as has my mother. No doubt Antonia shared with them the impressions she garnered of you during the time you spent together. Like you, I am extraordinarily pleased and relieved. We Romans celebrate the birthdays of mothers and sisters, wives and daughters, of grandmothers and granddaughters, aunts and nieces, but virtually never the anniversary of a retainer who may be a mistress. That my family commemorated yours is a wondrous sign they accept and approve you—not simply as my companion, but for whom you are: for your own character, your intrinsic self."

"Those words are a gift beyond comparison," I returned, deeply affected. "I have not wanted to admit, even to myself, that I have been desperately anxious about your family's opinion of me—uncertain whether their cordiality was genuine amity or mere social nicety."

The little book was arranged in categories: sea fish, pond fish, river fish; appropriate baits; the best and worst weather for catching specific types of fish; solutions for deterrents to successful fishing like wind, algae, waterfowl, dolphins and—the nemesis I had encountered—turtles that scare off fish in order to steal bait from hooks. Enraptured I perused, barely heeding Tiberius who made me alternately stand and sit as he undressed me and himself and turned down the bedcovers. As promised, Chloe had placed in the wardrobe a covered box, containing a satchel of meticulously wadded balls of lambswool and a flask of laser seed oil. On the shelf beside the box she had set a stack of wiping cloths. (In my own bedchamber she had installed an identical store.) Tiberius spread out one of the cloths to protect the bed, anointed himself with the oil, and saturated a wad of lambswool, all the while I continued to read. Finally he snatched the book away, skittered it across the floor, handed me the pessary and half growled, "If you do not take this, I shall thrust it into you myself! Hnn,…" he continued, now with anticipative tone and lascivious smile, "…how erotic that would be!"

Finding myself in libidinous agreement, I reclined upon the bed propped on my elbows, raised one knee to separate my legs a little, and exclaimed, "Proceed!"

That Tiberius' family had recognized the occasion at all, during this time of distress over Lucius, moved me immensely and bolstered my confidence they had accepted me. Consequently I began to yearn for a suitable reason and occasion to reciprocate their benevolence. As we were returning to our bed—now to retire for the night—I realized such an opportunity was right at hand. "Tiberius, might it be appropriate for me to prepare an artistic memento commemorating Lucius?" So I ventured as he was putting out the lamp. "Granted he has not yet perished; but if he does, I should like to have ready a tribute to present. I can always alter or discard it if he rallies. What a morbid suggestion: I loathe myself for making it."

"Wonderful insight and recommendation, my Lioness!" he returned as he lay down beside me. "Given the present circumstances, the suggestion is practical and entirely appropriate. A tribute of such nature cannot help being morbid: your natural compassion makes you recoil from it. Already I have begun work on an elegy in honor of Lucius. Otherwise I would have composed an epigram for your birthday. Will you forgive me?"

I drew my arms about him. "Why need you ask?"

For much of the next day I pondered a suitable artistic tribute to Lucius, and hoping all the while we would receive word his illness had abated. Coming across my unfinished tableau of the eagle that had perched atop our Rhodian farmhouse, I found my answer. I decided to represent Lucius as Ganymede, the prince of Dardania whom a great eagle transported to the heavens, there to join the immortals as the cupbearer of Zeus. The concept worked splendidly. The eagle we saw on Rhodes I had depicted with its body horizontal and wings extended vertically upward—poised to take flight. This rendering enabled me to create a credible sketch of a human figure, lying prone along the eagle's back and clinging to its neck. This figure I represented looking upward, beyond the eagle's head at a golden light, which emanated from the upper corner of the tableau as though from the heavens. The small size of the figure precluded the need for a high level of accuracy in Lucius' physiognomy. Never had I seen him, of course. The portrait I had created for Julia several years before had been derived from Tiberius' recollection of Lucius in his twelfth year. Nevertheless from my memory of that tableau, and from the statues of Lucius I had observed on my whirlwind tour of Rome with Antonia, I could mentally age his features and so conjecture his present appearance.

While working on this project, I found myself pondering a conundrum. Thrasyllus had maintained the eagle's appearance on our Rhodian prophesied the authority of Rome coming to rest upon our domicile. How could this come about, I wondered, now that Tiberius had withdrawn from public life? "Speculation is a waste of mental energy," he admonished me, after I recounted my musings during our afternoon rest. "Only the unfoldment of events will uncover that secret. Better to concentrate our attention upon issues at hand, which are plenteous and vexatious enough."

Several days later we received word that Lucius had perished on the day immediately following my birthday *[August 20, 2 CE]*. His remains were going to be cremated in Marseilles and then transported to Rome. The most notable men of Marseilles and military tribunes from the garrison were to serve as honor guard. Tiberius and I began working sedulously—he on his poetic **Lament for Lucius Caesar** and I on my Ganymede tableau—from early morning until the flickering of lamplight strained our eyes. We wanted to complete the preparation of our tributes before the cortège arrived. Tiberius resorted to the Palatine the following afternoon, to receive Augustus' intentions for the funeral: everyone's place in the procession and the paeans to be delivered. The emperor insisted Tiberius join the rest of the family in meeting the cortège at the city gate and escorting it to their mausoleum. This gesture immensely pleased Tiberius. His participation would be a highly conspicuous demonstration of reconciliation with his stepfather and with Lucius' brother Gaius. Tiberius accordingly set Chloris to work fashioning mourning garments for him: a tunic of solid black and toga the hue of slate.

The ship carrying the cortège docked at Ostia six days before the Calends of September *[August 27]*. On that same day I sent Augustus my completed Ganymede tableau. He responded with a note thanking me profusely, and expressing hope I would come forth to view the funeral as an observer. On the morrow, military legates bore the cortège to the barracks outside the city walls. Tiberius passed that night on the Palatine, to join his family the next morning in the procession to the mausoleum. The ceremony took place at the fifth hour *[10:00 a.m.]*. The senate had proclaimed a day of mourning with all regular business suspended. Longus and his wife Rutilia—a plump, red-haired woman every whit as loquacious as he—came to collect me half an hour before, as Tiberius had asked them to escort me. I donned a dark blue chiton Chloris and Leda had managed to finish just in time for the occasion, and over this garment draped Phoebe's shawl. No one paid our party any attention, for the crowd was subdued and somber as befitted the circumstance.

We arrived to find the procession already at the propylaeum of the mausoleum, the funerary urn on a pedestal in its center, and members of the family grouped along each side with military honor guards standing behind them. A murmur did ripple through the onlookers when, after Augustus and then an auburn-haired youth about the age of Drusus had each delivered a short eulogy, Tiberius stepped forward to read his **Lament**. After he finished, two young women escorted a husky pubescent boy, as he carried the urn into the great tomb with the family following. The crowd dissipated as quietly as it had assembled.

Longus and Rutilia invited me for luncheon, which I declined. At home I picked at a single slice of milk-soaked, cassia-dusted bread. Owing to the mournfulness of the event I had just witnessed, I had little appetite. Not expecting to see Tiberius for the remainder of the day, I retired to the library to write in my journal. In midafternoon, however, while I was contemplating calling for an early bath, Alcmene brought me a note in Tiberius' hand: would I please repair the Palatine and bring my harp? With a surge of new energy I leaped to my feet, and told Alcmene to accompany me to my suite. There with her assistance I washed my face, cleaned my teeth, and had my hair rebound.

The stocky, gray-haired manservant who met me upon my arrival at the Palatine introduced himself as Caesar's steward Diodomedes. He escorted me to a grand sitting room in the private sector on the long side of the peristyle, to the immediate right of the stairway we had ascended for our supper with the family. Everyone there present seemed more tired than grief-stricken, with the exception of one of the two young women who had escorted the urn into the mausoleum. She was sitting on a settee, weeping bitterly. Beside her were the other young woman, and the boy who had carried the urn.

Augustus smiled wearily but cordially as I entered. "After spending the last three hours receiving senators, bureaucrats, military officers, retainers, relatives seen once a year or less frequently, we are all desperate for intelligent conversation and nerve-soothing company. Thank you for coming here this afternoon to provide us with both."

"My sincerest of condolences to each of you," I replied earnestly as I curtsied.

"Little comfort are the condolences of a harlot!" the weeping girl blurted from her corner.

"Pina!" Augustus ejaculated. Now I realized the girl was his younger granddaughter Agrippina. She had blue-gray eyes like her grandfather's although not as piercing, and sandy hair like Antonia's albeit not as curly.

Managing to remain unruffled, I said—and with genuine compassion, I am pleased to write— "She is understandably overwrought, and has my special sympathy."

On hearing my words Agrippina stormed out of the room, wailing and clenching her fists. The other girl followed her in silence. The boy—brown haired and eyed with merging brows like Augustus'—came over and stood before me breathing heavily. Red-faced, teeth bared, hands outstretched with fingers spread like tentacles, he appeared as though poised to strangle me. He was nearly as tall as I, broad shouldered, thickly boned, and quite muscular. Becoming frightened I cringed, and crossed my arms before my face in defense. Augustus and Tiberius rose abruptly from their chairs, from a settee Drusus and the auburn youth who had delivered the eulogy. The youth seized the boy by one wrist, and with the words, "Come, let us comfort your sister!" led him out of the room. This utterance revealed my assailant was Marcus Vipsanius Agrippa Postumus, Augustus' youngest grandson.

Augustus himself closed his eyes, sighed, and asked in a voice heavy with wearied exasperation, "Are you all right?"

"Yes, Caesar," I replied breathlessly.

"You have my most profound apologies for the inexcusable conduct of my grandchildren. Let me caution you. Never be alone in this house: keep an attendant with you at all times." Tension was mounting in his voice. "Did you... uh...uh,...alas, you must excuse me!"

He bolted from his chair toward a doorway, Livia and Diodomedes hastening after him. We heard a gag, a retch, the spatter of liquid, and then the closing of a door. Now I became far more anguished than all the while Postumus had threatened me. Lightheaded, my heart pounding, my breath short, I made my way to the very chair from which Augustus had fled. There I sat down trembling, clenching an armrest with my right hand and my harp with the left. Why, I was wondering with exasperation, after all the vomiting I had done during my pregnancy, did even so much as overhearing the process still unsettle me? Even Sannio noticed my distress. He emerged from his corner and sat facing me, his tail striking the floor with soft thuds.

"Are you taken ill?" Antonia inquired in a worried tone, half rising from her chair.

Tiberius came over and started to rub my back slowly. "She has never been able to abide seeing or hearing another person vomit," he explained. "Here, surrender me this before you drop it," he added as he extracted the harp from my shaking hand. I closed my eyes and breathed deeply, fighting to regain my composure.

"You upset our dear guest with your puking, Uncle!" I heard Antonia chide.

Opening my eyes I saw Augustus standing before me, greenish pale but otherwise unperturbed and actually jovial. He took my chin in one hand and cleared his throat. "Forgive me if I distressed you," he said solicitously. "A chronically nervous digestion causes me to vomit frequently. You could never endure living with me. Often I wonder how Livia stomachs it."

Some moments of silence ensued while everyone grasped the bad pun. Then Tiberius rolled his eyes; Drusus pointed his thumb downward as if at an unsatisfactory gladiator; Antonia exclaimed, "Really now, Uncle;" but Livia, who was emerging from the doorway, merely smiled.

The humor helped calm me and I sighed with relief. "Recovered?" Augustus inquired, now smiling ingratiatingly. I nodded and returned his smile. "Livia and I can empathize with you. She dreads and recoils from fire and I from lightning as ardently as you do from vomiting. It is a tribute to her inestimable courage, that on hearing a fire has broken out within the city she purposely travels to the site, there to encourage the efforts of firefighters and offer consolation and assistance to the victims."

"I can endure being present at a fire, so long as I do not feel it is threatening to engulf me," Livia remarked as she approached the company.

Augustus released my chin, backed away and seated himself on the settee Agrippina and her companions had vacated. Livia joined her husband, and Tiberius settled back into his chair. Diodomedes arrived with a tumbler which he handed to Augustus. "Warmed goat's milk with a dusting of cassia," Augustus explained. "Settles and revitalizes." *The very remedy that Ialyssian physician had recommended for my nausea,* I reflected. "Now what I was endeavoring to ask you," Augustus continued as he sipped the draught, "before this other unpleasantness arose," (another chorus of groans and hisses emanated from the family) "is whether you were able to witness the obsequies."

"Yes—they were beautiful and touching. The people standing near to me were silent and somber with respect and empathy. For certain all Rome is sharing your grief."

"Your attendance and comments are deeply appreciated."

The young woman who had accompanied Agrippina reentered the parlor, approached Augustus and curtsied to him. "Pina has fallen asleep," she said quietly, "and Nero is mollifying Postumus." From her words I determined the auburn-haired youth was Antonia's elder son. "If it please you, I should like to depart to my own house and there seek the consolation of my mother."

"Go, my child, our hearts with you," Augustus replied, "and our thanks for attending Agrippina." He returned his intense gaze to me. "She was Lucius' betrothed: Aemilia Lepida, descendant of the great statesman Lucius Cornelius Sulla, and distant cousin to that treacherous mountebank who married and corrupted my elder granddaughter. Thank you again for your representation of Lucius as Ganymede. Do I have your permission, allowing Longus to produce copies for sale?"

"But of course; it is my gift to you, Sir, for you to do with as you please," I answered, bewildered by his request.

Raising his eyebrows slightly he regarded me with the piercing, admonishing, yet paternal, look of a knowledgeable mentor cautioning an ingénue. "The design remains yours forever. It should never be reproduced without your consent, no matter who owns the tableau upon which it is represented. Never forget this point of law, my dear; it exists to protect such unique talents as yours."

"Thank you," I said frankly, returning his gaze with what I hoped was a look of gratitude.

"Six grandchildren have been born to me," he continued, his tone now rueful. "One died in infancy, his loss particularly poignant because he was Livia's grandson as well as mine. Now a second has been taken, whom I had destined to play a significant role in the future of the Roman state as well as this family. Of those who remain: he who is of highest importance, because I have designated him to succeed me as head of both state and family, is worrisome because his physical health is fragile. Another languishes in exile, a convicted felon like her mother—who of the two children I begot had to be the one that survived!" This final phrase he uttered with a sudden snarl of sarcasm, and a flash of anger in his brilliant eyes. "Mother and daughter alike are flagrant transgressors of laws my jurists and I meticulously designed to ensure the stability of our society, and for which I labored long and arduously to obtain passage by the senate."

He lowered his eyes; and his manner once again became poignantly morose. "My two youngest grandchildren, as you have seen, are of excitable and potentially violent temperament. Is it any wonder I suffer from agitation that disrupts my digestion?" He looked up at me once again. "Tiberius and Antonia tell me you are an accomplished harpist. Livia is quite correct: your endowments appear limitless. We ask that you now play for us, and with your music assuage the penetrating thrusts of anxiety and sorrow."

Tiberius handed me my harp. As I tuned it Sannio began to howl, sending a subdued ripple of laughter through the company and prompting Diodomedes to escort the mastiff from the room by the scruff of his neck. "See, neither your playing nor mine aggravates him, but simply the instrument's sound." I said to Antonia. For perhaps an hour I played and sang as I had years earlier for Alexias: dance melodies and folk songs and lullabies I had learned on Rhodes, and the few I remembered from my childhood. I was fervent with gratitude and joyous peace; for despite what Tiberius had already told me, only now at this gathering did I fully come to recognize and actually feel quite tangibly his family's acceptance of me. While preoccupied with their own bereavement of monumental proportion, they had commiserated with my peculiar peccadillo about vomiting and set to heartening me with compassion and humor. Augustus had confessed to me his anguish about his grandchildren. The emperor himself, whose private secrets were inextricably intertwined with those of the state, felt comfortable sharing them with me. To my immense satisfaction my mood infected my music, resulting in a performance elegant and vibrant and yet sufficiently quiescent to befit the occasion. As on that Rhodian afternoon with Alexias, my present audience sat in pensively reflective silence while I played and for some time after I had ceased.

The red-gold blaze of late afternoon sun had begun to creep through the windows from the peristyle. Diodomedes whispered something to Livia, who nodded and then revealed the intent of the steward's utterance. "Tiberius, will you be remaining for supper?" she asked.

"No," he replied, "I feel it is best we return home. This day has been grueling for us all." He rose to his feet, approached my chair and, taking my hand, helped me stand as well. Of his decision I was glad because I remained without appetite, although throughout the day I had hardly eaten anything.

"I quite agree," Augustus said. Leaving his settee he ambled toward the door through which he had fled earlier. Turning to face the company he continued, "In fact I hereby bid everyone good evening as I retire early, tomorrow being another day of routine business." His countenance was clearly drawn with fatigue. Tiberius bowed and I curtsied. Augustus nodded wearily, but then brightened. "What do you think of my fishing manual?" he inquired.

"Most informative, and a pure joy to read." I answered.

He said nothing, but returned that disarming smile of his before disappearing through the doorway. Now Antonia spoke. "With Uncle I concur. It is time I checked on my Tiberius, to see what sort of unimaginable predicament he has gotten into." She came over and hugged me. "Thank you for your superb music."

"Diodomedes, all will sup in their respective quarters." Livia said. The steward bowed and departed. A serving woman brought my shawl, which Antonia helped me don. Tiberius and I repeated our obeisances to Livia, who in return hugged us each. Drusus bowed as we took our leave.

"Watching you this afternoon was ineffably gratifying," Tiberius remarked while I bathed. "You were poised and gracious, noticeably at ease and affable; and my family was equally congenial toward you. There is no longer any question: they have accepted you, not only with tolerance but with affinity and affection. You quite obviously reciprocate their feelings."

"Only with Thrasyllus and Aka have I felt as comfortable and appreciated as I did today," I returned, "the hostility of Agrippina and her brother notwithstanding. Their antipathy did not disturb me—not only because I realized they were grief-stricken, but because everyone else was extraordinarily amiable, caring and...well, accepting. Those were highly personal reflections your stepfather shared with me this afternoon."

"Such is the manner in which members of any family ought to behave toward one another. You are fast becoming one of us, Clytia. Now: what did you think of my *Lament for Lucius Caesar*?"

"Will you first promise not to drown me in here?"

"Was it that dreadful?"

"Labored, stilted, and rather pompous. You are far better at composing epigrams than elegies, my beloved."

"For certain. My prose is equally lugubrious."

"Your family appreciated your effort notwithstanding."

"Oh, I never presumed they would not. And by allowing me to read the piece in public, my stepfather provided an overt affirmation of reconciliation between us."

...the manner in which members of a family ought to behave toward one another... fast becoming one of us... Echoing through my consciousness as I lay abed that night, these phrases induced a singular excitement and caused sleep to flee. For the first time in my life I no longer felt myself an outcast loved only by a fellow outcast. This family—the most prestigious in the known world—had freely offered me their affection and had accepted mine in return, without the condescension, criticism, and ridicule with which my own kin had always afflicted me. I felt rejuvenated, reborn, with a sense of belonging and unconditional acceptance I had never known. Even Thrasyllus, for whom I had utmost esteem and affection, had often made me feel defensively obligated to account for thoughts and actions—not in any malicious sense, but as a jejune pupil deferring to the enlarged understanding of my mentor.

...I never presumed they would not. Here was another proof of the underlying empathy between Tiberius and his family. Mine would have castigated me mercilessly—claimed I had embarrassed them beyond reparation—had I read aloud a composition of literary inferiority. But the affinity of Tiberius' family for him seemed unremarkable, in comparison to what they had extended me. He was one of their own. I was an interloper: a stranger not even a member of their race, and possibly presumed a courtesan as well. Yet they had welcomed me

without hesitation or stipulation or cavil. Perhaps this was the specific import of the recent meteor for Tiberius and me.

The week following Lucius' funeral burgeoned with activity and discovery. The very next morning I repaired to my studio, and began recording the impressions of respect the funeral had left upon me: the dense yet orderly assemblage of spectators, the muted colors of their garments appropriate to the occasion, the solemnity in the facial features of the man who had stood next to me. Presently a noisily jubilant Longus arrived with my original *Lion of Nemea*. Norenas had fallen for my ruse, I reflected with a certain smug satisfaction; although I was actually far more relieved to have the painting back than to exult over the success of the deceit. A startling revelation awaited me. Longus had sent the elder Myronides to effect the exchange, his purpose being to keep Norenas from realizing Longus and the remainder of the gallery staff knew about the pilfering arrangement. On this mission, Myronides had discovered it was not Norenas himself but his wife, who had conceived the artifice and insisted upon its implementation.

Later that afternoon I expressed my assumption that since Norenas was wed he was no longer trying to find me—if he had endeavored to do so in the first place. Tiberius responded with a warning that immediately dissolved my euphoria. Such complacency I should sedulously avoid. Although married, Norenas may still aspire to locate and harm Clytia Eupistide in retribution for her having abandoned him. Moreover should he discover Galatea Aristoclide exposed his wife's artistic chicanery, he may seek vengeance for that. "The wisdom of an accomplished politician," I commented in return, reflectively and gratefully. For once instead of castigating myself over my naiveté, I rejoiced at having received this precaution.

After spending the following morning on our veranda, peering at the city around apartment buildings, I finally mustered sufficient temerity to return to the Palatine rooftop on the morrow. Nausicaa I brought along to help carry my paint chest and palettes. We did not encounter a single member of the family: only guards and servants who recognized and saluted me accordingly, plus several household cats. On that first day we brought a satchel of biscuits and cheese. Taking note, Diodomedes advised we had no further need: his staff would provide us with any victuals we desired. Nausicaa sat silently in the belvedere and exulted in the views, while I filled two palettes with the colors and shapes of the city.

"Everyone is busy, busy, busy: my mother and stepfather with affairs of state, Antonia with the children and the house, the guards and servants with their duties," Tiberius exclaimed when after my second visit I mentioned the lack of encounters. "Once the Ludi Romani start they will be all the busier, attending religious ceremonies and performances and games. Hardly a life of ease my family lives. You caught a glimpse of it while I was regent and then imperial legate to Rhodes; and that latter was merely a token magistracy. Convivial gatherings are few and far between—and fondly cherished—because opportunities for them are so scarce. Antonia usually dines with the young members; but my mother and stepfather grab their meals whenever they can manage, and often while pursuing other matters: preparing for meetings or religious observances, evaluating petitions, dictating correspondence or speeches—even when bathing or dressing or traveling in their litters."

Tiberius became busy as well. It was customary—in fact virtually obligatory—for Roman aristocrats even of private station to devote their mornings to receiving callers. Tiberius proved to be no exception. During forenoons I scrupulously avoided the atrium area, while he greeted a coterie like that Augustus had described: relatives, retainers, well-wishers—even the political enemy Lucius Scribonius Libo, who behind a facade of amity was clearly gloating over Tiberius' enforced withdrawal from public life.

Petitions and petitioners arrived as well. One appeal came from the wife of a praetorian on behalf of her father. He had served as a centurion in the Germanic campaigns of Tiberius' brother, and had witnessed Nero's fatal accident. At present this veteran was slowly recovering from an extended illness, which his physician had anticipated he would not survive. The news of Tiberius' recall had delighted the veteran, leaving him jubilant and invigorated. The daughter respectfully inquired whether Tiberius might consider visiting her father; or finding that objectionable, send a letter or make some other small gesture to further the invalid's morale. Tiberius gave considerable thought to an appropriate response and elicited my opinion. To send a gift, or to visit the veteran in person, might create speculation Tiberius was endeavoring to rally a faction. To send a mere letter, however, seemed coldly dismissive. My suggestion Tiberius compose the man an epigram elicited a kiss to my forehead.

Another plea Tiberius chose to honor came from a bricklayer. A pair of bullies had duped his daughter of five years into consuming red squill. The ensuing ordeal had ravaged the girl's digestion. Her father solicited from Tiberius a monetary loan, to defray the devastating and escalating expenses of medical treatment. He promised repayment in full, no matter if this took the remainder of his life and he must render some installments in kind. Considering himself unworthy of direct audience with Tiberius, the petitioner had delivered his request to Canulus our ostiarius. As a pledge of honesty and sincerity he had left his trowel, scarifier, and iron stamp for impressing his insignia on his bricks. Tiberius was pensive and reflective as he examined the tools, turning each carefully in his hands. At length he called out to whatever servant was within earshot of the office to fetch Chloe and Demetrius. In quiet tones instructed them to carry the tools to the bricklayer's home, assess the little girl's condition and establish a treatment program, arrange to check on her regularly, and pay any costs associated with her recovery.

I took great delight in viewing the religious procession that opened the Ludi Romani: the festival honoring the god Jupiter and the citizenry of Rome. The day was that preceding the Nones of September *[9/4]*. There had been festivals on Rhodes, of course. Having to forego these after removing to the farm left me feeling starved in a way. Moreover, I had never witnessed an Italian pageant. My mother and her aunt had always decried these events as unnecessary and dissipate frivolities—a squandering of money, a waste of time, diversion of attention from the administration of government and transaction of business. Never mind the celebrations usually took place only in mornings, and regular transactions resumed later in those same mornings and in the afternoons. And never mind our family was hardly affected by government or business matters any festival disrupted or postponed.

Tiberius insisted I take Ajax and Androcles as my bodyguards and Alcmene as my attendant. Being seen with servants already known as members of his household would reveal my association with him. As I had anticipated, he opted to remain at home. After all he loathed public appearances, and avoided them whenever his presence was not absolutely required. Although the Forum was but a short walk from the house we left directly at dawn, to insure finding a place to stand with an unobstructed view. We managed to ensconce ourselves in the portico of the Basilica Aemilia.

The procession originated at the base of the Capitoline Hill and proceeded along the Sacred Way, through the Forum toward the Circus Maximus. There first approached an army of lictores, each bearing on his left shoulder a fascis: that bundle of elmwood rods enclosing an ax and bound with a strap of red leather, signifying the authority of a magistrate or priest. There followed the Flamen Dialis—the chief priest of Jupiter—whom I easily identified by his saffron-colored toga and white conical hat. The woman beside him I presumed was his wife the Flaminica. Behind them walked six senatorial magistrates, distinguished by their purple-bordered togas. Tiberius later explained they were the aediles, responsible for the keeping in repair the public buildings and streets of Rome and for the exhibition of games.

Augustus followed, riding in a gilded chariot drawn by four white horses. He wore a purple toga embroidered with gold stars. Tiberius described this as the toga picta, worn by the principal pontiff on ceremonial occasions. Accompanying Augustus on foot was a group of senators: the college of pontiffs, Tiberius said, of whom Augustus was president. To them was entrusted the superintendence of all religious observances and rituals, whether public or private. An ox-drawn cart followed the pontiffs, holding a bullock, a pig, and two cockerels: the animals to be sacrificed for consecration of the event. At the end of the procession, acolytes escorted images of various Roman deities, carried on small litters or drawn in carts. Tiberius later identified the acolytes as representatives of the various trade guilds.

Ambling homeward with my small retinue, I considered the pleasant satisfaction I had derived from being jostled amid that crowd. To evade the possibility however remote of a member or acquaintance of my family recognizing me, I had kept my himation drawn tightly over my head and about my face to conceal my hair and as much of my visage as possible. Some people had smiled at me while others had sneered. Some had politely stepped aside to allow me place, while others had brusquely shoved ahead of me. Some had stared speculatively and exchanged whispers, while others had looked at me briefly and turned away with obvious indifference.

In the end, nobody had paid me a high level of attention. Even the most extensive of encounters had been little more than passing glances and nods. Basking in this anonymity as if in a warm glow, I recalled having the same feeling during my travels to large cities like Ephesus and Alexandria where I was certain nobody knew me. A twinge of sadness, however, crept into my reverie as I considered that Tiberius could never enjoy obscurity no matter how privately he lived. My appreciation for his love of solitude deepened significantly. Now to my dismay the satisfying warmth of contentment escalated into the burning heat of anger, as recollections of my mother's attitude toward my recognition intruded into my thought. She had demanded I become famous: a household name. Yet once I had started to achieve acclaim in academic circles, she and her aunt had berated me incessantly for exhibiting frowardness unbecoming a woman and for seeking notoriety to satisfy unabashed self-centeredness.

My anger promptly dissipated when upon arriving home, I discovered and immediately accepted an invitation from Antonia. She asked me to accompany her with her sisters to a theatrical performance, which was being presented as part of the Ludi Romani at the Theater of Marcellus four days hence. Afterward we would take a luncheon at her sister Prima's house. Antonia would collect me at half past the third hour *[8:30 a.m.]*. The remainder of the present day and the morning of next, I passed sketching and painting my recollections of the procession. What I aspired to capture in colors and shapes, was the jubilant, almost flippant vitality of the celebration in contrast to the staid solemnity of Lucius' funeral.

Marinus, the praetorian prefect Scapula, and Vescularius Atticus newly arrived from Rhodes, began harassing Tiberius with an invitation to accompany them to a forthcoming gladiatorial exhibition. Fights to the death between men and other men or between men and wild beasts, was the one form of Roman public entertainment I dreaded the prospect of having to view. Then Tiberius relieved my anxiety. He explained that gladiatorial combats, mock hunts, and wrestling matches were restricted to the eyes of men. The doomed performers were felonious slaves serving convictions.

On the morrow I repaired to the Palatine. As before we encountered only servants, guards, and cats; but from the belvedere, Nausicaa and I observed a heat of chariot races in the Circus Maximus. Briefly I wondered whether Antonia was attending the event without having invited me. With a surge of self-annoyance and dismay at having entertained such a sense of self-importance I put the consideration out of thought, rejoiced over the prospect of accompanying Antonia to the theater, and exulted in being able to view the races from my present vantage point. The competition was dynamically colorful—a painter's delight, as the three palettes I filled attested. The stadium was bedecked with streaming banners, the teams and their drivers with vibrant trappings. The spectators in their variegated clothing created the impression of a multichrome liquid overspreading the white bleachers.

The next day, while Tiberius was at his gladiatorial show I returned to the Palatine roof once again, for what proved to be a disappointing and ultimately distressing visit. There were no chariot races or even exercises. Warming weather was starting to create a haze, blurring the outlines and colors of the city. At departure Nausicaa and I were proceeding along the ground floor colonnade toward the exit to the transverse corridor, when we encountered Agrippina and Postumus coming toward us. I halted, lowered my eyes, and curtsied; Nausicaa followed my example.

As I straightened, Agrippina spat in my face. "If I ran this household instead of Livia and Antonia, a harlot like you would never be allowed to set foot inside the entrance!" she snarled.

More surprised than agitated or angered, I found myself verbally stymied, unable to respond. Hardly did I wish to retort with what might be construed a breach of etiquette; these were, after all, the grandchildren of the emperor. Nausicaa wiped my face with her kerchief. Her action allowed me to compose myself and find my tongue. "Your grandfather himself invited me to sketch and paint here," I said calmly and steadily. "I am your former stepfather's ward, and not a harlot. Never in my life have I solicited or offered sexual favors in return for money."

"My grandfather allows you your way because he lets Livia rule him! And no matter what you call yourself, you still are what you are: the filthy whore for whom Tiberius abandoned our mother! Insolence becomes your sort. Do not dare try to defend or justify your sleazy, parasitic self to my brother and me ever again; and do not try to befriend us. Just stay clear!" Abruptly turning her back to us, she proceeded on her way. I worried her brother might assault me as he had on the day of the funeral; but after glowering at me for a moment with teeth once again bared, he turned and hastened after his sister like a puppy catching up with its master.

"So intent was she upon execrating me, she did not notice how she belittled her grandfather with her insinuation he lets your mother dominate him." So I commented at supper, to Tiberius and Marinus who had invited himself.

"I cannot offer an accurate assessment of her character, or of her brother's," Tiberius mused. "Both were small children when I departed for Rhodes; and I have only peripherally encountered either since our return.

"Do you think she will turn the rest of your family against me?"

"She is not going to change their opinions of your person, which we already know are favorable. The potential danger from her hostility, is that it may prompt my stepfather to decide I have too visible a companion. No matter how steadfastly we maintain you are my ward, gossip-mongers are going to insinuate you are my mistress. You know I loathe the prospect of making you housebound again, especially in Rome with all she has to offer. If we return to Rhodes or retire elsewhere so soon after coming here, we stand to create the impression I failed to achieve reconciliation with my family. My stepfather is certain to support you. The manner in which Agrippina treated you is egregiously unfair, unbecoming a young woman of her position, unacceptable for any member of our family, and sets a dreadful example for her brother. When you are with Antonia tomorrow, be sure you relate all this to her."

"Everyone is her sworn enemy, actively plotting her undoing," Antonia responded to my description of my encounter with Agrippina. "Unless she decides you are her friend. Then all at once you are a fellow target of those sworn enemies. That is why she is so protective of her younger brother. She got the notion of Livia as dominatrix from Julia her mother, and from her grandmother Scribonia—my uncle's former wife, who always thought she deserved Livia's position and acclaim. Pina is convinced the discovery of Julia's adultery with my brother, their plot against my uncle, and the consequences they suffered, are all somehow Livia's doing. That my uncle places high value on Livia's political insights and seeks them daily heightens Pina's suspicions. She is jealous, moreover, because my daughter is married while she is not, and thinks Livia is behind this as well. The marriage was purely a matter of state and did not imply favoritism at all. My uncle wanted to send Gaius to his embassy with the dignity of having a wife.

"As you noticed, young Marcus Agrippa whom we call Postumus has quite a temper. This is very distressing to my uncle, because the tutors and philosophers he has engaged to calm Postumus have met with little success. Of course Agrippina makes their task all the harder by urging her own insinuations upon her brother. You might manage to befriend or at least keep him at bay by talking about angling, which is an overwhelming passion for him. Otherwise it is best you heed Agrippina's warning and keep your distance as much as you can. This matter I shall discuss with my uncle for sure. Moreover I shall speak with my elder son, to whom Pina is betrothed. He will stop her from harassing you and with ease, since she worships the very air he breathes. That he is Livia's grandson, and that Livia urged their match, does not seem to perturb Agrippina at all," she added with a giggle. "You have not actually been introduced to my sons, have you? High time you were." We had reached our destination. "When our excursion is over, I shall bring you to the Palatine for you to make their acquaintance. I must warn you, however: you will likely find quite dreadful Tiberius Drusus my younger. He is so offensive that Livia—his own grandmother—cannot abide being in the same room with him."

How can young Tiberius' mother and grandmother be so pejorative of him? I wondered to myself.

Antonia's sisters proved as affable, candid, and unaffected as she. Prima so strongly resembled the images of her father I had observed over the years, that on first seeing her I had to suppress a startle. Like him she was tall and broad shouldered, heavily boned, with hair as tightly curled as Antonia's but nut brown in color. After our initial exchange of greetings she promptly explained her sobriquet. Her real name, of course, was Antonia. Upon the birth of her younger sister, her mother started calling her Prima because she was the first

Antonia. Prima's body was slightly distended in the middle stage of pregnancy. Of this she spoke forthrightly as well. Sixteen years after bearing her husband a son—the notorious Gnaeus Domitius Ahenobarbus whom Gaius Caesar had thrown off his staff—Prima suddenly became fecund again. After delivering a daughter two years ago—and now approaching her forty-first year—she was expecting yet another child. Quite incredible, did I not agree?

Prima introduced her two older sisters—the daughters of Octavia by her first husband—who were as diminutive as Prima was statuesque. Marcella the elder—petite and lithe, with dark eyes and hair streaked with gray—was reserved with a touch of melancholy. And appreciatively so, considering the ordeal with which her husband Iullus and cousin Julia had afflicted her. The younger sister Claudia—equally short of stature but stockier than Marcella—had the latter's same dark eyes; however they sparkled more effusively.

The Theater of Marcellus was by far the largest edifice of its kind I had ever seen. It was overlaid with the same pink marble as the Porticus Octaviae, and appointed with statues of great Greek and Italian playwrights. The production was a well-polished and hysterically funny rendering of *Pseudolus*, the lighthearted satire on marriage by the renowned Titus Maccius Plautus. The subsequent luncheon consisted of salad greens, slices of cold roast fowl, and plain barley bread. Quite clearly, ordinary fare was the preference of the imperial family.

Since Antonia had described me to her sisters in advance of our encounter, they already knew me as Tiberius' ward, the sophista Pythia of Naples, the decorative artist Eutychus of Rhodes, a harpist, and an angler. Speaking for the company, Marcella echoed the sentiments Antonia had expressed to me during our luncheon on the belvedere, declaring the four sisters found meeting a woman with unusual achievements a refreshing delight. When they gathered by themselves, Prima said, all they shared were complaints about their husbands and children.

All laughed sympathetically when Antonia described my brush with Agrippina; and Claudia reassured me Agrippina treated everyone else the same way. Pulchra—Claudia's daughter by her first husband—was among the exceptions whom Agrippina considered friends: hence Agrippina was insistent Claudia was endeavoring to undermine the girls' relationship. Antonia passed about my practice cloth with the painting of moths. After the gasps and adulations had subsided, Claudia inquired whether I was willing to produce a wedding veil with a painted design for Pulchra when the time came for her to be married. When I declared that I would do so with pleasure and honor, she replied that I should consider the commission a pleasure but not an honor, since she by no means wished me to regard her as my superior.

When we arrived at the Palatine, Antonia led me to the peristyle section, then through the colonnade spanning the backside of the house. There were no rooms along this corridor, which served only to connect the two longer sides of the peristyle rectangle. We proceeded up a corner staircase to a set of rooms on the longer side, lying across the peristyle from the rest of the house. This was the apartment Augustus had prepared, for Antonia and her husband Nero Claudius Drusus to occupy when they were in Rome. They had never acquired a separate house of their own, having lived for the most part of their married life in Lyons the capital of Gaul. There Nero had served first as military commander and later the provincial governor.

We entered the sitting room. Seated at a table strewn with open scrolls were Drusus, the auburn-haired youth who had attended Postumus on the day of Lucius' funeral, a younger boy with the same auburn hair, another boy about the same age but dark and swarthy and wearing a skullcap, and finally a tall gray-haired man of about Augustus' age. Drusus, the swarthy boy, and the man rose and stood beside the table. The auburn boy remained seated with a vacuous look on his face. The auburn youth bounded over to us and bowed. Antonia said, "Galatea Aristoclide, my elder son Nero Claudius Drusus Germanicus."

As he straightened, I discovered how disarmingly engaging he was. His hazel eyes twinkled with a hint of mischief, and his smile conveyed the sense he was overjoyed to make one's acquaintance. "Warmest welcome to the lady about whom we keep hearing the most wondrous reports!" he exclaimed. Gesturing to the table, he now spoke in a quietly respectful tone. "Our tutor of history, Titus Livius of Padua." This introduction made my heart beat rapidly with excitement. As I curtsied the renowned historian bowed.

Brightening anew, Germanicus continued the introductions. "My first cousin Drusus Claudius Nero you already know." My stepson bowed, smiling. "Tiberius Claudius Drusus is my little brother." Young Tiberius continued to stare vacantly until Germanicus commanded, "Stand up and bow!" The boy clambered awkwardly to his feet, upsetting his chair in the process. As he bowed he broke wind, long and loudly. Antonia glanced at me with a pained look; Germanicus closed his eyes; Drusus shook his head slowly; the swarthy boy appeared to sigh. Taking no notice or at least unperturbed by these responses, Tiberius began to stare again and to drool from his mouth as well. Drusus started to fan the air with one hand. From off the table he picked up a kerchief and hurled it at young Tiberius. The boy mopped his face with a questioning hesitation, as though struggling to remember and implement extraordinarily difficult instructions.

Germanicus introduced the swarthy boy. "Our friend Marcus Julius Herod Agrippa, prince of Judaea, who takes lessons with us." Before this grandson of Herod the Great, and nephew to the three rulers currently ruling the now divided Judaea, I began a second curtsy. Antonia noticed my motion, and with a precautionary glance and wave of her hand forestalled it. Herod Agrippa bowed to me. Then Livius said something to the two boys. Promptly they set about closing and gathering the tablets and scrolls with noticeable diligence, until young Tiberius fell over the chair he had overturned.

"Recall what I told you earlier," Antonia murmured to me.

"We were studying the victories of Hannibal and his brother Hasdrubal during the second Carthaginian War, and how the strategies of Scipio Africanus eventually reversed them." Germanicus continued vibrantly. "Be on your guard, Lady Galatea! Having heard you are a redoubtable scholar, we may hunt you down to join the ranks of our tutors!"

"Which I shall with delight," I answered, by now knowing right well to omit the word *honor*.

Antonia took my hand in hers and smiled warmly. "Thank you again for accompanying me today." Once more I curtsied to Livius; all the pupils except young Tiberius bowed again; I started for the door. As I exited the room, I overheard Antonia say to Germanicus in a somber tone, "I need to have serious words with you about Agrippina."

Upon returning home, I found my textile collection had arrived from Rhodes that very afternoon. What abysmal timing, I thought. Had this cargo come a day earlier, I could have shown Antonia and her sisters a well-finished example of my painting on fabric instead of that practice piece. Briefly I considered sending a completed item to Antonia—or to Livia, especially since Tiberius had promised her one. Nevertheless I decided to wait. Sooner or later an opportunity to display my handiwork in its finer forms must present itself. Belaboring the matter in the meantime might result in my being deemed a nuisance and a braggart.

Since I was not home to direct him, Valens had had the stevedores deliver the three trunks to my sitting room. Consequently there was barely enough space for me to turn about. I sent Nausicaa after menservants to remove the trunks to my studio. Menon had duly sent the report I had requested. To my relief it was placidly unremarkable. Everyone was content and well. The weather was salubrious. The impending harvest was not going to produce noticeable profits, but definitely yield enough to sustain the occupants of the farm through the forthcoming winter and pay the annual taxes on the property.

I was planning to start unpacking the collection the next morning, until Tiberius scuttled my intentions over breakfast. Still recovering from the speculative glances, the obvious whispering, the contrived and obsequious greetings, and simply from being on display at his gladiatorial exhibition three days earlier, he was not in the pleasantest of moods. As a show of loyalty to his family he must definitely attend the public events on the final day of the Ludi Romani, as these were dedicated to Caesar the Dictator. Three days thereafter the two-day celebration of Augustus' birthday would commence, and Tiberius must be on hand for this as well. In the meanwhile, to evade the possibility of being dragged off to another event not incumbent upon him, Tiberius was going to follow his parents' recommendation and take me to visit his grandmother. I should have my women assemble sufficient clothing and accessories for ten days, and promptly. Rather a long time, I thought, to impose upon an elderly lady in her eighty-second year; but I said nothing.

Since the journey would take the better part of a day, Tiberius wanted to depart as soon as possible. Drusus was going to accompany us. Tiberius intended to spend this sojourn counseling his son about the responsibilities which would become incumbent upon him when he came of age in a few weeks. If Drusus wanted to attend any of the forthcoming Ludi Romani events he was assuredly out of luck, since a father's orders are irresistible. So again I reflected without making any remark.

Because Tiberius had not yet acquired a carriage of his own, Livia lent the use of hers. We were taking Gallina and Valens as our attendants. Tiberius said I must make certain to bring my harp and a sizable supply of painting materials; whereupon the misgivings I was entertaining faded before excited anticipation. Although I had grown up in Italy, my only travels within her borders had been those innumerable trips across the uninteresting coastal plain between Naples and my family's retreat in the Campanian hills, and the recent hasty journey by night from Ostia to Rome.

We had to depart before dawn, since carriages and wagons are not allowed on the city streets of Rome during daylight hours. Drusus was duly aboard the carriage, his valet in the servants' wagon. I assumed we were going to use the Appian Road: the broad, javelin-straight military artery designed for the rapid conveyance of troops and ordnance from Rome to Brindisi. It runs directly from Rome through the Alban Hills and Pontine Marshes to Terracina near the coast, and then turns inland directly to Fondi. Instead, the itinerary Tiberius selected took us back toward Ostia, and then southward along the seashore.

While we traveled, Tiberius outlined to Drusus the types of contracts into which a Roman youth would be expected to enter after coming of age: ownership and maintenance of property; marriage and hence guardianship of the persons and properties of wife and children; and patronage, whereby a stronger individual agreed to promote the interests of a weaker in return for specific services. This is critically important to politicians as the method whereby loyalties are established. For a time I listened with genuine interest, but eventually found my attention diverted by the splendid scenery. The coastline we traversed is a veritable zigzag of rocky jetties, which extending into the sea formed coves and small bays between them. At times the roadway traversed the edges of high, sheer cliffs; at others along low, grassy berms or sandy dunes rising barely a cubit above the level of the beach.

After Ostia we passed two seashore towns: Laurento and Lavinium [Pratica di Mare]. Between them, farms and villas lay on either side of the road. By midafternoon I was hungry and—more significantly—in need of a latrine. Not to worry, Tiberius reassured me after I whispered my condition: we were about to halt at Anzio. Presently we turned through a gate in a high wall and down a drive in a small park, to a sprawling, rectangular villa surfaced with pale pink stucco.

While the building itself was large but unimposing its locale was not, for it stood on a rolling berm overlooking a cove. To the south the berm curved outward into a long and broad jetty, with high white cliffs descending precipitously into the water and surmounted by a small lighthouse. All rooms opened to a capacious central nymphaeum, lit from above by a circular clerestory. Each room gave out as well onto a broad exterior colonnade. This feature, conjoined with the physical orientation of the house, provided every room except for those in work areas with a view of the sea. Besides a sitting room, two bedrooms, bath and latrine, our suite had its own dining room and pantry and two servants' rooms. The interior walls were adorned with paintings and mosaics representative of the locale: seashore and harbor scenes, varieties of fish and crustaceans, mythologic sea creatures like the hippocamp, sea legends like the birth of Aphrodite.

The peristyle held a fishpond, surrounded by small statues and potted plants. At its far end this garden opened to an expansive veranda, from which stairs embedded in the berm descended to the beach. The potted shrubs, statuary, and the pergola which provided the veranda with decoration and shade, were carefully placed and manicured so they did not obstruct the perspective on the sea. The same held true for the ornamental bushes and trees planted about the perimeter of the house. Further to preserve the aesthetics, the stable and barracks for the guards were tucked away toward the mainland in a copse of trees. This villa was one of his family's favorite retreats, Tiberius remarked. Here we were going to spend the greater portion of our sojourn, and impose upon his grandmother for only two days before returning to Rome.

For the next rapturous week, when not in Tiberius' arms I sat in the villa's library, perusing classics from its ample collection while he expounded to Drusus the details of contract law. With them I strolled along the beach; or else I sat on the veranda painting, sketching, practicing embroidery (a skill I had begun to neglect in favor of painting on fabrics) or strumming my harp, while father and son conversed about topics many and varied. These sessions revealed Drusus' avid interest in architecture.

At other times I left father and son alone—as on those afternoons when I watched from the veranda as they cavorted in the warm cerulean waters, unable to join them because I had never learned to swim; or on the morning Gallina and I and a manservant attached to the villa explored the pleasant town of Anzio. A resort for wealthy Romans, it boasted a racetrack, amphitheater, theater, art gallery, shops with exotic and expensive wares—all diminutive versions of those found in Rome. The harbor held as many pleasure boats as fishing vessels.

The best natural model the place had to offer was the promontory at the end of the cove. The berm itself was a treeless, grassy monotony. On the very first evening of our stay, I started to record the colors of sunset on the clouds, the cliff, the beach, and the water, and continued on the evening thereafter. The changing hues I found evocative of metals and represented them accordingly: the warm glow of gold and copper, the green and tan of bronze, the blue and gray of steel, the black of iron. By day I reviewed and refined the piece, working rapidly and sedulously from the inspiration the scene evoked. By lunchtime on our fourth day at the villa, I had a completed tableau.

Later that same afternoon I decided with equally ardent determination to depict the villa itself, as a rehearsal for the project I intended to pursue upon returning to Rome: to represent the panorama of the city apparent from atop the Palatine. Heretofore I had not painted edifices or cityscapes in earnest, because I had lacked viable models. From the veranda of our townhouse in Rhodes, most buildings were too distant for reproduction in detail. Of the immediately proximate homes of neighbors one could only see portions. During my travels I had not spent sufficient time in any particular place to do more than sketch renowned edifices like the Parthenon, the Mausoleum of Halicarnassus, the Serapeion and Pharos lighthouse of Alexandria. Architecture of even the slightest aesthetic did not exist on the farm. In fanciful landscapes I had depicted idealized buildings, from temples to amphitheaters to stadia to farmhouses—but at a distance, so they did not require much detail or even accuracy.

At an edge of the plaza spreading before the villa I had a manservant place a chair, where I could see the building's front as well as one side. Sitting wrapped in a gauzy veil to protect my visage from sun and insects and eyes of roving guards, I drew the outline of the edifice. The next morning I completed this sketch and began to apply colors. By the time Gallina came to advise me Master insisted I join him in our chambers, I felt I had completed a satisfactory practice vignette: simplistic, lacking finer detail, but properly proportioned and shaded. On the morning following, however, the representation appeared quite wrong: two-dimensional and flaccid, as though the building's front and side were pieces of cloth affixed one beside the other upon a wall. That same afternoon, after Gallina and I had returned from our tour of Anzio, I carried the painting to the front of the villa at precisely the same hour in which I had completed it. The perspectives and proportions, the shadows and shadings and colors, all seemed to have been accurately recorded. Why, then, did the piece appear unnatural?

Sitting on the veranda the morning thereafter, I attempted a rendering of the villa's rear facade. It proceeded no better than my representation of the building's front, and left me puzzled and frustrated. Nor was I alone in my mood, for near to noon angry shouts emanated from within the villa. They died down, resumed, and once again subsided. A sullen and angry Drusus emerged, strode across the veranda to its edge and looked out on the sea, paying no heed to me. A seagull lighted some distance from us on the veranda's waist-high enclosure wall. Drusus seized one of my paint vials and hurled it at the bird with great force. Red paint splattered gull, wall, and the stairs to the beach. The vial fell onto the stairs and shattered.

"Why will you not hear me out?" shouted an aggravated Tiberius as he entered the veranda. "You would do well to apply the energy you are expending on opposing the concept to understanding it!"

Drusus whirled about to face him. "One cannot resist one's destiny, but one can alter one's destiny!" Now I perceived the reason behind the quarrel. Drusus continued, "You repudiate my mother and subject me to a life of misery under Julia's tutelage. Then you ship off to Rhodes for nearly a decade. Now that you have finally returned, all you can do is spout the nonsensical, contradictory philosophical falderal you picked up there! Why did you not apply the energy you expended on absorbing that nonsense, to defending your marriage to Mamma and the integrity of our home?"

"You are every bit as stupid as you are insolent! Had I done what you just recommended, Patruus would have breached amicitia with me for certain! Imagine what course your destiny would have taken after that!"

"By your own conduct you accomplished precisely the same result: surrendered your wife, your political position and adherents, your credibility with the populace and their respect for you. How do you think it feels, to be the son of a laughingstock?"

"Oh, you prefer I had defied Caesar Augustus outrightly, and provoked him to breach amicitia! What, pray tell, would you be doing today? Standing here on this, his estate? Studying ethics with Athenodorus of Alexandria, history with Livius of Padua, composition and rhetoric with Verrius Flaccus—not to mention *architecture*..." he drawled the last word slowly and emphatically "... with Cocceius Auctus and Valerius of Ostia and venerable old Vitruvius Pollio? What sort of a career would you be anticipating? Certainly not admission to the senate. And do you assume any professional architect would put his reputation at risk by agreeing to apprentice you?"

"Grandmother Livia would have intervened on my behalf!"

"What makes you so cocksure? Her influence has its limits, of which she is right well aware and takes care not to overstep!"

"You both need to compose yourselves!" I interjected, realizing I was leaving myself open to rebuttal and possible reprimand. Hardly was it my place to intervene in a dispute, between a father and his son whose mother I was not. Nevertheless they held their peace, each eying me with a quizzical look that was almost comical.

Then Drusus' eye fell upon my sketch. "That has to be the most ludicrously ridiculous portrayal of a building ever produced," he sneered. "And you will go on to extort exorbitant royalties from Lucilius Longus' gullible customers for such trash!"

"You will not speak to her in that tone of voice and with such disrespectful imputations!" Tiberius retorted.

"Why not, Father? She is only your mistress, and not even an Italian. And the truth is the truth: this picture is a hunk of excrement. So is the one she did on the villa's front!"

"I WILL NOT HAVE YOU SPEAK DEGRADINGLY OF HER PERSON OR HER ENDEAVORS!" Tiberius' roar was earsplitting.

"Enough!" I cried with a clap of my hands. "Shame upon the two of you, exchanging silly insults like a pair of schoolboys!" Again the silence and perplexed expression. "Drusus, I know this rendering is far inferior to my usual work!" So I continued, my tone still intense. "You have an immensely better comprehension of architecture than I. Instead of decrying my representations of buildings, why do you not offer me knowledgeable suggestions for improving them?"

"To do so would be to manifest a modicum of maturity," Tiberius grumbled sarcastically. Drusus' face reddened. He pursed his lips and shut his eyes.

"Oh, hush: your behavior is as puerile as your son's!" I chided. Tiberius startled, rolled his eyes, but said nothing.

Seizing this opportunity to calm and instruct, I lowered my voice and softened its timbre. "Drusus, I realize you would absolutely exult in pursuit of a career as an architect or an engineer. Nevertheless, for you to become a senator is inevitable. This is the aspect of your destiny you cannot resist or alter. Here, however, is how you can adjust and improve the character that aspect assumes. When Gaius succeeds to his grandfather's position he will be in need of a loyal associate, with appropriate expertise to counsel him effectively about the building projects he contemplates. The same associate must be able to evaluate accurately the capabilities of architects and engineers, whom he would recommend to Gaius for designation to implement those projects. Not only membership but popularity in the senate will be equally critical for this adviser, enabling him to propound such proposals to that body and secure their passage into law. Why not make yourself that loyal associate? Use the skills of patronage your father is teaching you, to solidify your amicitia with Gaius and cultivate that of other senators and future senators—and let architecture be the purpose behind that patronage. Privately you could become a patron to architects themselves, promoting their services to the public as Senator Longus promotes the works of his client artists.

"As for the separation of your parents: your father pursued the course he deemed most correct under the circumstances. We have all, at one time or another, taken actions that cause grief to others—some trivial, some devastating, most unintentional. I think your father explained quite well the dilemma he faced when he divorced your mother: a disrupted home, or complete destruction of your chances for a successful career in any vocation. Had that breach of amicitia occurred, you would have ended up neither senator nor architect, but an outcast like Gaius Gracchus."

I recalled the incident with Miranda and the cloak Alexias had sent her. The response on this occasion was remarkably similar. Without uttering a word, his face expressionless, Drusus seated himself on the bench beside me and fixed his gaze on the unfinished sketch. I smiled at Tiberius, who beckoned me with his head. Drusus took no notice as I rose from the bench. Taking my hand, Tiberius whispered, "Come, let us walk along the beach." As we headed to the stairs two menservants arrived with buckets, rags, and brushes for scrubbing the paint off where it had spattered. Seeing Drusus' valet Jason peering from the doorway, I beckoned him. In subdued tones I asked him to fetch, from the sitting room of our quarters, my vignette of the villa's front and carry it to his charge.

While we strolled, a dejected Tiberius elaborated upon the quarrel he had had with his son. During Tiberius' absence from Rome, Livia had been recommending Drusus to political allies upon whose influence and support she knew Drusus could rely to advance his political career. Drusus felt Tiberius had been remiss in not doing this himself. Distance was no object: Tiberius could have accomplished the task through correspondence as easily as through conversation. Now with Drusus' coming of age imminent, how could Tiberius possibly expect to forge those essential alignments on short notice, and as a private citizen with no active involvement in political affairs?

Tiberius had countered that with his reputation having been sullied over the past four years, at present he had notoriously few adherents to promote Drusus' interests but detractors aplenty to subvert them. To his father's surprise, Drusus retorted that Tiberius had never been without an adherence sufficiently powerful to sway political opinion: otherwise his enemies could not have convinced Gaius to fear him. "He is developing sound political insights," Tiberius concluded with an obvious surge of pride.

"His tantrum took me quite by surprise. Ordinarily he is so reticent."

Tiberius nodded. "His outburst was justified," he continued, now glum again. "I myself did practically nothing to prepare the way for his emergence into public life. Will I make the same mistake regarding Alcimus?"

"Alcimus is hardly destined to become a Roman senator," I said with a gentle laugh as I leaned against his arm.

"True; but how will I make the appropriate introductions for him, in whatever path of life he pursues? I have no connections with guilds or trade organizations. And what about my own character? Will self-absorption—preoccupation with the course my own life is taking—lead me to ignore the paternal duties I owe Alcimus, even as I did with Drusus?"

Because I could sense the urgency of Tiberius' need for reassurance, I did not mention we had had previous discussions of this matter. Instead I replied, "By the time it becomes necessary to establish professional and social connections for Alcimus, you will have long been recognized as a private philanthropist instead of a jaded politician. Now, as for your fears you will neglect either son: well, my love, you can count upon me not to let you do so!"

He smiled wistfully. "Spoken like a true wife," he said as he drew the arm against which I had been leaning across my shoulders. His manner and tone resumed their melancholy. "Drusus' horoscope reveals a future of prominence, but always overshadowed by someone of higher prestige—and short-lived. I cannot help but wonder if this portends an early death for him. Recall Thrasyllus' prediction. You and I both will be bereaved of a child unique to each of ourselves. At least we can take comfort that the forecast excludes Alcimus."

"And Thrasyllus added that those children destined to bereave us do not necessarily have to be human offspring. Perhaps Drusus—like his father—will become disillusioned with public life, retire therefrom, and become a patron to aspiring architects."

The gray, white, and red seagull, darting across our path toward the water's edge and taking flight, reminded me of the outburst which had brought about the bird's peculiar coloration. Suddenly a premonition, almost vividly tangible in its intensity, seized me. A display of Drusus' temper was indeed going to prove harmful to him, and fulfill for Tiberius the prophecy of bereavement of the child uniquely his. The prospect sent a tremble through me. Mentally I reiterated my belief in the presence and governance of Underlying Good, hoping to acquire a sense of peace and persuasion my presage was wrong.

Tiberius felt me shudder. "Are you all right?" he asked.

As succinctly as I could manage, I explained my concern a display of temper might someday lead to trouble for Drusus, and left the matter there. My premonition about the prophecy I could not bring myself to disclose. Tiberius' response was casually dismissive. "The exuberance of youthful emotion is doing battle with Drusus' rational side. He remains embittered over my withdrawal to Rhodes, all the while he understands and appreciates I left him in Rome for his own good. We must expect the rational to prevail as he matures. I shall keep watch to insure it does."

Years later my presage proved both accurate and horrific. Even then I kept it to myself. There are times when withholding a secret from one's spouse is a far greater act of love than unhesitant and candid disclosure.

Upon our return we found stairs and veranda cleansed of the paint, and the servants calmly laying luncheon on the table beneath the pergola as if nothing had happened. Drusus was still seated on his bench, his eyes fixated upon my two vignettes of the villa. He ignored our attempts at persuading him to join us, for the delectable preparation of ray sautéed in caper sauce with a side dish of asparagus. A particular pleasure of Anzio was the wide variety of fresh fish and crustaceans, drawn in abundance from the teeming waters offshore. Nor did Drusus pay any heed to the plate of food which, at my behest, one of the attendants prepared and placed on the bench beside him. But all at once, when Tiberius and I were about halfway through our meal, Drusus stood upright, seized the plate, carried it to the table, and seated himself.

"Mistress Galatea, I believe I have found the solution to your difficulty!" he exclaimed with a beaming smile as he dug into his repast. "Everything in nature is curved and undulating—even rigid components like bones and rocks and tree trunks. Therefore, anything natural casts a curved and undulating shadow. Not so a building. It consists of lines and planes and angles laid out in great precision. The shadows of a building, then, and of other man-made structures like monuments, are likewise angular and planar. Behold, here is a perfect example!" He pointed to the shadow cast by the edge of the pergola, and near to it that of the trunk of a potted shrub. And correct he was. The shadow of the little tree trunk was clearly irregular and feathery, but that of the structure sharp and straight.

Drusus continued his discourse with enthusiasm growing. "Curved constructions like arches and urns cast curved shadows; but these are circles and portions of circles rather than irregular undulations. Like angles and planes, they conform to precise geometric dimensions. Undoubtedly you have studied Euclid." I nodded. "So when you draw the shadow of a curved structure, you have to envision a circle first. Now, what happens when an object, whether natural or man-made, casts a shadow upon a building? That shadow assumes the geometry of the surface upon which it falls, which will be either a plane, or a cylinder in the case of a column. The shadow of a tree on the side of a building is a two-dimensional plane with the outline of the tree." He took an asparagus stalk from his plate and held it horizontally alongside his water tumbler. "And see here, how the shadow cast on a circular object becomes part of the circle?" He was absolutely correct.

"Also, there are three architectural oddities you might find useful to know about. The long side of a large rectangular edifice like a basilica or temple dips in the distance out of sight. For this very reason the stoops running along the longer sides of the Parthenon are curved upward at either end, so a person standing at one edge can see the other. Secondly: columns when viewed from a distance appear to bulge in the center. Again the Parthenon holds the solution: its columns are slightly concave. Today's architects compensate for these anomalies when designing new structures. Finally: an array of buildings receding into the distance appears to curve ever so slightly toward the center of the viewer's line of vision. Oh, and I apologize for my disrespectful behavior toward you, and for breaking your paint vial."

"My feelings are unhurt. Moreover I brought spare vials and an ample supply of red paint." Quite readily I smiled, as I was gaining a fondness for Drusus. To my dismay, the terrible foreboding about his temper reemerged. Although confident he liked me in return, I also sensed his apology for his tantrum was not entirely sincere.

I passed the remainder of that day, all of the next, and the morning of the third applying Drusus' recommendations to the two vignettes. The results were eminently satisfying to my youthful instructor as well as to me, as both renderings assumed the desired realism. He had been correct, I noted, about horizontal declination. Looking along the villa's exterior colonnade from the front, I could not see the farther end of its floor. I had to leave the vignettes behind at the villa, wet and not entirely finished, in the afternoon when we departed for Fondi. The villa's steward assured me he would send the paintings to Rome as soon as they had dried. Although I was eager to see Fondi and of course to meet Tiberius' grandmother, I knew right well I was going to miss Anzio: its grand vista over land and sea, its warmly caressing breezes, its light that was brilliantly coruscant over water but shifted to softly pastel over land. Nuances of this sort had not been apparent from our Rhodian townhouse or farm, because their perspectives on the sea were limited or distant.

Nearing Terracina, we passed the promontory of Circeii. Purportedly the abode of Circe the nymph who turned the companions of Odysseus into beasts, it befits its legend with its appearance, rising ominously dark and shadowy from the sea glowing fiery in the late afternoon sun. At Terracina we picked up the Appian Road where it turns eastward to Fondi. Away from the coast, the land rose gradually until it leveled into a plain ringed by low mountains. We passed grainfields, orchards, vineyards, pastures in which goats or sheep were starting to gather into huddles for the approaching night. The hues and shadings were darker, deeper, more intense than those of Anzio—much like, in fact, those of the Rhodian farm.

We did not enter Fondi proper, but just before reaching that town turned into a side road leading into the hills. Twilight was falling when we halted before a diminutive villa faced with flagstones. As we lighted from the carriage, we could see in the far distance the very top of the setting sun: an immense red orb sinking into a darkened bay. The entryway led directly to a small square peristyle, in the center of which stood a huge planter filled with blooming flowers. The youthful steward who greeted us said Lady Alfidia had already retired for the night; but he had both bath and a supper of chicken ragout prepared for us. Tiberius asked that we be shown to our quarters and the victuals brought there. The steward led us across the peristyle to a stretch of rooms along the villa's left side. Tiberius he escorted to the leftmost, me to the room in the center, and Drusus to the one at our right. The bath, he explained, lay farther to the right just before the wing's intersection with the villa's rear side. "Why do I always end up with the room next to the bath?" Drusus moaned—actually with good-natured mock exasperation—after the steward had departed with our servants. Although proportionate to the villa's overall size, the guest section was cramped, crowded, and stuffy after the expansive suite we had occupied at Anzio.

When we emerged into the peristyle the next morning, a serving woman reminiscent of Phoebe advised that Lady Alfidia was awaiting us on the veranda. With a curtsy she beckoned us to follow her. The veranda lay not behind but beside the villa, on the opposite side from our quarters. Its orientation provided a view of the mountains to the rear, of the plain and beyond that the sea to the front. The house and veranda stood on a gentle rise, within a walled park landscaped with an abundance of flowering plants and shrubs. The veranda too was crowded with pots and planters of flowers. I noted several heliotropes of different hues.

Beneath a pergola strewn with a morning-glory vine, Drusus was already seated at table beside the great-grandmother whom he quite strongly resembled. Alfidia was petite like Livia but very slender. She had thick white hair, and watery hazel eyes which she must wipe persistently with a kerchief. Her pale crêpe skin had a translucent quality reminiscent of myrrhine glass. Her kindly smile revealed she still had a fair number of teeth, although they were understandably discolored from age. Her head and hands shook slightly but continually, and her voice quavered as she spoke.

After returning Tiberius' embrace and kisses, she acknowledged my curtsy with a smile and words of welcome and bade me sit beside her. While we partook of the assortment of fruit on the charger at the table's center, she spoke nary a word to me. First she inquired after the family in Rome: was everyone well (yes). What a terrible tragedy to befall Lucius (agreed). Apart from that were there any special tidings about anyone (no). Was Tiberius Drusus' deportment improving at all (no).

News of the relatives at Fondi was somewhat more interesting. It had taken a grandiose public ceremony of recognition to induce Alfidia's brother, to retire from the municipal council because his snoring disrupted its sessions. His son—Alfidia's nephew—had made a fool of himself by berating in public a fellow councilman, who had challenged logistics the nephew was presenting to justify an aqueduct expansion project. It turned out the nephew had the wrong report: logistics for construction of a new bridge. The nephew redeemed his reputation and salvaged his political alignment with the challenger by sponsoring a public banquet and an Atellan farce satirizing his gaffe. The greatest topic of general concern at present in Fondi was the lack of rain, a matter of understandable import to farmers.

Next, Alfidia asked Drusus whether he was excited about his impending coming of age (yes). Did he feel prepared (no). Was not his father teaching him well (yes, but instruction no matter how good is no substitute for experience). Was Drusus still pursuing his studies of architecture (most certainly, with a quick glance at me). When did he anticipate starting military service (come the spring, most likely, he and Nero who now insists upon being called Germanicus shall commence training together). Was marriage on his horizon (not immediately).

Alfidia closed her rheumy eyes and dozed. The rest of us munched our fruit in silence, waiting to see whether she would awaken. Within a few minutes she did, daubed her eyes, and with renewed vigor directed her attention to Tiberius. With relief indescribable she was rejoicing to have him back in Italy safe and sound. How was he getting on with his stepfather (actually fairly amicably, now that Tiberius had agreed to remain a private citizen). Did he miss being a public figure (not at all—Alfidia remarked she was hardly surprised). Had he any aspirations or plans for his new life (to devote his energies and resources primarily to aiding the sick, but also to advancing the careers of selected artists and other entrepreneurs whose works he felt particularly merited promotion).

Alfidia raised her chin, in what proved a signal to her Phoebe and a younger serving woman. They approached and helped Alfidia to her feet; the younger woman handed her a cane. Slowly the trio made their way back into the house. After a few moments' hesitation I too rose and caught up with them, since I needed the privy as well. From our guestroom I retrieved my paints and palettes, as I wanted to record the riot of colors and shapes the profusion of blooming plants provided. Back on the veranda, the breakfast had been cleared away and the table cleaned. Tiberius and Drusus were wandering in the garden behind the house, chatting affably with a man of about Augustus' age whom I presumed was a relative or neighbor.

Beside Alfidia's chair stood two baskets: the one empty, the other piled with large and densely matted wads of wool. Reaching into the latter, she retrieved a carder and a mass of wool. This she proceeded to card, pausing every so often to feel the texture of the newly combed fibers. Those with which she was satisfied she dropped into the empty basket. When I began to sketch a flower-laden planter, she asked me what I was doing. After a brief description of my process, I complimented her on the abundance of blossoms in her dwelling. She had them maintained, she explained, on account of her eyesight. Everything appeared blurred as if she were looking through a gauze curtain, a wall of translucent glass, a sheet of ice, one of these wads of wool. Shadings and colors were what she could best perceive. She could make out large shapes and some of their general characteristics but no details. For example she could tell I was moderately tall, broadly built, and had black hair; but she could not discern my facial features.

She asked me to tell her about myself, which I did while she carded and I painted. Of course I withheld the quintessential secrets of my relationship with Tiberius: his gift to me of the Rhodian farm, our association with Thrasyllus, and of course our marriage and offspring. For a time she listened without interrupting me. Before I finished she returned the carder to the basket of uncombed wool, and sat with her eyes closed and her hands folded in her lap. So she continued in silence for some time after I had concluded my tale, leading me to wonder whether she had fallen asleep, until she reached up and wiped her eyes. As I sat looking at a brilliant red rose in full bloom, a thought struck me. With my rag I wiped away my sketch of the planter with its small details, and began a rendering of the rose large enough to fill the entire palette. Tiberius arrived with Drusus and the visitor. He was Publius Alfidius Sabinus, the nephew Alfidia had described earlier.

The servants laid the table for luncheon, which proved to be a ragout of lamb. To Tiberius I turned with a pleading look; but before either he or I could say anything, Alfidia perceived my cringe and asked what was wrong. Fearful of causing offense I hesitated; whereupon Tiberius interjected I could not eat lamb because it made me ill. Immediately Alfidia beckoned her steward: what other viands had he ready to offer her lady guest? Pork sausage or trout both purchased fresh that morning in Fondi, or eggs from the villa's hennery, all of which could be quickly cooked. Much as the trout appealed, having had quite a fill of fish at Anzio and tired of eggs in general, I chose the sausage. Promptly served it was, atop a bed of long green beans. Impelled by a recollection of my mother and her aunt, who would have become livid because I had not only confessed a peculiar peccadillo but accepted a remedy, I started to apologize. The entire company interrupted me with assurances my self-reproach was unnecessary.

Following luncheon, Alfidia retired to her bedchamber while the rest of us remained on the veranda. Alfidia's characterization of her eyesight had given me an idea. Loosening a lock of my hair, I drew it across my face and looked at the rose through the veil of strands. Surely enough, I could make out the blossom's basic shape and color but no details. And so I began a process. First I would study the rose carefully with my eyes unobstructed, then with my hair drawn over my eyes. From memory I applied to the palette the details and shading of the rose as perceived through my hair. Viewed in sight unobscured, the rendering was a grotesquerie of unrealistically intense outlines, vivid colors and sharp shadings, reminiscent of those strange plants that grow at the bottom of the sea. Looking through my hair, however, I could see emerging an accurate representation of a rose.

Aspiring to present the completed tableau to Alfidia before our departure for Rome the next morning, I worked on it sedulously, frenetically. Fortunately Tiberius and his cousin were immersed in a discussion of local politics, to which Drusus was listening attentively but with obvious boredom. Consequently none of them paid any attention to my strange articulations of my hair, and the equally strange image I was producing. I did not retire for afternoon respite, and only put the work aside for a bath, a supper of morels and other vegetables in milky sauce, and a brief harp recital. As night began to fall, I asked the steward if there was a dayroom in which I might continue my endeavor. He escorted me to a library quite spare of books, and brought in extra lamps to insure me adequate light. Then he showed me the kitchen, where he suggested I bring the finished piece to let the room's natural warmth facilitate its drying. Well into the second watch of the night I worked, and duly left the result in the kitchen. Come the morning, to my satisfaction I found it nearly dry, and the Phoebe replicate staring at it befuddled until I showed her the procedure for viewing it properly.

When I presented the vignette to Alfidia, I made sure she held it by the edges—not only because the paint was still slightly wet, but so her hands did not obstruct any portion of her perspective. As she sat holding it her lower lip began to tremble, and her eyes to stream with more effluence than usual. Five years had elapsed and maybe more, she said, since she had been able to discern the elegant details of a rose. A wondrous gift, from one who was endowed with wondrous gifts—not only artistic and musical talent but intuition, generosity, and compassion.

Now she had a gift to present me in return, she continued as gingerly she placed the tableau on the table. Like me she had watched her childhood acquaintances marry one after another, while her father rejected suitor after suitor. Scion of a family long significant in the municipal council of Fondi and himself a prominent member, Marcus Alfidius had aspired to establish a political presence at Rome in the hope of eventually gaining admission to the senate—if not for himself then for his descendants. To accomplish this purpose he had sought a patron, who would make his name known to the Roman political elite and to the populace as well. Throughout this quest, Alfidius had kept his daughter unmarried—hence available to solidify through wedlock the arrangement he sought.

At length when Alfidia was in her eighteenth year, her father achieved his aspiration. He had made the acquaintance of Marcus Livius Drusus Claudianus, then a childless widower desirous not only of offspring, but of monies with which to finance his campaigns for election to the senatorial magistracies. The two men struck a bargain: Livius Drusus would make the essential introductions for Alfidius at Rome, in return for the hand of Alfidius' daughter and use of his funds. Alfidia was sixteen years her husband's junior—the same chronological difference, I reflected, between Tiberius and me. During her enforced spinsterhood as in mine, some of her contemporaries had snickered and others had pitied. All had thrust aside former feelings and offered sincere heartfelt congratulations, on learning of Alfidia's betrothal to a Roman nobleman with a stellar ancestry and personal renown of his own.

Alfidia never fell passionately in love with her spouse as Livia did with Augustus. Nor did Alfidia have reason to believe her husband was fervently enamored of her. Nevertheless their union was not unhappy. Drusus Claudianus treated Alfidia with kindness and respect, which she gratefully reciprocated. They had four children, all born prematurely. Only the eldest survived; and she inherited her mother's unfortunate pathology. Alfidia shared a humorous reminiscence about her husband. From his adoptive father he had inherited a garden, located on Rome's Esquiline Hill. Titus Caecilius Atticus Pomponianus, the grandfather of Tiberius' first wife, aspired to purchase the garden—but not for the price upon which Drusus Claudianus insisted. The great orator and statesman Marcus Tullius Cicero, who was a close friend of Atticus, tried to persuade Claudianus to lower his demand and accept Atticus' offer. For nearly a year the three negotiated, but hardly with the dignified reserve one might expect from men of education and refinement. They haggled as snidely and vociferously as a trio of fishwives, Alfidia asserted. Drusus Claudianus ended up selling the garden for his desired price, to the enormously wealthy freedman Vedius Pollio. He incorporated the plot into his own Esquiline estate, which lay adjacent. Eventually her father's garden reverted to Livia in a way, through

Pollio's bequest of his Esquiline properties to Augustus. Today the Porticus Livia stands thereon.

After a chuckle and a wipe of her eyes, Alfidia resumed her narrative. When Livia quit the marriage her parents had arranged for her, and espoused her father's former political enemy—the man who had designated Drusus Claudianus for execution and precipitated his suicide—Alfidia became grief-stricken and outraged beyond measure. How could her only child renounce the principles for which her husband had fought and died? And how could the son-in-law so carefully chosen acquiesce to this insurrection—even naming his usurper guardian of his sons, the grandsons of Marcus Livius Drusus Claudianus? Alfidia returned to Fondi, resolved never to speak to Livia again. Her father and brother followed, to escape the violence in which Augustus' regime was born. Both were content to exchange the pedestrian safety of a municipal council for the potentially fatal glory of the Roman senate. On one of his extensive estates, Alfidia's brother built for her the little villa in which she resided today.

Twenty years elapsed, through which Alfidia execrated Livia, Augustus, and Tiberius' father. Then one day, while strolling upon the very veranda where we were sitting, Alfidia observed four fishing vessels and two trade ships upon the distant bay. She took note of grain fields undulating in the wind, of pastures white with sheep, of orchards and vineyards pendant with fruit, of recently born children cavorting at play. A thought coming to her strong and sure sent a tremor down her back. The man responsible for the present peace and prosperity unprecedented in Roman history was in love with, married to, and caring for her daughter. Moreover he was raising that daughter's sons—Alfidia's grandsons—with unparalleled political advantages. Meanwhile Alfidia, seething with resentment, was depriving herself of her only child and of her grandchildren out of reverence for a husband and son-in-law both long deceased. It was quite an epiphany. At once Alfidia sent to Livia and Augustus a letter soliciting reconciliation; they promptly came to visit her at Fondi; and when she appeared in the city forum for the festival of the goddess Pomona, leaning upon her present son-in-law's arm, her own brother joined the rest of the populace in gaping and gasping with astonishment. Smiling to the startled onlookers, she asserted the time had come for letting bygones be bygones.

Alfidia continued that she had sensed, very acutely, the intense bitterness I harbored about my past. From the experience she had just finished describing, she had learned a false sense of what is right creates a genuine wrong. For two decades, Alfidia's pointless veneration of two dead men's outmoded political principles had kept her from appreciating and enjoying her only living child. And was not Alfidia actually dishonoring her late husband by excoriating his daughter from a misguided sense of right? Although my family's mistreatment of me was hardly justifiable, it had not necessarily arisen because they were intrinsically evil or because they considered me to be so. More likely they were confused and deluded, even as Alfidia had been about the type of respect she owed her husband and child. This was her gift to me. Although it could not diminish the pain of my memories, it might help make them easier to bear, and hopefully set me on the path to pity and perhaps even forgive my forebears.

A false sense of right begets a genuine wrong. Years ago in Rhodes, Thrasyllus had urged me to pity and forgive my family. I did not succeed, because I believed my family were fully conscious—very well aware—of the glaring wrongness of their abusive treatment of me, their absurd standards of morality, their disdain and contempt for other people, their incessant dissatisfaction with their lives and insistence they were entitled to better than what they had received. Despite this recognition, they had perpetuated these evils anyway. How can one pity, let alone forgive, those who practice wrong knowingly and deliberately?

The notion my family had been acting from a deluded sense of right brought about a significant change in my sentiments. From deep within my consciousness, I recognized a burning desire for revenge: for seeing my family heartbroken with remorse, or writhing from the same torments they had imposed upon me. Living with oppressive conclusions—that your daughter is incorrigible beyond redemption, that everyone else in the world leads a more advantaged life, that nobody else in the world recognizes let alone appreciates your matchless intellect, your superior morality, the godlike characteristics of your son—surely must be unspeakably painful. Here was the vengeance: present, palpable, and actively afflictive. For a time I seethed with scornful gratification. My family had lived surrounded and confronted by realities they had deliberately and stolidly refused to accept: the realities that their mores were distorted and oppressive, that no one's life is charmed, that my father was not an intellect unsurpassed by any other on earth, that my brother was indolent and spoiled, that I was not monstrous.

Why should I pity my family for the self-engendered sufferings they so richly deserved? After some further contemplation it occurred to me, that even as my kin had been self-deceived by their false sense of right, so had I been self-deceived: blinded by my failure to recognize they had afflicted me from an honest if misplaced desire to fulfill their false sense of right. Suddenly the long elusive pity became tangible. My gloating over my family's self-imposed misery dissipated—and to my relief, as I had begun to hate myself for harboring this disdainful satisfaction. Tranquil joy crept over me, as my change in sentiment toward my kin conjoined with immeasurable gratitude to Alfidia for inducing it.

Nevertheless a certain disappointment left my elation hollow. The misguided righteousness of their intentions notwithstanding, my family had thoroughly enjoyed—yea, delighted—in watching me suffer from the torments with which they and others had smitten me. The simile would be an unnaturally cruel magistrate exulting over the misery of convicts suffering under penalties rightly prescribed by law. I still wanted my family to recognize, admit, and repent their wrong. At last I had managed somewhat to pity, but certainly not to forgive.

So I reflected during our return journey to Rome. We did not enter the circuitous seashore route at Terracina but continued on the direct Appian Road, which here veered northward through the Pontine Marshes. Low fingers of land covered with rushes, sedge grasses, toadstools, and an occasional stand of scrubby trees, lay interspersed amid great pools of murky brown water. Patches of green or yellow scum floated atop some of the pools. A man-made canal, filled with the same smutty water, paralleled the road. Tiberius remarked we were fortunate the dearth of recent rain had left the roadway entirely dry, allowing us to advance quickly through the marsh. Such was not usually the case: the road was often flooded. The drainage canal, constructed on Augustus' orders, was not proving as effective at controlling inundations as hoped. The air was fetid and malodorous. Clouds of insects hung suspended in the air. According to one tradition these marshes, rather than the jetty at Terracina, were the abode of the nymph Circe who had changed men into lions, wolves, and pigs. Wild pigs we did see, along with turtles and snakes, and waterfowl which, to escape the commotion of our carriage, with wings flapping contrived to run across the surface of the waters.

We emerged from the marshes at the outskirts of Aricia, where we halted for about half an hour at a military waystation. The commandant and his staff treated us with deferential aplomb: there was none of the blustering adulation civilians usually bestow upon members of the emperor's family, and which Tiberius so ardently loathed. Thereafter we traversed rolling and occasionally steep gradients through the Alban Hills, where forested slopes descended into limpid slate-colored lakes. From the want of rain, Drusus remarked, water levels were low and the region lacking in its usually lustrous verdure. Once again, Tiberius had timed the journey impeccably—a skill no doubt arising from outlining and executing military maneuvers. We negotiated the potentially hazardous pitches of the Alban Hills as daylight waned, and arrived at Rome well after dark.

A letter from Thrasyllus was awaiting us. Alcimus, now in his eighth month, had just begun to crawl. Phoenix had already been crawling for a good month. The adults in the household had become especially careful as to where they stepped. Thrasylla and Miranda were admonished to store any belongings they valued well above the floor. The two boys and the household cats had taken a great interest in one another, since all were at the same eye level and employing four-footed locomotion. One day when things seemed too quiet, Briseis became concerned and went on a search. She came across the two babes lying asleep on the nursery floor, each with a sleeping cat nestled against him. A pity, she had declared, I was not on hand to record the scene.

The reference to Miranda made me think of Alexias, so I asked Tiberius whether he knew what had become of our former servant in the aftermath of Lucius Caesar's death. A good question, Tiberius acknowledged. For certain, ownership of Alexius had ceded to Augustus along with the rest of Lucius' property. He promised to find out for sure come the morrow.

On that morrow Tiberius proceeded to a military review, and I went to my studio to unpack my textile collection at long last. During this operation I contemplated future artistic endeavors. To the Palatine I aspired to return, there to record the city on as many tableaux as required to create an unbroken panorama. For certain, however, I first needed more experience at depicting buildings. This necessity was glaringly obvious from my two paintings of the villa at Anzio, which I discovered in my studio. The villa's steward had duly forwarded them. Although implementation of Drusus' recommendations had improved them immensely, they were still amateurish and unrefined.

How to go about obtaining the necessary practice posed a quandary. From the Palatine the details of individual structures were indiscernible, being too far distant. From our veranda one could see uninteresting apartment houses aplenty, but only portions of the more elaborate public edifices. To attain unobstructed views of chosen subjects, it appeared I must sit at the edges of streets or in plazas and arouse the inevitable curiosity of passersby. Would Tiberius and his family allow me this level of exposure, so long as I kept myself well veiled and surrounded by bodyguards and did not converse with any of the onlookers? I could of course reassume the guise of Eutychus. A male artist painting at a street corner would attract attention, but not nearly so much as a woman in the same role.

Coming upon a shawl of deep green linen upon which I had painted one of the Guardian Trees in bloom, I reflected that my present environs severely lacked suitable models to be derived from nature. Now having my collection of textiles, I wanted to resume painting designs upon them. This form of art I felt should be confined to representations of foliage and animals and geologic formations. The notion of a garment with a building depicted upon it seemed garish and gauche.

Our own small peristyle was severely lacking in the aesthetic I was contemplating, despite the improvements I had ordered: the foliage pruned, and the little reflection pool repaired and filled. There was no roof garden on our veranda, only the rectangular wood planter with the heliotropes. The peristyle and roof garden on the Palatine were beautiful and complex; but they still lacked the height of trees and the ever-changing scintillations of the light filtering through their canopy, the abundance and spontaneity of color and shape and shadow in plants left to spread naturally across an expanse of ground, the glistening of water in ponds or streams, the heady fragrances of forest and field, the startling sudden appearances of wildlife.

Tiberius did not return home for luncheon. Nor did I expect him, and so had bread and cheese brought to the studio. Alcmene was drying me after my bath when Tiberius arrived and promptly dismissed her. He was in one of his wearily pensive moods from having been on display.

He undressed and settled himself into the bath basin. At his request I poured water from a bucket heating on the brazier, into the bath until he said he was satisfied with the temperature. A brooding silence reigned while I donned the clean garments Alcmene had left for me, and he sat tracing patterns on the water's surface with a strigil. As he began to apply the instrument to his chest, his mood brightened. Alexias, he had learned, had taken a passionate interest in medicine while serving as Lucius' valet. So it was from him Miranda acquired her inclination toward pharmaceuticals, I interjected. Tiberius smiled and nodded as he continued. Having noted this interest, Lucius had apprenticed Alexias to a physician with a respected public practice in Marseilles, during the prince's brief and fatal sojourn in that city. An appropriate decision; for given his limited literacy and servile status, Alexias could hardly pursue an academic course of study at the University of Marseilles. Augustus, now Alexias' owner, was resolved to free him once the apprenticeship was satisfied. Tiberius stopped his movements and sighed, his demeanor again doleful. Through childhood and youth, he mused, Lucius had exhibited little more than arrogant willfulness and peevish condescension. The provision he made for Alexias had demonstrated a noble side of character. Such a terrible futility death had overtaken Lucius before his better attributes could be fully revealed.

After another brief silence he looked up at me and smiled ingenuously. In an offhand manner as if nothing were amiss he declared we were invited to sup on the Palatine, two days hence on the eve of Augustus' birthday. The celebrant had a particularly special request for a gift. He desired I should play my harp and sing for him.

We gathered in the formal dining room adjacent to the sitting room where we had assembled after Lucius' funeral. Tiberius and I were not the only familial guests. Augustus' cousin Quintus Pedius and his wife Laelia were visiting from Velletri. Germanicus and Drusus were on hand as well, but not Agrippina, Postumus, or the younger Tiberius. I presented Livia the green Guardian Tree shawl, which she accepted with great enthusiasm and the remainder of the company marveled over. Augustus said someday I should demonstrate how I managed such remarkable techniques.

Livia thereupon told the puzzled visitors I was the renowned Eutychus of Rhodes. She went on to explain the marketing purpose of my pseudonym, and in conclusion declared they had better keep it all secret. Pedius and Laelia both startled. Then Laelia exclaimed excitedly that they owned two reproductions of my works: a still life, and a trio of fantastically colored butterflies. No fantasy, I returned: a species of butterfly so hued actually nests and breeds in a remote river valley on Rhodes. Suddenly, panic shot through me like a lightning bolt: would Laelia take offense at my correction? Inside my head, the voice of my mother was shouting her usual contradictory instructions: *You must never, ever correct another even if you know the person is wrong,* versus *Why did you let that poor individual continue in error instead of revealing the truth?* But all Laelia did was smile warmly and say, "How fascinating!"

We dined on broiled red mullet—Livia's particular passion, her husband remarked—together with asparagus, the tasty dark bread, and of course the ubiquitous elecampane. Once again the conversation was lighthearted and non-confrontational. How was Drusus proceeding with preparations for his coming of age? A stellar pupil, Tiberius replied, readily grasping the concepts and responsibilities of entering into contracts: the primary purpose of his new legal status. Had I enjoyed the trip to Anzio and Fondi? Immeasurably! Memories of the scenery still leave me breathless. With all aspects of the excursion so wondrous, I could not decide which to describe first. Nonna (Alfidia) and I became fast friends, Drusus averred. He went on to describe how I had painted what appeared a grotesquerie to everyone else, but proved a wondrous delight to Alfidia, who through her clouded eyes perceived a rose in bloom.

Had Tiberius received any petitions for charitable relief? He related the two to which he had attended prior to our excursion: the veteran, and the bricklayer's daughter. The veteran's daughter had sent a long note of thanks. Tiberius' epigram had so raised her father's morale, that after several readings and rereadings he had quit his bed, and spent nearly two hours romping with his grandchildren on his bedchamber floor. Just this morning the bricklayer had stopped by the house. When the ostiarius offered him audience with Tiberius he refused, and asked only that Tiberius be informed the little girl was responding well to Chloe's treatments.

A request that arrived during our absence, and which Tiberius was going to honor for sure, had come from an aspiring decorative artist seeking seed money to establish his own wall painting business. Tiberius would finance a competitor to Eutychus of Rhodes? So Augustus bantered. Eutychus of Rhodes need not fear competition, Tiberius replied; *his* work stands on its own proven merit. Of course one cannot determine how many clients have purchased copies of Eutychus' works from the Gallery of the Four Winds simply to relieve their ears, he added; whereupon I kicked his shin. While rubbing it he asserted I was picking up bad habits from Antonia, who proceeded to punch his shoulder.

How were Pedius and Laelia faring with their grandson, Antonia inquired. Not well, Pedius replied wistfully. June just passed marked the ninth anniversary of the boy's birth. With each succeeding year he has become more difficult to manage. His inability to hear or to speak had rendered him absolutely incapable of learning rules of etiquette and properly restrained conduct. His own frustration over his condition is leading to more and more temper tantrums, prolonged periods of pining and weeping, and obstinate resistance to any efforts by family and servants to direct his behavior. His mentors are unable to assess the types and levels of knowledge and comprehension he possesses. *I ought to tell them about Miranda,* I thought. *Surely they would appreciate hearing how Miranda had been similarly obstreperous, and Briseis had overcome this propensity after observing and cultivating Miranda's interest in pharmaceuticals. __ No, no, no!* came that contradictory voice: *It is intrusive of you to offer such information, particularly to people you have only just met. __ But should they learn I possessed this knowledge and withheld it from them, will they not think ill of me?* Fortuitously, Tiberius brought my mental wrestling match to an abrupt end by expounding Miranda's history himself.

Feeling at this point a sudden and uncanny surge of self-confidence, I initiated conversation with Augustus. Did he still have the ivory statue of Alexander the Great? Yes, in his rooftop study where he continues to regard it with highest esteem. I explained how I had chosen it for him during my visit to Alexandria, because I knew he was an admirer of that intrepid young Macedonian king. After complimenting me on my selection he declared it attested not only to my artistic noesis, but to my sensitivity and consideration of the inclinations and partialities of others.

Next I extolled Drusus for his interest in architecture, and described to the company how his advice had been pivotal to my representation of buildings. With lowered eyes, reddened cheeks, and a bashful smile, Drusus acknowledged my praise. I went on to expound my present aspiration—the panorama of the city—and the predicament I faced with regard to its execution. How could I obtain essential practice at depicting buildings without attracting boundless unwanted attention? Augustus resolved both of my quandaries with a simple question. Had I considered the Gardens of Maecenas? There I could paint an edifice—the villa—along with an abundance of foliage, in absolute privacy on days the park was closed to the public.

When the conversation shifted to Germanicus' pursuit of astronomy, I mentioned my particular fascination with meteors. He responded that he loathed meteors over all other celestial objects because they invariably presage disaster. A decade later he still had vivid memories of observing, as a young boy, the great display of meteors that had preceded his father's horrid death. Far more recently, had not a meteor foretold the disaster that had befallen his cousin Lucius? Surprisingly unafraid—and after reiterating my sympathies for the two unfortunates—I contested Germanicus' notion. Meteors denote change, I averred, but not necessarily evil. At the time of my life when personal anguish was highest—when I was most desperate for consolation and appreciation—the appearance of a meteor foretold the beginning of my acquaintance with Tiberius.

"Some might label that a disaster beyond any comparison," Antonia rejoined. Tiberius said nothing in return, but proceeded to crumble a bread crust above her head, showering her hair, neck, and bodice with crumbs. After a few moments she uttered a yowl and began to brush herself and her couch vigorously. "Really now, children," Augustus groused. The melancholy of Germanicus, who was reclining beside her, dissolved into a fit of laughter. As if cued by this levity Sannio came over, laid his head on my lap, and refused to budge although Augustus thrice clapped his hands and ordered him hence. By then everyone was tittering, including the manservant who dragged Sannio away.

We withdrew to the adjacent sitting room, to which for dessert a chef brought a tray of assorted candied fruits. While playing my harp I reflected that I ought to discuss, with Tiberius, the engagement of a music master to enlarge my repertoire. After I finished the gaming board was brought out. While we were playing, those contradictory misgivings came roaring back into my mind. Had I breached etiquette and protocol, by soliciting whether Augustus appreciated the artifact I had procured for him? He had thanked me with obvious gratitude, and confessed pleasure at learning I knew of and respected his admiration for Alexander the Great. Were his responses sincere, or polite dissembling to cover umbrage?

Had I talked too much about my own interests: in painting tableaux of buildings, which had elicited the offer of the Gardens of Maecenas; in meteors, about which I had debated with Germanicus? Did my audience think me a compliment-hungry braggart? My mother would have maintained this was unequivocally true, had she been privy to my conversations that evening. But had I kept quiet she would have berated me for my reticence. My distraction was evident in my game. As I threw one Dog after another, more contradictions yelled. *Your pathetic performance is an unfathomable embarrassment,* versus *Play well, and you will be thought impudent.* Smiling, I made light of my inadequate playing: after all, someone has to finish last. Ever so predictably, Antonia chided Tiberius for training me poorly.

All at once the house reverberated with a loud report. Windows and doors rattled and lamps flickered. From the peristyle colonnade emanated a moaning, which increased in volume and pitch. Another report followed. Diodomedes went into the colonnade, where he conversed briefly with someone—presumably a fellow servant or a guard. Returning to the room, he announced the Sirocco had begun to blow. "An unwelcome visitor, precisely in time my birthday," Augustus grumbled as the moaning escalated into a shriek. Tiberius decided it were best we leave immediately before conditions worsened; traveling by night in a Sirocco, one ran the risk of being struck by blowing debris indiscernible in the dark. Before we departed, Augustus offered what seemed as much a command as a question. We were going to attend the chariot races in honor of his birthday on the morrow, were we not? "For certain, Sirocco notwithstanding," Tiberius replied.

Sleep eluded me that night. I lay listening to the wind shake the window shutters, and fighting the urge to toss and turn lest I disturb Tiberius. Eventually I was unable to lie still any longer. I arose and located my dressing gown in the half-light emanating from the sitting room, into which I wandered as I donned the garment. After removing one of the burning lamps from the stand, I started to head downstairs to the library. There I hoped to find, in the writings of some philosopher, a refuge from the contradictions I kept pondering or a mechanism for halting their intrusion. When I entered the colonnade, however, the wind immediately extinguished my lamp. After setting it on the sill of the open archway before me, I gazed at the open sky above the peristyle. The Sirocco was blowing in a haze, to which the lights of the city imparted their usual yellowish glow. Only the brightest stars were visible. At times it seemed as though the wind was actually moving them.

Oh depart from me, leave me alone! Ever since receiving Tiberius' tongue-lashing that winter's evening on Rhodes, I had striven to suppress my familial recollections. For a fair amount of time I had managed quite well. Why had these contradictory directives suddenly begun to intrude anew, and with such virulence? Hardly could I tell Tiberius about them. He would become wroth with me for continuing to ruminate about my family. I needed to vomit—not physically, for I felt perfectly well without the slightest trace of nausea. But mentally, emotionally, I was overflowing—yea, bursting—with frustration, anger, and grief. After abating somewhat, the wind began to blow with renewed intensity. As the pitch and volume of its sound increased, I leaned on the archway sill and shouted across the peristyle with all my might: not in a scream but a low-pitched, guttural bellow. So I did twice more when new gusts arose, presuming the shriek of the wind would drown the sound of my wails. So forceful these were, they left me coughing and gasping for air, my throat raw with irritation.

My outcries were overheard after all. Within moments of the third, Androcles who was on guard duty that night appeared beside me. Nestor, Alcmene, and Tiberius followed. Was I all right? I said nothing but only nodded as I covered my face with my hands. Tiberius thanked and dismissed the servants. His having to shout above the wind made me realize how loud my own cries must have been. By one wrist he led me back into our sitting room and lowered me onto the settee. After seating himself beside me he pulled my hands away from my face and held them, as he looked at me with tender solicitation, even as he had on that evening in Rhodes following my altercation with Timoleon. "What by all the gods is wrong?" he demanded.

"Telling you would anger you," I replied dolefully.

He rolled his eyes. "Your family—again!" he concluded petulantly. "Well, better you tell me your ruminations than wake the whole house and possibly the neighbors, bawling like a heifer in heat."

And so plaintively and contritely, I described the contradictions with which I had struggled that evening. My voice grew hoarse as I spoke, and I had to keep clearing my throat. As I proceeded with my narrative, Tiberius to my amazement began to smile. By the time I finished he was gently laughing. "Did you not perceive you were thinking like a military commander, a magistrate, or a ruler? Had you not yourself averred, that I carefully evaluated and discussed with my military council the potential outcomes of various battle strategies before deciding which to pursue? Does not my stepfather do precisely the same before proposing new legislation or implementing a new policy or project? The mental grappling you are experiencing occurs when one comes to recognize, rely upon, and truly trust one's own determinations. Your family had contorted this natural and healthy proclivity into a means of oppression. Trying to keep you under their control, they strove to suppress your innate ability to make independent decisions: hence their exaggerated, contradictory, and invariably pejorative reactions whenever you followed your own judgments.

"Down the future you must anticipate having to consider new choices, and in that process face dilemmas and confusions. Furthermore, you should expect to make wrong decisions. For these regret may be appropriate; but never, ever the remorse and self-condemnation your family urged. The human does not exist who does not err—your own kin included, no matter how hard they may have tried to convince you they were exceptions to this rule."

Now I laughed. He kissed my hands, and continuing to hold them resumed his pleasant discourse. "Clytia, I am immeasurably pleased to see this development in your character. It reassures me you can and will make carefully considered decisions with regard to the rearing of our son. Nevertheless you must beware not to allow your family's castigations, of this natural and acceptable inclination to weigh and assess options before you, to distort or hinder its operation. The more you let fear or self-condemnation intrude upon your considerations, the greater the likelihood of your making mistakes. And perhaps a good way for you to keep those recollections from clouding your judgments, would be for you to revel in the satisfaction your family's efforts to prevent you from pursuing your own decisions has failed. Had their endeavors succeeded, you and I would not be having our present conversation."

"Thank you, thank you, my dearest Scorpion!" I burbled.

He looked at me quizzically. "You have not used that epithet in years, although I call you my Lioness all the time."

"On the last occasion I had used it, I did so inappropriately and you justifiably took offense. Since then I have read and reflected upon discourses

516

about scorpions. Although they can be aggressive attackers, they sting only to protect themselves, their lairs, and their young—never for the deliberate purpose of exacting vengeance upon their perceived assailants. Hardly do they rejoice in the sufferings of their victims. Reading the Syrian medicinal from Gaius, I actually came across scorpion venom as an ingredient in remedies for pain and weakness of the joints.

"Your sting, my dearest, has been your wresting me from my family's control and keeping them from discovering me. It has been the wise counsels and patient forbearance you have imparted over the years, while I wrestled with the memories of maltreatment, and strove to overcome bad habits I had derived from those afflictions and from my family's obtuse mores. Now you have assured me I can make independent decisions without feeling the fear and guilt my family had associated with them. Well and fine if my kindred are stung with frustration, over my failure to achieve their unreachable expectations and over my ultimate escape from their clutches. And if they are not, no matter either. At last my desire to see them suffer for having afflicted me is dissipating."

He took me in his arms and held me in silence, stroking my hair with one hand. When he spoke again, his voice was husky with emotion. "I had imagined you had presented me with every conceivable reason for loving you. Now you have provided yet another."

Turning my face upward, I smiled into his. "Do you not yet realize after all these years, that your inspiration and correction, molding and shaping my character, evoked and revealed those reasons for loving me?"

While we kissed, a great gust of wind penetrated the shutter with enough force to blow out all the lamps on the stand. Now we both laughed. "Perhaps a sign from the heavens that we ought to be back in bed," Tiberius said with finality. "No point in relighting the lamps," he called out on hearing Nestor fumbling for a flint. In the darkness I was unable to see the way to the bedchamber or anything else. Tiberius could of course, and got me back into our bed without mishap.

Come the morning, I was unable to speak above a whisper. Chloe administered a syrup dark and pungent. "This formula Master's mother favors for relieving quinsy and soreness of throat," she honked encouragingly. Viscous and sweet with a slightly smoky flavor, the medicine worked immediately, tingling my throat with pleasant warmth as it numbed the soreness.

"Your condition serves you right well, after all your shouting into the Sirocco," Tiberius teased as we prepared to depart for the Circus Maximus. He insisted I bring a stylus and tablet to communicate with our companions in writing. In our litter he handed me a purse of betting money. We shared a box with Longus, Rutilia, and Marinus, all of whom commiserated good-naturedly about my condition. They blamed it on the Sirocco without eliciting any further explanation, and threatened to chastise me roundly if I dared utter a single word. I could not have made myself heard above the wind anyway. My comrades frequently had to shout. They had me point to the color on which I elected to bet. I chose White; the other selections were Blue, Green, and Scarlet. So passionate are the Romans about their circus factions, Rutilia managed to interject during a brief lull in the wind, that extended families and even whole neighborhoods adhere to particular colors as vehemently as to their ancestral customs and tutelary deities.

The stadium attendants had saturated the track with water, to keep the Sirocco from turning it into a dust storm blinding horses, drivers, and spectators. The event opened with the entry into the arena, of a procession similar to that of the Ludi Romani. Not Augustus this time but two magistrates rode in the triumphal car: the aediles responsible for arranging the event. As the cavalcade wound its way about the track, the spectators rose to their feet and cheered. Many waved kerchiefs representing the colors of their chosen teams. The gilt chariot halted before Augustus' box. One of the aediles dropped a white kerchief onto the track to signify the start of the races, and the crowd took their seats.

Either agitated or invigorated by the wind, the horses pranced and pitched and reared as their grooms led them to the starting line, which had been traced across the track in chalk. Standing by their charges, these attendants struggled with pats and strokes to instill calm. Gusts snapped banners ripping some of them, and threatened to unbind our hair and tear our garments from our bodies. Each race entailed seven circuits around the stadium. To keep count of the laps, one of seven gold dolphins on a superstructure in the center of the arena was tipped head downward when a circuit was completed. We each bet a denarius on our chosen color to place first, an aes to place second, a sesterce for third. Marinus and I profited handsomely from the first two heats, as White came in second in the first race; then first in the second, third, and fourth. Thereafter we not only lost our winnings but depleted our reserves; for White turned disastrously lackluster, finishing last in the next five races and third in the final tenth. Between the fourth and fifth races, and later between the eighth and ninth, teams of desultores competed. Each drove a pair of horses at full gallop. The riders stood straddled with one foot on the back of each of their mounts, or leaped from one horse to the other.

We were served a platter of finger-foods for our luncheon: pasties topped with meat or fish or cheese, small sausages, assorted cooked vegetables, figs and sweet pastries. My companions urged Augustus' preferred Ligurian wine upon me for drink and with good reason, for it soothes the throat as well as the stomach. Owing to the difficulty of making oneself heard above the wind, conversations were sporadic and tersely abbreviated.

The morning thereafter I was in my studio when Fulgens brought me two letter tablets. The one was from Antonia. She and her sisters were considering mounting a special exhibition in the Porticus Octaviae, to commemorate its forthcoming twenty-fifth anniversary. For certain I must join them and contribute my incomparable artistic expertise. Claudia had agreed to host the first meeting about the exhibition at her home the Friday forthcoming.

The second tablet bore a seal with the impression of a frog. The communiqué was from Gaius Maecenas Acer, manager of the Villa Maecenatis and freedman of its former owner (whose signet the frog was, Tiberius told me later). Having received a letter directly from Caesar Augustus recommending Galatea Aristoclide to view, sketch, and paint the villa and gardens on days of closure, Acer and his staff stood ready to welcome and accommodate. The grounds were open to the public on Wednesdays and Saturdays, and on specially designated holidays like the birthday of Caesar. Immediately I replied. The birthday of Augustus, falling on a Sunday that year, had directly followed a regular public day. Not wishing to burden Acer right after an extended period of visitation, I inquired whether I might visit the gardens on the forthcoming Thursday. Acer sent an affirmative reply that same afternoon: I was welcome at the Gardens of Maecenas on any day of my choice, from the second hour when the staff reported for their work.

In the meanwhile I found the chariot race had left quite an impression upon me: one of great dynamically flowing and rippling force. This had been manifest in the undulating muscles of the horses and their drivers, the shuddering of harness tack, the glint and flashing of light off the metal of vehicles in motion, the fluttering of plumes and scarves, the taut grimaces of the charioteers as they maneuvered their teams vying for position. In my studio I began to record my memories of these hues and shapes and images, reflecting with admiration on how the charioteers had controlled their teams and raced them effectively amid the onslaught of the Sirocco.

On my third day of pursuing this endeavor, a thought struck me with great urgency. Unable to continue painting, I put down my brush and sat staring at my palette without seeing it, my mind lost in contemplation. For years I had been struggling to reconcile my notion of Underlying Good, to the presence and prevalence of human adversity and its consequent sufferings. If Good is the governing Principle of the universe, whence arises adversity? If from ignorance of that Principle, whence arises the ignorance? From my present considerations, I found myself finally beginning to understand what I had read and heard and tried to accept on faith alone: that adversity leads us to improve our physical circumstances, our behaviors, our ethics and morals, our perspectives on situations facing us, our views of and interactions with our fellow man. In short, adversity forces us to strive all the harder to reach that excellence within ourselves of which Aristotle wrote—even as the Sirocco had compelled those charioteers to manage their teams all the more diligently. Socrates, I remembered reading, tenaciously refused to answer his shrewish wife Xanthippe with anger and oppression. Instead he relished the self-discipline requisite to bestow nothing except kindness upon her. In the end she mellowed into congeniality, and bore him three sons.

As I mused, my contemplations seemed to grow more and more momentous. My heart began to pound from the sense of wonderment building in my consciousness. I asked myself: could I walk up to my mother today, and with absolute sincerity say, *Thank you for the myriad, the excessive, the physically and emotionally torturous and even life-threatening abuses you heaped upon me; for without them I would never have become the individual I now am?* My answer to myself—a firm, confident *Yes!* —left me awestruck, exultant, breathless with an oddly restrained yet escalating excitement. At long last I had managed to forgive my family!

Or had I? My next thought brought me back to a dismal reality. Should the scenario I had envisioned truly take place—should I actually have occasion to thank my mother for the maltreatment which had brought me to my present state—she would take credit for having driven me to my achievements against my resistant will, and never attribute them to the strength of my own character. Now dejected, I picked up my brush. The paint on it and on the palette had begun to crust over, because I had been so long considering what I had hoped was an end to a protracted philosophical quest. The forgiveness I so desperately craved, and which had seemed finally to have come within my reach, remained as elusive and enigmatic as ever.

I started to clean the brush. The dried paint made the task stubborn; but after a while, as I continued to work the cleaning oil through the bristles, the clots began to loosen and break apart. Presently I noticed an uncanny parallel between what was happening to the brush, and the changes my life with Tiberius had wrought in my perspectives about my family. Were not my anger and bitterness, befuddlement and dismay over my adversities, yielding to gratitude for the benefits they had engendered? Was not the determination my family had mistreated me from a perverted sense of right sweeping away my desire to avenge myself on them and gloat over their sufferings? Xanthippe had not yielded readily to Socrates' kindness; yet he had persisted, trusting the goodness of his endeavor to prevail. Unless I trust the inherent goodness of my aspiration after forgiveness to prevail, and unless I rejoice in the benefactions I presently enjoy, my adherence to and confidence in Underlying Good is vain hypocrisy.

By the time I had wiped the oil from the brush and placed it in its storage box, my gloom had lifted into a calm earnest. Nevertheless while we were resting together following sex, Tiberius commented I was unwontedly reticent and asked what was amiss. Briefly, tersely as I could manage—not only because I did not want to irritate him but because my voice was still healing—I described my frustration over my inability to forgive. All the while he lay on his back, shaking his head from side to side, pursing his lips and rolling his eyes. When I had finished, and he began his reply with the words, "Will you ever, EVER," I assumed he was going to conclude with *stop ruminating about your family?* Instead he finished with, "stop being so harsh on yourself?"

On the day I had chosen for my visit to the Gardens of Maecenas, I took Ajax and Nausicaa as my attendants. My paints and palettes I left at home—not only on account of the Sirocco, but because I wished to spend this visit exploring as much of the estate as possible. Later I would choose which elements to depict. A high wall of red bricks enclosed the park. Acer was a pleasant little man, with hair bleached and skin darkened by the sun. He admitted us through a set of thick wooden gates. Beside these stood an armed guard, whose brilliant blue livery attested to Augustus' ownership of the property.

Looking about, I recognized trees and plants with which I was familiar from Rhodes and my parents' Campanian retreat; but having learned the names of but few of these flora, I asked Acer to identify them as we proceeded on our tour. First to catch my attention was a stand of Roman pines, their deep-brown corrugated trunks soaring upward into their dark-green cloud-shaped canopy, their heady fragrance filling the air beneath them. Acer identified olive and oak, hemlock and willow, acanthus and ligustrum, rose and rhododendron, jasmine and spearmint, and a bounty of others. The names of a few I already knew, like laurel from the trees before Augustus' residence, and dogwood which in spring had decorated the fields of our farm with blossoms. From Acer's litany I came to discover the Guardian Trees were a sycamore, an oak, and a hawthorn.

My guide pointed out fascinating imports the likes of which I had never seen: yews from Gaul with dark-green needle-like leaves, citrus trees, red-barked cedars, an immense date palm from Syria, tamarind trees from Nubia, camellia shrubs and an azedarach tree from China. Some wildlife was present: songbirds and squirrels, rabbits and woodchucks—not nearly as abundantly as on the Rhodian farm, but certainly in numbers greater than I had expected given the garden's urban locale. Cats were on hand as well, to control vermin. Throughout the park a large staff of gardeners was hard at work, keeping the foliage at bay with hoes, rakes, and shears. From time to time we encountered mounted guards.

On our Rhodian promontory the menservants had kept the network of hardened dirt and gravel paths, and the few pieces of statuary, free of brambles and fallen branches and stinging plants. Otherwise they had left the foliage untouched. The result had been a dynamic and ever-fluctuating embroidery of natural growth. This had assumed different colors and hues and shadings and shapes from season to season and year to year, effecting changes even in static elements like boulders, the pond, and the Guardian Trees.

In the Gardens of Maecenas, the plants were meticulously arranged in groupings evocative of rooms in a house. Apparently, hardly anything was allowed to germinate spontaneously. Everything was deliberately placed to catch the eye with contrasts of color and shape: a small red-leafed plum in the center of a crescent of willows, their image captured in a reflection pool; a pergola hedged with oleander and shaded by laurel; olives and azaleas ringing a fountain; rhododendron dotting the edge of the shade cast by the pines. Ground coverings were monotonously uniform—here a spread of grass or clover, there one of ivy—with nothing interspersed. There were no stray sprigs, no fallen logs and branches, no tangled underbrush. Everything was trimmed and manicured like a tailored garment. Small plants like poppies and larkspur and feverfew and germander—and, yes, heliotrope—which in their natural setting splashed color across field and forest floor, were here confined to urns set along the garden's flagstone walks. The only flora that appeared to be allowed spontaneous germination was an occasional orchid, nestled in a crack in a retaining wall or at the point of separation where a tree branch emerged from its trunk.

The park was undeniably aesthetic, but unnatural and forced. For this reason none of its landscapes appealed to me. Not that I regarded the excursion a waste by any means; for it inspired me to merge elements of what I had observed with memories of wilder environs to create imaginary scenes. Moreover I had perceived natural models in specific plants and blooms, their individuality unaffected by the artificiality of the garden's design. My favorite feature of the garden turned out to be its large pond. Ironically enough the intervention of the gardeners had created an admittedly artificial, yet dynamic and palpitating artistic masterpiece. The ponds I knew from Campania and Rhodes had been drab and unaesthetic, despite their support of fish, frogs, turtles, and waterfowl. Dark and still, they had reflected the sun only when it was at certain angles. Their edges were ringed with mud and dense stands of reeds and rushes. Some of these grew within the waters themselves and swallowed, amid their dusty greens tans and browns, the delicate pastels offered by flags. In late summer, cress and water docks spread a green scum across the waters' surfaces. Sometimes the waters themselves stank and bred fierce biting flies.

The pond in the Gardens of Maecenas was edged with pink, white, and pale brown gravel, which maintained the essential moisture of the soil along with the cleanliness of visitors' feet. There were no rushes. Only a single, obviously manicured stand of reeds grew in the shade of an oak. Along a sunnier edge grew flags. Although at the end of their season the lingering blooms, unencumbered by reedy competitors, displayed an iridescence almost luminous. Somewhat subdued by the surrounding thickets, the Sirocco created ripples on the surface of the dark waters, reflecting sunlight in shimmering coruscations. And on that same surface, instead of scum there spread the leafy green pads of waterlilies. Their star-shaped blossoms bobbing on the waves—some white, some pink, some blue, some golden—had the translucence of alabaster.

We saw no turtles. To Nausicaa's delight, however, a frog with green and gray mottling sat balanced upon a lily pad, studying us with eyes like glass knobs, his throat undulating like a bellows. A pair of white swans, gliding slowly across an open expanse of water, added elegance to the scene. Presently there was a commotion within a nearby clump of oleander. A family of ducks emerged and waddled to the pond: first the colorful drake with his green head, reddish-brown neck, white flanks touched with brown and black; then the hen whose movements revealed a vibrant blue underwing beneath a surface mottling of brown and tan; and finally six puffy brown ducklings. I asked Acer whether the pond contained fish. Yes, he said; in fact, Caesar himself occasionally comes here to angle. He then added with an air of caution, that to prevent unauthorized angling when the park was open to the public, the official answer was no fish were present. I assured him my companions and I would keep the secret.

The villa itself was very much as I had originally envisioned the residence of Augustus. The immense, three-story structure was faced with travertine. Each floor of its exterior was wrapped in a broad colonnade, with marble statues standing between the columns along the front of the first floor. We ascended eight broad travertine steps. Through a pair of high wooden doors, arched at their top and elaborately carved with human representations of the Four Winds, we entered an inner foyer three stories in height. Illumination proceeded from windows embedded in the walls above the entryway and directly opposite. On the second and third floors, balconies adorned with ornately sculpted friezes traversed the wall opposite the entrance. The foyer and balconies were decorated with statuary, their walls with painted panels representing trees and shrubs, grasses and flowers. The ceiling of the foyer was painted with human representations of the Four Seasons. All this was quite appropriate, I mused, for a mansion set amidst a garden.

Acer showed us those portions of the first floor immediately adjacent to the foyer. To our left, a series of interconnecting rooms housed Maecenas' collection of art and sculpture. To our right lay a large reception room, and beyond it a great hall for the giving of concerts and lectures. The remainder of the first floor, Acer explained, held two formal dining rooms, a library, offices, and artists' studios. There was a stairway, well illumined by windows, in each of the building's corners. The second floor was devoted to living quarters, including apartments for guests, and for the resident artists and writers whose careers Maecenas and his wife Terentia had sponsored and promoted. Servant quarters were on the third floor, along with some workrooms. Other work areas lay in a partially subterranean basement. Like the home of Augustus and our Rhodian townhouse, the villa was constructed against a hillside.

Acer led us through the foyer to the peristyle. As in my current domicile and in the private section of Augustus,' a colonnade skirted the interior perimeter of each floor. Nearly a quarter of the peristyle was devoted to a great fountain. From the mouths of two lions' heads atop columns set in relief on one wall of the house, water cascaded into a broad shallow basin. This was inlaid with mosaic and genuine seashells, to resemble the sea floor with its fish and shellfish and odd plants. The remainder of the peristyle was paved with multicolored flagstones, and adorned with the predictable shrubs, small trees, potted flowering plants, statues, and benches. In one corner, beneath an arbor of flowering vines, stood a stone table and benches for outdoor dining. Although the villa was presently unoccupied, a permanent staff of servants kept it ready for use. Augustus occasionally entertained dignitaries here, and when suffering from respiratory distress took up residence himself—to partake of the Esquiline breezes, said to be the most salubrious in all Rome.

As we took our leave I thanked Acer for the tour, and asked if I might apply to return with my painting accessories. He congenially reassured me I needed no further appointments, but was perfectly welcome to arrive unannounced whenever I pleased. Journeying homeward, I began with growing excitement to lay mental plans for yet another artistic endeavor. Using the peristyle I had just observed and that on the Palatine for models, I would develop and implement a design for the remodeling of our own. And once the Sirocco ceased, I would assess the Palatine roof garden for ideas to enhance our veranda. After all, as lady of our house I had a right, privilege, and responsibility to cultivate the aesthetics of the place.

"If these be your intentions," Tiberius drawled after I had outlined my goal to him that afternoon, "you should be prepared to hurry. You may not have much time to realize your plans." I returned a puzzled look. "What do you think of the Villa Maecenatis?" he continued with a hint of banter in his voice.

"Stunning—almost enchanting," I answered, now all the more puzzled.

"What do you think of our taking up residence there?"

Now utterly astounded, I could do nothing more than gasp and gape wide-eyed.

Tiberius' mood waxed serious as he elaborated. Located near the Forum area and at the junction of five streets, our present home gave him much more visibility and ready accessibility to the public than befit someone in a private station. Petitions and petitioners, he said, were continuing to arrive in distressingly burgeoning numbers. He had thought his abandonment of public life would diminish this volume, and had been looking forward to reprieve from the interviews with strangers which his shyness had always made so difficult. Furthermore, as a private citizen he could hardly endorse someone for public office or recommend another for a military post; however, a considerable number of the petitions were of such character. Was a political party forming about him after all? This development Augustus would surely interpret as an abrogation of Tiberius' agreement to take no part in public affairs, even though the emperor understood Tiberius was not encouraging the process. And finally: Tiberius simply did not have the time to consider every request. He was becoming concerned lest suppliants turned away would wreak damage upon his already fragile reputation, spreading accusations of hardheartedness and indifference.

At the very time I had been touring the gardens and villa of Maecenas, Tiberius had been on the Palatine, petitioning Augustus to let him occupy the estate because it offered so much more seclusion than did Tiberius' present residence. At the villa, Tiberius' interactions with people could be strictly controlled. Passersby cannot casually drop in as at the Carinae house; for even now on days the park is open to the public, the residence is not. Tiberius will require anyone seeking an interview submit a request in writing—exceptions of course being family members, and friends of whose identity Tiberius will apprise the villa's staff and guards. He will make amply clear as well, that he will only consider petitions for philanthropic intervention such as aid to the sick and to worthy indigents or endowments for artists, scholars, physicians, and the like. Any request with even the remotest suggestion of a political purpose he will emphatically and unequivocally reject. This was the rationale he had offered Augustus for his request. He had not apprised his stepfather of his other, equally urgent motive: seclusion in which the revelation of our marriage and son to the family might be made discreetly, and kept secret from the public as long as necessary.

Antonia duly collected me the next morning, for the meeting with her sisters about the art exhibition. We assembled at the Aventine Hill home of Claudia and her second husband Paullus Aemilius Lepidus. (Her deceased first husband had been Livia's cousin Marcus Valerius Messalla Appianus.) This antiquated ancestral dwelling of the senatorial Aemilii Lepidi imparted a very tangible sense of history. Crepuscular and shadowy, the centuries-old house adhered to a pattern characteristic of early Roman domestic architecture, with a great atrium directly in the center and small rooms of various purposes skirting its perimeter. Most daily activities took place in the atrium, our meeting being no exception. We sat in a grouping of chairs and settees in one corner of the large, dusky room.

There were two additional participants beside the four sisters and me. One was a delicate, gray-haired woman named Atia. Her introduction as Augustus' aunt I thought I had misunderstood, until she explained she was indeed two years her nephew's junior. Her dark-haired companion was her daughter Marcia, about Antonia's age. Prima elaborated that Lucius Marcius Philippus—Atia's husband and Marcia's father—was in fact Augustus' stepbrother: the son of Augustus' mother's second husband by his first wife. Everyone laughed as I exhaled sharply and shook my head. The complexity of the Caesars' familial ties was beginning to boggle my mind.

Discussion began with concurrence the exhibit should open on the forthcoming anniversary of Octavia's birth—the sixth day before the Ides of March *[3/10]*. The first theme proposed, and which I assumed for certain would be chosen, was scenes from the *Aeneid*. Publius Vergilius Maro had been engaged in composing this epic at the very time the portico was first opened. Octavia herself had consistently supported the poet financially, and awarded him a special donative for the reference he made in his work to her deceased son—the present company's brother Marcus Claudius Marcellus, for whom the theater was named. In the end, however, the sisters rejected this topic as predictable and redundant and hence unlikely to encourage large attendance. The same if not more so, they decided, for scenes from the *Iliad* or *Odyssey*.

After further discussion, everyone concurred the exhibition ought to be empire-wide in scope. Marcia suggested representations of famous natural phenomena in Italy and the provinces. This was also rejected, as more appropriate for the Porticus Vipsaniae: funded and built at the behest of Agrippa's sister Polla, and devoted to the geography and topography of the empire. What about an exhibition of the works of a single artist, say of the painters Timomachus of Byzantium or Apelles of Cos, or of the sculptor Pheidias of Athens—or the works of a specific family of artists: the sculptor Cephisodotus of Athens, his son the unparalleled Praxiteles, and Praxiteles' sons Cephisodotus and Timarchides? So Claudia urged. A good thought, all agreed. But the task of locating pieces in multitudinous collections, and arranging for them to be borrowed or copied, could prove formidably time-consuming and prevent the exhibit from opening on the chosen date.

My companions pressured me for a recommendation. I resisted, asserting that since I did not feel it my place to offer one, I had come unprepared. Finally after they continued to press me, I suggested contacting the governors of all the provinces and asking them to send three of the finest artworks which best represented or characterized their particular domains—be these originals or copies; be they paintings, sculptures, mosaics, or models of large works like buildings. Another intriguing but impractical notion was the consensus. It might work well for the ten provinces under the administration of governors appointed by the senate, since peace and prosperity and civilization prevailed in these locales. But in those provinces controlled by the military governors who answered directly to the emperor, there was likely little art to be found. In most of these regions the native populations are boorish and agrestic, their artistic creations barbarous, uncouth, and few in number. Moreover the governors might resent having to fulfill an unanticipated requirement which could prove difficult for them, and which they may consider frivolous in the face of difficulties far more severe. Already these administrators were burdened with unstable borders, rebellious hostile natives, and the task of imposing Roman government processes upon peoples unfamiliar with and potentially resistant to these.

Right away the miserable contradictions began to infringe upon my conscience. *My suggestion was preposterous and impractical; it was complicated and confusing to my hearers; in offering it at all I had either been unacceptably froward, or had naively yielded to a solicitation not entirely sincere.* Now prepared to resist this onslaught, I promptly shoved the intrusion aside and mentally shouted, *Marcia and Claudia were not offended when the company rejected their notions!*

To my pleasant surprise, Prima credited my proposal for prompting her suggestion: solicit from the municipal councils of the twenty largest cities in Italy and three in Sicily, their four finest artworks whether paintings or sculptures. This notion met with everyone's approval. Each of the four sisters agreed to contact four Italian cities, Atia to write the remaining four, Marcia to address the three Sicilian. Again to my immense annoyance the inner voice began to complain: *Why had I not been invited to write some of the cities?* And again, I mentally fought back. Here was a circumstance, in which the familial connections of my hostesses were indispensable—familial connections I lacked. How could I expect to introduce myself to a municipal council? As the Greek ward Tiberius brought back with him from Rhodes? For a recipient of charity to approach a governing body as an equal to the emperor's nieces would be the acme of presumption. As a pupil of the artist Eutychus of Rhodes? As Eutychus himself? Suppose some compulsive decurion, having never heard of Eutychus or Galatea, decided our identities warranted investigation?

When I returned home Tiberius announced Augustus had approved our occupancy of the Villa Maecenatis; and he—Tiberius—wanted to repair there directly after Drusus' coming of age. Since he must devote his attention exclusively to the forthcoming ceremony, which was now nine days away, he was entrusting supervision of the move to me. What was there to fear, he asked with a grin when I returned a look of terror. Demetrius had spent this very day arranging with Acer for the transfer of our staff to the villa. Upkeep of the Carinae house after our departure would become the responsibility of Diodomedes. Our servants would move all our belongings. My duty as lady of our household was to insure everything once unpacked at the villa—as well as the furnishings already in situ—were arranged according to our taste, pleasure, and aesthetic sense. Drusus was coming to reside at the Carinae for this final week before his rite of passage. Tiberius was relying upon me to keep the transfer process quiet, orderly, and unobtrusive, so as not to jangle the youth's already frayed nerves.

The transition was not nearly as difficult as I had anticipated. Only two regions of the villa required my supervision. One was the master male and female quarters on the second floor. Here our servants, already knowing our preferences for arrangement of furniture and other appointments, for the organization of our wardrobes, executed these requirements with minimal intervention on my part. The other venue I must address was an artist studio on the first floor—one of four—which I selected because it had the best illumination. Into it I had the contents of my Carinae studio moved, including my *Lion of Nemea* and *Zeus Descending to Danae*. Since the villa was neither my property nor Tiberius,' to have them hung somewhere seemed a froward and inappropriate encroachment. He agreed. The lovers vignettes I had transferred to my new studio as well. The *Lion* and *Danae* I placed on easels, but the vignettes I left sequestered in their packing crate. For a man to display erotic art in his personal environs was perfectly acceptable; but for a woman other than a bona fide prostitute, doing so was disdained as abominable and even unnatural.

The private quarters overlooked the most scenic portion of the garden. Beyond the glimmering pond, tall trees obstructed the view of the city buildings. In addition to its bedchamber, my suite included a sitting room with a pantry, a separate dressing room with an immense closet, a bath with its own water tap and brazier, a privy, and two servants' rooms. The wall paintings were maritime in theme: mollusks, cuttlefish, sea urchins, and octopi on a sandy ocean floor; a school of fish; an eel cavorting with a ray; a trio of leaping dolphins; fishermen casting nets from a ship; others tallying a catch and mending their nets on a beach; a fanciful seaside villa; a calm, sunlit expanse of blue sky and water; the foaming gray and white clouds and billows of an ocean storm.

Tiberius' suite was arranged in the same pattern as mine, and adorned with scenes from the *Odyssey*. In the sitting room were the great wooden horse standing in silhouette amid the burning city of Troy; Odysseus and his companions putting out the single eye of the drunken Cyclops who had devoured their comrades; their flight from the cannibals of Laestrygonia; the circumvention of Scylla and Charybdis; the jaded wanderer identifying himself upon his return to Ithaca by shooting with the bow of Eurytus an arrow through the handles of twelve axes; the lightning bolt of Zeus striking Eupeithes the suitor of Odysseus' wife Penelope, as he prepares to mount an assault against her newly-arrived husband. The bedchamber was adorned with erotic scenes of the epic: Odysseus with amorous advances persuading the nymph Circe to restore to human form his followers she has turned into swine; the hero listening to the fatally seductive songs of the half-woman/half-bird Sirens while tied to his ship's mast so he cannot respond to them, his men rowing unperturbed because he has stopped their ears with wax; his scorning the lovelorn nymph Calypso as he gazes eastward toward his homeland; the faithful Penelope unraveling by night the shroud she is allegedly weaving for her father-in-law, thereby evading her promise to select a new husband upon completing the garment; Penelope embracing and kissing Odysseus when at long last they are reunited. Fortuitously the bath and dressing room were less elaborately adorned, the former with seascapes and the latter with island landscapes. In the dressing room I was able to have Ajax hang the lovers vignettes without creating visual havoc.

A parlor lying between the sitting rooms of the two suites struck me as an odd superfluity, until Tiberius explained Gaius Maecenas' relationship with his wife Terentia had been notoriously volatile. Twice they had divorced, only to reconsider and remarry. The parlor had given them distance when they were in disagreement and neutral ground upon which to resolve differences, without restricting access to one another in times of passionate concord. Its walls were decorated with bucolic scenes real and imaginary: a shepherd dozing on a hillside while his dogs guard his flock; satyrs dancing while Pan plays his pipes; anglers fishing in a stream; a sacrifice upon a rustic altar fashioned from a tree; a pair of lovers caressing in a bower; Artemis leading a group of hunters by night.

All of the rooms had expansive windows and doors, which opened to the interior corridor and the exterior colonnade in order to catch the famous Esquiline breezes. At this time, however, they were shuttered fast against the Sirocco. Shafts of sunlight pierced the spaces between the slats, and danced about as the blasts of wind shook the blinds.

During that final week, except for when we bathed and slept together, I was never alone with Tiberius for more than what seemed like fleeting moments. The better part of each day he passed with Drusus and I spent at the villa—even on a Wednesday when the gardens were open, because the house was not accessible to the public. That same Wednesday, the onset of another menses—again exactly two months since the last—raised my hopes a bimonthly regularity was being established. By the Friday following, all the bustle and confusion had come to an end. At supper I pronounced the villa ready for our occupancy. With countenance radiant and eyes moist with pride, Tiberius declared Drusus well prepared for and worthy to assume the toga virilis on the forthcoming Sunday. Drusus did not answer but lowered his eyes and half smiled, conveying a slightly sardonic air. Shyness, I thought with compassion, having seen Tiberius respond similarly to compliments ever since I had known him. And how easily these reactions could be misinterpreted as expressions of contempt.

In our bedchamber Saturday afternoon, Tiberius outlined specific instructions for me to follow the next day. During the second hour, a troop of relatives was going to assemble at the house: Drusus' first cousins Germanicus and Tiberius; Agrippina and Postumus, who were in fact Drusus' aunt and uncle since his mother Vipsania was their much older sister; Livia and Drusus' maternal grandmother Caecilia Attica the mother of Vipsania; and of course Vipsania herself with all but the youngest of the five sons she had borne her second husband—Drusus' brothers. So reflected, and momentarily wondered how he might react upon learning he had yet another.

Tiberius and this entourage would lead Drusus in a festive procession through the city streets to the Capitoline. I should remain out of sight until their departure, after which I was free to journey to the Capitoline by litter. Unfortunately I could not be present for the sacrifice and prayers in the Temple of Jupiter Capitolinus, not being a relative. And being a woman I could not attend the games—boxing and wrestling matches—which Tiberius was offering after the ceremony. Nevertheless as a member of the general public, I was welcome to witness the actual donning of the toga virilis, and hear the introduction Tiberius was going to deliver on the Capitoline plaza. Afterward I should not return to the Carinae house, but proceed directly to the Villa Maecenatis.

A fairly sizable crowd had gathered about the base and on the stairs ascending the slope of the Capitoline Hill. Presently the family party emerged from the temple's interior to its colonnaded porch. For the first time I beheld Tiberius' former wife: a diminutive woman with an oval face of pleasant mien, and the same warm brown hair as her son's. She wore a cream-colored veil over a stola of light blue. Tiberius' garments were completely white: there was no vertical purple stripe on his tunic to indicate senatorial rank, no broad purple border on his toga attesting to public office. A slight commotion sent a murmur through the crowd. Augustus emerged from the coterie of relatives and retainers with whom Antonia and I were standing, and took his place beside Livia on the porch. Here was an explicit demonstration, that Augustus' disgruntlement with Tiberius did not extend to their personal relationship and was not a breach of amicitia. More significantly, the emperor's gesture displayed his commitment to the promotion of Drusus' political career, which Tiberius as a private citizen could not foster. Together, Tiberius and Vipsania removed Drusus' toga iuventus characterized by its narrow purple border, and robed him in the solid white toga of manhood.

Turning to face the spectators, Tiberius delivered his address. "My fellow citizens, I give you Drusus (he pronounced the name with particular emphasis) Claudius Nero. He is well prepared to assume and well capable of executing the responsibilities which fall to him as he comes of age. His paternal lineage descends from the Sabine leader Attus Clausus, whom you all know was a founding father of the Roman race. Through his paternal grandfather he is descended from Gaius Claudius Nero, whose defeat of Hannibal's forces proved decisive in ending the second war with Carthage favorably for Rome. Through his paternal grandmother Drusus is descended from the great censor Appius Claudius Caecus to whom the Roman senate owes its code of ethics, and from Marcus Livius Drusus Claudianus the adoptive son of the heroically reforming plebeian tribune. His maternal grandparents, although of ancestry less renowned, are themselves brilliantly illustrious, being Marcus Vipsanius Agrippa and Caecilia Attica. This my son is stolidly committed to understanding and advancing the best interests of the Roman people. Celebrate with me, ye men of Rome, at the contests of wrestlers and boxers which follow this ceremony in the Saepta Julia." The crowd burst into cheers and applause.

There was a distinct detachment in Tiberius' manner: not of indifference and certainly not of estrangement or hostility toward his son, but of calm and joyous surrender of Drusus to his new independence. So I reflected as the litter bore me to the Villa Maecenatis. Exiting the vehicle before the gleaming front steps, I became aware of a change. The Sirocco had ceased. A light, fresh, intermittent breeze from the west was beginning to dissipate the haze. The afternoon sun, filtering through what haze still lingered, was bathing the landscape in golden light. Delighting in this refreshment, I could not resist spending the next hour wandering the gardens. When at length I entered the villa's foyer, a delicium advised me Master was awaiting me in the library. As I entered the room— cavernous yet stuffy, owing to the great mass of books it contained—he looked up from the star charts he was examining. His eyes were sparkling, and his smile and manner expressed the restrained joy of someone marveling at a wondrous discovery. With his hand he beckoned me to shut the door and sit beside him.

"Clytia, I feel rejuvenated," he said quietly and almost rapturously as he took my right hand in both of his. "Watching Nero—pardon me, who now calls himself Germanicus—watching him prepare to escort Drusus from the Saepta Julia to the Palatine I found myself cleansed, of that lingering compunction my leaving Drusus under my mother's tutelage during my sojourn on Rhodes had deprived him of a proper upbringing. Watching my son return this afternoon to my stepfather's home—the milieu in which Drusus was reared and to which he is bound more firmly than I—filled me with a clear and calm satisfaction. I am only Caesar's stepson; but Drusus is nephew to the intended successor Gaius. To Germanicus my stepfather's grandnephew Drusus is first cousin, and likewise to Germanicus' sister Livilla who is Gaius' wife. These lines of kinship, amid which Drusus matured and which he thoroughly understands, guarantee him a more prodigious place in Roman politics and a marriage commensurate with his stature than I could achieve for him. His horoscope, which I have just recast, bears this out. As for Vipsania: when I beheld her today she was merely a pleasant but distant memory. Your presence in my heart and home has thoroughly quenched my residual longings for her, and my remorse for having repudiated her. Nevertheless, recalling the experience of losing her has left me steadfast, unwavering, in my resolve never to let any person or circumstance or argument or condition no matter how urgent—not even my stepfather and his Chimera—persuade me to release you so long as you will have me!"

"Remember my promise of always and forever," I replied earnestly, returning his smile. I did not mention the immense relief I had felt, upon observing there were no tears in his eyes as he beheld Vipsania. As he raised my hand to his face and kissed it, I found myself unable to resist disclosing an idea I had been considering for several days but hesitating to propound. "Tiberius, now that you have made peace with your family regarding your political aspirations, why should we risk alienating them anew with pressure to accept your non-Italian wife and son? Why do we not simply return to Rhodes—the city, I mean, not the farm; or repair to Alexandria, to Aphrodisias, or to Antioch, where eastern mores abound? There your living openly, with me ostensibly your mistress and Alcimus our bastard, would be entirely acceptable—or at least far more so than in Italy. Eventually your testament will establish the legitimacy of our relationship and of our son."

"Well considered, my Lioness: once more your keen insights show themselves forth. Nevertheless I insist we follow that recommendation only as a last resort, after we have exhausted every conceivable effort to persuade my family to recognize and accept you as my wife and Alcimus as our legitimate son. Politics has nothing to do with this. The approval of my family I crave for no reason other than they are my family."

A feeling akin to remorse swept through my consciousness—rueful and pitying, desperate to console and ameliorate—carrying not the guilt of remorse but its emotional barbs nonetheless. Tiberius' aspiration I appreciated only too well—and too painfully. Tears flooded my eyes as I flung my arms about him and thrust my head beneath his chin. "I understand, my love," I murmured emphatically, "most assuredly I understand!"

The intensity of my response seemed momentarily to take him by surprise, but then he gently enfolded me in his embrace. "I know you do," he said softly and compassionately. "How could you not? And I thank you." He began to stroke my hair. "Now I understand the import last August's meteor—the one foretelling disaster for Lucius Caesar—had for me. Events are clearly aligning themselves toward fulfillment of my monumental change. This I am confident will take the form of a new life as a private person with a new wife and a new child—a life approved by my family and accepted by Roman society without cavil."

During the ensuing autumn I embarked upon the lifestyle my mother had consistently decried as wasteful and frivolous, all the while she envied and begrudged those who led it and coveted it for herself. Thanks to the skills of Pallas the barber, Florentinus the cobbler, Chloris the seamstress and her daughter Leda the cosmetician, the accents of jewelry I had Phoebe send from Rhodes and Tiberius authorized Chloris to obtain for me new, I was coiffed and dressed in the heights of current fashion and elegance. Under the tutelage of yet another Phoebe—Agrippina's music mistress whom Augustus sent to instruct me—I enhanced my prowess at the harp along with my repertoire.

Antonia and her sisters began taking me to salons conducted by society ladies, always introducing me as Tiberius' ward with the bogus history he had created for me. The intellectual intent of these sessions surprised me. I had always assumed they consisted of nothing more than social interactions—the exchange of personal news and gossip. Although these elements were certainly present, the primary purpose of the gatherings turned out to be examination and discussion of artistic or philosophical or literary topics, if only on a superficial level.

On an afternoon in mid-October, Tiberius and I attended a pleasant concert by a flute and harp ensemble at the Theater of Marcellus. This was the first public event at which we appeared together since our arrival in Rome. Ajax and Androcles accompanied us as our bodyguards, Alcmene and Nestor as our personal attendants. As I anticipated, many people stared and some exchanged whispers while others offered bows and curtsies and verbal greetings. A week later we returned to the same venue for a stunning performance of Sophocles' *Philoctetes.*

Augustus and Livia continued to invite Tiberius and me to supper on the Palatine whenever their schedules allowed. Sextus Appuleius and Quinctilia invited us to dine with them one evening, Longus and Rutilia on another, Marcella's elder daughter Agrippina and her husband Haterius on yet another. (Remember, Friend Reader, the elder Agrippa was Marcella's first husband and Augustus' daughter's second.)

Aulus Plautius Silvanus and his wife Urgulania had us to luncheon at the ancestral home of the Claudii Nerones. The Silvani were the age of Longus and Rutilia—older than Tiberius but younger than Livia. After a simple meal of clear fish and vegetable soup and barley bread, they showed me what little there was to see of the house. It was an atrium-centered dwelling like the home of Claudia; but being smaller in scale it was bright and airy instead of cavernous and shadowy. We saw only four attendants. Tiberius later explained Aulus was struggling financially: hence the simplicity of the meal he offered, and his lack of servants. His progenitors' mismanagement of their family assets had left barely enough to meet the minimum property qualification required for membership in the senate. Tiberius and Livia were letting Aulus occupy the house rent-free in return for its upkeep, lest Aulus be forced to forfeit his place in the senate because he could not pay the tax incumbent upon its members. I commented the reward seemed equitable for Aulus' loyalty to Tiberius in the face of Augustus' disapproval. Tiberius corrected me promptly. He and his mother were not bestowing benefits because Aulus Silvanus—like Longus, Vescularius, Marinus, and Quirinius Cyrenius who was now Gaius' advisor—had chosen to support Tiberius specifically against Augustus' disgruntlement over Tiberius' retirement to Rhodes. The Plautii Silvani had been retainers of the Claudii Nerones for many generations. This adherence, being multi-generational, demanded unflagging loyalty from both sides. Consequently it transcended both alignments and disagreements between particular members of either. Urgulania, not really comprehending this conceit, mistakenly believed Livia regarded her a special friend.

From Livia Ocellina we received and accepted an invitation to an elaborate formal dinner. The large number of guests, being neither relatives nor retainers, made Tiberius uncomfortable. One cannot easily tell who may be a lurking enemy, he remarked to me afterward. Having to recline rather than sit at table added to his distress. He found amusing, however, my reaction to the three viands offered: wild boar, gazelle, and peacock. While the other guests marveled and fawned over their flavors as exotic, I found them commonplace. With wild boar I was already familiar, since Nicanor had hunted it on the Rhodian farm—along with venison which the gazelle tasted like, and pheasant to which the peacock seemed identical.

On another evening I got to serve as hostess, when Tiberius honored with supper his Roman supporters late of Rhodes: Longus and Rutilia, Vescularius and Nevidia, and Marinus. My menu selection of grilled swordfish, a mélange of fennel, morels, and dasheens, met with everyone's approval as reminiscent of the fare we all had relished on Rhodes.

To my surprise, every single one of these encounters I enjoyed thoroughly. The patient and kindly counsel Tiberius imparted, after I yelled myself hoarse on the eve of Augustus' birthday, dispelled those horrific misgivings my family had instilled in me about my social behaviors. No longer obstructed by these distorted scruples, the finishing of Demas flowed readily and naturally into mind and conduct. I found myself at ease, poised, and readily conversant. Not even on Rhodes—and certainly never in Naples—had I experienced so active a social life. When I commented about this to Tiberius, he replied we were sedentary and introverted compared with most Romans of wealth and position. Salons and supper parties, at which to see and be seen, were tools for the idle privileged class to aid their struggle against boredom. His tarnished reputation was keeping us from being awash in invitations.

I also started to frequent, on my own and at a leisurely pace, public buildings and parks Antonia had shown me during our morning tour of the city. Surprisingly enough my favorite turned out not to be the Porticus Octaviae with its extensive art collection, but the Porticus Liviae. It seemed to hold a special meaning for me because it had been dedicated in conjunction with Tiberius' triumph. The portico's construction encourages admission of light and circulation of air through the wide trellised walkway bordering a colonnade with high vaulted ceilings, at all times of the day and even in cloudy weather. Broad and sloping eaves prevent penetration of direct sunlight with its consequent heat, and also of driving rain. The portico's lapidary was my favorite exhibit in all Rome. The gemstones are fraught with colors and hues, with scintilla adding fascination as the daylight shifted.

The week following Drusus' coming of age celebration I spent sketching various views of the Villa Maecenatis' exterior—from the gardens on the days they were closed, and from the peristyle on days they were open. At the end of this period I was satisfied with the improvements to my technique of depicting edifices—confident it was adequate for rendering buildings observed from a distant perspective, which obscured finer details. On the three consecutive days following I returned to the Palatine, where I began work on my panorama in earnest. The cessation of the Sirocco had left the air clear and pristine and slightly golden, as is typical for October. I wanted to take advantage of these conditions to complete the sketches on the small palettes before the shortening days, lengthening shadows, and drizzle of the winter months compromised the views. Those days I intended to spend in my studio, copying my depictions onto an expansive palette and refining characteristics, hues, and shadings.

My first two visits were unremarkable. As usual I encountered none of the family—only guards and servants with whom I was unfamiliar, but who knew me right well and greeted me by name. A girl about Nausicaa's age brought us luncheon. On the third day I assumed she was the cause of the slight commotion behind me, until Phaedra my attendant on this occasion suddenly whispered "Mistress!" in an urgent tone as she crumpled into a low curtsy. Turning about, I discovered Augustus standing at the entrance to the belvedere. After setting down my palette as I rose to my feet, I curtsied while returning his smile.

Without taking his eyes off me he said in a deliberate tone, "I will speak with your mistress privately," whereupon Phaedra withdrew into the roof garden beyond earshot. Seating himself on one of the belvedere benches, he motioned for me to sit immediately beside him. "May I see?" he asked, gesturing to the tableau on which I had been working. It represented the view across the Forum Boarium to the Tiber Island, the Theater of Marcellus and Porticus Octaviae and the Theater of Pompeius beyond. "Quite pleasing," he declared. "Not amateurish at all, although you are a novice at depicting buildings. Your artistic talent awes me. That you manage to produce such phenomenal representations with minimal formal training defies credibility. How long do you think completion of your panorama will take?"

"To tell the truth, Caesar, that will depend upon how many small tableaux of the various vistas I can complete before the onset of winter suppresses natural illumination."

"And threatens to sicken you with chilblains if you persist in sitting up here in the cold." After a pause, during which he continued to gaze and smile at me rather reflectively, he said, "Your return to my Syracuse delights me inestimably."

I returned a puzzled look.

"You do not realize that since you first started coming here to sketch, I have observed you from my study over there." So my attendance had not gone unnoticed after all on those previous visits when I had presumed it was. "Then your excursion to Anzio and Fondi, and after that the Sirocco, kept you away," he continued. "I missed your sweet presence bitterly."

As he spoke, his manner became increasingly disarming. His gaze, his movements, his tone of voice, were pleasantly engaging, warmly solicitous—I even dare write enticing. Finally after a pause and a glance at Phaedra, he said in an undertone, "Please accompany me to my retreat. I shall repair there first, leaving you here. Let several minutes pass, and then send your woman on an errand for an hour; or better yet find a pretext for sending her home. I shall have you escorted there after we finish. Once your maid has gone, come to me. The discretion of our tryst is assured. Family and servants know never to disturb me in this office except for the direst of emergencies. The doors I keep bolted; and as an added safeguard the couch—ostensibly for my napping—is segregated from the main room in a shuttered cubicle."

How does one resist an overture for sex from the most famous and powerful man in the known world—a man already legendary in his own time, and guaranteed similar respect and admiration from generations yet unborn? With the most effective, albeit not entirely foolproof, weapon a woman has. My heart was pounding as I smiled back wistfully, hoping to convey the impression I was flattered and even interested. Gently I replied, "Although your offer entices me strongly, I regret having to decline because I am *in my days* as the grannies often say."

Fortuitously he nodded acceptance of this excuse I was menstruating— which I was not, and which he could have ordered investigated. "Be warned, then," he replied, smiling all the more salaciously, "you can expect me to persist." He patted my knee and departed for his enclosure.

"Now we have to tell him about our marriage no matter what the consequences, or the chances are he will never let you alone!" Tiberius expostulated after I described my experience. "All his life he has been a womanizer. Given his present age and the fragility of his health, he probably can no longer penetrate; but he can still engage in fumbling and fondling and fellatio. From that very first conversation with me, which you surreptitiously witnessed, we learned he suspects you are my mistress. The state of matrimony, however, he holds sacrosanct for foreigners as well as for Italians. Let me handle this business. Until it is settled, I recommend you not venture to the Palatine unless with me."

I could not have agreed more, even if refraining from the Palatine meant postponing the panorama until the spring or abandoning it altogether. And so I began to wander the estate's gardens seeking ideas for alternative projects. Noticing the pond still held an abundance of waterlily blooms, I enthusiastically set about recording these in anticipation of painting them on textiles over the winter. While pursuing this endeavor during the next several days, I found myself pondering Augustus' proposition with dismay and alarm. Although fully confident I could never, ever, bring myself to be unfaithful to Tiberius, I could not dispel a strong titillation his stepfather's offer had aroused in me. For days I forcibly banished the notion from my thoughts and felt terribly guilty when it came rushing back, until the morning I lay dreaming the man stirring at my side was Augustus rather than Tiberius. To my relief I found the latter unperturbed and actually amused after I confessed my infatuation.

"I should expect you to feel an attraction for him. He is phenomenally charismatic and persuasive in all elements of character. How else do you suppose he has been so successful at convincing the world his monarchy is not a monarchy? You need not worry about future advances from him, for I spoke with him yesterday."

"How did he take the disclosure?"

Tiberius, who had been lying on his back, rolled onto his side toward me. He wore that mischievous smile he always assumed when thoroughly satisfied with the outcome of a confrontation. "You will find out anon. In the meanwhile," he took me in his arms anew, "I thank you for your fidelity."

"There can be no other way," I replied fervently. "Always and forever."

An imperial letter tablet awaited me when I returned from the pond at noon.

Imperator Caesar Augustus to Clytia Neronis, greeting.

You likely think me a lecherous old hypocrite, having invited you to engage in the very act my own legislation against adultery stringently condemns. The strength of your character and quickness of your mind are to be extolled. You managed to refuse me without disclosing your marriage before you had secured Tiberius' permission for doing so. Nor did you let my rank and reputation intimidate you into yielding to me against your will and principles.

You and Tiberius are both well aware, that as a matter of public policy I strongly oppose intermarriage between Italians and other races. Hence I cannot make public my approval of yours— at least not at this time. Nonetheless I eschew condemning your union outrightly, especially while I am promoting reconciliation with Tiberius. Therefore I request you continue to keep your marriage secret—representing yourself ostensibly as Tiberius' ward and Antonia's friend—until such time the revelation of your marriage becomes viable. Tiberius and I together shall ponder and deduce an appropriate mechanism for this disclosure. For the sake of your child we cannot hesitate or dally, but must expeditiously derive a conclusion. We hardly want your son maturing in ignorance of his true parentage, and with more affection for a foster family than for his own.

I have discussed this course of action with Tiberius, and he is in agreement. To preclude the possibility of premature revelation from some and inevitable contention from others, we shall conceal this matter from the members of our family with two exceptions. Antonia we have already taken into our confidence, to her inestimable delight. Livia too we shall inform, but not until January when we can surprise her on her birthday. We trust you will keep this counsel as well.

Sincerely I hope these words dispel any misgivings you may have had about returning to my Syracuse, where henceforth you can rest assured your chastity will be honored.

When I had finished reading the letter aloud to him, Tiberius broke into guffaws. "You never cease to astound me, my Lioness. Innumerable Roman politicians and foreign potentates have tried assiduously but failed to accomplish what you just did: render Caesar Augustus defensive and conciliatory."

"Dare I return to his rooftop?"

"Most wholeheartedly I recommend you do. Your continued absence might cause offense, leading him to renege his endorsement of our marriage."

And so the day thereafter, having finished sketching the waterlilies, I repaired back to the belvedere where Antonia joined me for luncheon. Apart from telling me my news was wonderful and I should rest assured she would keep it secret, she said nothing more about my marriage or the incident with her uncle. Instead we discussed another matter that had started to concern me, and Tiberius had urged me to consult Antonia about. The birthday of my youthful nemesis Agrippina was four days before the Nones of February *[2/2]*. Although the event was still some time distant, I had begun to wonder what sort of present could I possibly offer without offending the recipient.

Antonia reassured me I was hardly the only person who found Agrippina difficult to please. "You are either a friend of unassailable loyalty, or a bitter and dangerous enemy. Even assigning servants to her is challenging. You should anticipate her sneering at whatever gift you present, be it the treasure of Croesus!"

A sudden inspiration struck me. Agrippina adored Germanicus. Hence I proposed, "What if I were to paint a little portrait of Nero Germanicus on a pendant for her to wear about her neck?"

"A brilliant idea," Antonia returned ebulliently, "with which Nero is sure to comply. I can hardly wait to see the look on Pina's face when the gift is presented." Antonia's smile had become sly.

The next afternoon I returned to the belvedere. Seeing Augustus approach, I banished Nausicaa into the roof garden beyond hearing.

"Welcome back," he said quietly, his smile and manner now demure but still engaging.

"Thank you for allowing me to return here, Caesar," I replied, lowering my eyes as I curtsied.

"You were never forbidden. Thank you for forgiving my inappropriate advances."

Without question he was embarrassed; and suddenly he was candid and vulnerable instead of authoritarian and unassailable. With a surge of sincere compassion I raised my eyes to his and returned his smile. "There is nothing to forgive. How could you be expected to know of the marriage Tiberius and I successfully conceal from our own servants? Fearing to offend and distress you by disclosing it, we abetted your ignorance."

As he seated himself, he gestured for me to take a different bench. He gazed at me in silence, with a somewhat mournful expression on his face, until at length the intensity of those brilliant blue-gray eyes drove me to lower mine again. "Learning of your marriage, and of the integrity and courage you and Tiberius have demonstrated in keeping it covert, has heightened my respect for you both. You are truly a model of ideal womanhood: beautiful, perceptive, poised, patient, devoted, forbearing, and chaste. Yet I still find you disarming, devastatingly desirable—even more than I did before your recent revelation. Why does my admission alarm you?"

He had noted my growing discomfiture. "Hardly I wish to become a rival to Livia for your affections," I said reticently, feeling a rush of warmth and nervously knotting and unknotting my fingers as I spoke.

"You I find desirable; Livia I love," he returned definitively. "There you have the difference, which given your intelligence you can easily grasp. And I hope you might find me desirable in return, even while you devotedly love Tiberius."

Relieved by this clarification and amused by his vanity, I raised my eyes—and I must admit—returned a coquettish look and smile. "Truthfully, Caesar, I find you extraordinarily desirable." Although my own attraction to him embarrassed me, being able to confess it removed the lingering guilt I was still harboring.

"Ah, splendid! Now the character of our relationship can be defined." He extended his right hand.

"Friend?"

"Friend indeed," I replied as I placed my hand in his.

And so began a unique and rewarding association, the memories of which remain clear and inspiring. Cooperation from the weather allowed me to pursue the panorama project through the remainder of October and into November. Occasional brief overnight rains abating at dawn were insufficient to break the escalating drought, but left the air of daytime clear and pristine without dust and haze. On almost every one of my visits Augustus came to chat, always sitting at a respectable distance from me within the belvedere and fully in sight of my serving woman.

Some of our conversations were quite weighty, as when we discussed Atomism. So vehemently did he challenge this philosophy as preposterous poppycock that I—a critic of the persuasion in my own right—found myself defending some of its doctrines. After listening attentively and respectfully to my exposition of Underlying Good, he pronounced it brilliantly considered and worthy of further evaluation. He was confident my methodology was tapping the Force which holds stars and planets in their courses and regulates the seasons of Earth. Nevertheless he recommended replacing the term Good with Order because good is relative: what is good for you is precisely the opposite for your enemy.

For the most part, however, our conversations were casual, lighthearted, and extemporaneous inquiries and comments about one another: our likes and dislikes, minutiae from our respective personal histories and our present everyday activities, observations of and discussions about our respective peculiarities and characteristics. We challenged each other's self-deprecations with complimentary alternatives. Like Eupistus the physician Augustus admired my teeth, since his own were small, widely-spaced, and streaked with discolorations that refused to yield to dentifrice. His self-consciousness about his shortness of stature I countered with the assurance he would never have the inclination to stoop—about which I was starting to remind Tiberius with increasing frequency and counteraccusations of sounding like a nagging wife. Commiserating with me about my neurosis over vomiting, he was confident it arose from my having been accused and terrorized whenever my brother puked. Lightning induced the same sort of shrinking panic in him, he said, ever since in his early adulthood, a bolt had struck and killed the torchbearer preceding his litter while he was traveling in a thunderstorm. Livia reacted identically whenever she felt threatened by fire, after having been caught and singed in that flash conflagration of the woods outside Sparta.

One day Augustus reassured me that despite his official eschewal of interracial marriage, he was relieved and delighted Tiberius had found love again after the misery of being wed to Julia—especially with a partner as intelligent, engaging, and obviously devoted as I. He continued with a warning, which lent a clearer perspective to his conversation with Tiberius on which I had eavesdropped. For himself and for members of his family there come times, when their affinities and affections must yield to the needs of his regime. Already I was experiencing the imposition of having to keep secret my marriage and child. I should be prepared for other circumstances to arise, requiring sacrifices more severe. Although Augustus would make every endeavor to avoid or mitigate such afflictions as fully as possible, there may come occasions when these efforts will fail or cannot be made in the first place. The Sword of Damocles is very real, he said, and as much a threat to human happiness as to life itself. This conversation made me realize Augustus' love and consideration for his family were much deeper than I had originally assumed.

Early in his rise to power he had learned—from his own experiences and from the insights of Livia—that moderation and conciliation are almost invariably more effective, at diffusing the enmity of one's personal and political enemies and procuring their acquiescence, than are violence and repression. The latter certainly have their place, but must be applied very judiciously and only in last resort; for they can easily augment the hostility their use is intended to suppress. Year after year, decade after decade, Augustus had seen pardon and forgiveness induce opponents to turn about completely, and start supporting him or at least become neutral.

Nevertheless, there will always be some adversaries who refuse to yield. For him the prime example was the Scribonii Libones; for me my family and Agrippina. Once you have recognized a mistake you have made, have corrected and apologized for it, these implacable enemies will continue to hold it against you. Any efforts you undertake to cultivate their approval or to defend and justify yourself, prompt them to judge you insecure. Reacting to them with disdain or hostility of your own only heightens theirs. Nonchalant indifference to their accusations—allowing your record to stand for itself—offers a far more effective way of diffusing these insinuations. A humorous response is even better, if you can manage to think of one. Some twelve years ago, during a junket to Gaul for reviewing the reorganization of administration in that province, Augustus discharged from his entourage a young military legate. He was being insolent to superiors, permitting and even encouraging rowdy behavior among his subordinates. The impudent youth confronted Augustus: how was he expected to explain the dismissal to his father? Instead of responding that the boy should have thought about this consequence before engaging in the misconduct which precipitated his discharge—the retort I might likely have given—Augustus had replied, *Simply tell your father I was not to your liking.* Thoroughly nonplussed, the youth retreated without uttering another word.

Another particularly memorable discussion began with an exchange about the alterations of our respective identities. Who would we be today, had we remained precisely who we were at birth? Augustus had been born Gaius Octavius Thurinus into a family of Italian landed gentry—ancient and immensely wealthy but of little political significance. Voluntarily accepting the testamentary adoption from his maternal granduncle the Dictator—the brother of his maternal grandmother—had made him Gaius Julius Caesar Octavianus. Had he declined the bequest, he mused while gazing into the distance with a nostalgic smile, his greatest worries today would be not enough rain or too much, not enough harvest or too much. He would be married to a pleasant, docile, minimally educated, and utterly uninspiring daughter of a fellow landowner— never knowing but hence never missing his intense love for Livia, the comforting satisfaction she reciprocated his ardor, her profound intellectualism from which arose her acute insights into politics and other aspects of human nature, her uproarious sense of humor. Likely he would be enjoying untroubled digestion and sound sleep at night, both of which were forfeit to the stupendous mental pressures and emotional tensions of his present responsibilities.

What would have become of the Roman state had he rejected his testamentary adoption, I inquired uneasily. He sighed and closed his eyes; his smile fled and his demeanor became deliberative. He answered slowly, obviously thinking through his response as he gave it. Unless Antonius or another political strongman managed to establish a workable system, the chaos and bloodshed of the Republic's political and economic disorder would have continued and worsened. Eventually the provinces would have either broken away of their own accord or been conquered by other powers. Ultimately Rome herself would have been subdued by who knows what opponent: the rebounded Egypt Cleopatra aspired to bring about, Parthia, the Germans, the Pannonians, even a province or another Italian city. A pity, he continued after another sigh and with obvious sadness, that Antonius had been unwilling to share power. He had very sound and practical political ideas, and genuine altruism toward the people he governed. Had they not ended up fighting one another to the death, Antonius and Augustus might have developed a successful diarchy, patterned after the constitutional distribution of power between the two consuls. A system of this type would have precluded the still lingering objections to the monarchic characteristic of the present regime.

Listening to his respectful commentary about his former opponent, I recalled with a sudden surge of anger how my mother and her aunt used to denigrate—vehemently and persistently—people who disagreed with their opinions and notions, and gloat triumphantly over misfortunes befalling the resented. Struggling to keep from sounding petulant, I proceeded to describe how the designation Pythia had been forced upon me so my brother did not have to trouble himself with the extra effort of pronouncing my real name; how I had become Daphne the ward to thwart my family from finding me and turning me back into Pythia; and subsequently my becoming Galatea the allegedly absentee farm owner, to shield me not only from my kin but from enemies of Tiberius. After some reflection, Augustus reminded me my birth identity had not changed at all. Daphne and Galatea were merely ruses, disguises—costumes concealing Clytia from those who would destroy her true self. He agreed with my conclusion that placating my family had been a hopeless prospect, but doubted it would have led me to madness or suicide. The inherent steeliness of my character would have prevented me from succumbing to self-destruction. Instead, he felt, I would have become increasingly eccentric—forlorn or irascible and most definitely reclusive—distancing myself from my persecutors by rendering them uneasy and apprehensive in my presence.

After another thoughtful pause he continued. Every parent—he being no exception—wrongs his or her children in some fashion at one time or another. Genuinely tragic, however, is the parent who refuses to acknowledge and repent those imprecations. Tragic, he repeated—not despicable. Although through intervening years I have pondered, cherished, and shared this assessment, at this first hearing remorse cut my psyche like a razor. Tears filled my eyes and ran down my cheeks, flustering my comrade, who nervously daubed my eyes with his kerchief as he inquired what he had done to upset me. After some deep breaths to compose myself, I explained how I had been trying unsuccessfully for years to forgive my family, and loathing myself for my inability to do so.

To this very day, his answer echoes through my mind as though it were only just spoken. "Do you not see, Clytia? You cannot forgive your family because you love them. You are baffled, confused, and frustrated, because you cannot fathom those you love hurting you so deeply in return. For this very same reason I cannot forgive my daughter and granddaughter their efforts to wrest my power from me. Their turning against me has left an agony more intense and enduring than any physical ailment or injury could inflict. Having to punish them to avoid abrogating my own laws exacerbates that pain. What a burden you have carried, my dear, striving through all these years to accomplish the impossible! But now have been separated from your family for nearly a decade. Try to dismiss your memories of them as you would a bad dream. You are a member of our family now. Pina and her silly remonstrances aside, we assuredly love you, and are poised to protect and promote your happiness and best interests."

I remember listening to him transfixed—yea, enraptured. His words brought more than guidance and reassurance. For the first time in my life I sensed a bonding I had never known from my own kin. Quitting my bench I seated myself at his side, flung my arms about him and held myself close against him without uttering a word—forgetting in my exuberance that to touch his person without first receiving his assent was to commit an act of sacrilege. It occurred to me later that he had thoroughly enjoyed my gesture. Tiberius assured me my assessment was entirely correct.

SATURNALIA INTERLUDE

Day-to-day life in the Villa Maecenatis required some serious acclimation on my part. The sheer size of the place was intimidating. My domiciles for the first two decades of my life had consisted of an alcove and a countryside hovel. Consequently the townhouse and suburban villa and subsequently the farmhouse on Rhodes—and certainly the Carinae house in Rome—had seemed expansive. Their spaces were limited and cramped, however, in comparison with the number and size of the rooms in my newest habitat. Under my own roof lay an art gallery replete with original pieces by legendary artists—including a small sculpture of Apollo rendered by no less a master than Pheidias of Athens, and an almost surreal seascape by my own exemplar Zeuxis of Heraclea.

The collection of the villa's library rivaled that of the Academia Norenas in size, and assuredly surpassed it in caliber. There were thorough collections in virtually every academic area: mathematics and science, philosophy and politics, literature and rhetoric, art and music. Well protected were original manuscripts of the *Anabasis* by Thucydides, of the *Poetics* by Aristotle, and of the third *Philippic* by Demosthenes. In their own separate alcove were stored manuscripts by the two late, great Roman poets Publius Vergilius Maro and Quintus Horatius Flaccus, whom Maecenas had engaged to extol Augustus' regime—along with the correspondence between the poets, their patron, and the emperor they glorified. At times I almost felt as if we were dwelling on holy ground, intruding upon the habitat of immortals.

The parlor separating Tiberius' suite from mine proved an annoying detriment to intimacy. It was flanked on either side by the sitting rooms of our respective suites: hence our bedrooms were separated by three intervening chambers. At least in the Carinae house and earlier in our houses on Rhodes, our suites had been directly adjacent to one another. Tiberius called this offending space the Zone of Neutrality, after a region in which two hostile armies by mutual agreement do not engage one another in combat. Upon rising from his bed in the morning, I had to traverse this wasteland in order to dress for the day, since my clothes and accessories and implements of my toilette were all kept on the female side.

Similarly when we bathed together, as we did on most afternoons, I must either arrange for a change of garments to be brought to Tiberius' quarters beforehand or for his clothes to be brought to my domain; otherwise one of us had to go traipsing across the Zone of Neutrality in a dressing gown. Presently we had a small collection of clothes and accessories stored in one another's dressing rooms. These aggregations required continual replenishment. Furthermore some essential items—the right cosmetic or hair ribbon, girdle or fibula, scarf, cloak, sandals or shoes—quite often were not on hand and had to be retrieved from beyond the void.

After our first week of residence, Tiberius had a dining table and chairs moved into the parlor for us to take our meals there, rather than in one of the two immense and highly ornate dining rooms on the ground floor. Since it well fit the parlor's sylvan theme, I had the planter box of heliotropes here installed. These usages proved well-conceived, softening the Zone of Neutrality with a bit of cozy familiarity that made negotiating the expanse a little less pernicious.

In the studio I had chosen to make my own, I set about painting models from the villa's environs onto textiles. My first endeavor in this genre was to represent—on a swath of fine, soft wool—a vine laden with blossoms of various pastels. Once hemmed, the textile became the creation I had envisioned: a small, soft blanket. I finished but did not undertake to embroider its edge, lest I fail to complete it in time for its intended purpose. Antonia's sister Prima was due to deliver sometime in December; and I wanted to have a suitable gift ready for the occasion.

I also began transferring, to the gigantesque palette I had procured from Longus for this purpose, the individual portions of the panorama. To keep the gallery curator and other members of the staff from determining Eutychus of Rhodes and I were one in the same, Tiberius and I perpetuated the ruse I was the artist's pupil and hence emulator of his style. The last of the individual segments of the panorama I completed directly on Tiberius' birthday. Afterward I remained on the Palatine, to celebrate both birthday and concluded project with a supper of red mullet and the casting of dice. The Ludi Plebeii were in progress. From viewing the opening street procession I had abstained, for I was busy with my project. Being patrician, neither Augustus nor Tiberius could attend any of the associated events. Nor could I: this celebration of Rome's non-aristocratic populace was exclusively for them. The Livii were plebeian, and the Antonii: hence to acknowledge the intent of the festival, Livia with Prima and Antonia had attended a theatrical performance and chariot race. Although intrigued that the Romans had a provision in their culture for curbing elitism, as spouse and guest of elites I kept this reflection to myself. Alone with Tiberius later, I did disclose it to him. He extolled both my insight and my discretion. Later that night before falling asleep, I reflected upon the pleasantness of the evening's festivity, in contrast to the drudgery of those ghastly pastry parties with which my family had acknowledged my birthdays. These celebrations had been driven by a sense of rote duty—like the following of an incomprehensible and unbelieved religious ritual because the neglect of it engenders discomfiture. The prevalent emotion had always been resentment, for the inconvenience the obligation imposed and for my blatant lack of gratitude. At Tiberius' event familial affection was palpably ingenuous and tangible, although no specific declaration was made.

That same November my menses began to occur regularly—at or very near to intervals of twenty-nine days. This indication of normality so relieved me of underlying fear a new growth might be developing, that acquaintances noticed and commented there was at once new calmness and ebullience about me.

Through the remainder of November and first week of December I returned repeatedly to the Palatine—now not to the belvedere but to the quarters of Antonia. Here I executed the portrait of Germanicus, for which he thoroughly enjoyed sitting. My association with Antonia had blossomed into a pleasant and intimate friendship—my first acquaintance of this nature with a member of my own sex since my girlhood affiliation with Photis. Spontaneously and unannounced, Antonia had started seeking me at the Villa Maecenatis and I called upon her on the Palatine, neither of us ever feeling the other was imposing. Oftentimes Antonia accompanied me on one of my junkets about the city.

Only occasionally did we discuss weighty, thought-provoking subjects like philosophical notions. For the most part our conversations were similar to those I had exchanged with Augustus on the belvedere—mostly the mundane minutiae of everyday life, but with feminine nuances. We would talk about the weather, the health and behaviors of family members and servants, our personal food preferences and those of Antonia's kin, how to dress for a specific event, the exasperating qualities inherent in men.

To Antonia I felt comfortable disclosing details of my relationship with Tiberius—how we became acquainted, the intensity of our reciprocated love, the growth in one another's characters our connection impelled and continued to impel, our high frequency of sex and our sedulous efforts to avert its consequences. That last comment elicited a wistful chuckle from my companion. She and Nero had shared a vigorously active sex life, as her seven pregnancies attested. Before, during, and since their marriage she had not entertained the slightest desire for another man, and was content to remain celibate for the rest of her life. To satisfy residual yearnings for her husband, she immersed herself in romances. This literary genre I had explored only tangentially, because my parents and my father's fellow academicians had so sharply condemned it as obscene. Now I borrowed Antonia's copy of the *Milesian Sketches* by Aristides and started to enjoy what I had missed.

On the Calends of that December, Tiberius and I were part of a great host of relatives and retainers, who accompanied Augustus to a lecture on philosophy by his longtime friend and mentor Areus Didymus of Alexandria. Afterward we attended a formal dinner on the Palatine to celebrate Areus—a delightfully engaging man. While traveling there in our litter I suddenly remembered that initial family supper, during which Tiberius had revealed my alternative identity as Pythia of Naples with published critiques of Atomism. Suppose one of his kindred introduced me as such to Areus, especially before a crowd of people who knew me barely or not at all? How was I going to explain myself? Tiberius laughed when I voiced my terror. How little I still understood his family. Never would they disclose information of discrete nature without my consent. How unlike my kin, who would not hesitate to embarrass me and enjoy my distress.

Areus' talk I found interesting but strikingly simplistic—especially for a thinker who was ordinarily more profound. The argument he presented was that the brutal antagonism of the Skeptic philosopher Aenesidemus of Cnossus, toward those who unwaveringly embrace the principles of any philosophical system as unchallengeable doctrine, constitutes a doctrine unto itself. This line of reasoning was indicative of a trend in contemporary philosophical study, which I had first noticed at the Rhodes Academy. Aficionados were concentrating upon indicating commonalities and drawing comparisons between established philosophical precepts, or else organizing those precepts into categories. No one seemed to be putting forth much in the way of original philosophical ideas or concepts. Little wonder I had grown disillusioned with academics.

Tiberius and I spent the entire week of Saturnalia at the sprawling villa of Ad Gallinas Albas: Livia's farm in the countryside some nine miles north of Rome at the outskirts of Veii. As on the trip to Anzio we took Gallina and Valens as our personal attendants. Tiberius ordered distribution of a donative, a festive dinner, and minimal work responsibilities for the remainder of our staff in our absence. The atmosphere at the farm was lighthearted and jovial.

Conversations were forthright, candid, and punctuated with humor. It was a time of relief and respite and reflection—of freedom from the routine of senate sessions, from the obligations of religious rites and other public ceremonies, from the hearing and consideration of petitions—although the arrival of several messages did necessitate Augustus sequester himself to review them and respond.

Antonia and her sisters did not join us. Nor did Agrippina. Prima's confinement was imminent, so she wanted all her sisters about her. Agrippina, who doted on infants and young children, had demanded to accompany Antonia. In Agrippina's eyes, caring for a newborn cousin presented a far graver and more urgent responsibility than defending her brother from the rest of the family. So Augustus remarked with a chuckle, but not without a nuance of pride in his granddaughter's maternal inclinations. Moreover the company of her cousins Pulchra and Iulla was certain to give Agrippina a pleasanter Saturnalia than sulking by herself at the farm.

Postumus, Germanicus, Drusus, and the younger Tiberius accompanied us, as did the three young Asiatic vassal princes. Right away all the youths decided to band together, and pursue their activities as a group apart from everyone else. They took their meals in the same hall as the rest of us, but at their own table and often at different hours. And so for the first three days, until other guests arrived, Tiberius and I dined only with Livia and Augustus.

The details of this excursion I shall never forget. In keeping with the presumption I was Tiberius' ward, he and I were assigned separate but adjacent quarters on the second floor of the main house. This edifice stands on a bluff above the Tiber, which our rooms directly overlooked. Across its banks in the distance we could see the pale gray walls of Rome, the variegated colors of the roofs of buildings, and the white upper portions of the more elevated buildings including the Temple of Capitoline Jupiter. Scarcely had we settled into our chambers, when an eager Livia insisted upon escorting me on a tour of the house and its environs.

As we walked about she related anecdotes about the farm. It was a part of the patrimony of the Livii Drusi, who through successive generations had kept it under active cultivation down to the present day. Livia's father had named it Ad Gallinas Albas for the strain of white-feathered fowl raised there, regarding which Livia described two particularly striking experiences. During her first pregnancy, aspiring to determine the sort of child she was destined to bear, she took an egg from under one of the setting hens. Through successive days she and her serving women warmed the egg in their hands, until it hatched a vibrant and strapping white cockerel with a fine red crest atop his head. An accurate prophecy, did I not agree? she inquired. Vigorously I nodded while returning her smile. Meanwhile Tiberius, who had accompanied us, covered his eyes with one hand while his cheeks and ears reddened.

Laurel proliferated on the farm. Livia showed me the villa's great summer dayroom, closed off for the present season because it was sunken to preserve coolness. Its walls were painted to represent the estate's formal garden with the laurel groves extending beyond. As we proceeded through one of those groves, Livia recounted another prodigy associated with the farm. It had occurred at the time her divorce from Tiberius' father was being finalized. Alighting from her carriage before the villa's entrance, she heard a raucous cry. Barely above her head, an eagle was soaring with a pullet from the villa's flock struggling in its talons. After making several swoops the eagle released its victim, which Livia managed to catch. In her beak the pullet was clutching a laurel sprig. The pullet proved unharmed and was returned to the coop. She matured into a sturdy and fecund setting hen, who survived for fifteen years and became a matriarch of the flock. Reverence for her was palpable in the conduct of her fellow hens as well as her own numerous offspring.

Livia recognized the laurel as a dwarf variety with small dark and glossy leaves, and branches that shimmer rather than bend in the wind. She placed the strain under the special care of her gardeners; and it flourished rapidly and abundantly. Eventually one of the horticulturists in the service of Maecenas informed Livia this species of laurel was a highly uncommon variety. Because of its rarity, its particular beauty, and the omen associated with it, Augustus and Tiberius with their own hands had cut branches from the stands for fashioning into the victory crowns they wore for their triumphs. Livia showed me the special laurel, the trees of which reached no higher than my head.

The farm's primary crop was a red fig, which matured in early autumn. This year's yield had been abundant, although not excessive like the plums of Augustus' cousin Lucius Pinarius Scarpus. Livia attributed her lesser harvest to the lack of substantial rains since July. Indeed, evidence of drought abounded in the stark grayness of the foliage, punctuated here and there with a fleeting patch of faded crimson or tan. None of the rich reds, browns, deep greens and blues of well-watered winters was to be seen.

That first evening, over a supper of roast fowl fresh from the flock, Tiberius in keeping with the spirit of the holiday proposed a verbal game. He, Augustus, and Livia should each describe an encounter with the populace during the past year, which was at once harrowing and amusing. Then I must decide which I considered most memorable and why. Tiberius began with an account of a petition he had received just the preceding week. A cobbler had requested an interview to discuss financial assistance for care of his widowed mother. The written plea had seemed so poignant and genuine that Tiberius agreed to receive the man, presuming the mother was physically ill and in need of medical treatment and nursing care. However when directly questioned about his mother's health, the shoemaker replied she was hale and hearty and strong as a heifer. What he was seeking from Tiberius was a continuing stipend, for the purchase and maintenance of a caged bird to distract and entertain Grannie. She was becoming increasingly irascible with age, and had started to harass her son's wife and their children so virulently they were threatening to leave him. Struggling to retain his composure against conflicting urges either to rail at the man or burst into guffaws, Tiberius managed to state sedately that while he sympathized with the petitioner's plight, to conserve his assets he must restrict his donations to the support of failing humans.

Augustus proceeded next. On Sunday and Wednesday and Friday mornings he received petitioners in the reception area of his home—a practice I quite well remembered Tiberius pursuing at our Rhodian townhouse. During the past summer, a man approached him pale and trembling. The look on the petitioner's face was not so much one of reverence, but rather of befuddled trepidation. The man kept extending and then retracting the hand in which he clasped his entreaty, as though he were trying to affix it to something swaying. The image that flashed into Augustus' mind he could not help but express; for had he not he would certainly have begun to laugh, and ended up disconcerting the poor man all the more. As he reached forward and extracted the scroll from the tightly-clenched and oscillating hand, Augustus advised the hapless petitioner he looked as though he were endeavoring to offer a denarius to an elephant.

One of Livia's charities was the donation of dowries to indigent brides, who aspired to improve their personal condition and that of their families through marriage, and whose characters she had assessed as worthy of her benefaction. On rare occasions she interviewed a petitioner and her family in their own residence, to ascertain whether an orderly and fastidious household indicated the applicant could be expected to make a diligent and industrious wife. In July she had canvassed the daughter of a day laborer at his apartment in the Suburra. Lying across the Tiber from the rest of Rome, this poverty-stricken, crime-ridden district was home to the most impecunious of citizens—along with social misfits who could anticipate being driven out of regions deemed more respectable because of their wealth. Fearful and elusive themselves since most were fugitives from creditors, the more upright denizens of the region habitually and deliberately ignored the activities of their eccentric or felonious neighbors.

Livia had traveled to this locale with a heavily armed escort surrounding her litter. She was exiting the tenement in which her prospective beneficiary resided, when on the street before it there began to pass a small retinue of men, women, and children—all of them stark naked except for insufficiently concealing loincloths on the adults. While Livia stood on the stoop, struggling not to stare agape with incredulity, the horrified father of the bride hurriedly explained the group was a local company of nudists. They never bothered anybody, never engaged in displays or acts of outright lewdness, and always responded very pleasantly to the young children who predictably inquired about their absence of dress. On balmy days like the present they gathered in the nearby public park, to avail themselves of the sun before proceeding to the public bath. Meanwhile the commander of Livia's bodyguard accosted the entourage brandishing his sword, nearly trampling the group with his horse, and shouting. Did they realize whose sacrosanct eyes they had violated, and that their offense was punishable by death? While the nudists gaped back abashed, confused, and frightened, Livia composed herself and called out to leave the assemblage alone. To a woman of her disposition, she asserted, the sight of naked men was no different from that of statues. The nudist leader crossed his hands over his groin and bowed, and motioned to his companions to emulate him. Traveling through the empire with her husband, Livia had observed many strange customs and bizarre sights; but none could compare, she felt quite certain, with receiving obeisance from a troupe of nudists.

Now I must provide my answer: which scenario did I find the most memorable, and why? After some reflection in silence upon the three accounts, I chose Augustus.' As I had listened to each narrative, I explained, I had deliberately conjured a mental image of what was being described: a stipend-supported bird, a monetary offering to an elephant, or a gaggle of people unclothed. Of the three, the funded elephant had left the strongest and most lingering impression upon my conscience.

Early the next day, Tiberius went horseback riding with the youths and boys. Augustus retired to the library, to deal with a message from Publius Octavius the present prefect of Egypt regarding an administrative problem. Consequently I sought out Livia. She was weaving in a room set aside for this purpose, replete with baskets and distaffs filled with wool and flax fibers and spindles wound with thread. Her hands moved with the precision of machinery, producing a flawless textile without any of the variation in tension between the individual warp threads that had always been my shortcoming. Taking care to keep my manner jocular, I described how I passed years in abject frustration while my family refused to allow me a loom, only to discover once provided with one that I could not manipulate it successfully. After laughing gently at my narration, Livia invited me to sit beside her and make a few passes with her shuttle. The predictable result ensued. Each warp I produced had a different tension, and none was satisfactory. Nevertheless, I felt none of the embarrassment or dejection I had endured when Timoxena and Phoebe had endeavored to teach me weaving. In fact I now found the process tediously repetitive and dull.

While she corrected the aberrations I had left in her textile, Livia inquired whether I had come upon any models for my artwork in the short time I had been on her farm. Indeed I had, I responded brightly. On our excursion, which had taken us along the bank of the Tiber, we had come upon a weathered wood pinnacle altar. Although I had seen pictures of these structures, which Italian farmers and shepherds fashion out of trees, this was my first time to observe a genuine one. A lambskin and a sheaf of grain hanging from a crossbeam near the apex, and surrounding soil reddish-brown from absorbing blood, were proof the altar was currently in use by the denizens of the farm.

Here the river curved slightly. Where it straightened a bit farther upstream, we had crossed it on a low brick bridge. The center of the bridge was adorned with a column of travertine, topped with a basalt sculpture of an urn. When we approached this area on our return, I discovered the pathway actually ran atop a culvert where it passed the altar. Built with the same architecture as the bridge and of the same brick, the culvert formed a man-made berm spanning an eddy created by the river's curve. The scene was replete with architectural dynamism. Culvert and bridge stood at right angles to each other. The pediments veering downward into the water, with altar and column soaring skyward, imbued the scene with vertical and linear energy. This nuance was complemented by the river's horizontal flow, the circular inferences of the eddy's currents, and the arches of the structures. I aspired to complete two tableaux: the one depicting the altar, the other the column and bridge.

Why then, Livia queried, was I not taking advantage of the unseasonably warm and clear weather to reproduce those vistas, instead of wasting my time watching her pursue an activity that evoked frustration and unhappy memories for me? Not that she did not enjoy my company: that assumption I should never make. Nonetheless I should not let a sense of duty or protocol impel me to forgo an opportunity to engage the special ability with which I was endowed. And as if some cosmic plan were unfolding, a manservant arrived to announce Master desired Lady's presence in the library. Had not Tiberius told me Augustus frequently sought her opinions on matters of state? Now I was without excuse for lingering with her instead of recording the scenes I had described. So Livia admonished me as she departed.

Although the weather was unseasonably warm and balmy, I had brought with me from Rome my heavy himation of densely woven dark blue wool, lest a change should set in. Before setting out I wrapped myself in this garment, so I did not have to carry it on my arm. Our man Valens I sought out and engaged to help me transport my accouterments: palettes and paints, brushes and rags, easel and stool. Where the Tiber curved away from the culvert, the bank on the opposite descended gently into a natural beach about fifteen cubits at its widest point. This was my destination. By the time we reached it I was sweltering, and shed the himation after Valens departed.

So engrossed I became in the panorama before me, that I took notice neither of passage of time nor of my physique. The arrival of a mounted guard with a satchel of victuals—compliments of Lady Livia, he said—made me realize I was not only hungry, but in need of relieving myself so urgently I knew I could never reach the villa in time. Recalling my experience with the same predicament while in the moth glade on Rhodes, I located the closest clump of shrubbery dense enough to conceal me. It turned out to be a stand of the favored laurel. Although I recoiled from the notion of profaning it, the forces of nature overruled my reservation. Casting my himation over a low-hanging branch formed a tent, under which I executed the necessary function. All the while I salved my conscience with the mental argument I had at least aspired not to sully the laurel; and I blessed its presence for providing me the privacy my situation so desperately demanded. Had not Tiberius assured me, on the far sadder but no less urgent occasion of Xanthothrix' euthanasia, that doing what is most right under the circumstances incurs neither blame nor regret? Nevertheless I resolved never to tell him about the present incident—and I never did.

Now I was glad for having hauled that lugubrious himation with me, not only for the concealment it had provided but for its warmth. As I munched the boiled eggs and cooked vegetables Livia had sent, I realized that while sitting still and painting without an overwrap, I had become chilled. Would I become ill, I wondered as I huddled beneath the himation, now grateful for its weight. After my brief meal I walked up and down the beach a bit until I felt comfortably warm. Then I returned to my painting, until the lowering sun obscured my subjects in shadow and the air became noticeably cooler quite quickly. Valens I had ordered to call for me at this time of the day; and duly arrive he did. To avoid further chill I proceeded to the villa at a brisk pace, hoping I had managed to ward off a body cold. Hardly did I relish the embarrassment of taking ill while a guest at Livia's farm. Carrying only my palettes atop the box with my brushes and paints, I quickly outdistanced poor Valens whom I had encumbered with stool, easel, and rags.

Awakening at dawn the next morning, I detected no change in my physical condition. Hence I arose and dressed myself without the assistance of Gallina, lest the ensuing commotion wake Tiberius. Because the daylight hours of winter are short, I wanted to take as much advantage of them as possible to complete my project while the weather remained cooperative. I told Valens to have Gallina bring me victuals at noon, to preclude worrying Livia or any other member of the family about whether I was fed. I also made plans to interrupt my work at intervals, and repair to the villa or one of its outbuildings to relieve myself.

As we neared the altar, what I had thought at first was the whistling of wind turned out to be music of plaintive and haunting quality. A shepherd was leaning against the altar, playing his pipes. Beside him on ground newly bloodied lay the headless carcass of a kid, its feet bound together with a thong. Drops of blood were falling intermittently from the animal's head, which was affixed to the crossbeam near the summit of the altar: presumably the shepherd had used his staff to accomplish this feat. Upon seeing Valens and me, the shepherd promptly left off his playing. As if in a single motion he affixed his pipes to a leather thong on his belt, picked up his staff in one hand and his sacrifice in the other, and headed into the woods. Before I could call out to him, inviting him to remain and continue his music so intriguing, he had disappeared traceless like a fleeting specter. At once I began adding him to my scene while the image he had left remained fresh and vibrant in my mind.

As I painted, I became aware of irritation developing in my nostrils and sinuses. Feeling otherwise well, I decided if this were the only consequence of my sitting perspiring in the elements without an overwrap, I could count myself fortunate. I had just finished devouring the lentil and vegetable soup from the covered tureen Gallina had delivered, when I saw men carrying some sort of baggage along the pathway in my direction. They proved to be Augustus, Postumus, and five menservants laden with poles, lines, buckets and baskets, and stools upon which to sit: the accouterments of fishing. At the center of the bridge they halted.

"Will you join us in angling?" Augustus called out to me jovially.

"But certainly!" Notwithstanding I had forsworn angling because of the miserable memories it evoked, I could hardly refuse the present invitation. The party finished crossing the bridge and descended the riverbank to the beach. Turtles, sunning themselves at the water's edge, dove into the shallows as the group approached.

"I will not angle with *her*!" Postumus shouted upon reaching the beach. He clenched his fists and stamped one foot, as little mute Miranda had when frustrated.

"Then you shall return to the villa, listen to Tiberius attentively, and follow his instructions without another remonstrative word or act," Augustus returned sternly. Postumus reddened and stared at me, chest heaving and teeth bared; but he said nothing.

As we were tethering lines to poles and hooks to lines, and affixing meat scraps from one of the pots for bait, Postumus' demeanor shifted markedly. With diligence and facility he prepared his own pole, and then assisted one of the menservants who was struggling with his. All the while he babbled cheerily if inanely about how he hoped the fish were good and hungry, how angling refreshes one's spirits and refocuses one's mind, how mankind would suffer starvation were it not for the dedication of fishermen to their vocation. After casting his line he quieted down and admonished the rest of us to do the same, lest we scare off the fish with our loud talk.

With a toss of his head, Augustus motioned I should withdraw with him to a slight distance from Postumus, just out of earshot. "Tiberius was teaching the young men military sword maneuvers," he began in an undertone. Dejection was clear in his voice despite its quietude. "When unable to master one of the moves, Marcus became wild with fury. It took my insistence that he join me at angling—his favorite pastime—to calm him down." We cast our lines into the river. "My grandson!" he continued, now in a distressed whisper. "He entered his fourteenth year this past September: three days before the Ides [9/11], when you and Tiberius were in Anzio."

The response I murmured— "Hardly do I expect he would have allowed us at his celebration,"—elicited a slight and fleeting smile.

"In less than two short years he will come of age. Conjecture him as an adult, and holding my office." Augustus' tone became trepidatious. "Now with Lucius gone, should Gaius prove unable to fulfill his responsibilities, I want my authority to devolve upon Nero Germanicus. However our fisherman here as Gaius' brother has the stronger hereditary claim. Confounded turtles!" he concluded, raising his voice slightly. The rapid succession of brief tugs we were feeling on our lines confirmed these creatures were busy at our hooks. One of the menservants seized a handful of bait from its container, carried it to the end of the beach upriver from where we were standing, and there dropped it into the shallows. A technique anglers utilize for drawing turtles away from baited hooks, and which I did not particularly favor because I had found it can distract the fish as well.

"Marcus, you must stop lifting your line as soon as you feel a pull, but wait to see if it remains taut!" Augustus called out to Postumus.

A turtle nibbles the bait, while a fish swallows it whole and swims off. Hence the experienced angler knows not to raise his line upon first feeling a tug, but only when the tension persists. Postumus was not following this rule but repeatedly raising his line, and finding nothing at its end but slightly masticated bait. His increasingly abrupt motions and the grimaces on his reddening face betrayed his growing agitation. "No matter how long I wait it is not enough!" he bellowed. And as if to make matters all the worse, at the very moment my own forbearance paid off. The pull on my line had not only continued but grown noticeably strong and steady. I hauled in the line. A moderately sized trout was flapping at its end. Postumus flung his own pole to the ground and trampled it with his feet.

From my less than happy days of angling in Campania, I recalled a friendly old man: the father of the lady who made those horrid birthday pastries. He had taught me a technique for judging whether I had a turtle or a fish. I turned my pole over to the manservant who had cast the bait. While he dislodged my catch from the hook and flung it into a waiting vat of water, I scoured the ground for a short but stout twig. On finding one I approached Postumus and curtsied with lowered eyes. "Master Marcus, it grieves me to watch those miserable turtles ruin this occasion for you—the dirty little scoundrels! Let us see if we can outsmart them." While he looked at me bewildered—perhaps too astonished at my effrontery in approaching him to repel me—I secured the twig to his line about a cubit above the hook. After affixing fresh bait, I picked up the pole and cast the line into the river. The twig of course floated on the water's surface. The pole I handed back to Postumus. "If the twig submerges, start counting to seven, saying your name between each number so you do not count too fast. If the twig reappears before you reach seven, you definitely have a turtle; but if it remains underwater after you have finished counting, you should have a fish." Still silent and flabbergasted, he affixed his gaze to the twig.

The manservant handed me my pole, on the hook of which he had placed fresh bait. I cast the line back into the river, but neglected to take account of any tugs on it because I was assiduously watching Postumus' twig. It submerged, only to resurface immediately. "Do not raise your line," cautioned Augustus, who was watching that twig as well. It dipped and promptly rebounded four more times in rapid succession. Postumus left the line in the water without having to be prompted. On its fifth plunge the twig stayed down. "Let it be, let it be," Augustus urged. "Do not hasten to pull up, but wait and see what happens."

Suddenly the line became extremely taught and remained so, curving the top of the pole into the semblance of a sickle. "Pull up, now pull up!" Augustus and I cried, virtually in unison. The catch was a great gray freshwater mullet. "You could feed nearly our whole family with that," Augustus declared as another manservant helped a beaming Postumus remove the fish from the hook.

When this operation was over, Postumus approached Augustus and me. He did not smile, and kept turning his gaze from one of us to the other with the awestruck look of someone who has discovered something phenomenal. Then he bowed to me and asserted, "I no longer care what my sister says about you. She is utterly wrong. You are a wonderful lady, and I like you! Now I am going to go catch more fish! How fine it feels to get revenge on those horrid turtles!" Augustus rolled his eyes.

After handing my pole back to the manservant, I returned to my painting. As the afternoon progressed, Postumus with my turtle-thwarting mechanism successfully took a trout, a barbel, a perch, and another gray mullet. Quite condescendingly he poked fun at his grandfather, whose lesser catch included only two perch, a trout, and a little goby which he returned to the river. I reflected upon the dramatics I had and continued to witness. Mental or emotional instability is certainly no respecter of rank. A child so afflicted can be born into the most ordinary of families. For Augustus, however, this problem—magnified and escalated by his political position—was a significant threat to the safety and stability of his family, of his regime, and ultimately of the empire's entire populace. Some lingering disappointment—or even, dare I say, resentment—which I had been entertaining over Tiberius' insistence our marriage be morganatic, was now dissipating into relief and gratitude. His foresight in making this demand assured Alcimus' protection from the certainly distressing and potentially fatal effects of dynastic rivalry.

Postumus' ebullience lent our return to the villa, amid the red-gold light and elongated shadows of the descending sun, the jubilation of a triumph. To my immense surprise and apparently that of Augustus as well, the triumphator himself insisted upon carrying the box with my brushes and paint vials as though they were the requisite triumphal offering to Jupiter. From the hillock overlooking the villa we beheld a carriage newly arrived at its entrance. A woman's voice, echoing through the villa's halls, enabled us to identify the newcomers before we even laid eyes upon them. They were the loud and flamboyant Livia Ocellina, her husband Gaius Sulpicius Galba, and his two young sons by his previous wife (who had died of dropsy, Tiberius told me later). Earlier that afternoon another set of guests had arrived. They were Claudia's husband Paullus Aemilius Lepidus, and his grandchildren Aemilia Lepida and Lucius Aemilius Paullus. Cornelia the deceased elder daughter of Augustus' former wife Scribonia had been the elder Paullus' first wife. Their son was the treasonous Lucius Aemilius Paullus who had married (and presumably corrupted) Augustus' granddaughter Julia. Hence the grandchildren Paullus brought were the emperor's great-grandchildren.

Everyone was gathered in the villa's spacious reception room. The gaudily dressed, coiffed, and ribboned Ocellina sailed toward us like a barge bedecked for a wedding party. After dropping a hasty and perfunctory curtsy to Augustus without even looking at his face, she took both my hands in hers. "So you are the pupil of the artist who created that magnificent work of art!" Releasing one hand, with the other she led (the better word might be dragged) me over to where Livia was seated holding the Guardian Tree shawl I had given her. "I must have one as well!" Ocellina asserted. Be warned I shall not let you rest, but harass you mercilessly until you have obtained it for me!"

On the floor in the center of the room, those two little great-grandchildren and a delicium were building a tower with a set of painted wood blocks. Postumus rushed over and—still clutching my paint box—with a mighty kick demolished the structure, sending the blocks skittering across the floor in every direction. Little Lucius Paullus (he was about three years of age) burst into tears and ran to his grandfather for solace. His older sister and the delicium sat looking at the ruins in silent sorrow.

The youngest Galba—Servius, whose fifth birthday we would celebrate several days hence—sauntered toward Postumus with an officious air. "Why did you commit so nasty an act?" he demanded.

"Because it pleased me," Postumus snarled contentiously.

Impelled as if by instinct—without hesitating to consider whether my action was appropriate or what its consequences might be—I turned to Postumus with an ingratiating smile. "Here, let me relieve you of this, which you were so very kind to carry," I said solicitously, as I cautiously extracted my box from his clasp before he could send it flying as well. "Equeleus is waiting to assist you in cleaning and dressing your fine catch of fish!" I continued, referring to one of the menservants who had accompanied us. After Postumus had bounded off with Equeleus, I said to the delicium, "Why not see if you can build a new tower, grander than the other?"

At that very moment more guests arrived: Quintus Pedius, Laelia, and their deafmute grandson who hid behind his grandfather. After saluting his host and hostess, Pedius apologized for the absence of his son and daughter-in-law: they were seriously preoccupied with care for their newborn daughter. The little girl Aemilia approached the deafmute and extended her hand. He backed away abruptly, shaking his head, frowning, and protruding his lower lip. When Amelia persisted, the boy darted from the reception room and across the atrium toward the villa's front door. As Pedius and a manservant pursued, Laelia urged the aggrieved Amelia not to take offense: Pedillus was shy and frightened because he could not hear or speak. A few moments later Pedius returned, gripping the wrist of the squirming and kicking and biting Pedillus. After a bow, Pedius apologized that he and Laelia must excuse themselves for some time to their appointed quarters.

On the morrow the weather retained its unseasonable warmth. Nevertheless the gathering of slow-moving dark clouds along the western horizon indicated change was on the way, and prompted me to don the thick himation. Being warmed from the walk, I shed this garment upon reaching my destination. A flock of magpies, feasting on the remnants of bait and fish offal, flew off as I approached the beach. One of these birds I added to my depiction of the travertine column.

Around midmorning a cheery procession passed by. Germanicus, Drusus, and two of the young vassal princes—Mithridates of the Bosporus and Antiochus III of Commagene—appeared. They were leading a quartet of ponies along the path above the culvert. Aemilia and her brother Lucius were sitting on the back of one animal, the Galba brothers on the second, Tiberius Drusus and Mithridates' younger brother Cotys on the third, Postumus alone on the fourth. All were squealing with delight. The scene brought to mind that afternoon at the Rhodian farm, when Tiberius and Thrasyllus had led Miranda and Thrasylla about on our donkey Asellus. With this pleasant memory came a twinge of sad frustration. How long must Tiberius and I wait, for the right time and circumstance to be reunited with Alcimus? And would Alcimus accept Tiberius and me? Would our son forge emotional bonds with his foster family and come to regard his parents as strangers?

Perhaps fortuitously, my musings were brought to a sudden and quite unanticipated end. The pony cavalcade had scarcely crossed the river and disappeared around the curve just past the bridge, when Pedillus came running along the pathway apparently as fast as his legs could carry him. After tearing across the bridge and down the berm he started to careen across the beach, eying the pediments of the bridge as though intending to hide amid them. But when he saw what I was doing, he came to an abrupt halt.

Now a manservant came striding on the path, glancing frantically about. When he reached the center of the bridge I called out, "He is here with me," taking care not to raise my head or make any other show of recognition lest it induce the boy to bolt. Being deaf he could not hear my outcry; however the servant did. He slowed his pace to a stop, smiling and swinging his arms with relief. After a few moments' halt he proceeded slowly and stealthily down the berm to the beach, where he assumed a squatting position in the shadows behind me. His skulking, quite palpably, was to draw near to his charge without inducing the latter to run off. The effort may well have been unnecessary, as the boy's attention remained affixed upon my easel. The servant called out an apology for the intrusion, to which I responded there had been no offense. As though entranced the boy followed every movement of my hand, as I dipped brushes into paint vials and spread the colors across the tableau. Presently the pony brigade trundled across the bridge en route back to the villa. Pedillus noticed them, not from their noise but from the moving shadow they cast across our venue. After gazing at them with obvious ennui he resumed watching me. The contemptuous look on his face faded back into one of rapt concentration.

Meanwhile the loquacious manservant explained, with far many more words than necessary, the cause of the incident just transpired. The deafmute was obstreperous and antisocial—quite understandably. Surely anyone could appreciate the frustration, arising from a compromised ability to communicate with others and to comprehend their intentions in turn. The present preoccupation of Pedillus' parents with his newly born and sickly baby sister was adding to his distress. His grandparents had brought him to Ad Gallinas with hopes interaction with children close to his own age, in the convivial atmosphere of Saturnalia, might calm and cheer him. The strategy was proving unsuccessful. The boy was exhibiting nothing but belligerence, toward the other children and the adults who were endeavoring to elicit his participation in festive activities. The pony ride was the most recent example. With smiles and hand gestures the company had invited Pedillus to join them. The manservant had endeavored to place the boy behind Postumus on the same beast. These efforts had precipitated the elopement I had witnessed.

Eventually I perceived Pedillus had been standing beside me for quite some time—nearly half an hour, perhaps. Yet he seemed indefatigable. I slid to the edge of my stool farther from him, nudged him to get his attention, and pointed to indicate he should sit beside me. After accepting my offer with an expressionless face, he promptly resumed gazing at my easel. Gallina arrived with my lunch of chicken and vegetable pasties. These I shared with my observer, who devoured his portion with gusto without diverting his eyes from the tableau. I insisted Gallina remain with us to watch Pedillus. Dismissing the harried manservant granted a reprieve to my ears as well as his person.

My self-congratulatory pride at having escaped the ravages of a cold was fading fast. I found myself shivering, and could feel the inflammation in my head worsening and descending steadily into my throat and chest. Soon my nose became runny, and I began to sneeze and cough. So engrossed had I been with Pedillus, that I had not noticed my body becoming steadily chilled once the warmth from my walk had worn off. Meanwhile the gray cloudbank had enlarged, filling the western sky with the similitude of a mountain range. Despite the deterioration of the weather and of my health—or really more on account of both—I resolved to complete as much of the two tableaux as I could in situ so long as my physique and the elements held out. Accordingly I wrapped myself my himation and—with assistance readily proffered by my newfound admirer—kept moving easel and stool to ensure I was sitting in the sun. By the time Valens arrived I was well ready to quit, for my symptoms now included stiff joints, chills, and lightheadedness.

When Pedillus saw us start to pack up, he began a silent temper tantrum: clenching his fists, shaking his head violently and stamping his feet. "Be prepared to grab him, as he may decide to run off," I cautioned Gallina and Valens. Actually it was I who prevented the anticipated dash. After seizing Pedillus' left hand with my right, with my left hand I pointed at the sun, and then indicated it was setting by turning my forefinger downward. Grabbing the edge of my himation I drew it snugly across my chest, and shook myself in an exaggeration of shivering. Pointing thereafter to my mouth, I mimicked chewing to indicate it was time to eat. Finally I pointed toward the villa and then picked up my stool, shoved one side gently into Pedillus' free hand, placed his hand I was holding upon the opposite edge, and released him. Far less calamity would arise if he ran off with the stool than with my paint box. Yet run off he did not. He stood holding the stool and staring straight ahead, as though pondering the implications of my action. Then he looked up at me and, for the first time that afternoon, smiled. Smiling back, I jerked my head toward the villa as I picked up the two tableaux. Valens seized my easel, Gallina my paint box and wiping rags. The four of us proceeded to our destination, Pedillus carrying that stool as proudly as Postumus had the paint box on the previous day.

As our journey progressed, I began to wonder whether I was going to reach the villa alive. I felt chilled to the bone, and utterly drained of strength and energy. Every joint in my body ached. My throat was raw; swallowing had become difficult. My chest hurt from coughing. Frequent and violent sneezes were leaving me dizzy. Once I had finally dragged myself to my quarters, Tiberius ordered Gallina to get me into the hottest bathwater I could abide, then into at least a pair of heavy shifts and directly to bed. I began a litany of apology and self-reproach: having carelessly abandoned my overwrap—not only today but several days earlier—I was now an embarrassment to him and an encumbrance to his family. He rolled his eyes and interrupted my oration: did I assume I was the only member of the human race, who had ever made a mistake of this type and endured its consequences? He would report my condition to family and guests, along with the stupidity I had exhibited in allowing myself to fall victim to the elements.

It took three shifts to make me comfortable. I had just crawled gratefully into the bed, the linens of which Gallina had thoughtfully warmed by holding them before the brazier, when there was a knock on the chamber door. The visitor was Livia. She had with her a small tumbler. With a kindly smile she inquired whether I should care to try her favorite remedy for sore throat and quinsy. This was the same syrup Chloe had administered, after I had shouted myself hoarse into the Sirocco. After relating that incident, over which Livia and I both laughed, I asked her of what the medicine consisted. Mostly of Attic honey, she replied, mixed with the charred flesh of forest swallow chicks (hence its smokiness), and a great variety of spices and herbs. Livia urged me to consider eating some food easily swallowed, perhaps broth and polenta. Her suggestion I immediately embraced, for it made me realize I was in fact hungry. I started to order Gallina to fetch those victuals, but Livia stopped me. She would have a resident servant prepare and deliver my supper; Gallina had done enough for the day.

The next morning I awoke feeling hardly any better. The room was warm from the brazier, but at the same time stuffy, damp, and clammy. It was also quite dark, for the windows were shut fast. The reason was apparent as soon as I had Gallina open them to clear the stuffiness. The sky was heavily overcast, and the air filled with a blowing mist so thick we could not see across the Tiber. I sent Gallina to elicit another dose of the cough syrup—from a servant and not from Livia herself, I specified—and to prepare my favored repast of cassia-dusted milk-soaked bread with the milk heated. Well, Livia herself returned with both articles. While she administered the syrup, Livia announced she had some cheering news to help promote my recovery. Overnight, Prima had been safely delivered of a healthy baby daughter. Domitia Lepida they had named her. Prima sent me special thanks for the blanket I had prepared, and conjectured I must be clairvoyant. How else did I know to create a floral design so particularly appropriate for a little girl?

While I slowly and arduously munched my bread and struggled to swallow it, Livia declared with a combination of compassion and amusement that her husband had contracted the very affliction I was enduring. He was wondering if I by chance might care to keep his company in the hearth room of the villa's kitchen. Hardly aesthetic surroundings, but more salubriously warm than any other area of the villa. There I could sit in a chair or recline on a cot, whichever I preferred.

Dear Reader, do you assume I gave refusal even the slightest consideration? With profuse thanks I accepted the offer, opting for the chair. After Livia left I arose from my bed as quickly as my condition allowed, eased and cleansed myself, rinsed my face and mouth, and had Gallina brush my hair and braid it anew. One of the three blankets on my bed she draped around me, and handed me a clean kerchief. Aching and wobbly, leaning on Gallina's arm, I made my way to my destination ever so slowly. Although we passed a goodly number of servants, all of whom wished me sympathy and speedy recovery, none of the family or guests was about. The reason I discovered presently.

Owing to its purely utilitarian purpose, the hearth room was utterly devoid of decoration. Nevertheless there was a comfortingly wholesome quality about it. Fires in the pair of hearths crackled cheerily, and made variegated patterns of light to dance upon the walls. There were pleasant odors of food in preparation. The chair awaiting me had been softened and warmed with a lining of blankets, which I drew about my shoulders and over my lap and legs. Augustus lay on a cot beneath his own heap of blankets. The upper portion of his body was slightly elevated on pillows behind his back. Like me he was clad in multiple tunics, and had a blanket wrapped about his shoulders. From his puffy eyes, raw and red nose, and gravelly voice I gathered he also felt as miserable as I. Nonetheless he greeted me ebulliently, and offered regrets I was sharing an ailment he had assumed was uniquely his own. Puzzled by his remark, I repeated my account of how I had succumbed to my own folly. At least down the future I could, by taking appropriate precautions, evade the conditions which had induced my affliction. So he commented in return. He was not so fortunate. Whenever the weather assumed its present state, he invariably came down with a full body cold; and he had yet to find a means of preventing this inevitability.

For the remainder of the morning we did not converse, owing to the soreness of our throats and congestion of our heads and chests. We rested in a sort of half-doze, catching each other's eyes and exchanging smiles whenever one of us coughed or sneezed. I sent Gallina after my harp, on which I strummed melodies slow and mellow for which Augustus whispered his thanks. I too found the music soothing, as concentrating upon it distracted me from my physical discomfort. Presently Tiberius arrived, wearing a cook's apron and head wrap. With him were Diodomedes and two other menservants. One of the latter carried a covered serving dish, the other a pair of bowls, several spoons, and napkins. These they set upon the low table between my chair and Augustus' cot.

Now I realized why I had not seen any family members or guests earlier on. During Saturnalia most Roman families designate a day, on which the menfolk serve a meal to their servants. Tiberius had told me about this practice but never carried it out. Instead he had compensated our staff with monetary donations and lengthy reprieves from their duties. Augustus croaked I ought to paint a portrait of Tiberius in his present attire, and keep it in reserve should ever I have a necessity for blackmailing him. The suggestion elicited a gale of giggles, which the congestion in my chest perverted into a fit of choking and gagging. Served me right, Tiberius exclaimed. Diodomedes promptly filled a tumbler with water, from which he helped me to drink and so assuage my distress. He told Augustus' manservant, Gallina, and the two waiters they should accompany Master Tiberius to the dining room; he—Diodomedes—would serve us our dinner. The dish was a stew of capon and paste in a milky sauce, delicately flavored with hints of lovage, coriander, and pepper: a mild, easily digested repast which I found immensely satisfying and a little invigorating.

While we dined, an utterly marvelous incident took place. Pedillus wandered into our chamber, carrying one of my tableaux: the representation of the rustic altar above the culvert. At the actual locale, a small portion of the villa house was visible far in the distance to the viewer's left. This area of the tableau I had not yet completed. What Pedillus showed me left me momentarily breathless with amazement. To the left of the altar was a depiction of the villa segment. Larger than in reality, it appeared as though it were immediately adjacent to the altar. Standing in a row above the structure were three human figures, each nearly as tall as the building beneath. Individually the additions were rather crude and simplistic. They were disproportional with respect to each other and to the other elements of the tableau, and monochromatic in red paint. Rather than spoiling the scene, however, this disparate addition imbued it with a hauntingly fantastic character—like a vision one recalls from a dream. The building segment seemed to evoke a shrine, and the human figures caryatids surmounting it.

I peered into Pedillus' face to get his attention, pointed to the additions, moved my hand horizontally several times to imitate brush strokes, and then pointed directly at Pedillus' chest while keeping an inquiring look on my face. Perceiving the meaning of my gestures, he nodded vigorously: he had painted the addenda. His face bore the earnest, solicitous look of a pupil seeking from his master a favorable evaluation of an assignment. Cautioning Augustus the paint was wet, I handed him the tableau. He studied it pensively while I described Pedillus' deed and my evaluation of his handiwork. The discomfited Diodomedes rattled off an apology: since family and servants both were preoccupied with the meal presently being served, the boy had managed to elude supervision and invade my quarters undetected. Augustus handed the tableau back to me. After some moments of reflective silence, in a quiet tone he ordered Diodomedes to fetch Pedius and Laelia.

Before the steward could depart, I interjected a countermand. Prior to seeking out Pedillus' grandparents, Diodomedes should fetch my paint box and one of the two large palettes I had brought but not yet used. So fixated I was on the plan unfolding in my mind, that only after Diodomedes left did I consider, with a sudden pang of trepidation, the man whose order I had amended was not only my host but ruler of the entire civilized world. Not perturbed in the least, Augustus leaned back upon his pillows and shut his eyes. I smiled at Pedillus, and again by pointing invited him to seat himself on the floor beside my chair. He compiled without hesitation, smiling in return.

Diodomedes brought my requested paraphernalia. Along the edges of the palette, with a pencil I quickly sketched entities I knew Pedillus had seen on the farm: a duck and a pony which he had observed while at the culvert with me, one of the barnyard dogs, a cat from the ever-present resident clowder, and a cockerel from among the many that strutted and crowed in the chicken pens. From the larger storage jars I filled five vials of paint: one of each with a primary color, another with black, the last with white. Mixing these in the center of the palette, I showed my intrigued and delighted pupil how to create new colors and shades by blending the paints in various combinations. Beginning with the duck, I demonstrated how to embellish the sketch with details, applying different hues to represent the variegated shadings of the feathers. After each step of the process I looked at him inquisitively, hoping to elicit an acknowledgment he understood; and every time he nodded his comprehension. I handed him the palette, directed him to place it on the floor, handed him the paint vials and the brush, and set him at work.

Presently an apron-clad Pedius arrived—without Laelia whose chattering, he said, had precluded his or Diodomedes' getting her attention. By now the boy was thoroughly engrossed in his project, concentrating quite contentedly, his tongue protruding slightly from the left corner of his mouth. While Pedius looked on in amazement, I explained his grandson was recording with impressive accuracy his observation of genuine ducks at the culvert the previous day. Pedius departed hastily, and returned leading Laelia by one hand. I assured them Pedillus was making a commendable attempt to depict the duck's mottling. If the result seemed clumsy and unskilled, this was only due to the boy's lack of training. Now Augustus spoke up, not without considerable effort. He suggested lessons in art may do much more toward calming Pedillus and rendering him tractable, than displays of stolid indifference or the application of harsh discipline toward his displays of bad temper.

Pedius and Laelia departed, conversing in excited murmurs. The warmth and quietude of the morning hours returned. Gallina and the manservant who had earlier attended Augustus arrived to relieve Diodomedes. The man stirred the two hearth fires and added more charcoal. Since Augustus fell asleep I did not play my harp, and just sat watching Pedillus paint. Presently I began to wonder whether I could manage to instruct him in artistic techniques. The thought came to me to close my hand gently about his in which he held the brush and guide his strokes. Although nonplussed at first, he did not resist my intervention. When he saw the improved results, he acknowledged his comprehension by smiling up at me. After he had completed the duck, I showed him how to wipe away the accumulated paint from the mixing area with a rag, to apply oil from the cruse in my paint box to a pristine section of the rag, clean his brush therewith, and begin afresh.

Pedillus started on the cat. By now I was becoming seriously fatigued. The appeal of a long hot bath and soft warm bed was increasing precipitously. The room began steadily to darken, as the wintertime daylight faded with its usual rapidity. The attendant manservant stirred and fed the fires anew, and lit the trio of lamps hanging on a stand. Augustus awoke and beckoned the man, who helped him rise from his cot and make his way toward the privy. Barely but fortuitously I succeeded in suppressing another giggle. Augustus' legs and feet were bound for warmth in sheaths of wool cloth. These greaves, together with the layering of multiple tunics, made the sovereign of Rome resemble one of those cloth dolls I used to make for sick and indigent children on Rhodes.

Now I began to wonder how I was going to persuade Pedillus, without precipitating a tantrum, that the hour for him to quit was at hand. Another inspiration struck. I dispatched Gallina to find a shallow container—a box, a basket, or a bowl—large enough to hold six paint vials, two brushes, and a rag. She returned with a suitable basket. Again I closed my hand around Pedillus,' and now stayed his motions. Already he had begun to depict the shadings of the cat's musculature—a task difficult with furred animals because the homogeneity of their coats masks the details of their morphology. He returned a look querulous and somewhat alarmed. With my other hand I pointed to the darkened window and then to the lamp stand. Then I made motions to indicate splashing and the stroking of a strigil, opened my mouth and pointed at it, and finally laid my cheek against my open palm and shut my eyes. To my relief he caught my meaning: it was time to prepare for bath, supper, and sleep. I extracted the brush from his hand, cleaned it with an oiled portion of the rag, and laid it in the basket. Next I replenished the paint vials, capped them with stoppers and placed them beside the brush. Lastly I filled the empty vial with oil from my cruse, stopped the vial and set it in the basket. Finally I added another brush and a folded, unused rag. Pedillus beamed with delight, as he perceived he now had his own painting accouterments.

After another especially hot bath, another supper of polenta and broth, and another dose of Livia's cough medicine, I fell asleep immediately. The next morning I was definitely improved, but nevertheless—to my immense regret—still too weak, woozy, and congested to participate in the birthday celebration for young Servius Galba. Back to the hearth room my servants brought me. Augustus was already there. He was as congested and red-eyed as on the previous day, but considerably more chipper. Instead of lying on a cot, he sat in a chair as did I. Over a breakfast of fruit compote we exchanged pleasantries, good wishes for one another's health, and complaints about the weather. Although the mist had dispersed, the air remained penetratingly cold and damp, the wind blustery, and the skies darkly overcast with lowering clouds.

Augustus called for a gaming board. A basket of hazelnuts served as our betting currency. We had barely started to gamble when Pedillus arrived carrying his paint basket, his loquacious manservant with the palette. No longer an aimless wanderer, Pedillus now had a fixed purpose. He set right to work on the unfinished cat, completed it in practically no time at all, and without hesitation turned to the dog. His servant repeatedly tried to engage Gallina and Augustus' man in chitchat, until Augustus growled they must all hold their peace.

Luncheon consisted of bread rolls and potted cow's milk cheese—which Pedillus and I devoured with relish, but Augustus tried to resist on the ground our breakfast had satiated his appetite. Livia adamantly refused to leave the room until he partook of at least some of the lunch, since he needed the nourishment to regain his health. "Little wonder the wags aver Caesar rules the world but Livia rules Caesar," he mused defeatedly as he dug in. Afterward, Pedillus returned to his painting. Upon finishing off the dog with amazing swiftness and accuracy he turned to the pony. Augustus and I resumed our gambling. As usual my play began badly but steadily improved.

Somewhat later, little Servius Galba came with Ocellina his stepmother to pay his respects. Although on this very day he had just entered his sixth year, his comportment and speech were masterfully polished and facile. After bowing and wishing for our speedy recovery, he expressed his regret that we had been unable to attend his birthday celebration. He showed us the abacus he had received at that event, and proclaimed he anticipated putting it to good use helping him master his numbers. Turning his attention to Pedillus, Servius declared he pitied Pedillus for not being able to hear or speak and so forgave his absence from the day's festivities, and was happy to see Pedillus had found a pastime gladdening and calming to him. Augustus, who had been smiling amusedly throughout the entire oration, remarked to Ocellina that she and her husband were assuredly raising a naturally born politician. *[Servius Sulpicius Galba succeeded Nero Claudius Caesar as emperor in 68 CE.]*

Although still achy and congested the next morning—our last at Ad Gallinas—I felt sufficiently recovered to take breakfast with the other women. I was the last to arrive; and as I did, the entire table burst into applause. While I looked from face to smiling face bemused, Livia said, "We commend you for the astounding contributions you have made to the fellowship of our family during this holiday sojourn."

"Fellowship?" I replied, still at a loss. "What could I possibly have contributed in the way of fellowship, having passed the majority of my days apart from everyone else—first out of doors painting, and thereafter in consequence of my own folly languishing in sickness?"

"Now, now," Livia chided, "no self-recrimination. You may not have taken ill, had I not urged you to paint those outdoor scenes. And did you not cheer The Great Grumbler while sharing his affliction? Accomplished the virtually impossible feat of befriending Postumus? And above all: though your art, uncovered the secret for reaching the mind of Pedillus—slashed the Gordian Knot his own progenitors have endeavored in vain to untie?"

In late afternoon, following luncheon of eggs beaten together with morels and subsequently afternoon respite, all the guests—including Tiberius and me—departed the villa. Lurching in our carriage under my heap of shifts and blankets, I uttered nary a word. When Tiberius asked if I was quiet because my throat hurt, I smiled and nodded. In truth I was lost in my thoughts— reflecting, ruminating, pondering. My mother used to harangue me incessantly for never contributing enough to our family—albeit she hardly ever offered specific descriptions of the contributions expected of me. With great anxiety I would struggle to be a better scholar, a better housekeeper, more acquiescent and obliging to my family's demands—only to learn such were not the anticipated contributions and suffer consequent vituperation. During the week just past, I had not so much as entertained the thought—let alone outlined a plan— for cultivating the approval of Tiberius' kin by making some sort of tangible contribution to their family. Yet this was precisely what I had done, and simply by being myself. Acting upon and carrying out impulses and inclinations natural to me, I had wrought those achievements Livia had enumerated.

Alas, my Reader, I have belabored the events of a single week. The episode, however, marked a significant turning point in my character. Gone was the lingering sense I could only win the approval of others by being more than myself. This once ever-present tension was now ebbing from my psyche, yielding to a proper, healthy self-appreciation, and to calm joy.

TRANSFIGURATION

January was a prodigious month for the first family. Nineteen days before the Calends of February *[January 14, 3 CE]* would have been the fortieth birth anniversary of Tiberius' brother. Later in the month—four days before the Calends *[January 29]*—Lucius Caesar would have entered his twentieth year. Tiberius cautioned me not to offer condolences to his mother or to Augustus. They, like him, preferred keeping their bereavements to themselves.

Seventeen days before the Calends of February *[January 16]* marked thirty years since the senate conferred upon Gaius Julius Caesar Octavianus the honorary cognomen of Augustus. He commemorated the occasion with a military review in the Saepta Julia, followed by a gladiatorial exhibition— both of which Tiberius attended but I as a woman could not. Nor did Livia invite me to the reception she held for the wives of senators in honor of her husband's event—an exclusion for which she apologized profusely. It was strictly a matter of Roman politics, she explained, at which I as a Greek would have been awkwardly out of place. Tiberius told me later the intent of his mother's fête was to remind the Roman aristocracy, that after five centuries of ruling Rome they were no longer in charge. Now I was assuredly relieved to have been excluded.

The very next day was the fortieth anniversary of the marriage of Livia and Augustus. Tiberius and I shared in their celebration on the Palatine, over a quiet and simple supper of baked sole fish, brown bread, and asparagus another favorite of Augustus.

For this entire month I practically ensconced myself in my studio, spending as much time there as I could manage. The Ad Gallinas tableaux I was determined to finish in time to present them to Livia on her birthday—the third day before the Calends of February *[January 30]*. I was also engaged in refining with finishing retouches my tableau of the city of Rome. Antonia and her sisters wanted to display this accomplishment—as the work of Eutychus Rhodou, of course—at their forthcoming exhibition in the Porticus Octaviae. Although the event was not scheduled to open until March, I wanted to get the panorama done so I could return to my preferred medium of painting on textiles. Furthermore, I aspired to finish the tableau of racing chariots I had started upon the previous September.

Livia's anniversary was her sixtieth. Tiberius and I waited until the eighth hour *[1:00 p.m.]* before departing for the Palatine. This was the time Augustus and Antonia had selected to disband well-wishers and other family members, so the four of us might be alone with Livia. We greeted her in the sitting room of the apartment she and Augustus shared. While Livia examined the tableaux with unabashed delight, Antonia motioned to the servants to withdraw. Livia looked up from her chair, now clearly puzzled. Augustus took the tableaux from her and said quietly, "We have another—and extraordinarily special—gift for you, my wife."

Antonia smiled broadly, took a deep breath, paused a moment, and then with controlled excitement said, "Tiberius and Clytia are married, and..."

Here she paused again, for Livia gasped and interrupted her. "Oh my dears!" Smiling ecstatically she extended her arms toward me. Perceiving her intent, I approached and embraced her. After kissing me on either cheek, she closed her fingers about my silver and ruby ring. "Am I correct in assuming this is your wedding jewel? You need to place it on the proper finger!" Gently she wriggled the ring off the third finger of my right hand, and onto the corresponding digit of my left.

As Livia released me, Antonia said, "There is yet more."

Tiberius somewhat somberly completed the disclosure. "We have a son. In three weeks he will be one full year of age. We left him on Rhodes under the tutelage of friends: a Platonic scholar and his family."

"Another grandchild, my Livia," Augustus interjected brightly. "And you thought you had seen your last."

Livia's smile faded as her visage assumed an enraptured mien. After a short silence she asked, "What did you name him?"

"Alcimus," Tiberius answered.

Livia nodded. "From Nero. Why did you not bring him with you?"

"He strongly resembles you, Mammah. Imagine the ensuant controversy."

On hearing Tiberius' explanation, Livia startled. Her reaction prompted Augustus to laugh. "A wise precaution," he said.

Livia turned her gaze, now imploring, to Tiberius and me. "Nonetheless, you cannot leave him much longer in the care of friends, unaware of his parentage and true identity. Husband, we must find a suitable way to reunite the boy with his parents, and soon!" Her voice had assumed an admonishing, didactic tenor, although gently modulated.

"Agreed," Augustus responded. "Hence I hereby grant Tiberius permission to bring the scholar—with his family and the boy—to reside at the Villa Maecenatis. As one of his philanthropies, Tiberius will sponsor and promote the academic and literary endeavors of this,...this,..."

"Thrasyllus Balbilusides of Alexandria," Tiberius interjected.

"This Thrasyllus And So Forth. The transition of your son to you his parents will be accomplished easily and discreetly. As for his resemblance to Livia: let us not mention it at all, until someone broaches the subject. Should that happen, we can maintain the resemblance is purely coincidental."

Here Livia interjected. "The young son of my retainer Marcus Salvius Otho strongly resembles Tiberius. Not to worry, Clytia: Tiberius was on Rhodes when that boy was conceived. But here is an example of accidental similarity."

Augustus continued. "You must be prepared, however, just in case circumstances arise that force you to admit the truth. You married on Rhodes but concealed your union upon coming to Rome, because you knew I vehemently disapprove of intermarriage between Italians and other races. For my part I am prepared to maintain, that although I shall continue to eschew such unions, legally I can do nothing to prevent them. Tiberius' espousal of a Greek wife will be yet another element, of the gross insubordination he let make shambles of his political and military career."

"What about your family's younger members?" I ventured gingerly. "How do you think Drusus will react upon learning he has a brother? Agrippina will probably hate me more than ever, and try to persuade Postumus to abandon his newfound affinity for me. Will they spread malicious gossip? And young Tiberius Drusus: can he be trusted not to babble obtusely about our marriage and son?"

"We are not going to reveal your secret to them, any more than to strangers, until absolutely we must. Having raised Drusus myself," here Augustus cast an aggravated glance at Tiberius, "I am inclined to think his character may benefit from helping to rear a little brother, and that he will be amenable once reassured his patrimony will remain his alone. He and Nero Germanicus will be departing for military training at Marseilles anyway, come the new year. We all know Pina is never content unless she is miserable. At least she will be forced to stop calling you a whore. And nobody takes the utterances of Marcus Postumus or of Tiberius Drusus seriously. You must make up your mind not to take umbrage at anything they say to you or about you, with regard to this or any other matter. As for the spread of gossip: remember who we are. We select for servants, and for hirelings like secretaries and the children's tutors—and above all for our friends and confidants—only those upon whom we can depend to be unassailable circumspect.

"Be forewarned nonetheless. Speculative innuendo about your relationship with Tiberius is circulating already, and will certainly proliferate once somebody notices your boy resembles Livia. Do not let yourself become alarmed or outraged. Above all do not react, as doing so will incite more gossip. People throughout the world speak ill of our entire family every day, spreading malicious rumors and lies. Do you notice any of us losing sleep on that account?"

Recalling the execrations my mother, her aunt, and my fiancé's father used to heap upon the imperial family without considering the validity of these aspersions, I vigorously nodded my understanding.

"Now let us cease from this dreary line of discussion, and rejoice over the newest addition to our family!" Augustus' tone was no less imperative than when he had been cautioning us about disclosure.

"What are you cogitating—mulling over?" Tiberius asked in regard to my pensive silence, as our litter bore us homeward.

"How your stepfather can be so compassionately benign, and yet so virulently ruthless with regard to the same issue, continues to amaze me. He approved disclosure of our marriage and child, and eased my qualms about the insinuations it will engender; yet he made clear his intention to excoriate it as proof of your insubordination."

"His Chimera at work. You are feeling her bite for the first time. We know full well my stepfather privately approves of you and of our marriage; but publicly, officially, he cannot. He cannot credibly discourage fellow Italians from contracting interracial marriages without castigating that of his own stepson. Today we won a Pyrrhic victory, my love. One can anticipate an outcome no better when locked in combat with the Chimera. To be reunited with our son, we must endure being denounced by my family as rebellious and insubordinate outcasts, if only ostensibly."

The next day was Antonia's thirty-eighth anniversary. Her sisters were going to celebrate it with a luncheon at the home of Prima. Recalling Antonia's interest in my sketch cloth during our first supper together, I had been planning since that occasion to make her a gift of a headscarf, in the center of which I had painted a trio of moths lighted upon an acacia branch. Accordingly when we arrived home, I ransacked my textile collection from Rhodes for the piece. Having located it, I decided it was unsuitable for presentation to Antonia, for it was clumsily and amateurishly executed in comparison to my present work. It was, after all, one of my earliest attempts at fabric painting.

Nonetheless when I expressed my misgiving to Tiberius, and asked if he thought we could procure an alternative gift on such short notice, he insisted I proceed with my original intention. The early works of any artist are going to appear crude and naïve beside later endeavors which bear the results of experience and practice. No one coming to tomorrow's gathering is capable of producing an artifact equivalent in caliber to that scarf, despite the shortcomings only I can perceive. He anticipated—yea, virtually guaranteed—Antonia was going to be delighted with it. In addition to not being overly critical of myself, I should not belittle my strengths and talents, but continually respect, cherish, and strive to enhance them.

Before I departed for Antonia's fête, Tiberius admonished me once again not to denigrate the headscarf. As he had predicted, Antonia was euphoric about it. A goodly number of guests was in attendance. Nearly every woman was accompanied by at least one daughter. Claudia brought her Pulchra, Marcella her two: Iulla, and Vipsania the wife of Haterius. Present as well were Atia, her daughter Marcia and Marcia's daughter Numantina, Quinctilia the wife of Augustus' nephew Sextus Appuleius and her daughter Appuleia. Prima of course had four-year-old Domitia, and newly born Lepida whom I held in my arms, wrapped in the blanket I had painted to honor her birth. Livia alone was without a daughter. Instead she had brought a visibly sulking Agrippina.

The young girls dined a table of their own. Amid the couches at the matrons' table a chair had been set specifically for me. The main course was a side of lamb, lying upon a bed of fennels, leeks, and dasheens. My bowels tightened with panic but only momentarily; for a waiter plunked before me a plate upon which lay a squab, a mound of tiny beets, and a puffy baked pastry. Not infrequently Agrippina looked up from her couch in my direction, sneered, and uttered words that induced her peers to stare and giggle. Their conduct brought to mind those young women who had ridiculed me in my youth—and to my surprise, did not distress me at all. Reflecting on this matter before sleep that night, I suddenly realized I had forgiven my tormentors of long ago. Silly girls, just emerging into womanhood, lack appreciation and compassion for the foibles and eccentricities of others—the insights into the diversities of human nature which experience alone can bring about. They consequently seek the comfort of conformity when assessing associates. My upbringing had rendered me so very awkward, so utterly devoid of poise and social grace—bookish, erudite, ignorant of the popular trends my contemporaries followed, unfashionably dressed and coiffed, and of course blatantly celibate. Was there any wonder I received the scorn of those whose rearing had been conventional?

As for Agrippina: her I sincerely pitied. The perspectives on her character Antonia and Augustus had provided made me perceive myself a catalyst, impelling elements of a tortured psyche to emerge. Owing to her grandfather's— yea, her entire family's—unique and untouchable position in politics and society, Agrippina had grown up sheltered and sequestered from the rest of the world. Apart from her siblings and cousins, she had no friends of her own. She had never known her father Agrippa, who died in her third year of life. From her mother she had learned to loathe her stepfather Tiberius—more likely, I suspect from what he had told me, from Julia's display of ambivalence toward him than from words of outright scorn. Presently that doting and indulgent mother was ripped away—declared a traitor to her people, a disgrace to her family, and worse. For having plotted against her own father, she was deemed a parricide and hence an unnatural being. Now while the mother languished in exile a convicted felon, the former stepfather Agrippina had been taught to disdain was salvaging his reputation and assuaging Augustus' disaffection toward him. And here was I, protégé of that former stepfather, finding favor with the rest of Agrippina's family, as was he for having introduced me to them.

A distinct sense of having been cleansed—yea, rarefied—came over me. The old stumbling block of resentment, crowding and darkening my conscience since childhood, had partially dissolved. At last I had come to understand what impelled youthful mockers past and present to scorn and shun me. Rancor toward my family, however, remained unabated. Not yet could I fathom why they would raise me to be so blatantly nonconforming that I became a target of ridicule, and then persecute me because I was ridiculed. Nevertheless, I resolved not to let this lingering bitterness diminish my euphoria over the accomplishment I had realized this day. To forgive those who had denigrated me because they had misconstrued my character, was a milestone in my quest to forgive all adversaries.

Directly after breakfast the next morning—the Calends of February— Tiberius bade me join him in the office he utilized for correspondence. He summoned Demetrius, and Acer the villa's manager. To them he announced he was preparing to bring to reside at the villa, two espoused couples with four children between them. Arbindus and Briseis now had a second son, whom they were letting everyone call Leonidas because no one could say his Gallic name. The Gauls have a consonant in their language which no Greek or Italian is able to pronounce *[W]*. It sounds vaguely like *oueh* or *ouhrreh*. Arbindus is a Latin corruption and extension of something akin to *oh-oueh-en*, meaning young fighter *[Owen].*

Appropriate guest quarters must be made ready. Continuing, Tiberius admitted to having swelled the villa's personnel with the addition of servants from his Carinae household. How many attendants could the newcomers bring, without straightening accommodations and working conditions for the staff? Eight or ten perhaps, no more than fifteen, Demetrius ventured after a thoughtful silence. Acer nodded agreement.

After the stewards departed Tiberius had me transcribe a letter to Thrasyllus, outlining a detailed plan for the transfer of the sage and his family—including Alcimus— along with that of Arbindus to Rome. They may bring as many as fifteen attendants. Tiberius urged that owing to their age, Phoebe and Menon should remain on the farm in retirement. Miranda they should keep with them and not include her in Thrasyllus' train, lest her deficiency render her disruptive in new environs. Rhathines still belonged to Aka as her slave. Tiberius with my sanction welcomed her to leave him on the farm as well, instead of returning him to Commagene. Surely this venerable and sedulous physician, now in his seventy-first year, had earned a calm retirement. Tiberius was recommending I as owner retain Nicanor as supervisor of the estate and its workers. In conclusion Tiberius stated he must be advised, not only of the dates of arrival, but of how many people and how much baggage to expect, so he could have appropriate transport vehicles waiting in Ostia.

Aside to me, Tiberius remarked he was sure Nicanor would be more than happy with his new role. Indeed, Nicanor had taken one of the farmworkers as a concubine: a widow with two grown sons. He was thoroughly enjoying life on the farm: cultivating, harvesting, hunting with his hounds, and indulging his new spouse's grandchildren in lieu of his own. Whether Nicanor had grandchildren by his daughter Penelope he could not ascertain, since her master Cassander Haidou had disallowed all contact with Tiberius' household. Nicanor's son Ajax, being homosexual, was unlikely to beget offspring.

After sealing the letter and entrusting it to Fulgens for delivery, Tiberius said I ought to consider what I should like done about my art collection on the Rhodian farm. My original purpose in leaving it behind—that Alcimus may grow up amid my artwork—was now obsolete. Although Tiberius felt assured Nicanor and his fellow servants would continue to admire my efforts, keeping the entire conglomerate unavailable to anyone else seemed a terrible waste. What did I think about leaving a few favorite selections behind and transferring the rest to Italy? At present there was no room in the villa's gallery to display the collection; however there likely was sufficient room for it at Ad Gallinas, and certainly at Anzio. Of course I could always cede everything to Longus, who would be ecstatic.

Now I pondered for a time in silence. Preoccupied with adjusting to life in Rome, with cultivating Tiberius' family, and at present over the prospect of being reunited with Alcimus, I had actually forgotten all about the Rhodian collection. For now we should merely leave the entire caboodle in place, I decided. Nicanor and his staff were at hand to insure its protection from fire or other types of destruction. Alcimus was still far too young, even to understand let alone to appreciate it. We should concentrate on facilitating his adjustment to living with us instead of Thrasyllus. Once that is accomplished, I shall attend to the artwork.

Tiberius smiled benevolently, amorously. Alcimus could not have asked for a more caring mother, he said as he took my hand. But I must not tarry overly long about that art collection; the longer I wait, the longer I deprive the world of its splendors. As I kissed his hand in which he held mine, an old and too familiar sense of self-loathing crept into my consciousness. The inner voice of my mother was hounding me once again. *How presumptuous of you to accept his compliments. Your character as a parent and abilities as an artist cannot possibly merit such praise. You are too naïve to recognize he was simply being obsequious.*

This time I fought back with a vengeance. Mentally I shouted, *Unequivocally wrong you are; and let me show you why! Without cavil I am a caring mother; for I aspire to ascertain and implement what is best for my child, instead of exploiting him for my personal benefit and satisfaction! Moreover I am an accomplished and acclaimed artist, and not a self-congratulatory pretender like my father! Why should it seem strange, out of place, unnatural, for this man who loves me—this man who fathered that child on me and encouraged the development of my artistic skills—to compliment me? And would he not appreciate my accepting his accolades?* The voice ceased immediately, and in new situations of this nature, permanently I can retrospectively acknowledge. Never since have I felt uncomfortable accepting praise of which I am genuinely worthy. Tiberius was unaware of this mental turmoil churning within my consciousness, for "Thank you, my dearest." was my only reply.

The day following was Agrippina's birthday *[February 2]*. Since it was a Saturday and nobody was preoccupied with business, the entire immediate family celebrated with a luncheon. Pulchra, Numantina, Appuleia, Iulla, and the Aemilia Lepida once betrothed to Lucius Caesar, were invited as well. While observing Agrippina's reaction, as she removed the pendant with my portrait of Germanicus from its cloth pouch, Antonia and I had to bite our lips and hold our breaths to keep from bursting out in laughter. Agrippina looked up abruptly, wide-eyed and open-mouthed as though she had witnessed some other-worldly phenomenon. Then her eyes narrowed; her mouth closed and its corners turned downward. Without uttering a word she returned the pendant to its pouch. When Augustus insisted an expression of gratitude was in order, Agrippina immediately rose from her chair and strode from the room in silence—but not without taking the pendant with her. Now Antonia and I smiled broadly at one another. Germanicus started to follow Agrippina, but Augustus told him to let her be. While returning to the Villa Maecenatis I found myself musing that Agrippina, who hated me, was an Aquarian like my mother who hated me. But Livia and Antonia, both born under the same sign, had become my devoted friends. Moreover Agrippina hated most everyone, not just me. Here was proof of Thrasyllus' assertion back on Rhodes, that not all Aquarians are my enemies. Now more than ever I was resolved to make Alcimus my friend, and with confidence this endeavor could be accomplished.

About a week thereafter, we received an enthusiastic reply from Thrasyllus. Nicanor and his bride Lois were amply pleased with their responsibility of managing the farm. Phoebe and Menon were grateful to have Miranda with them in their retirement. Miranda was presently helping with delight to care for Lois' newborn granddaughter. Thrasyllus' packet included an effusive expression of gratitude, written in Rhathines' own hand. Thus the company headed for Rome would consist of Alcimus and the family of Arbindus, Thrasyllus and his family, and four of their six servants. Thrasyllus presumed (and rightly) that I would not object to the eldest servile couple remaining on the farm as companions to Rhathines.

Our joyous anticipation was short-lived. Within a few days a second letter arrived from Thrasyllus. Since both the stars and the numerological table had predicted a baleful outcome for the journey, he was postponing departure until the prognostications turned benign. After several more days a third message revealed the reason for the unfavorable forecast, and the wisdom of Thrasyllus for heeding it. Rhathines had determined Aka was once again pregnant. With an imperative consistent with her royal upbringing, she was demanding to be relocated to Alexandria and there placed under the care of the premier physicians at the Museion. Thrasyllus had to admit he found himself agreeing with her importunity. After the grim outcome of the last birth, both parents wanted the present gravidity scrutinized and evaluated as assiduously and expertly as possible.

Alcimus was and would continue to be well cared for on the farm. There was nothing Thrasyllus and Aka could do for him that our servants could not do far better. Thrasylla their daughter was going to remain there as well. As inexorable as her mother, Thrasylla was refusing to be separated from her playmates. Thrasyllus and Aka were going to leave their six servants on Rhodes: from the royal house of Commagene they would elicit a staff for their new quarters. At least monthly and more frequently if possible, Thrasyllus would journey to Rhodes to insure everything was in order. To this pledge he was undeviatingly committed. Tiberius concurred, for he still wanted to bring Alcimus to Rome as a member of Thrasyllus' household. To transport Alcimus separately with his own set of servants would raise too many of the wrong sort of questions.

Thrasyllus' baleful forecast had yet another element. That winter's weather had continued unseasonably warm and dry. Sunny days had abounded. There was no rain, only a very occasional day of mist like we had had at Ad Gallinas. On the day before the first anniversary of Alcimus' birth, strong northeasterly winds began to blow, bringing clouds aplenty with some lightning and thunder but still no rain—a Euroclydon without the usual drenching.

Three nights later we were abruptly roused from sleep by what at first I thought was thunder. The noise proved to be pounding on the door to Tiberius' suite. It loudened, now on our bedchamber door. Demetrius cried out, "Master! Master Tiberius! You must arise at once! The Palatine is engulfed in flames!"

Tiberius was out the door before I could finish wrapping myself in my dressing gown. The villa's cavernous foyer was bright from the light of myriad lamps. A phalanx of servants was waiting, queued on either side of the open exterior doors. I joined Demetrius, Acer, and ten armed guards on the front steps. Through the darkness of the gardens an undulating constellation of lights was hastening toward the villa. Presently a mounted escort, about half of whose members were holding torches, drew up before the entryway with a familiar carriage in their midst. Behind the vehicle were Germanicus and Drusus on horses, each with a passenger—young Tiberius behind his brother, and Postumus behind my stepson. To Drusus I called out, "Is your father on the Palatine?" and immediately felt exceedingly and embarrassedly stupid. Where else would Tiberius have gone?

"Yes: he is directing the evacuation," replied Augustus as he exited the carriage assisted by two of the villa's guards.

"And we are going back there to help!" Germanicus called out as he slid his brother to the ground. Drusus did the same with Postumus. Meanwhile

Antonia had emerged from the carriage, her head wrapped in my moth scarf. She was helping a noticeably distraught Livia, over whose head and shoulders my Guardian Tree shawl was draped, alight from the vehicle. The reason for Livia's distress was quite apparent, from the cinders she and her two companions had on their heads and shoulders. Having just escaped fire, Livia was suffering the same agitation I experienced when forced to witness vomiting. Antonia and Augustus began slowly to lead her up the steps. Now Agrippina exited the carriage.

"Company regroup: to the Palatine forth!" the escort commander ordered. The posse comitatus reined their mounts back into formation and departed.

Tiberius Drusus began to howl, "The gods have mercy upon us, the g-g-gods have m-m-mercy up-p-pon us-s-s!" This was the first time I noticed he stuttered. Livia's trembling became more intense. Her face paled; she choked and leaned forward. Fearing she was going to vomit, I felt my muscles tighten, my teeth clench. My heart began to pound and my knees become wobbly. Lightheaded, I felt impelled to run and at the same time to remain transfixed. *You must not succumb, you cannot succumb!* I kept shouting to myself mentally, all the while struggling to acknowledge the presence and dominance of Underlying Good.

"Shut your miserable mouth!" Agrippina snarled at Tiberius Drusus to no avail.

Antonia beckoned me to take Livia's hand, then turned to face her younger son and raised her own hand as if to strike him. "Stifle yourself, or I shall smack you into the Outer Ether!" she shouted. Tiberius Drusus looked up at her with that vacuous gaze of his, but complied with her demand.

"The glories of motherhood!" Augustus murmured.

In the end my terror proved groundless. Livia raised her head, inhaled several deep breaths, smiled wanly at me, and began slowly to ascend the steps. Although relieved I did not have to witness her vomiting, I still craved solitude in which to calm down, and surmised Livia did as well. Accordingly as we entered the villa I cried out, "Stand aside: she needs to breathe freely and not feel crowded!" The servants waiting in the foyer backed away. From a stand I removed a lamp. "Fetch us more lights, and summon Chloe!" I added as I led the newcomers from the foyer into the reception room adjoining the concert hall. "Here you can sit in quietude," I said, carefully modulating my voice into a gentle timbre as Augustus lowered the still shaking Livia onto a settee. Seating myself beside her, I took each of her hands in one of mine. She gripped tightly. Her hands continued to shake, as did mine. Two menservants entered, the one carrying a lampstand and the other gingerly balancing a trio of burning lamps. These three along with mine, when hung on the stand, cast an oval pool of light around the settee, and faint blurry shadows on the walls of the otherwise darkened reception room.

Chloe arrived, bearing a pair of tumblers. One she handed to Livia with a curtsy, the other to me. They contained an infusion of peppermint leaves, a favorite of Chloe's for soothing upset stomachs and jangled nerves. In a tremulous voice Livia thanked her as she took the tumbler. Chloe curtsied again and departed. Augustus gently nudged Livia on the shoulder to move towards me, into the center of the settee. He seated himself at her side and drew his arms about her. She rested her head on his chest beneath his chin as she continued to sip the infusion. Their gestures of intimacy made me feel obliged to depart, and I started to rise from the settee. As if he had read my thoughts, Augustus said, "Please do not feel you must leave us, as we show our affection for one another. We deeply value your understanding and compassionate help, your efforts to calm and cheer." Livia smiled again with obvious relief. She said nothing but reached over, and with her free hand seized mine and squeezed it anew—now with amity instead of anguish.

I have no idea for how long the three of us sat together in that oval of light. Livia and I finished our draughts, and placed our empty tumblers on the low table before the settee. From time to time the sounds of footfalls and voices emanated from the foyer and died away. Eventually those noises began again, the door opened, and a smiling Antonia peeked into the reception room. "All have escaped safe and sound," she said joyously, "including the animals." Thereupon Sannio burst past her and toward our settee. He was covered with wet ash, which he proceeded to deposit upon the three of us by means of a vigorous shake.

"Aigh!" Livia exclaimed. She heaved a great sigh, and then burst out laughing. "The gods be thanked everyone is all right!" she continued cheerily as she brushed Sannio's detritus from her bosom and lap. "And thanks again to you and your pharmakeutria for your efforts, Clytia! I am ever so well refreshed!"

Tiberius stood in the doorway behind Antonia. "The brigades worked most assiduously, and extinguished the fire well before it could burn the house to the ground. The precise extent of the damage we were unable to determine in the darkness. Antiochus and the Cimmerian princes, along with all of their servants, we installed in the Carinae. The balance of your household is here, dispersed throughout the villa wherever we were able to find space for them. Diodomedes and Acer are in the process of deciding who should remain to attend you. The remainder they will send to Ad Gallinas. Meanwhile, the resident staff has readied your quarters and drawn baths for you."

"Of which we are most desperately in need, thanks to Sannio—including you my poor Clytia, and Sannio himself," said Augustus as he rose from the settee. He extended his hand to Livia, who before taking it turned and hugged me tightly.

"You were truly wondrous tonight, my Lioness, comforting my mother as you did," Tiberius said while we bathed.

"I daresay I would have been far from wondrous had she actually vomited," I murmured distractedly as I traced patterns in the ash floating on the surface of the bathwater. A proposition kept churning about in my mind despite my best efforts to ignore it. To present it at this time of anguish, chagrin, and uncertainty seemed terribly selfish of me. Nevertheless I had to succumb. "Tiberius, without question there is insufficient room to accommodate Thrasyllus' entire entourage here at the villa, now that your family is staying with us. Might you not reconsider having Alcimus sent to us alone? We could have Rhathines attend him on the voyage, then return directly to Rhodes once he has delivered his charge. Surely there are enough servants at hand here to accommodate one more resident, especially with the overflow from the Palatine. Arbindus and his family can remain on Rhodes until the present crisis has passed and all are restored to their rightful demesnes."

"Remember, we have Agrippina and Tiberius Drusus residing with us now. I thought we aspired to keep our marriage and son secret from them as long as possible."

"They are going to find out sooner or later. Recall the concerns your mother expressed, when we told her about Alcimus on her birthday. He is fully a year old. The longer we keep him ignorant of his true parentage, the less inclined he may be to accept it. Who can predict how long your family must remain here until their house is rebuilt?"

Tiberius nodded thoughtfully. "Your point is well taken; however, there is another element to be considered. In return for keeping Alcimus, I promised to bring Thrasyllus to Rome as soon as I saw my way clear for doing so. If I bring Alcimus here without Thrasyllus, I shall be in breach of patronage." Suddenly he sat upright, sloshing the water. "You and I are both fools for not thinking of this alternative sooner. I shall ask my mother to let me install Thrasyllus and his train at Ad Gallinas. To Thrasyllus I shall explain he will still be on a farm, but at least on a farm barely ten miles from Rome. Moreover he must only abide there temporarily. Once the Palatine house is restored and my family quits this villa, he will reside here in their place."

"Will there be enough room at Ad Gallinas, with servants from the Palatine lodged there?"

"Have you forgotten we have plenty of other properties to which they can be moved?" Every so often, the sheer immensity and extent of Tiberius' family's possessions escaped my comprehension.

After our bath we returned to bed. When I awoke, the room was brilliant with sunlight and I was alone. While dressing me, Phaedra confirmed my assumption Tiberius had gone to investigate the extent of the damage on the Palatine. Continuing, she said Master had told her to ask that I utilize the rear staircases exclusively, and take care to avoid the reception and office areas of the villa since Lord Caesar and Lady Livia will be conducting public business in those venues. *Even in the face of personal calamity the relentless demands of the Chimera must be met,* I mused while departing for my studio.

Now the portent of the eagle on our housetop became palpable. Indeed the authority of Rome had taken refuge in our domicile.

Armed guards had been stationed throughout the villa, even along my circuitous route. So accustomed had I become to seeing them they no longer perturbed me, as had the praetorians when first installed in the townhouse on Rhodes. The entire day I spent working on the panorama tableau, even while munching the bread and cold sausage morsels I had delivered for my luncheon. After our bath, Tiberius and I supped alone in our parlor on a surprisingly pleasing ragout of kid. He reported the upper story of the Palatine house had suffered significant damage and probably must be rebuilt entirely. The ground floor rooms were intact, but badly marred from smoke and heat and from the water used to extinguish the flames. The laurel trees flanking the main entrance to the house were heaps of charred ash, and the two adjacent temples burned all the way to their foundations.

A serving woman I did not recognize, and so presumed was a member of the Palatine household, brought a note from Antonia. She and her sisters had decided to assemble, on the morrow at the fourth hour *[9:00 a.m.]* at the Porticus Octaviae, to review the submissions for the forthcoming exhibit and begin assessing how they should be arranged for viewing. I was welcome to share her litter or journey alone in mine, whichever I preferred. I opted for her company.

We found that twenty-two of the twenty-four cities had responded, so eighty-eight artworks were at the portico. The two outliers—Fiesole and Syracuse—had sent word theirs were forthcoming and should arrive before the year's end. The Palatine conflagration had left Pappus the curator fraught with anxiety about the possibility of fire erupting at the portico. Accordingly he had engaged watchmen with barrels of water at the ready, attending the storage areas by day and night. A wide range of quality and style was represented—in paintings, in ceramic and metal sculptures and reliefs, and in artifacts like weapons and ceremonial tableware. There were a few originals by grand masters, and a fair number of copies. These included a Eutychus of Rhodes! from the city of Benevento: my *Arrow-stricken Achilles*. This submission prompted me to discuss with my companions, whether displaying the copy could possibly embarrass the municipal council of Benevento. The original at Longus' gallery might be known to viewers of the exhibition. In the end we decided the copy being representative of Benevento should no more embarrass that city, than the copy of Praxiteles' Hermes in the portico's permanent collection should embarrass Rome because the original can be seen at Olympia.

To our immense delight, most offerings were the efforts of artists indigenous to the participating cities and characteristic of their locales. Perhaps a third of such contributions were antiquities, practically all of these Etruscan. We spent the morning evaluating the sizes, shapes, and colorings of each piece, recording our observations on tablets. Afterward we adjourned to a room especially reserved for our luncheon of fish and vegetable ragout. In the afternoon we completed a slow and meticulous tour of the exhibition hall, deciding from the notations we had made in the morning where each piece should be displayed. Our calculations included allowance for the artifacts not yet received—including my panorama.

The Villa Maecenatis and its grounds seemed afire with the red-gold light and dark shadows of the lowering sun, when Antonia's litter turned through the gates. It was the day of Lupercalia: the Roman festival of fecundity in fields, flocks, and humans. Fortuitously the grotto of Faunus on the Palatine, in which the rites are celebrated, had escaped the ravages of the fire. As part of the ritual, two youths clad only in goatskin loincloths are anointed with the blood of the sacrificial goats, then cleansed with milk and required to laugh. Thereafter the pair runs through the region of the Palatine in which the earliest dwellings of Rome had been built: the sector of the hill overlooking the Forum. The youths carry strips of hide cut from the sacrificial animals, and with these strike every woman they can reach during their run. The touch of the thong Is presumed to purify the physique and stimulate fertility. The thongs are called februa, from the archaic Latin verb februare: to purify. Hence the day of the festival was designated Februdies, and February the month in which it falls. Germanicus and

Drusus had been the youths chosen for this year's festival. Antonia and I had been laughing together, about how the two of us were far more interested in obviating fertility than inducing it. As I was exiting the litter, I felt something traverse my backside. Turning about I beheld Germanicus sporting his goat hide loincloth beneath his cloak and tunic, brandishing his februum and grinning mischievously.

Tiberius had already bathed. As I did, he delivered the disappointing news that Augustus had rejected our request to install Thrasyllus at Ad Gallinas at this particular time. The three vassal princes were going to be moved to Ad Gallinas, and the Carinae house given over to the architects and engineers and artisans engaged to reconstruct the Palatine mansion. When he turned Tiberius down, Augustus had made clear he appreciated and shared our concern, that the longer we postponed taking Alcimus into our custody the more difficult the transition might be for him. Nevertheless we must anticipate the eventual revelation, that Tiberius while on Rhodes had taken a Greek wife and begotten on her a half-Italian son, will be controversial for at least some family members and for the general public assuredly. Augustus felt it better, for his immediate family and for ours, to defray having to weather the forthcoming tumult until the present duress of restoring and reoccupying the Palatine house had passed.

Daily life at the villa did not change much with the imperial family in residence. Encounters with its members were even less frequent than on my excursions to the Palatine rooftop, where Augustus had so often been present. But since no regular business was transacted on Saturdays, the entire family did usually assemble for supper and gaming on Friday evenings, in one or other of the villa's two great dining rooms. Postumus and Tiberius Drusus continued to be excluded from these gatherings, and not because of their manners. Tiberius had explained to me that by tradition in upscale Italian households, prepubescent children dined separately from the adults.

On that first Friday Agrippina endeavored to join the two lads, until Augustus mandated she take her place at the adult table. Now in her seventeenth year, Agrippina was well beyond the age of segregation. Her condescending aversions of her eyes, her scowls, her refusals to answer my questions but respond immediately when others posed the same queries, kept me biting my inner lip so not to laugh. Her grandfather failed to find her posturing quite so amusing. Slamming his fist on the table, he growled, "You are a guest in this villa, and will show respect and deference toward its mistress!"

"Then I shall return to taking my meals with my brother and our ridiculous cousin, whose company I far prefer anyway," she returned with snooty condescension.

She rose to depart; whereupon Augustus seized her by the wrist. "Given the prominence of our family, you have no choice but to treat every person you encounter with civility—including those you cannot abide or whom you know despise you." So he hissed through clenched teeth, as he lowered her back onto the couch she had been sharing with Antonia. "It is high time you acknowledge and accept this responsibility."

At that meal and henceforth, Agrippina reclined at table with a visage devoid of expression. She neither initiated nor participated in any conversations, and replied tersely to direct inquiries—including mine—in steadily measured tones.

During the final two weeks of that year I threw myself unflaggingly into finalizing the panorama—as much to distract myself from fretting about having to postpone reunion with Alcimus as to satisfy myself the tableau was complete and represented the very highest quality of my artistic work. Although the exhibit was not scheduled to open until six days before the Ides of March *[3/10]*, I aspired to finish my endeavor by the year's end, so as not to inconvenience the exhibitors by presenting the piece for hanging at the last minute. Thursday mornings I spent with Antonia and her sisters at the Porticus Octaviae, deciding where each piece in the exhibition should be placed or hung for display. My deadline for finishing my contribution I missed, but only slightly. On the morning of New Year's Day I applied the final brush stroke and left the tableau to dry, quitting my studio with the pleasantly satiated feeling that accompanies accomplishment of a goal with the satisfaction one hoped to realize.

That New Year opened on a Friday. Since the day following was the ordinary weekly holiday, everyone was relaxed and nonchalant over the prospect of two consecutive days of respite. The weather continued clear, balmy, and unusually warm as it had been throughout the winter. I was cleaning my brushes when Nausicaa arrived in my studio. She announced Lady Livia desired that upon completion of my present task, I should repair the villa's kitchen. It lay on the first floor, right nearby to the artist studios, but in a detached wing which could be closed off to protect the main building from fire and from being inundated with cooking odors. On arriving I found Livia, Antonia, and Agrippina, clad in cook's aprons and head wraps like those Tiberius had worn at Ad Gallinas. While binding me the same garb, Livia explained that on New Year's Day, in honor of the goddess Juno Lucina the women of Roman households feed their servants, even as the men do to honor Saturn during his festival. I responded that although I was familiar with the custom, this was the first occasion on which I had been asked to participate; and I regarded the invitation a special honor.

"What honor?" Antonia retorted. "You have not been invited but drafted! Is this not a family tradition, and you one of ours?" Agrippina scowled but said nothing.

The atmosphere in the kitchen was heady with the fragrance of roasting meat. The blackamoor chef Scourus and his assistants were sedulously engaged in the preparation of the repast. My companions and I distributed plates, spoons, and tumblers along the long parallel tables in the adjoining refectory. We filled jugs with water, wine, and mead, and set them in the middle of the tables. Then we heaped bread rolls into baskets and interspersed them among the jugs. At noon, the servants began to file in and take their seats. The delicia—every one of them clothed for a change—repaired to a table especially reserved for them. To another table set at right angles to the rest, Scourus' staff brought a charger piled with sliced pork, fowl, and fish, two large bowls filled with a mixture of cooked carrots, beets, and turnips. Once everyone was settled, Livia called for silence. She then recited a prayer to Juno Lucina. Afterward, Antonia asked me to help her with the meat platter. Livia and Agrippina each seized a bowl of vegetables. Each recipient was allowed to take as much of whatever he or she liked. When the contents of charger and bowls were depleted we repaired to the kitchen, where Scourus replenished our supply.

By the time everyone had been served I was ravenous myself, and beginning to wonder what arrangements had been made for our own luncheon. Seeing my companions returning to the kitchen I followed, and found them loading a covered meat charger and vegetable bowl onto a little cart, the likes of which the serving staff regularly employed to transport food to the villa's dining rooms. Another cart was already stocked with a breadbasket and two beverage jugs. We trundled our cargo to the winter dining room, where we found our menfolk. On seeing us they burst into laughter, and then into applause. The table being already set, all we must do was place the serving vessels in the center and uncover them. At each woman's place was a little object. Livia's was a new shuttle for her loom, Agrippina's a little box of carved wood containing ivory sewing needles of different sizes, Antonia's a recently published romance. My gift was a bundle of the charcoal pencils I use for sketching, bound about with a ribbon of pink my favorite color. Another tradition of New Year's Day. After the ladies of the household had waited upon their servants, they were presented in turn with gifts pertinent to their own particular skills and pastimes. Yet another custom to which Tiberius had never strictly adhered; for he preferred giving me presents spontaneously—whenever the inclination struck him—rather than waiting for specific occasions.

That evening we finalized the New Year with a supper of bread slices soaked in egg, sautéed, and finally sprinkled with pepper. Augustus demanded a harp recital of me before we adjourned to the game board. From Agrippina's music mistress Phoebe I had learned traditional Italian folksongs and currently popular ditties, the likes of both my audience sang jubilantly to my musical accompaniment. The next day was a regular Saturday, with everybody reviewing impending tasks and organizing schedules for the week forthcoming. While the ordinary people of Rome were enjoying a second day of leisure, the first family was sequestered in work. So I mused, when before descending to my studio I gazed out the windows of our parlor at the visitors wandering the gardens.

With only ten days left before the art exhibit was to open, Antonia and I journeyed daily to the Porticus Octaviae. There the planners considered the exhibit in various lights: morning, afternoon, sunny, cloudy (a condition we simulated by covering the windows with gray cloth), at sunset, in lamplight. We arranged and rearranged the collection until it met with everyone's satisfaction. The pieces we were awaiting duly arrived—including the panorama by Eutychus of Rhodes which had finally dried. Prima inquired how I might respond, if asked why no one ever seems to have met or even beheld Eutychus in person, and why he is hardly known even in Rhodes. Being a deafmute he is notoriously shy and eschews all contact with the public, I replied. He lives on the isolated hillside farm formerly the refuge of Tiberius. The owner ceded the lease of the property to Eutychus after Tiberius departed. Being under exclusive contract to Lucilius Longus, Eutychus is not well known outside the circle of Longus' clientèle. Well contrived explanations, all agreed.

In the afternoon of the day before the opening of the exhibit, members of the family toured it after Pappus had closed the Porticus Octaviae to the public early. Tiberius and I traveled there in our own litter, which delivered us to a side entrance to evade notice. Marcella and Claudia were already present with their respective daughters, Marcella's son-in-law Haterius, Claudia's husband Paullus Aemilius Lepidus, and her son Marcus Valerius Barbatus Appianus by her previous spouse now deceased. Next came Marcia with her husband and daughter. Prima arrived with her husband, their son and elder daughter. Heard well before her actual appearance was Livia Ocellina, who came with her spouse and elder stepson.

Marcia's parents Atia and Lucius Marcius Philippus arrived with a trio of houseguests: Quintus Pedius, Laelia, and Pedillus. On catching sight of me my erstwhile pupil ran over, then stopped abruptly and bowed. His demeanor surprised me so utterly and pleasantly, I quite involuntarily returned a curtsy.

Then I took one of his hands in mine and led him about the exhibit, pointing with my other hand to details in the various paintings. As we proceeded he was noticeably attentive, calm and cooperative—quite unlike the frenzied, desperate little maniac he had been at Ad Gallinas.

Last to appear were Augustus and Livia, Germanicus, Drusus, and Agrippina. After everyone had viewed the exhibit, the planners remained behind with Augustus, to join Pappus the curator, two augurs, and twelve lictores for a brief rehearsal of the opening ceremony. Pedillus I now restored to his grandparents, and without precipitating a tantrum. A small temporary altar had been erected in the courtyard. In the event of rain which seemed unlikely, the altar could be moved to the colonnade enclosing the courtyard. After assembling in Pappus' office we would line up in pairs and proceed to the altar—the augurs leading, then the lictores, Augustus and Pappus next in line, the four daughters of Octavia, and finally Atia, Marcia, and I bringing up the rear. On reaching the altar our pairs would divide, and each member stand on his or her respective side of the altar: Marcia and Atia would stand together. After the sacrificial fowl had been killed and the auspices taken, Augustus would make a short speech and declare the exhibition open. He suggested that following the ceremony the planners should mingle with visitors to the exhibit, offering information and answering questions. We all six consented, and with elan.

Almost incredibly, the morrow brought the same nasty, joint-chilling blowing mist we had endured at Ad Gallinas during Saturnalia. Phaedra dressed me in a chiton of light wool, crimson in color and embroidered with a white key—one of Chloris' more elegant creations for my winter wardrobe. About my neck Phaedra fastened the strand of large white pearls Chloris had come across, and secured Tiberius' permission to purchase as highly complementary to my wardrobe. The pearls felt warm and smooth. I loved their gentle sensation upon my skin, the understated yet stunning elegance their simplicity imparted. Wearing them on this occasion, I felt instilled with a subtle and uncanny enthusiasm that somehow, in some fashion, the event was going to prove particularly propitious for me. While Phaedra was applying makeup to my eyelids, cheeks, and lips, Tiberius arrived and confirmed my intuition. He had just finished casting the horoscope for the day's event. A startling but eminently satisfying discovery was in store for all involved, he said. Phaedra concluded her task by selecting two coverings: the heavy himation of deep blue wool (it had been cleaned since its use at Ad Gallinas), and a white veil of lighter wool. Their colors completed my costume quite aesthetically. The himation was, of course, for protection against the elements, the veil for wearing inside the portico.

Reclining beside Antonia in her litter, I shivered and drew the himation more closely about me, grateful for its weight. The veil I carried in a satchel. At the same side entrance we had utilized the day before, a heatedly excited Pappus met us. Despite the weather, large crowds were waiting in the courtyard and on the street before the main entrance for the exhibit to open. The altar had duly been moved under the shelter of the colonnade at the rear of the portico. Other family members began to arrive. Everyone who had been to the previous day's viewing was present. Augustus' nephews Sextus and Marcus Appuleius came also, with their respective wives Quinctilia and Caecilia, and Appuleia the daughter of Sextus and Quinctilia. (Marcus and Caecilia were childless.) Understandably absent were Postumus and Tiberius Drusus. Attendants escorted those who were not participating in the ceremony to the section of the colonnade especially cordoned off for them. This sector, which held the entrance to the exhibit hall, extended between the altar and the entry to the colonnade through which our procession was to emerge. Consequently we must pass by the family to reach the altar. A most convenient arrangement, I thought. It relieved the portico staff from the onus of having to irritate spectators by clearing them from our path of travel, lest they obstruct our passage by thronging us.

After a sequence of prayers, the half of which I did not understand because they were uttered in archaic Latin, the augurs sacrificed their victims and pronounced the auspices favorable. Augustus delivered his speech which, as he had promised, was brief. Predictably he extolled his late sister as a model Roman matron. Patient, gentle, uncomplaining in adversity, Octavia had been a dutiful and faithful wife, a devoted mother, and a purveyor of charity within and without her home. In addition to five children of her own, Octavia had raised the four children her second husband had begotten on other wives. Quite appreciably, Augustus did not specify these offspring were the notorious Iullus Antonius, and the three children his father Marcus Antonius had sired on Queen Cleopatra.

Despite the myriad demands of managing a household—compounded in later years by a struggle with rapidly failing health—Octavia had managed time and energy to promote the careers of writers and artists. Today their works glorify Rome, and bring pleasure and enlightenment to the people of that city and of all the world. Octavia's daughters follow her example, in domestic life, and in artistic patronage as evidenced in the exhibit opening this morning. Here Augustus identified his nieces, beginning with Marcella the eldest: he extended his right hand toward each as he spoke her name. In conclusion he declared they were assisted in their efforts by Atia and Marcia their kinswomen, and Galatea Aristoclide their devoted friend.

Now a diminutive man with fine features and white hair, clad in chiton and himation, approached the podium. Opening a scroll, he proceeded to read six brief epigrams in Greek with Latin translations following. The poems extolled the late Octavia, her children living and dead, and her contributions to the good of humanity. With a sudden thrill of delight, I realized that I knew him by reputation: Crinagoras of Mytilene, whose works I had read in Tiberius' libraries on Rhodes and at the Villa Maecenatis.

Our family group disbanded. Of its members only we the planners, the Appuleii who had not yet seen the exhibit, and Agrippina, Iulla, and Numantina who wanted to socialize with Appuleia, entered the exhibit hall. After half an hour or so the general public was allowed in. Everyone was complimentary; many were inquisitive. The question most commonly asked was how we had arrived at the exhibit's theme. By consensus after consideration of many different ideas, was our answer. As noontide neared I found myself growing pleasantly hungry, and looking forward to the luncheon being prepared for us. At about this time I noticed a young woman clad in Greek costume, darting about the exhibit with great elan. The look on her face as she viewed the various articles mingled rapture with reverence. From time to time she approached a portly Greek man and an older Greek woman, and spoke to them with excited ebullience before moving on to another part of the exhibit. Her companions quite obviously did not share her enthusiasm, for they seemed bored and even annoyed with her commentaries. Nor did they appear to be viewing the offerings; or if they were, they were doing so very cursorily. Every time the young woman caught my attention, her confrères were conversing in the main walkway with their backs to the displays.

Eventually this trio drew near to where I was standing, between an Etruscan bronze statue of a mounted warrior and a landscape by Zeuxis of Heraclea— contributions from the city of Fiesole. The young woman came closest to me. She had wispy brown hair and a broad, flat face evocative of the stiff Greek portraiture prevalent five centuries ago. I smiled at her as I stepped aside to let her view the Zeuxis without obstruction. In her ecstasy over the painting she took no notice of me. Since my attention was focused upon her, in turn I paid none to her associates until I heard a voice all too familiar.

"No, no Philo, this one is Tiberius' floozy. Not even the likes of him could stoop so low, as to find attractive that sleazy, abominable, parricidal turd we have to acknowledge as your sister." Only then did I realize the older woman and the young man were my mother and brother!

Immediately and involuntarily—more driven by instinct than rationale—I drew my veil (for which I had exchanged the himation) across my face, hung my head, and turned toward the wall. I felt as though a great rock had struck me, driving the breath from my lungs and knocking me off balance. Heart pounding, knees wobbling, throat and lungs constricted, lightheaded and fearful of fainting, I leaned my forehead against the wall and pressed my hands to it. Struggling to retain presence of mind, inhaling and exhaling deep shuddering breaths, I concentrated upon keeping my face well concealed beneath my veil to preclude my being recognized after all.

A different familiar voice rang out. "You will be thanked to keep your adverse opinions about our family and acquaintances to yourself!" Agrippina enjoined with her usual snarl.

"Aha, the truth hurts!" my mother scoffed in return.

A hand closed about each of my upper arms and a head rested between my shoulders: those of Claudia, who was considerably shorter than I. "Come," she said softly. Quickly yet very gently she led me away from the area of confrontation, and on a circuitous path to avoid a direct encounter with the assailants. Although we were at some distance, and my veil still obscured most of my face, I managed to see that Antonia, Marcella, and Marcia had joined Agrippina. I also noted the look of smug satisfaction on my mother's face as she observed my discomfiture. As Claudia and I continued our trek, from behind us I heard Marcella demand, "Why are you visiting our mother's portico, if you harbor such blatant contempt for us?"

Atia met us at the doorway to the exhibit hall. "She was just delivered a devastating revilement," Claudia explained as the three of us exited into the colonnade. The cold and misty air chilled but refreshed me, so my head began to clear. My companions led me to Pappus' office, where they seated me and wrapped my himation about me since I was shivering. The curator, understandably alarmed, asked what had happened, and Claudia apprised him. After pouring liquid from a jug into a tumbler which he handed me, he departed hastily for the exhibit hall. The contents of the tumbler turned out to be mead, for which I was grateful.

My intense reaction had been evoked by what my mother had said about Tiberius—her insinuation he was despicable but not sufficiently debased to find me attractive—and of course by the epithets she had subsequently applied to me. From their conversation, however, I discovered Claudia and Atia assumed I had taken umbrage at being called Tiberius' floozy. Although the mead was beginning to relax me, I remained too agitated to offer a corrective explanation.

As I was finishing my draught, we heard a hubbub of excited voices emanating from the colonnade. Marcella burst through the door, followed by Antonia and then Pappus.

"What a harridan!" a red-faced Antonia was exclaiming. "I cannot recall ever having encountered such degrading effrontery so aggressively delivered!" She turned toward Claudia, Atia, and me. "Did you hear how she answered Marcella?"

We three shook our heads. Claudia replied, "No; by then we were out of earshot."

Marcella said, "She sneered back at me, 'This is a public venue, is it not?' I was caught off guard and could not readily think of an answer. It seemed as though that shrew knew precisely what to say to befuddle me."

Antonia interjected, "Shaking and struggling to keep my voice from quavering, I managed to say, 'Yes this is a public venue indeed, but one in which decorum and respect are required.'"

Marcella spoke again. "That little sylph who had been flitting to and fro through the exhibit rushed over, wrapped her hands about the shrew's arm and said something in lowered tones. Although we could not hear the words, to judge from the worried expression on the young woman's face they must have been a plea to desist. But the shrew brushed off the sylph's hands as abruptly and indifferently as if she were divesting herself of insects, and continued her verbal assault. 'Decorum and respect toward a whore—how characteristic of your ilk.'

"Marcia, Antonia, and I stood there aghast, too flabbergasted to think of a response. Meanwhile Pappus beckoned two portico attendants and a guard, all of whom had been watching the dramatics. 'You and your party shall leave,' he told the shrew firmly. 'Come along, my dears,' our adversary said, now in a mockingly solicitous tone, addressing the sylph and that young man who was with them but loudly enough for the entire exhibit hall to hear. 'We are being put out onto the street for bringing the truth to light.'"

Antonia spoke again. "The sylph uttered a cry of anguish, prostrated herself before us and exclaimed plaintively, 'Oh, most gracious and noble Ladies— daughters of the late lamented Octavia and nieces of Caesar—I humbly beg your mercy and indulgence!' She lifted her head from the floor, presenting a tear-streaked face. 'My husband and his mother brought me here—strongly against their inclinations and at great expense to themselves—because I was longing so very, very desperately to see your exhibition. Please, please, will you grant them leave to wait somewhere in comfort while I finish viewing? I promise to be quick, not to cause any disturbance, and not to return once I depart!'

"We stood looking at one another, as if asking how we could possibly refuse. Finally Marcella and Marcia nodded; and I, fighting to keep my tone calm and controlled said, 'Very well, so long as we have surety there will be no further disruption.' Then Pappus here had the guard and one attendant escort the shrew and her son—who throughout the altercation did not utter a single word, but stood gaping inanely like my own Tiberius—out of the exhibit hall. The other attendant Pappus put with the sylph."

Now Pappus spoke. "That bitch and her fat pup I had sent to an unused studio, in a section of the portico where traffic is minimal—ensuring them the least opportunity possible for proclaiming their gross maledictions to passersby. I even had a serving of mead and biscuits brought to pacify them. And do you know, she had the unmitigated effrontery to say, 'We never partake of that beverage!' 'Suit yourself,' I answered as I took my leave. Amphitryon I assigned to their young woman, more to prevent the crowd from accosting her than to keep her behavior in line."

"As you can well imagine, every pair of eyes in the exhibit hall was upon us," Marcella continued. "Hence Prima and Marcia did not come here with Antonia and me. We left them behind with the girls" (by whom of course she meant Agrippina, Numantina, Appuleia, and Iulla) "to restore order, while the two of us escaped so we could compose ourselves."

"By your leave, Ladies, I ought to return to the exhibit and assist with that restoration of order," Pappus interrupted, bowing as he spoke.

"Yes; and our thanks goes with you," Marcella said. After Pappus left she added, "I cannot recall ever having seen Antonia so agitated."

"Never have I encountered such an abrasive individual—and so readily responsive with invective!" Antonia exclaimed. "She had an immediate, and supremely vituperative, rejoinder for absolutely everything we said or did!"

At long last I found my tongue. Staring at the floor I murmured without forethought, "She has always contrived to find precisely the right words to belittle anyone who confronts or contradicts her."

A collective gasp wafted through the room. Claudia, seated beside me, squeezed my hand. "You know this woman?" she asked with incredulity clear in her tone.

After swallowing hard I continued measuredly, "That very woman is my mother: she who drove me to seek sanctuary with Tiberius."

Another collective gasp, more forceful than the preceding. Claudia murmured, "By all the gods!"

There ensued a short period of silence, which Atia broke. "Little wonder you reacted so intensely," she said quietly.

More silence, then Antonia: "Do you care to remain here, or prefer to return home? If you choose to leave, we shall certainly not hold that decision against you."

My appetite had fled. Now I dreaded the prospect of the luncheon, to which I had earlier been looking forward with relish. The mead had left me feeling slightly sluggish. Almost overwhelmingly I craved solitude in which to sort out the events that had just transpired. "To return home I should like," I said meekly. Thereupon Antonia stepped to the doorway and called out to an unseen attendant, "Fetch my litter to the entrance appointed us."

The isolation I desired on this occasion was far different from the dark and restrictive confines of an alcove, in which to wonder and ponder what shortcomings and deficiencies in my character kept me at loggerheads with my family—kept them from appreciating my opinions, kept them from perceiving what I wanted more than anything in life was reconciliation. Now I needed the openness of air and expanse. On reaching the Zone of Neutrality I had the doors giving onto the gardens opened, a chair placed near and a small brazier beside it, a blanket bought and wrapped about me. There I sat, watching the gray mist cast its pallor upon the seemingly lifeless winter foliage—and ruminating.

Imagine, oh Dearest Reader, what abject horror had seized me when I realized my brother had apparently recognized me; that the changes to my appearance and bearing had been insufficient to disguise me. Or had they? My mother had promptly rejected my brother's identification; and for this I was hugely relieved. Nevertheless the epithets with which she referred to me had left me devastated, as did her comment about Tiberius. Him of course she hated merely because he was prominent and wealthy. More excruciatingly painful I found her assumption I was someone else. She would not or could not entertain the possibility, that I had found my way into Tiberius' affections and the charmed circle of his family and associates.

Heretofore, altercations with my family had always left me bewildered, grief-stricken, and remorseful. Why did my kin persist in misinterpreting my intentions and behaviors—in persecuting me for deeds they misconstrued while never allowing me to make amends? For how many countless years had I repeated this query to myself? But now this self-questioning fled as I considered my achievements, what I had become: lady of this renowned estate, an accomplished and well recognized artist earning lucrative royalties, a personal friend of the emperor himself and well-liked by the majority of his kin, and—

most gratifying of all—wife to a man who returned my intense love for him and mother of his child. All these I had achieved, not because my mother had accepted and cultivated my natural endowments and inclinations, but because she had sought relentlessly to suppress or pervert those leanings and I had defied her efforts. As self-deprecation yielded to self-assurance and remorse to anger I found myself more keenly chagrined and embittered than I could remember having been, after the most virulent of squabbles with my family. To no avail I kept reminding myself the bounties of my present life would never have come to pass, had I not resisted and ultimately abandoned my kin. The diatribe my mother delivered this day had utterly destroyed the faint and weary hope I had been fostering about possibly managing to forgive her.

Nevertheless I found myself considering my brother in a different light. Him I had always dismissed as a slow-witted and oafish chump, too muddleheaded from our family's incessant coddling to figure anything out for himself. Yet today he had readily noticed and correctly identified me. Furthermore he had a wife! Either she and her family were as asinine as he and ours, or he had matured into a better person than I had expected him to become. Sincerely hoping the latter assessment was the correct one, I rejoiced in discovering I was not so contemptuous of Philo as I had assumed. That he remained abjectly deferential to our mother was clearly evident from his immediate compliance, after she rejected his conclusion he had discovered me. If you and your kin had been urgently seeking a person for nearly a decade, and suddenly you thought you had come upon that individual, would you not encourage any relative who challenged your conclusion to have a second look and reconsider? For his emasculation I truly pitied Philo and did not scorn him.

My thoughts reverted to my mother. The aching, unrequited yearning for her approval, the longing to hear or read the words, *Well done, my daughter, you leave me proud!* —the thin hope this desire might someday be fulfilled—had fled my consciousness, leaving only the despair of its continued elusion. This day's encounter verified my mother truly did not want to see me successful, distinguished, and prosperous. All she wanted was to continue condemning me, to persist in excoriating me for failing to reach a non-existent standard of achievement. To my surprise and dismay, I now longed once again to exact vengeance: to watch with relish while my mother suffered for having afflicted me through half my lifetime, with humiliation and unnecessary guilt.

What had become of Underlying Good? The more I tried to claim its presence and governance, the more than ever it seemed a remote philosophical abstraction inapplicable and useless. For certain I could see no element of good in my mother whatsoever. What little I had perceived in my brother was being stultified, suppressed, overwhelmed, by our mother's overweening malevolence. And was not the goodness I had just associated with myself no more than the arrogant condescension of pride in accomplishment, and of self-pitying justification for resentment and even revenge?

Slowly I became aware of someone standing before me. It was Alcmene, my attendant for the afternoon. More than usually trepidatious, she gingerly reported Lady Laelia and her grandson had just arrived at the villa inquiring to see me. Should she (Alcmene) advise them I was indisposed? Her message transformed me utterly. Casting off my blanket, I leaped to my feet with such verve that Alcmene took several steps backward. Her reaction alerted me to regain poise quickly. After inhaling deeply and exhaling slowly, I was able to respond in steady tones. No, she should not dismiss my callers: I would receive them. I was about to have them escorted to the smaller reception room directly adjacent to the art gallery. Then the thought struck me irresistibly, to have them await me in my studio instead. I hastened into my suite, where Alcmene joined me after sending the messenger away. With her assistance I rinsed my mouth, retouched my makeup, tucked loosened locks of hair back into their bands, and straightened my clothes—all at madcap pace. Briskly but not too hurriedly lest I arrive winded and flustered, I traversed the colonnade and descended the stairs to my destination.

When I arrived, Laelia was admiring my **Lion of Nemea,** and Pedillus was wandering about the studio observing but not touching the tableaux on their easels and textiles on their racks. Laelia gently seized her grandson about the shoulders and turned him so he noticed me. Now he bent forward with a bow. With a smile and nod I acknowledged his gesture, and with a sweep of my hand invited him to resume scrutinizing my work.

While he did, Laelia joyously related what had transpired in Pedillus' life since the Saturnalia. Upon their return to Velletri from Ad Gallinas, her husband had promptly set about locating a local decorative artist who felt willing and able to teach a deafmute. As his artistic skills developed, Pedillus' demeanor improved. More and more he had begun to show the characteristics I noted the previous evening at the art exhibit: contentment, alertness, tractability. For the first time in his life his family was able to teach him fundamentals of etiquette, as evinced by his bows to me. Quite frequently he volunteered to help with the care of his baby sister. There were still tantrums, still episodes of anger and frustration—quite appreciable, I interjected, given the boy's impairment.

Nonetheless, Laelia continued, these outbreaks were definitely becoming less frequent.

Having finished his brief tour of my studio, Pedillus returned to where his grandmother and I were sitting. Laelia retrieved a cloth satchel that had been leaning against the leg of her chair, and from it removed a tableau. It was a collage of the same animals I had originally sketched for Pedillus to paint at Ad Gallinas: duck, cockerel, cat, dog, and pony. All were depicted in proper proportion amid scenery. The cat, dog, and pony were standing on a grassy hillock beneath a tree in which the cockerel was perched, while the duck swam on a rivulet in the foreground. The scene was imposed upon a background of pale blue sky.

With an earnestly inquiring look on my face, I pointed to the tableau and then tapped all my fingers against my chest: was Pedillus willing to give the piece to me? Catching my meaning he nodded enthusiastically, then pulled the tableau out of Laelia's hands and pushed it into mine. To express my thanks I curtsied. Casting about mentally for a gift with which to reciprocate, I asked Laelia whether frogs could be found on their estate or in its environs. She gave an affirmative reply; so from my collection I selected a partially completed tableau of the frog in the Villa Maecenatis' pond. This piece I handed to Pedillus, who laughed silently upon seeing its subject. I pressed my finger against his chest, then pointed to the tableau and mimicked brush strokes with my hand. During this procedure I instructed Laelia. On returning home she should have another frog located for Pedillus, to serve as a model from which he could complete the tableau.

Laelia picked up the empty satchel from the floor and handed it to Pedillus, who duly inserted the frog tableau. When she turned her gaze to me there were tears in her eyes. She sighed abruptly, and then spoke solemnly. Was I a nymph or goddess in disguise? Who besides a divinity could effect such a healing transformation in her grandson? I assured her I was an ordinary mortal with faults aplenty—no more divine than Caesar, who rather than I had been the one to urge cultivation of Pedillus' artistic inclinations. Nonetheless I did like to wonder and consider, whether some benign cosmic Force had driven Pedillus to me on the banks of the Tiber at Ad Gallinas and impelled me to notice his interest in my art.

A host of conflicting emotions churned within my conscience, making me fearful of losing my self-control in the presence of my two callers. Desperate once again for solitude, I lied to Laelia that I felt a headache coming on and blamed it on the weather. Pointing to my forehead, I grimaced; then I folded my hands, laid my head on them, and shut my eyes. Pedillus caught my meaning: I had a headache and wanted to lie down. Bending down I drew my arms about him, felt his tighten about me, and detected a kiss to my cheek. We released one another; I tweaked Pedillus' cheek; then Laelia embraced me. We exited the studio without any fuss from Pedillus. I ordered the servant attending the hallway to have my guests' litter fetched to the villa's front, and escort the guests themselves to the foyer. While mounting the stairway after they departed, I found myself mentally thanking Underlying Good, for my ability through sign language to communicate so effectively with this unfortunate boy.

The Zone of Neutrality had been unaltered since my departure. The doors to the balcony were still open, the chair still before them with the blanket lying across it. Nevertheless the brazier beside the chair was aglow with new charcoal: clearly Alcmene had anticipated my return. The brief experience that had just unfolded in my studio set me to ruminating anew. In the course of a few hours I had gone from being designated a whore, and a *sleazy, abominable, parricidal turd*, to a goddess. So why, then, did I continue to feel sullied and scorned as inadequate—still desperate to defend and justify myself to my family, and now desirous to return vengeance for the sufferings they had inflicted upon me? Why could I not simply dismiss their criticism as nonsensical, especially now I had received yet another—and particularly glowing—approbation from a relative of Augustus? Underlying Good was alternating in my mind between distantly elusive and intangible when I contemplated the encounter with my mother, and palpably apparent as an active Force transforming Pedillus' life with me the instrument of that transformation.

As I gazed out upon the gardens, the hue of the gray mist deepened and the trees became silhouettes: daylight was waning. Suddenly my blanket became warmer. Tiberius had come up behind my chair and drawn his arms about me. I leaned my head back against his chest and closed my eyes.

"Antonia gave a full account of what happened at the exhibit, and Laelia of what transpired here this afternoon." His voice was quiet and deep with emotion. "Ah, my poor Clytia! Until now I never fully comprehended the extent to which your family brutalized you. Little wonder you have struggled and fought so arduously, to put your memories into proper perspective and gain peace of mind. And despite the trauma you incurred at the exhibit, you willingly received Laelia and Pedillus with composure and grace—even joyousness—as though nothing were amiss. Laelia was stunned, when just before her departure for Velletri my mother related to her what befell you this morning. You are truly a lioness of incredible fortitude, for the likes of which I have not begun to give you sufficient credit. And what a fool I have been, losing patience with your struggles or making light of your ordeal! May someday that generous heart of yours find a way to forgive me."

"There is nothing to forgive," I murmured as I began to weep with silent convulsive sobs, like those I had emitted upon learning Tiberius had forgiven me for trading insults with Timoleon before half the Academy of Rhodes. "Until now you did not fully understand what I endured." Turning my head upward I looked him in the face, smiled, and all at once started to laugh while continuing to weep. "Your admission brings me unspeakable happiness and solacing ease, my love. And for the first time in my life, I am feeling sorry for myself without any sense of guilt!"

Looking down at me, he raised his eyebrows quizzically. "Only a woman can contrive to laugh and cry simultaneously." He drew me to my feet and held me close against him. "Go right ahead and pity yourself, for you have earned that privilege. By all the gods, how cold you are! You are shivering, and your hands are like lumps of ice. Whatever possessed you to sit here with this door wide open to weather so foul? Did you not learn anything from your Saturnalia affliction?"

"I felt desperate for draughts of fresh air, as though I were strangling, suffocating." So engrossed I had been in my pondering, I had failed to notice that despite blanket and brazier I had become chilled. "Into a hot bath I shall get myself as soon as one can be drawn. Alcmene!"

"Our regular bath is already prepared and awaiting us in my suite, according to the time of day," Tiberius interjected. "Did you not hear Nestor banging about?"

"No—I suppose I was too distressed and lost in thought."

"Quite understandable. Alcmene, go and advise my mother that Lady here is fatigued and still shaken, but recovering her self-assurance and calm. For our supper, have something prepared which is at once highly nutritive and soothing; consult Chloe if necessary." Alcmene curtsied and departed. "My entire family is deeply concerned about today's events and their effect upon you," Tiberius continued as he escorted me to the bathroom. His words touched me deeply. While we were undressing I started to weep once more. "Why these new tears my dearest one? Has something I have said or done distressed you?"

"My family never gave me support, protection, vindication, or consolation in untoward circumstances. Today your family provided them, continues to provide them; and I remain grateful far beyond my ability to express. Even Agrippina, who hates me, came to my defense this morning."

He chuckled as he helped me into the bath. "Agrippina does not hate you. If truly she did she would not have intervened at all, but left you to contend with the situation on your own."

For supper we were brought the pleasing dish of chicken and paste in milky sauce that was served to Augustus and me in the hearth room at Ad Gallinas. Although I anticipated having to force myself to eat, I found the repast quite appealing and nurturing. Warmed and comforted—physically by bath and meal, emotionally by Tiberius' tender reassurances of his own and his family's concern for me—I drifted promptly and contentedly to sleep, and did not awaken until rather late the next morning. Phaedra while dressing me said Tiberius had already departed to call upon several families with sick folk to whom he was providing assistance. On finishing she told me Lord Caesar wished to see me in his office.

The villa had three offices on its ground floor. The largest, from which Maecenas while alive had conducted his patronage of artistic endeavors, Acer presently used for administration of the physical maintenance of the villa and its grounds. The second, which Maecenas had devoted to his personal affairs, Tiberius had taken over for his private matters; although for the interim he had surrendered this space to his mother and moved his own business upstairs into his sitting room. The third and smallest but most elegantly appointed office, Maecenas had kept specifically for Augustus to utilize whenever he sojourned at the villa. On entering this gorgeous little room, I found Agrippina with her grandfather. With lowered eyes I curtsied to her and said, "Thank you for coming to my defense yesterday."

"Let us get this matter correct: because of you I had to come to the defense of my family," she growled back at me.

"Pina!" Augustus interjected sternly. "A retainer has thanked you for intervening on her behalf! You will follow the protocols incumbent upon a proper patron and graciously accept her gratitude!"

Agrippina's face reddened. After several more moments of glowering at me she murmured sullenly, "You are welcome." Turning on her heel, she walked stridently from the room with clenched fists. Her grandfather's face assumed a look of wary concern as he watched her leave.

"I sincerely regret she hates me," I ventured after Agrippina had slammed the door behind her.

"If she really hated you, she would not have come to your aid in the first place." Precisely what Tiberius had asserted the previous evening; however, hearing this reassurance from Augustus put to final rest the lingering qualms I had been entertaining. With a wave of one hand, he motioned for me to take a seat on the intricately carved settee facing his desk. After several moments of silence he spoke pensively, looking downward at the stylus with which he was toying. "Yesterday you had a very, very grievous encounter. Nothing strikes me as more monstrously unnatural than a parent, who loathes a child with such abject hatred as your mother apparently harbors for you. Never, ever, shall I forgive my daughter her attempt to wrest my authority from me; but never, ever shall I cease to love her."

He sighed, placed the stylus on the desk, and turned his steely gaze directly at me. "Every member of my family, who saw or heard what happened at the exhibit, shares my sympathy for you. Down the future, however, we cannot have you react as you did, should you reencounter your mother's scorn. While this may not ever happen, you should be prepared in case it does. Suppose your mother reconsiders, concludes your brother correctly identified you after all, and launches an exposé? Or your brother, convinced he was right despite your mother's rejection of his assessment, decides to investigate you further? And how would you respond should a relative, or an acquaintance of your family you have long forgotten, approach and say, 'So, daughter of...' what is your mother's name?"

"Anthe Eupistou."

"'...daughter of Anthe Eupistou, is this how you repay your mother all the selfless personal sacrifices she made, the goodness she bestowed unconditionally upon you—by running away from the haven she provided and prostituting yourself to a ne'er-do-well the likes of Tiberius Nero?'"

Although his suggestion dejected me, I was sincerely grateful for the alert it carried. Nodding my comprehension, I managed a wan smile. "Quite frankly, I do fear a possible repetition of yesterday's scene."

"The humility and forthright honesty of your admission are most commendable. Your own mother's failure to recognize you yesterday proves the bogus identity and history Tiberius has created for you are highly credible. The charade will not continue to work, however, should you show the slightest sign of discomposure if someone asserts you are your mother's degenerate daughter. You need to be able to say with unruffled aplomb and confidence, *I am not who you think I am, but rather Galatea Aristoclide late of Rhodes. Apparently I resemble the person you presumed I was.* You will not succeed, until you find a way to keep those agonizing memories of your mother's abuse from unnerving you. Gossip and speculation about yesterday's event are spreading rapidly."

Closing my eyes, I winced. "I am so terribly, terribly sorry!"

"Certainly you are. Now please, do not castigate yourself. Inured as this family is to unsavory epithets and scurrilous innuendo, I cannot recall any of us who has not given way to our emotions in public at one time or another. I myself broke down and wept right before a full senate when the verdict against Julia was read. But returning to what happened at the exhibit: fortuitously it appears the general assumption was that you reacted not to the defamation your mother heaped on you as her daughter, but to her having called you Tiberius' whore. This ruse our publicists will maintain. It works quite well, making you appear defensive of your chastity as Tiberius' ward and not his strumpet. Nevertheless I have asked Tiberius to take you for a sojourn to his ancestral villa at Palestrina, until the sensation over this incident dies down. Moreover I have engaged Areus Didymus of Alexandria, whose lecture you attended not very long ago, to give you counsel before you depart."

His mood became reflective, reminiscent. "When we received the word Tiberius' brother had been injured beyond hope of survival, Livia sequestered herself in her bedchamber. For three days she did not take food or drink. She may have let herself die had I not intervened. The philosophical guidance Areus offered helps her surmount her grief to this day. I urge you to consult her also. You need to put your torturous memories into proper perspective, and mitigate the agony they invoke. Although indisputably excruciating, they are still only memories. As I have said before: you are no longer a member of your mother's family but of ours, and we all love you. Now go see if you can find Livia."

With the assistance of a delicium I came upon Livia weaving, in the artist's studio directly adjacent to mine. She smiled warmly as I entered. "My husband told me to expect you: come sit here beside me." Now her smile fled. She shut her eyes and took several deep breaths before proceeding in a somber tone. "My Nero was in his thirtieth year—just entering the prime of his life, already an accomplished military commander and anticipating a brilliant political career— when he was cut down by that terrible accident. Do you know what happened?"

"Yes. His horse lost its footing and rolled on him, crushing his entire side."

Livia swallowed hard. "For the second time in my life I had to endure losing a child. The death of an infant directly after birth has remained poignant, because this was the only child Caesar and I engendered together. The loss was easier to bear than Nero's, however, because the babe did not live long enough to leave memories. In fact to forestall these, my husband and I insisted we not be told the gender. Of Nero I had wonderful memories aplenty. These recollections—together with a conjecture of him crushed and bloodied— overwhelmed my conscience. I lost all sense of time, of where I was or what I did. I was not even aware of passing my natural excreta during those three days of solitude, although discovery of my chamber pot full yet lidded showed I had executed my functions in normal fashion.

"I recall becoming gradually conscious of Caesar shaking me and calling my name: 'Livia, Livia! Look at me! Pay heed to me!' 'Yes, yes,' was all I could mutter as I emerged from my trance, to find I was sitting on the edge of my bed. He was standing before me, pouring water from a pitcher into a tumbler. 'Here,' he said softly; but as he pressed the tumbler to my lips, I refused it. Now he spoke vehemently. 'Confound it, Livia, you have not taken drink or nourishment for three days! You are destroying yourself and that I will not have! I hereby invoke my prerogative as your spouse, your paterfamilias, the superior partner in our marriage compact, to command you quit this path of self-annihilation at once!'

"He sat on the bed beside me and with his free arm drew me against him. 'Livia,' he continued, his voice now mild but still urgent, 'you know I love you immeasurably. Right now I am suffering the loss of someone I loved very, very much as well. Do not compound my grief by taking yourself from me, my wife most cherished.' On hearing those tender words I began to weep. I took the water and then the broth he had brought, which he administered from its cruse with a spoon. While feeding me, he explained he had arranged for Areus to counsel me and insisted I accept the philosopher's guidance.

"First we must travel to Pavia, from whence we escorted the funerary cortege to Rome. Through that journey I felt as though I had turned to stone, especially as I beheld the funeral pyres the cities and towns through which we passed had lit in Nero's commemoration. Nothing seemed more devastating than to recognize those fires were meant for me.

"Putting Areus' requirements into practice proved far from easy, and demanded considerable self-discipline. Areus bade me surround myself with mementos of Nero: toys, books, garments, tools he employed (his stylus for example). He had me ponder Nero's pleasures: his favorite foods, favorite colors, favorite pastimes, his fondness for Antonia and their children. It was at Areus' suggestion that Caesar and I invited Antonia and her children to reside with us permanently. At first merely thinking about these reminders, let alone seeing and touching them, heightened rather than alleviated my grief. As time passed, however, I found Areus' recommendations effective, albeit only to a point. Memories of Nero, the company of his widow and children, the constant reminder my husband and another son equally beloved are still with me, provide no more than bittersweet comfort; for they cannot restore Nero or my unnamed babe." She paused her weaving, holding the shuttle in her left hand. Tears trickled from her eyes.

"My sincerest apology!" I exclaimed. "Your effort to help me is upsetting you!"

Livia took a deep breath, and with the forefinger of her left hand brushed away her tears. "You caused no offense." She looked at me and smiled ruefully. "May my experience serve to warn you, not to expect more of Areus than he is capable of presenting. Those painful memories of your mother's mistreatment cannot be eradicated, any more than my deceased children can be restored to me. All Areus can provide is methodology for coping with your pain."

While mounting the stairway to our quarters I paused abruptly, riveted by a sudden and particularly perceptive reflection upon the horoscope Tiberius had cast the preceding day. He had predicted a startling but satisfying discovery for all involved with the art exhibit. Without question there had been a plenitude of discoveries startling and satisfying. Startled I was to see my brother married, startled to find myself still devastated by my mother's contempt for me, yet satisfied and relieved I was that she had failed to recognize me. Firsthand I had observed the members of Tiberius' family startled by my mother's obstreperous conduct, by the virulence of her hatred, by the passive acquiescence of Philo. The commiseration and guidance of Tiberius and his kin, in the aftermath of the incident at the exhibit, convinced me they were satisfied as well, now that the mystery surrounding my obsession with my mother had been lifted for them.

More than ever I was appreciating the gentle counsel with which Tiberius had prepared me to face the possibility of miscarriage. His own mother had suffered this grave disappointment. She had managed to cope by reminding herself there were no memories of this child. Had Anthe miscarried the laments would have been endless, and the cause somehow attributed to me. Whenever a woman of her acquaintance miscarried, she had gloated. So I reflected, growing hot with anger as I entered the Zone of Neutrality. Rather than remaining there, I withdrew to my sitting room because it promised more privacy than the parlor. Feeling unwontedly fatigued I laid down upon the daybed, and continued to ruminate.

Memories. Livia's evoked the oxymoron of sorrow-laden joy. Her memories brought her peace, if only a limited sense thereof. A similar attitude for myself, I remained unable to embrace. Why could I not dismiss my family's abuses as one does a bad dream? No matter how hard I tried to suppress them, these recollections kept resurfacing in my conscience, bringing with them abject hatred and craving for revenge. Had I not kept reminding myself—over and over, year after year—that without the importunities of my family, I would never have come to know Tiberius and his kin, let alone received their commiseration? For this I was grateful, immeasurably grateful! Why did this gratitude keep failing to put my familial memories into proper perspective? Was I truly incapable of expressing sufficient gratitude, even as my mother had always maintained?

In the morning of the Ides of March *[3/15]*, Tiberius and I met with Areus Didymus in the library of the philosopher's modest home near the Caelian Hill. Areus was about Augustus' age: a stocky man with brown hair and beard streaked with white, and vibrant hazel eyes that conveyed a sense of profound knowledge and acute insight. He listened patiently and attentively as I related my history, right up to the encounter with my mother and brother at the art exhibit. The narration lasted a good two hours. Tiberius from time to time inserted a clarifying comment or embellishment. Areus agreed to keep secret our marriage and son.

"Why do you wish to punish your mother?" the philosopher inquired after my discourse was over.

Startled and dismayed by his question, I responded with another. "Sir, did the narrative I just delivered not make the reason amply clear?"

"Allow me to rephrase. What benefit—what manifestation of Underlying Good—do you expect to derive from afflicting your mother?"

"I want her to understand how deeply she has hurt me."

"For that she needs to be educated, not punished."

"Sir, I spent half my life trying to educate her: to convince her I am not the lazy, slovenly, disrespectful wretch she maintains I am to this day!" Agitation was beginning to make me shake, to speak in strained tones.

"Your mother has no desire to change her judgment of you. If she did, she would have accepted rather than challenge your brother's recognition of you at the art exhibit."

"Precisely what I concluded," I croaked as I began to weep, once more with those silent convulsive sobs.

Areus continued steadily "Genuine vengeance has an altruistic element, presenting its recipients the options of altering their conduct or suffering consequences for not. As we speak, Caesar is sacrificing in the temple to Mars the Avenger on this the anniversary of his father's assassination. When he made avenging that murder his political agenda, the younger Caesar gave opponents—his father's and his own—the choices of supporting his cause or at least desisting from hostility, or of sustaining political and very possibly personal annihilation. Your mother will not or cannot entertain the notion she misjudged you. Afflicting her will not dispel but reinforce her pernicious image of you. Retribution that confers punishment alone, without offering its recipient the alternative of reformation, is ethically reprehensible—hardly a course of action you would care to pursue."

I nodded, unable to respond verbally.

"You must learn to live with the perpetual and agonizing knowledge your mother will never cease to disdain you—to regard you as uncooperative, lazy, rebellious, and ungrateful. That knowledge is an open wound in your psyche that cannot be healed, only salved." Uncanny, I thought, that Areus should use the same simile Tiberius had when he consoled me over Timoleon. The philosopher continued, "Every time you find yourself in despair over your mother's disfavor, you should remind yourself her maledictions and mistreatments drove you to seek refuge with Tiberius. You owe the happiness you enjoy today to the misery she inflicted upon you."

These words incensed me. Through clenched teeth I declared, fretfully and vehemently, "Year after year, I have pondered that very line of reasoning! Instead of bringing me comfort, it makes me feel I should be grateful for my mother's abuse and forgive her. Well, I cannot bring myself to thank or forgive; and I despise this ethical inadequacy in myself!"

"There is no ethical inadequacy. Your resentment is entirely natural and appreciable. Furthermore, resentment is probably not so much what you feel as strongly as frustration and grief. You are not alone. My father, who owned and managed a lucrative shipping business in Alexandria, decried my decision to become a sophistos. How could I expect abstractions about the workings of the universe, and the contemplations of philosophers long dead, to put food on our family's table? Nor did he arrange marriage for me. Like you, I wrestled with contradictory feelings about this deliberate neglect of paternal obligation. Its intent angered and grieved me sorely, even while I was grateful because it allowed me to marry for love. My father persisted with his hostility for two decades, shunning along with me my wife and the three grandchildren we gave him, never speaking a civil word to or about us. Eventually—after I had gained recognition in my chosen vocation—my father relented and began interacting cordially with my family and me. In the end, however, he disinherited me altogether, and left only tiny token amounts to my sons and daughter. The balance of his considerable fortune went entirely to my identical twin brother, who thought my setback both amusing and well deserved. Why my father reverted puzzles and chagrins me to this day, twenty-five years after his death.

"Trying to force yourself to forgive your mother is a pointless waste of effort. What she did to you is inexcusable, unpardonable, and will remain inexcusable and unpardonable unless she repents and recants. In order to forgive, you must diffuse and dispel the anger you harbor toward her. Anger is a venom we generate within ourselves. It poisons us, not its objects. Let me return, now, to a proposition I started to advance earlier. When a man purchases a rare and expensive artifact, does he not hold it in higher esteem than the ordinary, commonplace articles of his household? And if he drains his coffers to procure that superlative, will he not cherish it more intensely than would someone who inherited it, who received it as a gift, or who was sufficiently wealthy to acquire it without incurring financial hardship? Here is my directive to you. Every time you find yourself ruminating about your mother in anger, I want you to catch your breath. Then deliberately tell yourself enduring her abuse was the price you paid for the life you presently enjoy with Tiberius. Without question that price was exorbitant. But consider how much more you value your association with Tiberius and his family than does our splenetic Agrippina, who acquired her connection with them by birth."

From that meeting I came away almost dreamy with serenity. Tiberius commented upon my demeanor immediately, Augustus during supper that evening. Through the subsequent two weeks Tiberius and I spent at the diminutive Palestrina villa with its elegant formal garden, set amid the narrow defiles of the Alban hills, I remained nearly rapturous with newfound peace. Tiberius seemed more loving and lovable than ever, our personal attendants Alcmene and Nestor never more attentive, the villa's resident servants and the townspeople of picturesque hillside Palestrina remarkably convivial. Did I not perceive, Tiberius asked one evening, the loveliness inhered not outside of me, but within?

The villa lies between the modern town and the ancient citadel, to which Tiberius took me one day. The view I found breathtaking. To the one side rose the white ridge of Soracte; to the opposite the plain of the Pontine Marshes stretched to the horizon.

The same persistently dry and usually balmy weather, which had made the winter pleasantly and deceptively mild and caused the Palatine house to burn, was rendering the spring unseasonably cold. Lacking warmth and moisture to stimulate growth, the foliage retained the dull gray and brown hues of hibernation and offered little artistic endeavor. Nevertheless from time to time I did come across minuscule points of green, pushing their way upward through the lackluster litter of the ground, or emerging from dark tips or buds on the branches of trees. A sketch of these I completed with greater zeal than I had similar models in the past. Their newness of life, emerging patiently and determinedly despite adverse conditions, conveyed not a sense of adversity but of triumph—a striking parallel to the change in sentiment Areus had urged upon me.

The region seemed to burgeon with artistic inspiration. Many a morning I passed in the city's immense Temple of Fortune, reveling in its grand and exquisite mosaics representing scenes of the Nile. Details of one I reproduced on a pair of vignettes: a rhinoceros comically stranded upon a rock amid floodwaters, and a group of black-skinned Ethiopians stalking a leopard with bows and arrows. Well imagine then my surprise, Dear Reader, that afternoon when Tiberius groused he had little love for either the villa or its locale. The narrow and winding defiles so intriguing to me, he found stifling and disconcerting. For him the sinuous landscape evoked images of troops entrapped in ambush, frantic for an elusive escape route. He longed for vistas viewed from remote vantages, having acquired this inclination during our years on the promontory of the Rhodian farm. The Palestrina estate was nearby to Rome, but inconvenient to reach through the mountain passes. Drusus his son shared his antipathy. Nevertheless they were loath dispossess themselves of this patrimony of the Claudii Nerones. Tiberius felt the villa could be put to best use as a place to retire servants incapacitated by age, injury, or illness.

During our return to Rome on the final day of March, a steady wind piled heavy lowering clouds into the sky. Overnight I awakened to the sound and scent of abundant precipitation—not the suffocating mist that had brought occasional minimal moisture to a winter's day, but a steady and penetrating rain. The Calends of April was a triple feast day for the goddesses Venus, Fortune, and Concord, venerating fertility and prosperity from sexual intercourse conducted within the moral boundary of marriage. The rites—sacrifices, chants and prayers—were incumbent upon the pontiffs and on all Roman matrons: hence Augustus as chief pontiff and Livia as chief matron officiated. The ceremony was held at the Temple of Concord in the main Forum. Being neither pontiff nor matron, Tiberius could not participate. He persuaded me not to attend as a spectator, especially since owing to the rain the usual preliminary procession was being foregone. In his bedchamber we commemorated this religious observance with the physical activity it consecrated.

The drenching weather persisted throughout April and elicited some strongly contradictory emotions. To be sure, everyone was grateful for the broken drought—for the promises of bountiful crops to sustain life and of luxuriant blossoms and foliage to beautify it. Along with their benefits, however, the rains brought increasing restlessness and frustration. We felt ourselves confined—yea, trapped—in the Villa Maecenatis. Any venture out of doors promised a soggy and slippery excursion. Rebuilding of the Palatine house had to be suspended. Clothing, bedding, bath towels, all felt cold and clammy. Despite the implementation of braziers, nothing could be made fully dry. For this very same reason I had to refrain from painting.

Through that relentlessly wet April I found myself noticing, more and more, the negative characteristics of Tiberius' family. When a break in her schedule offered a rare and usually brief period of respite, Livia invited me to join her, either in the library, or in her studio where I practiced my embroidery while she wove. We discussed subjects from the sublime to the banal—from the most subtle elements of philosophy and politics, art and literature, to the rigors of managing households and farms and husbands and children. Our conversations I enjoyed immensely, for Livia was extraordinarily learned and a sharply incisive thinker. Nevertheless I found she could be stubbornly opinionated and narrow-minded—politely respectful of my ideas and conclusions, but doggedly resistant to reevaluating let alone changing her own.

Augustus, who had so eagerly engaged me in conversation during my visits to the Palatine rooftop, now passed me in the villa's hallways without even glancing in my direction; or he acknowledged my greetings with an indifferent grunt.

Agrippina continued to be sullenly polite to me in the presence of others; but when she encountered me by herself, or when Postumus was with her but no one else, she was unflaggingly contemptuous. She developed the habit of walking past me with eyes averted, ignoring my greetings and then breaking into loud snickering behind me. Postumus proved worse. Encountering him alone one day, I commented in a pleasant tone it was a pity no one could go fishing on account of the rain. He clenched one fist, raised it before my face, bared his teeth, and growled, "You will not speak to me unless I speak to you first!" So much for the friendship I had assumed we cultivated at Ad Gallinas. As I curtsied and hastily backed away, I remembered Augustus had precautioned me never to be alone in the house when Postumus was about. Fortunately Phaedra was with me and a manservant with Postumus. Now keenly aware Postumus was unstable and potentially dangerous, I followed Augustus' counsel and thereafter never ventured forth from my quarters without an attendant.

Postumus and Agrippina I never saw in the villa's library, where I frequently came upon Tiberius' son Drusus and Antonia's two sons his cousins. All three were avid learners, with whom I enjoyed exchanging knowledge and insights. But Germanicus, who had originally struck me as eminently personable and affable, started to impress me as overly arrogant—too full of himself—excessively confident about and impressed with achievements and capabilities of which had minimal understanding or mastery. This conduct in turn made me annoyed at Antonia: why did she not perceive Germanicus' hauteur and endeavor to curb it? She was ready enough to castigate and reprimand the bumbling and flubbing of his younger brother. Indeed Tiberius Drusus, whom the rest of the family scorned, surprised me in quite the opposite manner. He was a diligent pupil with a keenly intellectual mind and a broad range of interests, and an ability to retain information and grasp concepts beyond the ken of many adults. Nonetheless, our encounters caused me fully to appreciate his family's distaste for him. His tendencies to drool while staring vacuously, to break out into loud and lengthy guffaws for no apparent reason, to ramble in effete and pointless conversations, made remaining in his presence for any length of time quite a trying experience.

Drusus my unacknowledged stepson was invariably polite and gracious to me. At three different times, however, on entering our parlor I overheard from Tiberius' quarters his voice and Drusus' raised in heated argument. On one occasion I heard Livia as well, and was able to make out the words of a shout from Tiberius: "Have you a better suggestion for a bride? Be glad her family is willing to accept you!" The prospective bride, Tiberius told me later, was the Aemilia Lepida who had been affianced to the late Lucius Caesar. The betrothal would be solemnized upon Drusus' return from military training, for which he was scheduled to depart on the Calends of May. The date for the nuptials was yet to be determined.

Everyone seemed annoying in one way or another—if not to me directly, then to somebody else. Why was I suddenly overly sensitive to the faults and shortcomings of Tiberius' kin? Was it from having to be sequestered with them on account of the weather? Was it a natural outcome of lengthening acquaintance and increasing familiarity? Why this complete reversal of the equanimity I had acquired from Areus?

We got some relief from our doldrums after the Ides passed, and the household began to bustle with preparations for sending Drusus and Germanicus to their military training at Marseilles. Tiberius spent quite a lot of time with the two youths, advising them of what they could expect from their commanding officers and how they should conduct themselves. One night he remarked to me in private, that he hoped military discipline might induce Drusus to abandon his irascibility and Germanicus his cockiness. So he had been contemplating those aggravating traits as well.

Before sleep that night I recalled, with resentment all too familiar, my parents reiterating I had no right to feel annoyance toward anyone, and irritations I harbored were proof of my abject selfishness. Tiberius' insistence he had not stopped loving me while angry about my confronting Timoleon, had continued to surprise me for years. While now lay I abed mulling these concerns, a sudden wave of determination surged through me. Ceasing abruptly to ruminate about my progenitors' imputations, I proceeded to challenge them. *What human is without shortcomings which inflame and vex the shortcomings of other humans, no matter how much love is exchanged between them?* With this recognition both the resentment and the surprise faded, and the calm I had felt at Palestrina returned.

Marcella and Iulla were preparing to depart for Marseilles as well, to their home in that city. They would quit Ostia along with Drusus and Germanicus on the same day—the Calends of May—but not on the same ship. The youths were going to travel by military transport, the mother and daughter on a monoreme. During the week preceding Marcella sent me a note, asking whether I was willing to sell her one of my—pardon me, one of Eutychus Rhodou's original paintings. In response I offered to send her one gratis from my collection on Rhodes, or produce one altogether new once the weather relented: all she must do was specify a subject or genre. No, no, no, she answered: she wanted one from which copies had been made and sold. Then should a visitor to her home confess to having the same article, she could boast hers was the original.

Accordingly I contacted Longus for an appointment. A day later, Marcella and I met with him in his office at the Gallery of the Four Winds. After we had exchanged greetings, Marcella asked which of my originals on display was currently generating the most orders for copies. A black cat chasing speckled black and orange moths, Longus replied. *Carbo, represented chasing creatures he never actually saw.* Longus rang for an attendant, whom he ordered to fetch the piece. After a brief examination, Marcella emphatically declared it was for certain the one she wanted. Impossible, Longus countered: he could hardly surrender the original when orders for copies were flourishing.

Now I intervened. I had other pieces to offer as replacements—completed articles I could retrieve from Rhodes, or the chariot tableau on which I intended to resume work once the weather relented. Was it not preferable the cat/moth piece be taken off the market at the height of its popularity? If copies continue to be produced they will eventually become ubiquitous, and render the representation commonplace and boring. Moreover their limited number will increase the value of the extant copies. Shaking his head, Longus remarked to Marcella that he continued to marvel a woman could possess such amazing aptitude for the art business.

Marcella also demanded Antonia cede her my headscarf with moths; and Antonia's adamant refusal led to vociferous quarrels. One of these reverberated through the entire villa and even outside. Guards and groundskeepers momentarily paused their activities to listen. Augustus subsequently delivered a tongue-lashing which left both nieces comically crestfallen like a pair of bawled-out schoolgirls. In the end it was actually I who settled the dispute, privately with Antonia but in favor of Marcella. That scarf, I reminded Antonia, had been an early experiment both in depicting the moths and painting on textiles. It did not represent my best work at either endeavor. From Rhodes I could procure several superior vignettes of moths for Antonia to consider. To a scarf or palla or other garment of her choice I could transfer any of these scenes, or base an entirely new composition on elements thereof. Since both Antonia and I resided in Rome, consulting with her face-to-face about a project of this character would more easily guarantee an outcome to her satisfaction, than attempting to achieve a similar result for Marcella by sending messages to and from Marseilles. "Did you assume my kin are exempt from engaging in infantile behavior?" Tiberius posed his question with a roll of his eyes, after I had described my achievement as a peace negotiator.

The travelers departed amid torrential rain. On the very next day the weather cleared. The evening thereafter, Tiberius and I supped alone. Livia, Antonia, and Agrippina were participating in the nightlong festival of the Good Goddess—patroness of chastity and fecundity in women. Her mystical rites were sedulously shielded from men and non-Italians. Augustus was taking advantage of the womenfolk's absence to dine with Postumus and Tiberius Drusus—at great risk to his chronically nervous stomach, he had joked to us earlier. Through the ensuing week, the air heated rapidly to a pleasant warmth that persisted throughout the month. Just enough occasional rain fell—usually overnight—to keep natural moisture at a salubrious level.

You need not imagine the results. By the end of May the gardens were replete with shoots and leaves and burgeoning blossoms, their colors and fragrances a feast for the senses. Young wildlife abounded. Feral kittens, bird chicks, baby rabbits and squirrels, peered from nests or scurried into them from before my feet. Most vibrant of all was the pond. The flags created an impenetrable wall of pale green with a rainbow spread across its top. The swans bred cygnets, the ducks ducklings. The water at times appeared boiling from fish breaching its surface. The frog was back on his lily pad dais, inflating and deflating the great ball of his throat to attract the lady friends who must have been present but whom we never observed.

The sizes, abundance, and intensity of coloration in the waterlilies made the group I had painted so admiringly the previous autumn seem paltry and insipid. Accordingly I began a new tableau, and gave the earlier one to Longus. He was overjoyed to acquire a new Eutychus Rhodou original, replacing the one of which Marcella had relieved him and refreshing his stock of models for reproduction. Of course I did not frequent the gardens on the days they were open to the public. Moreover, I either departed the pond or avoided it in the first place whenever Postumus ventured there to angle.

Most of my time between forays to the gardens I passed in my studio. There I set about transferring images I had recorded or memorized—not only from the villa's environs but from Ad Gallinas and Palestrina and Rhodes—to my textile collection. From time to time I had enlarged it with new purchases since receiving the original from Rhodes. Now I decided to cease adding to it, in favor of a new project. My goal was to paint a design on every piece, and thereafter decide upon a use for each article—whether to fashion it into a garment, a blanket, a decorative covering for furniture, a curtain to cover a window or divide a room or conceal a storage area. The work progressed steadily, rapidly, and successfully; for the temperature and humidity of the air were precisely right for allowing the paint to dry properly.

Toward the end of May I ran out of room in which to work. An empty studio lay on the other side of mine from Livia's. From Acer I solicited and received permission to utilize this room for storing completed pieces. Thereafter I engaged Ajax to construct additional drying racks—absolutely his favorite task, he assured me. One of my endeavors was the headscarf with moths I had promised Antonia. At my request Thrasyllus had duly sent three well-executed vignettes, from which Antonia selected a quartet of moths in flight above a cascade of water.

With sedulous determination I returned to my *Charioteers* tableau, which I finally finished just before the Ides of June. Tiberius forbade my lending it to Longus for display in the Gallery of the Four Winds. Why should Longus have the pleasure of viewing this original masterwork daily? To be sure, Tiberius wanted Longus to see the work, to produce and sell copies of it—no more than ten, and those all numbered. For this purpose Longus must send copyists to the villa, to work under the direct supervision of myself or a properly instructed attendant. Tiberius was determined to forestall a repetition of what happened with my *Zeus Descending to Danae* and *Lion of Nemea*: surreptitious substitution of a copy for the original. These pieces and the *Charioteers* he had placed on easels in Zone of Neutrality. Why should they languish in my storage studio? They could always be moved there when Longus or a copier called.

Now that the weather allowed, I resumed frequenting the various public venues of Rome whenever the inclination struck me. Three days before the Ides of June *[6/11]* I actually participated, for the first time, in a Roman festival. It was a feast of Mater Matuta, divine patroness of extended families. Matrons celebrated the goddess with a sequence of prayers, first for their nieces and nephews and thereafter for their own children. Only a matron who had been married no more than once was permitted to place the commemorative wreath on the statue of the goddess. The honor went this year to Prima. Although I traveled with Livia and Antonia to the Forum Boarium, I honored their recommendation to keep separate from them, lest I become an attraction and divert participants from the purpose of the feast. Accordingly when my fellow passengers exited their litters, I tarried behind. Then while everyone's attention was focused on my companions, I managed to slip out of my vehicle and into the temple unnoticed. As usual I enjoyed the vibrancy of color and movement that characterize events of this sort, while I contemplated its spiritual implications.

I also continued to accompany Tiberius or Antonia to cultural or social events. One which left a particularly lasting impression upon me was a poetry reading Marcia and her mother Atia hosted. There were two guests of honor. The one was Crinagoras of Mytilene, the other Publius Ovidius Naso. Both poets I was most delighted to meet in person, but Ovidius in particular. Throughout his poetry I had perceived a profound respect for womanhood— from the coquettish but confident guidelines of his *Art of Love* to the profound intellectualism and emotionalism of his *Heroides*. The latter are letters of the poet's own composition, which he ascribes to the womenfolk of legendary heroes. Of his eight students who delivered estimable samples of their own works, three were women—one the master poet's own stepdaughter. Naso himself proved quite the disappointment. He proved tremendously impressed with his own abilities and achievements, and equally condescending and dismissive toward those of others. Marcia introduced me as the sole pupil of the elusive decorator Eutychus of Rhodes and an accomplished painter in my own right. Naso responded with the lowered eyelids, curled lip, and shrug of bored indifference. When I complimented him for the esteem he held for women, he superciliously inquired why I found his attitude surprising.

My pace of life was frenetic through spring and early summer. At the time I persuaded myself, that I was expanding and perfecting my abilities as an artist by exploring what seemed an infinitude of amenities the world's foremost city had to offer. In retrospect I now realize my intensity was a hedge against the frustration, of having to postpone being reunited with Alcimus for what was beginning to seem an eternity. With the weather now cooperative, work on the Palatine house resumed in earnest. Given the extent of the damage, however, the architects did not anticipate completion until well into autumn. According to Thrasyllus' most recent correspondence, Alcimus was starting to walk while holding onto furnishings or the hands of adults. I had missed seeing my child take his first steps! Would I also miss hearing him utter his first words? And underlying those vexations was the ever-present despair of knowing Alcimus was condemned to live on a figurative precipice. He must never come to know my family, nor they him. As for his father's: privately they had accepted him with joy. Before the public, however, they must treat him as an outcast.

A sharp reminder, of the diametric difference portended for Alcimus between the private and public attitudes of his father's kin, came with the announcement Augustus made during a supper in the final week of June. On the following Saturday, when the gardens were open to the public, Augustus intended to stroll the venue weather permitting. Everyone should be ready by the fifth hour *[10:00 a.m.]*. Then turning to me, Augustus declared he sincerely regretted Tiberius and I must be excluded. Far more puzzled than hurt, I smiled acquiescently and proceeded with my meal as though nothing were amiss. But later, as soon as we were alone, I sought an explanation from Tiberius. From time to time, on days the weather was salubrious and the park open to the public, Augustus would meander about the gardens greeting the visitors. Members of his family, as well as any of the special friends he occasionally invited to accompany him, all had to dress decorously. Tiberius was uninvited because, so far as the public was concerned, he remained out of favor with Augustus. And I as Tiberius' ward was solely his concern, neither of Augustus nor his family.

Now I was thoroughly confused. Why were we rejected from this present activity? Had not Tiberius participated in the funeral of Lucius Caesar? Had not Tiberius and I attended the chariot race honoring Augustus' birthday, as well as the lecture and reception the emperor had hosted for Areus Didymus? Had not Augustus come forward and stood beside Livia at Drusus' coming of age? Had he not allowed—yea, sanctioned—my participation in the planning of the art exhibit, and invited Tiberius to its opening ceremony? After a dejected sigh Tiberius continued his explanation with dogged patience. At Drusus' fête,

Augustus had made his appearance to suppress speculation he and Livia were at odds, and to make clear his intention to promote the political career of her grandson. As for the other occasions I enumerated: by our participation, we had rendered honor and glory to Augustus. But for Augustus to invite us on one of his strolls would be for him to grant honor and glory to us.

Standing in our parlor on the morrow, Tiberius and I watched the company emerge from the villa's main entrance. Augustus carrying the ornately carved cane Tiberius had sent him from Rhodes, and Livia wrapped in her newly cleaned Guardian Tree shawl, were reassurances our rejection was not at all personal. Augustus was in magisterial garb, Antonia in a yellow palla edged with a grass-green border, Agrippina in an unadorned palla of pink. Postumus was present also, draped in the traditional toga of youth with its narrow purple stripe. The escort included Augustus' German bodyguard, our own Androcles and Ajax, and the guards Paris and Niger from the villa's regular staff. We could see people smiling, bowing, waving, applauding. Occasionally a faint cry of *Hail, Caesar!* reached us. Some stopped to say a few words of greeting, others to engage in lengthy conversations: likely expositions on how the government could be better managed, Tiberius remarked wryly. Two different women presented writing tablets to Livia: probably petitions I presumed and Tiberius agreed.

Leaning against him, my arm about his waist and his about mine, I apologized for rewording a question I had posed many a time before. What sort of confusing, convoluted life were we about to offer Alcimus, facing pro forma rejection by his kin while receiving their affection in secret? Tiberius kissed my forehead, and in a gentle tone replied we were going to provide our son the best life possible under the circumstances facing us, however these may unfold. Although this assertion did not quell my fears and qualms about Alcimus' future, it lessened a sense of parental inadequacy my contemplations of his life prospects had been urging upon me. Tiberius kissed my forehead again, and drew me toward his suite.

While we undressed one another, I became aware of a new and particularly compelling perspective taking hold in my conscience. It was so overwhelming, I could not fully fathom it at first, and realized I needed time to ponder and clarify it for myself. Hence I mentioned nothing of it to Tiberius while we lay abed resting from our exertions, and certainly not to the rest of the family during luncheon. Afterward I repaired to my studio, where I did not paint a single stroke but spent the entire afternoon thinking.

Now I found myself relieved—even pleased—to have been excluded from Augustus' stroll. Being able to pass the morning coupling with my beloved was eminently more pleasurable and satisfying, than receiving the stares and obeisances of strangers as one of the emperor's elect. More than two years had passed since I had sat in my bed on the Rhodian farm, considering how the fortune and renown of my alter-ego Eutychus had changed neither my character nor my physical requirements. Now it seemed that deduction was assuming a larger dimension.

The perception dawning upon me, was that there is nothing wrong with being ordinary! Such is the natural condition of humankind. Ordinary people constitute the world's majority. Some are rich, others poor; some are learned, others ignorant; some are free, others servile. Lack of celebrity is the commonality they all share. People recognized as extraordinary are oddities, anomalies. And except for individuals whose fame arises from criminality, the extraordinary are servants of the ordinary! Augustus as ruler, Tiberius as military strategist and commander, he and Livia as patrons, Areus as mentor, Ovidius Naso as poet, Longus as art maven, and quite frankly Eutychus as decorator—all are servants, supplying their clientèle with governance, protection, assistance, guidance, poetic inspiration, and artistic beauty.

My family had repeatedly castigated me for not attaining sufficient renown to become a household name. This burden of guilt I had never relinquished. Even my incessant reminders to myself, that I was famous as the artist Eutychus and somewhat renowned as the sophista Pythia of Naples, had failed to bring relief. Why? Because these accolades celebrated fictions rather than my own identity.

From my childhood I had entertained a mystique about notables—fantasizing I belonged to a celebrated set myself, or else was the best friend of someone who did. Without question the latter aspiration had been fulfilled, and most repletely. A man whose birth had automatically given him distinction as a Roman aristocrat, and who had augmented his fame with personal accomplishments, had taken me as his consort. The very emperor had taken me as his friend. I enjoyed acceptance and approval if not outright friendship from the majority of their kin. Yet even as Tiberius' chosen mate, I had continued to feel an outsider—an interloper intruding upon a charmed circle to which I did not belong naturally. Now this despairing sense of exclusion was yielding to one of joyous belonging. For the first time in my life, I was happy and content to be a member of the uncelebrated majority. The sensation was intriguing, exciting, and wondrously satisfying.

During that afternoon's bath, I described my new insights to Tiberius with jubilation. He listened patiently, smiling all the while. As I finished, an insight struck me so strongly that I sat upright and sloshed the bathwater. Taking his hands in mine, gazing earnestly into his face, I confessed his yearning to be ordinary, unnoticed, one of a crowd, had always puzzled me. Now I thoroughly understood and appreciated his unrequited desire. He drew me to him and held me, without uttering a word, until the cooling of the water forced a quick finish to our bath. We spent the remainder of the evening in a reverie, exchanging smiles, caresses, and kisses. The bond between us had strengthened, suddenly and significantly. At the very end of June, Augustus announced another stroll with regrets Tiberius and I could not participate. My flippant and nonchalant reply, that for the exclusion I was planning amply to compensate Tiberius in our bedchamber, surprised everybody including me.

After the Nones of July *[7/7]*, the weather turned excruciatingly hot and damp. Not even the renowned breezes of the Esquiline offered relief, being themselves steamy. Tiberius and I began sleeping apart, in our own suites. The number of visitors to the gardens dwindled significantly. Nobody was moving about any more than was absolutely necessary. Work on the Palatine house slowed, and had to be suspended during midday hours. Games, festivals, and cultural events were canceled. For certain I had little inclination to explore the city's public venues. The wildlife of the garden was sedentary, and could often be seen panting. Presently the water in the pond began to feel almost like bathwater, and stinging insects started to hang in the air above it. There was rain nearly every day, but in the form of brief showers. These cooled the air only slightly while significantly augmenting its sticky humidity.

After nearly a week of heat torture—on the birth anniversary of Caesar the Dictator, to be exact *[July 12]*—Augustus announced we should all make ready to board the Galatea for a cruise southward. A fair number of administrative matters requiring his direct intervention had developed at Naples. At the close of this business we would set sail at once for the family's retreat on Capri, there to pass in relaxation and leisure pursuits the month named for him. So we might leave Rome as soon as possible, there would be no inviting relatives or retainers and waiting for them to respond. Anyone who felt slighted upon learning of our departure was welcome to join us later.

That same evening, once we were alone, I confessed to Tiberius a growing trepidation about being in close quarters with Agrippina and Postumus. A wise concern but not to worry, Tiberius reassured me. He would recommend his stepfather assign us accommodations as far away from these adversaries as possible—although Augustus likely had already considered this strategy. The problem of Agrippina was resolved the next morning, unwittingly by Agrippina herself. She demanded to spend the summer with her cousin Pulchra instead—as she put it—of suffering the supreme boredom of a cruise and of *that forbidding villa*. Claudia was entirely agreeable; so off to their house Agrippina went: to the relief of all except Postumus and Tiberius Drusus, neither of whom seemed aware she was gone. Despite Augustus' intense urgency, nearly another week elapsed before we were ready to depart. Augustus must continue actively to govern even while on vacation. To support his work, a small staff of secretaries, notaries, and other essential clerks had to be assembled.

Tiberius and I faced having hurriedly to decide which servants to take with us. We could not employ our usual traveling companions Valens and Gallina because the latter was prone to seasickness. Nor could we take Nestor and Alcmene, as there would be no one to substitute for them on their Sabbaths. I hardly wanted to separate Phaedra from her spouse of two weeks: Rufus, one of the villa's gardeners. Alexandra disallowed Nausicaa as not yet sufficiently experienced as a personal servant to attend me without the supervision of a superior. This left Chloe, of whose medical expertise Tiberius did not wish to deprive the Villa Maecenatis. The yacht already had a shipboard physician who would disembark and attend us on Capri. In the end, Tiberius prevailed upon Alexandra to give me Nausicaa. He maintained I felt sufficiently comfortable with her expertise to extend her this opportunity for testing it, and I would not take offense at any fumbles she committed. Moreover Nausicaa could observe and consult the maidservants of Livia and Antonia for guidance. Tiberius took Nausicaa's brother Nomius, who had become a satisfactorily competent valet.

The more popular and efficient method of reaching Ostia from Rome was by river barge on the Tiber. Augustus nevertheless preferred traveling overland, as Tiberius had when we first arrived from Rhodes. Transferring as sizable train as his, between land conveyances and a barge at the landings in either city, was certain to draw notice. Accordingly we departed in the predawn twilight of a morning already brilliant with white heat haze. Ours was a procession of four vehicles. Augustus, Livia, and Antonia with their attendants rode in the first carriage, Tiberius and I with our attendants in the second, Postumus and Tiberius Drusus with the more of the serving staff in the third, the remaining servants in a wagon with our luggage. An escort of mounted praetorians joined us directly outside the city gate. On nearing Ostia we did not proceed to the main wharf, but turned down a side road on the outskirts of the city to a cove where a launch was docked. Anchored nearby, at the entrance to the cove, was a military escort ship. In the distance we could see the yacht, lying at the outer edge of the harbor with a second escort at her side.

I cannot recall a single occasion when my mother, observing the Galatea in the waters off Naples, did not decry her as a floating mansion devoted solely to decadent sybaritic luxury—a frivolous waste of money extorted from an overtaxed populace. In actuality, most of the yacht was devoted to governance: reception rooms, a banqueting hall, offices, archives, accommodations for visiting dignitaries, government functionaries, praetorians, and their servants. Moreover the yacht had a resident staff of her own: sailors, rowers, maintenance personnel, and cooks. The family area at the ship's rear—decorated with carvings, inlays, and mosaics—was quite compact.

Aft on the upper deck, a library, dayroom, and dining room with pantry, lay on either side of a central hallway. This opened onto a delightful covered veranda at the very rear of the ship. Descending a stairway to the sleeping quarters directly below the day complex, we encountered another central hallway with suites of rooms on both sides. This corridor was bisected by two narrow perpendicular hallways, with windows at either end providing light and ventilation. The central passageway ended at a locked door, through which the other regions of the ship could be reached. The bath and latrine lay adjacent to this terminus. Each room had a door opening onto the corridor. A steward named Casper, waiting at the base of the stairs with tablet and stylus in hand, greeted us cordially and took note of which suite each member of the family chose to occupy.

Tiberius selected a suite of three of adjoining rooms: a central sitting room flanked on either side by a bedroom with a servant's alcove. We concurred that owing to the heat, our sleeping separately was definitely the preferable option. Separate quarters also served to help conceal the true character of our relationship from servants and family members whom we wished to keep unaware. There were no furnishings. Tiberius summoned Casper, introduced him to Nomius and Nausicaa, and left the three to appoint the suite.

The air was cooler on the sea than on land, but not significantly. After breakfast on the veranda, Tiberius took me on a tour of the ship. Thereafter we returned to the veranda where, when not chatting with the rest of the family, I sat gazing out at the water and pondering the thoughts it evoked. On my first ocean voyage—from Italy to Rhodes—the sea churned by the Sirocco had induced a mental image of an immense textile forever under creation, being woven through eternity on a great cosmic loom. During later sailings—particularly that which returned us to Italy—the weaving was complete: the sea was a seamless undulating blanket, upon which the sky kept painting and repainting patterns and hues. On this hot July day, however, the sea struck me as a blank palette waiting to be filled with depiction. Owing to lack of wind, wave action was minimal. The thick white haze spread an opaque pallor over the water, obscuring objects beneath the surface. No seabirds or dolphins appeared to escort the yacht: presumably the weather was rendering lethargic even this wildlife. The only potential models I had were the two escort ships bearing praetorians. Accordingly I sent Nausicaa for my paint box, and on her return started to sketch one of these vessels.

Hardly had I begun, however, when I felt a sharp tap on my shoulder. Postumus was standing before me, grinning. Quite congenitally he asked whether I should like to join Patruus and him. At the rail I saw Augustus baiting a hook. Beside him were two attendants with buckets, poles, and lines. So Agrippina was indeed the catalyst for Postumus' hostility toward me, I mentally noted as I put down pencil and palette and hastened to join my fellow anglers. Augustus caught nothing, I caught nothing; but Postumus—certainly to my relief and I presume to his grandfather's as well—hooked an ink fish. He guffawed most heartily when it spurted all over him the substance for which it is named.

No hardened, dry sea rations on this voyage. We dined on turbot and fresh asparagus for luncheon, served right on the veranda—even to Postumus and Tiberius Drusus, albeit at their own table on the side of the veranda farthest from ours. Now the hottest portion of the day was approaching. Tiberius suggested and everyone agreed, the veranda was likely a preferable venue for postprandial respite than the stuffy sleeping quarters below deck. Hence we remained on the veranda through the afternoon, sitting or reclining on the chairs and settees—except for Tiberius Drusus, whom an attendant escorted to the library at Livia's behest. A notary arrived with a stylus and set of tablets, and spent the afternoon conferring with Augustus in muffled tones. I returned to my sketch on which I worked intermittently, and to my contemplations which I pursued unremittingly.

The dynamism that had thrilled me on my previous voyages was distinctly lacking from the present. Reflecting upon this dearth of inspiration, I suddenly realized my childhood and adolescent obsession with the weaving of textiles had left me entirely. No, I did not feel a frustrated aspirant at weaving who had voluntarily—and regretfully—set aside her cherished ambition upon discovering her ineptitude at the required skill. The fascination with weaving was gone altogether. Embroidering and painting on textiles had superseded the yearning to create them.

Nevertheless the resentment toward my mother remained, unabated and now even exacerbated. Forcing me to live among weavers and observe their craft, blatantly refusing to allow me a loom but making sure to tell me each time a neighbor acquired one for a daughter, calling me ungrateful and degenerate when my unrequited desire distressed me: these abuses were now grieving and angering me anew. Yes, yes, pursuant to Areus' instructions I considered my present environs and companions, and acknowledged with gratitude these circumstances were well worth the price of enduring my mother's mistreatment. But this salve for the wound in my soul was not working. Fully confident I felt, that had the motive behind my mother's aspersions been truly didactic—genuinely intended to improve my character—I would have forgiven her by now. But such had never been her motive. After years and years of trying I still could not come to terms, with the knowledge she had deliberately and premeditatedly afflicted me and enjoyed observing my consequent anguish.

And so with these considerations I ruined for myself what could have been a pleasurable, calming afternoon. Although warm, the sea breeze was refreshing to skin, nostrils, and lungs. Wherever the sun struck the veranda, servants lowered awnings to create shade. None of my companions, apart from Augustus and his notary, engaged in serious pursuits. Antonia read a romance. Tiberius and Livia played at a gaming board for a short while, but presently left off and sat gazing at the expanse of sea. Intermittently they chatted about innocuous matters: petitioners and their foibles, acquaintances and relatives, the overall success of the art exhibit, the rebuilding of the Palatine house. Postumus fished with sufficient success to leave him contented and forestall a temper tantrum.

I was a little surprised when supper was brought before we had bathed. Presently Livia dispelled this trivial mystery. While we were dining on a ragout of vegetables and sea scallops, she told me to repair the bathroom directly after the meal. On arriving with Nausicca, I found Livia in the process of being undressed by her attendant. Antonia, already nude, was sitting in the rectangular bath. Although submerged, the basin had slightly raised sides to prevent the water from sloshing out when the yacht rolled or pitched. It was decorated with mosaics of marine plants and animals, which the moving water animated; and it was just large enough to hold the three of us comfortably. The water, cool and salt, was very refreshing. Livia explained that in torrid weather, a cold bath directly before retiring made sleeping in the hot and narrow confines of our suites a bit more tolerable.

Here I sat—I the ordinary—with the wife and niece of the emperor, the three of us stark naked. We chatted, splashed, cavorted, and giggled like a trio of urchins at a street fountain, until outside in the corridor the emperor himself bellowed we should get out of there so the men could have their turn. To dispel the salt our attendants collected fresh water from a vat into pitchers, and poured it over us after we had stepped out of the bath. Without any prompting from me Nausicaa wet her fingers, then ran them over my scalp and through my hair. She had remembered I favored this procedure for cooling and cleansing my head in hot weather. Observing this operation, Livia and Antonia ordered their women to do the same.

My two companions retired to their chambers immediately after our bath; but I crept back up to the veranda to view the sunset amid the haze. Would I see once again the glorious variety of smoky hues Tiberius and I had beheld from the deck of the Phoenix? Disappointment was in store for me. The haze was so uniform and thick, that through it the sun appeared a medallion glowing yellowish-red as if molten, the redness deepening as it approached the horizon. The haze itself did not glow, but merely changed from white to light gray to a darker bluish gray as the sun descended. The seawater reflected the image of the sun, and darkened in the same manner as the sky. There were no clouds, catching the sun's rays at differing angles to create varying patterns, textures, and colors in the sky and cast them upon the water's surface.

As the top of the sun was disappearing below the horizon, and I was preparing to depart the veranda, I saw the yacht's oars suddenly rise. The escort ships followed suit. At first I assumed the oarsmen might be changing shifts, until I saw an anchor being lowered from the yacht's side. I asked the manservant in attendance on the veranda the reason for the halt. Because the haze was so dense, he replied as he pointed skyward, no stars were visible for the boatmen to use as guideposts. They must wait until the waning moon had risen. And surely enough: when a call of nature woke me later in the night, as I made my way to the latrine I could feel the ship once again underway. On returning to my bedchamber I looked through the window and beheld the gibbous moon, not white but deep yellow, her outline blurred and her surface features obscured.

Directly after we had finished our breakfast fruit the next morning, Tiberius drew me back below deck to our suite. He wanted to engage in sex before our quarters became too hot for this type of exertion. Afterward in the bathroom we rinsed one another with cool water, while Nomius stood guard to insure no one discovered us. Returning to the veranda, we found the yacht again at rest and a monotreme at her side. *A highly placed government functionary had brought a matter requiring the emperor's immediate attention.* So I thought to myself, as nonchalantly as if a roofer had arrived to repair a leaky gutter. The lithe fleet monoreme seemed to exude the dynamism so distinctly lacking from the rest of our environs. Much as I would have enjoyed sketching her, the sudden emergence of a different subject deterred me.

While I was observing the monoreme, a window directly above the waterline opened in the yacht's side. A trio of attendants poked their heads out, and looked directly downward at the water. After a brief conversation, the men cast a net before them. A school of fish had gathered between the yacht and the monoreme, undoubtedly attracted by the shade or by the illusion of shelter the boats cast. The movements of the fish created slight ripples, and changes of shading beneath the surface. After a few minutes, the men drew up their burgeoning net. Its contents, which proved to be smelts, flipped about glistening and glinting like a heap of living silver. Fortuitously the crewmembers repeated their operation thrice. The duration of their effort enabled me to complete a sketch hasty and rudimentary, yet sufficiently complete to allow for easy addition of details later.

And so I did after another cold luncheon, this time of chilled tuna and salad greens. Augustus did not share our meal but dined with his visitors. He joined us about half an hour later. The monotreme had pulled away, and the yacht and her escorts resumed their course. Augustus dozed, Livia embroidered, Antonia continued with her romance. I worked alternately on my escort ship and smelt-fishers tableaux. When Postumus and Tiberius Drusus started to quarrel, Tiberius herded them into the library with the comment, "Since you care to be belligerent, come learn the lessons and discipline of military history." We dined that evening on those smelts, lightly sautéed in seasoned oil with long beans—quite delicious.

"Does hot weather make you insatiable?" I demanded of Tiberius as he drew me below deck for another round of postprandial sex the following morning. "You were the same in the heat at Anzio last year!"

"Not hot weather but you render me so!" he returned as he finished undressing me and hastily shed his own garments. "Now I am vacationing, with no petitioners, critics, retainers, sycophants, gossip-mongers, enemies, or defenders to distract me from indulging my relentless desire for you! And do you not love it?" he concluded as he anointed himself with laser oil.

Lying down on his bed, I inserted my pessary and said, "Your lioness is waiting for you to tame her!"

That entire third day was essentially a copy of the preceding afternoon. Even the two troublesome youths settled into contented ennui. We supped on red mullet, brown bread, and steamed fennel. On the fourth morning of our journey we arose to find the yacht anchored at the outer limit of the Naples harbor. Our escorts were hard at work, chasing off vessels which endeavored to approach without proper authorization. While we were breakfasting on the veranda, a launch drew up alongside the yacht. A servant reported the entire municipal council of Naples was aboard. "Could they not have given me the chance to get fully awake and properly dressed?" Augustus groaned. "On the other hand," he continued, "perhaps they are to be commended for their wisdom, in getting the welcoming ceremony over before the day gets any hotter. Who wants to stand listening to the same dull repetitive speeches extolling one's character and achievement while sweltering in toga and shoes?"

We rested on the veranda after lunch of boiled eggs, sliced cucumbers, and bread rolls. Without question the yacht's culinary crew had gone ashore for supplies. Much as I had enjoyed the various fish dishes we had consumed since the beginning of our voyage, I welcomed this reprieve from them. Contentedly planning to return to one of my sketches after a short doze, I stretched out in my chair and closed my eyes. Presently I heard a call of "Clytia, Clytia!" With a start I glanced about the veranda, and determined from the angle of the sun I had been asleep for perhaps an hour. My two palettes, which I had laid in my lap, were now atop my paint box on the floor beside my chair. Presumably a servant had placed them there to prevent their slipping off my lap. The only member of the family I saw was Antonia, sitting in a chair and looking up from her romance. Again the call, "Clytia, dear Clytia!" The voice was Augustus.' A manservant approached, bowed, and said, "My Lady, Caesar beckons you join him and Lady Livia in the dayroom."

They were sitting at a table stacked with writing tablets. "Ah, here she be!" Augustus exclaimed as I entered. "We have been examining the matters the Neapolitan council referred to our consideration," he continued as I seated myself in an empty chair beside the table. "One may be from your mother." Picking up one of the tablets, he read, "Widow Anthe Eupistou seeks a donative, for repayment of a lien against property which cannot be sold." He looked up at me, his merging brows knit in puzzlement. "Property which cannot be sold? This sounds rather bizarre."

"My mother grubbed up money by any means she could," I mused. "What is meant by property which cannot be sold, I cannot even fathom an explanation."

"Why does the request come from her and not your brother, whom I presume as her curator authorized the loan?"

"Perhaps the petitioner is not my mother after all, but someone else with the same name," I ventured. "Sincerely I hope nothing adverse has happened to my brother," I added, and honestly. Although I still considered Philo an inane wonk on account of an upbringing over which he had no control, I assuredly did not hate him or wish him any sort of misfortune.

"Well, we shall soon find out. Since the petition is from a woman, I am handing it over to Livia."

"And I am inviting you to attend the interview," Livia said. "Are you not curious to see what this is all about?"

"Burningly so," I replied. Indeed my interest was very much aroused. "I wonder whether my mother will recognize me on this occasion."

"You will have to remain absolutely unruffled and not so much as flinch, should she berate you or speak derogatorily about you," said Augustus. "Do you feel you can manage such self-control?"

"I am prepared to hold my breath and clench my teeth and endure whatever she says about me.'

"Pretend she is decrying someone else and not you," Livia said. "In actuality that would be true. Not the real you, but the false view of you she has conjured in her own mind is the object of her resentment."

My self-confidence soared to new heights. "Thank you for that reminder!" I exclaimed. "Now I am actually eager to hear what derogations she has in store for me!"

"I have two other petitions, both straightforward. One is a request for a dowry, the other for assistance with medical expenses. And both are from Italians. Your mother is not a Roman citizen or the widow of a Roman citizen, is she?"

"Not unless unknown to me she married a Roman citizen after my father died. That seems highly unlikely, since she always disdained Italians as her inferiors."

"She could have married a Greek with half citizenship," Augustus interjected.

"The matter of citizenship is going to be the first question I put to her," Livia continued. "If lacking this qualification, what makes her think she is entitled to my charity?"

"She has always presumed she is entitled to whatever she craves, that anybody who possesses something she craves has no right to it, and that being denied anything she craves—even by Nature herself—is a gross injustice!" Vehemently I responded as I felt myself grow warm with resentment.

"Fortunately for us in this heat, I can dispense with visiting the petitioners' domiciles: the local praetor has already done so." Livia picked up the tablet from which Augustus had read and looked it over. "He attests to the genuine need and worthiness of the bride and of the invalid. About your mother's request he has misgivings and recommends thorough interrogation." She put the tablet back on the table and smiled at me slyly, her eyes twinkling with a hint of mischief. "I am going to schedule all three interviews for tomorrow morning, and conduct Anthe's last—primarily because I am confident it is going to take longer than either of the others, but also because I want to make her wait her turn. Let her sit in the heat and stew about not being seen first."

Augustus smiled. "You never imagined my wife could be such a rascal, did you?"

"If introducing you becomes necessary, I shall present you as my Greek language interpreter," Livia said reassuringly.

"As if she requires one," her husband quipped.

Tiberius joined us. "Fetch me something for a headache—tincture of spirea, preferably," he said to the attendant manservant before slumping into an empty chair. He drew and exhaled a deep breath. "Trying to teach military history to your respective grandsons is tantamount to self-immolation!" he exclaimed. "I was attempting an explanation of the *Anabasis* of Thucydides. Postumus sat in a pout without the slightest indication of comprehension. And Tiberius Drusus kept interrupting, alternating between bombastic digressions about people and places and deities and other details in the text, comments about the writer's syntax, and questions about the plans we are making for his birthday!" *[August 1]*

"This Thursday next," Augustus said. "By then we should be well out of this hellhole. Have we given thoughts to a gift?"

"How about a set of intensive lessons in comportment?" Tiberius grumbled. With a nod of thanks he took the spirea from the manservant.

"That has been tried and retried," Augustus said wearily. "Summon Lady Antonia," he ordered the servant. "What plans have you in mind for Tiberius Drusus' birthday celebration?" he asked when she arrived.

"Fie on me, Uncle! Between the heat and the bustle of preparing for this cruise, I forgot all about my own son's birthday!"

"You are hardly alone," Augustus mused. "Young Tiberius' birthday always seems to sneak up on us unawares." He turned his gaze to me. "Do you think you might be able to finish your picture of the escort ship by next Thursday?"

"Not as a painting but only as a sketch, and not with any profound detail. I fear there is insufficient time to apply paint, let alone allow it to dry."

"Never mind profound detail or paint: consider the recipient!" Augustus returned. "All we need is a halfway decent representation."

"That I feel certain I can have ready," I replied confidently. To tell the truth I welcomed this incentive, for I was beginning to empathize with Agrippina: a cruise can very quickly become boring.

The rest of that Sunday afternoon I spent immersed in my project. It developed better than I had anticipated, because the escort ships provided me with ever-present models. To rest my eyes from time to time, I gazed out upon the activities of the Naples harbor as best I could through the haze. Sailors and fishermen were plying their boats, stevedores lading and unlading. Some merchants were procuring shipments of goods they had ordered, others selling their wares to customers in the wharfside marketplace. Ordinary people these were: the unknown, unrecognized, uncelebrated, and critically essential mainstay of the human race.

Raising my eyes to the hills, I thought I managed to discern just barely the buildings of the Academia Norenas. A mistake indeed, for the appreciation for common folk in which I had been exulting became tainted by recollections of my parents' elitism. Were not members of the Greek intelligentsia a superior species of humanity, not to be sullied by association with racial and intellectual inferiors? Should not have rulership of the world been entrusted to them, rather than to belligerent and vulgar Italians? And was not my father an unspeakable genius, whose superiority eluded even the others of his milieu? My parents had craved adulation, and felt significantly slighted when praise or notice to which they felt entitled was not forthcoming. Conversely, having to behave like peers—or worse yet like subordinates—among people they considered their equals or inferiors, my parents considered sullying, demeaning. Hence their rationale for avoiding social occasions, which in turn kept me from learning proper skills at interaction.

Now here I sat amid genuine elite; and what did I find? Strong familial affection for sure, along with disagreements, bereavements, rebellious children, difficult grandchildren, bodily afflictions—the very same problems one encounters in the humblest of homes. And do you know, Dear Reader, I found myself truly pitying my mother. She had lived under the delusion that elitism is the solution to everyday problems.

A fishing vessel drew too near the yacht, and was intercepted by one of the escort ships. After some questioning, the praetorians granted the fishing crew permission to shout greetings to Augustus from their deck. *Privacy is an elusive commodity for the truly elite,* I reflected. My mother may well have enjoyed being gushed over; but was she ready to endure the spread of speculative and malicious innuendo about herself and her kin? Recalling her own vituperative assessments—not only of Augustus and his family but of other elites as well—I wondered whether my mother even realized she could be a target of similar invective, were she in a position of prominence.

We dined that evening on white grouper. The waiter reported one of the shipboard chefs had struck an intriguing bargain, with the Neapolitan fishmonger from whom he had purchased the commodity. In return for being allowed to announce his catch had been selected for the emperor, the fishmonger had lent his kitchen to the chef for the cooking of the grouper. That way the heat would not be imparted to the yacht. *Now all of Naples knows what we were having for supper* I thought, corroborating my assessment of the elite's lack of privacy.

During our bath, Livia asked me whether I had developed any last minute misgivings about attending the morrow's interview with my mother. No, I replied with a chuckle. Rather, I was looking forward to seeing what sort of absurdity my mother had to offer.

Although I retired that evening feeling very much at ease, sleep eluded me. Standing before the window of my cabin, looking at the harbor and city lights through the yellow glow with which they illuminated the haze, I mentally scrutinized my thoughts and emotions for the source of this present malaise. What I discovered dismayed me. With contentment I was presuming my mother's request was going to be preposterous, and Livia was going to deny it outrightly while I sat by and gloated. What I did not want to recognize was the possibility the plea was legitimate, that Livia would feel obliged to grant it, that the pejoratives I had uttered about my mother would be belied, and—worst of all—that I would begrudge my mother the fulfillment of her petition. For certain my mother had always taken pleasure in my failures and distresses and resented my successes and joys. Reciprocating in kind, however, would make me her moral equal; and this equivalence I most assuredly did not desire.

The opportunity to hold myself superior to those vicious standards of my kindred was at hand. With a surge of determination, I resolved not to let it elude me. If Underlying Good is the governing Principle of the universe, then aspiration to be fair and unprejudiced toward my mother's petition is a manifestation of that Principle and must be fulfilled. With my vision blurred by tears, with the city lights distorted by the haze, I could not tell for certain whether the flash I detected was simply a glint off a wave or a distant ship—or a meteor.

After returning to bed I still did not sleep, so excited and elated was I by my ethical achievement. Nevertheless at dawn I arose refreshed. For my costume that day I selected a waterish blue chiton Cloris had fashioned, of linen loosely woven for coolness. On its left front just below knee line I had painted a trio of waterlilies. For my overwrap I chose a veil of the same fabric and weave—unadorned because the painting supplied sufficient ornamentation, and ocher in color to match one of the waterlilies. Once this couture so carefully considered was completed, it occurred to me I ought to have first determined what Livia was wearing, to ensure I was not dressed more ornately than she. Accordingly I sent Nausicaa to inquire of Livia's maid Malthace, and learned to my relief Livia had opted for a mauve stola and pale gray veil both highly embellished with embroidery. Not at all hungry—from surfeit of grouper the evening before, I presumed—at the breakfast table I consumed only a tumbler of water. To Livia I confessed that in view of all I had said the day before, I anticipated being terribly embarrassed if my mother's petition turned out to be acceptable. Not to worry, she replied: my willingness to admit misjudgment she approved.

Malthace accompanied us to the yacht's formal audience hall. There two toga-clad men—one a magistrate—awaited us, along with a young woman and five praetorians. Livia introduced the magistrate as the Neapolitan praetor Aulus Poppaeus Sabinus, then the rest of her retinue without their names. The man in the plain toga was her legal consultant, the woman her stenographer, and I her Greek language interpreter. In the audience chamber we took our places on a dais: Livia in the center chair, the stenographer to the right so Livia could see what was being transcribed, myself on Livia's left. Malthace sat behind us at the rear of the dais. A trio of benches filled the lower region of the room extending before us. The door through which we had entered was behind us. Poppaeus took his place beside another door, which opened to our left. Once everyone was settled, Livia nodded to Poppaeus. He opened his door to the petitioners, who had arrived by launch and were waiting in the adjacent reception area.

As anticipated the first two interviews proceeded quickly, for the requests were straightforward and refreshingly meritorious. The plea for assistance with medical expenses was made by the wife of a carpenter, who had become too afflicted with palsy to continue plying his trade. Indeed this poor man was so stricken he could barely speak. He attended the interview nonetheless, lying on a cot which his two sons carried. His wife maintained they were only seeking temporary support, until the elder son could complete the apprenticeship in which he was presently enrolled, and thereafter begin rejuvenating the family business. This son in turn offered to repay the monies once he had achieved financial independence. The quaking father managed to convey his approval by vigorously nodding his already shaking head. After commending the carpenter for attending the meeting in his condition, to prove his family's need was genuine, Livia assented to the request. Remuneration she would not require, but adherence to the understanding her aid was to be temporary she would. The elder son must report to her the completion of his apprenticeship, and agree to inspections by her agent of the financial condition of his business. Once its earnings were adequate to support the family, her assistance would end.

The petition for a dowry came from a widow who presented herself with her daughter. Her husband had been a mate on a fishing vessel. He had drowned after becoming entangled in netting while attempting to save two fellow sailors, who had been washed overboard when a sudden storm overwhelmed the boat. The chagrined owner and his wife had invited the widow and her daughter to reside in their own home, where over time their son and the widow's daughter grew enamored of one another. The youth and his parents had agreed to accept the girl without a dowry. Nevertheless her mother hoped Livia might be willing to grant one anyway, that the daughter may have an endowment entirely and inalienably hers: not only insuring her financial security but reinforcing her identity and individuality. Livia responded with a rhetorical question: how could she possibly refuse so well purposed a request? 350,000 sesterces would be her reward. Without uttering a word the widow shut her eyes, clasped her hands before her, and sank to her knees as though in prayer before a goddess. The daughter, who had sat silent through the interview, began to weep openly and presently blurted out, "Thank you, oh thank you, thank you!"

"You are truly fortunate to have so caring a mother," Livia returned gently. Myself I found genuinely happy for the girl, and at the same time envious of her. She had a possession I would never embrace: the supportive affection of her mother. Not even the wealth, power, and privilege of the Caesars could provide me with this wondrous gift.

Finally Malthace stepped down from the dais and gently roused the mother, and Poppaeus escorted the pair from the chamber. Rising from her chair, Livia ordered a short recess. For this I was quite glad, because it enabled me to collect my thoughts and abandon the pessimistic slough into which they had slipped. Moreover I needed to use the nearby privy. Livia faced the same necessity, from which even the most elite of elites are not exempt. As we reentered the audience hall, to compose myself I took a deep breath and held it as long as possible. Although I kept telling myself I did not care whether my mother and brother recognized me or not, whether they defamed me or not, I found myself fighting against the anger, the sorrow, the frustration their rejection of me had never ceased to engender.

My mother entered the hall bearing the dour expression of sullen anger she had always worn, when forced to comply with requirements at which she chafed. My brother followed her, looking duller and more docile than ever. To me my mother paid no heed. Nor did my brother, although he gazed directly at me. Most likely my mother's insistence he had misidentified me at the Porticus Octaviae kept him from recognizing me here. Well I knew she was so domineering of him—and he so acquiescent to her—she invariably challenged and he readily abandoned any notion he managed to conceive through independent reasoning of his own.

"The showing of respect is in order!" intoned Poppaeus. My mother scowled at him but duly curtsied to Livia, and my brother bowed. None of the earlier petitioners had needed to be reminded of this requirement.

Livia acknowledged their obeisance with a slight nod. "You may seat yourselves," she said in a gracious tone. From the stenographer she took a tablet—no doubt the one with the particulars of the petition—and perused it while my mother continued to scowl. Raising her head, Livia inquired, "Who among your kindred is a Roman citizen?"

"None," my mother returned with supercilious hauteur.

"Why, then, do you consider yourself entitled to my charity?" Livia's tone was still gracious.

"As residents of Naples we pay taxes to your government." More hauteur.

"And our government in return provides your family and all Neapolitans with water and sewage, public baths for your health and cleanliness, public parks and entertainments for your enjoyment, fire brigades to protect your property, police and armies to protect your persons, magistrates to insure justice is rendered you."

Once again I held my breath, now to keep from giggling. My mother, the consummate expert at demeaning the assertions of others, had finally met her match. "We are sorry to have wasted your time," she retorted disdainfully as she rose to her feet.

"You were not given leave to depart!" Livia returned sharply. Now clearly nonplussed, my mother plunked herself back down on the bench beside my brother. He had not budged since the interview began but sat staring open-mouthed and uncomprehendingly, as though the proceedings were being conducted in a language he did not understand. Livia addressed him, "Young man, why are you not making this request on behalf of your mother? Are you not her legal curator?" He remained silent, his look still vacuous. "Young man, can you not answer my question?" Impatience was clear in Livia's tone.

Philo cleared his throat. "Ah,...ahem,...nah." He rubbed one palm across his face. "I support her petition," he finally mumbled perfunctorily, as though he had been coached in anticipation of this question—which he undoubtedly had.

Livia perused the tablet again. "Your request is for funds enabling you to repay a loan you took, against a piece of property you claim cannot be sold. What do you mean by this? Why can you not sell the property and use the proceeds to pay off the loan—or simply surrender to foreclosure?"

My mother shut her eyes as though suddenly in pain. After a long silence she finally murmured, "The property does not belong to us."

"Does not belong to you? How did you contrive to borrow against property you do not own?" The pitch of Livia's voice rose slightly, betraying her incredulity.

After another long silence: "My late husband was, and at present my son here is, its curator."

"But to whom does it belong?"

My brother stretched his arms above his head and yawned long and loudly, almost in a shout. Livia stared at him amazed. My mother glared back defiantly, as though Livia had no right to deem my brother's behavior anything but acceptable.

Livia repeated her question. "Who owns the property?"

My mother responded reticently, as though resentful yet fearful of Livia's question. "My husband was a sophistos at an academy here in Naples. He obtained the higher education required for his profession at the Museion in Alexandria. During his course of study a dormitory, in which the Museion provided housing for students from abroad, caught fire and claimed a number of lives. Among them was another advanced student and his wife. Their young daughter, only in her second year of life, survived. When the Museion administration contacted the father's family, they denied any knowledge of his marriage and refused to acknowledge or accept the child. Assuming responsibility for the accident, the Museion offered a monetary stipend for the orphan's upkeep to anyone willing to accept her as a ward. Since my husband and I were eager for children, he procured custody of the girl and the stipend. About a decade later, after we were settled in Naples and blessed with a child of our own, we used a portion of the stipend to purchase a pleasant property in the countryside near the city of Nola."

As I write these words, I sit trembling. My heart pounds as intensely as it did while I sat listening to this revelation. The family who had raised me so abusively were not my blood kindred! Little wonder they had esteemed my presumed brother so much more highly than I. And who were my real kin? Would I ever find out? Growing hot and lightheaded I started to fan myself with one hand, thinking it better to be noticed for this than for fainting. Within seconds Malthace was standing beside me, fanning me with a wooden paddle and handing me a tumbler of water. Her interruption could not have been more timely or salubrious. After the draught of water and several deep breaths, my self-control was restored and strengthened—and quite fortuitously, in preparation for what I was about to hear next.

"Did you adopt the girl?" Livia inquired.

"No: we saw no reason for doing so."

"Then the property you purchased remained legally hers. What led you to presume you had the right to use monies specified for her upkeep and dowry to suit your own ends?"

Anthe—to whom I can no longer refer as my mother! —now assumed an air of righteous indignation. "We considered those funds compensation for raising her," she returned arrogantly. "Why should she alone enjoy their advantages? The purchase enabled our entire family—the girl included—to partake of the benefits the property provided."

"Does your ward reside with you?"

"No. She disappeared from our domicile nearly a decade ago."

"Did she know the property belonged to her?"

"No. We intentionally led her to believe she was our natural daughter and Philo here her natural brother."

"Why?"

"So she could not use her status as our ward against us. Her natural family will never know how fortunate they were for having rejected her. She was willful and insolent, slovenly and lazy. Because she had a brilliant mind, my husband—despite her unrelenting resistance—managed at length to educate her sufficiently to become a sophista. Since so few women achieve this status, she could have become world renowned had she applied herself diligently to academics. But this she did not, and therefore remained unrecognized."

How very wrong you are, you bitch! Now from fury I was hot again, still trembling but clearheaded. No less an academician than Thrasyllus of Alexandria has read and quoted the writings of Pythia of Naples! Areus had been quite correct. Despite her very vocal insistence to the contrary, Anthe had never wanted to see me successful and celebrated, lest she be forced to stop harassing me.

Anthe continued, "We arranged a marriage for her with a splendid young man, as immensely wealthy as he was profoundly intellectual." I choked and had to clear my throat; fortunately no one paid any heed. "His father, in fact, was the benefactor after whom the academy at which my husband taught is named. The slut ran off while plans for the wedding were being laid. We suspected she went after a married cavalry soldier with whom she had been corresponding. In retrospect I suppose letting her write him was a mistake. At the time, however, he was paying her to create lesson plans for his children, and we were pleased she was finally contributing to our household finances. When we attempted to contact this man, we were informed he was killed in action on the German front."

Tiberius' ruse had worked!

"A terrible misfortune," Livia said in a respectful tone. "So the property near Nola was going to serve as your ward's dowry," she continued.

"Oh, no! The groom and his father were willing to accept her without a dowry. We did not want to give her control of the property, for fear she would drive us off it."

"For what purpose did you utilize it?"

"As a retreat from the unhealthy air of Naples. Poor Philo here from childhood has suffered miserably from acute respiratory distress." Even as Anthe was speaking these words, Philo emitted a loud and raucous snort and then proceeded to pick his nose. "Surely you understand our need, as your own husband suffers the same ailment."

"Caesar my husband does not find the environs of Nola therapeutic for his respiratory afflictions."

Did Livia have to deliver this rejoinder? Anthe's entire body shook as though from a sudden blow. Her sullen expression changed to one of mortified embarrassment and thence to suppressed fury. Meanwhile I must once again inhale deeply and hold my breath to keep from bursting out in laughter. Livia's jaw and the cords in her neck tightened as she fought the same impulse. She too took a deep breath and exhaled before speaking again.

"Since your ward has quite palpably abandoned her property, and so many years ago, by now its ownership should have legally reverted to your son as its curator. Why, then, do you claim you cannot sell it?"

Anthe appeared pain-stricken once again. She lowered her eyes, folded her hands in her lap, and sat in silence. Livia repeated the question. At length, without raising her eyes, Anthe murmured, "The contract with the Museion specifies any portion of the stipend unused for the orphan's upkeep must revert to that institution."

"What was the original amount of the stipend?"

"Seventy-five Greek talents."

"Quite adequate; yet there is nothing left of it?" Incredulity was clear in Livia's voice.

"Only the property. The balance went to feed, clothe, and rear that ingrate!"

The balance went to mortgages on city and country houses, shop-fashioned clothing, private tutors for Philo, entertainments to divert him and expensive foodstuffs to indulge him! Little wonder there was no money for my dowry. The Eupistodoi had purloined for their own use the fund to which I alone was entitled. So I reflected as my body temperature rose once again. My chest tightened, as though compressed by that figurative great rock. Diverting my eyes to the floor, I forced myself to take deep regular breaths.

Livia had paused, to confer in subdued tones with the legal specialist. They separated, and Livia addressed Anthe anew.

"At last the reason you cannot sell the property is clear." Livia's tone was confidently conclusive. "If your ward is legally married and continues to claim ownership, your son is not its curator because this office has automatically devolved upon her husband. If she is deceased or has decided to abandon the property, it cedes to the Museion. Now: if your ward is alive and unmarried and continues to claim ownership, then your son is indeed curator. But should he in this capacity sell the property, the proceeds remain your ward's possession. They cannot be used to satisfy a financial obligation your son as curator incurred for purposes of your own. Did you not review the legal ramifications of offering the property as collateral?"

"There was no time to delve into arcane and convoluted legalities! We needed the money immediately!"

Livia showed no reaction to the outburst. "For what reason?"

Anthe exhaled sharply and pursed her lips in exasperation. "Last month my daughter-in-law—Philo's wife of less than two years—decided to leave him. Her father—that dirty bastard—initiated a lawsuit against us because we did not immediately repay her dowry!"

"How much do you owe?"

"375,000 sesterces."

"A suitable amount for a dowry. Did you offer to repay it in installments?"

"We lack the means even to make installments. My poor Philo has never been able to procure steady employment. Over the past five years he has worked only sporadically."

"Young man, what is your profession?"

"He is a stonemason."

"Can he not answer for himself?"

Anthe glowered, and Philo stared as though bewildered. *So he finally overcame his inanity sufficiently at least to learn a trade*, I reflected.

"In a large and flourishing city like Naples you cannot find steady work as a stonemason?" Livia continued in a modulated yet incredulous tenor.

"He could not even secure a regular apprenticeship, but had to settle for an abbreviated, truncated course of training," Anthe replied petulantly. "It appears we do not know the right people," she added, now testily. *Such is what comes*, I thought, *from holding yourself aloof from all others and refusing to socialize.*

Livia addressed Philo. "Did your father-in-law not employ you in some capacity? What is his trade?"

"He is a wall decorator." Philo finally spoke up. *Hence the daughter's interest in art*, I reasoned.

"Has he additional children or other relatives living with him besides your estranged wife?"

"Two younger children," Anthe replied.

"Are they of age?"

After a sullen silence, Anthe finally answered, "No."

"Hardly a surprise, then, he should demand the dowry be repaid at once," Livia mused aloud. "With his daughter back in his household, he must have needed immediate funds to feed and clothe her."

Anthe's face grew red with rage, and the pitch of her voice lowered. "Do you not understand, we used the dowry for the same purposes—to put food in that ditz' mouth and clothes on her back? To satisfy her frivolous obsession with painting we had to buy her reproductions, and engage an art instructor to give her lessons. We took her on a costly excursion to Rome for a particular exhibition. There she put on a display of histrionics that humiliated Philo and me beyond imagination. Can you not comprehend what we endured to keep her happy in her marriage? Nothing, nothing sufficed. My poor Philo here was devastated when she announced she could no longer abide being in our presence."

"Frictions within a marriage are often better resolved when a partner alters personal behaviors the spouse finds objectionable, than by trying to force or bribe the offended spouse to tolerate such conduct." As she spoke, Livia directed her eyes at Philo who was scratching his crotch. "The same holds true for one seeking to acquire or retain work. Irritating an employer can only react against one's own best interests."

Anthe sat scowling while Philo continued his operation.

"Without earnings from your son, how do you manage to meet your everyday living expenses?" The harshening of Livia's tone revealed her escalating frustration.

"Barely, with my husband's pension from his former employer."

"Have you no other assets against which you could have borrowed?"

"None! We are forced to live in a miserable, cramped, dingy apartment above a shop on the Potters' Street, in the filthiest, noisiest section of Naples! Had that ungrateful, parricidal jade married the man we chose for her—and had she continued to earn royalties from teaching and publishing as the sophista my husband labored so scrupulously to make her—we would not have had to sell the fine house in which we raised her!"

"If your circumstances are as straitened as you imply, why are you not residing on the property against which you borrowed? Surely the services of stonemasons are required in its region. Why do you maintain a separate dwelling in Naples?

"The rental of our apartment in Naples is paid by my husband's former employer as part of the pension settlement," Anthe replied almost triumphantly.

Livia nodded comprehendingly. "Have you considered leasing out the country property and applying the rental monies toward the repayment of your obligation?"

"We already have a tenant. After my husband died, the only way we could pay the taxes on the place was by renting it."

Who in his right mind, I wondered, *would voluntarily rent a worthless strip of barren, inarable scrubland?*

"To what entity are they paid?"

"The city of Nola."

Again Livia nodded her comprehension. "For what purpose is the tenant utilizing the property?" she continued. "You may have justification for raising the rental amount."

"I have no idea. We cannot afford to make the trip there to investigate."

"How, then, did you procure the tenant?"

"Through a broker—a fine young man whom my Philo here was fortunate enough to befriend."

"Did he not apprise you of how the tenant intended to use your tract?"

"We felt no need to ask him that question; and we have not seen him since he delivered the signed lease."

"Do you not have relatives to whom you can turn for assistance?"

"My aged maiden aunt, who makes her home with Philo and me, is destitute."

So Euethia was still alive! I mentally noted, not without surprise. Then with a twinge of cynicism, I wondered to what extent she had contributed to the breakup of Philo's marriage.

"All the rest of our kin reside in Colosse," Anthe continued, "We have not been in touch with them for more than thirty years. Our relationship was never harmonious."

"Then you cannot expect them to assist you with this matter."

"No."

What happened to the beneficence of Norenas? He must have abandoned the Eupistodoi after I abandoned his son. What was left of his donations had to have been squandered.

After another sullen silence, Anthe waxed vehement once again. "Do you not understand we are desperate? Are you going to aid us or not?"

"You will be thanked to lower your voice." The unruffled manner in which Livia delivered her rebuke left Anthe rattled. "We need to determine who at present is the actual curator of the property," Livia continued. "I shall set agents at work to find this out. Should your son prove not to be the curator, the rents will accrue to whichever party is—along with responsibility for the taxes."

"Suppose that selfish, self-centered, malicious strumpet, on learning she owns the property, drives our tenant off?"

"What advantage could she possibly derive from doing so, when the rent defrays the taxes?" At Livia's conundrum Anthe glared with indignation, but remained silent.

Once again Livia conferred with the legal consultant. Now he spoke. "The curator of a property does have the option, not to implement recommendations from the owner that the curator deems disadvantageous. Should your son prove to be the legal curator, he may choose to retain the tenant. Your ward will have no say in the matter."

For a brief moment Anthe's visage brightened, presumably at the prospect I might not have my way in this imaginary scenario.

The consultant continued. "Should our investigation determine your son is not curator after all, then the rightful administrator—your ward's husband if she is married, or otherwise the Museion—will of course have the prerogative to remove the tenant. This curator will be obligated for ensuring the taxes are paid."

"Retaining the rental income appears the better choice for whomever rightfully controls the property," Livia concluded. "What is your ward's name?"

"Clytia."

"And her surname?"

"Eupistide."

Anthe's tone was superciliously sneering, as if to imply Livia's inquiry was ludicrously mindless.

"After your husband, of course, to lead her to believe she was your natural daughter. What was her natural father's name?"

"I do not remember."

"Do you recall the name of the cavalry commander with whom she corresponded?"

"Most definitely: Decimus Calvinius Valens."

"In what year did your ward depart your domicile?" Livia continued her inquiry.

"The same in which your son departed for Rhodes—in fact, she left us at the very time he left you."

"An odd coincidence, but no more than that." Livia's tone was dismissive. Another admirable forestalling tactic, to preclude Anthe from drawing a connection between Tiberius' flight and mine, and possibly leading my brother to decide he had recognized me after all. "I presume the municipal bank is the lienholder."

"No! The bank rejected us! We had to resort to a usurer!" More righteous indignation. No remorse or shame or embarrassment because the bank deemed her proposition a poor risk.

"Your situation is more than desperate. It is downright perilous, and not only from a financial standpoint. Leading your ward to believe she was your natural daughter, for the purpose of seizing control of her assets, is an act of outright embezzlement—a crime, bearing the punishments of property forfeiture and imprisonment or relegation. Your ward has every right to sue you for the dupery you perpetrated on her. If we manage to locate her, we shall have no alternative but to inform her of your deception. If she remains undiscoverable, the property will revert to the Museion. Then that institution will have the same right to sue you."

Anthe's reddened face turned white with fear. "My husband...my deceased husband...he demanded unrelentingly that we lead her to believe she was our daughter!" she sputtered. *A fictitious defense for sure,* I thought. *Eupistus never demanded anything of Anthe; the paternity charade was her idea.*

"Your ward, or the Museion, stand little to gain financially from suing you, since you have no assets to forfeit. Hopefully, neither is so mean-spirited to sue you purely for the sake of revenge."

"You may rest assured, both are!" Anthe growled indignantly. "What are we to do?"

"If you anticipate being sued, you must be prepared to pay fines in addition to the debt you presently owe." Livia replied straightforwardly, showing no reaction to the emotional display. "Therefore you, Philo, need to procure employment of any sort you can, and as quickly as you can. This should not be terribly difficult in a prosperous city like Naples, so long as you are not selective about what work you find available. If you cannot work as a stonemason, then become a stevedore, a ship's mate, a day laborer, a courier, a janitor—whatever you must. Once you find employment, being a diligent and accommodating worker will be incumbent upon you. You must avoid giving your employer any incentive for dismissing you. What is the name of your usurer?"

"Alexander Simonides."

"Do you know of him?" Livia asked Poppaeus.

"Yes. A notoriously devious and obnoxious scoundrel, barely ahead of the law."

"Haul him before your tribunal, along with Mistress Anthe and Philo here. Rule he has to accept repayment of their loan in installments, and at a fixed interest rate of two percent only."

"With pleasure for sure!" Poppaeus returned boisterously.

"The size and frequency of those installments—monthly, bimonthly, quarterly—I leave to your discretion, as they will depend upon the level of income Philo is able to procure. If his salary proves insufficient to meet the installment amount you decide upon as reasonable, I shall supply the difference. At the end of every quarter, Philo must have his employer confirm he is still employed and not in danger of being dismissed."

"And what recourse will we have if Philo does find himself dismissed—or if he cannot find work in the first place?" Anthe's tone was now superciliously argumentative.

"He is always welcome to apply at my brickyards near Atella. Have Praetor Poppaeus contact me, and I shall provide a letter of introduction for Philo to present the director." Livia replied mildly, unruffled by Anthe's challenge.

"Brickyards!" Anthe exclaimed in a disdainful undertone.

"Persons in your situation cannot afford to be choosy," Livia returned, still mild. "I should think brickyards a natural milieu for a stonemason."

Anthe shifted about uncomfortably on the bench, her visage again sullen; but she said nothing.

"We must allow a reasonable length of time for the proposed plan of action to be completed," Livia continued, again addressing Poppaeus. "Nevertheless, we cannot allow it to be prolonged indefinitely. If you are unable to finalize arrangements before the Calends of September, convene a hearing to determine cause and remedy for the delay. Should you feel a need for my intervention before or at that time, do not hesitate to seek it. For the present, this matter is concluded."

Poppaeus rose to his feet and bowed. For several moments Anthe remained seated with a perplexed expression on her face, as though she did not understand the interview was over and nothing remained to be said. At length her mien resumed its sullenness. She arose, nudging Philo with her hand as she did. With lowered eyes and protruding lower lip she curtsied abruptly. After Philo finally bowed hesitantly, Poppaeus escorted them through the exit.

"By all the gods, what an interview!" I heard Livia exclaim as the room reeled about me, filled with pale light, and disappeared.

Awakening with the pungent odor of camphor filling my nostrils, I momentarily imagined I was lying on the examining table of the Ialyssian physician Eupistus. As my consciousness cleared and my eyes focused, I realized I was on one of the benches in the audience chamber. "She is coming around," said a male voice I did not recognize. Turning my head I beheld a gray-headed man in physician's garb, holding the vial of camphor. "Breathe deeply and regularly, Lady, in…" he inhaled, "…and out," he exhaled. "Come along, in…" he inhaled and I did as well, "…and out," we exhaled simultaneously. "Very good, that is the way. Are you nauseous? No, no, do not speak. Continue your deep breathing, just nod yes or turn your head no." Turn my head I did. Although my stomach felt as though it had that rock in it, I did not feel as though I were going to vomit. The man took my right hand. "Can you sit up?" Endeavoring to pull myself upright, I was overcome by lightheadedness and fell back upon the bench. "I suspect this confounded heat got to her," the man said to Livia.

"I do not believe she has eaten anything today," Livia replied. With gratitude I realized her remark was to keep my attendant unaware of the emotional agitation I had just undergone. "Our shipboard physician Marcianus," she added for my benefit.

"Tsk, tsk, tsk, shame on you!" Marcianus chided. "You cannot neglect your nourishment, just because hot weather makes you lose your appetite. I recommend we remove her to the infirmary for at least the remainder of the day."

"Oh no, no, Sir! Please, let me return to the veranda!" Plaintively but emphatically I protested as I struggled anew to raise myself. "Here, Malthace, help me to sit!" With the maidservant's assistance I pulled myself upright. "I feel desperately in need of open air. As soon as I arrive there, I shall eat something—I promise!"

"Indeed good for her to be in fresh air, and drinking water aplenty," Marcianus conceded.

Mathace supported me on one side and Livia on the other as we proceeded aft through the yacht's corridors. Yet once we reached the veranda I did not remain, but bolted headlong down the staircase to our sleeping quarters. "Go with her, the both of you, and do not leave her unattended for a moment!" I heard Livia command, presumably addressing servants I had not noticed. *She cares enough about me to insure I do not commit suicide,* I noted mentally as I flung myself face downward upon my bed. Gratefully I acknowledged her words as evidence of Underlying Good, the existence of which I desperately kept reiterating.

Recollections of the interview were coming almost like physical blows—as though ocean waves or great gusts of wind were striking me. Not only had I been scorned and tortured by the guardians appointed me: I had been outrightly rejected by my own kin! Little wonder Euethia used to preach I should never have been born, that out of altruism unsurpassed Anthe and Eupistus had chosen to rear me contrary to their better interests. Now I felt more demeaned than ever I had while living with and enduring the scorn of the Eupistodoi. To no avail I kept reminding myself I was loved and respected by Augustus the potentate and Thrasyllus the intellect.

Without cavil I had embraced the pseudo-identities Tiberius had created for me—Daphne Hipparchide and subsequently Galatea Aristoclide—to conceal me from the family who had led me to believe I was one of their own. But to discover Clytia Eupistide was also a nonentity induced a frantic bewilderment, a disconsolate despair, a terrifying feeling I was at once both alive and dead. Despite my antipathy toward the Eupistodoi, having to believe I was one of them had imparted a sense of identity. Now I realized the Eupistodoi had not even considered me a slave, whose humanity even the most cruel or indifferent of owners must acknowledge. To my foster family I had been a mere tool—an impersonal, inanimate object to be exploited in any way they saw fit, with no more regard for human feeling than a farmer imputes to a sickle or plow.

Anthe had exploited me to satisfy a longing for offspring—more likely to show off to neighbors and relatives than to rear with maternal devotion. Then

Philo's birth canceled her need for me in this capacity. Thereafter she had endeavored to indulge her obsession with wealth and renown—advantages she had steadfastly maintained meant nothing to her—by driving me to become the greatest of the great: a sophista unmatched by all others who went before or would come after me, familiar to and revered by every person on earth. Through deceit she had taken control of assets rightfully mine, and with them purchased that scrappy piece of land to suit her pleasure—all the while alleging I was her natural daughter for whose dowry there were no funds. Little wonder she had kept me unmarried: to prevent control of my stipend—and hence of her cherished retreat—from ceding to my husband.

Suddenly I wondered whether I owed my very life to the Museion's caveat for reversion of ownership. But for that provision I might have been deliberately abandoned on some country roadside and said to have wandered off, or deliberately drowned while bathing and alleged to have slipped and hit my head during a reckless cavort. After all I was still a young child when Philo's birth canceled my function as cherished offspring. For certain I would never have been administered a poison, the effects of which resembled natural illness. Neither Anthe nor Euethia possessed the necessary knowledge or skills, nor the means and connections for hiring an unscrupulous pharmakeutria to perform such a task.

My head began to ache as I contemplated these morbid ideas. I rolled onto my back and shut my eyes. For nearly a lifetime I had grappled with anger and embitterment toward the Eupistodoi. Guilt had haunted me for harboring such resentment, because I had assumed they were my kin and therefore hating them was a moral offense. Now the guilt was gone, and in its place a strong sense of self-justification. What rational person would not have taken umbrage at being afflicted in the manner I was?

Anthe's present predicament was the consequence of her own folly. To keep myself from gloating over her situation, I redirected my musings to the morning's great revelation. With a sense of unsettled urgency surging within my consciousness, I started to wonder who my real parents were and why their kindred had spurned me. *Who was I? Who am I?* This lack of tangible identity brought on a strange and almost sickening disheartenment, as though to confirm Euethia's assertion my birth and existence were undeserved. I likened myself to a piece of driftwood or a sea plant uprooted, tossing willy-nilly on the waves without hope of refuge or security. How appropriately they had named me Clytia.

"Who am I?" I heard myself murmur as someone's hand closed about one of mine.

"Leave us." Tiberius' tone was level and straightforward: he was addressing whoever was attending me.

Although the room reeled a little as I sat upright, I sensed full possession of my faculties and consciousness. Casting my arms about Tiberius and pressing my face into his shoulder, I repeated my inquiry in a plaintive wail: "Who am I?!"

He drew his arms about me and stroked my hair. Gently yet emphatically he replied, "You are Clytia Neronis my beloved wife, mother of Tiberius Claudius Alcimus my beloved son."

For a moment I felt very much like the abject ingrate Anthe and Euethia had always accused me of being, although I knew full well such was not what Tiberius implied. "True, oh true, my love: so you have made me! But who is the person you transformed? What is my birth name? Who am I—who was I? From what stock did I spring; and why did they reject me?"

Relaxing his embrace, he turned so we were sitting side by side on the bed. From its far end he retrieved a bowl of polenta with a spoon protruding from its midst, and held it before me. "Eat!" he ordered.

"No—I have a prodigious headache," I groaned.

"Of course you do. You are empty, and you have been through a grueling that would deplete the energy of a Titan. Nomius!" The servant opened the door to the antechamber. "Fetch Lady a tincture of spirea." Nomius shut the door, and Tiberius shoved the spoon into my mouth. "It is my legal and moral privilege, as your husband, to demand you take this nourishment!" *The very same approach Augustus had applied to Livia,* I reflected as I swallowed the dollop of polenta. Immediately it loosened the knot in my stomach, so willingly I took the rest. "We have set about finding out who you are," he declared as he continued to feed me. "What office did my mother's protégé Quintus Ostorius Scapula assume on this present month's Calends?"

"Prefect of Egypt," I replied between mouthfuls. My spirits started to lift as I anticipated the course his conversation was going to take.

"My mother has already dictated orders for him to initiate a thorough examination of all the Museion's records relevant to that fire: its victims, the remedial actions taken, and the persons involved therewith—particularly the advanced student Eupistus from Colosse."

Having finished the polenta, I once again threw my arms about him and held him tightly, not uttering a word, until a knock of the door impelled us to separate and sit side by side again. The caller proved to be Marcianus with the spirea. After the physician departed I spoke again, the tenor of my voice intensifying as I selected words to express the urgency I was feeling. "I need to be among people, reminding myself I am no less a member of the human race than any of them."

Tiberius nodded, and patted my hand as he rose to leave. "Fetch water for me to cleanse my face and mouth, and prepare to brush and rebind my hair," I ordered Nausicaa as I headed for the privy. My toiletries completed I ascended the stairs, moving slowly and breathing deeply and hoping I could manage to retain my composure. Doing so proved impossible after all. As soon as I entered the veranda Antonia embraced me, and I began to weep. Fortunately I just shed tears and did not break into sobs, not even those silent ones. Daubing my eyes with her kerchief, Antonia led me to where Tiberius was sitting with Livia, and with Augustus in whose piercing eyes compassion seemed clearly evident.

"My dear, what a discovery!" Augustus began as Antonia, gently pushing downward on my shoulders lowered me into a vacant chair. "No, no: do not fight those tears to which you are so very well entitled. You have undergone transfiguration: a rite of passage the likes of which each of us present here has traversed. There is no need for me to describe my transfiguration, for you are acquainted with my origins from landed gentry with little political significance. Livia has further transfigured me. She is sensitive to the feelings of others— mine included—and patient with their shortcomings. Over the years she has gently guided my judgments away from anger and callous indifference, and toward affability, moderation, and forgiveness.

Livia's early life was entirely typical for a woman of her heritage. Being the daughter of a senator, she dutifully married the senator her father selected for her husband, dutifully bore two sons who would become senators, dutifully supported her husband's political agenda despite the physical hardships and dangers it imposed upon her—until the opportunity for transfiguration presented itself. She created quite a public controversy, leaving her first husband with his long and well recognized senatorial lineage to wed me—the political and social upstart—purely for love." As he spoke these words, Augustus gently took Livia's hand in his. She smiled sweetly and her cheeks colored slightly. "Now she occupies a position integral to my system of government. Protectress to the interest of women and exemplar of marital fidelity is an indispensable and permanent institution, which will devolve upon Livia's granddaughter—my own grandson's wife—when he succeeds me."

Augustus diverted his gaze to his niece. "While yet in her mother's womb, Antonia went from being the symbol of her parents' unity to that of her father's breach, not only with her mother but with me and with his nationality. Years later Antonia underwent transfiguration from a deliriously happy, pampered, and fecund wife to a reclusive and grieving widow, and then to another essential member of my regime. By tradition, responsibility for managing my personal household and matters pertaining to it falls to Livia as my wife: but Antonia, assuming those burdens, has relieved Livia to perform the tasks her new role requires. Antonia's responsibilities exceed those of ordinary housewives—even the spouses of senators—for they include oversight of the vassal princes residing with us. Their transformation from barbaric churlishness to civilized gentility Antonia is achieving masterfully, even as she labors to bring about the transfiguration of her bumbling son.

"Life as a prominent senator seemed inevitable for Tiberius, as much before as after his parents' separation, until he chose to transfigure himself. He bore the brunt of my wrath, of Marcus Lollius' slanders and the unfounded suspicions they raised in Gaius, of public disdain and ridicule, of threats against his very life, to bring about his conversion into what he is today. The private philanthropist is so very more conducive to his character than the politician. Tiberius and Livia alike transfigure the lives of the petitioners who seek their interventions and benefactions.

"My transfiguration of the Roman state affects innumerable persons none of us will ever encounter. And as for you, my dear: with dutiful persistence you tried to fulfill the impossible expectations your foster family set for you, and endured the abuse they heaped upon you. Those afflictions were actually salutary, eliciting the strengths and excellences of your character. Finding yourself unable to satisfy your guardians, you courageously fled them and eluded their efforts to find you. You began a new life of love with Tiberius, despite the uncertainties and hardships and outright danger to which it exposed you. You, dearest one, stood by Tiberius through the turmoil of his transfiguration, supporting his change with your loyalty and bravery, forbearance and love. With humility you accepted and fulfilled the finishing he required of you, improving your appearance and bearing. You came to recognize, and have prolifically cultivated, the marvelous artistic talent you never realized you had. With phenomenal courage and determination you fought and overcame the dangerous condition of sterility, arising from your guardians' neglect of your physical health, and persevered to bring an uncertain pregnancy to fruition.

"Your true origins may remain undiscoverable. For the present you employ pseudonyms to evade recognition. Your marriage and the existence of your son are unknown except to a very few. None of these obfuscations affects your identity. They do not alter the woman into whom you have made yourself: the loving wife and mother, the poised gracious and engaging companion, the learned intellectual, the gifted artist. Your transfiguration bases your identity—includes you among those who throughout history have transformed their lives and the lives of others.

"Thanks to you a new transfiguration is unfolding for Antonia as she emerges from seclusion, to accompany you at public events and to plan one as well—the art exhibition. What you accomplished for my little cousin Pedillus is nothing short of miraculous. Your identity is secure. You are, and will remain forever, one of us—one of this family of transfigured and agents of transfiguration.

"We look after our own. All of us present here today have agreed upon a decision. To ameliorate the shock of what unfolded in your life this morning, arrangements to bring your son and the family with whom he resides to Rome will be implemented, directly upon our return from our current sojourn. I have already sent Diodomedes orders to expedite the rebuilding of our townhouse, even if work must be done at night. If that dwelling is not ready by the time we arrive back and we must remain at the Villa Maecenatis, we shall install your party at Ad Gallinas and move our Asiatic princes to my estate at Tivoli. They can enjoy riding and hunting amid the hills."

His words woke within my consciousness a sense of corrective explication and adjustment—powerful, yet quieting and stabilizing. I felt neither the exaggerated joy nor the self-deprecating gratitude, of one who receives an unanticipated blessing and considers it undeserved. My weeping abated. Not groveling contritely with lowered eyes and murmuring voice, but returning Augustus' gaze with calm self-assurance, I smiled and said simply and forthrightly, "Thank you! Thank you all!"

"Our pleasure assuredly," Augustus returned.

"Indeed!" Livia interjected buoyantly. "And I am feeling quite transfigured myself, having discovered I do not share a grandchild with that horrid woman after all!"

Augustus continued, "Now to help you dispel the effects of this morning's ordeal, we have arranged a little entertainment to cheer you." While speaking he motioned to a manservant, who departed the veranda and promptly returned with a small troupe of acrobats. One was carrying an armful of differently colored leather balls, which he proceeded to juggle. Another started to walk about the veranda on his hands, his knees bent above his head and his groin tightly covered. The remaining five assumed a sequence of different positions while standing upon one another's shoulders. After they had finished, one man left the veranda and returned with a trio of small white dogs. He directed them through a series of tricks—chasing their tails, walking on their hind legs, turning backward flips, vaulting sidewise over one other, one riding on the other's back. A notary's arrival with a message in the middle of the performance required Augustus to leave, the demands of government being relentless. After a respite the hand walker had resumed his stance. He clapped his feet as Augustus passed by.

Laughing with delight, I enthusiastically applauded the concluded dog act. As the trainer was guiding his charges away, the remainder of the troupe reassembled—including the juggler who had put aside his balls, and the hand walker who had reassumed his normal posture. The dog man returned carrying a flute. After he had sounded two notes, the company sang *Pierced with Flares from Eros' Bow, My Heart with Ardor for You Glows*—my very favorite Rhodian folk song. As we applauded their performance, Tiberius disclosed he had remembered my affinity for the piece and apprised the performers.

As they prepared to sing again, the light of day darkened abruptly. A powerful gust of wind disheveled hair and clothing, caused the entertainers and the servants and even the praetorians standing at attention to stumble, and set the yacht to rocking precipitously. Heavy rain followed immediately, sending everybody scurrying for enclosure. Although the servants attempted to shield us by lowering and tethering the awnings, they could not complete their operation in time to keep us from becoming well doused. Assembled in the dayroom, we concurred our best recourse was to bathe at once and thereafter take supper.

While thunder was rumbling during our bath, Livia said she anticipated her husband would not be joining us for our repast. Her remark reminded me that lightning storms unnerved Augustus. Outside the shuttered windows of our quarters the rain pelted, lightning flashed and thunder rattled. Having the windows shut made the air stuffy, even with the doors to the central corridor open for ventilation. Nevertheless, being sequestered from all the ruckus churning beyond the walls imparted me an especially strong sense of shelter and protection. I felt as thoroughly hidden as though in a secret cavern deep in the bowels of the earth, where no enemy or any other discord could possibly find me.

The meal was not served until the storm had abated. Livia's prognostication of her husband's absence proved true. Although I did not presume to inquire, I concluded swordfish had been deliberately selected for the entree because it was known to be my favorite. The yacht still rocked, but now pleasantly. Rapidly I grew so drowsy, that I barely managed to finish my food. Thereafter I begged to be excused, apologizing profusely and asserting I meant no offense. "Why do you assume you are causing offence?" Livia inquired bemusedly. "Given what you endured during the course of this day, how could you not be exhausted by now?" Turning to Antonia and Tiberius, Livia continued, "She is still feeling the effects of her turgid upbringing. Her foster mother would have castigated her roundly for being oscitant."

They understand—they understand—THEY UNDERSTAND!! At last this fact was becoming palpably real to me. Until now I had harbored the notion not even Tiberius could fully appreciate the torments, arising from the self-doubt and self-loathing the Eupistodoi had instilled in me. Now that incertitude, that misgiving, that persistent despair from feeling misunderstood and misjudged, was gone. *They understand!* While I descended the staircase to my quarters, while Nausicaa prepared me for bed, while I lay listening an occasional rumble of now distant thunder, I felt as though I were in a consoling dream from which I would emerge back into a reality of agony. *No!* I kept mentally forcing myself to acknowledge as my surroundings faded with the onset of sleep. *No! The agony has become the dream, and the consolation reality!*

Abruptly I awoke, and with a feeling I had slept for merely a few minutes. Presently I realized this presumption was false. There were no footfalls or voices to be heard. The only illumination in my chamber was that outlining the door, from the lamps hanging in the hallway. The lack of light emanating from the adjacent servant's alcove indicated Nausicca had retired. The yacht had ceased her rocking. My bedroom had cooled, and was noticeably but pleasantly damp. A familiar and appealing sensation began to infiltrate my nostrils: fog. Fumbling in the limited light, I managed to locate lamp and flint. With the room better illumined, I found and wrapped myself in my dressing gown. Knowing the main hallways were kept lit throughout the night, I extinguished the lamp and left it on the dressing table before I exited the chamber. Quietly I treaded through the central corridor and up the staircase to the dayrooms. The praetorian standing guard at the top of the stairs snapped to attention.

To my dismay I found the veranda in utter darkness, since all the awnings had been lowered. But as I was turning to leave, a manservant arrived with a lamp and towel. Readily he obliged, when I asked him to raise one of the awnings so I might inhale the fog. He hung his lamp on one of the stands, and with the towel dried a chair for me to sit upon. In the mist I perceived a silhouette permeated with points of light: one of the escort ships with lamps burning, backlit by the glow penetrating the fog from the harbor and city. Closing my eyes I breathed the cleansing vapors with relish, while I contemplated the discourse Augustus had delivered that afternoon.

His speech was having quite an effect upon me, succeeding where Areus had not. At last I was willing to concede, that without the vicissitudes of my life with the Eupistodoi—their verbal and physical abuses, their distorted aspirations and ideals, the bad habits and inappropriate behaviors I had developed from association with and resistance to that family—I likely would never have detected let alone cultivated those latent strengths and abilities Augustus had extolled. For a time I found myself fancying my first acknowledgment of Underlying Good—on my hot, dusty birthday in Campania a decade ago—had set into motion some cosmic action which aligned events specifically to bring about my transformation. More likely, I reflected with amusement while conjuring a more realistic explanation, that epiphany had sharpened my awareness of opportunities for improving my condition and solidified my determination to take advantage of these.

My anger toward the Eupistodoi not only remained but intensified, now that I understood how they had deceived and exploited me. Nevertheless my guilt for harboring that anger was gone. Gone as well was the painful, unrequited disappointment that had dogged me because I had continually failed to achieve the impossible goals, set by those malingerers who had led me to believe they were my family. No longer did I feel frustrated by inability to diffuse my anger toward my tormentors, let alone forgive them. Moreover now that I understood the reason for their contempt, I was finding its memories easier to bear.

We look after our own. Augustus' words echoed through my mind like a clarion call. During my youth, Anthe and Euethia had continually insisted I was nothing more than a nuisance to the few friends I had managed to cultivate: the girl Photis, the confirmed bachelor sophistos Praumetis, students who had passed through the Academia Norenas including of course the *weird Roman soldier.* As each relationship had developed my guardians assured me I was an intruder, seeking affection to which I was not entitled. They had maintained I was forcing myself upon people who did not reciprocate my feelings—who in fact resented my overtures but were too polite to say so outrightly and shun me as I deserved. Consequently I had always felt myself an interloper in relationships—even with Tiberius despite our marriage; for I had continued to harbor a latent fear he might someday tire of me and cast me away. And despite Augustus' declaration on the Palatine, that he and his family loved me as one of their own, I had continued to feel an outsider among them.

Tiberius is as much in love with you as you are with him! For nearly a decade, through his words and actions he has demonstrated, over and over again, he is as committed to your prosperity and happiness as you are to his, and pledged as much as you to your unity with one another. Moreover his family have approved you as Tiberius' wife and accepted your son, over and above their political objections to interracial marriage. They have welcomed you as one of their own, and extolled you for bringing benefits to them. Why do you not accept them in return, instead of torturing yourself with persistent and indefensible doubts? You must embrace this family that has embraced you, for you have none other!

Clenching fists and teeth, I mentally shrieked those words at myself. And while doing so I began to feel refreshed, uplifted, and healed both emotionally and physically—as though a chronic ailment I had taught myself to ignore had started to remit.

Had I just experienced a monumental change, which Thrasyllus had failed to detect when he cast my horoscope before Tiberius and I quit Rhodes? No, I decided after further reflection. Much had been revealed, but nothing had really changed. I had always been the daughter of my natural parents, and since early childhood the ward of the Eupistodoi. Toward the latter I was no less embittered than before the great discovery. Neither Tiberius nor his family—with the possible albeit not for certain exception of Agrippina and Postumus—had ever harbored ambivalence toward me. But Augustus' oration—particularly his description of my transforming effect upon Antonia and his promise to hasten the reunion of Tiberius and me with our son—had finally obliterated that sense of alienation, which quite palpably no one besides me (and maybe Agrippina although not for sure) had been harboring.

One might call this a significant change. Nevertheless I prefer to use Augustus' words—transformation and transfiguration—to describe what had happened to me. I did not feel corrected or otherwise altered, but assuredly enhanced. Without the slightest compunction I had joyed over the gift of the acrobats' performance—a gift the family who claimed me as one of theirs had provided specifically to cheer me. Having noted out of the corner of one eye, Livia watching me with a look of contented assurance, I recognized and accepted she was pleased to see me recovering. And what Augustus had said about my influence upon Antonia made me feel useful as a friend ought to be, and not parasitic as the Eupistodoi had always insisted I was.

To my surprise I started to feel as though I had been useful to Philo—a sensation I found most gratifying, and not at all in a vengeful way. Philo had presented himself at the interview exactly as I had recalled and often described him: unresponsive and uncouth, exhibiting the very vileness Anthe had incessantly attributed to me. Yet during the interim of years since my flight, some circumstance or some person—perhaps even Anthe herself—had motivated Philo to learn and master a skill. Hence he did not lack the ability to apply himself. Nor was he entirely without appealing characteristics. Two years ago, for a reason which at the time made sense, that decorator had approved him as a son-in-law and scrimped up the money for a dowry.

Philo had no perception of how the repressive cosseting of his mother and her aunt was obfuscating and enervating his strengths of body, mind, and character. Chronically unemployable and now divorced, he was undoubtedly being reassured his plight was everyone else's fault but not his own. *A life ruined*, I reflected with a renewed surge of anger toward Anthe and Euethia. Honestly and sincerely, I hoped the desperate situation into which his mother and great-aunt had led him, and the solution Livia proposed, would open Philo's eyes to the terrible deceit his family had perpetrated upon him and so bring about his transfiguration.

My thoughts reverted to my natural kin. They could not have possibly rejected me for my character, having never so much as laid eyes on me. Anthe said they had refused to acknowledge my parents' marriage as well as my birth. Presuming Anthe had told the truth, I must have been a lovechild, born to a couple whose affinity for one another had impelled them to marry—or if not, then to cohabit—and generate a child in opposition to parental intentions. This conclusion I found fascinating and strangely satisfying. Apparently I was the outcome of a couple's commitment to giving their love precedence over familial demands.

My parents must have been rebels, opposing the marital intentions their families had outlined for them. Of course I had been a rebel, challenging and resisting the nonsense the Eupistodoi endeavored to force upon me, and eventually delivering the penultimate defiance of fleeing them. Tiberius had been a rebel, abandoning the vocational path for which not only his family but his ancestry and his societal position had predestined him.

Not surprisingly the Eupistodoi were continuing to deprecate my character, as they had for most of my life. Yet while Tiberius' family had been dismayed and angered by his act of rebellion, they had not allowed it to alter or diminish their respect and affection for him as an individual. The enforced confinement to Rhodes had been intended as a reprimand, but also to protect Tiberius from the potentially fatal consequences of being regarded a viable rival to Gaius. Continuing the reprimand—and demonstrating he had no tolerance for insubordination even from members of his own family—Augustus had made Tiberius' release from confinement and return to Rome contingent upon agreement not to participate in public affairs. Nevertheless Augustus did not in any way restrict or interfere with Tiberius' personal activities: his attending to petitioners, his pursuit of astrology, his marriage outside his race. Rather, the emperor had commended these pursuits as better suited than politics to Tiberius' temperament.

What a duo of examples to compare! The Eupistodoi had persecuted me for rejecting their ideals: called me unnatural, depraved, perversely lacking in affection and gratitude. The response of Tiberius' family to his rebellion had shown me the better alternative. Suppose down the future our son rebelled in some fashion against Tiberius and me. Intervention to correct and discipline might or might not be appropriate: the withholding of affection or delivery of abuse for the sake of spite could never be. Our responsibility as parents will be to recommend and when necessary outline a pathway for his life, suitable to his talents, his inclinations, the particular social and financial circumstances into which he will fall. We must mentor and guide and help with recovery from mistakes, but never interfere with his fundamental human right to make his own decisions about his life or penalize him for exercising that right. Before long, Alcimus was going to reenter our lives. The time was at hand to forsake the traumas of the past, and by devoting undivided attention and energy to addressing properly the present and future be as useful to our son as we could manage.

Once again I became sleepy—not as I did earlier from exhaustion induced by turmoil, but with the intense calm that accompanies a sense of accomplishment. Returning to our quarters I entered not my bedchamber but Tiberius.' Moving gingerly so not to wake him I laid down at his side. Within moments I felt his arms enclose me and his lips press against mine.

By the time we awakened the fog had lifted. The sky was filled with gray clouds, the air damp but pleasantly cool. I wondered whether Augustus' comments the previous day, about Antonia's emergence from seclusion, impelled her to propose over breakfast that she and I explore the wharf of Naples together. How we could maintain anonymity became the next matter of discussion. She liked my suggestion we exchange costumes: she dressed in one of my chitons with hair bound in Greek fashion, while I wore a stola of hers and had my hair arranged in Roman mode. Then Tiberius reminded us a pair of mysterious women emerging from the Galatea's launch was certain to attract attention. We decided to follow the recommendation he offered: dress in servants' livery, and accompany the yacht's kitchen crew when they went ashore for supplies.

This company found our mission delightfully amusing—as did Nausicaa, Antonia's maidservant Felicia, and the four praetorians who accompanied us in plainclothes.

The guards maintained discreet distances and credibly pretended to be minding their own business. We wandered through the narrow streets and alleyways crowded with ware-filled shops and stalls, raucous tradesmen and equally strident customers. Antonia did not purchase anything, but reveled in the sights and sounds and smells and the very dirt from which ordinarily she was sedulously shielded. She confessed this was her first visit to the Neapolitan wharf, and she was enjoying it thoroughly. My guardians had taken me several times when I was a small child. After Philo's birth, however, they never brought me near the place, and decried my longing to revisit it the excessive and immoral boldness of a hussy. Antonia proposed they must have feared Philo might learn something about the real world and real life. I purchased a bolt of linen, suitable for a himation or palla. It was the color of polished copper: an unusual shade for sure, and hence the reason it was rather expensive. Nevertheless its appeal I could not resist. Passing through the Potters' section we found it cleaner and quieter, its buildings brighter and more spacious than in most of the region— hardly as deplorable as Anthe had made it out to be.

As we were boarding the Galatea, Tiberius banteringly demanded to know how I could justify procuring a new textile when I had not yet finished sorting through the morass I already possessed. When I gave craving hopeless and incurable as my excuse, he rolled his eyes and Antonia giggled. We lunched on eggs beaten together with onions and oysters—without Augustus, who was attending a repast the municipal council was holding in his honor, and whose digestion onions and oysters threatened anyway.

Antonia dominated our luncheon conversation. With elan unabashed she described our adventure, punching or kicking Tiberius whenever he interrupted her narrative with his usual guying. Having thoroughly enjoyed the excursion myself, I was feeling placidly contented and increasingly assuaged with relief, as the tribulations of the previous day and night faded into memory. Sex that afternoon conveyed an exceptionally sweet and soothing exchange of mutual approbation and commitment; for now I was reveling in gratitude for the assertion Tiberius had made the day before. Clytia Neronis, wife to Tiberius Claudius Nero and mother of Tiberius Claudius Alcimus, was the only identity I possessed for certain. It was wondrous, and all I needed.

While we lay resting I began to dream. In bright daylight I was standing in at the entrance to the Campanian property from the public roadway. With me were Livia, Tiberius, and a stripling lad who I realized represented Alcimus down the future. Anthe, Euethia, and Philo appeared, hastening toward us on the road. The two women were livid with indignation.

"Who do you think you are, bringing visitors to our villa without consulting me?" Anthe demanded hotly.

"They are my family, which you are not; and they have asked to see this unpleasant memento of my childhood." So I replied with perfect composure.

"I will allow nothing of the sort," Anthe returned, her choler waxing. "How typically inconsiderate and self-centered of you, to presume you might escort total strangers about the place—not only without first obtaining my permission, but without allowing me to supervise the tour."

Throughout this upbraiding, Euethia vigorously nodded wholehearted approval while Philo stared with his usual vacuity.

"As the property has been proven mine, I may exercise and enjoy the privilege of showing it to whomever I please." Again I spoke with unruffled confidence, which Euethia proceeded to decry as impertinence indicative of the lowest grade of humanity. Anthe said nothing in return, but began to stride aggressively toward the property's gate to block our access—in the very ungainly manner for which she would have berated me soundly.

All at once a great fog emerged, and like a wall separated Anthe and her companions from me and mine. Imbued with a strange luminosity, it scintillated like gossamer in the wind. Nevertheless it was thoroughly opaque: those on either side could neither see nor hear the persons on the other. My party and I proceeded through the gate, and along the path up the hill to where the house stood. We discovered the building a barren white ruin, evocative of a weather-bleached skeleton. Only then did I notice the land itself was utterly devoid of anything living. The trees were gone, the shrubs, the grass, the very weeds and brambles. Only dry, hardened tan soil strewn with rocks remained. The pond in which I had fished was nothing more than a dusty shallow depression in this desert. But directly beyond the wall enclosing the demesne, lush verdure lay all around.

With a start I awoke, to discover the walls and ceiling of our chamber sparkling with coruscations of sunlight reflected off the waves. The orientation of the yacht had shifted, allowing the capture of these glitters. Observing them, I felt intrigued by the coincidence of their appearance with the corrective described above. Fascination became awe, which set me to trembling and stirring a bit. My movement roused Tiberius, who asked if I were all right. Excitedly I described the dream, and with élan increasing my interpretation of it.

Although my recollections of life with the Eupistodoi were as vivid as ever, they now rankled but minimally. These memories were no more than bad dreams, from which one emerges with relief they were only dreams—remembered sometimes with bewilderment and sometimes with amusement but never with distress. The memory of my life with my foster family was a barren wasteland, to be abandoned for the replete reality of the genuine world—not to be continuously cultivated; certainly not to be imposed upon the family of which I was now a member; and above all not transmitted to my posterity.

In the extraordinarily unlikely event an Eupistodou might someday recognize me and offer genuine apologies and amends, I would of course graciously and gratefully accept them. Diminishing in my conscience, however, was the desperate longing for such rapprochement, and the smoldering frustration because it was not forthcoming. Disappearing as well was the lingering desire I had battled for so long: my wish to see the Eupistodoi miserable with remorse for having mistreated me. At long last I was managing to abandon my lifelong struggle to pardon the unpardonable. How ironically this surrender had not come with a brilliant flourish and tremulous éclat, but as naturally as unobtrusively as breathing.

Since the weather had cooled, our company returned to the customary habit of bathing before supper. Noting my quietude, Livia inquired whether something was troubling me. Not yet ready to articulate what I was contemplating, I assured her nothing was amiss and I was simply physically and emotionally fatigued—no lie, for in fact I was. But the question Augustus posed, during our supper of roasted fowl from the Neapolitan markets, brown bread and sliced sweet capsicum peppers, elicited an emphatic response.

"Well, my Clytia, have you given any thought to your newly discovered possession?"

"Presuming you mean the property near Nola, I propose ceding it to Anthe."

There was a collective gasp. "Are you all right?" Tiberius inquired incredulously. He placed his hand on my forehead as though to determine whether I was feverish.

"Throughout history, in every known society including our own, land has been regarded as an invaluable asset to oneself and one's descendants," Augustus replied in a rather didactic tone.

"So long as that land is a genuine asset!" I retorted. Catching myself, reminding myself to whom I was speaking, I lowered my voice and continued in far meeker deportment. "With all due respect: what use could I possibly have for a minuscule and eroded stretch of rocks, weeds, briers, dust, and miserable memories, when I already own the replete and productive farm on Rhodes?"

"Suppose the tenant or another has improved the condition of the Campanian property?"

"It is far too small to be a viable farm. The Rhodian tract is ten times larger at least and under full cultivation; yet it is no more than self-sustaining."

"The Campanian property may never be viable as a farm. However, if the tenant has turned it into an attractive country retreat—the use for which Anthe intended it but never had the funds to realize—its value could have soared."

My rationale was becoming more and more clearly defined, and my determination firmer. "The place is tiny—maybe twice the size of the Gardens of Maecenas. It cannot be worth terribly much, even if in pristine condition—which I certainly hope is not the case. Why? Because the higher the value of the land, the higher the taxes on it. Right now the income from renting the property pays the taxes. Suppose I acknowledge ownership and subsequently lose the tenant. Then I shall have to pay the taxes directly out of my own coffers, or go through the trouble of procuring another tenant. Forfeiture to the Museion transfers this problem to them—and unfairly, in my opinion. Since the property is so small, I rather suspect the trouble of keeping track of the tenant and the taxes from afar will outweigh any financial benefit either the Museion or I could derive from it."

"You would show Anthe such altruism after she afflicted you so sorely? You are entitled to sue her for defrauding you."

Strongly I suspected Augustus' line of questioning was rhetorical—a test of my character. It roused me to put into words the new perspective I had gained. My intensity returned. Folding my arms, I rested them on the table before me and leaned forward, shifting my eyes to each member of my audience as I spoke. "Sue her for what? Recovery of the original 75 talents? She has no assets to surrender. Require she, her son, and her aunt be sold as slaves? I wonder whether their purchase prices combined would equal the amount they pilfered. They have no refined skills: the very household chores they performed and complained about were incompetently executed. Garnishing Philo's wages until the debt is paid may obligate him to me for the remainder of his life. I do not need the 75 talents. And furthermore: I hardly want such cruelties as deliberate enslavement or prolonged indebtedness weighing upon my conscience.

"Remember: I know Anthe far, far better than any of you. Neither suing her nor prolonging her present financial predicament will impel her to regret her ill treatment of me, nor heal the painful wounds she afflicted upon my psyche. Nor will duress stimulate her to abandon her frivolous spending habits. The present solution Livia has outlined will not be permanent. Anthe will get into another financial impasse, then another and thereafter another. Each time she will come whining back to Livia or the praetor for rescue, always maintaining her predicaments are everyone else's fault but never hers. Moreover, suing Anthe will make me visible to her. The satisfaction of discovering what became of me after I fled her domicile I do not care to give her.

"With utmost respect for the program Livia has delineated, I urge offering the property to Anthe with two caveats. First off she may not retain the tract, but must sell it and apply the proceeds toward her debt. Secondly being neither a Roman citizen herself nor wife to a Roman citizen, she may never again solicit financial assistance from Livia or from any Roman magistrate elected or appointed. If you lead her to believe these requirements will impose some sort of hardship on me, I can virtually guarantee she will accept them!"

A brief silence ensued. Augustus, who had been watching me as though mildly intrigued, raised his eyebrows and drawled pensively. "The art of forfeiture: losing what is of lesser value but comfortably obvious, to gain that which is worthier but not as immediately tangible. For three decades and more I have observed politicians and bureaucrats struggle—oftentimes vainly—to embrace this concept. You have seen the same in military circles," he added as he turned to Tiberius, who nodded. Shifting his steely gaze back to me, Augustus continued, "And you, my dear, came by it ever so naturally—proving all the more you are one of us, one of our kind. Livia, my Livia, I presume you have ordered an assessment of the property."

"Oh yes."

"The place cannot not be entirely worthless. If its value proves less than what Anthe owes, she must accept it as partial remediation of her debt. In the meanwhile, let us put this and all other matters of serious concern out of mind. As of now, we are vacationing! Come the morrow we set sail for Capri, there to remain for the duration of the month named in my honor."

Following supper the gaming board was brought out. I prevailed as that evening's overall winner with five Venus throws.

While we were breakfasting the next morning, the yacht set sail. The air was clear and comfortably tepid, the sky intensely blue. Off waves of similar hue the sunlight glanced in blinding flashes. The dolphins were back, glimmering almost golden as they leapt. The morning I passed in finalizing my sketch of the escort ship. The product turned out better than I had anticipated. Throughout its development, the uninterrupted presence of the actual escorts had provided me with models continually.

While we were lunching on biscuits and boiled eggs, the craggy hills of Capri began to loom larger and larger on the horizon. We proceeded along the coastline, where verdant vales lay between jagged cliffs rising directly out of the sea. After passing a port bustling with fishing and pleasure craft, we halted in a cove at the farthest end of the island. There a monotreme was already at anchor. A launch set forth from the dock on the beach and pulled alongside the yacht. Our servants departed first, to ensure our quarters were in order. After about an hour we boarded the launch, which transported us to the dock where a carriage awaited. On a sinuous road, lined with vegetation ablaze with blossoms, we ascended one of the rocky promontories delineating the cove's boundaries. Across its end spread the great villa that was our destination.

The villa was about the size of the one at Anzio if not larger, and square rather than rectangular. Its exterior had an intriguing facade, with rocks of varying colors embedded in tan stucco. Water was collected in a great cistern, as on the Rhodian farm. Only about a third of the villa—the section directly overlooking the cove—was devoted to the family. The remaining portions, as on the yacht, consisted of offices and meeting rooms, and of lodging for guests, clerical staff, praetorians, and visiting officials. I had not realized, until now, that similar accommodations at the Anzio villa were the reason it was so immense. The presence of these functionaries, along with the monoreme, belied Augustus' affirmation of pure vacation. His Chimera never relented from her demands.

Even in its administrative areas, though, the villa was designed for relaxation. Its rooms were spacious and airy and—as at Anzio—decorated with mosaics and paintings oceanic in theme. A semicircular colonnade at the promontory's end precisely matched its curvature. Here was a place to stroll or sit, while enjoying sea breezes and spectacular views of land, cove, and the Bay of Naples. The colonnade enclosed a garden where, on that very evening of our arrival, Augustus held a delightful feast for his government staff. The fare was octopus simmered with vegetables and paste in seasoned broth: a local delicacy, said to enhance one's physical vitality and libido. A jocular discussion of this attribute prompted Augustus to quip, that while at his age no remedy could be guaranteed successful he was still willing to try any. Actually he did not partake of the repast, having dined ahead of time on his favorite black bread and potted cow's milk cheese.

The very next morning, Tiberius announced he was determined to teach me the wondrous skill I had never acquired: swimming. He led me to a section of beach in the cove, where when I stood in water reaching no higher than my waist. That first day he taught me nothing more than how to stay afloat on my back.

The day following—the Calends of August—was the birthday of Tiberius Drusus. We gave him a little party in the garden, where Livia sat near the exit to the colonnade in case she had to escape. Young Tiberius was quite taken with my sketch of the escort ship. He examined it assiduously, turning it to different angles and not uttering a word until—prompted by Antonia—he distractedly stammered thanks without taking his eyes from the tableau. The arrival of pastries turned the promising art aficionado into Philo. Casting the sketch aside he lunged at the platter with rapture unabashed. After a while I began to dread a repetition of what Philo had done on that fateful birthday of mine in Campania—until the ever-watchful Antonia slapped his hand and declared he had had absolutely enough.

So began the month which remains one of the most pleasurable reminiscences of my life. The island proved a place of seemingly endless fascination. It was indeed the artist's idyll I had always heard it to be, if not more. On the third day following our arrival a light white haze overspread what had been dazzling blue skies. Briefly I was disappointed, until I realized the overcast moderated into soft pastels the colors of our surroundings—the sky, the sea, the foliage abounding with flowers of every conceivable shape and color, the rocks of eroded hillsides, the villa without and within. As you have likely concluded, Dear Reader, I passed many an hour recording that myriad of hues. Many an evening after supper I played my harp while we sat in garden or colonnade, watching the setting sun turn water and sky fiery, and then to those smoky shades of rose, bronze, and slate, which I recalled from our voyages through the Sirocco and from our stay at Anzio.

Testy and irritating as we all had been through the rains of April, is how relaxed and easygoing we now became. Every morning during the first week of our sojourn, in pre-dawn twilight Tiberius and I repaired to the cove. Our purpose was to complete the day's lesson in swimming before the sun became sufficiently intense to tan my skin. Once I was able to remain afloat on my back without sinking he instructed me in floating prone, raising my head to inhale and immersing it to exhale in a stream of bubbles. Kicks and arm strokes followed. By the end of that week I was reasonably adept at paddling myself about. Tiberius cautioned me never to swim in unfamiliar waters, lest I encounter a riptide or some other dangerous condition—and never without a companion present who could aid me in difficulty. We continued to frequent the cove beach to swim purely for pleasure, if not early in the morning then just before sunset, for the remainder of the month. One day he penned an epigram extolling my efforts:

Sleek and graceful as the dolphin, Apollo's scion,
The sea nymph glides glimmering through the waves;
The sea foam parts before her, frothing in envy
Of resplendent loveliness rivaling its daughter's.
*[Greek legend maintained Aphrodite, goddess of beauty and amatory love,
was born of sea foam.]*

Every day without fail, Tiberius repaired to the library to pore over star charts; and every day he found nothing remarkable. The cerulean forces, he said, appeared to be vacationing right along with those terrestrial.

Tiberius also pursued his other favored pastime of visiting and rendering assistance to the sick and their families. He asked me to accompany him on one of these trips and bring my harp. Our destination was the inn at the center of the port village past which we had sailed. Imagine my start, when I found its main gathering room hung with Eutychus of Rhodes reproductions!! They were six Greek legendary scenes: Bellerophon astride Pegasus, Phryxis and Helle astride the ram of golden fleece, Atlas supporting the world on his shoulders, Admetus with his chariot harnessed to lions and boars, Icarus falling from the sky, and the once notorious Lion of Nemea.

The invalid was the innkeeper's wife, who was recovering from a miscarriage. The couple occupied a pleasant apartment adjoining the rear of the inn. They had two children, who sat at my feet and gazed up at me open-mouthed while I played and sang for about half an hour. Tiberius introduced me as a friend of his sister-in-law Antonia. On our journey back to the villa Tiberius explained he did not introduce me as Eutychus' pupil, lest our hosts start asking me questions about my *teacher* and I must conjure answers ad libitum.

Augustus and I resumed our candid conversations. Capri was a place of special meaning for him. When he started to relate the circumstances whereby he had acquired ownership of the island. I interrupted him, confessing Tiberius had already told me about the dying oak springing back to life within days of Augustus' arrival. "A holly oak, to be precise; and it is still alive. Come, let me show you." As we headed to the garden, he explained that he had leased the villa in which the phenomenon had occurred. Following the auspicious incident he had promptly purchased the place. Over the years he had implemented enlargements and improvements, which had rendered the villa practically unrecognizable from when he had first acquired it. The holly was immense. The vibrant deep green of its leaves, and the lack of dried leaves and branches within its foliage, attested to its health. During the course of our stay on Capri,

I painted two vignettes of the tree. One was placed in the villa's library. The other Augustus took with him back to Rome, to be placed in his study.

With considerable pride Augustus showed me the two collections he kept at the villa. The one was a store of antique weapons and armaments. "Had any been used in the Trojan War?" I wondered aloud while admiring the spiral relief on a bronze shield covered with a patina of dark green tarnish. "I like to assume they were," Augustus returned reflectively. His other congeries were as grotesque as intriguing. They were skeletal remains—mostly the skulls—of bizarre creatures, which he had discovered on the island in the grottoes and in rock outcroppings in the cliffs above the coves. Once having overcome my initial revulsion I painstakingly studied the skulls and other bones, conjectured how muscles and skin must have overlaid them, and made sketches accordingly. These efforts revealed two goats with long flat faces suggestive of a trowel, a squirrel as big as a housecat, a small and oddly elongated lion, and a diminutive hippopotamus (of all creatures!) perhaps the size of Sannio. There was a host of fearsome-looking fish some of which had fangs, a goodly assortment of weird shells, and a large sea creature vaguely resembling a dolphin. Augustus' favorite was a bona fide monster. It was slightly bigger than an eagle, had the head and teeth of a lizard, the body and limbs of a bat, and a thin sinuous tail longer than its body [the pterosaur Eudimorphodon]. "Could it be possible," Augustus speculated, "that harpies are neither divine nor mythological but materially mortal after all, and this the remains of one?"

The possibility of a connection between the real world, and that which we consider spectral, must have fired my imagination unawares. During wakefulness several nights later, I heard eerie calls emanating from the sea. They sounded uncannily like female voices, wailing as though in mourning. I arose and hastened onto the exterior colonnade, where presently Tiberius joined me. "Are we actually hearing the cries of Sirens?" I asked as my skin began to crawl. With a chuckle he replied. "The local inhabitants are quite fond of assuring newcomers the sounds are indeed the singing of Sirens. Being heard only at this time of year renders them all the more mysterious. Nevertheless they are simply the voices of migrating orca whales calling to one another."

The denizens of Capri have a flippant, saucy side—the character trait that inclined them to dupe gullible tourists with disconcerting but harmless fibs. The convivial and carefree insouciance with which the locals go about their daily business—putting off to another day and time whatever did not absolutely have to be accomplished immediately—had once prompted Augustus to call them a population of do-nothings. One morning Antonia suggested she and I spend the entire day at the port village. When we exited the litter at the entry gate, Antonia gave the bearers leave to go about as they pleased, so long as they checked back from time to time to see whether we were ready to depart.

There was not terribly much to see: shops offering wares for everyday use, greengrocers, fishmongers, two taverns, the inn with the Eutychus reproductions, and a temple to Neptune. Nevertheless I enjoyed our foray immensely. The simplicity of the place was wonderfully refreshing. Wandering through the forum, about the streets, along the wharf where fishermen were mending their nets and tending their boats, and at the public bathing beach, we were greeted cordially and as though we were as ordinary as the shopkeepers and fishermen. There was no adulation, no fawning, no speculative stares and whispering. We lunched at one of the taverns on conch cooked with fennel—a local specialty. Our attendants and praetorians sat at an adjacent table. The other patrons glanced at us and some of them smiled, before returning their attention back to their own repasts as indifferently as though they had observed a group of strangers utterly unknown. The staff treated us with pleasant courtesy but extended us no greater deference than to anyone else.

Antonia had brought her harp to Capri. She proved to be more accomplished at playing it than she had led me to believe. We spent many a delightful afternoon together, improvising duets. Antonia was also phenomenally adept at the art of embroidery. I watched intrigued as she separated threads into their component fibers, then stretched and anchored these across established designs, to represent the veins of leaves or the subtle stria of petals or feathers. When I voiced my admiration, she pointed out the difference between our hands and fingers. Mine are somewhat short, and broad. Hers despite her statuesque build were long and slender, and hence more suited than mine to maneuvering delicate fibers into intricate patterns.

The conversations I shared with Antonia, candid and intimate, tightened the bond of friendship between us. We shared notions as trivial as our favorite colors: hers yellow, mine pink; our favorite foods: hers lamb (she laughed at my grimace), mine swordfish; our favorite pastimes: mine drawing and painting, hers embroidering and reading romances. She commiserated with my growing frustration over my prolonged separation from Alcimus. Thrasyllus' most recent letter reported Alcimus was walking about freely, and had started to talk—to say a few single words on his own, and to repeat back whole phrases spoken to him. I had missed seeing my son's first steps, and now hearing his first speech.

Antonia in turn confided to me the grave concerns she harbored for her children down the future. Would Germanicus' cocky arrogance induce his cousin and brother-in-law Gaius to consider him a potential political enemy, either before or after Gaius had assumed Augustus' position? Would Livilla be able to carry out the services to the regime Livia presently performed, as willingly and successfully as did Livia? Would Tiberius Drusus as an adult be an incorrigible buffoon, a lifelong embarrassment to his family? Antonia adamantly refused to let me disparage my maternal concerns as mere trivialities beside hers. What could be more legitimate than a mother's desire to be reunited with her child, and to insure his future wellbeing whatever pattern that must take?

On Capri even Tiberius Drusus and Postumus seemed more agreeable—the former less obtuse, the latter less threatening. This villa, like that of Maecenas, had a large and replete library; and as at the Villa Maecenatis, it became the younger Tiberius' favorite resort. With polite poise he would ask me questions about philosophy or literature or sciences. And when one or more of his elders engaged me in discussions of these topics, young Tiberius for the most part listened attentively and did not interrupt. There were fewer otiose interjections, and far less effete yammering. Postumus spent the greater part of his days fishing, and after a few initial tantrums started shrugging off disappointing catches as angler's angst. Twice he watched Tiberius and me when we swam at the cove beach, and complimented me on my neophyte efforts. But during our third session together he jumped into the water, attempted to hold my head under, then initiated a fistfight with Tiberius for stopping him. Thereafter Tiberius and I conspired, with Nomius and with Postumus' valet Albinus, to distract Postumus from going to the cove when we wanted to swim or lure him away when he was already there.

Livia no longer struck me as arrogantly imperious but as drivingly benign. She confessed that until the actual encounter with Anthe, she had neither fully understood nor appreciated the virulence of the emotional agony with which the Eupistodoi had afflicted me. On a day near to the middle of the month, instead of insisting I come before her, she sought me in the garden where I was sketching the vista across the bay. She was carrying two tablets.

"I have received from Poppaeus the assessor's findings," she began as she seated herself beside me and opened one of the tablets. "The property turns out to be worth just about what is owed the usurer. The tenant has kept the house in good repair, but allowed the condition of the land to deteriorate immeasurably. This is the reason the valuation is so low. The neighbors are chafing about the purported use of the place as a secluded rendezvous site for a group of male lovers." She looked at me with a mischievous smirk. "Could the broker—that *fine young man* who befriended Philo—be one of them?"

"Hardly would it surprise me," I mused. "Philo has been so pampered and protected and dominated by his mother and great-aunt, he is likely to feel comfortable with effeminacy and intimidated by genuine virility."

"At any rate, I presume you still wish to surrender the property."

"Most assuredly: I want neither the scruffy place nor the scruffy tenant."

Livia opened the other tablet and handed it to me. "What do you think of this letter I have drafted?"

> Livia Caesaris to Philo Eupistides and his mother Anthe, Greetings.
>
> The assessor appointed by Aulus Poppaeus Sabinus, Praetor of the City of Naples, has valued at 382,500 sesterces the property against which you illicitly borrowed. This amount is sufficient to repay your obligation—in kind if the property is ceded to your creditor directly, or in cash if it is sold.
>
> Discovery of your former ward alive and legally married establishes her husband as curator. Not wishing to retain the property, they approve surrender of its ownership to you. We strongly encourage you to accept their offer; for down the future neither I nor any government agency will entertain further petitions from you for financial remediation. To preserve the anonymity of the ward and her spouse, Tiberius Claudius Nero will serve as curator ex officio for this transfer of ownership.

"As splendid as I expected," I said with great sincerity as I returned the tablet. "Succinct and forthright; yet it speaks volumes. Anthe will be ever so frustrated, on discovering she can neither come crawling back to you for aid nor find out what became of me and whom I married."

"Then you approve the letter?"

"Oh most wholeheartedly! I only hope Anthe accepts its terms."

"If she does not, she will be stuck with her debt. Then you will sell the property for whatever price moves it promptly, even if that price is below the assessed value. After all you are not interested in making a profit off of it."

The sharp insights of Livia, so highly esteemed by Augustus, I reflected as I nodded my understanding with a heartfelt smile.

On the morning of my birthday, I awoke to find myself alone in bed. While dressing me, Nausicaa said Tiberius had gone to call upon another sick client. After breakfasting by myself in our suite, I repaired to Augustus' gallery of bones to finish fleshing out the little hippopotamus. Only the servants were about. In response to my inquiry, one of them told me Augustus and Livia were in the villa's administrative area addressing a matter of state, and Antonia was busy with Tiberius Drusus. Not seeing Postumus either, I assumed he was fishing at the cove. There were no decorations in the villa, as there had been for the birthday of Tiberius Drusus. Perhaps since I was not a member of the family by birth, it was felt I did not merit decorations in their domicile. So I mused as I sat sketching, not without a bit of hurt. Close to midday, Tiberius finally appeared and insisted I accompany him to see yet another invalid. This time I need not bring my harp. When I complained about starting to feel hungry he replied that he was as well, but our visit was going to be brief.

The litter transported us to the dock in the cove, where we boarded a small but wide boat. It had a cloth canopy to shield us from the sun. After skirting a short distance of the coastline, the boat turned directly toward the cliffs. I assumed we were going to enter a rivulet leading inland, until all at once a boatman collapsed the canopy, and we passed through a natural arch into a grotto. Here the water actually glowed with blue light! And as if that were not enough, Tiberius' hand and forearm when thrust into the water appeared coated with silver. The mysterious illumination, he said, was somehow related to the light of day, for it waned at nightfall and when clouds passed overhead.

Along a beach of sorts at the grotto's widest point, there extended a man-made stone veranda. It was replete with tables and benches covered with cushions, and statues of Nereids draped with banners aplenty. Our boat pulled up to a stone dock upon which we disembarked. The entire family was awaiting us—even Postumus and Tiberius Drusus, who were seated as always at a separate table some distance from the main. The surfaces I expected to be damp and clammy, but found they were not. Holding warm on a brazier was a luncheon of fresh crustaceans: a much favored local delicacy, which we peeled and munched with delight. As the steward began laying the table, Tiberius suddenly moved behind me. I felt something hard and cool strike my chest just above the top of my chiton. It was a large stone, transparently blue like the waters of the grotto, suspended from a chain of gold and silver links. And just like those waters, the stone glimmered and scintillated with the vibrantly shifting light. To my skin the necklace imparted a soothing sense much like that of my pearls, but with coolness rather than warmth.

Augustus said the family had been discussing, ever since our arrival on Capri, whether to show me this marine nymphaeum sooner or keep it as a birthday surprise. Now aware of the Azure Cave as they called it, I should feel free to come here whenever I like and bring my paints and palettes. All I need do is ask a steward at the villa to ready litter and boat. Wiping tears of jubilation from my eyes with Tiberius' kerchief, I burbled my reply. Keeping the grotto secret until our sojourn was half over limited the number of times I could return before we must depart for Rome. Nevertheless the birthday surprise was well worth the wait.

Return to the Azure Cave I did, many more times during the remainder of that month. Some trips I made with paints and palettes, and my only companion a thoroughly delighted Nausicaa. Those marvelously vibrant blues, greens, pale yellows and whites, even grays and occasional reds, all shone with jewel-like luminosity which I labored intently to reproduce. On other occasions I repaired there with Tiberius, with Antonia, with both, and with the entire family—for reading, conversing, gaming, or simply resting and letting the beauty of the environs refresh our senses.

We all grew mellow, through the salubriously warm days and sultry nights and delectable local dishes of that waning August. A message from Thrasyllus added to our euphoria. Directly on my birthday, Aka had delivered a son—a month premature, but still robustly healthy. Thrasyllus was now making ready the transition to Italy of their entire household, and of Alcimus with his.

The only disappointment marring the rapture we felt was the prospect of its coming to an end. Augustus wanted to quit Capri no later than the Calends of September, to insure himself several days upon returning to Rome to prepare for the Ludi Romani. Presumably at Anthe's insistence, Philo had accepted Livia's proposal. Poppaeus advised his first tribunal for September was scheduled for the Calends. If the date suited us, he would place our case first on his docket. We agreed; and Augustus set the eve of that appointment for our departure.

The steady drizzle which fell all that day, Augustus declared a particularly favorable omen for a pleasant journey and safe return. His prognosis concurred with the numerological forecast Tiberius had made the day before. The rain also helped mollify our regret over having to leave Capri. Had the weather remained idyllic, departure would have been tortuously difficult. We set sail in midafternoon to reach Naples before nightfall, since the stars were not likely to be visible thereafter. Having to take our supper of grilled whiting in the yacht's enclosed dining room instead of on her veranda, was an additional reminder the serene repose of summer was over and the business of autumn waited to be addressed.

On the morrow the harbor was enveloped in fog. Standing on the veranda inhaling the vapors, I watched the launch emerge from the mist and draw alongside the yacht to collect Tiberius for his mission. At the very moment the launch was disappearing into it, the fog for a brief moment became a brilliant pale yellow before reverting to its somber grayness. This sudden penetration of sunlight reminded me of the similar incident long ago, which had occurred while Phoebe was bringing me to discover Tiberius' true identity. Was today's event as favorable an omen as the former?

On retreating to the dayroom, I found Antonia embroidering alone. Augustus and Livia, she said, were in the administrative sector with their secretaries, already reviewing the roster of meetings and appointments to be addressed upon our return. Why, Antonia continued, was I so fond of fog? Her question forced me to define my partiality once and for all. I described how fog's quietude calmed my nerves. Its cooling vapors refreshed my skin while soothing and cleansing nostrils, sinuses, and lungs. This physical reinvigoration in turn impelled clearer mental perspectives. Ideas and aspirations became more definitive, concerns and difficulties less threatening.

In my life, fog always seemed to appear whenever I was poised to make a significant commitment. Amid a fog, Tiberius and I had recognized our relationship not as a passing whim but a permanent commitment to one another. Amid a fog he had asked for my hand in marriage. And barely a month ago, on this very yacht, amid a fog I had abandoned my lingering sense of commitment to the Eupistodoi—that ineffectual wavering between desire for vengeance and hope for forgiveness and reconciliation. In that same fog I had reaffirmed my commitment to Tiberius, to the child with which he had blessed me, and to his family who had accepted me as one of their own and committed themselves to my prosperity. "So what commitment does this morning's fog elicit?" Antonia inquired jocularly. "None I have discerned so far," I confessed. "We have yet to witness its pledge."

Even as I spoke the fog was dissipating, to reveal a slightly hazy sky patched with fluffy gray and white clouds. The humid air rapidly grew very warm and made the dayroom oppressive, so Antonia and I exited to the veranda. Anon we were joined by Livia, and shortly thereafter by an impatient Augustus who had hoped to be under sail by now. Tiberius had been gone for well over an hour. Why was a mere transfer of ownership taking so long? At length the launch arrived. The yacht's sails raised and her oars dropped. We were underway before Tiberius reached the veranda.

When he did arrive, he slumped into a chair as though bone weary. For several moments he remained silent, his eyes closed and his hands in his lap. Finally he sighed and murmured, "What an encounter!"

"They quarreled about the offer," Augustus ventured.

"Not at all." Tiberius opened his eyes, sat upright, and continued forthrightly. "While Poppaeus read off the terms of the agreement, Philo stood at my side before the tribunal, staring openmouthed as though he did not comprehend a single word. After I handed him the stylus he stood gaping at it in his hand, until Poppaeus instructed him to sign his name beneath mine on the document. Throughout this process Anthe stood to one side scowling, but did not utter a sound. However once the business was over, as we were preparing to exit the courtroom she approached me, curtsied, and quite graciously asked if she might have a word. Poppaeus had a notary escort the two of us and my praetorians to an antechamber.

"She spoke nervously, hesitantly, choosing her words carefully. 'Most beneficent Tiberius Nero, do you...are you...Sir, have you made the acquaintance of our Clytia?' 'I have had that wondrous pleasure,' I returned, struggling against the temptation to challenge the *our Clytia* and wondering whether my response would evoke a scornful rejoinder. It did not. Still cautious she continued, 'Did she by chance disclose to you why she fled our domicile?'

"'You set for her standards of academic achievement you knew she could not possibly meet, and heaped recrimination upon her without mercy when she fell short of those unattainable expectations. You neglected her physical appearance, refinement of her social skills, and worst of all her health. The aberrant gynecological condition you ignored nearly killed her. Fortuitously her husband engaged a capable midwife who was able to detect, arrest, and reverse the deterioration.'

"Now Anthe waxed indignant. 'The gods be thanked she survived,' she scoffed dismissively, as though I had described your recovery from a skinned knee. 'We had no reason to suspect the condition was life-threatening, and deemed the infrequency of her menses a blessing for her. Primping and etiquette can be learned at any time of life. We feared teaching them to Clytia while she was completing her education would distract her from her studies and induce vanity. Clytia had the potential to become a sophista, and acquire the fame and wealth which accrue to such unique women. She steadfastly resisted our efforts to prepare her for this career, and received our purposeful rebukes in return.

We raised Clytia in the same manner my father raised my brother and me. His chastisements I accepted with gratitude. They forced me to evaluate and improve upon my motives and aspirations, my viewpoints and actions.'

"'The upbringing that worked on the parent will not necessarily work on the child,' I returned evenly. 'Each of us has a nature all our own. My son Drusus is hardly the individual I was at his age. Your relationship with Clytia may have been far more harmonious, had you employed a method of upbringing better suited to her particular character.'

"'In other words, you are saying we should have pampered and indulged her!'

"'Not at all,' I countered, managing to remain placid and successfully resisting the urge to include, *as you pampered and indulged your son.* 'I only submit that corrective processes, when excessively and unnecessarily harsh, elicit defiance and rebellion instead of respectful and willing compliance. Mistress Anthe, allow me to tell you a brief story.' I proceeded to relate the incident when you"—here he glanced at Augustus— "dismissed that insubordinate legate, up to the point when the youth defiantly demanded how he could explain the discharge to his father. Then I put to Anthe the question, 'What, pray tell, would have been your response?'

"'Why I would have told that boy his question was entirely out of line, and he fully deserved whatever punishment his father chose to inflict upon him!'

"After concluding the story with your reply of, *Tell your father I was not to your liking,* I elaborated upon its effect. 'The nexus of this story has utterly eluded you, Mistress Anthe. Caesar understood the dismissal itself sufficed as a reprimand for the infraction. Had he delivered the rejoinder you recommended, he would have turned that youth into a potentially lifelong enemy. Now with Clytia: you persistently went beyond what was necessary to correct and adjust her behavior. You aggrieved her and blasted her self-respect with egregious humiliation and personal degradation. The present discovery, that you led her to believe she was your natural daughter so you could embezzle her patrimony, gives her cause for yet greater resentment. Quite palpably the rigorous upbringing for which you credit your father failed to instill in you a sense of ethics. The cruel and deceitful methods you perpetrated upon Clytia have made her your lifelong enemy.'

"By now Anthe was red-faced and trembling with fury—not surprisingly, in consideration of what I had just said. 'The country retreat was intended for the pleasure of our entire family, Clytia included! Why should she alone enjoy the benefits of her stipend, and the Eupistodoi have no compensation? We sheltered, fed, clothed, and reared her; and for our efforts she returned nothing but insolence. She owes us that property! You accuse us of having abused her. Well she abused us, with her blatant defiance and ingratitude!'

"Struggling to maintain my composure I continued, 'The original stipend was intended specifically for Clytia's maintenance, and should have been budgeted accordingly. Its amount was quite substantial. Had you determined it inadequate to meet her needs, you could have requested an increase from the Museion. However you would have had to justify your petition, with proof the monies were being used exclusively for Clytia's upkeep. Legally, Clytia owes you nothing. She had every right to retain that property for herself, leaving you to struggle with the debt you incurred by fraudulently presenting her possession as collateral. She still has the right to demand a full accounting—to ascertain whether there were other ways in which her stipend was utilized apart from its original purpose, and to sue you for recovery of squandered funds. Yet she chooses not to invoke those rights. She ceded the property to you, when she could have sold it for her own profit or forfeited it to the Museion. Such is hardly the conduct of a defiant ingrate!'

"I expected another scathing rebuttal. But after glowering at me in silence for a rather prolonged space of time, Anthe lowered her eyes and assumed a morose expression. 'How do you come to know Clytia so well?' she asked petulantly, without looking up. I gave no response. 'What sort of man did she marry—Greek? Italian? What is his profession? Can he afford to maintain her in comfortable circumstances?' I continued to hold my peace. 'You are not going to tell me anything about her, are you?' she finally concluded irascibly as she raised her eyes to glare at me once more.

"'Mistress Anthe,' I replied steadily, 'Clytia took flight to exclude you from her life. From that time until this very day she has been striving to exclude you from her memories. You need to do likewise. And remember: Clytia does not want you to discover her whereabouts or her new identity. Should you attempt to seek these out, her husband and his family will intervene to thwart your efforts; and you are likely to find their obstruction very, very hurtful.'

"She lowered her eyes again. When, after another long pause, she raised them they were brimming with tears. Slowly and now plaintively she said, 'Will you please tell Clytia that we—my son here, my aunt, and I myself—wish her happiness and prosperity, and that we all still love her and miss her terribly?' 'I shall for certain, Mistress Anthe,' I returned as gently as I could, suppressing the temptation to add, *although I sincerely doubt she will believe you.* Anthe daubed her eyes with the hem of her veil as she drew it across her face. She curtsied to me again, and then hastened to the door without uttering another word. Her son, who had stood by expressionless and silent throughout the entire conversation, followed her like an obedient dog without casting a glance at me or the notary."

For a time the five of us sat silent, reflecting upon Tiberius' account. Presently Augustus said, "A rebuke well deserved and well delivered."

Tiberius' narrative left me unsettled, nonplussed. "Never have I known Anthe to weep for any reason apart from anger at me—certainly never for repentance," I pondered aloud.

"Perhaps she was simply frustrated because she could not rebut my imprecations of her and my defense of you," Tiberius returned sardonically.

"Nor do I recall her speaking reverentially of her father on any occasion," I continued. "She persistently described him as obdurately authoritarian, unrelentingly and oftentimes purposelessly afflictive."

"As she was to you," said Livia.

New and intriguing insights were emerging within my conscience. "She hardly ever mentioned her brother," I added. "The few times she did, she invariably denounced him as a shiftless and frowzy oaf."

"As her son is today," Tiberius rejoined.

Another pensive silence followed, which Tiberius broke. Rising from his chair, he bowed to the company and said, "I beg you excuse me, while I go below to shed this overlay," tugging at his toga as he spoke the final word. He took my hand and drew me to my feet. "Come along and assist me, my dearest."

"Plan upon helping him remove his other garments, and all of yours as well," Augustus quipped with a sly smile and wink.

Sex was not Tiberius' intent. "I anticipated you might wish to be alone," he said as we entered his bedchamber.

"You must have read my thoughts," I returned gratefully as I helped him remove his toga. "I was starting to feel crowded upon, and—to my surprise—slightly resentful of your family despite their benevolence. The uncanny manner, in which their conclusions about Anthe were paralleling mine, I found rather unsettling."

"If you like, I shall make excuses for you at luncheon and have victuals sent to you here—on condition you assure me you will eat them and not neglect your nourishment.

"You have that promise, my love."

He took both my hands in his and raised them to his lips, recognizing that in my present mood I would have found an embrace or even a kiss to my forehead overly intrusive. After he departed I lay down on the bed. Listening to the soft rush of the yacht through the water, and the distant nearly inaudible thudding of the hortator's hammers, I was once again in my alcove—but now feeling its calming quietude without the bitter anguish of previous retreats, as new insights about Anthe started to flood my conscience.

Areus had denounced revenge as ethically reprehensible, futile and poisonous—unless it impels reform. Tiberius' rebuke had served vengeance upon Anthe this morning. But did the tears she had shed indicate genuine remorse? Had they rather arisen from frustration and self-pity? Tiberius had denounced her malicious and deceitful treatment of me, shown preposterous her declaration I was a defiant ingrate, and refused to disclose my present whereabouts and condition.

Vengeance had been served. Had it dispelled my own sharp memories of the emotional and physical distress Anthe had inflicted upon me, or assuaged their lingering pain? Not in the least. Nevertheless my perspective had shifted. Gone was the lingering bewilderment: the questioning why Anthe had treated me so cruelly. I had always assumed she had brutalized me premeditatedly, and for no other purpose than to aggrieve. Now I understood she had employed the only model for childrearing she understood. Her imprecations were intended didactically; and she had assumed the umbrages I took were resistance to this intent. From Tiberius' description of her failure to grasp the moral lesson from Augustus' dismissal of the military tribune, I gathered she lacked the capacity to determine when she had gone too far.

Corollaries to my conclusion started coming to thought. Having decided her brother had been favored and indulged over her, Anthe had raised Philo in what she thought was the same fashion. The brother, however, had matured into an intrepid and dynamic entrepreneur, extraordinarily successful at managing and enlarging the family's fulling enterprise. Anthe had cosseted Philo excessively. Either she did not know when to cease, or believed her brother had been indulged far more than he actually was.

Anthe's brother had married the daughter of a Colossian weaver and fathered two sons upon her. Suddenly I recalled a single occasion long forgotten. Anthe had remarked with great bitterness, that her father had proclaimed his daughter-in-law's proficiency at weaving a benchmark for Anthe and Euethia to match. Here was the reason both women had denounced my fascination with textiles and weaving! It had lain before me for half a lifetime, obscured by my own anguish and resentment.

There was a knock on my chamber door. From the anteroom, Nausicaa called out she had brought my lunch. It proved to be a savory, traditionally

Neapolitan ragout of crab meat and vegetables. Among the contents were rounds of parsnips and carrots sliced crosswise. These reminded me of coins, and in turn prompted a reflection upon Anthe's financial habits. Incessantly she had complained there was never enough income to meet basic household needs. Nevertheless she had maintained a townhouse and country retreat as indispensable necessities, and castigated not only me but her husband when either of us dared suggest either one or both could be dispensed with.

The short-lived financial reprieve Publius Norenas had provided my flight had cut short. Thereafter Anthe had reverted to coercion and deception and outright theft, extorting her daughter-in-law's dowry as she had my stipend. Apparently she could no more curtail her profligate spending than she could refrain from harassing me or mollycoddling Philo. More plausible than ever seemed that rumor, which Thrasyllus had said circulated through the academic community at the time of Eupistus' sudden demise: the allegation Anthe had overwhelmed her spouse with unrelenting pressure—driving him to become the sophistos of unsurpassable fame and wealth, for which he lacked the intellectual capacity and personal charisma to achieve.

A subsequent visit to the privy revealed I had started to menstruate. This discovery in turn engendered reflections upon Anthe's neglect of my gynecological health—if neglect, indeed, was the proper word. With a touch of amusement I asked myself what woman, who endured a menses every month, would not envy one who underwent that process only sporadically? Hardly ever had the Eupistodoi discussed my infrequency. Conversations regarding matters even remotely related to sex were scrupulously avoided, because they invariably sent Euethia into a prolonged frenzy of shrieking about blatant prurience. Consultation with a midwife about my condition was consequently out of the question. Owing to the perpetual mismanagement of household funds, the services of a midwife or physician or pharmakeutria had always presaged hardship. Treatments of Philo's ailments invariably took precedence over mine, not only because he was pampered, but also—I now considered with a pang of harsh reality—because he was one of the Eupistodoi while I was not.

The vengeance served this morning had indeed impelled reform—maybe or maybe not in Anthe, but for certain in me! After all those passing years, I had finally forgiven the Eupistodoi! What is forgiveness but the cancellation of a debt? I had confused it with pardon: the permissive indulgence of wrongdoing which encourages repetition of the offense. This misunderstanding explained why, after physically separating myself from the Eupistodoi, I had persisted in ruminating upon and reassessing their abuses—struggling all the while to refrain from doing so and thoroughly annoying Tiberius in the process. I had been trying to explain the inexplicable, to find justification for the unjustifiable.

Suddenly I was once again clearheaded, and now imbued with a strong sense of determination. After downing my stew with relish, I rose and opened the door to the hallway. There I asked attendant manservant to have a bath drawn for me and my maid summoned. I selected a clean, rose-colored chiton, on the lower left front of which I had painted an orchid with a bouquet of white blossoms—a costume far more becoming than the plain and shabby yellow chiton I had worn that morning. When Nausicaa began to brush out my hair, I asked her to rebind it in a fashion she considered particularly spiffy. After she had finished this task with delight, I had her adorn my face with makeup, apply a drop of night jasmine perfume to the nape of my neck, then finish my couture with a gauzy white veil and my newly acquired aquamarine necklace.

Aspiring to make an entrance poised and dignified, I slowly ascended the staircase. At its top I paused to inhale deeply before traversing the veranda to where the family was gathered. On seeing me Tiberius leaped from his settee and hastened to intercept, taking both of my hands in his. My stolidity vanished. Once again awestruck, I began to weep. Releasing his hands, I threw my arms about him and pressed my face against his shoulder. "I have forgiven them, my love—forgiven the Eupistodoi their mistreatment of me!" I exclaimed, trembling again as the full significance of my declaration stirred my sentiments.

Suddenly I was blinded: Tiberius was daubing my face with his kerchief. "Ah! Finally I am rid of that shadow-family—those lemures who have haunted and tainted our life together! You have displayed to their fullest the attributes of your epithet, my Lioness!" He escorted me to where the rest of the family was seated and gazing at me quizzically. A little embarrassed after my outburst—and wondrously, incredulously lilted with relief—I started to laugh. Tiberius rolled his eyes. "What I have said before I shall say over and over again: only a woman can contrive to weep and laugh simultaneously. MaY I present you the new Clytia: emancipated, free at last from the enslavement of her past, purified, restored, healed,..."

"Transfigured!" Augustus concluded the pronouncement.

INTERLUDE OF DAEMONS

We dropped anchor at the outskirts of Ostia's harbor about an hour after dawn. As a result we missed the window of opportunity for slipping into Rome relatively unnoticed, before daybreak started bringing people into the streets. Augustus was far from pleased with the two options he must weigh. Entering the city at midday, whether by river barge or by quitting his carriage for a litter at the city's gate, was certain to cause a great disruption of traffic and business. But remaining on the yacht until nightfall posed the possibility of a day wasted in idleness, foreshortening his time to prepare for the Ludi Romani. Meanwhile our escort ships were hard at work as they had been at Naples, intercepting the onlookers drawing too near. The all too familiar inner voice tried to insinuate blame for these inconveniences lay with me. Had we not halted in Naples to transfer my property, we would have reached Ostia in the night and Augustus would not be annoyed. Well, Dear Reader: unhesitatingly, quite effortlessly, but most aggressively I retorted mentally, *Hold your peace! Caesar willingly allowed the stopover in Naples because he wished to help me! He wanted that property transfer to occur!*

In the end Augustus decided fetch from Rome the secretary he had left in charge of overseeing his appointments, the three notaries he had assigned to reviewing legal matters that arose in his absence, as many of the six aediles as could be gathered to discuss the Ludi Romani, his tailor with his costume for the opening ceremony of the games, and finally Diodomedes with the architect who was directing the restoration of the Palatine house for a report on its condition. Did any of us recommend additions to in this posse comitatus? Livia decided to send for her secretary and couturier, Tiberius for Demetrius to report on conditions at the Villa Maecenentis. Anticipating arrival at around noon, Augustus sent orders to the kitchen crew to prepare luncheon for his non-servile guests in the smaller of the yacht's two formal dining rooms, for the others in the servants' refectory. The fare was a congealed mold of lobster on a bed of lettuce—an elegant presentation for visitors and staff alike.

The afternoon left me alone with Antonia, as the other adults were busy with their guests. She could not read or embroider and I could not sketch, because all the requisite materials had been packed. Therefore we just chatted on the veranda while watching the bustling of the harbor. After a while the door to the enclosure flew open. Postumus tore across the veranda, red-faced, grimacing, and growling. He kicked some of the furniture and tossed a cushion from one of the settees into the water. It took the efforts of all three praetorians who had rushed after him to restrain and carry him off howling, kicking, and pounding.

Tiberius Drusus ambled onto the veranda with his jerky, apelike limp. Antonia asked him if he knew what had precipitated the tirade. Ingenuously and guilelessly, Tiberius Drusus stuttered the explanation. On receiving orders from Augustus, disallowing any more fishing from the yacht, Postumus' valet Albinus had offered to help Postumus find a different activity for passing the afternoon. Thereupon Tiberius Drusus had spoken up and recommended Postumus join him in the library to read history, as it is far more enjoyable than angling anyway. Throwing back her head and raising her hands in frustration, Antonia demanded of her son whether he possessed any tact whatsoever. He stared back at her blandly, uncomprehendingly, until she murmured he should return to the library and read his history and keep out of her sight. I summoned the courage to say I presumed horoscopes had been cast for Postumus and Tiberius Drusus. Indeed they had, Antonia returned. Most incredibly, she mused, they portended significant public roles for both youths.

A sudden disquiet caused me to shudder, as though from a physical chill. Was the family being excessively harsh with Postumus and Tiberius Drusus, I wondered, as the Eupistodoi had with me? Would these two recalcitrants respond more readily to gentle correction than to punitive; or would mildness only augment their fractiousness? I had been inclined to think of Tiberius' family as unassailably veracious, despite my occasional disaffections with them. Now I perceived them no less vulnerable to errors of judgment and irrational emotional responses than the rest of us. Their mistakes, however, carried the potential of being far, far more consequential than those of ordinary persons.

How does a parent determine which approach is appropriate? Or how does one know when one has applied sufficient discipline and needs to stop, before the reprimands elicit counterproductive rage, anguish, or rebellious indifference? Would Tiberius and I manage to strike the appropriate balance with Alcimus? Hopefully my present awareness of this necessity would enable me to apply it properly down the future.

The contingent from Rome departed in midafternoon, and about an hour after them the staff of secretaries and notaries and stenographers who had accompanied us on our vacation. Thereafter Augustus told us to bathe, dress well, and repair to the smaller formal dining room in which he had hosted the aediles for luncheon. He had ordered a festive supper of roast suckling pig, to honor the yacht's captain Favorinus: a statuesque, bald-headed, leathern-skinned man, very gracious despite his formidable physique. The guests included Favorinus' officers, and the principals of the yacht's domestic staff like Casper the steward and Marcianus the physician.

Amid those smokey pastels of sunset over water we boarded the launch and sailed to the cove. Here a messenger informed us our carriages had been detained. A horse had stumbled and injured its leg, forcing the caravan to halt while a replacement was fetched. By the time the train arrived, night had fallen. Once inside these vehicles we sat in a pleasant sort of stupor, dozing and making occasional brief, idle conversations. On reaching the Villa Maecenatis—where Sannio barked us a prolonged and vociferous welcome—we all retired directly to our bedchambers. The day had seemed long and arduous even though our physical exertions had been minimal.

The next morning a cantankerous Augustus departed to attend a meeting of his Probouleutic Committee. This was a congress of senators and representatives of the imperial administration, for the purpose of apprising each body of concerns affecting the other. Tiberius sequestered himself in the makeshift office of his sitting room, there to review with Fulgens the heap of correspondence that had accumulated during our absence. Livia and Antonia were heading to the Palatine to assess the restoration of the house, and asked if I cared to come along. How, Friend Reader, could I have possibly refused?

The house was fragrant with the clean, refreshing odors of new construction—wood freshly hewn and planed, wet plaster, wet paint, tilled soil. Landscapers were replanting the peristyle garden, making it more extensive than before; and plumbers were at work repairing its fountain. The walls of the central corridor had been restored with their original design: flowering vines superimposed on an ivory background, separated into panels representing window frames to create the illusion of a colonnade opening upon a garden. Most of the rooms in the house, Livia said, had been returned to their former condition: these we would examine anon. First off, however, she wanted to visit the public reception area, where the more significant changes had been ordered. On entering the central court we found its light enhanced: the clerestory had been enlarged. The majority of wall paintings in the court, representing marble and alabaster inlays, had wholly or partially survived the fire and were in the process of being cleaned or restored. One near the exterior stairway, having been severely damaged, was being repainted with the depiction of a balance scale: Augustus' birth sign of Libra.

The nearest of the three parallel rooms—the one immediately to our right—had been completely refurbished. The new décor brought much needed brightness to this room, in which deep blues and grays had formerly predominated. Against a beige background were depicted narrow wood columns, descending from a broad architrave to a broader plinth below. In the foreground were large stone orthostates represented with a thick garland of leaves, flowers and fruits extending between them. From the garland there appeared to hang aspects of pastoral life: bouquets of flowers, cornucopiae of fruits, a shepherd's lyre, a shepherd's crook, an ox's head. Above the painted architrave ran a delightful mural depicting life in rural Egypt, as the hippopotamus and crocodile in the river attested. The two artists working on this rendering, without uttering a word descended their scaffolding and stood before us with their heads lowered. When I surmised aloud the frieze on the Altar of Augustan Peace must have been the model for the garland decoration, Livia returned an approving smile.

Since the walls in the other two reception rooms were undergoing restoration without alterations to their original décor, Livia gave each a quick and cursory glance. Of far greater interest, she said, was the dining room. Smoke, soot, and the water employed to extinguish the fire, had extensively damaged these walls. Now they were being completely restored. As we approached I noticed rose instead of yellow now dominated the walls, inducing a mellow glow and corroborating instead of controverting the tesserae of the floor.

The artist working on a pictorial panel turned about as we entered, and proved to be the elder Myronides. He rushed toward me, sank to his knees, took my right hand in both of his and pressed it to his forehead. When he looked up at me still holding my hand, his face was tear-streaked. "Oh my Lady!" he gasped. "How can I thank you and your teacher enough for forgiving my travesty against you, thereby allowing me to continue pursuit of my craft?" Rising to his feet he released my hand and gestured to the panel on which he had been working. "As I replicate your magnificent work on Caesar's walls—revering with every stroke of my brush your benevolent and magnanimous character—I marvel as well at the prowess with which you emulate your teacher's artistic skill and style." Only then did I notice he had been copying, on a far larger scale than the original, my scene of the shepherd at the rustic altar above the culvert at Ad Gallinas! To one side, resting upon an easel was the original, on which I had adjusted Pedillus' addenda to match my style of representation.

Transfixed I stood, open-mouthed, benumbed by surprise. After letting me stare for a time, Livia placed one of her hands on either side of my head and turned it to the right. The panel on that wall held a reproduction of my painting of the Doric column and urn, at the bridge adjacent to that culvert. And beside it stood an easel with the original. I gasped, held my breath, and then exhaled it in a low cry. Finally I found my tongue, albeit stuttering like Tiberius Drusus. "I...I...am wo-wo-wordless! Am-am-amazed! I had assumed these were destroyed in the fire!"

Livia proceeded to explain. "Since we could not settle upon a suitable place for displaying them in this house, my husband and I had them sent back to Ad Gallinas and hung in the library there. That decision proved their salvation. Now come along over here." She led me to the wall opposite the Doric column. Its panel depicted a copse of three laurel trees. The panel had been reproduced from a study I had created from memory of the laurel groves of Ad Gallinas, the Guardian Trees serving as my model. My intent was eventually to reproduce the design on fabric. No original was at hand. Again I stood staring transfixed, wordless. After a congenial laugh Livia said, "We had your chief steward pilfer the tableau from the Villa Maecenatis while you were with us on Capri. Myronides was instructed to complete the copy before the others, so the original could be returned before you arrived back in Rome and discovered it missing."

I followed my companions through the rest of the house, half stupefied with wonderment. The very emperor and his wife had chosen my artwork, to adorn the walls of a room in which they would receive and entertain dignitaries and vassals from the world over. Furthermore, my patrons acknowledged the tableaux as my own—not the works of my fictitious teacher! How could I possibly deserve such an honor; and how could I possibly express sufficient gratitude? Suddenly an inner voice practically shouted, *You just did! You expressed your thanks, and your benefactors heard you! Nothing more is required!*

In the private quarters of Augustus and Livia, servants were installing new furniture. Livia checked on a painting in Augustus' bedchamber to insure it had been appropriately restored, and invited me to have a look. The painting depicted the god Apollo as an Asiatic deity. Naked to the waist, his long hair braided and cascading down his back and shoulders, his blue and golden chlamys stretched across his lap, he is seated on a stool beside the omphalos: the marble boss in his temple at Delphi, said to be the navel of the earth. He holds his lyre in his left hand and supports it upon his knee. Livia said it was not a copy but an original her husband had commissioned after the defeat of Cleopatra, acknowledging the supremacy of enlightenment over all provinces and nations. The artist, now deceased, was an Alexandrian named Hermagoras, recommended to Augustus by the Areus Didymus. Livia nodded approvingly when I responded that I had observed other works by Hermagoras when I visited Alexandria.

As we traveled back to the Villa Maecenatis, Livia said in her usual, slightly imperious manner, "You will be a member of my train at tomorrow's opening of the Ludi Romani, will you not?"

Although once again taken aback, I won the battle to maintain my poise and managed to reply steadily. "Absolutely! My sincerest thanks for your invitation!" Then I posed a question, for which I immediately berated myself over its stupidity. "How shall I dress?"

"Comparably to the way you dressed for the art exhibition," Livia returned forthrightly. "You and your couturier will find something well suited." If she thought my query ridiculous, she gave no indication.

Now I posed what I thought was a far more sensible question. "May I be so bold to ask why the copyist was informed the Ad Gallinas scenes were my work and not that of my alleged teacher?"

"Really now, Clytia! You are far more intelligent than to make so ludicrous an inquiry. How could Eutychus, living in seclusion on Rhodes, accurately paint scenes of Italy? We had to explain rationally why the style of those tableaux was so similar to work attributed to him." As I buried my face in my hands, she jabbed me gently with her elbow. "Oh come, come! Do you presume you are the only person who has ever posed a question without thinking it through first?" Yet I was not feeling devastatingly and mortifyingly embarrassed, as I always had when in similar situations previously. Instead I found my gaffe quite humorous, and laughed as I uncovered my face.

Livia excused herself to lunch in her quarters with her secretary, while they continued to review her forthcoming appointments. Augustus was still with his committee, and Tiberius had gone to visit a sick person. While dining with Antonia alone, I plucked up the courage to ask her why Livia had invited me to be part of her retinue, after Augustus had excluded Tiberius and me from his garden strolls. Antonia complimented my insight, and after a sigh gave an explanation. By including me in her entourage, Livia was making an unspoken declaration to the public that she did not share her husband's antipathy toward Tiberius. In alarm I dropped my spoon into its bowl, causing the lentil and onion soup we were consuming to spatter on the table.

"By no means do I wish to become a cause of friction between Livia and Caesar!" I declared emphatically and embarrassedly, as with my napkin I started to mop up the mess I had made. The attendant manservant rushed to assist.

Antonia chuckled. "Have you not by now perceived, that including you as an organizer of the art exhibit had conveyed the very same notion Livia is about to put forth? The disgruntlement with Tiberius is my uncle's alone, and is purely political."

"About time I comprehended this precept," I grumbled. "After all, I have had it presented to me over and over for the past year."

On returning to my suite I sent Gallina after the barber Pallas, the couturier Chloris and her cosmetician daughter Leda, for all to prepare my appearance for the forthcoming event. After reviewing a number of different combinations we narrowed our choices to two: the waterish blue chiton with waterlilies and ocher veil I had worn for Livia's interview with Anthe, or the rose chiton with the orchid. In the end we chose the waterlilies as better fitting the present season: in September waterlilies are blooming profusely while orchids are mostly dormant. For jewelry I selected the aquamarine pendant I had received for my birthday, as it well matched the hue of the chiton. Leda cheerfully assured her she would have ready, for my toilette the next morning, color for my eyelids to complement my selected costume.

As we were finalizing these preparations, Tiberius arrived. "Be prepared to answer questions about that design," he cautioned, pointing to the waterlilies. "Recall Ocellina at Saturnalia last. Maintain your teacher Eutychus executed it, and under an exclusive contract with me." Seeing my quizzical look he continued didactically, "If you admit to completing it yourself, every woman you meet tomorrow will be pressing you to create one for her—as thereafter will all the relatives and friends to whom she shows it off!"

My response took me by surprise as much as it did Tiberius. "Is it necessary to continue ascribing my artwork to a fictitious man? Sappho published her poetry under her own name; and for that matter so did Pythia of Naples her critiques of Atomism. What great calamity would arise, if owners and purveyors of works by Eutychus of Rhodes were suddenly to learn the artist was actually a woman named Galatea Aristoclide? Another fiction, granted, as I am not about to utilize Clytia Eupistide and certainly not Clytia Neronis. But at least a fiction of proper gender—and a tangible person, not a dubitable recluse."

"Imagine how foolish such a disclosure would make Longus appear. You cannot expect him to cooperate, and may even lose his patronage of your work were you to suggest such a course."

"Well suppose then I take credit for my textile paintings alone?"

"Are you prepared to fulfill orders in a timely manner? Before very long, you are going to be concentrating your energies upon reacquainting yourself with our son and assuming the duties of rearing him."

"Suppose I keep my prices discouragingly high?"

"Then are you prepared for the ensuing challenges? *Preposterous! Are you serious? Can you not give me a special discount?* Consider the ensuing gossip. *That ward or mistress or whatever she is to Tiberius is a greedy little mercenary!*"

Unable to refute his arguments, I nodded my acquiescence. Yet the desire to have my work recognized as my own remained firm. Nothing was to be accomplished by brooding about this matter. Down the future, opportunities for having my efforts credited to me may present themselves suddenly and subtly—or they may not. To be on the alert for such happenings I resolved, but not to waste energy complaining because none seemed forthcoming.

Agrippina was not going to return to the Villa Maecenatis. She had asked Augustus—perhaps more correctly, importuned him—to let her remain with her cousin Claudia Pulchra until the Palatine house was ready for occupancy; and he had given her leave provided Claudia her hostess remained willing to keep her. There seemed little sense in moving her to the villa for an abbreviated time, only to move her again almost immediately.

Agrippina, Pulchra, and Numantina were among the ladies of Livia's entourage at the opening of the Ludi Romani. The three girls behaved very civilly toward me, and did not engage in snide snickering as at Antonia's birthday celebration. We sat in an area at the edge of the Rostrum that had been especially cordoned off for us. As we were entering this reserve, a woman in the crowd threw Agrippina a rose and shouted, "We love you, Darling; and we love your mother and sister and want them back!" Agrippina curtsied demurely; but as she walked to her seat, her face assumed a look of fierce defiance.

The rest of our coterie included, quite predictably, Antonia, Claudia, Prima, Atia and Marcia, Livia Ocellina. Also present were the wives of the consuls and other magistrates, and—quite noticeably, I thought—Rutilia, Nevidia, and Urgulania the wife of Aulus Plautius Silvanus. The husbands of all three, of course, were staunch retainers of Tiberius. Nevidia greeted me warmly and said her daughters sent me their regards—particularly Attica, the younger who continued to revere me as a paragon. In all there were about twenty-five of us. True to Tiberius' prediction, many of our companions noticed the waterlilies and several asked how they might obtain similar designs. Do you know, Dear Reader: instead of dutifully supplying the caveat Tiberius had specified, I readily gave the price of the waterlilies at 95,000 sesterces! Moreover I found myself adding that the artist was like me a pupil of Eutychus Rhodou, and that smaller, less complex designs might be available for less money. Anyone interested should send a written request to me—Galatea Aristoclide—at the Villa Maecenatis.

Although I enjoyed watching the opening ceremony, I did not find it as enthralling as the previous year's. The Romans hold pageants and games for every conceivable occasion, public or private: religious holidays, assumptions of office, weddings, funerals, comings of age. All this festivity I had come to regard as commonplace.

Four days later, in the company of Tiberius, Longus, and Rutilia, I attended a stiff and turgid adaptation of the tragedy of the Trojan women at the Theater of Marcellus. The play, offered as a component of the Ludi Romani, emphasized harshness in the Greeks and resilience in the race from which the Romans claim descent. Although I realized the work was biased in favor of its intended audience, as a Greek I felt it grossly misrepresented my race as unnecessarily and arbitrarily cruel. The piece was written by none other than the elderly orator and historian Gaius Asinius Pollio: the father of Vipsania's present husband.

In keeping with Roman theatrical tradition, to offset the ruefulness of the tragedy a comedy mime was presented afterward. The mimic characters and plot were transparently obvious: the disaffection between Augustus and Tiberius, and the response of the imperial family to the Palatine fire. A brown ram (Tiberius) continually butted heads with a white ram (Augustus). Presently the brown ram strode offstage in a huff, ignoring the pleas of the white ram and a brown ewe (Livia) for him to remain. The white ram ranted for a time, shaking his fists and stamping his feet, but eventually turned his back. Anon the brown ram returned and on his knees implored the white ram, who continued to stand with his back turned. Suddenly the white ram reeled about and ran his brown counterpart offstage.

Several times the brown ram cautiously poked his head out from the wing, only to withdraw it abruptly when the white ram grimaced and stamped one foot at him. Meanwhile the brown ewe cajoled the white ram with a variety of techniques: tearfully begging, kissing and caressing, railing angrily. Finally the white ram flung his hands in the air to indicate exasperation. Then with one finger he beckoned the brown. Slowly, with his head bowed in apparent contrition, the brown ram shuffled onstage. He had proceeded only a short distance before the white ram sharply clapped his hands and, pointing one finger, remanded the brown to a stool near the corner of the stage where he had entered. The brown ram sat down, crossed his legs, propped his elbow on one knee and his chin on his fist. He gazed at the audience with a look of frustrated puzzlement, as though wondering whether there was any way out of his predicament at all.

Now three boys clad in yellow, red, and black ran onstage and started flitting about, waving banners with colors the same as their costumes. They of course represented the fire. The white ram seized the ewe's hand, and together they dashed toward the brown ram. The remainder of the company followed: a white ewe (Antonia), two white lambs (Agrippina and Postumus), and a third lamb mottled brown and white. He ran with a distinct limp: Tiberius Drusus, his coloration representing the intermarriage of Augustus' kin with Livia's. Once the entire band had reached the brown ram's side of the stage, the white ram seated himself upon the stool back-to-back with the brown. The two started shoving their bums about as though trying to dislodge one another. Finally the brown ewe demanded they desist, shaking her finger as if at a pair of small children. The rams turned until they were sitting side by side, facing the audience. Both assumed the posture and countenance the brown ram had displayed earlier: elbow on knee, chin on fist, a visage of quizzical perplexity. The scrim was drawn. The audience, who had been laughing hysterically, burst into applause.

Right from its beginning I found this Atellan farce thoroughly funny, and hated myself because I did. The family who had embraced, consoled, and inspired me was the object of this public derision. What was wrong with me, I kept wondering, that I should find it amusing? With little success I had struggled not to laugh. Yet Tiberius, sitting beside me, had roared with laughter. So did Longus, and Rutilia with such force she gave herself a stitch. Glancing at the imperial box, I noted Augustus, Livia, Antonia and her sisters, all laughing heartily as well. My assumption was their laughter was a sham, to conceal from the public their umbrage and embarrassment. But the hilarity continued through supper, as the mime was reviewed scene by scene. Now I understood everyone had thoroughly enjoyed the diversion without any offense whatsoever.

And after the discussion and laughter about the mime had ended, Antonia and Livia began to mimic the faces I had made upon seeing my paintings reproduced on the walls of the Palatine house. Their antics set Augustus and Tiberius to laughing once more, and to chiding me about my reaction. For what I believe was the first time in my life, I thoroughly enjoyed being the object of derision, because I knew it was meant kindly, playfully, and not to aggrieve. Briefly I presumed Agrippina would have approved the razzing I was receiving. Then I wondered why I had even considered this matter at all, and directly banished it from my thoughts.

As I started to fall asleep that night, the notion I should have been represented in the mime as Tiberius' companion suddenly came to mind. The unmitigated arrogance of this sentiment so appalled me, that I abruptly sat upright in bed and cried out, disturbing Tiberius in the process. He inquired whether I was ill, and I assured him I was not but had merely awakened startled from a bizarre dream. I laid back down, kissing him as I did. My inclusion in the mime would have had no bearing whatsoever upon the story presented, but would have drawn unnecessary and possibly unwelcome attention to me. So I reflected as in a calming contentment I drifted into sleep.

Over breakfast the next morning, I raised the matter of a birthday gift for Postumus. The occasion was forthcoming in four days, on the second before the Ides *[September 11]*. Tiberius and I had missed it the previous year, having been at Anzio. I recommended my newly completed tableaux of the yacht's kitchen crew netting smelts. My suggestion elicited a vigorous protest: this tableau was far too fine an offering for the intended recipient. Postumus would better appreciate a basket trap or bait bucket from a purveyor of angling paraphernalia. Furthermore, Tiberius wanted the smelt tableau for his private collection. But since the entire matter meant so very much to me, he would procure a suitable gift for Postumus.

As I went about the pleasurable task of unpacking and reviewing the sketches and paintings I had completed during our vacation, I became aware of a bewildering emptiness starting to pervade my psyche. The notion Augustus was annoyed with me because the transfer of my property to Eupistodoi had delayed our arrival in Ostia. The necessity I continue attributing my artwork to a male alter ego. The presumption I belonged in a play because it represented acquaintances of mine, even though I was not cogent to the plot in the least. Taking offense because that play satirized my friends—yea, my family! Wondering whether Agrippina would be disappointed for not being able to see me derided. All my life I had brooded over intimations of this nature, hating myself for entertaining them and trying to rationalize why I did. Yet within the past week I had started to dismiss these suggestions readily and confidently, giving them little further thought if any at all.

This abrupt change in perspective proved so unsettling and distracting, that within an hour I found myself unable to concentrate on my present efforts. I returned to the Zone of Neutrality, and there penned a letter to Areus Didymus requesting an interview. Afterward I went for a walk in the gardens. They were closed to the public, the day being Sunday. Wandering rather aimlessly, paying little heed to my environs, I continued to puzzle over the new void in my sentiments. Postumus was angling at the pond. Although his valet was present, I did not venture near.

Despite my intense affection for Tiberius' family and profound gratitude for all they had done for me, I was eager to have them out of the villa and back on the Palatine. Then Tiberius and I could be reunited with our son. So I mused, without feeling at all guilty about wishing them gone. Nevertheless my insouciance over this matter heightened the bewilderment with which I was wrestling. None of the family was about when I returned from my stroll. Back at the Zone of Neutrality. Gallina I sent after milk-soaked bread strips for my luncheon. Along with this repast she delivered a letter tablet. The message was from Areus: could I please come that very afternoon at the eighth hour? *[1:00 p.m.]*

It was already a quarter hour past the seventh. After bolting my food I hastened to my suite, calling for water to cleanse my face and mouth. No time to improve my wardrobe. My plain chiton of cream colored homespun would have to do, along with the shabby pink veil I had worn in the garden. Lacking time for brushing and rebinding my hair, I had Alcmene enclose it in a white headscarf. She I appointed to accompany me on my junket, and sent Gallina to have the litter brought around. It was waiting at the villa's front by the time Alcmene and I reached the vestibule.

Areus greeted me warmly and with obvious sympathy. From my letter he had gathered I was in considerable distress and urgently in need of counsel. After introducing his wife Hypatia, he escorted Alcmene and me to his office. Hypatia accompanied us, proving her husband a stickler for rectitude. For a man to receive two strange women alone in his own domicile was a blatant and scandalmongering impropriety. Through the next hour I described in detail all that had unfolded in my life with regard to Anthe that summer, concluding with my *transfiguration* and my forgiveness of the Eupistodoi.

Since that final epiphany I had been endeavoring to correct bad habits or behaviors in myself upon detecting them, and thereafter give them no further consideration. Such conduct—utterly unprecedented in my life—was baffling and disconcerting me. Why was I not engaging in deep and critical self-recrimination and self-examination, to determine what deficiencies in my character had impelled me to obey those inappropriate impulses? Areus asked me to specify what I meant by deficiencies. I recited the litany of matters about which I felt I should be gravely concerned and was not: lack of personal recognition, derision, wishing Tiberius' family out of my home.

During my discourse Areus began to smile reflectively. When I had finished, he asked me to define a daemon. My several offerings—a silly superstition, a figment of one's imagination, a malicious fear-inducing bogey—he said were correct, but did not include the particular explanation he was seeking. A daemon, he elaborated, is the personification as a spiritual being of an experience which exerts profound and continuing influence upon an individual. Consider, Areus said, my assertion I had ceased longing for reconciliation with Anthe. In actuality I had achieved reconciliation. Anthe may not be reconciled to me. She may still think me a slothful self-centered ingrate. However, her harboring this opinion no longer mattered to me. My accepting her for whom she was, and what she had been to me, had reconciled me to her.

Anthe had persuaded me all my mistakes and blunders were consequences of dire, unforgivable, and irredeemable moral inadequacies in my nature. Desperate to prove her accusations untrue, I had pondered and ruminated and agonized over them at length. From these deliberations I had hoped to derive some way of convincing Anthe I was repentant and willing to reform, or else that she was mistaken about me. Anthe's continual refusal to accept my pleas drove me into deeper self-doubt and self-condemnation, greater yearning to be understood and greater despair I never would be. These misgivings were the daemons with which Anthe had afflicted me.

Areus returned to the scruples I had described, and one by one showed me how they represented the false sense of responsibility Anthe had imposed upon me. Regarding the yen for recognition of my artwork or my inclusion in the mime: Areus rightly surmised Anthe had called me lackadaisical about my studies and my personal demeanor when a teacher commended a fellow student instead of me, or when an acquaintance praised the beauty and virtue of someone else's daughter. On the matter of ridicule: surely Anthe had insisted fault lay entirely with me when I became the object of derision; and she had contrived to blame me when a member of her family—particularly her son—was mocked. As for my eagerness to have Tiberius' family out of my home and reinstalled in theirs: Areus correctly surmised Anthe had denounced, as disrespectful and even unnaturally unaffectionate, the fretfulness I had displayed when crammed with the rest of my foster family into their *villa of elegance on our unsurpassable country property*. He spoke those final words with such sarcasm, I could not help but laugh.

Concluding, Areus remarked most of his clients sought his counsel because they were emotionally burdened. I had consulted him because I had been unburdened. This sensation I was finding discomfiting because it was so entirely foreign to me. My repudiation of Anthe's overbearing influence had enabled me to perceive, that errors of thought and action once recognized need to be rectified, but thereafter cast aside without further consideration and not puzzled or rued over time and again. The daemons, however, were screaming that I should be agonizing, should be condemning myself. So long as I continued to ignore this clamor, it would cease in due time. The process I could hasten by finding, claiming, and rejoicing in any good to be derived from identifying and correcting a mistake I had made—perhaps the protection of myself or another from danger, the determination of a better plan of action for some endeavor, an enhancement of personal character, a saving of money.

During our journey homeward I felt neither euphoric nor serenely tranquil but placidly neutral. But as I was ascending the villa's front steps, I suddenly felt wonderstruck. *This elegant residence is your home, and you its lady.* So I pondered as slowly I entered the premises. The place was bustling with activity. Augustus had toured the Palatine house and decided it was ready for occupancy. His serving staff and ours were busy organizing and packing up belongings. Although glad they were leaving since their departure harbingered reunion with my son, I had to admit I was going to miss my erstwhile boarders. My erstwhile boarders: the emperor of Rome and his immediate family. This family—replete above all others in power, prestige, and wealth—had accepted me as one of their own, and undertaken special efforts to promote my wellbeing. Their undisguised unfeigned affection and devotion continued to exceed my greatest expectations. A year had passed since they had welcomed me into their midst and undertaken my tutelage. Why was I still astonished?

I found myself reflecting with similar fascination, upon the other elements of the charmed life I had come to lead in consequence of fleeing the Eupistodoi. These flooded my conscience, one after another, as I ascended the stairs to our quarters. Foremost were Tiberius' unconditional love and loyalty, his patient forbearance of my tortured emotions and pent-up rage, the restoration of my gynecologic health that resulted in the birth of a child. There were also the gift of the Rhodian farm, the discovery and cultivation of my artistic and musical talents, refinement and finishing of my manners, my travels. Had I not contemplated these boons, over and over, year after year, despairing of ever feeling or expressing sufficient gratitude? Now I was viewing the benefits as tangible, concrete, congenial, and efficacious. Although mystifying, the sensation was neither woeful nor disheartening by any means. On the contrary, it was refreshingly uplifting.

Tiberius was awaiting me mildly agitated, far more worried than angry. What emotional emergency had erupted, sufficiently dire to send me hastening off to Areus alone and unannounced, even before I had had the opportunity to discuss it with my own spouse? After recounting my interview with the philosopher, I declared that I now did have a matter of urgency to discuss with my own spouse. As I described my newly vibrant awareness of and appreciation for all the benefactions our life together had brought me, Tiberius began to smile. "Clytia, behold your daemons!" he exclaimed after I had finished. "Are they not splendid? Do they not burgeon with the gratitude of which you had always presumed yourself incapable? Anthe's daemons had kept you from perceiving your own. Now that you are banishing hers, yours are at last coming clear."

ENDINGS AND BEGINNINGS

Over breakfast on the day following my interview with Areus, I asked Tiberius whether it might be appropriate for me to assist in the transition of his family back to their own domicile. If I took over supervision of the packing and transport of their goods, Livia and Antonia could repair to the Palatine and make sure everything arrived in good order and got placed where it should.

"Behold your daemon!" Tiberius exclaimed. "Hearken to what it is saying! As lady of this house, you wish to insure it remains well ordered during and after the present changeover. Moreover you recognize my mother and Antonia harbor the same desire for their residence."

Indeed both women accepted my offer appreciatively, expressing their thanks and goodbyes with effusive hugging and kissing.

Members of the family's domestic staff who had served at the Villa Maecenatis returned to the Palatine with each shipment of belongings. One group took Sannio with them. Since I saw neither Postumus nor Tiberius Drusus nor their respective valets all that morning, I concluded these menservants had escorted their charges to their destination. Luncheon I took alone with Tiberius. He had invited Augustus who was still at the villa; but the emperor, sequestered in his office, had declined. After postprandial repose the transfer operation resumed. By late afternoon it was complete, and Diodomedes went to inform Augustus. Acer set his domestic staff to straightening and thoroughly cleaning the villa's guest quarters. For a while I remained to watch. This was the first occasion on which I thoroughly scrutinized the area. It enabled me to consider what I might want rearranged, removed, or added, in anticipation of Thrasyllus' arrival and occupancy.

On leaving this environ, I asked a passing serving woman whether Caesar was still in his office. No, he had quit the villa more than an hour ago. Momentarily I felt piqued. Why had Augustus not sent word he was leaving, that I might come before him and bid a respectful goodbye face to face? Furthermore, did he not owe Tiberius and me a word of thanks for our hospitality? Then promptly and readily, my perspective adjusted. By now did I not know Augustus well enough, to appreciate he did not waste time and effort on unnecessary platitudes? Since he regarded me a member of his family, he palpably did not care I had missed his departure and presumed I did not either.

That very afternoon prior to our bath, Tiberius dictated another letter to Thrasyllus, advising we were now in a position to receive him and all his charges.

Without the presence of Tiberius' family and the consequent enlarged serving staff, the villa seemed a cold and cavernous wasteland. On the morrow I consulted with Acer and Demetrius about the need for converting a section of the guest quarters into a nursery. Ten adults were anticipated, and six children, the eldest (Thrasylla) being of school age and the youngest (Balbilus) newly born. Intermediate were four toddlers: three walking and one crawling. (This retinue included Alcimus, the two sons of Arbindus and Briseis, and the little daughter of Aka's wetnurse.) "We must anticipate their getting into everything," Acer concluded my discourse with a grin. Since Maecenas and Terentia never had children, he continued, the resident staff was about to embark upon an unprecedented adventure. Demetrius recommended his wife Alexandra to direct the necessary changes—the installation of juvenile furnishings, and the securing of objects at risk for ravagement by little fingers.

Postumus never did receive the birthday present Tiberius had acquired: a handheld fishnet. Tiberius would save it for giving on another occasion, perhaps Saturnalia. When the time had arrived for Postumus to depart the villa and its pond for the Palatine, he had thrown a tantrum during which he had bitten his valet on the hand. For punishment, Augustus had denied Postumus his birthday celebration. Relieved at having evaded this potentially volatile obligation for yet another year, Tiberius took me to the Theater of Marcellus. We witnessed a Pyrrhic dance pantomime, mounted as part of the Ludi Romani. The troupe consisted of boys and girls whose features were distinctly Asiatic. Tiberius later explained they were indeed children of Asiatic nobility, brought to Rome especially for this performance. The regular childhood education of Asiatic nobles included training in this dance form, which had originated in their homeland. The subject of the pantomime was the *Judgment of Paris.*

Not Livia Ocellina as Tiberius and I had anticipated, but rather Cornelia the wife of the consul Lucius Volusius Saturninus sent me an inquiry regarding the waterlily design. What would be the price of a single blossom painted on a garment, or a trio like that on my chiton but one third the size? "See what comes of making your specialty seem too readily available?" Tiberius chided. "Had you followed my counsel and declared your designs an exclusive purview of my stepfather's family, you would not be facing this present predicament." For the remainder of that morning and most of the afternoon I sat in my studio, berating myself for the egotism of flaunting my craft, and casting about for plausible strategies to limit the number of orders I might actually receive. Prohibitive pricing and prolonged completion times were the only solutions I could fathom.

Responding to Cornelia, I ascribed the craft to a pupil of Eutychus of Rhodes for whom I served as agent. The minimum cost of a painted design, no matter how small, was 70,000 sesterces. The specific amount charged, moreover, would depend upon the size and complexity of the design, as well as the material and weave of the fabric since some are more difficult to paint than others. Would she kindly provide this information were she were still interested? In conclusion I asserted a large or particularly elaborate project might take as long as six months to finish, assuming the artist agreed to undertake it at all. "Thinking worthy of a seasoned politician or general," Tiberius now complimented me. "If you cannot find justification for turning down a petition or the terms of a treaty, give the supplicant incentive for voluntarily withdrawing the request or refining it better to suit you."

Several days thereafter, Antonia and I attended another poetry reading, about which I was initially very trepidatious. Our hostess was Pompeia, the wife of the younger Lucius Scribonius Libo: well known as ambivalent to Augustus, and the Nerones' archenemy. Not a cause for concern, Antonia reassured me after I had confessed my misgiving. The enmity was not between Pompeia and me but our respective spouses: let us leave the squabbling to them. The granddaughter of the legendary Gnaeus Pompeius Magnus and daughter of his reprobate son Sextus proved a congenial soul, so unaffected and easygoing that one could not help but relax in her presence. Practically all the participants were familiar to me: the coterie of poets flocking about the snooty Publius Ovidius Naso, the genuine intellectuals and the dilettantes who fancied themselves intellectuals, the socialites who cared little or nothing about the syllabus but very much about whom they saw and who saw them. Consequently the affair seemed commonplace and dull, despite the excellence of the poetry delivered. Such is the life of the leisured few which the workaday multitude envy, and would not if they knew how truly boring that life truly is. So I reflected as I exchanged greetings and conversations mostly perfunctory and idle.

Cornelia was present. Polite yet clearly vexed she confronted me: why did painting on clothes cost so outrageously much and take so very long to complete? Having anticipated these very inquiries, I was prepared and able to reply with calm assurance. The artist charges high fees, I explained, because painting on fabric is horrendously nerve-wracking. This particular type of artistry demands extraordinary control and precision. Mistakes are not readily correctable and can prove indelible. Should a brush slip or dribble, should paint bleed from the design along the fibers of the textile, the effects cannot be reversed. A single mishap can ruin an entire garment. And because the artist must proceed slowly and gingerly, projects cannot be rushed to meet prescribed deadlines. For this very reason the artist limits the number of orders accepted, so clients are not kept waiting ludicrously long. Cornelia said she appreciated my enlightening her, and hoped there would be no offense if she held off ordering. Although I warmly assured her no offense would be taken whatsoever, I felt disappointed nonetheless. Secretly I had been cherishing the hope my explanations might somehow persuade her to commission a textile painting.

On the final day of the Ludi Romani *[September 19]* we received a letter from Thrasyllus. Its chronology revealed his entourage was presently in transit, and due to arrive ten days before the Calends of October *[September 22]*—the day directly preceding Augustus' birthday. With only four days left for preparation, my first impulse was to panic. I could not turn immediately to Tiberius, who was at the Saepta Julia attending the gladiatorial combat commemorating Caesar the Dictator.

Sit down quietly and compose yourself, the thought came strongly. *You are the lady of his household and every whit capable of acting accordingly.* Sit down I did, in my favorite chair by the doors of our parlor overlooking the gardens, the heliotrope planter at my feet. After a few minutes another thought struck: I had not examined the guest quarters at all since I had ordered their revamping. The ensuing week I had spent fussing about my studio with the tableaux from Capri, in the gardens painting a study of some blossoming oleanders with which I planned to revitalize my heavy blue himation, and of course at the poetry reading. Which of the three guest suites had been adapted I did not even know, having left that decision to Alexandra.

After hastening to the area, I discovered Alexandra to her credit had not selected the largest suite, with its panels representing the violent Oresteia legend. She had chosen one of the two second largest, the walls of which were painted with cityscapes. While still in the colonnade as I approached my destination, I overheard her remark she was worried I would be dismayed with the results of her efforts. Presumably she was recalling the tongue-lashing I had delivered at the onset of our acquaintance, and coolness I had exhibited toward her during our foray to the Gallery of the Four Winds. She proceeded to ask her companion how many servants the newcomers were bringing, and whether they wished these attendants lodged with them in the suite or in the regular servants' quarters on the villa's third floor. The confrère, who turned out to be Acer, replied he did not know the answers to her queries.

Alexandra cast a doleful look at me as she curtsied when I entered the suite. She went on to explain that she had originally considered the other suite of similar size because its walls were painted with scenes of farm life. Acer, however, had suggested those depictions might make the children homesick, whereas the city scenes represented their new environment.

She proceeded to show me her handiwork. From the colonnade one entered a great parlor, illuminated by windows overlooking the gardens. Smaller rooms lay along either side of the parlor. One of these rooms was the bath. Quite intelligently, Alexandra had turned the room beside the bath into a nursery, replete not only with linens and bassinets but with toys: a ball of leather and two of striped cloth, a cloth baby doll, a little wagon filled with painted building blocks, a hobbyhorse. Two rooms adjacent to the nursery Alexandra had designated children's bedrooms, and the remainder for servants. The rooms along the opposite side of the parlor comprised a matrimonial suite, a dining room, and two more servants rooms.

The praise I bestowed on her efforts elicited another curtsy. Lowering myself onto one of the parlor chairs, I confessed to having overheard her question about the disposition of servants. The scholar, I said, was bringing six servants: three couples, one of whom had a child. Was there space to house all of these servants on the villa's third floor? Acer assured me there was. Satisfied, I proceeded to elaborate my desire for the rooms in the apartment that Alexandra had designated for servants. The anticipated retinue was going to include a manumitted Gallic couple with two children of their own, in addition to the Greek scholar with his wife and three children. Consequently a second matrimonial chamber was required. Another room I should like converted into a study for the scholar, from which he could escape the inevitable ruckus. Since the children were all quite young, the nursery and bedchambers Alexandra had appointed appeared sufficient accommodation for them. This provision left the room closest to the parlor's entry unaccounted for. I recommended it be used by night as the station for the servants on duty. And why not turn it by day into a dining room just for the children? Here they could spill and slop to their hearts' content without offending adult sensibilities. This final suggestion elicited a delighted smile from Alexandra and a chuckle from Acer.

"Can all this be accomplished in four days?" I concluded sheepishly.

"But of course, Lady," Acer asserted. "Having these clear directives, all we must do is move furniture."

Four of Thrasyllus' six servants had been on Rhodes: the other two were from the staff acquired from Commagene for service in Alexandria. The four from Rhodes had cooperated on the farm with Briseis and Arbindus to meet the needs of all the children; but so had Phoebe and Menon, Rhathines, Nicanor and Lois, and farm workers when called upon. To address this loss of assistance, I asked Alexandra and Acer if between them they could cull four servants from their respective staffs, to provide service as nannies. If necessary, I was willing to dispense with one or two of my attendants and perform by myself some of the tasks they ordinarily executed. "No need, Lady," Alexandra replied with yet another curtsy, and that slight smile which always seemed to convey a nuance of derision. She had two women and a youth in mind, who at present had little assigned them and could easily assume more work. Acer added he could supply another woman to bring the number to four.

Before dawn on the anticipated day of arrival, Demetrius departed for Ostia with crew and wagon for transporting the travelers' belongings. The travelers themselves Demetrius would bring by river barge rather than carriage, so they need not wait until nightfall to enter Rome. Tiberius gave Demetrius permission to find lodging for himself and his crew should the ship be delayed. Over breakfast I confessed to being so excited I could scarcely think. Tiberius averred he shared my sentiment most keenly. Together we made a final check of the guest quarters, although we already knew they were well in order: the inspection was more to preoccupy ourselves than to find reasons for implementing change. Tiberius' departure to conduct an interview with a petitioner actually left me feeling slightly envious. A definitive purpose upon which to concentrate had offered him a concrete distraction from the malaise of anticipation. After sitting for some time in my studio without doing anything, I went out into the gardens. There I wandered aimlessly, until a ground wasp's sting on my left foot sent me hobbling and wincing back toward the villa. Fortuitously one of the mounted guards came upon me in my distress. Placing me on his steed, he gave me a quick lift to my destination.

So I did not have to climb the stairs to my quarters, I had the guard and a resident serving woman help me into the concert hall reception room and send for Chloe. After assessing my condition, the pharmakeutria told the woman to stay with me; then she herself departed hastily. I was glad for the companion, as I was starting to feel lightheaded. When I told her of my sensation, she stood behind me and gently grasped my shoulders. Quite soon Chloe returned, accompanied by two of the largest menservants on the staff. The men lifted the chair in which I was sitting. Then our party proceeded up the stairs to my suite.

Awaiting us in my bathroom was Alexandra's younger daughter Calypso. She had with her a basin, various implements, several jars, a bolt of cloth, and a wooden crutch. Chloe filled the basin with water, mixed in some salts from one of the jars, and placed the basin on the brazier which she told Calypso to ignite and stoke. Once the water was heated she had me soak my foot, until the flesh softened sufficiently to let her easily remove the stinger with a tongs. From another jar she applied a generous spread of ointment, which helped immensely to relieve the pain. Then she wrapped the cloth about the already swollen foot, leaving it looking about three times its natural size. While instructing me on use of the crutch, she cautioned me to remain as sedentary as possible for the next several days until the swelling subsided. For right now, bedrest was in order.

The tincture of spirea Chloe gave me must have had another additive. Immediately upon lying down I fell asleep, and did not awaken until just before sunset. My left foot was aching and throbbing virulently. Phaedra and Gallina were at hand. The former joyously announced our houseguests had arrived and were settling into their quarters; Master was with them. Chloe was there as well, Gallina continued, to assess any medicinal needs the newcomers might have. She had given my present attendants instructions for bathing me. They limped me back to the bathroom, undressed and unbandaged and lowered me into the tub. My foot almost glowed with a patchwork of black and red mottling. After I had finished bathing and the women had helped me out, I sat on the bathroom bench while they dried and dressed me.

When my toilette was nearing its finish, Phaedra abruptly departed. Several minutes later she returned, bearing a large jar of water. She placed it on the floor in front of me and told me to immerse my injured foot. The water was startlingly cold and its sensation excruciating, inducing from me a low guttural cry of pain. Phaedra was prompt with an explanation. A vat of water was kept buried in the floor of the villa's root cellar—the building's coldest region—for whatever reason or occasion might demand exceptionally cool water. This special liquid was not dispersed frivolously. In my case it was being used to curtail and reduce the swelling. Chloe had said I should steep my foot for ten minutes, for which purpose Phaedra would monitor the clepsydra in the parlor. After she left I sat in silence, staring at my variegated foot, until the cold water chilled my whole body and made me ask Gallina for an overwrap.

All the while I soaked and ached and shivered, I contemplated anew the elitism of my situation. I had a resident pharmakeutria at hand to address my affliction, and servants aplenty to assist with my recovery. How did people of ordinary circumstances, who did not have a resident pharmakeutria and servants aplenty, cope with indispositions? As best they could, I answered myself. Of course Anthe would have lambasted me for letting myself get stung in the first place, I mused, now with genuine amusement instead of anger. Suddenly I found myself acknowledging that Alcimus too was going to enjoy the advantages of material wealth. As he matured I must watch out for, and be prepared to address, any signs he was letting riches dupe him into indolence, extravagance, indifference to the less prosperous or—worse yet—contempt for them.

Phaedra's return put an end to my reflections. By now my foot was almost numb. Phaedra gently lifted it from the water cruse, dried it, applied more salve and a clean bandage. Thereafter she and Gallina helped me back to the Zone of Neutrality. To my surprise, Tiberius was waiting to take supper with me. I had assumed he would either be dining with his family since it was the eve of Augustus' birthday, or else with Thrasyllus. Augustus was indisposed: sneezing, wheezing, and coughing with the respiratory distress that often afflicted him in this season. Thrasyllus had insisted my own indisposition should not cause me to be left to dine alone. Furthermore the children, weary from their journey and bewildered by their new surroundings, were becoming fretful and in need of bed. In the morning we could become reacquainted.

And so we did. Directly from breakfast Tiberius departed for the games which the aristocratic youth of Rome were mounting for Augustus' birthday: foot races, wrestling matches, and *The Game of Troy*. While Chloe was drying and dressing my foot after another cold-water soak, Phaedra brought word from our newcomers. They inquired whether I was able and willing to receive their entire company in my quarters. Most assuredly, I replied with elation. From my bathroom and through the intervening rooms of my suite to the parlor I hobbled, Chloe all the while scolding and restraining me from moving too quickly for the good of my foot.

Among the adults there was no difference in appearance and bearing, from when I had last seen them the year previous. Not surprisingly, however, the changes in the children were significant. Precocious Thrasylla, now in her sixth year and getting leggy, was mastering poise and etiquette. Forthrightly she approached me, curtsied, addressed me as Mistress Galatea, said she regretted I was not feeling well, asserted she had missed me on Rhodes, and concluded with the hope she might be permitted to acquire a pet during her stay in my home. We would look into that possibility, I assured her. Thrasylla proceeded to introduce her baby brother Balbilus, who was sound asleep. A Commagenean serving woman unfamiliar to me was holding him. When I inquired whether she was the wetnurse, she nodded her head without answering. The infant Arbindus was supporting on one arm began to squirm and fret. Arbindus lowered him to the floor, where he began to crawl about giggling. Thrasylla spoke up and identified him as Leonidas. I asked his Gallic name, and predictably could not pronounce it: something like Le-oueh-leh-lehen *[Lewellyn]*. Arbindus said it meant the same as the boy's Greek sobriquet.

Now Briseis came forward, holding a toddler's hand in each of hers. The slightly taller one with blonde hair and blue eyes was unmistakably Phoenix. As I shifted my eyes to the other, my breath began to shorten and my heart to pound. For the first time since his infancy, I beheld the son I had borne Tiberius. To my amazement and immense relief, he did not resemble Livia nearly so strongly as he had when newly born. His eyes were still shaped very much like hers, but his pupils were darker. His face now seemed longer, his cheeks less plump, and his chin broader than those of Livia or Tiberius. His hair was auburn, but of a distinctly darker hue than Tiberius' and wavier than his—no doubt the influence of my hair. These changes in appearance heartened me. They should make easier than anticipated, the presentation of Alcimus as fathered by the fictitious rake from whom Tiberius was sheltering me. Much as I longed to embrace my son, I knew doing so would only intimidate him since in his eyes I was a total stranger. Nothing but the passage of time could make him feel comfortable in my presence. I only caught a momentary glimpse of him and of Phoenix anyway, because both boys upon seeing me promptly withdrew behind Briseis.

Following this brief introduction, Briseis and Arbindus escorted the children back to their domain, leaving Aka and Thrasyllus with me. Before I could utter another word the sage insisted I describe, in my own words, the life-changing experience Tiberius said I had undergone in Naples. Accordingly I related the information about my past that Livia's interview with Anthe had brought to light, and the personal transfiguration it had impelled in me. When I had finished, Thrasyllus remarked there were yet more revelations ahead for me. My horoscope showed I was undergoing a period of discovery, destined not so much to alter my life and character as to enlarge them.

As we retired that evening, Tiberius revealed he had made incumbent upon Briseis and Arbindus the same tight discretion regarding our marriage that we had required of Alcmene and Nestor. Since Augustus, Livia, and Antonia were privy to the secret, from them Arbindus and Briseis could anticipate inquiries or comments indicative of that knowledge. Arbindus and Briseis should be prepared to receive Livia in their quarters: after all, Alcimus was her grandson. Best not to bring him to the Palatine, lest the resemblance—albeit slight—still be noticed and induce questions. To the unapprised we were going to maintain Alcimus was an orphan whom Thrasyllus rescued. Both servants had assured him with ebullience of their willingness to comply.

That eventful day was a Monday. For the next several I puzzled over the prognostication Thrasyllus had indicated for me. Come Thursday its meaning began to come clear. On that morning Chloe pronounced my foot healed, and said I could resume my normal activities. Then after some hesitation she leaned over me and whispered trepidatiously, "The one little boy is yours, is he not?" Feeling the figurative rock strike my chest, I could do nothing more than lower my eyes. As I inhaled sharply and looked up at her imploringly, she took my hand in hers. "Fear and fret not: your secret is safe with me."

Directly I sent Chloe to the guest quarters, to inquire whether I might pay a visit. She promptly returned with an affirmation. Upon my arrival Aka and Thrasyllus alike insisted I was welcome to show up unannounced whenever I pleased, so long as I would not take offense should they have to turn me away for any reason. Thrasylla was taking lessons from her father in the study Alexandra and Acer had prepared for him. In the nursery, Balbilus lay babbling in his bassinet. Alcimus, Phoenix, and little Leonidas were contentedly playing with a male delicium, and with the wetnurse's little daughter who was about Leonidas' age. Although all but the delicium were clad in tunics, their bottoms were bare. Within a few moments I understood why. As soon as Alcimus started to squat and press, a statuesque Negress emerged as though from nowhere and strode across the nursery floor. She seized Alcimus by one hand, whisked him into a corner, plunked him onto a waiting pot, and stood before him to insure he stayed put until his business was finished. The Negress I recognized as Amera, wife to Scourus the cook. Briseis answered affirmatively, when I inquired whether Amera was one of the nannies Alexandra had appointed. Tiberius arrived and requested I be excused. His mother had sent word she wanted to see the two of us on the Palatine. Our litter was waiting at the villa's entrance.

Livia received us in the office she maintained for her business, on the first floor of the private sector of the house directly below her living quarters.

Although poised and controlled as usual, she was clearly excited. She had the report of the investigation she had ordered Quintus Ostorius Scapula to conduct, regarding the circumstances surrounding the deaths of my parents. The findings, she said, were very, very startling.

The Museion had appointed a committee to investigate the fire that had claimed my parents' lives. The minutes of this committee revealed my father's name was Marcus Ennius and my mother's Varilla. Both appellatives were Italian: I was not Greek after all! The tragic event had occurred seven days before the Ides of March in the 728th year since the founding of Rome *[March 9, 25 BCE]*. My parents and a female servant were among fourteen people who had died while attempting to escape the engulfed building. The rescuers discovered me—unconscious and barely breathing—beneath my father's charred body. The distribution of the debris and condition of his corpse indicated he had deliberately overlain me, acting as a human shield when a ceiling collapsed.

The student sophistos Eupistus Evandrides of Colosse was a member of the Museion's investigative committee. He volunteered to contact my father's next of kin in Calabria, regarding disposition of the remains and custody of the surviving child. According to the minutes, Eupistus presented the committee with an incensed letter from Marcus Ennius' father, denying knowledge of his son's wife and daughter and averring he would accept neither the living girl nor her mother's remains. The minutes continued that Eupistus had arranged for interment of the mother and servant in Alexandria's municipal cemetery, together with the remains of five other victims whose next of kin could not be identified or reached. He also agreed to take custody of the girl as his ward.

With the thoroughness expected of a highly-placed member of the imperial administration, Scapula had sought corroborating evidence. Investigation of the cemetery records proved inconclusive. The ashes of all the victims had been interred in three communal urns, making the precise number of bodies therein impossible to determine. There was no way to tell whether the remains of Varilla and her servant had been included. But Scapula had also dispatched an investigator to Calabria, to ascertain whether the family of the deceased Marcus Ennius would either affirm or dispute the Museion's record.

Aggrieved and dismayed, my father's elder brother Lucius Ennius challenged the report unequivocally. Marcus Ennius and Varilla had married in Reggio Calabria, half a year before their departure for Alexandria. The family had not only known of their daughter's birth, but rejoiced over it. Following the fire, four funerary urns had been delivered. Each was clearly labeled to account for Marcus, Varilla, their babe of twenty months, and their servant. Lucius had escorted Scapula's investigator from the reception room to the family crypt, where indeed the four urns reposed unmistakably marked.

Lucius had allowed his father, whose namesake he was, to be present at the interview with the investigator. Privily, however, the younger Lucius had recommended the investigator not question the elder, whose cognitive abilities were slowed and blunted by old age. Nevertheless as the investigator was reentering the reception room after visiting the crypt, the senior Lucius Ennius suddenly blurted out he had assuredly not written any such letter. When my uncle Lucius asked whether the inquiry implied his niece was still alive, the investigator responded he did not know. His answer was honest, because Scapula seldom gave his staff explanations for his orders, and never when they originated from Livia unless she gave specific permission.

Livia recommended she contact the Ennii as soon as possible, lest they launch an investigation of their own and uncover information we were striving to keep secret. What did Tiberius and I think of her sending the Ennii a letter, advising them she had ordered the investigation as part of a probe into the origins of Tiberius' ward? Probably the best course of action, Tiberius replied.

Suddenly I was horror-stricken. Was our marriage void, I inquired in panic, given my name was on our contracts was Clytia Eupistide? Not at all, Tiberius replied calmly while Livia smiled wittingly. Our uninterrupted cohabitation as man and wife over successive years trumped the written contracts. Moreover these had been executed in full faith and confidence, that my name when affixed had actually been Eupistide.

The euphoria arising from these discoveries about my next of kin—and my relief on learning the discoveries did not compromise my marriage—quickly deteriorated into dismay and seething anger. Bad enough the Eupistodoi had harassed and tortured me, had lied about my identity to gain control of my stipend so they might squander it. Now I was facing the knowledge they had not rescued, but kidnapped me for that stipend. Thirty years later their fraud caused me to make an utter fool of myself before the emperor and his family, with my grieving and whining and carrying on like a ninny about not knowing who I was. Yet surprisingly, this resentment faded as rapidly as it had come on. Far, far more important to me were the potential ramifications of the discovery upon Tiberius and Alcimus. At present we were maintaining Alcimus and I were Tiberius' Greek wards. We had anticipated eventually disclosing I was Tiberius' Greek wife and Alcimus his half-Italian son.

Full Italian parentage conferred full Roman citizenship: the rights to vote and stand for election to public office as well as to own property unrestricted, to marry a female Roman citizen, and to appeal judicial decisions to the emperor. Alcimus was legally the equal of his half-brother Drusus; yet the morganatic character of my marriage to Tiberius left Drusus superior to Alcimus in wealth and prestige. Would Alcimus come to resent this inequality? Would the Ennii as well? How would the Ennii react, upon learning they were maritally aligned with Tiberius and Livia? Would they demand perks and privileges, public and political visibility? Or rather, would they recoil from having such prominence thrust upon them? Would they object to being involuntarily associated with Tiberius' tarnished reputation? Reggio Calabria was a hotbed of antipathy toward him, because the Scribonii Libones were that city's senatorial patrons. My thoughts I voiced to my companions, who commiserated with my concerns but could not dispel them. Only the unfolding of events could dictate how we must respond to the questions I raised. Dealing with each matter as it presented itself was laborious and worrisome enough, without the added effort and distress of speculation about the future.

At luncheon that very afternoon, Tiberius and I received another extraordinary surprise. Thrasyllus declared he knew of the Ennii quite well—not personally but by reputation. They were wealthy Calabrian landowners—collaterally related to Quintus Ennius the renowned Italian poet of old, and proud of that connection. The modern-day Ennii were profoundly respected in academic circles for their financial patronage, of smaller institutions of higher learning and of specific endeavors by individual scholars. No, they had not underwritten Thrasyllus' redaction of the works of Plato, recently completed on our Rhodian farm. So Thrasyllus laughingly forestalled a possible query from Tiberius or me. He continued with an urgent but respectful appeal. If the Ennii replied to Livia that they wished to meet me, might I be willing to let Thrasyllus make this introduction? More than mere curiosity was behind his request. Now in Rome and aspiring to establish a philosophic academy, Thrasyllus was hoping to elicit patrons besides Tiberius to fund this project. With a roll of his eyes and in a voice poignant with relief, Tiberius uttered thanks.

Tiberius and I returned to our quarters for afternoon respite, and yet two more surprises. One was Alexandra, putting away clean clothing in my dressing room—and grouping the garments according to their color as I required rather than by weight as she preferred. After a curtsy she explained her presence in a low and slightly sullen monotone. Since Chloe was a pharmakeutria, Alexandra had appointed her one of the nannies for the children. Rather than betray to yet another servant the true nature of my relationship with Master Tiberius, Alexandra herself had in turn assumed Chloe's position as my attendant. Taking her by the hand I smiled warmly, and complimented her discretion regarding my personal life along with her perspicacious choice of Chloe for a nanny. But there was no need for Chloe's services in that capacity, I continued, as Briseis the Gallic freedwoman was herself a pharmakeutria. Let Chloe return to my service: I trusted Alexandra's judgment to select another, eminently suitable candidate for a nanny. Her stony expression relaxed a bit with relief as she curtsied once again. After she had departed without speaking another word, I found myself neither vexed by her blatant display of dislike for me, nor particularly relieved not to have her once again my attendant.

The other surprise was lying on the table in the parlor: a cloth satchel with a letter tablet beside it. The message was from Cornelia Saturnini, the consul's wife who had expressed interest in my textile painting—and whom I had presumed thoroughly discouraged by my explanation for high prices and prolonged production times. The satchel contained a newly completed stola. Cornelia wrote she wished to commission a representation of flowers on its lower left front. The size of the design did not matter; nor did it necessarily have to depict waterlilies. The length of time to completion was of no concern, so long as a finished product was eventually delivered. The only constraint upon the artist was not to exceed 85,000 sesterces, the maximum Cornelia's husband was willing to let her spend.

With no hesitation whatsoever I started to compose an acceptance, until Tiberius interrupted my writing with a question. Should I not first inspect the garment, to make sure it could be successfully painted upon? Now having decided to become an entrepreneur, I must abide by the standards I had set for myself: not to produce more than what was agreed upon for the remuneration specified, and to work at a calm pace without the pressure of a deadline. But I also owed any client delivery of a superlative product within a reasonable period of time: hence I should take care not to accept a project which could compromise or prevent such fulfillment. Following this admonition I put down my letter tablet, and proceeded closely to scrutinize the stola. It was woven of fine yellow wool, wonderfully soft but abundant with tiny hairs. Retrieving my tablet, I erased my immediate and unqualified acceptance of the project and in its stead penned a warning. Owing to the fuzzy surface of the fabric, blurring of edges and outlines in the design cannot be avoided. Did Cornelia wish me to proceed with the garment supplied, or replace it with one of smoother texture?

Within a week, Livia received a stirring and heartfelt response from Lucius Ennius. He and his entire family had shed tears of joy, upon learning I was not only alive but under the care of no lesser personages than herself and Tiberius.

If the Ennii provided for my travel and accommodations, would I be willing to visit them in Calabria? Now, now, we have serious matters to address. So Tiberius admonished as I bounced in my chair clapping my hands and Livia smiled amusedly at my élan. We must decide what we can tell the Ennii and what we must withhold, especially since we had not yet determined whether they were inclined to spread gossip.

The Ennii were bound to inquire what had prompted the investigation that uncovered my connection to them. The answer of course was Anthe's confession. Since Livia kept the details of appeals for her charity strictly confidential, we must prepare a plausible response that would not violate this ethic. To the satisfaction of all we agreed to say Livia's inquiry into a different matter, the particulars of which cannot be disclosed, prompted an investigation into ways the Museion had compensated victims of the fire and their families.

For certain we should not disclose I was married to Tiberius. The rationale for making our union public had not yet arisen. We did not yet know whether the Ennii could be trusted, to keep it secret until we ourselves felt comfortable letting it be known. We consequently decided to retain the charade that I was Tiberius' ward. The Ennii now knew the Museion had remanded me to the tutelage of the Eupistodoi. Consequently we could no longer hold to the original conceit Tiberius had concocted, maintaining I had grown up in Alexandria and there married a rake. To whom, moreover, could we attribute the dowry with which we were alleging my fictitious spouse had absconded? Supposed the Ennii asked for the husband's name and we supplied a falsity; then subsequently the Ennii tried to contact this person—or worse yet set out to sue him for recovery of the pilfered dowry? Alcimus portended yet another challenge. How could we explain his name without generating suspicion he was Tiberius' son? To present him for now as the wall decorator's son, but subsequently admit he was Tiberius,' stood to render us ludicrously silly. Yet since he was a descendant of the Ennii, not to tell them of his existence seemed unequivocally unethical.

The three of us sat pondering these stumbling blocks, in a silence so profound the nearly imperceptible drip of the clepsydra became clearly audible. Devoid as my companions of ideas for introducing me credibly, I stopped trying to evoke any and mentally embraced the presence of Underlying Good. If being reunited with my natural kin and establishing my genuine identity at long last were manifestations of this Principle, they could not be obstructed. Suddenly a scenario began to unfold in my mind, steadily as though it were a script already written; and as it proceeded, I voiced it to my fellows.

Decimus Calvinius Valens, whose acquaintance I had made during his brief enrollment at the Academia Norenas, and who after departing that institution had corresponded with me, eventually helped me flee the Eupistodoi. He sent me to Alexandria, where a married couple who were friends of his sheltered me. They introduced me to an unwed acquaintance of theirs: Tiberius Claudius Alcimus, a freedman of Tiberius Nero. He was and still is an agent of the imperial government. My new companion and I promptly fell in love and married. No dowry was involved because my husband willingly accepted me without one. Several years later he received the assignment abroad in which he is presently engaged. Extraordinarily sensitive and secretive, it necessitated we abandon our home and confrères in Alexandria and—for all intents and purposes—utterly obliterate our true identities.

In his capacity as imperial legate of Rhodes and as my husband's patron, Tiberius had assumed tutelage of me and my infant son while my spouse was operating under cover. To enhance our concealment, Tiberius had created my pseudonym of Galatea Aristoclide and my bogus personal history. Bringing my son and me to Rome was actually another aspect of Tiberius' obfuscation. He felt most people were likely to presume an undercover operative would keep his family carefully sequestered—not give them visibility as Tiberius' wards. My son's full name cannot be disclosed because it would identify his father. In the infrequent, furtive correspondence my husband and I manage to exchange, we agreed our boy could be called Alcimus Alcimedes and nothing more.

Tiberius looked at me with raised eyebrows. Just how did I expect to guarantee the Ennii would keep all of this secret, especially if old Lucius Ennius were doddering? The same way we deter our servants from spreading gossip, I responded: by conjoining flattery with fear. Because the Ennii are my family we are taking them into our confidence; however they must take warning. If they disclose our secrets, we shall have no option but to discredit them utterly—compromise their ability to procure services, enter into contracts, sponsor protégés, or offer endowments. Thus I replied through clenched teeth, and a steely grin which I relaxed before continuing.

Now Tiberius drew a rhetorical question. Had he not asserted time and again I was a natural politician? "Indisputably one of ours," his mother replied. She proceeded with an objection to Tiberius Claudius Alcimus: we should avoid any inferences directly associating me with her son. Livia continued with a much simpler, equally credible, and far more intriguing version of my scenario. The man who had made my acquaintance at the

Academia Norenas, corresponded with me thereafter, engineered my escape from the Eupistodoi, and ultimately married me, is a covert agent of the government. This characterization can be made safely, because no one had recognized Tiberius while he was attending the Academia Norenas. The cavalry commander later killed on the German front is another fiction concealing the agent's real identity. On accepting his present assignment, my husband had petitioned Livia to arrange protective custody for me. Livia had accordingly asked Tiberius to obfuscate me as his Greek ward and one of his private charities. Quite understandably my husband's real name cannot and will not be disclosed. Moreover the particulars of his mission and the pseudonyms he employs are secret even to me, for they carry the potential for my being taken hostage by enemies he has been engaged to thwart.

Livia paused. Her brows tightened slightly into a frown as she stared at the floor like Tiberius when lost in thought. She resumed speaking in a pensive, rueful tone. We had not yet ascertained how discreet the Ennii are—how well they can be entrusted with secrets. To them we were going to represent me with the same pseudonym by which I was known in Rome, but with a different identity. Little harm could arise if a rumor started circulating through the capital, that Augustus was guarding the wife of some secretive government agent under the pretext of Tiberius' charity. About Alcimus, however, I must say nothing. Consider the consequences, should the Ennii make his existence known while we were keeping it secret even from members of Caesar's family. We must nonetheless assume the Ennii were going to inquire whether I had children. In response I need not lie, only maintain I was not at liberty to disclose this information lest it compromise my husband's security and my own.

During the ensuing week, while the meeting with the Ennii was being arranged, my emotions alternated between joyous anticipation and nervous trepidation. Suppose the Ennii took an immediate dislike to me or I to them? Suppose we found their discretion could not be relied upon? Underlying Good will be present and must prevail, I kept reminding myself. And behold, I was blessed with the distraction of my art. Cornelia sent word she was agreeable to any design I felt appropriate for her yellow stola, so long as I stayed within the budget she had allotted. After a morning of deliberation in my studio I decided a grouping of flags would suit the stola, the garment's fuzziness lending itself to the natural translucency of these flowers.

Livia was immeasurably pleased and relieved to learn Thrasyllus aspired to meet the Ennii, since there was no question he could be trusted to maintain

717

our charade. For Tiberius to serve as my escort would presumably violate his agreement to refrain from any sort of participation in government affairs. Livia had, after all, launched the entire investigation as an inquiry into Egyptian matters of state. Furthermore Tiberius' appearance near Reggio Calabria— the client city of the Scribonii Libones—could very well ignite a furor of outrage. In one serious conversation with Thrasyllus and me prior to our journey, Tiberius pressed us to investigate whether the Ennii regarded him with hostility. For the present they did not realize they were aligned with him by our marriage. In anticipation of eventually lifting the secrecy from our union, Tiberius desired to know what sort of reaction from the Ennii we must prepare for.

Our departure was set for the early morning of a Friday, the fifth day before the Ides of October *[10/11]*. By river barge we would travel to Ostia, and there board a monotreme. She would get us to Reggio Calabria no later than Sunday morning and very possibly earlier. The Ennii were prepared to meet our ship, and accommodate us at their estate on the city's outskirts. Once again I chose Nausicaa to attend me. While she and Phaedra were dressing me by lamplight, since dawn was just beginning to illuminate the sky, Tiberius announced Thrasyllus had asked us to breakfast in his quarters. The sage was quite excited because his forecasts, both astrological and numerological, portended a particularly fruitful and satisfying journey.

During our voyage I conversed with Thrasyllus about many topics, but never felt obliged to explain or defend my conclusions. Without any impulse to record my observations, I sat watching the waves change color and shape, the dolphins appear and reappear to escort the ship. In fact, although I had brought my accoutrements, I did not sketch or paint at all. Instead I followed Antonia's example and perused one of the romances of Aristides Mileteou. It was a sorrowful tale of forbidden love between a man and woman of Babylon, who exchanged their tryst through a hole in the wall that separated their families' properties.

The possibility that the Ennii and I might dislike one another no longer distressed me. They were entitled to their opinions and I to mine. If we found one another distasteful, we would simply part company and not plan any future encounters. Although I accepted the shrimp for our luncheon, without any guilt or embarrassment I demanded an alternative to the lamb shank presented for our supper. The variant turned out to be baked smelts. After befuddling the server by inquiring whether the smelts had been netted from the monoreme during our transit (they had not), I explained to Thrasyllus my reason for posing the question. He chuckled at my insouciance and guiltless assertiveness, both of which he attributed to my transfiguration. No longer was I hearing the inner voice of Anthe, accusing me of being slothful and unproductive, overbearing and obstreperous—demanding that to which I was not entitled while stridently resisting what I deserved.

The monoreme, constructed for speed, was capable of traveling up to three times faster than the imperial yacht. The steady and westerly wind was highly favorable. Since the skies were clear and the stars visible, we did not need to halt during the night. As a result we docked in Reggio Calabria sooner than anticipated: at dusk on the day following our departure. Having already bathed and supped, we spent the night on the ship. Hardly had we finished breakfasting the next morning, when an officer of the monoreme announced our host's carriage had arrived.

The city of Reggio Calabria I found strikingly beautiful. Buildings and gardens, elegantly designed and decorated, stood along broad avenues shaded by great spreading trees. All were carefully ordered like those of Rhodes, in the strict rectangular grids ordained by Hippodamus of Miletus. Such environs attested a wealthy and sophisticated populace. Presently the carriage exited one of the city gates and continued down a road. Like most Roman arteries it was bordered with tombs and funerary stelae, which became less prevalent as our distance from the city increased. At length the carriage turned down a sinuous side road, which wound up a gently rising hill to a stately but sprawling farm spread across the apex.

The man waiting to greet us appeared likely to be in his sixth decade. He was slightly portly, had brown eyes, and straight dark brown hair broadly streaked with gray. To Thrasyllus, who alighted from the carriage first, he gave a long, low bow of profound respect. As I started to descend, our host took my left hand in his right to assist me. When I had reached the ground, he seized my right hand with his left. For maybe as long as a minute he stood holding both my hands and gazing at me as though bemused. Finally he said, in a voice hoarse and quavering with emotion, "Without question you are Clytia, for you are the very image of Varilla your mother."

This revelation about my appearance overwhelmed me, with a sense of identity more tangibly concrete than I had hitherto fathomed. All the self-assurance I presumed to have achieved, and on which I had been priding myself, dissipated utterly. My heart began to pound, and my breath to come in sharp irregular gasps. Tears momentarily blinded my eyes before cascading down my cheeks. Nevertheless I did not burst into sobs, but stood looking at our host in silence as though dumbstruck. My mouth remained agape and my jaw trembling, even after he had added, "I am your uncle Lucius Ennius: your father's elder brother." He spoke tenderly, obviously commiserate of my surging emotions as well as stirred by his own.

"A most affecting moment for you both," Thrasyllus asserted compassionately. His words broke my stagnation. Although I still could not find my tongue, I did manage a wan smile.

Uncle Lucius' aplomb rebounded as well. Releasing my left hand he pointed to a servant standing beside the villa's entrance. "My man will show you to your quarters," he said forthrightly, turning his face from mine to Thrasyllus' as he spoke. The manservant bowed. Looking again at me and now smiling, Lucius continued, "Please allow me the privilege of escorting you to yours. There you can relax and recover your equanimity. Send word when you feel ready to meet the rest of us Ennii—but not before." From the villa's spacious atrium we proceeded partway down a rambling corridor. Then through a door in its wall we entered another, much smaller atrium predictably decorated with statuary and planters. My quarters consisted of a trio of rooms to the right. Thrasyllus' were an identical set to our left. A bath and privy lay between them, along the perpendicular wall facing the entryway. A maidservant was waiting in my suite, on the walls of which hung detailed charcoal sketches of various flowers. The maid curtsied as I entered.

I had anticipated needing to remain alone for considerable time, garnering sufficient emotional fortitude to face my family without forfeiting my self-control. But as I acknowledged the serving woman's obeisance and introduced her to Nausicaa, I suddenly became aware such preparation was unnecessary. The rush of sentiment that overcame me upon meeting my uncle had vanished. Now I was excited about becoming better acquainted with him and getting to know my other relatives. And although I anticipated sorrow when the fate of my parents was discussed, and anger regarding my abduction by the Eupistodoi, I harbored neither anguish nor trepidation about facing these feelings.

While proceeding to the privy, I had the resident servant Aureola procure a basin of water for cleaning my mouth and washing my face. After completing this process I set Nausicaa to adjusting my hair. Aureola I sent to advise my uncle I was ready to meet the family as soon as they cared to receive me. Meanwhile a pair of menservants delivered my luggage. While I sat watching Nausicaa and Aureola unpack and store my belongings—from time to time giving them specific advice as to where I wanted something put—I considered a very significant and rewarding lacuna in my conscience. The need for an alcove in which to brood and grieve, to struggle with the contradiction of taking comfort from self-pity and self-hatred for seeking that comfort, had fled!

Before the women had finished their task my uncle arrived to collect me. I followed him into the little atrium, where Thrasyllus was waiting to accompany us. As we proceeded down the main hallway in a direction away from the villa's entrance, my uncle apprised us of whom we were about to meet. Waiting to greet us, he said, were his wife Caesonia, their daughters Ennia and Lucinda and son Lucius, Lucinda's husband Gnaeus Latorius, and the younger Lucius' wife Scribonia. She was not one of the Libones, he was quick to add, having astutely deduced the reason I suddenly stopped short. At hand as well, he continued—now in a rather warning tone—was his aged father, whose mental acuity was only intermittent.

The corridor terminated at a circular nymphaeum, large and airy and ringed by a circular colonnade. Outside, a tree-studded hillside descended to a flowing stream. As we arrived my Uncle Lucius excitedly announced, "With honor and profound respect I present the renowned Platonic scholar Thrasyllus Balbilusides. And with rapturous joy our own Ennia Clytia—known to the Roman public as Galatea—the long-lost daughter of my brother Marcus!" Those who were seated rose to their feet and burst into applause—except for a white-haired man who continued to sit, watching with an air of studious puzzlement as though struggling to comprehend what the fuss was all about. One by one the others came forward. Each identified himself or herself, bowed or curtsied before Thrasyllus, then embraced and kissed me.

This ceremony ended, my uncle bade everyone be seated. I could not comply, however, because by holding my hand he kept me standing at his side. He drew me before the old man, who gazed up at us rather inquisitively as we approached. My uncle spoke slowly and with a gentle urgency. "Papa, this is the now grown daughter of Marcus and Varilla. Do you remember, we learned she survived the fire?" My grandfather showed no sign of comprehension, but lowered his eyes to stare straight ahead at nothing in particular. As my uncle and I took our seats, he posed an inquiry. Before having me relate my life story, might he better acquaint me with the members of my family? Readily I assented.

He embarked upon an exposition of everyone's age and marital status and occupation. My aged grandfather Lucius was in his eighty-first year. His namesake son—my uncle Lucius—was himself in his sixty-first year: older than I had assumed. Caesonia my uncle's wife was in her fifty-ninth year, and their marriage in its forty-second. Ennia their eldest child was in her thirty-eighth year, and married for nearly two decades to a sophistos who taught at the great Academy of Syracuse in Sicily—once the purview of Archimedes. They had two daughters, both partial to academics and enrolled as students in their father's institution. The elder was in her eighteenth year, recently married to a student pursuing the advanced curriculum to become a sophistos. The younger, just entering her fourteenth year, was hoping for a similar match. Ennia had come alone from Syracuse to meet me, because neither father nor daughters could be persuaded to leave in the middle of the school term.

The third generation Lucius Ennius—my uncle's son—was in his thirty-fifth year, his wife Scribonia in her twenty-ninth. Both resided on the farm with their son of eleven years, and identical twin daughters in their ninth year. Lucinda my youngest cousin—four years my junior—also dwelt on the farm with her husband Latorius. They had a son in his eighth year and another in his fourth. The younger boy they had named Marcus in honor of my father. All three of my uncle's children strongly resembled him. Scribonia my cousin Lucius' wife—petite with fine fair hair and blue eyes—had a birdlike delicacy. Lucinda's Gnaeus Latorius was precisely the opposite. Tall and broad shouldered, with tightly curled brown hair and twinkling brown eyes, he bore a striking resemblance to the long dead Marcus Antonius.

The Ennii derived a substantial income from three truck farms. Profits were used to fulfill requests for financial support, from academies too small to be financially self-sustaining, from individual scholars engaged in specific projects, and from victims of dire and uncontrollable circumstances such as destruction of property by flood or fire. Every application was carefully evaluated for merit and scrutinized for the possibility of fraud. For his entire adult life, my uncle by himself had directed both farm operations and endowments, as had his father and grandfather. Within the past decade, however, the number of petitions for assistance had soared beyond the ability of a single person to manage. My uncle attributed the burgeoning interest in academic pursuits, to the political peace and economic prosperity Augustus' stabilization of the government had wrought. To ensure farm and funding projects alike would receive adequate management in his old age and beyond, Uncle Lucius was grooming Latorius his son-in-law to assume administration of the agrarian functions, and Lucius Ennius his son to manage the financial conferrals.

My uncle's tone assumed a somber tenor. My father, had he survived, would be in his fifty-seventh year, my mother in her fifty-fourth. My grandfather—for so long a patron of academics, so proud of his family's connection to the poet Quintus Ennius—had exulted in his younger son's decision to become a sophistos. A year's study at the Academy in Syracuse had brought my father two extraordinary acquaintances. The one was a mathematician, who recommended my father to the Museion for admission to their program of advanced studies. The other was a young female student from Capua, whose parents had agreed to gratify her academic proclivities by sending her to the academy for a single year. Her father, although the owner of a pottery factory in Capua, was nonetheless an aficionado of higher learning. He was proud to be a distant cousin of Lucius Varius Rufus: the late celebrated panegyrist of Caesar the Dictator, who together with his friend Publius Vergilius Maro had introduced the aspiring poet Quintus Horatius Flaccus to Augustus and Maecenas.

My heart began to pound anew. Following Vergilius' untimely death from sunstroke, Maecenas had appointed Varius to redact the late poet's unfinished work. In Maecenas' personal library I had read, not only Varius' own writings but the original manuscript of Vergilius' *Aeneid* with Varius' edits, all without ever realizing I was related. Although excited by this discovery I held my peace, caring neither to interrupt my uncle, nor explain my connection to the imperial family any sooner than was absolutely necessary.

My uncle continued his narration. Like the Ennii albeit not as extensively, my maternal grandfather Marcus Varius had provided financial support to needful smaller institutions of higher learning. He gave his surviving daughter—my mother's elder sister—in marriage to a kindred spirit: a widowed Pompeian truck farmer who eventually endowed a large academy in Naples. The sensation of the rock striking my chest caused me to sit abruptly upright. Breathlessly I blurted out the inevitable question. "Was the Pompeian's name Norenas?"

"Why, yes," my uncle returned with quizzical surprise.

Now the room began to reel and fill with pale light; however it did not disappear. After covering my face with my own hands, I started to feel gentle touches on my shoulders and forearms. A chorus of worried voices inquired if I were suddenly taken ill. After I had inhaled and exhaled several deep breaths the room settled down, and I assured everyone I was quite well. Nevertheless as I removed my hands from my face, my cousin Ennia declared it ashen. Still breathing a bit heavily, I turned to my uncle and asked if with due respect I might interrupt his narrative with my own, since doing so would explain the strange and extreme reaction I had just displayed. He assented readily, and apparently a little surprised I had sought his permission.

Before beginning my account, I vehemently insisted the information I was about to disclose must be kept absolutely secret. The most casual, innocuous, oblique reference to anything I was about to reveal could seriously endanger me and my newfound kindred alike. My uncle smiled. How little I yet understood about those newfound kindred, he remarked. Keeping counsel was second nature to this family, who were accustomed to holding in strictest confidence the details of the manifold requests they received for financial assistance. Fortified by this reassurance, I was able to proceed without confusion or misgiving.

The miserable years with my foster family I took care to relate as succinctly and stolidly as I could, to keep my account from turning petulant and maudlin. Nevertheless my audience reacted with gasps and hisses, tongue clickings and grunts, arising from incredulity and infuriation. The description of my betrothal elicited laughter as well. Here I had to pause. Again I covered my face and took several deep breaths. In a tremulous voice I confessed to being overcome with dismay, to learn the fiancé I had scorned and ultimately fled was my own first cousin! He was not, my uncle promptly and emphatically interjected. My aunt Varia was but Lucius Norenas' stepmother! Moreover she no longer is, for she and Publius Norenas were divorced well before he and his son entered my life. My reaction of slumping on my settee, head thrown back and arms dangling, set my audience to laughing sympathetically.

Upon reaching the period of my elopement, I proceeded to alter the fiction upon which with Tiberius and Thrasyllus I had originally agreed. My purpose was to bring the story closer to the actual truth, so I could better remember what I related. Accordingly I explained how Tiberius and I became acquainted at the Academia Norenas while he was registered there, concealed by a false identity under which he corresponded with me for the two years thereafter. When he retired to Rhodes, Tiberius invited me to accompany him as his ward, under a pseudonym to prevent the Eupistodoi from tracing me. Further to obscure my identity, Tiberius invented the story he was sheltering me from an abusive wall decorator husband. During that sojourn, my benefactor and I made the acquaintance of the renowned Thrasyllus (at whom I smiled and nodded). We also befriended a significant functionary of the imperial administration, who eventually took me as his wife. This conceit meshed nicely with the story Tiberius had spread, about marrying off his presumed ward Daphne Hipparchide before quitting the city of Rhodes for the farm.

Upon receiving his current assignment, which is covert, my husband returned me to the protective custody of Tiberius while the latter was imperial legate to Rhodes. Owing to the secrecy of my husband's present function, his identity most absolutely cannot be revealed under any circumstances. Nor can I disclose whether we have children, lest this information be used to identify or blackmail my spouse.

Now Thrasyllus spoke for the first time. Was the present company familiar with the work of decorative artist Eutychus of Rhodes? The round of denials left me slightly startled and dismayed. All listened raptly as Thrasyllus continued with a succinct description, of how Tiberius came to recognize and cultivate my disposition for drawing and painting, and Longus to market my endeavors under my male pseudonym. Now a collective gasp arose from the company. Stuttering a bit from excitement, my uncle averred Fannia his mother—my grandmother now deceased—had pursued drawing for a pastime. Breathlessly I inquired whether the sketches in my quarters were hers, and my uncle responded with an affirmation. Suddenly I was fully conscious my grandmother's sketches were hanging throughout the villa. Earlier I had noticed them, of course, but with the nonchalant indifference that ignorance impels. A reverential awe crept over me. Closing my eyes, I declared I was deeply moved and grateful to discover Fannia had bequeathed me the incomparable legacy of artistic ability. Now my uncle, with demeanor still solemn, asked the predictable question: was I willing to send the Ennii one of my pieces? Most gladly, I reassured him earnestly. With lowered eyes he responded in a quiet voice hoarse with emotion. Surely a tangible example, of the wondrous talent I had inherited from his mother, would help him bear the unabated anguish her suicide continues to impose upon him.

A pensive silence ensued, after which my uncle returned to his narrative. Each year of my parents' study at the Museion had brought my grandparents on both sides new joy and pride. My father was a stellar student. So was my mother, in the classes she took purely for her personal pleasure. The faculty urged her to consider pursuing the full curriculum and becoming a sophista. These encouragements she respectfully declined, maintaining her primary interests in life were to help her husband succeed in his career, to bear him as many children as he wanted and she was able, and to impart them not only actual knowledge but respect and appreciation for that knowledge. She was popular as well with the other advanced students and their spouses—always ready to assist with housekeeping, minding a child, administering a dose of medicine, or commiserating with frustrations. My birth, in the second year of my father's course of study, had brought the Museion community as much delight as it had my family.

Once again I interrupted my uncle. On precisely what day was I born, I asked pressingly. Returning another quizzical look, he slowly gave the answer as fourteen days before the Calends of September. With a wistful smile I thanked him and apologized for the intrusion. My regret he dismissed, as perfectly appreciable from someone who had never known the date of her birth. Thereupon I explained the reason for my inquiry: to determine whether the Eupistodoi had celebrated my birthday each year on a bogus anniversary they had concocted, which would render wrong all astrological calculations made for me hitherto. Ironically enough (and to my immense relief!) they had commemorated my birth with scrupulous attention to its accuracy. Nevertheless they had secured custody of me through fraud. Another example of their contradictory ethics, I scoffed with bitter irony. Of my birth's occurrence they had surely known, having been members of the Museion's student population at the time. Eupistus, I now realized, had entered the program for advanced studies in the year after my father had. Anthe surely took particular notice of my birth, because she was presumed barren at the time it occurred. Envy had always impelled her to obsess over events beneficial to others, which she either craved for herself or felt the recipients did not deserve.

Unruffled by my digression as though it had never occurred, my uncle resumed his account. So impressed was the Museion's faculty with my father's erudition and insights, they invited him to join their ranks upon completion of his curriculum—a considerable honor and tribute to a student's achievement and future promise. My father would have assumed his new position in the September directly following the second anniversary of my birth, but for the fatal fire of the preceding March. Another reason for which Anthe may have fixated upon me. She would have coveted for Eupistus the position my father had been offered.

The families of both my parents were understandably devastated by the report of the fire. Varius my maternal grandfather had expressed profuse condolences, but thereafter renounced any further association with the Ennii. Not a breach of amicitia, my uncle replied to my query: the Varii had duly and fairly acknowledged the tragedy was not directly the fault of the Ennii. Nonetheless there was no denying, my mother's marriage to my father had brought her an untimely and grisly death. Chagrin overcame the Ennii as well. During the year following the fire they had sedulously immersed themselves in their daily routines, striving to distance themselves from the catastrophe. On its anniversary, however, my reticent grandmother Fannia drowned herself in the brook we could see from where we were gathered. Within days of her funeral, my grandfather began to exhibit a marked increase in irascibility, forgetfulness, and dreaminess, along with an inclination to draw bizarre conclusions about events present and past. Eventually his mentality deteriorated into its present state of bemusement punctuated with rare moments of lucidity.

Here my uncle ceased speaking. He lowered his eyes and sat in a melancholy silence which the rest of us shared. At length, my cousin Lucinda quietly asked if I should like to visit the crypt in which my parents' remains were interred. "Please at a later time," I replied. "For that inspection, I must fortify myself emotionally."

Another pensive silence ensued, which my cousin Lucius broke with the question I had expected to hear sooner. What had prompted an investigation of the fire after a lapse of nearly thirty years? The explanation I had rehearsed with Tiberius and Livia, of an inquiry into the Museion's compensation of the fire's victims, proved eminently satisfactory. Now my eldest cousin Ennia declared she was flabbergasted and horrified at what she had just heard. The Eupistodoi had engineered my kidnapping to satisfy their yearning for a child, and then gone on to abuse me. Was there no penalty to impose, no recompense to exact? None, I replied. Eupistus was long dead. Hardly did I care to give Anthe the satisfaction of finding out what had become of me. Vengeance had already been served, my uncle concluded reflectively.

Two menservants arrived. One announced luncheon was laid. The pair proceeded to help my grandfather rise slowly to his feet. The rest of us followed. Once standing my grandfather turned toward me, pointed a finger, and loudly proclaimed I looked exactly like Varilla my mother. The entire company stood in yet another somber silence as the attendants helped my grandfather through the door. Afterward my uncle heaved a sigh. Finally brightening, he commented no one was certain how to address me. Ideally I should be called Ennia or Ennilla; but never having known this nomenclature, I could not be expected to respond readily to it. Did I wish to be called Galatea? Truthfully, I replied, I preferred the name Clytia even though the Eupistodoi had given it to me. Again my uncle startled. He grasped my hand tightly. The Eupistodoi had not bestowed the name Clytia on me, he exclaimed: my mother had! The contractions of her body during the birth process had induced a mental picture, of her child being transported into life on undulating ocean waves.

The room reeled about me, filled with pale light, and disappeared.

Quite palpably I was unconscious for only a few moments. I awoke as my uncle was laying me on the settee I had vacated, and ordering his companions to stand aside to allow me air. After taking a few deep breaths, I sat up without any difficulty and apologized for my faint. No need, no need, my uncle insisted soothingly as he seated himself beside me and took my hand. The morning could not have been anything short of arduous for me emotionally. His words were seconded by nods and a chorus of murmurs from the group. All would understand, my uncle continued, if I preferred to withdraw to my quarters instead of joining the company for luncheon. The great feast they were planning for me could even be postponed until the morrow. Now I looked up abruptly. Well that Uncle Lucius had mentioned a feast, I said, for I must warn my hosts that I cannot consume lamb. My uncle startled, and turned his gaze from me to the other family members. "Precisely like Varilla!" he exclaimed. Then facing me anew he patted my hand and said congenially, "Your mother could never abide lamb either."

On standing up, I wobbled. Scribonia and Lucinda rushed to support me. Leaning upon them, I returned to my quarters. Here I thanked them for their assistance, and then said I sensed an urgency to be alone for a while. Most understandable, both women concurred. Nevertheless I must promise, Lucinda continued, not to dismiss my attendants but keep them within earshot in case I required further aid. After I had duly promised and the sisters-in-law had left, I sat down on the bed feeling extraordinarily weary physically, mentally, and emotionally. Within a few minutes, however, this heaviness dissipated. Noticing I was hungry, I sent Aureola for a bowl of broth and a bread roll. Further invigorated by the little repast, I did not pass the time sleeping as I had anticipated but wrote in my journal instead.

The sunlight was beginning to turn golden when Nausicaa approached to announce I had visitors. Lucinda and Scribonia had returned, and Ennia with them, to inquire after my condition and see if I might care to join them for a bath. With delight I accepted their invitation immediately. Nausicaa gathered clean garments for me. We followed our hostesses into the main hallway, and then down another corridor to a spacious bathroom, decorated with mosaics in geometric patterns. While our respective attendants were drying us, Lucinda declared a surprise awaited me in the adjoining dressing room. Here my companions dressed me in a Roman stola. Then in keeping with traditional Italian fashion they pulled my hair away from my face, piled it upon the crown of my head, and bound it there with a fillet. Outside their domain I may have to maintain I was Greek and dress the part; but while with my family I could and should wear the costume of my own true race. *My own true race,* I reflected as a strong confidence—a feeling of firmness unassailable and peaceful—took hold in my psyche. *At last I know my people, my flesh and blood; and they have accepted as one of theirs!* So I pondered with an ineffable and calming joy, while I followed my cousins to the dining room. My long elusive sense of identity was growing in strength and coherence.

We dined upon roasted kid and beets braised with leeks. For perhaps the first time I found this viand thoroughly appetizing. Thrasyllus delivered a paean on Tiberius. Extolled were his passion for higher learning and patronage of its promulgators, his devotion to charity especially toward the sick and their families, his commitment to care honorably and respectably for those whose tutelage was entrusted to him. This last disposition was well exemplified by my own physical safety, health, contentment, and chastity, all meticulously and scrupulously maintained. In response my uncle stated he and his family felt themselves in a quandary. Without question they were unfathomably grateful and beholden to Tiberius for rescuing me from the Eupistodoi. This act had set in motion the sequence of events, which had culminated in the exposure of the terrible fraud of my kidnapping, the wondrous revelation to my family I was still alive, my present reunification with my rightful kin.

My uncle continued. Through successive generations the Ennii had carefully distanced themselves from politics both local and federal, lest such involvement compromise in some fashion their promotion of academic causes. The dissension between Tiberius and Augustus and their respective political adherents was of no interest to the Ennii. Nonetheless the climate of intense hostility toward Tiberius, presently pervading Calabria, necessitated the Ennii maintain an outward appearance of stolid indifference if not outright enmity toward him. All hoped Tiberius would understand and forgive.

My initial reactions were deep disappointment, and fear my kindred's ambivalence toward Tiberius would delay and even compromise our ability to make known our marriage. Then a surge of annoyance induced me to pose a rude question. Publius Sulpicius Quirinius Cyrenius, defying Augustus and public opinion alike, had unfalteringly and conspicuously supported Tiberius through his time of disgrace. This adherence did not prevent Augustus from appointing Cyrenius to be Gaius Caesar's chief of staff. Others had remained overtly loyal to Tiberius without compromising their credibility or suffering adverse consequences. Might not the Ennii take courage from these examples, and defy without fear the prevalent antagonism toward Tiberius?

The company fell silent. My uncle returned a look of great gravity. After a deep breath he slowly explained that retribution from the Scribonii Libones was a very real and urgent threat, greatly feared throughout the region. In Rome these actions were held in check by defiance from other aristocrats. Over Calabria, however, the Libones presided unchallenged. The inhabitant of this region who opposed them for any reason no matter how inconsequential, could anticipate having his reputation devastated and his livelihood destroyed. Chastened and chagrined I lowered my eyes, and uttered an apology which my uncle sympathetically declared unnecessary. How could I, residing in Rome, possibly understand local conditions?

But that night, after I had returned to my chambers and was preparing for bed, I reflected upon my uncle's determination to remain ostensibly ambivalent toward Tiberius. After deciding to discuss my misgivings with Areus upon returning to Rome, I expected to fall asleep. Instead I lay tossing and turning, unable to dispel the resentment that overwhelmed me—resentment toward the Libones for their hostility to Tiberius, toward my uncle for his acquiescence, even toward Tiberius' late father for his breach of amicitia that had antagonized the Libones in the first place.

At length I rose, entered the sitting room of my suite, and gazed out the window at the little peristyle. The full moon, hanging in the sky just past zenith, was sending down a cascade of pale bluish-white light. I imagined the fields and orchards of the farm, and the beautiful buildings of Reggio Calabria, bathed in the same chaste illumination. Suddenly I considered the moon was shedding her lovely light indiscriminately: upon me, upon the Ennii, upon Tiberius and his family, upon the Scribonii Libones. She could not but treat us as equals. From this observation I took a great lesson in leveling. Neither the Libones, nor the Ennii, nor Tiberius' family and kin, nor I, were deliberately and purposely purveying intentional malice. We were all humans promoting our own agendas, and doing whatever was necessary to keep the contrary agendas of others from causing us harm. The Libones I must respect as fellow humans with virtues as well as faults. The splendor of Reggio Calabria I surmised—correctly, I would ascertain from my uncle on the morrow—must be the result of their patronage. Little wonder Augustus had relegated his elder granddaughter to this city. She was, after all, descended from the Libones.

Anthe's influence once again, I thought with a rush of anger and disgust. Anyone whose opinions or actions she disapproved or disagreed with, she vociferously denounced as irredeemably evil and without right to existence. This very prejudice I had been harboring toward the Libones. Becoming uncomfortably warm and slightly nauseous, I found the sitting room's exterior door and stepped through it into the peristyle. My resentment toward the Libones had fled. Distressing me now was my continued inability to shed the undesirable habits and attitudes the Eupistodoi had instilled in me. Why was forgetting these inclinations proving so formidably difficult?

The roof of the villa beyond the peristyle, serving as a stationary perspective, enabled me to watch the moon progress ever so slowly along her trajectory. Whenever her brightness began to distress my eyes, I averted them to a small statuary group of dancing fauns at the center of the peristyle. Each time I beheld the group, it was more deeply immersed in shadow. When the moon finally disappeared beyond the rooftop, the statues became completely enshrouded and barely visible. There stood the answer to my perplexity. These untoward recollections were surfacing in my conscience to be identified and corrected, but then remanded to the shadows of memory. There they will remain not necessarily forgotten, but no longer an influence upon my thoughts and actions—even as the statuary group was still slightly discernible in the darkness, but devoid of the moon's intense illumination that had revealed every detail. My physical discomfiture fled. On returning to my bedchamber I fell asleep immediately, to awaken refreshed at cockcrow.

After breakfast, my female cousins took me on a tour of the farm. Since the grain and flax harvests were over, our wagon passed fields of beige stubble extending to the horizon. Presently we came upon similarly extensive vineyards in the height of their harvest, and fruit orchards where pears and olives were being picked. Farther along, workers were digging dasheens, beets, leeks, carrots, and turnips; others were removing bean pods from their vines. I was well familiar with these processes, having observed them occasionally in Campania and regularly on the Rhodian farm. Never before, however, had I seen production on so immense a scale. Veritable armies of workers were loading produce into waiting caravans of wagons. Continuing, we came upon pasturage across which the animals appeared like nodules dotting a green carpet: white sheep, gray goats, red pigs, brown cattle. Here and there were barns for wintertime shelter and feeding. Into one, workmen were unloading a wagonload of hay bales and grain amphorae. As our journey concluded we passed a trio of four-story dormitories for housing the farm workers, and a sprawling building beside the stream. This edifice I rightly identified as housing the cistern for both dormitories and villa.

While we jostled along in our wagon, my companions exulted over my present life, plying me with comments and questions to which I had to respond gingerly. *Being the wife of a covert government agent must be incomparably exciting!*

___ *Harrowing is a far better description. We live a life of deceptive secrecy, breach of which can be life-threatening.* ___ *What sort of man is Tiberius Nero?* ___ *Aloof and reticent, but respectful, gracious, and generous.* ___ *Has he made advances to you?* (A chorus of giggles followed this inquiry.) *His conduct toward me has been nothing short of exemplary.* ___ *What a special privilege to be personally acquainted with the family of Caesar Augustus!* ___ *They are as human as the rest of us, and burdened not only with their own human woes but those of half the rest of humanity.* ___ *Rome must be a fabulous place in which to live, with so much to see and do!* ___ *Too much! Attend one event, and you end up ruing having to miss three others. And then there are the crowds, the noise, the dirt, the malodorous air, the perpetual risk of fire, the petty crime.*

Upon our return my uncle asked if I might care to visit the crypt. Yes, I replied solemnly. Although I had been dreading the experience, I knew eventually I must endure it or be considered parricidal. The chamber was subterranean: down a flight of stairs at the far end of one of the villa's many corridors. There was a profusion of vessels, because this venue held the remains of generations of Ennii. My uncle guided me to a shelf upon which stood a pair of urns, each with a charcoal portrait sketch before it. Gazing upon these, I was essentially viewing my parents for the first time, having been separated from them at far too young an age to remember them in life. Not surprisingly my father strongly resembled my uncle; and as the Ennii had unanimously averred, my mother strongly resembled me.

I had anticipated being overwhelmed with an emotion of some sort: joy at beholding my parents at last, grief over their demise, bitterness over my enforced and uncontrollable separation from them, even a grim impulse to join them in death. Instead to my surprise I felt a sort of compassionate indifference. Although sincerely regretful about their fate, I was merely looking upon a pair of strangers long deceased. When I surmised the sketches were the work of my Grandmother Fannia, my uncle could only nod in reply. His visage was taut and his throat constricted in sorrow. With his mother and my parents he had interacted and loved. They had been integral elements of his life, ripped away from him under tragic circumstances. To me they were just names and sketches and funerary urns. Years went by before I realized, upon recalling this entire incident, that I had never thought to ask my uncle what my parents' birthdays were.

Aggravated over my perceived indifference, I closed my eyes and stood with head bowed until I felt my uncle gently nudge my shoulder. He raised his lamp before the diminutive urn standing beside my mother's. In a hoarse whisper he said that on learning I was alive, he and his son had discussed opening the urn to ascertain its actual contents. They had reconsidered, however, lest it held human remains. Now I shuddered with chagrin, disgust, and anger. Presented to the Ennii to deceive them into assuming I was dead, this urn may hold the ashes of a child or the partial remains of an adult, never to be restored to rightful kindred. Noting my reaction, my uncle to my immeasurable relief escorted me to the exit.

Luncheon consisted only of boiled eggs, an assortment of cheeses, biscuits, and salad greens. It was intentionally light, my uncle explained, in anticipation of the feast to be held in my honor at evening. The fare suited me quite well, as my visit to the crypt had left me with little appetite. Nevertheless the victuals elicited a vociferous complaint from one of the twin daughters of my cousin Lucius and his Scribonia. The offender was informed she must hold her peace or leave hungry. Her departure with clenched fists and protruding lower lip elicited congenial chuckles from the adults. My little cousin's generally amiable behavior had already attested she was not, like Agrippina, consistently obstreperous. This was only an isolated incident.

After postprandial respite, the ladies of the house invited me to join them in the clothes-making chamber. Aureola led me to an immense room in which Caesonia and another serving woman were each working a loom. Lucinda, Ennia, and two more serving women were stitching garments; Scribonia was supervising her daughters at spinning thread. The objector to the luncheon was concentrating contentedly upon her present task. She showed no indication either of resentment or of remorse. No mention was made of her earlier defiance.

Ennia inquired whether I wove and sewed. Sheepishly I confessed that I performed neither of these operations, but then added I did embroider. Why should I create garments, Scribonia interjected vociferously, when Rome offered activities of far greater interest? She and her fellow kinswomen fashioned clothing as much to pass the time of day as to dress their household. Several times I considered telling them about my failed efforts at weaving, and about my endeavors at painting on textiles. Nevertheless I could not bring myself to do so. Already my education as a sophista, my alleged marriage to a covert operative, and my association with the imperial family, had rendered me exceptional in my kinswomen's eyes. I craved their acceptance as an equal, not a pretentious superior. Hence I remained mostly silent while I sat smiling, and genuinely enjoying their chatter about neighbors and servants and farm conditions. When asked if I were bored I emphatically denied, and noted with relief the ingenuousness of my response palpably convinced my listeners it was honest.

The feast that evening was indeed exceptional: a fattened veal, an assortment of cooked vegetables, hearty brown bread rolls, fruit pasties for dessert. Only the children took breakfast the next morning; the adults remained thoroughly satiated.

Over the next several days I was introduced to the routine of the farm. Every morning after breakfast the adults assembled in the villa's library, and the children gathered in a fully appointed classroom immediately adjacent. While the latter took lessons from a resident Greek schoolmaster, their parents with my uncle presiding engaged in readings and ponderings and discussions of intellectual topics. Thrasyllus and I attended these sessions. At the beginning of the first, my uncle—hardly surprisingly—asked Thrasyllus to cast everyone's horoscope. Thrasyllus had to decline, because the library lacked the requisite charts and tables. If given each person's time and place of birth, he would gladly perform the prognostications upon returning to Rome.

Then would Thrasyllus be willing to enlighten his audience with an exposition of a philosophical matter? The sage proceeded to explain the rationale he had employed in his recently completed redaction of the works of Plato. This great philosopher's thirty-six writings fall readily into nine tetralogies. Plato had maintained the pursuit of philosophy required investigation of three elements: dialectic, physics, and ethics. The works in each tetralogy are thematically consistent with one of these components. According to Plato the human soul has three aspects: cognitive, spirited, and appetitive. Philosophy cultivates these propensities into virtues. Hence dialectic raises the cognitive to wisdom, physics directs the spirited into courage, and ethics guides the appetitive into temperance. The nine tetralogies fall naturally into groupings of three, each associated with one of these three virtues. The trios in turn are united by the virtue of justice. This order reflects the mathematical order of the universe, discovered and set forth by Pythagoras. Three, four, and nine are perfect numbers, representing the triangle, the square, and the cube. The product of three and three is nine, that of three and four is twelve; the product of three and twelve is thirty-six and so is that of four and nine.

After uttering oohs and gasps of wonderment, our audience asked Thrasyllus for an explanation of Plato's philosophy. Thrasyllus responded with a cursory and highly encapsulated description of the great master's complex doctrine. Every element of the material world—every person, every animal, every object—is the manifestation of an incorporeal form, immortal and perfect. The man or woman who strives unceasingly to express absolute goodness through discipline of thought and action, gains an increasing consciousness of the underlying immortal perfection. This advancing metaphysical comprehension in turn promotes harmony in the material world: temperance in individual behavior;

concord, philanthropy, ethics and justice in society; excellence in academics, craftsmanship, art, music, and professional endeavors.

Thrasyllus' discourse made perfect sense to me. But although the remainder of his audience listened to it attentively, they quite palpably were left befuddled. The next morning they turned their attention back to Aristotle's *Poetics*, which they had been reading and pondering before our arrival. The conclusions enthusiastically shared were rational, but shallow and sophomoric. Although appreciative and promotive of advanced learning, the Ennii themselves possessed little more than rudimentary education. Noting this I took special care to keep my remarks cursory, lest I offend with a carelessly spontaneous display of erudition. Thrasyllus, I noticed, did so as well. The morning thereafter my uncle insisted they temporarily leave off the *Poetics* and start aggressively reading Aristophanes' *The Birds*. A pantomime performance was going to be given in Reggio Calabria, as part of the games celebrating the marriage of a decurion's daughter. The event was to fall on the day set for Thrasyllus and me to depart. For a send-off, my uncle wanted everyone to attend the play. Afterward we would dine at the city's finest inn before escorting us to our monoreme.

The afternoon activities of the Ennii were devoted to activities traditionally associated with their respective genders. The men and boys scrutinized and addressed physical conditions on the farm: which fields should lie fallow and which should be sown, what structures required repair, whether a pond should be dredged, and the like. The menfolk reviewed and considered requests for financial support: from academics, sick folk, and victims of emergencies like fire or crop blight. Of course they maintained the financial records for the farm operations and the charity.

Upon the women and girls fell the responsibility of maintaining the villa itself. They ensured the serving staff kept the house clean and made requisite repairs, planned menus with the kitchen staff, supervised the production of footwear, participated in the production of clothing and household textiles like towels, napkins, and bedsheets. They kept careful accounting of expenditures, which they reported to my uncle and to Latorius. As on our Rhodian farm, virtually all household appointments like furniture and crockery were produced on the premises. On occasion, however, the women approached Uncle Lucius for money to purchase some special item. I joined them on a merry excursion to Reggio Calabria, on the afternoon that followed Thrasyllus' discourse on Plato. To my immense enjoyment we scoured the textile region for decorative fabrics, to replace faded draperies in the reception room where applicants for financial aid were interviewed.

My kinswomen also pursued social activities traditionally regarded as incumbent upon their sex. On the day after our junket to Reggio Calabria, the afternoon was predictably devoted to measuring and preparing the newly acquired fabrics for fashioning into draperies. On the subsequent morning we visited the farm workers' dormitory. There we cheered a man recuperating from injuries and two little children sick with the croup, congratulated a young woman delivered earlier that morning of a son, and heard petitions. A couple sought permission to wed. A mother requested arbitration on behalf of her daughter, whom two other girls kept bullying. Because his son was too puny for the physical rigors of farm husbandry, a father asked whether the Ennii might be willing to train the boy as a household servant. The next day we visited a neighboring farm with gifts, to congratulate the proprietor and his daughter who that very morning had sent word of her betrothal.

The mime of **The Birds** was little more than decent. Similarly mediocre I found the meal of tuna baked with dasheens and long beans, which we partook in a private dining room at the inn. The Ennii, however, were enthralled by performance and meal alike. Quite understandable, I commented to Thrasyllus while we stood on the deck of the monoreme, watching the buildings of Reggio Calabria redden in the lowering sun as they receded into the distance. Unacquainted with the superlative theater and cuisine of Rome, the Ennii could hardly compare them with the offerings of Reggio Calabria. My excursion had been admittedly stressful at times, but for the most part enjoyable and certainly very busy. When my cousin Lucinda asked why I had not made any drawings during my visit, I replied that everyone had kept me so pleasantly occupied, I never even had a chance to unpack the pencils and paints and palettes I had brought along. I promised to create depictions from my memories and send them from Rome.

My explanation to Lucinda was but a half-truth. Hardly could I confess, that my encounter with my newly discovered relatives had actually enervated my artistic inspiration. So I reflected while sitting upon that deck throughout the following day, watching sea and sky and birds and dolphins without inclination to sketch them. The life of the Ennii seemed pleasant enough. Their interaction with one another appeared genuinely cordial. Their days were replete with satisfying activity, calm and relatively untroubled. Their wealth, obviating concern for basic needs, allowed them time and means for pursuing without conscience any pastime that appealed. If only superficially imbued with learning, they were nonetheless intensely appreciative of it and devoted to its promulgation. But for the Eupistodoi kidnapping me, I would have shared the placidly contented life of the Ennii, knowing neither an alternative way of living nor feeling any impetus to seek one.

Or would I have? To be sure, much of my higher learning had been forced upon me by the Eupistodoi. But suppose as one of the Ennii, I had reached through my own volition the same level of academic knowledge I presently possessed? Would I have come to disdain my kin as unlearned and boring? And would visits to Reggio Calabria and other cities have left me craving the excitements of urban life, scorning the isolation and repetitiveness of the farm? Admittedly I had hardly scorned life on the Rhodian farm, and before that the several months of confinement to the townhouse. Those circumstances, however, had been imbued with unparalleled excitement by the potential endangerment to our very existence the rift between Tiberius and Augustus had implied.

Quite simultaneously, those harrowing circumstances on Rhodes were enriched by the discovery and cultivation of my artistic capabilities. Although confident the Ennii would have encouraged pursuit of my talent, I seriously doubt they would have considered having my efforts commercially marketed. In summation: by comparison to my life experience, that of the Ennii was unequivocally dull. Cruelty and conflict, rage and sorrow, had made my life with the Eupistodoi miserable but certainly unique. Undeniably I owed my present life to the chicanery and abuse my foster family had perpetrated. To my immense and most happy surprise, I realized I was finally starting to feel the gratitude Areus had urged upon me—gratitude for the superior life the imprecations of the Eupistodoi had driven me to seek and find.

My uncle's fear of alienating the Scribonii Libones had been worrying me, lest it compromise Tiberius' ability to disclose I was his wife and Alcimus our son. Nevertheless my hopes were soaring. As you well know, Dear Reader, I had been anticipating Tiberius' monumental change was going to entail the complete dissolution of any and all political influence he carried, and his subsequent emergence into respect and popularity as a private citizen and philanthropist. Our ability to disclose our marriage and our son's true paternity must be imminent.

These ponderings I shared with Thrasyllus, who responded with an admittedly well merited rebuke. How could I presume the scenario I had outlined was for certain the form Tiberius' monumental change was going to take? Thrasyllus himself could not divine the character of the impending change, for the stars were persistently mute. I should be prepared to accept the possibility marriage and paternity must remain forever obscured. "Oh come along now, no self-castigation: give me instead a smile." So he chided perkily, after I had lowered my eyes and head in self-reproach. Did I not recall his telling me one can alter the pattern one's destiny takes but cannot alter the destiny itself? Still morose, I nodded. Before our departure for Calabria, Thrasyllus had cast my horoscope along with those of Tiberius and Alcimus. Mine presaged a significant change, which without question had just materialized as the acquaintance of my genuine family. For Tiberius the long-awaited monumental change was imminent. In the aftermath of its occurrence, Alcimus and I were destined to bring Tiberius continually calming peace and euphoric joy.

Thrasyllus continued. Suppose Tiberius' monumental change requires we keep our marriage secret, for a season or even for a lifetime? We can certainly make ourselves miserable over this necessity. Or else, thrusting aside querulousness as wasteful of time and energy of thought, we can direct our efforts toward surmounting difficulties the requirement will impose upon us. There is a parable, which Stoic writers are fond of repeating: maybe I know it. A man responding to his destiny may be likened to a dog tied to a cart. He who tries to resist gets dragged along relentlessly and is miserable. But he who trots along cooperatively not only remains calm and contented throughout the journey, but at its end may receive a tangible reward for his forbearance—for the dog perhaps a biscuit; presumably but not necessarily a commodity more ethereal for the man. Again I smiled contritely, and confessed to being familiar with the parable but negligent in applying its inference. So my philosophical outlook needed refreshment and strengthening, Thrasyllus averred. Does not everyone's from time to time?

The levity of his reply I found pleasantly reassuring; but after his next sentence I jumped up from my chair, ran to his, and cast my arms about him. My uncle had agreed to underwrite Thrasyllus' endeavor to establish an academy of higher learning at Rome. While all subjects would be taught, the philosophical research of faculty and advanced students would consist of investigating the potential use of astrological calculations—not only for predicting the futures and fortunes of men, but for implementing the methodology of didactics, ethics, and physics Plato had promulgated. Thrasyllus continued jocularly, that the discourse he had delivered on this subject quite palpably had made more of an impression on the Ennii than he had realized. Furthermore my uncle's willingness to support a protégé of Tiberius was either outstandingly courageous, or evidence the Libones were not so formidable a threat after all.

The very next day after my return to Rome, I began two sketches of the Ennii farm while my memories remained fresh. One was of pear pickers: a man in a tree handing a fruit to a colleague standing on the ground with a loaded basket at his feet. The other scene depicted the villa, set upon its hill, from a distance sufficiently safe to preclude my having to render much detail. My stepson's derogation of my representations of buildings still made me leery. Over the next week I painted these tableaux. Because I lacked actual models, they turned out disappointingly simplistic: hardly my best work. Eventually I sketched anew both scenes in pencil on fresh palettes. The abundance of lines produced a more complex and hence satisfying result.

The sketches completed, I wrapped them for dispatch to the Ennii. Tiberius said I should send at least one painting as well, since Thrasyllus had persuaded them my renown as Eutychus lay in this medium. Most certainly not the painted equivalents of the sketches, I protested, since with these I was highly dissatisfied. I suggested procuring a copy of something from Longus. Tiberius returned an unequivocal no: as my kindred the Ennii deserved an original, not a deception. He suggested my **Zeus Descending to Danae**. This recommendation annoyed me. The **Danae** I had particularly cherished since its rescue from Myronides and Lucius Norenas. "Absolutely not," I returned emphatically. "How about the **Smelt Fishers?**"

"Most assuredly no!" he snarled back.

"The stars or gods or Underlying Good or whatever is appropriate be thanked, that Thrasyllus did not disclose I painted on fabrics as well as palettes." So I mused aloud as we poked about my storage studio for something suitable with which we were both willing to part.

"Have you nothing in complete condition?" he demanded querulously. Indeed the tableaux on hand were unfinished renderings of foliage and wildlife, representing only as much as was necessary for use as models for textile paintings.

Finally we came across the plum tree of the Gardens of Maecenas in bloom, surrounded by hemlocks, with the reflection pool in the foreground mirroring the scene. "Finish it about the edges and send it off," Tiberius commanded. "And do not forget to sign it," he added imperatively. When I protested it was the only version I had, he inquired in a sarcastic tone whether I remembered I could always paint another come the spring.

Later in the day, the laughter we shared over our tiff made our embraces during afternoon repose all the more tender and loving. Jocularly we concluded we had been long overdue for the type of petty and pointless argument that defines a genuine marriage.

While he agreed with Thrasyllus' admonition we should not make any conclusive assumptions, Tiberius shared my confidence his monumental change was going to be an absolute and categorical immersion in private life. There appeared to be firm indications. One was my uncle's willingness to support Thrasyllus without concern for alienating the Libones. Another was the enervation in Rome of the minimal political adherence Tiberius had retained, during and immediately following his enforced exile on Rhodes. Cyrenius, the most influential of his primary supporters, was far from Rome as Gaius Caesar's chief of staff. The demonstrative adherence of Longus, Marinus, and Vescularius Atticus was being looked upon as having accomplished its purpose, now that Augustus and Gaius had relented sufficiently to let Tiberius return to Rome. Tiberius had not resumed an active membership in the senate upon being recalled. Any senators who had remained clandestinely loyal no longer had incentive for aligning themselves with him to subserve political ends. Tiberius remained highly popular in military circles, but as the veteran commander who had set examples to be honored and followed, rather than an active leader with a dynamic following possibly poised to impose martial law. Furthermore Tiberius was now himself a retainer—obligated to Atticus, Marinus, Longus, and Cyrenius for their unflagging and outspoken support through his nadir, and to Augustus and Gaius for their begrudging clemency. Nevertheless, Tiberius advised we maintain the secrecy of our marriage until his monumental change had actually taken place and we had ascertained its character for certain. With him on this point I agreed. Basing so significant an action as disclosing our marriage, upon a mere assumption of what pattern our future was going to follow, could prove a fatal mistake.

Our hopeful anticipation was abruptly dissolved by a horrific message that arrived from Augustus.

Tiberius' presumption Gaius would fall victim to his own gullibility appeared to have proven true. After drawing his peace negotiations with Parthia to a close in June, Gaius had led an invasion force into Armenia. His mission was to suppress a revolt the pro-Parthian faction had raised against the puppet he had installed on the Armenian throne a year earlier. The operation proved slow and difficult. On the seventh day before the Ides of September *[9/7]*, Gaius' army laid siege to a mountain fort in which a large force of rebels had ensconced themselves. After three days the fort's commandant sent Gaius a request to engage in dialogue, outside the fortress under a flag of truce. Anticipating negotiations for a surrender, Gaius complied. Although the precise details of what transpired thereafter were still sketchy—something to do with the treasure of the King of Parthia—what was definite is that the man had managed to lure Gaius away from his bodyguard and then stab him. Gaius survived the attack. While the physicians present with the Roman force dressed the wound, a wagon

741

was prepared. As hastily as possible, Gaius was transported under military escort to the nearest Roman-occupied town some eighty miles distant.

Since passage though the high and jagged mountains of Armenia was slow and difficult, the news had taken a full week to reach Gaius' headquarters in Syria. A deputation promptly quit Antioch to investigate precisely what had happened and what remediation was required. Just today, a full month after the dreadful event, their report had finally reached Rome. Gaius had attained his destination and was resting—weak and uncomfortable but already exhibiting signs of healing, under the care of the garrison's medical component. Three superlative physicians—one from Antioch and two from the medical complex of Hippocrates on Cos—had been dispatched to the prince. As soon as he was sufficiently recovered, Gaius would be transported to Antioch. For all anyone knew the offending fort was still under siege.

"Where were the portents?" I demanded of Thrasyllus after we had barged into his apartment to deliver the news.

Putting a finger to his lips, the sage hushed us: the children were napping. He motioned for us to take the settee, then consulted his charts. Presently he looked up and said quietly, "The portent was already delivered."

"That meteor of a year ago!" Tiberius exclaimed in an urgent undertone. "Now I remember it presaged danger for Gaius and Lucius alike! Because Lucius' death followed immediately, I must have forgotten the implication for Gaius; or assuming I had misinterpreted it, I put it out of mind. Clytia, my stepfather, and I—all three of us witnessed that meteor. How does it affect us mutually?"

Thrasyllus continued to examine his diagrams. At length he spoke again. "The matter has been resolved. The danger the meteor implied for Gaius has been revealed and addressed: he is recuperating in safety. The same held true for Lucius, in the most tragic way possible. He might have lived, had he heeded the warnings his own body presented him. As for the rest of you who observed the meteor: somehow it is tied to Tiberius' monumental change, and to significant changes for Clytia and for Caesar."

"Now more than ever I am persuaded my monumental change is going to be my utter demise as a public figure," Tiberius exclaimed over our supper of pork sausages and a medley of vegetables. "Lucius' death did not impel my stepfather to coerce me into a public position of some sort. The authority of Rome has quit my domicile. Now Gaius has survived a life-threatening experience: surely his position as designated successor is secured. How much stronger need the indications be?"

With the tacit cooperation of Briseis, Tiberius and I began the task of gradually and surreptitiously acclimating Alcimus to ourselves. Acer willingly allowed Alcimus, along with Briseis' son Phoenix, the run of the villa. Nearly every day Briseis brought the boys to the Zone of Neutrality, to play with the toys we had placed there. The paintings displayed on easels got removed to my storage studio.

Tiberius and I carefully coordinated our schedules, so one if not both of us could be present. Livia too managed a few visits. We played with the boys, told or read them stories, took them on romps through the gardens when the weather was salubrious and the grounds closed to the public. Servants took all the children to the gardens on public days, to gain experience interacting with strangers. The staff also conducted excursions to the kitchen garden, for encounters with the barnyard animals and participation in picking vegetables.

We also visited the children in their quarters. All were too young for conversation, except for Thrasylla who thoroughly enjoyed showing off her erudition. Alcimus and Phoenix could repeat words and phrases spoken to them. They could identify objects but not their characteristics, knowing a ball to be a ball but having no idea what was meant by a red ball. Physical needs—hunger, thirst, pain, need of the potty—they expressed in incomplete phrases or with gestures. They could pronounce neither *Galatea* nor *Tiberius*. We achieved success with *Gala* and *Nero*. Hardly could we present me as Clytia, lest they babble the name to those from whom it must still be kept secret.

Briseis began bringing Alcimus to my studio, sometimes with Phoenix but more frequently alone. He would sit watching me paint or draw, while I talked to him about what I was doing. Under Briseis' watchful eye lest he damage something or injure himself, I allowed him to poke about the accouterments of the studio. When he started exhibiting signs of boredom Briseis would promptly withdraw him, lest he cease to enjoy these visits and start dreading them. One morning Alcimus wandered into my studio followed by Amera rather than Briseis. The visit was entirely spontaneous, and Amera offered profuse apologies for the interruption. To dismiss her concern nonchalantly demanded considerable self-control of me; for I was almost delirious with the sheer joy of seeing my son accept me unabashedly. When I told Tiberius about the incident later that day, he rejoiced with me albeit not without a bit of jealousy. Briseis had been doing the same for Tiberius as she had for me, taking Alcimus alone to Tiberius at his office (which he had reclaimed from Livia), or in the villa's library. So far, Alcimus had not by his own volition sought out Tiberius as he had me.

Thrasyllus and Aka were invited with us to Friday night suppers on the Palatine. The first of these occasions was to celebrate Tiberius' birthday, on the eve of the actual anniversary. I was surprised to see Thrasyllus nervous. Wed to royalty and revered as an intellectual unsurpassed, he was nevertheless intimidated in the presence of Augustus. The emperor for his part was intrigued by this legendary scholar, as were Livia and Antonia, Drusus and Germanicus. The entire company, but Augustus especially, pummeled Thrasyllus with inquiries about every conceivable subject: astrology, numerology, ethics, the various schools of philosophy, art, music, literature, phenomena of the natural world. A subsequent evening's discussion was not surprisingly devoted to Thrasyllus' redaction of Plato. Another explored the subject of meteors; a third whether deceptions are unethical when they are perpetrated to achieve altruistic ends.

Tiberius introduced Thrasyllus to Longus, and inquired whether the senator might willingly assist the philosopher in finding a physical site in which to establish his school. Since he was still ostensibly in disfavor with Augustus, Tiberius was convinced this effort was doomed to failure should he undertake it. Longus accepted the task most enthusiastically.

With Antonia I attended a recitation hosted by her sister Claudia, and delivered by Gaius Julius Hyginus the curator of the Palatine Library. His *Genealogiae*—from which he fortuitously read only selections—was assuredly the most simplistically puerile, insipidly asinine rendering of Greek theogony I had ever encountered. Philo Eupistides, Lucius Norenas, the schoolboys I once tutored, had offered more sophisticated interpretations. Struggling to maintain my composure, I felt torn between urges to break down in tears or burst out in laughter. The tightened lips and squinted eyes of Antonia and her sisters, as we exchanged glances, showed they shared my mortification. We verbalized it to one another—mostly in groans—after Hyginus and the other guests had left. Claudia clarified the matter, declaring Hyginus fancied himself a scholar when he was only a cataloger of books.

With Cornelia's flag design I continued quite slowly, working on it first off in mornings for seldom more than two hours, and not every day. Such was not a deliberate tactic to delay completion. Inspiration came upon me early, and was short-lived. Once it faded, I found myself unable to produce satisfactory results. Stop I must, and turn to other pursuits. Anew I reviewed my textile collection, coordinating its contents with the various designs I had recorded on tableaux in anticipation of future fabric painting projects. The scenes from the Ennius farm I began to repaint in proper detail, not with the intention of giving them away but of keeping them for mementoes of my journey. Dutifully I practiced my harp, and started once again to compose music: simple pieces to play for Alcimus and his confreres.

Late one morning a very agitated Briseis came to my studio seeking Alcimus. He had disappeared from the nursery more than an hour earlier, just when Briseis and the male nanny Aminocles were distracted and aggravated with Phoenix for defecating on the floor. The residential areas of the villa, the offices and workrooms, had all been searched unsuccessfully. Already the residence quarters of the servants were still being investigated. Concern was raised that Alcimus had wandered from the building into the gardens. Acer had notified the guard commander, who set his men on a search. All were worried Alcimus might have escaped the estate altogether, into the public streets.

Within a few minutes Demetrius joined us, calm and smiling. A search party of serving women had found Alcimus safe and sound, but could not pry him loose from where he had installed himself. With Demetrius was a maidservant I did not recognize. She curtsied, introduced herself as Chrysanthe, and asked whether I was willing to accompany her. Trying to describe what had happened, she said, portended to be far more complicated and confusing than simply showing me. Briseis must come too, she added. Chrysanthe escorted us to the servant residence quarters on the villa's third floor, into one of the chambers, past four neatly-made beds to a door in the far wall. It opened to a wardrobe alcove, filled with shelves on which clothes were stacked. In the middle of the alcove a wizened white-haired woman sat working a loom. And on the floor beside her, watching in obvious entrancement, sat Alcimus.

The old woman paid us no heed, until she looked away from her loom to smile at Alcimus and saw us in the doorway. Grasping the loom's frame she struggled to stand up, until I said she should desist. Chrysanthe introduced the woman as her great-grandmother, whose name turned out to be Clytia! Besides afflicting her with catarrh, cold weather stiffened and enfeebled this Clytia's arthritic knees and feet, making ascending and descending stairs painfully difficult. Therefore with the onset of autumn, her loom was brought upstairs from the workroom area and placed in the warmer alcove. In a quavering voice, Clytia declared she was quite flattered to have so ardent a male admirer at her age. She apologized for the consternation to the household his adherence to her had engendered. Briseis seized Alcimus' hand and tried to draw him away; whereupon he initiated a tantrum. "Please let him stay," Clytia the weaver insisted gently. "Chrysanthe will check on him regularly. Sooner or later he must get hungry or fall asleep. Then nabbing him will be easy."

Morning after morning thereafter, Alcimus would play in the nursery or peristyle for a time, then suddenly rise up and proceed to Clytia's station. When he could not be coaxed away for luncheon, Chrysanthe brought his victuals along with Clytia's. The latter kept watch on him and, when she noticed Nature starting to call, directed him to her chamber pot. With these orders he complied most dutifully. Some afternoons he fell asleep on her floor. On other days he forewent his nap to observe her weaving without interruption. When evening approached and Clytia put her work away, she would tell Alcimus it was time for her bath and supper and for his as well, but he was welcome to visit her in the morning. Only on hearing that promise did he willingly leave with Chrysanthe or one of the nannies.

One afternoon, Tiberius posed a weighty question. Had I given any further thought to the disposition of my art collection still on the Rhodian farm? In truth I had not, I admitted. Preoccupied with my introduction to the Ennii, with the discoveries about my background they had revealed, with my present art projects, and above all with becoming reacquainted with our son, I had once again let the collection slip my mind. Tiberius explained he intended to approach his mother about housing the collection at Ad Gallinas, with every confidence she would assent. Her farm's proximity to Rome would provide easy access to the collection. Attributed to Eutychus of Rhodes, my works would not provoke controversy, speculation, or need for special explanation—except, of course, for distinctly personal items. These we must retain somewhere in our private quarters. He could not fathom why Livia might refuse the request; but if she did, Tiberius would have the entire collection placed in Palestrina. The property being exclusively his precluded any necessity for permissions or explanations. Perhaps having my artwork there would diminish his dislike for the place.

While he was speaking, I suddenly felt a surge of empathy for the household staff on Rhodes. Should they complain about missing the collection, what sort of compensation can I offer them? Rolling his eyes, Tiberius declared I was as usual considerate of others to a fault. The collection is mine to do with as I please, and not my servants' possession. If they miss it, the onus of finding a solution is theirs. They can always procure copies of my works. Furthermore I ought to consider leasing out the farmhouse, once removal of the collection precluded the possibility of damage from careless or cavalier tenants. Why not add rental monies to the hedge fund I had created for paying the taxes on the property in years of inadequate harvests?

At supper on the first Friday of December, Augustus announced he and Livia had decided to spend this year's Saturnalia at Baia, warming and loosening their cold-stiffened joints in the mineral hot springs of that locale. For certain we must join them and bring Alcimus. Our son could be passed off as a member of Thrasyllus' family since they had also been invited. There was going to be an abundance of children of all ages. Prima, Claudia, Marcia, and Augustus' nephews Sextus and Marcus Appuleius were coming with their families. So were Atia and her husband Lucius Marcius Philippus, Pedius and Laelia and very likely Pedillus. From Fondi we could expect Alfidia, her nephew Publius Alfidius Sabinus and his wife Bonilla, their daughter and son-in-law and that couple's two little girls. We would put into port at Formia to collect them. Augustus had designated Alfidius imperial governor of Sicily for the forthcoming magisterial year, and we were going to celebrate that appointment. In fact, Alfidius and his family would not return to Fondi but proceed directly from Baia to Syracuse.

We should prepare to head for Ostia and board the Galatea one week from the morrow: the nineteenth day before the Calends of January *[December 14]*. After Tiberius remarked Thrasyllus' birthday was the day preceding—the Ides itself—Augustus designated that for our departure: we would fête Thrasyllus at sea. Could the yacht and villa accommodate such a large crowd, I inquired and immediately feared I had been unacceptably froward. Augustus not only laughed, but commended me for posing a well-considered question. In addition to the usual contingent of government functionaries, praetorians, and crewmembers, the Galatea could accommodate as many as forty guests and their attendants. She had quarters I had not seen.

About this impending journey I was quite excited, for I had vague but pleasant memories of Baia: of the turquoise sea, the bounty of fountains, the ornate and colorful buildings, and of course the warm and effervescent waters of the public bath. Eupistus and Anthe had taken me there once in my early childhood. A resort for the wealthy and notable of Rome, Baia became an object of Anthe's scorn as soon as she determined she possessed neither the means nor the celebrity to win acceptance there. Tiberius promised to take me about the town but not to the bath, where we were bound to be bombarded with embarrassingly probing inquiries. Augustus' villa enclosed its own mineral spring of which we would avail ourselves.

Again we designated Nomius and Nausicaa our personal servants. Just as Nausicaa and Gallina were finalizing the packing of my trunk—on the third day before we were to depart—a perturbed Tiberius strode into my quarters and announced Augustus had canceled the trip. As my attendants started to moan and cluck pityingly, he brusquely ordered them out. He sank into a chair and sat staring at the floor. Finally he sighed, raised his eyes, and spoke in measured tones. Gaius had sent word he was relinquishing all of his titles and powers, upon expiration of the current magisterial year on the final day of December.

Like his grandfather, Gaius had been afflicted since childhood with chronically weak health. His fragile constitution, aggravated by the still festering stab wound he had sustained the previous autumn, was compromising his ability to carry out his current responsibilities. But furthermore and immensely worse: having determined he lacked the necessary mental competence to execute suitably the responsibilities of Augustus' office, Gaius had renounced his grandfather's indication of him to become the next emperor. Having found the hot dry climate of Syria ameliorative to his physique, Gaius had decided to retire as a private citizen to Heliopolis and there pursue his passion for horticulture.

In consequence the Saturnalia became a rather glum affair. Tiberius ordered a donative and extra leisure time for the servants as had been his wont on Rhodes, for he and Thrasyllus could not possibly wait tables for such a large staff. We presented Alcimus and Phoenix each with a toy boat for floating in the bath, Thrasylla with a necklace of painted wood beads. Ajax our carpenter/bodyguard had fashioned these gifts of wood at Tiberius' behest, and I had painted them. We received no invitations to dine on the Palatine; however right on the second day of the festival, Thrasyllus was summoned there. He returned in a state of troubled reticence—the absolute opposite of his usual joviality. His coolness, moreover, persisted for several weeks, fading very gradually and not altogether. He repeatedly reassured Tiberius and me he was merely preoccupied with setting up his academy, which he anticipated inaugurating come the New Year. Indeed, he and Longus had finally located and rented reasonably suitable quarters: a spacious apartment not far from the Saepta Julia.

Decades would pass before Thrasyllus finally confided, to Tiberius and me, what had perturbed him. Augustus had compelled him to perform the very sort of calculation astrologers were morally and ethically forbidden: to determine whether death was imminent for Augustus or for Gaius—and worse yet without Gaius' permission for this prognostication. For Augustus no impending death, Thrasyllus found. For Gaius yes, but only if he wandered far from his rightful domicile.

On the sixth day of that Saturnalia, Livia came to the Villa Maecenatis with presents for the children. For the boys a toy drum and trumpet; a wooden caged bird that clapped its beak, wings, and tail when one pulled the string between its legs; a wooden Trojan horse on a wheeled platform, with a compartment on its back that opened to reveal Greek soldiers. For Thrasylla a book of Greek verses, easy to read and appropriate for a young girl. Livia apologized for her weary somberness, which she attributed to the strain her husband was under. Whether Augustus had shared with her Thrasyllus' grim forecast for Gaius she never revealed. Tiberius said nothing to her about housing my art collection at Ad Gallinas. His silence on this matter I fully appreciated.

Augustus was now in his sixty-fifth year, and without an immediately viable successor to his office. Germanicus his closest suitable male blood relative was still too young and insufficiently trained to succeed Augustus, should the latter suddenly become incapacitated or drop dead. Once again Augustus required a regent—someone aligned with his family, and whose unassailable loyalty and willingness eventually to yield control to Germanicus could be depended upon—but whom? Prima's husband Domitius Ahenobarbus? His unsavory personal traits like animal cruelty aside, he was a provenly effective administrator and military leader. The military maneuvers he had performed on the Rhine frontier during Tiberius' Rhodian retirement confirmed these abilities unequivocally. Quirinius Cyrenius, presently Gaius' chief of staff? Augustus could bind him closer to the family by giving him Antonia or Agrippina in marriage.

Publius Quinctilius Varus, the equally competent imperial legate of Syria? His sister was the wife of Augustus' nephew Sextus Appuleius. Varus himself had married Vipsania's sister: Agrippa's second daughter by Caecilia Attica. Their son—now like Germanicus and Drusus in military training—was betrothed to Claudia's daughter Pulchra.

And what about Tiberius himself? Thrasyllus kept insisting Tiberius' monumental change was at hand. What must become of our relationship, should that change turn out to be reappointment to the regency? Must we divorce so Tiberius could wed Antonia or Agrippina? My concern was ludicrous, Tiberius scoffed. How, he demanded, could the regency possibly be a monumental change for him, when he had already held that position? Hardly could he foresee Augustus entrusting him with this assignment for a second time, after he had abandoned it. Augustus would have to face the embarrassment of renouncing his present denunciation—ostensibly, officially, for public consideration—of Tiberius as an insubordinate to the regime.

Suppose Augustus did redesignate Tiberius regent after all? There was no need for maritally reinforcing such an appointment, since Tiberius was already bound by blood to the eventual successor Germanicus. A tie of this character had not been in place when Tiberius was appointed regent for Gaius: hence the enforced marriage to Julia. And finally—here Tiberius assumed his mischievous scorpion grin—Augustus could press us to divorce all he wanted; but not even he had legal authority to compel us so long as we both refused. Here is where

749

Tiberius and Julia had made their mistake, of yielding to Augustus' importunity instead of invoking their individual rights to self-determination.

He reminded me of the horoscope Thrasyllus had cast prior to our departure from Rhodes. Unquestionably the first element had been fulfilled. While separated from his parents, Alcimus had undergone a period of flux of which he would have no recollection. Now the second element—Tiberius' monumental change—was at hand. The third and final aspect to follow was mitigation. What could that imply beside tranquility, contentment, and assuagement from the tumults of our pasts?

Tiberius' optimism as to what the future held for us imbued me with a lighthearted momentum. This in turn impelled a surge of artistic productivity and excellence. Through the remainder of that December and the January following I worked on Cornelia's stola, finished in fine detail the two scenes of the Ennius farm, and painted a little portrait of Alcimus to give Livia on her birthday. Unable to envision a suitable offering for Antonia's birthday, I combed my studio and textile collection. Finally I came across another sketch swatch painted with moths, like the one Antonia and Livia had admired that very first time I supped with them on the Palatine. The fabric, although not identical, was similar in texture and color to the moth-themed headscarf I had completed for Antonia, replacing the one with which Marcella had absconded. After washing and drying the swatch I finished its edges with embroidery, to create a kerchief well matching the headscarf.

Deciding upon a gift appropriate for Agrippina, whose birthday fell three days after Antonia's, cost me several sleepless nights. Could I possibly produce another artwork which—like the portrait of Germanicus I had presented the previous year—she would feel constrained not to scorn? Finally I recalled the familial letter Tiberius had received on Rhodes, in which Antonia had written of Livilla deriding Agrippina for playing with dolls. Was Agrippina still partial to dolls? Might she appreciate a little cloth doll, like those I used to create for sick or indigent Rhodian children? I sent an inquiry to Antonia, and on reading her response felt the metaphorical rock impress my chest. Long after Agrippina had stopped actually playing with her dolls, she had retained them with great fondness in a collection. The Palatine fire had destroyed the entire cache.

Neither the desire to honor Agrippina's birthday, nor my persistent if presumably hopeless aspiration to turn her disdain for me into approval, impelled the excellence of the artifact I produced. Pity sincere and genuine over Agrippina's loss of her collection drove my creation of an infant likeness, far more lifelike than any cloth doll I had completed previously. No doubt my recollection of Alcimus in infancy for my model, and my now developed skill at painting on textiles, had wrought improvements over my previous results. Nevertheless, an overwhelming desire to ameliorate Agrippina's sorrow seemed the primary impetus behind the superior product.

As I worked on this project, I found myself recalling how Anthe and Euethia used to castigate me as pitiless. The roast burned, the milk soured, the cat killed Philo's toad, the mortgage payment was due: yet I showed no pity for these disasters. Now I asked myself: when Anthe suffered a genuine loss, had I felt pity? Being honestly able to answer yes relieved me, of yet another imaginary guilt long suppressed but not totally forgotten. Despite the abuse she had heaped on me year after year, I pitied Anthe the loss of her husband and the predicaments into which her persistent silliness had brought her. Despite the dislike for me which Agrippina continued to make amply clear, I pitied her the loss of her dolls. How, then, could anyone presume I was pitiless?

After the doll was finished, and the paint with which I had depicted its facial features drying, I rummaged through my textile collection for a suitable swaddling cloth. Finding nothing, I summoned Chloris the dressmaker to my studio, showed her the new *baby*, and inquired if she could create an appropriate covering in time for Agrippina's birthday. Her eyes sparkled as she curtsied. She would make the time, even if she had to stay up nights. Many a year had passed since she had been asked to swaddle a babe.

True to our anticipation, we received an invitation to celebrate in the larger of the two formal dining rooms in the Villa Maecenatis—neither on Livia's birthday, nor on Antonia's the following day, nor on Agrippina's, but for luncheon on the February Calends. This year it fell on a Friday, the favored day for celebrations since there was no impending business on Saturday. Thrasyllus and Aka were invited. We must for certain bring all the children. *An indication of Augustus' distress,* I reflected. Observing young children, for their artlessness and guileless innocence, brought him respite from emotional turmoil. To keep unapprised attendees from questioning why we were giving Livia a portrait of one of those children late of Rhodes, we had her gift and Antonia's delivered directly to them on their actual birthdays instead of presenting them at the celebration itself. Agrippina was accordingly told to expect hers on her birthday as well.

Augustus was oddly mellow, not with contentment but in a world-weary way—like a man who has ceased struggling against adversity and resigned himself to it. As we started to dine on the favored entree of red mullet, together with carrots and peas in a milky sauce, Augustus revealed he had successfully persuaded Gaius to return to Italy. Now that the team of architects and builders who had restored the Palatine had quit the Carinae house, it was ready for Gaius and Livilla to occupy. Augustus earnestly hoped that after rest, continued proper medical treatment, reassurance of his ability to govern and perhaps further education in this discipline, Gaius would at least agree to serve as regent for Germanicus if he could not be persuaded to reassume his former position as successor-designate.

With a slight chuckle Augustus added that Gaius' wife Livilla had likely been more effective than Augustus himself, in prevailing upon Gaius to return home. So long as she presumed Gaius' junket had a projected end, Livilla enjoyed being pampered and adulated by both Roman and foreign dignitaries and their wives. But now the prospect of spending the remainder of her life gardening in Syria was nothing short of dreadful. On hearing Livilla mentioned Agrippina assumed a scowl, which she retained until her grandfather noted her expression and scowled back at her.

Tiberius and I laughed over Agrippina's stiffly formal acknowledgment of the doll. *Vipsania Agrippina, granddaughter of Caesar, has accepted your unnecessary gift in honor of her birthday.* Antonia subsequently disclosed she had apprised Agrippina, that learning about the destruction of the doll collection had motivated me. Agrippina had stood in silence holding my doll, trembling and shedding tears. *Why should that woman care my dolls got burned up?* she had finally managed to sneer, albeit in choked tones. During two subsequent suppers on the Palatine that February I caught, out of the corner of my eye, glimpses of her looking at me with an expression suggestive of remorse. But as soon as I met her gaze directly and smiled at her, she immediately averted her eyes and assumed a sulky countenance.

By the Ides of February I had completed Cornelia's stola, which I sent to her with an invoice for the full 85,000 sesterces her husband had allowed. The difficulty of painting on all those fine hairs had prompted me to charge above my minimum of 70,000. Cornelia immediately returned her payment with a barrage of compliments. *What a delight to receive the finished article in time for celebrating the New Year. It is an exquisite piece of workmanship, far exceeding my expectations. Production did not take nearly as long as anticipated. Would the artist be willing to create something similar for my sister?* In my note of thanks for her remuneration, I promised to determine if and when a new endeavor could be initiated.

Because I had agreed to complete Cornelia's project for money, the efforts I had put into it had been especially painstaking. Consequently I craved a reprieve before assuming an equivalently onerous assignment. Furthermore my mind was preoccupied with other issues. With Tiberius' monumental change imminent I was steeling myself mentally and emotionally, in case it caught us off guard and unprepared by assuming a form we had never anticipated. More tangibly: the second anniversary of Alcimus' birth was approaching. Since he was too young to understand its implication, did we really need to celebrate it? "Why should we not let him enjoy being a center of attention for an afternoon?" Tiberius responded to my consideration.

Having in mind the ideal birthday gift—or so I presumed—I summoned Ajax to my studio. Could he possibly fashion a loom suitable for Alcimus: diminutive and simple to operate, yet highly durable? Not such a good idea, Ajax responded after some thought. The mechanism for changing the direction of the warp between passes of the shuttle might prove frustrating to operate, as well as a painful trap for little fingers. So too the beater bar for compressing the threads. Nonetheless he would give the idea further consideration. When I was back in the studio about a week later, Ajax returned with Chrysanthe. She carried a rectangular frame, with pegs extending along either of its narrower sides. Cords of yarn were strung from the pegs across the center of the frame. Chrysanthe picked up a wood shuttle shaped rather like a dasheen. Through hole at one end, a strand of yarn was threaded. She showed me how to create a simple weave by passing the shuttle over one warp thread and under the next, and then repeating the procedure alternately in the opposite direction: thrusting the shuttle under threads it had previously gone over, and over those it had previously passed under.

Ajax cautioned me. Despite its simplicity, the peg loom may require more precision and patient repetition than Alcimus possessed at his age. The gift would hardly be a waste, however, as it could be merely put aside until the boy was older. Whether Alcimus took to the loom or not, hopefully he would enjoy a toy Ajax had invented. It was rectangle of finished wood, with rounded corners and an oval opening extending lengthwise across its center. A block of wood, fitted into grooves along the edges of the opening, could be slid back and forth from one end of the opening to the other. The curved ends of the opening prevented the block from reaching them, and squeezing fingers in the process. "A simulated loom shuttle!" I remarked joyously, as though I had made a marvelous discovery.

Before Ajax and Chrysanthe arrived I had been working on a new project I had initiated: painting a white blossoming tea shrub upon the swath of copper colored linen I had purchased in Naples. After the pair had left I could not

753

resume my artistic endeavor, but only sit and think about Ajax. This avowed homosexual's admirable understanding of and appreciation for children had taken me by surprise. One might have presumed Ajax' aberrant sexual inclination would have prompted him to recoil from children. Instead he reveled in them, and clearly had their best interests at heart. How inclined we humans are to let one another's distasteful qualities becloud our identification of better traits.

My reflections elicited a stern warning from Tiberius after I shared them with him. Although a loyal servant, an unexcelled carpenter, a pleasant person, and an insightful devotee of children, Ajax was still a man of deviant character. Excessive appreciation for Ajax' worthwhile qualities could blind me to indications he may be attempting to lure Alcimus—or any other boys or men for that matter, free or servile—toward homosexuality. Ever I must be alert to and cautious about Ajax' intentions. Chastened I thanked him for the admonition, but added I could hardly bring myself to hate Ajax. Tiberius returned he would have sold Ajax long ago had he hated or feared the man. Ajax' sexual orientation, not his person, was the objectionable to be guarded against.

On Alcimus' birthday I had Briseis prepare a party, in the nursery beginning at noon. No one from the Palatine was able to come. The chest cold with which Augustus was struggling had taken a turn for the worse that morning, leaving him too ill to attend any of the business he had scheduled for the day. Livia had to substitute for him, while Antonia addressed the matters Livia had originally planned to handle. For a gift the family had sent a little cloak of fine bright red wool, with which Alcimus appeared quite pleased. Thrasyllus and Aka participated in the fete. Their gift to Alcimus—a tambourine—I deemed quite appropriate for a child entering his third year, although I pitied the servants its effect along with the trumpet and drum upon their ears. Scourus the chef—the nanny Amera's husband—prepared an assortment of appetizing pastries. These goodies prompted me to relate—jocundly, without bitterness, and to the sincere amusement of the adults present—my recollection of those tasteless, grease-laden, puke-inducing pastries with which my foster family had celebrated birthdays.

Alcimus was mildly intrigued by the peg loom but far more taken with the sliding block. So was Phoenix, whose attempt to get the toy away from Alcimus precipitated a noisy altercation. Briseis promptly intervened. Today was Alcimus' special day, she explained, just like the special day Phoenix had enjoyed not terribly long ago. Alcimus had been given the block slide as a gift for his special day, even as Phoenix on his occasion had received the puzzle board Uncle Ajax had made. And being Alcimus' special helper anyway, Phoenix could take pleasure from making sure Alcimus enjoyed his celebration and his gifts. *Already Briseis is grooming Phoenix to become Alcimus' valet*, I mused silently. The party lasted barely two hours. By then tears were beginning to flow once again: not from anger but from the exasperation of sheer exhaustion. The adult guests departed, leaving Briseis and her nanny colleagues to settle the celebrant and his cohorts down to nap.

Precisely one week later we began to receive, every several days, word of Gaius' return to Italy. He had quit Heliopolis for Antioch on Alcimus' birthday. To publicize he was now a private citizen, he had booked passage for Livilla and himself on an ordinary merchant vessel bound for Italy. On its fourth day at sea this ship put into port at Limyra on the coast of Lycia: not to unlade or lade wares, but because her chief passenger had taken gravely ill. Gaius was transported to the infirmary at the local barracks. Three days later, on the ninth day before the New Year, he expired *[February 21, 4 CE]*. The physicians who attended him in his final hours concurred, his health had been too weak to bear the ordinary rigors of travel. He should have lingered longer in Heliopolis, and not considered journeying to Italy until better recovered.

Sitting in my studio, trying to think of a special gift for Augustus, I found myself wondering why this terrible misfortune had occurred. The resignation of a successor was an aggravating but not necessarily insurmountable setback to a government. The loss of a beloved grandson, upon whom so much hope had been lavished, was irredeemable. All the more devastating was the occurrence of Gaius' death, less than three years after that of his brother Lucius. Augustus was now facing the fact his insistence had wrought Gaius' demise. One could only imagine the consequent emotional distress. For perhaps the first time, a strong contempt—almost a loathing—for Augustus surged through my conscience. Why was he so abjectly selfish, so self-righteous, that he could not discern Gaius' objection to journeying before sufficiently strengthened was a plea for his very life? And what was wrong with Gaius for not standing his ground, especially now he was a private citizen? I recalled the many times Tiberius, in the tone of weary resignation he often assumed when discussing his stepfather, reminded me how impossible Augustus was to resist. No member of his family had ever opposed him without enduring suffering of some sort.

Suddenly I recognized a blatant and uncharitable condescension I had been harboring. Not only had I been begrudging Augustus his relentless imperativeness: his family I had been viewing with a harsh double standard. Those who acquiesced to Augustus—Tiberius included—I had been scorning as pusillanimous. Yet relatives like Julia and her namesake daughter—both of whom had suffered terrible reprisal for resisting the emperor—I had been disdaining as disrespectfully parricidal and well deserving of their punishments.

Now earnestly forgiving, I felt the resentment dissipate from me in physical sensation—as though my body discharged an unhealthy vapor or humor. Augustus I started to pity, sincerely and grievously, for the anguish which must have been weighing upon his conscience. From the sense of his character I had gained during our rooftop conversations, I was persuaded he assuredly recognized his importunity had brought about Gaius' demise. Clearly the rightful domicile Thrasyllus had predicted for Gaius' safety was Syria. Driven by his own relentlessness, however, Augustus had made up his mind this safe haven could only be Italy; and he had persuaded Gaius accordingly.

Now I suggested my *Lion of Nemea* or *Charioteers* as a consolatory gift for Augustus. Tiberius forbade me unequivocally. Those masterworks must remain in our domicile for Alcimus to behold, and come to appreciate as he matured. Surely I had another work suitable for Augustus. Ironically, Tiberius had not been so possessive of the *Zeus Descending to Danae* when he recommended I surrender it to the Ennii. We are all entitled to changes of opinion and mood.

Descending the stairs to my studio, I could not think of anything tangible in my collection. An idea began to take shape in my mind, firmly and surprisingly forcefully. I found a blank palette, about the same size as the one on which I had depicted Lucius Caesar as Ganymede being carried to the heavens on the divine eagle. In the center of the blank I sketched Pegasus soaring skyward, from the viewer's left to right, with a youth (Gaius) astride his back. Before, beside and behind Pegasus I drew flying cupids. In the upper right I depicted a bearded Jupiter seated on his throne, to his right Venus standing with two more cupids, and to his left Lucius Caesar holding a chalice in his role as Ganymede. My inspiration was the sculpted group in the Temple of Mars the Avenger, which represents that divinity with Venus at his right and the deified Caesar the Dictator at his left.

So not to compromise its quality, I did not rush this design. Nevertheless it developed quickly. Moreover to my immense relief and satisfaction, it appeared to represent the best of my artistic ability. By noon the basic sketch was finished. When Phaedra came to summon me for luncheon, I asked her to send biscuits and cheese to the studio. These I proceeded munch while beginning to fill in the details of musculature and visages. In the afternoon, Amera brought Alcimus and Phoenix for a visit. With each stroke of charcoal, I explained how it enhanced the scene: see the way this line helps show the horse is moving, this next that the man's hair is streaming in the wind, these little dashes that the horse's wings are made of feathers. The project so energized me, I felt neither the need for afternoon rest nor enervation at the day's ending, which I did not even notice until darkness enshrouding the studio forced me to light a lamp. I might even have continued by lamplight had Alcmene not intruded, to advise me Master was demanding I leave off and retire for the night.

Back in our parlor, I found Tiberius at once exasperated and amused by my unrelenting zeal. He had already bathed and supped. My own meal of kid and vegetable stew—Scourus' culinary opposite of Euethia's horror—was holding warm on the brazier.

After a night of sound sleep I woke refreshed at first light, and hastened to my dressing room. With the assistance of a somnambulant Nausicaa, I donned one of the shabby paint-splattered chitons reserved for my purpose at hand. Beginning with the divinities, I painted them in pale but iridescent shades of yellow and white—deliberately rendering their features indistinct so they appeared to be humanized figures of light. The front of Pegasus and his cupid escorts I represented similarly; but the horse's rear I colored with the more earthy hues of cream, tan, light gray, and a bit of brown. The gradation symbolized the ascent from the material realm to the spiritual. The rider's skin I gave the warm hue of healthiest flesh, his face a nuance of luminosity as he beholds his destination; and I made sure he had Gaius' sand-colored hair. The entire scene I decided to impose upon a simple background of pristine blue. Doing so not only obviated the necessity of adding more details such as earth and sea, but enhanced the sense of apotheosis: a flight through the sky. When Aminocles brought Alcimus and Phoenix that afternoon, I questioned them about the colors as I mixed them on my paint palette or applied them to the scene: which goes here, now which goes there? To my surprise and immense delight, Alcimus by pointing correctly identified all he was shown. Phoenix, however, could offer no more than a good guess each time he was asked.

Again I worked through the entire day, taking the same luncheon victuals and foregoing afternoon repose. By evening the entire work was finished except for an area of background at the bottom. Come the morrow I completed the tableau, filling in what was left of the background and adjusting some fine details here and there. By noon the piece was finished; and I carried it to the kitchen for quick drying. Luncheon and afternoon respite I took with Tiberius, who remarked it was high time I joined him. Lioness-like I responded, audibly and physically, in our bed.

Now why was I suddenly so pensive, he queried later while we were bathing: had I caught Thrasyllus' affliction? My confession to having been thinking about Augustus elicited a roll of eyes. Continuing, I maintained that I could not recall ever having completed a painting of such excellence in so short a period of time. The impetus to accomplish that goal had been a relentlessness beyond comprehension—beyond my ability to construe let alone describe. I felt as though I had touched the daemon of Augustus' inexorability. So integral was this to his character, the daily fulfillment of its demands defined his very existence. Little wonder he was mystified and grieved by the inability of his nearest and dearest to emulate or even appreciate such drive. Tiberius raised his eyebrows, then leaned over and kissed my forehead.

New Year's Eve arrived. Since Augustus was mourning Gaius we could not expect an invitation to celebrate on the Palatine. Tiberius and I supped on a roast of pork with Thrasyllus and Aka in their quarters. The astrologer's markedly increased reticence made the both of us uncomfortable, despite his profuse apologies and assurance his distraction had absolutely nothing to do with anyone present. Thrasyllus insisted he was still preoccupied with the details of establishing his academy. He proceeded meticulously to describe how he and his manservants had spent the preceding week, removing volumes from his study at the Villa Maecenatis to the new school library, and combing the stores and stalls of booksellers for more. Thrasyllus had also sent to my Rhodian farm for the books he had left in storage there. Not having heard from Lucius Ennius since our visit to his farm, Thrasyllus had finally mustered the temerity to approach him for funds to purchase school furniture: shelving, desks and the like. My uncle had duly responded with a substantial donative.

We anticipated passing New Year's Day in the manner we spent most holidays—lounging about while letting our servants enjoy a reprieve from their duties—until in midmorning, Tiberius received an urgent summons to the Palatine. The day being at once a Saturday and a holiday, the gardens were open to the public; and because the weather was unseasonably warm and salubrious there were many visitors. Some milled about impatiently while others stood and gawked, behind the implied boundaries the guards created to allow Tiberius' litter and its escort to pass. This exhibition of privilege and rank I found distinctly annoying: for the visitors, whose pleasure had to be interrupted as they were herded together like sheep; for the guards, who had to keep bystanders at their distance and endure the complaints of some; for Tiberius, who loathed being an object of scrutiny and speculation.

In the territory of the Germans, Maroboduus the dynamic young chieftain of the Marcomanni had been remarkably successful in subjugating other tribes of his race to his control. This achievement portended the emergence of a unified German kingdom, from what had been conglomeration of aggressive but mutually independent entities. Augustus desired Tiberius' assessment of this development, and of its implications for Roman military strategy in the area. Tiberius had taken with him my rendering of Gaius' apotheosis. On returning home he reported Augustus had contemplated the tableau during a rather lengthy silence. Then after a sigh, the emperor quietly remarked he expected no less excellence nor compassion from me.

Tiberius said Augustus had told him to ask me, whether I were willing to allow Longus to market copies of the Gaius tableau—a request to which I consented without hesitation. Augustus never thanked me directly either verbally or in writing for this painting; yet I felt honored rather than slighted by his omission. The emperor himself considered me so much a friend, so much an intimate, that he could rest confident I did not require a visible acknowledgment of his gratitude. I never saw either my original of Gaius' apotheosis, or my representation of his brother Lucius as Ganymede, displayed in any of Augustus' domiciles. Only when reflecting on this matter years later did I ask Tiberius whether he knew whatever became of those two paintings. My query surprised him. Had I never learned, never been apprised, that Augustus had had them placed before their corresponding funerary urns in his family mausoleum? What venue for their display could be more appropriate?

From the Palatine, Tiberius brought the New Year's gifts Livia had prepared for the children. For each of the three elder boys was a shovel and pail for digging in the gardens once the weather allowed; for little Leonidas a wooden rattle painted to resemble a piglet; for Thrasylla a strand of colored glass beads. Thrasylla promptly cast into the toybox the necklace of wooden beads Ajax had made for her, declaring it the stuff of babies and its successor befitting a girl of her maturity. In anticipation of Gaius' funeral, Germanicus and Drusus had arrived from Gaul, as had Marcella and all three of her children: Lucius, Gaius and Iulla. Germanicus and Drusus were staying on the Palatine, where Tiberius had already spent the afternoon with them. Marcella and her offspring went to reside with her sister Claudia.

Claudia reminded everyone the anniversary of the art exhibit at the Porticus Octaviae was precisely one week away. Time was at hand to discuss closing and dismantling it, especially now that Marcella was present to participate. Were the planners agreeable to meeting at her house for luncheon on the morrow? We all assented, unanimously grateful, I believe, for this distraction from the bereavement, and worse yet the uncertain future with which the death of Gaius was confronting the family.

It was agreed that whoever solicited contributions from particular cities should assume the responsibility, of thanking those same cities for their participation and ensuring their entries were safely returned. This consensus of course excluded me, since I had not contacted any cities in the first place. Therefore to have a role in helping out, I volunteered to oversee the disassembly of the exhibit at the portico, ensuring everything was well packed and properly addressed. This offer won warm acceptance, which my next did not. When I suggested leaving my panorama of Rome to become part of the portico's permanent exhibition, my colleagues glanced at one another uncomfortably. Then Prima remarked reticently, that for a decision of this character the approval of Pappus the curator must be secured. Her meaning was amply clear: my work did not meet the artistic standard of the permanent collection. So I replied, as my audience shifted about contritely. No offense was intended, Claudia offered cautiously. None was taken, I responded reassuringly. Representing buildings was the weakest of my artistic skills. Then waxing contrite, I apologized for having been so presumptuous. A successful decorative artist I was without question; but being such did not make me a grand master. That some elements of my style were similar to those of Zeuxis of Heraclea hardly made my work the equal of his.

My remorse was fleeting. It dissipated upon my reminding myself no human being is exempt from uttering nonsense, or from presuming to be in some way superior to what he or she actually is. What a contrast to my past, when I had spent hours, days, weeks and even months and years ruing such gaffes. "Forget that past!" Tiberius chided after I had related my reflections to him while we bathed. Why was I wasting time and mental energy, measuring the better person I had become against the person I once was? Was it not more worthwhile to direct that time and energy exclusively to being the better person? As for the panorama: Tiberius concurred it hardly represented my best work. Nonetheless I ought to consider retaining it as a memento of the exhibition, and offer Longus the opportunity to copy it. That the original had been displayed in the exhibition, Longus would make a selling point for the reproductions. And of course I could always give Longus the original outrightly, if I could not abide keeping it.

My task at the Porticus Octaviae lasted four days, was pleasantly diverting, and could not have occurred at a more opportune time. All the children fell ill, first with a stomach ailment which disappeared once its victim vomited, and subsequently with the croup. The volatility of that spring's weather— brief periods of sweltering warmth alternating with lengthy chills sufficient to produce overnight frost—proved deleterious to the health of many adults as well, Augustus among them. Barely did he recover from one ailment before contracting another. He had overcome his chest cold, but now once again had catarrh.

When not consulting with his stepfather about the German situation, Tiberius filled his days visiting sick folks. Usually he took Chloe with him. The reply she gave, after I marveled neither she nor Tiberius had contracted anything, rather intrigued me. I had expected her to boast—and not without justification—about her sedulous devotion to her craft of maintaining health as well as promoting recovery. Instead she asserted that sincere and unselfish desire to comfort and heal the sick provides sound protection from their ailments. *An unwitting acknowledgment of Underlying Good*, I thought to myself quite contentedly.

In the end I not only kept the panorama, but reveled with relief I had not disposed of it. Within the span of a few days I had gone from loathing the piece as a blatant example of inferior workmanship to cherishing it as a memento. The experiences it evoked had changed my life inexorably. Augustus' nieces had accepted me as a colleague in the planning and mounting of their exhibition. Augustus himself had befriended me while I sat in his roof garden preparing the panorama. The exhibition itself had set in motion the chain of events, which led to the revelation of the Eupistodoi's fraud, my solution to it, the abandonment of my seething resentment toward them, and the discovery of my true genealogy. To this day I view the painting as an intriguing paradox, of how something superficially banal and contemptable can represent the most inspiring and lifechanging aspects of one's existence. Longus accepted with euphoria my offer to let him copy the piece. He readily agreed to my limit of ten numbered reproductions, and to sending Myronides to execute the work in my storage studio.

Not until the third week of March did the liburna bearing Gaius' ashes and honor guard reach Ostia. Both the cremation and the subsequent departure of the ship had been subjected to repeated postponements on account of bad weather. Augustus set the Calends of April as the date for the funeral.

The obsequies followed the same pattern as for Gaius' brother Lucius. On this occasion, however, I stood with Thrasyllus and Aka among the invited guests rather than with the spectators. Antonia introduced me as Tiberius' ward Galatea to her daughter Claudia Livilla, the widow of the decedent. Petite and lithe, with ivory skin, black hair, and dark limpid eyes, Livilla seemed almost an animate sculpture representing some artist's idealization of young womanhood.

Her girlhood ugliness, which I had endeavored to attenuate in the portraits I had created on Rhodes, was now superseded by striking beauty. Livilla curtsied to me, and graciously expressed thanks for my condolences in forthright but modulated tones. Germanicus conducted the funeral because Augustus was still ill, and had to watch the proceedings lying in his litter. The paean Tiberius delivered ex tempore—succinct yet thorough, laudatory but not obsequious— was a significant improvement over the turgid written lament he had presented for Lucius Caesar. Throughout the ceremony Agrippina sobbed bitterly and manifestly, adamantly refusing comfort from all who offered. Livilla presented quite the contrast, standing silently with lowered eyes and demure visage. Yet despite the niceties of her demeanor—her aplomb, her poise, her courtesy— there was a subtle, nearly indefinable, peculiarity about Livilla which made me uncomfortable. Almost I felt as though nuances of dishonesty and hypocrisy underlay the refined behaviors she displayed—rather like our infanticidal servant Pericalles, but hardly the same.

The ceremony over, Augustus promptly had himself whisked off homeward. Livia polled the family group: did we care to gather on the Palatine as we had after Lucius' funeral, or simply return to our individual homes? Everyone chose the latter option except for Tiberius. He elected to repair the Palatine, to spend additional time with Drusus and Germanicus during the remainder of their furlough in Rome: in three days they must return to Marseilles. Tiberius did not insist they seek him at the Villa Maecenatis, although as father to the one and uncle to the other, his doing would have been the exercise not only of privilege but of expectation. Rightfully, as he told me later, I surmised his purpose was to avoid any risk of having to explain Alcimus.

That Calends of April marked the fourth anniversary of my investigation of the Rhodian farm and decision to purchase it—although I felt as though eons had passed since that event. So I remarked to Tiberius, who concurred. On that farm we had sought refuge from disgrace and peril, never anticipating there to find the joy of my restored gynecologic health followed by the birth of our son.

As the month progressed the weather at last became stable and tepid. There were quite a few rainy days, as is typical for the season; but those which were clear were gloriously so. The extent of daylight was now noticeably longer. Everyone's health rebounded, as did invitations to suppers on the Palatine. We had received none throughout March, and quite understandably. One could assuredly pardon Augustus for not feeling sociable, given his illnesses, his grief over the death of Gaius, the military instability of the German theater, and the need to find a regent for Germanicus. Livilla had succeeded me as the primary target of Agrippina's sneers and scowls. So I noted with mild amusement, and compassion toward the new victim. Livilla still treated me politely and deferentially.

The foliage, long abeyant because of the prolonged cold, at last began to sprout and bloom. One of the earliest to blossom was the red-leafed plum tree. Eagerly I set about painting it, to replace the representation Tiberius had insisted I send the Ennii. The new depiction proved superior to the former, not only because my style was more developed but because the tree was more efflorescent this year than last.

Once again Briseis and the other nannies brought the children into the gardens. Phoenix and Alcimus were now talking generatively rather than imitatively: putting forth original ideas and not just responding to those others offered. Every other sentence was a question: why this, why that? They pursued the tossing or rolling of balls, racing one another across expanses of grass, floating their toy boats in the pond or peristyle fountains, and sometimes throwing rocks into the water until stopped by their duennas. They played hide and seek amid the shrubbery and *helped* the gardeners, who indulged them with simple assignments like gathering prunings into piles.

Little Leonidas, who was just learning to walk, could not keep pace with his fellows when they romped about the gardens, and hence was not included in their excursions. He did follow his confreres about, when they played in the villa's peristyle garden. I admired his persistence. He could only take a few halting steps, before his legs gave way and forced him to fall to his knees or onto his fanny. Without the slightest frustration he would raise himself on hands and knees, haul himself upright, and repeat the procedure. In a section of the peristyle well secluded and shaded by bushes, Ajax constructed a large shallow box, which the gardeners filled with a clean mix of soil, sand, and crushed pine needles. Ajax had had the foresight to construct a cover as well, to keep the contents dry and free of vermin, and to obstruct the household clowder from utilizing the box as a latrine. With their shovels and pails the boys created gardens, roadways, rivers, harbors, and even buildings. The single time Leonidas entered the box he promptly sat down in the dirt, seized a handful, and endeavored to stuff it into his mouth. Thereafter Leonidas was allowed to watch his comrades from outside the dirt box but not set foot therein.

Although she occasionally participated with the boys in their activities, Thrasylla had little inclination to do so. Most often I saw her slowly strolling the gardens with Nausicaa's younger sister Calypso, whom she had befriended. Thrasylla's strong intellectual leanings intrigued Calypso. Moreover Thrasylla craved an audience, which Calypso provided. She would listen fascinated, to Thrasylla's earnest if sophomoric expositions on history, literature, art, natural science, and grammatical constructions.

From his wetnurse's arms, or from his bassinet woven of Egyptian reeds, bright eyed Balbilus would watch the goings-on for a time. Before long, however, he would start fussing because he was hungry or wet and have to be taken back inside the villa; or he would simply fall asleep to think through the hubbub he had observed.

The spirits of Balbilus' father lifted considerably at this time. Notices Longus had posted at his Gallery of the Four Winds, about the academy Thrasyllus was endeavoring to launch, had netted applications from nineteen prospective students: fifteen at the intermediate level and four aspiring sophistoi. Tiberius too was lighthearted. He thoroughly enjoyed advising his stepfather on military matters in the capacity purely of a counselor, free of the responsibilities associated with an actual command.

During that April I received and accepted invitations to three salons offered by society ladies—one of them Livia Ocellina. All three events were excruciatingly boring. No poet or musician or artist or intellectual was presented. Nor was any program devoted to the examination of a particular topic or discipline. Children were either bragged or complained about, husbands almost exclusively the latter. There was much speculative gossip about presumed marital frictions, illicit sexual liaisons, gluttony, winebibbing, unseemly personal habits and traits, extravagant dress. Notably and extraordinarily gratifying for me, however, was my having been invited directly: a proof of my acceptance in Roman high society.

At the final occasion—Ocellina's in fact—Cornelia Saturnini showed up wearing the stola I had painted for her, even though the late April weather was too warm for its wool fabric. Upon catching sight of me, Cornelia immediately and quite vociferously displayed the design, and credited me for having negotiated with the artist for its completion. The consequence was ever so predictable. Cornelia was surrounded with admirers; and I was barraged repeatedly with the question, *Can a similar product be completed for me?* Over and over I delivered the same pitch I had given Cornelia six months earlier: *Send a written request to me, Galatea Aristoclide, at the Villa Maecenatis, and I shall contact the artist. Pricing and length of time to completion will depend upon the type of design desired. The artist reserves the right to refuse any order or postpone its acceptance, and will not guarantee a specific date for completion.*

At this gathering's close, as Antonia and I were preparing to board our respective litters, Lucilius Longus' wife Rutilia approached us with a mischievous smile. What did I think about joining her, in mounting a salon to consider the life and work of the renowned, reclusive, mute decorative artist Eutychus of Rhodes? Being his *pupil* (she deliberately cleared her throat and winked), I was well suited to deliver a presentation. Rutilia was willing to offer her home, unless I should prefer to host the event at the Villa Maecenatis. At supper on the Palatine the following evening Antonia related Rutilia's suggestion, to the merriment and encouragement of all present except for Agrippina.

As that April drew toward its end Tiberius went daily to the Palatine, departing directly after breakfast each morning and not returning until late afternoon. Moreover he became markedly reticent, and had trouble sleeping. Whenever I asked him what was wrong he readily apologized for his quietude. He was merely preoccupied, he assured me, with the German situation that was becoming increasingly acute. But then, on the final day of the month, the real reason for Tiberius' distraction was revealed. It changed our lives prodigiously—yea, monumentally.

The day was a Wednesday. The very weather seemed ominous: uncomfortably humid, with dark, heavily overcast skies threatening rain. After Tiberius left for the Palatine, I decided any efforts I made at painting would be futile since they could not possibly dry in the damp. Accordingly I repaired not to my studio but to the peristyle, where I knew the children were present. Alcimus and Phoenix were in the dirt box, from which Amera was distracting Leonidas and the daughter of the wetnurse by tossing a ball. Thrasylla was lecturing a fascinated if befuddled Calypso about the asterism Praesippe. Balbilus was babbling contentedly in his bassinet. Although the air was not particularly warm, while walking I felt heated; and my garments clung uncomfortably to my skin. Yet as I seated myself in the dining pergola, a sudden chill coursed through me. Although I attributed the sensation to clamminess of body and clothing from perspiration, its brief occurrence left me with an odd sense of foreboding.

Presently Alcmene hastened toward me, carrying my tattered pink veil. While wrapping the garment about me she explained, with the usual agitation she displayed toward matters she considered urgent, that Caesar had sent a litter for me and it was waiting at the villa's entrance. With my head lowered, the veil drawn over as much of my face as possible without obscuring my vision, I descended the front steps through the corridor of guards holding back the onlookers, to the litter awaiting me. The Palatine ostiarius said I should proceed to Syracuse. Knowing by this he meant Augustus' rooftop study I ascended the appropriate staircase, and arrived before the First Citizen of Rome huffing and puffing, perspiring and disheveled.

Present with Augustus were Tiberius, Livia, and Antonia, but no one else—not a notary, secretary, stenographer, nor even a servant. Augustus was seated behind his desk, Livia and Tiberius each on an ancillary chair, Antonia on a settee. As I took my place beside her amid a murmur of salutations, she helped me remove my veil. Augustus rose, turned to the credenza behind him, poured water from a jug into a tumbler, and handed the tumbler to me. Grateful for the refreshment I began to drink deeply, but stopped abruptly upon noting everyone wore a somber expression and had not uttered a word since greeting me. At the same time the significance of the venue struck me. We were sequestered in Augustus' private sanctuary, where our conversations could not be accidentally overheard.

My stomach tightened and my throat constricted, causing me to cough. Antonia rubbed my back. Augustus reseated himself and set his eyes upon me. Never before had his intense gaze seemed so piercing. Terror surged in me momentarily, as I began to surmise the purpose of the gathering. Then a calm and defiant fortitude followed. While taking another sip of my draught, I returned Augustus' gaze with an almost insolent confidence. Then I said steadily, "You have designated Tiberius regent for Germanicus. Now you want me to accept divorce, so Tiberius can wed Antonia or Agrippina! Well, Sir, I absolutely and unequivocally refuse!"

To my surprise, Augustus lowered his eyes. While watching him, awaiting his answer, I heard Tiberius shift in his chair, and felt Antonia take my hand in hers. When Augustus resumed looking at me his gaze was unmistakably softer, and actually rather abashed as though my words had stung. After a sigh he spoke in slow, measured, almost pleading tones. "Clytia...our ever-perceptive Clytia...you are nearly correct. Tiberius has agreed to become my adoptive son, and successor to my office in lieu of my grandson Gaius. Tiberius will adopt Germanicus to become his successor in turn. You need not fear divorce, for which I did not press you. Tiberius most explicitly made his acceptance of my request conditional upon retaining you as his wife. Without cavil I agreed. All I ask of you, is your cooperation in maintaining—perhaps permanently—the subterfuge you are Tiberius' Greek ward. Your son may not discover his true identity until the reading of Tiberius' will unveils it."

Those words might have left me numb and disjointed with relief, blubbering with gratitude for the exemption from divorce. Instead my defiance remained. It did not arise from the prospect of continuing the charade, or of postponing the revelation of Alcimus' paternity: Tiberius and I had discussed and prepared for these contingencies even before we left Rhodes. A different ancestry—my own—impelled the challenge with which I responded. "Why not instead reveal who I truly am: one of the Ennii, an Italian, a member of the race you are endeavoring to preserve unadulterated? You are striving to stimulate marriage between Italians. Why not maintain Tiberius, believing I was Greek, took me as his ostensible ward and surreptitious mistress? When my genuine background was uncovered, Tiberius did not hesitate to marry me and acknowledge our presumed bastard. Will not this scenario render Tiberius, as your intended successor and afterward as prince himself, a more credible exemplar for intra-Italian marriage than a twice-divorced bachelor?"

All the while I spoke, Augustus nodded with averted eyes. When I finished he affixed his gaze on me anew, now with a pensive demeanor. "We considered this course of action, but rejected it because the Ennii are adamantly politically neutral. How would we placate them, should they raise objections to one of their own succeeding to Livia's position? Furthermore your mother's sister was married for a time to Publius Norenas. Our intelligence has determined he died this winter past. Imagine, however, the ensuing scandal, should Lucius Norenas expose you as his former fiancée after you and Tiberius make public your marriage.

"More seriously: the neutrality of the Ennii has earned them the hostility of the Scribonii Libones. Being the dominant family of Calabria, the Libones resent the refusal of the Ennii to become their retainers. Well you know the Libones are virulent opponents of Tiberius. Nor have they ever been terribly fond of me, even while I was married to one of them. Nonetheless they have been exulting for nearly half a century over their alignment to my political position, through their blood relationship to my daughter and her children. Now the death of Gaius has devastated that connection, wreaking far greater attrition than did the demise of Gaius' brother or the disgraces of his mother and sister. The only link the Libones will have to my position, is the betrothal and eventual marriage of Agrippina to Germanicus; for I am not preparing Postumus to assume a role in political affairs.

"I anticipate having to offer the Libones concessions, to deter their fomenting opposition to my decision. For this very reason I am also going to adopt Postumus because he is descended from the Libones, although he will not be an active participant in governmental proceedings and certainly not designated a successor. You well understand that marriages in our milieu reinforce political alliances. For Tiberius, whom the Libones already regard as an enemy, to reveal he is married to a woman whose family the Libones also consider adversarial, will make the task of mollifying them all the more difficult if not impossible. Your son presents another possible opponent for the Libones. Never mind your marriage is morganatic and you have foreordained your son to be strictly a private citizen. Should his existence become known, he will have the potential for attracting political adherents. This same development I envision for Postumus.

"Consider as well, the effect disclosing your marriage would have upon you. Are you prepared and inclined to spend your days as Livia does hers? Once you are known as Tiberius' wife, you will be overwhelmed with petitions and requests for intervention and expected to respond to all. The time left for you to engage in painting will be minimal, if not precluded altogether."

By now I was nodding my comprehension. My defiance had lessened considerably but not disappeared entirely.

Augustus continued. "We need to convey the impression Tiberius has shifted his priorities to his new office, thereby curtailing the amount of time and attention he once devoted to charitable activities as a private citizen. You of course are chief among those charities; therefore you and Tiberius must ostensibly separate. Only ostensibly!" He had noticed my startle. "After Tiberius has taken up residence here on the Palatine, you will continue to reside at the Villa Maecenatis as his ward. When invited to sup with us here, you can remain for the night. Whenever we quit Rome for vacation Tiberius will accompany us, and so will you as our invited guest. Tiberius will be among us too, when the oppressive air of the Palatine drives us to seek relief at the Villa Maecenatis amid the breezes of the Esquiline. If and when the public becomes aware of your son, we shall maintain he is the offspring of the estranged husband from whom Tiberius shielded you. Rumors Tiberius is his father are certain to spread, with the boy's similarity in appearance to Livia cited as evidence. Fortuitously the resemblance is not so strong, that our publicists cannot dismiss it as coincidental. Otherwise we should have to remove the two of you from Rome altogether."

Relief poured through my conscience like a warm liquid; yet my temerity remained. "And where would you have sent us?" I asked Augustus archly.

"Ad Gallinas, Palestrina, Ariccia, Velletri, Tuscolo—any place upon which the two of you agree, provided it is sufficiently close to Rome for Tiberius to reach easily."

Finally I smiled. "Thank you for not forcing Tiberius and me apart," I said, now quite mollified. "Your accommodation of our marriage leaves me more than agreeable to comply with the charade you have proposed. At long last I have ceased loathing myself for engaging in deception. Since early childhood, deception has been my way of life, my means of survival."

Augustus glanced about his audience. "Truly one of our kind," he asserted. Rising again to his feet he said, his tone now distinctly authoritative, "This matter satisfactorily concluded, you are all dismissed."

The four of us—Livia, Antonia, Tiberius, and I—clambered down the staircase without exchanging a word. This stony silence persisted between Tiberius and me as we journeyed together in his litter back to the Villa Maecenatis. But as we walked through the foyer he took my hand and gently said, "We need to consult Thrasyllus. Let us hope he is here and has not gone to his new academy."

The sage's apartment was in a noisy ruckus, as the children were being fed lunch. To our relief we found Thrasyllus was indeed present, having sought refuge in his study. He was partaking from a platter of meat pasties, which he offered to share with us and we refused because neither of us had any appetite. Although I sat down in a chair, Tiberius stood before Thrasyllus, and very agitatedly recounted what had transpired on the Palatine.

"Your monumental change," Thrasyllus concluded, calmly and confidently.

"What change? As much as ever I am my stepfather's lackey! Why could I not refuse him—tell him he must come up with an alternate strategy for the succession? Farther than ever I have moved from becoming the private citizen I so desperately wish to be!"

Thrasyllus remained unruffled. "Hitherto you have always held exalted but subordinate positions within your stepfather's regime: a military commander, and a magistrate with extraordinary powers. You were never indicated to be what he is—until today. From this adoption you will acquire a new name and paternity. Eventually you will assume the position of highest authority recognized by the Roman constitution. Thereafter you will be answerable to no man: only to the laws. This is your monumental change. It is also your destiny, which you cannot alter. Now sit down and compose yourself!"

"My destiny indeed! How can succession to my stepfather's position be right for me, when for my entire life the holding of any public office has chafed and discomfited me? My destiny is to succumb unresisting to my stepfather's dictates and whims like a stupid unsuspecting ox being led to the slaughter, and end up fretting and chafing in the tasks to which he appoints me—all the while hating and castigating myself for my spinelessness!"

Thrasyllus wiped his hands and mouth on a napkin and rose from his chair. Turning his back to us, he scrutinized the collection of scrolls and tablets on the shelves behind his desk. As he searched, he spoke. "For the past decade you have been trying to become a private citizen. What has your effort accomplished? Your life put at risk, your family aggrieved, and you made a public laughingstock. But hardly has your endeavor turned you into a private citizen."

He selected a small scroll and proceeded to unroll it across the desk. "This is the record of the first prognostication I made for the two of you, back when we were newly acquainted on Rhodes. It states your glory, Tiberius, will overspread the world like the light of the sun; and Clytia will honor and support you with devotion like her namesake flower turning her face to the sun. You will always be together, yet you will always be separate. This second element of the prophecy has already been fulfilled, by Tiberius having to reside on the Palatine and Clytia to maintain a false identity. She has already contentedly accepted this destiny for herself—like the dog trotting cheerfully along with the cart to which he is tethered. You, Tiberius, are the dog being dragged: futilely resisting, and making himself miserable in consequence. You are familiar with that simile, are you not? Clytia knows it."

"Yes, yes, I have read it many times. So I am supposed to rejoice and exult every time my stepfather importunes me, and comply with enthusiastic contentment because I lack the fortitude and determination to refuse him."

"Will you stop wallowing in self-pity long enough to consider today's developments from your stepfather's perspective? Your abortive design to turn yourself into a private citizen thoroughly disaffected him toward you—caused him to scorn you as recklessly and irresponsibly insubordinate. Why did he put his disgruntlement aside and ask you to become his successor? Because he has accepted and acknowledged you alone are best qualified and can best be trusted, properly to continue his life's work after he has departed this world. He had to swallow his pride, annoyance, and concern about the example your rebelliousness set. Doing so required considerable humility from a man of authority unsurpassed."

"How are you so certain this is my monumental change, when there were no portents—no meteors, no lightning, no unusual flights of birds, no oddities in sacrificial victims?"

"The indications were given long ago on Rhodes—and quite manifestly too as I recall—when the imminence of the change was first discerned. Recall the glowing tunic and the eagle. What you are experiencing now is their fulfillment."

"Surely those refer to the fire, when the authority of Rome took refuge in my domicile."

"Took refuge it did—and never left."

Having run out of counterarguments Tiberius rolled his eyes, rose to his feet, and strode from the room without a word or even a glance to Thrasyllus or me. Thrasyllus sighed and said, "He will recover. Right now I recommend you see to him."

"So I shall. Thank you for your patient counsels."

The apartment was now absolutely silent. On my way out I stopped by the nursery. All the boys were asleep; and Thrasylla was working the peg loom originally intended for Alcimus. In the Zone of Neutrality, Tiberius was standing before the door giving onto the gardens—precisely where I had sat after Anthe excoriated me at the art exhibition. Rain had begun to fall. On drawing directly beside him, I realized he was weeping. He took me in his arms and held me close against him. Presently his sobbing diminished and then ceased altogether. He kissed my forehead and softly said, "Come, let us lie down together." He did not elicit sex, but wanted only to sleep in my arms. Upon awakening he smiled at me, then tugged at the collar of his tunic and exclaimed, "Whew! Clammy! I could use a bath; how about you?" His mood had shifted diametrically.

Through the ensuing month of May, daily life at the Villa Maecenatis proceeded essentially unaltered. Tiberius did not immediately take up residence on the Palatine. Unless specifically summoned there he spent his mornings in his office with Fulgens his secretary, considering petitions. Only now instead of simply reviewing these matters and Tiberius' decisions about them, the two were making the necessary preparations to transfer management of the entire operation to Fulgens. Tiberius and I continued to pass our afternoons together. We supped sometimes alone, most often with Thrasyllus and his family, and thrice on the Palatine.

Frequent rains persisted through the first week of that month. Thereafter the weather became clear and warm, inducing what plants had remained dormant to bloom. The gardens became a riot of shapes, colors, and fragrances. The tea shrub burgeoned, giving me a model better than I had originally recorded. Consequently I was able to enlarge and embellish the depiction on the copper-colored linen beyond my original anticipation. By the third week of the month, as this project was drawing to its end, I began casting about for another and found myself torn with indecision. Tired of depicting plants, I longed to paint a detailed portrait of Alcimus. Plants bloom year after year. Whatever I missed in the gardens this season would reappear come the following. Once a child emerges from his present point of maturity to the next, the endearments of the previous stage are forever lost. Still, not to avail myself of the foliage proliferation while it lasted seemed strangely irresponsible. So I kept reiterating to myself, while my distraction rendered the preliminary sketches I made of my son highly unsatisfactory.

Tiberius suggested a portrayal of the villa amid its verdure—a representation long overdue, he added. At first I objected on the ground I was not terribly adept at rendering buildings. Were not the derogations of my efforts by his son Drusus, and the rejection of my panorama by Antonia's sisters, ample proof of their inadequacy? An incentive to improve my technique, he countered rather testily. My new undertaking proved more pleasant than I had anticipated. Beneath the stand of pines I found a place fragrant and well shaded, in which to sit and behold a most interesting vista of the villa. My vantage directly faced the southern corner of the building, from which the front extended to my left, and to my right the side embedded against the slope of the hill.

As I began to sketch, a sort of contented resignation came over me. *This splendid edifice is going to remain my home,* I kept reminding myself. Yes, there was disappointment. Gone were the hopes Tiberius and I had entertained for our future: the tumults of his political past forgiven and forgotten for new life in private philanthropy, disclosure once and for all of my genuine identity without fear of adverse repercussions, recognition and acceptance of Alcimus' true ancestries paternal and maternal. Nevertheless, nothing substantive had changed between Tiberius and me. Acceptance of his new position had done no more than engender some superficial inconveniences. We must continue to maintain our charade of custodian and ward; but we were still married. Abiding in different residences was bound to make intimacy more difficult to come by; but the prospect of arcane encounters offered a titillating excitement.

While I sketched, the children cavorted about the gardens. Their gambols gave me an idea for another painting project. Depicting the children playing in the peristyle would enable me to represent the villa from a different aspect, and include Alcimus in the scene. The notion prompted me to ponder. Clinging to the goodness that inhered in my life—goodness the present disappointments and frustrations did not alter—had left me receptive to this new inspiration. Underlying Good is ever unfolding, ever renewing. Identification and acceptance of present good prepares the human mind to recognize the new forms goodness assumes.

Thrasylla's birthday fell three days before the Calends of June *[May 30]*. We feted her with a luncheon at which Calypso was the guest of honor. Tiberius quite appreciably asked to be excused. His absence Thrasylla did not seem to notice. She roused the anger of her parents by professing immense disappointment with the pair of caged sparrows I presented her: they proved a paltry substitute for the dog she craved to romp with. Patiently but firmly, I advised her the villa belonged not to any of its present occupants but to Caesar. To him we all must answer should the dog damage the building or gardens. After some moments of reflection, Thrasylla's demeanor brightened. She declared that given such circumstances she would gladly accept the sparrows, happy to have pets of any kind at last.

Arriving at the Zone of Neutrality I overheard bustling in my quarters, where my maids were engaged in routine housekeeping. On entering Tiberius' suite for afternoon repose I found him awaiting me still clothed, sitting on the edge of the bed and staring moodily at the floor. The rock of trepidation began to weigh upon my chest as I sat beside him. Turning to face me he took both my hands in his, and gazed at me with a rueful countenance.

"Conditions on the German frontier are rapidly deteriorating for Rome. Maroboduus has been steadily enlarging and unifying his kingdom into a well-organized and forceful opposition. What tribes have remained independent—successful at resisting his efforts to overtake them—continue to mount aggressions of their own against us. Roman morale is extremely low. The present commander-in-chief Marcus Vinicius admits the situation is beyond his ability to address. His subordinate commanders and the soldiery agree, and are clamoring for him to be replaced or superseded."

Tiberius sighed. Averting his gaze from me back to the floor indicated he was lost in thought, searching for the best words to convey his intentions. In measured tones he spoke again. "My stepfather wants me to overweigh Vinicius—assume direct command of the Roman forces on the German front. With him I am entirely in agreement. How can I respond as a distant adviser in Rome, to occurrences requiring immediate intervention? Only from observation of situations firsthand, as they emerge, can effective remedial strategies be formulated."

He tightened his grip on my hands as he resumed looking at me, his expression now wistfully pleading. "Clytia, I may have to be absent from Italy for years. Moreover I shall be in danger, albeit not as much as the soldier in the front line of a battle, or as we were during my confinement to Rhodes. Nonetheless there is always risk to one's person in a military setting."

At a loss for words, I could only nod my comprehension. I was not angry, nor fearful, nor sorrowed, but numbly acquiescent.

"I shall not be departing until July. My stepfather wants first to finalize my adoption. Before he can do so I must adopt Germanicus. He cannot be legally regarded my stepfather's grandson unless I adopt him before my stepfather adopts me. Since Germanicus is of age, he must appear before the praetor to accept his new status. At present he is completing field maneuvers, and not free to depart for Italy before the third week of June. Hence I asked my mother and stepfather if I might take you and Alcimus to Ad Gallinas for the interim preceding Germanicus' arrival. Both approved most heartily. We shall take Nestor and Alcmene, Arbindus and Briseis, Phoenix and Leonidas. My mother has notified the farm's chief steward to make ready for us. I have advised Thrasyllus and Aka. They assured me of their understanding and wished us a vacation filled with bliss."

"They said nothing to me at the party; nor did Briseis."

"I asked them not to, so I might inform you. Now, are you tired; do you wish to sleep?"

"No," I replied truthfully.

"Then I recommend you go supervise your maids, who at my behest are packing clothing and accessories for you to take. My own attendants I shall immediately set to doing the same for me, so we may depart before dawn tomorrow morning. We shall have greater inclination for lovemaking and ample time for it once we reach the farm."

If Tiberius did not inform my women of the purpose of our journey, they assuredly surmised its intent. From my wardrobe they had chosen the most flatteringly seductive garments and accouterments. To complement these selections, Leda the cosmetician had prepared a small collection of subtly evocative shades. Chloe called me to one corner, where she discreetly showed me my box of contraceptives fully replenished. Observing these preparations and contemplating the activities they were intended to promote made my libido soar until I could no longer wait. That very afternoon I engaged Tiberius in our bath, right in the water. Since we could not apply contraceptives, we deliberately halted before reaching climax. This interruption left us trembling with sensual excitement. While we were drying one another afterward—paying special attention to each other's erogenous areas and laughing about the venue I had chosen for seduction—he called me Εμή Λαγνεία [Eme Lagneia - My Lusty One] instead of Εμή Λέαινα [Eme Leaina - My Lioness].

Tiberius continued to employ my new epithet—and most appropriately— through the three subsequent weeks we passed at Ad Gallinas. This sojourn was one of the most intensely erotic episodes of my life. Not once did I touch the paints and palettes I had brought along. We made love passionately and frequently—almost daily and sometimes more than once in a day—amid the deep shade of the laurel terraces (not at the spot I had profaned!), again in our bathwater, most often abed in the suite we shared overlooking the Tiber. It had been Tiberius' during the Saturnalia we spent at the villa, when we had maintained separate quarters to deceive the relatives. Tiberius did not care the villa's staff knew our relationship was amatory, or whether they suspected Alcimus was his son. Never mind he had a mistress: what Roman aristocrat did not? No one was going to spread gossip, lest it elicit reproach and consequences from Livia.

Thanks to the friendly cooperativeness of the villa's personnel, Alcimus and Phoenix participated in farming activities they had been too young to pursue while still in Rhodes. Instead of merely watching the milking of a goat, they were invited to pull her teats. Instead of observing the feeding of the chickens, they were engaged to help distribute the grain. Collecting eggs became a particularly delectable pursuit. They *assisted* a carpenter—fetched materials for him and mimicked his efforts—at repairing a chicken coop. Alcimus duly found a weaver—Nympha by name—who not only let him watch her but helped him pass the shuttle through the warp.

The joy we were sharing—the bliss Thrasyllus and Aka had wished upon us—was nevertheless nervous and frenetic; for it was overshadowed by the melancholy of our forthcoming separation. In quiet pensive moments—while strolling along the villa's pathways, resting after sex, sitting on the balcony of our suite gazing at the rooftops of Rome, or watching the sun turn the Tiber golden while I strummed my harp—Tiberius counseled me for coping with his absence. Seek, he told me, the consolation of his mother, of Antonia and her sisters. All had had to endure the dreadful uncertainty, of wondering whether their husbands while engaged in military operations were safe or even alive. The enforced celibacy I was about to endure was not uniquely mine. Consider Antonia and Marcella, both widowed. Furthermore, was he himself not facing the same challenge?

To keep myself from moping and succumbing to self-pity I should pursue my regular activities, and undertake new projects with determination and vigor. Closest attention must be given to the development of Alcimus. I must prepare to take the initiative on guiding him, and on intervening to subvert undesirable activities or traits. After all, I am going to be the only parent he has directly at hand. Upon our return to Rome, I should see about extracting Alcimus from the household of Thrasyllus and integrating him into my own.

Eleven days before the Calends of July *[June 21]*, we received word from Livia that Germanicus had reached Rome. Augustus had designated the sixth day before the Calends *[June 26]* for the dual adoption, and the evening thereafter for Tiberius' departure to the German front. Not wanting to quit the farm any sooner than we absolutely must, Tiberius set the eve of the adoption for our return to Rome. The hours preceding we passed entwined in one another's arms, kissing, caressing, weeping, drying one another's eyes, and exchanging reassurances. He presented me with a gift, which at first sight made me squeal with salacious laughter before eliciting tears anew. From a linen satchel he withdrew a phallus, reproduced with meticulous and accurate detail in highly polished acacia wood. "It is the next best to me," he said ruefully. "Use it to calm and satisfy your natural desires; and as you do, reflect upon my unshakeable love for you."

When preparing to depart we asked Nestor and Alcmene to join Arbindus and Briseis in their carriage, instead of traveling with us in ours as they had when we came to the farm. Both complied without a word, fully realizing Tiberius wanted to be alone with me. As we were boarding, Tiberius told the coachman to proceed first to the Palatine. During the journey back to Rome we exchanged not a word, but sat holding hands in melancholy silence. When the carriage halted he threw his arms about me, drew me tight against him and kissed me repeatedly. My face became wet with his tears.

"This moment has to be our farewell!" he exclaimed hoarsely. "Be strong, my Lioness: be true to your character! The both of us have succumbed to the Chimera—allowed her to capture and enslave us unawares. Not even our son has escaped her oppression, being forced to live ignorant of his true identity. The arcane subtlety of her wiles and machinations challenges and evades human comprehension. We cannot escape or resist her, only salve and mitigate her afflictions as best we can. To you I must entrust the task of buffering and diverting the blows she directs at Alcimus. Physical distance cannot rupture the love we share. We are only going out of sight, not out of one another's lives."

On returning to the Villa Maecenatis, I discovered all of Tiberius' personal belongings had been removed from his quarters. The suite seemed cavernous and barren—imbued with the impersonal sterility of abandonment. I sat down on the bed in a state of mind I find difficult to describe. Although physically tired, I did not care to sleep. Although emotionally overwrought, I felt no urge to weep. Drained of all energy both physical and mental, I was unable to focus my thoughts even upon Underlying Good. From its satchel I removed the wood phallus and sat gently stroking it, as so often I had its genuine counterpart. Fill my bed with pillows, embrace them with the replica between my legs, and masturbate. This scenario offered a drearily paltry substitute for the intimacy I must forgo, into an unforeseeable future which seemed an endless eternity. Now tears of self-pity began to sting my eyes. I closed them, clenched my teeth, and tightened my hand about the phallus. *It is the next best to me,* echoed through my mind. Other women have endured: now I must stop being a ninny and emulate them.

Suddenly a great horror seized me with an almost physical tangibility—as though some monstrous bird had grasped me in its talons. For more than a year my menses had occurred with absolute regularity. The present onset was nearly a week overdue. Was the uterine growth developing anew? Faint, shaking, and short of breath, I feebly called out, "Fetch Briseis!" and immediately wondered with despair whether anyone had heard me. Someone had. After frantically returning the phallus to its sack, I was struggling to my feet with the intention of stumbling out to the parlor to find an attendant, when Briseis arrived.

"No, Lady, no, no, no!" Her assertion was as compassionate as it was confident. "There cannot be another growth. The large amount laser you have been consuming will have suppressed it. Chloe and I are going to continue administering laser to you in Master Tiberius' absence. The dosage will be lower than what is necessary for contraception, but adequate to forestall a new growth. Your menses is unquestionably delayed for a different reason."

"What, then?"

"Lady, your parting from Master Tiberius cannot help being grievous for you." Briseis' tone was now cautious but still compassionate. "Severe distress can delay a menses or even prevent it from occurring altogether. And if I may be so bold: you are now in your thirtieth year, are you not?"

"I am."

"Although you are yet a bit young, you may be approaching the time in your life when menses cease altogether—particularly given your tumultuous gynecologic history. Do you find yourself becoming suddenly and inexplicably warm from time to time?"

"Not that I have noticed."

She nodded comprehendingly. "There remains the possibility you are once again with child."

"How can that be, when I have been consuming laser?" Although my tone was testy, I was more incredulous than annoyed.

Briseis motioned to the bed with one hand and asked, "May I?" indicating she wished to seat herself beside me. I nodded, and she took her place. "Lady," she continued now earnestly, "Chloe and I have consistently and carefully sought for you the finest, purest, most potent laser available. But the overall reliability of this contraceptive is fading rapidly. The laser plant resists cultivation and only grows in the wild. Overharvesting without allowing time for adequate regrowth has wiped out entire stands, and severely weakened the strains of those which remain. Whenever Chloe and I knew we had a mediocre variety—for example when we could not obtain Cyrenian and had to resort to Syrian— we increased your dosage. Nevertheless the threat of failure has always been present—ever a possibility we were unable to determine when we had a less than adequate batch." Her next words she whispered. "Lady, if you wish to obviate the possibility of pregnancy, I can administer pennyroyal. No one else needs to know—not even Chloe."

"No!" I responded, also in a whisper but emphatically, as my skin crept in revulsion at the prospect. Then aloud I said, "Thank you: now I wish once again to be alone." Briseis rose, curtsied, and departed.

Once again with child. Sporadically I slept, waking with a mingling of excitement and dread. With what more wondrous token of our shared love could Tiberius have left me? Yet this development stood to make him a laughingstock, precisely when his new position required he appear irreproachable—confirming rumors the ward he had been ostensibly sheltering in chastity was actually his mistress, and eliciting snickers over how the forces of nature uncovered his charade. We could resort to another lie, maintaining this child was the offspring of Thrasyllus and Aka. But how could this be fair to Thrasyllus and Aka, let alone the babe? At least the false paternity we had given Alcimus was intangible. Moreover those servants who were not already privy to the true nature of my relationship with Tiberius, would now know and must be consigned to silence. Could every single one be trusted not to break that silence? Not all were of the household of Tiberius. What about the villa's permanent staff who answered to Acer?

And what were the potential dangers to my physique? Practically my entire pregnancy with Alcimus I had passed lying abed with my feet elevated, fearful the slightest movement might induce miscarriage. Now that I was older, was the risk thereof greater? If complications set in, would I survive? Taking several deep breaths, I forced myself to relax. Only the passage of time could reveal the reason for my delayed menses. Not until the cause was known could an appropriate course of action be considered. For the interim the task Tiberius had assigned me, of migrating Alcimus from the household of Thrasyllus into my own, offered a most welcome distraction from rumination about my gynecological condition.

In predawn twilight I fell back asleep. When I awoke the sun was high in the sky. After availing myself of the latrine, I wandered into my dressing room.

Here Gallina, Phaedra, and Alcmene were unpacking and sorting through the articles I had taken to Ad Gallinas. I ordered the women to start moving each and every one of my belongings across the parlor into Master Tiberius' suite. Everything: clothes, accessories, paints, palettes, books, writing tablets.

Phaedra I sent to fetch Arbindus and Briseis. When they arrived I escorted them to a corner of the Zone of Neutrality—out of earshot from my maidservants. In lowered tones but with unabashed confidence, I declared my wish for them to take up residence, with their boys and mine, in what had been my quarters. This intervening parlor we would continue to utilize for dining and the children's play. The thought of offering an explanation did not cross my mind. Briseis, however, immediately surmised my intention. "You are doing well, Lady, to remove your son from his foster family while he is still too young to develop a strong affinity for them which could be hard to break." The three of us proceeded to the quarters of Thrasyllus, who turned out to have gone to his academy. Aka, however, was present. She echoed Briseis in support of my design, and assured me her husband would agree. That he did, in a note I received about an hour later.

By then I had returned to Tiberius' suite and sent for Acer. Not wanting to disclose the reason for the new arrangement, I dissembled that Thrasyllus and Aka found they needed more room. The two suites adjacent to theirs I wanted kept free, for use by Augustus and his family or other guests. Briseis and Arbindus I wanted placed in my former quarters, because its murals were less intimidating for children than the *Odyssey* scenes in the male suite. Hardly could I add that I cherished this venue for myself because it evoked memories of lying in Tiberius' embrace.

Over the next several days Acer had furniture moved and arranged, turning what had been my sitting room into a bedroom for the boys, and the Zone of Neutrality into a dynamic center of familial activity: for meals, play, storytelling and so forth. Alcimus and Phoenix quite understandably demanded to know why they were being relocated. They received the explanation that they were becoming such big boys, we had to give them more space in which to continue growing.

Five days before the Nones of July *[7/3]*, a note arrived from Tiberius. He had arrived safely. As he rode his horse into the great military camp at Augst, the soldiery had broken into loud cheers. That he missed me sorely went without saying. In response I wrote a detailed account of the new living arrangements I had mandated, including my specific rationale for moving myself into his former suite.

779

Still no menses. Standing behind me one morning, Briseis encircled my abdomen with her hands and forearms. Had I felt nauseous at all, she inquired. Indeed I had not.

I started spending most of my waking hours—and his—with Alcimus. Since he and Phoenix were inseparable, I treated them as equals: sketching them while they played together, telling them stories, answering their *Why?* questions, coaching them on numbers, colors, the Greek and Latin alphabets. They were amazingly trilingual: fluent in Greek, Latin, and Gaelic, since Briseis and Arbindus conversed with them in all three tongues. Calling upon the family of Thrasyllus became a delightful adventure, as did visiting me in my studio and Uncle Ajax in his carpentry shop. There were two venues, to which one boy would go but not the other. As much as he liked Scourus the cook, Alcimus found the culinary arts terribly dull. Phoenix, however, was intrigued by them. Contrariwise, Phoenix fretted throughout his first visit with Clytia the aged weaver and refused to accompany us subsequently. Alcimus insisted upon visiting Clytia daily and had to be pacified when he could not.

During the children's naptimes I resumed, with almost obsessive determination, my work on the two tableaux of the Villa Maecenatis—foregoing my own afternoon respite because it brought memories of lying with Tiberius. This I reported to him; and he wrote back a lovingly tender commendation. The possibility I might be pregnant I did not yet mention. Until I knew for sure, I did not care to distress him about this matter.

Precisely one week after Tiberius' departure—on Friday evening four days before the Nones of July *[7/4]*—I was invited to supper on the Palatine, along with Thrasyllus and Aka. Agrippina was not present, having gone to visit Pulchra; and Antonia's daughter Livilla had taken to her bed with a sedative for menstrual cramps. Augustus wanted to take advantage of their absence to inquire freely how I was faring without Tiberius. First I recounted my relocation activities, to my audience's immense enjoyment. Thereafter I announced my conclusion, that brooding over my separation from Tiberius could do nothing more than render me miserable. Consequently I had resolved to immerse myself in distractions while awaiting his return to Rome in triumph. Augustus raised his eyebrows and reiterated, "One of our own."

At that same supper Augustus advised us Titus Livius was making ready to deliver a recitation, of the most recently completed portion of his monumental history of Rome. Upon this endeavor the historian had been working, under Augustus' patronage, for the past three decades. A selection of senators, foreign dignitaries, members of the intelligentsia, and patrons of the literary arts was going to be invited to this present reading. The venue was going to be the lecture hall of the Villa Maecenatis, as it was ideal both in size and dignity to accommodate this elite audience. Our inclusion among the invitees went without saying. The event was going to take place the morning of the fourth Thursday of July—nine days before the Calends of August *[July 24]*. Acer and his people were already coordinating with the imperial publicists on the preparations.

Another week passed without menses. Briseis repeated the process of embracing my abdomen. She also lifted each of my breasts as though to ascertain their weight. Nothing conclusive yet. Although I had filled my bed with pillows and hugged them nightly, I could not bring myself to make use of the phallus. Doing so I felt might profane an unborn child—not physically, but certainly in my conscience.

A society lady whom I did not know at all invited me to attend a delightful salon, at which she and fellow attendees read epigrams they had composed. Antonia and her sisters were present. So was Rutilia, who became wroth with me because I wore a deep green chiton trimmed with an embroidered key border of ivory. "Why are you not wearing one of your paintings?" she demanded in a tense undertone.

"Because I do not wish to become a center of attention, and because I am too busy with other projects right now to accept any new commissions!" I returned in a similar tenor. My answer was as honest as it was deceptive. Indeed I was preoccupied with attending to Alcimus and completing the two villa tableaux, but also with awaiting the determination of my gynecological condition.

During the subsequent week I completed the representation of the villa's exterior. The peristyle scene was taking longer because it required more meticulous detail: the ornamental plants and statuary in close proximity to the viewer's eye, together with the great fountain and the pergola and of course the children at play. The weather turned seasonably torrid: hot and hazy, with humidity that hurt one's lungs and stillness that made one feel engulfed in a blanket. Augustus, who had difficulty breathing in these conditions, became once again a resident of the Villa Maecenatis and beneficiary of the minimal breeze the Esquiline was offering. The rest of the family remained on the Palatine. Either they had sounder constitutions or weaker minds—he was not sure of which, the emperor joked.

Briseis continued to measure my abdomen and lift my breasts each morning. On Thursday she pronounced both tummy and bosom perceptively enlarged. After dressing I collected my paints and unfinished peristyle tableau and headed for that locale. All the children were splashing naked in the fountain, under the careful supervision of Arbindus, Briseis, Amera, and Aminocles. No chances were being taken that someone might slip and crack a skull or choke with water. In the pergola, Augustus was busy with a notary. After seating myself at a discreet distance and opening my paint box, I found myself utterly devoid of motivation. The long wait to ascertain my condition was wearing on me. I closed the box and sat watching the children.

After a while, a slight stir of activity within the pergola caught my attention. The notary, who had risen to his feet, was gathering his tablets. After bowing to Augustus he turned to depart. I resumed watching the children until I felt someone sit down beside me and take my hand. My new companion was Augustus. I smiled, albeit rather halfheartedly. Raising his eyebrows he said, "You are uncharacteristically glum. Tiberius' absence must surely be wearing upon you."

Closing my eyes, I sighed heavily. Momentarily I considered keeping secret the great concern I was harboring, and merely affirming his supposition since it was absolutely accurate. Nonetheless I felt driven to confess my greater distress, even though I dreaded the reaction it might provoke. Opening my eyes I said cautiously, "There is a strong possibility I am with child."

True to my expectation his manner hardened. He let go of my hand. His intense eyes narrowed and seemed almost to glimmer with irritation. "Were you not employing a contraceptive?" he demanded sternly.

Fortunately I was prepared for this question and responded humbly but steadily. "Yes: assiduously. Both of us were utilizing laser, which is recognized as the most effective contraceptive known. My pharmakeutriae have informed me, however, that laser is no longer as reliable as once it was."

"Did they offer an explanation?"

"Overharvesting has weakened its strains."

He looked toward the children in the fountain and nodded slowly. "When will you be certain about your condition?"

"Most likely within a week."

"Have you advised Tiberius?"

"No. Not wanting to alarm him unnecessarily, I have been awaiting confirmation."

Another nod. He still did not look at me. "You understand there will be extraordinarily serious repercussions should this become public knowledge."

"For certain the innuendo." Now in falsetto I intoned, *Tiberius impregnated his ward, the estranged wife of another man!*" and then in sardonic tenor continued, "precisely when he must more than ever be above suspicion. I shudder to imagine how the Scribonii Libones might make use of that tidbit."

"More a feast than a tidbit. We shall assuredly have to send you away from Rome. In due time we may be able to bring you back here, maintaining your second child the result of a short-lived period of reconciliation with your bogus husband—unless your new offspring resembles Tiberius too strongly for us to obfuscate his paternity as we are able for Alcimus."

"Already I have a secretive place to which I can retreat: my farm on Rhodes. You yourself advised me not to dispose of it. Now your counsel is proving its worth."

He resumed looking at me with his steely gaze. "I was thinking of locating you somewhere in Italy. Why distance yourself from Tiberius any more than absolutely necessary?"

My exasperation mounted. This was evident in the tone of my response, despite my effort to remain respectful. "Should we not seek Tiberius' opinion—determine where he prefers I go into hiding?"

He lowered his eyes and nodded. "Indeed we should." Raising his eyes with a gaze milder, less intimidating, he took my hand again. "You are a survivor, my Clytia, whom Tiberius so appropriately calls his Lioness. You will prevail against any and all difficulties the future unfolds for you." For a brief period of silence during which he continued holding my hand, he looked at me with an almost earnest solicitousness—as though he craved assurance I understood his compliment. Without changing his demeanor he spoke again. "You will consider I hope, leaving behind for my family to enjoy, a few of the artistic treasures you created during your sojourn with us."

His abrupt change to the topic of conversation left me nonplussed. "Select for yourselves whatever you desire—the entire collection should you like," I returned wistfully, almost distractedly.

"No," he returned a bit sharply, squeezing my hand. "I am asking you to consider leaving behind only those items you consider dispensable—duplicates, or articles with which you are not entirely satisfied. If you find none, you find none."

Three mornings thereafter I awoke nauseous, reached for my chamber pot, retched but ejected nothing. This event sent Nausicaa, who had been my night attendant, scurrying across the parlor for Briseis. "Lady, I sent Nausicaa to fetch Chloe," Briseis said as she sat on my bed and gently slid her hand across my still heaving abdomen. "The signs are becoming increasingly certain."

Chloe arrived bearing a tumbler and a shallow bowl. The tumbler contained peppermint infusion. She sat down on the bed to my left. "Drink slowly lest you induce retching anew," she cautioned. "Give the solution ample time to work. After the nausea has abated, Briseis and I will examine you thoroughly."

By the time I finished the draught my stomach was settled. "The nausea is gone, Chloe," I said. "Please proceed, as I eagerly await your assessment.

She rose to her feet, took my left hand in her right, and placed her left hand in the middle of my back. "Here now, lie down on your back, slowly, easily."

Briseis got up as Chloe lowered me. I was already naked, having slept unclothed because of the hot weather. The two women examined my breasts, abdomen, and vagina, after the manner of the Ialyssian physician Eupistus but far more gently. When they had finished and set me upright again, Chloe asked whether I felt I could urinate. I replied affirmatively, so she and Briseis helped me to my feet. Chloe handed me the empty bowl she had brought with her. She instructed me to take it to the latrine, fill it privily, and then leave the specimen for her and Briseis to examine there. A significant and much appreciated difference, from having to supply the specimen in my examiner's presence and watch while he scrutinized it.

"There is no longer any question, Lady," said Chloe as the pair reentered my bedchamber, both smiling joyously. "Our heartiest of congratulations!"

"You must be quite elated," Briseis offered.

"Yes and no," I said ruefully, for a serious concern had entered my mind. "Will I have to remain bedridden, as during my previous pregnancy?"

"A wise precaution in view of your age and gynecological history," Chloe returned while Briseis nodded.

"Caesar informed me he will require I quit Rome should I prove pregnant, to forestall the inevitable gossip. How can I comply if I must keep myself immobile?"

Chloe, who had reseated herself at my left side, rubbed her hand on my thigh in a gesture of reassurance. "You can travel anywhere in the world, Lady, so long as preparations are made in advance to keep you horizontal and minimally jostled. For this reason a sea voyage is less threatening than a journey overland. But fear not! Whether by sea or by land, with proper accommodations invalids and wounded soldiers are safely transported regularly."

Returning to Rhodes presents no danger, I reflected with a surge of relief. All I said, however, was "The rest of the villa's staff must not know—not even my personal attendants."

Briseis who had remained standing before me said, "We can maintain you suffered a sunstroke while in the gardens. Hot weather slows recovery from this affliction, and necessitates the patient be kept as immobile as possible."

Chloe nodded vigorously. "Before anyone starts to wonder why you have not recovered, you will have departed here. Where is Caesar planning to send you?"

"The locale has not yet been decided." I answered distractedly, since another concern had struck me. "More immediately: if I must start immobilizing myself, will I have to miss the recitation to be delivered in the lecture hall downstairs three days hence? It is a rare opportunity—to be cherished for a lifetime. To be so close and yet to miss it offers a sore and permanent disappointment. And how will I attend to the materials in my studios? Must I be carried there and returned here sitting in a chair, as when I was stung by the wasp?"

Briseis and Chloe regarded one another cognitively for several moments. Finally Chloe said, "At this early stage you can sit upright for periods of time provided you remain immobile, and that you lie down immediately should you start to feel fatigued or otherwise uncomfortable. You can walk about the house slowly and carefully, provided you do not make any more excursions than are absolutely necessary and always have an attendant with you. Once you reach your fifth month, however, you must stay strictly bedridden." Briseis nodded her agreement.

"Thank you, I shall be sure to comply. Now I should like a cooling bath and change of my bedlinens."

"A proper prescription," Chloe said, rising once again to her feet. "We shall go and inform your attendants of our bogus diagnosis and recommendations for your recovery."

Gallina and Phaedra had replaced Nausicaa. Although I found their *Oh, Lady! Poor Lady!* distinctly annoying, I took care not to show my disgruntlement. Having been led to believe I was ill, their concern was sincere. Awaiting me in my sitting room, after I had finished my bath, was a bowl of broth and a large fluffy roll: Chloe and Briseis wanted to insure I ate. Although the roll appealed and I consumed it, the broth seemed unappetizingly greasy. This portion of the repast I returned to the kitchen with Gallina, in favor of a tumbler of warm milk sprinkled with cassia. Despite my lack of appetite I was able to finish the breakfast without adverse consequence. A ruckus began in the parlor, where the nannies were preparing to take the boys outside. Suddenly I overheard Alcimus ask plaintively, "Where is Mistress Gala?"

Tears stung my eyes. Would the party be gone, I wondered, by the time I had crept to the door? My woe immediately shifted to joy when I heard Briseis reply, "Mistress Gala is sick and abed. After you come in, you can visit her and cheer her up."

In fact I did feel like lying down, but did not until I had written two essentially identical messages—the one to Tiberius, the other to Augustus. *My pharmakeutriae have confirmed I am with child, but assured me I can travel safely if properly accommodated. Therefore unless a more suitable proposal is offered, I intend to forestall gossip by retiring to my farm on Rhodes.* As I was handing the tablets to Fulgens for delivery, I wondered what could have possessed me to address not only my spouse but the emperor himself in so assertive a fashion. When I awoke from my nap, Phaedra brought me a tablet with the imperial seal. Augustus replied that so long as the journey to Rhodes presented no danger for me and Tiberius approved, his only objection to my retiring there was that he and the rest of his family could not visit me easily.

Suddenly I began to ask myself, *Why not remain in Italy, near to the Caesars and to the Ennii, the both of whom have accepted me as one of their own? Why not stay near these folk, upon whom I could reply for prompt and unassailably effective assistance with any problems I encountered?* In our last conversation Augustus had raised a good point. Why should I render myself unnecessarily difficult for Tiberius to reach? Yet the draw of the Rhodian farm seemed inexorable. Why?

My contemplation was interrupted by the noise of the children arriving. The knocker at my door proved to be Alcimus, who was very cautiously carrying a vase full of fresh posies. Phaedra reassured me Rufus her gardener spouse had approved the flowers for picking. After hugs and kisses and the placing of the vase on the night table, Alcimus bowed. Clearly someone was teaching him manners. *Can he continue to learn refinement on an isolated hillside with uncultivated farm workers for acquaintances?* I wondered. *Why not?* I answered myself. *Will not I be his teacher and mentor? Cannot I assert my influence over that of strangers? What will prevent us, as Alcimus and his sibling grow older, from traveling to the cities of Rhodes and beyond and availing ourselves of their cultural offerings? We are going to live on the farm, not be imprisoned there. The place may be far from Rome; but is it not all the closer to Athens, Ephesus, and Alexandria?*

The noise outside my quarters dwindled into quiet as the children settled down for their naps. Although my suite was well cross-ventilated with openings to both the exterior and interior colonnades, the physically larger Zone of Neutrality was still less oppressive in the heat of the day. Slowly and gingerly I made my way past toys and cushions, to where my favorite chair still stood by the door open to the exterior colonnade. The foliage of the gardens appeared monochromatic and lackluster in the white heat haze, until I noticed a trio of saplings at the edge of a copse. Although much younger, smaller in size and of different species, they reminded me strongly of the Guardian trees.

Suddenly I understood why the Rhodian farm was calling me. It defined my identity as Tiberius' wife. There we had exchanged our vows of marriage. There I had been at hand at the time his reputation and very life were most endangered—to provide him daily with the encouragement of unflagging loyalty, the solace of love, the gritty determination to survive. There with his approval and support I had perfected my artistic skills. There his concern and care and demand for intervention had enabled me to overcome the physical aberration—long ignored or sneered at—which had compromised my ability to bear children and eventually became life-threatening. There in consequence of that healing I conceived and bore our first child. Now there I shall repair to bear our second. Tiberius must approve my removal to Rhodes—surely he must. And if he does not, I shall start a wifely argument! This final conjecture brought a twinge of joyous amusement.

Phaedra cautiously drew before me, curtsied and announced I had visitors: Thrasyllus and Aka. With her assistance I arose from my chair, turned to greet my callers, and asked them to join me in my sitting room. As we entered Thrasyllus asserted he and Aka were gravely concerned, having been informed I was taken quite ill. After thanking and dismissing Phaedra I apprised my guests of my condition, of the necessity for my quitting Rome, of my motivations for withdrawing to Rhodes, and of the necessity they keep all these matters absolutely secret. Aka jumped to her feet with a squeal, threw her arms about me and pummeled my cheek with kisses.

Thrasyllus smiled broadly, offered congratulations and reassurance of confidentiality, and joked Tiberius had left me with the best remembrance one could conceive. Did I wish him to cast my horoscope? Yes most certainly, I replied once Aka and I had ceased groaning over his pun. After they had departed and I had lain down to rest, I reflected upon the fact I had accepted Thrasyllus' offer of prognostication primarily out of politeness. What was the point of determining what the future may or may not promise, and then deliberating let alone agonizing over it? Only after it became the present could the difficulties it brought be effectively addressed.

Two mornings later I had the entire contents of both my studios brought to the Zone of Neutrality. What artwork to take with me or to leave behind I must decide. By noon I had made up my mind—far sooner than I had anticipated. Augustus' assumption about duplicates had proven quite correct. There was a goodly number of multiple representations of similar themes—scenes and plantings of the Gardens of Maecenas, vistas of Capri and other locales we had visited, portrayals of human and animal activities. There were actually only seven unique items: the crew of the Galatea harvesting smelts shipside, the exterior of the Villa Maecenatis and the scene of the children playing in its peristyle both just completed, the *Lion of Nemea* and *Zeus Descending to Danae* that had to be rescued from Lucius Norenas, the *Charioteers*, and finally the panorama of Rome.

While at first I had intended unequivocally to have all of these shipped to Rhodes, in the end I chose only the panorama and the *Charioteers*. Consideration of the youthful audience who would be beholding my artwork on Rhodes impelled my decision to leave the others behind. To very young children the *Lion of Nemea* could present a terrifying prospect. The tale of a god, descending as a shower of gold upon a maiden for the purpose of deflowering her, was assuredly sordid and even smacked of blasphemy. Accordingly I indicated these to remain in Rome.

Alcimus and Phoenix and certainly Leonidas were too young to remember the Villa Maecenatis: hence its depictions could not possibly hold any significance for them. Nor could the *Smelt Fishers*, since the boys had never witnessed the taking of fish. Accordingly I designated these three tableaux for Augustus, confident the smelts scene would bring him a chuckle. The painting of the peristyle, which included Alcimus, must certainly go to Livia. Did not her need for a representation of her youngest grandchild far surpass mine since I was taking him with me?

With this thought I retrieved the two tableaux of the Villa Maecenatis. In the lower right corner of each, I painted the signature of Galatea Aristoclide. Thereafter I set Gallina to indicating, with ribbons I had cut from a strip of cloth, the tableaux finished and unfinished I wished to have transported to Rhodes. In this shipment I included a special memento: Pedillus' animal assemblage. I also decided to have all my painting accouterments—paints, brushes, blank palettes, easels and drying racks—shipped as well. Having expended considerable time, money, and effort—my own and that of others—upon the purchasing or construction of these accessories, I was hardly inclined to acquire new ones. Upon finishing I sent Gallina for Acer. He agreed to crate and ship everything I had indicated and advise Augustus the balance was at his disposal.

My collection of unfinished and unpainted textiles required a different solution from that of my paintings. It had dwindled to about one third the size it had been when I had it shipped from Rhodes to Rome, after I had extracted pieces for painting or for Chloris the couturier to fashion into garments. But now it seemed wasteful to ship the fabric paintings I had so painstakingly completed to an isolated farm, where no one but myself and my servants would be present to view them. After summoning Chloris I instructed her to fashion, into usable Roman costumes, any textiles with completed designs as well as those to which designs had not yet been affixed. When done she should present the garments to the members of Tiberius' family and household. Only those with partially completed paintings I wanted sent to Rhodes.

The next morning Chloe came to my quarters with the same pair of burly menservants who had carried me seated in the aftermath of the wasp's sting. They delivered me in my chair to the lecture hall while it was yet empty, thereby precluding this unusual mode of entry from attracting the attention of other attendees. The bearers placed me in a corner to the immediate right of the dais, where there would be no traffic.

Although Titus Livius stood with his back to me, I could hear him perfectly. The recitation was a pure delight. His lucid and highly explicative style of writing I resolved to emulate; for it caught and held the listener's attention whether the subject matter was of interest or not. He covered the Second Punic War, during which the Carthaginians inflicted resounding defeats upon the Roman armies and invaded Italy, but Roman military strategy rebounding in Italy and Spain ultimately dismantled the Carthaginian empire. Writing respectfully and admiringly of the Carthaginian leaders, rather than denigrating them as miscreants or exploitative opportunists, Livius rendered the Roman success all the more striking. He laid particular emphasis upon a pair of consular colleagues—Gaius Claudius Nero and Marcus Livius Drusus—whose generalship rallied Roman forces after their devastating defeat at Cannae and resulted in the expulsion of the Carthaginians from Italy. The historian's intent, of course, was to praise the ancestry of Augustus' family. Yet while listening to this accolade I began to tremble with a strange excitement. For perhaps the first time in my life, two figures of history ceased to be names in a book and became tangible human beings. And these two acclaimed consuls were ancestors of my own children!

My chair bearers discreetly waited until the hall had emptied before they carried me out. The parlor being empty, I presumed the children were either in the gardens or in the peristyle. As Gallina helped me rise from the chair, I told her to have Fulgens give each carrier a denarius. Both thanked me, bowed, and departed. To my surprise Gallina said I had guests. When she opened my sitting room door, I found Antonia, her sisters Prima and Claudia, their great-aunt Atia and cousin Marcia awaiting me with a luncheon of cold cooked fowl, bread rolls and fruit. They responded with surprise and dismay to my assertion I anticipated removing to Rhodes. How could they easily visit me at such a distance? I explained my particular fondness for Rhodes. On that island I had become known to Tiberius and made the recipient of his kindness, which had rescued me from domestic plight and eventually led to my acquaintance with the present company. Claudia assured me she and her sisters were my friends forever, no matter how distant my abode from theirs. My response was that Tiberius liked to say we are out of one another's sight but not out of our lives. All approved.

Although the next five days were filled with preoccupying activities, they seemed an anxiety-filled eternity as I awaited Tiberius' answer to my letter. Bed- and chair-ridden in my quarters and inspired by his recitation, I resumed reading the published portion of Titus Livius' great Roman history. Ironically enough I had begun its perusal on Rhodes, but put it aside after coming to Rome and letting other pursuits distract me.

Now more than ever the presence of the little boys brought refreshing delight. Alcimus and Phoenix understandably inquired whether I was sick, and showed immense relief when I responded that I was only very, very tired. Thrasyllus came with my horoscope. He pronounced it ambiguous, indicating a concurrent ending and beginning. What ambiguity, I demanded somewhat scoffingly. My sojourn in Rome was ending, and within me new life was beginning. The prognostication may have more than merely superficial implication, the sage replied with his usual patience.

Livia visited me one morning. Her demeanor had a quiet sweetness—earnest and reflective—which confirmed her assertion the discovery of my condition had moved her beyond her ability to put into words. She gently but insistently demanded my reassurance—which I fervently gave—that I would diligently keep her informed of my children's development and seek her guidance in rearing them. Aka called daily, as did Antonia. Both were effervescent with excitement the first two days. On the third day, when they happened to arrive together, I bantered the cause of their persistent euphoria must surely be the prospect of being rid of me. Their ensuing horror was quite comical, as both protested vigorously they were ecstatic about my condition and not my impending departure.

Tiberius' reply was militaristically succinct, straightforward, and commanding. Unequivocally he agreed I should return to the Rhodian farm. In a communique sent concurrently with mine, he had advised his mother and stepfather of this decision and asked them to arrange my transportation. The servants he had selected to accompany me were Nestor and Alcmene, Arbindus and Briseis of course. He also designated Valens and Gallina, Scourus and Amera. Moreover I must assuredly take Chloe at least for my journey, and not hesitate to retain her at the farm should I feel a need for her expertise there. Under no circumstances should Ajax and his lover Androcles be returned to Rhodes.

The task of informing the chosen attendants of their impending transfers and making the corresponding arrangements, Tiberius had delegated to Demetrius. This onus I should not assume. My only obligation with regard to my relocation was to arrange for the disposition of my artwork. With no other matter was I to concern myself, apart from reaching my destination safely, and there maintaining my health and wellbeing and those of Alcimus and his emergent sibling. Tiberius' final sentence I found more touching than any saccharine recitation of passion I could have imagined. *Incumbent upon you is the protection of yourself, and of our two children whom I love as much as you and Drusus and more than anyone else.*

Accompanying the letter was a small vial. Opening it I discovered a shock of hair, reddish brown with a few strands of gray interspersed—Tiberius' own. I rang for a servant and Phaedra responded. Since she had not been apprised of my pregnancy, I asked her to send Briseis or Chloe to me: Phaedra I surmised would simply assume I desired medicine. My conclusion proved correct. Chloe duly arrived somewhat alarmed and asked what was ailing me. After reassuring her I was as well as could be expected in my present condition, I inquired whether she knew what a bulla was. When she affirmed that she did, I requested she procure one for me. She left on her errand with elation. About an hour later she returned with an amulet of solid silver suspended from a silver chain.

Alcimus' bulla, still on Rhodes, was fashioned out of leather. To accept a silver bulla for his sibling would be unfair to him. Should I send Chloe after a second bulla wrought of the world's most precious metal? Or should I simply have her exchange the silver bulla for one of plain leather? Pursuing the second course could make me appear hypocritical, since I did wear a silver ring. Then I thought further about my ring. It had been a gift from a lover to his beloved: Tiberius' expression of his gratitude for my companionship, loyalty, support, and the self-sacrifices these had required of me. The ensuing moral perspective left me pleasantly calm. After thanking Chloe for honoring our unborn with a present of such high value, I continued with a request she exchange it for a bulla of plain leather. Silver, I maintained, is a gift to be earned. Given unconditionally it might evoke extravagance and entitlement in its recipient.

Another week passed and quite fleetingly, as I directed the implementation of my plans for transferring my belongings. Nearly every day I had at least one visitor. Thrasyllus, Aka, and Antonia continued to call almost daily, inquiring how I felt and whether I wanted their assistance with any matter. Prima, Claudia, and Marcia visited—individually, not as a group. Livia came on the day preceding the Nones of August *[8/4]*. She and Augustus, who with the advent of more moderate weather returned to the Palatine, had decided to postpone quitting Rome for vacation until after my departure for Rhodes. Given my condition they did not want me to make an unnecessary journey to a resort, to which they themselves had no intention of repairing so long as they must leave me behind in Rome.

There was an abrupt change in Gallina's demeanor. Ordinarily quiet but cheerful, she suddenly became sullen and even irascible. One morning she started to brush out my hair so roughly, my scalp hurt. When I objected she threw the brush into my lap, told me to dress my hair myself, and departed my quarters slamming the doors behind her. Conscientious of my condition I very deliberately and meticulously calmed myself, acknowledging the presence of Underlying Good in my consciousness and Gallina's. Once my anger and hurt feelings sublimated, and I could think clearly and not react emotionally, I rang my gong. Phaedra responded. I told her to seek Chloe and together with her find Gallina. Thereafter all three must come to me. My hair still unbound, I made my way from bedchamber to sitting room. When the trio arrived I told them to seat themselves.

Quietly and sedately, I asked Gallina what was distressing her. In an angry tone she refused to answer in the presence of the others. In reply I asserted that I feared being alone with her, lest her state of mind tempt her to do me physical violence. Then she would tell me nothing, she snarled. Still managing to remain unruffled but also now stern, I explained her uncharacteristically surly behavior aggrieved me but worried me more. If she did not disclose the reason for her misconduct, I saw no choice but to refer her to Demetrius for disciplinary action. Her features tightened into a grimace. After several moments of silence she burst into tears. She confessed to being upset about having to remove to Rhodes. She loved Rome: its crowds, its bustle, its burgeoning markets. The prospect of living on an isolated farm was devastating her. Why, she demanded angrily, of all the servants in the household had I chosen her and her husband to accompany me? Why not Phaedra and Rufus, who were younger and more adaptable to new environs?

At once I comprehended the misconception under which she was laboring. Master Tiberius rather than I had made the selection of servants, I explained. Although I could have stopped here, I felt impelled to elaborate. Although Tiberius had not disclosed the reason for his choice, I could surmise it was because Phaedra was his slave but Rufus was owned by Acer. Why an exchange had not been negotiated, I did not know. Perhaps Master Tiberius felt the maturity of Gallina and Valens made them a particular asset to me in my solitude—not that this possibility was meant to decry Phaedra I added, throwing what I hoped was a reassuring glance at her. Whatever Tiberius' motive, I was utterly disinclined to challenge his wishes with regard to the disposition of his staff. Nonetheless I could assure Gallina she need not anticipate being confined to the farm. It was not all that far from the cities of Rhodes and Ialyssos. Although unquestionably miniscule by comparison with those of Rome, their markets were replete with unusual goods because of the island's proximity to the Orient. The Rhodian markets' smaller size made such wares all the more apparent. In conclusion I suggested Gallina proceed to Rhodes with the expectation of finding at least one worthwhile element, to be respected or enjoyed or cherished in some fashion. After a dejected sigh Gallina murmured she would endeavor to implement my recommendation, and then apologized for her inappropriate behavior.

Other servants began to stop by and wish me well, upon being informed of my imminent departure. The most memorable encounter was with Demetrius and Alexandra. With them came Nomius and Calypso. Nausicaa was attending me at the time of their visit. Everyone wore an ingenuous smile. Demetrius declared they felt privileged to have known and served me. He and his son bowed; his two daughters curtsied. Then Alexandra after some hesitation strode over to my chair and threw her arms about me.

Augustus and Livia visited me together three days before the Ides *[August 11]*. They had specified and ordered the arrangements and accommodations for my travel. Rather than bumping along in a carriage, I would be taken by barge down the Tiber to Ostia. Awaiting me there would be a monotreme fitted with a hammock specially tethered to remain relatively stationary, so it neither rocked in tandem with the ship nor swayed from its own momentum. Arriving at Rhodes, I had no option but to reach the farm by carriage. Such a vehicle, equipped with a similar sort of hammock, would meet me at the dock. All preparations were in place: I could leave on the morrow if I wished. Nevertheless my visitors hoped I was agreeable to setting my departure for the thirteenth day before the Calends of September *[August 20]*, that they might celebrate my birthday the day preceding. Without hesitation I agreed. Then I presented Livia the peristyle tableau. After waxing ecstatic she asked whether I would be willing to send her from Rhodes, representations of Alcimus as he grew and of course of his sibling. Already my intention, I replied.

"Be safe, my dear, and be judicious." Augustus said wistfully as they prepared to leave. "Hasten slowly."

In the letter I composed for Tiberius that evening, I explained my reason for not writing sooner was not to distract him until I had concrete information to report. Continuing, I supplied the date of my intended departure and reason I was lingering in Rome for an extra week. During that extra week, Antonia and her sisters called several times again. Aka and Thrasyllus continued to call daily. The numerological table Thrasyllus cast for me assured a safe, calm, and expeditious journey.

Longus and Rutilia were unable to visit me. At the end of July they had quit Italy for Lyons, there to reunite with their two sons whose military service had ended. Nevertheless the copyist Myronides called, with a purse of 200 aurei in royalties and a characteristically wordy letter from Longus. Augustus had informed him of my impending departure. Aside from effusive regrets I must be separated from Tiberius and that Rutilia and he could not be in Rome to see me off, Longus expressed hope I would continue to pursue my painting endeavors and provide him more originals for copying. Making Myronides wait, I wrote a brief response assuring Longus I intended to continue my artistic endeavors but nothing else. Hardly was I going to commit myself to orders I may prove unable to fulfill, being preoccupied with matters more urgent.

A letter arrived from Phoebe, written at the behest of Nicanor who did not trust his own literacy. Tiberius had contacted the staff at the farm to make ready for me. All preparations were complete, and everyone was thoroughly delighted with the prospect of my return. There was adequate room to accommodate the new servants who were to accompany me.

To Alcimus and Phoenix, Briseis and I continuously reiterated we were about to travel by ship back home. There we would once again see Mistress Phoebe, Miranda, Masters Menon and Nicanor and Rhathines. Thrasylla, Balbilus, Melissa the wetnurse's daughter, and their parents would not be joining us. Someday, however, they would visit us or we would visit them. In the meantime there would be new friends to meet and play with. Gallina to my relief mellowed, and made preparation for the transfer with an air of gracious resignation.

With my paints and tableaux and textiles, journal and writing implements all packed for shipping, there was little else for me to do during that remaining week but reflect upon and ponder the momentous effects my three-year sojourn in Rome had wrought in my life and character. The most significant of course were the discovery of my genuine family, and of the terrible—yea, criminal—deceptions the Eupistodoi had perpetrated upon us without remorse, as though doing so were their privilege. Cruel and avaricious, determined to hold themselves as well as others to obtusely excessive and even unnatural standards, the Eupistodoi—so I decided—were not worth any further consideration from me. Was this not forgiveness in its purest, most absolute sense—that of obliteration?

My contemplations shifted to my true kindred, the Ennii. Their lack of vindictiveness toward the Eupistodoi had set for me a profound example of forgiveness. I had little reason to doubt they would have taken me under their care. Why, then, had I not sought their tutelage, especially after Augustus had urged me to remain in Italy? Because I had found tediously boring their ingenuous manner and their artless, superficial intellectuality. Living with them, I would become condescendingly argumentative and rebellious. Gentle and altruistic, they hardly deserved such contentiousness in return for their generosity.

As for Tiberius' family, their respect and affection for my person was incontestable. But from their public and political standpoint, I was a discomforting and dangerous appendage—an embarrassment poised to bring awkward and potentially disastrous consequences if revealed. Should a need to abandon me arise, they most certainly would hasten to carry it out despite personal regret.

Would I miss the abundant intellectual and cultural activities of Rome—the public exhibits, the concerts and lectures and plays, the social gatherings? Not really. Having partaken freely of this sumptuous repast, I felt thoroughly satisfied and even satiated. Once I had asked Antonia what had become of Maecenas' widow Terentia, whom we had never encountered at any gatherings we attended. Having had her fill of such activities, Terentia retired to Veii after her husband's death. There she began, and to the present continues devoting her energies to educating the local children. Well could I appreciate her sentiments. My memories of similar experiences were now in place, to broaden and enrich the education I would eventually impart to my own children.

And how would I explain to those children who their father was, and why he must remain unknown to them? While they were yet small I could simply tell them he was far, far away doing wondrous works; but as they grew older, they were bound to demand more thorough explications. Mentally I began to develop an elaborate charade. To our children I would identify Tiberius as Alcimedes. This indigenously Greek pattern of nomenclature would imply my son's paternal grandfather was called Alcimus. In a sense it was absolutely accurate; for after all, Alcimus' paternal grandfather had borne the name Nero. By sending gifts and eventually correspondence as Alcimedes, Tiberius could establish himself as an elusive but nonetheless viable presence. Identifying him as a covert agent of the government—very close to the emperor and engaged in sensitive espionage—could explain not only his evasion of his family, but the reason I as an accomplished artist had no portraits of him about.

Presently and quite abruptly I put a halt to those plans for the distant future. Why waste time and mental energy constructing a scenario which might prove utterly useless when the time to implement it arrived? A far more immediate concern was renewing itself in my conscience. How could I endure prolonged periods of celibacy after a decade of intense sexual activity? *Even as widows and other military wives cope with these very difficulties,* I reiterated to myself. *What makes your situation unique? If others can manage their lives under such conditions, so can you! Make Antonia your ensample!*

A brief missive arrived from Tiberius. Although he had approved the delay of my departure so his family could celebrate my birthday, he cautioned me not to postpone my journey any further. The bigger I became with child, the more travel might likely become arduous for me and dangerous to the unborn. He insisted we resolve to let our love and devotion—for one another and for our children—bring us joy and inspiration every morning, and peace and contentment every night. He advised me to apprise my uncle Lucius Ennius of my impending move, stating its purpose was to bring me closer to my undercover agent husband. Should Lucius receive unsolicited news I had quit Rome, he surely must wonder what had become of me.

As the day of my departure neared, I began to perceive in myself a calm assurance of ability to surmount every challenge the future seemed to portend. This confidence found explicit expression during the celebration of my birthday. The festivities began first thing in the morning, with the servants decorating the Zone of Neutrality while Alcimus, Phoenix, Leonidas, and Melissa *assisted* most enthusiastically. Guests began to arrive toward noon. First to come were Thrasyllus and Aka with their children. Their gift was a hamper of baby paraphernalia—swaddling, blankets, rattles and the like—already secured in a chest to be stowed with my luggage. The next to appear was Claudia, then Atia and Marcia, and after them Prima with her two little daughters.

Antonia arrived, and with her a clown whom she introduced as Rusticulus. He was her family's gift, she explained jocularly, to cheer the children and wear them out so they would sleep throughout the morrow's journey. Rusticulus' bucolic sobriquet and costume had been deliberately selected to evoke the environment we were about to enter. He set right to work, performing tricks of legerdemain with a ball, a feather, and a coin. Presently he removed from his satchel a hand puppet representing a donkey, whose whispers into his master's ear evoked a lively conversation about the necessity for children to mind their parents. Suddenly Rusticulus leapt to his feet and bowed, for Livia had entered the room. As she embraced me a group of servants began laying the table for luncheon. Briseis spoke in an undertone to Rusticulus, who nodded. Then clapping his hands, he announced to the children their meal was awaiting them in the peristyle. He gathered them into a line, and with the discipline of a military revue marched them out the door.

We adults feasted on swordfish and asparagus, and the fluffy rolls I had come to relish. All favorite foods of mine, and for certain carefully selected for the occasion; yet I would not miss them on Rhodes at all, since Tiberius had appointed Scourus to accompany me. Dessert was stellar: a cake saturated with a mixture of fruit juice and honey and topped with an assortment of glazed fruits. Just as we were being served this delicacy, Augustus arrived. His entrance prompted Livia to jest how typical of a man to show up just in time for the sweets. Actually he did not partake of the confection. At his beckoning two menservants laid before my feet a chest bound with a leather harness. "Seventy-five gold talents," he said. "We need not admonish you to guard it carefully. And well you know, you can rely upon us to supply you with any necessity you might need."

Of course I was deeply moved, that Augustus should remember and restore the amount of my pilfered stipend. Instead of whimpering my gratitude for a benefaction utterly undeserved—the type of response the Eupistodoi had always required of me—I replied with a comfortable self-assurance and aplomb that came as naturally as breathing. "My dear friends and family, I thank you for the myriad benefactions you have bestowed upon me. You welcomed me into your midst, promoted my artistry, found for me my true identity, patiently endured and ultimately healed my wounded psyche. With impunity and gratitude I shall continue to seek your assistance as my needs arise. But neither upon you nor upon Tiberius shall I wholly depend. Who knows what unforeseen circumstances might prevent any of you rendering aid, no matter how strong your desire to provide it? Upon my proficiencies alone must I rely—my assessments, my judgments, my decisions; and I alone must face and address the consequences they engender. May the Governance of the Universe grant me the moral strength and foresight to make right decisions, and the humility neither to rue nor to excuse mistakes but to accept, acknowledge, and correct them."

While I spoke, Augustus gazed at me pensively. When I had finished he said in measured tones, "Tiberius rightly calls Clytia his Lioness. The male lion goes off to defend his territory, leaving his mate entirely alone—dependent solely upon her own instincts and ingenuity to protect, nurture, and properly rear his offspring. Self-reliance is an admirable quality in a man, and in a woman inestimable. And now for our Lioness we have yet one more gift, for which we must put her to work." He nodded to Arbindus who opened the door to the colonnade. Lucilius Longus and his wife Rutilia swept into the parlor. With them was Nigrinus the young curator of the Villa Maecenatis art gallery. A trio of attendants followed. One carried the **Lion of Nemea** tableau, the second the **Zeus Descending to Danae**, and the third an easel sufficiently low for me to reach while seated.

After Longus had delivered me a prolonged and vigorous handshake and Rutilia practically smothered me with kisses, Nigrinus bowed and spoke. "My Lady, last week I had the honor of receiving a visit from Caesar and Senator Longus. Both assured me these two great paintings are your own work, rather than that of your master Eutychus. We ask that you affix your signature to both.

While Nigrinus was speaking his companions set the **Lion** on the easel before me. The signature of Eutychus Rhodou had been scraped away without disturbing the paint beneath it. Nigrinus himself opened the paint box and dipped a fine brush into a vial of dark blue paint. For a moment I sat trembling, breathing laboriously, clutching the brush white-knuckled, looking at the tableau through a prism of tears. My own art was being openly acknowledged as mine. Although I expected to remain benumbed for some time, this state within only a few moments gave way to a strong and clear determination. Flicking away my tears with the fingers of my free hand I smiled, and painted *Galatea Aristoclide* in the lower right corner. Nigrinus' attendants set the **Danae** before me. As I proceeded with this signature, Nigrinus spoke again. "Your representation of our domicile, which already bears your signature, Caesar has donated for display in our gallery. The two pieces you have just signed will be placed there as well."

My task completed, the entire company—from the sovereign of half the world to the menials serving us—broke into cheers and applause. While Briseis handed pieces of the cake to all, Augustus announced he and Longus had struck a bargain. From the artwork I was leaving behind, Augustus and Livia and any interested members of their family would select whatever pieces they desired. Thereafter, Longus would take possession of the rest.

Antonia remained at the Villa Maecenatis for the remainder of the day and spent the night. We talked well into the third watch, reminiscing about my Italian sojourn. Come the morning she accompanied me to Ostia on the Tiber barge, insisting repeatedly she could not thank me enough for bringing her out of her self-imposed seclusion. Upon boarding the monoreme I found myself welcoming my seclusion, and not merely because I was relieved of Antonia's prattling. Glad to be alone, I was starting to feel ready and even looking forward to confronting the challenges of the future. My self-confidence was soaring. A monarch I was, a ruler of my own realm: my farm, my servants, my children, my life. And with being a ruler came the obligation to be firm but scrupulously fair, to assume full responsibility for decisions right and wrong, to promote strengths in myself and those answerable to me, to rectify deficiencies and ultimately obliterate them. With no less a model than Caesar Augustus, could I fail?

TO BE CONTINUED

www.ingramcontent.com/pod-product-compliance
Lightning Source LLC
Chambersburg PA
CBHW031016030726
47497CB00004B/884